Charles John Huffam Dickens (7 February 1812 – 9 June 1870) was an English writer and social critic. He created some of the world's best-known fictional characters and is regarded by many as the greatest novelist of the Victorian era. His works enjoyed unprecedented popularity during his lifetime, and by the 20th century critics and scholars had recognised him as a literary genius. His novels and short stories are still widely read today.

Born in Portsmouth, Dickens left school to work in a factory when his father was incarcerated in a debtors' prison. Despite his lack of formal education, he edited a weekly journal for 20 years, wrote 15 novels, five novellas, hundreds of short stories and non-fiction articles, lectured and performed readings extensively, was an indefatigable letter writer, and campaigned vigorously for children's rights, education, and other social reforms. (Source: Wikipedia)

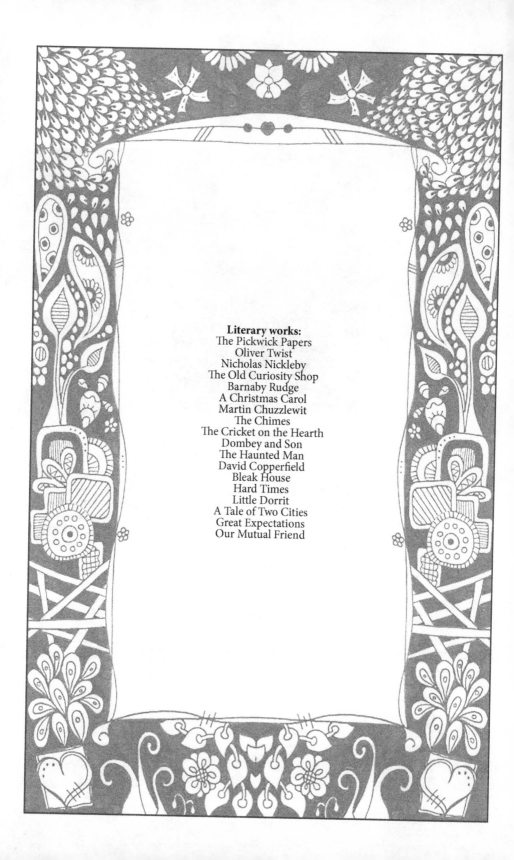

Literary works:
The Pickwick Papers
Oliver Twist
Nicholas Nickleby
The Old Curiosity Shop
Barnaby Rudge
A Christmas Carol
Martin Chuzzlewit
The Chimes
The Cricket on the Hearth
Dombey and Son
The Haunted Man
David Copperfield
Bleak House
Hard Times
Little Dorrit
A Tale of Two Cities
Great Expectations
Our Mutual Friend

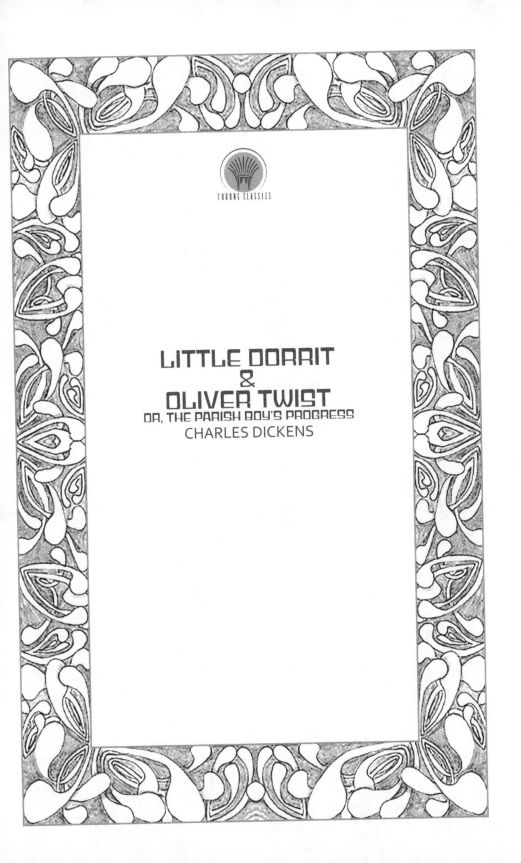

THRONE CLASSICS

LITTLE DORRIT
&
OLIVER TWIST
OR, THE PARISH BOY'S PROGRESS
CHARLES DICKENS

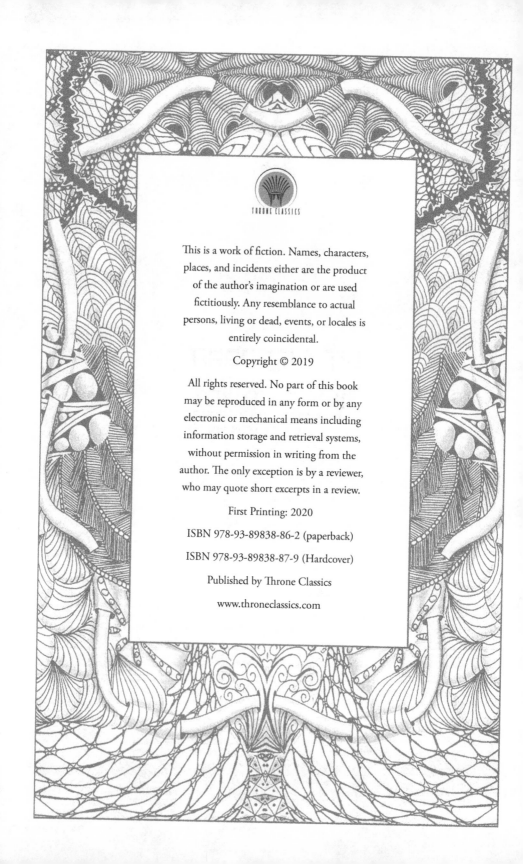

First Printing: 2020

ISBN 978-93-89838-86-2 (paperback)

ISBN 978-93-89838-87-9 (Hardcover)

Published by Throne Classics

www.throneclassics.com

Contents

LITTLE DORRIT
&
OLIVER TWIST
OR, THE PARISH BOY'S PROGRESS

LITTLE DORRIT

PREFACE TO THE 1857 EDITION

I have been occupied with this story, during many working hours of two years. I must have been very ill employed, if I could not leave its merits and demerits as a whole, to express themselves on its being read as a whole. But, as it is not unreasonable to suppose that I may have held its threads with a more continuous attention than anyone else can have given them during its desultory publication, it is not unreasonable to ask that the weaving may be looked at in its completed state, and with the pattern finished.

If I might offer any apology for so exaggerated a fiction as the Barnacles and the Circumlocution Office, I would seek it in the common experience of an Englishman, without presuming to mention the unimportant fact of my having done that violence to good manners, in the days of a Russian war, and of a Court of Inquiry at Chelsea. If I might make so bold as to defend that extravagant conception, Mr Merdle, I would hint that it originated after the Railroad-share epoch, in the times of a certain Irish bank, and of one or two other equally laudable enterprises. If I were to plead anything in mitigation of the preposterous fancy that a bad design will sometimes claim to be a good and an expressly religious design, it would be the curious coincidence that it has been brought to its climax in these pages, in the days of the public examination of late Directors of a Royal British Bank. But, I submit myself to suffer judgment to go by default on all these counts, if need be, and to accept the assurance (on good authority) that nothing like them was ever known in this land.

Some of my readers may have an interest in being informed whether or no any portions of the Marshalsea Prison are yet standing. I did not know, myself, until the sixth of this present month, when I went to look. I found the outer front courtyard, often mentioned here, metamorphosed into a butter shop; and I then almost gave up every brick of the jail for lost. Wandering, however, down a certain adjacent 'Angel Court, leading to Bermondsey', I came to 'Marshalsea Place:' the houses in which I recognised, not only as the great block of the former prison, but as preserving the rooms that arose in my mind's-eye when I became Little Dorrit's biographer. The smallest boy I ever conversed with, carrying the largest baby I ever saw, offered a supernaturally intelligent explanation of the locality in its old uses, and was very nearly correct. How this young Newton (for such I judge him to be) came by his information, I don't know; he was a quarter of a century too young to know anything about it of himself. I pointed to the window of the room where Little Dorrit was born, and where her father lived so long, and asked him what was the name of the lodger who tenanted that apartment at present? He said, 'Tom Pythick.' I asked him who was Tom Pythick? and he said, 'Joe Pythick's uncle.'

A little further on, I found the older and smaller wall, which used to enclose the pent-up inner prison where nobody was put, except for ceremony. But, whosoever goes into Marshalsea Place, turning out of Angel Court, leading to Bermondsey, will find his feet on the very paving-stones of the extinct Marshalsea jail; will see its narrow yard to the right and to the left, very little altered if at all, except that the walls were lowered when the place got free; will look upon rooms in which the debtors lived; and will stand among the crowding ghosts of many miserable years.

In the Preface to Bleak House I remarked that I had never had so many readers. In the Preface to its next successor, Little Dorrit, I have still to repeat the same words. Deeply sensible of the affection and confidence that have grown up between us, I add to this Preface, as I added to that, May we meet again!

London May 1857

BOOK THE FIRST: POVERTY

CHAPTER 1. Sun and Shadow

Thirty years ago, Marseilles lay burning in the sun, one day.

A blazing sun upon a fierce August day was no greater rarity in southern France then, than at any other time, before or since. Everything in Marseilles, and about Marseilles, had stared at the fervid sky, and been stared at in return, until a staring habit had become universal there. Strangers were stared out of countenance by staring white houses, staring white walls, staring white streets, staring tracts of arid road, staring hills from which verdure was burnt away. The only things to be seen not fixedly staring and glaring were the vines drooping under their load of grapes. These did occasionally wink a little, as the hot air barely moved their faint leaves.

There was no wind to make a ripple on the foul water within the harbour, or on the beautiful sea without. The line of demarcation between the two colours, black and blue, showed the point which the pure sea would not pass; but it lay as quiet as the abominable pool, with which it never mixed. Boats without awnings were too hot to touch; ships blistered at their moorings; the stones of the quays had not cooled, night or day, for months. Hindoos, Russians, Chinese, Spaniards, Portuguese, Englishmen, Frenchmen, Genoese, Neapolitans, Venetians, Greeks, Turks, descendants from all the builders of Babel, come to trade at Marseilles, sought the shade alike—taking refuge in any hiding-place from a sea too intensely blue to be looked at, and a sky of purple, set with one great flaming jewel of fire.

The universal stare made the eyes ache. Towards the distant line of Italian coast, indeed, it was a little relieved by light clouds of mist, slowly rising from the evaporation of the sea, but it softened nowhere else. Far away the staring roads, deep in dust, stared from the hill-side, stared from the hollow, stared from the interminable plain. Far away the dusty vines overhanging wayside cottages, and the monotonous wayside avenues of parched trees without shade, drooped beneath the stare of earth and sky. So did the horses with drowsy bells, in long files of carts, creeping slowly towards the interior; so did their recumbent drivers, when they were awake, which rarely happened; so did the exhausted labourers in the fields. Everything that lived or grew, was oppressed by the glare; except the lizard, passing swiftly over rough stone walls, and the cicala, chirping his dry hot chirp, like a rattle. The very dust was scorched brown, and something quivered in the atmosphere as if the air itself were panting.

Blinds, shutters, curtains, awnings, were all closed and drawn to keep out the stare. Grant it but a chink or keyhole, and it shot in like a white-hot arrow. The churches were the freest from it. To come out of the twilight of pillars and arches—dreamily dotted with winking lamps, dreamily peopled with ugly old shadows piously dozing, spitting, and begging—was to plunge into a fiery river, and swim for life to the nearest strip of shade. So, with people lounging and lying wherever shade was, with but little hum of tongues or barking of dogs, with occasional jangling of discordant church bells and rattling of vicious drums, Marseilles, a fact to be strongly smelt and tasted, lay broiling in the sun one day.

In Marseilles that day there was a villainous prison. In one of its chambers, so repulsive a place that even the obtrusive stare blinked at it, and left it to such refuse of reflected light as it could find for itself, were two men. Besides the two men, a notched and disfigured bench, immovable from the wall, with a draught-board rudely hacked upon it with a knife, a set of draughts, made of old buttons and soup bones, a set of dominoes, two mats, and two or three wine bottles. That was all the chamber held, exclusive of rats and other unseen vermin, in addition to the seen vermin, the two men.

It received such light as it got through a grating of iron bars fashioned like a pretty large window, by means of which it could be always inspected from the gloomy staircase on which the grating gave. There was a broad strong ledge of stone to this grating where the bottom of it was let into the masonry, three or four feet above the ground. Upon it, one of the two men lolled, half sitting and half lying, with his knees drawn up, and his feet and shoulders planted against the opposite sides of the aperture. The bars were wide enough apart to admit of his thrusting his arm through to the elbow; and so he held on negligently, for his greater ease.

A prison taint was on everything there. The imprisoned air, the imprisoned light, the imprisoned damps, the imprisoned men, were all deteriorated by confinement. As the captive men were faded and haggard, so the iron was rusty, the stone was slimy, the wood was rotten, the air was faint, the light was dim. Like a well, like a vault, like a tomb, the prison had no knowledge of the brightness outside, and would have kept its polluted atmosphere intact in one of the spice islands of the Indian ocean.

The man who lay on the ledge of the grating was even chilled. He jerked his great cloak more heavily upon him by an impatient movement of one shoulder, and growled, 'To the devil with this Brigand of a Sun that never shines in here!'

He was waiting to be fed, looking sideways through the bars that he might see the further down the stairs, with much of the expression of a wild beast in similar expectation. But his eyes, too close together, were not so nobly set in his head as those of the king of beasts are in his, and they were sharp rather than bright—pointed weapons with little surface to betray them. They had no depth or change; they glittered, and they opened and shut. So far, and waiving their use to himself, a clockmaker could have made a better pair. He had a hook nose, handsome after its kind, but too high between the eyes by probably just as much as his eyes were too near to one another. For the rest, he was large and tall in frame, had thin lips, where his thick moustache showed them at all, and a quantity of dry hair, of no definable colour, in its shaggy state, but shot with red. The hand with which he held the grating (seamed all over the back with ugly scratches newly healed), was unusually small and plump; would have been unusually white but for the prison grime.

The other man was lying on the stone floor, covered with a coarse brown coat.

'Get up, pig!' growled the first. 'Don't sleep when I am hungry.'

'It's all one, master,' said the pig, in a submissive manner, and not without cheerfulness; 'I can wake when I will, I can sleep when I will. It's all the same.'

As he said it, he rose, shook himself, scratched himself, tied his brown coat loosely round his neck by the sleeves (he had previously used it as a coverlet), and sat down upon the pavement yawning, with his back against the wall opposite to the grating.

'Say what the hour is,' grumbled the first man.

'The mid-day bells will ring—in forty minutes.' When he made the little pause, he had looked round the prison-room, as if for certain information.

'You are a clock. How is it that you always know?'

'How can I say? I always know what the hour is, and where I am. I was brought in here at night, and out of a boat, but I know where I am. See here! Marseilles harbour;' on his knees on the pavement, mapping it all out with a swarthy forefinger; 'Toulon (where the galleys are), Spain over there, Algiers over there. Creeping away to the left here, Nice. Round by the Cornice to Genoa. Genoa Mole and Harbour. Quarantine Ground. City there; terrace gardens blushing with the bella donna. Here, Porto Fino. Stand out for Leghorn. Out again for Civita Vecchia, so away to—hey! there's no room for Naples;' he had got to the wall by this time; 'but it's all one; it's in there!'

He remained on his knees, looking up at his fellow-prisoner with a lively look for a prison. A sunburnt, quick, lithe, little man, though rather thickset. Earrings in his brown ears, white teeth lighting up his grotesque brown face, intensely black hair clustering about his brown throat, a ragged red shirt open at his brown breast. Loose, seaman-like trousers, decent shoes, a long red cap, a red sash round his waist, and a knife in it.

'Judge if I come back from Naples as I went! See here, my master! Civita Vecchia, Leghorn, Porto Fino, Genoa, Cornice, Off Nice (which is in there), Marseilles, you and me. The apartment of the jailer and his keys is where I put this thumb; and here at my wrist they keep the national razor in its case—the guillotine locked up.'

The other man spat suddenly on the pavement, and gurgled in his throat.

Some lock below gurgled in its throat immediately afterwards, and then a door crashed. Slow steps began ascending the stairs; the prattle of a sweet little voice mingled with the noise they made; and the prison-keeper appeared carrying his daughter, three or four years old, and a basket.

'How goes the world this forenoon, gentlemen? My little one, you see, going round with me to have a peep at her father's birds. Fie, then! Look at the birds, my pretty, look at the birds.'

He looked sharply at the birds himself, as he held the child up at the grate, especially at the little bird, whose activity he seemed to mistrust. 'I have brought your bread, Signor John Baptist,' said he (they all spoke in French, but the little man was an Italian); 'and if I might recommend you not to game—'

'You don't recommend the master!' said John Baptist, showing his teeth as he smiled.

'Oh! but the master wins,' returned the jailer, with a passing look of no particular liking at the other man, 'and you lose. It's quite another thing. You get husky bread and sour drink by it; and he gets sausage of Lyons, veal in savoury jelly, white bread, strachino cheese, and good wine by it. Look at the birds, my pretty!'

'Poor birds!' said the child.

The fair little face, touched with divine compassion, as it peeped shrinkingly through the grate, was like an angel's in the prison. John Baptist rose and moved towards it, as if it had a good attraction for him. The other bird remained as before, except for an impatient glance at the basket.

'Stay!' said the jailer, putting his little daughter on the outer ledge of the grate, 'she shall feed the birds. This big loaf is for Signor John Baptist. We must break it to get it through into the cage. So, there's a tame bird to kiss the little hand! This sausage in a vine leaf is for Monsieur Rigaud. Again—this veal in savoury jelly is for Monsieur Rigaud. Again—these three white little loaves are for Monsieur Rigaud. Again, this cheese—again, this wine—again, this tobacco—all for Monsieur Rigaud. Lucky bird!'

The child put all these things between the bars into the soft, Smooth, well-shaped hand, with evident dread—more than once drawing back her own and looking at the man with her fair brow roughened into an expression half of fright and half of anger. Whereas she had put the lump of coarse bread into the swart, scaled, knotted hands of John Baptist (who had scarcely as much nail on his eight fingers and two thumbs as would have made out one for Monsieur Rigaud), with ready confidence; and, when he kissed her hand, had herself passed it caressingly over his face. Monsieur Rigaud, indifferent to this distinction, propitiated the father by laughing and nodding at the daughter as often as she gave him anything; and, so soon as he had all his viands about him in convenient nooks of the ledge on which he rested, began to eat with an appetite.

When Monsieur Rigaud laughed, a change took place in his face, that was more remarkable than prepossessing. His moustache went up under his nose, and his nose came down over his moustache, in a very sinister and cruel manner.

'There!' said the jailer, turning his basket upside down to beat the crumbs out, 'I have expended all the money I received; here is the note of it, and that's a thing accomplished. Monsieur Rigaud, as I expected yesterday, the President will look for the pleasure of your society at an hour after mid-day, to-day.'

'To try me, eh?' said Rigaud, pausing, knife in hand and morsel in mouth.

'You have said it. To try you.'

'There is no news for me?' asked John Baptist, who had begun, contentedly, to munch his bread.

The jailer shrugged his shoulders.

'Lady of mine! Am I to lie here all my life, my father?'

'What do I know!' cried the jailer, turning upon him with southern quickness, and gesticulating with both his hands and all his fingers, as if he were threatening to tear him to pieces. 'My friend, how is it possible for me to tell how long you are to lie here? What do I know, John Baptist Cavalletto? Death of my life! There are prisoners here sometimes, who are not in such a devil of a hurry to be tried.'

He seemed to glance obliquely at Monsieur Rigaud in this remark; but Monsieur Rigaud had already resumed his meal, though not with quite so quick an appetite as before.

'Adieu, my birds!' said the keeper of the prison, taking his pretty child in his arms, and dictating the words with a kiss.

18

'Adieu, my birds!' the pretty child repeated.

Her innocent face looked back so brightly over his shoulder, as he walked away with her, singing her the song of the child's game:

'Who passes by this road so late?

Compagnon de la Majolaine!

Who passes by this road so late?

Always gay!'

that John Baptist felt it a point of honour to reply at the grate, and in good time and tune, though a little hoarsely:

'Of all the king's knights 'tis the flower,

Compagnon de la Majolaine!

Of all the king's knights 'tis the flower,

Always gay!'

Which accompanied them so far down the few steep stairs, that the prison-keeper had to stop at last for his little daughter to hear the song out, and repeat the Refrain while they were yet in sight. Then the child's head disappeared, and the prison-keeper's head disappeared, but the little voice prolonged the strain until the door clashed.

Monsieur Rigaud, finding the listening John Baptist in his way before the echoes had ceased (even the echoes were the weaker for imprisonment, and seemed to lag), reminded him with a push of his foot that he had better resume his own darker place. The little man sat down again upon the pavement with the negligent ease of one who was thoroughly accustomed to pavements; and placing three hunks of coarse bread before himself, and falling to upon a fourth, began contentedly to work his way through them as if to clear them off were a sort of game.

Perhaps he glanced at the Lyons sausage, and perhaps he glanced at the veal in savoury jelly, but they were not there long, to make his mouth water; Monsieur Rigaud soon dispatched them, in spite of the president and tribunal, and proceeded to suck his fingers as clean as he could, and to wipe them on his vine leaves. Then, as he paused in his drink to contemplate his fellow-prisoner, his moustache went up, and his nose came down.

'How do you find the bread?'

'A little dry, but I have my old sauce here,' returned John Baptist, holding up his knife.

'How sauce?'

'I can cut my bread so—like a melon. Or so—like an omelette. Or so—like a fried fish. Or so—like Lyons sausage,' said John Baptist, demonstrating the various cuts on the bread he held, and soberly chewing what he had in his mouth.

'Here!' cried Monsieur Rigaud. 'You may drink. You may finish this.'

It was no great gift, for there was mighty little wine left; but Signor Cavalletto, jumping to his feet, received the bottle gratefully, turned it upside down at his mouth, and smacked his lips.

'Put the bottle by with the rest,' said Rigaud.

The little man obeyed his orders, and stood ready to give him a lighted match; for he was now rolling his tobacco into cigarettes by the aid of little squares of paper which had been brought in with it.

'Here! You may have one.'

'A thousand thanks, my master!' John Baptist said in his own language, and with the quick conciliatory manner of his own countrymen.

Monsieur Rigaud arose, lighted a cigarette, put the rest of his stock into a breast-pocket, and stretched himself out at full length upon the bench. Cavalletto sat down on the pavement, holding one of his ankles in each hand, and smoking peacefully. There seemed to be some uncomfortable attraction of Monsieur Rigaud's eyes to the immediate neighbourhood of that part of the pavement where the thumb had been in the plan. They were so drawn in that direction, that the Italian more than once followed them to and back from the pavement in some surprise.

'What an infernal hole this is!' said Monsieur Rigaud, breaking a long pause. 'Look at the light of day. Day? the light of yesterday week, the light of six months ago, the light of six years ago. So slack and dead!'

It came languishing down a square funnel that blinded a window in the staircase wall, through which the sky was never seen—nor anything else.

'Cavalletto,' said Monsieur Rigaud, suddenly withdrawing his gaze from this funnel to which they had both involuntarily turned their eyes, 'you know me for a gentleman?'

'Surely, surely!'

'How long have we been here?'

'I, eleven weeks, to-morrow night at midnight. You, nine weeks and three days, at five this afternoon.'

'Have I ever done anything here? Ever touched the broom, or spread the mats, or rolled them up, or found the draughts, or collected the dominoes, or put my hand to any kind of work?'

'Never!'

'Have you ever thought of looking to me to do any kind of work?'

John Baptist answered with that peculiar back-handed shake of the right forefinger which is the most expressive negative in the Italian language.

'No! You knew from the first moment when you saw me here, that I was a gentleman?'

'ALTRO!' returned John Baptist, closing his eyes and giving his head a most vehement toss. The word being, according to its Genoese emphasis, a confirmation, a contradiction, an assertion, a denial, a taunt, a compliment, a joke, and fifty other things, became in the present instance, with a significance beyond all power of written expression, our familiar English 'I believe you!'

'Haha! You are right! A gentleman I am! And a gentleman I'll live, and a gentleman I'll die! It's my intent to be a gentleman. It's my game. Death of my soul, I play it out wherever I go!'

He changed his posture to a sitting one, crying with a triumphant air:

'Here I am! See me! Shaken out of destiny's dice-box into the company of a mere smuggler;—shut up with a poor little contraband trader, whose papers are wrong, and whom the police lay hold of besides, for placing his boat (as a means of getting beyond the frontier) at the disposition of other little people whose papers are wrong; and he instinctively recognises my position, even by this light and in this place. It's well done! By Heaven! I win, however the game goes.'

Again his moustache went up, and his nose came down.

'What's the hour now?' he asked, with a dry hot pallor upon him, rather difficult of association with merriment.

'A little half-hour after mid-day.'

'Good! The President will have a gentleman before him soon. Come! Shall I tell you on what accusation? It must be now, or never, for I shall not return here. Either I shall go free, or I shall go to be made ready for shaving. You know where they keep the razor.'

Signor Cavalletto took his cigarette from between his parted lips, and showed more momentary discomfiture than might have been expected.

'I am a'—Monsieur Rigaud stood up to say it—'I am a cosmopolitan gentleman. I own no particular country. My father was Swiss—Canton de Vaud. My mother was French by blood, English by birth. I myself was born in Belgium. I am a citizen of the world.'

His theatrical air, as he stood with one arm on his hip within the folds of his cloak, together with his manner of disregarding his companion and addressing the opposite wall instead, seemed to intimate that he was rehearsing for the President, whose examination he was shortly to undergo, rather than troubling himself merely to enlighten so small a person as John Baptist Cavalletto.

'Call me five-and-thirty years of age. I have seen the world. I have lived here, and lived there, and lived like a gentleman everywhere. I have been treated and respected as a gentleman universally. If you try to prejudice me by making out that I have lived by my wits—how do your lawyers live—your politicians—your intriguers—your men of the Exchange?'

He kept his small smooth hand in constant requisition, as if it were a witness to his gentility that had often done him good service before.

'Two years ago I came to Marseilles. I admit that I was poor; I had been ill. When your lawyers, your politicians, your intriguers, your men of the Exchange fall ill, and have not scraped money together, they become poor. I put up at the Cross of Gold,—kept then by Monsieur Henri Barronneau—sixty-five at least, and in a failing state of health. I had lived in the house some four months when Monsieur Henri Barronneau had the misfortune to die;— at any rate, not a rare misfortune, that. It happens without any aid of mine, pretty often.'

John Baptist having smoked his cigarette down to his fingers' ends, Monsieur Rigaud had the magnanimity to throw him another. He lighted the second at the ashes of the first, and smoked on, looking sideways at his companion, who, preoccupied with his own case, hardly looked at him.

'Monsieur Barronneau left a widow. She was two-and-twenty. She had gained a reputation for beauty, and (which is often another thing) was beautiful. I continued to live at the Cross of Gold. I married Madame Barronneau. It is not for me to say whether there was any great disparity in such a match. Here I stand, with the contamination of a jail upon me; but it is possible that you may think me better suited to her than her former husband was.'

He had a certain air of being a handsome man—which he was not; and a certain air of being a well-bred man—which he was not. It was mere swagger and challenge; but in this particular, as in many others, blustering assertion goes for proof, half over the world.

'Be it as it may, Madame Barronneau approved of me. That is not to prejudice me, I hope?'

His eye happening to light upon John Baptist with this inquiry, that little man briskly shook his head in the negative, and repeated in an argumentative tone under his breath, altro, altro, altro, altro—an infinite number of times.

'Now came the difficulties of our position. I am proud. I say nothing in defence of pride, but I am proud. It is also my character to govern. I can't submit; I must govern. Unfortunately, the property of Madame Rigaud was settled upon herself. Such was the insane act of her late husband. More unfortunately still, she had relations. When a wife's relations interpose against a husband who is a gentleman, who is proud, and who must govern, the consequences are inimical to peace. There was yet another source of difference between us. Madame Rigaud was unfortunately a little vulgar. I sought to improve her manners and ameliorate her general tone; she (supported in this likewise by her relations) resented my endeavours. Quarrels began to arise between us; and, propagated and exaggerated by the slanders of the relations of Madame Rigaud, to become notorious to the neighbours. It has been said that I treated Madame Rigaud with cruelty. I may have been seen to slap her face—nothing more. I have a light hand; and if I have been seen apparently to correct Madame Rigaud in that manner, I have done it almost playfully.'

If the playfulness of Monsieur Rigaud were at all expressed by his smile at this point, the relations of Madame Rigaud might have said that they would have much preferred his correcting that unfortunate woman seriously.

'I am sensitive and brave. I do not advance it as a merit to be sensitive and brave, but it is my character. If the male relations of Madame Rigaud had put themselves forward openly, I should have known how to deal with them. They knew that, and their machinations were conducted in secret; consequently, Madame Rigaud and I were brought into frequent and unfortunate collision. Even when I wanted any little sum of money for my personal expenses, I could not obtain it without collision—and I, too, a man whose character it is to govern! One night, Madame Rigaud and myself were walking amicably—I may say like lovers—on a height overhanging the sea. An evil star occasioned Madame Rigaud to advert to her relations; I reasoned with her on that subject, and remonstrated on the want of duty and devotion manifested in her allowing herself to be influenced by their jealous animosity towards her husband. Madame Rigaud retorted; I retorted; Madame Rigaud grew warm; I grew warm, and provoked her. I admit it. Frankness is a part of my character. At length, Madame Rigaud, in an access of fury that I must ever deplore, threw herself upon me with screams of passion (no doubt those that were overheard at some distance), tore my clothes, tore my hair, lacerated my hands, trampled and trod the dust, and finally leaped over, dashing herself to death upon the rocks below. Such is the train of incidents which malice has perverted into my endeavouring to force from Madame Rigaud a relinquishment of her rights; and, on her persistence in a refusal to make the concession I required, struggling with her—assassinating her!'

He stepped aside to the ledge where the vine leaves yet lay strewn about, collected two or three, and stood wiping his hands upon them, with his back to the light.

'Well,' he demanded after a silence, 'have you nothing to say to all that?'

'It's ugly,' returned the little man, who had risen, and was brightening his knife upon his shoe, as he leaned an arm against the wall.

'What do you mean?'

John Baptist polished his knife in silence.

'Do you mean that I have not represented the case correctly?'

'Al-tro!' returned John Baptist. The word was an apology now, and stood for 'Oh, by no means!'

'What then?'

'Presidents and tribunals are so prejudiced.'

'Well,' cried the other, uneasily flinging the end of his cloak over his shoulder with an oath, 'let them do their worst!'

'Truly I think they will,' murmured John Baptist to himself, as he bent his head to put his knife in his sash.

Nothing more was said on either side, though they both began walking to and fro, and necessarily crossed at every turn. Monsieur Rigaud sometimes stopped, as if he were going to put his case in a new light, or make some irate remonstrance; but Signor Cavalletto continuing to go slowly to and fro at a grotesque kind of jog-trot pace with his eyes turned downward, nothing came of these inclinings.

By-and-by the noise of the key in the lock arrested them both. The sound of voices succeeded, and the tread of feet. The door clashed, the voices and the feet came on, and the prison-keeper slowly ascended the stairs, followed by a guard of soldiers.

'Now, Monsieur Rigaud,' said he, pausing for a moment at the grate, with his keys in his hands, 'have the goodness to come out.'

'I am to depart in state, I see?'

'Why, unless you did,' returned the jailer, 'you might depart in so many pieces that it would be difficult to get you together again. There's a crowd, Monsieur Rigaud, and it doesn't love you.'

He passed on out of sight, and unlocked and unbarred a low door in the corner of the chamber. 'Now,' said he, as he opened it and appeared within, 'come out.'

There is no sort of whiteness in all the hues under the sun at all like the whiteness of Monsieur Rigaud's face as it was then. Neither is there any expression of the human countenance at all like that expression in every little line of which the frightened heart is seen to beat. Both are conventionally compared with death; but the difference is the whole deep gulf between the struggle done, and the fight at its most desperate extremity.

He lighted another of his paper cigars at his companion's; put it tightly between his teeth; covered his head with a soft slouched hat; threw the end of his cloak over his shoulder again; and walked out into the side gallery on which the door opened, without taking any further notice of Signor Cavalletto. As to that little man himself, his whole attention had become absorbed in getting near the door and looking out at it. Precisely as a beast might approach the opened gate of his den and eye the freedom beyond, he passed those few moments in watching and peering, until the door was closed upon him.

There was an officer in command of the soldiers; a stout, serviceable, profoundly calm man, with his drawn sword in his hand, smoking a cigar. He very briefly directed the placing of Monsieur Rigaud in the midst of the party, put himself with consummate indifference at their head, gave the word 'march!' and so they all went jingling down the staircase. The door clashed—the key turned—and a ray of unusual light, and a breath of unusual air, seemed to have passed through the jail, vanishing in a tiny wreath of smoke from the cigar.

Still, in his captivity, like a lower animal—like some impatient ape, or roused bear of the smaller species—the prisoner, now left solitary, had jumped upon the ledge, to lose no glimpse of this departure. As he yet stood clasping the grate with both hands, an uproar broke upon his hearing; yells, shrieks, oaths, threats, execrations, all comprehended in it, though (as in a storm) nothing but a raging swell of sound distinctly heard.

Excited into a still greater resemblance to a caged wild animal by his anxiety to know more, the prisoner leaped nimbly down, ran round the chamber, leaped nimbly up again, clasped the grate and tried to shake it, leaped down and ran, leaped up and listened, and never rested until the noise, becoming more and more distant, had died away. How many better prisoners have worn their noble hearts out so; no man thinking of it; not even the beloved of their souls realising it; great kings and governors, who had made them captive, careering in the sunlight jauntily, and men cheering them on. Even the said great personages dying in bed, making exemplary ends and sounding speeches; and polite history, more servile than their instruments, embalming them!

At last, John Baptist, now able to choose his own spot within the compass of those walls for the exercise of his faculty of going to sleep when he would, lay down upon the bench, with his face turned over on his crossed arms, and slumbered. In his submission, in his lightness, in his good humour, in his short-lived passion, in his easy contentment with hard bread and hard stones, in his ready sleep, in his fits and starts, altogether a true son of the land that gave him birth.

The wide stare stared itself out for one while; the Sun went down in a red, green, golden glory; the stars came out in the heavens, and the fire-flies mimicked them in the lower air, as men may feebly imitate the goodness of a better order of beings; the long dusty roads and the interminable plains were in repose—and so deep a hush was on the sea, that it scarcely whispered of the time when it shall give up its dead.

CHAPTER 2 Fellow Travellers

No more of yesterday's howling over yonder to-day, Sir; is there?'

'I have heard none.'

24

'Then you may be sure there is none. When these people howl, they howl to be heard.'

'Most people do, I suppose.'

'Ah! but these people are always howling. Never happy otherwise.'

'Do you mean the Marseilles people?'

'I mean the French people. They're always at it. As to Marseilles, we know what Marseilles is. It sent the most insurrectionary tune into the world that was ever composed. It couldn't exist without allonging and marshonging to something or other—victory or death, or blazes, or something.'

The speaker, with a whimsical good humour upon him all the time, looked over the parapet-wall with the greatest disparagement of Marseilles; and taking up a determined position by putting his hands in his pockets and rattling his money at it, apostrophised it with a short laugh.

'Allong and marshong, indeed. It would be more creditable to you, I think, to let other people allong and marshong about their lawful business, instead of shutting 'em up in quarantine!'

'Tiresome enough,' said the other. 'But we shall be out to-day.'

'Out to-day!' repeated the first. 'It's almost an aggravation of the enormity, that we shall be out to-day. Out! What have we ever been in for?'

'For no very strong reason, I must say. But as we come from the East, and as the East is the country of the plague—'

'The plague!' repeated the other. 'That's my grievance. I have had the plague continually, ever since I have been here. I am like a sane man shut up in a madhouse; I can't stand the suspicion of the thing. I came here as well as ever I was in my life; but to suspect me of the plague is to give me the plague. And I have had it—and I have got it.'

'You bear it very well, Mr Meagles,' said the second speaker, smiling.

'No. If you knew the real state of the case, that's the last observation you would think of making. I have been waking up night after night, and saying, now I have got it, now it has developed itself, now I am in for it, now these fellows are making out their case for their precautions. Why, I'd as soon have a spit put through me, and be stuck upon a card in a collection of beetles, as lead the life I have been leading here.'

'Well, Mr Meagles, say no more about it now it's over,' urged a cheerful feminine voice.

'Over!' repeated Mr Meagles, who appeared (though without any ill-nature) to be in that peculiar state of mind in which the last word spoken by anybody else is a new injury. 'Over! and why should I say no more about it because it's over?'

It was Mrs Meagles who had spoken to Mr Meagles; and Mrs Meagles was, like Mr Meagles, comely and healthy, with a pleasant English face which had been looking at homely things for five-and-fifty years or more, and shone with a bright reflection of them.

'There! Never mind, Father, never mind!' said Mrs Meagles. 'For goodness sake content yourself with Pet.'

'With Pet?' repeated Mr Meagles in his injured vein. Pet, however, being close behind him, touched him on the shoulder, and Mr Meagles immediately forgave Marseilles from the bottom of his heart.

Pet was about twenty. A fair girl with rich brown hair hanging free in natural ringlets. A lovely girl, with a frank face, and wonderful eyes; so large, so soft, so bright, set to such perfection in her kind good head. She was round and fresh and dimpled and spoilt, and there was in Pet an air of timidity and dependence which was the best weakness in the world, and gave her the only crowning charm a girl so pretty and pleasant could have been without.

'Now, I ask you,' said Mr Meagles in the blandest confidence, falling back a step himself, and handing his daughter a step forward to illustrate his question: 'I ask you simply, as between man and man, you know, DID you ever hear of such damned nonsense as putting Pet in quarantine?'

'It has had the result of making even quarantine enjoyable.'

'Come!' said Mr Meagles, 'that's something to be sure. I am obliged to you for that remark. Now, Pet, my darling, you had better go along with Mother and get ready for the boat. The officer of health, and a variety of humbugs in cocked hats, are coming off to let us out of this at last: and all we jail-birds are to breakfast together in something approaching to a Christian style again, before we take wing for our different destinations. Tattycoram, stick you close to your young mistress.'

He spoke to a handsome girl with lustrous dark hair and eyes, and very neatly dressed, who replied with a half curtsey as she passed off in the train of Mrs Meagles and Pet. They crossed the bare scorched terrace all three together, and disappeared through a staring white archway. Mr Meagles's companion, a grave dark man of forty, still stood looking towards this archway after they were gone; until Mr Meagles tapped him on the arm.

'I beg your pardon,' said he, starting.

'Not at all,' said Mr Meagles.

They took one silent turn backward and forward in the shade of the wall, getting, at the height on which the quarantine barracks are placed, what cool refreshment of sea breeze there was at seven in the morning. Mr Meagles's companion resumed the conversation.

'May I ask you,' he said, 'what is the name of—'

'Tattycoram?' Mr Meagles struck in. 'I have not the least idea.'

'I thought,' said the other, 'that—'

'Tattycoram?' suggested Mr Meagles again.

'Thank you—that Tattycoram was a name; and I have several times wondered at the oddity of it.'

'Why, the fact is,' said Mr Meagles, 'Mrs Meagles and myself are, you see, practical people.'

'That you have frequently mentioned in the course of the agreeable and interesting conversations we have had together, walking up and down on these stones,' said the other, with a half smile breaking through the gravity of his dark face.

'Practical people. So one day, five or six years ago now, when we took Pet to church at the

Foundling—you have heard of the Foundling Hospital in London? Similar to the Institution for the Found Children in Paris?'

'I have seen it.'

'Well! One day when we took Pet to church there to hear the music—because, as practical people, it is the business of our lives to show her everything that we think can please her—Mother (my usual name for Mrs Meagles) began to cry so, that it was necessary to take her out. "What's the matter, Mother?" said I, when we had brought her a little round: "you are frightening Pet, my dear." "Yes, I know that, Father," says Mother, "but I think it's through my loving her so much, that it ever came into my head." "That ever what came into your head, Mother?" "O dear, dear!" cried Mother, breaking out again, "when I saw all those children ranged tier above tier, and appealing from the father none of them has ever known on earth, to the great Father of us all in Heaven, I thought, does any wretched mother ever come here, and look among those young faces, wondering which is the poor child she brought into this forlorn world, never through all its life to know her love, her kiss, her face, her voice, even her name!" Now that was practical in Mother, and I told her so. I said, "Mother, that's what I call practical in you, my dear."'

The other, not unmoved, assented.

'So I said next day: Now, Mother, I have a proposition to make that I think you'll approve of. Let us take one of those same little children to be a little maid to Pet. We are practical people. So if we should find her temper a little defective, or any of her ways a little wide of ours, we shall know what we have to take into account. We shall know what an immense deduction must be made from all the influences and experiences that have formed us—no parents, no child-brother or sister, no individuality of home, no Glass Slipper, or Fairy Godmother. And that's the way we came by Tattycoram.'

'And the name itself—'

'By George!' said Mr Meagles, 'I was forgetting the name itself. Why, she was called in the Institution, Harriet Beadle—an arbitrary name, of course. Now, Harriet we changed into Hattey, and then into Tatty, because, as practical people, we thought even a playful name might be a new thing to her, and might have a softening and affectionate kind of effect, don't you see? As to Beadle, that I needn't say was wholly out of the question. If there is anything that is not to be tolerated on any terms, anything that is a type of Jack-in-office insolence and absurdity, anything that represents in coats, waistcoats, and big sticks our English holding on by nonsense after every one has found it out, it is a beadle. You haven't seen a beadle lately?'

'As an Englishman who has been more than twenty years in China, no.'

'Then,' said Mr Meagles, laying his forefinger on his companion's breast with great animation, 'don't you see a beadle, now, if you can help it. Whenever I see a beadle in full fig, coming down a street on a Sunday at the head of a charity school, I am obliged to turn and run away, or I should hit him. The name of Beadle being out of the question, and the originator of the Institution for these poor foundlings having been a blessed creature of the name of Coram, we gave that name to Pet's little maid. At one time she was Tatty, and at one time she was Coram, until we got into a way of mixing the two names together, and now she is always Tattycoram.'

'Your daughter,' said the other, when they had taken another silent turn to and fro, and, after standing for a moment at the wall glancing down at the sea, had resumed their walk, 'is your only child, I know, Mr Meagles. May I ask you—in no impertinent curiosity, but because I have had so much pleasure in your society, may never in this labyrinth of a world exchange a quiet word with you again, and wish to preserve an accurate remembrance of you and yours—may I ask you, if I have not gathered from your good wife that you have had other children?'

'No. No,' said Mr Meagles. 'Not exactly other children. One other child.'

'I am afraid I have inadvertently touched upon a tender theme.'

'Never mind,' said Mr Meagles. 'If I am grave about it, I am not at all sorrowful. It quiets me for a moment, but does not make me unhappy. Pet had a twin sister who died when we could just see her eyes—exactly like Pet's—above the table, as she stood on tiptoe holding by it.'

'Ah! indeed, indeed!'

'Yes, and being practical people, a result has gradually sprung up in the minds of Mrs Meagles and myself which perhaps you may—or perhaps you may not—understand. Pet and her baby sister were so exactly alike, and so completely one, that in our thoughts we have never been able to separate them since. It would be of no use to tell us that our dead child was a mere infant. We have changed that child according to the changes in the child spared to us and always with us. As Pet has grown, that child has grown; as Pet has become more sensible and womanly, her sister has become more sensible and womanly by just the same degrees. It would be as hard to convince me that if I was to pass into the other world to-morrow, I should not, through the mercy of God, be received there by a daughter, just like Pet, as to persuade me that Pet herself is not a reality at my side.'

'I understand you,' said the other, gently.

'As to her,' pursued her father, 'the sudden loss of her little picture and playfellow, and her early association with that mystery in which we all have our equal share, but which is not often so forcibly presented to a child, has necessarily had some influence on her character. Then, her mother and I were not young when we married, and Pet has always had a sort of grown-up life with us, though we have tried to adapt ourselves to her. We have been advised more than once when she has been a little ailing, to change climate and air for her as often as we could—especially at about this time of her life—and to keep her amused. So, as I have no need to stick at a bank-desk now (though I have been poor enough in my time I assure you, or I should have married Mrs Meagles long before), we go trotting about the world. This is how you found us staring at the Nile, and the Pyramids, and the Sphinxes, and the Desert, and all the rest of it; and this is how Tattycoram will be a greater traveller in course of time than Captain Cook.'

'I thank you,' said the other, 'very heartily for your confidence.'

'Don't mention it,' returned Mr Meagles, 'I am sure you are quite welcome. And now, Mr Clennam, perhaps I may ask you whether you have yet come to a decision where to go next?'

'Indeed, no. I am such a waif and stray everywhere, that I am liable to be drifted where any current may set.'

'It's extraordinary to me—if you'll excuse my freedom in saying so—that you don't go straight to London,' said Mr Meagles, in the tone of a confidential adviser.

'Perhaps I shall.'

'Ay! But I mean with a will.'

'I have no will. That is to say,'—he coloured a little,—'next to none that I can put in action now. Trained by main force; broken, not bent; heavily ironed with an object on which I was never consulted and which was never mine; shipped away to the other end of the world before I was of age, and exiled there until my father's death there, a year ago; always grinding in a mill I always hated; what is to be expected from me in middle life? Will, purpose, hope? All those lights were extinguished before I could sound the words.'

'Light 'em up again!' said Mr Meagles.

'Ah! Easily said. I am the son, Mr Meagles, of a hard father and mother. I am the only child of parents who weighed, measured, and priced everything; for whom what could not be weighed, measured, and priced, had no existence. Strict people as the phrase is, professors of a stern religion, their very religion was a gloomy sacrifice of tastes and sympathies that were never their own, offered up as a part of a bargain for the security of their possessions. Austere faces, inexorable discipline, penance in this world and terror in the next—nothing graceful or gentle anywhere, and the void in my cowed heart everywhere—this was my childhood, if I may so misuse the word as to apply it to such a beginning of life.'

'Really though?' said Mr Meagles, made very uncomfortable by the picture offered to his imagination. 'That was a tough commencement. But come! You must now study, and profit by, all that lies beyond it, like a practical man.'

'If the people who are usually called practical, were practical in your direction—'

'Why, so they are!' said Mr Meagles.

'Are they indeed?'

'Well, I suppose so,' returned Mr Meagles, thinking about it. 'Eh? One can but be practical, and Mrs Meagles and myself are nothing else.'

'My unknown course is easier and more helpful than I had expected to find it, then,' said Clennam, shaking his head with his grave smile. 'Enough of me. Here is the boat.'

The boat was filled with the cocked hats to which Mr Meagles entertained a national objection; and the wearers of those cocked hats landed and came up the steps, and all the impounded travellers congregated together. There was then a mighty production of papers on the part of the cocked hats, and a calling over of names, and great work of signing, sealing, stamping, inking, and sanding, with exceedingly blurred, gritty, and undecipherable results. Finally, everything was done according to rule, and the travellers were at liberty to depart whithersoever they would.

They made little account of stare and glare, in the new pleasure of recovering their freedom, but flitted across the harbour in gay boats, and reassembled at a great hotel, whence the sun was excluded by closed lattices, and where bare paved floors, lofty ceilings, and resounding corridors tempered the intense heat. There, a great table in a great room was soon profusely covered with a superb repast; and the quarantine quarters became bare indeed, remembered among dainty dishes, southern fruits, cooled wines, flowers from Genoa, snow from the mountain tops, and all the colours of the rainbow flashing in the mirrors.

'But I bear those monotonous walls no ill-will now,' said Mr Meagles. 'One always begins to forgive a place as soon as it's left behind; I dare say a prisoner begins to relent towards his prison, after he is let out.'

They were about thirty in company, and all talking; but necessarily in groups. Father and Mother Meagles sat with their daughter between them, the last three on one side of the table: on the opposite side sat Mr Clennam; a tall French gentleman with raven hair and beard, of a swart and terrible, not to say genteelly diabolical aspect, but who had shown himself the mildest of men; and a handsome young Englishwoman, travelling quite alone, who had a proud observant face, and had either withdrawn herself from the rest or been avoided by the rest—nobody, herself excepted perhaps, could have quite decided which. The rest of the party were of the usual materials: travellers on business, and travellers for pleasure; officers from India on leave; merchants in the Greek and Turkey trades; a clerical English husband in a meek strait-waistcoat, on a wedding trip with his young wife; a majestic English mama and papa, of the patrician order, with a family of three growing-up daughters, who were keeping a journal for the confusion of their fellow-creatures; and a deaf old English mother, tough in travel, with a very decidedly grown-up daughter indeed, which daughter went sketching about the universe in the expectation of ultimately toning herself off into the married state.

The reserved Englishwoman took up Mr Meagles in his last remark.

'Do you mean that a prisoner forgives his prison?' said she, slowly and with emphasis.

'That was my speculation, Miss Wade. I don't pretend to know positively how a prisoner might feel. I never was one before.'

'Mademoiselle doubts,' said the French gentleman in his own language, 'it's being so easy to forgive?'

'I do.'

Pet had to translate this passage to Mr Meagles, who never by any accident acquired any knowledge whatever of the language of any country into which he travelled. 'Oh!' said he. 'Dear me! But that's a pity, isn't it?'

'That I am not credulous?' said Miss Wade.

'Not exactly that. Put it another way. That you can't believe it easy to forgive.'

'My experience,' she quietly returned, 'has been correcting my belief in many respects, for some years. It is our natural progress, I have heard.'

'Well, well! But it's not natural to bear malice, I hope?' said Mr Meagles, cheerily.

'If I had been shut up in any place to pine and suffer, I should always hate that place and wish to burn it down, or raze it to the ground. I know no more.'

'Strong, sir?' said Mr Meagles to the Frenchman; it being another of his habits to address individuals of all nations in idiomatic English, with a perfect conviction that they were bound to understand it somehow. 'Rather forcible in our fair friend, you'll agree with me, I think?'

The French gentleman courteously replied, 'Plait-il?' To which Mr Meagles returned with much satisfaction, 'You are right. My opinion.'

The breakfast beginning by-and-by to languish, Mr Meagles made the company a speech. It was short enough and sensible enough, considering that it was a speech at all, and hearty.

It merely went to the effect that as they had all been thrown together by chance, and had all preserved a good understanding together, and were now about to disperse, and were not likely ever to find themselves all together again, what could they do better than bid farewell to one another, and give one another good-speed in a simultaneous glass of cool champagne all round the table? It was done, and with a general shaking of hands the assembly broke up for ever.

The solitary young lady all this time had said no more. She rose with the rest, and silently withdrew to a remote corner of the great room, where she sat herself on a couch in a window, seeming to watch the reflection of the water as it made a silver quivering on the bars of the lattice. She sat, turned away from the whole length of the apartment, as if she were lonely of her own haughty choice. And yet it would have been as difficult as ever to say, positively, whether she avoided the rest, or was avoided.

The shadow in which she sat, falling like a gloomy veil across her forehead, accorded very well with the character of her beauty. One could hardly see the face, so still and scornful, set off by the arched dark eyebrows, and the folds of dark hair, without wondering what its expression would be if a change came over it. That it could soften or relent, appeared next to impossible. That it could deepen into anger or any extreme of defiance, and that it must change in that direction when it changed at all, would have been its peculiar impression upon most observers. It was dressed and trimmed into no ceremony of expression. Although not an open face, there was no pretence in it. 'I am self-contained and self-reliant; your opinion is nothing to me; I have no interest in you, care nothing for you, and see and hear you with indifference'— this it said plainly. It said so in the proud eyes, in the lifted nostril, in the handsome but compressed and even cruel mouth. Cover either two of those channels of expression, and the third would have said so still. Mask them all, and the mere turn of the head would have shown an unsubduable nature.

Pet had moved up to her (she had been the subject of remark among her family and Mr Clennam, who were now the only other occupants of the room), and was standing at her side.

'Are you'—she turned her eyes, and Pet faltered—'expecting any one to meet you here, Miss Wade?'

'I? No.'

'Father is sending to the Poste Restante. Shall he have the pleasure of directing the messenger to ask if there are any letters for you?'

'I thank him, but I know there can be none.'

'We are afraid,' said Pet, sitting down beside her, shyly and half tenderly, 'that you will feel quite deserted when we are all gone.'

'Indeed!'

'Not,' said Pet, apologetically and embarrassed by her eyes, 'not, of course, that we are any company to you, or that we have been able to be so, or that we thought you wished it.'

'I have not intended to make it understood that I did wish it.'

'No. Of course. But—in short,' said Pet, timidly touching her hand as it lay impassive on the sofa between them, 'will you not allow Father to tender you any slight assistance or service? He will be very glad.'

'Very glad,' said Mr Meagles, coming forward with his wife and Clennam. 'Anything short of speaking the language, I shall be delighted to undertake, I am sure.'

'I am obliged to you,' she returned, 'but my arrangements are made, and I prefer to go my own way in my own manner.'

'Do you?' said Mr Meagles to himself, as he surveyed her with a puzzled look. 'Well! There's character in that, too.'

'I am not much used to the society of young ladies, and I am afraid I may not show my appreciation of it as others might. A pleasant journey to you. Good-bye!'

She would not have put out her hand, it seemed, but that Mr Meagles put out his so straight before her that she could not pass it. She put hers in it, and it lay there just as it had lain upon the couch.

'Good-bye!' said Mr Meagles. 'This is the last good-bye upon the list, for Mother and I have just said it to Mr Clennam here, and he only waits to say it to Pet. Good-bye! We may never meet again.'

'In our course through life we shall meet the people who are coming to meet us, from many strange places and by many strange roads,' was the composed reply; 'and what it is set to us to do to them, and what it is set to them to do to us, will all be done.'

There was something in the manner of these words that jarred upon Pet's ear. It implied that what was to be done was necessarily evil, and it caused her to say in a whisper, 'O Father!' and to shrink childishly, in her spoilt way, a little closer to him. This was not lost on the speaker.

'Your pretty daughter,' she said, 'starts to think of such things. Yet,' looking full upon her, 'you may be sure that there are men and women already on their road, who have their business to do with you, and who will do it. Of a certainty they will do it. They may be coming hundreds, thousands, of miles over the sea there; they may be close at hand now; they may be coming, for anything you know or anything you can do to prevent it, from the vilest sweepings of this very town.'

With the coldest of farewells, and with a certain worn expression on her beauty that gave it, though scarcely yet in its prime, a wasted look, she left the room.

Now, there were many stairs and passages that she had to traverse in passing from that part of the spacious house to the chamber she had secured for her own occupation. When she had almost completed the journey, and was passing along the gallery in which her room was, she heard an angry sound of muttering and sobbing. A door stood open, and within she saw the attendant upon the girl she had just left; the maid with the curious name.

She stood still, to look at this maid. A sullen, passionate girl! Her rich black hair was all about her face, her face was flushed and hot, and as she sobbed and raged, she plucked at her lips with an unsparing hand.

'Selfish brutes!' said the girl, sobbing and heaving between whiles. 'Not caring what becomes of me! Leaving me here hungry and thirsty and tired, to starve, for anything they care! Beasts! Devils! Wretches!'

'My poor girl, what is the matter?'

She looked up suddenly, with reddened eyes, and with her hands suspended, in the act of pinching her neck, freshly disfigured with great scarlet blots. 'It's nothing to you what's the matter. It don't signify to any one.'

'O yes it does; I am sorry to see you so.'

'You are not sorry,' said the girl. 'You are glad. You know you are glad. I never was like this but twice over in the quarantine yonder; and both times you found me. I am afraid of you.'

'Afraid of me?'

'Yes. You seem to come like my own anger, my own malice, my own—whatever it is—I don't know what it is. But I am ill-used, I am ill-used, I am ill-used!' Here the sobs and the tears, and the tearing hand, which had all been suspended together since the first surprise, went on together anew.

The visitor stood looking at her with a strange attentive smile. It was wonderful to see the fury of the contest in the girl, and the bodily struggle she made as if she were rent by the Demons of old.

'I am younger than she is by two or three years, and yet it's me that looks after her, as if I was old, and it's she that's always petted and called Baby! I detest the name. I hate her! They make a fool of her, they spoil her. She thinks of nothing but herself, she thinks no more of me than if I was a stock and a stone!' So the girl went on.

'You must have patience.'

'I won't have patience!'

'If they take much care of themselves, and little or none of you, you must not mind it.'

I will mind it.'

'Hush! Be more prudent. You forget your dependent position.'

'I don't care for that. I'll run away. I'll do some mischief. I won't bear it; I can't bear it; I shall die if I try to bear it!'

The observer stood with her hand upon her own bosom, looking at the girl, as one afflicted with a diseased part might curiously watch the dissection and exposition of an analogous case.

The girl raged and battled with all the force of her youth and fulness of life, until by little and little her passionate exclamations trailed off into broken murmurs as if she were in pain. By corresponding degrees she sank into a chair, then upon her knees, then upon the ground beside the bed, drawing the coverlet with her, half to hide her shamed head and wet hair in it, and half, as it seemed, to embrace it, rather than have nothing to take to her repentant breast.

'Go away from me, go away from me! When my temper comes upon me, I am mad. I know I might keep it off if I only tried hard enough, and sometimes I do try hard enough, and at other times I don't and won't. What have I said! I knew when I said it, it was all lies. They think I am being taken care of somewhere, and have all I want. They are nothing but good to me. I love them dearly; no people could ever be kinder to a thankless creature than they always are to me. Do, do go away, for I am afraid of you. I am afraid of myself when I feel my temper coming, and I am as much afraid of you. Go away from me, and let me pray and cry myself better!'

The day passed on; and again the wide stare stared itself out; and the hot night was on

Marseilles; and through it the caravan of the morning, all dispersed, went their appointed ways. And thus ever by day and night, under the sun and under the stars, climbing the dusty hills and toiling along the weary plains, journeying by land and journeying by sea, coming and going so strangely, to meet and to act and react on one another, move all we restless travellers through the pilgrimage of life.

CHAPTER 3. Home

It was a Sunday evening in London, gloomy, close, and stale. Maddening church bells of all degrees of dissonance, sharp and flat, cracked and clear, fast and slow, made the brick-and-mortar echoes hideous. Melancholy streets, in a penitential garb of soot, steeped the souls of the people who were condemned to look at them out of windows, in dire despondency. In every thoroughfare, up almost every alley, and down almost every turning, some doleful bell was throbbing, jerking, tolling, as if the Plague were in the city and the dead-carts were going round. Everything was bolted and barred that could by possibility furnish relief to an overworked people. No pictures, no unfamiliar animals, no rare plants or flowers, no natural or artificial wonders of the ancient world—all taboo with that enlightened strictness, that the ugly South Sea gods in the British Museum might have supposed themselves at home again. Nothing to see but streets, streets, streets. Nothing to breathe but streets, streets, streets. Nothing to change the brooding mind, or raise it up. Nothing for the spent toiler to do, but to compare the monotony of his seventh day with the monotony of his six days, think what a weary life he led, and make the best of it—or the worst, according to the probabilities.

At such a happy time, so propitious to the interests of religion and morality, Mr Arthur Clennam, newly arrived from Marseilles by way of Dover, and by Dover coach the Blue-eyed Maid, sat in the window of a coffee-house on Ludgate Hill. Ten thousand responsible houses surrounded him, frowning as heavily on the streets they composed, as if they were every one inhabited by the ten young men of the Calender's story, who blackened their faces and bemoaned their miseries every night. Fifty thousand lairs surrounded him where people lived so unwholesomely that fair water put into their crowded rooms on Saturday night, would be corrupt on Sunday morning; albeit my lord, their county member, was amazed that they failed to sleep in company with their butcher's meat. Miles of close wells and pits of houses, where the inhabitants gasped for air, stretched far away towards every point of the compass. Through the heart of the town a deadly sewer ebbed and flowed, in the place of a fine fresh river. What secular want could the million or so of human beings whose daily labour, six days in the week, lay among these Arcadian objects, from the sweet sameness of which they had no escape between the cradle and the grave—what secular want could they possibly have upon their seventh day? Clearly they could want nothing but a stringent policeman.

Mr Arthur Clennam sat in the window of the coffee-house on Ludgate Hill, counting one of the neighbouring bells, making sentences and burdens of songs out of it in spite of himself, and wondering how many sick people it might be the death of in the course of the year. As the hour approached, its changes of measure made it more and more exasperating. At the quarter, it went off into a condition of deadly-lively importunity, urging the populace in a voluble manner to Come to church, Come to church, Come to church! At the ten minutes, it became aware that the congregation would be scanty, and slowly hammered out in low spirits, They won't come, they won't come, they won't come! At the five minutes, it abandoned hope, and shook every house in the neighbourhood for three hundred seconds, with one dismal swing per second, as a groan of despair.

'Thank Heaven!' said Clennam, when the hour struck, and the bell stopped.

But its sound had revived a long train of miserable Sundays, and the procession would not stop with the bell, but continued to march on. 'Heaven forgive me,' said he, 'and those who trained me. How I have hated this day!'

There was the dreary Sunday of his childhood, when he sat with his hands before him, scared out of his senses by a horrible tract which commenced business with the poor child by asking him in its title, why he was going to Perdition?—a piece of curiosity that he really, in a frock and drawers, was not in a condition to satisfy—and which, for the further attraction of his infant mind, had a parenthesis in every other line with some such hiccupping reference as 2 Ep. Thess. c. iii, v. 6 & 7. There was the sleepy Sunday of his boyhood, when, like a military deserter, he was marched to chapel by a picquet of teachers three times a day, morally handcuffed to another boy; and when he would willingly have bartered two meals of indigestible sermon for another ounce or two of inferior mutton at his scanty dinner in the flesh. There was the interminable Sunday of his nonage; when his mother, stern of face and unrelenting of heart, would sit all day behind a Bible—bound, like her own construction of it, in the hardest, barest, and straitest boards, with one dinted ornament on the cover like the drag of a chain, and a wrathful sprinkling of red upon the edges of the leaves—as if it, of all books! were a fortification against sweetness of temper, natural affection, and gentle intercourse. There was the resentful Sunday of a little later, when he sat down glowering and glooming through the tardy length of the day, with a sullen sense of injury in his heart, and no more real knowledge of the beneficent history of the New Testament than if he had been bred among idolaters. There was a legion of Sundays, all days of unserviceable bitterness and mortification, slowly passing before him.

'Beg pardon, sir,' said a brisk waiter, rubbing the table. 'Wish see bed-room?'

'Yes. I have just made up my mind to do it.'

'Chaymaid!' cried the waiter. 'Gelen box num seven wish see room!'

'Stay!' said Clennam, rousing himself. 'I was not thinking of what I said; I answered mechanically. I am not going to sleep here. I am going home.'

'Deed, sir? Chaymaid! Gelen box num seven, not go sleep here, gome.'

He sat in the same place as the day died, looking at the dull houses opposite, and thinking, if the disembodied spirits of former inhabitants were ever conscious of them, how they must pity themselves for their old places of imprisonment. Sometimes a face would appear behind the dingy glass of a window, and would fade away into the gloom as if it had seen enough of life and had vanished out of it. Presently the rain began to fall in slanting lines between him and those houses, and people began to collect under cover of the public passage opposite, and to look out hopelessly at the sky as the rain dropped thicker and faster. Then wet umbrellas began to appear, draggled skirts, and mud. What the mud had been doing with itself, or where it came from, who could say? But it seemed to collect in a moment, as a crowd will, and in five minutes to have splashed all the sons and daughters of Adam. The lamplighter was going his rounds now; and as the fiery jets sprang up under his touch, one might have fancied them astonished at being suffered to introduce any show of brightness into such a dismal scene.

Mr Arthur Clennam took up his hat and buttoned his coat, and walked out. In the country, the rain would have developed a thousand fresh scents, and every drop would have had its bright association with some beautiful form of growth or life. In the city, it developed only foul stale smells, and was a sickly, lukewarm, dirt-stained, wretched addition to the gutters.

He crossed by St Paul's and went down, at a long angle, almost to the water's edge, through some of the crooked and descending streets which lie (and lay more crookedly and closely then) between the river and Cheapside. Passing, now the mouldy hall of some obsolete Worshipful Company, now the illuminated windows of a Congregationless Church that seemed to be waiting for some adventurous Belzoni to dig it out and discover its history; passing silent warehouses and wharves, and here and there a narrow alley leading to the river, where a wretched little bill, FOUND DROWNED, was weeping on the wet wall; he came at last to the house he sought. An old brick house, so dingy as to be all but black, standing by itself within a gateway. Before it, a square court-yard where a shrub or two and a patch of grass were as rank (which is saying much) as the iron railings enclosing them were rusty; behind it, a jumble of roots. It was a double house, with long, narrow, heavily-framed windows. Many years ago, it had had it in its mind to slide down sideways; it had been propped up, however, and was leaning on some half-dozen gigantic crutches: which gymnasium for the neighbouring cats, weather-stained, smoke-blackened, and overgrown with weeds, appeared in these latter days to be no very sure reliance.

'Nothing changed,' said the traveller, stopping to look round. 'Dark and miserable as ever. A light in my mother's window, which seems never to have been extinguished since I came home twice a year from school, and dragged my box over this pavement. Well, well, well!'

He went up to the door, which had a projecting canopy in carved work of festooned jack-towels and children's heads with water on the brain, designed after a once-popular monumental pattern, and knocked. A shuffling step was soon heard on the stone floor of the hall, and the door was opened by an old man, bent and dried, but with keen eyes.

He had a candle in his hand, and he held it up for a moment to assist his keen eyes. 'Ah, Mr Arthur?' he said, without any emotion, 'you are come at last? Step in.'

Mr Arthur stepped in and shut the door.

'Your figure is filled out, and set,' said the old man, turning to look at him with the light raised again, and shaking his head; 'but you don't come up to your father in my opinion. Nor yet your mother.'

'How is my mother?'

'She is as she always is now. Keeps her room when not actually bedridden, and hasn't been out of it fifteen times in as many years, Arthur.' They had walked into a spare, meagre dining-room. The old man had put the candlestick upon the table, and, supporting his right elbow with his left hand, was smoothing his leathern jaws while he looked at the visitor. The visitor offered his hand. The old man took it coldly enough, and seemed to prefer his jaws, to which he returned as soon as he could.

'I doubt if your mother will approve of your coming home on the Sabbath, Arthur,' he said, shaking his head warily.

'You wouldn't have me go away again?'

'Oh! I? I? I am not the master. It's not what I would have. I have stood between your father and mother for a number of years. I don't pretend to stand between your mother and you.'

'Will you tell her that I have come home?'

'Yes, Arthur, yes. Oh, to be sure! I'll tell her that you have come home. Please to wait here. You won't find the room changed.' He took another candle from a cupboard, lighted it, left the first on the table, and went upon his errand. He was a short, bald old man, in a high-shouldered black coat and waistcoat, drab breeches, and long drab gaiters. He might, from his dress, have been either clerk or servant, and in fact had long been both. There was nothing about him in the way of decoration but a watch, which was lowered into the depths of its proper pocket by an old black ribbon, and had a tarnished copper key moored above it, to show where it was sunk. His head was awry, and he had a one-sided, crab-like way with him, as if his foundations had yielded at about the same time as those of the house, and he ought to have been propped up in a similar manner.

'How weak am I,' said Arthur Clennam, when he was gone, 'that I could shed tears at this reception! I, who have never experienced anything else; who have never expected anything else.'

He not only could, but did. It was the momentary yielding of a nature that had been disappointed from the dawn of its perceptions, but had not quite given up all its hopeful yearnings yet. He subdued it, took up the candle, and examined the room. The old articles of furniture were in their old places; the Plagues of Egypt, much the dimmer for the fly and smoke plagues of London, were framed and glazed upon the walls. There was the old cellaret with nothing in it, lined with lead, like a sort of coffin in compartments; there was the old dark closet, also with nothing in it, of which he had been many a time the sole contents, in days of punishment, when he had regarded it as the veritable entrance to that bourne to which the tract had found him galloping. There was the large, hard-featured clock on the sideboard, which he used to see bending its figured brows upon him with a savage joy when he was behind-hand with his lessons, and which, when it was wound up once a week with an iron handle, used to sound as if it were growling in ferocious anticipation of the miseries into which it would bring him. But here was the old man come back, saying, 'Arthur, I'll go before and light you.'

Arthur followed him up the staircase, which was panelled off into spaces like so many mourning tablets, into a dim bed-chamber, the floor of which had gradually so sunk and settled, that the fire-place was in a dell. On a black bier-like sofa in this hollow, propped up behind with one great angular black bolster like the block at a state execution in the good old times, sat his mother in a widow's dress.

She and his father had been at variance from his earliest remembrance. To sit speechless himself in the midst of rigid silence, glancing in dread from the one averted face to the other, had been the peacefullest occupation of his childhood. She gave him one glassy kiss, and four stiff fingers muffled in worsted. This embrace concluded, he sat down on the opposite side of her little table. There was a fire in the grate, as there had been night and day for fifteen years. There was a kettle on the hob, as there had been night and day for fifteen years. There was a little mound of damped ashes on the top of the fire, and another little mound swept together under the grate, as there had been night and day for fifteen years. There was a smell of black dye in the airless room, which the fire had been drawing out of the crape and stuff of the widow's dress for fifteen months, and out of the bier-like sofa for fifteen years.

'Mother, this is a change from your old active habits.'

'The world has narrowed to these dimensions, Arthur,' she replied, glancing round the room. 'It is well for me that I never set my heart upon its hollow vanities.'

The old influence of her presence and her stern strong voice, so gathered about her son, that he felt conscious of a renewal of the timid chill and reserve of his childhood.

'Do you never leave your room, mother?'

'What with my rheumatic affection, and what with its attendant debility or nervous weakness—names are of no matter now—I have lost the use of my limbs. I never leave my room. I have not been outside this door for—tell him for how long,' she said, speaking over her shoulder.

'A dozen year next Christmas,' returned a cracked voice out of the dimness behind.

'Is that Affery?' said Arthur, looking towards it.

The cracked voice replied that it was Affery: and an old woman came forward into what doubtful light there was, and kissed her hand once; then subsided again into the dimness.

'I am able,' said Mrs Clennam, with a slight motion of her worsted-muffled right hand toward a chair on wheels, standing before a tall writing cabinet close shut up, 'I am able to attend to my business duties, and I am thankful for the privilege. It is a great privilege. But no more of business on this day. It is a bad night, is it not?'

'Yes, mother.'

'Does it snow?'

'Snow, mother? And we only yet in September?'

'All seasons are alike to me,' she returned, with a grim kind of luxuriousness. 'I know nothing of summer and winter, shut up here. The Lord has been pleased to put me beyond all that.' With her cold grey eyes and her cold grey hair, and her immovable face, as stiff as the folds of her stony head-dress,—her being beyond the reach of the seasons seemed but a fit sequence to her being beyond the reach of all changing emotions.

On her little table lay two or three books, her handkerchief, a pair of steel spectacles newly taken off, and an old-fashioned gold watch in a heavy double case. Upon this last object her son's eyes and her own now rested together.

'I see that you received the packet I sent you on my father's death, safely, mother.'

'You see.'

'I never knew my father to show so much anxiety on any subject, as that his watch should be sent straight to you.'

'I keep it here as a remembrance of your father.'

'It was not until the last, that he expressed the wish; when he could only put his hand upon it, and very indistinctly say to me "your mother." A moment before, I thought him wandering in his mind, as he had been for many hours—I think he had no consciousness of pain in his short illness—when I saw him turn himself in his bed and try to open it.'

'Was your father, then, not wandering in his mind when he tried to open it?'

'No. He was quite sensible at that time.'

Mrs Clennam shook her head; whether in dismissal of the deceased or opposing herself to her son's opinion, was not clearly expressed.

'After my father's death I opened it myself, thinking there might be, for anything I knew, some memorandum there. However, as I need not tell you, mother, there was nothing but the old silk watch-paper worked in beads, which you found (no doubt) in its place between the cases, where I found and left it.'

Mrs Clennam signified assent; then added, 'No more of business on this day,' and then added, 'Affery, it is nine o'clock.'

Upon this, the old woman cleared the little table, went out of the room, and quickly returned with a tray on which was a dish of little rusks and a small precise pat of butter, cool, symmetrical, white, and plump. The old man who had been standing by the door in one attitude during the whole interview, looking at the mother up-stairs as he had looked at the son down-stairs, went out at the same time, and, after a longer absence, returned with another tray on which was the greater part of a bottle of port wine (which, to judge by his panting, he had brought from the cellar), a lemon, a sugar-basin, and a spice box. With these materials and the aid of the kettle, he filled a tumbler with a hot and odorous mixture, measured out and compounded with as much nicety as a physician's prescription. Into this mixture Mrs Clennam dipped certain of the rusks, and ate them; while the old woman buttered certain other of the rusks, which were to be eaten alone. When the invalid had eaten all the rusks and drunk all the mixture, the two trays were removed; and the books and the candle, watch, handkerchief, and spectacles were replaced upon the table. She then put on the spectacles and read certain passages aloud from a book—sternly, fiercely, wrathfully—praying that her enemies (she made them by her tone and manner expressly hers) might be put to the edge of the sword, consumed by fire, smitten by plagues and leprosy, that their bones might be ground to dust, and that they might be utterly exterminated. As she read on, years seemed to fall away from her son like the imaginings of a dream, and all the old dark horrors of his usual preparation for the sleep of an innocent child to overshadow him.

She shut the book and remained for a little time with her face shaded by her hand. So did the old man, otherwise still unchanged in attitude; so, probably, did the old woman in her dimmer part of the room. Then the sick woman was ready for bed.

'Good night, Arthur. Affery will see to your accommodation. Only touch me, for my hand is tender.' He touched the worsted muffling of her hand—that was nothing; if his mother had been sheathed in brass there would have been no new barrier between them—and followed the old man and woman down-stairs.

The latter asked him, when they were alone together among the heavy shadows of the dining-room, would he have some supper?

'No, Affery, no supper.'

'You shall if you like,' said Affery. 'There's her tomorrow's partridge in the larder—her first this year; say the word and I'll cook it.'

No, he had not long dined, and could eat nothing.

'Have something to drink, then,' said Affery; 'you shall have some of her bottle of port, if you like. I'll tell Jeremiah that you ordered me to bring it you.'

No; nor would he have that, either.

'It's no reason, Arthur,' said the old woman, bending over him to whisper, 'that because I am afeared of my life of 'em, you should be. You've got half the property, haven't you?'

'Yes, yes.'

'Well then, don't you be cowed. You're clever, Arthur, an't you?'

He nodded, as she seemed to expect an answer in the affirmative.

'Then stand up against them! She's awful clever, and none but a clever one durst say a word to her. He's a clever one—oh, he's a clever one!—and he gives it her when he has a mind to't, he does!'

'Your husband does?'

'Does? It makes me shake from head to foot, to hear him give it her. My husband, Jeremiah Flintwinch, can conquer even your mother. What can he be but a clever one to do that!'

His shuffling footstep coming towards them caused her to retreat to the other end of the room. Though a tall, hard-favoured, sinewy old woman, who in her youth might have enlisted in the Foot Guards without much fear of discovery, she collapsed before the little keen-eyed crab-like old man.

'Now, Affery,' said he, 'now, woman, what are you doing? Can't you find Master Arthur something or another to pick at?'

Master Arthur repeated his recent refusal to pick at anything.

'Very well, then,' said the old man; 'make his bed. Stir yourself.' His neck was so twisted that the knotted ends of his white cravat usually dangled under one ear; his natural acerbity and energy, always contending with a second nature of habitual repression, gave his features a swollen and suffused look; and altogether, he had a weird appearance of having hanged himself at one time or other, and of having gone about ever since, halter and all, exactly as some timely hand had cut him down.

'You'll have bitter words together to-morrow, Arthur; you and your mother,' said Jeremiah. 'Your having given up the business on your father's death—which she suspects, though we have left it to you to tell her—won't go off smoothly.'

'I have given up everything in life for the business, and the time came for me to give up that.'

'Good!' cried Jeremiah, evidently meaning Bad. 'Very good! only don't expect me to stand between your mother and you, Arthur. I stood between your mother and your father, fending off this, and fending off that, and getting crushed and pounded betwixt em; and I've done with such work.'

'You will never be asked to begin it again for me, Jeremiah.'

40

'Good. I'm glad to hear it; because I should have had to decline it, if I had been. That's enough—as your mother says—and more than enough of such matters on a Sabbath night. Affery, woman, have you found what you want yet?'

She had been collecting sheets and blankets from a press, and hastened to gather them up, and to reply, 'Yes, Jeremiah.' Arthur Clennam helped her by carrying the load himself, wished the old man good night, and went up-stairs with her to the top of the house.

They mounted up and up, through the musty smell of an old close house, little used, to a large garret bed-room. Meagre and spare, like all the other rooms, it was even uglier and grimmer than the rest, by being the place of banishment for the worn-out furniture. Its movables were ugly old chairs with worn-out seats, and ugly old chairs without any seats; a threadbare patternless carpet, a maimed table, a crippled wardrobe, a lean set of fire-irons like the skeleton of a set deceased, a washing-stand that looked as if it had stood for ages in a hail of dirty soapsuds, and a bedstead with four bare atomies of posts, each terminating in a spike, as if for the dismal accommodation of lodgers who might prefer to impale themselves. Arthur opened the long low window, and looked out upon the old blasted and blackened forest of chimneys, and the old red glare in the sky, which had seemed to him once upon a time but a nightly reflection of the fiery environment that was presented to his childish fancy in all directions, let it look where it would.

He drew in his head again, sat down at the bedside, and looked on at Affery Flintwinch making the bed.

'Affery, you were not married when I went away.'

She screwed her mouth into the form of saying 'No,' shook her head, and proceeded to get a pillow into its case.

'How did it happen?'

'Why, Jeremiah, o' course,' said Affery, with an end of the pillow-case between her teeth.

'Of course he proposed it, but how did it all come about? I should have thought that neither of you would have married; least of all should I have thought of your marrying each other.'

'No more should I,' said Mrs Flintwinch, tying the pillow tightly in its case.

'That's what I mean. When did you begin to think otherwise?'

'Never begun to think otherwise at all,' said Mrs Flintwinch.

Seeing, as she patted the pillow into its place on the bolster, that he was still looking at her as if waiting for the rest of her reply, she gave it a great poke in the middle, and asked, 'How could I help myself?'

'How could you help yourself from being married!'

'O' course,' said Mrs Flintwinch. 'It was no doing o' mine. I'd never thought of it. I'd got something to do, without thinking, indeed! She kept me to it (as well as he) when she could go about, and she could go about then.'

'Well?'

'Well?' echoed Mrs Flintwinch. 'That's what I said myself. Well! What's the use of considering? If them two clever ones have made up their minds to it, what's left for me to do? Nothing.'

'Was it my mother's project, then?'

'The Lord bless you, Arthur, and forgive me the wish!' cried Affery, speaking always in a low tone. 'If they hadn't been both of a mind in it, how could it ever have been? Jeremiah never courted me; t'ant likely that he would, after living in the house with me and ordering me about for as many years as he'd done. He said to me one day, he said, "Affery," he said, "now I am going to tell you something. What do you think of the name of Flintwinch?" "What do I think of it?" I says. "Yes," he said, "because you're going to take it," he said. "Take it?" I says. "Jere-mi-ah?" Oh! he's a clever one!'

Mrs Flintwinch went on to spread the upper sheet over the bed, and the blanket over that, and the counterpane over that, as if she had quite concluded her story.

'Well?' said Arthur again.

'Well?' echoed Mrs Flintwinch again. 'How could I help myself? He said to me, "Affery, you and me must be married, and I'll tell you why. She's failing in health, and she'll want pretty constant attendance up in her room, and we shall have to be much with her, and there'll be nobody about now but ourselves when we're away from her, and altogether it will be more convenient. She's of my opinion," he said, "so if you'll put your bonnet on next Monday morning at eight, we'll get it over."' Mrs Flintwinch tucked up the bed.

'Well?'

'Well?' repeated Mrs Flintwinch, 'I think so! I sits me down and says it. Well!—Jeremiah then says to me, "As to banns, next Sunday being the third time of asking (for I've put 'em up a fortnight), is my reason for naming Monday. She'll speak to you about it herself, and now she'll find you prepared, Affery." That same day she spoke to me, and she said, "So, Affery, I understand that you and Jeremiah are going to be married. I am glad of it, and so are you, with reason. It is a very good thing for you, and very welcome under the circumstances to me. He is a sensible man, and a trustworthy man, and a persevering man, and a pious man." What could I say when it had come to that? Why, if it had been—a smothering instead of a wedding,' Mrs Flintwinch cast about in her mind with great pains for this form of expression, 'I couldn't have said a word upon it, against them two clever ones.'

'In good faith, I believe so.'

'And so you may, Arthur.'

'Affery, what girl was that in my mother's room just now?'

'Girl?' said Mrs Flintwinch in a rather sharp key.

'It was a girl, surely, whom I saw near you—almost hidden in the dark corner?'

'Oh! She? Little Dorrit? She's nothing; she's a whim of—hers.' It was a peculiarity of Affery Flintwinch that she never spoke of Mrs Clennam by name. 'But there's another sort of girls than that about. Have you forgot your old sweetheart? Long and long ago, I'll be bound.'

'I suffered enough from my mother's separating us, to remember her. I recollect her very well.'

'Have you got another?'

'No.'

'Here's news for you, then. She's well to do now, and a widow. And if you like to have her, why you can.'

'And how do you know that, Affery?'

'Them two clever ones have been speaking about it.—There's Jeremiah on the stairs!' She was gone in a moment.

Mrs Flintwinch had introduced into the web that his mind was busily weaving, in that old workshop where the loom of his youth had stood, the last thread wanting to the pattern. The airy folly of a boy's love had found its way even into that house, and he had been as wretched under its hopelessness as if the house had been a castle of romance. Little more than a week ago at Marseilles, the face of the pretty girl from whom he had parted with regret, had had an unusual interest for him, and a tender hold upon him, because of some resemblance, real or imagined, to this first face that had soared out of his gloomy life into the bright glories of fancy. He leaned upon the sill of the long low window, and looking out upon the blackened forest of chimneys again, began to dream; for it had been the uniform tendency of this man's life—so much was wanting in it to think about, so much that might have been better directed and happier to speculate upon—to make him a dreamer, after all.

CHAPTER 4. Mrs Flintwinch has a Dream

When Mrs Flintwinch dreamed, she usually dreamed, unlike the son of her old mistress, with her eyes shut. She had a curiously vivid dream that night, and before she had left the son of her old mistress many hours. In fact it was not at all like a dream; it was so very real in every respect. It happened in this wise.

The bed-chamber occupied by Mr and Mrs Flintwinch was within a few paces of that to which Mrs Clennam had been so long confined. It was not on the same floor, for it was a room at the side of the house, which was approached by a steep descent of a few odd steps, diverging from the main staircase nearly opposite to Mrs Clennam's door. It could scarcely be said to be within call, the walls, doors, and panelling of the old place were so cumbrous; but it was within easy reach, in any undress, at any hour of the night, in any temperature. At the head of the bed and within a foot of Mrs Flintwinch's ear, was a bell, the line of which hung ready to Mrs Clennam's hand. Whenever this bell rang, up started Affery, and was in the sick room before she was awake.

Having got her mistress into bed, lighted her lamp, and given her good night, Mrs Flintwinch went to roost as usual, saving that her lord had not yet appeared. It was her lord himself who became—unlike the last theme in the mind, according to the observation of most philosophers—the subject of Mrs Flintwinch's dream.

It seemed to her that she awoke after sleeping some hours, and found Jeremiah not yet abed. That she looked at the candle she had left burning, and, measuring the time like King Alfred the Great, was confirmed by its wasted state in her belief that she had been asleep for some considerable period. That she arose thereupon, muffled herself up in a wrapper, put on her shoes, and went out on the staircase, much surprised, to look for Jeremiah.

The staircase was as wooden and solid as need be, and Affery went straight down it without any of those deviations peculiar to dreams. She did not skim over it, but walked down it, and guided herself by the banisters on account of her candle having died out. In one corner of the hall, behind the house-door, there was a little waiting-room, like a well-shaft, with a long narrow window in it as if it had been ripped up. In this room, which was never used, a light was burning.

Mrs Flintwinch crossed the hall, feeling its pavement cold to her stockingless feet, and peeped in between the rusty hinges on the door, which stood a little open. She expected to see Jeremiah fast asleep or in a fit, but he was calmly seated in a chair, awake, and in his usual health. But what—hey?—Lord forgive us!—Mrs Flintwinch muttered some ejaculation to this effect, and turned giddy.

For, Mr Flintwinch awake, was watching Mr Flintwinch asleep. He sat on one side of the small table, looking keenly at himself on the other side with his chin sunk on his breast, snoring. The waking Flintwinch had his full front face presented to his wife; the sleeping Flintwinch was in profile. The waking Flintwinch was the old original; the sleeping Flintwinch was the double, just as she might have distinguished between a tangible object and its reflection in a glass, Affery made out this difference with her head going round and round.

If she had had any doubt which was her own Jeremiah, it would have been resolved by his impatience. He looked about him for an offensive weapon, caught up the snuffers, and, before applying them to the cabbage-headed candle, lunged at the sleeper as though he would have run him through the body.

'Who's that? What's the matter?' cried the sleeper, starting.

Mr Flintwinch made a movement with the snuffers, as if he would have enforced silence on his companion by putting them down his throat; the companion, coming to himself, said, rubbing his eyes, 'I forgot where I was.'

'You have been asleep,' snarled Jeremiah, referring to his watch, 'two hours. You said you would be rested enough if you had a short nap.'

'I have had a short nap,' said Double.

'Half-past two o'clock in the morning,' muttered Jeremiah. 'Where's your hat? Where's your coat? Where's the box?'

'All here,' said Double, tying up his throat with sleepy carefulness in a shawl. 'Stop a minute. Now give me the sleeve—not that sleeve, the other one. Ha! I'm not as young as I was.' Mr Flintwinch had pulled him into his coat with vehement energy. 'You promised me a second glass after I was rested.'

'Drink it!' returned Jeremiah, 'and—choke yourself, I was going to say—but go, I mean.' At the same time he produced the identical port-wine bottle, and filled a wine-glass.

'Her port-wine, I believe?' said Double, tasting it as if he were in the Docks, with hours to spare. 'Her health.'

He took a sip.

'Your health!'

He took another sip.

'His health!'

He took another sip.

'And all friends round St Paul's.' He emptied and put down the wine-glass half-way through this ancient civic toast, and took up the box. It was an iron box some two feet square, which he carried under his arms pretty easily. Jeremiah watched his manner of adjusting it, with jealous eyes; tried it with his hands, to be sure that he had a firm hold of it; bade him for his life be careful what he was about; and then stole out on tiptoe to open the door for him. Affery, anticipating the last movement, was on the staircase. The sequence of things was so ordinary and natural, that, standing there, she could hear the door open, feel the night air, and see the stars outside.

But now came the most remarkable part of the dream. She felt so afraid of her husband, that being on the staircase, she had not the power to retreat to her room (which she might easily have done before he had fastened the door), but stood there staring. Consequently when he came up the staircase to bed, candle in hand, he came full upon her. He looked astonished, but said not a word. He kept his eyes upon her, and kept advancing; and she, completely under his influence, kept retiring before him. Thus, she walking backward and he walking forward, they came into their own room. They were no sooner shut in there, than Mr Flintwinch took her by the throat, and shook her until she was black in the face.

'Why, Affery, woman—Affery!' said Mr Flintwinch. 'What have you been dreaming of? Wake up, wake up! What's the matter?'

'The—the matter, Jeremiah?' gasped Mrs Flintwinch, rolling her eyes.

'Why, Affery, woman—Affery! You have been getting out of bed in your sleep, my dear! I come up, after having fallen asleep myself, below, and find you in your wrapper here, with the nightmare. Affery, woman,' said Mr Flintwinch, with a friendly grin on his expressive countenance, 'if you ever have a dream of this sort again, it'll be a sign of your being in want of physic. And I'll give you such a dose, old woman—such a dose!'

Mrs Flintwinch thanked him and crept into bed.

CHAPTER 5. Family Affairs

As the city clocks struck nine on Monday morning, Mrs Clennam was wheeled by Jeremiah Flintwinch of the cut-down aspect to her tall cabinet. When she had unlocked and opened it, and had settled herself at its desk, Jeremiah withdrew—as it might be, to hang himself more effectually—and her son appeared.

'Are you any better this morning, mother?'

She shook her head, with the same austere air of luxuriousness that she had shown overnight when speaking of the weather. 'I shall never be better any more. It is well for me, Arthur, that I know it and can bear it.'

Sitting with her hands laid separately upon the desk, and the tall cabinet towering before her, she looked as if she were performing on a dumb church organ. Her son thought so (it was an old thought with him), while he took his seat beside it.

She opened a drawer or two, looked over some business papers, and put them back again. Her severe face had no thread of relaxation in it, by which any explorer could have been guided to the gloomy labyrinth of her thoughts.

'Shall I speak of our affairs, mother? Are you inclined to enter upon business?'

'Am I inclined, Arthur? Rather, are you? Your father has been dead a year and more. I have been at your disposal, and waiting your pleasure, ever since.'

'There was much to arrange before I could leave; and when I did leave, I travelled a little for rest and relief.'

She turned her face towards him, as not having heard or understood his last words.

'For rest and relief.'

She glanced round the sombre room, and appeared from the motion of her lips to repeat the words to herself, as calling it to witness how little of either it afforded her.

'Besides, mother, you being sole executrix, and having the direction and management of the estate, there remained little business, or I might say none, that I could transact, until you had had time to arrange matters to your satisfaction.'

'The accounts are made out,' she returned. 'I have them here. The vouchers have all been examined and passed. You can inspect them when you like, Arthur; now, if you please.'

'It is quite enough, mother, to know that the business is completed. Shall I proceed then?'

'Why not?' she said, in her frozen way.

'Mother, our House has done less and less for some years past, and our dealings have been progressively on the decline. We have never shown much confidence, or invited much; we have attached no people to us; the track we have kept is not the track of the time; and we have been left far behind. I need not dwell on this to you, mother. You know it necessarily.'

'I know what you mean,' she answered, in a qualified tone.

'Even this old house in which we speak,' pursued her son, 'is an instance of what I say. In my father's earlier time, and in his uncle's time before him, it was a place of business—really a place of business, and business resort. Now, it is a mere anomaly and incongruity here, out of date and out of purpose. All our consignments have long been made to Rovinghams' the commission-merchants; and although, as a check upon them, and in the stewardship of my father's resources, your judgment and watchfulness have been actively exerted, still those qualities would have influenced my father's fortunes equally, if you had lived in any private dwelling: would they not?'

'Do you consider,' she returned, without answering his question, 'that a house serves no purpose, Arthur, in sheltering your infirm and afflicted—justly infirm and righteously afflicted—mother?'

'I was speaking only of business purposes.'

'With what object?'

'I am coming to it.'

'I foresee,' she returned, fixing her eyes upon him, 'what it is. But the Lord forbid that I should repine under any visitation. In my sinfulness I merit bitter disappointment, and I accept it.'

'Mother, I grieve to hear you speak like this, though I have had my apprehensions that you would—'

'You knew I would. You knew me,' she interrupted.

Her son paused for a moment. He had struck fire out of her, and was surprised. 'Well!' she said, relapsing into stone. 'Go on. Let me hear.'

'You have anticipated, mother, that I decide for my part, to abandon the business. I have done with it. I will not take upon myself to advise you; you will continue it, I see. If I had any influence with you, I would simply use it to soften your judgment of me in causing you this disappointment: to represent to you that I have lived the half of a long term of life, and have never before set my own will against yours. I cannot say that I have been able to conform myself, in heart and spirit, to your rules; I cannot say that I believe my forty years have been profitable or pleasant to myself, or any one; but I have habitually submitted, and I only ask you to remember it.'

Woe to the suppliant, if such a one there were or ever had been, who had any concession to look for in the inexorable face at the cabinet. Woe to the defaulter whose appeal lay to the tribunal where those severe eyes presided. Great need had the rigid woman of her mystical religion, veiled in gloom and darkness, with lightnings of cursing, vengeance, and destruction, flashing through the sable clouds. Forgive us our debts as we forgive our debtors, was a prayer too poor in spirit for her. Smite Thou my debtors, Lord, wither them, crush them; do Thou as I would do, and Thou shalt have my worship: this was the impious tower of stone she built up to scale Heaven.

'Have you finished, Arthur, or have you anything more to say to me? I think there can be nothing else. You have been short, but full of matter!'

'Mother, I have yet something more to say. It has been upon my mind, night and day, this long time. It is far more difficult to say than what I have said. That concerned myself; this concerns us all.'

'Us all! Who are us all?'

'Yourself, myself, my dead father.'

She took her hands from the desk; folded them in her lap; and sat looking towards the fire, with the impenetrability of an old Egyptian sculpture.

'You knew my father infinitely better than I ever knew him; and his reserve with me yielded to you. You were much the stronger, mother, and directed him. As a child, I knew it as well as I know it now. I knew that your ascendancy over him was the cause of his going to China to take care of the business there, while you took care of it here (though I do not even now know whether these were really terms of separation that you agreed upon); and that it was your will that I should remain with you until I was twenty, and then go to him as I did. You will not be offended by my recalling this, after twenty years?'

'I am waiting to hear why you recall it.'

He lowered his voice, and said, with manifest reluctance, and against his will:

'I want to ask you, mother, whether it ever occurred to you to suspect—'

At the word Suspect, she turned her eyes momentarily upon her son, with a dark frown. She then suffered them to seek the fire, as before; but with the frown fixed above them, as if the sculptor of old Egypt had indented it in the hard granite face, to frown for ages.

'—that he had any secret remembrance which caused him trouble of mind—remorse? Whether you ever observed anything in his conduct suggesting that; or ever spoke to him upon it, or ever heard him hint at such a thing?'

'I do not understand what kind of secret remembrance you mean to infer that your father was a prey to,' she returned, after a silence. 'You speak so mysteriously.'

'Is it possible, mother,' her son leaned forward to be the nearer to her while he whispered it, and laid his hand nervously upon her desk, 'is it possible, mother, that he had unhappily wronged any one, and made no reparation?'

Looking at him wrathfully, she bent herself back in her chair to keep him further off, but gave him no reply.

'I am deeply sensible, mother, that if this thought has never at any time flashed upon you, it must seem cruel and unnatural in me, even in this confidence, to breathe it. But I cannot shake it off. Time and change (I have tried both before breaking silence) do nothing to wear it out. Remember, I was with my father. Remember, I saw his face when he gave the watch into my keeping, and struggled to express that he sent it as a token you would understand, to you. Remember, I saw him at the last with the pencil in his failing hand, trying to write some word for you to read, but to which he could give no shape. The more remote and cruel this vague suspicion that I have, the stronger the circumstances that could give it any semblance of probability to me. For Heaven's sake, let us examine sacredly whether there is any wrong entrusted to us to set right. No one can help towards it, mother, but you.'

Still so recoiling in her chair that her overpoised weight moved it, from time to time, a little on its wheels, and gave her the appearance of a phantom of fierce aspect gliding away from him, she interposed her left arm, bent at the elbow with the back of her hand towards her face, between herself and him, and looked at him in a fixed silence.

'In grasping at money and in driving hard bargains—I have begun, and I must speak of such things now, mother—some one may have been grievously deceived, injured, ruined. You were the moving power of all this machinery before my birth; your stronger spirit has been infused into all my father's dealings for more than two score years. You can set these doubts at rest, I think, if you will really help me to discover the truth. Will you, mother?'

He stopped in the hope that she would speak. But her grey hair was not more immovable in its two folds, than were her firm lips.

'If reparation can be made to any one, if restitution can be made to any one, let us know it and make it. Nay, mother, if within my means, let me make it. I have seen so little happiness come of money; it has brought within my knowledge so little peace to this house, or to any one belonging to it, that it is worth less to me than to another. It can buy me nothing that will not be a reproach and misery to me, if I am haunted by a suspicion that it darkened my father's last hours with remorse, and that it is not honestly and justly mine.'

There was a bell-rope hanging on the panelled wall, some two or three yards from the cabinet. By a swift and sudden action of her foot, she drove her wheeled chair rapidly back to it and pulled it violently—still holding her arm up in its shield-like posture, as if he were striking at her, and she warding off the blow.

A girl came hurrying in, frightened.

'Send Flintwinch here!'

In a moment the girl had withdrawn, and the old man stood within the door. 'What! You're hammer and tongs, already, you two?' he said, coolly stroking his face. 'I thought you would be. I was pretty sure of it.'

'Flintwinch!' said the mother, 'look at my son. Look at him!'

'Well, I am looking at him,' said Flintwinch.

She stretched out the arm with which she had shielded herself, and as she went on, pointed at the object of her anger.

'In the very hour of his return almost—before the shoe upon his foot is dry—he asperses his father's memory to his mother! Asks his mother to become, with him, a spy upon his father's transactions through a lifetime! Has misgivings that the goods of this world which we have painfully got together early and late, with wear and tear and toil and self-denial, are so much plunder; and asks to whom they shall be given up, as reparation and restitution!'

Although she said this raging, she said it in a voice so far from being beyond her control that it was even lower than her usual tone. She also spoke with great distinctness.

'Reparation!' said she. 'Yes, truly! It is easy for him to talk of reparation, fresh from journeying and junketing in foreign lands, and living a life of vanity and pleasure. But let him look at me, in prison, and in bonds here. I endure without murmuring, because it is appointed that I shall so make reparation for my sins. Reparation! Is there none in this room? Has there been none here this fifteen years?'

Thus was she always balancing her bargains with the Majesty of heaven, posting up the entries to her credit, strictly keeping her set-off, and claiming her due. She was only remarkable in this, for the force and emphasis with which she did it. Thousands upon thousands do it, according to their varying manner, every day.

'Flintwinch, give me that book!'

The old man handed it to her from the table. She put two fingers between the leaves, closed the book upon them, and held it up to her son in a threatening way.

'In the days of old, Arthur, treated of in this commentary, there were pious men, beloved of the Lord, who would have cursed their sons for less than this: who would have sent them forth, and sent whole nations forth, if such had supported them, to be avoided of God and man, and perish, down to the baby at the breast. But I only tell you that if you ever renew that theme with me, I will renounce you; I will so dismiss you through that doorway, that you had better have been motherless from your cradle. I will never see or know you more. And if, after all, you were to come into this darkened room to look upon me lying dead, my body should bleed, if I could make it, when you came near me.'

In part relieved by the intensity of this threat, and in part (monstrous as the fact is) by a general impression that it was in some sort a religious proceeding, she handed back the book to the old man, and was silent.

'Now,' said Jeremiah; 'premising that I'm not going to stand between you two, will you let me ask (as I have been called in, and made a third) what is all this about?'

'Take your version of it,' returned Arthur, finding it left to him to speak, 'from my mother. Let it rest there. What I have said, was said to my mother only.'

'Oh!' returned the old man. 'From your mother? Take it from your mother? Well! But your mother mentioned that you had been suspecting your father. That's not dutiful, Mr Arthur. Who will you be suspecting next?'

'Enough,' said Mrs Clennam, turning her face so that it was addressed for the moment to the old man only. 'Let no more be said about this.'

'Yes, but stop a bit, stop a bit,' the old man persisted. 'Let us see how we stand. Have you told Mr Arthur that he mustn't lay offences at his father's door? That he has no right to do it? That he has no ground to go upon?'

'I tell him so now.'

'Ah! Exactly,' said the old man. 'You tell him so now. You hadn't told him so before, and you tell him so now. Ay, ay! That's right! You know I stood between you and his father so long, that it seems as if death had made no difference, and I was still standing between you. So I will, and so in fairness I require to have that plainly put forward. Arthur, you please to hear that you have no right to mistrust your father, and have no ground to go upon.'

He put his hands to the back of the wheeled chair, and muttering to himself, slowly wheeled his mistress back to her cabinet. 'Now,' he resumed, standing behind her: 'in case I should go away leaving things half done, and so should be wanted again when you come to the other half and get into one of your flights, has Arthur told you what he means to do about the business?'

'He has relinquished it.'

'In favour of nobody, I suppose?'

Mrs Clennam glanced at her son, leaning against one of the windows. He observed the look and said, 'To my mother, of course. She does what she pleases.'

'And if any pleasure,' she said after a short pause, 'could arise for me out of the disappointment of my expectations that my son, in the prime of his life, would infuse new youth and strength into it, and make it of great profit and power, it would be in advancing an old and faithful servant. Jeremiah, the captain deserts the ship, but you and I will sink or float with it.'

Jeremiah, whose eyes glistened as if they saw money, darted a sudden look at the son, which seemed to say, 'I owe you no thanks for this; you have done nothing towards it!' and then told the mother that he thanked her, and that Affery thanked her, and that he would never desert her, and that Affery would never desert her. Finally, he hauled up his watch from its depths, and said, 'Eleven. Time for your oysters!' and with that change of subject, which involved no change of expression or manner, rang the bell.

But Mrs Clennam, resolved to treat herself with the greater rigour for having been supposed to be unacquainted with reparation, refused to eat her oysters when they were brought. They looked tempting; eight in number, circularly set out on a white plate on a tray covered with a white napkin, flanked by a slice of buttered French roll, and a little compact glass of cool wine and water; but she resisted all persuasions, and sent them down again— placing the act to her credit, no doubt, in her Eternal Day-Book.

This refection of oysters was not presided over by Affery, but by the girl who had appeared when the bell was rung; the same who had been in the dimly-lighted room last night. Now that he had an opportunity of observing her, Arthur found that her diminutive figure, small features, and slight spare dress, gave her the appearance of being much younger than she was. A woman, probably of not less than two-and-twenty, she might have been passed in the street for little more than half that age. Not that her face was very youthful, for in truth there was more consideration and care in it than naturally belonged to her utmost years; but she was so little and light, so noiseless and shy, and appeared so conscious of being out of place among the three hard elders, that she had all the manner and much of the appearance of a subdued child.

In a hard way, and in an uncertain way that fluctuated between patronage and putting down, the sprinkling from a watering-pot and hydraulic pressure, Mrs Clennam showed an interest in this dependent. Even in the moment of her entrance, upon the violent ringing of the bell, when the mother shielded herself with that singular action from the son, Mrs Clennam's eyes had had some individual recognition in them, which seemed reserved for her. As there are degrees of hardness in the hardest metal, and shades of colour in black itself, so, even in the asperity of Mrs Clennam's demeanour towards all the rest of humanity and towards Little Dorrit, there was a fine gradation.

Little Dorrit let herself out to do needlework. At so much a day—or at so little—from eight to eight, Little Dorrit was to be hired. Punctual to the moment, Little Dorrit appeared; punctual to the moment, Little Dorrit vanished. What became of Little Dorrit between the two eights was a mystery.

Another of the moral phenomena of Little Dorrit. Besides her consideration money, her daily contract included meals. She had an extraordinary repugnance to dining in company; would never do so, if it were possible to escape. Would always plead that she had this bit of work to begin first, or that bit of work to finish first; and would, of a certainty, scheme and plan—not very cunningly, it would seem, for she deceived no one—to dine alone. Successful in this, happy in carrying off her plate anywhere, to make a table of her lap, or a box, or the ground, or even as was supposed, to stand on tip-toe, dining moderately at a mantel-shelf; the great anxiety of Little Dorrit's day was set at rest.

It was not easy to make out Little Dorrit's face; she was so retiring, plied her needle in such removed corners, and started away so scared if encountered on the stairs. But it seemed to be a pale transparent face, quick in expression, though not beautiful in feature, its soft hazel eyes excepted. A delicately bent head, a tiny form, a quick little pair of busy hands, and a shabby dress—it must needs have been very shabby to look at all so, being so neat—were Little Dorrit as she sat at work.

For these particulars or generalities concerning Little Dorrit, Mr Arthur was indebted in the course of the day to his own eyes and to Mrs Affery's tongue. If Mrs Affery had had any will or way of her own, it would probably have been unfavourable to Little Dorrit. But as 'them two clever ones'—Mrs Affery's perpetual reference, in whom her personality was swallowed up—were agreed to accept Little Dorrit as a matter of course, she had nothing for it but to follow suit. Similarly, if the two clever ones had agreed to murder Little Dorrit by candlelight, Mrs Affery, being required to hold the candle, would no doubt have done it.

In the intervals of roasting the partridge for the invalid chamber, and preparing a baking-dish of beef and pudding for the dining-room, Mrs Affery made the communications above set forth; invariably putting her head in at the door again after she had taken it out, to enforce resistance to the two clever ones. It appeared to have become a perfect passion with Mrs Flintwinch, that the only son should be pitted against them.

In the course of the day, too, Arthur looked through the whole house. Dull and dark he found it. The gaunt rooms, deserted for years upon years, seemed to have settled down into a gloomy lethargy from which nothing could rouse them again. The furniture, at once spare and lumbering, hid in the rooms rather than furnished them, and there was no colour in all the house; such colour as had ever been there, had long ago started away on lost sunbeams— got itself absorbed, perhaps, into flowers, butterflies, plumage of birds, precious stones, what not. There was not one straight floor from the foundation to the roof; the ceilings were so fantastically clouded by smoke and dust, that old women might have told fortunes in them better than in grouts of tea; the dead-cold hearths showed no traces of having ever been warmed but in heaps of soot that had tumbled down the chimneys, and eddied about in little dusky whirlwinds when the doors were opened. In what had once been a drawing-room, there were a pair of meagre mirrors, with dismal processions of black figures carrying black garlands, walking round the frames; but even these were short of heads and legs, and one undertaker-like Cupid had swung round on its own axis and got upside down, and another had fallen off altogether. The room Arthur Clennam's deceased father had occupied for business purposes, when he first remembered him, was so unaltered that he might have been imagined still to keep it invisibly, as his visible relict kept her room up-stairs; Jeremiah Flintwinch still going between them negotiating.

His picture, dark and gloomy, earnestly speechless on the wall, with the eyes intently looking at his son as they had looked when life departed from them, seemed to urge him awfully to the task he had attempted; but as to any yielding on the part of his mother, he had now no hope, and as to any other means of setting his distrust at rest, he had abandoned hope a long time. Down in the cellars, as up in the bed-chambers, old objects that he well remembered were changed by age and decay, but were still in their old places; even to empty beer-casks hoary with cobwebs, and empty wine-bottles with fur and fungus choking up their throats. There, too, among unusual bottle-racks and pale slants of light from the yard above, was the strong room stored with old ledgers, which had as musty and corrupt a smell as if they were regularly balanced, in the dead small hours, by a nightly resurrection of old book-keepers.

The baking-dish was served up in a penitential manner on a shrunken cloth at an end of the dining-table, at two o'clock, when he dined with Mr Flintwinch, the new partner. Mr Flintwinch informed him that his mother had recovered her equanimity now, and that he need not fear her again alluding to what had passed in the morning. 'And don't you lay offences at your father's door, Mr Arthur,' added Jeremiah, 'once for all, don't do it! Now, we have done with the subject.'

Mr Flintwinch had been already rearranging and dusting his own particular little office, as if to do honour to his accession to new dignity. He resumed this occupation when he was replete with beef, had sucked up all the gravy in the baking-dish with the flat of his knife, and had drawn liberally on a barrel of small beer in the scullery. Thus refreshed, he tucked up his shirt-sleeves and went to work again; and Mr Arthur, watching him as he set about it, plainly saw that his father's picture, or his father's grave, would be as communicative with him as this old man.

'Now, Affery, woman,' said Mr Flintwinch, as she crossed the hall. 'You hadn't made Mr Arthur's bed when I was up there last. Stir yourself. Bustle.'

But Mr Arthur found the house so blank and dreary, and was so unwilling to assist at another implacable consignment of his mother's enemies (perhaps himself among them) to mortal disfigurement and immortal ruin, that he announced his intention of lodging at the coffee-house where he had left his luggage. Mr Flintwinch taking kindly to the idea of getting rid of him, and his mother being indifferent, beyond considerations of saving, to most domestic arrangements that were not bounded by the walls of her own chamber, he easily carried this point without new offence. Daily business hours were agreed upon, which his mother, Mr Flintwinch, and he, were to devote together to a necessary checking of books and papers; and he left the home he had so lately found, with depressed heart.

But Little Dorrit?

The business hours, allowing for intervals of invalid regimen of oysters and partridges, during which Clennam refreshed himself with a walk, were from ten to six for about a fortnight. Sometimes Little Dorrit was employed at her needle, sometimes not, sometimes appeared as a humble visitor: which must have been her character on the occasion of his arrival. His original curiosity augmented every day, as he watched for her, saw or did not see her, and speculated about her. Influenced by his predominant idea, he even fell into a habit of discussing with himself the possibility of her being in some way associated with it. At last he resolved to watch Little Dorrit and know more of her story.

CHAPTER 6. The Father of the Marshalsea

Thirty years ago there stood, a few doors short of the church of Saint George, in the borough of Southwark, on the left-hand side of the way going southward, the Marshalsea Prison. It had stood there many years before, and it remained there some years afterwards; but it is gone now, and the world is none the worse without it.

It was an oblong pile of barrack building, partitioned into squalid houses standing back to back, so that there were no back rooms; environed by a narrow paved yard, hemmed in by high walls duly spiked at top. Itself a close and confined prison for debtors, it contained within it a much closer and more confined jail for smugglers. Offenders against the revenue laws, and defaulters to excise or customs who had incurred fines which they were unable to pay, were supposed to be incarcerated behind an iron-plated door closing up a second prison, consisting of a strong cell or two, and a blind alley some yard and a half wide, which formed the mysterious termination of the very limited skittle-ground in which the Marshalsea debtors bowled down their troubles.

Supposed to be incarcerated there, because the time had rather outgrown the strong cells and the blind alley. In practice they had come to be considered a little too bad, though in theory they were quite as good as ever; which may be observed to be the case at the present day with other cells that are not at all strong, and with other blind alleys that are stone-blind. Hence the smugglers habitually consorted with the debtors (who received them with open arms), except at certain constitutional moments when somebody came from some Office, to go through some form of overlooking something which neither he nor anybody else knew anything about. On these truly British occasions, the smugglers, if any, made a feint of walking into the strong cells and the blind alley, while this somebody pretended to do his something: and made a reality of walking out again as soon as he hadn't done it—neatly epitomising the administration of most of the public affairs in our right little, tight little, island.

There had been taken to the Marshalsea Prison, long before the day when the sun shone on Marseilles and on the opening of this narrative, a debtor with whom this narrative has some concern.

He was, at that time, a very amiable and very helpless middle-aged gentleman, who was going out again directly. Necessarily, he was going out again directly, because the Marshalsea lock never turned upon a debtor who was not. He brought in a portmanteau with him, which he doubted its being worth while to unpack; he was so perfectly clear—like all the rest of them, the turnkey on the lock said—that he was going out again directly.

He was a shy, retiring man; well-looking, though in an effeminate style; with a mild voice, curling hair, and irresolute hands—rings upon the fingers in those days—which nervously wandered to his trembling lip a hundred times in the first half-hour of his acquaintance with the jail. His principal anxiety was about his wife.

'Do you think, sir,' he asked the turnkey, 'that she will be very much shocked, if she should come to the gate to-morrow morning?'

The turnkey gave it as the result of his experience that some of 'em was and some of 'em wasn't. In general, more no than yes. 'What like is she, you see?' he philosophically asked: 'that's what it hinges on.'

'She is very delicate and inexperienced indeed.'

'That,' said the turnkey, 'is agen her.'

'She is so little used to go out alone,' said the debtor, 'that I am at a loss to think how she will ever make her way here, if she walks.'

'P'raps,' quoth the turnkey, 'she'll take a ackney coach.'

'Perhaps.' The irresolute fingers went to the trembling lip. 'I hope she will. She may not think of it.'

'Or p'raps,' said the turnkey, offering his suggestions from the the top of his well-worn wooden stool, as he might have offered them to a child for whose weakness he felt a compassion, 'p'raps she'll get her brother, or her sister, to come along with her.'

'She has no brother or sister.'

'Niece, nevy, cousin, serwant, young 'ooman, greengrocer.—Dash it! One or another on 'em,' said the turnkey, repudiating beforehand the refusal of all his suggestions.

'I fear—I hope it is not against the rules—that she will bring the children.'

'The children?' said the turnkey. 'And the rules? Why, lord set you up like a corner pin, we've a reg'lar playground o' children here. Children! Why we swarm with 'em. How many a you got?'

'Two,' said the debtor, lifting his irresolute hand to his lip again, and turning into the prison.

The turnkey followed him with his eyes. 'And you another,' he observed to himself, 'which makes three on you. And your wife another, I'll lay a crown. Which makes four on you. And another coming, I'll lay half-a-crown. Which'll make five on you. And I'll go another seven and sixpence to name which is the helplessest, the unborn baby or you!'

He was right in all his particulars. She came next day with a little boy of three years old, and a little girl of two, and he stood entirely corroborated.

'Got a room now; haven't you?' the turnkey asked the debtor after a week or two.

'Yes, I have got a very good room.'

'Any little sticks a coming to furnish it?' said the turnkey.

'I expect a few necessary articles of furniture to be delivered by the carrier, this afternoon.'

'Missis and little 'uns a coming to keep you company?' asked the turnkey.

'Why, yes, we think it better that we should not be scattered, even for a few weeks.'

'Even for a few weeks, of course,' replied the turnkey. And he followed him again with his eyes, and nodded his head seven times when he was gone.

The affairs of this debtor were perplexed by a partnership, of which he knew no more than that he had invested money in it; by legal matters of assignment and settlement, conveyance here and conveyance there, suspicion of unlawful preference of creditors in this direction, and of mysterious spiriting away of property in that; and as nobody on the face of the earth could be more incapable of explaining any single item in the heap of confusion than the debtor himself, nothing comprehensible could be made of his case. To question him in detail, and endeavour to reconcile his answers; to closet him with accountants and sharp practitioners, learned in the wiles of insolvency and bankruptcy; was only to put the case out at compound interest and incomprehensibility. The irresolute fingers fluttered more and more ineffectually about the trembling lip on every such occasion, and the sharpest practitioners gave him up as a hopeless job.

'Out?' said the turnkey, 'he'll never get out, unless his creditors take him by the shoulders and shove him out.'

He had been there five or six months, when he came running to this turnkey one forenoon to tell him, breathless and pale, that his wife was ill.

'As anybody might a known she would be,' said the turnkey.

'We intended,' he returned, 'that she should go to a country lodging only to-morrow. What am I to do! Oh, good heaven, what am I to do!'

'Don't waste your time in clasping your hands and biting your fingers,' responded the practical turnkey, taking him by the elbow, 'but come along with me.'

The turnkey conducted him—trembling from head to foot, and constantly crying under his breath, What was he to do! while his irresolute fingers bedabbled the tears upon his face—up one of the common staircases in the prison to a door on the garret story. Upon which door the turnkey knocked with the handle of his key.

'Come in!' cried a voice inside.

The turnkey, opening the door, disclosed in a wretched, ill-smelling little room, two hoarse, puffy, red-faced personages seated at a rickety table, playing at all-fours, smoking pipes, and drinking brandy.

'Doctor,' said the turnkey, 'here's a gentleman's wife in want of you without a minute's loss of time!'

The doctor's friend was in the positive degree of hoarseness, puffiness, red-facedness, all-fours, tobacco, dirt, and brandy; the doctor in the comparative—hoarser, puffier, more red-faced, more all-fourey, tobaccoer, dirtier, and brandier. The doctor was amazingly shabby, in a torn and darned rough-weather sea-jacket, out at elbows and eminently short of buttons (he had been in his time the experienced surgeon carried by a passenger ship), the dirtiest white trousers conceivable by mortal man, carpet slippers, and no visible linen. 'Childbed?' said the doctor. 'I'm the boy!' With that the doctor took a comb from the chimney-piece and stuck his hair upright—which appeared to be his way of washing himself—produced a professional chest or case, of most abject appearance, from the cupboard where his cup and saucer and coals were, settled his chin in the frowsy wrapper round his neck, and became a ghastly medical scarecrow.

The doctor and the debtor ran down-stairs, leaving the turnkey to return to the lock, and made for the debtor's room. All the ladies in the prison had got hold of the news, and were in the yard. Some of them had already taken possession of the two children, and were hospitably carrying them off; others were offering loans of little comforts from their own scanty store; others were sympathising with the greatest volubility. The gentlemen prisoners, feeling themselves at a disadvantage, had for the most part retired, not to say sneaked, to their rooms; from the open windows of which some of them now complimented the doctor with whistles as he passed below, while others, with several stories between them, interchanged sarcastic references to the prevalent excitement.

It was a hot summer day, and the prison rooms were baking between the high walls. In the debtor's confined chamber, Mrs Bangham, charwoman and messenger, who was not a prisoner (though she had been once), but was the popular medium of communication with the outer world, had volunteered her services as fly-catcher and general attendant. The walls and ceiling were blackened with flies. Mrs Bangham, expert in sudden device, with one hand fanned the patient with a cabbage leaf, and with the other set traps of vinegar and sugar in gallipots; at the same time enunciating sentiments of an encouraging and congratulatory nature, adapted to the occasion.

'The flies trouble you, don't they, my dear?' said Mrs Bangham. 'But p'raps they'll take your mind off of it, and do you good. What between the buryin ground, the grocer's, the waggon-stables, and the paunch trade, the Marshalsea flies gets very large. P'raps they're sent as a consolation, if we only know'd it. How are you now, my dear? No better? No, my dear, it ain't to be expected; you'll be worse before you're better, and you know it, don't you? Yes. That's right! And to think of a sweet little cherub being born inside the lock! Now ain't it pretty, ain't that something to carry you through it pleasant? Why, we ain't had such a thing happen here, my dear, not for I couldn't name the time when. And you a crying too?' said Mrs Bangham, to rally the patient more and more. 'You! Making yourself so famous! With the flies a falling into the gallipots by fifties! And everything a going on so well! And here if there ain't,' said Mrs Bangham as the door opened, 'if there ain't your dear gentleman along with Dr Haggage! And now indeed we are complete, I think!'

The doctor was scarcely the kind of apparition to inspire a patient with a sense of absolute completeness, but as he presently delivered the opinion, 'We are as right as we can be, Mrs Bangham, and we shall come out of this like a house afire;' and as he and Mrs Bangham took possession of the poor helpless pair, as everybody else and anybody else had always done, the means at hand were as good on the whole as better would have been. The special feature in Dr Haggage's treatment of the case, was his determination to keep Mrs Bangham up to the mark. As thus:

'Mrs Bangham,' said the doctor, before he had been there twenty minutes, 'go outside and fetch a little brandy, or we shall have you giving in.'

'Thank you, sir. But none on my accounts,' said Mrs Bangham.

'Mrs Bangham,' returned the doctor, 'I am in professional attendance on this lady, and don't choose to allow any discussion on your part. Go outside and fetch a little brandy, or I foresee that you'll break down.'

'You're to be obeyed, sir,' said Mrs Bangham, rising. 'If you was to put your own lips to it, I think you wouldn't be the worse, for you look but poorly, sir.'

'Mrs Bangham,' returned the doctor, 'I am not your business, thank you, but you are mine. Never you mind me, if you please. What you have got to do, is, to do as you are told, and to go and get what I bid you.'

Mrs Bangham submitted; and the doctor, having administered her potion, took his own. He repeated the treatment every hour, being very determined with Mrs Bangham. Three or four hours passed; the flies fell into the traps by hundreds; and at length one little life, hardly stronger than theirs, appeared among the multitude of lesser deaths.

'A very nice little girl indeed,' said the doctor; 'little, but well-formed. Halloa, Mrs Bangham! You're looking queer! You be off, ma'am, this minute, and fetch a little more brandy, or we shall have you in hysterics.'

By this time, the rings had begun to fall from the debtor's irresolute hands, like leaves from a wintry tree. Not one was left upon them that night, when he put something that chinked into the doctor's greasy palm. In the meantime Mrs Bangham had been out on an errand to a neighbouring establishment decorated with three golden balls, where she was very well known.

'Thank you,' said the doctor, 'thank you. Your good lady is quite composed. Doing charmingly.'

'I am very happy and very thankful to know it,' said the debtor, 'though I little thought once, that—'

'That a child would be born to you in a place like this?' said the doctor. 'Bah, bah, sir, what does it signify? A little more elbow-room is all we want here. We are quiet here; we don't get badgered here; there's no knocker here, sir, to be hammered at by creditors and bring a man's heart into his mouth. Nobody comes here to ask if a man's at home, and to say he'll stand on the door mat till he is. Nobody writes threatening letters about money to this place. It's freedom, sir, it's freedom! I have had to-day's practice at home and abroad, on a march, and aboard ship, and I'll tell you this: I don't know that I have ever pursued it under such quiet circumstances as here this day. Elsewhere, people are restless, worried, hurried about, anxious respecting one thing, anxious respecting another. Nothing of the kind here, sir. We have done all that—we know the worst of it; we have got to the bottom, we can't fall, and what have we found? Peace. That's the word for it. Peace.' With this profession of faith, the doctor, who was an old jail-bird, and was more sodden than usual, and had the additional and unusual stimulus of money in his pocket, returned to his associate and chum in hoarseness, puffiness, red-facedness, all-fours, tobacco, dirt, and brandy.

Now, the debtor was a very different man from the doctor, but he had already begun to travel, by his opposite segment of the circle, to the same point. Crushed at first by his imprisonment, he had soon found a dull relief in it. He was under lock and key; but the lock and key that kept him in, kept numbers of his troubles out. If he had been a man with strength of purpose to face those troubles and fight them, he might have broken the net that held him, or broken his heart; but being what he was, he languidly slipped into this smooth descent, and never more took one step upward.

When he was relieved of the perplexed affairs that nothing would make plain, through having them returned upon his hands by a dozen agents in succession who could make neither beginning, middle, nor end of them or him, he found his miserable place of refuge a quieter refuge than it had been before. He had unpacked the portmanteau long ago; and his elder children now played regularly about the yard, and everybody knew the baby, and claimed a kind of proprietorship in her.

'Why, I'm getting proud of you,' said his friend the turnkey, one day. 'You'll be the oldest inhabitant soon. The Marshalsea wouldn't be like the Marshalsea now, without you and your family.'

The turnkey really was proud of him. He would mention him in laudatory terms to new-comers, when his back was turned. 'You took notice of him,' he would say, 'that went out of the lodge just now?'

New-comer would probably answer Yes.

'Brought up as a gentleman, he was, if ever a man was. Ed'cated at no end of expense. Went into the Marshal's house once to try a new piano for him. Played it, I understand, like one o'clock—beautiful! As to languages—speaks anything. We've had a Frenchman here in his time, and it's my opinion he knowed more French than the Frenchman did. We've had an Italian here in his time, and he shut him up in about half a minute. You'll find some characters behind other locks, I don't say you won't; but if you want the top sawyer in such respects as I've mentioned, you must come to the Marshalsea.'

When his youngest child was eight years old, his wife, who had long been languishing away—of her own inherent weakness, not that she retained any greater sensitiveness as to her place of abode than he did—went upon a visit to a poor friend and old nurse in the country, and died there. He remained shut up in his room for a fortnight afterwards; and an attorney's clerk, who was going through the Insolvent Court, engrossed an address of condolence to him, which looked like a Lease, and which all the prisoners signed. When he appeared again he was greyer (he had soon begun to turn grey); and the turnkey noticed that his hands went often to his trembling lips again, as they had used to do when he first came in. But he got pretty well over it in a month or two; and in the meantime the children played about the yard as regularly as ever, but in black.

Then Mrs Bangham, long popular medium of communication with the outer world, began to be infirm, and to be found oftener than usual comatose on pavements, with her basket of purchases spilt, and the change of her clients ninepence short. His son began to supersede Mrs Bangham, and to execute commissions in a knowing manner, and to be of the prison prisonous, of the streets streety.

Time went on, and the turnkey began to fail. His chest swelled, and his legs got weak, and he was short of breath. The well-worn wooden stool was 'beyond him,' he complained. He sat in an arm-chair with a cushion, and sometimes wheezed so, for minutes together, that he couldn't turn the key. When he was overpowered by these fits, the debtor often turned it for him.

'You and me,' said the turnkey, one snowy winter's night when the lodge, with a bright fire in it, was pretty full of company, 'is the oldest inhabitants. I wasn't here myself above seven year before you. I shan't last long. When I'm off the lock for good and all, you'll be the Father of the Marshalsea.'

The turnkey went off the lock of this world next day. His words were remembered and repeated; and tradition afterwards handed down from generation to generation—a Marshalsea generation might be calculated as about three months—that the shabby old debtor with the soft manner and the white hair, was the Father of the Marshalsea.

And he grew to be proud of the title. If any impostor had arisen to claim it, he would have shed tears in resentment of the attempt to deprive him of his rights. A disposition began to be perceived in him to exaggerate the number of years he had been there; it was generally understood that you must deduct a few from his account; he was vain, the fleeting generations of debtors said.

All new-comers were presented to him. He was punctilious in the exaction of this ceremony. The wits would perform the office of introduction with overcharged pomp and politeness, but they could not easily overstep his sense of its gravity. He received them in his poor room (he disliked an introduction in the mere yard, as informal—a thing that might happen to anybody), with a kind of bowed-down beneficence. They were welcome to the Marshalsea, he would tell them. Yes, he was the Father of the place. So the world was kind enough to call him; and so he was, if more than twenty years of residence gave him a claim to the title. It looked small at first, but there was very good company there—among a mixture—necessarily a mixture—and very good air.

It became a not unusual circumstance for letters to be put under his door at night, enclosing half-a-crown, two half-crowns, now and then at long intervals even half-a-sovereign, for the Father of the Marshalsea. 'With the compliments of a collegian taking leave.' He received the gifts as tributes, from admirers, to a public character. Sometimes these correspondents assumed facetious names, as the Brick, Bellows, Old Gooseberry, Wideawake, Snooks, Mops, Cutaway, the Dogs-meat Man; but he considered this in bad taste, and was always a little hurt by it.

In the fulness of time, this correspondence showing signs of wearing out, and seeming to require an effort on the part of the correspondents to which in the hurried circumstances of departure many of them might not be equal, he established the custom of attending collegians of a certain standing, to the gate, and taking leave of them there. The collegian under treatment, after shaking hands, would occasionally stop to wrap up something in a bit of paper, and would come back again calling 'Hi!'

He would look round surprised. 'Me?' he would say, with a smile.

By this time the collegian would be up with him, and he would paternally add, 'What have you forgotten? What can I do for you?'

'I forgot to leave this,' the collegian would usually return, 'for the Father of the Marshalsea.'

'My good sir,' he would rejoin, 'he is infinitely obliged to you.' But, to the last, the irresolute hand of old would remain in the pocket into which he had slipped the money during two or three turns about the yard, lest the transaction should be too conspicuous to the general body of collegians.

One afternoon he had been doing the honours of the place to a rather large party of collegians, who happened to be going out, when, as he was coming back, he encountered one from the poor side who had been taken in execution for a small sum a week before, had 'settled' in the course of that afternoon, and was going out too. The man was a mere Plasterer in his working dress; had his wife with him, and a bundle; and was in high spirits.

'God bless you, sir,' he said in passing.

'And you,' benignantly returned the Father of the Marshalsea.

They were pretty far divided, going their several ways, when the Plasterer called out, 'I say!—sir!' and came back to him.

'It ain't much,' said the Plasterer, putting a little pile of halfpence in his hand, 'but it's well meant.'

The Father of the Marshalsea had never been offered tribute in copper yet. His children often had, and with his perfect acquiescence it had gone into the common purse to buy meat that he had eaten, and drink that he had drunk; but fustian splashed with white lime, bestowing halfpence on him, front to front, was new.

'How dare you!' he said to the man, and feebly burst into tears.

The Plasterer turned him towards the wall, that his face might not be seen; and the action was so delicate, and the man was so penetrated with repentance, and asked pardon so honestly, that he could make him no less acknowledgment than, 'I know you meant it kindly. Say no more.'

'Bless your soul, sir,' urged the Plasterer, 'I did indeed. I'd do more by you than the rest of 'em do, I fancy.'

'What would you do?' he asked.

'I'd come back to see you, after I was let out.'

'Give me the money again,' said the other, eagerly, 'and I'll keep it, and never spend it. Thank you for it, thank you! I shall see you again?'

'If I live a week you shall.'

They shook hands and parted. The collegians, assembled in Symposium in the Snuggery that night, marvelled what had happened to their Father; he walked so late in the shadows of the yard, and seemed so downcast.

CHAPTER 7. The Child of the Marshalsea

The baby whose first draught of air had been tinctured with Doctor Haggage's brandy, was handed down among the generations of collegians, like the tradition of their common parent. In the earlier stages of her existence, she was handed down in a literal and prosaic sense; it being almost a part of the entrance footing of every new collegian to nurse the child who had been born in the college.

'By rights,' remarked the turnkey when she was first shown to him, 'I ought to be her godfather.'

The debtor irresolutely thought of it for a minute, and said, 'Perhaps you wouldn't object to really being her godfather?'

'Oh! I don't object,' replied the turnkey, 'if you don't.'

Thus it came to pass that she was christened one Sunday afternoon, when the turnkey, being relieved, was off the lock; and that the turnkey went up to the font of Saint George's Church, and promised and vowed and renounced on her behalf, as he himself related when he came back, 'like a good 'un.'

This invested the turnkey with a new proprietary share in the child, over and above his former official one. When she began to walk and talk, he became fond of her; bought a little arm-chair and stood it by the high fender of the lodge fire-place; liked to have her company when he was on the lock; and used to bribe her with cheap toys to come and talk to him. The child, for her part, soon grew so fond of the turnkey that she would come climbing up the lodge-steps of her own accord at all hours of the day. When she fell asleep in the little armchair by the high fender, the turnkey would cover her with his pocket-handkerchief; and when she sat in it dressing and undressing a doll which soon came to be unlike dolls on the other side of the lock, and to bear a horrible family resemblance to Mrs Bangham—he would contemplate her from the top of his stool with exceeding gentleness. Witnessing these things, the collegians would express an opinion that the turnkey, who was a bachelor, had been cut out by nature for a family man. But the turnkey thanked them, and said, 'No, on the whole it was enough to see other people's children there.'

At what period of her early life the little creature began to perceive that it was not the habit of all the world to live locked up in narrow yards surrounded by high walls with spikes at the top, would be a difficult question to settle. But she was a very, very little creature indeed, when she had somehow gained the knowledge that her clasp of her father's hand was to be always loosened at the door which the great key opened; and that while her own light steps were free to pass beyond it, his feet must never cross that line. A pitiful and plaintive look, with which she had begun to regard him when she was still extremely young, was perhaps a part of this discovery.

With a pitiful and plaintive look for everything, indeed, but with something in it for only him that was like protection, this Child of the Marshalsea and the child of the Father of the Marshalsea, sat by her friend the turnkey in the lodge, kept the family room, or wandered about the prison-yard, for the first eight years of her life. With a pitiful and plaintive look for her wayward sister; for her idle brother; for the high blank walls; for the faded crowd they shut in; for the games of the prison children as they whooped and ran, and played at hide-and-seek, and made the iron bars of the inner gateway 'Home.'

Wistful and wondering, she would sit in summer weather by the high fender in the lodge, looking up at the sky through the barred window, until, when she turned her eyes away, bars of light would arise between her and her friend, and she would see him through a grating, too.

'Thinking of the fields,' the turnkey said once, after watching her, 'ain't you?'

'Where are they?' she inquired.

'Why, they're—over there, my dear,' said the turnkey, with a vague flourish of his key. 'Just about there.'

'Does anybody open them, and shut them? Are they locked?'

The turnkey was discomfited. 'Well,' he said. 'Not in general.'

'Are they very pretty, Bob?' She called him Bob, by his own particular request and instruction.

'Lovely. Full of flowers. There's buttercups, and there's daisies, and there's'—the turnkey hesitated, being short of floral nomenclature—'there's dandelions, and all manner of games.'

'Is it very pleasant to be there, Bob?'

'Prime,' said the turnkey.

'Was father ever there?'

'Hem!' coughed the turnkey. 'O yes, he was there, sometimes.'

'Is he sorry not to be there now?'

'N-not particular,' said the turnkey.

'Nor any of the people?' she asked, glancing at the listless crowd within. 'O are you quite sure and certain, Bob?'

At this difficult point of the conversation Bob gave in, and changed the subject to hard-bake: always his last resource when he found his little friend getting him into a political, social, or theological corner. But this was the origin of a series of Sunday excursions that these two curious companions made together. They used to issue from the lodge on alternate Sunday afternoons with great gravity, bound for some meadows or green lanes that had been elaborately appointed by the turnkey in the course of the week; and there she picked grass and flowers to bring home, while he smoked his pipe. Afterwards, there were tea-gardens, shrimps, ale, and other delicacies; and then they would come back hand in hand, unless she was more than usually tired, and had fallen asleep on his shoulder.

In those early days, the turnkey first began profoundly to consider a question which cost him so much mental labour, that it remained undetermined on the day of his death. He decided to will and bequeath his little property of savings to his godchild, and the point arose how could it be so 'tied up' as that only she should have the benefit of it? His experience on the lock gave him such an acute perception of the enormous difficulty of 'tying up' money with any approach to tightness, and contrariwise of the remarkable ease with which it got loose, that through a series of years he regularly propounded this knotty point to every new insolvent agent and other professional gentleman who passed in and out.

'Supposing,' he would say, stating the case with his key on the professional gentleman's waistcoat; 'supposing a man wanted to leave his property to a young female, and wanted to tie it up so that nobody else should ever be able to make a grab at it; how would you tie up that property?'

'Settle it strictly on herself,' the professional gentleman would complacently answer.

'But look here,' quoth the turnkey. 'Supposing she had, say a brother, say a father, say a husband, who would be likely to make a grab at that property when she came into it—how about that?'

'It would be settled on herself, and they would have no more legal claim on it than you,' would be the professional answer.

'Stop a bit,' said the turnkey. 'Supposing she was tender-hearted, and they came over her. Where's your law for tying it up then?'

The deepest character whom the turnkey sounded, was unable to produce his law for tying such a knot as that. So, the turnkey thought about it all his life, and died intestate after all.

But that was long afterwards, when his god-daughter was past sixteen. The first half of that space of her life was only just accomplished, when her pitiful and plaintive look saw her father a widower. From that time the protection that her wondering eyes had expressed towards him, became embodied in action, and the Child of the Marshalsea took upon herself a new relation towards the Father.

At first, such a baby could do little more than sit with him, deserting her livelier place by the high fender, and quietly watching him. But this made her so far necessary to him that he became accustomed to her, and began to be sensible of missing her when she was not there. Through this little gate, she passed out of childhood into the care-laden world.

What her pitiful look saw, at that early time, in her father, in her sister, in her brother, in the jail; how much, or how little of the wretched truth it pleased God to make visible to her; lies hidden with many mysteries. It is enough that she was inspired to be something which was not what the rest were, and to be that something, different and laborious, for the sake of the rest. Inspired? Yes. Shall we speak of the inspiration of a poet or a priest, and not of the heart impelled by love and self-devotion to the lowliest work in the lowliest way of life!

With no earthly friend to help her, or so much as to see her, but the one so strangely assorted; with no knowledge even of the common daily tone and habits of the common members of the free community who are not shut up in prisons; born and bred in a social condition, false even with a reference to the falsest condition outside the walls; drinking from infancy of a well whose waters had their own peculiar stain, their own unwholesome and unnatural taste; the Child of the Marshalsea began her womanly life.

No matter through what mistakes and discouragements, what ridicule (not unkindly meant, but deeply felt) of her youth and little figure, what humble consciousness of her own babyhood and want of strength, even in the matter of lifting and carrying; through how much weariness and hopelessness, and how many secret tears; she drudged on, until recognised as useful, even indispensable. That time came. She took the place of eldest of the three, in all things but precedence; was the head of the fallen family; and bore, in her own heart, its anxieties and shames.

At thirteen, she could read and keep accounts, that is, could put down in words and figures how much the bare necessaries that they wanted would cost, and how much less they had to buy them with. She had been, by snatches of a few weeks at a time, to an evening school outside, and got her sister and brother sent to day-schools by desultory starts, during three or four years. There was no instruction for any of them at home; but she knew well—no one better—that a man so broken as to be the Father of the Marshalsea, could be no father to his own children.

To these scanty means of improvement, she added another of her own contriving. Once, among the heterogeneous crowd of inmates there appeared a dancing-master. Her sister had a great desire to learn the dancing-master's art, and seemed to have a taste that way. At thirteen years old, the Child of the Marshalsea presented herself to the dancing-master, with a little bag in her hand, and preferred her humble petition.

'If you please, I was born here, sir.'

'Oh! You are the young lady, are you?' said the dancing-master, surveying the small figure and uplifted face.

'Yes, sir.'

'And what can I do for you?' said the dancing-master.

'Nothing for me, sir, thank you,' anxiously undrawing the strings of the little bag; 'but if, while you stay here, you could be so kind as to teach my sister cheap—'

'My child, I'll teach her for nothing,' said the dancing-master, shutting up the bag. He was as good-natured a dancing-master as ever danced to the Insolvent Court, and he kept his word. The sister was so apt a pupil, and the dancing-master had such abundant leisure to bestow upon her (for it took him a matter of ten weeks to set to his creditors, lead off, turn the Commissioners, and right and left back to his professional pursuits), that wonderful progress was made. Indeed the dancing-master was so proud of it, and so wishful to display it before he left to a few select friends among the collegians, that at six o'clock on a certain fine morning, a minuet de la cour came off in the yard—the college-rooms being of too confined proportions for the purpose—in which so much ground was covered, and the steps were so conscientiously executed, that the dancing-master, having to play the kit besides, was thoroughly blown.

The success of this beginning, which led to the dancing-master's continuing his instruction after his release, emboldened the poor child to try again. She watched and waited months for a seamstress. In the fulness of time a milliner came in, and to her she repaired on her own behalf.

'I beg your pardon, ma'am,' she said, looking timidly round the door of the milliner, whom she found in tears and in bed: 'but I was born here.'

Everybody seemed to hear of her as soon as they arrived; for the milliner sat up in bed, drying her eyes, and said, just as the dancing-master had said:

'Oh! You are the child, are you?'

'Yes, ma'am.'

'I am sorry I haven't got anything for you,' said the milliner, shaking her head.

'It's not that, ma'am. If you please I want to learn needle-work.'

'Why should you do that,' returned the milliner, 'with me before you? It has not done me much good.'

'Nothing—whatever it is—seems to have done anybody much good who comes here,' she returned in all simplicity; 'but I want to learn just the same.'

'I am afraid you are so weak, you see,' the milliner objected.

'I don't think I am weak, ma'am.'

'And you are so very, very little, you see,' the milliner objected.

'Yes, I am afraid I am very little indeed,' returned the Child of the Marshalsea; and so began to sob over that unfortunate defect of hers, which came so often in her way. The milliner—who was not morose or hard-hearted, only newly insolvent—was touched, took her in hand with goodwill, found her the most patient and earnest of pupils, and made her a cunning work-woman in course of time.

In course of time, and in the very self-same course of time, the Father of the Marshalsea gradually developed a new flower of character. The more Fatherly he grew as to the Marshalsea, and the more dependent he became on the contributions of his changing family, the greater stand he made by his forlorn gentility. With the same hand that he pocketed a collegian's half-crown half an hour ago, he would wipe away the tears that streamed over his cheeks if any reference were made to his daughters' earning their bread. So, over and above other daily cares, the Child of the Marshalsea had always upon her the care of preserving the genteel fiction that they were all idle beggars together.

The sister became a dancer. There was a ruined uncle in the family group—ruined by his brother, the Father of the Marshalsea, and knowing no more how than his ruiner did, but accepting the fact as an inevitable certainty—on whom her protection devolved. Naturally a retired and simple man, he had shown no particular sense of being ruined at the time when that calamity fell upon him, further than that he left off washing himself when the shock was announced, and never took to that luxury any more. He had been a very indifferent musical amateur in his better days; and when he fell with his brother, resorted for support to playing a clarionet as dirty as himself in a small Theatre Orchestra. It was the theatre in which his niece became a dancer; he had been a fixture there a long time when she took her poor station in it; and he accepted the task of serving as her escort and guardian, just as he would have accepted an illness, a legacy, a feast, starvation—anything but soap.

To enable this girl to earn her few weekly shillings, it was necessary for the Child of the Marshalsea to go through an elaborate form with the Father.

'Fanny is not going to live with us just now, father. She will be here a good deal in the day, but she is going to live outside with uncle.'

'You surprise me. Why?'

'I think uncle wants a companion, father. He should be attended to, and looked after.'

'A companion? He passes much of his time here. And you attend to him and look after him, Amy, a great deal more than ever your sister will. You all go out so much; you all go out so much.'

This was to keep up the ceremony and pretence of his having no idea that Amy herself went out by the day to work.

'But we are always glad to come home, father; now, are we not? And as to Fanny, perhaps besides keeping uncle company and taking care of him, it may be as well for her not quite to live here, always. She was not born here as I was, you know, father.'

'Well, Amy, well. I don't quite follow you, but it's natural I suppose that Fanny should prefer to be outside, and even that you often should, too. So, you and Fanny and your uncle, my dear, shall have your own way. Good, good. I'll not meddle; don't mind me.'

To get her brother out of the prison; out of the succession to Mrs Bangham in executing commissions, and out of the slang interchange with very doubtful companions consequent upon both; was her hardest task. At eighteen he would have dragged on from hand to mouth, from hour to hour, from penny to penny, until eighty. Nobody got into the prison from whom he derived anything useful or good, and she could find no patron for him but her old friend and godfather.

'Dear Bob,' said she, 'what is to become of poor Tip?' His name was Edward, and Ted had been transformed into Tip, within the walls.

The turnkey had strong private opinions as to what would become of poor Tip, and had even gone so far with the view of averting their fulfilment, as to sound Tip in reference to the expediency of running away and going to serve his country. But Tip had thanked him, and said he didn't seem to care for his country.

'Well, my dear,' said the turnkey, 'something ought to be done with him. Suppose I try and get him into the law?'

'That would be so good of you, Bob!'

The turnkey had now two points to put to the professional gentlemen as they passed in and out. He put this second one so perseveringly that a stool and twelve shillings a week were at last found for Tip in the office of an attorney in a great National Palladium called the Palace Court; at that time one of a considerable list of everlasting bulwarks to the dignity and safety of Albion, whose places know them no more.

Tip languished in Clifford's Inns for six months, and at the expiration of that term sauntered back one evening with his hands in his pockets, and incidentally observed to his sister that he was not going back again.

'Not going back again?' said the poor little anxious Child of the Marshalsea, always calculating and planning for Tip, in the front rank of her charges.

'I am so tired of it,' said Tip, 'that I have cut it.'

Tip tired of everything. With intervals of Marshalsea lounging, and Mrs Bangham succession, his small second mother, aided by her trusty friend, got him into a warehouse, into a market garden, into the hop trade, into the law again, into an auctioneers, into a brewery, into a stockbroker's, into the law again, into a coach office, into a waggon office, into the law again, into a general dealer's, into a distillery, into the law again, into a wool house, into a dry goods house, into the Billingsgate trade, into the foreign fruit trade, and into the docks. But whatever Tip went into, he came out of tired, announcing that he had cut it. Wherever he went, this foredoomed Tip appeared to take the prison walls with him, and to set them up in such trade or calling; and to prowl about within their narrow limits in the old slip-shod, purposeless, down-at-heel way; until the real immovable Marshalsea walls asserted their fascination over him, and brought him back.

Nevertheless, the brave little creature did so fix her heart on her brother's rescue, that while he was ringing out these doleful changes, she pinched and scraped enough together to ship him for Canada. When he was tired of nothing to do, and disposed in its turn to cut even that, he graciously consented to go to Canada. And there was grief in her bosom over parting with him, and joy in the hope of his being put in a straight course at last.

'God bless you, dear Tip. Don't be too proud to come and see us, when you have made your fortune.'

'All right!' said Tip, and went.

But not all the way to Canada; in fact, not further than Liverpool. After making the voyage to that port from London, he found himself so strongly impelled to cut the vessel, that he resolved to walk back again. Carrying out which intention, he presented himself before her at the expiration of a month, in rags, without shoes, and much more tired than ever.

At length, after another interval of successorship to Mrs Bangham, he found a pursuit for himself, and announced it.

'Amy, I have got a situation.'

'Have you really and truly, Tip?'

'All right. I shall do now. You needn't look anxious about me any more, old girl.'

'What is it, Tip?'

'Why, you know Slingo by sight?'

'Not the man they call the dealer?'

'That's the chap. He'll be out on Monday, and he's going to give me a berth.'

'What is he a dealer in, Tip?'

'Horses. All right! I shall do now, Amy.'

She lost sight of him for months afterwards, and only heard from him once. A whisper passed among the elder collegians that he had been seen at a mock auction in Moorfields, pretending to buy plated articles for massive silver, and paying for them with the greatest liberality in bank notes; but it never reached her ears. One evening she was alone at work—standing up at the window, to save the twilight lingering above the wall—when he opened the door and walked in.

She kissed and welcomed him; but was afraid to ask him any questions. He saw how anxious and timid she was, and appeared sorry.

'I am afraid, Amy, you'll be vexed this time. Upon my life I am!'

'I am very sorry to hear you say so, Tip. Have you come back?'

'Why—yes.'

'Not expecting this time that what you had found would answer very well, I am less surprised and sorry than I might have been, Tip.'

'Ah! But that's not the worst of it.'

'Not the worst of it?'

'Don't look so startled. No, Amy, not the worst of it. I have come back, you see; but—don't look so startled—I have come back in what I may call a new way. I am off the volunteer list altogether. I am in now, as one of the regulars.'

'Oh! Don't say you are a prisoner, Tip! Don't, don't!'

'Well, I don't want to say it,' he returned in a reluctant tone; 'but if you can't understand me without my saying it, what am I to do? I am in for forty pound odd.'

For the first time in all those years, she sunk under her cares. She cried, with her clasped hands lifted above her head, that it would kill their father if he ever knew it; and fell down at Tip's graceless feet.

It was easier for Tip to bring her to her senses than for her to bring him to understand that the Father of the Marshalsea would be beside himself if he knew the truth. The thing was incomprehensible to Tip, and altogether a fanciful notion. He yielded to it in that light only, when he submitted to her entreaties, backed by those of his uncle and sister. There was no want of precedent for his return; it was accounted for to the father in the usual way; and the collegians, with a better comprehension of the pious fraud than Tip, supported it loyally.

This was the life, and this the history, of the child of the Marshalsea at twenty-two. With a still surviving attachment to the one miserable yard and block of houses as her birthplace and home, she passed to and fro in it shrinkingly now, with a womanly consciousness that she was pointed out to every one. Since she had begun to work beyond the walls, she had found it necessary to conceal where she lived, and to come and go as secretly as she could, between the free city and the iron gates, outside of which she had never slept in her life. Her original timidity had grown with this concealment, and her light step and her little figure shunned the thronged streets while they passed along them.

Worldly wise in hard and poor necessities, she was innocent in all things else. Innocent, in the mist through which she saw her father, and the prison, and the turbid living river that flowed through it and flowed on.

This was the life, and this the history, of Little Dorrit; now going home upon a dull September evening, observed at a distance by Arthur Clennam. This was the life, and this the history, of Little Dorrit; turning at the end of London Bridge, recrossing it, going back again, passing on to Saint George's Church, turning back suddenly once more, and flitting in at the open outer gate and little court-yard of the Marshalsea.

CHAPTER 8. The Lock

Arthur Clennam stood in the street, waiting to ask some passer-by what place that was. He suffered a few people to pass him in whose face there was no encouragement to make the inquiry, and still stood pausing in the street, when an old man came up and turned into the courtyard.

He stooped a good deal, and plodded along in a slow pre-occupied manner, which made the bustling London thoroughfares no very safe resort for him. He was dirtily and meanly dressed, in a threadbare coat, once blue, reaching to his ankles and buttoned to his chin, where it vanished in the pale ghost of a velvet collar. A piece of red cloth with which that phantom had been stiffened in its lifetime was now laid bare, and poked itself up, at the back of the old man's neck, into a confusion of grey hair and rusty stock and buckle which altogether nearly poked his hat off. A greasy hat it was, and a napless; impending over his eyes, cracked and crumpled at the brim, and with a wisp of pocket-handkerchief dangling out below it. His trousers were so long and loose, and his shoes so clumsy and large, that he shuffled like an elephant; though how much of this was gait, and how much trailing cloth and leather, no one could have told. Under one arm he carried a limp and worn-out case, containing some wind instrument; in the same hand he had a pennyworth of snuff in a little packet of whitey-brown paper, from which he slowly comforted his poor blue old nose with a lengthened-out pinch, as Arthur Clennam looked at him.

To this old man crossing the court-yard, he preferred his inquiry, touching him on the shoulder. The old man stopped and looked round, with the expression in his weak grey eyes of one whose thoughts had been far off, and who was a little dull of hearing also.

'Pray, sir,' said Arthur, repeating his question, 'what is this place?'

'Ay! This place?' returned the old man, staying his pinch of snuff on its road, and pointing at the place without looking at it. 'This is the Marshalsea, sir.'

'The debtors' prison?'

'Sir,' said the old man, with the air of deeming it not quite necessary to insist upon that designation, 'the debtors' prison.'

He turned himself about, and went on.

'I beg your pardon,' said Arthur, stopping him once more, 'but will you allow me to ask you another question? Can any one go in here?'

'Any one can go in,' replied the old man; plainly adding by the significance of his emphasis, 'but it is not every one who can go out.'

'Pardon me once more. Are you familiar with the place?'

'Sir,' returned the old man, squeezing his little packet of snuff in his hand, and turning upon his interrogator as if such questions hurt him. 'I am.'

'I beg you to excuse me. I am not impertinently curious, but have a good object. Do you know the name of Dorrit here?'

'My name, sir,' replied the old man most unexpectedly, 'is Dorrit.'

Arthur pulled off his hat to him. 'Grant me the favour of half-a-dozen words. I was wholly unprepared for your announcement, and hope that assurance is my sufficient apology for having taken the liberty of addressing you. I have recently come home to England after a long absence. I have seen at my mother's—Mrs Clennam in the city—a young woman working at her needle, whom I have only heard addressed or spoken of as Little Dorrit. I have felt sincerely interested in her, and have had a great desire to know something more about her. I saw her, not a minute before you came up, pass in at that door.'

The old man looked at him attentively. 'Are you a sailor, sir?' he asked. He seemed a little disappointed by the shake of the head that replied to him. 'Not a sailor? I judged from your sunburnt face that you might be. Are you in earnest, sir?'

'I do assure you that I am, and do entreat you to believe that I am, in plain earnest.'

'I know very little of the world, sir,' returned the other, who had a weak and quavering voice. 'I am merely passing on, like the shadow over the sun-dial. It would be worth no man's while to mislead me; it would really be too easy—too poor a success, to yield any satisfaction. The young woman whom you saw go in here is my brother's child. My brother is William Dorrit; I am Frederick. You say you have seen her at your mother's (I know your mother befriends her), you have felt an interest in her, and you wish to know what she does here. Come and see.'

He went on again, and Arthur accompanied him.

'My brother,' said the old man, pausing on the step and slowly facing round again, 'has been here many years; and much that happens even among ourselves, out of doors, is kept from him for reasons that I needn't enter upon now. Be so good as to say nothing of my niece's working at her needle. Be so good as to say nothing that goes beyond what is said among us. If you keep within our bounds, you cannot well be wrong. Now! Come and see.'

Arthur followed him down a narrow entry, at the end of which a key was turned, and a strong door was opened from within. It admitted them into a lodge or lobby, across which they passed, and so through another door and a grating into the prison. The old man always plodding on before, turned round, in his slow, stiff, stooping manner, when they came to the turnkey on duty, as if to present his companion. The turnkey nodded; and the companion passed in without being asked whom he wanted.

The night was dark; and the prison lamps in the yard, and the candles in the prison windows faintly shining behind many sorts of wry old curtain and blind, had not the air of making it lighter. A few people loitered about, but the greater part of the population was within doors. The old man, taking the right-hand side of the yard, turned in at the third or fourth doorway, and began to ascend the stairs. 'They are rather dark, sir, but you will not find anything in the way.'

He paused for a moment before opening a door on the second story. He had no sooner turned the handle than the visitor saw Little Dorrit, and saw the reason of her setting so much store by dining alone.

She had brought the meat home that she should have eaten herself, and was already warming it on a gridiron over the fire for her father, clad in an old grey gown and a black cap, awaiting his supper at the table. A clean cloth was spread before him, with knife, fork, and spoon, salt-cellar, pepper-box, glass, and pewter ale-pot. Such zests as his particular little phial of cayenne pepper and his pennyworth of pickles in a saucer, were not wanting.

She started, coloured deeply, and turned white. The visitor, more with his eyes than by the slight impulsive motion of his hand, entreated her to be reassured and to trust him.

'I found this gentleman,' said the uncle—'Mr Clennam, William, son of Amy's friend—at the outer gate, wishful, as he was going by, of paying his respects, but hesitating whether to come in or not. This is my brother William, sir.'

'I hope,' said Arthur, very doubtful what to say, 'that my respect for your daughter may explain and justify my desire to be presented to you, sir.'

70

'Mr Clennam,' returned the other, rising, taking his cap off in the flat of his hand, and so holding it, ready to put on again, 'you do me honour. You are welcome, sir;' with a low bow. 'Frederick, a chair. Pray sit down, Mr Clennam.'

He put his black cap on again as he had taken it off, and resumed his own seat. There was a wonderful air of benignity and patronage in his manner. These were the ceremonies with which he received the collegians.

'You are welcome to the Marshalsea, sir. I have welcomed many gentlemen to these walls. Perhaps you are aware—my daughter Amy may have mentioned that I am the Father of this place.'

'I—so I have understood,' said Arthur, dashing at the assertion.

'You know, I dare say, that my daughter Amy was born here. A good girl, sir, a dear girl, and long a comfort and support to me. Amy, my dear, put this dish on; Mr Clennam will excuse the primitive customs to which we are reduced here. Is it a compliment to ask you if you would do me the honour, sir, to—'

'Thank you,' returned Arthur. 'Not a morsel.'

He felt himself quite lost in wonder at the manner of the man, and that the probability of his daughter's having had a reserve as to her family history, should be so far out of his mind.

She filled his glass, put all the little matters on the table ready to his hand, and then sat beside him while he ate his supper. Evidently in observance of their nightly custom, she put some bread before herself, and touched his glass with her lips; but Arthur saw she was troubled and took nothing. Her look at her father, half admiring him and proud of him, half ashamed for him, all devoted and loving, went to his inmost heart.

The Father of the Marshalsea condescended towards his brother as an amiable, well-meaning man; a private character, who had not arrived at distinction. 'Frederick,' said he, 'you and Fanny sup at your lodgings to-night, I know. What have you done with Fanny, Frederick?'

'She is walking with Tip.'

'Tip—as you may know—is my son, Mr Clennam. He has been a little wild, and difficult to settle, but his introduction to the world was rather'—he shrugged his shoulders with a faint sigh, and looked round the room—'a little adverse. Your first visit here, sir?'

'My first.'

'You could hardly have been here since your boyhood without my knowledge. It very seldom happens that anybody—of any pretensions—any pretensions—comes here without being presented to me.'

'As many as forty or fifty in a day have been introduced to my brother,' said Frederick, faintly lighting up with a ray of pride.

'Yes!' the Father of the Marshalsea assented. 'We have even exceeded that number. On a fine Sunday in term time, it is quite a Levee—quite a Levee. Amy, my dear, I have been trying half the day to remember the name of the gentleman from Camberwell who was introduced to me last Christmas week by that agreeable coal-merchant who was remanded for six months.'

'I don't remember his name, father.'

'Frederick, do you remember his name?'

Frederick doubted if he had ever heard it. No one could doubt that Frederick was the last person upon earth to put such a question to, with any hope of information.

'I mean,' said his brother, 'the gentleman who did that handsome action with so much delicacy. Ha! Tush! The name has quite escaped me. Mr Clennam, as I have happened to mention handsome and delicate action, you may like, perhaps, to know what it was.'

'Very much,' said Arthur, withdrawing his eyes from the delicate head beginning to droop and the pale face with a new solicitude stealing over it.

'It is so generous, and shows so much fine feeling, that it is almost a duty to mention it. I said at the time that I always would mention it on every suitable occasion, without regard to personal sensitiveness. A—well—a—it's of no use to disguise the fact—you must know, Mr Clennam, that it does sometimes occur that people who come here desire to offer some little— Testimonial—to the Father of the place.'

To see her hand upon his arm in mute entreaty half-repressed, and her timid little shrinking figure turning away, was to see a sad, sad sight.

'Sometimes,' he went on in a low, soft voice, agitated, and clearing his throat every now and then; 'sometimes—hem—it takes one shape and sometimes another; but it is generally— ha—Money. And it is, I cannot but confess it, it is too often—hem—acceptable. This gentleman that I refer to, was presented to me, Mr Clennam, in a manner highly gratifying to my feelings, and conversed not only with great politeness, but with great—ahem—information.' All this time, though he had finished his supper, he was nervously going about his plate with his knife and fork, as if some of it were still before him. 'It appeared from his conversation that he had a garden, though he was delicate of mentioning it at first, as gardens are—hem—are not accessible to me. But it came out, through my admiring a very fine cluster of geranium— beautiful cluster of geranium to be sure—which he had brought from his conservatory. On my taking notice of its rich colour, he showed me a piece of paper round it, on which was written, "For the Father of the Marshalsea," and presented it to me. But this was—hem—not all. He made a particular request, on taking leave, that I would remove the paper in half an hour. I—ha—I did so; and I found that it contained—ahem—two guineas. I assure you, Mr Clennam, I have received—hem—Testimonials in many ways, and of many degrees of value, and they have always been—ha—unfortunately acceptable; but I never was more pleased than with this—ahem—this particular Testimonial.'

Arthur was in the act of saying the little he could say on such a theme, when a bell began to ring, and footsteps approached the door. A pretty girl of a far better figure and much more developed than Little Dorrit, though looking much younger in the face when the two were observed together, stopped in the doorway on seeing a stranger; and a young man who was with her, stopped too.

'Mr Clennam, Fanny. My eldest daughter and my son, Mr Clennam. The bell is a signal for visitors to retire, and so they have come to say good night; but there is plenty of time, plenty of time. Girls, Mr Clennam will excuse any household business you may have together. He knows, I dare say, that I have but one room here.'

'I only want my clean dress from Amy, father,' said the second girl.

'And I my clothes,' said Tip.

Amy opened a drawer in an old piece of furniture that was a chest of drawers above and a bedstead below, and produced two little bundles, which she handed to her brother and sister. 'Mended and made up?' Clennam heard the sister ask in a whisper. To which Amy answered 'Yes.' He had risen now, and took the opportunity of glancing round the room. The bare walls had been coloured green, evidently by an unskilled hand, and were poorly decorated with a few prints. The window was curtained, and the floor carpeted; and there were shelves and pegs, and other such conveniences, that had accumulated in the course of years. It was a close, confined room, poorly furnished; and the chimney smoked to boot, or the tin screen at the top of the fireplace was superfluous; but constant pains and care had made it neat, and even, after its kind, comfortable.

All the while the bell was ringing, and the uncle was anxious to go. 'Come, Fanny, come, Fanny,' he said, with his ragged clarionet case under his arm; 'the lock, child, the lock!'

Fanny bade her father good night, and whisked off airily. Tip had already clattered down-stairs. 'Now, Mr Clennam,' said the uncle, looking back as he shuffled out after them, 'the lock, sir, the lock.'

Mr Clennam had two things to do before he followed; one, to offer his testimonial to the Father of the Marshalsea, without giving pain to his child; the other to say something to that child, though it were but a word, in explanation of his having come there.

'Allow me,' said the Father, 'to see you down-stairs.'

She had slipped out after the rest, and they were alone. 'Not on any account,' said the visitor, hurriedly. 'Pray allow me to—' chink, chink, chink.

'Mr Clennam,' said the Father, 'I am deeply, deeply—' But his visitor had shut up his hand to stop the clinking, and had gone down-stairs with great speed.

He saw no Little Dorrit on his way down, or in the yard. The last two or three stragglers were hurrying to the lodge, and he was following, when he caught sight of her in the doorway of the first house from the entrance. He turned back hastily.

'Pray forgive me,' he said, 'for speaking to you here; pray forgive me for coming here at all! I followed you to-night. I did so, that I might endeavour to render you and your family some service. You know the terms on which I and my mother are, and may not be surprised that I have preserved our distant relations at her house, lest I should unintentionally make her jealous, or resentful, or do you any injury in her estimation. What I have seen here, in this short time, has greatly increased my heartfelt wish to be a friend to you. It would recompense me for much disappointment if I could hope to gain your confidence.'

She was scared at first, but seemed to take courage while he spoke to her.

'You are very good, sir. You speak very earnestly to me. But I—but I wish you had not watched me.'

He understood the emotion with which she said it, to arise in her father's behalf; and he respected it, and was silent.

'Mrs Clennam has been of great service to me; I don't know what we should have done without the employment she has given me; I am afraid it may not be a good return to become secret with her; I can say no more to-night, sir. I am sure you mean to be kind to us. Thank you, thank you.'

'Let me ask you one question before I leave. Have you known my mother long?'

'I think two years, sir,—The bell has stopped.'

'How did you know her first? Did she send here for you?'

'No. She does not even know that I live here. We have a friend, father and I—a poor labouring man, but the best of friends—and I wrote out that I wished to do needlework, and gave his address. And he got what I wrote out displayed at a few places where it cost nothing, and Mrs Clennam found me that way, and sent for me. The gate will be locked, sir!'

She was so tremulous and agitated, and he was so moved by compassion for her, and by deep interest in her story as it dawned upon him, that he could scarcely tear himself away. But the stoppage of the bell, and the quiet in the prison, were a warning to depart; and with a few hurried words of kindness he left her gliding back to her father.

But he remained too late. The inner gate was locked, and the lodge closed. After a little fruitless knocking with his hand, he was standing there with the disagreeable conviction upon him that he had got to get through the night, when a voice accosted him from behind.

'Caught, eh?' said the voice. 'You won't go home till morning. Oh! It's you, is it, Mr Clennam?'

The voice was Tip's; and they stood looking at one another in the prison-yard, as it began to rain.

'You've done it,' observed Tip; 'you must be sharper than that next time.'

'But you are locked in too,' said Arthur.

'I believe I am!' said Tip, sarcastically. 'About! But not in your way. I belong to the shop, only my sister has a theory that our governor must never know it. I don't see why, myself.'

'Can I get any shelter?' asked Arthur. 'What had I better do?'

'We had better get hold of Amy first of all,' said Tip, referring any difficulty to her as a matter of course.

'I would rather walk about all night—it's not much to do—than give that trouble.'

'You needn't do that, if you don't mind paying for a bed. If you don't mind paying, they'll make you up one on the Snuggery table, under the circumstances. If you'll come along, I'll introduce you there.'

As they passed down the yard, Arthur looked up at the window of the room he had lately left, where the light was still burning. 'Yes, sir,' said Tip, following his glance. 'That's the governor's. She'll sit with him for another hour reading yesterday's paper to him, or something of that sort; and then she'll come out like a little ghost, and vanish away without a sound.'

'I don't understand you.'

'The governor sleeps up in the room, and she has a lodging at the turnkey's. First house there,' said Tip, pointing out the doorway into which she had retired. 'First house, sky parlour. She pays twice as much for it as she would for one twice as good outside. But she stands by the governor, poor dear girl, day and night.'

This brought them to the tavern-establishment at the upper end of the prison, where the collegians had just vacated their social evening club. The apartment on the ground-floor in which it was held, was the Snuggery in question; the presidential tribune of the chairman, the pewter-pots, glasses, pipes, tobacco-ashes, and general flavour of members, were still as that convivial institution had left them on its adjournment. The Snuggery had two of the qualities popularly held to be essential to grog for ladies, in respect that it was hot and strong; but in the third point of analogy, requiring plenty of it, the Snuggery was defective; being but a cooped-up apartment.

The unaccustomed visitor from outside, naturally assumed everybody here to be prisoners—landlord, waiter, barmaid, potboy, and all. Whether they were or not, did not appear; but they all had a weedy look. The keeper of a chandler's shop in a front parlour, who took in gentlemen boarders, lent his assistance in making the bed. He had been a tailor in his time, and had kept a phaeton, he said. He boasted that he stood up litigiously for the interests of the college; and he had undefined and undefinable ideas that the marshal intercepted a 'Fund,' which ought to come to the collegians. He liked to believe this, and always impressed the shadowy grievance on new-comers and strangers; though he could not, for his life, have explained what Fund he meant, or how the notion had got rooted in his soul. He had fully convinced himself, notwithstanding, that his own proper share of the Fund was three and ninepence a week; and that in this amount he, as an individual collegian, was swindled by the marshal, regularly every Monday. Apparently, he helped to make the bed, that he might not lose an opportunity of stating this case; after which unloading of his mind, and after announcing (as it seemed he always did, without anything coming of it) that he was going to write a letter to the papers and show the marshal up, he fell into miscellaneous conversation with the rest. It was evident from the general tone of the whole party, that they had come to regard insolvency as the normal state of mankind, and the payment of debts as a disease that occasionally broke out.

In this strange scene, and with these strange spectres flitting about him, Arthur Clennam looked on at the preparations as if they were part of a dream. Pending which, the long-initiated Tip, with an awful enjoyment of the Snuggery's resources, pointed out the common kitchen fire maintained by subscription of collegians, the boiler for hot water supported in like manner, and other premises generally tending to the deduction that the way to be healthy, wealthy, and wise, was to come to the Marshalsea.

The two tables put together in a corner, were, at length, converted into a very fair bed; and the stranger was left to the Windsor chairs, the presidential tribune, the beery atmosphere, sawdust, pipe-lights, spittoons and repose. But the last item was long, long, long, in linking itself to the rest. The novelty of the place, the coming upon it without preparation, the sense of being locked up, the remembrance of that room up-stairs, of the two brothers, and above all of the retiring childish form, and the face in which he now saw years of insufficient food, if not of want, kept him waking and unhappy.

Speculations, too, bearing the strangest relations towards the prison, but always concerning the prison, ran like nightmares through his mind while he lay awake. Whether coffins were kept ready for people who might die there, where they were kept, how they were kept, where people who died in the prison were buried, how they were taken out, what forms were observed, whether an implacable creditor could arrest the dead? As to escaping, what chances there were of escape? Whether a prisoner could scale the walls with a cord and grapple, how he would descend upon the other side? whether he could alight on a housetop, steal down a staircase, let himself out at a door, and get lost in the crowd? As to Fire in the prison, if one were to break out while he lay there?

And these involuntary starts of fancy were, after all, but the setting of a picture in which three people kept before him. His father, with the steadfast look with which he had died, prophetically darkened forth in the portrait; his mother, with her arm up, warding off his suspicion; Little Dorrit, with her hand on the degraded arm, and her drooping head turned away.

What if his mother had an old reason she well knew for softening to this poor girl! What if the prisoner now sleeping quietly—Heaven grant it!—by the light of the great Day of judgment should trace back his fall to her. What if any act of hers and of his father's, should have even remotely brought the grey heads of those two brothers so low!

A swift thought shot into his mind. In that long imprisonment here, and in her own long confinement to her room, did his mother find a balance to be struck? 'I admit that I was accessory to that man's captivity. I have suffered for it in kind. He has decayed in his prison: I in mine. I have paid the penalty.'

When all the other thoughts had faded out, this one held possession of him. When he fell asleep, she came before him in her wheeled chair, warding him off with this justification. When he awoke, and sprang up causelessly frightened, the words were in his ears, as if her voice had slowly spoken them at his pillow, to break his rest: 'He withers away in his prison; I wither away in mine; inexorable justice is done; what do I owe on this score!'

CHAPTER 9. Little Mother

The morning light was in no hurry to climb the prison wall and look in at the Snuggery windows; and when it did come, it would have been more welcome if it had come alone, instead of bringing a rush of rain with it. But the equinoctial gales were blowing out at sea, and the impartial south-west wind, in its flight, would not neglect even the narrow Marshalsea. While it roared through the steeple of St George's Church, and twirled all the cowls in the neighbourhood, it made a swoop to beat the Southwark smoke into the jail; and, plunging down the chimneys of the few early collegians who were yet lighting their fires, half suffocated them.

Arthur Clennam would have been little disposed to linger in bed, though his bed had been in a more private situation, and less affected by the raking out of yesterday's fire, the kindling of to-day's under the collegiate boiler, the filling of that Spartan vessel at the pump, the sweeping and sawdusting of the common room, and other such preparations. Heartily glad to see the morning, though little rested by the night, he turned out as soon as he could distinguish objects about him, and paced the yard for two heavy hours before the gate was opened.

The walls were so near to one another, and the wild clouds hurried over them so fast, that it gave him a sensation like the beginning of sea-sickness to look up at the gusty sky. The rain, carried aslant by flaws of wind, blackened that side of the central building which he had visited last night, but left a narrow dry trough under the lee of the wall, where he walked up and down among the waifs of straw and dust and paper, the waste droppings of the pump, and the stray leaves of yesterday's greens. It was as haggard a view of life as a man need look upon.

Nor was it relieved by any glimpse of the little creature who had brought him there. Perhaps she glided out of her doorway and in at that where her father lived, while his face was turned from both; but he saw nothing of her. It was too early for her brother; to have seen him once, was to have seen enough of him to know that he would be sluggish to leave whatever frowsy bed he occupied at night; so, as Arthur Clennam walked up and down, waiting for the gate to open, he cast about in his mind for future rather than for present means of pursuing his discoveries.

At last the lodge-gate turned, and the turnkey, standing on the step, taking an early comb at his hair, was ready to let him out. With a joyful sense of release he passed through the lodge, and found himself again in the little outer court-yard where he had spoken to the brother last night.

There was a string of people already straggling in, whom it was not difficult to identify as the nondescript messengers, go-betweens, and errand-bearers of the place. Some of them had been lounging in the rain until the gate should open; others, who had timed their arrival with greater nicety, were coming up now, and passing in with damp whitey-brown paper bags from the grocers, loaves of bread, lumps of butter, eggs, milk, and the like. The shabbiness of these attendants upon shabbiness, the poverty of these insolvent waiters upon insolvency, was a sight to see. Such threadbare coats and trousers, such fusty gowns and shawls, such squashed hats and bonnets, such boots and shoes, such umbrellas and walking-sticks, never were seen in Rag Fair. All of them wore the cast-off clothes of other men and women, were made up of patches and pieces of other people's individuality, and had no sartorial existence of their own proper. Their walk was the walk of a race apart. They had a peculiar way of doggedly slinking round the corner, as if they were eternally going to the pawnbroker's. When they coughed, they coughed like people accustomed to be forgotten on doorsteps and in draughty passages, waiting for answers to letters in faded ink, which gave the recipients of those manuscripts great mental disturbance and no satisfaction. As they eyed the stranger in passing, they eyed him with borrowing eyes—hungry, sharp, speculative as to his softness if they were accredited to him, and the likelihood of his standing something handsome. Mendicity on commission stooped in their high shoulders, shambled in their unsteady legs, buttoned and pinned and darned and dragged their clothes, frayed their button-holes, leaked out of their figures in dirty little ends of tape, and issued from their mouths in alcoholic breathings.

As these people passed him standing still in the court-yard, and one of them turned back to inquire if he could assist him with his services, it came into Arthur Clennam's mind that he would speak to Little Dorrit again before he went away. She would have recovered her first surprise, and might feel easier with him. He asked this member of the fraternity (who had two red herrings in his hand, and a loaf and a blacking brush under his arm), where was the nearest place to get a cup of coffee at. The nondescript replied in encouraging terms, and brought him to a coffee-shop in the street within a stone's throw.

'Do you know Miss Dorrit?' asked the new client.

The nondescript knew two Miss Dorrits; one who was born inside—That was the one! That was the one? The nondescript had known her many years. In regard of the other Miss Dorrit, the nondescript lodged in the same house with herself and uncle.

This changed the client's half-formed design of remaining at the coffee-shop until the nondescript should bring him word that Dorrit had issued forth into the street. He entrusted the nondescript with a confidential message to her, importing that the visitor who had waited on her father last night, begged the favour of a few words with her at her uncle's lodging; he obtained from the same source full directions to the house, which was very near; dismissed the nondescript gratified with half-a-crown; and having hastily refreshed himself at the coffee-shop, repaired with all speed to the clarionet-player's dwelling.

There were so many lodgers in this house that the doorpost seemed to be as full of bell-handles as a cathedral organ is of stops. Doubtful which might be the clarionet-stop, he was considering the point, when a shuttlecock flew out of the parlour window, and alighted on his hat. He then observed that in the parlour window was a blind with the inscription, MR CRIPPLES's ACADEMY; also in another line, EVENING TUITION; and behind the blind was a little white-faced boy, with a slice of bread-and-butter and a battledore. The window being accessible from the footway, he looked in over the blind, returned the shuttlecock, and put his question.

'Dorrit?' said the little white-faced boy (Master Cripples in fact). 'Mr Dorrit? Third bell and one knock.'

The pupils of Mr Cripples appeared to have been making a copy-book of the street-door, it was so extensively scribbled over in pencil. The frequency of the inscriptions, 'Old Dorrit,' and 'Dirty Dick,' in combination, suggested intentions of personality on the part Of Mr Cripples's pupils. There was ample time to make these observations before the door was opened by the poor old man himself.

'Ha!' said he, very slowly remembering Arthur, 'you were shut in last night?'

'Yes, Mr Dorrit. I hope to meet your niece here presently.'

'Oh!' said he, pondering. 'Out of my brother's way? True. Would you come up-stairs and wait for her?'

'Thank you.'

Turning himself as slowly as he turned in his mind whatever he heard or said, he led the way up the narrow stairs. The house was very close, and had an unwholesome smell. The little staircase windows looked in at the back windows of other houses as unwholesome as itself, with poles and lines thrust out of them, on which unsightly linen hung; as if the inhabitants were angling for clothes, and had had some wretched bites not worth attending to. In the back garret—a sickly room, with a turn-up bedstead in it, so hastily and recently turned up that the blankets were boiling over, as it were, and keeping the lid open—a half-finished breakfast of coffee and toast for two persons was jumbled down anyhow on a rickety table.

There was no one there. The old man mumbling to himself, after some consideration, that Fanny had run away, went to the next room to fetch her back. The visitor, observing that she held the door on the inside, and that, when the uncle tried to open it, there was a sharp adjuration of 'Don't, stupid!' and an appearance of loose stocking and flannel, concluded that the young lady was in an undress. The uncle, without appearing to come to any conclusion, shuffled in again, sat down in his chair, and began warming his hands at the fire; not that it was cold, or that he had any waking idea whether it was or not.

'What did you think of my brother, sir?' he asked, when he by-and-by discovered what he was doing, left off, reached over to the chimney-piece, and took his clarionet case down.

'I was glad,' said Arthur, very much at a loss, for his thoughts were on the brother before him; 'to find him so well and cheerful.'

'Ha!' muttered the old man, 'yes, yes, yes, yes, yes!'

Arthur wondered what he could possibly want with the clarionet case. He did not want it at all. He discovered, in due time, that it was not the little paper of snuff (which was also on the chimney-piece), put it back again, took down the snuff instead, and solaced himself with a pinch. He was as feeble, spare, and slow in his pinches as in everything else, but a certain little trickling of enjoyment of them played in the poor worn nerves about the corners of his eyes and mouth.

'Amy, Mr Clennam. What do you think of her?'

'I am much impressed, Mr Dorrit, by all that I have seen of her and thought of her.'

'My brother would have been quite lost without Amy,' he returned. 'We should all have been lost without Amy. She is a very good girl, Amy. She does her duty.'

Arthur fancied that he heard in these praises a certain tone of custom, which he had heard from the father last night with an inward protest and feeling of antagonism. It was not that they stinted her praises, or were insensible to what she did for them; but that they were lazily habituated to her, as they were to all the rest of their condition. He fancied that although they had before them, every day, the means of comparison between her and one another and themselves, they regarded her as being in her necessary place; as holding a position towards them all which belonged to her, like her name or her age. He fancied that they viewed her, not as having risen away from the prison atmosphere, but as appertaining to it; as being vaguely what they had a right to expect, and nothing more.

Her uncle resumed his breakfast, and was munching toast sopped in coffee, oblivious of his guest, when the third bell rang. That was Amy, he said, and went down to let her in; leaving the visitor with as vivid a picture on his mind of his begrimed hands, dirt-worn face, and decayed figure, as if he were still drooping in his chair.

She came up after him, in the usual plain dress, and with the usual timid manner. Her lips were a little parted, as if her heart beat faster than usual.

'Mr Clennam, Amy,' said her uncle, 'has been expecting you some time.'

'I took the liberty of sending you a message.'

'I received the message, sir.'

'Are you going to my mother's this morning? I think not, for it is past your usual hour.'

'Not to-day, sir. I am not wanted to-day.'

'Will you allow Me to walk a little way in whatever direction you may be going? I can then speak to you as we walk, both without detaining you here, and without intruding longer here myself.'

She looked embarrassed, but said, if he pleased. He made a pretence of having mislaid his walking-stick, to give her time to set the bedstead right, to answer her sister's impatient knock at the wall, and to say a word softly to her uncle. Then he found it, and they went down-stairs; she first, he following; the uncle standing at the stair-head, and probably forgetting them before they had reached the ground floor.

Mr Cripples's pupils, who were by this time coming to school, desisted from their morning recreation of cuffing one another with bags and books, to stare with all the eyes they had at a stranger who had been to see Dirty Dick. They bore the trying spectacle in silence, until the mysterious visitor was at a safe distance; when they burst into pebbles and yells, and likewise into reviling dances, and in all respects buried the pipe of peace with so many savage ceremonies, that, if Mr Cripples had been the chief of the Cripplewayboo tribe with his war-paint on, they could scarcely have done greater justice to their education.

In the midst of this homage, Mr Arthur Clennam offered his arm to Little Dorrit, and Little Dorrit took it. 'Will you go by the Iron Bridge,' said he, 'where there is an escape from the noise of the street?' Little Dorrit answered, if he pleased, and presently ventured to hope that he would 'not mind' Mr Cripples's boys, for she had herself received her education, such as it was, in Mr Cripples's evening academy. He returned, with the best will in the world, that Mr Cripples's boys were forgiven out of the bottom of his soul. Thus did Cripples unconsciously become a master of the ceremonies between them, and bring them more naturally together than Beau Nash might have done if they had lived in his golden days, and he had alighted from his coach and six for the purpose.

The morning remained squally, and the streets were miserably muddy, but no rain fell as they walked towards the Iron Bridge. The little creature seemed so young in his eyes, that there were moments when he found himself thinking of her, if not speaking to her, as if she were a child. Perhaps he seemed as old in her eyes as she seemed young in his.

'I am sorry to hear you were so inconvenienced last night, sir, as to be locked in. It was very unfortunate.'

It was nothing, he returned. He had had a very good bed.

'Oh yes!' she said quickly; 'she believed there were excellent beds at the coffee-house.' He noticed that the coffee-house was quite a majestic hotel to her, and that she treasured its reputation.

'I believe it is very expensive,' said Little Dorrit, 'but my father has told me that quite beautiful dinners may be got there. And wine,' she added timidly.

'Were you ever there?'

'Oh no! Only into the kitchen to fetch hot water.'

To think of growing up with a kind of awe upon one as to the luxuries of that superb establishment, the Marshalsea Hotel!

'I asked you last night,' said Clennam, 'how you had become acquainted with my mother. Did you ever hear her name before she sent for you?'

'No, sir.'

'Do you think your father ever did?'

'No, sir.'

He met her eyes raised to his with so much wonder in them (she was scared when the encounter took place, and shrunk away again), that he felt it necessary to say:

'I have a reason for asking, which I cannot very well explain; but you must, on no account, suppose it to be of a nature to cause you the least alarm or anxiety. Quite the reverse. And you think that at no time of your father's life was my name of Clennam ever familiar to him?'

'No, sir.'

He felt, from the tone in which she spoke, that she was glancing up at him with those parted lips; therefore he looked before him, rather than make her heart beat quicker still by embarrassing her afresh.

Thus they emerged upon the Iron Bridge, which was as quiet after the roaring streets as though it had been open country. The wind blew roughly, the wet squalls came rattling past them, skimming the pools on the road and pavement, and raining them down into the river. The clouds raced on furiously in the lead-coloured sky, the smoke and mist raced after them, the dark tide ran fierce and strong in the same direction. Little Dorrit seemed the least, the quietest, and weakest of Heaven's creatures.

'Let me put you in a coach,' said Clennam, very nearly adding 'my poor child.'

She hurriedly declined, saying that wet or dry made little difference to her; she was used to go about in all weathers. He knew it to be so, and was touched with more pity; thinking of the slight figure at his side, making its nightly way through the damp dark boisterous streets to such a place of rest.

'You spoke so feelingly to me last night, sir, and I found afterwards that you had been so generous to my father, that I could not resist your message, if it was only to thank you; especially as I wished very much to say to you—' she hesitated and trembled, and tears rose in her eyes, but did not fall.

'To say to me—?'

'That I hope you will not misunderstand my father. Don't judge him, sir, as you would judge others outside the gates. He has been there so long! I never saw him outside, but I can understand that he must have grown different in some things since.'

'My thoughts will never be unjust or harsh towards him, believe me.'

'Not,' she said, with a prouder air, as the misgiving evidently crept upon her that she might seem to be abandoning him, 'not that he has anything to be ashamed of for himself, or that I have anything to be ashamed of for him. He only requires to be understood. I only ask for him that his life may be fairly remembered. All that he said was quite true. It all happened just as he related it. He is very much respected. Everybody who comes in, is glad to know him. He is more courted than anyone else. He is far more thought of than the Marshal is.'

If ever pride were innocent, it was innocent in Little Dorrit when she grew boastful of her father.

'It is often said that his manners are a true gentleman's, and quite a study. I see none like them in that place, but he is admitted to be superior to all the rest. This is quite as much why they make him presents, as because they know him to be needy. He is not to be blamed for being in need, poor love. Who could be in prison a quarter of a century, and be prosperous!'

What affection in her words, what compassion in her repressed tears, what a great soul of fidelity within her, how true the light that shed false brightness round him!

'If I have found it best to conceal where my home is, it is not because I am ashamed of him. God forbid! Nor am I so much ashamed of the place itself as might be supposed. People are not bad because they come there. I have known numbers of good, persevering, honest people come there through misfortune. They are almost all kind-hearted to one another. And it would be ungrateful indeed in me, to forget that I have had many quiet, comfortable hours there; that I had an excellent friend there when I was quite a baby, who was very very fond of me; that I have been taught there, and have worked there, and have slept soundly there. I think it would be almost cowardly and cruel not to have some little attachment for it, after all this.'

She had relieved the faithful fulness of her heart, and modestly said, raising her eyes appealingly to her new friend's, 'I did not mean to say so much, nor have I ever but once spoken about this before. But it seems to set it more right than it was last night. I said I wished you had not followed me, sir. I don't wish it so much now, unless you should think—indeed I don't wish it at all, unless I should have spoken so confusedly, that—that you can scarcely understand me, which I am afraid may be the case.'

He told her with perfect truth that it was not the case; and putting himself between her and the sharp wind and rain, sheltered her as well as he could.

'I feel permitted now,' he said, 'to ask you a little more concerning your father. Has he many creditors?'

'Oh! a great number.'

'I mean detaining creditors, who keep him where he is?'

'Oh yes! a great number.'

'Can you tell me—I can get the information, no doubt, elsewhere, if you cannot—who is the most influential of them?'

Little Dorrit said, after considering a little, that she used to hear long ago of Mr Tite Barnacle as a man of great power. He was a commissioner, or a board, or a trustee, 'or something.' He lived in Grosvenor Square, she thought, or very near it. He was under Government—high in the Circumlocution Office. She appeared to have acquired, in her infancy, some awful impression of the might of this formidable Mr Tite Barnacle of Grosvenor Square, or very near it, and the Circumlocution Office, which quite crushed her when she mentioned him.

'It can do no harm,' thought Arthur, 'if I see this Mr Tite Barnacle.'

The thought did not present itself so quietly but that her quickness intercepted it. 'Ah!' said Little Dorrit, shaking her head with the mild despair of a lifetime. 'Many people used to think once of getting my poor father out, but you don't know how hopeless it is.'

She forgot to be shy at the moment, in honestly warning him away from the sunken wreck he had a dream of raising; and looked at him with eyes which assuredly, in association with her patient face, her fragile figure, her spare dress, and the wind and rain, did not turn him from his purpose of helping her.

'Even if it could be done,' said she—'and it never can be done now—where could father live, or how could he live? I have often thought that if such a change could come, it might be anything but a service to him now. People might not think so well of him outside as they do there. He might not be so gently dealt with outside as he is there. He might not be so fit himself for the life outside as he is for that.'

Here for the first time she could not restrain her tears from falling; and the little thin hands he had watched when they were so busy, trembled as they clasped each other.

'It would be a new distress to him even to know that I earn a little money, and that Fanny earns a little money. He is so anxious about us, you see, feeling helplessly shut up there. Such a good, good father!'

He let the little burst of feeling go by before he spoke. It was soon gone. She was not accustomed to think of herself, or to trouble any one with her emotions. He had but glanced away at the piles of city roofs and chimneys among which the smoke was rolling heavily, and at the wilderness of masts on the river, and the wilderness of steeples on the shore, indistinctly mixed together in the stormy haze, when she was again as quiet as if she had been plying her needle in his mother's room.

'You would be glad to have your brother set at liberty?'

'Oh very, very glad, sir!'

'Well, we will hope for him at least. You told me last night of a friend you had?'

His name was Plornish, Little Dorrit said.

And where did Plornish live? Plornish lived in Bleeding Heart Yard. He was 'only a plasterer,' Little Dorrit said, as a caution to him not to form high social expectations of Plornish. He lived at the last house in Bleeding Heart Yard, and his name was over a little gateway.

Arthur took down the address and gave her his. He had now done all he sought to do for the present, except that he wished to leave her with a reliance upon him, and to have something like a promise from her that she would cherish it.

'There is one friend!' he said, putting up his pocketbook. 'As I take you back—you are going back?'

'Oh yes! going straight home.'

'—As I take you back,' the word home jarred upon him, 'let me ask you to persuade yourself that you have another friend. I make no professions, and say no more.'

'You are truly kind to me, sir. I am sure I need no more.'

They walked back through the miserable muddy streets, and among the poor, mean shops, and were jostled by the crowds of dirty hucksters usual to a poor neighbourhood. There was nothing, by the short way, that was pleasant to any of the five senses. Yet it was not a common passage through common rain, and mire, and noise, to Clennam, having this little, slender, careful creature on his arm. How young she seemed to him, or how old he to her; or what a secret either to the other, in that beginning of the destined interweaving of their stories, matters not here. He thought of her having been born and bred among these scenes, and shrinking through them now, familiar yet misplaced; he thought of her long acquaintance with the squalid needs of life, and of her innocence; of her solicitude for others, and her few years, and her childish aspect.

They were come into the High Street, where the prison stood, when a voice cried, 'Little mother, little mother!' Little Dorrit stopping and looking back, an excited figure of a strange kind bounced against them (still crying 'little mother'), fell down, and scattered the contents of a large basket, filled with potatoes, in the mud.

'Oh, Maggy,' said Little Dorrit, 'what a clumsy child you are!'

Maggy was not hurt, but picked herself up immediately, and then began to pick up the potatoes, in which both Little Dorrit and Arthur Clennam helped. Maggy picked up very few potatoes and a great quantity of mud; but they were all recovered, and deposited in the basket. Maggy then smeared her muddy face with her shawl, and presenting it to Mr Clennam as a type of purity, enabled him to see what she was like.

She was about eight-and-twenty, with large bones, large features, large feet and hands, large eyes and no hair. Her large eyes were limpid and almost colourless; they seemed to be very little affected by light, and to stand unnaturally still. There was also that attentive listening expression in her face, which is seen in the faces of the blind; but she was not blind, having one tolerably serviceable eye. Her face was not exceedingly ugly, though it was only redeemed from being so by a smile; a good-humoured smile, and pleasant in itself, but rendered pitiable by being constantly there. A great white cap, with a quantity of opaque frilling that was always flapping about, apologised for Maggy's baldness, and made it so very difficult for her old black bonnet to retain its place upon her head, that it held on round her neck like a gipsy's baby. A commission of haberdashers could alone have reported what the rest of her poor dress was made of, but it had a strong general resemblance to seaweed, with here and there a gigantic tea-leaf. Her shawl looked particularly like a tea-leaf after long infusion.

Arthur Clennam looked at Little Dorrit with the expression of one saying, 'May I ask who this is?' Little Dorrit, whose hand this Maggy, still calling her little mother, had begun to fondle, answered in words (they were under a gateway into which the majority of the potatoes had rolled).

'This is Maggy, sir.'

'Maggy, sir,' echoed the personage presented. 'Little mother!'

'She is the grand-daughter—' said Little Dorrit.

'Grand-daughter,' echoed Maggy.

'Of my old nurse, who has been dead a long time. Maggy, how old are you?'

'Ten, mother,' said Maggy.

'You can't think how good she is, sir,' said Little Dorrit, with infinite tenderness.

'Good she is,' echoed Maggy, transferring the pronoun in a most expressive way from herself to her little mother.

'Or how clever,' said Little Dorrit. 'She goes on errands as well as any one.' Maggy laughed. 'And is as trustworthy as the Bank of England.' Maggy laughed. 'She earns her own living entirely. Entirely, sir!' said Little Dorrit, in a lower and triumphant tone. 'Really does!'

'What is her history?' asked Clennam.

'Think of that, Maggy?' said Little Dorrit, taking her two large hands and clapping them together. 'A gentleman from thousands of miles away, wanting to know your history!'

'My history?' cried Maggy. 'Little mother.'

84

'She means me,' said Little Dorrit, rather confused; 'she is very much attached to me. Her old grandmother was not so kind to her as she should have been; was she, Maggy?'

Maggy shook her head, made a drinking vessel of her clenched left hand, drank out of it, and said, 'Gin.' Then beat an imaginary child, and said, 'Broom-handles and pokers.'

'When Maggy was ten years old,' said Little Dorrit, watching her face while she spoke, 'she had a bad fever, sir, and she has never grown any older ever since.'

'Ten years old,' said Maggy, nodding her head. 'But what a nice hospital! So comfortable, wasn't it? Oh so nice it was. Such a Ev'nly place!'

'She had never been at peace before, sir,' said Little Dorrit, turning towards Arthur for an instant and speaking low, 'and she always runs off upon that.'

'Such beds there is there!' cried Maggy. 'Such lemonades! Such oranges! Such d'licious broth and wine! Such Chicking! Oh, AIN'T it a delightful place to go and stop at!'

'So Maggy stopped there as long as she could,' said Little Dorrit, in her former tone of telling a child's story; the tone designed for Maggy's ear, 'and at last, when she could stop there no longer, she came out. Then, because she was never to be more than ten years old, however long she lived—'

'However long she lived,' echoed Maggy.

'—And because she was very weak; indeed was so weak that when she began to laugh she couldn't stop herself—which was a great pity—'

(Maggy mighty grave of a sudden.)

'—Her grandmother did not know what to do with her, and for some years was very unkind to her indeed. At length, in course of time, Maggy began to take pains to improve herself, and to be very attentive and very industrious; and by degrees was allowed to come in and out as often as she liked, and got enough to do to support herself, and does support herself. And that,' said Little Dorrit, clapping the two great hands together again, 'is Maggy's history, as Maggy knows!'

Ah! But Arthur would have known what was wanting to its completeness, though he had never heard of the words Little mother; though he had never seen the fondling of the small spare hand; though he had had no sight for the tears now standing in the colourless eyes; though he had had no hearing for the sob that checked the clumsy laugh. The dirty gateway with the wind and rain whistling through it, and the basket of muddy potatoes waiting to be spilt again or taken up, never seemed the common hole it really was, when he looked back to it by these lights. Never, never!

They were very near the end of their walk, and they now came out of the gateway to finish it. Nothing would serve Maggy but that they must stop at a grocer's window, short of their destination, for her to show her learning. She could read after a sort; and picked out the fat figures in the tickets of prices, for the most part correctly. She also stumbled, with a large balance of success against her failures, through various philanthropic recommendations to Try our Mixture, Try our Family Black, Try our Orange-flavoured Pekoe, challenging competition at the head of Flowery Teas; and various cautions to the public against spurious establishments and adulterated articles. When he saw how pleasure brought a rosy tint into Little Dorrit's face when Maggy made a hit, he felt that he could have stood there making a library of the grocer's window until the rain and wind were tired.

The court-yard received them at last, and there he said goodbye to Little Dorrit. Little as she had always looked, she looked less than ever when he saw her going into the Marshalsea lodge passage, the little mother attended by her big child.

The cage door opened, and when the small bird, reared in captivity, had tamely fluttered in, he saw it shut again; and then he came away.

CHAPTER 10. Containing the whole Science of Government

The Circumlocution Office was (as everybody knows without being told) the most important Department under Government. No public business of any kind could possibly be done at any time without the acquiescence of the Circumlocution Office. Its finger was in the largest public pie, and in the smallest public tart. It was equally impossible to do the plainest right and to undo the plainest wrong without the express authority of the Circumlocution Office. If another Gunpowder Plot had been discovered half an hour before the lighting of the match, nobody would have been justified in saving the parliament until there had been half a score of boards, half a bushel of minutes, several sacks of official memoranda, and a family-vault full of ungrammatical correspondence, on the part of the Circumlocution Office.

This glorious establishment had been early in the field, when the one sublime principle involving the difficult art of governing a country, was first distinctly revealed to statesmen. It had been foremost to study that bright revelation and to carry its shining influence through the whole of the official proceedings. Whatever was required to be done, the Circumlocution Office was beforehand with all the public departments in the art of perceiving—HOW NOT TO DO IT.

Through this delicate perception, through the tact with which it invariably seized it, and through the genius with which it always acted on it, the Circumlocution Office had risen to overtop all the public departments; and the public condition had risen to be—what it was.

It is true that How not to do it was the great study and object of all public departments and professional politicians all round the Circumlocution Office. It is true that every new premier and every new government, coming in because they had upheld a certain thing as necessary to be done, were no sooner come in than they applied their utmost faculties to discovering How not to do it. It is true that from the moment when a general election was over, every returned man who had been raving on hustings because it hadn't been done, and who had been asking the friends of the honourable gentleman in the opposite interest on pain of impeachment to tell him why it hadn't been done, and who had been asserting that it must be done, and who had been pledging himself that it should be done, began to devise, How it was not to be done. It is true that the debates of both Houses of Parliament the whole session through, uniformly tended to the protracted deliberation, How not to do it. It is true that the royal speech at the opening of such session virtually said, My lords and gentlemen, you have a considerable stroke of work to do, and you will please to retire to your respective chambers, and discuss, How not to do it. It is true that the royal speech, at the close of such session, virtually said, My lords and gentlemen, you have through several laborious months been considering with great loyalty and patriotism, How not to do it, and you have found out;

and with the blessing of Providence upon the harvest (natural, not political), I now dismiss you. All this is true, but the Circumlocution Office went beyond it.

Because the Circumlocution Office went on mechanically, every day, keeping this wonderful, all-sufficient wheel of statesmanship, How not to do it, in motion. Because the Circumlocution Office was down upon any ill-advised public servant who was going to do it, or who appeared to be by any surprising accident in remote danger of doing it, with a minute, and a memorandum, and a letter of instructions that extinguished him. It was this spirit of national efficiency in the Circumlocution Office that had gradually led to its having something to do with everything. Mechanicians, natural philosophers, soldiers, sailors, petitioners, memorialists, people with grievances, people who wanted to prevent grievances, people who wanted to redress grievances, jobbing people, jobbed people, people who couldn't get rewarded for merit, and people who couldn't get punished for demerit, were all indiscriminately tucked up under the foolscap paper of the Circumlocution Office.

Numbers of people were lost in the Circumlocution Office. Unfortunates with wrongs, or with projects for the general welfare (and they had better have had wrongs at first, than have taken that bitter English recipe for certainly getting them), who in slow lapse of time and agony had passed safely through other public departments; who, according to rule, had been bullied in this, over-reached by that, and evaded by the other; got referred at last to the Circumlocution Office, and never reappeared in the light of day. Boards sat upon them, secretaries minuted upon them, commissioners gabbled about them, clerks registered, entered, checked, and ticked them off, and they melted away. In short, all the business of the country went through the Circumlocution Office, except the business that never came out of it; and its name was Legion.

Sometimes, angry spirits attacked the Circumlocution Office. Sometimes, parliamentary questions were asked about it, and even parliamentary motions made or threatened about it by demagogues so low and ignorant as to hold that the real recipe of government was, How to do it. Then would the noble lord, or right honourable gentleman, in whose department it was to defend the Circumlocution Office, put an orange in his pocket, and make a regular field-day of the occasion. Then would he come down to that house with a slap upon the table, and meet the honourable gentleman foot to foot. Then would he be there to tell that honourable gentleman that the Circumlocution Office not only was blameless in this matter, but was commendable in this matter, was extollable to the skies in this matter. Then would he be there to tell that honourable gentleman that, although the Circumlocution Office was invariably right and wholly right, it never was so right as in this matter. Then would he be there to tell that honourable gentleman that it would have been more to his honour, more to his credit, more to his good taste, more to his good sense, more to half the dictionary of commonplaces, if he had left the Circumlocution Office alone, and never approached this matter. Then would he keep one eye upon a coach or crammer from the Circumlocution Office sitting below the bar, and smash the honourable gentleman with the Circumlocution Office account of this matter. And although one of two things always happened; namely, either that the Circumlocution Office had nothing to say and said it, or that it had something to say of which the noble lord, or right honourable gentleman, blundered one half and forgot the other; the Circumlocution Office was always voted immaculate by an accommodating majority.

Such a nursery of statesmen had the Department become in virtue of a long career of this nature, that several solemn lords had attained the reputation of being quite unearthly prodigies of business, solely from having practised, How not to do it, as the head of the Circumlocution Office. As to the minor priests and acolytes of that temple, the result of all this was that they stood divided into two classes, and, down to the junior messenger, either believed in the Circumlocution Office as a heaven-born institution that had an absolute right to do whatever it liked; or took refuge in total infidelity, and considered it a flagrant nuisance.

The Barnacle family had for some time helped to administer the Circumlocution Office. The Tite Barnacle Branch, indeed, considered themselves in a general way as having vested rights in that direction, and took it ill if any other family had much to say to it. The Barnacles were a very high family, and a very large family. They were dispersed all over the public offices, and held all sorts of public places. Either the nation was under a load of obligation to the Barnacles, or the Barnacles were under a load of obligation to the nation. It was not quite unanimously settled which; the Barnacles having their opinion, the nation theirs.

The Mr Tite Barnacle who at the period now in question usually coached or crammed the statesman at the head of the Circumlocution Office, when that noble or right honourable individual sat a little uneasily in his saddle by reason of some vagabond making a tilt at him in a newspaper, was more flush of blood than money. As a Barnacle he had his place, which was a snug thing enough; and as a Barnacle he had of course put in his son Barnacle Junior in the office. But he had intermarried with a branch of the Stiltstalkings, who were also better endowed in a sanguineous point of view than with real or personal property, and of this marriage there had been issue, Barnacle junior and three young ladies. What with the patrician requirements of Barnacle junior, the three young ladies, Mrs Tite Barnacle nee Stiltstalking, and himself, Mr Tite Barnacle found the intervals between quarter day and quarter day rather longer than he could have desired; a circumstance which he always attributed to the country's parsimony.

For Mr Tite Barnacle, Mr Arthur Clennam made his fifth inquiry one day at the Circumlocution Office; having on previous occasions awaited that gentleman successively in a hall, a glass case, a waiting room, and a fire-proof passage where the Department seemed to keep its wind. On this occasion Mr Barnacle was not engaged, as he had been before, with the noble prodigy at the head of the Department; but was absent. Barnacle Junior, however, was announced as a lesser star, yet visible above the office horizon.

With Barnacle junior, he signified his desire to confer; and found that young gentleman singeing the calves of his legs at the parental fire, and supporting his spine against the mantel-shelf. It was a comfortable room, handsomely furnished in the higher official manner; an presenting stately suggestions of the absent Barnacle, in the thick carpet, the leather-covered desk to sit at, the leather-covered desk to stand at, the formidable easy-chair and hearth-rug, the interposed screen, the torn-up papers, the dispatch-boxes with little labels sticking out of them, like medicine bottles or dead game, the pervading smell of leather and mahogany, and a general bamboozling air of How not to do it.

The present Barnacle, holding Mr Clennam's card in his hand, had a youthful aspect, and the fluffiest little whisker, perhaps, that ever was seen. Such a downy tip was on his callow chin, that he seemed half fledged like a young bird; and a compassionate observer might have urged that, if he had not singed the calves of his legs, he would have died of cold. He had a superior eye-glass dangling round his neck, but unfortunately had such flat orbits to his eyes and such limp little eyelids that it wouldn't stick in when he put it up, but kept tumbling out against his waistcoat buttons with a click that discomposed him very much.

'Oh, I say. Look here! My father's not in the way, and won't be in the way to-day,' said Barnacle Junior. 'Is this anything that I can do?'

(Click! Eye-glass down. Barnacle Junior quite frightened and feeling all round himself, but not able to find it.)

'You are very good,' said Arthur Clennam. 'I wish however to see Mr Barnacle.'

'But I say. Look here! You haven't got any appointment, you know,' said Barnacle Junior.

(By this time he had found the eye-glass, and put it up again.)

'No,' said Arthur Clennam. 'That is what I wish to have.'

'But I say. Look here! Is this public business?' asked Barnacle junior.

(Click! Eye-glass down again. Barnacle Junior in that state of search after it that Mr Clennam felt it useless to reply at present.)

'Is it,' said Barnacle junior, taking heed of his visitor's brown face, 'anything about— Tonnage—or that sort of thing?'

(Pausing for a reply, he opened his right eye with his hand, and stuck his glass in it, in that inflammatory manner that his eye began watering dreadfully.)

'No,' said Arthur, 'it is nothing about tonnage.'

'Then look here. Is it private business?'

'I really am not sure. It relates to a Mr Dorrit.'

'Look here, I tell you what! You had better call at our house, if you are going that way. Twenty-four, Mews Street, Grosvenor Square. My father's got a slight touch of the gout, and is kept at home by it.'

(The misguided young Barnacle evidently going blind on his eye-glass side, but ashamed to make any further alteration in his painful arrangements.)

'Thank you. I will call there now. Good morning.' Young Barnacle seemed discomfited at this, as not having at all expected him to go.

'You are quite sure,' said Barnacle junior, calling after him when he got to the door, unwilling wholly to relinquish the bright business idea he had conceived; 'that it's nothing about Tonnage?'

'Quite sure.'

With such assurance, and rather wondering what might have taken place if it had been anything about tonnage, Mr Clennam withdrew to pursue his inquiries.

Mews Street, Grosvenor Square, was not absolutely Grosvenor Square itself, but it was very near it. It was a hideous little street of dead wall, stables, and dunghills, with lofts over coach-houses inhabited by coachmen's families, who had a passion for drying clothes and decorating their window-sills with miniature turnpike-gates. The principal chimney-sweep of that fashionable quarter lived at the blind end of Mews Street; and the same corner contained an establishment much frequented about early morning and twilight for the purchase of wine-bottles and kitchen-stuff. Punch's shows used to lean against the dead wall in Mews Street, while their proprietors were dining elsewhere; and the dogs of the neighbourhood made appointments to meet in the same locality. Yet there were two or three small airless houses at the entrance end of Mews Street, which went at enormous rents on account of their being abject hangers-on to a fashionable situation; and whenever one of these fearful little coops was to be let (which seldom happened, for they were in great request), the house agent advertised it as a gentlemanly residence in the most aristocratic part of town, inhabited solely by the elite of the beau monde.

If a gentlemanly residence coming strictly within this narrow margin had not been essential to the blood of the Barnacles, this particular branch would have had a pretty wide selection among, let us say, ten thousand houses, offering fifty times the accommodation for a third of the money. As it was, Mr Barnacle, finding his gentlemanly residence extremely inconvenient and extremely dear, always laid it, as a public servant, at the door of the country, and adduced it as another instance of the country's parsimony.

Arthur Clennam came to a squeezed house, with a ramshackle bowed front, little dingy windows, and a little dark area like a damp waistcoat-pocket, which he found to be number twenty-four, Mews Street, Grosvenor Square. To the sense of smell the house was like a sort of bottle filled with a strong distillation of Mews; and when the footman opened the door, he seemed to take the stopper out.

The footman was to the Grosvenor Square footmen, what the house was to the Grosvenor Square houses. Admirable in his way, his way was a back and a bye way. His gorgeousness was not unmixed with dirt; and both in complexion and consistency he had suffered from the closeness of his pantry. A sallow flabbiness was upon him when he took the stopper out, and presented the bottle to Mr Clennam's nose.

'Be so good as to give that card to Mr Tite Barnacle, and to say that I have just now seen the younger Mr Barnacle, who recommended me to call here.'

The footman (who had as many large buttons with the Barnacle crest upon them on the flaps of his pockets, as if he were the family strong box, and carried the plate and jewels about with him buttoned up) pondered over the card a little; then said, 'Walk in.' It required some judgment to do it without butting the inner hall-door open, and in the consequent mental confusion and physical darkness slipping down the kitchen stairs. The visitor, however, brought himself up safely on the door-mat.

Still the footman said 'Walk in,' so the visitor followed him. At the inner hall-door, another bottle seemed to be presented and another stopper taken out. This second vial appeared to be filled with concentrated provisions and extract of Sink from the pantry. After a skirmish in the narrow passage, occasioned by the footman's opening the door of the dismal dining-room with confidence, finding some one there with consternation, and backing on the visitor with disorder, the visitor was shut up, pending his announcement, in a close back parlour. There he had an opportunity of refreshing himself with both the bottles at once, looking out at a low blinding wall three feet off, and speculating on the number of Barnacle families within the bills of mortality who lived in such hutches of their own free flunkey choice.

Mr Barnacle would see him. Would he walk up-stairs? He would, and he did; and in the drawing-room, with his leg on a rest, he found Mr Barnacle himself, the express image and presentment of How not to do it.

Mr Barnacle dated from a better time, when the country was not so parsimonious and the Circumlocution Office was not so badgered. He wound and wound folds of white cravat round his neck, as he wound and wound folds of tape and paper round the neck of the country. His wristbands and collar were oppressive; his voice and manner were oppressive. He had a large watch-chain and bunch of seals, a coat buttoned up to inconvenience, a waistcoat buttoned up to inconvenience, an unwrinkled pair of trousers, a stiff pair of boots. He was altogether splendid, massive, overpowering, and impracticable. He seemed to have been sitting for his portrait to Sir Thomas Lawrence all the days of his life.

'Mr Clennam?' said Mr Barnacle. 'Be seated.'

Mr Clennam became seated.

'You have called on me, I believe,' said Mr Barnacle, 'at the Circumlocution—' giving it the air of a word of about five-and-twenty syllables—'Office.'

'I have taken that liberty.'

Mr Barnacle solemnly bent his head as who should say, 'I do not deny that it is a liberty; proceed to take another liberty, and let me know your business.'

'Allow me to observe that I have been for some years in China, am quite a stranger at home, and have no personal motive or interest in the inquiry I am about to make.'

Mr Barnacle tapped his fingers on the table, and, as if he were now sitting for his portrait to a new and strange artist, appeared to say to his visitor, 'If you will be good enough to take me with my present lofty expression, I shall feel obliged.'

'I have found a debtor in the Marshalsea Prison of the name of Dorrit, who has been there many years. I wish to investigate his confused affairs so far as to ascertain whether it may not be possible, after this lapse of time, to ameliorate his unhappy condition. The name of Mr Tite Barnacle has been mentioned to me as representing some highly influential interest among his creditors. Am I correctly informed?'

It being one of the principles of the Circumlocution Office never, on any account whatever, to give a straightforward answer, Mr Barnacle said, 'Possibly.'

'On behalf of the Crown, may I ask, or as private individual?'

'The Circumlocution Department, sir,' Mr Barnacle replied, 'may have possibly recommended—possibly—I cannot say—that some public claim against the insolvent estate of a firm or copartnership to which this person may have belonged, should be enforced. The question may have been, in the course of official business, referred to the Circumlocution Department for its consideration. The Department may have either originated, or confirmed, a Minute making that recommendation.'

'I assume this to be the case, then.'

'The Circumlocution Department,' said Mr Barnacle, 'is not responsible for any gentleman's assumptions.'

'May I inquire how I can obtain official information as to the real state of the case?'

'It is competent,' said Mr Barnacle, 'to any member of the—Public,' mentioning that obscure body with reluctance, as his natural enemy, 'to memorialise the Circumlocution Department. Such formalities as are required to be observed in so doing, may be known on application to the proper branch of that Department.'

'Which is the proper branch?'

'I must refer you,' returned Mr Barnacle, ringing the bell, 'to the Department itself for a formal answer to that inquiry.'

'Excuse my mentioning—'

'The Department is accessible to the—Public,' Mr Barnacle was always checked a little by that word of impertinent signification, 'if the—Public approaches it according to the official forms; if the—Public does not approach it according to the official forms, the—Public has itself to blame.'

Mr Barnacle made him a severe bow, as a wounded man of family, a wounded man of place, and a wounded man of a gentlemanly residence, all rolled into one; and he made Mr Barnacle a bow, and was shut out into Mews Street by the flabby footman.

Having got to this pass, he resolved as an exercise in perseverance, to betake himself again to the Circumlocution Office, and try what satisfaction he could get there. So he went back to the Circumlocution Office, and once more sent up his card to Barnacle junior by a messenger who took it very ill indeed that he should come back again, and who was eating mashed potatoes and gravy behind a partition by the hall fire.

He was readmitted to the presence of Barnacle junior, and found that young gentleman singeing his knees now, and gaping his weary way on to four o'clock.

'I say. Look here. You stick to us in a devil of a manner,' Said Barnacle junior, looking over his shoulder.

'I want to know—'

'Look here. Upon my soul you mustn't come into the place saying you want to know, you know,' remonstrated Barnacle junior, turning about and putting up the eye-glass.

'I want to know,' said Arthur Clennam, who had made up his mind to persistence in one short form of words, 'the precise nature of the claim of the Crown against a prisoner for debt, named Dorrit.'

'I say. Look here. You really are going it at a great pace, you know. Egad, you haven't got an appointment,' said Barnacle junior, as if the thing were growing serious.

'I want to know,' said Arthur, and repeated his case.

Barnacle junior stared at him until his eye-glass fell out, and then put it in again and stared at him until it fell out again. 'You have no right to come this sort of move,' he then observed with the greatest weakness. 'Look here. What do you mean? You told me you didn't know whether it was public business or not.'

'I have now ascertained that it is public business,' returned the suitor, 'and I want to know'—and again repeated his monotonous inquiry.

Its effect upon young Barnacle was to make him repeat in a defenceless way, 'Look here! Upon my SOUL you mustn't come into the place saying you want to know, you know!' The effect of that upon Arthur Clennam was to make him repeat his inquiry in exactly the same words and tone as before. The effect of that upon young Barnacle was to make him a wonderful spectacle of failure and helplessness.

'Well, I tell you what. Look here. You had better try the Secretarial Department,' he said at last, sidling to the bell and ringing it. 'Jenkinson,' to the mashed potatoes messenger, 'Mr Wobbler!'

Arthur Clennam, who now felt that he had devoted himself to the storming of the Circumlocution Office, and must go through with it, accompanied the messenger to another floor of the building, where that functionary pointed out Mr Wobbler's room. He entered that apartment, and found two gentlemen sitting face to face at a large and easy desk, one of whom was polishing a gun-barrel on his pocket-handkerchief, while the other was spreading marmalade on bread with a paper-knife.

'Mr Wobbler?' inquired the suitor.

Both gentlemen glanced at him, and seemed surprised at his assurance.

'So he went,' said the gentleman with the gun-barrel, who was an extremely deliberate speaker, 'down to his cousin's place, and took the Dog with him by rail. Inestimable Dog. Flew at the porter fellow when he was put into the dog-box, and flew at the guard when he was taken out. He got half-a-dozen fellows into a Barn, and a good supply of Rats, and timed the Dog. Finding the Dog able to do it immensely, made the match, and heavily backed the Dog. When the match came off, some devil of a fellow was bought over, Sir, Dog was made drunk, Dog's master was cleaned out.'

'Mr Wobbler?' inquired the suitor.

The gentleman who was spreading the marmalade returned, without looking up from that occupation, 'What did he call the Dog?'

'Called him Lovely,' said the other gentleman. 'Said the Dog was the perfect picture of the old aunt from whom he had expectations. Found him particularly like her when hocussed.'

'Mr Wobbler?' said the suitor.

Both gentlemen laughed for some time. The gentleman with the gun-barrel, considering it, on inspection, in a satisfactory state, referred it to the other; receiving confirmation of his views, he fitted it into its place in the case before him, and took out the stock and polished that, softly whistling.

'Mr Wobbler?' said the suitor.

'What's the matter?' then said Mr Wobbler, with his mouth full.

'I want to know—' and Arthur Clennam again mechanically set forth what he wanted to know.

'Can't inform you,' observed Mr Wobbler, apparently to his lunch. 'Never heard of it. Nothing at all to do with it. Better try Mr Clive, second door on the left in the next passage.'

'Perhaps he will give me the same answer.'

'Very likely. Don't know anything about it,' said Mr Wobbler.

The suitor turned away and had left the room, when the gentleman with the gun called out 'Mister! Hallo!'

He looked in again.

'Shut the door after you. You're letting in a devil of a draught here!'

A few steps brought him to the second door on the left in the next passage. In that room he found three gentlemen; number one doing nothing particular, number two doing nothing particular, number three doing nothing particular. They seemed, however, to be more directly concerned than the others had been in the effective execution of the great principle of the office, as there was an awful inner apartment with a double door, in which the Circumlocution Sages appeared to be assembled in council, and out of which there was an imposing coming of papers, and into which there was an imposing going of papers, almost constantly; wherein another gentleman, number four, was the active instrument.

'I want to know,' said Arthur Clennam,—and again stated his case in the same barrel-organ way. As number one referred him to number two, and as number two referred him to number three, he had occasion to state it three times before they all referred him to number four, to whom he stated it again.

Number four was a vivacious, well-looking, well-dressed, agreeable young fellow—he was a Barnacle, but on the more sprightly side of the family—and he said in an easy way, 'Oh! you had better not bother yourself about it, I think.'

'Not bother myself about it?'

'No! I recommend you not to bother yourself about it.'

This was such a new point of view that Arthur Clennam found himself at a loss how to receive it.

'You can if you like. I can give you plenty of forms to fill up. Lots of 'em here. You can have a dozen if you like. But you'll never go on with it,' said number four.

'Would it be such hopeless work? Excuse me; I am a stranger in England.'

'I don't say it would be hopeless,' returned number four, with a frank smile. 'I don't express an opinion about that; I only express an opinion about you. I don't think you'd go on with it. However, of course, you can do as you like. I suppose there was a failure in the performance of a contract, or something of that kind, was there?'

'I really don't know.'

'Well! That you can find out. Then you'll find out what Department the contract was in, and then you'll find out all about it there.'

'I beg your pardon. How shall I find out?'

'Why, you'll—you'll ask till they tell you. Then you'll memorialise that Department (according to regular forms which you'll find out) for leave to memorialise this Department. If you get it (which you may after a time), that memorial must be entered in that Department, sent to be registered in this Department, sent back to be signed by that Department, sent back to be countersigned by this Department, and then it will begin to be regularly before that Department. You'll find out when the business passes through each of these stages by asking at both Departments till they tell you.'

'But surely this is not the way to do the business,' Arthur Clennam could not help saying.

This airy young Barnacle was quite entertained by his simplicity in supposing for a moment that it was. This light in hand young Barnacle knew perfectly that it was not. This touch and go young Barnacle had 'got up' the Department in a private secretaryship, that he might be ready for any little bit of fat that came to hand; and he fully understood the Department to be a politico-diplomatic hocus pocus piece of machinery for the assistance of the nobs in keeping off the snobs. This dashing young Barnacle, in a word, was likely to become a statesman, and to make a figure.

'When the business is regularly before that Department, whatever it is,' pursued this bright young Barnacle, 'then you can watch it from time to time through that Department. When it comes regularly before this Department, then you must watch it from time to time through this Department. We shall have to refer it right and left; and when we refer it anywhere, then you'll have to look it up. When it comes back to us at any time, then you had better look us up. When it sticks anywhere, you'll have to try to give it a jog. When you write to another Department about it, and then to this Department about it, and don't hear anything satisfactory about it, why then you had better—keep on writing.'

Arthur Clennam looked very doubtful indeed. 'But I am obliged to you at any rate,' said he, 'for your politeness.'

'Not at all,' replied this engaging young Barnacle. 'Try the thing, and see how you like it. It will be in your power to give it up at any time, if you don't like it. You had better take a lot of forms away with you. Give him a lot of forms!' With which instruction to number two, this sparkling young Barnacle took a fresh handful of papers from numbers one and three, and carried them into the sanctuary to offer to the presiding Idol of the Circumlocution Office.

Arthur Clennam put his forms in his pocket gloomily enough, and went his way down the long stone passage and the long stone staircase. He had come to the swing doors leading into the street, and was waiting, not over patiently, for two people who were between him and them to pass out and let him follow, when the voice of one of them struck familiarly on his ear. He looked at the speaker and recognised Mr Meagles. Mr Meagles was very red in the face—redder than travel could have made him—and collaring a short man who was with him, said, 'come out, you rascal, come Out!'

It was such an unexpected hearing, and it was also such an unexpected sight to see Mr Meagles burst the swing doors open, and emerge into the street with the short man, who was of an unoffending appearance, that Clennam stood still for the moment exchanging looks of surprise with the porter. He followed, however, quickly; and saw Mr Meagles going down the street with his enemy at his side. He soon came up with his old travelling companion, and touched him on the back. The choleric face which Mr Meagles turned upon him smoothed when he saw who it was, and he put out his friendly hand.

'How are you?' said Mr Meagles. 'How d'ye do? I have only just come over from abroad. I am glad to see you.'

'And I am rejoiced to see you.'

'Thank'ee. Thank'ee!'

'Mrs Meagles and your daughter—?'

'Are as well as possible,' said Mr Meagles. 'I only wish you had come upon me in a more prepossessing condition as to coolness.'

Though it was anything but a hot day, Mr Meagles was in a heated state that attracted the attention of the passersby; more particularly as he leaned his back against a railing, took off his hat and cravat, and heartily rubbed his steaming head and face, and his reddened ears and neck, without the least regard for public opinion.

'Whew!' said Mr Meagles, dressing again. 'That's comfortable. Now I am cooler.'

'You have been ruffled, Mr Meagles. What is the matter?'

'Wait a bit, and I'll tell you. Have you leisure for a turn in the Park?'

'As much as you please.'

'Come along then. Ah! you may well look at him.' He happened to have turned his eyes towards the offender whom Mr Meagles had so angrily collared. 'He's something to look at, that fellow is.'

He was not much to look at, either in point of size or in point of dress; being merely a short, square, practical looking man, whose hair had turned grey, and in whose face and forehead there were deep lines of cogitation, which looked as though they were carved in hard wood. He was dressed in decent black, a little rusty, and had the appearance of a sagacious master in some handicraft. He had a spectacle-case in his hand, which he turned over and over while he was thus in question, with a certain free use of the thumb that is never seen but in a hand accustomed to tools.

'You keep with us,' said Mr Meagles, in a threatening kind of Way, 'and I'll introduce you presently. Now then!'

Clennam wondered within himself, as they took the nearest way to the Park, what this unknown (who complied in the gentlest manner) could have been doing. His appearance did not at all justify the suspicion that he had been detected in designs on Mr Meagles's pocket-handkerchief; nor had he any appearance of being quarrelsome or violent. He was a quiet, plain, steady man; made no attempt to escape; and seemed a little depressed, but neither ashamed nor repentant. If he were a criminal offender, he must surely be an incorrigible hypocrite; and if he were no offender, why should Mr Meagles have collared him in the Circumlocution Office? He perceived that the man was not a difficulty in his own mind alone, but in Mr Meagles's too; for such conversation as they had together on the short way to the Park was by no means well sustained, and Mr Meagles's eye always wandered back to the man, even when he spoke of something very different.

At length they being among the trees, Mr Meagles stopped short, and said:

'Mr Clennam, will you do me the favour to look at this man? His name is Doyce, Daniel Doyce. You wouldn't suppose this man to be a notorious rascal; would you?'

'I certainly should not.' It was really a disconcerting question, with the man there.

'No. You would not. I know you would not. You wouldn't suppose him to be a public offender; would you?'

'No.'

'No. But he is. He is a public offender. What has he been guilty of? Murder, manslaughter, arson, forgery, swindling, house-breaking, highway robbery, larceny, conspiracy, fraud? Which should you say, now?'

'I should say,' returned Arthur Clennam, observing a faint smile in Daniel Doyce's face, 'not one of them.'

'You are right,' said Mr Meagles. 'But he has been ingenious, and he has been trying to turn his ingenuity to his country's service. That makes him a public offender directly, sir.'

Arthur looked at the man himself, who only shook his head.

'This Doyce,' said Mr Meagles, 'is a smith and engineer. He is not in a large way, but he is well known as a very ingenious man. A dozen years ago, he perfects an invention (involving a very curious secret process) of great importance to his country and his fellow-creatures. I won't say how much money it cost him, or how many years of his life he had been about it, but he brought it to perfection a dozen years ago. Wasn't it a dozen?' said Mr Meagles, addressing Doyce. 'He is the most exasperating man in the world; he never complains!'

'Yes. Rather better than twelve years ago.'

'Rather better?' said Mr Meagles, 'you mean rather worse. Well, Mr Clennam, he addresses himself to the Government. The moment he addresses himself to the Government, he becomes a public offender! Sir,' said Mr Meagles, in danger of making himself excessively hot again, 'he ceases to be an innocent citizen, and becomes a culprit. He is treated from that instant as a man who has done some infernal action. He is a man to be shirked, put off, brow-beaten, sneered at, handed over by this highly-connected young or old gentleman, to that highly-connected young or old gentleman, and dodged back again; he is a man with no rights in his own time, or his own property; a mere outlaw, whom it is justifiable to get rid of anyhow; a man to be worn out by all possible means.'

It was not so difficult to believe, after the morning's experience, as Mr Meagles supposed.

'Don't stand there, Doyce, turning your spectacle-case over and over,' cried Mr Meagles, 'but tell Mr Clennam what you confessed to me.'

'I undoubtedly was made to feel,' said the inventor, 'as if I had committed an offence. In dancing attendance at the various offices, I was always treated, more or less, as if it was a very bad offence. I have frequently found it necessary to reflect, for my own self-support, that I really had not done anything to bring myself into the Newgate Calendar, but only wanted to effect a great saving and a great improvement.'

'There!' said Mr Meagles. 'Judge whether I exaggerate. Now you'll be able to believe me when I tell you the rest of the case.'

With this prelude, Mr Meagles went through the narrative; the established narrative, which has become tiresome; the matter-of-course narrative which we all know by heart. How, after interminable attendance and correspondence, after infinite impertinences, ignorances, and insults, my lords made a Minute, number three thousand four hundred and seventy-two, allowing the culprit to make certain trials of his invention at his own expense. How the trials were made in the presence of a board of six, of whom two ancient members were too blind to see it, two other ancient members were too deaf to hear it, one other ancient member was too lame to get near it, and the final ancient member was too pig-headed to look at it. How there were more years; more impertinences, ignorances, and insults. How my lords then made a Minute, number five thousand one hundred and three, whereby they resigned the business to the Circumlocution Office. How the Circumlocution Office, in course of time, took up the business as if it were a bran new thing of yesterday, which had never been heard of before; muddled the business, addled the business, tossed the business in a wet blanket. How the impertinences, ignorances, and insults went through the multiplication table. How there was a reference of the invention to three Barnacles and a Stiltstalking, who knew nothing about it; into whose heads nothing could be hammered about it; who got bored about it, and reported physical impossibilities about it. How the Circumlocution Office, in a Minute, number eight thousand seven hundred and forty, 'saw no reason to reverse the decision at which my lords had arrived.' How the Circumlocution Office, being reminded that my lords had arrived at no decision, shelved the business. How there had been a final interview with the head of the Circumlocution Office that very morning, and how the Brazen Head had spoken, and had been, upon the whole, and under all the circumstances, and looking at it from the various points of view, of opinion that one of two courses was to be pursued in respect of the business: that was to say, either to leave it alone for evermore, or to begin it all over again.

'Upon which,' said Mr Meagles, 'as a practical man, I then and there, in that presence, took Doyce by the collar, and told him it was plain to me that he was an infamous rascal and treasonable disturber of the government peace, and took him away. I brought him out of the office door by the collar, that the very porter might know I was a practical man who appreciated the official estimate of such characters; and here we are!'

If that airy young Barnacle had been there, he would have frankly told them perhaps that the Circumlocution Office had achieved its function. That what the Barnacles had to do, was to stick on to the national ship as long as they could. That to trim the ship, lighten the ship, clean the ship, would be to knock them off; that they could but be knocked off once; and that if the ship went down with them yet sticking to it, that was the ship's look out, and not theirs.

'There!' said Mr Meagles, 'now you know all about Doyce. Except, which I own does not improve my state of mind, that even now you don't hear him complain.'

'You must have great patience,' said Arthur Clennam, looking at him with some wonder, 'great forbearance.'

'No,' he returned, 'I don't know that I have more than another man.'

'By the Lord, you have more than I have, though!' cried Mr Meagles.

Doyce smiled, as he said to Clennam, 'You see, my experience of these things does not begin with myself. It has been in my way to know a little about them from time to time. Mine is not a particular case. I am not worse used than a hundred others who have put themselves in the same position—than all the others, I was going to say.'

'I don't know that I should find that a consolation, if it were my case; but I am very glad that you do.'

'Understand me! I don't say,' he replied in his steady, planning way, and looking into the distance before him as if his grey eye were measuring it, 'that it's recompense for a man's toil and hope; but it's a certain sort of relief to know that I might have counted on this.'

He spoke in that quiet deliberate manner, and in that undertone, which is often observable in mechanics who consider and adjust with great nicety. It belonged to him like his suppleness of thumb, or his peculiar way of tilting up his hat at the back every now and then, as if he were contemplating some half-finished work of his hand and thinking about it.

'Disappointed?' he went on, as he walked between them under the trees. 'Yes. No doubt I am disappointed. Hurt? Yes. No doubt I am hurt. That's only natural. But what I mean when I say that people who put themselves in the same position are mostly used in the same way—'

'In England,' said Mr Meagles.

'Oh! of course I mean in England. When they take their inventions into foreign countries, that's quite different. And that's the reason why so many go there.'

Mr Meagles very hot indeed again.

'What I mean is, that however this comes to be the regular way of our government, it is its regular way. Have you ever heard of any projector or inventor who failed to find it all but inaccessible, and whom it did not discourage and ill-treat?'

'I cannot say that I ever have.'

'Have you ever known it to be beforehand in the adoption of any useful thing? Ever known it to set an example of any useful kind?'

'I am a good deal older than my friend here,' said Mr Meagles, 'and I'll answer that. Never.'

'But we all three have known, I expect,' said the inventor, 'a pretty many cases of its fixed determination to be miles upon miles, and years upon years, behind the rest of us; and of its being found out persisting in the use of things long superseded, even after the better things were well known and generally taken up?'

They all agreed upon that.

'Well then,' said Doyce, with a sigh, 'as I know what such a metal will do at such a temperature, and such a body under such a pressure, so I may know (if I will only consider), how these great lords and gentlemen will certainly deal with such a matter as mine. I have no right to be surprised, with a head upon my shoulders, and memory in it, that I fall into the ranks with all who came before me. I ought to have let it alone. I have had warning enough, I am sure.'

With that he put up his spectacle-case, and said to Arthur, 'If I don't complain, Mr Clennam, I can feel gratitude; and I assure you that I feel it towards our mutual friend. Many's the day, and many's the way in which he has backed me.'

'Stuff and nonsense,' said Mr Meagles.

Arthur could not but glance at Daniel Doyce in the ensuing silence. Though it was evidently in the grain of his character, and of his respect for his own case, that he should abstain from idle murmuring, it was evident that he had grown the older, the sterner, and the poorer, for his long endeavour. He could not but think what a blessed thing it would have been for this man, if he had taken a lesson from the gentlemen who were so kind as to take a nation's affairs in charge, and had learnt How not to do it.

Mr Meagles was hot and despondent for about five minutes, and then began to cool and clear up.

'Come, come!' said he. 'We shall not make this the better by being grim. Where do you think of going, Dan?'

'I shall go back to the factory,' said Dan.

'Why then, we'll all go back to the factory, or walk in that direction,' returned Mr Meagles cheerfully. 'Mr Clennam won't be deterred by its being in Bleeding Heart Yard.'

'Bleeding Heart Yard?' said Clennam. 'I want to go there.'

'So much the better,' cried Mr Meagles. 'Come along!'

As they went along, certainly one of the party, and probably more than one, thought that Bleeding Heart Yard was no inappropriate destination for a man who had been in official correspondence with my lords and the Barnacles—and perhaps had a misgiving also that Britannia herself might come to look for lodgings in Bleeding Heart Yard some ugly day or other, if she over-did the Circumlocution Office.

CHAPTER 11. Let Loose

A late, dull autumn night was closing in upon the river Saone. The stream, like a sullied looking-glass in a gloomy place, reflected the clouds heavily; and the low banks leaned over here and there, as if they were half curious, and half afraid, to see their darkening pictures in the water. The flat expanse of country about Chalons lay a long heavy streak, occasionally made a little ragged by a row of poplar trees against the wrathful sunset. On the banks of the river Saone it was wet, depressing, solitary; and the night deepened fast.

One man slowly moving on towards Chalons was the only visible figure in the landscape. Cain might have looked as lonely and avoided. With an old sheepskin knapsack at his back, and a rough, unbarked stick cut out of some wood in his hand; miry, footsore, his shoes and gaiters trodden out, his hair and beard untrimmed; the cloak he carried over his shoulder, and the clothes he wore, sodden with wet; limping along in pain and difficulty; he looked as if the clouds were hurrying from him, as if the wail of the wind and the shuddering of the grass were directed against him, as if the low mysterious plashing of the water murmured at him, as if the fitful autumn night were disturbed by him.

He glanced here, and he glanced there, sullenly but shrinkingly; and sometimes stopped and turned about, and looked all round him. Then he limped on again, toiling and muttering.

'To the devil with this plain that has no end! To the devil with these stones that cut like knives! To the devil with this dismal darkness, wrapping itself about one with a chill! I hate you!'

And he would have visited his hatred upon it all with the scowl he threw about him, if he could. He trudged a little further; and looking into the distance before him, stopped again.

'I, hungry, thirsty, weary. You, imbeciles, where the lights are yonder, eating and drinking, and warming yourselves at fires! I wish I had the sacking of your town; I would repay you, my children!'

But the teeth he set at the town, and the hand he shook at the town, brought the town no nearer; and the man was yet hungrier, and thirstier, and wearier, when his feet were on its jagged pavement, and he stood looking about him.

There was the hotel with its gateway, and its savoury smell of cooking; there was the cafe with its bright windows, and its rattling of dominoes; there was the dyer's with its strips of red cloth on the doorposts; there was the silversmith's with its earrings, and its offerings for altars; there was the tobacco dealer's with its lively group of soldier customers coming out pipe in mouth; there were the bad odours of the town, and the rain and the refuse in the kennels, and the faint lamps slung across the road, and the huge Diligence, and its mountain of luggage, and its six grey horses with their tails tied up, getting under weigh at the coach office. But no small cabaret for a straitened traveller being within sight, he had to seek one round the dark corner, where the cabbage leaves lay thickest, trodden about the public cistern at which women had not yet left off drawing water. There, in the back street he found one, the Break of Day. The curtained windows clouded the Break of Day, but it seemed light and warm, and it announced in legible inscriptions with appropriate pictorial embellishment of billiard cue and ball, that at the Break of Day one could play billiards; that there one could find meat, drink, and lodgings, whether one came on horseback, or came on foot; and that it kept good wines, liqueurs, and brandy. The man turned the handle of the Break of Day door, and limped in.

He touched his discoloured slouched hat, as he came in at the door, to a few men who occupied the room. Two were playing dominoes at one of the little tables; three or four were seated round the stove, conversing as they smoked; the billiard-table in the centre was left alone for the time; the landlady of the Daybreak sat behind her little counter among her cloudy bottles of syrups, baskets of cakes, and leaden drainage for glasses, working at her needle.

Making his way to an empty little table in a corner of the room behind the stove, he put down his knapsack and his cloak upon the ground. As he raised his head from stooping to do so, he found the landlady beside him.

'One can lodge here to-night, madame?'

'Perfectly!' said the landlady in a high, sing-song, cheery voice.

'Good. One can dine—sup—what you please to call it?'

'Ah, perfectly!' cried the landlady as before.

'Dispatch then, madame, if you please. Something to eat, as quickly as you can; and some wine at once. I am exhausted.'

'It is very bad weather, monsieur,' said the landlady.

'Cursed weather.'

'And a very long road.'

'A cursed road.'

His hoarse voice failed him, and he rested his head upon his hands until a bottle of wine was brought from the counter. Having filled and emptied his little tumbler twice, and having broken off an end from the great loaf that was set before him with his cloth and napkin, soup-plate, salt, pepper, and oil, he rested his back against the corner of the wall, made a couch of the bench on which he sat, and began to chew crust, until such time as his repast should be ready.

There had been that momentary interruption of the talk about the stove, and that temporary inattention to and distraction from one another, which is usually inseparable in such a company from the arrival of a stranger. It had passed over by this time; and the men had done glancing at him, and were talking again.

'That's the true reason,' said one of them, bringing a story he had been telling, to a close, 'that's the true reason why they said that the devil was let loose.' The speaker was the tall Swiss belonging to the church, and he brought something of the authority of the church into the discussion—especially as the devil was in question.

The landlady having given her directions for the new guest's entertainment to her husband, who acted as cook to the Break of Day, had resumed her needlework behind her counter. She was a smart, neat, bright little woman, with a good deal of cap and a good deal of stocking, and she struck into the conversation with several laughing nods of her head, but without looking up from her work.

'Ah Heaven, then,' said she. 'When the boat came up from Lyons, and brought the news that the devil was actually let loose at Marseilles, some fly-catchers swallowed it. But I? No, not I.'

'Madame, you are always right,' returned the tall Swiss. 'Doubtless you were enraged against that man, madame?'

'Ay, yes, then!' cried the landlady, raising her eyes from her work, opening them very wide, and tossing her head on one side. 'Naturally, yes.'

'He was a bad subject.'

'He was a wicked wretch,' said the landlady, 'and well merited what he had the good fortune to escape. So much the worse.'

'Stay, madame! Let us see,' returned the Swiss, argumentatively turning his cigar between his lips. 'It may have been his unfortunate destiny. He may have been the child of circumstances. It is always possible that he had, and has, good in him if one did but know how to find it out. Philosophical philanthropy teaches—'

The rest of the little knot about the stove murmured an objection to the introduction of that threatening expression. Even the two players at dominoes glanced up from their game, as if to protest against philosophical philanthropy being brought by name into the Break of Day.

'Hold there, you and your philanthropy,' cried the smiling landlady, nodding her head more than ever. 'Listen then. I am a woman, I. I know nothing of philosophical philanthropy. But I know what I have seen, and what I have looked in the face in this world here, where I find myself. And I tell you this, my friend, that there are people (men and women both, unfortunately) who have no good in them—none. That there are people whom it is necessary to detest without compromise. That there are people who must be dealt with as enemies of the human race. That there are people who have no human heart, and who must be crushed like savage beasts and cleared out of the way. They are but few, I hope; but I have seen (in this world here where I find myself, and even at the little Break of Day) that there are such people. And I do not doubt that this man—whatever they call him, I forget his name—is one of them.'

The landlady's lively speech was received with greater favour at the Break of Day, than it would have elicited from certain amiable whitewashers of the class she so unreasonably objected to, nearer Great Britain.

'My faith! If your philosophical philanthropy,' said the landlady, putting down her work, and rising to take the stranger's soup from her husband, who appeared with it at a side door, 'puts anybody at the mercy of such people by holding terms with them at all, in words or deeds, or both, take it away from the Break of Day, for it isn't worth a sou.'

As she placed the soup before the guest, who changed his attitude to a sitting one, he looked her full in the face, and his moustache went up under his nose, and his nose came down over his moustache.

'Well!' said the previous speaker, 'let us come back to our subject. Leaving all that aside, gentlemen, it was because the man was acquitted on his trial that people said at Marseilles that the devil was let loose. That was how the phrase began to circulate, and what it meant; nothing more.'

'How do they call him?' said the landlady. 'Biraud, is it not?'

'Rigaud, madame,' returned the tall Swiss.

'Rigaud! To be sure.'

The traveller's soup was succeeded by a dish of meat, and that by a dish of vegetables. He ate all that was placed before him, emptied his bottle of wine, called for a glass of rum, and smoked his cigarette with his cup of coffee. As he became refreshed, he became overbearing; and patronised the company at the Daybreak in certain small talk at which he assisted, as if his condition were far above his appearance.

The company might have had other engagements, or they might have felt their inferiority, but in any case they dispersed by degrees, and not being replaced by other company, left their new patron in possession of the Break of Day. The landlord was clinking about in his kitchen; the landlady was quiet at her work; and the refreshed traveller sat smoking by the stove, warming his ragged feet.

'Pardon me, madame—that Biraud.'

'Rigaud, monsieur.'

'Rigaud. Pardon me again—has contracted your displeasure, how?'

The landlady, who had been at one moment thinking within herself that this was a handsome man, at another moment that this was an ill-looking man, observed the nose coming down and the moustache going up, and strongly inclined to the latter decision. Rigaud was a criminal, she said, who had killed his wife.

'Ay, ay? Death of my life, that's a criminal indeed. But how do you know it?'

'All the world knows it.'

'Hah! And yet he escaped justice?'

'Monsieur, the law could not prove it against him to its satisfaction. So the law says. Nevertheless, all the world knows he did it. The people knew it so well, that they tried to tear him to pieces.'

'Being all in perfect accord with their own wives?' said the guest. 'Haha!'

The landlady of the Break of Day looked at him again, and felt almost confirmed in her last decision. He had a fine hand, though, and he turned it with a great show. She began once more to think that he was not ill-looking after all.

'Did you mention, madame—or was it mentioned among the gentlemen—what became of him?'

The landlady shook her head; it being the first conversational stage at which her vivacious earnestness had ceased to nod it, keeping time to what she said. It had been mentioned at the Daybreak, she remarked, on the authority of the journals, that he had been kept in prison for his own safety. However that might be, he had escaped his deserts; so much the worse.

The guest sat looking at her as he smoked out his final cigarette, and as she sat with her head bent over her work, with an expression that might have resolved her doubts, and brought her to a lasting conclusion on the subject of his good or bad looks if she had seen it. When she did look up, the expression was not there. The hand was smoothing his shaggy moustache.

'May one ask to be shown to bed, madame?'

Very willingly, monsieur. Hola, my husband! My husband would conduct him up-stairs. There was one traveller there, asleep, who had gone to bed very early indeed, being overpowered by fatigue; but it was a large chamber with two beds in it, and space enough for twenty. This the landlady of the Break of Day chirpingly explained, calling between whiles, 'Hola, my husband!' out at the side door.

My husband answered at length, 'It is I, my wife!' and presenting himself in his cook's cap, lighted the traveller up a steep and narrow staircase; the traveller carrying his own cloak and knapsack, and bidding the landlady good night with a complimentary reference to the pleasure of seeing her again to-morrow. It was a large room, with a rough splintery floor, unplastered rafters overhead, and two bedsteads on opposite sides. Here 'my husband' put down the candle he carried, and with a sidelong look at his guest stooping over his knapsack, gruffly gave him the instruction, 'The bed to the right!' and left him to his repose. The landlord, whether he was a good or a bad physiognomist, had fully made up his mind that the guest was an ill-looking fellow.

The guest looked contemptuously at the clean coarse bedding prepared for him, and, sitting down on the rush chair at the bedside, drew his money out of his pocket, and told it over in his hand. 'One must eat,' he muttered to himself, 'but by Heaven I must eat at the cost of some other man to-morrow!'

As he sat pondering, and mechanically weighing his money in his palm, the deep breathing of the traveller in the other bed fell so regularly upon his hearing that it attracted his eyes in that direction. The man was covered up warm, and had drawn the white curtain at his head, so that he could be only heard, not seen. But the deep regular breathing, still going on while the other was taking off his worn shoes and gaiters, and still continuing when he had laid aside his coat and cravat, became at length a strong provocative to curiosity, and incentive to get a glimpse of the sleeper's face.

The waking traveller, therefore, stole a little nearer, and yet a little nearer, and a little nearer to the sleeping traveller's bed, until he stood close beside it. Even then he could not see his face, for he had drawn the sheet over it. The regular breathing still continuing, he put his smooth white hand (such a treacherous hand it looked, as it went creeping from him!) to the sheet, and gently lifted it away.

'Death of my soul!' he whispered, falling back, 'here's Cavalletto!'

The little Italian, previously influenced in his sleep, perhaps, by the stealthy presence at his bedside, stopped in his regular breathing, and with a long deep respiration opened his eyes.

At first they were not awake, though open. He lay for some seconds looking placidly at his old prison companion, and then, all at once, with a cry of surprise and alarm, sprang out of bed.

'Hush! What's the matter? Keep quiet! It's I. You know me?' cried the other, in a suppressed voice.

But John Baptist, widely staring, muttering a number of invocations and ejaculations, tremblingly backing into a corner, slipping on his trousers, and tying his coat by the two sleeves round his neck, manifested an unmistakable desire to escape by the door rather than renew the acquaintance. Seeing this, his old prison comrade fell back upon the door, and set his shoulders against it.

'Cavalletto! Wake, boy! Rub your eyes and look at me. Not the name you used to call me—don't use that—Lagnier, say Lagnier!'

John Baptist, staring at him with eyes opened to their utmost width, made a number of those national, backhanded shakes of the right forefinger in the air, as if he were resolved on negativing beforehand everything that the other could possibly advance during the whole term of his life.

'Cavalletto! Give me your hand. You know Lagnier, the gentleman. Touch the hand of a gentleman!'

Submitting himself to the old tone of condescending authority, John Baptist, not at all steady on his legs as yet, advanced and put his hand in his patron's. Monsieur Lagnier laughed; and having given it a squeeze, tossed it up and let it go.

'Then you were—' faltered John Baptist.

'Not shaved? No. See here!' cried Lagnier, giving his head a twirl; 'as tight on as your own.'

John Baptist, with a slight shiver, looked all round the room as if to recall where he was. His patron took that opportunity of turning the key in the door, and then sat down upon his bed.

'Look!' he said, holding up his shoes and gaiters. 'That's a poor trim for a gentleman, you'll say. No matter, you shall see how soon I'll mend it. Come and sit down. Take your old place!'

John Baptist, looking anything but reassured, sat down on the floor at the bedside, keeping his eyes upon his patron all the time.

'That's well!' cried Lagnier. 'Now we might be in the old infernal hole again, hey? How long have you been out?'

'Two days after you, my master.'

'How do you come here?'

'I was cautioned not to stay there, and so I left the town at once, and since then I have changed about. I have been doing odds and ends at Avignon, at Pont Esprit, at Lyons; upon the Rhone, upon the Saone.' As he spoke, he rapidly mapped the places out with his sunburnt hand upon the floor.

'And where are you going?'

'Going, my master?'

'Ay!'

John Baptist seemed to desire to evade the question without knowing how. 'By Bacchus!' he said at last, as if he were forced to the admission, 'I have sometimes had a thought of going to Paris, and perhaps to England.'

'Cavalletto. This is in confidence. I also am going to Paris and perhaps to England. We'll go together.'

The little man nodded his head, and showed his teeth; and yet seemed not quite convinced that it was a surpassingly desirable arrangement.

'We'll go together,' repeated Lagnier. 'You shall see how soon I will force myself to be recognised as a gentleman, and you shall profit by it. It is agreed? Are we one?'

'Oh, surely, surely!' said the little man.

'Then you shall hear before I sleep—and in six words, for I want sleep—how I appear before you, I, Lagnier. Remember that. Not the other.'

'Altro, altro! Not Ri——' Before John Baptist could finish the name, his comrade had got his hand under his chin and fiercely shut up his mouth.

'Death! what are you doing? Do you want me to be trampled upon and stoned? Do you want to be trampled upon and stoned? You would be. You don't imagine that they would set upon me, and let my prison chum go? Don't think it!'

There was an expression in his face as he released his grip of his friend's jaw, from which his friend inferred that if the course of events really came to any stoning and trampling, Monsieur Lagnier would so distinguish him with his notice as to ensure his having his full share of it. He remembered what a cosmopolitan gentleman Monsieur Lagnier was, and how few weak distinctions he made.

'I am a man,' said Monsieur Lagnier, 'whom society has deeply wronged since you last saw me. You know that I am sensitive and brave, and that it is my character to govern. How has society respected those qualities in me? I have been shrieked at through the streets. I have been guarded through the streets against men, and especially women, running at me armed with any weapons they could lay their hands on. I have lain in prison for security, with the place of my confinement kept a secret, lest I should be torn out of it and felled by a hundred blows. I have been carted out of Marseilles in the dead of night, and carried leagues away from it packed in straw. It has not been safe for me to go near my house; and, with a beggar's pittance in my pocket, I have walked through vile mud and weather ever since, until my feet are crippled— look at them! Such are the humiliations that society has inflicted upon me, possessing the qualities I have mentioned, and which you know me to possess. But society shall pay for it.'

All this he said in his companion's ear, and with his hand before his lips.

'Even here,' he went on in the same way, 'even in this mean drinking-shop, society pursues me. Madame defames me, and her guests defame me. I, too, a gentleman with manners and accomplishments to strike them dead! But the wrongs society has heaped upon me are treasured in this breast.'

To all of which John Baptist, listening attentively to the suppressed hoarse voice, said from time to time, 'Surely, surely!' tossing his head and shutting his eyes, as if there were the clearest case against society that perfect candour could make out.

'Put my shoes there,' continued Lagnier. 'Hang my cloak to dry there by the door. Take my hat.' He obeyed each instruction, as it was given. 'And this is the bed to which society consigns me, is it? Hah. Very well!'

As he stretched out his length upon it, with a ragged handkerchief bound round his wicked head, and only his wicked head showing above the bedclothes, John Baptist was rather strongly reminded of what had so very nearly happened to prevent the moustache from any more going up as it did, and the nose from any more coming down as it did.

'Shaken out of destiny's dice-box again into your company, eh? By Heaven! So much the better for you. You'll profit by it. I shall need a long rest. Let me sleep in the morning.'

John Baptist replied that he should sleep as long as he would, and wishing him a happy night, put out the candle. One might have supposed that the next proceeding of the Italian would have been to undress; but he did exactly the reverse, and dressed himself from head to foot, saving his shoes. When he had so done, he lay down upon his bed with some of its coverings over him, and his coat still tied round his neck, to get through the night.

When he started up, the Godfather Break of Day was peeping at its namesake. He rose, took his shoes in his hand, turned the key in the door with great caution, and crept downstairs. Nothing was astir there but the smell of coffee, wine, tobacco, and syrups; and madame's little counter looked ghastly enough. But he had paid madame his little note at it over night, and wanted to see nobody—wanted nothing but to get on his shoes and his knapsack, open the door, and run away.

He prospered in his object. No movement or voice was heard when he opened the door; no wicked head tied up in a ragged handkerchief looked out of the upper window. When the sun had raised his full disc above the flat line of the horizon, and was striking fire out of the long muddy vista of paved road with its weary avenue of little trees, a black speck moved along the road and splashed among the flaming pools of rain-water, which black speck was John Baptist Cavalletto running away from his patron.

CHAPTER 12. Bleeding Heart Yard

In London itself, though in the old rustic road towards a suburb of note where in the days of William Shakespeare, author and stage-player, there were Royal hunting-seats—howbeit no sport is left there now but for hunters of men—Bleeding Heart Yard was to be found; a place much changed in feature and in fortune, yet with some relish of ancient greatness about it. Two or three mighty stacks of chimneys, and a few large dark rooms which had escaped being walled and subdivided out of the recognition of their old proportions, gave the Yard a character. It was inhabited by poor people, who set up their rest among its faded glories, as Arabs of the desert pitch their tents among the fallen stones of the Pyramids; but there was a family sentimental feeling prevalent in the Yard, that it had a character.

As if the aspiring city had become puffed up in the very ground on which it stood, the ground had so risen about Bleeding Heart Yard that you got into it down a flight of steps which formed no part of the original approach, and got out of it by a low gateway into a maze of shabby streets, which went about and about, tortuously ascending to the level again. At this end of the Yard and over the gateway, was the factory of Daniel Doyce, often heavily beating like a bleeding heart of iron, with the clink of metal upon metal.

The opinion of the Yard was divided respecting the derivation of its name. The more practical of its inmates abided by the tradition of a murder; the gentler and more imaginative inhabitants, including the whole of the tender sex, were loyal to the legend of a young lady of former times closely imprisoned in her chamber by a cruel father for remaining true to her own true love, and refusing to marry the suitor he chose for her. The legend related how that the young lady used to be seen up at her window behind the bars, murmuring a love-lorn song of which the burden was, 'Bleeding Heart, Bleeding Heart, bleeding away,' until she died. It was objected by the murderous party that this Refrain was notoriously the invention of a tambour-worker, a spinster and romantic, still lodging in the Yard. But, forasmuch as all favourite legends must be associated with the affections, and as many more people fall in love than commit murder—which it may be hoped, howsoever bad we are, will continue until the end of the world to be the dispensation under which we shall live—the Bleeding Heart, Bleeding Heart, bleeding away story, carried the day by a great majority. Neither party would listen to the antiquaries who delivered learned lectures in the neighbourhood, showing the Bleeding Heart to have been the heraldic cognisance of the old family to whom the property had once belonged. And, considering that the hour-glass they turned from year to year was filled with the earthiest and coarsest sand, the Bleeding Heart Yarders had reason enough for objecting to be despoiled of the one little golden grain of poetry that sparkled in it.

Down in to the Yard, by way of the steps, came Daniel Doyce, Mr Meagles, and Clennam. Passing along the Yard, and between the open doors on either hand, all abundantly garnished with light children nursing heavy ones, they arrived at its opposite boundary, the gateway. Here Arthur Clennam stopped to look about him for the domicile of Plornish, plasterer, whose name, according to the custom of Londoners, Daniel Doyce had never seen or heard of to that hour.

It was plain enough, nevertheless, as Little Dorrit had said; over a lime-splashed gateway in the corner, within which Plornish kept a ladder and a barrel or two. The last house in Bleeding Heart Yard which she had described as his place of habitation, was a large house, let off to various tenants; but Plornish ingeniously hinted that he lived in the parlour, by means of a painted hand under his name, the forefinger of which hand (on which the artist had depicted a ring and a most elaborate nail of the genteelest form) referred all inquirers to that apartment.

Parting from his companions, after arranging another meeting with Mr Meagles, Clennam went alone into the entry, and knocked with his knuckles at the parlour-door. It was opened presently by a woman with a child in her arms, whose unoccupied hand was hastily rearranging the upper part of her dress. This was Mrs Plornish, and this maternal action was the action of Mrs Plornish during a large part of her waking existence.

Was Mr Plornish at home? 'Well, sir,' said Mrs Plornish, a civil woman, 'not to deceive you, he's gone to look for a job.'

'Not to deceive you' was a method of speech with Mrs Plornish. She would deceive you, under any circumstances, as little as might be; but she had a trick of answering in this provisional form.

'Do you think he will be back soon, if I wait for him?'

'I have been expecting him,' said Mrs Plornish, 'this half an hour, at any minute of time. Walk in, sir.'

Arthur entered the rather dark and close parlour (though it was lofty too), and sat down in the chair she placed for him.

'Not to deceive you, sir, I notice it,' said Mrs Plornish, 'and I take it kind of you.'

He was at a loss to understand what she meant; and by expressing as much in his looks, elicited her explanation.

'It ain't many that comes into a poor place, that deems it worth their while to move their hats,' said Mrs Plornish. 'But people think more of it than people think.'

Clennam returned, with an uncomfortable feeling in so very slight a courtesy being unusual, Was that all! And stooping down to pinch the cheek of another young child who was sitting on the floor, staring at him, asked Mrs Plornish how old that fine boy was?

'Four year just turned, sir,' said Mrs Plornish. 'He is a fine little fellow, ain't he, sir? But this one is rather sickly.' She tenderly hushed the baby in her arms, as she said it. 'You wouldn't mind my asking if it happened to be a job as you was come about, sir, would you?' asked Mrs Plornish wistfully.

She asked it so anxiously, that if he had been in possession of any kind of tenement, he would have had it plastered a foot deep rather than answer No. But he was obliged to answer No; and he saw a shade of disappointment on her face, as she checked a sigh, and looked at the low fire. Then he saw, also, that Mrs Plornish was a young woman, made somewhat slatternly in herself and her belongings by poverty; and so dragged at by poverty and the children together, that their united forces had already dragged her face into wrinkles.

'All such things as jobs,' said Mrs Plornish, 'seems to me to have gone underground, they do indeed.' (Herein Mrs Plornish limited her remark to the plastering trade, and spoke without reference to the Circumlocution Office and the Barnacle Family.)

'Is it so difficult to get work?' asked Arthur Clennam.

'Plornish finds it so,' she returned. 'He is quite unfortunate. Really he is.'

Really he was. He was one of those many wayfarers on the road of life, who seem to be afflicted with supernatural corns, rendering it impossible for them to keep up even with their lame competitors. A willing, working, soft hearted, not hard-headed fellow, Plornish took his fortune as smoothly as could be expected; but it was a rough one. It so rarely happened that anybody seemed to want him, it was such an exceptional case when his powers were in any request, that his misty mind could not make out how it happened. He took it as it came, therefore; he tumbled into all kinds of difficulties, and tumbled out of them; and, by tumbling through life, got himself considerably bruised.

'It's not for want of looking after jobs, I am sure,' said Mrs Plornish, lifting up her eyebrows, and searching for a solution of the problem between the bars of the grate; 'nor yet for want of working at them when they are to be got. No one ever heard my husband complain of work.'

Somehow or other, this was the general misfortune of Bleeding Heart Yard. From time to time there were public complaints, pathetically going about, of labour being scarce—which certain people seemed to take extraordinarily ill, as though they had an absolute right to it on their own terms—but Bleeding Heart Yard, though as willing a Yard as any in Britain, was never the better for the demand. That high old family, the Barnacles, had long been too busy with their great principle to look into the matter; and indeed the matter had nothing to do with their watchfulness in out-generalling all other high old families except the Stiltstalkings.

While Mrs Plornish spoke in these words of her absent lord, her lord returned. A smooth-cheeked, fresh-coloured, sandy-whiskered man of thirty. Long in the legs, yielding at the knees, foolish in the face, flannel-jacketed, lime-whitened.

'This is Plornish, sir.'

'I came,' said Clennam, rising, 'to beg the favour of a little conversation with you on the subject of the Dorrit family.'

Plornish became suspicious. Seemed to scent a creditor. Said, 'Ah, yes. Well. He didn't know what satisfaction he could give any gentleman, respecting that family. What might it be about, now?'

'I know you better,' said Clennam, smiling, 'than you suppose.'

Plornish observed, not smiling in return, And yet he hadn't the pleasure of being acquainted with the gentleman, neither.

'No,' said Arthur, 'I know your kind offices at second hand, but on the best authority; through Little Dorrit.—I mean,' he explained, 'Miss Dorrit.'

'Mr Clennam, is it? Oh! I've heard of you, Sir.'

'And I of you,' said Arthur.

'Please to sit down again, Sir, and consider yourself welcome.—Why, yes,' said Plornish, taking a chair, and lifting the elder child upon his knee, that he might have the moral support of speaking to a stranger over his head, 'I have been on the wrong side of the Lock myself, and in that way we come to know Miss Dorrit. Me and my wife, we are well acquainted with Miss Dorrit.'

'Intimate!' cried Mrs Plornish. Indeed, she was so proud of the acquaintance, that she had awakened some bitterness of spirit in the Yard by magnifying to an enormous amount the sum for which Miss Dorrit's father had become insolvent. The Bleeding Hearts resented her claiming to know people of such distinction.

'It was her father that I got acquainted with first. And through getting acquainted with him, you see—why—I got acquainted with her,' said Plornish tautologically.

'I see.'

'Ah! And there's manners! There's polish! There's a gentleman to have run to seed in the Marshalsea jail! Why, perhaps you are not aware,' said Plornish, lowering his voice, and speaking with a perverse admiration of what he ought to have pitied or despised, 'not aware that Miss Dorrit and her sister dursn't let him know that they work for a living. No!' said Plornish, looking with a ridiculous triumph first at his wife, and then all round the room. 'Dursn't let him know it, they dursn't!'

'Without admiring him for that,' Clennam quietly observed, 'I am very sorry for him.'

The remark appeared to suggest to Plornish, for the first time, that it might not be a very fine trait of character after all. He pondered about it for a moment, and gave it up.

'As to me,' he resumed, 'certainly Mr Dorrit is as affable with me, I am sure, as I can possibly expect. Considering the differences and distances betwixt us, more so. But it's Miss Dorrit that we were speaking of.'

'True. Pray how did you introduce her at my mother's!'

Mr Plornish picked a bit of lime out of his whisker, put it between his lips, turned it with his tongue like a sugar-plum, considered, found himself unequal to the task of lucid explanation, and appealing to his wife, said, 'Sally, you may as well mention how it was, old woman.'

'Miss Dorrit,' said Sally, hushing the baby from side to side, and laying her chin upon the little hand as it tried to disarrange the gown again, 'came here one afternoon with a bit of writing, telling that how she wished for needlework, and asked if it would be considered any ill-conwenience in case she was to give her address here.' (Plornish repeated, her address here, in a low voice, as if he were making responses at church.) 'Me and Plornish says, No, Miss Dorrit, no ill-conwenience,' (Plornish repeated, no ill-conwenience,) 'and she wrote it in, according. Which then me and Plornish says, Ho Miss Dorrit!' (Plornish repeated, Ho Miss Dorrit.) 'Have you thought of copying it three or four times, as the way to make it known in more places than one? No, says Miss Dorrit, I have not, but I will. She copied it out according, on this table, in a sweet writing, and Plornish, he took it where he worked, having a job just then,' (Plornish repeated job just then,) 'and likewise to the landlord of the Yard; through which it was that Mrs Clennam first happened to employ Miss Dorrit.' Plornish repeated, employ Miss Dorrit; and Mrs Plornish having come to an end, feigned to bite the fingers of the little hand as she kissed it.

'The landlord of the Yard,' said Arthur Clennam, 'is—'

'He is Mr Casby, by name, he is,' said Plornish, 'and Pancks, he collects the rents. That,' added Mr Plornish, dwelling on the subject with a slow thoughtfulness that appeared to have no connection with any specific object, and to lead him nowhere, 'that is about what they are, you may believe me or not, as you think proper.'

'Ay?' returned Clennam, thoughtful in his turn. 'Mr Casby, too! An old acquaintance of mine, long ago!'

Mr Plornish did not see his road to any comment on this fact, and made none. As there truly was no reason why he should have the least interest in it, Arthur Clennam went on to the present purport of his visit; namely, to make Plornish the instrument of effecting Tip's release, with as little detriment as possible to the self-reliance and self-helpfulness of the young man, supposing him to possess any remnant of those qualities: without doubt a very wide stretch of supposition. Plornish, having been made acquainted with the cause of action from the Defendant's own mouth, gave Arthur to understand that the Plaintiff was a 'Chaunter'— meaning, not a singer of anthems, but a seller of horses—and that he (Plornish) considered that ten shillings in the pound 'would settle handsome,' and that more would be a waste of money. The Principal and instrument soon drove off together to a stable-yard in High Holborn, where a remarkably fine grey gelding, worth, at the lowest figure, seventy-five guineas (not taking into account the value of the shot he had been made to swallow for the improvement of his form), was to be parted with for a twenty-pound note, in consequence of his having run away last week with Mrs Captain Barbary of Cheltenham, who wasn't up to a horse of his courage, and who, in mere spite, insisted on selling him for that ridiculous sum: or, in other words, on giving him away. Plornish, going up this yard alone and leaving his Principal outside, found a gentleman with tight drab legs, a rather old hat, a little hooked stick, and a blue neckerchief (Captain Maroon of Gloucestershire, a private friend of Captain Barbary); who happened to be there, in a friendly way, to mention these little circumstances concerning the remarkably fine grey gelding to any real judge of a horse and quick snapper-up of a good thing, who might look in at that address as per advertisement. This gentleman, happening also to be the Plaintiff in the Tip case, referred Mr Plornish to his solicitor, and declined to treat with Mr Plornish, or even to endure his presence in the yard, unless he appeared there with a twenty-pound note: in which case only, the gentleman would augur from appearances that he meant business, and might be induced to talk to him. On this hint, Mr Plornish retired to communicate with his Principal, and presently came back with the required credentials. Then said Captain Maroon, 'Now, how much time do you want to make the other twenty in? Now, I'll give you a month.' Then said Captain Maroon, when that wouldn't suit, 'Now, I'll tell what I'll do with you. You shall get me a good bill at four months, made payable at a banking-house, for the other twenty!' Then said Captain Maroon, when that wouldn't suit, 'Now, come; Here's the last I've got to say to you. You shall give me another ten down, and I'll run my pen clean through it.' Then said Captain Maroon when that wouldn't suit, 'Now, I'll tell you what it is, and this shuts it up; he has used me bad, but I'll let him off for another five down and a bottle of wine; and if you mean done, say done, and if you don't like it, leave it.' Finally said Captain Maroon, when that wouldn't suit either, 'Hand over, then!'—And in consideration of the first offer, gave a receipt in full and discharged the prisoner.

'Mr Plornish,' said Arthur, 'I trust to you, if you please, to keep my secret. If you will undertake to let the young man know that he is free, and to tell him that you were employed to compound for the debt by some one whom you are not at liberty to name, you will not only do me a service, but may do him one, and his sister also.'

'The last reason, sir,' said Plornish, 'would be quite sufficient. Your wishes shall be attended to.'

'A Friend has obtained his discharge, you can say if you please. A Friend who hopes that for his sister's sake, if for no one else's, he will make good use of his liberty.'

'Your wishes, sir, shall be attended to.'

'And if you will be so good, in your better knowledge of the family, as to communicate freely with me, and to point out to me any means by which you think I may be delicately and really useful to Little Dorrit, I shall feel under an obligation to you.'

'Don't name it, sir,' returned Plornish, 'it'll be ekally a pleasure an a—it'l be ekally a pleasure and a—' Finding himself unable to balance his sentence after two efforts, Mr Plornish wisely dropped it. He took Clennam's card and appropriate pecuniary compliment.

He was earnest to finish his commission at once, and his Principal was in the same mind. So his Principal offered to set him down at the Marshalsea Gate, and they drove in that direction over Blackfriars Bridge. On the way, Arthur elicited from his new friend a confused summary of the interior life of Bleeding Heart Yard. They was all hard up there, Mr Plornish said, uncommon hard up, to be sure. Well, he couldn't say how it was; he didn't know as anybody could say how it was; all he know'd was, that so it was. When a man felt, on his own back and in his own belly, that poor he was, that man (Mr Plornish gave it as his decided belief) know'd well that he was poor somehow or another, and you couldn't talk it out of him, no more than you could talk Beef into him. Then you see, some people as was better off said, and a good many such people lived pretty close up to the mark themselves if not beyond it so he'd heerd, that they was 'improvident' (that was the favourite word) down the Yard. For instance, if they see a man with his wife and children going to Hampton Court in a Wan, perhaps once in a year, they says, 'Hallo! I thought you was poor, my improvident friend!' Why, Lord, how hard it was upon a man! What was a man to do? He couldn't go mollancholy mad, and even if he did, you wouldn't be the better for it. In Mr Plornish's judgment you would be the worse for it. Yet you seemed to want to make a man mollancholy mad. You was always at it—if not with your right hand, with your left. What was they a doing in the Yard? Why, take a look at 'em and see. There was the girls and their mothers a working at their sewing, or their shoe-binding, or their trimming, or their waistcoat making, day and night and night and day, and not more than able to keep body and soul together after all—often not so much. There was people of pretty well all sorts of trades you could name, all wanting to work, and yet not able to get it. There was old people, after working all their lives, going and being shut up in the workhouse, much worse fed and lodged and treated altogether, than—Mr Plornish said manufacturers, but appeared to mean malefactors. Why, a man didn't know where to turn himself for a crumb of comfort. As to who was to blame for it, Mr Plornish didn't know who was to blame for it. He could tell you who suffered, but he couldn't tell you whose fault it was. It wasn't his place to find out, and who'd mind what he said, if he did find out? He only know'd that it wasn't put right by them what undertook that line of business, and that it didn't come right of itself. And, in brief, his illogical opinion was, that if you couldn't do nothing for him, you had better take nothing from him for doing of it; so far as he could make out, that was about what it come to. Thus, in a prolix, gently-growling, foolish way, did Plornish turn the tangled skein of his estate about and about, like a blind man who was trying to find some beginning or end to it; until they reached the prison gate. There, he left his Principal alone; to wonder, as he rode away, how many thousand Plornishes there might be within a day or two's journey of the Circumlocution Office, playing sundry curious variations on the same tune, which were not known by ear in that glorious institution.

CHAPTER 13. Patriarchal

The mention of Mr Casby again revived in Clennam's memory the smouldering embers of curiosity and interest which Mrs Flintwinch had fanned on the night of his arrival. Flora Casby had been the beloved of his boyhood; and Flora was the daughter and only child of wooden-headed old Christopher (so he was still occasionally spoken of by some irreverent spirits who had had dealings with him, and in whom familiarity had bred its proverbial result perhaps), who was reputed to be rich in weekly tenants, and to get a good quantity of blood out of the stones of several unpromising courts and alleys.

After some days of inquiry and research, Arthur Clennam became convinced that the case of the Father of the Marshalsea was indeed a hopeless one, and sorrowfully resigned the idea of helping him to freedom again. He had no hopeful inquiry to make at present, concerning Little Dorrit either; but he argued with himself that it might—for anything he knew—it might be serviceable to the poor child, if he renewed this acquaintance. It is hardly necessary to add

113

that beyond all doubt he would have presented himself at Mr Casby's door, if there had been no Little Dorrit in existence; for we all know how we all deceive ourselves—that is to say, how people in general, our profounder selves excepted, deceive themselves—as to motives of action.

With a comfortable impression upon him, and quite an honest one in its way, that he was still patronising Little Dorrit in doing what had no reference to her, he found himself one afternoon at the corner of Mr Casby's street. Mr Casby lived in a street in the Gray's Inn Road, which had set off from that thoroughfare with the intention of running at one heat down into the valley, and up again to the top of Pentonville Hill; but which had run itself out of breath in twenty yards, and had stood still ever since. There is no such place in that part now; but it remained there for many years, looking with a baulked countenance at the wilderness patched with unfruitful gardens and pimpled with eruptive summerhouses, that it had meant to run over in no time.

'The house,' thought Clennam, as he crossed to the door, 'is as little changed as my mother's, and looks almost as gloomy. But the likeness ends outside. I know its staid repose within. The smell of its jars of old rose-leaves and lavender seems to come upon me even here.'

When his knock at the bright brass knocker of obsolete shape brought a woman-servant to the door, those faded scents in truth saluted him like wintry breath that had a faint remembrance in it of the bygone spring. He stepped into the sober, silent, air-tight house—one might have fancied it to have been stifled by Mutes in the Eastern manner—and the door, closing again, seemed to shut out sound and motion. The furniture was formal, grave, and quaker-like, but well-kept; and had as prepossessing an aspect as anything, from a human creature to a wooden stool, that is meant for much use and is preserved for little, can ever wear. There was a grave clock, ticking somewhere up the staircase; and there was a songless bird in the same direction, pecking at his cage, as if he were ticking too. The parlour-fire ticked in the grate. There was only one person on the parlour-hearth, and the loud watch in his pocket ticked audibly.

The servant-maid had ticked the two words 'Mr Clennam' so softly that she had not been heard; and he consequently stood, within the door she had closed, unnoticed. The figure of a man advanced in life, whose smooth grey eyebrows seemed to move to the ticking as the fire-light flickered on them, sat in an arm-chair, with his list shoes on the rug, and his thumbs slowly revolving over one another. This was old Christopher Casby—recognisable at a glance—as unchanged in twenty years and upward as his own solid furniture—as little touched by the influence of the varying seasons as the old rose-leaves and old lavender in his porcelain jars.

Perhaps there never was a man, in this troublesome world, so troublesome for the imagination to picture as a boy. And yet he had changed very little in his progress through life. Confronting him, in the room in which he sat, was a boy's portrait, which anybody seeing him would have identified as Master Christopher Casby, aged ten: though disguised with a haymaking rake, for which he had had, at any time, as much taste or use as for a diving-bell; and sitting (on one of his own legs) upon a bank of violets, moved to precocious contemplation by the spire of a village church. There was the same smooth face and forehead, the same calm blue eye, the same placid air. The shining bald head, which looked so very large because it shone so much; and the long grey hair at its sides and back, like floss silk or spun glass, which looked so very benevolent because it was never cut; were not, of course, to be seen in the boy as in the old man. Nevertheless, in the Seraphic creature with the haymaking rake, were clearly to be discerned the rudiments of the Patriarch with the list shoes.

Patriarch was the name which many people delighted to give him. Various old ladies in the neighbourhood spoke of him as The Last of the Patriarchs. So grey, so slow, so quiet, so impassionate, so very bumpy in the head, Patriarch was the word for him. He had been accosted in the streets, and respectfully solicited to become a Patriarch for painters and for sculptors; with so much importunity, in sooth, that it would appear to be beyond the Fine Arts to remember the points of a Patriarch, or to invent one. Philanthropists of both sexes had asked who he was, and on being informed, 'Old Christopher Casby, formerly Town-agent to Lord Decimus Tite Barnacle,' had cried in a rapture of disappointment, 'Oh! why, with that head, is he not a benefactor to his species! Oh! why, with that head, is he not a father to the orphan and a friend to the friendless!' With that head, however, he remained old Christopher Casby, proclaimed by common report rich in house property; and with that head, he now sat in his silent parlour. Indeed it would be the height of unreason to expect him to be sitting there without that head.

Arthur Clennam moved to attract his attention, and the grey eyebrows turned towards him.

'I beg your pardon,' said Clennam, 'I fear you did not hear me announced?'

'No, sir, I did not. Did you wish to see me, sir?'

'I wished to pay my respects.'

Mr Casby seemed a feather's weight disappointed by the last words, having perhaps prepared himself for the visitor's wishing to pay something else. 'Have I the pleasure, sir,' he proceeded—'take a chair, if you please—have I the pleasure of knowing—? Ah! truly, yes, I think I have! I believe I am not mistaken in supposing that I am acquainted with those features? I think I address a gentleman of whose return to this country I was informed by Mr Flintwinch?'

'That is your present visitor.'

'Really! Mr Clennam?'

'No other, Mr Casby.'

'Mr Clennam, I am glad to see you. How have you been since we met?'

Without thinking it worth while to explain that in the course of some quarter of a century he had experienced occasional slight fluctuations in his health and spirits, Clennam answered generally that he had never been better, or something equally to the purpose; and shook hands with the possessor of 'that head' as it shed its patriarchal light upon him.

'We are older, Mr Clennam,' said Christopher Casby.

'We are—not younger,' said Clennam. After this wise remark he felt that he was scarcely shining with brilliancy, and became aware that he was nervous.

'And your respected father,' said Mr Casby, 'is no more! I was grieved to hear it, Mr Clennam, I was grieved.'

Arthur replied in the usual way that he felt infinitely obliged to him.

'There was a time,' said Mr Casby, 'when your parents and myself were not on friendly terms. There was a little family misunderstanding among us. Your respected mother was rather jealous of her son, maybe; when I say her son, I mean your worthy self, your worthy self.'

His smooth face had a bloom upon it like ripe wall-fruit. What with his blooming face, and that head, and his blue eyes, he seemed to be delivering sentiments of rare wisdom and virtue. In like manner, his physiognomical expression seemed to teem with benignity. Nobody could have said where the wisdom was, or where the virtue was, or where the benignity was; but they all seemed to be somewhere about him.

'Those times, however,' pursued Mr Casby, 'are past and gone, past and gone. I do myself the pleasure of making a visit to your respected mother occasionally, and of admiring the fortitude and strength of mind with which she bears her trials, bears her trials.'

When he made one of these little repetitions, sitting with his hands crossed before him, he did it with his head on one side, and a gentle smile, as if he had something in his thoughts too sweetly profound to be put into words. As if he denied himself the pleasure of uttering it, lest he should soar too high; and his meekness therefore preferred to be unmeaning.

'I have heard that you were kind enough on one of those occasions,' said Arthur, catching at the opportunity as it drifted past him, 'to mention Little Dorrit to my mother.'

'Little—? Dorrit? That's the seamstress who was mentioned to me by a small tenant of mine? Yes, yes. Dorrit? That's the name. Ah, yes, yes! You call her Little Dorrit?'

No road in that direction. Nothing came of the cross-cut. It led no further.

'My daughter Flora,' said Mr Casby, 'as you may have heard probably, Mr Clennam, was married and established in life, several years ago. She had the misfortune to lose her husband when she had been married a few months. She resides with me again. She will be glad to see you, if you will permit me to let her know that you are here.'

'By all means,' returned Clennam. 'I should have preferred the request, if your kindness had not anticipated me.'

Upon this Mr Casby rose up in his list shoes, and with a slow, heavy step (he was of an elephantine build), made for the door. He had a long wide-skirted bottle-green coat on, and a bottle-green pair of trousers, and a bottle-green waistcoat. The Patriarchs were not dressed in bottle-green broadcloth, and yet his clothes looked patriarchal.

He had scarcely left the room, and allowed the ticking to become audible again, when a quick hand turned a latchkey in the house-door, opened it, and shut it. Immediately afterwards, a quick and eager short dark man came into the room with so much way upon him that he was within a foot of Clennam before he could stop.

'Halloa!' he said.

Clennam saw no reason why he should not say 'Halloa!' too.

'What's the matter?' said the short dark man.

'I have not heard that anything is the matter,' returned Clennam.

'Where's Mr Casby?' asked the short dark man, looking about.

'He will be here directly, if you want him.'

'I want him?' said the short dark man. 'Don't you?'

This elicited a word or two of explanation from Clennam, during the delivery of which the short dark man held his breath and looked at him. He was dressed in black and rusty iron grey; had jet black beads of eyes; a scrubby little black chin; wiry black hair striking out from his head in prongs, like forks or hair-pins; and a complexion that was very dingy by nature, or very dirty by art, or a compound of nature and art. He had dirty hands and dirty broken nails, and looked as if he had been in the coals; he was in a perspiration, and snorted and sniffed and puffed and blew, like a little labouring steam-engine.

'Oh!' said he, when Arthur told him how he came to be there. 'Very well. That's right. If he should ask for Pancks, will you be so good as to say that Pancks is come in?' And so, with a snort and a puff, he worked out by another door.

Now, in the old days at home, certain audacious doubts respecting the last of the Patriarchs, which were afloat in the air, had, by some forgotten means, come in contact with Arthur's sensorium. He was aware of motes and specks of suspicion in the atmosphere of that time; seen through which medium, Christopher Casby was a mere Inn signpost, without any Inn—an invitation to rest and be thankful, when there was no place to put up at, and nothing whatever to be thankful for. He knew that some of these specks even represented Christopher as capable of harbouring designs in 'that head,' and as being a crafty impostor. Other motes there were which showed him as a heavy, selfish, drifting Booby, who, having stumbled, in the course of his unwieldy jostlings against other men, on the discovery that to get through life with ease and credit, he had but to hold his tongue, keep the bald part of his head well polished, and leave his hair alone, had had just cunning enough to seize the idea and stick to it. It was said that his being town-agent to Lord Decimus Tite Barnacle was referable, not to his having the least business capacity, but to his looking so supremely benignant that nobody could suppose the property screwed or jobbed under such a man; also, that for similar reasons he now got more money out of his own wretched lettings, unquestioned, than anybody with a less nobby and less shining crown could possibly have done. In a word, it was represented (Clennam called to mind, alone in the ticking parlour) that many people select their models, much as the painters, just now mentioned, select theirs; and that, whereas in the Royal Academy some evil old ruffian of a Dog-stealer will annually be found embodying all the cardinal virtues, on account of his eyelashes, or his chin, or his legs (thereby planting thorns of confusion in the breasts of the more observant students of nature), so, in the great social Exhibition, accessories are often accepted in lieu of the internal character.

Calling these things to mind, and ranging Mr Pancks in a row with them, Arthur Clennam leaned this day to the opinion, without quite deciding on it, that the last of the Patriarchs was the drifting Booby aforesaid, with the one idea of keeping the bald part of his head highly polished: and that, much as an unwieldy ship in the Thames river may sometimes be seen heavily driving with the tide, broadside on, stern first, in its own way and in the way of everything else, though making a great show of navigation, when all of a sudden, a little coaly steam-tug will bear down upon it, take it in tow, and bustle off with it; similarly the cumbrous Patriarch had been taken in tow by the snorting Pancks, and was now following in the wake of that dingy little craft.

The return of Mr Casby with his daughter Flora, put an end to these meditations. Clennam's eyes no sooner fell upon the subject of his old passion than it shivered and broke to pieces.

Most men will be found sufficiently true to themselves to be true to an old idea. It is no proof of an inconstant mind, but exactly the opposite, when the idea will not bear close comparison with the reality, and the contrast is a fatal shock to it. Such was Clennam's case. In his youth he had ardently loved this woman, and had heaped upon her all the locked-up wealth of his affection and imagination. That wealth had been, in his desert home, like Robinson Crusoe's money; exchangeable with no one, lying idle in the dark to rust, until he poured it out for her. Ever since that memorable time, though he had, until the night of his arrival, as completely dismissed her from any association with his Present or Future as if she had been dead (which she might easily have been for anything he knew), he had kept the old fancy of the Past unchanged, in its old sacred place. And now, after all, the last of the Patriarchs coolly walked into the parlour, saying in effect, 'Be good enough to throw it down and dance upon it. This is Flora.'

Flora, always tall, had grown to be very broad too, and short of breath; but that was not much. Flora, whom he had left a lily, had become a peony; but that was not much. Flora, who had seemed enchanting in all she said and thought, was diffuse and silly. That was much. Flora, who had been spoiled and artless long ago, was determined to be spoiled and artless now. That was a fatal blow.

This is Flora!

'I am sure,' giggled Flora, tossing her head with a caricature of her girlish manner, such as a mummer might have presented at her own funeral, if she had lived and died in classical antiquity, 'I am ashamed to see Mr Clennam, I am a mere fright, I know he'll find me fearfully changed, I am actually an old woman, it's shocking to be found out, it's really shocking!'

He assured her that she was just what he had expected and that time had not stood still with himself.

'Oh! But with a gentleman it's so different and really you look so amazingly well that you have no right to say anything of the kind, while, as to me, you know—oh!' cried Flora with a little scream, 'I am dreadful!'

The Patriarch, apparently not yet understanding his own part in the drama under representation, glowed with vacant serenity.

'But if we talk of not having changed,' said Flora, who, whatever she said, never once came to a full stop, 'look at Papa, is not Papa precisely what he was when you went away, isn't it cruel and unnatural of Papa to be such a reproach to his own child, if we go on in this way much longer people who don't know us will begin to suppose that I am Papa's Mama!'

That must be a long time hence, Arthur considered.

'Oh Mr Clennam you insincerest of creatures,' said Flora, 'I perceive already you have not lost your old way of paying compliments, your old way when you used to pretend to be so sentimentally struck you know—at least I don't mean that, I—oh I don't know what I mean!' Here Flora tittered confusedly, and gave him one of her old glances.

The Patriarch, as if he now began to perceive that his part in the piece was to get off the stage as soon as might be, rose, and went to the door by which Pancks had worked out, hailing that Tug by name. He received an answer from some little Dock beyond, and was towed out of sight directly.

'You mustn't think of going yet,' said Flora—Arthur had looked at his hat, being in a ludicrous dismay, and not knowing what to do: 'you could never be so unkind as to think of going, Arthur—I mean Mr Arthur—or I suppose Mr Clennam would be far more proper—but I am sure I don't know what I am saying—without a word about the dear old days gone for ever, when I come to think of it I dare say it would be much better not to speak of them and it's highly probable that you have some much more agreeable engagement and pray let Me be the last person in the world to interfere with it though there was a time, but I am running into nonsense again.'

Was it possible that Flora could have been such a chatterer in the days she referred to? Could there have been anything like her present disjointed volubility in the fascinations that had captivated him?

'Indeed I have little doubt,' said Flora, running on with astonishing speed, and pointing her conversation with nothing but commas, and very few of them, 'that you are married to some Chinese lady, being in China so long and being in business and naturally desirous to settle and extend your connection nothing was more likely than that you should propose to a Chinese lady and nothing was more natural I am sure than that the Chinese lady should accept you and think herself very well off too, I only hope she's not a Pagodian dissenter.'

'I am not,' returned Arthur, smiling in spite of himself, 'married to any lady, Flora.'

'Oh good gracious me I hope you never kept yourself a bachelor so long on my account!' tittered Flora; 'but of course you never did why should you, pray don't answer, I don't know where I'm running to, oh do tell me something about the Chinese ladies whether their eyes are really so long and narrow always putting me in mind of mother-of-pearl fish at cards and do they really wear tails down their back and plaited too or is it only the men, and when they pull their hair so very tight off their foreheads don't they hurt themselves, and why do they stick little bells all over their bridges and temples and hats and things or don't they really do it?' Flora gave him another of her old glances. Instantly she went on again, as if he had spoken in reply for some time.

'Then it's all true and they really do! good gracious Arthur!—pray excuse me—old habit—Mr Clennam far more proper—what a country to live in for so long a time, and with so many lanterns and umbrellas too how very dark and wet the climate ought to be and no doubt actually is, and the sums of money that must be made by those two trades where everybody carries them and hangs them everywhere, the little shoes too and the feet screwed back in infancy is quite surprising, what a traveller you are!'

In his ridiculous distress, Clennam received another of the old glances without in the least knowing what to do with it.

'Dear dear,' said Flora, 'only to think of the changes at home Arthur—cannot overcome it, and seems so natural, Mr Clennam far more proper—since you became familiar with the Chinese customs and language which I am persuaded you speak like a Native if not better for you were always quick and clever though immensely difficult no doubt, I am sure the tea chests alone would kill me if I tried, such changes Arthur—I am doing it again, seems so natural, most improper—as no one could have believed, who could have ever imagined Mrs Finching when I can't imagine it myself!'

'Is that your married name?' asked Arthur, struck, in the midst of all this, by a certain warmth of heart that expressed itself in her tone when she referred, however oddly, to the youthful relation in which they had stood to one another. 'Finching?'

'Finching oh yes isn't it a dreadful name, but as Mr F. said when he proposed to me which he did seven times and handsomely consented I must say to be what he used to call on liking twelve months, after all, he wasn't answerable for it and couldn't help it could he, Excellent man, not at all like you but excellent man!'

Flora had at last talked herself out of breath for one moment. One moment; for she recovered breath in the act of raising a minute corner of her pocket-handkerchief to her eye, as a tribute to the ghost of the departed Mr F., and began again.

'No one could dispute, Arthur—Mr Clennam—that it's quite right you should be formally friendly to me under the altered circumstances and indeed you couldn't be anything else, at least I suppose not you ought to know, but I can't help recalling that there was a time when things were very different.'

'My dear Mrs Finching,' Arthur began, struck by the good tone again.

'Oh not that nasty ugly name, say Flora!'

'Flora. I assure you, Flora, I am happy in seeing you once more, and in finding that, like me, you have not forgotten the old foolish dreams, when we saw all before us in the light of our youth and hope.'

'You don't seem so,' pouted Flora, 'you take it very coolly, but however I know you are disappointed in me, I suppose the Chinese ladies—Mandarinesses if you call them so—are the cause or perhaps I am the cause myself, it's just as likely.'

'No, no,' Clennam entreated, 'don't say that.'

'Oh I must you know,' said Flora, in a positive tone, 'what nonsense not to, I know I am not what you expected, I know that very well.'

In the midst of her rapidity, she had found that out with the quick perception of a cleverer woman. The inconsistent and profoundly unreasonable way in which she instantly went on, nevertheless, to interweave their long-abandoned boy and girl relations with their present interview, made Clennam feel as if he were light-headed.

'One remark,' said Flora, giving their conversation, without the slightest notice and to the great terror of Clennam, the tone of a love-quarrel, 'I wish to make, one explanation I wish to offer, when your Mama came and made a scene of it with my Papa and when I was called down into the little breakfast-room where they were looking at one another with your Mama's parasol between them seated on two chairs like mad bulls what was I to do?'

'My dear Mrs Finching,' urged Clennam—'all so long ago and so long concluded, is it worth while seriously to—'

'I can't Arthur,' returned Flora, 'be denounced as heartless by the whole society of China without setting myself right when I have the opportunity of doing so, and you must be very well aware that there was Paul and Virginia which had to be returned and which was returned without note or comment, not that I mean to say you could have written to me watched as I was but if it had only come back with a red wafer on the cover I should have known that it meant Come to Pekin Nankeen and What's the third place, barefoot.'

'My dear Mrs Finching, you were not to blame, and I never blamed you. We were both too young, too dependent and helpless, to do anything but accept our separation.—Pray think how long ago,' gently remonstrated Arthur.

'One more remark,' proceeded Flora with unslackened volubility, 'I wish to make, one more explanation I wish to offer, for five days I had a cold in the head from crying which I passed entirely in the back drawing-room—there is the back drawing-room still on the first floor and still at the back of the house to confirm my words—when that dreary period had passed a lull succeeded years rolled on and Mr F. became acquainted with us at a mutual friend's, he was all attention he called next day he soon began to call three evenings a week and to send in little things for supper it was not love on Mr F.'s part it was adoration, Mr F. proposed with the full approval of Papa and what could I do?'

'Nothing whatever,' said Arthur, with the cheerfulest readiness, 'but what you did. Let an old friend assure you of his full conviction that you did quite right.'

'One last remark,' proceeded Flora, rejecting commonplace life with a wave of her hand, 'I wish to make, one last explanation I wish to offer, there was a time ere Mr F. first paid attentions incapable of being mistaken, but that is past and was not to be, dear Mr Clennam you no longer wear a golden chain you are free I trust you may be happy, here is Papa who is always tiresome and putting in his nose everywhere where he is not wanted.'

With these words, and with a hasty gesture fraught with timid caution—such a gesture had Clennam's eyes been familiar with in the old time—poor Flora left herself at eighteen years of age, a long long way behind again; and came to a full stop at last.

Or rather, she left about half of herself at eighteen years of age behind, and grafted the rest on to the relict of the late Mr F.; thus making a moral mermaid of herself, which her once boy-lover contemplated with feelings wherein his sense of the sorrowful and his sense of the comical were curiously blended.

For example. As if there were a secret understanding between herself and Clennam of the most thrilling nature; as if the first of a train of post-chaises and four, extending all the way to Scotland, were at that moment round the corner; and as if she couldn't (and wouldn't) have walked into the Parish Church with him, under the shade of the family umbrella, with the Patriarchal blessing on her head, and the perfect concurrence of all mankind; Flora comforted her soul with agonies of mysterious signalling, expressing dread of discovery. With the sensation of becoming more and more light-headed every minute, Clennam saw the relict of the late Mr F. enjoying herself in the most wonderful manner, by putting herself and him in their old places, and going through all the old performances—now, when the stage was dusty, when the scenery was faded, when the youthful actors were dead, when the orchestra was empty, when the lights were out. And still, through all this grotesque revival of what he remembered as having once been prettily natural to her, he could not but feel that it revived at sight of him, and that there was a tender memory in it.

The Patriarch insisted on his staying to dinner, and Flora signalled 'Yes!' Clennam so wished he could have done more than stay to dinner—so heartily wished he could have found the Flora that had been, or that never had been—that he thought the least atonement he could make for the disappointment he almost felt ashamed of, was to give himself up to the family desire. Therefore, he stayed to dinner.

Pancks dined with them. Pancks steamed out of his little dock at a quarter before six, and bore straight down for the Patriarch, who happened to be then driving, in an inane manner, through a stagnant account of Bleeding Heart Yard. Pancks instantly made fast to him and hauled him out.

'Bleeding Heart Yard?' said Pancks, with a puff and a snort. 'It's a troublesome property. Don't pay you badly, but rents are very hard to get there. You have more trouble with that one place than with all the places belonging to you.'

Just as the big ship in tow gets the credit, with most spectators, of being the powerful object, so the Patriarch usually seemed to have said himself whatever Pancks said for him.

'Indeed?' returned Clennam, upon whom this impression was so efficiently made by a mere gleam of the polished head that he spoke the ship instead of the Tug. 'The people are so poor there?'

'You can't say, you know,' snorted Pancks, taking one of his dirty hands out of his rusty iron-grey pockets to bite his nails, if he could find any, and turning his beads of eyes upon his employer, 'whether they're poor or not. They say they are, but they all say that. When a man says he's rich, you're generally sure he isn't. Besides, if they are poor, you can't help it. You'd be poor yourself if you didn't get your rents.'

'True enough,' said Arthur.

'You're not going to keep open house for all the poor of London,' pursued Pancks. 'You're not going to lodge 'em for nothing. You're not going to open your gates wide and let 'em come free. Not if you know it, you ain't.'

Mr Casby shook his head, in Placid and benignant generality.

'If a man takes a room of you at half-a-crown a week, and when the week comes round hasn't got the half-crown, you say to that man, Why have you got the room, then? If you haven't got the one thing, why have you got the other? What have you been and done with your money? What do you mean by it? What are you up to? That's what you say to a man of that sort; and if you didn't say it, more shame for you!' Mr Pancks here made a singular and startling noise, produced by a strong blowing effort in the region of the nose, unattended by any result but that acoustic one.

'You have some extent of such property about the east and north-east here, I believe?' said Clennam, doubtful which of the two to address.

'Oh, pretty well,' said Pancks. 'You're not particular to east or north-east, any point of the compass will do for you. What you want is a good investment and a quick return. You take it where you can find it. You ain't nice as to situation—not you.'

There was a fourth and most original figure in the Patriarchal tent, who also appeared before dinner. This was an amazing little old woman, with a face like a staring wooden doll too cheap for expression, and a stiff yellow wig perched unevenly on the top of her head, as if the child who owned the doll had driven a tack through it anywhere, so that it only got fastened on. Another remarkable thing in this little old woman was, that the same child seemed to have damaged her face in two or three places with some blunt instrument in the nature of a spoon; her countenance, and particularly the tip of her nose, presenting the phenomena of several dints, generally answering to the bowl of that article. A further remarkable thing in this little old woman was, that she had no name but Mr F.'s Aunt.

She broke upon the visitor's view under the following circumstances: Flora said when the first dish was being put on the table, perhaps Mr Clennam might not have heard that Mr F. had left her a legacy? Clennam in return implied his hope that Mr F. had endowed the wife whom he adored, with the greater part of his worldly substance, if not with all. Flora said, oh yes, she didn't mean that, Mr F. had made a beautiful will, but he had left her as a separate legacy, his Aunt. She then went out of the room to fetch the legacy, and, on her return, rather triumphantly presented 'Mr F.'s Aunt.'

The major characteristics discoverable by the stranger in Mr F.'s Aunt, were extreme severity and grim taciturnity; sometimes interrupted by a propensity to offer remarks in a deep warning voice, which, being totally uncalled for by anything said by anybody, and traceable to no association of ideas, confounded and terrified the Mind. Mr F.'s Aunt may have thrown in these observations on some system of her own, and it may have been ingenious, or even subtle: but the key to it was wanted.

The neatly-served and well-cooked dinner (for everything about the Patriarchal household promoted quiet digestion) began with some soup, some fried soles, a butter-boat of shrimp sauce, and a dish of potatoes. The conversation still turned on the receipt of rents. Mr F.'s Aunt, after regarding the company for ten minutes with a malevolent gaze, delivered the following fearful remark:

'When we lived at Henley, Barnes's gander was stole by tinkers.'

Mr Pancks courageously nodded his head and said, 'All right, ma'am.' But the effect of this mysterious communication upon Clennam was absolutely to frighten him. And another circumstance invested this old lady with peculiar terrors. Though she was always staring, she never acknowledged that she saw any individual. The polite and attentive stranger would desire, say, to consult her inclinations on the subject of potatoes. His expressive action would be hopelessly lost upon her, and what could he do? No man could say, 'Mr F.'s Aunt, will you permit me?' Every man retired from the spoon, as Clennam did, cowed and baffled.

There was mutton, a steak, and an apple-pie—nothing in the remotest way connected with ganders—and the dinner went on like a disenchanted feast, as it truly was. Once upon a time Clennam had sat at that table taking no heed of anything but Flora; now the principal heed he took of Flora was to observe, against his will, that she was very fond of porter, that she combined a great deal of sherry with sentiment, and that if she were a little overgrown, it was upon substantial grounds. The last of the Patriarchs had always been a mighty eater, and he disposed of an immense quantity of solid food with the benignity of a good soul who was feeding some one else. Mr Pancks, who was always in a hurry, and who referred at intervals to a little dirty notebook which he kept beside him (perhaps containing the names of the defaulters he meant to look up by way of dessert), took in his victuals much as if he were coaling; with a good deal of noise, a good deal of dropping about, and a puff and a snort occasionally, as if he were nearly ready to steam away.

All through dinner, Flora combined her present appetite for eating and drinking with her past appetite for romantic love, in a way that made Clennam afraid to lift his eyes from his plate; since he could not look towards her without receiving some glance of mysterious meaning or warning, as if they were engaged in a plot. Mr F.'s Aunt sat silently defying him with an aspect of the greatest bitterness, until the removal of the cloth and the appearance of the decanters, when she originated another observation—struck into the conversation like a clock, without consulting anybody.

Flora had just said, 'Mr Clennam, will you give me a glass of port for Mr F.'s Aunt?'

'The Monument near London Bridge,' that lady instantly proclaimed, 'was put up arter the Great Fire of London; and the Great Fire of London was not the fire in which your uncle George's workshops was burned down.'

Mr Pancks, with his former courage, said, 'Indeed, ma'am? All right!' But appearing to be incensed by imaginary contradiction, or other ill-usage, Mr F.'s Aunt, instead of relapsing into silence, made the following additional proclamation:

'I hate a fool!'

She imparted to this sentiment, in itself almost Solomonic, so extremely injurious and personal a character by levelling it straight at the visitor's head, that it became necessary to lead Mr F.'s Aunt from the room. This was quietly done by Flora; Mr F.'s Aunt offering no resistance, but inquiring on her way out, 'What he come there for, then?' with implacable animosity.

When Flora returned, she explained that her legacy was a clever old lady, but was sometimes a little singular, and 'took dislikes'—peculiarities of which Flora seemed to be proud rather than otherwise. As Flora's good nature shone in the case, Clennam had no fault to find with the old lady for eliciting it, now that he was relieved from the terrors of her presence; and they took a glass or two of wine in peace. Foreseeing then that the Pancks would shortly get under weigh, and that the Patriarch would go to sleep, he pleaded the necessity of visiting his mother, and asked Mr Pancks in which direction he was going?

'Citywards, sir,' said Pancks.

'Shall we walk together?' said Arthur.

'Quite agreeable,' said Pancks.

Meanwhile Flora was murmuring in rapid snatches for his ear, that there was a time and that the past was a yawning gulf however and that a golden chain no longer bound him and that she revered the memory of the late Mr F. and that she should be at home to-morrow at half-past one and that the decrees of Fate were beyond recall and that she considered nothing so improbable as that he ever walked on the north-west side of Gray's-Inn Gardens at exactly four o'clock in the afternoon. He tried at parting to give his hand in frankness to the existing Flora—not the vanished Flora, or the mermaid—but Flora wouldn't have it, couldn't have it, was wholly destitute of the power of separating herself and him from their bygone characters. He left the house miserably enough; and so much more light-headed than ever, that if it had not been his good fortune to be towed away, he might, for the first quarter of an hour, have drifted anywhere.

When he began to come to himself, in the cooler air and the absence of Flora, he found Pancks at full speed, cropping such scanty pasturage of nails as he could find, and snorting at intervals. These, in conjunction with one hand in his pocket and his roughened hat hind side before, were evidently the conditions under which he reflected.

'A fresh night!' said Arthur.

'Yes, it's pretty fresh,' assented Pancks. 'As a stranger you feel the climate more than I do, I dare say. Indeed I haven't got time to feel it.'

'You lead such a busy life?'

'Yes, I have always some of 'em to look up, or something to look after. But I like business,' said Pancks, getting on a little faster. 'What's a man made for?'

'For nothing else?' said Clennam.

Pancks put the counter question, 'What else?' It packed up, in the smallest compass, a weight that had rested on Clennam's life; and he made no answer.

'That's what I ask our weekly tenants,' said Pancks. 'Some of 'em will pull long faces to me, and say, Poor as you see us, master, we're always grinding, drudging, toiling, every minute we're awake. I say to them, What else are you made for? It shuts them up. They haven't a word to answer. What else are you made for? That clinches it.'

'Ah dear, dear, dear!' sighed Clennam.

'Here am I,' said Pancks, pursuing his argument with the weekly tenant. 'What else do you suppose I think I am made for? Nothing. Rattle me out of bed early, set me going, give me as short a time as you like to bolt my meals in, and keep me at it. Keep me always at it, and I'll keep you always at it, you keep somebody else always at it. There you are with the Whole Duty of Man in a commercial country.'

When they had walked a little further in silence, Clennam said: 'Have you no taste for anything, Mr Pancks?'

'What's taste?' drily retorted Pancks.

'Let us say inclination.'

'I have an inclination to get money, sir,' said Pancks, 'if you will show me how.' He blew off that sound again, and it occurred to his companion for the first time that it was his way of laughing. He was a singular man in all respects; he might not have been quite in earnest, but that the short, hard, rapid manner in which he shot out these cinders of principles, as if it were done by mechanical revolvency, seemed irreconcilable with banter.

'You are no great reader, I suppose?' said Clennam.

'Never read anything but letters and accounts. Never collect anything but advertisements relative to next of kin. If that's a taste, I have got that. You're not of the Clennams of Cornwall, Mr Clennam?'

'Not that I ever heard of.'

'I know you're not. I asked your mother, sir. She has too much character to let a chance escape her.'

'Supposing I had been of the Clennams of Cornwall?'

'You'd have heard of something to your advantage.'

'Indeed! I have heard of little enough to my advantage for some time.'

'There's a Cornish property going a begging, sir, and not a Cornish Clennam to have it for the asking,' said Pancks, taking his note-book from his breast pocket and putting it in again. 'I turn off here. I wish you good night.'

'Good night!' said Clennam. But the Tug, suddenly lightened, and untrammelled by having any weight in tow, was already puffing away into the distance.

They had crossed Smithfield together, and Clennam was left alone at the corner of Barbican. He had no intention of presenting himself in his mother's dismal room that night, and could not have felt more depressed and cast away if he had been in a wilderness. He turned slowly down Aldersgate Street, and was pondering his way along towards Saint Paul's, purposing to come into one of the great thoroughfares for the sake of their light and life, when a crowd of people flocked towards him on the same pavement, and he stood aside against a shop to let them pass. As they came up, he made out that they were gathered around a something that was carried on men's shoulders. He soon saw that it was a litter, hastily made of a shutter or some such thing; and a recumbent figure upon it, and the scraps of conversation in the crowd, and a muddy bundle carried by one man, and a muddy hat carried by another, informed him that an accident had occurred. The litter stopped under a lamp before it had passed him half-a-dozen paces, for some readjustment of the burden; and, the crowd stopping too, he found himself in the midst of the array.

'An accident going to the Hospital?' he asked an old man beside him, who stood shaking his head, inviting conversation.

'Yes,' said the man, 'along of them Mails. They ought to be prosecuted and fined, them Mails. They come a racing out of Lad Lane and Wood Street at twelve or fourteen mile a hour, them Mails do. The only wonder is, that people ain't killed oftener by them Mails.'

'This person is not killed, I hope?'

'I don't know!' said the man, 'it an't for the want of a will in them Mails, if he an't.' The speaker having folded his arms, and set in comfortably to address his depreciation of them Mails to any of the bystanders who would listen, several voices, out of pure sympathy with the sufferer, confirmed him; one voice saying to Clennam, 'They're a public nuisance, them Mails, sir;' another, 'I see one on 'em pull up within half a inch of a boy, last night;' another, 'I see one on 'em go over a cat, sir—and it might have been your own mother;' and all representing, by implication, that if he happened to possess any public influence, he could not use it better than against them Mails.

'Why, a native Englishman is put to it every night of his life, to save his life from them Mails,' argued the first old man; 'and he knows when they're a coming round the corner, to tear him limb from limb. What can you expect from a poor foreigner who don't know nothing about 'em!'

'Is this a foreigner?' said Clennam, leaning forward to look.

In the midst of such replies as 'Frenchman, sir,' 'Porteghee, sir,' 'Dutchman, sir,' 'Prooshan, sir,' and other conflicting testimony, he now heard a feeble voice asking, both in Italian and in French, for water. A general remark going round, in reply, of 'Ah, poor fellow, he says he'll never get over it; and no wonder!' Clennam begged to be allowed to pass, as he understood the poor creature. He was immediately handed to the front, to speak to him.

'First, he wants some water,' said he, looking round. (A dozen good fellows dispersed to get it.) 'Are you badly hurt, my friend?' he asked the man on the litter, in Italian.

126

'Yes, sir; yes, yes, yes. It's my leg, it's my leg. But it pleases me to hear the old music, though I am very bad.'

'You are a traveller! Stay! See, the water! Let me give you some.'

They had rested the litter on a pile of paving stones. It was at a convenient height from the ground, and by stooping he could lightly raise the head with one hand and hold the glass to his lips with the other. A little, muscular, brown man, with black hair and white teeth. A lively face, apparently. Earrings in his ears.

'That's well. You are a traveller?'

'Surely, sir.'

'A stranger in this city?'

'Surely, surely, altogether. I am arrived this unhappy evening.'

'From what country?'

'Marseilles.'

'Why, see there! I also! Almost as much a stranger here as you, though born here, I came from Marseilles a little while ago. Don't be cast down.' The face looked up at him imploringly, as he rose from wiping it, and gently replaced the coat that covered the writhing figure. 'I won't leave you till you shall be well taken care of. Courage! You will be very much better half an hour hence.'

'Ah! Altro, Altro!' cried the poor little man, in a faintly incredulous tone; and as they took him up, hung out his right hand to give the forefinger a back-handed shake in the air.

Arthur Clennam turned; and walking beside the litter, and saying an encouraging word now and then, accompanied it to the neighbouring hospital of Saint Bartholomew. None of the crowd but the bearers and he being admitted, the disabled man was soon laid on a table in a cool, methodical way, and carefully examined by a surgeon who was as near at hand, and as ready to appear as Calamity herself. 'He hardly knows an English word,' said Clennam; 'is he badly hurt?'

'Let us know all about it first,' said the surgeon, continuing his examination with a businesslike delight in it, 'before we pronounce.'

After trying the leg with a finger, and two fingers, and one hand and two hands, and over and under, and up and down, and in this direction and in that, and approvingly remarking on the points of interest to another gentleman who joined him, the surgeon at last clapped the patient on the shoulder, and said, 'He won't hurt. He'll do very well. It's difficult enough, but we shall not want him to part with his leg this time.' Which Clennam interpreted to the patient, who was full of gratitude, and, in his demonstrative way, kissed both the interpreter's hand and the surgeon's several times.

'It's a serious injury, I suppose?' said Clennam.

'Ye-es,' replied the surgeon, with the thoughtful pleasure of an artist contemplating the work upon his easel. 'Yes, it's enough. There's a compound fracture above the knee, and a dislocation below. They are both of a beautiful kind.' He gave the patient a friendly clap on the shoulder again, as if he really felt that he was a very good fellow indeed, and worthy of all commendation for having broken his leg in a manner interesting to science.

'He speaks French?' said the surgeon.

'Oh yes, he speaks French.'

'He'll be at no loss here, then.—You have only to bear a little pain like a brave fellow, my friend, and to be thankful that all goes as well as it does,' he added, in that tongue, 'and you'll walk again to a marvel. Now, let us see whether there's anything else the matter, and how our ribs are?'

There was nothing else the matter, and our ribs were sound. Clennam remained until everything possible to be done had been skilfully and promptly done—the poor belated wanderer in a strange land movingly besought that favour of him—and lingered by the bed to which he was in due time removed, until he had fallen into a doze. Even then he wrote a few words for him on his card, with a promise to return to-morrow, and left it to be given to him when he should awake.

All these proceedings occupied so long that it struck eleven o'clock at night as he came out at the Hospital Gate. He had hired a lodging for the present in Covent Garden, and he took the nearest way to that quarter, by Snow Hill and Holborn.

Left to himself again, after the solicitude and compassion of his last adventure, he was naturally in a thoughtful mood. As naturally, he could not walk on thinking for ten minutes without recalling Flora. She necessarily recalled to him his life, with all its misdirection and little happiness.

When he got to his lodging, he sat down before the dying fire, as he had stood at the window of his old room looking out upon the blackened forest of chimneys, and turned his gaze back upon the gloomy vista by which he had come to that stage in his existence. So long, so bare, so blank. No childhood; no youth, except for one remembrance; that one remembrance proved, only that day, to be a piece of folly.

It was a misfortune to him, trifle as it might have been to another. For, while all that was hard and stern in his recollection, remained Reality on being proved—was obdurate to the sight and touch, and relaxed nothing of its old indomitable grimness—the one tender recollection of his experience would not bear the same test, and melted away. He had foreseen this, on the former night, when he had dreamed with waking eyes, but he had not felt it then; and he had now.

He was a dreamer in such wise, because he was a man who had, deep-rooted in his nature, a belief in all the gentle and good things his life had been without. Bred in meanness and hard dealing, this had rescued him to be a man of honourable mind and open hand. Bred in coldness and severity, this had rescued him to have a warm and sympathetic heart. Bred in a creed too darkly audacious to pursue, through its process of reserving the making of man in the image of his Creator to the making of his Creator in the image of an erring man, this had rescued him to judge not, and in humility to be merciful, and have hope and charity.

And this saved him still from the whimpering weakness and cruel selfishness of holding that because such a happiness or such a virtue had not come into his little path, or worked well for him, therefore it was not in the great scheme, but was reducible, when found in appearance, to the basest elements. A disappointed mind he had, but a mind too firm and healthy for such unwholesome air. Leaving himself in the dark, it could rise into the light, seeing it shine on others and hailing it.

Therefore, he sat before his dying fire, sorrowful to think upon the way by which he had come to that night, yet not strewing poison on the way by which other men had come to it. That he should have missed so much, and at his time of life should look so far about him for any staff to bear him company upon his downward journey and cheer it, was a just regret. He looked at the fire from which the blaze departed, from which the afterglow subsided, in which the ashes turned grey, from which they dropped to dust, and thought, 'How soon I too shall pass through such changes, and be gone!'

To review his life was like descending a green tree in fruit and flower, and seeing all the branches wither and drop off, one by one, as he came down towards them.

'From the unhappy suppression of my youngest days, through the rigid and unloving home that followed them, through my departure, my long exile, my return, my mother's welcome, my intercourse with her since, down to the afternoon of this day with poor Flora,' said Arthur Clennam, 'what have I found!'

His door was softly opened, and these spoken words startled him, and came as if they were an answer:

'Little Dorrit.'

CHAPTER 14. Little Dorrit's Party

Arthur Clennam rose hastily, and saw her standing at the door. This history must sometimes see with Little Dorrit's eyes, and shall begin that course by seeing him.

Little Dorrit looked into a dim room, which seemed a spacious one to her, and grandly furnished. Courtly ideas of Covent Garden, as a place with famous coffee-houses, where gentlemen wearing gold-laced coats and swords had quarrelled and fought duels; costly ideas of Covent Garden, as a place where there were flowers in winter at guineas a-piece, pine-apples at guineas a pound, and peas at guineas a pint; picturesque ideas of Covent Garden, as a place where there was a mighty theatre, showing wonderful and beautiful sights to richly-dressed ladies and gentlemen, and which was for ever far beyond the reach of poor Fanny or poor uncle; desolate ideas of Covent Garden, as having all those arches in it, where the miserable children in rags among whom she had just now passed, like young rats, slunk and hid, fed on offal, huddled together for warmth, and were hunted about (look to the rats young and old, all ye Barnacles, for before God they are eating away our foundations, and will bring the roofs on our heads!); teeming ideas of Covent Garden, as a place of past and present mystery, romance, abundance, want, beauty, ugliness, fair country gardens, and foul street gutters; all confused together,—made the room dimmer than it was in Little Dorrit's eyes, as they timidly saw it from the door.

At first in the chair before the gone-out fire, and then turned round wondering to see her, was the gentleman whom she sought. The brown, grave gentleman, who smiled so pleasantly, who was so frank and considerate in his manner, and yet in whose earnestness there was something that reminded her of his mother, with the great difference that she was earnest in asperity and he in gentleness. Now he regarded her with that attentive and inquiring look before which Little Dorrit's eyes had always fallen, and before which they fell still.

'My poor child! Here at midnight?'

'I said Little Dorrit, sir, on purpose to prepare you. I knew you must be very much surprised.'

'Are you alone?'

'No sir, I have got Maggy with me.'

Considering her entrance sufficiently prepared for by this mention of her name, Maggy appeared from the landing outside, on the broad grin. She instantly suppressed that manifestation, however, and became fixedly solemn.

'And I have no fire,' said Clennam. 'And you are—' He was going to say so lightly clad, but stopped himself in what would have been a reference to her poverty, saying instead, 'And it is so cold.'

Putting the chair from which he had risen nearer to the grate, he made her sit down in it; and hurriedly bringing wood and coal, heaped them together and got a blaze.

'Your foot is like marble, my child;' he had happened to touch it, while stooping on one knee at his work of kindling the fire; 'put it nearer the warmth.' Little Dorrit thanked him hastily. It was quite warm, it was very warm! It smote upon his heart to feel that she hid her thin, worn shoe.

Little Dorrit was not ashamed of her poor shoes. He knew her story, and it was not that. Little Dorrit had a misgiving that he might blame her father, if he saw them; that he might think, 'why did he dine to-day, and leave this little creature to the mercy of the cold stones!' She had no belief that it would have been a just reflection; she simply knew, by experience, that such delusions did sometimes present themselves to people. It was a part of her father's misfortunes that they did.

'Before I say anything else,' Little Dorrit began, sitting before the pale fire, and raising her eyes again to the face which in its harmonious look of interest, and pity, and protection, she felt to be a mystery far above her in degree, and almost removed beyond her guessing at; 'may I tell you something, sir?'

'Yes, my child.'

A slight shade of distress fell upon her, at his so often calling her a child. She was surprised that he should see it, or think of such a slight thing; but he said directly:

'I wanted a tender word, and could think of no other. As you just now gave yourself the name they give you at my mother's, and as that is the name by which I always think of you, let me call you Little Dorrit.'

'Thank you, sir, I should like it better than any name.'

'Little Dorrit.'

'Little mother,' Maggy (who had been falling asleep) put in, as a correction.

'It's all the same, Maggy,' returned Little Dorrit, 'all the same.'

'Is it all the same, mother?'

'Just the same.'

Maggy laughed, and immediately snored. In Little Dorrit's eyes and ears, the uncouth figure and the uncouth sound were as pleasant as could be. There was a glow of pride in her big child, overspreading her face, when it again met the eyes of the grave brown gentleman. She wondered what he was thinking of, as he looked at Maggy and her. She thought what a good father he would be. How, with some such look, he would counsel and cherish his daughter.

'What I was going to tell you, sir,' said Little Dorrit, 'is, that my brother is at large.'

Arthur was rejoiced to hear it, and hoped he would do well.

'And what I was going to tell you, sir,' said Little Dorrit, trembling in all her little figure and in her voice, 'is, that I am not to know whose generosity released him—am never to ask, and am never to be told, and am never to thank that gentleman with all my grateful heart!'

He would probably need no thanks, Clennam said. Very likely he would be thankful himself (and with reason), that he had had the means and chance of doing a little service to her, who well deserved a great one.

'And what I was going to say, sir, is,' said Little Dorrit, trembling more and more, 'that if I knew him, and I might, I would tell him that he can never, never know how I feel his goodness, and how my good father would feel it. And what I was going to say, sir, is, that if I knew him, and I might—but I don't know him and I must not—know that!—I would tell him that I shall never any more lie down to sleep without having prayed to Heaven to bless him and reward him. And if I knew him, and I might, I would go down on my knees to him, and take his hand and kiss it and ask him not to draw it away, but to leave it—O to leave it for a moment—and let my thankful tears fall on it; for I have no other thanks to give him!'

Little Dorrit had put his hand to her lips, and would have kneeled to him, but he gently prevented her, and replaced her in her chair. Her eyes, and the tones of her voice, had thanked him far better than she thought. He was not able to say, quite as composedly as usual, 'There, Little Dorrit, there, there, there! We will suppose that you did know this person, and that you might do all this, and that it was all done. And now tell me, Who am quite another person—who am nothing more than the friend who begged you to trust him—why you are out at midnight, and what it is that brings you so far through the streets at this late hour, my slight, delicate,' child was on his lips again, 'Little Dorrit!'

'Maggy and I have been to-night,' she answered, subduing herself with the quiet effort that had long been natural to her, 'to the theatre where my sister is engaged.'

'And oh ain't it a Ev'nly place,' suddenly interrupted Maggy, who seemed to have the power of going to sleep and waking up whenever she chose. 'Almost as good as a hospital. Only there ain't no Chicking in it.'

Here she shook herself, and fell asleep again.

'We went there,' said Little Dorrit, glancing at her charge, 'because I like sometimes to know, of my own knowledge, that my sister is doing well; and like to see her there, with my own eyes, when neither she nor Uncle is aware. It is very seldom indeed that I can do that, because when I am not out at work, I am with my father, and even when I am out at work, I hurry home to him. But I pretend to-night that I am at a party.'

As she made the confession, timidly hesitating, she raised her eyes to the face, and read its expression so plainly that she answered it.

'Oh no, certainly! I never was at a party in my life.'

She paused a little under his attentive look, and then said, 'I hope there is no harm in it. I could never have been of any use, if I had not pretended a little.'

She feared that he was blaming her in his mind for so devising to contrive for them, think for them, and watch over them, without their knowledge or gratitude; perhaps even with their reproaches for supposed neglect. But what was really in his mind, was the weak figure with its strong purpose, the thin worn shoes, the insufficient dress, and the pretence of recreation and enjoyment. He asked where the suppositious party was? At a place where she worked, answered Little Dorrit, blushing. She had said very little about it; only a few words to make her father easy. Her father did not believe it to be a grand party—indeed he might suppose that. And she glanced for an instant at the shawl she wore.

'It is the first night,' said Little Dorrit, 'that I have ever been away from home. And London looks so large, so barren, and so wild.' In Little Dorrit's eyes, its vastness under the black sky was awful; a tremor passed over her as she said the words.

'But this is not,' she added, with the quiet effort again, 'what I have come to trouble you with, sir. My sister's having found a friend, a lady she has told me of and made me rather anxious about, was the first cause of my coming away from home. And being away, and coming (on purpose) round by where you lived and seeing a light in the window—'

Not for the first time. No, not for the first time. In Little Dorrit's eyes, the outside of that window had been a distant star on other nights than this. She had toiled out of her way, tired and troubled, to look up at it, and wonder about the grave, brown gentleman from so far off, who had spoken to her as a friend and protector.

'There were three things,' said Little Dorrit, 'that I thought I would like to say, if you were alone and I might come up-stairs. First, what I have tried to say, but never can—never shall—'

'Hush, hush! That is done with, and disposed of. Let us pass to the second,' said Clennam, smiling her agitation away, making the blaze shine upon her, and putting wine and cake and fruit towards her on the table.

'I think,' said Little Dorrit—'this is the second thing, sir—I think Mrs Clennam must have found out my secret, and must know where I come from and where I go to. Where I live, I mean.'

'Indeed!' returned Clennam quickly. He asked her, after short consideration, why she supposed so.

'I think,' replied Little Dorrit, 'that Mr Flintwinch must have watched me.'

And why, Clennam asked, as he turned his eyes upon the fire, bent his brows, and considered again; why did she suppose that?

'I have met him twice. Both times near home. Both times at night, when I was going back. Both times I thought (though that may easily be my mistake), that he hardly looked as if he had met me by accident.'

'Did he say anything?'

'No; he only nodded and put his head on one side.'

'The devil take his head!' mused Clennam, still looking at the fire; 'it's always on one side.'

He roused himself to persuade her to put some wine to her lips, and to touch something to eat—it was very difficult, she was so timid and shy—and then said, musing again:

'Is my mother at all changed to you?'

'Oh, not at all. She is just the same. I wondered whether I had better tell her my history. I wondered whether I might—I mean, whether you would like me to tell her. I wondered,' said Little Dorrit, looking at him in a suppliant way, and gradually withdrawing her eyes as he looked at her, 'whether you would advise me what I ought to do.'

'Little Dorrit,' said Clennam; and the phrase had already begun, between these two, to stand for a hundred gentle phrases, according to the varying tone and connection in which it was used; 'do nothing. I will have some talk with my old friend, Mrs Affery. Do nothing, Little Dorrit—except refresh yourself with such means as there are here. I entreat you to do that.'

'Thank you, I am not hungry. Nor,' said Little Dorrit, as he softly put her glass towards her, 'nor thirsty.—I think Maggy might like something, perhaps.'

'We will make her find pockets presently for all there is here,' said Clennam: 'but before we awake her, there was a third thing to say.'

'Yes. You will not be offended, sir?'

'I promise that, unreservedly.'

'It will sound strange. I hardly know how to say it. Don't think it unreasonable or ungrateful in me,' said Little Dorrit, with returning and increasing agitation.

'No, no, no. I am sure it will be natural and right. I am not afraid that I shall put a wrong construction on it, whatever it is.'

'Thank you. You are coming back to see my father again?'

'Yes.'

'You have been so good and thoughtful as to write him a note, saying that you are coming to-morrow?'

'Oh, that was nothing! Yes.'

'Can you guess,' said Little Dorrit, folding her small hands tight in one another, and looking at him with all the earnestness of her soul looking steadily out of her eyes, 'what I am going to ask you not to do?'

'I think I can. But I may be wrong.'

'No, you are not wrong,' said Little Dorrit, shaking her head. 'If we should want it so very, very badly that we cannot do without it, let me ask you for it.'

'I Will,—I Will.'

'Don't encourage him to ask. Don't understand him if he does ask. Don't give it to him. Save him and spare him that, and you will be able to think better of him!'

Clennam said—not very plainly, seeing those tears glistening in her anxious eyes—that her wish should be sacred with him.

'You don't know what he is,' she said; 'you don't know what he really is. How can you, seeing him there all at once, dear love, and not gradually, as I have done! You have been so good to us, so delicately and truly good, that I want him to be better in your eyes than in anybody's. And I cannot bear to think,' cried Little Dorrit, covering her tears with her hands, 'I cannot bear to think that you of all the world should see him in his only moments of degradation.'

'Pray,' said Clennam, 'do not be so distressed. Pray, pray, Little Dorrit! This is quite understood now.'

'Thank you, sir. Thank you! I have tried very much to keep myself from saying this; I have thought about it, days and nights; but when I knew for certain you were coming again, I made up my mind to speak to you. Not because I am ashamed of him,' she dried her tears quickly, 'but because I know him better than any one does, and love him, and am proud of him.'

Relieved of this weight, Little Dorrit was nervously anxious to be gone. Maggy being broad awake, and in the act of distantly gloating over the fruit and cakes with chuckles of anticipation, Clennam made the best diversion in his power by pouring her out a glass of wine, which she drank in a series of loud smacks; putting her hand upon her windpipe after every one, and saying, breathless, with her eyes in a prominent state, 'Oh, ain't it d'licious! Ain't it hospitally!' When she had finished the wine and these encomiums, he charged her to load her basket (she was never without her basket) with every eatable thing upon the table, and to take especial care to leave no scrap behind. Maggy's pleasure in doing this and her little mother's pleasure in seeing Maggy pleased, was as good a turn as circumstances could have given to the late conversation.

'But the gates will have been locked long ago,' said Clennam, suddenly remembering it. 'Where are you going?'

'I am going to Maggy's lodging,' answered Little Dorrit. 'I shall be quite safe, quite well taken care of.'

'I must accompany you there,' said Clennam, 'I cannot let you go alone.'

'Yes, pray leave us to go there by ourselves. Pray do!' begged Little Dorrit.

She was so earnest in the petition, that Clennam felt a delicacy in obtruding himself upon her: the rather, because he could well understand that Maggy's lodging was of the obscurest sort. 'Come, Maggy,' said Little Dorrit cheerily, 'we shall do very well; we know the way by this time, Maggy?'

'Yes, yes, little mother; we know the way,' chuckled Maggy. And away they went. Little Dorrit turned at the door to say, 'God bless you!' She said it very softly, but perhaps she may have been as audible above—who knows!—as a whole cathedral choir.

Arthur Clennam suffered them to pass the corner of the street before he followed at a distance; not with any idea of encroaching a second time on Little Dorrit's privacy, but to satisfy his mind by seeing her secure in the neighbourhood to which she was accustomed. So diminutive she looked, so fragile and defenceless against the bleak damp weather, flitting along in the shuffling shadow of her charge, that he felt, in his compassion, and in his habit of considering her a child apart from the rest of the rough world, as if he would have been glad to take her up in his arms and carry her to her journey's end.

In course of time she came into the leading thoroughfare where the Marshalsea was, and then he saw them slacken their pace, and soon turn down a by-street. He stopped, felt that he had no right to go further, and slowly left them. He had no suspicion that they ran any risk of being houseless until morning; had no idea of the truth until long, long afterwards.

But, said Little Dorrit, when they stopped at a poor dwelling all in darkness, and heard no sound on listening at the door, 'Now, this is a good lodging for you, Maggy, and we must not give offence. Consequently, we will only knock twice, and not very loud; and if we cannot wake them so, we must walk about till day.'

Once, Little Dorrit knocked with a careful hand, and listened. Twice, Little Dorrit knocked with a careful hand, and listened. All was close and still. 'Maggy, we must do the best we can, my dear. We must be patient, and wait for day.'

It was a chill dark night, with a damp wind blowing, when they came out into the leading street again, and heard the clocks strike half-past one. 'In only five hours and a half,' said Little Dorrit, 'we shall be able to go home.' To speak of home, and to go and look at it, it being so near, was a natural sequence. They went to the closed gate, and peeped through into the court-yard. 'I hope he is sound asleep,' said Little Dorrit, kissing one of the bars, 'and does not miss me.'

The gate was so familiar, and so like a companion, that they put down Maggy's basket in a corner to serve for a seat, and keeping close together, rested there for some time. While the street was empty and silent, Little Dorrit was not afraid; but when she heard a footstep at a distance, or saw a moving shadow among the street lamps, she was startled, and whispered, 'Maggy, I see some one. Come away!' Maggy would then wake up more or less fretfully, and they would wander about a little, and come back again.

As long as eating was a novelty and an amusement, Maggy kept up pretty well. But that period going by, she became querulous about the cold, and shivered and whimpered. 'It will soon be over, dear,' said Little Dorrit patiently. 'Oh it's all very fine for you, little mother,' returned Maggy, 'but I'm a poor thing, only ten years old.' At last, in the dead of the night, when the street was very still indeed, Little Dorrit laid the heavy head upon her bosom, and soothed her to sleep. And thus she sat at the gate, as it were alone; looking up at the stars, and seeing the clouds pass over them in their wild flight—which was the dance at Little Dorrit's party.

'If it really was a party!' she thought once, as she sat there. 'If it was light and warm and beautiful, and it was our house, and my poor dear was its master, and had never been inside these walls. And if Mr Clennam was one of our visitors, and we were dancing to delightful music, and were all as gay and light-hearted as ever we could be! I wonder—' Such a vista of wonder opened out before her, that she sat looking up at the stars, quite lost, until Maggy was querulous again, and wanted to get up and walk.

Three o'clock, and half-past three, and they had passed over London Bridge. They had heard the rush of the tide against obstacles; and looked down, awed, through the dark vapour on the river; had seen little spots of lighted water where the bridge lamps were reflected, shining like demon eyes, with a terrible fascination in them for guilt and misery. They had shrunk past homeless people, lying coiled up in nooks. They had run from drunkards. They had started from slinking men, whistling and signing to one another at bye corners, or running away at full speed. Though everywhere the leader and the guide, Little Dorrit, happy for once in her youthful appearance, feigned to cling to and rely upon Maggy. And more than once some voice, from among a knot of brawling or prowling figures in their path, had called out to the rest to 'let the woman and the child go by!'

So, the woman and the child had gone by, and gone on, and five had sounded from the steeples. They were walking slowly towards the east, already looking for the first pale streak of day, when a woman came after them.

'What are you doing with the child?' she said to Maggy.

She was young—far too young to be there, Heaven knows!—and neither ugly nor wicked-looking. She spoke coarsely, but with no naturally coarse voice; there was even something musical in its sound.

'What are you doing with yourself?' retorted Maggy, for want of a better answer.

'Can't you see, without my telling you?'

'I don't know as I can,' said Maggy.

'Killing myself! Now I have answered you, answer me. What are you doing with the child?'

The supposed child kept her head drooped down, and kept her form close at Maggy's side.

'Poor thing!' said the woman. 'Have you no feeling, that you keep her out in the cruel streets at such a time as this? Have you no eyes, that you don't see how delicate and slender she is? Have you no sense (you don't look as if you had much) that you don't take more pity on this cold and trembling little hand?'

She had stepped across to that side, and held the hand between her own two, chafing it. 'Kiss a poor lost creature, dear,' she said, bending her face, 'and tell me where's she taking you.'

Little Dorrit turned towards her.

'Why, my God!' she said, recoiling, 'you're a woman!'

'Don't mind that!' said Little Dorrit, clasping one of her hands that had suddenly released hers. 'I am not afraid of you.'

'Then you had better be,' she answered. 'Have you no mother?'

'No.'

'No father?'

'Yes, a very dear one.'

'Go home to him, and be afraid of me. Let me go. Good night!'

'I must thank you first; let me speak to you as if I really were a child.'

'You can't do it,' said the woman. 'You are kind and innocent; but you can't look at me out of a child's eyes. I never should have touched you, but I thought that you were a child.' And with a strange, wild cry, she went away.

No day yet in the sky, but there was day in the resounding stones of the streets; in the waggons, carts, and coaches; in the workers going to various occupations; in the opening of early shops; in the traffic at markets; in the stir of the riverside. There was coming day in the flaring lights, with a feebler colour in them than they would have had at another time; coming day in the increased sharpness of the air, and the ghastly dying of the night.

They went back again to the gate, intending to wait there now until it should be opened; but the air was so raw and cold that Little Dorrit, leading Maggy about in her sleep, kept in motion. Going round by the Church, she saw lights there, and the door open; and went up the steps and looked in.

'Who's that?' cried a stout old man, who was putting on a nightcap as if he were going to bed in a vault.

'It's no one particular, sir,' said Little Dorrit.

'Stop!' cried the man. 'Let's have a look at you!'

This caused her to turn back again in the act of going out, and to present herself and her charge before him.

'I thought so!' said he. 'I know you.'

'We have often seen each other,' said Little Dorrit, recognising the sexton, or the beadle, or the verger, or whatever he was, 'when I have been at church here.'

'More than that, we've got your birth in our Register, you know; you're one of our curiosities.'

'Indeed!' said Little Dorrit.

'To be sure. As the child of the—by-the-bye, how did you get out so early?'

'We were shut out last night, and are waiting to get in.'

'You don't mean it? And there's another hour good yet! Come into the vestry. You'll find a fire in the vestry, on account of the painters. I'm waiting for the painters, or I shouldn't be here, you may depend upon it. One of our curiosities mustn't be cold when we have it in our power to warm her up comfortable. Come along.'

He was a very good old fellow, in his familiar way; and having stirred the vestry fire, he looked round the shelves of registers for a particular volume. 'Here you are, you see,' he said, taking it down and turning the leaves. 'Here you'll find yourself, as large as life. Amy, daughter of William and Fanny Dorrit. Born, Marshalsea Prison, Parish of St George. And we tell people that you have lived there, without so much as a day's or a night's absence, ever since. Is it true?'

'Quite true, till last night.'

'Lord!' But his surveying her with an admiring gaze suggested Something else to him, to wit: 'I am sorry to see, though, that you are faint and tired. Stay a bit. I'll get some cushions out of the church, and you and your friend shall lie down before the fire. Don't be afraid of not going in to join your father when the gate opens. I'll call you.'

He soon brought in the cushions, and strewed them on the ground.

'There you are, you see. Again as large as life. Oh, never mind thanking. I've daughters of my own. And though they weren't born in the Marshalsea Prison, they might have been, if I had been, in my ways of carrying on, of your father's breed. Stop a bit. I must put something under the cushion for your head. Here's a burial volume, just the thing! We have got Mrs Bangham in this book. But what makes these books interesting to most people is—not who's in 'em, but who isn't—who's coming, you know, and when. That's the interesting question.'

Commendingly looking back at the pillow he had improvised, he left them to their hour's repose. Maggy was snoring already, and Little Dorrit was soon fast asleep with her head resting on that sealed book of Fate, untroubled by its mysterious blank leaves.

This was Little Dorrit's party. The shame, desertion, wretchedness, and exposure of the great capital; the wet, the cold, the slow hours, and the swift clouds of the dismal night. This was the party from which Little Dorrit went home, jaded, in the first grey mist of a rainy morning.

CHAPTER 15. Mrs Flintwinch has another Dream

The debilitated old house in the city, wrapped in its mantle of soot, and leaning heavily on the crutches that had partaken of its decay and worn out with it, never knew a healthy or a cheerful interval, let what would betide. If the sun ever touched it, it was but with a ray, and that was gone in half an hour; if the moonlight ever fell upon it, it was only to put a few patches on its doleful cloak, and make it look more wretched. The stars, to be sure, coldly watched it when the nights and the smoke were clear enough; and all bad weather stood by it with a rare fidelity. You should alike find rain, hail, frost, and thaw lingering in that dismal enclosure when they had vanished from other places; and as to snow, you should see it there for weeks, long after it had changed from yellow to black, slowly weeping away its grimy life. The place had no other adherents. As to street noises, the rumbling of wheels in the lane merely rushed in at the gateway in going past, and rushed out again: making the listening Mistress Affery feel as if she were deaf, and recovered the sense of hearing by instantaneous flashes. So with whistling, singing, talking, laughing, and all pleasant human sounds. They leaped the gap in a moment, and went upon their way.

The varying light of fire and candle in Mrs Clennam's room made the greatest change that ever broke the dead monotony of the spot. In her two long narrow windows, the fire shone sullenly all day, and sullenly all night. On rare occasions it flashed up passionately, as she did; but for the most part it was suppressed, like her, and preyed upon itself evenly and slowly. During many hours of the short winter days, however, when it was dusk there early in the afternoon, changing distortions of herself in her wheeled chair, of Mr Flintwinch with his wry neck, of Mistress Affery coming and going, would be thrown upon the house wall that was over the gateway, and would hover there like shadows from a great magic lantern. As the room-ridden invalid settled for the night, these would gradually disappear: Mistress Affery's magnified shadow always flitting about, last, until it finally glided away into the air, as though she were off upon a witch excursion. Then the solitary light would burn unchangingly, until it burned pale before the dawn, and at last died under the breath of Mrs Affery, as her shadow descended on it from the witch-region of sleep.

Strange, if the little sick-room fire were in effect a beacon fire, summoning some one, and that the most unlikely some one in the world, to the spot that must be come to. Strange, if the little sick-room light were in effect a watch-light, burning in that place every night until an appointed event should be watched out! Which of the vast multitude of travellers, under the sun and the stars, climbing the dusty hills and toiling along the weary plains, journeying by land and journeying by sea, coming and going so strangely, to meet and to act and react on one another; which of the host may, with no suspicion of the journey's end, be travelling surely hither?

Time shall show us. The post of honour and the post of shame, the general's station and the drummer's, a peer's statue in Westminster Abbey and a seaman's hammock in the bosom of the deep, the mitre and the workhouse, the woolsack and the gallows, the throne and the guillotine—the travellers to all are on the great high road, but it has wonderful divergencies, and only Time shall show us whither each traveller is bound.

On a wintry afternoon at twilight, Mrs Flintwinch, having been heavy all day, dreamed this dream:

She thought she was in the kitchen getting the kettle ready for tea, and was warming herself with her feet upon the fender and the skirt of her gown tucked up, before the collapsed fire in the middle of the grate, bordered on either hand by a deep cold black ravine. She thought that as she sat thus, musing upon the question whether life was not for some people a rather dull invention, she was frightened by a sudden noise behind her. She thought that she had been similarly frightened once last week, and that the noise was of a mysterious kind—a sound of rustling and of three or four quick beats like a rapid step; while a shock or tremble was communicated to her heart, as if the step had shaken the floor, or even as if she had been touched by some awful hand. She thought that this revived within her certain old fears of hers that the house was haunted; and that she flew up the kitchen stairs without knowing how she got up, to be nearer company.

Mistress Affery thought that on reaching the hall, she saw the door of her liege lord's office standing open, and the room empty. That she went to the ripped-up window in the little room by the street door to connect her palpitating heart, through the glass, with living things beyond and outside the haunted house. That she then saw, on the wall over the gateway, the shadows of the two clever ones in conversation above. That she then went upstairs with her shoes in her hand, partly to be near the clever ones as a match for most ghosts, and partly to hear what they were talking about.

'None of your nonsense with me,' said Mr Flintwinch. 'I won't take it from you.'

Mrs Flintwinch dreamed that she stood behind the door, which was just ajar, and most distinctly heard her husband say these bold words.

'Flintwinch,' returned Mrs Clennam, in her usual strong low voice, 'there is a demon of anger in you. Guard against it.'

'I don't care whether there's one or a dozen,' said Mr Flintwinch, forcibly suggesting in his tone that the higher number was nearer the mark. 'If there was fifty, they should all say, None of your nonsense with me, I won't take it from you—I'd make 'em say it, whether they liked it or not.'

'What have I done, you wrathful man?' her strong voice asked.

'Done?' said Mr Flintwinch. 'Dropped down upon me.'

'If you mean, remonstrated with you—'

'Don't put words into my mouth that I don't mean,' said Jeremiah, sticking to his figurative expression with tenacious and impenetrable obstinacy: 'I mean dropped down upon me.'

'I remonstrated with you,' she began again, 'because—'

'I won't have it!' cried Jeremiah. 'You dropped down upon me.'

'I dropped down upon you, then, you ill-conditioned man,' (Jeremiah chuckled at having forced her to adopt his phrase,) 'for having been needlessly significant to Arthur that morning. I have a right to complain of it as almost a breach of confidence. You did not mean it—'

'I won't have it!' interposed the contradictory Jeremiah, flinging back the concession. 'I did mean it.'

'I suppose I must leave you to speak in soliloquy if you choose,' she replied, after a pause that seemed an angry one. 'It is useless my addressing myself to a rash and headstrong old man who has a set purpose not to hear me.'

'Now, I won't take that from you either,' said Jeremiah. 'I have no such purpose. I have told you I did mean it. Do you wish to know why I meant it, you rash and headstrong old woman?'

'After all, you only restore me my own words,' she said, struggling with her indignation. 'Yes.'

'This is why, then. Because you hadn't cleared his father to him, and you ought to have done it. Because, before you went into any tantrum about yourself, who are—'

'Hold there, Flintwinch!' she cried out in a changed voice: 'you may go a word too far.'

The old man seemed to think so. There was another pause, and he had altered his position in the room, when he spoke again more mildly:

'I was going to tell you why it was. Because, before you took your own part, I thought you ought to have taken the part of Arthur's father. Arthur's father! I had no particular love for Arthur's father. I served Arthur's father's uncle, in this house, when Arthur's father was not much above me—was poorer as far as his pocket went—and when his uncle might as soon have left me his heir as have left him. He starved in the parlour, and I starved in the kitchen; that was the principal difference in our positions; there was not much more than a flight of breakneck stairs between us. I never took to him in those times; I don't know that I ever took to him greatly at any time. He was an undecided, irresolute chap, who had everything but his orphan life scared out of him when he was young. And when he brought you home here, the wife his uncle had named for him, I didn't need to look at you twice (you were a good-looking woman at that time) to know who'd be master. You have stood of your own strength ever since. Stand of your own strength now. Don't lean against the dead.'

'I do not—as you call it—lean against the dead.'

'But you had a mind to do it, if I had submitted,' growled Jeremiah, 'and that's why you drop down upon me. You can't forget that I didn't submit. I suppose you are astonished that I should consider it worth my while to have justice done to Arthur's father? Hey? It doesn't matter whether you answer or not, because I know you are, and you know you are. Come, then, I'll tell you how it is. I may be a bit of an oddity in point of temper, but this is my temper—I can't let anybody have entirely their own way. You are a determined woman, and a clever woman; and when you see your purpose before you, nothing will turn you from it. Who knows that better than I do?'

'Nothing will turn me from it, Flintwinch, when I have justified it to myself. Add that.'

'Justified it to yourself? I said you were the most determined woman on the face of the earth (or I meant to say so), and if you are determined to justify any object you entertain, of course you'll do it.'

'Man! I justify myself by the authority of these Books,' she cried, with stern emphasis, and appearing from the sound that followed to strike the dead-weight of her arm upon the table.

'Never mind that,' returned Jeremiah calmly, 'we won't enter into that question at present. However that may be, you carry out your purposes, and you make everything go down before them. Now, I won't go down before them. I have been faithful to you, and useful to you, and I am attached to you. But I can't consent, and I won't consent, and I never did consent, and I never will consent to be lost in you. Swallow up everybody else, and welcome. The peculiarity of my temper is, ma'am, that I won't be swallowed up alive.'

Perhaps this had originally been the mainspring of the understanding between them. Descrying thus much of force of character in Mr Flintwinch, perhaps Mrs Clennam had deemed alliance with him worth her while.

'Enough and more than enough of the subject,' said she gloomily.

'Unless you drop down upon me again,' returned the persistent Flintwinch, 'and then you must expect to hear of it again.'

Mistress Affery dreamed that the figure of her lord here began walking up and down the room, as if to cool his spleen, and that she ran away; but that, as he did not issue forth when she had stood listening and trembling in the shadowy hall a little time, she crept up-stairs again, impelled as before by ghosts and curiosity, and once more cowered outside the door.

'Please to light the candle, Flintwinch,' Mrs Clennam was saying, apparently wishing to draw him back into their usual tone. 'It is nearly time for tea. Little Dorrit is coming, and will find me in the dark.'

Mr Flintwinch lighted the candle briskly, and said as he put it down upon the table:

'What are you going to do with Little Dorrit? Is she to come to work here for ever? To come to tea here for ever? To come backwards and forwards here, in the same way, for ever?'

'How can you talk about "for ever" to a maimed creature like me? Are we not all cut down like the grass of the field, and was not I shorn by the scythe many years ago: since when I have been lying here, waiting to be gathered into the barn?'

'Ay, ay! But since you have been lying here—not near dead—nothing like it—numbers of children and young people, blooming women, strong men, and what not, have been cut down and carried; and still here are you, you see, not much changed after all. Your time and mine may be a long one yet. When I say for ever, I mean (though I am not poetical) through all our time.' Mr Flintwinch gave this explanation with great calmness, and calmly waited for an answer.

'So long as Little Dorrit is quiet and industrious, and stands in need of the slight help I can give her, and deserves it; so long, I suppose, unless she withdraws of her own act, she will continue to come here, I being spared.'

'Nothing more than that?' said Flintwinch, stroking his mouth and chin.

'What should there be more than that! What could there be more than that!' she ejaculated in her sternly wondering way.

Mrs Flintwinch dreamed, that, for the space of a minute or two, they remained looking at each other with the candle between them, and that she somehow derived an impression that they looked at each other fixedly.

'Do you happen to know, Mrs Clennam,' Affery's liege lord then demanded in a much lower voice, and with an amount of expression that seemed quite out of proportion to the simple purpose of his words, 'where she lives?'

'No.'

'Would you—now, would you like to know?' said Jeremiah with a pounce as if he had sprung upon her.

'If I cared to know, I should know already. Could I not have asked her any day?'

'Then you don't care to know?'

'I do not.'

Mr Flintwinch, having expelled a long significant breath said, with his former emphasis, 'For I have accidentally—mind!—found out.'

'Wherever she lives,' said Mrs Clennam, speaking in one unmodulated hard voice, and separating her words as distinctly as if she were reading them off from separate bits of metal that she took up one by one, 'she has made a secret of it, and she shall always keep her secret from me.'

'After all, perhaps you would rather not have known the fact, any how?' said Jeremiah; and he said it with a twist, as if his words had come out of him in his own wry shape.

'Flintwinch,' said his mistress and partner, flashing into a sudden energy that made Affery start, 'why do you goad me? Look round this room. If it is any compensation for my long confinement within these narrow limits—not that I complain of being afflicted; you know I never complain of that—if it is any compensation to me for long confinement to this room, that while I am shut up from all pleasant change I am also shut up from the knowledge of some things that I may prefer to avoid knowing, why should you, of all men, grudge me that belief?'

'I don't grudge it to you,' returned Jeremiah.

'Then say no more. Say no more. Let Little Dorrit keep her secret from me, and do you keep it from me also. Let her come and go, unobserved and unquestioned. Let me suffer, and let me have what alleviation belongs to my condition. Is it so much, that you torment me like an evil spirit?'

'I asked you a question. That's all.'

'I have answered it. So, say no more. Say no more.' Here the sound of the wheeled chair was heard upon the floor, and Affery's bell rang with a hasty jerk.

More afraid of her husband at the moment than of the mysterious sound in the kitchen, Affery crept away as lightly and as quickly as she could, descended the kitchen stairs almost as rapidly as she had ascended them, resumed her seat before the fire, tucked up her skirt again, and finally threw her apron over her head. Then the bell rang once more, and then once more, and then kept on ringing; in despite of which importunate summons, Affery still sat behind her apron, recovering her breath.

At last Mr Flintwinch came shuffling down the staircase into the hall, muttering and calling 'Affery woman!' all the way. Affery still remaining behind her apron, he came stumbling down the kitchen stairs, candle in hand, sidled up to her, twitched her apron off, and roused her.

'Oh Jeremiah!' cried Affery, waking. 'What a start you gave me!'

'What have you been doing, woman?' inquired Jeremiah. 'You've been rung for fifty times.'

'Oh Jeremiah,' said Mistress Affery, 'I have been a-dreaming!'

Reminded of her former achievement in that way, Mr Flintwinch held the candle to her head, as if he had some idea of lighting her up for the illumination of the kitchen.

'Don't you know it's her tea-time?' he demanded with a vicious grin, and giving one of the legs of Mistress Affery's chair a kick.

'Jeremiah? Tea-time? I don't know what's come to me. But I got such a dreadful turn, Jeremiah, before I went—off a-dreaming, that I think it must be that.'

'Yoogh! Sleepy-Head!' said Mr Flintwinch, 'what are you talking about?'

'Such a strange noise, Jeremiah, and such a curious movement. In the kitchen here—just here.'

Jeremiah held up his light and looked at the blackened ceiling, held down his light and looked at the damp stone floor, turned round with his light and looked about at the spotted and blotched walls.

'Rats, cats, water, drains,' said Jeremiah.

Mistress Affery negatived each with a shake of her head. 'No, Jeremiah; I have felt it before. I have felt it up-stairs, and once on the staircase as I was going from her room to ours in the night—a rustle and a sort of trembling touch behind me.'

'Affery, my woman,' said Mr Flintwinch grimly, after advancing his nose to that lady's lips as a test for the detection of spirituous liquors, 'if you don't get tea pretty quick, old woman, you'll become sensible of a rustle and a touch that'll send you flying to the other end of the kitchen.'

This prediction stimulated Mrs Flintwinch to bestir herself, and to hasten up-stairs to Mrs Clennam's chamber. But, for all that, she now began to entertain a settled conviction that there was something wrong in the gloomy house. Henceforth, she was never at peace in it after daylight departed; and never went up or down stairs in the dark without having her apron over her head, lest she should see something.

What with these ghostly apprehensions and her singular dreams, Mrs Flintwinch fell that evening into a haunted state of mind, from which it may be long before this present narrative descries any trace of her recovery. In the vagueness and indistinctness of all her new experiences and perceptions, as everything about her was mysterious to herself she began to be mysterious to others: and became as difficult to be made out to anybody's satisfaction as she found the house and everything in it difficult to make out to her own.

She had not yet finished preparing Mrs Clennam's tea, when the soft knock came to the door which always announced Little Dorrit. Mistress Affery looked on at Little Dorrit taking off her homely bonnet in the hall, and at Mr Flintwinch scraping his jaws and contemplating her in silence, as expecting some wonderful consequence to ensue which would frighten her out of her five wits or blow them all three to pieces.

After tea there came another knock at the door, announcing Arthur. Mistress Affery went down to let him in, and he said on entering, 'Affery, I am glad it's you. I want to ask you a question.' Affery immediately replied, 'For goodness sake don't ask me nothing, Arthur! I am frightened out of one half of my life, and dreamed out of the other. Don't ask me nothing! I don't know which is which, or what is what!'—and immediately started away from him, and came near him no more.

Mistress Affery having no taste for reading, and no sufficient light for needlework in the subdued room, supposing her to have the inclination, now sat every night in the dimness from which she had momentarily emerged on the evening of Arthur Clennam's return, occupied with crowds of wild speculations and suspicions respecting her mistress and her husband and the noises in the house. When the ferocious devotional exercises were engaged in, these speculations would distract Mistress Affery's eyes towards the door, as if she expected some dark form to appear at those propitious moments, and make the party one too many.

Otherwise, Affery never said or did anything to attract the attention of the two clever ones towards her in any marked degree, except on certain occasions, generally at about the quiet hour towards bed-time, when she would suddenly dart out of her dim corner, and whisper with a face of terror to Mr Flintwinch, reading the paper near Mrs Clennam's little table:

'There, Jeremiah! Now! What's that noise?'

Then the noise, if there were any, would have ceased, and Mr Flintwinch would snarl, turning upon her as if she had cut him down that moment against his will, 'Affery, old woman, you shall have a dose, old woman, such a dose! You have been dreaming again!'

CHAPTER 16. Nobody's Weakness

The time being come for the renewal of his acquaintance with the Meagles family, Clennam, pursuant to contract made between himself and Mr Meagles within the precincts of Bleeding Heart Yard, turned his face on a certain Saturday towards Twickenham, where Mr Meagles had a cottage-residence of his own. The weather being fine and dry, and any English road abounding in interest for him who had been so long away, he sent his valise on by the coach, and set out to walk. A walk was in itself a new enjoyment to him, and one that had rarely diversified his life afar off.

He went by Fulham and Putney, for the pleasure of strolling over the heath. It was bright and shining there; and when he found himself so far on his road to Twickenham, he found himself a long way on his road to a number of airier and less substantial destinations. They had risen before him fast, in the healthful exercise and the pleasant road. It is not easy to walk alone in the country without musing upon something. And he had plenty of unsettled subjects to meditate upon, though he had been walking to the Land's End.

First, there was the subject seldom absent from his mind, the question, what he was to do henceforth in life; to what occupation he should devote himself, and in what direction he had best seek it. He was far from rich, and every day of indecision and inaction made his inheritance a source of greater anxiety to him. As often as he began to consider how to increase this inheritance, or to lay it by, so often his misgiving that there was some one with an unsatisfied claim upon his justice, returned; and that alone was a subject to outlast the longest walk. Again, there was the subject of his relations with his mother, which were now upon an equable and peaceful but never confidential footing, and whom he saw several times a week. Little Dorrit was a leading and a constant subject: for the circumstances of his life, united to those of her own story, presented the little creature to him as the only person between whom and himself there were ties of innocent reliance on one hand, and affectionate protection on the other; ties of compassion, respect, unselfish interest, gratitude, and pity. Thinking of her, and of the possibility of her father's release from prison by the unbarring hand of death—the only change of circumstance he could foresee that might enable him to be such a friend to her as he wished to be, by altering her whole manner of life, smoothing her rough road, and giving her a home—he regarded her, in that perspective, as his adopted daughter, his poor child of the Marshalsea hushed to rest. If there were a last subject in his thoughts, and it lay towards Twickenham, its form was so indefinite that it was little more than the pervading atmosphere in which these other subjects floated before him.

He had crossed the heath and was leaving it behind when he gained upon a figure which had been in advance of him for some time, and which, as he gained upon it, he thought he knew. He derived this impression from something in the turn of the head, and in the figure's action of consideration, as it went on at a sufficiently sturdy walk. But when the man—for it was a man's figure—pushed his hat up at the back of his head, and stopped to consider some object before him, he knew it to be Daniel Doyce.

'How do you do, Mr Doyce?' said Clennam, overtaking him. 'I am glad to see you again, and in a healthier place than the Circumlocution Office.'

'Ha! Mr Meagles's friend!' exclaimed that public criminal, coming out of some mental combinations he had been making, and offering his hand. 'I am glad to see you, sir. Will you excuse me if I forget your name?'

'Readily. It's not a celebrated name. It's not Barnacle.'

'No, no,' said Daniel, laughing. 'And now I know what it is. It's Clennam. How do you do, Mr Clennam?'

'I have some hope,' said Arthur, as they walked on together, 'that we may be going to the same place, Mr Doyce.'

'Meaning Twickenham?' returned Daniel. 'I am glad to hear it.'

They were soon quite intimate, and lightened the way with a variety of conversation. The ingenious culprit was a man of great modesty and good sense; and, though a plain man, had been too much accustomed to combine what was original and daring in conception with what was patient and minute in execution, to be by any means an ordinary man. It was at first difficult to lead him to speak about himself, and he put off Arthur's advances in that direction by admitting slightly, oh yes, he had done this, and he had done that, and such a thing was of his making, and such another thing was his discovery, but it was his trade, you see, his trade; until, as he gradually became assured that his companion had a real interest in his account of himself, he frankly yielded to it. Then it appeared that he was the son of a north-country blacksmith, and had originally been apprenticed by his widowed mother to a lock-maker; that he had 'struck out a few little things' at the lock-maker's, which had led to his being released from his indentures with a present, which present had enabled him to gratify his ardent wish to bind himself to a working engineer, under whom he had laboured hard, learned hard, and lived hard, seven years. His time being out, he had 'worked in the shop' at weekly wages seven or eight years more; and had then betaken himself to the banks of the Clyde, where he had studied, and filed, and hammered, and improved his knowledge, theoretical and practical, for six or seven years more. There he had had an offer to go to Lyons, which he had accepted; and from Lyons had been engaged to go to Germany, and in Germany had had an offer to go to St Petersburg, and there had done very well indeed—never better. However, he had naturally felt a preference for his own country, and a wish to gain distinction there, and to do whatever service he could do, there rather than elsewhere. And so he had come home. And so at home he had established himself in business, and had invented and executed, and worked his way on, until, after a dozen years of constant suit and service, he had been enrolled in the Great British Legion of Honour, the Legion of the Rebuffed of the Circumlocution Office, and had been decorated with the Great British Order of Merit, the Order of the Disorder of the Barnacles and Stiltstalkings.

'It is much to be regretted,' said Clennam, 'that you ever turned your thoughts that way, Mr Doyce.'

'True, sir, true to a certain extent. But what is a man to do? if he has the misfortune to strike out something serviceable to the nation, he must follow where it leads him.'

'Hadn't he better let it go?' said Clennam.

'He can't do it,' said Doyce, shaking his head with a thoughtful smile. 'It's not put into his head to be buried. It's put into his head to be made useful. You hold your life on the condition that to the last you shall struggle hard for it. Every man holds a discovery on the same terms.'

'That is to say,' said Arthur, with a growing admiration of his quiet companion, 'you are not finally discouraged even now?'

'I have no right to be, if I am,' returned the other. 'The thing is as true as it ever was.'

When they had walked a little way in silence, Clennam, at once to change the direct point of their conversation and not to change it too abruptly, asked Mr Doyce if he had any partner in his business to relieve him of a portion of its anxieties?

'No,' he returned, 'not at present. I had when I first entered on it, and a good man he was. But he has been dead some years; and as I could not easily take to the notion of another when I lost him, I bought his share for myself and have gone on by myself ever since. And here's another thing,' he said, stopping for a moment with a good-humoured laugh in his eyes, and laying his closed right hand, with its peculiar suppleness of thumb, on Clennam's arm, 'no inventor can be a man of business, you know.'

'No?' said Clennam.

'Why, so the men of business say,' he answered, resuming the walk and laughing outright. 'I don't know why we unfortunate creatures should be supposed to want common sense, but it is generally taken for granted that we do. Even the best friend I have in the world, our excellent friend over yonder,' said Doyce, nodding towards Twickenham, 'extends a sort of protection to me, don't you know, as a man not quite able to take care of himself?'

Arthur Clennam could not help joining in the good-humoured laugh, for he recognised the truth of the description.

'So I find that I must have a partner who is a man of business and not guilty of any inventions,' said Daniel Doyce, taking off his hat to pass his hand over his forehead, 'if it's only in deference to the current opinion, and to uphold the credit of the Works. I don't think he'll find that I have been very remiss or confused in my way of conducting them; but that's for him to say—whoever he is—not for me.'

'You have not chosen him yet, then?'

'No, sir, no. I have only just come to a decision to take one. The fact is, there's more to do than there used to be, and the Works are enough for me as I grow older. What with the books and correspondence, and foreign journeys for which a Principal is necessary, I can't do all. I am going to talk over the best way of negotiating the matter, if I find a spare half-hour between this and Monday morning, with my—my Nurse and protector,' said Doyce, with laughing eyes again. 'He is a sagacious man in business, and has had a good apprenticeship to it.'

After this, they conversed on different subjects until they arrived at their journey's end. A composed and unobtrusive self-sustainment was noticeable in Daniel Doyce—a calm knowledge that what was true must remain true, in spite of all the Barnacles in the family ocean, and would be just the truth, and neither more nor less when even that sea had run dry—which had a kind of greatness in it, though not of the official quality.

As he knew the house well, he conducted Arthur to it by the way that showed it to the best advantage. It was a charming place (none the worse for being a little eccentric), on the road by the river, and just what the residence of the Meagles family ought to be. It stood in a garden, no doubt as fresh and beautiful in the May of the Year as Pet now was in the May of her life; and it was defended by a goodly show of handsome trees and spreading evergreens, as Pet was by Mr and Mrs Meagles. It was made out of an old brick house, of which a part had been altogether pulled down, and another part had been changed into the present cottage; so there was a hale elderly portion, to represent Mr and Mrs Meagles, and a young picturesque, very pretty portion to represent Pet. There was even the later addition of a conservatory sheltering itself against it, uncertain of hue in its deep-stained glass, and in its more transparent portions flashing to the sun's rays, now like fire and now like harmless water drops; which might have stood for Tattycoram. Within view was the peaceful river and the ferry-boat, to moralise to all the inmates saying: Young or old, passionate or tranquil, chafing or content, you, thus runs the current always. Let the heart swell into what discord it will, thus plays the rippling water on the prow of the ferry-boat ever the same tune. Year after year, so much allowance for the drifting of the boat, so many miles an hour the flowing of the stream, here the rushes, there the lilies, nothing uncertain or unquiet, upon this road that steadily runs away; while you, upon your flowing road of time, are so capricious and distracted.

The bell at the gate had scarcely sounded when Mr Meagles came out to receive them. Mr Meagles had scarcely come out, when Mrs Meagles came out. Mrs Meagles had scarcely come out, when Pet came out. Pet scarcely had come out, when Tattycoram came out. Never had visitors a more hospitable reception.

'Here we are, you see,' said Mr Meagles, 'boxed up, Mr Clennam, within our own home-limits, as if we were never going to expand—that is, travel—again. Not like Marseilles, eh? No allonging and marshonging here!'

'A different kind of beauty, indeed!' said Clennam, looking about him.

'But, Lord bless me!' cried Mr Meagles, rubbing his hands with a relish, 'it was an uncommonly pleasant thing being in quarantine, wasn't it? Do you know, I have often wished myself back again? We were a capital party.'

This was Mr Meagles's invariable habit. Always to object to everything while he was travelling, and always to want to get back to it when he was not travelling.

'If it was summer-time,' said Mr Meagles, 'which I wish it was on your account, and in order that you might see the place at its best, you would hardly be able to hear yourself speak for birds. Being practical people, we never allow anybody to scare the birds; and the birds, being practical people too, come about us in myriads. We are delighted to see you, Clennam (if you'll allow me, I shall drop the Mister); I heartily assure you, we are delighted.'

'I have not had so pleasant a greeting,' said Clennam—then he recalled what Little Dorrit had said to him in his own room, and faithfully added 'except once—since we last walked to and fro, looking down at the Mediterranean.'

'Ah!' returned Mr Meagles. 'Something like a look out, that was, wasn't it? I don't want a military government, but I shouldn't mind a little allonging and marshonging—just a dash of it—in this neighbourhood sometimes. It's Devilish still.'

Bestowing this eulogium on the retired character of his retreat with a dubious shake of the head, Mr Meagles led the way into the house. It was just large enough, and no more; was as pretty within as it was without, and was perfectly well-arranged and comfortable. Some traces of the migratory habits of the family were to be observed in the covered frames and furniture, and wrapped-up hangings; but it was easy to see that it was one of Mr Meagles's whims to have the cottage always kept, in their absence, as if they were always coming back the day after to-morrow. Of articles collected on his various expeditions, there was such a vast miscellany that it was like the dwelling of an amiable Corsair. There were antiquities from Central Italy, made by the best modern houses in that department of industry; bits of mummy from Egypt (and perhaps Birmingham); model gondolas from Venice; model villages from Switzerland; morsels of tesselated pavement from Herculaneum and Pompeii, like petrified minced veal; ashes out of tombs, and lava out of Vesuvius; Spanish fans, Spezzian straw hats, Moorish slippers, Tuscan hairpins, Carrara sculpture, Trastaverini scarves, Genoese velvets and filigree, Neapolitan coral, Roman cameos, Geneva jewellery, Arab lanterns, rosaries blest all round by the Pope himself, and an infinite variety of lumber. There were views, like and unlike, of a multitude of places; and there was one little picture-room devoted to a few of the regular sticky old Saints, with sinews like whipcord, hair like Neptune's, wrinkles like tattooing, and such coats of varnish that every holy personage served for a fly-trap, and became what is now called in the vulgar tongue a Catch-em-alive O. Of these pictorial acquisitions Mr Meagles spoke in the usual manner. He was no judge, he said, except of what pleased himself; he had picked them up, dirt-cheap, and people had considered them rather fine. One man, who at any rate ought to know something of the subject, had declared that 'Sage, Reading' (a specially oily old gentleman in a blanket, with a swan's-down tippet for a beard, and a web of cracks all over him like rich pie-crust), to be a fine Guercino. As for Sebastian del Piombo there, you would judge for yourself; if it were not his later manner, the question was, Who was it? Titian, that might or might not be—perhaps he had only touched it. Daniel Doyce said perhaps he hadn't touched it, but Mr Meagles rather declined to overhear the remark.

When he had shown all his spoils, Mr Meagles took them into his own snug room overlooking the lawn, which was fitted up in part like a dressing-room and in part like an office, and in which, upon a kind of counter-desk, were a pair of brass scales for weighing gold, and a scoop for shovelling out money.

'Here they are, you see,' said Mr Meagles. 'I stood behind these two articles five-and-thirty years running, when I no more thought of gadding about than I now think of—staying at home. When I left the Bank for good, I asked for them, and brought them away with me. I mention it at once, or you might suppose that I sit in my counting-house (as Pet says I do), like the king in the poem of the four-and-twenty blackbirds, counting out my money.'

Clennam's eyes had strayed to a natural picture on the wall, of two pretty little girls with their arms entwined. 'Yes, Clennam,' said Mr Meagles, in a lower voice. 'There they both are. It was taken some seventeen years ago. As I often say to Mother, they were babies then.'

'Their names?' said Arthur.

'Ah, to be sure! You have never heard any name but Pet. Pet's name is Minnie; her sister's Lillie.'

'Should you have known, Mr Clennam, that one of them was meant for me?' asked Pet herself, now standing in the doorway.

'I might have thought that both of them were meant for you, both are still so like you. Indeed,' said Clennam, glancing from the fair original to the picture and back, 'I cannot even now say which is not your portrait.'

'D'ye hear that, Mother?' cried Mr Meagles to his wife, who had followed her daughter. 'It's always the same, Clennam; nobody can decide. The child to your left is Pet.'

The picture happened to be near a looking-glass. As Arthur looked at it again, he saw, by the reflection of the mirror, Tattycoram stop in passing outside the door, listen to what was going on, and pass away with an angry and contemptuous frown upon her face, that changed its beauty into ugliness.

'But come!' said Mr Meagles. 'You have had a long walk, and will be glad to get your boots off. As to Daniel here, I suppose he'd never think of taking his boots off, unless we showed him a boot-jack.'

'Why not?' asked Daniel, with a significant smile at Clennam.

'Oh! You have so many things to think about,' returned Mr Meagles, clapping him on the shoulder, as if his weakness must not be left to itself on any account. 'Figures, and wheels, and cogs, and levers, and screws, and cylinders, and a thousand things.'

'In my calling,' said Daniel, amused, 'the greater usually includes the less. But never mind, never mind! Whatever pleases you, pleases me.'

Clennam could not help speculating, as he seated himself in his room by the fire, whether there might be in the breast of this honest, affectionate, and cordial Mr Meagles, any microscopic portion of the mustard-seed that had sprung up into the great tree of the Circumlocution Office. His curious sense of a general superiority to Daniel Doyce, which seemed to be founded, not so much on anything in Doyce's personal character as on the mere fact of his being an originator and a man out of the beaten track of other men, suggested the idea. It might have occupied him until he went down to dinner an hour afterwards, if he had not had another question to consider, which had been in his mind so long ago as before he was in quarantine at Marseilles, and which had now returned to it, and was very urgent with it. No less a question than this: Whether he should allow himself to fall in love with Pet?

He was twice her age. (He changed the leg he had crossed over the other, and tried the calculation again, but could not bring out the total at less.) He was twice her age. Well! He was young in appearance, young in health and strength, young in heart. A man was certainly not old at forty; and many men were not in circumstances to marry, or did not marry, until they had attained that time of life. On the other hand, the question was, not what he thought of the point, but what she thought of it.

He believed that Mr Meagles was disposed to entertain a ripe regard for him, and he knew that he had a sincere regard for Mr Meagles and his good wife. He could foresee that to relinquish this beautiful only child, of whom they were so fond, to any husband, would be a trial of their love which perhaps they never yet had had the fortitude to contemplate. But the more beautiful and winning and charming she, the nearer they must always be to the necessity of approaching it. And why not in his favour, as well as in another's?

When he had got so far, it came again into his head that the question was, not what they thought of it, but what she thought of it.

Arthur Clennam was a retiring man, with a sense of many deficiencies; and he so exalted the merits of the beautiful Minnie in his mind, and depressed his own, that when he pinned himself to this point, his hopes began to fail him. He came to the final resolution, as he made himself ready for dinner, that he would not allow himself to fall in love with Pet.

There were only five, at a round table, and it was very pleasant indeed. They had so many places and people to recall, and they were all so easy and cheerful together (Daniel Doyce either sitting out like an amused spectator at cards, or coming in with some shrewd little experiences of his own, when it happened to be to the purpose), that they might have been together twenty times, and not have known so much of one another.

'And Miss Wade,' said Mr Meagles, after they had recalled a number of fellow-travellers. 'Has anybody seen Miss Wade?'

'I have,' said Tattycoram.

She had brought a little mantle which her young mistress had sent for, and was bending over her, putting it on, when she lifted up her dark eyes and made this unexpected answer.

'Tatty!' her young mistress exclaimed. 'You seen Miss Wade?—where?'

'Here, miss,' said Tattycoram.

'How?'

An impatient glance from Tattycoram seemed, as Clennam saw it, to answer 'With my eyes!' But her only answer in words was: 'I met her near the church.'

'What was she doing there I wonder!' said Mr Meagles. 'Not going to it, I should think.'

'She had written to me first,' said Tattycoram.

'Oh, Tatty!' murmured her mistress, 'take your hands away. I feel as if some one else was touching me!'

She said it in a quick involuntary way, but half playfully, and not more petulantly or disagreeably than a favourite child might have done, who laughed next moment. Tattycoram set her full red lips together, and crossed her arms upon her bosom.

'Did you wish to know, sir,' she said, looking at Mr Meagles, 'what Miss Wade wrote to me about?'

'Well, Tattycoram,' returned Mr Meagles, 'since you ask the question, and we are all friends here, perhaps you may as well mention it, if you are so inclined.'

'She knew, when we were travelling, where you lived,' said Tattycoram, 'and she had seen me not quite—not quite—'

'Not quite in a good temper, Tattycoram?' suggested Mr Meagles, shaking his head at the dark eyes with a quiet caution. 'Take a little time—count five-and-twenty, Tattycoram.'

She pressed her lips together again, and took a long deep breath.

'So she wrote to me to say that if I ever felt myself hurt,' she looked down at her young mistress, 'or found myself worried,' she looked down at her again, 'I might go to her, and be considerately treated. I was to think of it, and could speak to her by the church. So I went there to thank her.'

'Tatty,' said her young mistress, putting her hand up over her shoulder that the other might take it, 'Miss Wade almost frightened me when we parted, and I scarcely like to think of her just now as having been so near me without my knowing it. Tatty dear!'

Tatty stood for a moment, immovable.

'Hey?' cried Mr Meagles. 'Count another five-and-twenty, Tattycoram.'

She might have counted a dozen, when she bent and put her lips to the caressing hand. It patted her cheek, as it touched the owner's beautiful curls, and Tattycoram went away.

'Now there,' said Mr Meagles softly, as he gave a turn to the dumb-waiter on his right hand to twirl the sugar towards himself. 'There's a girl who might be lost and ruined, if she wasn't among practical people. Mother and I know, solely from being practical, that there are times when that girl's whole nature seems to roughen itself against seeing us so bound up in Pet. No father and mother were bound up in her, poor soul. I don't like to think of the way in which that unfortunate child, with all that passion and protest in her, feels when she hears the Fifth Commandment on a Sunday. I am always inclined to call out, Church, Count five-and-twenty, Tattycoram.'

Besides his dumb-waiter, Mr Meagles had two other not dumb waiters in the persons of two parlour-maids with rosy faces and bright eyes, who were a highly ornamental part of the table decoration. 'And why not, you see?' said Mr Meagles on this head. 'As I always say to Mother, why not have something pretty to look at, if you have anything at all?'

A certain Mrs Tickit, who was Cook and Housekeeper when the family were at home, and Housekeeper only when the family were away, completed the establishment. Mr Meagles regretted that the nature of the duties in which she was engaged, rendered Mrs Tickit unpresentable at present, but hoped to introduce her to the new visitor to-morrow. She was an important part of the Cottage, he said, and all his friends knew her. That was her picture up in the corner. When they went away, she always put on the silk-gown and the jet-black row of curls represented in that portrait (her hair was reddish-grey in the kitchen), established herself in the breakfast-room, put her spectacles between two particular leaves of Doctor Buchan's Domestic Medicine, and sat looking over the blind all day until they came back again. It was supposed that no persuasion could be invented which would induce Mrs Tickit to abandon her post at the blind, however long their absence, or to dispense with the attendance of Dr Buchan; the lucubrations of which learned practitioner, Mr Meagles implicitly believed she had never yet consulted to the extent of one word in her life.

In the evening they played an old-fashioned rubber; and Pet sat looking over her father's hand, or singing to herself by fits and starts at the piano. She was a spoilt child; but how could she be otherwise? Who could be much with so pliable and beautiful a creature, and not yield to her endearing influence? Who could pass an evening in the house, and not love her for the grace and charm of her very presence in the room? This was Clennam's reflection, notwithstanding the final conclusion at which he had arrived up-stairs.

In making it, he revoked. 'Why, what are you thinking of, my good sir?' asked the astonished Mr Meagles, who was his partner. 'I beg your pardon. Nothing,' returned Clennam. 'Think of something, next time; that's a dear fellow,' said Mr Meagles. Pet laughingly believed he had been thinking of Miss Wade. 'Why of Miss Wade, Pet?' asked her father. 'Why, indeed!' said Arthur Clennam. Pet coloured a little, and went to the piano again.

As they broke up for the night, Arthur overheard Doyce ask his host if he could give him half an hour's conversation before breakfast in the morning? The host replying willingly, Arthur lingered behind a moment, having his own word to add to that topic.

'Mr Meagles,' he said, on their being left alone, 'do you remember when you advised me to go straight to London?'

'Perfectly well.'

'And when you gave me some other good advice which I needed at that time?'

'I won't say what it was worth,' answered Mr Meagles: 'but of course I remember our being very pleasant and confidential together.'

'I have acted on your advice; and having disembarrassed myself of an occupation that was painful to me for many reasons, wish to devote myself and what means I have, to another pursuit.'

'Right! You can't do it too soon,' said Mr Meagles.

'Now, as I came down to-day, I found that your friend, Mr Doyce, is looking for a partner in his business—not a partner in his mechanical knowledge, but in the ways and means of turning the business arising from it to the best account.'

'Just so,' said Mr Meagles, with his hands in his pockets, and with the old business expression of face that had belonged to the scales and scoop.

'Mr Doyce mentioned incidentally, in the course of our conversation, that he was going to take your valuable advice on the subject of finding such a partner. If you should think our views and opportunities at all likely to coincide, perhaps you will let him know my available position. I speak, of course, in ignorance of the details, and they may be unsuitable on both sides.'

'No doubt, no doubt,' said Mr Meagles, with the caution belonging to the scales and scoop.

'But they will be a question of figures and accounts—'

'Just so, just so,' said Mr Meagles, with arithmetical solidity belonging to the scales and scoop.

'—And I shall be glad to enter into the subject, provided Mr Doyce responds, and you think well of it. If you will at present, therefore, allow me to place it in your hands, you will much oblige me.'

'Clennam, I accept the trust with readiness,' said Mr Meagles. 'And without anticipating any of the points which you, as a man of business, have of course reserved, I am free to say to you that I think something may come of this. Of one thing you may be perfectly certain. Daniel is an honest man.'

'I am so sure of it that I have promptly made up my mind to speak to you.'

'You must guide him, you know; you must steer him; you must direct him; he is one of a crotchety sort,' said Mr Meagles, evidently meaning nothing more than that he did new things and went new ways; 'but he is as honest as the sun, and so good night!'

Clennam went back to his room, sat down again before his fire, and made up his mind that he was glad he had resolved not to fall in love with Pet. She was so beautiful, so amiable, so apt to receive any true impression given to her gentle nature and her innocent heart, and make the man who should be so happy as to communicate it, the most fortunate and enviable of all men, that he was very glad indeed he had come to that conclusion.

But, as this might have been a reason for coming to the opposite conclusion, he followed out the theme again a little way in his mind; to justify himself, perhaps.

'Suppose that a man,' so his thoughts ran, 'who had been of age some twenty years or so; who was a diffident man, from the circumstances of his youth; who was rather a grave man, from the tenor of his life; who knew himself to be deficient in many little engaging qualities which he admired in others, from having been long in a distant region, with nothing softening near him; who had no kind sisters to present to her; who had no congenial home to make her known in; who was a stranger in the land; who had not a fortune to compensate, in any measure, for these defects; who had nothing in his favour but his honest love and his general wish to do right—suppose such a man were to come to this house, and were to yield to the captivation of this charming girl, and were to persuade himself that he could hope to win her; what a weakness it would be!'

He softly opened his window, and looked out upon the serene river. Year after year so much allowance for the drifting of the ferry-boat, so many miles an hour the flowing of the stream, here the rushes, there the lilies, nothing uncertain or unquiet.

Why should he be vexed or sore at heart? It was not his weakness that he had imagined. It was nobody's, nobody's within his knowledge; why should it trouble him? And yet it did trouble him. And he thought—who has not thought for a moment, sometimes?—that it might be better to flow away monotonously, like the river, and to compound for its insensibility to happiness with its insensibility to pain.

CHAPTER 17. Nobody's Rival

Before breakfast in the morning, Arthur walked out to look about him. As the morning was fine and he had an hour on his hands, he crossed the river by the ferry, and strolled along a footpath through some meadows. When he came back to the towing-path, he found the ferry-boat on the opposite side, and a gentleman hailing it and waiting to be taken over.

This gentleman looked barely thirty. He was well dressed, of a sprightly and gay appearance, a well-knit figure, and a rich dark complexion. As Arthur came over the stile and down to the water's edge, the lounger glanced at him for a moment, and then resumed his occupation of idly tossing stones into the water with his foot. There was something in his way of spurning them out of their places with his heel, and getting them into the required position, that Clennam thought had an air of cruelty in it. Most of us have more or less frequently derived a similar impression from a man's manner of doing some very little thing: plucking a flower, clearing away an obstacle, or even destroying an insentient object.

The gentleman's thoughts were preoccupied, as his face showed, and he took no notice of a fine Newfoundland dog, who watched him attentively, and watched every stone too, in its turn, eager to spring into the river on receiving his master's sign. The ferry-boat came over, however, without his receiving any sign, and when it grounded his master took him by the collar and walked him into it.

'Not this morning,' he said to the dog. 'You won't do for ladies' company, dripping wet. Lie down.'

Clennam followed the man and the dog into the boat, and took his seat. The dog did as he was ordered. The man remained standing, with his hands in his pockets, and towered between Clennam and the prospect. Man and dog both jumped lightly out as soon as they touched the other side, and went away. Clennam was glad to be rid of them.

The church clock struck the breakfast hour as he walked up the little lane by which the garden-gate was approached. The moment he pulled the bell a deep loud barking assailed him from within the wall.

'I heard no dog last night,' thought Clennam. The gate was opened by one of the rosy maids, and on the lawn were the Newfoundland dog and the man.

'Miss Minnie is not down yet, gentlemen,' said the blushing portress, as they all came together in the garden. Then she said to the master of the dog, 'Mr Clennam, sir,' and tripped away.

'Odd enough, Mr Clennam, that we should have met just now,' said the man. Upon which the dog became mute. 'Allow me to introduce myself—Henry Gowan. A pretty place this, and looks wonderfully well this morning!'

The manner was easy, and the voice agreeable; but still Clennam thought, that if he had not made that decided resolution to avoid falling in love with Pet, he would have taken a dislike to this Henry Gowan.

154

'It's new to you, I believe?' said this Gowan, when Arthur had extolled the place.

'Quite new. I made acquaintance with it only yesterday afternoon.'

'Ah! Of course this is not its best aspect. It used to look charming in the spring, before they went away last time. I should like you to have seen it then.'

But for that resolution so often recalled, Clennam might have wished him in the crater of Mount Etna, in return for this civility.

'I have had the pleasure of seeing it under many circumstances during the last three years, and it's—a Paradise.'

It was (at least it might have been, always excepting for that wise resolution) like his dexterous impudence to call it a Paradise. He only called it a Paradise because he first saw her coming, and so made her out within her hearing to be an angel, Confusion to him!

And ah! how beaming she looked, and how glad! How she caressed the dog, and how the dog knew her! How expressive that heightened colour in her face, that fluttered manner, her downcast eyes, her irresolute happiness! When had Clennam seen her look like this? Not that there was any reason why he might, could, would, or should have ever seen her look like this, or that he had ever hoped for himself to see her look like this; but still—when had he ever known her do it!

He stood at a little distance from them. This Gowan when he had talked about a Paradise, had gone up to her and taken her hand. The dog had put his great paws on her arm and laid his head against her dear bosom. She had laughed and welcomed them, and made far too much of the dog, far, far, too much—that is to say, supposing there had been any third person looking on who loved her.

She disengaged herself now, and came to Clennam, and put her hand in his and wished him good morning, and gracefully made as if she would take his arm and be escorted into the house. To this Gowan had no objection. No, he knew he was too safe.

There was a passing cloud on Mr Meagles's good-humoured face when they all three (four, counting the dog, and he was the most objectionable but one of the party) came in to breakfast. Neither it, nor the touch of uneasiness on Mrs Meagles as she directed her eyes towards it, was unobserved by Clennam.

'Well, Gowan,' said Mr Meagles, even suppressing a sigh; 'how goes the world with you this morning?'

'Much as usual, sir. Lion and I being determined not to waste anything of our weekly visit, turned out early, and came over from Kingston, my present headquarters, where I am making a sketch or two.' Then he told how he had met Mr Clennam at the ferry, and they had come over together.

'Mrs Gowan is well, Henry?' said Mrs Meagles. (Clennam became attentive.)

'My mother is quite well, thank you.' (Clennam became inattentive.) 'I have taken the liberty of making an addition to your family dinner-party to-day, which I hope will not be inconvenient to you or to Mr Meagles. I couldn't very well get out of it,' he explained, turning to the latter. 'The young fellow wrote to propose himself to me; and as he is well connected, I thought you would not object to my transferring him here.'

'Who is the young fellow?' asked Mr Meagles with peculiar complacency.

'He is one of the Barnacles. Tite Barnacle's son, Clarence Barnacle, who is in his father's Department. I can at least guarantee that the river shall not suffer from his visit. He won't set it on fire.'

'Aye, aye?' said Meagles. 'A Barnacle is he? We know something of that family, eh, Dan? By George, they are at the top of the tree, though! Let me see. What relation will this young fellow be to Lord Decimus now? His Lordship married, in seventeen ninety-seven, Lady Jemima Bilberry, who was the second daughter by the third marriage—no! There I am wrong! That was Lady Seraphina—Lady Jemima was the first daughter by the second marriage of the fifteenth Earl of Stiltstalking with the Honourable Clementina Toozellem. Very well. Now this young fellow's father married a Stiltstalking and his father married his cousin who was a Barnacle. The father of that father who married a Barnacle, married a Joddleby.—I am getting a little too far back, Gowan; I want to make out what relation this young fellow is to Lord Decimus.'

'That's easily stated. His father is nephew to Lord Decimus.'

'Nephew—to—Lord—Decimus,' Mr Meagles luxuriously repeated with his eyes shut, that he might have nothing to distract him from the full flavour of the genealogical tree. 'By George, you are right, Gowan. So he is.'

'Consequently, Lord Decimus is his great uncle.'

'But stop a bit!' said Mr Meagles, opening his eyes with a fresh discovery. 'Then on the mother's side, Lady Stiltstalking is his great aunt.'

'Of course she is.'

'Aye, aye, aye?' said Mr Meagles with much interest. 'Indeed, indeed? We shall be glad to see him. We'll entertain him as well as we can, in our humble way; and we shall not starve him, I hope, at all events.'

In the beginning of this dialogue, Clennam had expected some great harmless outburst from Mr Meagles, like that which had made him burst out of the Circumlocution Office, holding Doyce by the collar. But his good friend had a weakness which none of us need go into the next street to find, and which no amount of Circumlocution experience could long subdue in him. Clennam looked at Doyce; but Doyce knew all about it beforehand, and looked at his plate, and made no sign, and said no word.

'I am much obliged to you,' said Gowan, to conclude the subject. 'Clarence is a great ass, but he is one of the dearest and best fellows that ever lived!'

It appeared, before the breakfast was over, that everybody whom this Gowan knew was either more or less of an ass, or more or less of a knave; but was, notwithstanding, the most lovable, the most engaging, the simplest, truest, kindest, dearest, best fellow that ever lived. The process by which this unvarying result was attained, whatever the premises, might have been stated by Mr Henry Gowan thus: 'I claim to be always book-keeping, with a peculiar nicety, in every man's case, and posting up a careful little account of Good and Evil with him. I do this so conscientiously, that I am happy to tell you I find the most worthless of men to be the dearest old fellow too: and am in a condition to make the gratifying report, that there is much less difference than you are inclined to suppose between an honest man and a scoundrel.'

The effect of this cheering discovery happened to be, that while he seemed to be scrupulously finding good in most men, he did in reality lower it where it was, and set it up where it was not; but that was its only disagreeable or dangerous feature.

It scarcely seemed, however, to afford Mr Meagles as much satisfaction as the Barnacle genealogy had done. The cloud that Clennam had never seen upon his face before that morning, frequently overcast it again; and there was the same shadow of uneasy observation of him on the comely face of his wife. More than once or twice when Pet caressed the dog, it appeared to Clennam that her father was unhappy in seeing her do it; and, in one particular instance when Gowan stood on the other side of the dog, and bent his head at the same time, Arthur fancied that he saw tears rise to Mr Meagles's eyes as he hurried out of the room. It was either the fact too, or he fancied further, that Pet herself was not insensible to these little incidents; that she tried, with a more delicate affection than usual, to express to her good father how much she loved him; that it was on this account that she fell behind the rest, both as they went to church and as they returned from it, and took his arm. He could not have sworn but that as he walked alone in the garden afterwards, he had an instantaneous glimpse of her in her father's room, clinging to both her parents with the greatest tenderness, and weeping on her father's shoulder.

The latter part of the day turning out wet, they were fain to keep the house, look over Mr Meagles's collection, and beguile the time with conversation. This Gowan had plenty to say for himself, and said it in an off-hand and amusing manner. He appeared to be an artist by profession, and to have been at Rome some time; yet he had a slight, careless, amateur way with him—a perceptible limp, both in his devotion to art and his attainments—which Clennam could scarcely understand.

He applied to Daniel Doyce for help, as they stood together, looking out of window.

'You know Mr Gowan?' he said in a low voice.

'I have seen him here. Comes here every Sunday when they are at home.'

'An artist, I infer from what he says?'

'A sort of a one,' said Daniel Doyce, in a surly tone.

'What sort of a one?' asked Clennam, with a smile.

'Why, he has sauntered into the Arts at a leisurely Pall-Mall pace,' said Doyce, 'and I doubt if they care to be taken quite so coolly.'

Pursuing his inquiries, Clennam found that the Gowan family were a very distant ramification of the Barnacles; and that the paternal Gowan, originally attached to a legation abroad, had been pensioned off as a Commissioner of nothing particular somewhere or other, and had died at his post with his drawn salary in his hand, nobly defending it to the last extremity. In consideration of this eminent public service, the Barnacle then in power had recommended the Crown to bestow a pension of two or three hundred a-year on his widow; to which the next Barnacle in power had added certain shady and sedate apartments in the Palaces at Hampton Court, where the old lady still lived, deploring the degeneracy of the times in company with several other old ladies of both sexes. Her son, Mr Henry Gowan, inheriting from his father, the Commissioner, that very questionable help in life, a very small independence, had been difficult to settle; the rather, as public appointments chanced to be scarce, and his genius, during his earlier manhood, was of that exclusively agricultural character which applies itself to the cultivation of wild oats. At last he had declared that he would become a Painter; partly because he had always had an idle knack that way, and partly to grieve the souls of the Barnacles-in-chief who had not provided for him. So it had come to pass successively, first, that several distinguished ladies had been frightfully shocked; then, that portfolios of his performances had been handed about o' nights, and declared with ecstasy to be perfect Claudes, perfect Cuyps, perfect phaenomena; then, that Lord Decimus had bought his picture, and had asked the President and Council to dinner at a blow, and had said, with his own magnificent gravity, 'Do you know, there appears to me to be really immense merit in that work?' and, in short, that people of condition had absolutely taken pains to bring him into fashion. But, somehow, it had all failed. The prejudiced public had stood out against it obstinately. They had determined not to admire Lord Decimus's picture. They had determined to believe that in every service, except their own, a man must qualify himself, by striving early and late, and by working heart and soul, might and main. So now Mr Gowan, like that worn-out old coffin which never was Mahomet's nor anybody else's, hung midway between two points: jaundiced and jealous as to the one he had left: jaundiced and jealous as to the other that he couldn't reach.

Such was the substance of Clennam's discoveries concerning him, made that rainy Sunday afternoon and afterwards.

About an hour or so after dinner time, Young Barnacle appeared, attended by his eye-glass; in honour of whose family connections, Mr Meagles had cashiered the pretty parlour-maids for the day, and had placed on duty in their stead two dingy men. Young Barnacle was in the last degree amazed and disconcerted at sight of Arthur, and had murmured involuntarily, 'Look here! upon my soul, you know!' before his presence of mind returned.

Even then, he was obliged to embrace the earliest opportunity of taking his friend into a window, and saying, in a nasal way that was a part of his general debility:

'I want to speak to you, Gowan. I say. Look here. Who is that fellow?'

'A friend of our host's. None of mine.'

'He's a most ferocious Radical, you know,' said Young Barnacle.

'Is he? How do you know?'

'Ecod, sir, he was Pitching into our people the other day in the most tremendous manner. Went up to our place and Pitched into my father to that extent that it was necessary to order him out. Came back to our Department, and Pitched into me. Look here. You never saw such a fellow.'

'What did he want?'

'Ecod, sir,' returned Young Barnacle, 'he said he wanted to know, you know! Pervaded our Department—without an appointment—and said he wanted to know!'

The stare of indignant wonder with which Young Barnacle accompanied this disclosure, would have strained his eyes injuriously but for the opportune relief of dinner. Mr Meagles (who had been extremely solicitous to know how his uncle and aunt were) begged him to conduct Mrs Meagles to the dining-room. And when he sat on Mrs Meagles's right hand, Mr Meagles looked as gratified as if his whole family were there.

All the natural charm of the previous day was gone. The eaters of the dinner, like the dinner itself, were lukewarm, insipid, overdone—and all owing to this poor little dull Young Barnacle. Conversationless at any time, he was now the victim of a weakness special to the occasion, and solely referable to Clennam. He was under a pressing and continual necessity of looking at that gentleman, which occasioned his eye-glass to get into his soup, into his wine-glass, into Mrs Meagles's plate, to hang down his back like a bell-rope, and be several times disgracefully restored to his bosom by one of the dingy men. Weakened in mind by his frequent losses of this instrument, and its determination not to stick in his eye, and more and more enfeebled in intellect every time he looked at the mysterious Clennam, he applied spoons to his eyes, forks, and other foreign matters connected with the furniture of the dinner-table. His discovery of these mistakes greatly increased his difficulties, but never released him from the necessity of looking at Clennam. And whenever Clennam spoke, this ill-starred young man was clearly seized with a dread that he was coming, by some artful device, round to that point of wanting to know, you know.

It may be questioned, therefore, whether any one but Mr Meagles had much enjoyment of the time. Mr Meagles, however, thoroughly enjoyed Young Barnacle. As a mere flask of the golden water in the tale became a full fountain when it was poured out, so Mr Meagles seemed to feel that this small spice of Barnacle imparted to his table the flavour of the whole family-tree. In its presence, his frank, fine, genuine qualities paled; he was not so easy, he was not so natural, he was striving after something that did not belong to him, he was not himself. What a strange peculiarity on the part of Mr Meagles, and where should we find another such case!

At last the wet Sunday wore itself out in a wet night; and Young Barnacle went home in a cab, feebly smoking; and the objectionable Gowan went away on foot, accompanied by the objectionable dog. Pet had taken the most amiable pains all day to be friendly with Clennam, but Clennam had been a little reserved since breakfast—that is to say, would have been, if he had loved her.

When he had gone to his own room, and had again thrown himself into the chair by the fire, Mr Doyce knocked at the door, candle in hand, to ask him how and at what hour he proposed returning on the morrow? After settling this question, he said a word to Mr Doyce about this Gowan—who would have run in his head a good deal, if he had been his rival.

'Those are not good prospects for a painter,' said Clennam.

'No,' returned Doyce.

Mr Doyce stood, chamber-candlestick in hand, the other hand in his pocket, looking hard at the flame of his candle, with a certain quiet perception in his face that they were going to say something more.

'I thought our good friend a little changed, and out of spirits, after he came this morning?' said Clennam.

'Yes,' returned Doyce.

'But not his daughter?' said Clennam.

'No,' said Doyce.

There was a pause on both sides. Mr Doyce, still looking at the flame of his candle, slowly resumed:

'The truth is, he has twice taken his daughter abroad in the hope of separating her from

Mr Gowan. He rather thinks she is disposed to like him, and he has painful doubts (I quite agree with him, as I dare say you do) of the hopefulness of such a marriage.'

'There—' Clennam choked, and coughed, and stopped.

'Yes, you have taken cold,' said Daniel Doyce. But without looking at him.

'—There is an engagement between them, of course?' said Clennam airily.

'No. As I am told, certainly not. It has been solicited on the gentleman's part, but none has been made. Since their recent return, our friend has yielded to a weekly visit, but that is the utmost. Minnie would not deceive her father and mother. You have travelled with them, and I believe you know what a bond there is among them, extending even beyond this present life. All that there is between Miss Minnie and Mr Gowan, I have no doubt we see.'

'Ah! We see enough!' cried Arthur.

Mr Doyce wished him Good Night in the tone of a man who had heard a mournful, not to say despairing, exclamation, and who sought to infuse some encouragement and hope into the mind of the person by whom it had been uttered. Such tone was probably a part of his oddity, as one of a crotchety band; for how could he have heard anything of that kind, without Clennam's hearing it too?

The rain fell heavily on the roof, and pattered on the ground, and dripped among the evergreens and the leafless branches of the trees. The rain fell heavily, drearily. It was a night of tears.

If Clennam had not decided against falling in love with Pet; if he had had the weakness to do it; if he had, little by little, persuaded himself to set all the earnestness of his nature, all the might of his hope, and all the wealth of his matured character, on that cast; if he had done this and found that all was lost; he would have been, that night, unutterably miserable. As it was—

As it was, the rain fell heavily, drearily.

CHAPTER 18. Little Dorrit's Lover

Little Dorrit had not attained her twenty-second birthday without finding a lover. Even in the shallow Marshalsea, the ever young Archer shot off a few featherless arrows now and then from a mouldy bow, and winged a Collegian or two.

Little Dorrit's lover, however, was not a Collegian. He was the sentimental son of a turnkey. His father hoped, in the fulness of time, to leave him the inheritance of an unstained key; and had from his early youth familiarised him with the duties of his office, and with an ambition to retain the prison-lock in the family. While the succession was yet in abeyance, he assisted his mother in the conduct of a snug tobacco business round the corner of Horsemonger Lane (his father being a non-resident turnkey), which could usually command a neat connection within the College walls.

Years agone, when the object of his affections was wont to sit in her little arm-chair by the high Lodge-fender, Young John (family name, Chivery), a year older than herself, had eyed her with admiring wonder. When he had played with her in the yard, his favourite game had been to counterfeit locking her up in corners, and to counterfeit letting her out for real kisses. When he grew tall enough to peep through the keyhole of the great lock of the main door, he had divers times set down his father's dinner, or supper, to get on as it might on the outer side thereof, while he stood taking cold in one eye by dint of peeping at her through that airy perspective.

If Young John had ever slackened in his truth in the less penetrable days of his boyhood, when youth is prone to wear its boots unlaced and is happily unconscious of digestive organs, he had soon strung it up again and screwed it tight. At nineteen, his hand had inscribed in chalk on that part of the wall which fronted her lodgings, on the occasion of her birthday, 'Welcome sweet nursling of the Fairies!' At twenty-three, the same hand falteringly presented cigars on Sundays to the Father of the Marshalsea, and Father of the queen of his soul.

Young John was small of stature, with rather weak legs and very weak light hair. One of his eyes (perhaps the eye that used to peep through the keyhole) was also weak, and looked larger than the other, as if it couldn't collect itself. Young John was gentle likewise. But he was great of soul. Poetical, expansive, faithful.

Though too humble before the ruler of his heart to be sanguine, Young John had considered the object of his attachment in all its lights and shades. Following it out to blissful results, he had descried, without self-commendation, a fitness in it. Say things prospered, and they were united. She, the child of the Marshalsea; he, the lock-keeper. There was a fitness in that. Say he became a resident turnkey. She would officially succeed to the chamber she had rented so long. There was a beautiful propriety in that. It looked over the wall, if you stood on tip-toe; and, with a trellis-work of scarlet beans and a canary or so, would become a very Arbour. There was a charming idea in that. Then, being all in all to one another, there was even an appropriate grace in the lock. With the world shut out (except that part of it which would be shut in); with its troubles and disturbances only known to them by hearsay, as they would be described by the pilgrims tarrying with them on their way to the Insolvent Shrine; with the Arbour above, and the Lodge below; they would glide down the stream of time, in pastoral domestic happiness. Young John drew tears from his eyes by finishing the picture with a tombstone in the adjoining churchyard, close against the prison wall, bearing the following touching inscription: 'Sacred to the Memory Of JOHN CHIVERY, Sixty years Turnkey, and fifty years Head Turnkey, Of the neighbouring Marshalsea, Who departed this life, universally respected, on the thirty-first of December, One thousand eight hundred and eighty-six, Aged eighty-three years. Also of his truly beloved and truly loving wife, AMY, whose maiden name was DORRIT, Who survived his loss not quite forty-eight hours, And who breathed her last in the Marshalsea aforesaid. There she was born, There she lived, There she died.'

The Chivery parents were not ignorant of their son's attachment—indeed it had, on some exceptional occasions, thrown him into a state of mind that had impelled him to conduct himself with irascibility towards the customers, and damage the business—but they, in their turns, had worked it out to desirable conclusions. Mrs Chivery, a prudent woman, had desired her husband to take notice that their John's prospects of the Lock would certainly be strengthened by an alliance with Miss Dorrit, who had herself a kind of claim upon the College and was much respected there. Mrs Chivery had desired her husband to take notice that if, on the one hand, their John had means and a post of trust, on the other hand, Miss Dorrit had family; and that her (Mrs Chivery's) sentiment was, that two halves made a whole. Mrs Chivery, speaking as a mother and not as a diplomatist, had then, from a different point of view, desired her husband to recollect that their John had never been strong, and that his love had fretted and worried him enough as it was, without his being driven to do himself a mischief, as nobody couldn't say he wouldn't be if he was crossed. These arguments had so powerfully influenced the mind of Mr Chivery, who was a man of few words, that he had on sundry Sunday mornings, given his boy what he termed 'a lucky touch,' signifying that he considered such commendation of him to Good Fortune, preparatory to his that day declaring his passion and becoming triumphant. But Young John had never taken courage to make the declaration; and it was principally on these occasions that he had returned excited to the tobacco shop, and flown at the customers.

In this affair, as in every other, Little Dorrit herself was the last person considered. Her brother and sister were aware of it, and attained a sort of station by making a peg of it on which to air the miserably ragged old fiction of the family gentility. Her sister asserted the family gentility by flouting the poor swain as he loitered about the prison for glimpses of his dear. Tip asserted the family gentility, and his own, by coming out in the character of the aristocratic brother, and loftily swaggering in the little skittle ground respecting seizures by the scruff of the neck, which there were looming probabilities of some gentleman unknown executing on some little puppy not mentioned. These were not the only members of the Dorrit family who turned it to account. No, no. The Father of the Marshalsea was supposed to know nothing about the matter, of course: his poor dignity could not see so low. But he took the cigars, on Sundays, and was glad to get them; and sometimes even condescended to walk up and down the yard with the donor (who was proud and hopeful then), and benignantly to smoke one in his society. With no less readiness and condescension did he receive attentions from Chivery Senior, who always relinquished his arm-chair and newspaper to him, when he came into the Lodge during one of his spells of duty; and who had even mentioned to him, that, if he would like at any time after dusk quietly to step out into the fore-court and take a look at the street, there was not much to prevent him. If he did not avail himself of this latter civility, it was only because he had lost the relish for it; inasmuch as he took everything else he could get, and would say at times, 'Extremely civil person, Chivery; very attentive man and very respectful. Young Chivery, too; really almost with a delicate perception of one's position here. A very well conducted family indeed, the Chiveries. Their behaviour gratifies me.'

The devoted Young John all this time regarded the family with reverence. He never dreamed of disputing their pretensions, but did homage to the miserable Mumbo jumbo they paraded. As to resenting any affront from her brother, he would have felt, even if he had not naturally been of a most pacific disposition, that to wag his tongue or lift his hand against that sacred gentleman would be an unhallowed act. He was sorry that his noble mind should take offence; still, he felt the fact to be not incompatible with its nobility, and sought to propitiate and conciliate that gallant soul. Her father, a gentleman in misfortune—a gentleman of a fine spirit and courtly manners, who always bore with him—he deeply honoured. Her sister he considered somewhat vain and proud, but a young lady of infinite accomplishments, who could not forget the past. It was an instinctive testimony to Little Dorrit's worth and difference from all the rest, that the poor young fellow honoured and loved her for being simply what she was.

The tobacco business round the corner of Horsemonger Lane was carried out in a rural establishment one story high, which had the benefit of the air from the yards of Horsemonger Lane jail, and the advantage of a retired walk under the wall of that pleasant establishment. The business was of too modest a character to support a life-size Highlander, but it maintained a little one on a bracket on the door-post, who looked like a fallen Cherub that had found it necessary to take to a kilt.

From the portal thus decorated, one Sunday after an early dinner of baked viands, Young John issued forth on his usual Sunday errand; not empty-handed, but with his offering of cigars. He was neatly attired in a plum-coloured coat, with as large a collar of black velvet as his figure could carry; a silken waistcoat, bedecked with golden sprigs; a chaste neckerchief much in vogue at that day, representing a preserve of lilac pheasants on a buff ground; pantaloons so highly decorated with side-stripes that each leg was a three-stringed lute; and a hat of state very high and hard. When the prudent Mrs Chivery perceived that in addition to these adornments her John carried a pair of white kid gloves, and a cane like a little finger-post, surmounted by an ivory hand marshalling him the way that he should go; and when she saw him, in this heavy marching order, turn the corner to the right; she remarked to Mr Chivery, who was at home at the time, that she thought she knew which way the wind blew.

The Collegians were entertaining a considerable number of visitors that Sunday afternoon, and their Father kept his room for the purpose of receiving presentations. After making the tour of the yard, Little Dorrit's lover with a hurried heart went up-stairs, and knocked with his knuckles at the Father's door.

'Come in, come in!' said a gracious voice. The Father's voice, her father's, the Marshalsea's father's. He was seated in his black velvet cap, with his newspaper, three-and-sixpence accidentally left on the table, and two chairs arranged. Everything prepared for holding his Court.

'Ah, Young John! How do you do, how do you do!'

'Pretty well, I thank you, sir. I hope you are the same.'

'Yes, John Chivery; yes. Nothing to complain of.'

'I have taken the liberty, sir, of—'

'Eh?' The Father of the Marshalsea always lifted up his eyebrows at this point, and became amiably distraught and smilingly absent in mind.

'—A few cigars, sir.'

'Oh!' (For the moment, excessively surprised.) 'Thank you, Young John, thank you. But really, I am afraid I am too—No? Well then, I will say no more about it. Put them on the mantelshelf, if you please, Young John. And sit down, sit down. You are not a stranger, John.'

'Thank you, sir, I am sure—Miss;' here Young John turned the great hat round and round upon his left-hand, like a slowly twirling mouse-cage; 'Miss Amy quite well, sir?'

'Yes, John, yes; very well. She is out.'

'Indeed, sir?'

'Yes, John. Miss Amy is gone for an airing. My young people all go out a good deal. But at their time of life, it's natural, John.'

'Very much so, I am sure, sir.'

'An airing. An airing. Yes.' He was blandly tapping his fingers on the table, and casting his eyes up at the window. 'Amy has gone for an airing on the Iron Bridge. She has become

163

quite partial to the Iron Bridge of late, and seems to like to walk there better than anywhere.' He returned to conversation. 'Your father is not on duty at present, I think, John?'

'No, sir, he comes on later in the afternoon.' Another twirl of the great hat, and then Young John said, rising, 'I am afraid I must wish you good day, sir.'

'So soon? Good day, Young John. Nay, nay,' with the utmost condescension, 'never mind your glove, John. Shake hands with it on. You are no stranger here, you know.'

Highly gratified by the kindness of his reception, Young John descended the staircase. On his way down he met some Collegians bringing up visitors to be presented, and at that moment Mr Dorrit happened to call over the banisters with particular distinctness, 'Much obliged to you for your little testimonial, John!'

Little Dorrit's lover very soon laid down his penny on the tollplate of the Iron Bridge, and came upon it looking about him for the well-known and well-beloved figure. At first he feared she was not there; but as he walked on towards the Middlesex side, he saw her standing still, looking at the water. She was absorbed in thought, and he wondered what she might be thinking about. There were the piles of city roofs and chimneys, more free from smoke than on week-days; and there were the distant masts and steeples. Perhaps she was thinking about them.

Little Dorrit mused so long, and was so entirely preoccupied, that although her lover stood quiet for what he thought was a long time, and twice or thrice retired and came back again to the former spot, still she did not move. So, in the end, he made up his mind to go on, and seem to come upon her casually in passing, and speak to her. The place was quiet, and now or never was the time to speak to her.

He walked on, and she did not appear to hear his steps until he was close upon her. When he said 'Miss Dorrit!' she started and fell back from him, with an expression in her face of fright and something like dislike that caused him unutterable dismay. She had often avoided him before—always, indeed, for a long, long while. She had turned away and glided off so often when she had seen him coming toward her, that the unfortunate Young John could not think it accidental. But he had hoped that it might be shyness, her retiring character, her foreknowledge of the state of his heart, anything short of aversion. Now, that momentary look had said, 'You, of all people! I would rather have seen any one on earth than you!'

It was but a momentary look, inasmuch as she checked it, and said in her soft little voice, 'Oh, Mr John! Is it you?' But she felt what it had been, as he felt what it had been; and they stood looking at one another equally confused.

'Miss Amy, I am afraid I disturbed you by speaking to you.'

'Yes, rather. I—I came here to be alone, and I thought I was.'

'Miss Amy, I took the liberty of walking this way, because Mr Dorrit chanced to mention, when I called upon him just now, that you—'

She caused him more dismay than before by suddenly murmuring, 'O father, father!' in a heartrending tone, and turning her face away.

'Miss Amy, I hope I don't give you any uneasiness by naming Mr Dorrit. I assure you I found him very well and in the best of Spirits, and he showed me even more than his usual

164

kindness; being so very kind as to say that I was not a stranger there, and in all ways gratifying me very much.'

To the inexpressible consternation of her lover, Little Dorrit, with her hands to her averted face, and rocking herself where she stood as if she were in pain, murmured, 'O father, how can you! O dear, dear father, how can you, can you, do it!'

The poor fellow stood gazing at her, overflowing with sympathy, but not knowing what to make of this, until, having taken out her handkerchief and put it to her still averted face, she hurried away. At first he remained stock still; then hurried after her.

'Miss Amy, pray! Will you have the goodness to stop a moment? Miss Amy, if it comes to that, let me go. I shall go out of my senses, if I have to think that I have driven you away like this.'

His trembling voice and unfeigned earnestness brought Little Dorrit to a stop. 'Oh, I don't know what to do,' she cried, 'I don't know what to do!'

To Young John, who had never seen her bereft of her quiet self-command, who had seen her from her infancy ever so reliable and self-suppressed, there was a shock in her distress, and in having to associate himself with it as its cause, that shook him from his great hat to the pavement. He felt it necessary to explain himself. He might be misunderstood—supposed to mean something, or to have done something, that had never entered into his imagination. He begged her to hear him explain himself, as the greatest favour she could show him.

'Miss Amy, I know very well that your family is far above mine. It were vain to conceal it. There never was a Chivery a gentleman that ever I heard of, and I will not commit the meanness of making a false representation on a subject so momentous. Miss Amy, I know very well that your high-souled brother, and likewise your spirited sister, spurn me from a height. What I have to do is to respect them, to wish to be admitted to their friendship, to look up at the eminence on which they are placed from my lowlier station—for, whether viewed as tobacco or viewed as the lock, I well know it is lowly—and ever wish them well and happy.'

There really was a genuineness in the poor fellow, and a contrast between the hardness of his hat and the softness of his heart (albeit, perhaps, of his head, too), that was moving. Little Dorrit entreated him to disparage neither himself nor his station, and, above all things, to divest himself of any idea that she supposed hers to be superior. This gave him a little comfort.

'Miss Amy,' he then stammered, 'I have had for a long time—ages they seem to me— Revolving ages—a heart-cherished wish to say something to you. May I say it?'

Little Dorrit involuntarily started from his side again, with the faintest shadow of her former look; conquering that, she went on at great speed half across the Bridge without replying!

'May I—Miss Amy, I but ask the question humbly—may I say it? I have been so unlucky already in giving you pain without having any such intentions, before the holy Heavens! that there is no fear of my saying it unless I have your leave. I can be miserable alone, I can be cut up by myself, why should I also make miserable and cut up one that I would fling myself off that parapet to give half a moment's joy to! Not that that's much to do, for I'd do it for twopence.'

The mournfulness of his spirits, and the gorgeousness of his appearance, might have made him ridiculous, but that his delicacy made him respectable. Little Dorrit learnt from it what to do.

'If you please, John Chivery,' she returned, trembling, but in a quiet way, 'since you are so considerate as to ask me whether you shall say any more—if you please, no.'

'Never, Miss Amy?'

'No, if you please. Never.'

'O Lord!' gasped Young John.

'But perhaps you will let me, instead, say something to you. I want to say it earnestly, and with as plain a meaning as it is possible to express. When you think of us, John—I mean my brother, and sister, and me—don't think of us as being any different from the rest; for, whatever we once were (which I hardly know) we ceased to be long ago, and never can be any more. It will be much better for you, and much better for others, if you will do that instead of what you are doing now.'

Young John dolefully protested that he would try to bear it in mind, and would be heartily glad to do anything she wished.

'As to me,' said Little Dorrit, 'think as little of me as you can; the less, the better. When you think of me at all, John, let it only be as the child you have seen grow up in the prison with one set of duties always occupying her; as a weak, retired, contented, unprotected girl. I particularly want you to remember, that when I come outside the gate, I am unprotected and solitary.'

He would try to do anything she wished. But why did Miss Amy so much want him to remember that?

'Because,' returned Little Dorrit, 'I know I can then quite trust you not to forget to-day, and not to say any more to me. You are so generous that I know I can trust to you for that; and I do and I always will. I am going to show you, at once, that I fully trust you. I like this place where we are speaking better than any place I know;' her slight colour had faded, but her lover thought he saw it coming back just then; 'and I may be often here. I know it is only necessary for me to tell you so, to be quite sure that you will never come here again in search of me. And I am—quite sure!'

She might rely upon it, said Young John. He was a miserable wretch, but her word was more than a law for him.

'And good-bye, John,' said Little Dorrit. 'And I hope you will have a good wife one day, and be a happy man. I am sure you will deserve to be happy, and you will be, John.'

As she held out her hand to him with these words, the heart that was under the waistcoat of sprigs—mere slop-work, if the truth must be known—swelled to the size of the heart of a gentleman; and the poor common little fellow, having no room to hold it, burst into tears.

'Oh, don't cry,' said Little Dorrit piteously. 'Don't, don't! Good-bye, John. God bless you!'

'Good-bye, Miss Amy. Good-bye!'

And so he left her: first observing that she sat down on the corner of a seat, and not only rested her little hand upon the rough wall, but laid her face against it too, as if her head were heavy, and her mind were sad.

It was an affecting illustration of the fallacy of human projects, to behold her lover, with the great hat pulled over his eyes, the velvet collar turned up as if it rained, the plum-coloured coat buttoned to conceal the silken waistcoat of golden sprigs, and the little direction-post pointing inexorably home, creeping along by the worst back-streets, and composing, as he went, the following new inscription for a tombstone in St George's Churchyard:

'Here lie the mortal remains Of JOHN CHIVERY, Never anything worth mentioning, Who died about the end of the year one thousand eight hundred and twenty-six, Of a broken heart, Requesting with his last breath that the word AMY might be inscribed over his ashes, which was accordingly directed to be done, By his afflicted Parents.'

CHAPTER 19. The Father of the Marshalsea in two or three Relations

The brothers William and Frederick Dorrit, walking up and down the College-yard—of course on the aristocratic or Pump side, for the Father made it a point of his state to be chary of going among his children on the Poor side, except on Sunday mornings, Christmas Days, and other occasions of ceremony, in the observance whereof he was very punctual, and at which times he laid his hand upon the heads of their infants, and blessed those young insolvents with a benignity that was highly edifying—the brothers, walking up and down the College-yard together, were a memorable sight. Frederick the free, was so humbled, bowed, withered, and faded; William the bond, was so courtly, condescending, and benevolently conscious of a position; that in this regard only, if in no other, the brothers were a spectacle to wonder at.

They walked up and down the yard on the evening of Little Dorrit's Sunday interview with her lover on the Iron Bridge. The cares of state were over for that day, the Drawing Room had been well attended, several new presentations had taken place, the three-and-sixpence accidentally left on the table had accidentally increased to twelve shillings, and the Father of the Marshalsea refreshed himself with a whiff of cigar. As he walked up and down, affably accommodating his step to the shuffle of his brother, not proud in his superiority, but considerate of that poor creature, bearing with him, and breathing toleration of his infirmities in every little puff of smoke that issued from his lips and aspired to get over the spiked wall, he was a sight to wonder at.

His brother Frederick of the dim eye, palsied hand, bent form, and groping mind, submissively shuffled at his side, accepting his patronage as he accepted every incident of the labyrinthian world in which he had got lost. He held the usual screwed bit of whitey-brown paper in his hand, from which he ever and again unscrewed a spare pinch of snuff. That falteringly taken, he would glance at his brother not unadmiringly, put his hands behind him, and shuffle on so at his side until he took another pinch, or stood still to look about him—perchance suddenly missing his clarionet.

The College visitors were melting away as the shades of night drew on, but the yard was still pretty full, the Collegians being mostly out, seeing their friends to the Lodge. As the brothers paced the yard, William the bond looked about him to receive salutes, returned them by graciously lifting off his hat, and, with an engaging air, prevented Frederick the free from running against the company, or being jostled against the wall. The Collegians as a body were not easily impressible, but even they, according to their various ways of wondering, appeared to find in the two brothers a sight to wonder at.

'You are a little low this evening, Frederick,' said the Father of the Marshalsea. 'Anything the matter?'

'The matter?' He stared for a moment, and then dropped his head and eyes again. 'No, William, no. Nothing is the matter.'

'If you could be persuaded to smarten yourself up a little, Frederick—'

'Aye, aye!' said the old man hurriedly. 'But I can't be. I can't be. Don't talk so. That's all over.'

The Father of the Marshalsea glanced at a passing Collegian with whom he was on friendly terms, as who should say, 'An enfeebled old man, this; but he is my brother, sir, my brother, and the voice of Nature is potent!' and steered his brother clear of the handle of the pump by the threadbare sleeve. Nothing would have been wanting to the perfection of his character as a fraternal guide, philosopher and friend, if he had only steered his brother clear of ruin, instead of bringing it upon him.

'I think, William,' said the object of his affectionate consideration, 'that I am tired, and will go home to bed.'

'My dear Frederick,' returned the other, 'don't let me detain you; don't sacrifice your inclination to me.'

'Late hours, and a heated atmosphere, and years, I suppose,' said Frederick, 'weaken me.'

'My dear Frederick,' returned the Father of the Marshalsea, 'do you think you are sufficiently careful of yourself? Do you think your habits are as precise and methodical as— shall I say as mine are? Not to revert again to that little eccentricity which I mentioned just now, I doubt if you take air and exercise enough, Frederick. Here is the parade, always at your service. Why not use it more regularly than you do?'

'Hah!' sighed the other. 'Yes, yes, yes, yes.'

'But it is of no use saying yes, yes, my dear Frederick,' the Father of the Marshalsea in his mild wisdom persisted, 'unless you act on that assent. Consider my case, Frederick. I am a kind of example. Necessity and time have taught me what to do. At certain stated hours of the day, you will find me on the parade, in my room, in the Lodge, reading the paper, receiving company, eating and drinking. I have impressed upon Amy during many years, that I must have my meals (for instance) punctually. Amy has grown up in a sense of the importance of these arrangements, and you know what a good girl she is.'

The brother only sighed again, as he plodded dreamily along, 'Hah! Yes, yes, yes, yes.'

'My dear fellow,' said the Father of the Marshalsea, laying his hand upon his shoulder, and mildly rallying him—mildly, because of his weakness, poor dear soul; 'you said that before, and it does not express much, Frederick, even if it means much. I wish I could rouse you, my good Frederick; you want to be roused.'

'Yes, William, yes. No doubt,' returned the other, lifting his dim eyes to his face. 'But I am not like you.'

The Father of the Marshalsea said, with a shrug of modest self-depreciation, 'Oh! You might be like me, my dear Frederick; you might be, if you chose!' and forbore, in the magnanimity of his strength, to press his fallen brother further.

There was a great deal of leave-taking going on in corners, as was usual on Sunday nights;

and here and there in the dark, some poor woman, wife or mother, was weeping with a new Collegian. The time had been when the Father himself had wept, in the shades of that yard, as his own poor wife had wept. But it was many years ago; and now he was like a passenger aboard ship in a long voyage, who has recovered from sea-sickness, and is impatient of that weakness in the fresher passengers taken aboard at the last port. He was inclined to remonstrate, and to express his opinion that people who couldn't get on without crying, had no business there. In manner, if not in words, he always testified his displeasure at these interruptions of the general harmony; and it was so well understood, that delinquents usually withdrew if they were aware of him.

On this Sunday evening, he accompanied his brother to the gate with an air of endurance and clemency; being in a bland temper and graciously disposed to overlook the tears. In the flaring gaslight of the Lodge, several Collegians were basking; some taking leave of visitors, and some who had no visitors, watching the frequent turning of the key, and conversing with one another and with Mr Chivery. The paternal entrance made a sensation of course; and Mr Chivery, touching his hat (in a short manner though) with his key, hoped he found himself tolerable.

'Thank you, Chivery, quite well. And you?'

Mr Chivery said in a low growl, 'Oh! he was all right.' Which was his general way of acknowledging inquiries after his health when a little sullen.

'I had a visit from Young John to-day, Chivery. And very smart he looked, I assure you.'

So Mr Chivery had heard. Mr Chivery must confess, however, that his wish was that the boy didn't lay out so much money upon it. For what did it bring him in? It only brought him in wexation. And he could get that anywhere for nothing.

'How vexation, Chivery?' asked the benignant father.

'No odds,' returned Mr Chivery. 'Never mind. Mr Frederick going out?'

'Yes, Chivery, my brother is going home to bed. He is tired, and not quite well. Take care, Frederick, take care. Good night, my dear Frederick!'

Shaking hands with his brother, and touching his greasy hat to the company in the Lodge, Frederick slowly shuffled out of the door which Mr Chivery unlocked for him. The Father of the Marshalsea showed the amiable solicitude of a superior being that he should come to no harm.

'Be so kind as to keep the door open a moment, Chivery, that I may see him go along the passage and down the steps. Take care, Frederick! (He is very infirm.) Mind the steps! (He is so very absent.) Be careful how you cross, Frederick. (I really don't like the notion of his going wandering at large, he is so extremely liable to be run over.)'

With these words, and with a face expressive of many uneasy doubts and much anxious guardianship, he turned his regards upon the assembled company in the Lodge: so plainly indicating that his brother was to be pitied for not being under lock and key, that an opinion to that effect went round among the Collegians assembled.

But he did not receive it with unqualified assent; on the contrary, he said, No, gentlemen, no; let them not misunderstand him. His brother Frederick was much broken, no doubt, and it might be more comfortable to himself (the Father of the Marshalsea) to know that he was safe within the walls. Still, it must be remembered that to support an existence there during many years, required a certain combination of qualities—he did not say high qualities, but qualities—moral qualities. Now, had his brother Frederick that peculiar union of qualities? Gentlemen, he was a most excellent man, a most gentle, tender, and estimable man, with the simplicity of a child; but would he, though unsuited for most other places, do for that place? No; he said confidently, no! And, he said, Heaven forbid that Frederick should be there in any other character than in his present voluntary character! Gentlemen, whoever came to that College, to remain there a length of time, must have strength of character to go through a good deal and to come out of a good deal. Was his beloved brother Frederick that man? No. They saw him, even as it was, crushed. Misfortune crushed him. He had not power of recoil enough, not elasticity enough, to be a long time in such a place, and yet preserve his self-respect and feel conscious that he was a gentleman. Frederick had not (if he might use the expression) Power enough to see in any delicate little attentions and—and—Testimonials that he might under such circumstances receive, the goodness of human nature, the fine spirit animating the Collegians as a community, and at the same time no degradation to himself, and no depreciation of his claims as a gentleman. Gentlemen, God bless you!

Such was the homily with which he improved and pointed the occasion to the company in the Lodge before turning into the sallow yard again, and going with his own poor shabby dignity past the Collegian in the dressing-gown who had no coat, and past the Collegian in the sea-side slippers who had no shoes, and past the stout greengrocer Collegian in the corduroy knee-breeches who had no cares, and past the lean clerk Collegian in buttonless black who had no hopes, up his own poor shabby staircase to his own poor shabby room.

There, the table was laid for his supper, and his old grey gown was ready for him on his chair-back at the fire. His daughter put her little prayer-book in her pocket—had she been praying for pity on all prisoners and captives!—and rose to welcome him.

Uncle had gone home, then? she asked him, as she changed his coat and gave him his black velvet cap. Yes, uncle had gone home. Had her father enjoyed his walk? Why, not much, Amy; not much. No! Did he not feel quite well?

As she stood behind him, leaning over his chair so lovingly, he looked with downcast eyes at the fire. An uneasiness stole over him that was like a touch of shame; and when he spoke, as he presently did, it was in an unconnected and embarrassed manner.

'Something, I—hem!—I don't know what, has gone wrong with Chivery. He is not— ha!—not nearly so obliging and attentive as usual to-night. It—hem!—it's a little thing, but it puts me out, my love. It's impossible to forget,' turning his hands over and over and looking closely at them, 'that—hem!—that in such a life as mine, I am unfortunately dependent on these men for something every hour in the day.'

Her arm was on his shoulder, but she did not look in his face while he spoke. Bending her head she looked another way.

'I—hem!—I can't think, Amy, what has given Chivery offence. He is generally so—so very attentive and respectful. And to-night he was quite—quite short with me. Other people there too! Why, good Heaven! if I was to lose the support and recognition of Chivery and his brother officers, I might starve to death here.' While he spoke, he was opening and shutting his hands like valves; so conscious all the time of that touch of shame, that he shrunk before his own knowledge of his meaning.

'I—ha!—I can't think what it's owing to. I am sure I cannot imagine what the cause of it is. There was a certain Jackson here once, a turnkey of the name of Jackson (I don't think you can remember him, my dear, you were very young), and—hem!—and he had a—brother, and this—young brother paid his addresses to—at least, did not go so far as to pay his addresses to—but admired—respectfully admired—the—not daughter, the sister—of one of us; a rather distinguished Collegian; I may say, very much so. His name was Captain Martin; and he consulted me on the question whether it was necessary that his daughter—sister—should hazard offending the turnkey brother by being too—ha!—too plain with the other brother. Captain Martin was a gentleman and a man of honour, and I put it to him first to give me his—his own opinion. Captain Martin (highly respected in the army) then unhesitatingly said that it appeared to him that his—hem!—sister was not called upon to understand the young man too distinctly, and that she might lead him on—I am doubtful whether "lead him on" was Captain Martin's exact expression: indeed I think he said tolerate him—on her father's—I should say, brother's—account. I hardly know how I have strayed into this story. I suppose it has been through being unable to account for Chivery; but as to the connection between the two, I don't see—'

His voice died away, as if she could not bear the pain of hearing him, and her hand had gradually crept to his lips. For a little while there was a dead silence and stillness; and he remained shrunk in his chair, and she remained with her arm round his neck and her head bowed down upon his shoulder.

His supper was cooking in a saucepan on the fire, and, when she moved, it was to make it ready for him on the table. He took his usual seat, she took hers, and he began his meal. They did not, as yet, look at one another. By little and little he began; laying down his knife and fork with a noise, taking things up sharply, biting at his bread as if he were offended with it, and in other similar ways showing that he was out of sorts. At length he pushed his plate from him, and spoke aloud; with the strangest inconsistency.

'What does it matter whether I eat or starve? What does it matter whether such a blighted life as mine comes to an end, now, next week, or next year? What am I worth to anyone? A poor prisoner, fed on alms and broken victuals; a squalid, disgraced wretch!'

'Father, father!' As he rose she went on her knees to him, and held up her hands to him.

'Amy,' he went on in a suppressed voice, trembling violently, and looking at her as wildly as if he had gone mad. 'I tell you, if you could see me as your mother saw me, you wouldn't believe it to be the creature you have only looked at through the bars of this cage. I was young, I was accomplished, I was good-looking, I was independent—by God I was, child!—and people sought me out, and envied me. Envied me!'

'Dear father!' She tried to take down the shaking arm that he flourished in the air, but he resisted, and put her hand away.

'If I had but a picture of myself in those days, though it was ever so ill done, you would be proud of it, you would be proud of it. But I have no such thing. Now, let me be a warning! Let no man,' he cried, looking haggardly about, 'fail to preserve at least that little of the times of his prosperity and respect. Let his children have that clue to what he was. Unless my face, when I am dead, subsides into the long departed look—they say such things happen, I don't know—my children will have never seen me.'

'Father, father!'

'O despise me, despise me! Look away from me, don't listen to me, stop me, blush for me, cry for me—even you, Amy! Do it, do it! I do it to myself! I am hardened now, I have sunk too low to care long even for that.'

'Dear father, loved father, darling of my heart!' She was clinging to him with her arms, and she got him to drop into his chair again, and caught at the raised arm, and tried to put it round her neck.

'Let it lie there, father. Look at me, father, kiss me, father! Only think of me, father, for one little moment!'

Still he went on in the same wild way, though it was gradually breaking down into a miserable whining.

'And yet I have some respect here. I have made some stand against it. I am not quite trodden down. Go out and ask who is the chief person in the place. They'll tell you it's your father. Go out and ask who is never trifled with, and who is always treated with some delicacy. They'll say, your father. Go out and ask what funeral here (it must be here, I know it can be nowhere else) will make more talk, and perhaps more grief, than any that has ever gone out at the gate. They'll say your father's. Well then. Amy! Amy! Is your father so universally despised? Is there nothing to redeem him? Will you have nothing to remember him by but his ruin and decay? Will you be able to have no affection for him when he is gone, poor castaway, gone?'

He burst into tears of maudlin pity for himself, and at length suffering her to embrace him and take charge of him, let his grey head rest against her cheek, and bewailed his wretchedness. Presently he changed the subject of his lamentations, and clasping his hands about her as she embraced him, cried, O Amy, his motherless, forlorn child! O the days that he had seen her careful and laborious for him! Then he reverted to himself, and weakly told her how much better she would have loved him if she had known him in his vanished character, and how he would have married her to a gentleman who should have been proud of her as his daughter, and how (at which he cried again) she should first have ridden at his fatherly side on her own horse, and how the crowd (by which he meant in effect the people who had given him the twelve shillings he then had in his pocket) should have trudged the dusty roads respectfully.

Thus, now boasting, now despairing, in either fit a captive with the jail-rot upon him, and the impurity of his prison worn into the grain of his soul, he revealed his degenerate state to his affectionate child. No one else ever beheld him in the details of his humiliation. Little recked the Collegians who were laughing in their rooms over his late address in the Lodge, what a serious picture they had in their obscure gallery of the Marshalsea that Sunday night.

There was a classical daughter once—perhaps—who ministered to her father in his prison as her mother had ministered to her. Little Dorrit, though of the unheroic modern stock and mere English, did much more, in comforting her father's wasted heart upon her innocent breast, and turning to it a fountain of love and fidelity that never ran dry or waned through all his years of famine.

She soothed him; asked him for his forgiveness if she had been, or seemed to have been, undutiful; told him, Heaven knows truly, that she could not honour him more if he were the favourite of Fortune and the whole world acknowledged him. When his tears were dried, and he sobbed in his weakness no longer, and was free from that touch of shame, and had recovered his usual bearing, she prepared the remains of his supper afresh, and, sitting by his side, rejoiced to see him eat and drink. For now he sat in his black velvet cap and old grey gown, magnanimous again; and would have comported himself towards any Collegian who might have looked in to ask his advice, like a great moral Lord Chesterfield, or Master of the ethical ceremonies of the Marshalsea.

To keep his attention engaged, she talked with him about his wardrobe; when he was pleased to say, that Yes, indeed, those shirts she proposed would be exceedingly acceptable, for those he had were worn out, and, being ready-made, had never fitted him. Being conversational, and in a reasonable flow of spirits, he then invited her attention to his coat as it hung behind the door: remarking that the Father of the place would set an indifferent example to his children, already disposed to be slovenly, if he went among them out at elbows. He was jocular, too, as to the heeling of his shoes; but became grave on the subject of his cravat, and promised her that, when she could afford it, she should buy him a new one.

While he smoked out his cigar in peace, she made his bed, and put the small room in order for his repose. Being weary then, owing to the advanced hour and his emotions, he came out of his chair to bless her and wish her Good night. All this time he had never once thought of her dress, her shoes, her need of anything. No other person upon earth, save herself, could have been so unmindful of her wants.

He kissed her many times with 'Bless you, my love. Good night, my dear!'

But her gentle breast had been so deeply wounded by what she had seen of him that she was unwilling to leave him alone, lest he should lament and despair again. 'Father, dear, I am not tired; let me come back presently, when you are in bed, and sit by you.'

He asked her, with an air of protection, if she felt solitary?

'Yes, father.'

'Then come back by all means, my love.'

'I shall be very quiet, father.'

'Don't think of me, my dear,' he said, giving her his kind permission fully. 'Come back by all means.'

He seemed to be dozing when she returned, and she put the low fire together very softly lest she should awake him. But he overheard her, and called out who was that?

'Only Amy, father.'

'Amy, my child, come here. I want to say a word to you.'

He raised himself a little in his low bed, as she kneeled beside it to bring her face near him; and put his hand between hers. O! Both the private father and the Father of the Marshalsea were strong within him then.

'My love, you have had a life of hardship here. No companions, no recreations, many cares I am afraid?'

'Don't think of that, dear. I never do.'

'You know my position, Amy. I have not been able to do much for you; but all I have been able to do, I have done.'

'Yes, my dear father,' she rejoined, kissing him. 'I know, I know.'

'I am in the twenty-third year of my life here,' he said, with a catch in his breath that was not so much a sob as an irrepressible sound of self-approval, the momentary outburst of a noble consciousness. 'It is all I could do for my children—I have done it. Amy, my love, you are by far the best loved of the three; I have had you principally in my mind—whatever I have done for your sake, my dear child, I have done freely and without murmuring.'

Only the wisdom that holds the clue to all hearts and all mysteries, can surely know to what extent a man, especially a man brought down as this man had been, can impose upon himself. Enough, for the present place, that he lay down with wet eyelashes, serene, in a manner majestic, after bestowing his life of degradation as a sort of portion on the devoted child upon whom its miseries had fallen so heavily, and whose love alone had saved him to be even what he was.

That child had no doubts, asked herself no question, for she was but too content to see him with a lustre round his head. Poor dear, good dear, truest, kindest, dearest, were the only words she had for him, as she hushed him to rest.

She never left him all that night. As if she had done him a wrong which her tenderness could hardly repair, she sat by him in his sleep, at times softly kissing him with suspended breath, and calling him in a whisper by some endearing name. At times she stood aside so as not to intercept the low fire-light, and, watching him when it fell upon his sleeping face, wondered did he look now at all as he had looked when he was prosperous and happy; as he had so touched her by imagining that he might look once more in that awful time. At the thought of that time, she kneeled beside his bed again, and prayed, 'O spare his life! O save him to me! O look down upon my dear, long-suffering, unfortunate, much-changed, dear dear father!'

Not until the morning came to protect him and encourage him, did she give him a last kiss and leave the small room. When she had stolen down-stairs, and along the empty yard, and had crept up to her own high garret, the smokeless housetops and the distant country hills were discernible over the wall in the clear morning. As she gently opened the window, and looked eastward down the prison yard, the spikes upon the wall were tipped with red, then made a sullen purple pattern on the sun as it came flaming up into the heavens. The spikes had never looked so sharp and cruel, nor the bars so heavy, nor the prison space so gloomy and contracted. She thought of the sunrise on rolling rivers, of the sunrise on wide seas, of the sunrise on rich landscapes, of the sunrise on great forests where the birds were waking and the trees were rustling; and she looked down into the living grave on which the sun had risen, with her father in it three-and-twenty years, and said, in a burst of sorrow and compassion, 'No, no, I have never seen him in my life!'

CHAPTER 20. Moving in Society

If Young John Chivery had had the inclination and the power to write a satire on family pride, he would have had no need to go for an avenging illustration out of the family of his beloved. He would have found it amply in that gallant brother and that dainty sister, so steeped in mean experiences, and so loftily conscious of the family name; so ready to beg or borrow from the poorest, to eat of anybody's bread, spend anybody's money, drink from anybody's cup and break it afterwards. To have painted the sordid facts of their lives, and they throughout invoking the death's head apparition of the family gentility to come and scare their benefactors, would have made Young John a satirist of the first water.

Tip had turned his liberty to hopeful account by becoming a billiard-marker. He had troubled himself so little as to the means of his release, that Clennam scarcely needed to have been at the pains of impressing the mind of Mr Plornish on that subject. Whoever had paid him the compliment, he very readily accepted the compliment with his compliments, and there was an end of it. Issuing forth from the gate on these easy terms, he became a billiard-marker; and now occasionally looked in at the little skittle-ground in a green Newmarket coat (second-hand), with a shining collar and bright buttons (new), and drank the beer of the Collegians.

One solid stationary point in the looseness of this gentleman's character was, that he respected and admired his sister Amy. The feeling had never induced him to spare her a moment's uneasiness, or to put himself to any restraint or inconvenience on her account; but with that Marshalsea taint upon his love, he loved her. The same rank Marshalsea flavour was to be recognised in his distinctly perceiving that she sacrificed her life to her father, and in his having no idea that she had done anything for himself.

When this spirited young man and his sister had begun systematically to produce the family skeleton for the overawing of the College, this narrative cannot precisely state. Probably at about the period when they began to dine on the College charity. It is certain that the more reduced and necessitous they were, the more pompously the skeleton emerged from its tomb; and that when there was anything particularly shabby in the wind, the skeleton always came out with the ghastliest flourish.

Little Dorrit was late on the Monday morning, for her father slept late, and afterwards there was his breakfast to prepare and his room to arrange. She had no engagement to go out to work, however, and therefore stayed with him until, with Maggy's help, she had put everything right about him, and had seen him off upon his morning walk (of twenty yards or so) to the coffee-house to read the paper. She then got on her bonnet and went out, having been anxious to get out much sooner. There was, as usual, a cessation of the small-talk in the Lodge as she passed through it; and a Collegian who had come in on Saturday night, received the intimation from the elbow of a more seasoned Collegian, 'Look out. Here she is!'

She wanted to see her sister, but when she got round to Mr Cripples's, she found that both her sister and her uncle had gone to the theatre where they were engaged. Having taken thought of this probability by the way, and having settled that in such case she would follow them, she set off afresh for the theatre, which was on that side of the river, and not very far away.

Little Dorrit was almost as ignorant of the ways of theatres as of the ways of gold mines, and when she was directed to a furtive sort of door, with a curious up-all-night air about it, that appeared to be ashamed of itself and to be hiding in an alley, she hesitated to approach it; being further deterred by the sight of some half-dozen close-shaved gentlemen with their hats very strangely on, who were lounging about the door, looking not at all unlike Collegians. On her applying to them, reassured by this resemblance, for a direction to Miss Dorrit, they made way for her to enter a dark hall—it was more like a great grim lamp gone out than anything else—where she could hear the distant playing of music and the sound of dancing feet. A man so much in want of airing that he had a blue mould upon him, sat watching this dark place from a hole in a corner, like a spider; and he told her that he would send a message up to Miss Dorrit by the first lady or gentleman who went through. The first lady who went through had a roll of music, half in her muff and half out of it, and was in such a tumbled condition altogether, that it seemed as if it would be an act of kindness to iron her. But as she was very good-natured, and said, 'Come with me; I'll soon find Miss Dorrit for you,' Miss Dorrit's sister went with her, drawing nearer and nearer at every step she took in the darkness to the sound of music and the sound of dancing feet.

At last they came into a maze of dust, where a quantity of people were tumbling over one another, and where there was such a confusion of unaccountable shapes of beams, bulkheads, brick walls, ropes, and rollers, and such a mixing of gaslight and daylight, that they seemed to have got on the wrong side of the pattern of the universe. Little Dorrit, left to herself, and knocked against by somebody every moment, was quite bewildered, when she heard her sister's voice.

'Why, good gracious, Amy, what ever brought you here?'

'I wanted to see you, Fanny dear; and as I am going out all day to-morrow, and knew you might be engaged all day to-day, I thought—'

'But the idea, Amy, of you coming behind! I never did!' As her sister said this in no very cordial tone of welcome, she conducted her to a more open part of the maze, where various golden chairs and tables were heaped together, and where a number of young ladies were sitting on anything they could find, chattering. All these young ladies wanted ironing, and all had a curious way of looking everywhere while they chattered.

Just as the sisters arrived here, a monotonous boy in a Scotch cap put his head round a beam on the left, and said, 'Less noise there, ladies!' and disappeared. Immediately after which, a sprightly gentleman with a quantity of long black hair looked round a beam on the right, and said, 'Less noise there, darlings!' and also disappeared.

'The notion of you among professionals, Amy, is really the last thing I could have conceived!' said her sister. 'Why, how did you ever get here?'

'I don't know. The lady who told you I was here, was so good as to bring me in.'

'Like you quiet little things! You can make your way anywhere, I believe. I couldn't have managed it, Amy, though I know so much more of the world.'

It was the family custom to lay it down as family law, that she was a plain domestic little creature, without the great and sage experience of the rest. This family fiction was the family assertion of itself against her services. Not to make too much of them.

'Well! And what have you got on your mind, Amy? Of course you have got something on your mind about me?' said Fanny. She spoke as if her sister, between two and three years her junior, were her prejudiced grandmother.

'It is not much; but since you told me of the lady who gave you the bracelet, Fanny—'

The monotonous boy put his head round the beam on the left, and said, 'Look out there, ladies!' and disappeared. The sprightly gentleman with the black hair as suddenly put his head round the beam on the right, and said, 'Look out there, darlings!' and also disappeared. Thereupon all the young ladies rose and began shaking their skirts out behind.

'Well, Amy?' said Fanny, doing as the rest did; 'what were you going to say?'

'Since you told me a lady had given you the bracelet you showed me, Fanny, I have not been quite easy on your account, and indeed want to know a little more if you will confide more to me.'

'Now, ladies!' said the boy in the Scotch cap. 'Now, darlings!' said the gentleman with the black hair. They were every one gone in a moment, and the music and the dancing feet were heard again.

Little Dorrit sat down in a golden chair, made quite giddy by these rapid interruptions. Her sister and the rest were a long time gone; and during their absence a voice (it appeared to be that of the gentleman with the black hair) was continually calling out through the music, 'One, two, three, four, five, six—go! One, two, three, four, five, six—go! Steady, darlings! One, two, three, four, five, six—go!' Ultimately the voice stopped, and they all came back again, more or less out of breath, folding themselves in their shawls, and making ready for the streets. 'Stop a moment, Amy, and let them get away before us,' whispered Fanny. They were soon left alone; nothing more important happening, in the meantime, than the boy looking round his old beam, and saying, 'Everybody at eleven to-morrow, ladies!' and the gentleman with the black hair looking round his old beam, and saying, 'Everybody at eleven to-morrow, darlings!' each in his own accustomed manner.

When they were alone, something was rolled up or by other means got out of the way, and there was a great empty well before them, looking down into the depths of which Fanny said, 'Now, uncle!' Little Dorrit, as her eyes became used to the darkness, faintly made him out at the bottom of the well, in an obscure corner by himself, with his instrument in its ragged case under his arm.

The old man looked as if the remote high gallery windows, with their little strip of sky, might have been the point of his better fortunes, from which he had descended, until he had gradually sunk down below there to the bottom. He had been in that place six nights a week for many years, but had never been observed to raise his eyes above his music-book, and was confidently believed to have never seen a play. There were legends in the place that he did not so much as know the popular heroes and heroines by sight, and that the low comedian had 'mugged' at him in his richest manner fifty nights for a wager, and he had shown no trace of consciousness. The carpenters had a joke to the effect that he was dead without being aware of it; and the frequenters of the pit supposed him to pass his whole life, night and day, and Sunday and all, in the orchestra. They had tried him a few times with pinches of snuff offered over the rails, and he had always responded to this attention with a momentary waking up of manner that had the pale phantom of a gentleman in it: beyond this he never, on any occasion, had any other part in what was going on than the part written out for the clarionet; in private life, where there was no part for the clarionet, he had no part at all. Some said he was poor, some said he was a wealthy miser; but he said nothing, never lifted up his bowed head, never varied his shuffling gait by getting his springless foot from the ground. Though expecting now to be summoned by his niece, he did not hear her until she had spoken to him three or four times; nor was he at all surprised by the presence of two nieces instead of one, but merely said in his tremulous voice, 'I am coming, I am coming!' and crept forth by some underground way which emitted a cellarous smell.

'And so, Amy,' said her sister, when the three together passed out at the door that had such a shame-faced consciousness of being different from other doors: the uncle instinctively taking Amy's arm as the arm to be relied on: 'so, Amy, you are curious about me?'

She was pretty, and conscious, and rather flaunting; and the condescension with which she put aside the superiority of her charms, and of her worldly experience, and addressed her sister on almost equal terms, had a vast deal of the family in it.

'I am interested, Fanny, and concerned in anything that concerns you.'

'So you are, so you are, and you are the best of Amys. If I am ever a little provoking, I am sure you'll consider what a thing it is to occupy my position and feel a consciousness of being superior to it. I shouldn't care,' said the Daughter of the Father of the Marshalsea, 'if the others were not so common. None of them have come down in the world as we have. They are all on their own level. Common.'

Little Dorrit mildly looked at the speaker, but did not interrupt her. Fanny took out her handkerchief, and rather angrily wiped her eyes. 'I was not born where you were, you know, Amy, and perhaps that makes a difference. My dear child, when we get rid of Uncle, you shall know all about it. We'll drop him at the cook's shop where he is going to dine.'

They walked on with him until they came to a dirty shop window in a dirty street, which was made almost opaque by the steam of hot meats, vegetables, and puddings. But glimpses were to be caught of a roast leg of pork bursting into tears of sage and onion in a metal reservoir full of gravy, of an unctuous piece of roast beef and blisterous Yorkshire pudding, bubbling hot in a similar receptacle, of a stuffed fillet of veal in rapid cut, of a ham in a perspiration with the pace it was going at, of a shallow tank of baked potatoes glued together by their own richness, of a truss or two of boiled greens, and other substantial delicacies. Within, were a few wooden partitions, behind which such customers as found it more convenient to take away their dinners in stomachs than in their hands, Packed their purchases in solitude. Fanny opening her reticule, as they surveyed these things, produced from that repository a shilling and handed it to Uncle. Uncle, after not looking at it a little while, divined its object, and muttering 'Dinner? Ha! Yes, yes, yes!' slowly vanished from them into the mist.

'Now, Amy,' said her sister, 'come with me, if you are not too tired to walk to Harley Street, Cavendish Square.'

The air with which she threw off this distinguished address and the toss she gave to her new bonnet (which was more gauzy than serviceable), made her sister wonder; however, she expressed her readiness to go to Harley Street, and thither they directed their steps. Arrived at that grand destination, Fanny singled out the handsomest house, and knocking at the door, inquired for Mrs Merdle. The footman who opened the door, although he had powder on his head and was backed up by two other footmen likewise powdered, not only admitted Mrs Merdle to be at home, but asked Fanny to walk in. Fanny walked in, taking her sister with her; and they went up-stairs with powder going before and powder stopping behind, and were left in a spacious semicircular drawing-room, one of several drawing-rooms, where there was a parrot on the outside of a golden cage holding on by its beak, with its scaly legs in the air, and putting itself into many strange upside-down postures. This peculiarity has been observed in birds of quite another feather, climbing upon golden wires.

The room was far more splendid than anything Little Dorrit had ever imagined, and would have been splendid and costly in any eyes. She looked in amazement at her sister and would have asked a question, but that Fanny with a warning frown pointed to a curtained doorway of communication with another room. The curtain shook next moment, and a lady, raising it with a heavily ringed hand, dropped it behind her again as she entered.

The lady was not young and fresh from the hand of Nature, but was young and fresh from the hand of her maid. She had large unfeeling handsome eyes, and dark unfeeling handsome hair, and a broad unfeeling handsome bosom, and was made the most of in every particular. Either because she had a cold, or because it suited her face, she wore a rich white fillet tied over her head and under her chin. And if ever there were an unfeeling handsome chin that looked as if, for certain, it had never been, in familiar parlance, 'chucked' by the hand of man, it was the chin curbed up so tight and close by that laced bridle.

'Mrs Merdle,' said Fanny. 'My sister, ma'am.'

'I am glad to see your sister, Miss Dorrit. I did not remember that you had a sister.'

'I did not mention that I had,' said Fanny.

'Ah!' Mrs Merdle curled the little finger of her left hand as who should say, 'I have caught you. I know you didn't!' All her action was usually with her left hand because her hands were not a pair; and left being much the whiter and plumper of the two. Then she added: 'Sit down,' and composed herself voluptuously, in a nest of crimson and gold cushions, on an ottoman near the parrot.

'Also professional?' said Mrs Merdle, looking at Little Dorrit through an eye-glass.

Fanny answered No. 'No,' said Mrs Merdle, dropping her glass. 'Has not a professional air. Very pleasant; but not professional.'

'My sister, ma'am,' said Fanny, in whom there was a singular mixture of deference and hardihood, 'has been asking me to tell her, as between sisters, how I came to have the honour of knowing you. And as I had engaged to call upon you once more, I thought I might take the liberty of bringing her with me, when perhaps you would tell her. I wish her to know, and perhaps you will tell her?'

'Do you think, at your sister's age—' hinted Mrs Merdle.

'She is much older than she looks,' said Fanny; 'almost as old as I am.'

'Society,' said Mrs Merdle, with another curve of her little finger, 'is so difficult to explain to young persons (indeed is so difficult to explain to most persons), that I am glad to hear that. I wish Society was not so arbitrary, I wish it was not so exacting—Bird, be quiet!'

The parrot had given a most piercing shriek, as if its name were Society and it asserted its right to its exactions.

'But,' resumed Mrs Merdle, 'we must take it as we find it. We know it is hollow and conventional and worldly and very shocking, but unless we are Savages in the Tropical seas (I should have been charmed to be one myself—most delightful life and perfect climate, I am told), we must consult it. It is the common lot. Mr Merdle is a most extensive merchant, his transactions are on the vastest scale, his wealth and influence are very great, but even he—Bird, be quiet!'

The parrot had shrieked another shriek; and it filled up the sentence so expressively that Mrs Merdle was under no necessity to end it.

'Since your sister begs that I would terminate our personal acquaintance,' she began again, addressing Little Dorrit, 'by relating the circumstances that are much to her credit, I cannot object to comply with her request, I am sure. I have a son (I was first married extremely young) of two or three-and-twenty.'

Fanny set her lips, and her eyes looked half triumphantly at her sister.

'A son of two or three-and-twenty. He is a little gay, a thing Society is accustomed to in young men, and he is very impressible. Perhaps he inherits that misfortune. I am very impressible myself, by nature. The weakest of creatures—my feelings are touched in a moment.'

She said all this, and everything else, as coldly as a woman of snow; quite forgetting the sisters except at odd times, and apparently addressing some abstraction of Society; for whose behoof, too, she occasionally arranged her dress, or the composition of her figure upon the ottoman.

'So he is very impressible. Not a misfortune in our natural state I dare say, but we are not in a natural state. Much to be lamented, no doubt, particularly by myself, who am a child of nature if I could but show it; but so it is. Society suppresses us and dominates us—Bird, be quiet!'

The parrot had broken into a violent fit of laughter, after twisting divers bars of his cage with his crooked bill, and licking them with his black tongue.

'It is quite unnecessary to say to a person of your good sense, wide range of experience, and cultivated feeling,' said Mrs Merdle from her nest of crimson and gold—and there put up her glass to refresh her memory as to whom she was addressing,—'that the stage sometimes has a fascination for young men of that class of character. In saying the stage, I mean the people on it of the female sex. Therefore, when I heard that my son was supposed to be fascinated by a dancer, I knew what that usually meant in Society, and confided in her being a dancer at the Opera, where young men moving in Society are usually fascinated.'

She passed her white hands over one another, observant of the sisters now; and the rings upon her fingers grated against each other with a hard sound.

'As your sister will tell you, when I found what the theatre was I was much surprised and much distressed. But when I found that your sister, by rejecting my son's advances (I must add, in an unexpected manner), had brought him to the point of proposing marriage, my feelings were of the profoundest anguish—acute.'

She traced the outline of her left eyebrow, and put it right.

'In a distracted condition, which only a mother—moving in Society—can be susceptible of, I determined to go myself to the theatre, and represent my state of mind to the dancer. I made myself known to your sister. I found her, to my surprise, in many respects different from my expectations; and certainly in none more so, than in meeting me with—what shall I say—a sort of family assertion on her own part?' Mrs Merdle smiled.

'I told you, ma'am,' said Fanny, with a heightening colour, 'that although you found me in that situation, I was so far above the rest, that I considered my family as good as your son's; and that I had a brother who, knowing the circumstances, would be of the same opinion, and would not consider such a connection any honour.'

'Miss Dorrit,' said Mrs Merdle, after frostily looking at her through her glass, 'precisely what I was on the point of telling your sister, in pursuance of your request. Much obliged to you for recalling it so accurately and anticipating me. I immediately,' addressing Little Dorrit, '(for I am the creature of impulse), took a bracelet from my arm, and begged your sister to let me clasp it on hers, in token of the delight I had in our being able to approach the subject so far on a common footing.' (This was perfectly true, the lady having bought a cheap and showy article on her way to the interview, with a general eye to bribery.)

'And I told you, Mrs Merdle,' said Fanny, 'that we might be unfortunate, but we are not common.'

'I think, the very words, Miss Dorrit,' assented Mrs Merdle.

'And I told you, Mrs Merdle,' said Fanny, 'that if you spoke to me of the superiority of your son's standing in Society, it was barely possible that you rather deceived yourself in your suppositions about my origin; and that my father's standing, even in the Society in which he now moved (what that was, was best known to myself), was eminently superior, and was acknowledged by every one.'

'Quite accurate,' rejoined Mrs Merdle. 'A most admirable memory.'

'Thank you, ma'am. Perhaps you will be so kind as to tell my sister the rest.'

'There is very little to tell,' said Mrs Merdle, reviewing the breadth of bosom which seemed essential to her having room enough to be unfeeling in, 'but it is to your sister's credit. I pointed out to your sister the plain state of the case; the impossibility of the Society in which we moved recognising the Society in which she moved—though charming, I have no doubt; the immense disadvantage at which she would consequently place the family she had so high an opinion of, upon which we should find ourselves compelled to look down with contempt, and from which (socially speaking) we should feel obliged to recoil with abhorrence. In short, I made an appeal to that laudable pride in your sister.'

'Let my sister know, if you please, Mrs Merdle,' Fanny pouted, with a toss of her gauzy bonnet, 'that I had already had the honour of telling your son that I wished to have nothing whatever to say to him.'

'Well, Miss Dorrit,' assented Mrs Merdle, 'perhaps I might have mentioned that before. If I did not think of it, perhaps it was because my mind reverted to the apprehensions I had at the time that he might persevere and you might have something to say to him. I also mentioned to your sister—I again address the non-professional Miss Dorrit—that my son would have nothing in the event of such a marriage, and would be an absolute beggar. (I mention that merely as a fact which is part of the narrative, and not as supposing it to have influenced your sister, except in the prudent and legitimate way in which, constituted as our artificial system is, we must all be influenced by such considerations.) Finally, after some high words and high spirit on the part of your sister, we came to the complete understanding that there was no danger; and your sister was so obliging as to allow me to present her with a mark or two of my appreciation at my dressmaker's.'

Little Dorrit looked sorry, and glanced at Fanny with a troubled face.

'Also,' said Mrs Merdle, 'as to promise to give me the present pleasure of a closing interview, and of parting with her on the best of terms. On which occasion,' added Mrs Merdle, quitting her nest, and putting something in Fanny's hand, 'Miss Dorrit will permit me to say Farewell with best wishes in my own dull manner.'

The sisters rose at the same time, and they all stood near the cage of the parrot, as he tore at a claw-full of biscuit and spat it out, seemed to mock them with a pompous dance of his body without moving his feet, and suddenly turned himself upside down and trailed himself all over the outside of his golden cage, with the aid of his cruel beak and black tongue.

'Adieu, Miss Dorrit, with best wishes,' said Mrs Merdle. 'If we could only come to a Millennium, or something of that sort, I for one might have the pleasure of knowing a number of charming and talented persons from whom I am at present excluded. A more primitive state of society would be delicious to me. There used to be a poem when I learnt lessons, something about Lo the poor Indians whose something mind! If a few thousand persons moving in Society, could only go and be Indians, I would put my name down directly; but as, moving in Society, we can't be Indians, unfortunately—Good morning!'

They came down-stairs with powder before them and powder behind, the elder sister haughty and the younger sister humbled, and were shut out into unpowdered Harley Street, Cavendish Square.

'Well?' said Fanny, when they had gone a little way without speaking. 'Have you nothing to say, Amy?'

'Oh, I don't know what to say!' she answered, distressed. 'You didn't like this young man, Fanny?'

'Like him? He is almost an idiot.'

'I am so sorry—don't be hurt—but, since you ask me what I have to say, I am so very sorry, Fanny, that you suffered this lady to give you anything.'

'You little Fool!' returned her sister, shaking her with the sharp pull she gave her arm. 'Have you no spirit at all? But that's just the way! You have no self-respect, you have no becoming pride, just as you allow yourself to be followed about by a contemptible little Chivery of a thing,' with the scornfullest emphasis, 'you would let your family be trodden on, and never turn.'

'Don't say that, dear Fanny. I do what I can for them.'

'You do what you can for them!' repeated Fanny, walking her on very fast. 'Would you let a woman like this, whom you could see, if you had any experience of anything, to be as false and insolent as a woman can be—would you let her put her foot upon your family, and thank her for it?'

'No, Fanny, I am sure.'

'Then make her pay for it, you mean little thing. What else can you make her do? Make her pay for it, you stupid child; and do your family some credit with the money!'

They spoke no more all the way back to the lodging where Fanny and her uncle lived.

When they arrived there, they found the old man practising his clarionet in the dolefullest manner in a corner of the room. Fanny had a composite meal to make, of chops, and porter, and tea; and indignantly pretended to prepare it for herself, though her sister did all that in quiet reality. When at last Fanny sat down to eat and drink, she threw the table implements about and was angry with her bread, much as her father had been last night.

'If you despise me,' she said, bursting into vehement tears, 'because I am a dancer, why did you put me in the way of being one? It was your doing. You would have me stoop as low as the ground before this Mrs Merdle, and let her say what she liked and do what she liked, and hold us all in contempt, and tell us so to my face. Because I am a dancer!'

'O Fanny!'

'And Tip, too, poor fellow. She is to disparage him just as much as she likes, without any check—I suppose because he has been in the law, and the docks, and different things. Why, it was your doing, Amy. You might at least approve of his being defended.'

All this time the uncle was dolefully blowing his clarionet in the corner, sometimes taking it an inch or so from his mouth for a moment while he stopped to gaze at them, with a vague impression that somebody had said something.

'And your father, your poor father, Amy. Because he is not free to show himself and to speak for himself, you would let such people insult him with impunity. If you don't feel for yourself because you go out to work, you might at least feel for him, I should think, knowing what he has undergone so long.'

Poor Little Dorrit felt the injustice of this taunt rather sharply. The remembrance of last night added a barbed point to it. She said nothing in reply, but turned her chair from the table towards the fire. Uncle, after making one more pause, blew a dismal wail and went on again.

Fanny was passionate with the tea-cups and the bread as long as her passion lasted, and then protested that she was the wretchedest girl in the world, and she wished she was dead. After that, her crying became remorseful, and she got up and put her arms round her sister. Little Dorrit tried to stop her from saying anything, but she answered that she would, she must! Thereupon she said again, and again, 'I beg your pardon, Amy,' and 'Forgive me, Amy,' almost as passionately as she had said what she regretted.

'But indeed, indeed, Amy,' she resumed when they were seated in sisterly accord side by side, 'I hope and I think you would have seen this differently, if you had known a little more of Society.'

'Perhaps I might, Fanny,' said the mild Little Dorrit.

'You see, while you have been domestic and resignedly shut up there, Amy,' pursued her sister, gradually beginning to patronise, 'I have been out, moving more in Society, and may have been getting proud and spirited—more than I ought to be, perhaps?'

Little Dorrit answered 'Yes. O yes!'

'And while you have been thinking of the dinner or the clothes, I may have been thinking, you know, of the family. Now, may it not be so, Amy?'

Little Dorrit again nodded 'Yes,' with a more cheerful face than heart.

'Especially as we know,' said Fanny, 'that there certainly is a tone in the place to which you have been so true, which does belong to it, and which does make it different from other aspects of Society. So kiss me once again, Amy dear, and we will agree that we may both be right, and that you are a tranquil, domestic, home-loving, good girl.'

The clarionet had been lamenting most pathetically during this dialogue, but was cut short now by Fanny's announcement that it was time to go; which she conveyed to her uncle by shutting up his scrap of music, and taking the clarionet out of his mouth.

Little Dorrit parted from them at the door, and hastened back to the Marshalsea. It fell dark there sooner than elsewhere, and going into it that evening was like going into a deep trench. The shadow of the wall was on every object. Not least upon the figure in the old grey gown and the black velvet cap, as it turned towards her when she opened the door of the dim room.

'Why not upon me too!' thought Little Dorrit, with the door yet in her hand. 'It was not unreasonable in Fanny.'

CHAPTER 21. Mr Merdle's Complaint

Upon that establishment of state, the Merdle establishment in Harley Street, Cavendish Square, there was the shadow of no more common wall than the fronts of other establishments of state on the opposite side of the street. Like unexceptionable Society, the opposing rows of houses in Harley Street were very grim with one another. Indeed, the mansions and their inhabitants were so much alike in that respect, that the people were often to be found drawn up on opposite sides of dinner-tables, in the shade of their own loftiness, staring at the other side of the way with the dullness of the houses.

Everybody knows how like the street the two dinner-rows of people who take their stand by the street will be. The expressionless uniform twenty houses, all to be knocked at and rung at in the same form, all approachable by the same dull steps, all fended off by the same pattern of railing, all with the same impracticable fire-escapes, the same inconvenient fixtures in their heads, and everything without exception to be taken at a high valuation—who has not dined with these? The house so drearily out of repair, the occasional bow-window, the stuccoed house, the newly-fronted house, the corner house with nothing but angular rooms, the house with the blinds always down, the house with the hatchment always up, the house where the collector has called for one quarter of an Idea, and found nobody at home—who has not dined with these? The house that nobody will take, and is to be had a bargain—who does not know her? The showy house that was taken for life by the disappointed gentleman, and which does not suit him at all—who is unacquainted with that haunted habitation?

Harley Street, Cavendish Square, was more than aware of Mr and Mrs Merdle. Intruders there were in Harley Street, of whom it was not aware; but Mr and Mrs Merdle it delighted to honour. Society was aware of Mr and Mrs Merdle. Society had said 'Let us license them; let us know them.'

Mr Merdle was immensely rich; a man of prodigious enterprise; a Midas without the ears, who turned all he touched to gold. He was in everything good, from banking to building. He was in Parliament, of course. He was in the City, necessarily. He was Chairman of this, Trustee of that, President of the other. The weightiest of men had said to projectors, 'Now, what name have you got? Have you got Merdle?' And, the reply being in the negative, had said,

'Then I won't look at you.'

This great and fortunate man had provided that extensive bosom which required so much room to be unfeeling enough in, with a nest of crimson and gold some fifteen years before. It was not a bosom to repose upon, but it was a capital bosom to hang jewels upon. Mr Merdle wanted something to hang jewels upon, and he bought it for the purpose. Storr and Mortimer might have married on the same speculation.

Like all his other speculations, it was sound and successful. The jewels showed to the richest advantage. The bosom moving in Society with the jewels displayed upon it, attracted general admiration. Society approving, Mr Merdle was satisfied. He was the most disinterested of men,—did everything for Society, and got as little for himself out of all his gain and care, as a man might.

That is to say, it may be supposed that he got all he wanted, otherwise with unlimited wealth he would have got it. But his desire was to the utmost to satisfy Society (whatever that was), and take up all its drafts upon him for tribute. He did not shine in company; he had not very much to say for himself; he was a reserved man, with a broad, overhanging, watchful head, that particular kind of dull red colour in his cheeks which is rather stale than fresh, and a somewhat uneasy expression about his coat-cuffs, as if they were in his confidence, and had reasons for being anxious to hide his hands. In the little he said, he was a pleasant man enough; plain, emphatic about public and private confidence, and tenacious of the utmost deference being shown by every one, in all things, to Society. In this same Society (if that were it which came to his dinners, and to Mrs Merdle's receptions and concerts), he hardly seemed to enjoy himself much, and was mostly to be found against walls and behind doors. Also when he went out to it, instead of its coming home to him, he seemed a little fatigued, and upon the whole rather more disposed for bed; but he was always cultivating it nevertheless, and always moving in it—and always laying out money on it with the greatest liberality.

Mrs Merdle's first husband had been a colonel, under whose auspices the bosom had entered into competition with the snows of North America, and had come off at little disadvantage in point of whiteness, and at none in point of coldness. The colonel's son was Mrs Merdle's only child. He was of a chuckle-headed, high-shouldered make, with a general appearance of being, not so much a young man as a swelled boy. He had given so few signs of reason, that a by-word went among his companions that his brain had been frozen up in a mighty frost which prevailed at St John's, New Brunswick, at the period of his birth there, and had never thawed from that hour. Another by-word represented him as having in his infancy, through the negligence of a nurse, fallen out of a high window on his head, which had been heard by responsible witnesses to crack. It is probable that both these representations were of ex post facto origin; the young gentleman (whose expressive name was Sparkler) being monomaniacal in offering marriage to all manner of undesirable young ladies, and in remarking of every successive young lady to whom he tendered a matrimonial proposal that she was 'a doosed fine gal—well educated too—with no biggodd nonsense about her.'

A son-in-law with these limited talents, might have been a clog upon another man; but Mr Merdle did not want a son-in-law for himself; he wanted a son-in-law for Society. Mr Sparkler having been in the Guards, and being in the habit of frequenting all the races, and all the lounges, and all the parties, and being well known, Society was satisfied with its son-in-law. This happy result Mr Merdle would have considered well attained, though Mr Sparkler had been a more expensive article. And he did not get Mr Sparkler by any means cheap for Society, even as it was.

There was a dinner giving in the Harley Street establishment, while Little Dorrit was stitching at her father's new shirts by his side that night; and there were magnates from the Court and magnates from the City, magnates from the Commons and magnates from the Lords, magnates from the bench and magnates from the bar, Bishop magnates, Treasury magnates, Horse Guard magnates, Admiralty magnates,—all the magnates that keep us going, and sometimes trip us up.

'I am told,' said Bishop magnate to Horse Guards, 'that Mr Merdle has made another enormous hit. They say a hundred thousand pounds.'

Horse Guards had heard two.

Treasury had heard three.

Bar, handling his persuasive double eye-glass, was by no means clear but that it might be four. It was one of those happy strokes of calculation and combination, the result of which it was difficult to estimate. It was one of those instances of a comprehensive grasp, associated with habitual luck and characteristic boldness, of which an age presented us but few. But here was Brother Bellows, who had been in the great Bank case, and who could probably tell us more. What did Brother Bellows put this new success at?

Brother Bellows was on his way to make his bow to the bosom, and could only tell them in passing that he had heard it stated, with great appearance of truth, as being worth, from first to last, half-a-million of money.

Admiralty said Mr Merdle was a wonderful man, Treasury said he was a new power in the country, and would be able to buy up the whole House of Commons. Bishop said he was glad to think that this wealth flowed into the coffers of a gentleman who was always disposed to maintain the best interests of Society.

Mr Merdle himself was usually late on these occasions, as a man still detained in the clutch of giant enterprises when other men had shaken off their dwarfs for the day. On this occasion, he was the last arrival. Treasury said Merdle's work punished him a little. Bishop said he was glad to think that this wealth flowed into the coffers of a gentleman who accepted it with meekness.

Powder! There was so much Powder in waiting, that it flavoured the dinner. Pulverous particles got into the dishes, and Society's meats had a seasoning of first-rate footmen. Mr Merdle took down a countess who was secluded somewhere in the core of an immense dress, to which she was in the proportion of the heart to the overgrown cabbage. If so low a simile may be admitted, the dress went down the staircase like a richly brocaded Jack in the Green, and nobody knew what sort of small person carried it.

Society had everything it could want, and could not want, for dinner. It had everything to look at, and everything to eat, and everything to drink. It is to be hoped it enjoyed itself; for Mr Merdle's own share of the repast might have been paid for with eighteenpence. Mrs Merdle was magnificent. The chief butler was the next magnificent institution of the day. He was the stateliest man in the company. He did nothing, but he looked on as few other men could have done. He was Mr Merdle's last gift to Society. Mr Merdle didn't want him, and was put out of countenance when the great creature looked at him; but inappeasable Society would have him—and had got him.

The invisible countess carried out the Green at the usual stage of the entertainment, and the file of beauty was closed up by the bosom. Treasury said, Juno. Bishop said, Judith.

Bar fell into discussion with Horse Guards concerning courts-martial. Brothers Bellows and Bench struck in. Other magnates paired off. Mr Merdle sat silent, and looked at the table-cloth. Sometimes a magnate addressed him, to turn the stream of his own particular discussion towards him; but Mr Merdle seldom gave much attention to it, or did more than rouse himself from his calculations and pass the wine.

When they rose, so many of the magnates had something to say to Mr Merdle individually that he held little levees by the sideboard, and checked them off as they went out at the door.

Treasury hoped he might venture to congratulate one of England's world-famed capitalists and merchant-princes (he had turned that original sentiment in the house a few times, and it came easy to him) on a new achievement. To extend the triumphs of such men was to extend the triumphs and resources of the nation; and Treasury felt—he gave Mr Merdle to understand—patriotic on the subject.

'Thank you, my lord,' said Mr Merdle; 'thank you. I accept your congratulations with pride, and I am glad you approve.'

'Why, I don't unreservedly approve, my dear Mr Merdle. Because,' smiling Treasury turned him by the arm towards the sideboard and spoke banteringly, 'it never can be worth your while to come among us and help us.'

Mr Merdle felt honoured by the—

'No, no,' said Treasury, 'that is not the light in which one so distinguished for practical knowledge and great foresight, can be expected to regard it. If we should ever be happily enabled, by accidentally possessing the control over circumstances, to propose to one so eminent to—to come among us, and give us the weight of his influence, knowledge, and character, we could only propose it to him as a duty. In fact, as a duty that he owed to Society.'

Mr Merdle intimated that Society was the apple of his eye, and that its claims were paramount to every other consideration. Treasury moved on, and Bar came up.

Bar, with his little insinuating jury droop, and fingering his persuasive double eye-glass, hoped he might be excused if he mentioned to one of the greatest converters of the root of all evil into the root of all good, who had for a long time reflected a shining lustre on the annals even of our commercial country—if he mentioned, disinterestedly, and as, what we lawyers called in our pedantic way, amicus curiae, a fact that had come by accident within his knowledge. He had been required to look over the title of a very considerable estate in one of the eastern counties—lying, in fact, for Mr Merdle knew we lawyers loved to be particular, on the borders of two of the eastern counties. Now, the title was perfectly sound, and the estate was to be purchased by one who had the command of—Money (jury droop and persuasive eye-glass), on remarkably advantageous terms. This had come to Bar's knowledge only that day, and it had occurred to him, 'I shall have the honour of dining with my esteemed friend Mr Merdle this evening, and, strictly between ourselves, I will mention the opportunity.' Such a purchase would involve not only a great legitimate political influence, but some half-dozen church presentations of considerable annual value. Now, that Mr Merdle was already at no loss to discover means of occupying even his capital, and of fully employing even his active and vigorous intellect, Bar well knew: but he would venture to suggest that the question arose in his mind, whether one who had deservedly gained so high a position and so European a reputation did not owe it—we would not say to himself, but we would say to Society, to possess himself of such influences as these; and to exercise them—we would not say for his own, or for his party's, but we would say for Society's—benefit.

Mr Merdle again expressed himself as wholly devoted to that object of his constant consideration, and Bar took his persuasive eye-glass up the grand staircase. Bishop then came undesignedly sidling in the direction of the sideboard.

Surely the goods of this world, it occurred in an accidental way to Bishop to remark, could scarcely be directed into happier channels than when they accumulated under the magic touch of the wise and sagacious, who, while they knew the just value of riches (Bishop tried here to look as if he were rather poor himself), were aware of their importance, judiciously governed and rightly distributed, to the welfare of our brethren at large.

Mr Merdle with humility expressed his conviction that Bishop couldn't mean him, and with inconsistency expressed his high gratification in Bishop's good opinion.

Bishop then—jauntily stepping out a little with his well-shaped right leg, as though he said to Mr Merdle 'don't mind the apron; a mere form!' put this case to his good friend:

Whether it had occurred to his good friend, that Society might not unreasonably hope that one so blest in his undertakings, and whose example on his pedestal was so influential with it, would shed a little money in the direction of a mission or so to Africa?

Mr Merdle signifying that the idea should have his best attention, Bishop put another case:

Whether his good friend had at all interested himself in the proceedings of our Combined Additional Endowed Dignitaries Committee, and whether it had occurred to him that to shed a little money in that direction might be a great conception finely executed?

Mr Merdle made a similar reply, and Bishop explained his reason for inquiring.

Society looked to such men as his good friend to do such things. It was not that he looked to them, but that Society looked to them. Just as it was not Our Committee who wanted the Additional Endowed Dignitaries, but it was Society that was in a state of the most agonising uneasiness of mind until it got them. He begged to assure his good friend that he was extremely sensible of his good friend's regard on all occasions for the best interests of Society; and he considered that he was at once consulting those interests and expressing the feeling of Society, when he wished him continued prosperity, continued increase of riches, and continued things in general.

Bishop then betook himself up-stairs, and the other magnates gradually floated up after him until there was no one left below but Mr Merdle. That gentleman, after looking at the table-cloth until the soul of the chief butler glowed with a noble resentment, went slowly up after the rest, and became of no account in the stream of people on the grand staircase. Mrs Merdle was at home, the best of the jewels were hung out to be seen, Society got what it came for, Mr Merdle drank twopennyworth of tea in a corner and got more than he wanted.

Among the evening magnates was a famous physician, who knew everybody, and whom everybody knew. On entering at the door, he came upon Mr Merdle drinking his tea in a corner, and touched him on the arm.

Mr Merdle started. 'Oh! It's you!'

'Any better to-day?'

'No,' said Mr Merdle, 'I am no better.'

'A pity I didn't see you this morning. Pray come to me to-morrow, or let me come to you.'

'Well!' he replied. 'I will come to-morrow as I drive by.'

Bar and Bishop had both been bystanders during this short dialogue, and as Mr Merdle was swept away by the crowd, they made their remarks upon it to the Physician. Bar said, there was a certain point of mental strain beyond which no man could go; that the point varied with various textures of brain and peculiarities of constitution, as he had had occasion to notice in several of his learned brothers; but the point of endurance passed by a line's breadth, depression and dyspepsia ensued. Not to intrude on the sacred mysteries of medicine, he took it, now (with the jury droop and persuasive eye-glass), that this was Merdle's case? Bishop said that when he was a young man, and had fallen for a brief space into the habit of writing sermons on Saturdays, a habit which all young sons of the church should sedulously avoid, he had frequently been sensible of a depression, arising as he supposed from an over-taxed intellect, upon which the yolk of a new-laid egg, beaten up by the good woman in whose house he at that time lodged, with a glass of sound sherry, nutmeg, and powdered sugar acted like a charm. Without presuming to offer so simple a remedy to the consideration of so profound a professor of the great healing art, he would venture to inquire whether the strain, being by way of intricate calculations, the spirits might not (humanly speaking) be restored to their tone by a gentle and yet generous stimulant?

'Yes,' said the physician, 'yes, you are both right. But I may as well tell you that I can find nothing the matter with Mr Merdle. He has the constitution of a rhinoceros, the digestion of an ostrich, and the concentration of an oyster. As to nerves, Mr Merdle is of a cool temperament, and not a sensitive man: is about as invulnerable, I should say, as Achilles. How such a man should suppose himself unwell without reason, you may think strange. But I have found nothing the matter with him. He may have some deep-seated recondite complaint. I can't say. I only say, that at present I have not found it out.'

There was no shadow of Mr Merdle's complaint on the bosom now displaying precious stones in rivalry with many similar superb jewel-stands; there was no shadow of Mr Merdle's complaint on young Sparkler hovering about the rooms, monomaniacally seeking any sufficiently ineligible young lady with no nonsense about her; there was no shadow of Mr Merdle's complaint on the Barnacles and Stiltstalkings, of whom whole colonies were present; or on any of the company. Even on himself, its shadow was faint enough as he moved about among the throng, receiving homage.

Mr Merdle's complaint. Society and he had so much to do with one another in all things else, that it is hard to imagine his complaint, if he had one, being solely his own affair. Had he that deep-seated recondite complaint, and did any doctor find it out? Patience, in the meantime, the shadow of the Marshalsea wall was a real darkening influence, and could be seen on the Dorrit Family at any stage of the sun's course.

CHAPTER 22. A Puzzle

Mr Clennam did not increase in favour with the Father of the Marshalsea in the ratio of his increasing visits. His obtuseness on the great Testimonial question was not calculated to awaken admiration in the paternal breast, but had rather a tendency to give offence in that sensitive quarter, and to be regarded as a positive shortcoming in point of gentlemanly feeling. An impression of disappointment, occasioned by the discovery that Mr Clennam scarcely possessed that delicacy for which, in the confidence of his nature, he had been inclined to give him credit, began to darken the fatherly mind in connection with that gentleman. The father went so far as to say, in his private family circle, that he feared Mr Clennam was not a man of high instincts. He was happy, he observed, in his public capacity as leader and representative of the College, to receive Mr Clennam when he called to pay his respects; but he didn't find that he got on with him personally. There appeared to be something (he didn't know what it was) wanting in him. Howbeit, the father did not fail in any outward show of politeness, but, on the contrary, honoured him with much attention; perhaps cherishing the hope that, although not a man of a sufficiently brilliant and spontaneous turn of mind to repeat his former testimonial unsolicited, it might still be within the compass of his nature to bear the part of a responsive gentleman, in any correspondence that way tending.

In the threefold capacity, of the gentleman from outside who had been accidentally locked in on the night of his first appearance, of the gentleman from outside who had inquired into the affairs of the Father of the Marshalsea with the stupendous idea of getting him out, and of the gentleman from outside who took an interest in the child of the Marshalsea, Clennam soon became a visitor of mark. He was not surprised by the attentions he received from Mr Chivery when that officer was on the lock, for he made little distinction between Mr Chivery's politeness and that of the other turnkeys. It was on one particular afternoon that Mr Chivery surprised him all at once, and stood forth from his companions in bold relief.

Mr Chivery, by some artful exercise of his power of clearing the Lodge, had contrived to rid it of all sauntering Collegians; so that Clennam, coming out of the prison, should find him on duty alone.

'(Private) I ask your pardon, sir,' said Mr Chivery in a secret manner; 'but which way might you be going?'

'I am going over the Bridge.' He saw in Mr Chivery, with some astonishment, quite an Allegory of Silence, as he stood with his key on his lips.

'(Private) I ask your pardon again,' said Mr Chivery, 'but could you go round by Horsemonger Lane? Could you by any means find time to look in at that address?' handing him a little card, printed for circulation among the connection of Chivery and Co., Tobacconists, Importers of pure Havannah Cigars, Bengal Cheroots, and fine-flavoured Cubas, Dealers in Fancy Snuffs, &c. &c.

'(Private) It an't tobacco business,' said Mr Chivery. 'The truth is, it's my wife. She's wishful to say a word to you, sir, upon a point respecting—yes,' said Mr Chivery, answering Clennam's look of apprehension with a nod, 'respecting her.'

'I will make a point of seeing your wife directly.'

'Thank you, sir. Much obliged. It an't above ten minutes out of your way. Please to ask for Mrs Chivery!' These instructions, Mr Chivery, who had already let him out, cautiously called through a little slide in the outer door, which he could draw back from within for the inspection of visitors when it pleased him.

Arthur Clennam, with the card in his hand, betook himself to the address set forth upon it, and speedily arrived there. It was a very small establishment, wherein a decent woman sat behind the counter working at her needle. Little jars of tobacco, little boxes of cigars, a little assortment of pipes, a little jar or two of snuff, and a little instrument like a shoeing horn for serving it out, composed the retail stock in trade.

Arthur mentioned his name, and his having promised to call, on the solicitation of Mr Chivery. About something relating to Miss Dorrit, he believed. Mrs Chivery at once laid aside her work, rose up from her seat behind the counter, and deploringly shook her head.

'You may see him now,' said she, 'if you'll condescend to take a peep.'

With these mysterious words, she preceded the visitor into a little parlour behind the shop, with a little window in it commanding a very little dull back-yard. In this yard a wash of sheets and table-cloths tried (in vain, for want of air) to get itself dried on a line or two; and among those flapping articles was sitting in a chair, like the last mariner left alive on the deck of a damp ship without the power of furling the sails, a little woe-begone young man.

'Our John,' said Mrs Chivery.

Not to be deficient in interest, Clennam asked what he might be doing there?

'It's the only change he takes,' said Mrs Chivery, shaking her head afresh. 'He won't go out, even in the back-yard, when there's no linen; but when there's linen to keep the neighbours' eyes off, he'll sit there, hours. Hours he will. Says he feels as if it was groves!' Mrs Chivery shook her head again, put her apron in a motherly way to her eyes, and reconducted her visitor into the regions of the business.

'Please to take a seat, sir,' said Mrs Chivery. 'Miss Dorrit is the matter with Our John, sir; he's a breaking his heart for her, and I would wish to take the liberty to ask how it's to be made good to his parents when bust?'

Mrs Chivery, who was a comfortable-looking woman much respected about Horsemonger Lane for her feelings and her conversation, uttered this speech with fell composure, and immediately afterwards began again to shake her head and dry her eyes.

'Sir,' said she in continuation, 'you are acquainted with the family, and have interested yourself with the family, and are influential with the family. If you can promote views calculated to make two young people happy, let me, for Our John's sake, and for both their sakes, implore you so to do!'

'I have been so habituated,' returned Arthur, at a loss, 'during the short time I have known her, to consider Little—I have been so habituated to consider Miss Dorrit in a light altogether removed from that in which you present her to me, that you quite take me by surprise. Does she know your son?'

'Brought up together, sir,' said Mrs Chivery. 'Played together.'

'Does she know your son as her admirer?'

'Oh! bless you, sir,' said Mrs Chivery, with a sort of triumphant shiver, 'she never could have seen him on a Sunday without knowing he was that. His cane alone would have told it long ago, if nothing else had. Young men like John don't take to ivory hands a pinting, for nothing. How did I first know it myself? Similarly.'

'Perhaps Miss Dorrit may not be so ready as you, you see.'

'Then she knows it, sir,' said Mrs Chivery, 'by word of mouth.'

'Are you sure?'

'Sir,' said Mrs Chivery, 'sure and certain as in this house I am. I see my son go out with my own eyes when in this house I was, and I see my son come in with my own eyes when in this house I was, and I know he done it!' Mrs Chivery derived a surprising force of emphasis from the foregoing circumstantiality and repetition.

'May I ask you how he came to fall into the desponding state which causes you so much uneasiness?'

'That,' said Mrs Chivery, 'took place on that same day when to this house I see that John with these eyes return. Never been himself in this house since. Never was like what he has been since, not from the hour when to this house seven year ago me and his father, as tenants by the quarter, came!' An effect in the nature of an affidavit was gained from this speech by Mrs Chivery's peculiar power of construction.

'May I venture to inquire what is your version of the matter?'

'You may,' said Mrs Chivery, 'and I will give it to you in honour and in word as true as in this shop I stand. Our John has every one's good word and every one's good wish. He played with her as a child when in that yard a child she played. He has known her ever since. He went out upon the Sunday afternoon when in this very parlour he had dined, and met her, with appointment or without appointment; which, I do not pretend to say. He made his offer to her. Her brother and sister is high in their views, and against Our John. Her father is all for himself in his views and against sharing her with any one. Under which circumstances she has answered Our John, "No, John, I cannot have you, I cannot have any husband, it is not my intentions ever to become a wife, it is my intentions to be always a sacrifice, farewell, find another worthy of you, and forget me!" This is the way in which she is doomed to be a constant slave to them that are not worthy that a constant slave she unto them should be. This is the way in which Our John has come to find no pleasure but in taking cold among the linen, and in showing in that yard, as in that yard I have myself shown you, a broken-down ruin that goes home to his mother's heart!' Here the good woman pointed to the little window, whence her son might be seen sitting disconsolate in the tuneless groves; and again shook her head and wiped her eyes, and besought him, for the united sakes of both the young people, to exercise his influence towards the bright reversal of these dismal events.

She was so confident in her exposition of the case, and it was so undeniably founded on correct premises in so far as the relative positions of Little Dorrit and her family were concerned, that Clennam could not feel positive on the other side. He had come to attach to Little Dorrit an interest so peculiar—an interest that removed her from, while it grew out of, the common and coarse things surrounding her—that he found it disappointing, disagreeable, almost painful, to suppose her in love with young Mr Chivery in the back-yard, or any such person. On the other hand, he reasoned with himself that she was just as good and just as true in love with him, as not in love with him; and that to make a kind of domesticated fairy of her, on the penalty of isolation at heart from the only people she knew, would be but a weakness of his own fancy, and not a kind one. Still, her youthful and ethereal appearance, her timid manner, the charm of her sensitive voice and eyes, the very many respects in which she had interested him out of her own individuality, and the strong difference between herself and those about her, were not in unison, and were determined not to be in unison, with this newly presented idea.

He told the worthy Mrs Chivery, after turning these things over in his mind—he did that, indeed, while she was yet speaking—that he might be relied upon to do his utmost at all times to promote the happiness of Miss Dorrit, and to further the wishes of her heart if it were in his power to do so, and if he could discover what they were. At the same time he cautioned her against assumptions and appearances; enjoined strict silence and secrecy, lest Miss Dorrit should be made unhappy; and particularly advised her to endeavour to win her son's confidence and so to make quite sure of the state of the case. Mrs Chivery considered the latter precaution superfluous, but said she would try. She shook her head as if she had not derived all the comfort she had fondly expected from this interview, but thanked him nevertheless for the trouble he had kindly taken. They then parted good friends, and Arthur walked away.

The crowd in the street jostling the crowd in his mind, and the two crowds making a confusion, he avoided London Bridge, and turned off in the quieter direction of the Iron Bridge. He had scarcely set foot upon it, when he saw Little Dorrit walking on before him. It was a pleasant day, with a light breeze blowing, and she seemed to have that minute come there for air. He had left her in her father's room within an hour.

It was a timely chance, favourable to his wish of observing her face and manner when no one else was by. He quickened his pace; but before he reached her, she turned her head.

'Have I startled you?' he asked.

'I thought I knew the step,' she answered, hesitating.

'And did you know it, Little Dorrit? You could hardly have expected mine.'

'I did not expect any. But when I heard a step, I thought it—sounded like yours.'

'Are you going further?'

'No, sir, I am only walking here for a little change.'

They walked together, and she recovered her confiding manner with him, and looked up in his face as she said, after glancing around:

'It is so strange. Perhaps you can hardly understand it. I sometimes have a sensation as if it was almost unfeeling to walk here.'

'Unfeeling?'

'To see the river, and so much sky, and so many objects, and such change and motion. Then to go back, you know, and find him in the same cramped place.'

'Ah yes! But going back, you must remember that you take with you the spirit and influence of such things to cheer him.'

'Do I? I hope I may! I am afraid you fancy too much, sir, and make me out too powerful.

If you were in prison, could I bring such comfort to you?'

'Yes, Little Dorrit, I am sure of it.'

He gathered from a tremor on her lip, and a passing shadow of great agitation on her face, that her mind was with her father. He remained silent for a few moments, that she might regain her composure. The Little Dorrit, trembling on his arm, was less in unison than ever with Mrs Chivery's theory, and yet was not irreconcilable with a new fancy which sprung up within him, that there might be some one else in the hopeless—newer fancy still—in the hopeless unattainable distance.

They turned, and Clennam said, Here was Maggy coming! Little Dorrit looked up, surprised, and they confronted Maggy, who brought herself at sight of them to a dead stop. She had been trotting along, so preoccupied and busy that she had not recognised them until they turned upon her. She was now in a moment so conscience-stricken that her very basket partook of the change.

'Maggy, you promised me to stop near father.'

'So I would, Little Mother, only he wouldn't let me. If he takes and sends me out I must go. If he takes and says, "Maggy, you hurry away and back with that letter, and you shall have a sixpence if the answer's a good 'un," I must take it. Lor, Little Mother, what's a poor thing of ten year old to do? And if Mr Tip—if he happens to be a coming in as I come out, and if he says "Where are you going, Maggy?" and if I says, "I'm a going So and So," and if he says, "I'll have a Try too," and if he goes into the George and writes a letter and if he gives it me and says, "Take that one to the same place, and if the answer's a good 'un I'll give you a shilling," it ain't my fault, mother!'

Arthur read, in Little Dorrit's downcast eyes, to whom she foresaw that the letters were addressed.

'I'm a going So and So. There! That's where I am a going to,' said Maggy. 'I'm a going So and So. It ain't you, Little Mother, that's got anything to do with it—it's you, you know,' said Maggy, addressing Arthur. 'You'd better come, So and So, and let me take and give 'em to you.'

'We will not be so particular as that, Maggy. Give them me here,' said Clennam in a low voice.

'Well, then, come across the road,' answered Maggy in a very loud whisper. 'Little Mother wasn't to know nothing of it, and she would never have known nothing of it if you had only gone So and So, instead of bothering and loitering about. It ain't my fault. I must do what I am told. They ought to be ashamed of themselves for telling me.'

Clennam crossed to the other side, and hurriedly opened the letters. That from the father mentioned that most unexpectedly finding himself in the novel position of having been disappointed of a remittance from the City on which he had confidently counted, he took up his pen, being restrained by the unhappy circumstance of his incarceration during three-and-twenty years (doubly underlined), from coming himself, as he would otherwise certainly have done—took up his pen to entreat Mr Clennam to advance him the sum of Three Pounds Ten Shillings upon his I.O.U., which he begged to enclose. That from the son set forth that Mr Clennam would, he knew, be gratified to hear that he had at length obtained permanent employment of a highly satisfactory nature, accompanied with every prospect of complete success in life; but that the temporary inability of his employer to pay him his arrears of salary to that date (in which condition said employer had appealed to that generous forbearance in which he trusted he should never be wanting towards a fellow-creature), combined with the fraudulent conduct of a false friend and the present high price of provisions, had reduced him to the verge of ruin, unless he could by a quarter before six that evening raise the sum of eight pounds. This sum, Mr Clennam would be happy to learn, he had, through the promptitude of several friends who had a lively confidence in his probity, already raised, with the exception of a trifling balance of one pound seventeen and fourpence; the loan of which balance, for the period of one month, would be fraught with the usual beneficent consequences.

These letters Clennam answered with the aid of his pencil and pocket-book, on the spot; sending the father what he asked for, and excusing himself from compliance with the demand of the son. He then commissioned Maggy to return with his replies, and gave her the shilling of which the failure of her supplemental enterprise would have disappointed her otherwise.

When he rejoined Little Dorrit, and they had begun walking as before, she said all at once:

'I think I had better go. I had better go home.'

'Don't be distressed,' said Clennam, 'I have answered the letters. They were nothing. You know what they were. They were nothing.'

'But I am afraid,' she returned, 'to leave him, I am afraid to leave any of them. When I am gone, they pervert—but they don't mean it—even Maggy.'

'It was a very innocent commission that she undertook, poor thing. And in keeping it secret from you, she supposed, no doubt, that she was only saving you uneasiness.'

'Yes, I hope so, I hope so. But I had better go home! It was but the other day that my sister told me I had become so used to the prison that I had its tone and character. It must be so. I am sure it must be when I see these things. My place is there. I am better there, it is unfeeling in me to be here, when I can do the least thing there. Good-bye. I had far better stay at home!'

The agonised way in which she poured this out, as if it burst of itself from her suppressed heart, made it difficult for Clennam to keep the tears from his eyes as he saw and heard her.

'Don't call it home, my child!' he entreated. 'It is always painful to me to hear you call it home.'

'But it is home! What else can I call home? Why should I ever forget it for a single moment?'

'You never do, dear Little Dorrit, in any good and true service.'

'I hope not, O I hope not! But it is better for me to stay there; much better, much more dutiful, much happier. Please don't go with me, let me go by myself. Good-bye, God bless you. Thank you, thank you.'

He felt that it was better to respect her entreaty, and did not move while her slight form went quickly away from him. When it had fluttered out of sight, he turned his face towards the water and stood thinking.

She would have been distressed at any time by this discovery of the letters; but so much so, and in that unrestrainable way?

No.

When she had seen her father begging with his threadbare disguise on, when she had entreated him not to give her father money, she had been distressed, but not like this. Something had made her keenly and additionally sensitive just now. Now, was there some one in the hopeless unattainable distance? Or had the suspicion been brought into his mind, by his own associations of the troubled river running beneath the bridge with the same river higher up, its changeless tune upon the prow of the ferry-boat, so many miles an hour the peaceful flowing of the stream, here the rushes, there the lilies, nothing uncertain or unquiet?

He thought of his poor child, Little Dorrit, for a long time there; he thought of her going home; he thought of her in the night; he thought of her when the day came round again. And the poor child Little Dorrit thought of him—too faithfully, ah, too faithfully!—in the shadow of the Marshalsea wall.

CHAPTER 23. Machinery in Motion

Mr Meagles bestirred himself with such prompt activity in the matter of the negotiation with Daniel Doyce which Clennam had entrusted to him, that he soon brought it into business train, and called on Clennam at nine o'clock one morning to make his report.

'Doyce is highly gratified by your good opinion,' he opened the business by saying, 'and desires nothing so much as that you should examine the affairs of the Works for yourself, and entirely understand them. He has handed me the keys of all his books and papers—here they are jingling in this pocket—and the only charge he has given me is "Let Mr Clennam have the means of putting himself on a perfect equality with me as to knowing whatever I know. If it should come to nothing after all, he will respect my confidence. Unless I was sure of that to begin with, I should have nothing to do with him." And there, you see,' said Mr Meagles, 'you have Daniel Doyce all over.'

'A very honourable character.'

'Oh, yes, to be sure. Not a doubt of it. Odd, but very honourable. Very odd though. Now, would you believe, Clennam,' said Mr Meagles, with a hearty enjoyment of his friend's eccentricity, 'that I had a whole morning in What's-his-name Yard—'

'Bleeding Heart?'

'A whole morning in Bleeding Heart Yard, before I could induce him to pursue the subject at all?'

'How was that?'

'How was that, my friend? I no sooner mentioned your name in connection with it than he declared off.'

'Declared off on my account?'

'I no sooner mentioned your name, Clennam, than he said, "That will never do!" What did he mean by that? I asked him. No matter, Meagles; that would never do. Why would it never do? You'll hardly believe it, Clennam,' said Mr Meagles, laughing within himself, 'but it came out that it would never do, because you and he, walking down to Twickenham together, had glided into a friendly conversation in the course of which he had referred to his intention of taking a partner, supposing at the time that you were as firmly and finally settled as St Paul's Cathedral. "Whereas," says he, "Mr Clennam might now believe, if I entertained his proposition, that I had a sinister and designing motive in what was open free speech. Which I can't bear," says he, "which I really am too proud to bear.'"

'I should as soon suspect—'

'Of course you would,' interrupted Mr Meagles, 'and so I told him. But it took a morning to scale that wall; and I doubt if any other man than myself (he likes me of old) could have got his leg over it. Well, Clennam. This business-like obstacle surmounted, he then stipulated that before resuming with you I should look over the books and form my own opinion. I looked over the books, and formed my own opinion. "Is it, on the whole, for, or against?" says he. "For," says I. "Then," says he, "you may now, my good friend, give Mr Clennam the means of forming his opinion. To enable him to do which, without bias and with perfect freedom, I shall go out of town for a week." And he's gone,' said Mr Meagles; 'that's the rich conclusion of the thing.'

'Leaving me,' said Clennam, 'with a high sense, I must say, of his candour and his—'

'Oddity,' Mr Meagles struck in. 'I should think so!'

It was not exactly the word on Clennam's lips, but he forbore to interrupt his good-humoured friend.

'And now,' added Mr Meagles, 'you can begin to look into matters as soon as you think proper. I have undertaken to explain where you may want explanation, but to be strictly impartial, and to do nothing more.'

They began their perquisitions in Bleeding Heart Yard that same forenoon. Little peculiarities were easily to be detected by experienced eyes in Mr Doyce's way of managing his affairs, but they almost always involved some ingenious simplification of a difficulty, and some plain road to the desired end. That his papers were in arrear, and that he stood in need of assistance to develop the capacity of his business, was clear enough; but all the results of his undertakings during many years were distinctly set forth, and were ascertainable with ease. Nothing had been done for the purposes of the pending investigation; everything was in its genuine working dress, and in a certain honest rugged order. The calculations and entries, in his own hand, of which there were many, were bluntly written, and with no very neat precision; but were always plain and directed straight to the purpose. It occurred to Arthur that a far more elaborate and taking show of business—such as the records of the Circumlocution Office made perhaps—might be far less serviceable, as being meant to be far less intelligible.

Three or four days of steady application tendered him master of all the facts it was essential to become acquainted with. Mr Meagles was at hand the whole time, always ready to illuminate any dim place with the bright little safety-lamp belonging to the scales and scoop. Between them they agreed upon the sum it would be fair to offer for the purchase of a half-share in the business, and then Mr Meagles unsealed a paper in which Daniel Doyce had noted the amount at which he valued it; which was even something less. Thus, when Daniel came back, he found the affair as good as concluded.

'And I may now avow, Mr Clennam,' said he, with a cordial shake of the hand, 'that if I had looked high and low for a partner, I believe I could not have found one more to my mind.'

'I say the same,' said Clennam.

'And I say of both of you,' added Mr Meagles, 'that you are well matched. You keep him in check, Clennam, with your common sense, and you stick to the Works, Dan, with your—'

'Uncommon sense?' suggested Daniel, with his quiet smile.

'You may call it so, if you like—and each of you will be a right hand to the other. Here's my own right hand upon it, as a practical man, to both of you.'

The purchase was completed within a month. It left Arthur in possession of private personal means not exceeding a few hundred pounds; but it opened to him an active and promising career. The three friends dined together on the auspicious occasion; the factory and the factory wives and children made holiday and dined too; even Bleeding Heart Yard dined and was full of meat. Two months had barely gone by in all, when Bleeding Heart Yard had become so familiar with short-commons again, that the treat was forgotten there; when nothing seemed new in the partnership but the paint of the inscription on the door-posts, DOYCE AND CLENNAM; when it appeared even to Clennam himself, that he had had the affairs of the firm in his mind for years.

The little counting-house reserved for his own occupation, was a room of wood and glass at the end of a long low workshop, filled with benches, and vices, and tools, and straps, and wheels; which, when they were in gear with the steam-engine, went tearing round as though they had a suicidal mission to grind the business to dust and tear the factory to pieces. A communication of great trap-doors in the floor and roof with the workshop above and the workshop below, made a shaft of light in this perspective, which brought to Clennam's mind the child's old picture-book, where similar rays were the witnesses of Abel's murder. The noises were sufficiently removed and shut out from the counting-house to blend into a busy hum, interspersed with periodical clinks and thumps. The patient figures at work were swarthy with the filings of iron and steel that danced on every bench and bubbled up through every chink in the planking. The workshop was arrived at by a step-ladder from the outer yard below, where it served as a shelter for the large grindstone where tools were sharpened. The whole had at once a fanciful and practical air in Clennam's eyes, which was a welcome change; and, as often as he raised them from his first work of getting the array of business documents into perfect order, he glanced at these things with a feeling of pleasure in his pursuit that was new to him.

Raising his eyes thus one day, he was surprised to see a bonnet labouring up the step-ladder. The unusual apparition was followed by another bonnet. He then perceived that the first bonnet was on the head of Mr F.'s Aunt, and that the second bonnet was on the head of Flora, who seemed to have propelled her legacy up the steep ascent with considerable difficulty.

Though not altogether enraptured at the sight of these visitors, Clennam lost no time in opening the counting-house door, and extricating them from the workshop; a rescue which was rendered the more necessary by Mr F.'s Aunt already stumbling over some impediment, and menacing steam power as an Institution with a stony reticule she carried.

'Good gracious, Arthur,—I should say Mr Clennam, far more proper—the climb we have had to get up here and how ever to get down again without a fire-escape and Mr F.'s Aunt slipping through the steps and bruised all over and you in the machinery and foundry way too only think, and never told us!'

Thus, Flora, out of breath. Meanwhile, Mr F.'s Aunt rubbed her esteemed insteps with her umbrella, and vindictively glared.

'Most unkind never to have come back to see us since that day, though naturally it was not to be expected that there should be any attraction at our house and you were much more pleasantly engaged, that's pretty certain, and is she fair or dark blue eyes or black I wonder, not that I expect that she should be anything but a perfect contrast to me in all particulars for I am a disappointment as I very well know and you are quite right to be devoted no doubt though what I am saying Arthur never mind I hardly know myself Good gracious!'

By this time he had placed chairs for them in the counting-house. As Flora dropped into hers, she bestowed the old look upon him.

'And to think of Doyce and Clennam, and who Doyce can be,' said Flora; 'delightful man no doubt and married perhaps or perhaps a daughter, now has he really? then one understands the partnership and sees it all, don't tell me anything about it for I know I have no claim to ask the question the golden chain that once was forged being snapped and very proper.'

Flora put her hand tenderly on his, and gave him another of the youthful glances.

'Dear Arthur—force of habit, Mr Clennam every way more delicate and adapted to existing circumstances—I must beg to be excused for taking the liberty of this intrusion but I thought I might so far presume upon old times for ever faded never more to bloom as to call with Mr F.'s Aunt to congratulate and offer best wishes, A great deal superior to China not to be denied and much nearer though higher up!'

'I am very happy to see you,' said Clennam, 'and I thank you, Flora, very much for your kind remembrance.'

'More than I can say myself at any rate,' returned Flora, 'for I might have been dead and buried twenty distinct times over and no doubt whatever should have been before you had genuinely remembered Me or anything like it in spite of which one last remark I wish to make, one last explanation I wish to offer—'

'My dear Mrs Finching,' Arthur remonstrated in alarm.

'Oh not that disagreeable name, say Flora!'

'Flora, is it worth troubling yourself afresh to enter into explanations? I assure you none are needed. I am satisfied—I am perfectly satisfied.'

A diversion was occasioned here, by Mr F.'s Aunt making the following inexorable and awful statement:

'There's mile-stones on the Dover road!'

With such mortal hostility towards the human race did she discharge this missile, that Clennam was quite at a loss how to defend himself; the rather as he had been already perplexed in his mind by the honour of a visit from this venerable lady, when it was plain she held him in the utmost abhorrence. He could not but look at her with disconcertment, as she sat breathing bitterness and scorn, and staring leagues away. Flora, however, received the remark as if it had been of a most apposite and agreeable nature; approvingly observing aloud that Mr F.'s Aunt had a great deal of spirit. Stimulated either by this compliment, or by her burning indignation, that illustrious woman then added, 'Let him meet it if he can!' And, with a rigid movement of her stony reticule (an appendage of great size and of a fossil appearance), indicated that Clennam was the unfortunate person at whom the challenge was hurled.

'One last remark,' resumed Flora, 'I was going to say I wish to make one last explanation I wish to offer, Mr F.'s Aunt and myself would not have intruded on business hours Mr F. having been in business and though the wine trade still business is equally business call it what you will and business habits are just the same as witness Mr F. himself who had his slippers always on the mat at ten minutes before six in the afternoon and his boots inside the fender at ten minutes before eight in the morning to the moment in all weathers light or dark—would not therefore have intruded without a motive which being kindly meant it may be hoped will be kindly taken Arthur, Mr Clennam far more proper, even Doyce and Clennam probably more business-like.'

'Pray say nothing in the way of apology,' Arthur entreated. 'You are always welcome.'

'Very polite of you to say so Arthur—cannot remember Mr Clennam until the word is out, such is the habit of times for ever fled, and so true it is that oft in the stilly night ere slumber's chain has bound people, fond memory brings the light of other days around people—very polite but more polite than true I am afraid, for to go into the machinery business without so much as sending a line or a card to papa—I don't say me though there was a time but that is past and stern reality has now my gracious never mind—does not look like it you must confess.'

Even Flora's commas seemed to have fled on this occasion; she was so much more disjointed and voluble than in the preceding interview.

'Though indeed,' she hurried on, 'nothing else is to be expected and why should it be expected and if it's not to be expected why should it be, and I am far from blaming you or any one, When your mama and my papa worried us to death and severed the golden bowl—I mean bond but I dare say you know what I mean and if you don't you don't lose much and care just as little I will venture to add—when they severed the golden bond that bound us and threw us into fits of crying on the sofa nearly choked at least myself everything was changed and in giving my hand to Mr F. I know I did so with my eyes open but he was so very unsettled and in such low spirits that he had distractedly alluded to the river if not oil of something from the chemist's and I did it for the best.'

'My good Flora, we settled that before. It was all quite right.'

'It's perfectly clear you think so,' returned Flora, 'for you take it very coolly, if I hadn't known it to be China I should have guessed myself the Polar regions, dear Mr Clennam you are right however and I cannot blame you but as to Doyce and Clennam papa's property being about here we heard it from Pancks and but for him we never should have heard one word about it I am satisfied.'

'No, no, don't say that.'

'What nonsense not to say it Arthur—Doyce and Clennam—easier and less trying to me than Mr Clennam—when I know it and you know it too and can't deny it.'

'But I do deny it, Flora. I should soon have made you a friendly visit.'

'Ah!' said Flora, tossing her head. 'I dare say!' and she gave him another of the old looks.

'However when Pancks told us I made up my mind that Mr F.'s Aunt and I would come and call because when papa—which was before that—happened to mention her name to me and to say that you were interested in her I said at the moment Good gracious why not have her here then when there's anything to do instead of putting it out.'

'When you say Her,' observed Clennam, by this time pretty well bewildered, 'do you mean Mr F.'s—'

'My goodness, Arthur—Doyce and Clennam really easier to me with old remembrances—who ever heard of Mr F.'s Aunt doing needlework and going out by the day?'

'Going out by the day! Do you speak of Little Dorrit?'

'Why yes of course,' returned Flora; 'and of all the strangest names I ever heard the strangest, like a place down in the country with a turnpike, or a favourite pony or a puppy or a bird or something from a seed-shop to be put in a garden or a flower-pot and come up speckled.'

'Then, Flora,' said Arthur, with a sudden interest in the conversation, 'Mr Casby was so kind as to mention Little Dorrit to you, was he? What did he say?'

'Oh you know what papa is,' rejoined Flora, 'and how aggravatingly he sits looking beautiful and turning his thumbs over and over one another till he makes one giddy if one keeps one's eyes upon him, he said when we were talking of you—I don't know who began the subject Arthur (Doyce and Clennam) but I am sure it wasn't me, at least I hope not but you really must excuse my confessing more on that point.'

'Certainly,' said Arthur. 'By all means.'

'You are very ready,' pouted Flora, coming to a sudden stop in a captivating bashfulness, 'that I must admit, Papa said you had spoken of her in an earnest way and I said what I have told you and that's all.'

'That's all?' said Arthur, a little disappointed.

'Except that when Pancks told us of your having embarked in this business and with difficulty persuaded us that it was really you I said to Mr F.'s Aunt then we would come and ask you if it would be agreeable to all parties that she should be engaged at our house when required for I know she often goes to your mama's and I know that your mama has a very touchy temper Arthur—Doyce and Clennam—or I never might have married Mr F. and might have been at this hour but I am running into nonsense.'

'It was very kind of you, Flora, to think of this.'

Poor Flora rejoined with a plain sincerity which became her better than her youngest glances, that she was glad he thought so. She said it with so much heart that Clennam would have given a great deal to buy his old character of her on the spot, and throw it and the mermaid away for ever.

'I think, Flora,' he said, 'that the employment you can give Little Dorrit, and the kindness you can show her—'

'Yes and I will,' said Flora, quickly.

'I am sure of it—will be a great assistance and support to her. I do not feel that I have the right to tell you what I know of her, for I acquired the knowledge confidentially, and under circumstances that bind me to silence. But I have an interest in the little creature, and a respect for her that I cannot express to you. Her life has been one of such trial and devotion, and such quiet goodness, as you can scarcely imagine. I can hardly think of her, far less speak of her, without feeling moved. Let that feeling represent what I could tell you, and commit her to your friendliness with my thanks.'

Once more he put out his hand frankly to poor Flora; once more poor Flora couldn't accept it frankly, found it worth nothing openly, must make the old intrigue and mystery of it. As much to her own enjoyment as to his dismay, she covered it with a corner of her shawl as she took it. Then, looking towards the glass front of the counting-house, and seeing two figures approaching, she cried with infinite relish, 'Papa! Hush, Arthur, for Mercy's sake!' and tottered back to her chair with an amazing imitation of being in danger of swooning, in the dread surprise and maidenly flutter of her spirits.

The Patriarch, meanwhile, came inanely beaming towards the counting-house in the wake of Pancks. Pancks opened the door for him, towed him in, and retired to his own moorings in a corner.

'I heard from Flora,' said the Patriarch with his benevolent smile, 'that she was coming to call, coming to call. And being out, I thought I'd come also, thought I'd come also.'

The benign wisdom he infused into this declaration (not of itself profound), by means of his blue eyes, his shining head, and his long white hair, was most impressive. It seemed worth putting down among the noblest sentiments enunciated by the best of men. Also, when he said to Clennam, seating himself in the proffered chair, 'And you are in a new business, Mr Clennam? I wish you well, sir, I wish you well!' he seemed to have done benevolent wonders.

'Mrs Finching has been telling me, sir,' said Arthur, after making his acknowledgments; the relict of the late Mr F. meanwhile protesting, with a gesture, against his use of that respectable name; 'that she hopes occasionally to employ the young needlewoman you recommended to my mother. For which I have been thanking her.'

The Patriarch turning his head in a lumbering way towards Pancks, that assistant put up the note-book in which he had been absorbed, and took him in tow.

'You didn't recommend her, you know,' said Pancks; 'how could you? You knew nothing about her, you didn't. The name was mentioned to you, and you passed it on. That's what you did.'

'Well!' said Clennam. 'As she justifies any recommendation, it is much the same thing.'

'You are glad she turns out well,' said Pancks, 'but it wouldn't have been your fault if she had turned out ill. The credit's not yours as it is, and the blame wouldn't have been yours as it might have been. You gave no guarantee. You knew nothing about her.'

'You are not acquainted, then,' said Arthur, hazarding a random question, 'with any of her family?'

'Acquainted with any of her family?' returned Pancks. 'How should you be acquainted with any of her family? You never heard of 'em. You can't be acquainted with people you never heard of, can you? You should think not!'

All this time the Patriarch sat serenely smiling; nodding or shaking his head benevolently, as the case required.

'As to being a reference,' said Pancks, 'you know, in a general way, what being a reference means. It's all your eye, that is! Look at your tenants down the Yard here. They'd all be references for one another, if you'd let 'em. What would be the good of letting 'em? It's no satisfaction to be done by two men instead of one. One's enough. A person who can't pay, gets another person who can't pay, to guarantee that he can pay. Like a person with two wooden legs getting another person with two wooden legs, to guarantee that he has got two natural legs. It don't make either of them able to do a walking match. And four wooden legs are more troublesome to you than two, when you don't want any.' Mr Pancks concluded by blowing off that steam of his.

A momentary silence that ensued was broken by Mr F.'s Aunt, who had been sitting upright in a cataleptic state since her last public remark. She now underwent a violent twitch, calculated to produce a startling effect on the nerves of the uninitiated, and with the deadliest animosity observed:

'You can't make a head and brains out of a brass knob with nothing in it. You couldn't do it when your Uncle George was living; much less when he's dead.'

Mr Pancks was not slow to reply, with his usual calmness, 'Indeed, ma'am! Bless my soul! I'm surprised to hear it.' Despite his presence of mind, however, the speech of Mr F.'s Aunt produced a depressing effect on the little assembly; firstly, because it was impossible to disguise that Clennam's unoffending head was the particular temple of reason depreciated; and secondly, because nobody ever knew on these occasions whose Uncle George was referred to, or what spectral presence might be invoked under that appellation.

Therefore Flora said, though still not without a certain boastfulness and triumph in her legacy, that Mr F.'s Aunt was 'very lively to-day, and she thought they had better go.' But Mr F.'s Aunt proved so lively as to take the suggestion in unexpected dudgeon and declare that she would not go; adding, with several injurious expressions, that if 'He'—too evidently meaning Clennam—wanted to get rid of her, 'let him chuck her out of winder;' and urgently expressing her desire to see 'Him' perform that ceremony.

In this dilemma, Mr Pancks, whose resources appeared equal to any emergency in the Patriarchal waters, slipped on his hat, slipped out at the counting-house door, and slipped in again a moment afterwards with an artificial freshness upon him, as if he had been in the country for some weeks. 'Why, bless my heart, ma'am!' said Mr Pancks, rubbing up his hair in great astonishment, 'is that you? How do you do, ma'am? You are looking charming to-day! I am delighted to see you. Favour me with your arm, ma'am; we'll have a little walk together, you and me, if you'll honour me with your company.' And so escorted Mr F.'s Aunt down the private staircase of the counting-house with great gallantry and success. The patriarchal Mr Casby then rose with the air of having done it himself, and blandly followed: leaving his daughter, as she followed in her turn, to remark to her former lover in a distracted whisper (which she very much enjoyed), that they had drained the cup of life to the dregs; and further to hint mysteriously that the late Mr F. was at the bottom of it.

Alone again, Clennam became a prey to his old doubts in reference to his mother and Little Dorrit, and revolved the old thoughts and suspicions. They were all in his mind, blending themselves with the duties he was mechanically discharging, when a shadow on his papers caused him to look up for the cause. The cause was Mr Pancks. With his hat thrown back upon his ears as if his wiry prongs of hair had darted up like springs and cast it off, with his jet-black beads of eyes inquisitively sharp, with the fingers of his right hand in his mouth that he might bite the nails, and with the fingers of his left hand in reserve in his pocket for another course, Mr Pancks cast his shadow through the glass upon the books and papers.

Mr Pancks asked, with a little inquiring twist of his head, if he might come in again? Clennam replied with a nod of his head in the affirmative. Mr Pancks worked his way in, came alongside the desk, made himself fast by leaning his arms upon it, and started conversation with a puff and a snort.

'Mr F.'s Aunt is appeased, I hope?' said Clennam.

'All right, sir,' said Pancks.

'I am so unfortunate as to have awakened a strong animosity in the breast of that lady,' said Clennam. 'Do you know why?'

'Does she know why?' said Pancks.

'I suppose not.'

'I suppose not,' said Pancks.

He took out his note-book, opened it, shut it, dropped it into his hat, which was beside him on the desk, and looked in at it as it lay at the bottom of the hat: all with a great appearance of consideration.

'Mr Clennam,' he then began, 'I am in want of information, sir.'

'Connected with this firm?' asked Clennam.

'No,' said Pancks.

'With what then, Mr Pancks? That is to say, assuming that you want it of me.'

'Yes, sir; yes, I want it of you,' said Pancks, 'if I can persuade you to furnish it. A, B, C, D. DA, DE, DI, DO. Dictionary order. Dorrit. That's the name, sir?'

Mr Pancks blew off his peculiar noise again, and fell to at his right-hand nails. Arthur looked searchingly at him; he returned the look.

'I don't understand you, Mr Pancks.'

'That's the name that I want to know about.'

'And what do you want to know?'

'Whatever you can and will tell me.' This comprehensive summary of his desires was not discharged without some heavy labouring on the part of Mr Pancks's machinery.

'This is a singular visit, Mr Pancks. It strikes me as rather extraordinary that you should come, with such an object, to me.'

'It may be all extraordinary together,' returned Pancks. 'It may be out of the ordinary course, and yet be business. In short, it is business. I am a man of business. What business have I in this present world, except to stick to business? No business.'

With his former doubt whether this dry hard personage were quite in earnest, Clennam again turned his eyes attentively upon his face. It was as scrubby and dingy as ever, and as eager and quick as ever, and he could see nothing lurking in it that was at all expressive of a latent mockery that had seemed to strike upon his ear in the voice.

'Now,' said Pancks, 'to put this business on its own footing, it's not my proprietor's.'

'Do you refer to Mr Casby as your proprietor?'

Pancks nodded. 'My proprietor. Put a case. Say, at my proprietor's I hear name—name of young person Mr Clennam wants to serve. Say, name first mentioned to my proprietor by Plornish in the Yard. Say, I go to Plornish. Say, I ask Plornish as a matter of business for information. Say, Plornish, though six weeks in arrear to my proprietor, declines. Say, Mrs Plornish declines. Say, both refer to Mr Clennam. Put the case.'

'Well?'

'Well, sir,' returned Pancks, 'say, I come to him. Say, here I am.'

With those prongs of hair sticking up all over his head, and his breath coming and going very hard and short, the busy Pancks fell back a step (in Tug metaphor, took half a turn astern) as if to show his dingy hull complete, then forged a-head again, and directed his quick glance by turns into his hat where his note-book was, and into Clennam's face.

'Mr Pancks, not to trespass on your grounds of mystery, I will be as plain with you as I can. Let me ask two questions. First—'

'All right!' said Pancks, holding up his dirty forefinger with his broken nail. 'I see! "What's your motive?"'

'Exactly.'

'Motive,' said Pancks, 'good. Nothing to do with my proprietor; not stateable at present, ridiculous to state at present; but good. Desiring to serve young person, name of Dorrit,' said Pancks, with his forefinger still up as a caution. 'Better admit motive to be good.'

'Secondly, and lastly, what do you want to know?'

Mr Pancks fished up his note-book before the question was put, and buttoning it with care in an inner breast-pocket, and looking straight at Clennam all the time, replied with a pause and a puff, 'I want supplementary information of any sort.'

Clennam could not withhold a smile, as the panting little steam-tug, so useful to that unwieldy ship, the Casby, waited on and watched him as if it were seeking an opportunity of running in and rifling him of all he wanted before he could resist its manoeuvres; though there was that in Mr Pancks's eagerness, too, which awakened many wondering speculations in his mind. After a little consideration, he resolved to supply Mr Pancks with such leading information as it was in his power to impart him; well knowing that Mr Pancks, if he failed in his present research, was pretty sure to find other means of getting it.

He, therefore, first requesting Mr Pancks to remember his voluntary declaration that his proprietor had no part in the disclosure, and that his own intentions were good (two declarations which that coaly little gentleman with the greatest ardour repeated), openly told him that as to the Dorrit lineage or former place of habitation, he had no information to communicate, and that his knowledge of the family did not extend beyond the fact that it appeared to be now reduced to five members; namely, to two brothers, of whom one was single, and one a widower with three children. The ages of the whole family he made known to

Mr Pancks, as nearly as he could guess at them; and finally he described to him the position of the Father of the Marshalsea, and the course of time and events through which he had become invested with that character. To all this, Mr Pancks, snorting and blowing in a more and more portentous manner as he became more interested, listened with great attention; appearing to derive the most agreeable sensations from the painfullest parts of the narrative, and particularly to be quite charmed by the account of William Dorrit's long imprisonment.

'In conclusion, Mr Pancks,' said Arthur, 'I have but to say this. I have reasons beyond a personal regard for speaking as little as I can of the Dorrit family, particularly at my mother's house' (Mr Pancks nodded), 'and for knowing as much as I can. So devoted a man of business as you are—eh?'

For Mr Pancks had suddenly made that blowing effort with unusual force.

'It's nothing,' said Pancks.

'So devoted a man of business as yourself has a perfect understanding of a fair bargain. I wish to make a fair bargain with you, that you shall enlighten me concerning the Dorrit family when you have it in your power, as I have enlightened you. It may not give you a very flattering idea of my business habits, that I failed to make my terms beforehand,' continued Clennam; 'but I prefer to make them a point of honour. I have seen so much business done on sharp principles that, to tell you the truth, Mr Pancks, I am tired of them.'

Mr Pancks laughed. 'It's a bargain, sir,' said he. 'You shall find me stick to it.'

After that, he stood a little while looking at Clennam, and biting his ten nails all round; evidently while he fixed in his mind what he had been told, and went over it carefully, before the means of supplying a gap in his memory should be no longer at hand. 'It's all right,' he said at last, 'and now I'll wish you good day, as it's collecting day in the Yard. By-the-bye, though. A lame foreigner with a stick.'

'Ay, ay. You do take a reference sometimes, I see?' said Clennam.

'When he can pay, sir,' replied Pancks. 'Take all you can get, and keep back all you can't be forced to give up. That's business. The lame foreigner with the stick wants a top room down the Yard. Is he good for it?'

'I am,' said Clennam, 'and I will answer for him.'

'That's enough. What I must have of Bleeding Heart Yard,' said Pancks, making a note of the case in his book, 'is my bond. I want my bond, you see. Pay up, or produce your property! That's the watchword down the Yard. The lame foreigner with the stick represented that you sent him; but he could represent (as far as that goes) that the Great Mogul sent him. He has been in the hospital, I believe?'

'Yes. Through having met with an accident. He is only just now discharged.'

'It's pauperising a man, sir, I have been shown, to let him into a hospital?' said Pancks. And again blew off that remarkable sound.

'I have been shown so too,' said Clennam, coldly.

Mr Pancks, being by that time quite ready for a start, got under steam in a moment, and, without any other signal or ceremony, was snorting down the step-ladder and working into Bleeding Heart Yard, before he seemed to be well out of the counting-house.

Throughout the remainder of the day, Bleeding Heart Yard was in consternation, as the grim Pancks cruised in it; haranguing the inhabitants on their backslidings in respect of payment, demanding his bond, breathing notices to quit and executions, running down defaulters, sending a swell of terror on before him, and leaving it in his wake. Knots of people, impelled by a fatal attraction, lurked outside any house in which he was known to be, listening for fragments of his discourses to the inmates; and, when he was rumoured to be coming down the stairs, often could not disperse so quickly but that he would be prematurely in among them, demanding their own arrears, and rooting them to the spot. Throughout the remainder of the day, Mr Pancks's What were they up to? and What did they mean by it? sounded all over the Yard. Mr Pancks wouldn't hear of excuses, wouldn't hear of complaints, wouldn't hear of repairs, wouldn't hear of anything but unconditional money down. Perspiring and puffing and darting about in eccentric directions, and becoming hotter and dingier every moment, he lashed the tide of the yard into a most agitated and turbid state. It had not settled down into calm water again full two hours after he had been seen fuming away on the horizon at the top of the steps.

There were several small assemblages of the Bleeding Hearts at the popular points of meeting in the Yard that night, among whom it was universally agreed that Mr Pancks was a hard man to have to do with; and that it was much to be regretted, so it was, that a gentleman like Mr Casby should put his rents in his hands, and never know him in his true light. For (said the Bleeding Hearts), if a gentleman with that head of hair and them eyes took his rents into his own hands, ma'am, there would be none of this worriting and wearing, and things would be very different.

At which identical evening hour and minute, the Patriarch—who had floated serenely through the Yard in the forenoon before the harrying began, with the express design of getting up this trustfulness in his shining bumps and silken locks—at which identical hour and minute, that first-rate humbug of a thousand guns was heavily floundering in the little Dock of his exhausted Tug at home, and was saying, as he turned his thumbs:

'A very bad day's work, Pancks, very bad day's work. It seems to me, sir, and I must insist on making this observation forcibly in justice to myself, that you ought to have got much more money, much more money.'

CHAPTER 24. Fortune-Telling

Little Dorrit received a call that same evening from Mr Plornish, who, having intimated that he wished to speak to her privately, in a series of coughs so very noticeable as to favour the idea that her father, as regarded her seamstress occupation, was an illustration of the axiom that there are no such stone-blind men as those who will not see, obtained an audience with her on the common staircase outside the door.

'There's been a lady at our place to-day, Miss Dorrit,' Plornish growled, 'and another one along with her as is a old wixen if ever I met with such. The way she snapped a person's head off, dear me!'

The mild Plornish was at first quite unable to get his mind away from Mr F.'s Aunt. 'For,' said he, to excuse himself, 'she is, I do assure you, the winegariest party.'

At length, by a great effort, he detached himself from the subject sufficiently to observe:

'But she's neither here nor there just at present. The other lady, she's Mr Casby's daughter; and if Mr Casby an't well off, none better, it an't through any fault of Pancks. For, as to Pancks, he does, he really does, he does indeed!'

Mr Plornish, after his usual manner, was a little obscure, but conscientiously emphatic.

'And what she come to our place for,' he pursued, 'was to leave word that if Miss Dorrit would step up to that card—which it's Mr Casby's house that is, and Pancks he has a office at the back, where he really does, beyond belief—she would be glad for to engage her. She was a old and a dear friend, she said particular, of Mr Clennam, and hoped for to prove herself a useful friend to his friend. Them was her words. Wishing to know whether Miss Dorrit could come to-morrow morning, I said I would see you, Miss, and inquire, and look round there to-night, to say yes, or, if you was engaged to-morrow, when?'

'I can go to-morrow, thank you,' said Little Dorrit. 'This is very kind of you, but you are always kind.'

Mr Plornish, with a modest disavowal of his merits, opened the room door for her readmission, and followed her in with such an exceedingly bald pretence of not having been out at all, that her father might have observed it without being very suspicious. In his affable unconsciousness, however, he took no heed. Plornish, after a little conversation, in which he blended his former duty as a Collegian with his present privilege as a humble outside friend, qualified again by his low estate as a plasterer, took his leave; making the tour of the prison before he left, and looking on at a game of skittles with the mixed feelings of an old inhabitant who had his private reasons for believing that it might be his destiny to come back again.

Early in the morning, Little Dorrit, leaving Maggy in high domestic trust, set off for the Patriarchal tent. She went by the Iron Bridge, though it cost her a penny, and walked more slowly in that part of her journey than in any other. At five minutes before eight her hand was on the Patriarchal knocker, which was quite as high as she could reach.

She gave Mrs Finching's card to the young woman who opened the door, and the young woman told her that 'Miss Flora'—Flora having, on her return to the parental roof, reinvested herself with the title under which she had lived there—was not yet out of her bedroom, but she was to please to walk up into Miss Flora's sitting-room. She walked up into Miss Flora's sitting-room, as in duty bound, and there found a breakfast-table comfortably laid for two, with a supplementary tray upon it laid for one. The young woman, disappearing for a few moments, returned to say that she was to please to take a chair by the fire, and to take off her bonnet and make herself at home. But Little Dorrit, being bashful, and not used to make herself at home on such occasions, felt at a loss how to do it; so she was still sitting near the door with her bonnet on, when Flora came in in a hurry half an hour afterwards.

Flora was so sorry to have kept her waiting, and good gracious why did she sit out there in the cold when she had expected to find her by the fire reading the paper, and hadn't that heedless girl given her the message then, and had she really been in her bonnet all this time, and pray for goodness sake let Flora take it off! Flora taking it off in the best-natured manner in the world, was so struck with the face disclosed, that she said, 'Why, what a good little thing you are, my dear!' and pressed her face between her hands like the gentlest of women.

It was the word and the action of a moment. Little Dorrit had hardly time to think how kind it was, when Flora dashed at the breakfast-table full of business, and plunged over head and ears into loquacity.

'Really so sorry that I should happen to be late on this morning of all mornings because my intention and my wish was to be ready to meet you when you came in and to say that any one that interested Arthur Clennam half so much must interest me and that I gave you the heartiest welcome and was so glad, instead of which they never called me and there I still am snoring I dare say if the truth was known and if you don't like either cold fowl or hot boiled ham which many people don't I dare say besides Jews and theirs are scruples of conscience which we must all respect though I must say I wish they had them equally strong when they sell us false articles for real that certainly ain't worth the money I shall be quite vexed,' said Flora.

Little Dorrit thanked her, and said, shyly, bread-and-butter and tea was all she usually—

'Oh nonsense my dear child I can never hear of that,' said Flora, turning on the urn in the most reckless manner, and making herself wink by splashing hot water into her eyes as she bent down to look into the teapot. 'You are coming here on the footing of a friend and companion you know if you will let me take that liberty and I should be ashamed of myself indeed if you could come here upon any other, besides which Arthur Clennam spoke in such terms—you are tired my dear.'

'No, ma'am.'

'You turn so pale you have walked too far before breakfast and I dare say live a great way off and ought to have had a ride,' said Flora, 'dear dear is there anything that would do you good?'

'Indeed I am quite well, ma'am. I thank you again and again, but I am quite well.'

'Then take your tea at once I beg,' said Flora, 'and this wing of fowl and bit of ham, don't mind me or wait for me, because I always carry in this tray myself to Mr F.'s Aunt who breakfasts in bed and a charming old lady too and very clever, Portrait of Mr F. behind the door and very like though too much forehead and as to a pillar with a marble pavement and balustrades and a mountain, I never saw him near it nor not likely in the wine trade, excellent man but not at all in that way.'

Little Dorrit glanced at the portrait, very imperfectly following the references to that work of art.

'Mr F. was so devoted to me that he never could bear me out of his sight,' said Flora, 'though of course I am unable to say how long that might have lasted if he hadn't been cut short while I was a new broom, worthy man but not poetical manly prose but not romance.'

Little Dorrit glanced at the portrait again. The artist had given it a head that would have been, in an intellectual point of view, top-heavy for Shakespeare.

'Romance, however,' Flora went on, busily arranging Mr F.'s Aunt's toast, 'as I openly said to Mr F. when he proposed to me and you will be surprised to hear that he proposed seven times once in a hackney-coach once in a boat once in a pew once on a donkey at Tunbridge Wells and the rest on his knees, Romance was fled with the early days of Arthur Clennam, our parents tore us asunder we became marble and stern reality usurped the throne, Mr F. said very much to his credit that he was perfectly aware of it and even preferred that state of things accordingly the word was spoken the fiat went forth and such is life you see my dear and yet we do not break but bend, pray make a good breakfast while I go in with the tray.'

She disappeared, leaving Little Dorrit to ponder over the meaning of her scattered words. She soon came back again; and at last began to take her own breakfast, talking all the while.

'You see, my dear,' said Flora, measuring out a spoonful or two of some brown liquid that smelt like brandy, and putting it into her tea, 'I am obliged to be careful to follow the directions of my medical man though the flavour is anything but agreeable being a poor creature and it may be have never recovered the shock received in youth from too much giving way to crying in the next room when separated from Arthur, have you known him long?'

As soon as Little Dorrit comprehended that she had been asked this question—for which time was necessary, the galloping pace of her new patroness having left her far behind—she answered that she had known Mr Clennam ever since his return.

'To be sure you couldn't have known him before unless you had been in China or had corresponded neither of which is likely,' returned Flora, 'for travelling-people usually get more or less mahogany and you are not at all so and as to corresponding what about? that's very true unless tea, so it was at his mother's was it really that you knew him first, highly sensible and firm but dreadfully severe—ought to be the mother of the man in the iron mask.'

'Mrs Clennam has been kind to me,' said Little Dorrit.

'Really? I am sure I am glad to hear it because as Arthur's mother it's naturally pleasant to my feelings to have a better opinion of her than I had before, though what she thinks of me when I run on as I am certain to do and she sits glowering at me like Fate in a go-cart—shocking comparison really—invalid and not her fault—I never know or can imagine.'

'Shall I find my work anywhere, ma'am?' asked Little Dorrit, looking timidly about; 'can I get it?'

'You industrious little fairy,' returned Flora, taking, in another cup of tea, another of the doses prescribed by her medical man, 'there's not the slightest hurry and it's better that we should begin by being confidential about our mutual friend—too cold a word for me at least I don't mean that, very proper expression mutual friend—than become through mere formalities not you but me like the Spartan boy with the fox biting him, which I hope you'll excuse my bringing up for of all the tiresome boys that will go tumbling into every sort of company that boy's the tiresomest.'

Little Dorrit, her face very pale, sat down again to listen. 'Hadn't I better work the while?' she asked. 'I can work and attend too. I would rather, if I may.'

Her earnestness was so expressive of her being uneasy without her work, that Flora answered, 'Well my dear whatever you like best,' and produced a basket of white handkerchiefs. Little Dorrit gladly put it by her side, took out her little pocket-housewife, threaded the needle, and began to hem.

'What nimble fingers you have,' said Flora, 'but are you sure you are well?'

'Oh yes, indeed!'

Flora put her feet upon the fender, and settled herself for a thorough good romantic disclosure. She started off at score, tossing her head, sighing in the most demonstrative manner, making a great deal of use of her eyebrows, and occasionally, but not often, glancing at the quiet face that bent over the work.

'You must know my dear,' said Flora, 'but that I have no doubt you know already not only because I have already thrown it out in a general way but because I feel I carry it stamped in burning what's his names upon my brow that before I was introduced to the late Mr F. I had been engaged to Arthur Clennam—Mr Clennam in public where reserve is necessary Arthur here—we were all in all to one another it was the morning of life it was bliss it was frenzy it was everything else of that sort in the highest degree, when rent asunder we turned to stone in which capacity Arthur went to China and I became the statue bride of the late Mr F.'

Flora, uttering these words in a deep voice, enjoyed herself immensely.

'To paint,' said she, 'the emotions of that morning when all was marble within and Mr F.'s Aunt followed in a glass-coach which it stands to reason must have been in shameful repair or it never could have broken down two streets from the house and Mr F.'s Aunt brought home like the fifth of November in a rush-bottomed chair I will not attempt, suffice it to say that the hollow form of breakfast took place in the dining-room downstairs that papa partaking too freely of pickled salmon was ill for weeks and that Mr F. and myself went upon a continental tour to Calais where the people fought for us on the pier until they separated us though not for ever that was not yet to be.'

The statue bride, hardly pausing for breath, went on, with the greatest complacency, in a rambling manner sometimes incidental to flesh and blood.

'I will draw a veil over that dreamy life, Mr F. was in good spirits his appetite was good he liked the cookery he considered the wine weak but palatable and all was well, we returned to the immediate neighbourhood of Number Thirty Little Gosling Street London Docks and settled down, ere we had yet fully detected the housemaid in selling the feathers out of the spare bed Gout flying upwards soared with Mr F. to another sphere.'

His relict, with a glance at his portrait, shook her head and wiped her eyes.

'I revere the memory of Mr F. as an estimable man and most indulgent husband, only necessary to mention Asparagus and it appeared or to hint at any little delicate thing to drink and it came like magic in a pint bottle it was not ecstasy but it was comfort, I returned to papa's roof and lived secluded if not happy during some years until one day papa came smoothly blundering in and said that Arthur Clennam awaited me below, I went below and found him ask me not what I found him except that he was still unmarried still unchanged!'

The dark mystery with which Flora now enshrouded herself might have stopped other fingers than the nimble fingers that worked near her. They worked on without pause, and the busy head bent over them watching the stitches.

'Ask me not,' said Flora, 'if I love him still or if he still loves me or what the end is to be or when, we are surrounded by watchful eyes and it may be that we are destined to pine asunder it may be never more to be reunited not a word not a breath not a look to betray us all must be secret as the tomb wonder not therefore that even if I should seem comparatively cold to Arthur or Arthur should seem comparatively cold to me we have fatal reasons it is enough if we understand them hush!'

All of which Flora said with so much headlong vehemence as if she really believed it. There is not much doubt that when she worked herself into full mermaid condition, she did actually believe whatever she said in it.

'Hush!' repeated Flora, 'I have now told you all, confidence is established between us hush, for Arthur's sake I will always be a friend to you my dear girl and in Arthur's name you may always rely upon me.'

The nimble fingers laid aside the work, and the little figure rose and kissed her hand. 'You are very cold,' said Flora, changing to her own natural kind-hearted manner, and gaining greatly by the change. 'Don't work to-day. I am sure you are not well I am sure you are not strong.'

'It is only that I feel a little overcome by your kindness, and by Mr Clennam's kindness in confiding me to one he has known and loved so long.'

'Well really my dear,' said Flora, who had a decided tendency to be always honest when she gave herself time to think about it, 'it's as well to leave that alone now, for I couldn't undertake to say after all, but it doesn't signify lie down a little!'

'I have always been strong enough to do what I want to do, and I shall be quite well directly,' returned Little Dorrit, with a faint smile. 'You have overpowered me with gratitude, that's all. If I keep near the window for a moment I shall be quite myself.'

Flora opened a window, sat her in a chair by it, and considerately retired to her former place. It was a windy day, and the air stirring on Little Dorrit's face soon brightened it. In a very few minutes she returned to her basket of work, and her nimble fingers were as nimble as ever.

Quietly pursuing her task, she asked Flora if Mr Clennam had told her where she lived? When Flora replied in the negative, Little Dorrit said that she understood why he had been so delicate, but that she felt sure he would approve of her confiding her secret to Flora, and that she would therefore do so now with Flora's permission. Receiving an encouraging answer, she condensed the narrative of her life into a few scanty words about herself and a glowing eulogy upon her father; and Flora took it all in with a natural tenderness that quite understood it, and in which there was no incoherence.

When dinner-time came, Flora drew the arm of her new charge through hers, and led her down-stairs, and presented her to the Patriarch and Mr Pancks, who were already in the dining-room waiting to begin. (Mr F.'s Aunt was, for the time, laid up in ordinary in her chamber.) By those gentlemen she was received according to their characters; the Patriarch appearing to do her some inestimable service in saying that he was glad to see her, glad to see her; and Mr Pancks blowing off his favourite sound as a salute.

In that new presence she would have been bashful enough under any circumstances, and particularly under Flora's insisting on her drinking a glass of wine and eating of the best that was there; but her constraint was greatly increased by Mr Pancks. The demeanour of that gentleman at first suggested to her mind that he might be a taker of likenesses, so intently did he look at her, and so frequently did he glance at the little note-book by his side. Observing that he made no sketch, however, and that he talked about business only, she began to have suspicions that he represented some creditor of her father's, the balance due to whom was noted in that pocket volume. Regarded from this point of view Mr Pancks's puffings expressed injury and impatience, and each of his louder snorts became a demand for payment.

But here again she was undeceived by anomalous and incongruous conduct on the part of Mr Pancks himself. She had left the table half an hour, and was at work alone. Flora had 'gone to lie down' in the next room, concurrently with which retirement a smell of something to drink had broken out in the house. The Patriarch was fast asleep, with his philanthropic mouth open under a yellow pocket-handkerchief in the dining-room. At this quiet time, Mr Pancks softly appeared before her, urbanely nodding.

'Find it a little dull, Miss Dorrit?' inquired Pancks in a low voice.

'No, thank you, sir,' said Little Dorrit.

'Busy, I see,' observed Mr Pancks, stealing into the room by inches. 'What are those now, Miss Dorrit?'

'Handkerchiefs.'

'Are they, though!' said Pancks. 'I shouldn't have thought it.' Not in the least looking at them, but looking at Little Dorrit. 'Perhaps you wonder who I am. Shall I tell you? I am a fortune-teller.'

Little Dorrit now began to think he was mad.

'I belong body and soul to my proprietor,' said Pancks; 'you saw my proprietor having his dinner below. But I do a little in the other way, sometimes; privately, very privately, Miss Dorrit.'

Little Dorrit looked at him doubtfully, and not without alarm. 'I wish you'd show me the palm of your hand,' said Pancks. 'I should like to have a look at it. Don't let me be troublesome.'

He was so far troublesome that he was not at all wanted there, but she laid her work in her lap for a moment, and held out her left hand with her thimble on it.

'Years of toil, eh?' said Pancks, softly, touching it with his blunt forefinger. 'But what else are we made for? Nothing. Hallo!' looking into the lines. 'What's this with bars? It's a College! And what's this with a grey gown and a black velvet cap? it's a father! And what's this with a clarionet? It's an uncle! And what's this in dancing-shoes? It's a sister! And what's this straggling about in an idle sort of a way? It's a brother! And what's this thinking for 'em all? Why, this is you, Miss Dorrit!'

Her eyes met his as she looked up wonderingly into his face, and she thought that although his were sharp eyes, he was a brighter and gentler-looking man than she had supposed at dinner. His eyes were on her hand again directly, and her opportunity of confirming or correcting the impression was gone.

'Now, the deuce is in it,' muttered Pancks, tracing out a line in her hand with his clumsy finger, 'if this isn't me in the corner here! What do I want here? What's behind me?'

He carried his finger slowly down to the wrist, and round the wrist, and affected to look at the back of the hand for what was behind him.

'Is it any harm?' asked Little Dorrit, smiling.

'Deuce a bit!' said Pancks. 'What do you think it's worth?'

'I ought to ask you that. I am not the fortune-teller.'

'True,' said Pancks. 'What's it worth? You shall live to see, Miss Dorrit.'

Releasing the hand by slow degrees, he drew all his fingers through his prongs of hair, so that they stood up in their most portentous manner; and repeated slowly, 'Remember what I say, Miss Dorrit. You shall live to see.'

She could not help showing that she was much surprised, if it were only by his knowing so much about her.

'Ah! That's it!' said Pancks, pointing at her. 'Miss Dorrit, not that, ever!'

More surprised than before, and a little more frightened, she looked to him for an explanation of his last words.

'Not that,' said Pancks, making, with great seriousness, an imitation of a surprised look and manner that appeared to be unintentionally grotesque. 'Don't do that. Never on seeing me, no matter when, no matter where. I am nobody. Don't take on to mind me. Don't mention me. Take no notice. Will you agree, Miss Dorrit?'

'I hardly know what to say,' returned Little Dorrit, quite astounded. 'Why?'

'Because I am a fortune-teller. Pancks the gipsy. I haven't told you so much of your fortune yet, Miss Dorrit, as to tell you what's behind me on that little hand. I have told you—you shall live to see. Is it agreed, Miss Dorrit?'

'Agreed that I—am—to—'

'To take no notice of me away from here, unless I take on first. Not to mind me when I come and go. It's very easy. I am no loss, I am not handsome, I am not good company, I am only my proprietors grubber. You need do no more than think, "Ah! Pancks the gipsy at his fortune-telling—he'll tell the rest of my fortune one day—I shall live to know it." Is it agreed, Miss Dorrit?'

'Ye-es,' faltered Little Dorrit, whom he greatly confused, 'I suppose so, while you do no harm.'

'Good!' Mr Pancks glanced at the wall of the adjoining room, and stooped forward. 'Honest creature, woman of capital points, but heedless and a loose talker, Miss Dorrit.' With that he rubbed his hands as if the interview had been very satisfactory to him, panted away to the door, and urbanely nodded himself out again.

If Little Dorrit were beyond measure perplexed by this curious conduct on the part of her new acquaintance, and by finding herself involved in this singular treaty, her perplexity was not diminished by ensuing circumstances. Besides that Mr Pancks took every opportunity afforded him in Mr Casby's house of significantly glancing at her and snorting at her—which was not much, after what he had done already—he began to pervade her daily life. She saw him in the street, constantly. When she went to Mr Casby's, he was always there. When she went to Mrs Clennam's, he came there on any pretence, as if to keep her in his sight. A week had not gone by, when she found him to her astonishment in the Lodge one night, conversing with the turnkey on duty, and to all appearance one of his familiar companions. Her next surprise was to find him equally at his ease within the prison; to hear of his presenting himself among the visitors at her father's Sunday levee; to see him arm in arm with a Collegiate friend about the yard; to learn, from Fame, that he had greatly distinguished himself one evening at the social club that held its meetings in the Snuggery, by addressing a speech to the members of the institution, singing a song, and treating the company to five gallons of ale—report madly added a bushel of shrimps. The effect on Mr Plornish of such of these phenomena as he became an eye-witness of in his faithful visits, made an impression on Little Dorrit only second to that produced by the phenomena themselves. They seemed to gag and bind him. He could only stare, and sometimes weakly mutter that it wouldn't be believed down Bleeding Heart Yard that this was Pancks; but he never said a word more, or made a sign more, even to Little Dorrit. Mr Pancks crowned his mysteries by making himself acquainted with Tip in some unknown manner, and taking a Sunday saunter into the College on that gentleman's arm. Throughout he never took any notice of Little Dorrit, save once or twice when he happened to come close to her and there was no one very near; on which occasions, he said in passing, with a friendly look and a puff of encouragement, 'Pancks the gipsy—fortune-telling.'

Little Dorrit worked and strove as usual, wondering at all this, but keeping her wonder, as she had from her earliest years kept many heavier loads, in her own breast. A change had stolen, and was stealing yet, over the patient heart. Every day found her something more retiring than the day before. To pass in and out of the prison unnoticed, and elsewhere to be overlooked and forgotten, were, for herself, her chief desires.

To her own room too, strangely assorted room for her delicate youth and character, she was glad to retreat as often as she could without desertion of any duty. There were afternoon times when she was unemployed, when visitors dropped in to play a hand at cards with her father, when she could be spared and was better away. Then she would flit along the yard, climb the scores of stairs that led to her room, and take her seat at the window. Many combinations did those spikes upon the wall assume, many light shapes did the strong iron weave itself into, many golden touches fell upon the rust, while Little Dorrit sat there musing. New zigzags sprung into the cruel pattern sometimes, when she saw it through a burst of tears; but beautified or hardened still, always over it and under it and through it, she was fain to look in her solitude, seeing everything with that ineffaceable brand.

A garret, and a Marshalsea garret without compromise, was Little Dorrit's room. Beautifully kept, it was ugly in itself, and had little but cleanliness and air to set it off; for what embellishment she had ever been able to buy, had gone to her father's room. Howbeit, for this poor place she showed an increasing love; and to sit in it alone became her favourite rest.

Insomuch, that on a certain afternoon during the Pancks mysteries, when she was seated at her window, and heard Maggy's well-known step coming up the stairs, she was very much disturbed by the apprehension of being summoned away. As Maggy's step came higher up and nearer, she trembled and faltered; and it was as much as she could do to speak, when Maggy at length appeared.

'Please, Little Mother,' said Maggy, panting for breath, 'you must come down and see him. He's here.'

'Who, Maggy?'

'Who, o' course Mr Clennam. He's in your father's room, and he says to me, Maggy, will you be so kind and go and say it's only me.'

'I am not very well, Maggy. I had better not go. I am going to lie down. See! I lie down now, to ease my head. Say, with my grateful regard, that you left me so, or I would have come.'

'Well, it an't very polite though, Little Mother,' said the staring Maggy, 'to turn your face away, neither!'

Maggy was very susceptible to personal slights, and very ingenious in inventing them.

'Putting both your hands afore your face too!' she went on. 'If you can't bear the looks of a poor thing, it would be better to tell her so at once, and not go and shut her out like that, hurting her feelings and breaking her heart at ten year old, poor thing!'

'It's to ease my head, Maggy.'

'Well, and if you cry to ease your head, Little Mother, let me cry too. Don't go and have all the crying to yourself,' expostulated Maggy, 'that an't not being greedy.' And immediately began to blubber.

It was with some difficulty that she could be induced to go back with the excuse; but the promise of being told a story—of old her great delight—on condition that she concentrated her faculties upon the errand and left her little mistress to herself for an hour longer, combined with a misgiving on Maggy's part that she had left her good temper at the bottom of the staircase, prevailed. So away she went, muttering her message all the way to keep it in her mind, and, at the appointed time, came back.

'He was very sorry, I can tell you,' she announced, 'and wanted to send a doctor. And he's coming again to-morrow he is and I don't think he'll have a good sleep to-night along o' hearing about your head, Little Mother. Oh my! Ain't you been a-crying!'

'I think I have, a little, Maggy.'

'A little! Oh!'

'But it's all over now—all over for good, Maggy. And my head is much better and cooler, and I am quite comfortable. I am very glad I did not go down.'

Her great staring child tenderly embraced her; and having smoothed her hair, and bathed her forehead and eyes with cold water (offices in which her awkward hands became skilful), hugged her again, exulted in her brighter looks, and stationed her in her chair by the window. Over against this chair, Maggy, with apoplectic exertions that were not at all required, dragged the box which was her seat on story-telling occasions, sat down upon it, hugged her own knees, and said, with a voracious appetite for stories, and with widely-opened eyes:

'Now, Little Mother, let's have a good 'un!'

'What shall it be about, Maggy?'

'Oh, let's have a princess,' said Maggy, 'and let her be a reg'lar one. Beyond all belief, you know!'

Little Dorrit considered for a moment; and with a rather sad smile upon her face, which was flushed by the sunset, began:

'Maggy, there was once upon a time a fine King, and he had everything he could wish for, and a great deal more. He had gold and silver, diamonds and rubies, riches of every kind. He had palaces, and he had—'

'Hospitals,' interposed Maggy, still nursing her knees. 'Let him have hospitals, because they're so comfortable. Hospitals with lots of Chicking.'

'Yes, he had plenty of them, and he had plenty of everything.'

'Plenty of baked potatoes, for instance?' said Maggy.

'Plenty of everything.'

216

'Lor!' chuckled Maggy, giving her knees a hug. 'Wasn't it prime!'

'This King had a daughter, who was the wisest and most beautiful Princess that ever was seen. When she was a child she understood all her lessons before her masters taught them to her; and when she was grown up, she was the wonder of the world. Now, near the Palace where this Princess lived, there was a cottage in which there was a poor little tiny woman, who lived all alone by herself.'

'An old woman,' said Maggy, with an unctuous smack of her lips.

'No, not an old woman. Quite a young one.'

'I wonder she warn't afraid,' said Maggy. 'Go on, please.'

'The Princess passed the cottage nearly every day, and whenever she went by in her beautiful carriage, she saw the poor tiny woman spinning at her wheel, and she looked at the tiny woman, and the tiny woman looked at her. So, one day she stopped the coachman a little way from the cottage, and got out and walked on and peeped in at the door, and there, as usual, was the tiny woman spinning at her wheel, and she looked at the Princess, and the Princess looked at her.'

'Like trying to stare one another out,' said Maggy. 'Please go on, Little Mother.'

'The Princess was such a wonderful Princess that she had the power of knowing secrets, and she said to the tiny woman, Why do you keep it there? This showed her directly that the Princess knew why she lived all alone by herself spinning at her wheel, and she kneeled down at the Princess's feet, and asked her never to betray her. So the Princess said, I never will betray you. Let me see it. So the tiny woman closed the shutter of the cottage window and fastened the door, and trembling from head to foot for fear that any one should suspect her, opened a very secret place and showed the Princess a shadow.'

'Lor!' said Maggy.

'It was the shadow of Some one who had gone by long before: of Some one who had gone on far away quite out of reach, never, never to come back. It was bright to look at; and when the tiny woman showed it to the Princess, she was proud of it with all her heart, as a great, great treasure. When the Princess had considered it a little while, she said to the tiny woman, And you keep watch over this every day? And she cast down her eyes, and whispered, Yes. Then the Princess said, Remind me why. To which the other replied, that no one so good and kind had ever passed that way, and that was why in the beginning. She said, too, that nobody missed it, that nobody was the worse for it, that Some one had gone on, to those who were expecting him—'

'Some one was a man then?' interposed Maggy.

Little Dorrit timidly said Yes, she believed so; and resumed:

'—Had gone on to those who were expecting him, and that this remembrance was stolen or kept back from nobody. The Princess made answer, Ah! But when the cottager died it would be discovered there. The tiny woman told her No; when that time came, it would sink quietly into her own grave, and would never be found.'

'Well, to be sure!' said Maggy. 'Go on, please.'

'The Princess was very much astonished to hear this, as you may suppose, Maggy.'

('And well she might be,' said Maggy.)

'So she resolved to watch the tiny woman, and see what came of it. Every day she drove in her beautiful carriage by the cottage-door, and there she saw the tiny woman always alone by herself spinning at her wheel, and she looked at the tiny woman, and the tiny woman looked at her. At last one day the wheel was still, and the tiny woman was not to be seen. When the Princess made inquiries why the wheel had stopped, and where the tiny woman was, she was informed that the wheel had stopped because there was nobody to turn it, the tiny woman being dead.'

('They ought to have took her to the Hospital,' said Maggy, and then she'd have got over it.')

'The Princess, after crying a very little for the loss of the tiny woman, dried her eyes and got out of her carriage at the place where she had stopped it before, and went to the cottage and peeped in at the door. There was nobody to look at her now, and nobody for her to look at, so she went in at once to search for the treasured shadow. But there was no sign of it to be found anywhere; and then she knew that the tiny woman had told her the truth, and that it would never give anybody any trouble, and that it had sunk quietly into her own grave, and that she and it were at rest together.

'That's all, Maggy.'

The sunset flush was so bright on Little Dorrit's face when she came thus to the end of her story, that she interposed her hand to shade it.

'Had she got to be old?' Maggy asked.

'The tiny woman?'

'Ah!'

'I don't know,' said Little Dorrit. 'But it would have been just the same if she had been ever so old.'

'Would it raly!' said Maggy. 'Well, I suppose it would though.' And sat staring and ruminating.

She sat so long with her eyes wide open, that at length Little Dorrit, to entice her from her box, rose and looked out of window. As she glanced down into the yard, she saw Pancks come in and leer up with the corner of his eye as he went by.

'Who's he, Little Mother?' said Maggy. She had joined her at the window and was leaning on her shoulder. 'I see him come in and out often.'

'I have heard him called a fortune-teller,' said Little Dorrit. 'But I doubt if he could tell many people even their past or present fortunes.'

'Couldn't have told the Princess hers?' said Maggy.

Little Dorrit, looking musingly down into the dark valley of the prison, shook her head.

'Nor the tiny woman hers?' said Maggy.

'No,' said Little Dorrit, with the sunset very bright upon her. 'But let us come away from the window.'

CHAPTER 25. Conspirators and Others

The private residence of Mr Pancks was in Pentonville, where he lodged on the second-floor of a professional gentleman in an extremely small way, who had an inner-door within the street door, poised on a spring and starting open with a click like a trap; and who wrote up in the fan-light, RUGG, GENERAL AGENT, ACCOUNTANT, DEBTS RECOVERED.

This scroll, majestic in its severe simplicity, illuminated a little slip of front garden abutting on the thirsty high-road, where a few of the dustiest of leaves hung their dismal heads and led a life of choking. A professor of writing occupied the first-floor, and enlivened the garden railings with glass-cases containing choice examples of what his pupils had been before six lessons and while the whole of his young family shook the table, and what they had become after six lessons when the young family was under restraint. The tenancy of Mr Pancks was limited to one airy bedroom; he covenanting and agreeing with Mr Rugg his landlord, that in consideration of a certain scale of payments accurately defined, and on certain verbal notice duly given, he should be at liberty to elect to share the Sunday breakfast, dinner, tea, or supper, or each or any or all of those repasts or meals of Mr and Miss Rugg (his daughter) in the back-parlour.

Miss Rugg was a lady of a little property which she had acquired, together with much distinction in the neighbourhood, by having her heart severely lacerated and her feelings mangled by a middle-aged baker resident in the vicinity, against whom she had, by the agency of Mr Rugg, found it necessary to proceed at law to recover damages for a breach of promise of marriage. The baker having been, by the counsel for Miss Rugg, witheringly denounced on that occasion up to the full amount of twenty guineas, at the rate of about eighteen-pence an epithet, and having been cast in corresponding damages, still suffered occasional persecution from the youth of Pentonville. But Miss Rugg, environed by the majesty of the law, and having her damages invested in the public securities, was regarded with consideration.

In the society of Mr Rugg, who had a round white visage, as if all his blushes had been drawn out of him long ago, and who had a ragged yellow head like a worn-out hearth broom; and in the society of Miss Rugg, who had little nankeen spots, like shirt buttons, all over her face, and whose own yellow tresses were rather scrubby than luxuriant; Mr Pancks had usually dined on Sundays for some few years, and had twice a week, or so, enjoyed an evening collation of bread, Dutch cheese, and porter. Mr Pancks was one of the very few marriageable men for whom Miss Rugg had no terrors, the argument with which he reassured himself being twofold; that is to say, firstly, 'that it wouldn't do twice,' and secondly, 'that he wasn't worth it.' Fortified within this double armour, Mr Pancks snorted at Miss Rugg on easy terms.

Up to this time, Mr Pancks had transacted little or no business at his quarters in Pentonville, except in the sleeping line; but now that he had become a fortune-teller, he was often closeted after midnight with Mr Rugg in his little front-parlour office, and even after those untimely hours, burnt tallow in his bed-room. Though his duties as his proprietor's grubber were in no wise lessened; and though that service bore no greater resemblance to a bed of roses than was to be discovered in its many thorns; some new branch of industry made a constant demand upon him. When he cast off the Patriarch at night, it was only to take an anonymous craft in tow, and labour away afresh in other waters.

The advance from a personal acquaintance with the elder Mr Chivery to an introduction to his amiable wife and disconsolate son, may have been easy; but easy or not, Mr Pancks soon made it. He nestled in the bosom of the tobacco business within a week or two after his first appearance in the College, and particularly addressed himself to the cultivation of a good understanding with Young John. In this endeavour he so prospered as to lure that pining shepherd forth from the groves, and tempt him to undertake mysterious missions; on which he began to disappear at uncertain intervals for as long a space as two or three days together. The prudent Mrs Chivery, who wondered greatly at this change, would have protested against it as detrimental to the Highland typification on the doorpost but for two forcible reasons; one, that her John was roused to take strong interest in the business which these starts were supposed to advance—and this she held to be good for his drooping spirits; the other, that Mr Pancks confidentially agreed to pay her, for the occupation of her son's time, at the handsome rate of seven and sixpence per day. The proposal originated with himself, and was couched in the pithy terms, 'If your John is weak enough, ma'am, not to take it, that is no reason why you should be, don't you see? So, quite between ourselves, ma'am, business being business, here it is!'

What Mr Chivery thought of these things, or how much or how little he knew about them, was never gathered from himself. It has been already remarked that he was a man of few words; and it may be here observed that he had imbibed a professional habit of locking everything up. He locked himself up as carefully as he locked up the Marshalsea debtors. Even his custom of bolting his meals may have been a part of an uniform whole; but there is no question, that, as to all other purposes, he kept his mouth as he kept the Marshalsea door. He never opened it without occasion. When it was necessary to let anything out, he opened it a little way, held it open just as long as sufficed for the purpose, and locked it again. Even as he would be sparing of his trouble at the Marshalsea door, and would keep a visitor who wanted to go out, waiting for a few moments if he saw another visitor coming down the yard, so that one turn of the key should suffice for both, similarly he would often reserve a remark if he perceived another on its way to his lips, and would deliver himself of the two together. As to any key to his inner knowledge being to be found in his face, the Marshalsea key was as legible as an index to the individual characters and histories upon which it was turned.

That Mr Pancks should be moved to invite any one to dinner at Pentonville, was an unprecedented fact in his calendar. But he invited Young John to dinner, and even brought him within range of the dangerous (because expensive) fascinations of Miss Rugg. The banquet was appointed for a Sunday, and Miss Rugg with her own hands stuffed a leg of mutton with oysters on the occasion, and sent it to the baker's—not the baker's but an opposition establishment. Provision of oranges, apples, and nuts was also made. And rum was brought home by Mr Pancks on Saturday night, to gladden the visitor's heart.

The store of creature comforts was not the chief part of the visitor's reception. Its special feature was a foregone family confidence and sympathy. When Young John appeared at half-past one without the ivory hand and waistcoat of golden sprigs, the sun shorn of his beams by disastrous clouds, Mr Pancks presented him to the yellow-haired Ruggs as the young man he had so often mentioned who loved Miss Dorrit.

'I am glad,' said Mr Rugg, challenging him specially in that character, 'to have the distinguished gratification of making your acquaintance, sir. Your feelings do you honour. You are young; may you never outlive your feelings! If I was to outlive my own feelings, sir,' said

Mr Rugg, who was a man of many words, and was considered to possess a remarkably good address; 'if I was to outlive my own feelings, I'd leave fifty pound in my will to the man who would put me out of existence.'

Miss Rugg heaved a sigh.

'My daughter, sir,' said Mr Rugg. 'Anastatia, you are no stranger to the state of this young man's affections. My daughter has had her trials, sir'—Mr Rugg might have used the word more pointedly in the singular number—'and she can feel for you.'

Young John, almost overwhelmed by the touching nature of this greeting, professed himself to that effect.

'What I envy you, sir, is,' said Mr Rugg, 'allow me to take your hat—we are rather short of pegs—I'll put it in the corner, nobody will tread on it there—What I envy you, sir, is the luxury of your own feelings. I belong to a profession in which that luxury is sometimes denied us.'

Young John replied, with acknowledgments, that he only hoped he did what was right, and what showed how entirely he was devoted to Miss Dorrit. He wished to be unselfish; and he hoped he was. He wished to do anything as laid in his power to serve Miss Dorrit, altogether putting himself out of sight; and he hoped he did. It was but little that he could do, but he hoped he did it.

'Sir,' said Mr Rugg, taking him by the hand, 'you are a young man that it does one good to come across. You are a young man that I should like to put in the witness-box, to humanise the minds of the legal profession. I hope you have brought your appetite with you, and intend to play a good knife and fork?'

'Thank you, sir,' returned Young John, 'I don't eat much at present.'

Mr Rugg drew him a little apart. 'My daughter's case, sir,' said he, 'at the time when, in vindication of her outraged feelings and her sex, she became the plaintiff in Rugg and Bawkins. I suppose I could have put it in evidence, Mr Chivery, if I had thought it worth my while, that the amount of solid sustenance my daughter consumed at that period did not exceed ten ounces per week.'

'I think I go a little beyond that, sir,' returned the other, hesitating, as if he confessed it with some shame.

'But in your case there's no fiend in human form,' said Mr Rugg, with argumentative smile and action of hand. 'Observe, Mr Chivery! No fiend in human form!'

'No, sir, certainly,' Young John added with simplicity, 'I should be very sorry if there was.'

'The sentiment,' said Mr Rugg, 'is what I should have expected from your known principles. It would affect my daughter greatly, sir, if she heard it. As I perceive the mutton, I am glad she didn't hear it. Mr Pancks, on this occasion, pray face me. My dear, face Mr Chivery. For what we are going to receive, may we (and Miss Dorrit) be truly thankful!'

But for a grave waggishness in Mr Rugg's manner of delivering this introduction to the feast, it might have appeared that Miss Dorrit was expected to be one of the company. Pancks recognised the sally in his usual way, and took in his provender in his usual way. Miss Rugg, perhaps making up some of her arrears, likewise took very kindly to the mutton, and it rapidly diminished to the bone. A bread-and-butter pudding entirely disappeared, and a considerable amount of cheese and radishes vanished by the same means. Then came the dessert.

Then also, and before the broaching of the rum and water, came Mr Pancks's note-book. The ensuing business proceedings were brief but curious, and rather in the nature of a conspiracy. Mr Pancks looked over his note-book, which was now getting full, studiously; and picked out little extracts, which he wrote on separate slips of paper on the table; Mr Rugg, in the meanwhile, looking at him with close attention, and Young John losing his uncollected eye in mists of meditation. When Mr Pancks, who supported the character of chief conspirator, had completed his extracts, he looked them over, corrected them, put up his note-book, and held them like a hand at cards.

'Now, there's a churchyard in Bedfordshire,' said Pancks. 'Who takes it?'

'I'll take it, sir,' returned Mr Rugg, 'if no one bids.'

Mr Pancks dealt him his card, and looked at his hand again.

'Now, there's an Enquiry in York,' said Pancks. 'Who takes it?'

'I'm not good for York,' said Mr Rugg.

'Then perhaps,' pursued Pancks, 'you'll be so obliging, John Chivery?'

Young John assenting, Pancks dealt him his card, and consulted his hand again.

'There's a Church in London; I may as well take that. And a Family Bible; I may as well take that, too. That's two to me. Two to me,' repeated Pancks, breathing hard over his cards. 'Here's a Clerk at Durham for you, John, and an old seafaring gentleman at Dunstable for you, Mr Rugg. Two to me, was it? Yes, two to me. Here's a Stone; three to me. And a Still-born Baby; four to me. And all, for the present, told.'

When he had thus disposed of his cards, all being done very quietly and in a suppressed tone, Mr Pancks puffed his way into his own breast-pocket and tugged out a canvas bag; from which, with a sparing hand, he told forth money for travelling expenses in two little portions. 'Cash goes out fast,' he said anxiously, as he pushed a portion to each of his male companions, 'very fast.'

'I can only assure you, Mr Pancks,' said Young John, 'that I deeply regret my circumstances being such that I can't afford to pay my own charges, or that it's not advisable to allow me the time necessary for my doing the distances on foot; because nothing would give me greater satisfaction than to walk myself off my legs without fee or reward.'

This young man's disinterestedness appeared so very ludicrous in the eyes of Miss Rugg, that she was obliged to effect a precipitate retirement from the company, and to sit upon the stairs until she had had her laugh out. Meanwhile Mr Pancks, looking, not without some pity, at Young John, slowly and thoughtfully twisted up his canvas bag as if he were wringing its neck. The lady, returning as he restored it to his pocket, mixed rum and water for the party, not forgetting her fair self, and handed to every one his glass. When all were supplied, Mr Rugg rose, and silently holding out his glass at arm's length above the centre of the table, by that gesture invited the other three to add theirs, and to unite in a general conspiratorial clink. The ceremony was effective up to a certain point, and would have been wholly so throughout, if Miss Rugg, as she raised her glass to her lips in completion of it, had not happened to look at Young John; when she was again so overcome by the contemptible comicality of his disinterestedness as to splutter some ambrosial drops of rum and water around, and withdraw in confusion.

Such was the dinner without precedent, given by Pancks at Pentonville; and such was the busy and strange life Pancks led. The only waking moments at which he appeared to relax from his cares, and to recreate himself by going anywhere or saying anything without a pervading object, were when he showed a dawning interest in the lame foreigner with the stick, down Bleeding Heart Yard.

The foreigner, by name John Baptist Cavalletto—they called him Mr Baptist in the Yard—was such a chirping, easy, hopeful little fellow, that his attraction for Pancks was probably in the force of contrast. Solitary, weak, and scantily acquainted with the most necessary words of the only language in which he could communicate with the people about him, he went with the stream of his fortunes, in a brisk way that was new in those parts. With little to eat, and less to drink, and nothing to wear but what he wore upon him, or had brought tied up in one of the smallest bundles that ever were seen, he put as bright a face upon it as if he were in the most flourishing circumstances when he first hobbled up and down the Yard, humbly propitiating the general good-will with his white teeth.

It was uphill work for a foreigner, lame or sound, to make his way with the Bleeding Hearts. In the first place, they were vaguely persuaded that every foreigner had a knife about him; in the second, they held it to be a sound constitutional national axiom that he ought to go home to his own country. They never thought of inquiring how many of their own countrymen would be returned upon their hands from divers parts of the world, if the principle were generally recognised; they considered it particularly and peculiarly British. In the third place, they had a notion that it was a sort of Divine visitation upon a foreigner that he was not an Englishman, and that all kinds of calamities happened to his country because it did things that England did not, and did not do things that England did. In this belief, to be sure, they had long been carefully trained by the Barnacles and Stiltstalkings, who were always proclaiming to them, officially, that no country which failed to submit itself to those two large families could possibly hope to be under the protection of Providence; and who, when they believed it, disparaged them in private as the most prejudiced people under the sun.

This, therefore, might be called a political position of the Bleeding Hearts; but they entertained other objections to having foreigners in the Yard. They believed that foreigners were always badly off; and though they were as ill off themselves as they could desire to be, that did not diminish the force of the objection. They believed that foreigners were dragooned and bayoneted; and though they certainly got their own skulls promptly fractured if they showed any ill-humour, still it was with a blunt instrument, and that didn't count. They believed that foreigners were always immoral; and though they had an occasional assize at home, and now and then a divorce case or so, that had nothing to do with it. They believed that foreigners had no independent spirit, as never being escorted to the poll in droves by Lord Decimus Tite Barnacle, with colours flying and the tune of Rule Britannia playing. Not to be tedious, they had many other beliefs of a similar kind.

Against these obstacles, the lame foreigner with the stick had to make head as well as he could; not absolutely single-handed, because Mr Arthur Clennam had recommended him to the Plornishes (he lived at the top of the same house), but still at heavy odds. However, the Bleeding Hearts were kind hearts; and when they saw the little fellow cheerily limping about with a good-humoured face, doing no harm, drawing no knives, committing no outrageous immoralities, living chiefly on farinaceous and milk diet, and playing with Mrs Plornish's children of an evening, they began to think that although he could never hope to be an Englishman, still it would be hard to visit that affliction on his head. They began to accommodate themselves to his level, calling him 'Mr Baptist,' but treating him like a baby, and laughing immoderately at his lively gestures and his childish English—more, because he didn't mind it, and laughed too. They spoke to him in very loud voices as if he were stone deaf. They constructed sentences, by way of teaching him the language in its purity, such as were addressed by the savages to Captain Cook, or by Friday to Robinson Crusoe. Mrs Plornish was particularly ingenious in this art; and attained so much celebrity for saying 'Me ope you leg well soon,' that it was considered in the Yard but a very short remove indeed from speaking Italian. Even Mrs Plornish herself began to think that she had a natural call towards that language. As he became more popular, household objects were brought into requisition for his instruction in a copious vocabulary; and whenever he appeared in the Yard ladies would fly out at their doors crying 'Mr Baptist—tea-pot!' 'Mr Baptist—dust-pan!' 'Mr Baptist—flour-dredger!' 'Mr Baptist—coffee-biggin!' At the same time exhibiting those articles, and penetrating him with a sense of the appalling difficulties of the Anglo-Saxon tongue.

It was in this stage of his progress, and in about the third week of his occupation, that Mr Pancks's fancy became attracted by the little man. Mounting to his attic, attended by Mrs Plornish as interpreter, he found Mr Baptist with no furniture but his bed on the ground, a table, and a chair, carving with the aid of a few simple tools, in the blithest way possible.

'Now, old chap,' said Mr Pancks, 'pay up!'

He had his money ready, folded in a scrap of paper, and laughingly handed it in; then with a free action, threw out as many fingers of his right hand as there were shillings, and made a cut crosswise in the air for an odd sixpence.

'Oh!' said Mr Pancks, watching him, wonderingly. 'That's it, is it? You're a quick customer. It's all right. I didn't expect to receive it, though.'

Mrs Plornish here interposed with great condescension, and explained to Mr Baptist. 'E please. E glad get money.'

The little man smiled and nodded. His bright face seemed uncommonly attractive to Mr Pancks. 'How's he getting on in his limb?' he asked Mrs Plornish.

'Oh, he's a deal better, sir,' said Mrs Plornish. 'We expect next week he'll be able to leave off his stick entirely.' (The opportunity being too favourable to be lost, Mrs Plornish displayed her great accomplishment by explaining with pardonable pride to Mr Baptist, 'E ope you leg well soon.')

'He's a merry fellow, too,' said Mr Pancks, admiring him as if he were a mechanical toy. 'How does he live?'

'Why, sir,' rejoined Mrs Plornish, 'he turns out to have quite a power of carving them flowers that you see him at now.' (Mr Baptist, watching their faces as they spoke, held up his work. Mrs Plornish interpreted in her Italian manner, on behalf of Mr Pancks, 'E please. Double good!')

'Can he live by that?' asked Mr Pancks.

'He can live on very little, sir, and it is expected as he will be able, in time, to make a very good living. Mr Clennam got it him to do, and gives him odd jobs besides in at the Works next door—makes 'em for him, in short, when he knows he wants 'em.'

'And what does he do with himself, now, when he ain't hard at it?' said Mr Pancks.

'Why, not much as yet, sir, on accounts I suppose of not being able to walk much; but he goes about the Yard, and he chats without particular understanding or being understood, and he plays with the children, and he sits in the sun—he'll sit down anywhere, as if it was an arm-chair—and he'll sing, and he'll laugh!'

'Laugh!' echoed Mr Pancks. 'He looks to me as if every tooth in his head was always laughing.'

'But whenever he gets to the top of the steps at t'other end of the Yard,' said Mrs Plornish, 'he'll peep out in the curiousest way! So that some of us thinks he's peeping out towards where his own country is, and some of us thinks he's looking for somebody he don't want to see, and some of us don't know what to think.'

Mr Baptist seemed to have a general understanding of what she said; or perhaps his quickness caught and applied her slight action of peeping. In any case he closed his eyes and tossed his head with the air of a man who had sufficient reasons for what he did, and said in his own tongue, it didn't matter. Altro!

'What's Altro?' said Pancks.

'Hem! It's a sort of a general kind of expression, sir,' said Mrs Plornish.

'Is it?' said Pancks. 'Why, then Altro to you, old chap. Good afternoon. Altro!'

Mr Baptist in his vivacious way repeating the word several times, Mr Pancks in his duller way gave it him back once. From that time it became a frequent custom with Pancks the gipsy, as he went home jaded at night, to pass round by Bleeding Heart Yard, go quietly up the stairs, look in at Mr Baptist's door, and, finding him in his room, to say, 'Hallo, old chap! Altro!' To which Mr Baptist would reply with innumerable bright nods and smiles, 'Altro, signore, altro, altro, altro!' After this highly condensed conversation, Mr Pancks would go his way with an appearance of being lightened and refreshed.

CHAPTER 26. Nobody's State of Mind

If Arthur Clennam had not arrived at that wise decision firmly to restrain himself from loving Pet, he would have lived on in a state of much perplexity, involving difficult struggles with his own heart. Not the least of these would have been a contention, always waging within it, between a tendency to dislike Mr Henry Gowan, if not to regard him with positive repugnance, and a whisper that the inclination was unworthy. A generous nature is not prone to strong aversions, and is slow to admit them even dispassionately; but when it finds ill-will gaining upon it, and can discern between-whiles that its origin is not dispassionate, such a nature becomes distressed.

Therefore Mr Henry Gowan would have clouded Clennam's mind, and would have been far oftener present to it than more agreeable persons and subjects but for the great prudence of his decision aforesaid. As it was, Mr Gowan seemed transferred to Daniel Doyce's mind; at all events, it so happened that it usually fell to Mr Doyce's turn, rather than to Clennam's, to speak of him in the friendly conversations they held together. These were of frequent occurrence now; as the two partners shared a portion of a roomy house in one of the grave old-fashioned City streets, lying not far from the Bank of England, by London Wall.

Mr Doyce had been to Twickenham to pass the day. Clennam had excused himself. Mr Doyce was just come home. He put in his head at the door of Clennam's sitting-room to say Good night.

'Come in, come in!' said Clennam.

'I saw you were reading,' returned Doyce, as he entered, 'and thought you might not care to be disturbed.'

But for the notable resolution he had made, Clennam really might not have known what he had been reading; really might not have had his eyes upon the book for an hour past, though it lay open before him. He shut it up, rather quickly.

'Are they well?' he asked.

'Yes,' said Doyce; 'they are well. They are all well.'

Daniel had an old workmanlike habit of carrying his pocket-handkerchief in his hat. He took it out and wiped his forehead with it, slowly repeating, 'They are all well. Miss Minnie looking particularly well, I thought.'

'Any company at the cottage?'

'No, no company.'

'And how did you get on, you four?' asked Clennam gaily.

'There were five of us,' returned his partner. 'There was What's-his-name. He was there.'

'Who is he?' said Clennam.

'Mr Henry Gowan.'

'Ah, to be sure!' cried Clennam with unusual vivacity, 'Yes!—I forgot him.'

'As I mentioned, you may remember,' said Daniel Doyce, 'he is always there on Sunday.'

'Yes, yes,' returned Clennam; 'I remember now.'

Daniel Doyce, still wiping his forehead, ploddingly repeated. 'Yes. He was there, he was there. Oh yes, he was there. And his dog. He was there too.'

'Miss Meagles is quite attached to—the—dog,' observed Clennam.

'Quite so,' assented his partner. 'More attached to the dog than I am to the man.'

'You mean Mr—?'

'I mean Mr Gowan, most decidedly,' said Daniel Doyce.

There was a gap in the conversation, which Clennam devoted to winding up his watch.

'Perhaps you are a little hasty in your judgment,' he said. 'Our judgments—I am supposing a general case—'

'Of course,' said Doyce.

'Are so liable to be influenced by many considerations, which, almost without our knowing it, are unfair, that it is necessary to keep a guard upon them. For instance, Mr—'

'Gowan,' quietly said Doyce, upon whom the utterance of the name almost always devolved.

'Is young and handsome, easy and quick, has talent, and has seen a good deal of various kinds of life. It might be difficult to give an unselfish reason for being prepossessed against him.'

'Not difficult for me, I think, Clennam,' returned his partner. 'I see him bringing present anxiety, and, I fear, future sorrow, into my old friend's house. I see him wearing deeper lines into my old friend's face, the nearer he draws to, and the oftener he looks at, the face of his daughter. In short, I see him with a net about the pretty and affectionate creature whom he will never make happy.'

'We don't know,' said Clennam, almost in the tone of a man in pain, 'that he will not make her happy.'

'We don't know,' returned his partner, 'that the earth will last another hundred years, but we think it highly probable.'

'Well, well!' said Clennam, 'we must be hopeful, and we must at least try to be, if not generous (which, in this case, we have no opportunity of being), just. We will not disparage this gentleman, because he is successful in his addresses to the beautiful object of his ambition; and we will not question her natural right to bestow her love on one whom she finds worthy of it.'

'Maybe, my friend,' said Doyce. 'Maybe also, that she is too young and petted, too confiding and inexperienced, to discriminate well.'

'That,' said Clennam, 'would be far beyond our power of correction.'

Daniel Doyce shook his head gravely, and rejoined, 'I fear so.'

'Therefore, in a word,' said Clennam, 'we should make up our minds that it is not worthy of us to say any ill of Mr Gowan. It would be a poor thing to gratify a prejudice against him. And I resolve, for my part, not to depreciate him.'

'I am not quite so sure of myself, and therefore I reserve my privilege of objecting to him,' returned the other. 'But, if I am not sure of myself, I am sure of you, Clennam, and I know what an upright man you are, and how much to be respected. Good night, my friend and partner!' He shook his hand in saying this, as if there had been something serious at the bottom of their conversation; and they separated.

By this time they had visited the family on several occasions, and had always observed that even a passing allusion to Mr Henry Gowan when he was not among them, brought back the cloud which had obscured Mr Meagles's sunshine on the morning of the chance encounter at the Ferry. If Clennam had ever admitted the forbidden passion into his breast, this period might have been a period of real trial; under the actual circumstances, doubtless it was nothing—nothing.

Equally, if his heart had given entertainment to that prohibited guest, his silent fighting of his way through the mental condition of this period might have been a little meritorious. In the constant effort not to be betrayed into a new phase of the besetting sin of his experience, the pursuit of selfish objects by low and small means, and to hold instead to some high principle of honour and generosity, there might have been a little merit. In the resolution not even to avoid Mr Meagles's house, lest, in the selfish sparing of himself, he should bring any slight distress upon the daughter through making her the cause of an estrangement which he believed the father would regret, there might have been a little merit. In the modest truthfulness of always keeping in view the greater equality of Mr Gowan's years and the greater attractions of his person and manner, there might have been a little merit. In doing all this and much more, in a perfectly unaffected way and with a manful and composed constancy, while the pain within him (peculiar as his life and history) was very sharp, there might have been some quiet strength of character. But, after the resolution he had made, of course he could have no such merits as these; and such a state of mind was nobody's—nobody's.

Mr Gowan made it no concern of his whether it was nobody's or somebody's. He preserved his perfect serenity of manner on all occasions, as if the possibility of Clennam's presuming to have debated the great question were too distant and ridiculous to be imagined. He had always an affability to bestow on Clennam and an ease to treat him with, which might of itself (in the supposititious case of his not having taken that sagacious course) have been a very uncomfortable element in his state of mind.

'I quite regret you were not with us yesterday,' said Mr Henry Gowan, calling on Clennam the next morning. 'We had an agreeable day up the river there.'

So he had heard, Arthur said.

'From your partner?' returned Henry Gowan. 'What a dear old fellow he is!'

'I have a great regard for him.'

'By Jove, he is the finest creature!' said Gowan. 'So fresh, so green, trusts in such wonderful things!'

Here was one of the many little rough points that had a tendency to grate on Clennam's hearing. He put it aside by merely repeating that he had a high regard for Mr Doyce.

'He is charming! To see him mooning along to that time of life, laying down nothing by the way and picking up nothing by the way, is delightful. It warms a man. So unspoilt, so simple, such a good soul! Upon my life Mr Clennam, one feels desperately worldly and wicked in comparison with such an innocent creature. I speak for myself, let me add, without including you. You are genuine also.'

'Thank you for the compliment,' said Clennam, ill at ease; 'you are too, I hope?'

'So so,' rejoined the other. 'To be candid with you, tolerably. I am not a great impostor. Buy one of my pictures, and I assure you, in confidence, it will not be worth the money. Buy one of another man's—any great professor who beats me hollow—and the chances are that the more you give him, the more he'll impose upon you. They all do it.'

'All painters?'

'Painters, writers, patriots, all the rest who have stands in the market. Give almost any man I know ten pounds, and he will impose upon you to a corresponding extent; a thousand pounds—to a corresponding extent; ten thousand pounds—to a corresponding extent. So great the success, so great the imposition. But what a capital world it is!' cried Gowan with warm enthusiasm. 'What a jolly, excellent, lovable world it is!'

'I had rather thought,' said Clennam, 'that the principle you mention was chiefly acted on by—'

'By the Barnacles?' interrupted Gowan, laughing.

'By the political gentlemen who condescend to keep the Circumlocution Office.'

'Ah! Don't be hard upon the Barnacles,' said Gowan, laughing afresh, 'they are darling fellows! Even poor little Clarence, the born idiot of the family, is the most agreeable and most endearing blockhead! And by Jupiter, with a kind of cleverness in him too that would astonish you!'

'It would. Very much,' said Clennam, drily.

'And after all,' cried Gowan, with that characteristic balancing of his which reduced everything in the wide world to the same light weight, 'though I can't deny that the Circumlocution Office may ultimately shipwreck everybody and everything, still, that will probably not be in our time—and it's a school for gentlemen.'

'It's a very dangerous, unsatisfactory, and expensive school to the people who pay to keep the pupils there, I am afraid,' said Clennam, shaking his head.

'Ah! You are a terrible fellow,' returned Gowan, airily. 'I can understand how you have frightened that little donkey, Clarence, the most estimable of moon-calves (I really love him) nearly out of his wits. But enough of him, and of all the rest of them. I want to present you to my mother, Mr Clennam. Pray do me the favour to give me the opportunity.'

In nobody's state of mind, there was nothing Clennam would have desired less, or would have been more at a loss how to avoid.

'My mother lives in a most primitive manner down in that dreary red-brick dungeon at Hampton Court,' said Gowan. 'If you would make your own appointment, suggest your own day for permitting me to take you there to dinner, you would be bored and she would be charmed. Really that's the state of the case.'

What could Clennam say after this? His retiring character included a great deal that was simple in the best sense, because unpractised and unused; and in his simplicity and modesty, he could only say that he was happy to place himself at Mr Gowan's disposal. Accordingly he said it, and the day was fixed. And a dreaded day it was on his part, and a very unwelcome day when it came and they went down to Hampton Court together.

The venerable inhabitants of that venerable pile seemed, in those times, to be encamped there like a sort of civilised gipsies. There was a temporary air about their establishments, as if they were going away the moment they could get anything better; there was also a dissatisfied air about themselves, as if they took it very ill that they had not already got something much better. Genteel blinds and makeshifts were more or less observable as soon as their doors were opened; screens not half high enough, which made dining-rooms out of arched passages, and warded off obscure corners where footboys slept at nights with their heads among the knives and forks; curtains which called upon you to believe that they didn't hide anything; panes of glass which requested you not to see them; many objects of various forms, feigning to have no connection with their guilty secret, a bed; disguised traps in walls, which were clearly coal-cellars; affectations of no thoroughfares, which were evidently doors to little kitchens. Mental reservations and artful mysteries grew out of these things. Callers looking steadily into the eyes of their receivers, pretended not to smell cooking three feet off; people, confronting closets accidentally left open, pretended not to see bottles; visitors with their heads against a partition of thin canvas, and a page and a young female at high words on the other side, made believe to be sitting in a primeval silence. There was no end to the small social accommodation-bills of this nature which the gipsies of gentility were constantly drawing upon, and accepting for, one another.

Some of these Bohemians were of an irritable temperament, as constantly soured and vexed by two mental trials: the first, the consciousness that they had never got enough out of the public; the second, the consciousness that the public were admitted into the building. Under the latter great wrong, a few suffered dreadfully—particularly on Sundays, when they had for some time expected the earth to open and swallow the public up; but which desirable event had not yet occurred, in consequence of some reprehensible laxity in the arrangements of the Universe.

Mrs Gowan's door was attended by a family servant of several years' standing, who had his own crow to pluck with the public concerning a situation in the Post-Office which he had been for some time expecting, and to which he was not yet appointed. He perfectly knew that the public could never have got him in, but he grimly gratified himself with the idea that the public kept him out. Under the influence of this injury (and perhaps of some little straitness and irregularity in the matter of wages), he had grown neglectful of his person and morose in mind; and now beholding in Clennam one of the degraded body of his oppressors, received him with ignominy.

Mrs Gowan, however, received him with condescension. He found her a courtly old lady, formerly a Beauty, and still sufficiently well-favoured to have dispensed with the powder on her nose and a certain impossible bloom under each eye. She was a little lofty with him; so was another old lady, dark-browed and high-nosed, and who must have had something real about her or she could not have existed, but it was certainly not her hair or her teeth or her figure or her complexion; so was a grey old gentleman of dignified and sullen appearance; both of whom had come to dinner. But, as they had all been in the British Embassy way in sundry parts of the earth, and as a British Embassy cannot better establish a character with the Circumlocution Office than by treating its compatriots with illimitable contempt (else it would become like the Embassies of other countries), Clennam felt that on the whole they let him off lightly.

The dignified old gentleman turned out to be Lord Lancaster Stiltstalking, who had been maintained by the Circumlocution Office for many years as a representative of the Britannic Majesty abroad. This noble Refrigerator had iced several European courts in his time, and had done it with such complete success that the very name of Englishman yet struck cold to the stomachs of foreigners who had the distinguished honour of remembering him at a distance of a quarter of a century.

He was now in retirement, and hence (in a ponderous white cravat, like a stiff snow-drift) was so obliging as to shade the dinner. There was a whisper of the pervading Bohemian character in the nomadic nature of the service and its curious races of plates and dishes; but the noble Refrigerator, infinitely better than plate or porcelain, made it superb. He shaded the dinner, cooled the wines, chilled the gravy, and blighted the vegetables.

230

There was only one other person in the room: a microscopically small footboy, who waited on the malevolent man who hadn't got into the Post-Office. Even this youth, if his jacket could have been unbuttoned and his heart laid bare, would have been seen, as a distant adherent of the Barnacle family, already to aspire to a situation under Government.

Mrs Gowan with a gentle melancholy upon her, occasioned by her son's being reduced to court the swinish public as a follower of the low Arts, instead of asserting his birthright and putting a ring through its nose as an acknowledged Barnacle, headed the conversation at dinner on the evil days. It was then that Clennam learned for the first time what little pivots this great world goes round upon.

'If John Barnacle,' said Mrs Gowan, after the degeneracy of the times had been fully ascertained, 'if John Barnacle had but abandoned his most unfortunate idea of conciliating the mob, all would have been well, and I think the country would have been preserved.'

The old lady with the high nose assented; but added that if Augustus Stiltstalking had in a general way ordered the cavalry out with instructions to charge, she thought the country would have been preserved.

The noble Refrigerator assented; but added that if William Barnacle and Tudor Stiltstalking, when they came over to one another and formed their ever-memorable coalition, had boldly muzzled the newspapers, and rendered it penal for any Editor-person to presume to discuss the conduct of any appointed authority abroad or at home, he thought the country would have been preserved.

It was agreed that the country (another word for the Barnacles and Stiltstalkings) wanted preserving, but how it came to want preserving was not so clear. It was only clear that the question was all about John Barnacle, Augustus Stiltstalking, William Barnacle and Tudor Stiltstalking, Tom, Dick, or Harry Barnacle or Stiltstalking, because there was nobody else but mob. And this was the feature of the conversation which impressed Clennam, as a man not used to it, very disagreeably: making him doubt if it were quite right to sit there, silently hearing a great nation narrowed to such little bounds. Remembering, however, that in the Parliamentary debates, whether on the life of that nation's body or the life of its soul, the question was usually all about and between John Barnacle, Augustus Stiltstalking, William Barnacle and Tudor Stiltstalking, Tom, Dick, or Harry Barnacle or Stiltstalking, and nobody else; he said nothing on the part of mob, bethinking himself that mob was used to it.

Mr Henry Gowan seemed to have a malicious pleasure in playing off the three talkers against each other, and in seeing Clennam startled by what they said. Having as supreme a contempt for the class that had thrown him off as for the class that had not taken him on, he had no personal disquiet in anything that passed. His healthy state of mind appeared even to derive a gratification from Clennam's position of embarrassment and isolation among the good company; and if Clennam had been in that condition with which Nobody was incessantly contending, he would have suspected it, and would have struggled with the suspicion as a meanness, even while he sat at the table.

In the course of a couple of hours the noble Refrigerator, at no time less than a hundred years behind the period, got about five centuries in arrears, and delivered solemn political oracles appropriate to that epoch. He finished by freezing a cup of tea for his own drinking, and retiring at his lowest temperature.

Then Mrs Gowan, who had been accustomed in her days of a vacant arm-chair beside her to which to summon state to retain her devoted slaves, one by one, for short audiences as marks of her especial favour, invited Clennam with a turn of her fan to approach the presence. He obeyed, and took the tripod recently vacated by Lord Lancaster Stiltstalking.

'Mr Clennam,' said Mrs Gowan, 'apart from the happiness I have in becoming known to you, though in this odiously inconvenient place—a mere barrack—there is a subject on which I am dying to speak to you. It is the subject in connection with which my son first had, I believe, the pleasure of cultivating your acquaintance.'

Clennam inclined his head, as a generally suitable reply to what he did not yet quite understand.

'First,' said Mrs Gowan, 'now, is she really pretty?'

In nobody's difficulties, he would have found it very difficult to answer; very difficult indeed to smile, and say 'Who?'

'Oh! You know!' she returned. 'This flame of Henry's. This unfortunate fancy. There! If it is a point of honour that I should originate the name—Miss Mickles—Miggles.'

'Miss Meagles,' said Clennam, 'is very beautiful.'

'Men are so often mistaken on those points,' returned Mrs Gowan, shaking her head, 'that I candidly confess to you I feel anything but sure of it, even now; though it is something to have Henry corroborated with so much gravity and emphasis. He picked the people up at Rome, I think?'

The phrase would have given nobody mortal offence. Clennam replied, 'Excuse me, I doubt if I understand your expression.'

'Picked the people up,' said Mrs Gowan, tapping the sticks of her closed fan (a large green one, which she used as a hand-screen) on her little table. 'Came upon them. Found them out. Stumbled against them.'

'The people?'

'Yes. The Miggles people.'

'I really cannot say,' said Clennam, 'where my friend Mr Meagles first presented Mr Henry Gowan to his daughter.'

'I am pretty sure he picked her up at Rome; but never mind where—somewhere. Now (this is entirely between ourselves), is she very plebeian?'

'Really, ma'am,' returned Clennam, 'I am so undoubtedly plebeian myself, that I do not feel qualified to judge.'

'Very neat!' said Mrs Gowan, coolly unfurling her screen. 'Very happy! From which I infer that you secretly think her manner equal to her looks?'

Clennam, after a moment's stiffness, bowed.

'That's comforting, and I hope you may be right. Did Henry tell me you had travelled with them?'

'I travelled with my friend Mr Meagles, and his wife and daughter, during some months.' (Nobody's heart might have been wrung by the remembrance.)

'Really comforting, because you must have had a large experience of them. You see, Mr Clennam, this thing has been going on for a long time, and I find no improvement in it. Therefore to have the opportunity of speaking to one so well informed about it as yourself, is an immense relief to me. Quite a boon. Quite a blessing, I am sure.'

'Pardon me,' returned Clennam, 'but I am not in Mr Henry Gowan's confidence. I am far from being so well informed as you suppose me to be. Your mistake makes my position a very delicate one. No word on this topic has ever passed between Mr Henry Gowan and myself.'

Mrs Gowan glanced at the other end of the room, where her son was playing ecarte on a sofa, with the old lady who was for a charge of cavalry.

'Not in his confidence? No,' said Mrs Gowan. 'No word has passed between you? No. That I can imagine. But there are unexpressed confidences, Mr Clennam; and as you have been together intimately among these people, I cannot doubt that a confidence of that sort exists in the present case. Perhaps you have heard that I have suffered the keenest distress of mind from Henry's having taken to a pursuit which—well!' shrugging her shoulders, 'a very respectable pursuit, I dare say, and some artists are, as artists, quite superior persons; still, we never yet in our family have gone beyond an Amateur, and it is a pardonable weakness to feel a little—'

As Mrs Gowan broke off to heave a sigh, Clennam, however resolute to be magnanimous, could not keep down the thought that there was mighty little danger of the family's ever going beyond an Amateur, even as it was.

'Henry,' the mother resumed, 'is self-willed and resolute; and as these people naturally strain every nerve to catch him, I can entertain very little hope, Mr Clennam, that the thing will be broken off. I apprehend the girl's fortune will be very small; Henry might have done much better; there is scarcely anything to compensate for the connection: still, he acts for himself; and if I find no improvement within a short time, I see no other course than to resign myself and make the best of these people. I am infinitely obliged to you for what you have told me.'

As she shrugged her shoulders, Clennam stiffly bowed again. With an uneasy flush upon his face, and hesitation in his manner, he then said in a still lower tone than he had adopted yet:

'Mrs Gowan, I scarcely know how to acquit myself of what I feel to be a duty, and yet I must ask you for your kind consideration in attempting to discharge it. A misconception on your part, a very great misconception if I may venture to call it so, seems to require setting right. You have supposed Mr Meagles and his family to strain every nerve, I think you said—'

'Every nerve,' repeated Mrs Gowan, looking at him in calm obstinacy, with her green fan between her face and the fire.

'To secure Mr Henry Gowan?'

The lady placidly assented.

'Now that is so far,' said Arthur, 'from being the case, that I know Mr Meagles to be unhappy in this matter; and to have interposed all reasonable obstacles with the hope of putting an end to it.'

Mrs Gowan shut up her great green fan, tapped him on the arm with it, and tapped her smiling lips. 'Why, of course,' said she. 'Just what I mean.'

Arthur watched her face for some explanation of what she did mean.

'Are you really serious, Mr Clennam? Don't you see?'

Arthur did not see; and said so.

'Why, don't I know my son, and don't I know that this is exactly the way to hold him?' said Mrs Gowan, contemptuously; 'and do not these Miggles people know it, at least as well as I? Oh, shrewd people, Mr Clennam: evidently people of business! I believe Miggles belonged to a Bank. It ought to have been a very profitable Bank, if he had much to do with its management. This is very well done, indeed.'

'I beg and entreat you, ma'am—' Arthur interposed.

'Oh, Mr Clennam, can you really be so credulous?'

It made such a painful impression upon him to hear her talking in this haughty tone, and to see her patting her contemptuous lips with her fan, that he said very earnestly, 'Believe me, ma'am, this is unjust, a perfectly groundless suspicion.'

'Suspicion?' repeated Mrs Gowan. 'Not suspicion, Mr Clennam, Certainty. It is very knowingly done indeed, and seems to have taken you in completely.' She laughed; and again sat tapping her lips with her fan, and tossing her head, as if she added, 'Don't tell me. I know such people will do anything for the honour of such an alliance.'

At this opportune moment, the cards were thrown up, and Mr Henry Gowan came across the room saying, 'Mother, if you can spare Mr Clennam for this time, we have a long way to go, and it's getting late.' Mr Clennam thereupon rose, as he had no choice but to do; and Mrs Gowan showed him, to the last, the same look and the same tapped contemptuous lips.

'You have had a portentously long audience of my mother,' said Gowan, as the door closed upon them. 'I fervently hope she has not bored you?'

'Not at all,' said Clennam.

They had a little open phaeton for the journey, and were soon in it on the road home. Gowan, driving, lighted a cigar; Clennam declined one. Do what he would, he fell into such a mood of abstraction that Gowan said again, 'I am very much afraid my mother has bored you?' To which he roused himself to answer, 'Not at all!' and soon relapsed again.

In that state of mind which rendered nobody uneasy, his thoughtfulness would have turned principally on the man at his side. He would have thought of the morning when he first saw him rooting out the stones with his heel, and would have asked himself, 'Does he jerk me out of the path in the same careless, cruel way?' He would have thought, had this introduction to his mother been brought about by him because he knew what she would say, and that he could thus place his position before a rival and loftily warn him off, without himself reposing a word of confidence in him? He would have thought, even if there were no such design as that, had he brought him there to play with his repressed emotions, and torment him? The current of these meditations would have been stayed sometimes by a rush of shame, bearing a remonstrance to himself from his own open nature, representing that to shelter such suspicions, even for the passing moment, was not to hold the high, unenvious course he had

234

resolved to keep. At those times, the striving within him would have been hardest; and looking up and catching Gowan's eyes, he would have started as if he had done him an injury.

Then, looking at the dark road and its uncertain objects, he would have gradually trailed off again into thinking, 'Where are we driving, he and I, I wonder, on the darker road of life? How will it be with us, and with her, in the obscure distance?' Thinking of her, he would have been troubled anew with a reproachful misgiving that it was not even loyal to her to dislike him, and that in being so easily prejudiced against him he was less deserving of her than at first.

'You are evidently out of spirits,' said Gowan; 'I am very much afraid my mother must have bored you dreadfully.'

'Believe me, not at all,' said Clennam. 'It's nothing—nothing!'

CHAPTER 27. Five-and-Twenty

A frequently recurring doubt, whether Mr Pancks's desire to collect information relative to the Dorrit family could have any possible bearing on the misgivings he had imparted to his mother on his return from his long exile, caused Arthur Clennam much uneasiness at this period. What Mr Pancks already knew about the Dorrit family, what more he really wanted to find out, and why he should trouble his busy head about them at all, were questions that often perplexed him. Mr Pancks was not a man to waste his time and trouble in researches prompted by idle curiosity. That he had a specific object Clennam could not doubt. And whether the attainment of that object by Mr Pancks's industry might bring to light, in some untimely way, secret reasons which had induced his mother to take Little Dorrit by the hand, was a serious speculation.

Not that he ever wavered either in his desire or his determination to repair a wrong that had been done in his father's time, should a wrong come to light, and be reparable. The shadow of a supposed act of injustice, which had hung over him since his father's death, was so vague and formless that it might be the result of a reality widely remote from his idea of it. But, if his apprehensions should prove to be well founded, he was ready at any moment to lay down all he had, and begin the world anew. As the fierce dark teaching of his childhood had never sunk into his heart, so that first article in his code of morals was, that he must begin, in practical humility, with looking well to his feet on Earth, and that he could never mount on wings of words to Heaven. Duty on earth, restitution on earth, action on earth; these first, as the first steep steps upward. Strait was the gate and narrow was the way; far straiter and narrower than the broad high road paved with vain professions and vain repetitions, motes from other men's eyes and liberal delivery of others to the judgment—all cheap materials costing absolutely nothing.

No. It was not a selfish fear or hesitation that rendered him uneasy, but a mistrust lest Pancks might not observe his part of the understanding between them, and, making any discovery, might take some course upon it without imparting it to him. On the other hand, when he recalled his conversation with Pancks, and the little reason he had to suppose that there was any likelihood of that strange personage being on that track at all, there were times when he wondered that he made so much of it. Labouring in this sea, as all barks labour in cross seas, he tossed about and came to no haven.

The removal of Little Dorrit herself from their customary association, did not mend the matter. She was so much out, and so much in her own room, that he began to miss her and to find a blank in her place. He had written to her to inquire if she were better, and she had written back, very gratefully and earnestly telling him not to be uneasy on her behalf, for she was quite well; but he had not seen her, for what, in their intercourse, was a long time.

He returned home one evening from an interview with her father, who had mentioned that she was out visiting—which was what he always said when she was hard at work to buy his supper—and found Mr Meagles in an excited state walking up and down his room. On his opening the door, Mr Meagles stopped, faced round, and said:

'Clennam!—Tattycoram!'

'What's the matter?'

'Lost!'

'Why, bless my heart alive!' cried Clennam in amazement. 'What do you mean?'

'Wouldn't count five-and-twenty, sir; couldn't be got to do it; stopped at eight, and took herself off.'

'Left your house?'

'Never to come back,' said Mr Meagles, shaking his head. 'You don't know that girl's passionate and proud character. A team of horses couldn't draw her back now; the bolts and bars of the old Bastille couldn't keep her.'

'How did it happen? Pray sit down and tell me.'

'As to how it happened, it's not so easy to relate: because you must have the unfortunate temperament of the poor impetuous girl herself, before you can fully understand it. But it came about in this way. Pet and Mother and I have been having a good deal of talk together of late. I'll not disguise from you, Clennam, that those conversations have not been of as bright a kind as I could wish; they have referred to our going away again. In proposing to do which, I have had, in fact, an object.'

Nobody's heart beat quickly.

'An object,' said Mr Meagles, after a moment's pause, 'that I will not disguise from you, either, Clennam. There's an inclination on the part of my dear child which I am sorry for. Perhaps you guess the person. Henry Gowan.'

'I was not unprepared to hear it.'

'Well!' said Mr Meagles, with a heavy sigh, 'I wish to God you had never had to hear it. However, so it is. Mother and I have done all we could to get the better of it, Clennam. We have tried tender advice, we have tried time, we have tried absence. As yet, of no use. Our late conversations have been upon the subject of going away for another year at least, in order that there might be an entire separation and breaking off for that term. Upon that question, Pet has been unhappy, and therefore Mother and I have been unhappy.'

Clennam said that he could easily believe it.

'Well!' continued Mr Meagles in an apologetic way, 'I admit as a practical man, and I am sure Mother would admit as a practical woman, that we do, in families, magnify our troubles and make mountains of our molehills in a way that is calculated to be rather trying to people who look on—to mere outsiders, you know, Clennam. Still, Pet's happiness or unhappiness is quite a life or death question with us; and we may be excused, I hope, for making much of it. At all events, it might have been borne by Tattycoram. Now, don't you think so?'

'I do indeed think so,' returned Clennam, in most emphatic recognition of this very moderate expectation.

'No, sir,' said Mr Meagles, shaking his head ruefully. 'She couldn't stand it. The chafing and firing of that girl, the wearing and tearing of that girl within her own breast, has been such that I have softly said to her again and again in passing her, "Five-and-twenty, Tattycoram, five-and-twenty!" I heartily wish she could have gone on counting five-and-twenty day and night, and then it wouldn't have happened.'

Mr Meagles with a despondent countenance in which the goodness of his heart was even more expressed than in his times of cheerfulness and gaiety, stroked his face down from his forehead to his chin, and shook his head again.

'I said to Mother (not that it was necessary, for she would have thought it all for herself), we are practical people, my dear, and we know her story; we see in this unhappy girl some reflection of what was raging in her mother's heart before ever such a creature as this poor thing was in the world; we'll gloss her temper over, Mother, we won't notice it at present, my dear, we'll take advantage of some better disposition in her another time. So we said nothing. But, do what we would, it seems as if it was to be; she broke out violently one night.'

'How, and why?'

'If you ask me Why,' said Mr Meagles, a little disturbed by the question, for he was far more intent on softening her case than the family's, 'I can only refer you to what I have just repeated as having been pretty near my words to Mother. As to How, we had said Good night to Pet in her presence (very affectionately, I must allow), and she had attended Pet up-stairs—you remember she was her maid. Perhaps Pet, having been out of sorts, may have been a little more inconsiderate than usual in requiring services of her: but I don't know that I have any right to say so; she was always thoughtful and gentle.'

'The gentlest mistress in the world.'

'Thank you, Clennam,' said Mr Meagles, shaking him by the hand; 'you have often seen them together. Well! We presently heard this unfortunate Tattycoram loud and angry, and before we could ask what was the matter, Pet came back in a tremble, saying she was frightened of her. Close after her came Tattycoram in a flaming rage. "I hate you all three," says she, stamping her foot at us. "I am bursting with hate of the whole house."'

'Upon which you—?'

'I?' said Mr Meagles, with a plain good faith that might have commanded the belief of Mrs Gowan herself. 'I said, count five-and-twenty, Tattycoram.'

Mr Meagles again stroked his face and shook his head, with an air of profound regret.

'She was so used to do it, Clennam, that even then, such a picture of passion as you never saw, she stopped short, looked me full in the face, and counted (as I made out) to eight. But she couldn't control herself to go any further. There she broke down, poor thing, and gave the other seventeen to the four winds. Then it all burst out. She detested us, she was miserable with us, she couldn't bear it, she wouldn't bear it, she was determined to go away. She was younger than her young mistress, and would she remain to see her always held up as the only creature who was young and interesting, and to be cherished and loved? No. She wouldn't, she wouldn't, she wouldn't! What did we think she, Tattycoram, might have been if she had been caressed and cared for in her childhood, like her young mistress? As good as her? Ah! Perhaps fifty times as good. When we pretended to be so fond of one another, we exulted over her; that was what we did; we exulted over her and shamed her. And all in the house did the same. They talked about their fathers and mothers, and brothers and sisters; they liked to drag them up before her face. There was Mrs Tickit, only yesterday, when her little grandchild was with her, had been amused by the child's trying to call her (Tattycoram) by the wretched name we gave her; and had laughed at the name. Why, who didn't; and who were we that we should have a right to name her like a dog or a cat? But she didn't care. She would take no more benefits from us; she would fling us her name back again, and she would go. She would leave us that minute, nobody should stop her, and we should never hear of her again.'

Mr Meagles had recited all this with such a vivid remembrance of his original, that he was almost as flushed and hot by this time as he described her to have been.

'Ah, well!' he said, wiping his face. 'It was of no use trying reason then, with that vehement panting creature (Heaven knows what her mother's story must have been); so I quietly told her that she should not go at that late hour of night, and I gave her my hand and took her to her room, and locked the house doors. But she was gone this morning.'

'And you know no more of her?'

'No more,' returned Mr Meagles. 'I have been hunting about all day. She must have gone very early and very silently. I have found no trace of her down about us.'

'Stay! You want,' said Clennam, after a moment's reflection, 'to see her? I assume that?'

'Yes, assuredly; I want to give her another chance; Mother and Pet want to give her another chance; come! You yourself,' said Mr Meagles, persuasively, as if the provocation to be angry were not his own at all, 'want to give the poor passionate girl another chance, I know, Clennam.'

'It would be strange and hard indeed if I did not,' said Clennam, 'when you are all so forgiving. What I was going to ask you was, have you thought of that Miss Wade?'

'I have. I did not think of her until I had pervaded the whole of our neighbourhood, and I don't know that I should have done so then but for finding Mother and Pet, when I went home, full of the idea that Tattycoram must have gone to her. Then, of course, I recalled what she said that day at dinner when you were first with us.'

'Have you any idea where Miss Wade is to be found?'

'To tell you the truth,' returned Mr Meagles, 'it's because I have an addled jumble of a notion on that subject that you found me waiting here. There is one of those odd impressions in my house, which do mysteriously get into houses sometimes, which nobody seems to have picked up in a distinct form from anybody, and yet which everybody seems to have got hold of loosely from somebody and let go again, that she lives, or was living, thereabouts.' Mr Meagles handed him a slip of paper, on which was written the name of one of the dull by-streets in the Grosvenor region, near Park Lane.

'Here is no number,' said Arthur looking over it.

'No number, my dear Clennam?' returned his friend. 'No anything! The very name of the street may have been floating in the air; for, as I tell you, none of my people can say where they got it from. However, it's worth an inquiry; and as I would rather make it in company than alone, and as you too were a fellow-traveller of that immovable woman's, I thought perhaps—' Clennam finished the sentence for him by taking up his hat again, and saying he was ready.

It was now summer-time; a grey, hot, dusty evening. They rode to the top of Oxford Street, and there alighting, dived in among the great streets of melancholy stateliness, and the little streets that try to be as stately and succeed in being more melancholy, of which there is a labyrinth near Park Lane. Wildernesses of corner houses, with barbarous old porticoes and appurtenances; horrors that came into existence under some wrong-headed person in some wrong-headed time, still demanding the blind admiration of all ensuing generations and determined to do so until they tumbled down; frowned upon the twilight. Parasite little tenements, with the cramp in their whole frame, from the dwarf hall-door on the giant model of His Grace's in the Square to the squeezed window of the boudoir commanding the dunghills in the Mews, made the evening doleful. Rickety dwellings of undoubted fashion, but of a capacity to hold nothing comfortably except a dismal smell, looked like the last result of the great mansions' breeding in-and-in; and, where their little supplementary bows and balconies were supported on thin iron columns, seemed to be scrofulously resting upon crutches. Here and there a Hatchment, with the whole science of Heraldry in it, loomed down upon the street, like an Archbishop discoursing on Vanity. The shops, few in number, made no show; for popular opinion was as nothing to them. The pastrycook knew who was on his books, and in that knowledge could be calm, with a few glass cylinders of dowager peppermint-drops in his window, and half-a-dozen ancient specimens of currant-jelly. A few oranges formed the greengrocer's whole concession to the vulgar mind. A single basket made of moss, once containing plovers' eggs, held all that the poulterer had to say to the rabble. Everybody in those streets seemed (which is always the case at that hour and season) to be gone out to dinner, and nobody seemed to be giving the dinners they had gone to. On the doorsteps there were lounging footmen with bright parti-coloured plumage and white polls, like an extinct race of monstrous birds; and butlers, solitary men of recluse demeanour, each of whom appeared distrustful of all other butlers. The roll of carriages in the Park was done for the day; the street lamps were lighting; and wicked little grooms in the tightest fitting garments, with twists in their legs answering to the twists in their minds, hung about in pairs, chewing straws and exchanging fraudulent secrets. The spotted dogs who went out with the carriages, and who were so associated with splendid equipages that it looked like a condescension in those animals to come out without them, accompanied helpers to and fro on messages. Here and there was a retiring public-house which did not require to be supported on the shoulders of the people, and where gentlemen out of livery were not much wanted.

This last discovery was made by the two friends in pursuing their inquiries. Nothing was there, or anywhere, known of such a person as Miss Wade, in connection with the street they sought. It was one of the parasite streets; long, regular, narrow, dull and gloomy; like a brick and mortar funeral. They inquired at several little area gates, where a dejected youth stood spiking his chin on the summit of a precipitous little shoot of wooden steps, but could gain no information. They walked up the street on one side of the way, and down it on the other, what time two vociferous news-sellers, announcing an extraordinary event that had never happened and never would happen, pitched their hoarse voices into the secret chambers; but nothing came of it. At length they stood at the corner from which they had begun, and it had fallen quite dark, and they were no wiser.

It happened that in the street they had several times passed a dingy house, apparently empty, with bills in the windows, announcing that it was to let. The bills, as a variety in the funeral procession, almost amounted to a decoration. Perhaps because they kept the house separated in his mind, or perhaps because Mr Meagles and himself had twice agreed in passing, 'It is clear she don't live there,' Clennam now proposed that they should go back and try that house before finally going away. Mr Meagles agreed, and back they went.

They knocked once, and they rang once, without any response. 'Empty,' said Mr Meagles, listening. 'Once more,' said Clennam, and knocked again. After that knock they heard a movement below, and somebody shuffling up towards the door.

The confined entrance was so dark that it was impossible to make out distinctly what kind of person opened the door; but it appeared to be an old woman. 'Excuse our troubling you,' said Clennam. 'Pray can you tell us where Miss Wade lives?' The voice in the darkness unexpectedly replied, 'Lives here.'

'Is she at home?'

No answer coming, Mr Meagles asked again. 'Pray is she at home?'

After another delay, 'I suppose she is,' said the voice abruptly; 'you had better come in, and I'll ask.'

They were summarily shut into the close black house; and the figure rustling away, and speaking from a higher level, said, 'Come up, if you please; you can't tumble over anything.' They groped their way up-stairs towards a faint light, which proved to be the light of the street shining through a window; and the figure left them shut in an airless room.

'This is odd, Clennam,' said Mr Meagles, softly.

'Odd enough,' assented Clennam in the same tone, 'but we have succeeded; that's the main point. Here's a light coming!'

The light was a lamp, and the bearer was an old woman: very dirty, very wrinkled and dry. 'She's at home,' she said (and the voice was the same that had spoken before); 'she'll come directly.' Having set the lamp down on the table, the old woman dusted her hands on her apron, which she might have done for ever without cleaning them, looked at the visitors with a dim pair of eyes, and backed out.

The lady whom they had come to see, if she were the present occupant of the house, appeared to have taken up her quarters there as she might have established herself in an Eastern caravanserai. A small square of carpet in the middle of the room, a few articles of furniture that evidently did not belong to the room, and a disorder of trunks and travelling articles, formed the whole of her surroundings. Under some former regular inhabitant, the stifling little apartment had broken out into a pier-glass and a gilt table; but the gilding was as faded as last year's flowers, and the glass was so clouded that it seemed to hold in magic preservation all the fogs and bad weather it had ever reflected. The visitors had had a minute or two to look about them, when the door opened and Miss Wade came in.

She was exactly the same as when they had parted, just as handsome, just as scornful, just as repressed. She manifested no surprise in seeing them, nor any other emotion. She requested them to be seated; and declining to take a seat herself, at once anticipated any introduction of their business.

'I apprehend,' she said, 'that I know the cause of your favouring me with this visit. We may come to it at once.'

'The cause then, ma'am,' said Mr Meagles, 'is Tattycoram.'

'So I supposed.'

'Miss Wade,' said Mr Meagles, 'will you be so kind as to say whether you know anything of her?'

'Surely. I know she is here with me.'

'Then, ma'am,' said Mr Meagles, 'allow me to make known to you that I shall be happy to have her back, and that my wife and daughter will be happy to have her back. She has been with us a long time: we don't forget her claims upon us, and I hope we know how to make allowances.'

'You hope to know how to make allowances?' she returned, in a level, measured voice. 'For what?'

'I think my friend would say, Miss Wade,' Arthur Clennam interposed, seeing Mr Meagles rather at a loss, 'for the passionate sense that sometimes comes upon the poor girl, of being at a disadvantage. Which occasionally gets the better of better remembrances.'

The lady broke into a smile as she turned her eyes upon him. 'Indeed?' was all she answered.

She stood by the table so perfectly composed and still after this acknowledgment of his remark that Mr Meagles stared at her under a sort of fascination, and could not even look to Clennam to make another move. After waiting, awkwardly enough, for some moments, Arthur said:

'Perhaps it would be well if Mr Meagles could see her, Miss Wade?'

'That is easily done,' said she. 'Come here, child.' She had opened a door while saying this, and now led the girl in by the hand. It was very curious to see them standing together: the girl with her disengaged fingers plaiting the bosom of her dress, half irresolutely, half passionately; Miss Wade with her composed face attentively regarding her, and suggesting to an observer, with extraordinary force, in her composure itself (as a veil will suggest the form it covers), the unquenchable passion of her own nature.

'See here,' she said, in the same level way as before. 'Here is your patron, your master. He is willing to take you back, my dear, if you are sensible of the favour and choose to go. You can be, again, a foil to his pretty daughter, a slave to her pleasant wilfulness, and a toy in the house showing the goodness of the family. You can have your droll name again, playfully pointing you out and setting you apart, as it is right that you should be pointed out and set apart. (Your birth, you know; you must not forget your birth.) You can again be shown to this gentleman's daughter, Harriet, and kept before her, as a living reminder of her own superiority and her gracious condescension. You can recover all these advantages and many more of the same kind which I dare say start up in your memory while I speak, and which you lose in taking refuge with me—you can recover them all by telling these gentlemen how humbled and penitent you are, and by going back to them to be forgiven. What do you say, Harriet? Will you go?'

The girl who, under the influence of these words, had gradually risen in anger and heightened in colour, answered, raising her lustrous black eyes for the moment, and clenching her hand upon the folds it had been puckering up, 'I'd die sooner!'

Miss Wade, still standing at her side holding her hand, looked quietly round and said with a smile, 'Gentlemen! What do you do upon that?'

Poor Mr Meagles's inexpressible consternation in hearing his motives and actions so perverted, had prevented him from interposing any word until now; but now he regained the power of speech.

'Tattycoram,' said he, 'for I'll call you by that name still, my good girl, conscious that I meant nothing but kindness when I gave it to you, and conscious that you know it—'

'I don't!' said she, looking up again, and almost rending herself with the same busy hand.

'No, not now, perhaps,' said Mr Meagles; 'not with that lady's eyes so intent upon you, Tattycoram,' she glanced at them for a moment, 'and that power over you, which we see she exercises; not now, perhaps, but at another time. Tattycoram, I'll not ask that lady whether she believes what she has said, even in the anger and ill blood in which I and my friend here equally know she has spoken, though she subdues herself, with a determination that any one who has once seen her is not likely to forget. I'll not ask you, with your remembrance of my house and all belonging to it, whether you believe it. I'll only say that you have no profession to make to me or mine, and no forgiveness to entreat; and that all in the world that I ask you to do, is, to count five-and-twenty, Tattycoram.'

She looked at him for an instant, and then said frowningly, 'I won't. Miss Wade, take me away, please.'

The contention that raged within her had no softening in it now; it was wholly between passionate defiance and stubborn defiance. Her rich colour, her quick blood, her rapid breath, were all setting themselves against the opportunity of retracing their steps. 'I won't. I won't. I won't!' she repeated in a low, thick voice. 'I'd be torn to pieces first. I'd tear myself to pieces first!'

Miss Wade, who had released her hold, laid her hand protectingly on the girl's neck for a moment, and then said, looking round with her former smile and speaking exactly in her former tone, 'Gentlemen! What do you do upon that?'

'Oh, Tattycoram, Tattycoram!' cried Mr Meagles, adjuring her besides with an earnest hand. 'Hear that lady's voice, look at that lady's face, consider what is in that lady's heart, and think what a future lies before you. My child, whatever you may think, that lady's influence over you—astonishing to us, and I should hardly go too far in saying terrible to us to see—is founded in passion fiercer than yours, and temper more violent than yours. What can you two be together? What can come of it?'

'I am alone here, gentlemen,' observed Miss Wade, with no change of voice or manner. 'Say anything you will.'

'Politeness must yield to this misguided girl, ma'am,' said Mr Meagles, 'at her present pass; though I hope not altogether to dismiss it, even with the injury you do her so strongly before me. Excuse me for reminding you in her hearing—I must say it—that you were a mystery to all of us, and had nothing in common with any of us when she unfortunately fell in your way. I don't know what you are, but you don't hide, can't hide, what a dark spirit you have within you. If it should happen that you are a woman, who, from whatever cause, has a perverted delight in making a sister-woman as wretched as she is (I am old enough to have heard of such), I warn her against you, and I warn you against yourself.'

'Gentlemen!' said Miss Wade, calmly. 'When you have concluded—Mr Clennam, perhaps you will induce your friend—'

'Not without another effort,' said Mr Meagles, stoutly. 'Tattycoram, my poor dear girl, count five-and-twenty.'

'Do not reject the hope, the certainty, this kind man offers you,' said Clennam in a low emphatic voice. 'Turn to the friends you have not forgotten. Think once more!'

'I won't! Miss Wade,' said the girl, with her bosom swelling high, and speaking with her hand held to her throat, 'take me away!'

'Tattycoram,' said Mr Meagles. 'Once more yet! The only thing I ask of you in the world, my child! Count five-and-twenty!'

She put her hands tightly over her ears, confusedly tumbling down her bright black hair in the vehemence of the action, and turned her face resolutely to the wall. Miss Wade, who had watched her under this final appeal with that strange attentive smile, and that repressing hand upon her own bosom with which she had watched her in her struggle at Marseilles, then put her arm about her waist as if she took possession of her for evermore.

And there was a visible triumph in her face when she turned it to dismiss the visitors.

'As it is the last time I shall have the honour,' she said, 'and as you have spoken of not knowing what I am, and also of the foundation of my influence here, you may now know that it is founded in a common cause. What your broken plaything is as to birth, I am. She has no name, I have no name. Her wrong is my wrong. I have nothing more to say to you.'

This was addressed to Mr Meagles, who sorrowfully went out. As Clennam followed, she said to him, with the same external composure and in the same level voice, but with a smile that is only seen on cruel faces: a very faint smile, lifting the nostril, scarcely touching the lips, and not breaking away gradually, but instantly dismissed when done with:

'I hope the wife of your dear friend Mr Gowan, may be happy in the contrast of her extraction to this girl's and mine, and in the high good fortune that awaits her.'

CHAPTER 28. Nobody's Disappearance

Not resting satisfied with the endeavours he had made to recover his lost charge, Mr Meagles addressed a letter of remonstrance, breathing nothing but goodwill, not only to her, but to Miss Wade too. No answer coming to these epistles, or to another written to the stubborn girl by the hand of her late young mistress, which might have melted her if anything could (all three letters were returned weeks afterwards as having been refused at the house-door), he deputed Mrs Meagles to make the experiment of a personal interview. That worthy lady being unable to obtain one, and being steadfastly denied admission, Mr Meagles besought

Arthur to essay once more what he could do. All that came of his compliance was, his discovery that the empty house was left in charge of the old woman, that Miss Wade was gone, that the waifs and strays of furniture were gone, and that the old woman would accept any number of half-crowns and thank the donor kindly, but had no information whatever to exchange for those coins, beyond constantly offering for perusal a memorandum relative to fixtures, which the house-agent's young man had left in the hall.

Unwilling, even under this discomfiture, to resign the ingrate and leave her hopeless, in case of her better dispositions obtaining the mastery over the darker side of her character, Mr Meagles, for six successive days, published a discreetly covert advertisement in the morning papers, to the effect that if a certain young person who had lately left home without reflection, would at any time apply to his address at Twickenham, everything would be as it had been before, and no reproaches need be apprehended. The unexpected consequences of this notification suggested to the dismayed Mr Meagles for the first time that some hundreds of young persons must be leaving their homes without reflection every day; for shoals of wrong young people came down to Twickenham, who, not finding themselves received with enthusiasm, generally demanded compensation by way of damages, in addition to coach-hire there and back. Nor were these the only uninvited clients whom the advertisement produced. The swarm of begging-letter writers, who would seem to be always watching eagerly for any hook, however small, to hang a letter upon, wrote to say that having seen the advertisement, they were induced to apply with confidence for various sums, ranging from ten shillings to fifty pounds: not because they knew anything about the young person, but because they felt that to part with those donations would greatly relieve the advertiser's mind. Several projectors, likewise, availed themselves of the same opportunity to correspond with Mr Meagles; as, for example, to apprise him that their attention having been called to the advertisement by a friend, they begged to state that if they should ever hear anything of the young person, they would not fail to make it known to him immediately, and that in the meantime if he would oblige them with the funds necessary for bringing to perfection a certain entirely novel description of Pump, the happiest results would ensue to mankind.

Mr Meagles and his family, under these combined discouragements, had begun reluctantly to give up Tattycoram as irrecoverable, when the new and active firm of Doyce and Clennam, in their private capacities, went down on a Saturday to stay at the cottage until Monday. The senior partner took the coach, and the junior partner took his walking-stick.

A tranquil summer sunset shone upon him as he approached the end of his walk, and passed through the meadows by the river side. He had that sense of peace, and of being lightened of a weight of care, which country quiet awakens in the breasts of dwellers in towns. Everything within his view was lovely and placid. The rich foliage of the trees, the luxuriant grass diversified with wild flowers, the little green islands in the river, the beds of rushes, the water-lilies floating on the surface of the stream, the distant voices in boats borne musically towards him on the ripple of the water and the evening air, were all expressive of rest. In the occasional leap of a fish, or dip of an oar, or twittering of a bird not yet at roost, or distant barking of a dog, or lowing of a cow—in all such sounds, there was the prevailing breath of rest, which seemed to encompass him in every scent that sweetened the fragrant air. The long lines of red and gold in the sky, and the glorious track of the descending sun, were all divinely calm. Upon the purple tree-tops far away, and on the green height near at hand up which the shades were slowly creeping, there was an equal hush. Between the real landscape and its shadow in the water, there was no division; both were so untroubled and clear, and, while so fraught with solemn mystery of life and death, so hopefully reassuring to the gazer's soothed heart, because so tenderly and mercifully beautiful.

Clennam had stopped, not for the first time by many times, to look about him and suffer what he saw to sink into his soul, as the shadows, looked at, seemed to sink deeper and deeper into the water. He was slowly resuming his way, when he saw a figure in the path before him which he had, perhaps, already associated with the evening and its impressions.

Minnie was there, alone. She had some roses in her hand, and seemed to have stood still on seeing him, waiting for him. Her face was towards him, and she appeared to have been coming from the opposite direction. There was a flutter in her manner, which Clennam had never seen in it before; and as he came near her, it entered his mind all at once that she was there of a set purpose to speak to him.

She gave him her hand, and said, 'You wonder to see me here by myself? But the evening is so lovely, I have strolled further than I meant at first. I thought it likely I might meet you, and that made me more confident. You always come this way, do you not?'

As Clennam said that it was his favourite way, he felt her hand falter on his arm, and saw the roses shake.

'Will you let me give you one, Mr Clennam? I gathered them as I came out of the garden. Indeed, I almost gathered them for you, thinking it so likely I might meet you. Mr Doyce arrived more than an hour ago, and told us you were walking down.'

His own hand shook, as he accepted a rose or two from hers and thanked her. They were now by an avenue of trees. Whether they turned into it on his movement or on hers matters little. He never knew how that was.

'It is very grave here,' said Clennam, 'but very pleasant at this hour. Passing along this deep shade, and out at that arch of light at the other end, we come upon the ferry and the cottage by the best approach, I think.'

In her simple garden-hat and her light summer dress, with her rich brown hair naturally clustering about her, and her wonderful eyes raised to his for a moment with a look in which regard for him and trustfulness in him were strikingly blended with a kind of timid sorrow for him, she was so beautiful that it was well for his peace—or ill for his peace, he did not quite know which—that he had made that vigorous resolution he had so often thought about.

She broke a momentary silence by inquiring if he knew that papa had been thinking of another tour abroad? He said he had heard it mentioned. She broke another momentary silence by adding, with some hesitation, that papa had abandoned the idea.

At this, he thought directly, 'they are to be married.'

'Mr Clennam,' she said, hesitating more timidly yet, and speaking so low that he bent his head to hear her. 'I should very much like to give you my confidence, if you would not mind having the goodness to receive it. I should have very much liked to have given it to you long ago, because—I felt that you were becoming so much our friend.'

'How can I be otherwise than proud of it at any time! Pray give it to me. Pray trust me.'

'I could never have been afraid of trusting you,' she returned, raising her eyes frankly to his face. 'I think I would have done so some time ago, if I had known how. But I scarcely know how, even now.'

'Mr Gowan,' said Arthur Clennam, 'has reason to be very happy. God bless his wife and him!'

She wept, as she tried to thank him. He reassured her, took her hand as it lay with the trembling roses in it on his arm, took the remaining roses from it, and put it to his lips. At that time, it seemed to him, he first finally resigned the dying hope that had flickered in nobody's heart so much to its pain and trouble; and from that time he became in his own eyes, as to any similar hope or prospect, a very much older man who had done with that part of life.

He put the roses in his breast and they walked on for a little while, slowly and silently, under the umbrageous trees. Then he asked her, in a voice of cheerful kindness, was there anything else that she would say to him as her friend and her father's friend, many years older than herself; was there any trust she would repose in him, any service she would ask of him, any little aid to her happiness that she could give him the lasting gratification of believing it was in his power to render?

She was going to answer, when she was so touched by some little hidden sorrow or sympathy—what could it have been?—that she said, bursting into tears again: 'O Mr Clennam! Good, generous, Mr Clennam, pray tell me you do not blame me.'

'I blame you?' said Clennam. 'My dearest girl! I blame you? No!'

After clasping both her hands upon his arm, and looking confidentially up into his face, with some hurried words to the effect that she thanked him from her heart (as she did, if it be the source of earnestness), she gradually composed herself, with now and then a word of encouragement from him, as they walked on slowly and almost silently under the darkening trees.

'And, now, Minnie Gowan,' at length said Clennam, smiling; 'will you ask me nothing?'

'Oh! I have very much to ask of you.'

'That's well! I hope so; I am not disappointed.'

'You know how I am loved at home, and how I love home. You can hardly think it perhaps, dear Mr Clennam,' she spoke with great agitation, 'seeing me going from it of my own free will and choice, but I do so dearly love it!'

'I am sure of that,' said Clennam. 'Can you suppose I doubt it?'

'No, no. But it is strange, even to me, that loving it so much and being so much beloved in it, I can bear to cast it away. It seems so neglectful of it, so unthankful.'

'My dear girl,' said Clennam, 'it is in the natural progress and change of time. All homes are left so.'

'Yes, I know; but all homes are not left with such a blank in them as there will be in mine when I am gone. Not that there is any scarcity of far better and more endearing and more accomplished girls than I am; not that I am much, but that they have made so much of me!'

Pet's affectionate heart was overcharged, and she sobbed while she pictured what would happen.

'I know what a change papa will feel at first, and I know that at first I cannot be to him anything like what I have been these many years. And it is then, Mr Clennam, then more than at any time, that I beg and entreat you to remember him, and sometimes to keep him company when you can spare a little while; and to tell him that you know I was fonder of him when I left him, than I ever was in all my life. For there is nobody—he told me so himself when he talked to me this very day—there is nobody he likes so well as you, or trusts so much.'

A clue to what had passed between the father and daughter dropped like a heavy stone into the well of Clennam's heart, and swelled the water to his eyes. He said, cheerily, but not quite so cheerily as he tried to say, that it should be done—that he gave her his faithful promise.

'If I do not speak of mama,' said Pet, more moved by, and more pretty in, her innocent grief, than Clennam could trust himself even to consider—for which reason he counted the trees between them and the fading light as they slowly diminished in number—'it is because mama will understand me better in this action, and will feel my loss in a different way, and will look forward in a different manner. But you know what a dear, devoted mother she is, and you will remember her too; will you not?'

Let Minnie trust him, Clennam said, let Minnie trust him to do all she wished.

'And, dear Mr Clennam,' said Minnie, 'because papa and one whom I need not name, do not fully appreciate and understand one another yet, as they will by-and-by; and because it will be the duty, and the pride, and pleasure of my new life, to draw them to a better knowledge of one another, and to be a happiness to one another, and to be proud of one another, and to love one another, both loving me so dearly; oh, as you are a kind, true man! when I am first separated from home (I am going a long distance away), try to reconcile papa to him a little more, and use your great influence to keep him before papa's mind free from prejudice and in his real form. Will you do this for me, as you are a noble-hearted friend?'

Poor Pet! Self-deceived, mistaken child! When were such changes ever made in men's natural relations to one another: when was such reconcilement of ingrain differences ever effected! It has been tried many times by other daughters, Minnie; it has never succeeded; nothing has ever come of it but failure.

So Clennam thought. So he did not say; it was too late. He bound himself to do all she asked, and she knew full well that he would do it.

They were now at the last tree in the avenue. She stopped, and withdrew her arm. Speaking to him with her eyes lifted up to his, and with the hand that had lately rested on his sleeve trembling by touching one of the roses in his breast as an additional appeal to him, she said:

'Dear Mr Clennam, in my happiness—for I am happy, though you have seen me crying—I cannot bear to leave any cloud between us. If you have anything to forgive me (not anything that I have wilfully done, but any trouble I may have caused you without meaning it, or having it in my power to help it), forgive me to-night out of your noble heart!'

He stooped to meet the guileless face that met his without shrinking. He kissed it, and answered, Heaven knew that he had nothing to forgive. As he stooped to meet the innocent face once again, she whispered, 'Good-bye!' and he repeated it. It was taking leave of all his old hopes—all nobody's old restless doubts. They came out of the avenue next moment, arm-in-arm as they had entered it: and the trees seemed to close up behind them in the darkness, like their own perspective of the past.

The voices of Mr and Mrs Meagles and Doyce were audible directly, speaking near the garden gate. Hearing Pet's name among them, Clennam called out, 'She is here, with me.' There was some little wondering and laughing until they came up; but as soon as they had all come together, it ceased, and Pet glided away.

Mr Meagles, Doyce, and Clennam, without speaking, walked up and down on the brink of the river, in the light of the rising moon, for a few minutes; and then Doyce lingered behind, and went into the house. Mr Meagles and Clennam walked up and down together for a few minutes more without speaking, until at length the former broke silence.

'Arthur,' said he, using that familiar address for the first time in their communication, 'do you remember my telling you, as we walked up and down one hot morning, looking over the harbour at Marseilles, that Pet's baby sister who was dead seemed to Mother and me to have grown as she had grown, and changed as she had changed?'

'Very well.'

'You remember my saying that our thoughts had never been able to separate those twin sisters, and that, in our fancy, whatever Pet was, the other was?'

'Yes, very well.'

'Arthur,' said Mr Meagles, much subdued, 'I carry that fancy further to-night. I feel to-night, my dear fellow, as if you had loved my dead child very tenderly, and had lost her when she was like what Pet is now.'

'Thank you!' murmured Clennam, 'thank you!' And pressed his hand.

'Will you come in?' said Mr Meagles, presently.

'In a little while.'

Mr Meagles fell away, and he was left alone. When he had walked on the river's brink in the peaceful moonlight for some half an hour, he put his hand in his breast and tenderly took out the handful of roses. Perhaps he put them to his heart, perhaps he put them to his lips, but certainly he bent down on the shore and gently launched them on the flowing river. Pale and unreal in the moonlight, the river floated them away.

The lights were bright within doors when he entered, and the faces on which they shone, his own face not excepted, were soon quietly cheerful. They talked of many subjects (his partner never had had such a ready store to draw upon for the beguiling of the time), and so to bed, and to sleep. While the flowers, pale and unreal in the moonlight, floated away upon the river; and thus do greater things that once were in our breasts, and near our hearts, flow from us to the eternal seas.

CHAPTER 29. Mrs Flintwinch goes on Dreaming

The house in the city preserved its heavy dulness through all these transactions, and the invalid within it turned the same unvarying round of life. Morning, noon, and night, morning, noon, and night, each recurring with its accompanying monotony, always the same reluctant return of the same sequences of machinery, like a dragging piece of clockwork.

The wheeled chair had its associated remembrances and reveries, one may suppose, as every place that is made the station of a human being has. Pictures of demolished streets and altered houses, as they formerly were when the occupant of the chair was familiar with them, images of people as they too used to be, with little or no allowance made for the lapse of time since they were seen; of these, there must have been many in the long routine of gloomy days. To stop the clock of busy existence at the hour when we were personally sequestered from it, to suppose mankind stricken motionless when we were brought to a stand-still, to be unable to measure the changes beyond our view by any larger standard than the shrunken one of our own uniform and contracted existence, is the infirmity of many invalids, and the mental unhealthiness of almost all recluses.

What scenes and actors the stern woman most reviewed, as she sat from season to season in her one dark room, none knew but herself. Mr Flintwinch, with his wry presence brought to bear upon her daily like some eccentric mechanical force, would perhaps have screwed it out of her, if there had been less resistance in her; but she was too strong for him. So far as Mistress Affery was concerned, to regard her liege-lord and her disabled mistress with a face of blank wonder, to go about the house after dark with her apron over her head, always to listen for the strange noises and sometimes to hear them, and never to emerge from her ghostly, dreamy, sleep-waking state, was occupation enough for her.

There was a fair stroke of business doing, as Mistress Affery made out, for her husband had abundant occupation in his little office, and saw more people than had been used to come there for some years. This might easily be, the house having been long deserted; but he did receive letters, and comers, and keep books, and correspond. Moreover, he went about to other counting-houses, and to wharves, and docks, and to the Custom House, and to Garraway's Coffee House, and the Jerusalem Coffee House, and on 'Change; so that he was much in and out. He began, too, sometimes of an evening, when Mrs Clennam expressed no particular wish for his society, to resort to a tavern in the neighbourhood to look at the shipping news and closing prices in the evening paper, and even to exchange small socialities with mercantile Sea Captains who frequented that establishment. At some period of every day, he and Mrs Clennam held a council on matters of business; and it appeared to Affery, who was always groping about, listening and watching, that the two clever ones were making money.

The state of mind into which Mr Flintwinch's dazed lady had fallen, had now begun to be so expressed in all her looks and actions that she was held in very low account by the two clever ones, as a person, never of strong intellect, who was becoming foolish. Perhaps because her appearance was not of a commercial cast, or perhaps because it occurred to him that his having taken her to wife might expose his judgment to doubt in the minds of customers, Mr Flintwinch laid his commands upon her that she should hold her peace on the subject of her conjugal relations, and should no longer call him Jeremiah out of the domestic trio. Her frequent forgetfulness of this admonition intensified her startled manner, since Mr Flintwinch's habit of avenging himself on her remissness by making springs after her on the staircase, and shaking her, occasioned her to be always nervously uncertain when she might be thus waylaid next.

Little Dorrit had finished a long day's work in Mrs Clennam's room, and was neatly gathering up her shreds and odds and ends before going home. Mr Pancks, whom Affery had just shown in, was addressing an inquiry to Mrs Clennam on the subject of her health, coupled with the remark that, 'happening to find himself in that direction,' he had looked in to inquire, on behalf of his proprietor, how she found herself. Mrs Clennam, with a deep contraction of her brows, was looking at him.

'Mr Casby knows,' said she, 'that I am not subject to changes. The change that I await here is the great change.'

'Indeed, ma'am?' returned Mr Pancks, with a wandering eye towards the figure of the little seamstress on her knee picking threads and fraying of her work from the carpet. 'You look nicely, ma'am.'

'I bear what I have to bear,' she answered. 'Do you what you have to do.'

'Thank you, ma'am,' said Mr Pancks, 'such is my endeavour.'

'You are often in this direction, are you not?' asked Mrs Clennam.

'Why, yes, ma'am,' said Pancks, 'rather so lately; I have lately been round this way a good deal, owing to one thing and another.'

'Beg Mr Casby and his daughter not to trouble themselves, by deputy, about me. When they wish to see me, they know I am here to see them. They have no need to trouble themselves to send. You have no need to trouble yourself to come.'

'Not the least trouble, ma'am,' said Mr Pancks. 'You really are looking uncommonly nicely, ma'am.'

'Thank you. Good evening.'

The dismissal, and its accompanying finger pointed straight at the door, was so curt and direct that Mr Pancks did not see his way to prolong his visit. He stirred up his hair with his sprightliest expression, glanced at the little figure again, said 'Good evening, ma 'am; don't come down, Mrs Affery, I know the road to the door,' and steamed out. Mrs Clennam, her chin resting on her hand, followed him with attentive and darkly distrustful eyes; and Affery stood looking at her as if she were spell-bound.

Slowly and thoughtfully, Mrs Clennam's eyes turned from the door by which Pancks had gone out, to Little Dorrit, rising from the carpet. With her chin drooping more heavily on her hand, and her eyes vigilant and lowering, the sick woman sat looking at her until she attracted her attention. Little Dorrit coloured under such a gaze, and looked down. Mrs Clennam still sat intent.

'Little Dorrit,' she said, when she at last broke silence, 'what do you know of that man?'

'I don't know anything of him, ma'am, except that I have seen him about, and that he has spoken to me.'

'What has he said to you?'

'I don't understand what he has said, he is so strange. But nothing rough or disagreeable.'

'Why does he come here to see you?'

'I don't know, ma'am,' said Little Dorrit, with perfect frankness.

'You know that he does come here to see you?'

'I have fancied so,' said Little Dorrit. 'But why he should come here or anywhere for that, ma'am, I can't think.'

Mrs Clennam cast her eyes towards the ground, and with her strong, set face, as intent upon a subject in her mind as it had lately been upon the form that seemed to pass out of her view, sat absorbed. Some minutes elapsed before she came out of this thoughtfulness, and resumed her hard composure.

Little Dorrit in the meanwhile had been waiting to go, but afraid to disturb her by moving. She now ventured to leave the spot where she had been standing since she had risen, and to pass gently round by the wheeled chair. She stopped at its side to say 'Good night, ma'am.'

Mrs Clennam put out her hand, and laid it on her arm. Little Dorrit, confused under the touch, stood faltering. Perhaps some momentary recollection of the story of the Princess may have been in her mind.

'Tell me, Little Dorrit,' said Mrs Clennam, 'have you many friends now?'

'Very few, ma'am. Besides you, only Miss Flora and—one more.'

'Meaning,' said Mrs Clennam, with her unbent finger again pointing to the door, 'that man?'

'Oh no, ma'am!'

'Some friend of his, perhaps?'

'No ma'am.' Little Dorrit earnestly shook her head. 'Oh no! No one at all like him, or belonging to him.'

'Well!' said Mrs Clennam, almost smiling. 'It is no affair of mine. I ask, because I take an interest in you; and because I believe I was your friend when you had no other who could serve you. Is that so?'

'Yes, ma'am; indeed it is. I have been here many a time when, but for you and the work you gave me, we should have wanted everything.'

'We,' repeated Mrs Clennam, looking towards the watch, once her dead husband's, which always lay upon her table. 'Are there many of you?'

'Only father and I, now. I mean, only father and I to keep regularly out of what we get.'

'Have you undergone many privations? You and your father and who else there may be of you?' asked Mrs Clennam, speaking deliberately, and meditatively turning the watch over and over.

'Sometimes it has been rather hard to live,' said Little Dorrit, in her soft voice, and timid uncomplaining way; 'but I think not harder—as to that—than many people find it.'

'That's well said!' Mrs Clennam quickly returned. 'That's the truth! You are a good, thoughtful girl. You are a grateful girl too, or I much mistake you.'

'It is only natural to be that. There is no merit in being that,' said Little Dorrit. 'I am indeed.'

Mrs Clennam, with a gentleness of which the dreaming Affery had never dreamed her to be capable, drew down the face of her little seamstress, and kissed her on the forehead.

'Now go, Little Dorrit,' said she, 'or you will be late, poor child!'

In all the dreams Mistress Affery had been piling up since she first became devoted to the pursuit, she had dreamed nothing more astonishing than this. Her head ached with the idea that she would find the other clever one kissing Little Dorrit next, and then the two clever ones embracing each other and dissolving into tears of tenderness for all mankind. The idea quite stunned her, as she attended the light footsteps down the stairs, that the house door might be safely shut.

On opening it to let Little Dorrit out, she found Mr Pancks, instead of having gone his way, as in any less wonderful place and among less wonderful phenomena he might have been reasonably expected to do, fluttering up and down the court outside the house. The moment he saw Little Dorrit, he passed her briskly, said with his finger to his nose (as Mrs Affery distinctly heard), 'Pancks the gipsy, fortune-telling,' and went away. 'Lord save us, here's a gipsy and a fortune-teller in it now!' cried Mistress Affery. 'What next!'

She stood at the open door, staggering herself with this enigma, on a rainy, thundery evening. The clouds were flying fast, and the wind was coming up in gusts, banging some neighbouring shutters that had broken loose, twirling the rusty chimney-cowls and weather-cocks, and rushing round and round a confined adjacent churchyard as if it had a mind to blow the dead citizens out of their graves. The low thunder, muttering in all quarters of the sky at once, seemed to threaten vengeance for this attempted desecration, and to mutter, 'Let them rest! Let them rest!'

Mistress Affery, whose fear of thunder and lightning was only to be equalled by her dread of the haunted house with a premature and preternatural darkness in it, stood undecided whether to go in or not, until the question was settled for her by the door blowing upon her in a violent gust of wind and shutting her out. 'What's to be done now, what's to be done now!' cried Mistress Affery, wringing her hands in this last uneasy dream of all; 'when she's all alone by herself inside, and can no more come down to open it than the churchyard dead themselves!'

In this dilemma, Mistress Affery, with her apron as a hood to keep the rain off, ran crying up and down the solitary paved enclosure several times. Why she should then stoop down and look in at the keyhole of the door as if an eye would open it, it would be difficult to say; but it is none the less what most people would have done in the same situation, and it is what she did.

From this posture she started up suddenly, with a half scream, feeling something on her shoulder. It was the touch of a hand; of a man's hand.

The man was dressed like a traveller, in a foraging cap with fur about it, and a heap of cloak. He looked like a foreigner. He had a quantity of hair and moustache—jet black, except at the shaggy ends, where it had a tinge of red—and a high hook nose. He laughed at Mistress Affery's start and cry; and as he laughed, his moustache went up under his nose, and his nose came down over his moustache.

'What's the matter?' he asked in plain English. 'What are you frightened at?'

'At you,' panted Affery.

'Me, madam?'

'And the dismal evening, and—and everything,' said Affery. 'And here! The wind has been and blown the door to, and I can't get in.'

'Hah!' said the gentleman, who took that very coolly. 'Indeed! Do you know such a name as Clennam about here?'

'Lord bless us, I should think I did, I should think I did!' cried Affery, exasperated into a new wringing of hands by the inquiry.

'Where about here?'

'Where!' cried Affery, goaded into another inspection of the keyhole. 'Where but here in this house? And she's all alone in her room, and lost the use of her limbs and can't stir to help herself or me, and t'other clever one's out, and Lord forgive me!' cried Affery, driven into a frantic dance by these accumulated considerations, 'if I ain't a-going headlong out of my mind!'

Taking a warmer view of the matter now that it concerned himself, the gentleman stepped back to glance at the house, and his eye soon rested on the long narrow window of the little room near the hall-door.

'Where may the lady be who has lost the use of her limbs, madam?' he inquired, with that peculiar smile which Mistress Affery could not choose but keep her eyes upon.

'Up there!' said Affery. 'Them two windows.'

'Hah! I am of a fair size, but could not have the honour of presenting myself in that room without a ladder. Now, madam, frankly—frankness is a part of my character—shall I open the door for you?'

'Yes, bless you, sir, for a dear creetur, and do it at once,' cried Affery, 'for she may be a-calling to me at this very present minute, or may be setting herself a fire and burning herself to death, or there's no knowing what may be happening to her, and me a-going out of my mind at thinking of it!'

'Stay, my good madam!' He restrained her impatience with a smooth white hand. 'Business-hours, I apprehend, are over for the day?'

'Yes, yes, yes,' cried Affery. 'Long ago.'

'Let me make, then, a fair proposal. Fairness is a part of my character. I am just landed from the packet-boat, as you may see.' He showed her that his cloak was very wet, and that his boots were saturated with water; she had previously observed that he was dishevelled and sallow, as if from a rough voyage, and so chilled that he could not keep his teeth from chattering. 'I am just landed from the packet-boat, madam, and have been delayed by the weather: the infernal weather! In consequence of this, madam, some necessary business that I should otherwise have transacted here within the regular hours (necessary business because money-business), still remains to be done. Now, if you will fetch any authorised neighbouring somebody to do it in return for my opening the door, I'll open the door. If this arrangement should be objectionable, I'll—' and with the same smile he made a significant feint of backing away.

Mistress Affery, heartily glad to effect the proposed compromise, gave in her willing adhesion to it. The gentleman at once requested her to do him the favour of holding his cloak, took a short run at the narrow window, made a leap at the sill, clung his way up the bricks, and in a moment had his hand at the sash, raising it. His eyes looked so very sinister, as he put his leg into the room and glanced round at Mistress Affery, that she thought with a sudden coldness, if he were to go straight up-stairs to murder the invalid, what could she do to prevent him?

Happily he had no such purpose; for he reappeared, in a moment, at the house door. 'Now, my dear madam,' he said, as he took back his cloak and threw it on, 'if you have the goodness to—what the Devil's that!'

The strangest of sounds. Evidently close at hand from the peculiar shock it communicated to the air, yet subdued as if it were far off. A tremble, a rumble, and a fall of some light dry matter.

'What the Devil is it?'

'I don't know what it is, but I've heard the like of it over and over again,' said Affery, who had caught his arm.

He could hardly be a very brave man, even she thought in her dreamy start and fright, for his trembling lips had turned colourless. After listening a few moments, he made light of it.

'Bah! Nothing! Now, my dear madam, I think you spoke of some clever personage. Will you be so good as to confront me with that genius?' He held the door in his hand, as though he were quite ready to shut her out again if she failed.

'Don't you say anything about the door and me, then,' whispered Affery.

'Not a word.'

'And don't you stir from here, or speak if she calls, while I run round the corner.'

'Madam, I am a statue.'

Affery had so vivid a fear of his going stealthily up-stairs the moment her back was turned, that after hurrying out of sight, she returned to the gateway to peep at him. Seeing him still on the threshold, more out of the house than in it, as if he had no love for darkness and no desire to probe its mysteries, she flew into the next street, and sent a message into the tavern to Mr Flintwinch, who came out directly. The two returning together—the lady in advance, and Mr Flintwinch coming up briskly behind, animated with the hope of shaking her before she could get housed—saw the gentleman standing in the same place in the dark, and heard the strong voice of Mrs Clennam calling from her room, 'Who is it? What is it? Why does no one answer? Who is that, down there?'

CHAPTER 30. The Word of a Gentleman

When Mr and Mrs Flintwinch panted up to the door of the old house in the twilight, Jeremiah within a second of Affery, the stranger started back. 'Death of my soul!' he exclaimed. 'Why, how did you get here?'

Mr Flintwinch, to whom these words were spoken, repaid the stranger's wonder in full. He gazed at him with blank astonishment; he looked over his own shoulder, as expecting to see some one he had not been aware of standing behind him; he gazed at the stranger again, speechlessly, at a loss to know what he meant; he looked to his wife for explanation; receiving none, he pounced upon her, and shook her with such heartiness that he shook her cap off her head, saying between his teeth, with grim raillery, as he did it, 'Affery, my woman, you must have a dose, my woman! This is some of your tricks! You have been dreaming again, mistress. What's it about? Who is it? What does it mean! Speak out or be choked! It's the only choice I'll give you.'

Supposing Mistress Affery to have any power of election at the moment, her choice was decidedly to be choked; for she answered not a syllable to this adjuration, but, with her bare head wagging violently backwards and forwards, resigned herself to her punishment. The stranger, however, picking up her cap with an air of gallantry, interposed.

'Permit me,' said he, laying his hand on the shoulder of Jeremiah, who stopped and released his victim. 'Thank you. Excuse me. Husband and wife I know, from this playfulness. Haha! Always agreeable to see that relation playfully maintained. Listen! May I suggest that somebody up-stairs, in the dark, is becoming energetically curious to know what is going on here?'

This reference to Mrs Clennam's voice reminded Mr Flintwinch to step into the hall and call up the staircase. 'It's all right, I am here, Affery is coming with your light.' Then he said to the latter flustered woman, who was putting her cap on, 'Get out with you, and get up-stairs!' and then turned to the stranger and said to him, 'Now, sir, what might you please to want?'

'I am afraid,' said the stranger, 'I must be so troublesome as to propose a candle.'

'True,' assented Jeremiah. 'I was going to do so. Please to stand where you are while I get one.'

The visitor was standing in the doorway, but turned a little into the gloom of the house as Mr Flintwinch turned, and pursued him with his eyes into the little room, where he groped about for a phosphorus box. When he found it, it was damp, or otherwise out of order; and match after match that he struck into it lighted sufficiently to throw a dull glare about his groping face, and to sprinkle his hands with pale little spots of fire, but not sufficiently to light the candle. The stranger, taking advantage of this fitful illumination of his visage, looked intently and wonderingly at him. Jeremiah, when he at last lighted the candle, knew he had been doing this, by seeing the last shade of a lowering watchfulness clear away from his face, as it broke into the doubtful smile that was a large ingredient in its expression.

'Be so good,' said Jeremiah, closing the house door, and taking a pretty sharp survey of the smiling visitor in his turn, 'as to step into my counting-house.—It's all right, I tell you!' petulantly breaking off to answer the voice up-stairs, still unsatisfied, though Affery was there, speaking in persuasive tones. 'Don't I tell you it's all right? Preserve the woman, has she no reason at all in her!'

'Timorous,' remarked the stranger.

'Timorous?' said Mr Flintwinch, turning his head to retort, as he went before with the candle. 'More courageous than ninety men in a hundred, sir, let me tell you.'

'Though an invalid?'

'Many years an invalid. Mrs Clennam. The only one of that name left in the House now. My partner.'

Saying something apologetically as he crossed the hall, to the effect that at that time of night they were not in the habit of receiving any one, and were always shut up, Mr Flintwinch led the way into his own office, which presented a sufficiently business-like appearance. Here he put the light on his desk, and said to the stranger, with his wryest twist upon him, 'Your commands.'

'My name is Blandois.'

'Blandois. I don't know it,' said Jeremiah.

'I thought it possible,' resumed the other, 'that you might have been advised from Paris—'

'We have had no advice from Paris respecting anybody of the name of Blandois,' said Jeremiah.

'No?'

'No.'

Jeremiah stood in his favourite attitude. The smiling Mr Blandois, opening his cloak to get his hand to a breast-pocket, paused to say, with a laugh in his glittering eyes, which it occurred to Mr Flintwinch were too near together:

'You are so like a friend of mine! Not so identically the same as I supposed when I really did for the moment take you to be the same in the dusk—for which I ought to apologise; permit me to do so; a readiness to confess my errors is, I hope, a part of the frankness of my character—still, however, uncommonly like.'

'Indeed?' said Jeremiah, perversely. 'But I have not received any letter of advice from anywhere respecting anybody of the name of Blandois.'

'Just so,' said the stranger.

'Just so,' said Jeremiah.

Mr Blandois, not at all put out by this omission on the part of the correspondents of the house of Clennam and Co., took his pocket-book from his breast-pocket, selected a letter from that receptacle, and handed it to Mr Flintwinch. 'No doubt you are well acquainted with the writing. Perhaps the letter speaks for itself, and requires no advice. You are a far more competent judge of such affairs than I am. It is my misfortune to be, not so much a man of business, as what the world calls (arbitrarily) a gentleman.'

Mr Flintwinch took the letter, and read, under date of Paris, 'We have to present to you, on behalf of a highly esteemed correspondent of our Firm, M. Blandois, of this city,' &c. &c. 'Such facilities as he may require and such attentions as may lie in your power,' &c. &c. 'Also have to add that if you will honour M. Blandois' drafts at sight to the extent of, say Fifty Pounds sterling (50l.),' &c. &c.

'Very good, sir,' said Mr Flintwinch. 'Take a chair. To the extent of anything that our House can do—we are in a retired, old-fashioned, steady way of business, sir—we shall be happy to render you our best assistance. I observe, from the date of this, that we could not yet be advised of it. Probably you came over with the delayed mail that brings the advice.'

'That I came over with the delayed mail, sir,' returned Mr Blandois, passing his white hand down his high-hooked nose, 'I know to the cost of my head and stomach: the detestable and intolerable weather having racked them both. You see me in the plight in which I came out of the packet within this half-hour. I ought to have been here hours ago, and then I should not have to apologise—permit me to apologise—for presenting myself so unreasonably, and frightening—no, by-the-bye, you said not frightening; permit me to apologise again—the esteemed lady, Mrs Clennam, in her invalid chamber above stairs.'

Swagger and an air of authorised condescension do so much, that Mr Flintwinch had already begun to think this a highly gentlemanly personage. Not the less unyielding with him on that account, he scraped his chin and said, what could he have the honour of doing for Mr Blandois to-night, out of business hours?

'Faith!' returned that gentleman, shrugging his cloaked shoulders, 'I must change, and eat and drink, and be lodged somewhere. Have the kindness to advise me, a total stranger, where, and money is a matter of perfect indifference until to-morrow. The nearer the place, the better. Next door, if that's all.'

Mr Flintwinch was slowly beginning, 'For a gentleman of your habits, there is not in this immediate neighbourhood any hotel—' when Mr Blandois took him up.

'So much for my habits! my dear sir,' snapping his fingers. 'A citizen of the world has no habits. That I am, in my poor way, a gentleman, by Heaven! I will not deny, but I have no unaccommodating prejudiced habits. A clean room, a hot dish for dinner, and a bottle of not absolutely poisonous wine, are all I want tonight. But I want that much without the trouble of going one unnecessary inch to get it.'

'There is,' said Mr Flintwinch, with more than his usual deliberation, as he met, for a moment, Mr Blandois' shining eyes, which were restless; 'there is a coffee-house and tavern close here, which, so far, I can recommend; but there's no style about it.'

'I dispense with style!' said Mr Blandois, waving his hand. 'Do me the honour to show me the house, and introduce me there (if I am not too troublesome), and I shall be infinitely obliged.'

Mr Flintwinch, upon this, looked up his hat, and lighted Mr Blandois across the hall again. As he put the candle on a bracket, where the dark old panelling almost served as an extinguisher for it, he bethought himself of going up to tell the invalid that he would not be absent five minutes.

'Oblige me,' said the visitor, on his saying so, 'by presenting my card of visit. Do me the favour to add that I shall be happy to wait on Mrs Clennam, to offer my personal compliments, and to apologise for having occasioned any agitation in this tranquil corner, if it should suit her convenience to endure the presence of a stranger for a few minutes, after he shall have changed his wet clothes and fortified himself with something to eat and drink.'

Jeremiah made all despatch, and said, on his return, 'She'll be glad to see you, sir; but, being conscious that her sick room has no attractions, wishes me to say that she won't hold you to your offer, in case you should think better of it.'

'To think better of it,' returned the gallant Blandois, 'would be to slight a lady; to slight a lady would be to be deficient in chivalry towards the sex; and chivalry towards the sex is a part of my character!' Thus expressing himself, he threw the draggled skirt of his cloak over his shoulder, and accompanied Mr Flintwinch to the tavern; taking up on the road a porter who was waiting with his portmanteau on the outer side of the gateway.

The house was kept in a homely manner, and the condescension of Mr Blandois was infinite. It seemed to fill to inconvenience the little bar in which the widow landlady and her two daughters received him; it was much too big for the narrow wainscoted room with a bagatelle-board in it, that was first proposed for his reception; it perfectly swamped the little private holiday sitting-room of the family, which was finally given up to him. Here, in dry clothes and scented linen, with sleeked hair, a great ring on each forefinger and a massive show of watch-chain, Mr Blandois waiting for his dinner, lolling on a window-seat with his knees drawn up, looked (for all the difference in the setting of the jewel) fearfully and wonderfully like a certain Monsieur Rigaud who had once so waited for his breakfast, lying on the stone ledge of the iron grating of a cell in a villainous dungeon at Marseilles.

His greed at dinner, too, was closely in keeping with the greed of Monsieur Rigaud at breakfast. His avaricious manner of collecting all the eatables about him, and devouring some with his eyes while devouring others with his jaws, was the same manner. His utter disregard of other people, as shown in his way of tossing the little womanly toys of furniture about, flinging favourite cushions under his boots for a softer rest, and crushing delicate coverings with his big body and his great black head, had the same brute selfishness at the bottom of it. The softly moving hands that were so busy among the dishes had the old wicked facility of the hands that had clung to the bars. And when he could eat no more, and sat sucking his delicate fingers one by one and wiping them on a cloth, there wanted nothing but the substitution of vine-leaves to finish the picture.

On this man, with his moustache going up and his nose coming down in that most evil of smiles, and with his surface eyes looking as if they belonged to his dyed hair, and had had their natural power of reflecting light stopped by some similar process, Nature, always true, and never working in vain, had set the mark, Beware! It was not her fault, if the warning were fruitless. She is never to blame in any such instance.

Mr Blandois, having finished his repast and cleaned his fingers, took a cigar from his pocket, and, lying on the window-seat again, smoked it out at his leisure, occasionally apostrophising the smoke as it parted from his thin lips in a thin stream:

'Blandois, you shall turn the tables on society, my little child. Haha! Holy blue, you have begun well, Blandois! At a pinch, an excellent master in English or French; a man for the bosom of families! You have a quick perception, you have humour, you have ease, you have insinuating manners, you have a good appearance; in effect, you are a gentleman! A gentleman you shall live, my small boy, and a gentleman you shall die. You shall win, however the game goes. They shall all confess your merit, Blandois. You shall subdue the society which has grievously wronged you, to your own high spirit. Death of my soul! You are high spirited by right and by nature, my Blandois!'

To such soothing murmurs did this gentleman smoke out his cigar and drink out his bottle of wine. Both being finished, he shook himself into a sitting attitude; and with the concluding serious apostrophe, 'Hold, then! Blandois, you ingenious one, have all your wits about you!' arose and went back to the house of Clennam and Co.

He was received at the door by Mistress Affery, who, under instructions from her lord, had lighted up two candles in the hall and a third on the staircase, and who conducted him to Mrs Clennam's room. Tea was prepared there, and such little company arrangements had been made as usually attended the reception of expected visitors. They were slight on the greatest occasion, never extending beyond the production of the China tea-service, and the covering of the bed with a sober and sad drapery. For the rest, there was the bier-like sofa with the block upon it, and the figure in the widow's dress, as if attired for execution; the fire topped by the mound of damped ashes; the grate with its second little mound of ashes; the kettle and the smell of black dye; all as they had been for fifteen years.

Mr Flintwinch presented the gentleman commended to the consideration of Clennam and Co. Mrs Clennam, who had the letter lying before her, bent her head and requested him to sit. They looked very closely at one another. That was but natural curiosity.

'I thank you, sir, for thinking of a disabled woman like me. Few who come here on business have any remembrance to bestow on one so removed from observation. It would be idle to expect that they should have. Out of sight, out of mind. While I am grateful for the exception, I don't complain of the rule.'

Mr Blandois, in his most gentlemanly manner, was afraid he had disturbed her by unhappily presenting himself at such an unconscionable time. For which he had already offered his best apologies to Mr—he begged pardon—but by name had not the distinguished honour—

'Mr Flintwinch has been connected with the House many years.'

Mr Blandois was Mr Flintwinch's most obedient humble servant. He entreated Mr Flintwinch to receive the assurance of his profoundest consideration.

'My husband being dead,' said Mrs Clennam, 'and my son preferring another pursuit, our old House has no other representative in these days than Mr Flintwinch.'

'What do you call yourself?' was the surly demand of that gentleman. 'You have the head of two men.'

'My sex disqualifies me,' she proceeded with merely a slight turn of her eyes in Jeremiah's direction, 'from taking a responsible part in the business, even if I had the ability; and therefore Mr Flintwinch combines my interest with his own, and conducts it. It is not what it used to be; but some of our old friends (principally the writers of this letter) have the kindness not to forget us, and we retain the power of doing what they entrust to us as efficiently as we ever did. This however is not interesting to you. You are English, sir?'

'Faith, madam, no; I am neither born nor bred in England. In effect, I am of no country,' said Mr Blandois, stretching out his leg and smiting it: 'I descend from half-a-dozen countries.'

'You have been much about the world?'

'It is true. By Heaven, madam, I have been here and there and everywhere!'

'You have no ties, probably. Are not married?'

'Madam,' said Mr Blandois, with an ugly fall of his eyebrows, 'I adore your sex, but I am not married—never was.'

Mistress Affery, who stood at the table near him, pouring out the tea, happened in her dreamy state to look at him as he said these words, and to fancy that she caught an expression in his eyes which attracted her own eyes so that she could not get them away. The effect of this fancy was to keep her staring at him with the tea-pot in her hand, not only to her own great uneasiness, but manifestly to his, too; and, through them both, to Mrs Clennam's and Mr Flintwinch's. Thus a few ghostly moments supervened, when they were all confusedly staring without knowing why.

'Affery,' her mistress was the first to say, 'what is the matter with you?'

'I don't know,' said Mistress Affery, with her disengaged left hand extended towards the visitor. 'It ain't me. It's him!'

'What does this good woman mean?' cried Mr Blandois, turning white, hot, and slowly rising with a look of such deadly wrath that it contrasted surprisingly with the slight force of his words. 'How is it possible to understand this good creature?'

'It's not possible,' said Mr Flintwinch, screwing himself rapidly in that direction. 'She don't know what she means. She's an idiot, a wanderer in her mind. She shall have a dose, she shall have such a dose! Get along with you, my woman,' he added in her ear, 'get along with you, while you know you're Affery, and before you're shaken to yeast.'

Mistress Affery, sensible of the danger in which her identity stood, relinquished the tea-pot as her husband seized it, put her apron over her head, and in a twinkling vanished. The visitor gradually broke into a smile, and sat down again.

'You'll excuse her, Mr Blandois,' said Jeremiah, pouring out the tea himself, 'she's failing and breaking up; that's what she's about. Do you take sugar, sir?'

'Thank you, no tea for me.—Pardon my observing it, but that's a very remarkable watch!'

The tea-table was drawn up near the sofa, with a small interval between it and Mrs Clennam's own particular table. Mr Blandois in his gallantry had risen to hand that lady her tea (her dish of toast was already there), and it was in placing the cup conveniently within her reach that the watch, lying before her as it always did, attracted his attention. Mrs Clennam looked suddenly up at him.

'May I be permitted? Thank you. A fine old-fashioned watch,' he said, taking it in his hand. 'Heavy for use, but massive and genuine. I have a partiality for everything genuine. Such as I am, I am genuine myself. Hah! A gentleman's watch with two cases in the old fashion. May I remove it from the outer case? Thank you. Aye? An old silk watch-lining, worked with beads! I have often seen these among old Dutch people and Belgians. Quaint things!'

'They are old-fashioned, too,' said Mrs Clennam.

'Very. But this is not so old as the watch, I think?'

'I think not.'

'Extraordinary how they used to complicate these cyphers!' remarked Mr Blandois, glancing up with his own smile again. 'Now is this D. N. F.? It might be almost anything.'

'Those are the letters.'

Mr Flintwinch, who had been observantly pausing all this time with a cup of tea in his hand, and his mouth open ready to swallow the contents, began to do so: always entirely filling his mouth before he emptied it at a gulp; and always deliberating again before he refilled it.

'D. N. F. was some tender, lovely, fascinating fair-creature, I make no doubt,' observed Mr Blandois, as he snapped on the case again. 'I adore her memory on the assumption. Unfortunately for my peace of mind, I adore but too readily. It may be a vice, it may be a virtue, but adoration of female beauty and merit constitutes three parts of my character, madam.'

Mr Flintwinch had by this time poured himself out another cup of tea, which he was swallowing in gulps as before, with his eyes directed to the invalid.

'You may be heart-free here, sir,' she returned to Mr Blandois. 'Those letters are not intended, I believe, for the initials of any name.'

'Of a motto, perhaps,' said Mr Blandois, casually.

'Of a sentence. They have always stood, I believe, for Do Not Forget!'

'And naturally,' said Mr Blandois, replacing the watch and stepping backward to his former chair, 'you do not forget.'

Mr Flintwinch, finishing his tea, not only took a longer gulp than he had taken yet, but made his succeeding pause under new circumstances: that is to say, with his head thrown back and his cup held still at his lips, while his eyes were still directed at the invalid. She had that force of face, and that concentrated air of collecting her firmness or obstinacy, which represented in her case what would have been gesture and action in another, as she replied with her deliberate strength of speech:

'No, sir, I do not forget. To lead a life as monotonous as mine has been during many years, is not the way to forget. To lead a life of self-correction is not the way to forget. To be sensible of having (as we all have, every one of us, all the children of Adam!) offences to expiate and peace to make, does not justify the desire to forget. Therefore I have long dismissed it, and I neither forget nor wish to forget.'

Mr Flintwinch, who had latterly been shaking the sediment at the bottom of his tea-cup, round and round, here gulped it down, and putting the cup in the tea-tray, as done with, turned his eyes upon Mr Blandois as if to ask him what he thought of that?

'All expressed, madam,' said Mr Blandois, with his smoothest bow and his white hand on his breast, 'by the word "naturally," which I am proud to have had sufficient apprehension and appreciation (but without appreciation I could not be Blandois) to employ.'

'Pardon me, sir,' she returned, 'if I doubt the likelihood of a gentleman of pleasure, and change, and politeness, accustomed to court and to be courted—'

'Oh madam! By Heaven!'

'—If I doubt the likelihood of such a character quite comprehending what belongs to mine in my circumstances. Not to obtrude doctrine upon you,' she looked at the rigid pile of hard pale books before her, '(for you go your own way, and the consequences are on your own head), I will say this much: that I shape my course by pilots, strictly by proved and tried pilots, under whom I cannot be shipwrecked—can not be—and that if I were unmindful of the admonition conveyed in those three letters, I should not be half as chastened as I am.'

It was curious how she seized the occasion to argue with some invisible opponent. Perhaps with her own better sense, always turning upon herself and her own deception.

'If I forgot my ignorances in my life of health and freedom, I might complain of the life to which I am now condemned. I never do; I never have done. If I forgot that this scene, the Earth, is expressly meant to be a scene of gloom, and hardship, and dark trial, for the creatures who are made out of its dust, I might have some tenderness for its vanities. But I have no such tenderness. If I did not know that we are, every one, the subject (most justly the subject) of a wrath that must be satisfied, and against which mere actions are nothing, I might repine at the difference between me, imprisoned here, and the people who pass that gateway yonder. But I take it as a grace and favour to be elected to make the satisfaction I am making here, to know what I know for certain here, and to work out what I have worked out here. My affliction might otherwise have had no meaning to me. Hence I would forget, and I do forget, nothing. Hence I am contented, and say it is better with me than with millions.'

As she spoke these words, she put her hand upon the watch, and restored it to the precise spot on her little table which it always occupied. With her touch lingering upon it, she sat for some moments afterwards, looking at it steadily and half-defiantly.

Mr Blandois, during this exposition, had been strictly attentive, keeping his eyes fastened on the lady, and thoughtfully stroking his moustache with his two hands. Mr Flintwinch had been a little fidgety, and now struck in.

'There, there, there!' said he. 'That is quite understood, Mrs Clennam, and you have spoken piously and well. Mr Blandois, I suspect, is not of a pious cast.'

'On the contrary, sir!' that gentleman protested, snapping his fingers. 'Your pardon! It's a part of my character. I am sensitive, ardent, conscientious, and imaginative. A sensitive, ardent, conscientious, and imaginative man, Mr Flintwinch, must be that, or nothing!'

There was an inkling of suspicion in Mr Flintwinch's face that he might be nothing, as he swaggered out of his chair (it was characteristic of this man, as it is of all men similarly marked, that whatever he did, he overdid, though it were sometimes by only a hairsbreadth), and approached to take his leave of Mrs Clennam.

'With what will appear to you the egotism of a sick old woman, sir,' she then said, 'though really through your accidental allusion, I have been led away into the subject of myself and my infirmities. Being so considerate as to visit me, I hope you will be likewise so considerate as to overlook that. Don't compliment me, if you please.' For he was evidently going to do it. 'Mr Flintwinch will be happy to render you any service, and I hope your stay in this city may prove agreeable.'

Mr Blandois thanked her, and kissed his hand several times. 'This is an old room,' he remarked, with a sudden sprightliness of manner, looking round when he got near the door, 'I have been so interested that I have not observed it. But it's a genuine old room.'

'It is a genuine old house,' said Mrs Clennam, with her frozen smile. 'A place of no pretensions, but a piece of antiquity.'

'Faith!' cried the visitor. 'If Mr Flintwinch would do me the favour to take me through the rooms on my way out, he could hardly oblige me more. An old house is a weakness with me. I have many weaknesses, but none greater. I love and study the picturesque in all its varieties. I have been called picturesque myself. It is no merit to be picturesque—I have greater merits, perhaps—but I may be, by an accident. Sympathy, sympathy!'

'I tell you beforehand, Mr Blandois, that you'll find it very dingy and very bare,' said Jeremiah, taking up the candle. 'It's not worth your looking at.' But Mr Blandois, smiting him in a friendly manner on the back, only laughed; so the said Blandois kissed his hand again to Mrs Clennam, and they went out of the room together.

'You don't care to go up-stairs?' said Jeremiah, on the landing.

'On the contrary, Mr Flintwinch; if not tiresome to you, I shall be ravished!'

Mr Flintwinch, therefore, wormed himself up the staircase, and Mr Blandois followed close. They ascended to the great garret bed-room which Arthur had occupied on the night of his return. 'There, Mr Blandois!' said Jeremiah, showing it, 'I hope you may think that worth coming so high to see. I confess I don't.'

Mr Blandois being enraptured, they walked through other garrets and passages, and came down the staircase again. By this time Mr Flintwinch had remarked that he never found the visitor looking at any room, after throwing one quick glance around, but always found the visitor looking at him, Mr Flintwinch. With this discovery in his thoughts, he turned about on the staircase for another experiment. He met his eyes directly; and on the instant of their fixing one another, the visitor, with that ugly play of nose and moustache, laughed (as he had done at every similar moment since they left Mrs Clennam's chamber) a diabolically silent laugh.

As a much shorter man than the visitor, Mr Flintwinch was at the physical disadvantage of being thus disagreeably leered at from a height; and as he went first down the staircase, and was usually a step or two lower than the other, this disadvantage was at the time increased. He postponed looking at Mr Blandois again until this accidental inequality was removed by their having entered the late Mr Clennam's room. But, then twisting himself suddenly round upon him, he found his look unchanged.

'A most admirable old house,' smiled Mr Blandois. 'So mysterious. Do you never hear any haunted noises here?'

'Noises,' returned Mr Flintwinch. 'No.'

'Nor see any devils?'

'Not,' said Mr Flintwinch, grimly screwing himself at his questioner, 'not any that introduce themselves under that name and in that capacity.'

'Haha! A portrait here, I see.'

(Still looking at Mr Flintwinch, as if he were the portrait.)

'It's a portrait, sir, as you observe.'

'May I ask the subject, Mr Flintwinch?'

'Mr Clennam, deceased. Her husband.'

'Former owner of the remarkable watch, perhaps?' said the visitor.

Mr Flintwinch, who had cast his eyes towards the portrait, twisted himself about again, and again found himself the subject of the same look and smile. 'Yes, Mr Blandois,' he replied tartly. 'It was his, and his uncle's before him, and Lord knows who before him; and that's all I can tell you of its pedigree.'

'That's a strongly marked character, Mr Flintwinch, our friend up-stairs.'

'Yes, sir,' said Jeremiah, twisting himself at the visitor again, as he did during the whole of this dialogue, like some screw-machine that fell short of its grip; for the other never changed, and he always felt obliged to retreat a little. 'She is a remarkable woman. Great fortitude—great strength of mind.'

'They must have been very happy,' said Blandois.

'Who?' demanded Mr Flintwinch, with another screw at him.

Mr Blandois shook his right forefinger towards the sick room, and his left forefinger towards the portrait, and then, putting his arms akimbo and striding his legs wide apart, stood smiling down at Mr Flintwinch with the advancing nose and the retreating moustache.

'As happy as most other married people, I suppose,' returned Mr Flintwinch. 'I can't say. I don't know. There are secrets in all families.'

'Secrets!' cried Mr Blandois, quickly. 'Say it again, my son.'

'I say,' replied Mr Flintwinch, upon whom he had swelled himself so suddenly that Mr Flintwinch found his face almost brushed by the dilated chest. 'I say there are secrets in all families.'

'So there are,' cried the other, clapping him on both shoulders, and rolling him backwards and forwards. 'Haha! you are right. So there are! Secrets! Holy Blue! There are the devil's own secrets in some families, Mr Flintwinch!' With that, after clapping Mr Flintwinch on both shoulders several times, as if in a friendly and humorous way he were rallying him on a joke he had made, he threw up his arms, threw back his head, hooked his hands together behind it, and burst into a roar of laughter. It was in vain for Mr Flintwinch to try another screw at him. He had his laugh out.

'But, favour me with the candle a moment,' he said, when he had done. 'Let us have a look at the husband of the remarkable lady. Hah!' holding up the light at arm's length. 'A decided expression of face here too, though not of the same character. Looks as if he were saying, what is it—Do Not Forget—does he not, Mr Flintwinch? By Heaven, sir, he does!'

As he returned the candle, he looked at him once more; and then, leisurely strolling out with him into the hall, declared it to be a charming old house indeed, and one which had so greatly pleased him that he would not have missed inspecting it for a hundred pounds.

Throughout these singular freedoms on the part of Mr Blandois, which involved a general alteration in his demeanour, making it much coarser and rougher, much more violent and audacious than before, Mr Flintwinch, whose leathern face was not liable to many changes, preserved its immobility intact. Beyond now appearing perhaps, to have been left hanging a trifle too long before that friendly operation of cutting down, he outwardly maintained an equable composure. They had brought their survey to a close in the little room at the side of the hall, and he stood there, eyeing Mr Blandois.

'I am glad you are so well satisfied, sir,' was his calm remark. 'I didn't expect it. You seem to be quite in good spirits.'

'In admirable spirits,' returned Blandois. 'Word of honour! never more refreshed in spirits. Do you ever have presentiments, Mr Flintwinch?'

'I am not sure that I know what you mean by the term, sir,' replied that gentleman.

'Say, in this case, Mr Flintwinch, undefined anticipations of pleasure to come.'

'I can't say I'm sensible of such a sensation at present,' returned Mr Flintwinch with the utmost gravity. 'If I should find it coming on, I'll mention it.'

'Now I,' said Blandois, 'I, my son, have a presentiment to-night that we shall be well acquainted. Do you find it coming on?'

'N-no,' returned Mr Flintwinch, deliberately inquiring of himself. 'I can't say I do.'

'I have a strong presentiment that we shall become intimately acquainted.—You have no feeling of that sort yet?'

'Not yet,' said Mr Flintwinch.

Mr Blandois, taking him by both shoulders again, rolled him about a little in his former merry way, then drew his arm through his own, and invited him to come off and drink a bottle of wine like a dear deep old dog as he was.

Without a moment's indecision, Mr Flintwinch accepted the invitation, and they went out to the quarters where the traveller was lodged, through a heavy rain which had rattled on the windows, roofs, and pavements, ever since nightfall. The thunder and lightning had long ago passed over, but the rain was furious. On their arrival at Mr Blandois' room, a bottle of port wine was ordered by that gallant gentleman; who (crushing every pretty thing he could collect, in the soft disposition of his dainty figure) coiled himself upon the window-seat, while Mr Flintwinch took a chair opposite to him, with the table between them. Mr Blandois proposed having the largest glasses in the house, to which Mr Flintwinch assented. The bumpers filled, Mr Blandois, with a roystering gaiety, clinked the top of his glass against the bottom of Mr Flintwinch's, and the bottom of his glass against the top of Mr Flintwinch's, and drank to the intimate acquaintance he foresaw. Mr Flintwinch gravely pledged him, and drank all the wine he could get, and said nothing. As often as Mr Blandois clinked glasses (which was at every replenishment), Mr Flintwinch stolidly did his part of the clinking, and would have stolidly done his companion's part of the wine as well as his own: being, except in the article of palate, a mere cask.

In short, Mr Blandois found that to pour port wine into the reticent Flintwinch was, not to open him but to shut him up. Moreover, he had the appearance of a perfect ability to go on all night; or, if occasion were, all next day and all next night; whereas Mr Blandois soon grew indistinctly conscious of swaggering too fiercely and boastfully. He therefore terminated the entertainment at the end of the third bottle.

'You will draw upon us to-morrow, sir,' said Mr Flintwinch, with a business-like face at parting.

'My Cabbage,' returned the other, taking him by the collar with both hands, 'I'll draw upon you; have no fear. Adieu, my Flintwinch. Receive at parting;' here he gave him a southern embrace, and kissed him soundly on both cheeks; 'the word of a gentleman! By a thousand Thunders, you shall see me again!'

He did not present himself next day, though the letter of advice came duly to hand. Inquiring after him at night, Mr Flintwinch found, with surprise, that he had paid his bill and gone back to the Continent by way of Calais. Nevertheless, Jeremiah scraped out of his cogitating face a lively conviction that Mr Blandois would keep his word on this occasion, and would be seen again.

CHAPTER 31. Spirit

Anybody may pass, any day, in the thronged thoroughfares of the metropolis, some meagre, wrinkled, yellow old man (who might be supposed to have dropped from the stars, if there were any star in the Heavens dull enough to be suspected of casting off so feeble a spark), creeping along with a scared air, as though bewildered and a little frightened by the noise and bustle. This old man is always a little old man. If he were ever a big old man, he has shrunk into a little old man; if he were always a little old man, he has dwindled into a less old man. His coat is a colour, and cut, that never was the mode anywhere, at any period. Clearly, it was not made for him, or for any individual mortal. Some wholesale contractor measured Fate for five thousand coats of such quality, and Fate has lent this old coat to this old man, as one of a long unfinished line of many old men. It has always large dull metal buttons, similar to no other buttons. This old man wears a hat, a thumbed and napless and yet an obdurate hat, which has never adapted itself to the shape of his poor head. His coarse shirt and his coarse neckcloth have no more individuality than his coat and hat; they have the same character of not being his—of not being anybody's. Yet this old man wears these clothes with a certain unaccustomed air of being dressed and elaborated for the public ways; as though he passed the greater part of his time in a nightcap and gown. And so, like the country mouse in the second year of a famine, come to see the town mouse, and timidly threading his way to the town-mouse's lodging through a city of cats, this old man passes in the streets.

Sometimes, on holidays towards evening, he will be seen to walk with a slightly increased infirmity, and his old eyes will glimmer with a moist and marshy light. Then the little old man is drunk. A very small measure will overset him; he may be bowled off his unsteady legs with a half-pint pot. Some pitying acquaintance—chance acquaintance very often—has warmed up his weakness with a treat of beer, and the consequence will be the lapse of a longer time than usual before he shall pass again. For the little old man is going home to the Workhouse; and on his good behaviour they do not let him out often (though methinks they might, considering the few years he has before him to go out in, under the sun); and on his bad behaviour they shut him up closer than ever in a grove of two score and nineteen more old men, every one of whom smells of all the others.

Mrs Plornish's father,—a poor little reedy piping old gentleman, like a worn-out bird; who had been in what he called the music-binding business, and met with great misfortunes, and who had seldom been able to make his way, or to see it or to pay it, or to do anything at all with it but find it no thoroughfare,—had retired of his own accord to the Workhouse which was appointed by law to be the Good Samaritan of his district (without the twopence, which was bad political economy), on the settlement of that execution which had carried Mr Plornish to the Marshalsea College. Previous to his son-in-law's difficulties coming to that head, Old Nandy (he was always so called in his legal Retreat, but he was Old Mr Nandy among the Bleeding Hearts) had sat in a corner of the Plornish fireside, and taken his bite and sup out of the Plornish cupboard. He still hoped to resume that domestic position when Fortune should smile upon his son-in-law; in the meantime, while she preserved an immovable countenance, he was, and resolved to remain, one of these little old men in a grove of little old men with a community of flavour.

But no poverty in him, and no coat on him that never was the mode, and no Old Men's Ward for his dwelling-place, could quench his daughter's admiration. Mrs Plornish was as proud of her father's talents as she could possibly have been if they had made him Lord Chancellor. She had as firm a belief in the sweetness and propriety of his manners as she could possibly have had if he had been Lord Chamberlain. The poor little old man knew some pale and vapid little songs, long out of date, about Chloe, and Phyllis, and Strephon being wounded by the son of Venus; and for Mrs Plornish there was no such music at the Opera as the small internal flutterings and chirpings wherein he would discharge himself of these ditties, like a weak, little, broken barrel-organ, ground by a baby. On his 'days out,' those flecks of light in his flat vista of pollard old men,' it was at once Mrs Plornish's delight and sorrow, when he was strong with meat, and had taken his full halfpenny-worth of porter, to say, 'Sing us a song, Father.' Then he would give them Chloe, and if he were in pretty good spirits, Phyllis also—Strephon he had hardly been up to since he went into retirement—and then would Mrs Plornish declare she did believe there never was such a singer as Father, and wipe her eyes.

If he had come from Court on these occasions, nay, if he had been the noble Refrigerator come home triumphantly from a foreign court to be presented and promoted on his last tremendous failure, Mrs Plornish could not have handed him with greater elevation about Bleeding Heart Yard. 'Here's Father,' she would say, presenting him to a neighbour. 'Father will soon be home with us for good, now. Ain't Father looking well? Father's a sweeter singer than ever; you'd never have forgotten it, if you'd aheard him just now.' As to Mr Plornish, he had married these articles of belief in marrying Mr Nandy's daughter, and only wondered how it was that so gifted an old gentleman had not made a fortune. This he attributed, after much reflection, to his musical genius not having been scientifically developed in his youth. 'For why,' argued Mr Plornish, 'why go a-binding music when you've got it in yourself? That's where it is, I consider.'

Old Nandy had a patron: one patron. He had a patron who in a certain sumptuous way—an apologetic way, as if he constantly took an admiring audience to witness that he really could not help being more free with this old fellow than they might have expected, on account of his simplicity and poverty—was mightily good to him. Old Nandy had been several times to the Marshalsea College, communicating with his son-in-law during his short durance there; and had happily acquired to himself, and had by degrees and in course of time much improved, the patronage of the Father of that national institution.

Mr Dorrit was in the habit of receiving this old man as if the old man held of him in vassalage under some feudal tenure. He made little treats and teas for him, as if he came in with his homage from some outlying district where the tenantry were in a primitive state. It seemed as if there were moments when he could by no means have sworn but that the old man was an ancient retainer of his, who had been meritoriously faithful. When he mentioned him, he spoke of him casually as his old pensioner. He had a wonderful satisfaction in seeing him, and in commenting on his decayed condition after he was gone. It appeared to him amazing that he could hold up his head at all, poor creature. 'In the Workhouse, sir, the Union; no privacy, no visitors, no station, no respect, no speciality. Most deplorable!'

It was Old Nandy's birthday, and they let him out. He said nothing about its being his birthday, or they might have kept him in; for such old men should not be born. He passed along the streets as usual to Bleeding Heart Yard, and had his dinner with his daughter and son-in-law, and gave them Phyllis. He had hardly concluded, when Little Dorrit looked in to see how they all were.

'Miss Dorrit,' said Mrs Plornish, 'here's Father! Ain't he looking nice? And such voice he's in!'

Little Dorrit gave him her hand, and smilingly said she had not seen him this long time.

'No, they're rather hard on poor Father,' said Mrs Plornish with a lengthening face, 'and don't let him have half as much change and fresh air as would benefit him. But he'll soon be home for good, now. Won't you, Father?'

'Yes, my dear, I hope so. In good time, please God.'

Here Mr Plornish delivered himself of an oration which he invariably made, word for word the same, on all such opportunities. It was couched in the following terms:

'John Edward Nandy. Sir. While there's a ounce of wittles or drink of any sort in this present roof, you're fully welcome to your share on it. While there's a handful of fire or a mouthful of bed in this present roof, you're fully welcome to your share on it. If so be as there should be nothing in this present roof, you should be as welcome to your share on it as if it was something, much or little. And this is what I mean and so I don't deceive you, and consequently which is to stand out is to entreat of you, and therefore why not do it?'

To this lucid address, which Mr Plornish always delivered as if he had composed it (as no doubt he had) with enormous labour, Mrs Plornish's father pipingly replied:

'I thank you kindly, Thomas, and I know your intentions well, which is the same I thank you kindly for. But no, Thomas. Until such times as it's not to take it out of your children's mouths, which take it is, and call it by what name you will it do remain and equally deprive, though may they come, and too soon they can not come, no Thomas, no!'

Mrs Plornish, who had been turning her face a little away with a corner of her apron in her hand, brought herself back to the conversation again by telling Miss Dorrit that Father was going over the water to pay his respects, unless she knew of any reason why it might not be agreeable.

Her answer was, 'I am going straight home, and if he will come with me I shall be so glad to take care of him—so glad,' said Little Dorrit, always thoughtful of the feelings of the weak, 'of his company.'

'There, Father!' cried Mrs Plornish. 'Ain't you a gay young man to be going for a walk along with Miss Dorrit! Let me tie your neck-handkerchief into a regular good bow, for you're a regular beau yourself, Father, if ever there was one.'

With this filial joke his daughter smartened him up, and gave him a loving hug, and stood at the door with her weak child in her arms, and her strong child tumbling down the steps, looking after her little old father as he toddled away with his arm under Little Dorrit's.

They walked at a slow pace, and Little Dorrit took him by the Iron Bridge and sat him down there for a rest, and they looked over at the water and talked about the shipping, and the old man mentioned what he would do if he had a ship full of gold coming home to him (his plan was to take a noble lodging for the Plornishes and himself at a Tea Gardens, and live there all the rest of their lives, attended on by the waiter), and it was a special birthday of the old man. They were within five minutes of their destination, when, at the corner of her own street, they came upon Fanny in her new bonnet bound for the same port.

'Why, good gracious me, Amy!' cried that young lady starting. 'You never mean it!'

'Mean what, Fanny dear?'

'Well! I could have believed a great deal of you,' returned the young lady with burning indignation, 'but I don't think even I could have believed this, of even you!'

'Fanny!' cried Little Dorrit, wounded and astonished.

'Oh! Don't Fanny me, you mean little thing, don't! The idea of coming along the open streets, in the broad light of day, with a Pauper!' (firing off the last word as if it were a ball from an air-gun).

'O Fanny!'

'I tell you not to Fanny me, for I'll not submit to it! I never knew such a thing. The way in which you are resolved and determined to disgrace us on all occasions, is really infamous. You bad little thing!'

'Does it disgrace anybody,' said Little Dorrit, very gently, 'to take care of this poor old man?'

'Yes, miss,' returned her sister, 'and you ought to know it does. And you do know it does, and you do it because you know it does. The principal pleasure of your life is to remind your family of their misfortunes. And the next great pleasure of your existence is to keep low company. But, however, if you have no sense of decency, I have. You'll please to allow me to go on the other side of the way, unmolested.'

With this, she bounced across to the opposite pavement. The old disgrace, who had been deferentially bowing a pace or two off (for Little Dorrit had let his arm go in her wonder, when Fanny began), and who had been hustled and cursed by impatient passengers for stopping the way, rejoined his companion, rather giddy, and said, 'I hope nothing's wrong with your honoured father, Miss? I hope there's nothing the matter in the honoured family?'

'No, no,' returned Little Dorrit. 'No, thank you. Give me your arm again, Mr Nandy. We shall soon be there now.'

So she talked to him as she had talked before, and they came to the Lodge and found Mr Chivery on the lock, and went in. Now, it happened that the Father of the Marshalsea was sauntering towards the Lodge at the moment when they were coming out of it, entering the prison arm in arm. As the spectacle of their approach met his view, he displayed the utmost agitation and despondency of mind; and—altogether regardless of Old Nandy, who, making his reverence, stood with his hat in his hand, as he always did in that gracious presence—turned about, and hurried in at his own doorway and up the staircase.

Leaving the old unfortunate, whom in an evil hour she had taken under her protection, with a hurried promise to return to him directly, Little Dorrit hastened after her father, and, on the staircase, found Fanny following her, and flouncing up with offended dignity. The three came into the room almost together; and the Father sat down in his chair, buried his face in his hands, and uttered a groan.

'Of course,' said Fanny. 'Very proper. Poor, afflicted Pa! Now, I hope you believe me, Miss?'

'What is it, father?' cried Little Dorrit, bending over him. 'Have I made you unhappy, father? Not I, I hope!'

'You hope, indeed! I dare say! Oh, you'—Fanny paused for a sufficiently strong expression—'you Common-minded little Amy! You complete prison-child!'

He stopped these angry reproaches with a wave of his hand, and sobbed out, raising his face and shaking his melancholy head at his younger daughter, 'Amy, I know that you are innocent in intention. But you have cut me to the soul.'

'Innocent in intention!' the implacable Fanny struck in. 'Stuff in intention! Low in intention! Lowering of the family in intention!'

'Father!' cried Little Dorrit, pale and trembling. 'I am very sorry. Pray forgive me. Tell me how it is, that I may not do it again!'

'How it is, you prevaricating little piece of goods!' cried Fanny. 'You know how it is. I have told you already, so don't fly in the face of Providence by attempting to deny it!'

'Hush! Amy,' said the father, passing his pocket-handkerchief several times across his face, and then grasping it convulsively in the hand that dropped across his knee, 'I have done what I could to keep you select here; I have done what I could to retain you a position here. I may have succeeded; I may not. You may know it; you may not. I give no opinion. I have endured everything here but humiliation. That I have happily been spared—until this day.'

Here his convulsive grasp unclosed itself, and he put his pocket-handkerchief to his eyes again. Little Dorrit, on the ground beside him, with her imploring hand upon his arm, watched him remorsefully. Coming out of his fit of grief, he clenched his pocket-handkerchief once more.

'Humiliation I have happily been spared until this day. Through all my troubles there has been that—Spirit in myself, and that—that submission to it, if I may use the term, in those about me, which has spared me—ha—humiliation. But this day, this minute, I have keenly felt it.'

'Of course! How could it be otherwise?' exclaimed the irrepressible Fanny. 'Careering and prancing about with a Pauper!' (air-gun again).

'But, dear father,' cried Little Dorrit, 'I don't justify myself for having wounded your dear heart—no! Heaven knows I don't!' She clasped her hands in quite an agony of distress. 'I do nothing but beg and pray you to be comforted and overlook it. But if I had not known that you were kind to the old man yourself, and took much notice of him, and were always glad to see him, I would not have come here with him, father, I would not, indeed. What I have been so unhappy as to do, I have done in mistake. I would not wilfully bring a tear to your eyes, dear love!' said Little Dorrit, her heart well-nigh broken, 'for anything the world could give me, or anything it could take away.'

Fanny, with a partly angry and partly repentant sob, began to cry herself, and to say—as this young lady always said when she was half in passion and half out of it, half spiteful with herself and half spiteful with everybody else—that she wished she were dead.

The Father of the Marshalsea in the meantime took his younger daughter to his breast, and patted her head.

'There, there! Say no more, Amy, say no more, my child. I will forget it as soon as I can. I,' with hysterical cheerfulness, 'I—shall soon be able to dismiss it. It is perfectly true, my dear, that I am always glad to see my old pensioner—as such, as such—and that I do—ha—

extend as much protection and kindness to the—hum—the bruised reed—I trust I may so call him without impropriety—as in my circumstances, I can. It is quite true that this is the case, my dear child. At the same time, I preserve in doing this, if I may—ha—if I may use the expression—Spirit. Becoming Spirit. And there are some things which are,' he stopped to sob, 'irreconcilable with that, and wound that—wound it deeply. It is not that I have seen my good Amy attentive, and—ha—condescending to my old pensioner—it is not that that hurts me. It is, if I am to close the painful subject by being explicit, that I have seen my child, my own child, my own daughter, coming into this College out of the public streets—smiling! smiling!—arm in arm with—O my God, a livery!'

This reference to the coat of no cut and no time, the unfortunate gentleman gasped forth, in a scarcely audible voice, and with his clenched pocket-handkerchief raised in the air. His excited feelings might have found some further painful utterance, but for a knock at the door, which had been already twice repeated, and to which Fanny (still wishing herself dead, and indeed now going so far as to add, buried) cried 'Come in!'

'Ah, Young John!' said the Father, in an altered and calmed voice. 'What is it, Young John?'

'A letter for you, sir, being left in the Lodge just this minute, and a message with it, I thought, happening to be there myself, sir, I would bring it to your room.' The speaker's attention was much distracted by the piteous spectacle of Little Dorrit at her father's feet, with her head turned away.

'Indeed, John? Thank you.'

'The letter is from Mr Clennam, sir—it's the answer—and the message was, sir, that Mr Clennam also sent his compliments, and word that he would do himself the pleasure of calling this afternoon, hoping to see you, and likewise,' attention more distracted than before, 'Miss Amy.'

'Oh!' As the Father glanced into the letter (there was a bank-note in it), he reddened a little, and patted Amy on the head afresh. 'Thank you, Young John. Quite right. Much obliged to you for your attention. No one waiting?'

'No, sir, no one waiting.'

'Thank you, John. How is your mother, Young John?'

'Thank you, sir, she's not quite as well as we could wish—in fact, we none of us are, except father—but she's pretty well, sir.'

'Say we sent our remembrances, will you? Say kind remembrances, if you please, Young John.'

'Thank you, sir, I will.' And Mr Chivery junior went his way, having spontaneously composed on the spot an entirely new epitaph for himself, to the effect that Here lay the body of John Chivery, Who, Having at such a date, Beheld the idol of his life, In grief and tears, And feeling unable to bear the harrowing spectacle, Immediately repaired to the abode of his inconsolable parents, And terminated his existence by his own rash act.

'There, there, Amy!' said the Father, when Young John had closed the door, 'let us say no more about it.' The last few minutes had improved his spirits remarkably, and he was quite lightsome. 'Where is my old pensioner all this while? We must not leave him by himself any longer, or he will begin to suppose he is not welcome, and that would pain me. Will you fetch him, my child, or shall I?'

'If you wouldn't mind, father,' said Little Dorrit, trying to bring her sobbing to a close.

'Certainly I will go, my dear. I forgot; your eyes are rather red. There! Cheer up, Amy. Don't be uneasy about me. I am quite myself again, my love, quite myself. Go to your room, Amy, and make yourself look comfortable and pleasant to receive Mr Clennam.'

'I would rather stay in my own room, Father,' returned Little Dorrit, finding it more difficult than before to regain her composure. 'I would far rather not see Mr Clennam.'

'Oh, fie, fie, my dear, that's folly. Mr Clennam is a very gentlemanly man—very gentlemanly. A little reserved at times; but I will say extremely gentlemanly. I couldn't think of your not being here to receive Mr Clennam, my dear, especially this afternoon. So go and freshen yourself up, Amy; go and freshen yourself up, like a good girl.'

Thus directed, Little Dorrit dutifully rose and obeyed: only pausing for a moment as she went out of the room, to give her sister a kiss of reconciliation. Upon which, that young lady, feeling much harassed in her mind, and having for the time worn out the wish with which she generally relieved it, conceived and executed the brilliant idea of wishing Old Nandy dead, rather than that he should come bothering there like a disgusting, tiresome, wicked wretch, and making mischief between two sisters.

The Father of the Marshalsea, even humming a tune, and wearing his black velvet cap a little on one side, so much improved were his spirits, went down into the yard, and found his old pensioner standing there hat in hand just within the gate, as he had stood all this time. 'Come, Nandy!' said he, with great suavity. 'Come up-stairs, Nandy; you know the way; why don't you come up-stairs?' He went the length, on this occasion, of giving him his hand and saying, 'How are you, Nandy? Are you pretty well?' To which that vocalist returned, 'I thank you, honoured sir, I am all the better for seeing your honour.' As they went along the yard, the Father of the Marshalsea presented him to a Collegian of recent date. 'An old acquaintance of mine, sir, an old pensioner.' And then said, 'Be covered, my good Nandy; put your hat on,' with great consideration.

His patronage did not stop here; for he charged Maggy to get the tea ready, and instructed her to buy certain tea-cakes, fresh butter, eggs, cold ham, and shrimps: to purchase which collation he gave her a bank-note for ten pounds, laying strict injunctions on her to be careful of the change. These preparations were in an advanced stage of progress, and his daughter Amy had come back with her work, when Clennam presented himself; whom he most graciously received, and besought to join their meal.

'Amy, my love, you know Mr Clennam even better than I have the happiness of doing. Fanny, my dear, you are acquainted with Mr Clennam.' Fanny acknowledged him haughtily; the position she tacitly took up in all such cases being that there was a vast conspiracy to insult the family by not understanding it, or sufficiently deferring to it, and here was one of the conspirators. 'This, Mr Clennam, you must know, is an old pensioner of mine, Old Nandy, a very faithful old man.' (He always spoke of him as an object of great antiquity, but he was two or three years younger than himself.) 'Let me see. You know Plornish, I think? I think my daughter Amy has mentioned to me that you know poor Plornish?'

'O yes!' said Arthur Clennam.

'Well, sir, this is Mrs Plornish's father.'

'Indeed? I am glad to see him.'

'You would be more glad if you knew his many good qualities, Mr Clennam.'

'I hope I shall come to know them through knowing him,' said Arthur, secretly pitying the bowed and submissive figure.

'It is a holiday with him, and he comes to see his old friends, who are always glad to see him,' observed the Father of the Marshalsea. Then he added behind his hand, ('Union, poor old fellow. Out for the day.')

By this time Maggy, quietly assisted by her Little Mother, had spread the board, and the repast was ready. It being hot weather and the prison very close, the window was as wide open as it could be pushed. 'If Maggy will spread that newspaper on the window-sill, my dear,' remarked the Father complacently and in a half whisper to Little Dorrit, 'my old pensioner can have his tea there, while we are having ours.'

So, with a gulf between him and the good company of about a foot in width, standard measure, Mrs Plornish's father was handsomely regaled. Clennam had never seen anything like his magnanimous protection by that other Father, he of the Marshalsea; and was lost in the contemplation of its many wonders.

The most striking of these was perhaps the relishing manner in which he remarked on the pensioner's infirmities and failings, as if he were a gracious Keeper making a running commentary on the decline of the harmless animal he exhibited.

'Not ready for more ham yet, Nandy? Why, how slow you are! (His last teeth,' he explained to the company, 'are going, poor old boy.')

At another time, he said, 'No shrimps, Nandy?' and on his not instantly replying, observed, ('His hearing is becoming very defective. He'll be deaf directly.')

At another time he asked him, 'Do you walk much, Nandy, about the yard within the walls of that place of yours?'

'No, sir; no. I haven't any great liking for that.'

'No, to be sure,' he assented. 'Very natural.' Then he privately informed the circle ('Legs going.')

Once he asked the pensioner, in that general clemency which asked him anything to keep him afloat, how old his younger grandchild was?

'John Edward,' said the pensioner, slowly laying down his knife and fork to consider. 'How old, sir? Let me think now.'

The Father of the Marshalsea tapped his forehead ('Memory weak.')

'John Edward, sir? Well, I really forget. I couldn't say at this minute, sir, whether it's two and two months, or whether it's two and five months. It's one or the other.'

'Don't distress yourself by worrying your mind about it,' he returned, with infinite forbearance. ('Faculties evidently decaying—old man rusts in the life he leads!')

The more of these discoveries that he persuaded himself he made in the pensioner, the better he appeared to like him; and when he got out of his chair after tea to bid the pensioner good-bye, on his intimating that he feared, honoured sir, his time was running out, he made himself look as erect and strong as possible.

'We don't call this a shilling, Nandy, you know,' he said, putting one in his hand. 'We call it tobacco.'

'Honoured sir, I thank you. It shall buy tobacco. My thanks and duty to Miss Amy and Miss Fanny. I wish you good night, Mr Clennam.'

'And mind you don't forget us, you know, Nandy,' said the Father. 'You must come again, mind, whenever you have an afternoon. You must not come out without seeing us, or we shall be jealous. Good night, Nandy. Be very careful how you descend the stairs, Nandy; they are rather uneven and worn.' With that he stood on the landing, watching the old man down: and when he came into the room again, said, with a solemn satisfaction on him, 'A melancholy sight that, Mr Clennam, though one has the consolation of knowing that he doesn't feel it himself. The poor old fellow is a dismal wreck. Spirit broken and gone—pulverised—crushed out of him, sir, completely!'

As Clennam had a purpose in remaining, he said what he could responsive to these sentiments, and stood at the window with their enunciator, while Maggy and her Little Mother washed the tea-service and cleared it away. He noticed that his companion stood at the window with the air of an affable and accessible Sovereign, and that, when any of his people in the yard below looked up, his recognition of their salutes just stopped short of a blessing.

When Little Dorrit had her work on the table, and Maggy hers on the bedstead, Fanny fell to tying her bonnet as a preliminary to her departure. Arthur, still having his purpose, still remained. At this time the door opened, without any notice, and Mr Tip came in. He kissed Amy as she started up to meet him, nodded to Fanny, nodded to his father, gloomed on the visitor without further recognition, and sat down.

'Tip, dear,' said Little Dorrit, mildly, shocked by this, 'don't you see—'

'Yes, I see, Amy. If you refer to the presence of any visitor you have here—I say, if you refer to that,' answered Tip, jerking his head with emphasis towards his shoulder nearest Clennam, 'I see!'

'Is that all you say?'

'That's all I say. And I suppose,' added the lofty young man, after a moment's pause, 'that visitor will understand me, when I say that's all I say. In short, I suppose the visitor will understand that he hasn't used me like a gentleman.'

'I do not understand that,' observed the obnoxious personage referred to with tranquillity.

'No? Why, then, to make it clearer to you, sir, I beg to let you know that when I address what I call a properly-worded appeal, and an urgent appeal, and a delicate appeal, to an individual, for a small temporary accommodation, easily within his power—easily within his power, mind!—and when that individual writes back word to me that he begs to be excused, I consider that he doesn't treat me like a gentleman.'

The Father of the Marshalsea, who had surveyed his son in silence, no sooner heard this sentiment, than he began in angry voice:—

'How dare you—' But his son stopped him.

'Now, don't ask me how I dare, father, because that's bosh. As to the fact of the line of conduct I choose to adopt towards the individual present, you ought to be proud of my showing a proper spirit.'

'I should think so!' cried Fanny.

'A proper spirit?' said the Father. 'Yes, a proper spirit; a becoming spirit. Is it come to this that my son teaches me—me—spirit!'

'Now, don't let us bother about it, father, or have any row on the subject. I have fully made up my mind that the individual present has not treated me like a gentleman. And there's an end of it.'

'But there is not an end of it, sir,' returned the Father. 'But there shall not be an end of it. You have made up your mind? You have made up your mind?'

'Yes, I have. What's the good of keeping on like that?'

'Because,' returned the Father, in a great heat, 'you had no right to make up your mind to what is monstrous, to what is—ha—immoral, to what is—hum—parricidal. No, Mr Clennam, I beg, sir. Don't ask me to desist; there is a—hum—a general principle involved here, which rises even above considerations of—ha—hospitality. I object to the assertion made by my son. I—ha—I personally repel it.'

'Why, what is it to you, father?' returned the son, over his shoulder.

'What is it to me, sir? I have a—hum—a spirit, sir, that will not endure it. I,' he took out his pocket-handkerchief again and dabbed his face. 'I am outraged and insulted by it. Let me suppose the case that I myself may at a certain time—ha—or times, have made a—hum—an appeal, and a properly-worded appeal, and a delicate appeal, and an urgent appeal to some individual for a small temporary accommodation. Let me suppose that that accommodation could have been easily extended, and was not extended, and that that individual informed me that he begged to be excused. Am I to be told by my own son, that I therefore received treatment not due to a gentleman, and that I—ha—I submitted to it?'

His daughter Amy gently tried to calm him, but he would not on any account be calmed. He said his spirit was up, and wouldn't endure this.

Was he to be told that, he wished to know again, by his own son on his own hearth, to his own face? Was that humiliation to be put upon him by his own blood?

'You are putting it on yourself, father, and getting into all this injury of your own accord!' said the young gentleman morosely. 'What I have made up my mind about has nothing to do with you. What I said had nothing to do with you. Why need you go trying on other people's hats?'

'I reply it has everything to do with me,' returned the Father. 'I point out to you, sir, with indignation, that—hum—the—ha—delicacy and peculiarity of your father's position should strike you dumb, sir, if nothing else should, in laying down such—ha—such unnatural principles. Besides; if you are not filial, sir, if you discard that duty, you are at least—hum—not a Christian? Are you—ha—an Atheist? And is it Christian, let me ask you, to stigmatise and denounce an individual for begging to be excused this time, when the same individual may—ha—respond with the required accommodation next time? Is it the part of a Christian not to—hum—not to try him again?' He had worked himself into quite a religious glow and fervour.

'I see precious well,' said Mr Tip, rising, 'that I shall get no sensible or fair argument here to-night, and so the best thing I can do is to cut. Good night, Amy. Don't be vexed. I am very sorry it happens here, and you here, upon my soul I am; but I can't altogether part with my spirit, even for your sake, old girl.'

With those words he put on his hat and went out, accompanied by Miss Fanny; who did not consider it spirited on her part to take leave of Clennam with any less opposing demonstration than a stare, importing that she had always known him for one of the large body of conspirators.

When they were gone, the Father of the Marshalsea was at first inclined to sink into despondency again, and would have done so, but that a gentleman opportunely came up within a minute or two to attend him to the Snuggery. It was the gentleman Clennam had seen on the night of his own accidental detention there, who had that impalpable grievance about the misappropriated Fund on which the Marshal was supposed to batten. He presented himself as deputation to escort the Father to the Chair, it being an occasion on which he had promised to preside over the assembled Collegians in the enjoyment of a little Harmony.

'Such, you see, Mr Clennam,' said the Father, 'are the incongruities of my position here. But a public duty! No man, I am sure, would more readily recognise a public duty than yourself.'

Clennam besought him not to delay a moment.

'Amy, my dear, if you can persuade Mr Clennam to stay longer, I can leave the honours of our poor apology for an establishment with confidence in your hands, and perhaps you may do something towards erasing from Mr Clennam's mind the—ha—untoward and unpleasant circumstance which has occurred since tea-time.'

Clennam assured him that it had made no impression on his mind, and therefore required no erasure.

'My dear sir,' said the Father, with a removal of his black cap and a grasp of Clennam's hand, combining to express the safe receipt of his note and enclosure that afternoon, 'Heaven ever bless you!'

So, at last, Clennam's purpose in remaining was attained, and he could speak to Little Dorrit with nobody by. Maggy counted as nobody, and she was by.

CHAPTER 32. More Fortune-Telling

Maggy sat at her work in her great white cap with its quantity of opaque frilling hiding what profile she had (she had none to spare), and her serviceable eye brought to bear upon her occupation, on the window side of the room. What with her flapping cap, and what with her unserviceable eye, she was quite partitioned off from her Little Mother, whose seat was opposite the window. The tread and shuffle of feet on the pavement of the yard had much diminished since the taking of the Chair, the tide of Collegians having set strongly in the direction of Harmony. Some few who had no music in their souls, or no money in their pockets, dawdled about; and the old spectacle of the visitor-wife and the depressed unseasoned prisoner still lingered in corners, as broken cobwebs and such unsightly discomforts draggle in corners of other places. It was the quietest time the College knew, saving the night hours when the Collegians took the benefit of the act of sleep. The occasional rattle of applause upon the tables of the Snuggery, denoted the successful termination of a morsel of Harmony; or the responsive acceptance, by the united children, of some toast or sentiment offered to them by their Father. Occasionally, a vocal strain more sonorous than the generality informed the listener that some boastful bass was in blue water, or in the hunting field, or with the reindeer, or on the mountain, or among the heather; but the Marshal of the Marshalsea knew better, and had got him hard and fast.

As Arthur Clennam moved to sit down by the side of Little Dorrit, she trembled so that she had much ado to hold her needle. Clennam gently put his hand upon her work, and said, 'Dear Little Dorrit, let me lay it down.'

She yielded it to him, and he put it aside. Her hands were then nervously clasping together, but he took one of them.

'How seldom I have seen you lately, Little Dorrit!'

'I have been busy, sir.'

'But I heard only to-day,' said Clennam, 'by mere accident, of your having been with those good people close by me. Why not come to me, then?'

'I—I don't know. Or rather, I thought you might be busy too. You generally are now, are you not?'

He saw her trembling little form and her downcast face, and the eyes that drooped the moment they were raised to his—he saw them almost with as much concern as tenderness.

'My child, your manner is so changed!'

The trembling was now quite beyond her control. Softly withdrawing her hand, and laying it in her other hand, she sat before him with her head bent and her whole form trembling.

'My own Little Dorrit,' said Clennam, compassionately.

She burst into tears. Maggy looked round of a sudden, and stared for at least a minute; but did not interpose. Clennam waited some little while before he spoke again.

'I cannot bear,' he said then, 'to see you weep; but I hope this is a relief to an overcharged heart.'

'Yes it is, sir. Nothing but that.'

'Well, well! I feared you would think too much of what passed here just now. It is of no moment; not the least. I am only unfortunate to have come in the way. Let it go by with these tears. It is not worth one of them. One of them? Such an idle thing should be repeated, with my glad consent, fifty times a day, to save you a moment's heart-ache, Little Dorrit.'

She had taken courage now, and answered, far more in her usual manner, 'You are so good! But even if there was nothing else in it to be sorry for and ashamed of, it is such a bad return to you—'

'Hush!' said Clennam, smiling and touching her lips with his hand. 'Forgetfulness in you who remember so many and so much, would be new indeed. Shall I remind you that I am not, and that I never was, anything but the friend whom you agreed to trust? No. You remember it, don't you?'

'I try to do so, or I should have broken the promise just now, when my mistaken brother was here. You will consider his bringing-up in this place, and will not judge him hardly, poor fellow, I know!' In raising her eyes with these words, she observed his face more nearly than she had done yet, and said, with a quick change of tone, 'You have not been ill, Mr Clennam?'

'No.'

'Nor tried? Nor hurt?' she asked him, anxiously.

It fell to Clennam now, to be not quite certain how to answer. He said in reply:

'To speak the truth, I have been a little troubled, but it is over. Do I show it so plainly? I ought to have more fortitude and self-command than that. I thought I had. I must learn them of you. Who could teach me better!'

He never thought that she saw in him what no one else could see. He never thought that in the whole world there were no other eyes that looked upon him with the same light and strength as hers.

'But it brings me to something that I wish to say,' he continued, 'and therefore I will not quarrel even with my own face for telling tales and being unfaithful to me. Besides, it is a privilege and pleasure to confide in my Little Dorrit. Let me confess then, that, forgetting how grave I was, and how old I was, and how the time for such things had gone by me with the many years of sameness and little happiness that made up my long life far away, without marking it—that, forgetting all this, I fancied I loved some one.'

'Do I know her, sir?' asked Little Dorrit.

'No, my child.'

'Not the lady who has been kind to me for your sake?'

'Flora. No, no. Do you think—'

'I never quite thought so,' said Little Dorrit, more to herself than him. 'I did wonder at it a little.'

'Well!' said Clennam, abiding by the feeling that had fallen on him in the avenue on the night of the roses, the feeling that he was an older man, who had done with that tender part of life, 'I found out my mistake, and I thought about it a little—in short, a good deal—and got wiser. Being wiser, I counted up my years and considered what I am, and looked back, and looked forward, and found that I should soon be grey. I found that I had climbed the hill, and passed the level ground upon the top, and was descending quickly.'

If he had known the sharpness of the pain he caused the patient heart, in speaking thus! While doing it, too, with the purpose of easing and serving her.

'I found that the day when any such thing would have been graceful in me, or good in me, or hopeful or happy for me or any one in connection with me, was gone, and would never shine again.'

O! If he had known, if he had known! If he could have seen the dagger in his hand, and the cruel wounds it struck in the faithful bleeding breast of his Little Dorrit!

'All that is over, and I have turned my face from it. Why do I speak of this to Little Dorrit? Why do I show you, my child, the space of years that there is between us, and recall to you that I have passed, by the amount of your whole life, the time that is present to you?'

'Because you trust me, I hope. Because you know that nothing can touch you without touching me; that nothing can make you happy or unhappy, but it must make me, who am so grateful to you, the same.'

He heard the thrill in her voice, he saw her earnest face, he saw her clear true eyes, he saw the quickened bosom that would have joyfully thrown itself before him to receive a mortal wound directed at his breast, with the dying cry, 'I love him!' and the remotest suspicion of the truth never dawned upon his mind. No. He saw the devoted little creature with her worn shoes, in her common dress, in her jail-home; a slender child in body, a strong heroine in soul; and the light of her domestic story made all else dark to him.

'For those reasons assuredly, Little Dorrit, but for another too. So far removed, so different, and so much older, I am the better fitted for your friend and adviser. I mean, I am the more easily to be trusted; and any little constraint that you might feel with another, may vanish before me. Why have you kept so retired from me? Tell me.'

'I am better here. My place and use are here. I am much better here,' said Little Dorrit, faintly.

'So you said that day upon the bridge. I thought of it much afterwards. Have you no secret you could entrust to me, with hope and comfort, if you would!'

'Secret? No, I have no secret,' said Little Dorrit in some trouble.

They had been speaking in low voices; more because it was natural to what they said to adopt that tone, than with any care to reserve it from Maggy at her work. All of a sudden Maggy stared again, and this time spoke:

'I say! Little Mother!'

'Yes, Maggy.'

'If you an't got no secret of your own to tell him, tell him that about the Princess. She had a secret, you know.'

'The Princess had a secret?' said Clennam, in some surprise. 'What Princess was that, Maggy?'

'Lor! How you do go and bother a gal of ten,' said Maggy, 'catching the poor thing up in that way. Whoever said the Princess had a secret? I never said so.'

'I beg your pardon. I thought you did.'

'No, I didn't. How could I, when it was her as wanted to find it out? It was the little woman as had the secret, and she was always a spinning at her wheel. And so she says to her, why do you keep it there? And so the t'other one says to her, no I don't; and so the t'other one says to her, yes you do; and then they both goes to the cupboard, and there it is. And she wouldn't go into the Hospital, and so she died. You know, Little Mother; tell him that. For it was a reg'lar good secret, that was!' cried Maggy, hugging herself.

Arthur looked at Little Dorrit for help to comprehend this, and was struck by seeing her so timid and red. But, when she told him that it was only a Fairy Tale she had one day made up for Maggy, and that there was nothing in it which she wouldn't be ashamed to tell again to anybody else, even if she could remember it, he left the subject where it was.

However, he returned to his own subject by first entreating her to see him oftener, and to remember that it was impossible to have a stronger interest in her welfare than he had, or to be more set upon promoting it than he was. When she answered fervently, she well knew that, she never forgot it, he touched upon his second and more delicate point—the suspicion he had formed.

'Little Dorrit,' he said, taking her hand again, and speaking lower than he had spoken yet, so that even Maggy in the small room could not hear him, 'another word. I have wanted very much to say this to you; I have tried for opportunities. Don't mind me, who, for the matter of years, might be your father or your uncle. Always think of me as quite an old man. I know that all your devotion centres in this room, and that nothing to the last will ever tempt you away from the duties you discharge here. If I were not sure of it, I should, before now, have implored you, and implored your father, to let me make some provision for you in a more suitable place. But you may have an interest—I will not say, now, though even that might be—may have, at another time, an interest in some one else; an interest not incompatible with your affection here.'

She was very, very pale, and silently shook her head.

'It may be, dear Little Dorrit.'

'No. No. No.' She shook her head, after each slow repetition of the word, with an air of quiet desolation that he remembered long afterwards. The time came when he remembered it well, long afterwards, within those prison walls; within that very room.

'But, if it ever should be, tell me so, my dear child. Entrust the truth to me, point out the object of such an interest to me, and I will try with all the zeal, and honour, and friendship and respect that I feel for you, good Little Dorrit of my heart, to do you a lasting service.'

'O thank you, thank you! But, O no, O no, O no!' She said this, looking at him with her work-worn hands folded together, and in the same resigned accents as before.

'I press for no confidence now. I only ask you to repose unhesitating trust in me.'

'Can I do less than that, when you are so good!'

'Then you will trust me fully? Will have no secret unhappiness, or anxiety, concealed from me?'

'Almost none.'

'And you have none now?'

She shook her head. But she was very pale.

'When I lie down to-night, and my thoughts come back—as they will, for they do every night, even when I have not seen you—to this sad place, I may believe that there is no grief beyond this room, now, and its usual occupants, which preys on Little Dorrit's mind?'

She seemed to catch at these words—that he remembered, too, long afterwards—and said, more brightly, 'Yes, Mr Clennam; yes, you may!'

The crazy staircase, usually not slow to give notice when any one was coming up or down, here creaked under a quick tread, and a further sound was heard upon it, as if a little steam-engine with more steam than it knew what to do with, were working towards the room. As it approached, which it did very rapidly, it laboured with increased energy; and, after knocking at the door, it sounded as if it were stooping down and snorting in at the keyhole.

Before Maggy could open the door, Mr Pancks, opening it from without, stood without a hat and with his bare head in the wildest condition, looking at Clennam and Little Dorrit, over her shoulder. He had a lighted cigar in his hand, and brought with him airs of ale and tobacco smoke.

'Pancks the gipsy,' he observed out of breath, 'fortune-telling.'

He stood dingily smiling, and breathing hard at them, with a most curious air; as if, instead of being his proprietor's grubber, he were the triumphant proprietor of the Marshalsea, the Marshal, all the turnkeys, and all the Collegians. In his great self-satisfaction he put his cigar to his lips (being evidently no smoker), and took such a pull at it, with his right eye shut up tight for the purpose, that he underwent a convulsion of shuddering and choking. But even in the midst of that paroxysm, he still essayed to repeat his favourite introduction of himself, 'Pa-ancks the gi-ipsy, fortune-telling.'

'I am spending the evening with the rest of 'em,' said Pancks. 'I've been singing. I've been taking a part in White sand and grey sand. I don't know anything about it. Never mind. I'll take any part in anything. It's all the same, if you're loud enough.'

At first Clennam supposed him to be intoxicated. But he soon perceived that though he might be a little the worse (or better) for ale, the staple of his excitement was not brewed from malt, or distilled from any grain or berry.

'How d'ye do, Miss Dorrit?' said Pancks. 'I thought you wouldn't mind my running round, and looking in for a moment. Mr Clennam I heard was here, from Mr Dorrit. How are you, Sir?'

Clennam thanked him, and said he was glad to see him so gay.

'Gay!' said Pancks. 'I'm in wonderful feather, sir. I can't stop a minute, or I shall be missed, and I don't want 'em to miss me.—Eh, Miss Dorrit?'

He seemed to have an insatiate delight in appealing to her and looking at her; excitedly sticking his hair up at the same moment, like a dark species of cockatoo.

'I haven't been here half an hour. I knew Mr Dorrit was in the chair, and I said, "I'll go and support him!" I ought to be down in Bleeding Heart Yard by rights; but I can worry them to-morrow.—Eh, Miss Dorrit?'

His little black eyes sparkled electrically. His very hair seemed to sparkle as he roughened it. He was in that highly-charged state that one might have expected to draw sparks and snaps from him by presenting a knuckle to any part of his figure.

'Capital company here,' said Pancks.—'Eh, Miss Dorrit?'

She was half afraid of him, and irresolute what to say. He laughed, with a nod towards Clennam.

'Don't mind him, Miss Dorrit. He's one of us. We agreed that you shouldn't take on to mind me before people, but we didn't mean Mr Clennam. He's one of us. He's in it. An't you, Mr Clennam?—Eh, Miss Dorrit?'

The excitement of this strange creature was fast communicating itself to Clennam. Little Dorrit with amazement, saw this, and observed that they exchanged quick looks.

'I was making a remark,' said Pancks, 'but I declare I forget what it was. Oh, I know! Capital company here. I've been treating 'em all round.—Eh, Miss Dorrit?'

'Very generous of you,' she returned, noticing another of the quick looks between the two.

'Not at all,' said Pancks. 'Don't mention it. I'm coming into my property, that's the fact. I can afford to be liberal. I think I'll give 'em a treat here. Tables laid in the yard. Bread in stacks. Pipes in faggots. Tobacco in hayloads. Roast beef and plum-pudding for every one. Quart of double stout a head. Pint of wine too, if they like it, and the authorities give permission.—Eh, Miss Dorrit?'

She was thrown into such a confusion by his manner, or rather by Clennam's growing understanding of his manner (for she looked to him after every fresh appeal and cockatoo demonstration on the part of Mr Pancks), that she only moved her lips in answer, without forming any word.

'And oh, by-the-bye!' said Pancks, 'you were to live to know what was behind us on that little hand of yours. And so you shall, you shall, my darling.—Eh, Miss Dorrit?'

He had suddenly checked himself. Where he got all the additional black prongs from, that now flew up all over his head like the myriads of points that break out in the large change of a great firework, was a wonderful mystery.

'But I shall be missed;' he came back to that; 'and I don't want 'em to miss me. Mr Clennam, you and I made a bargain. I said you should find me stick to it. You shall find me stick to it now, sir, if you'll step out of the room a moment. Miss Dorrit, I wish you good night. Miss Dorrit, I wish you good fortune.'

He rapidly shook her by both hands, and puffed down stairs. Arthur followed him with such a hurried step, that he had very nearly tumbled over him on the last landing, and rolled him down into the yard.

'What is it, for Heaven's sake!' Arthur demanded, when they burst out there both together.

'Stop a moment, sir. Mr Rugg. Let me introduce him.'

With those words he presented another man without a hat, and also with a cigar, and also surrounded with a halo of ale and tobacco smoke, which man, though not so excited as himself, was in a state which would have been akin to lunacy but for its fading into sober method when compared with the rampancy of Mr Pancks.

'Mr Clennam, Mr Rugg,' said Pancks. 'Stop a moment. Come to the pump.'

They adjourned to the pump. Mr Pancks, instantly putting his head under the spout, requested Mr Rugg to take a good strong turn at the handle. Mr Rugg complying to the letter, Mr Pancks came forth snorting and blowing to some purpose, and dried himself on his handkerchief.

'I am the clearer for that,' he gasped to Clennam standing astonished. 'But upon my soul, to hear her father making speeches in that chair, knowing what we know, and to see her up in that room in that dress, knowing what we know, is enough to—give me a back, Mr Rugg—a little higher, sir,—that'll do.'

Then and there, on that Marshalsea pavement, in the shades of evening, did Mr Pancks, of all mankind, fly over the head and shoulders of Mr Rugg of Pentonville, General Agent, Accountant, and Recoverer of Debts. Alighting on his feet, he took Clennam by the button-hole, led him behind the pump, and pantingly produced from his pocket a bundle of papers.

Mr Rugg, also, pantingly produced from his pocket a bundle of papers.

'Stay!' said Clennam in a whisper. 'You have made a discovery.'

Mr Pancks answered, with an unction which there is no language to convey, 'We rather think so.'

'Does it implicate any one?'

'How implicate, sir?'

'In any suppression or wrong dealing of any kind?'

'Not a bit of it.'

'Thank God!' said Clennam to himself. 'Now show me.'

'You are to understand'—snorted Pancks, feverishly unfolding papers, and speaking in short high-pressure blasts of sentences, 'Where's the Pedigree? Where's Schedule number four, Mr Rugg? Oh! all right! Here we are.—You are to understand that we are this very day virtually complete. We shan't be legally for a day or two. Call it at the outside a week. We've been at it night and day for I don't know how long. Mr Rugg, you know how long? Never mind. Don't say. You'll only confuse me. You shall tell her, Mr Clennam. Not till we give you leave. Where's that rough total, Mr Rugg? Oh! Here we are! There sir! That's what you'll have to break to her. That man's your Father of the Marshalsea!'

CHAPTER 33. Mrs Merdle's Complaint

Resigning herself to inevitable fate by making the best of those people, the Miggleses, and submitting her philosophy to the draught upon it, of which she had foreseen the likelihood in her interview with Arthur, Mrs Gowan handsomely resolved not to oppose her son's marriage. In her progress to, and happy arrival at, this resolution, she was possibly influenced, not only by her maternal affections but by three politic considerations.

Of these, the first may have been that her son had never signified the smallest intention to ask her consent, or any mistrust of his ability to dispense with it; the second, that the pension bestowed upon her by a grateful country (and a Barnacle) would be freed from any little filial inroads, when her Henry should be married to the darling only child of a man in very easy circumstances; the third, that Henry's debts must clearly be paid down upon the altar-railing by his father-in-law. When, to these three-fold points of prudence there is added the fact that Mrs Gowan yielded her consent the moment she knew of Mr Meagles having yielded his, and that Mr Meagles's objection to the marriage had been the sole obstacle in its way all along, it becomes the height of probability that the relict of the deceased Commissioner of nothing particular, turned these ideas in her sagacious mind.

Among her connections and acquaintances, however, she maintained her individual dignity and the dignity of the blood of the Barnacles, by diligently nursing the pretence that it was a most unfortunate business; that she was sadly cut up by it; that this was a perfect fascination under which Henry laboured; that she had opposed it for a long time, but what could a mother do; and the like. She had already called Arthur Clennam to bear witness to this fable, as a friend of the Meagles family; and she followed up the move by now impounding the family itself for the same purpose. In the first interview she accorded to Mr Meagles, she slided herself into the position of disconsolately but gracefully yielding to irresistible pressure. With the utmost politeness and good-breeding, she feigned that it was she—not he—who had made the difficulty, and who at length gave way; and that the sacrifice was hers—not his. The same feint, with the same polite dexterity, she foisted on Mrs Meagles, as a conjuror might have forced a card on that innocent lady; and, when her future daughter-in-law was presented to her by her son, she said on embracing her, 'My dear, what have you done to Henry that has bewitched him so!' at the same time allowing a few tears to carry before them, in little pills, the cosmetic powder on her nose; as a delicate but touching signal that she suffered much inwardly for the show of composure with which she bore her misfortune.

Among the friends of Mrs Gowan (who piqued herself at once on being Society, and on maintaining intimate and easy relations with that Power), Mrs Merdle occupied a front row. True, the Hampton Court Bohemians, without exception, turned up their noses at Merdle as an upstart; but they turned them down again, by falling flat on their faces to worship his wealth. In which compensating adjustment of their noses, they were pretty much like Treasury, Bar, and Bishop, and all the rest of them.

To Mrs Merdle, Mrs Gowan repaired on a visit of self-condolence, after having given the gracious consent aforesaid. She drove into town for the purpose in a one-horse carriage irreverently called at that period of English history, a pill-box. It belonged to a job-master in a small way, who drove it himself, and who jobbed it by the day, or hour, to most of the old ladies in Hampton Court Palace; but it was a point of ceremony, in that encampment, that the whole equipage should be tacitly regarded as the private property of the jobber for the time being, and that the job-master should betray personal knowledge of nobody but the jobber in possession. So the Circumlocution Barnacles, who were the largest job-masters in the universe, always pretended to know of no other job but the job immediately in hand.

Mrs Merdle was at home, and was in her nest of crimson and gold, with the parrot on a neighbouring stem watching her with his head on one side, as if he took her for another splendid parrot of a larger species. To whom entered Mrs Gowan, with her favourite green fan, which softened the light on the spots of bloom.

'My dear soul,' said Mrs Gowan, tapping the back of her friend's hand with this fan after a little indifferent conversation, 'you are my only comfort. That affair of Henry's that I told you of, is to take place. Now, how does it strike you? I am dying to know, because you represent and express Society so well.'

Mrs Merdle reviewed the bosom which Society was accustomed to review; and having ascertained that show-window of Mr Merdle's and the London jewellers' to be in good order, replied:

'As to marriage on the part of a man, my dear, Society requires that he should retrieve his fortunes by marriage. Society requires that he should gain by marriage. Society requires that he should found a handsome establishment by marriage. Society does not see, otherwise, what he has to do with marriage. Bird, be quiet!'

For the parrot on his cage above them, presiding over the conference as if he were a judge (and indeed he looked rather like one), had wound up the exposition with a shriek.

'Cases there are,' said Mrs Merdle, delicately crooking the little finger of her favourite hand, and making her remarks neater by that neat action; 'cases there are where a man is not young or elegant, and is rich, and has a handsome establishment already. Those are of a different kind. In such cases—'

Mrs Merdle shrugged her snowy shoulders and put her hand upon the jewel-stand, checking a little cough, as though to add, 'why, a man looks out for this sort of thing, my dear.' Then the parrot shrieked again, and she put up her glass to look at him, and said, 'Bird! Do be quiet!'

'But, young men,' resumed Mrs Merdle, 'and by young men you know what I mean, my love—I mean people's sons who have the world before them—they must place themselves in a better position towards Society by marriage, or Society really will not have any patience with their making fools of themselves. Dreadfully worldly all this sounds,' said Mrs Merdle, leaning back in her nest and putting up her glass again, 'does it not?'

'But it is true,' said Mrs Gowan, with a highly moral air.

'My dear, it is not to be disputed for a moment,' returned Mrs Merdle; 'because Society has made up its mind on the subject, and there is nothing more to be said. If we were in a more primitive state, if we lived under roofs of leaves, and kept cows and sheep and creatures instead of banker's accounts (which would be delicious; my dear, I am pastoral to a degree, by nature), well and good. But we don't live under leaves, and keep cows and sheep and creatures. I perfectly exhaust myself sometimes, in pointing out the distinction to Edmund Sparkler.'

Mrs Gowan, looking over her green fan when this young gentleman's name was mentioned, replied as follows:

'My love, you know the wretched state of the country—those unfortunate concessions of John Barnacle's!—and you therefore know the reasons for my being as poor as Thingummy.'

'A church mouse?' Mrs Merdle suggested with a smile.

'I was thinking of the other proverbial church person—Job,' said Mrs Gowan. 'Either will do. It would be idle to disguise, consequently, that there is a wide difference between the position of your son and mine. I may add, too, that Henry has talent—'

'Which Edmund certainly has not,' said Mrs Merdle, with the greatest suavity.

'—and that his talent, combined with disappointment,' Mrs Gowan went on, 'has led him into a pursuit which—ah dear me! You know, my dear. Such being Henry's different position, the question is what is the most inferior class of marriage to which I can reconcile myself.'

Mrs Merdle was so much engaged with the contemplation of her arms (beautiful-formed arms, and the very thing for bracelets), that she omitted to reply for a while. Roused at length by the silence, she folded the arms, and with admirable presence of mind looked her friend full in the face, and said interrogatively, 'Ye-es? And then?'

'And then, my dear,' said Mrs Gowan not quite so sweetly as before, 'I should be glad to hear what you have to say to it.'

Here the parrot, who had been standing on one leg since he screamed last, burst into a fit of laughter, bobbed himself derisively up and down on both legs, and finished by standing on one leg again, and pausing for a reply, with his head as much awry as he could possibly twist it.

'Sounds mercenary to ask what the gentleman is to get with the lady,' said Mrs Merdle; 'but Society is perhaps a little mercenary, you know, my dear.'

'From what I can make out,' said Mrs Gowan, 'I believe I may say that Henry will be relieved from debt—'

'Much in debt?' asked Mrs Merdle through her eyeglass.

'Why tolerably, I should think,' said Mrs Gowan.

'Meaning the usual thing; I understand; just so,' Mrs Merdle observed in a comfortable sort of way.

'And that the father will make them an allowance of three hundred a-year, or perhaps altogether something more, which, in Italy-'

'Oh! Going to Italy?' said Mrs Merdle.

'For Henry to study. You need be at no loss to guess why, my dear. That dreadful Art—'

True. Mrs Merdle hastened to spare the feelings of her afflicted friend. She understood. Say no more!

'And that,' said Mrs Gowan, shaking her despondent head, 'that's all. That,' repeated Mrs Gowan, furling her green fan for the moment, and tapping her chin with it (it was on the way to being a double chin; might be called a chin and a half at present), 'that's all! On the death of the old people, I suppose there will be more to come; but how it may be restricted or locked up, I don't know. And as to that, they may live for ever. My dear, they are just the kind of people to do it.'

Now, Mrs Merdle, who really knew her friend Society pretty well, and who knew what Society's mothers were, and what Society's daughters were, and what Society's matrimonial market was, and how prices ruled in it, and what scheming and counter-scheming took place for the high buyers, and what bargaining and huckstering went on, thought in the depths of her capacious bosom that this was a sufficiently good catch. Knowing, however, what was expected of her, and perceiving the exact nature of the fiction to be nursed, she took it delicately in her arms, and put her required contribution of gloss upon it.

'And that is all, my dear?' said she, heaving a friendly sigh. 'Well, well! The fault is not yours. You have nothing to reproach yourself with. You must exercise the strength of mind for which you are renowned, and make the best of it.'

'The girl's family have made,' said Mrs Gowan, 'of course, the most strenuous endeavours to—as the lawyers say—to have and to hold Henry.'

'Of course they have, my dear,' said Mrs Merdle.

'I have persisted in every possible objection, and have worried myself morning, noon, and night, for means to detach Henry from the connection.'

'No doubt you have, my dear,' said Mrs Merdle.

'And all of no use. All has broken down beneath me. Now tell me, my love. Am I justified in at last yielding my most reluctant consent to Henry's marrying among people not in Society; or, have I acted with inexcusable weakness?'

In answer to this direct appeal, Mrs Merdle assured Mrs Gowan (speaking as a Priestess of Society) that she was highly to be commended, that she was much to be sympathised with, that she had taken the highest of parts, and had come out of the furnace refined. And Mrs Gowan, who of course saw through her own threadbare blind perfectly, and who knew that Mrs Merdle saw through it perfectly, and who knew that Society would see through it perfectly, came out of this form, notwithstanding, as she had gone into it, with immense complacency and gravity.

The conference was held at four or five o'clock in the afternoon, when all the region of Harley Street, Cavendish Square, was resonant of carriage-wheels and double-knocks. It had reached this point when Mr Merdle came home from his daily occupation of causing the British name to be more and more respected in all parts of the civilised globe capable of the appreciation of world-wide commercial enterprise and gigantic combinations of skill and capital. For, though nobody knew with the least precision what Mr Merdle's business was, except that it was to coin money, these were the terms in which everybody defined it on all ceremonious occasions, and which it was the last new polite reading of the parable of the camel and the needle's eye to accept without inquiry.

For a gentleman who had this splendid work cut out for him, Mr Merdle looked a little common, and rather as if, in the course of his vast transactions, he had accidentally made an interchange of heads with some inferior spirit. He presented himself before the two ladies in the course of a dismal stroll through his mansion, which had no apparent object but escape from the presence of the chief butler.

'I beg your pardon,' he said, stopping short in confusion; 'I didn't know there was anybody here but the parrot.'

However, as Mrs Merdle said, 'You can come in!' and as Mrs Gowan said she was just going, and had already risen to take her leave, he came in, and stood looking out at a distant window, with his hands crossed under his uneasy coat-cuffs, clasping his wrists as if he were taking himself into custody. In this attitude he fell directly into a reverie from which he was only aroused by his wife's calling to him from her ottoman, when they had been for some quarter of an hour alone.

'Eh? Yes?' said Mr Merdle, turning towards her. 'What is it?'

'What is it?' repeated Mrs Merdle. 'It is, I suppose, that you have not heard a word of my complaint.'

'Your complaint, Mrs Merdle?' said Mr Merdle. 'I didn't know that you were suffering from a complaint. What complaint?'

'A complaint of you,' said Mrs Merdle.

'Oh! A complaint of me,' said Mr Merdle. 'What is the—what have I—what may you have to complain of in me, Mrs Merdle?'

In his withdrawing, abstracted, pondering way, it took him some time to shape this question. As a kind of faint attempt to convince himself that he was the master of the house, he concluded by presenting his forefinger to the parrot, who expressed his opinion on that subject by instantly driving his bill into it.

'You were saying, Mrs Merdle,' said Mr Merdle, with his wounded finger in his mouth, 'that you had a complaint against me?'

'A complaint which I could scarcely show the justice of more emphatically, than by having to repeat it,' said Mrs Merdle. 'I might as well have stated it to the wall. I had far better have stated it to the bird. He would at least have screamed.'

'You don't want me to scream, Mrs Merdle, I suppose,' said Mr Merdle, taking a chair.

'Indeed I don't know,' retorted Mrs Merdle, 'but that you had better do that, than be so moody and distraught. One would at least know that you were sensible of what was going on around you.'

'A man might scream, and yet not be that, Mrs Merdle,' said Mr Merdle, heavily.

'And might be dogged, as you are at present, without screaming,' returned Mrs Merdle. 'That's very true. If you wish to know the complaint I make against you, it is, in so many plain words, that you really ought not to go into Society unless you can accommodate yourself to Society.'

Mr Merdle, so twisting his hands into what hair he had upon his head that he seemed to lift himself up by it as he started out of his chair, cried:

'Why, in the name of all the infernal powers, Mrs Merdle, who does more for Society than I do? Do you see these premises, Mrs Merdle? Do you see this furniture, Mrs Merdle? Do you look in the glass and see yourself, Mrs Merdle? Do you know the cost of all this, and who it's all provided for? And yet will you tell me that I oughtn't to go into Society? I, who shower money upon it in this way? I, who might always be said—to—to—to harness myself to a watering-cart full of money, and go about saturating Society every day of my life.'

'Pray, don't be violent, Mr Merdle,' said Mrs Merdle.

'Violent?' said Mr Merdle. 'You are enough to make me desperate. You don't know half of what I do to accommodate Society. You don't know anything of the sacrifices I make for it.'

'I know,' returned Mrs Merdle, 'that you receive the best in the land. I know that you move in the whole Society of the country. And I believe I know (indeed, not to make any ridiculous pretence about it, I know I know) who sustains you in it, Mr Merdle.'

'Mrs Merdle,' retorted that gentleman, wiping his dull red and yellow face, 'I know that as well as you do. If you were not an ornament to Society, and if I was not a benefactor to Society, you and I would never have come together. When I say a benefactor to it, I mean a person who provides it with all sorts of expensive things to eat and drink and look at. But, to tell me that I am not fit for it after all I have done for it—after all I have done for it,' repeated Mr Merdle, with a wild emphasis that made his wife lift up her eyelids, 'after all—all!—to tell me I have no right to mix with it after all, is a pretty reward.'

'I say,' answered Mrs Merdle composedly, 'that you ought to make yourself fit for it by being more degage, and less preoccupied. There is a positive vulgarity in carrying your business affairs about with you as you do.'

'How do I carry them about, Mrs Merdle?' asked Mr Merdle.

'How do you carry them about?' said Mrs Merdle. 'Look at yourself in the glass.'

Mr Merdle involuntarily turned his eyes in the direction of the nearest mirror, and asked, with a slow determination of his turbid blood to his temples, whether a man was to be called to account for his digestion?

'You have a physician,' said Mrs Merdle.

'He does me no good,' said Mr Merdle.

Mrs Merdle changed her ground.

'Besides,' said she, 'your digestion is nonsense. I don't speak of your digestion. I speak of your manner.'

'Mrs Merdle,' returned her husband, 'I look to you for that. You supply manner, and I supply money.'

'I don't expect you,' said Mrs Merdle, reposing easily among her cushions, 'to captivate people. I don't want you to take any trouble upon yourself, or to try to be fascinating. I simply request you to care about nothing—or seem to care about nothing—as everybody else does.'

'Do I ever say I care about anything?' asked Mr Merdle.

'Say? No! Nobody would attend to you if you did. But you show it.'

'Show what? What do I show?' demanded Mr Merdle hurriedly.

'I have already told you. You show that you carry your business cares an projects about, instead of leaving them in the City, or wherever else they belong to,' said Mrs Merdle. 'Or seeming to. Seeming would be quite enough: I ask no more. Whereas you couldn't be more occupied with your day's calculations and combinations than you habitually show yourself to be, if you were a carpenter.'

'A carpenter!' repeated Mr Merdle, checking something like a groan. 'I shouldn't so much mind being a carpenter, Mrs Merdle.'

'And my complaint is,' pursued the lady, disregarding the low remark, 'that it is not the tone of Society, and that you ought to correct it, Mr Merdle. If you have any doubt of my judgment, ask even Edmund Sparkler.' The door of the room had opened, and Mrs Merdle now surveyed the head of her son through her glass. 'Edmund; we want you here.'

Mr Sparkler, who had merely put in his head and looked round the room without entering (as if he were searching the house for that young lady with no nonsense about her), upon this followed up his head with his body, and stood before them. To whom, in a few easy words adapted to his capacity, Mrs Merdle stated the question at issue.

The young gentleman, after anxiously feeling his shirt-collar as if it were his pulse and he were hypochondriacal, observed, 'That he had heard it noticed by fellers.'

'Edmund Sparkler has heard it noticed,' said Mrs Merdle, with languid triumph. 'Why, no doubt everybody has heard it noticed!' Which in truth was no unreasonable inference; seeing that Mr Sparkler would probably be the last person, in any assemblage of the human species, to receive an impression from anything that passed in his presence.

'And Edmund Sparkler will tell you, I dare say,' said Mrs Merdle, waving her favourite hand towards her husband, 'how he has heard it noticed.'

'I couldn't,' said Mr Sparkler, after feeling his pulse as before, 'couldn't undertake to say what led to it—'cause memory desperate loose. But being in company with the brother of a doosed fine gal—well educated too—with no biggodd nonsense about her—at the period alluded to—'

'There! Never mind the sister,' remarked Mrs Merdle, a little impatiently. 'What did the brother say?'

'Didn't say a word, ma'am,' answered Mr Sparkler. 'As silent a feller as myself. Equally hard up for a remark.'

'Somebody said something,' returned Mrs Merdle. 'Never mind who it was.'

('Assure you I don't in the least,' said Mr Sparkler.)

'But tell us what it was.'

Mr Sparkler referred to his pulse again, and put himself through some severe mental discipline before he replied:

'Fellers referring to my Governor—expression not my own—occasionally compliment my Governor in a very handsome way on being immensely rich and knowing—perfect phenomenon of Buyer and Banker and that—but say the Shop sits heavily on him. Say he carried the Shop about, on his back rather—like Jew clothesmen with too much business.'

'Which,' said Mrs Merdle, rising, with her floating drapery about her, 'is exactly my complaint. Edmund, give me your arm up-stairs.'

Mr Merdle, left alone to meditate on a better conformation of himself to Society, looked out of nine windows in succession, and appeared to see nine wastes of space. When he had thus entertained himself he went down-stairs, and looked intently at all the carpets on the ground-floor; and then came up-stairs again, and looked intently at all the carpets on the first-floor; as if they were gloomy depths, in unison with his oppressed soul. Through all the rooms he wandered, as he always did, like the last person on earth who had any business to approach them. Let Mrs Merdle announce, with all her might, that she was at Home ever so many nights in a season, she could not announce more widely and unmistakably than Mr Merdle did that he was never at home.

At last he met the chief butler, the sight of which splendid retainer always finished him. Extinguished by this great creature, he sneaked to his dressing-room, and there remained shut up until he rode out to dinner, with Mrs Merdle, in her own handsome chariot. At dinner, he was envied and flattered as a being of might, was Treasuried, Barred, and Bishoped, as much as he would; and an hour after midnight came home alone, and being instantly put out again in his own hall, like a rushlight, by the chief butler, went sighing to bed.

CHAPTER 34. A Shoal of Barnacles

Mr Henry Gowan and the dog were established frequenters of the cottage, and the day was fixed for the wedding. There was to be a convocation of Barnacles on the occasion, in order that that very high and very large family might shed as much lustre on the marriage as so dim an event was capable of receiving.

To have got the whole Barnacle family together would have been impossible for two reasons. Firstly, because no building could have held all the members and connections of that illustrious house. Secondly, because wherever there was a square yard of ground in British occupation under the sun or moon, with a public post upon it, sticking to that post was a Barnacle. No intrepid navigator could plant a flag-staff upon any spot of earth, and take possession of it in the British name, but to that spot of earth, so soon as the discovery was known, the Circumlocution Office sent out a Barnacle and a despatch-box. Thus the Barnacles were all over the world, in every direction—despatch-boxing the compass.

But, while the so-potent art of Prospero himself would have failed in summoning the Barnacles from every speck of ocean and dry land on which there was nothing (except mischief) to be done and anything to be pocketed, it was perfectly feasible to assemble a good many Barnacles. This Mrs Gowan applied herself to do; calling on Mr Meagles frequently with new additions to the list, and holding conferences with that gentleman when he was not engaged (as he generally was at this period) in examining and paying the debts of his future son-in-law, in the apartment of scales and scoop.

One marriage guest there was, in reference to whose presence Mr Meagles felt a nearer interest and concern than in the attendance of the most elevated Barnacle expected; though he was far from insensible of the honour of having such company. This guest was Clennam. But Clennam had made a promise he held sacred, among the trees that summer night, and, in the chivalry of his heart, regarded it as binding him to many implied obligations. In forgetfulness of himself, and delicate service to her on all occasions, he was never to fail; to begin it, he answered Mr Meagles cheerfully, 'I shall come, of course.'

His partner, Daniel Doyce, was something of a stumbling-block in Mr Meagles's way, the worthy gentleman being not at all clear in his own anxious mind but that the mingling of Daniel with official Barnacleism might produce some explosive combination, even at a marriage breakfast. The national offender, however, lightened him of his uneasiness by coming down to Twickenham to represent that he begged, with the freedom of an old friend, and as a favour to one, that he might not be invited. 'For,' said he, 'as my business with this set of gentlemen was to do a public duty and a public service, and as their business with me was to prevent it by wearing my soul out, I think we had better not eat and drink together with a show of being of one mind.' Mr Meagles was much amused by his friend's oddity; and patronised him with a more protecting air of allowance than usual, when he rejoined: 'Well, well, Dan, you shall have your own crotchety way.'

To Mr Henry Gowan, as the time approached, Clennam tried to convey by all quiet and unpretending means, that he was frankly and disinterestedly desirous of tendering him any friendship he would accept. Mr Gowan treated him in return with his usual ease, and with his usual show of confidence, which was no confidence at all.

'You see, Clennam,' he happened to remark in the course of conversation one day, when they were walking near the Cottage within a week of the marriage, 'I am a disappointed man. That you know already.'

'Upon my word,' said Clennam, a little embarrassed, 'I scarcely know how.'

'Why,' returned Gowan, 'I belong to a clan, or a clique, or a family, or a connection, or whatever you like to call it, that might have provided for me in any one of fifty ways, and that took it into its head not to do it at all. So here I am, a poor devil of an artist.'

Clennam was beginning, 'But on the other hand—' when Gowan took him up.

'Yes, yes, I know. I have the good fortune of being beloved by a beautiful and charming girl whom I love with all my heart.'

('Is there much of it?' Clennam thought. And as he thought it, felt ashamed of himself.)

'And of finding a father-in-law who is a capital fellow and a liberal good old boy. Still, I had other prospects washed and combed into my childish head when it was washed and combed for me, and I took them to a public school when I washed and combed it for myself, and I am here without them, and thus I am a disappointed man.'

Clennam thought (and as he thought it, again felt ashamed of himself), was this notion of being disappointed in life, an assertion of station which the bridegroom brought into the family as his property, having already carried it detrimentally into his pursuit? And was it a hopeful or a promising thing anywhere?

'Not bitterly disappointed, I think,' he said aloud.

'Hang it, no; not bitterly,' laughed Gowan. 'My people are not worth that—though they are charming fellows, and I have the greatest affection for them. Besides, it's pleasant to show them that I can do without them, and that they may all go to the Devil. And besides, again, most men are disappointed in life, somehow or other, and influenced by their disappointment. But it's a dear good world, and I love it!'

'It lies fair before you now,' said Arthur.

'Fair as this summer river,' cried the other, with enthusiasm, 'and by Jove I glow with admiration of it, and with ardour to run a race in it. It's the best of old worlds! And my calling! The best of old callings, isn't it?'

'Full of interest and ambition, I conceive,' said Clennam.

'And imposition,' added Gowan, laughing; 'we won't leave out the imposition. I hope I may not break down in that; but there, my being a disappointed man may show itself. I may not be able to face it out gravely enough. Between you and me, I think there is some danger of my being just enough soured not to be able to do that.'

'To do what?' asked Clennam.

'To keep it up. To help myself in my turn, as the man before me helps himself in his, and pass the bottle of smoke. To keep up the pretence as to labour, and study, and patience, and being devoted to my art, and giving up many solitary days to it, and abandoning many pleasures for it, and living in it, and all the rest of it—in short, to pass the bottle of smoke according to rule.'

'But it is well for a man to respect his own vocation, whatever it is; and to think himself bound to uphold it, and to claim for it the respect it deserves; is it not?' Arthur reasoned. 'And your vocation, Gowan, may really demand this suit and service. I confess I should have thought that all Art did.'

'What a good fellow you are, Clennam!' exclaimed the other, stopping to look at him,

292

as if with irrepressible admiration. 'What a capital fellow! You have never been disappointed. That's easy to see.'

It would have been so cruel if he had meant it, that Clennam firmly resolved to believe he did not mean it. Gowan, without pausing, laid his hand upon his shoulder, and laughingly and lightly went on:

'Clennam, I don't like to dispel your generous visions, and I would give any money (if I had any), to live in such a rose-coloured mist. But what I do in my trade, I do to sell. What all we fellows do, we do to sell. If we didn't want to sell it for the most we can get for it, we shouldn't do it. Being work, it has to be done; but it's easily enough done. All the rest is hocus-pocus. Now here's one of the advantages, or disadvantages, of knowing a disappointed man. You hear the truth.'

Whatever he had heard, and whether it deserved that name or another, it sank into Clennam's mind. It so took root there, that he began to fear Henry Gowan would always be a trouble to him, and that so far he had gained little or nothing from the dismissal of Nobody, with all his inconsistencies, anxieties, and contradictions. He found a contest still always going on in his breast between his promise to keep Gowan in none but good aspects before the mind of Mr Meagles, and his enforced observation of Gowan in aspects that had no good in them. Nor could he quite support his own conscientious nature against misgivings that he distorted and discoloured himself, by reminding himself that he never sought those discoveries, and that he would have avoided them with willingness and great relief. For he never could forget what he had been; and he knew that he had once disliked Gowan for no better reason than that he had come in his way.

Harassed by these thoughts, he now began to wish the marriage over, Gowan and his young wife gone, and himself left to fulfil his promise, and discharge the generous function he had accepted. This last week was, in truth, an uneasy interval for the whole house. Before Pet, or before Gowan, Mr Meagles was radiant; but Clennam had more than once found him alone, with his view of the scales and scoop much blurred, and had often seen him look after the lovers, in the garden or elsewhere when he was not seen by them, with the old clouded face on which Gowan had fallen like a shadow. In the arrangement of the house for the great occasion, many little reminders of the old travels of the father and mother and daughter had to be disturbed and passed from hand to hand; and sometimes, in the midst of these mute witnesses, to the life they had had together, even Pet herself would yield to lamenting and weeping. Mrs Meagles, the blithest and busiest of mothers, went about singing and cheering everybody; but she, honest soul, had her flights into store rooms, where she would cry until her eyes were red, and would then come out, attributing that appearance to pickled onions and pepper, and singing clearer than ever. Mrs Tickit, finding no balsam for a wounded mind in Buchan's Domestic Medicine, suffered greatly from low spirits, and from moving recollections of Minnie's infancy. When the latter was powerful with her, she usually sent up secret messages importing that she was not in parlour condition as to her attire, and that she solicited a sight of 'her child' in the kitchen; there, she would bless her child's face, and bless her child's heart, and hug her child, in a medley of tears and congratulations, chopping-boards, rolling-pins, and pie-crust, with the tenderness of an old attached servant, which is a very pretty tenderness indeed.

But all days come that are to be; and the marriage-day was to be, and it came; and with it came all the Barnacles who were bidden to the feast.

There was Mr Tite Barnacle, from the Circumlocution Office, and Mews Street, Grosvenor Square, with the expensive Mrs Tite Barnacle nee Stiltstalking, who made the Quarter Days so long in coming, and the three expensive Miss Tite Barnacles, double-loaded with accomplishments and ready to go off, and yet not going off with the sharpness of flash and bang that might have been expected, but rather hanging fire. There was Barnacle junior, also from the Circumlocution Office, leaving the Tonnage of the country, which he was somehow supposed to take under his protection, to look after itself, and, sooth to say, not at all impairing the efficiency of its protection by leaving it alone. There was the engaging Young Barnacle, deriving from the sprightly side of the family, also from the Circumlocution Office, gaily and agreeably helping the occasion along, and treating it, in his sparkling way, as one of the official forms and fees of the Church Department of How not to do it. There were three other Young Barnacles from three other offices, insipid to all the senses, and terribly in want of seasoning, doing the marriage as they would have 'done' the Nile, Old Rome, the new singer, or Jerusalem.

But there was greater game than this. There was Lord Decimus Tite Barnacle himself, in the odour of Circumlocution—with the very smell of Despatch-Boxes upon him. Yes, there was Lord Decimus Tite Barnacle, who had risen to official heights on the wings of one indignant idea, and that was, My Lords, that I am yet to be told that it behoves a Minister of this free country to set bounds to the philanthropy, to cramp the charity, to fetter the public spirit, to contract the enterprise, to damp the independent self-reliance, of its people. That was, in other words, that this great statesman was always yet to be told that it behoved the Pilot of the ship to do anything but prosper in the private loaf and fish trade ashore, the crew being able, by dint of hard pumping, to keep the ship above water without him. On this sublime discovery in the great art How not to do it, Lord Decimus had long sustained the highest glory of the Barnacle family; and let any ill-advised member of either House but try How to do it by bringing in a Bill to do it, that Bill was as good as dead and buried when Lord Decimus Tite Barnacle rose up in his place and solemnly said, soaring into indignant majesty as the Circumlocution cheering soared around him, that he was yet to be told, My Lords, that it behoved him as the Minister of this free country, to set bounds to the philanthropy, to cramp the charity, to fetter the public spirit, to contract the enterprise, to damp the independent self-reliance, of its people. The discovery of this Behoving Machine was the discovery of the political perpetual motion. It never wore out, though it was always going round and round in all the State Departments.

And there, with his noble friend and relative Lord Decimus, was William Barnacle, who had made the ever-famous coalition with Tudor Stiltstalking, and who always kept ready his own particular recipe for How not to do it; sometimes tapping the Speaker, and drawing it fresh out of him, with a 'First, I will beg you, sir, to inform the House what Precedent we have for the course into which the honourable gentleman would precipitate us;' sometimes asking the honourable gentleman to favour him with his own version of the Precedent; sometimes telling the honourable gentleman that he (William Barnacle) would search for a Precedent; and oftentimes crushing the honourable gentleman flat on the spot by telling him there was no Precedent. But Precedent and Precipitate were, under all circumstances, the well-matched pair of battle-horses of this able Circumlocutionist. No matter that the unhappy honourable gentleman had been trying in vain, for twenty-five years, to precipitate William Barnacle into this—William Barnacle still put it to the House, and (at second-hand or so) to the country, whether he was to be precipitated into this. No matter that it was utterly irreconcilable with the nature of things and course of events that the wretched honourable gentleman could possibly produce a Precedent for this—William Barnacle would nevertheless thank the honourable gentleman for that ironical cheer, and would close with him upon that issue, and would tell him to his teeth that there Was NO Precedent for this. It might perhaps have been objected that the William Barnacle wisdom was not high wisdom or the earth it bamboozled would never have been made, or, if made in a rash mistake, would have remained blank mud. But Precedent and Precipitate together frightened all objection out of most people.

And there, too, was another Barnacle, a lively one, who had leaped through twenty places in quick succession, and was always in two or three at once, and who was the much-respected inventor of an art which he practised with great success and admiration in all Barnacle Governments. This was, when he was asked a Parliamentary question on any one topic, to return an answer on any other. It had done immense service, and brought him into high esteem with the Circumlocution Office.

And there, too, was a sprinkling of less distinguished Parliamentary Barnacles, who had not as yet got anything snug, and were going through their probation to prove their worthiness. These Barnacles perched upon staircases and hid in passages, waiting their orders to make houses or not to make houses; and they did all their hearing, and ohing, and cheering, and barking, under directions from the heads of the family; and they put dummy motions on the paper in the way of other men's motions; and they stalled disagreeable subjects off until late in the night and late in the session, and then with virtuous patriotism cried out that it was too late; and they went down into the country, whenever they were sent, and swore that Lord Decimus had revived trade from a swoon, and commerce from a fit, and had doubled the harvest of corn, quadrupled the harvest of hay, and prevented no end of gold from flying out of the Bank. Also these Barnacles were dealt, by the heads of the family, like so many cards below the court-cards, to public meetings and dinners; where they bore testimony to all sorts of services on the part of their noble and honourable relatives, and buttered the Barnacles on all sorts of toasts. And they stood, under similar orders, at all sorts of elections; and they turned out of their own seats, on the shortest notice and the most unreasonable terms, to let in other men; and they fetched and carried, and toadied and jobbed, and corrupted, and ate heaps of dirt, and were indefatigable in the public service. And there was not a list, in all the Circumlocution Office, of places that might fall vacant anywhere within half a century, from a lord of the Treasury to a Chinese consul, and up again to a governor-general of India, but as applicants for such places, the names of some or of every one of these hungry and adhesive Barnacles were down.

It was necessarily but a sprinkling of any class of Barnacles that attended the marriage, for there were not two score in all, and what is that subtracted from Legion! But the sprinkling was a swarm in the Twickenham cottage, and filled it. A Barnacle (assisted by a Barnacle) married the happy pair, and it behoved Lord Decimus Tite Barnacle himself to conduct Mrs Meagles to breakfast.

The entertainment was not as agreeable and natural as it might have been. Mr Meagles, hove down by his good company while he highly appreciated it, was not himself. Mrs Gowan was herself, and that did not improve him. The fiction that it was not Mr Meagles who had stood in the way, but that it was the Family greatness, and that the Family greatness had made a concession, and there was now a soothing unanimity, pervaded the affair, though it was never openly expressed. Then the Barnacles felt that they for their parts would have done with the Meagleses when the present patronising occasion was over; and the Meagleses felt the same for their parts. Then Gowan asserting his rights as a disappointed man who had his grudge against the family, and who, perhaps, had allowed his mother to have them there, as much in the hope it might give them some annoyance as with any other benevolent object, aired his pencil and his poverty ostentatiously before them, and told them he hoped in time to settle a crust of bread and cheese on his wife, and that he begged such of them as (more fortunate than himself) came in for any good thing, and could buy a picture, to please to remember the poor painter. Then Lord Decimus, who was a wonder on his own Parliamentary pedestal, turned out to be the windiest creature here: proposing happiness to the bride and bridegroom in a series of platitudes that would have made the hair of any sincere disciple and believer stand on end; and trotting, with the complacency of an idiotic elephant, among howling labyrinths of sentences which he seemed to take for high roads, and never so much as wanted to get out of. Then Mr Tite Barnacle could not but feel that there was a person in company, who would have disturbed his life-long sitting to Sir Thomas Lawrence in full official character, if such disturbance had been possible: while Barnacle junior did, with indignation, communicate to two vapid gentlemen, his relatives, that there was a feller here, look here, who had come to our Department without an appointment and said he wanted to know, you know; and that, look here, if he was to break out now, as he might you know (for you never could tell what an ungentlemanly Radical of that sort would be up to next), and was to say, look here, that he wanted to know this moment, you know, that would be jolly; wouldn't it?

The pleasantest part of the occasion by far, to Clennam, was the painfullest. When Mr and Mrs Meagles at last hung about Pet in the room with the two pictures (where the company were not), before going with her to the threshold which she could never recross to be the old Pet and the old delight, nothing could be more natural and simple than the three were. Gowan himself was touched, and answered Mr Meagles's 'O Gowan, take care of her, take care of her!' with an earnest 'Don't be so broken-hearted, sir. By Heaven I will!'

And so, with the last sobs and last loving words, and a last look to Clennam of confidence in his promise, Pet fell back in the carriage, and her husband waved his hand, and they were away for Dover; though not until the faithful Mrs Tickit, in her silk gown and jet black curls, had rushed out from some hiding-place, and thrown both her shoes after the carriage: an apparition which occasioned great surprise to the distinguished company at the windows.

The said company being now relieved from further attendance, and the chief Barnacles being rather hurried (for they had it in hand just then to send a mail or two which was in danger of going straight to its destination, beating about the seas like the Flying Dutchman, and to arrange with complexity for the stoppage of a good deal of important business otherwise in peril of being done), went their several ways; with all affability conveying to Mr and Mrs Meagles that general assurance that what they had been doing there, they had been doing at a sacrifice for Mr and Mrs Meagles's good, which they always conveyed to Mr John Bull in their official condescension to that most unfortunate creature.

A miserable blank remained in the house and in the hearts of the father and mother and Clennam. Mr Meagles called only one remembrance to his aid, that really did him good.

'It's very gratifying, Arthur,' he said, 'after all, to look back upon.'

'The past?' said Clennam.

'Yes—but I mean the company.'

It had made him much more low and unhappy at the time, but now it really did him good. 'It's very gratifying,' he said, often repeating the remark in the course of the evening. 'Such high company!'

CHAPTER 35. What was behind Mr Pancks on Little Dorrit's Hand

It was at this time that Mr Pancks, in discharge of his compact with Clennam, revealed to him the whole of his gipsy story, and told him Little Dorrit's fortune. Her father was heir-at-law to a great estate that had long lain unknown of, unclaimed, and accumulating. His right was now clear, nothing interposed in his way, the Marshalsea gates stood open, the Marshalsea walls were down, a few flourishes of his pen, and he was extremely rich.

In his tracking out of the claim to its complete establishment, Mr Pancks had shown a sagacity that nothing could baffle, and a patience and secrecy that nothing could tire. 'I little thought, sir,' said Pancks, 'when you and I crossed Smithfield that night, and I told you what sort of a Collector I was, that this would come of it. I little thought, sir, when I told you you were not of the Clennams of Cornwall, that I was ever going to tell you who were of the Dorrits of Dorsetshire.' He then went on to detail. How, having that name recorded in his note-book, he was first attracted by the name alone. How, having often found two exactly similar names, even belonging to the same place, to involve no traceable consanguinity, near or distant, he did not at first give much heed to this, except in the way of speculation as to what a surprising change would be made in the condition of a little seamstress, if she could be shown to have any interest in so large a property. How he rather supposed himself to have pursued the idea into its next degree, because there was something uncommon in the quiet little seamstress, which pleased him and provoked his curiosity. How he had felt his way inch by inch, and 'Moled it out, sir' (that was Mr Pancks's expression), grain by grain. How, in the beginning of the labour described by this new verb, and to render which the more expressive Mr Pancks shut his eyes in pronouncing it and shook his hair over them, he had alternated from sudden lights and hopes to sudden darkness and no hopes, and back again, and back again. How he had made acquaintances in the Prison, expressly that he might come and go there as all other comers and goers did; and how his first ray of light was unconsciously given him by Mr Dorrit himself and by his son; to both of whom he easily became known; with both of whom he talked much, casually ('but always Moleing you'll observe,' said Mr Pancks): and from whom he derived, without being at all suspected, two or three little points of family history which, as he began to hold clues of his own, suggested others. How it had at length become plain to Mr Pancks that he had made a real discovery of the heir-at-law to a great fortune, and that his discovery had but to be ripened to legal fulness and perfection. How he had, thereupon, sworn his landlord, Mr Rugg, to secrecy in a solemn manner, and taken him into Moleing partnership. How they had employed John Chivery as their sole clerk and agent, seeing to whom he was devoted. And how, until the present hour, when authorities mighty in the Bank and learned in the law declared their successful labours ended, they had confided in no other human being.

'So if the whole thing had broken down, sir,' concluded Pancks, 'at the very last, say the day before the other day when I showed you our papers in the Prison yard, or say that very day, nobody but ourselves would have been cruelly disappointed, or a penny the worse.'

Clennam, who had been almost incessantly shaking hands with him throughout the narrative, was reminded by this to say, in an amazement which even the preparation he had had for the main disclosure smoothed down, 'My dear Mr Pancks, this must have cost you a great sum of money.'

'Pretty well, sir,' said the triumphant Pancks. 'No trifle, though we did it as cheap as it could be done. And the outlay was a difficulty, let me tell you.'

'A difficulty!' repeated Clennam. 'But the difficulties you have so wonderfully conquered in the whole business!' shaking his hand again.

'I'll tell you how I did it,' said the delighted Pancks, putting his hair into a condition as elevated as himself. 'First, I spent all I had of my own. That wasn't much.'

'I am sorry for it,' said Clennam: 'not that it matters now, though. Then, what did you do?'

'Then,' answered Pancks, 'I borrowed a sum of my proprietor.'

'Of Mr Casby?' said Clennam. 'He's a fine old fellow.'

'Noble old boy; an't he?' said Mr Pancks, entering on a series of the dryest snorts. 'Generous old buck. Confiding old boy. Philanthropic old buck. Benevolent old boy! Twenty per cent. I engaged to pay him, sir. But we never do business for less at our shop.'

Arthur felt an awkward consciousness of having, in his exultant condition, been a little premature.

'I said to that boiling-over old Christian,' Mr Pancks pursued, appearing greatly to relish this descriptive epithet, 'that I had got a little project on hand; a hopeful one; I told him a hopeful one; which wanted a certain small capital. I proposed to him to lend me the money on my note. Which he did, at twenty; sticking the twenty on in a business-like way, and putting it into the note, to look like a part of the principal. If I had broken down after that, I should have been his grubber for the next seven years at half wages and double grind. But he's a perfect Patriarch; and it would do a man good to serve him on such terms—on any terms.'

Arthur for his life could not have said with confidence whether Pancks really thought so or not.

'When that was gone, sir,' resumed Pancks, 'and it did go, though I dribbled it out like so much blood, I had taken Mr Rugg into the secret. I proposed to borrow of Mr Rugg (or of Miss Rugg; it's the same thing; she made a little money by a speculation in the Common Pleas once). He lent it at ten, and thought that pretty high. But Mr Rugg's a red-haired man, sir, and gets his hair cut. And as to the crown of his hat, it's high. And as to the brim of his hat, it's narrow. And there's no more benevolence bubbling out of him, than out of a ninepin.'

'Your own recompense for all this, Mr Pancks,' said Clennam, 'ought to be a large one.'

'I don't mistrust getting it, sir,' said Pancks. 'I have made no bargain. I owed you one on that score; now I have paid it. Money out of pocket made good, time fairly allowed for, and Mr Rugg's bill settled, a thousand pounds would be a fortune to me. That matter I place in your hands. I authorize you now to break all this to the family in any way you think best.

Miss Amy Dorrit will be with Mrs Finching this morning. The sooner done the better. Can't be done too soon.'

This conversation took place in Clennam's bed-room, while he was yet in bed. For Mr Pancks had knocked up the house and made his way in, very early in the morning; and, without once sitting down or standing still, had delivered himself of the whole of his details (illustrated with a variety of documents) at the bedside. He now said he would 'go and look up Mr Rugg', from whom his excited state of mind appeared to require another back; and bundling up his papers, and exchanging one more hearty shake of the hand with Clennam, he went at full speed down-stairs, and steamed off.

Clennam, of course, resolved to go direct to Mr Casby's. He dressed and got out so quickly that he found himself at the corner of the patriarchal street nearly an hour before her time; but he was not sorry to have the opportunity of calming himself with a leisurely walk.

When he returned to the street, and had knocked at the bright brass knocker, he was informed that she had come, and was shown up-stairs to Flora's breakfast-room. Little Dorrit was not there herself, but Flora was, and testified the greatest amazement at seeing him.

'Good gracious, Arthur—Doyce and Clennam!' cried that lady, 'who would have ever thought of seeing such a sight as this and pray excuse a wrapper for upon my word I really never and a faded check too which is worse but our little friend is making me, not that I need mind mentioning it to you for you must know that there are such things a skirt, and having arranged that a trying on should take place after breakfast is the reason though I wish not so badly starched.'

'I ought to make an apology,' said Arthur, 'for so early and abrupt a visit; but you will excuse it when I tell you the cause.'

'In times for ever fled Arthur,' returned Mrs Finching, 'pray excuse me Doyce and Clennam infinitely more correct and though unquestionably distant still 'tis distance lends enchantment to the view, at least I don't mean that and if I did I suppose it would depend considerably on the nature of the view, but I'm running on again and you put it all out of my head.'

She glanced at him tenderly, and resumed:

'In times for ever fled I was going to say it would have sounded strange indeed for Arthur Clennam—Doyce and Clennam naturally quite different—to make apologies for coming here at any time, but that is past and what is past can never be recalled except in his own case as poor Mr F. said when he was in spirits Cucumber and therefore never ate it.'

She was making the tea when Arthur came in, and now hastily finished that operation.

'Papa,' she said, all mystery and whisper, as she shut down the tea-pot lid, 'is sitting prosingly breaking his new laid egg in the back parlour over the City article exactly like the Woodpecker Tapping and need never know that you are here, and our little friend you are well aware may be fully trusted when she comes down from cutting out on the large table overhead.'

Arthur then told her, in the fewest words, that it was their little friend he came to see; and what he had to announce to their little friend. At which astounding intelligence, Flora clasped her hands, fell into a tremble, and shed tears of sympathy and pleasure, like the good-natured creature she really was.

'For gracious sake let me get out of the way first,' said Flora, putting her hands to her ears and moving towards the door, 'or I know I shall go off dead and screaming and make everybody worse, and the dear little thing only this morning looking so nice and neat and good and yet so poor and now a fortune is she really and deserves it too! and might I mention it to Mr F.'s Aunt Arthur not Doyce and Clennam for this once or if objectionable not on any account.'

Arthur nodded his free permission, since Flora shut out all verbal communication. Flora nodded in return to thank him, and hurried out of the room.

Little Dorrit's step was already on the stairs, and in another moment she was at the door. Do what he could to compose his face, he could not convey so much of an ordinary expression into it, but that the moment she saw it she dropped her work, and cried, 'Mr Clennam! What's the matter?'

'Nothing, nothing. That is, no misfortune has happened. I have come to tell you something, but it is a piece of great good-fortune.'

'Good-fortune?'

'Wonderful fortune!'

They stood in a window, and her eyes, full of light, were fixed upon his face. He put an arm about her, seeing her likely to sink down. She put a hand upon that arm, partly to rest upon it, and partly so to preserve their relative positions as that her intent look at him should be shaken by no change of attitude in either of them. Her lips seemed to repeat 'Wonderful fortune?' He repeated it again, aloud.

'Dear Little Dorrit! Your father.'

The ice of the pale face broke at the word, and little lights and shoots of expression passed all over it. They were all expressions of pain. Her breath was faint and hurried. Her heart beat fast. He would have clasped the little figure closer, but he saw that the eyes appealed to him not to be moved.

'Your father can be free within this week. He does not know it; we must go to him from here, to tell him of it. Your father will be free within a few days. Your father will be free within a few hours. Remember we must go to him from here, to tell him of it!'

That brought her back. Her eyes were closing, but they opened again.

'This is not all the good-fortune. This is not all the wonderful good-fortune, my dear Little Dorrit. Shall I tell you more?'

Her lips shaped 'Yes.'

'Your father will be no beggar when he is free. He will want for nothing. Shall I tell you more? Remember! He knows nothing of it; we must go to him, from here, to tell him of it!'

She seemed to entreat him for a little time. He held her in his arm, and, after a pause, bent down his ear to listen.

'Did you ask me to go on?'

'Yes.'

'He will be a rich man. He is a rich man. A great sum of money is waiting to be paid over to him as his inheritance; you are all henceforth very wealthy. Bravest and best of children, I thank Heaven that you are rewarded!'

As he kissed her, she turned her head towards his shoulder, and raised her arm towards his neck; cried out 'Father! Father! Father!' and swooned away.

Upon which Flora returned to take care of her, and hovered about her on a sofa, intermingling kind offices and incoherent scraps of conversation in a manner so confounding, that whether she pressed the Marshalsea to take a spoonful of unclaimed dividends, for it would do her good; or whether she congratulated Little Dorrit's father on coming into possession of a hundred thousand smelling-bottles; or whether she explained that she put seventy-five thousand drops of spirits of lavender on fifty thousand pounds of lump sugar, and that she entreated Little Dorrit to take that gentle restorative; or whether she bathed the foreheads of Doyce and Clennam in vinegar, and gave the late Mr F. more air; no one with any sense of responsibility could have undertaken to decide. A tributary stream of confusion, moreover, poured in from an adjoining bedroom, where Mr F.'s Aunt appeared, from the sound of her voice, to be in a horizontal posture, awaiting her breakfast; and from which bower that inexorable lady snapped off short taunts, whenever she could get a hearing, as, 'Don't believe it's his doing!' and 'He needn't take no credit to himself for it!' and 'It'll be long enough, I expect, afore he'll give up any of his own money!' all designed to disparage Clennam's share in the discovery, and to relieve those inveterate feelings with which Mr F.'s Aunt regarded him.

But Little Dorrit's solicitude to get to her father, and to carry the joyful tidings to him, and not to leave him in his jail a moment with this happiness in store for him and still unknown to him, did more for her speedy restoration than all the skill and attention on earth could have done. 'Come with me to my dear father. Pray come and tell my dear father!' were the first words she said. Her father, her father. She spoke of nothing but him, thought of nothing but him. Kneeling down and pouring out her thankfulness with uplifted hands, her thanks were for her father.

Flora's tenderness was quite overcome by this, and she launched out among the cups and saucers into a wonderful flow of tears and speech.

'I declare,' she sobbed, 'I never was so cut up since your mama and my papa not Doyce and Clennam for this once but give the precious little thing a cup of tea and make her put it to her lips at least pray Arthur do, not even Mr F.'s last illness for that was of another kind and gout is not a child's affection though very painful for all parties and Mr F. a martyr with his leg upon a rest and the wine trade in itself inflammatory for they will do it more or less among themselves and who can wonder, it seems like a dream I am sure to think of nothing at all this morning and now Mines of money is it really, but you must know my darling love because you never will be strong enough to tell him all about it upon teaspoons, mightn't it be even best to try the directions of my own medical man for though the flavour is anything but agreeable still I force myself to do it as a prescription and find the benefit, you'd rather not why no my dear I'd rather not but still I do it as a duty, everybody will congratulate you some in earnest and some not and many will congratulate you with all their hearts but none more so I do assure you from the bottom of my own I do myself though sensible of blundering and being stupid, and will be judged by Arthur not Doyce and Clennam for this once so good-bye darling and God bless you and may you be very happy and excuse the liberty, vowing that the dress shall never be finished by anybody else but shall be laid by for a keepsake just as it is and called Little Dorrit though why that strangest of denominations at any time I never did myself and now I never shall!'

Thus Flora, in taking leave of her favourite. Little Dorrit thanked her, and embraced her, over and over again; and finally came out of the house with Clennam, and took coach for the Marshalsea.

It was a strangely unreal ride through the old squalid streets, with a sensation of being raised out of them into an airy world of wealth and grandeur. When Arthur told her that she would soon ride in her own carriage through very different scenes, when all the familiar experiences would have vanished away, she looked frightened. But when he substituted her father for herself, and told her how he would ride in his carriage, and how great and grand he would be, her tears of joy and innocent pride fell fast. Seeing that the happiness her mind could realise was all shining upon him, Arthur kept that single figure before her; and so they rode brightly through the poor streets in the prison neighbourhood to carry him the great news.

When Mr Chivery, who was on duty, admitted them into the Lodge, he saw something in their faces which filled him with astonishment. He stood looking after them, when they hurried into the prison, as though he perceived that they had come back accompanied by a ghost a-piece. Two or three Collegians whom they passed, looked after them too, and presently joining Mr Chivery, formed a little group on the Lodge steps, in the midst of which there spontaneously originated a whisper that the Father was going to get his discharge. Within a few minutes, it was heard in the remotest room in the College.

Little Dorrit opened the door from without, and they both entered. He was sitting in his old grey gown and his old black cap, in the sunlight by the window, reading his newspaper. His glasses were in his hand, and he had just looked round; surprised at first, no doubt, by her step upon the stairs, not expecting her until night; surprised again, by seeing Arthur Clennam in her company. As they came in, the same unwonted look in both of them which had already caught attention in the yard below, struck him. He did not rise or speak, but laid down his glasses and his newspaper on the table beside him, and looked at them with his mouth a little open and his lips trembling. When Arthur put out his hand, he touched it, but not with his usual state; and then he turned to his daughter, who had sat down close beside him with her hands upon his shoulder, and looked attentively in her face.

'Father! I have been made so happy this morning!'

'You have been made so happy, my dear?'

'By Mr Clennam, father. He brought me such joyful and wonderful intelligence about you! If he had not with his great kindness and gentleness, prepared me for it, father—prepared me for it, father—I think I could not have borne it.'

Her agitation was exceedingly great, and the tears rolled down her face. He put his hand suddenly to his heart, and looked at Clennam.

'Compose yourself, sir,' said Clennam, 'and take a little time to think. To think of the brightest and most fortunate accidents of life. We have all heard of great surprises of joy. They are not at an end, sir. They are rare, but not at an end.'

'Mr Clennam? Not at an end? Not at an end for—' He touched himself upon the breast, instead of saying 'me.'

'No,' returned Clennam.

'What surprise,' he asked, keeping his left hand over his heart, and there stopping in his speech, while with his right hand he put his glasses exactly level on the table: 'what such surprise can be in store for me?'

'Let me answer with another question. Tell me, Mr Dorrit, what surprise would be the most unlooked for and the most acceptable to you. Do not be afraid to imagine it, or to say what it would be.'

He looked steadfastly at Clennam, and, so looking at him, seemed to change into a very old haggard man. The sun was bright upon the wall beyond the window, and on the spikes at top. He slowly stretched out the hand that had been upon his heart, and pointed at the wall.

'It is down,' said Clennam. 'Gone!'

He remained in the same attitude, looking steadfastly at him.

'And in its place,' said Clennam, slowly and distinctly, 'are the means to possess and enjoy the utmost that they have so long shut out. Mr Dorrit, there is not the smallest doubt that within a few days you will be free, and highly prosperous. I congratulate you with all my soul on this change of fortune, and on the happy future into which you are soon to carry the treasure you have been blest with here—the best of all the riches you can have elsewhere—the treasure at your side.'

With those words, he pressed his hand and released it; and his daughter, laying her face against his, encircled him in the hour of his prosperity with her arms, as she had in the long years of his adversity encircled him with her love and toil and truth; and poured out her full heart in gratitude, hope, joy, blissful ecstasy, and all for him.

'I shall see him as I never saw him yet. I shall see my dear love, with the dark cloud cleared away. I shall see him, as my poor mother saw him long ago. O my dear, my dear! O father, father! O thank God, thank God!'

He yielded himself to her kisses and caresses, but did not return them, except that he put an arm about her. Neither did he say one word. His steadfast look was now divided between her and Clennam, and he began to shake as if he were very cold. Explaining to Little Dorrit that he would run to the coffee-house for a bottle of wine, Arthur fetched it with all the haste he could use. While it was being brought from the cellar to the bar, a number of excited people asked him what had happened; when he hurriedly informed them that Mr Dorrit had succeeded to a fortune.

On coming back with the wine in his hand, he found that she had placed her father in his easy chair, and had loosened his shirt and neckcloth. They filled a tumbler with wine, and held it to his lips. When he had swallowed a little, he took the glass himself and emptied it. Soon after that, he leaned back in his chair and cried, with his handkerchief before his face.

After this had lasted a while Clennam thought it a good season for diverting his attention from the main surprise, by relating its details. Slowly, therefore, and in a quiet tone of voice, he explained them as best he could, and enlarged on the nature of Pancks's service.

'He shall be—ha—he shall be handsomely recompensed, sir,' said the Father, starting up and moving hurriedly about the room. 'Assure yourself, Mr Clennam, that everybody concerned shall be—ha—shall be nobly rewarded. No one, my dear sir, shall say that he has an unsatisfied claim against me. I shall repay the—hum—the advances I have had from you, sir, with peculiar pleasure. I beg to be informed at your earliest convenience, what advances you have made my son.'

He had no purpose in going about the room, but he was not still a moment.

'Everybody,' he said, 'shall be remembered. I will not go away from here in anybody's debt. All the people who have been—ha—well behaved towards myself and my family, shall be rewarded. Chivery shall be rewarded. Young John shall be rewarded. I particularly wish, and intend, to act munificently, Mr Clennam.'

'Will you allow me,' said Arthur, laying his purse on the table, 'to supply any present contingencies, Mr Dorrit? I thought it best to bring a sum of money for the purpose.'

'Thank you, sir, thank you. I accept with readiness, at the present moment, what I could not an hour ago have conscientiously taken. I am obliged to you for the temporary accommodation. Exceedingly temporary, but well timed—well timed.' His hand had closed upon the money, and he carried it about with him. 'Be so kind, sir, as to add the amount to those former advances to which I have already referred; being careful, if you please, not to omit advances made to my son. A mere verbal statement of the gross amount is all I shall—ha—all I shall require.'

His eye fell upon his daughter at this point, and he stopped for a moment to kiss her, and to pat her head.

'It will be necessary to find a milliner, my love, and to make a speedy and complete change in your very plain dress. Something must be done with Maggy too, who at present is— ha—barely respectable, barely respectable. And your sister, Amy, and your brother. And my brother, your uncle—poor soul, I trust this will rouse him—messengers must be despatched to fetch them. They must be informed of this. We must break it to them cautiously, but they must be informed directly. We owe it as a duty to them and to ourselves, from this moment, not to let them—hum—not to let them do anything.'

This was the first intimation he had ever given, that he was privy to the fact that they did something for a livelihood.

He was still jogging about the room, with the purse clutched in his hand, when a great cheering arose in the yard. 'The news has spread already,' said Clennam, looking down from the window. 'Will you show yourself to them, Mr Dorrit? They are very earnest, and they evidently wish it.'

'I—hum—ha—I confess I could have desired, Amy my dear,' he said, jogging about in a more feverish flutter than before, 'to have made some change in my dress first, and to have bought a—hum—a watch and chain. But if it must be done as it is, it—ha—it must be done. Fasten the collar of my shirt, my dear. Mr Clennam, would you oblige me—hum—with a blue neckcloth you will find in that drawer at your elbow. Button my coat across at the chest, my love. It looks—ha—it looks broader, buttoned.'

With his trembling hand he pushed his grey hair up, and then, taking Clennam and his daughter for supporters, appeared at the window leaning on an arm of each. The Collegians cheered him very heartily, and he kissed his hand to them with great urbanity and protection.

When he withdrew into the room again, he said 'Poor creatures!' in a tone of much pity for their miserable condition.

Little Dorrit was deeply anxious that he should lie down to compose himself. On Arthur's speaking to her of his going to inform Pancks that he might now appear as soon as he would, and pursue the joyful business to its close, she entreated him in a whisper to stay with her until her father should be quite calm and at rest. He needed no second entreaty; and she prepared her father's bed, and begged him to lie down. For another half-hour or more he would be persuaded to do nothing but go about the room, discussing with himself the probabilities for and against the Marshal's allowing the whole of the prisoners to go to the windows of the official residence which commanded the street, to see himself and family depart for ever in a carriage—which, he said, he thought would be a Sight for them. But gradually he began to droop and tire, and at last stretched himself upon the bed.

She took her faithful place beside him, fanning him and cooling his forehead; and he seemed to be falling asleep (always with the money in his hand), when he unexpectedly sat up and said:

'Mr Clennam, I beg your pardon. Am I to understand, my dear sir, that I could—ha—could pass through the Lodge at this moment, and—hum—take a walk?'

'I think not, Mr Dorrit,' was the unwilling reply. 'There are certain forms to be completed; and although your detention here is now in itself a form, I fear it is one that for a little longer has to be observed too.'

At this he shed tears again.

'It is but a few hours, sir,' Clennam cheerfully urged upon him.

'A few hours, sir,' he returned in a sudden passion. 'You talk very easily of hours, sir! How long do you suppose, sir, that an hour is to a man who is choking for want of air?'

It was his last demonstration for that time; as, after shedding some more tears and querulously complaining that he couldn't breathe, he slowly fell into a slumber. Clennam had abundant occupation for his thoughts, as he sat in the quiet room watching the father on his bed, and the daughter fanning his face.

Little Dorrit had been thinking too. After softly putting his grey hair aside, and touching his forehead with her lips, she looked towards Arthur, who came nearer to her, and pursued in a low whisper the subject of her thoughts.

'Mr Clennam, will he pay all his debts before he leaves here?'

'No doubt. All.'

'All the debts for which he had been imprisoned here, all my life and longer?'

'No doubt.'

There was something of uncertainty and remonstrance in her look; something that was not all satisfaction. He wondered to detect it, and said:

'You are glad that he should do so?'

'Are you?' asked Little Dorrit, wistfully.

'Am I? Most heartily glad!'

'Then I know I ought to be.'

'And are you not?'

'It seems to me hard,' said Little Dorrit, 'that he should have lost so many years and suffered so much, and at last pay all the debts as well. It seems to me hard that he should pay in life and money both.'

'My dear child—' Clennam was beginning.

'Yes, I know I am wrong,' she pleaded timidly, 'don't think any worse of me; it has grown up with me here.'

The prison, which could spoil so many things, had tainted Little Dorrit's mind no more than this. Engendered as the confusion was, in compassion for the poor prisoner, her father, it was the first speck Clennam had ever seen, it was the last speck Clennam ever saw, of the prison atmosphere upon her.

He thought this, and forbore to say another word. With the thought, her purity and goodness came before him in their brightest light. The little spot made them the more beautiful.

Worn out with her own emotions, and yielding to the silence of the room, her hand slowly slackened and failed in its fanning movement, and her head dropped down on the pillow at her father's side. Clennam rose softly, opened and closed the door without a sound, and passed from the prison, carrying the quiet with him into the turbulent streets.

CHAPTER 36. The Marshalsea becomes an Orphan

And now the day arrived when Mr Dorrit and his family were to leave the prison for ever, and the stones of its much-trodden pavement were to know them no more.

The interval had been short, but he had greatly complained of its length, and had been imperious with Mr Rugg touching the delay. He had been high with Mr Rugg, and had threatened to employ some one else. He had requested Mr Rugg not to presume upon the place in which he found him, but to do his duty, sir, and to do it with promptitude. He had told Mr Rugg that he knew what lawyers and agents were, and that he would not submit to imposition. On that gentleman's humbly representing that he exerted himself to the utmost, Miss Fanny was very short with him; desiring to know what less he could do, when he had been told a dozen times that money was no object, and expressing her suspicion that he forgot whom he talked to.

Towards the Marshal, who was a Marshal of many years' standing, and with whom he had never had any previous difference, Mr Dorrit comported himself with severity. That officer, on personally tendering his congratulations, offered the free use of two rooms in his house for Mr Dorrit's occupation until his departure. Mr Dorrit thanked him at the moment, and replied that he would think of it; but the Marshal was no sooner gone than he sat down and wrote him a cutting note, in which he remarked that he had never on any former occasion had the honour of receiving his congratulations (which was true, though indeed there had not been anything particular to congratulate him upon), and that he begged, on behalf of himself and family, to repudiate the Marshal's offer, with all those thanks which its disinterested character and its perfect independence of all worldly considerations demanded.

Although his brother showed so dim a glimmering of interest in their altered fortunes that it was very doubtful whether he understood them, Mr Dorrit caused him to be measured for new raiment by the hosiers, tailors, hatters, and bootmakers whom he called in for himself; and ordered that his old clothes should be taken from him and burned. Miss Fanny and Mr Tip required no direction in making an appearance of great fashion and elegance; and the three passed this interval together at the best hotel in the neighbourhood—though truly, as Miss Fanny said, the best was very indifferent. In connection with that establishment, Mr Tip hired a cabriolet, horse, and groom, a very neat turn out, which was usually to be observed for two or three hours at a time gracing the Borough High Street, outside the Marshalsea court-yard. A modest little hired chariot and pair was also frequently to be seen there; in alighting from and entering which vehicle, Miss Fanny fluttered the Marshal's daughters by the display of inaccessible bonnets.

A great deal of business was transacted in this short period. Among other items, Messrs Peddle and Pool, solicitors, of Monument Yard, were instructed by their client Edward Dorrit, Esquire, to address a letter to Mr Arthur Clennam, enclosing the sum of twenty-four pounds nine shillings and eightpence, being the amount of principal and interest computed at the rate of five per cent. per annum, in which their client believed himself to be indebted to Mr Clennam. In making this communication and remittance, Messrs Peddle and Pool were further instructed by their client to remind Mr Clennam that the favour of the advance now repaid (including gate-fees) had not been asked of him, and to inform him that it would not have been accepted if it had been openly proffered in his name. With which they requested a stamped receipt, and remained his obedient servants. A great deal of business had likewise to be done, within the so-soon-to-be-orphaned Marshalsea, by Mr Dorrit so long its Father, chiefly arising out of applications made to him by Collegians for small sums of money. To these he responded with the greatest liberality, and with no lack of formality; always first writing to appoint a time at which the applicant might wait upon him in his room, and then receiving him in the midst of a vast accumulation of documents, and accompanying his donation (for he said in every such case, 'it is a donation, not a loan') with a great deal of good counsel: to the effect that he, the expiring Father of the Marshalsea, hoped to be long remembered, as an example that a man might preserve his own and the general respect even there.

The Collegians were not envious. Besides that they had a personal and traditional regard for a Collegian of so many years' standing, the event was creditable to the College, and made it famous in the newspapers. Perhaps more of them thought, too, than were quite aware of it, that the thing might in the lottery of chances have happened to themselves, or that something of the sort might yet happen to themselves some day or other. They took it very well. A few were low at the thought of being left behind, and being left poor; but even these did not grudge the family their brilliant reverse. There might have been much more envy in politer places. It seems probable that mediocrity of fortune would have been disposed to be less magnanimous than the Collegians, who lived from hand to mouth—from the pawnbroker's hand to the day's dinner.

They got up an address to him, which they presented in a neat frame and glass (though it was not afterwards displayed in the family mansion or preserved among the family papers); and to which he returned a gracious answer. In that document he assured them, in a Royal manner, that he received the profession of their attachment with a full conviction of its sincerity; and again generally exhorted them to follow his example—which, at least in so far as coming into a great property was concerned, there is no doubt they would have gladly imitated. He took the same occasion of inviting them to a comprehensive entertainment, to be given to the whole College in the yard, and at which he signified he would have the honour of taking a parting glass to the health and happiness of all those whom he was about to leave behind.

He did not in person dine at this public repast (it took place at two in the afternoon, and his dinners now came in from the hotel at six), but his son was so good as to take the head of the principal table, and to be very free and engaging. He himself went about among the company, and took notice of individuals, and saw that the viands were of the quality he had ordered, and that all were served. On the whole, he was like a baron of the olden time in a rare good humour. At the conclusion of the repast, he pledged his guests in a bumper of old Madeira; and told them that he hoped they had enjoyed themselves, and what was more, that they would enjoy themselves for the rest of the evening; that he wished them well; and that he bade them welcome. His health being drunk with acclamations, he was not so baronial after all but that in trying to return thanks he broke down, in the manner of a mere serf with a heart in his breast, and wept before them all. After this great success, which he supposed to be a failure, he gave them 'Mr Chivery and his brother officers;' whom he had beforehand presented with ten pounds each, and who were all in attendance. Mr Chivery spoke to the toast, saying, What you undertake to lock up, lock up; but remember that you are, in the words of the fettered African, a man and a brother ever. The list of toasts disposed of, Mr Dorrit urbanely went through the motions of playing a game of skittles with the Collegian who was the next oldest inhabitant to himself; and left the tenantry to their diversions.

But all these occurrences preceded the final day. And now the day arrived when he and his family were to leave the prison for ever, and when the stones of its much-trodden pavement were to know them no more.

Noon was the hour appointed for the departure. As it approached, there was not a Collegian within doors, nor a turnkey absent. The latter class of gentlemen appeared in their Sunday clothes, and the greater part of the Collegians were brightened up as much as circumstances allowed. Two or three flags were even displayed, and the children put on odds and ends of ribbon. Mr Dorrit himself, at this trying time, preserved a serious but graceful dignity. Much of his great attention was given to his brother, as to whose bearing on the great occasion he felt anxious.

'My dear Frederick,' said he, 'if you will give me your arm we will pass among our friends together. I think it is right that we should go out arm in arm, my dear Frederick.'

'Hah!' said Frederick. 'Yes, yes, yes, yes.'

'And if, my dear Frederick—if you could, without putting any great constraint upon yourself, throw a little (pray excuse me, Frederick), a little polish into your usual demeanour—'

'William, William,' said the other, shaking his head, 'it's for you to do all that. I don't know how. All forgotten, forgotten!'

'But, my dear fellow,' returned William, 'for that very reason, if for no other, you must positively try to rouse yourself. What you have forgotten you must now begin to recall, my dear Frederick. Your position—'

'Eh?' said Frederick.

'Your position, my dear Frederick.'

'Mine?' He looked first at his own figure, and then at his brother's, and then, drawing a long breath, cried, 'Hah, to be sure! Yes, yes, yes.'

'Your position, my dear Frederick, is now a fine one. Your position, as my brother, is a very fine one. And I know that it belongs to your conscientious nature to try to become worthy of it, my dear Frederick, and to try to adorn it. To be no discredit to it, but to adorn it.'

'William,' said the other weakly, and with a sigh, 'I will do anything you wish, my brother, provided it lies in my power. Pray be so kind as to recollect what a limited power mine is. What would you wish me to do to-day, brother? Say what it is, only say what it is.'

'My dearest Frederick, nothing. It is not worth troubling so good a heart as yours with.'

'Pray trouble it,' returned the other. 'It finds it no trouble, William, to do anything it can for you.'

William passed his hand across his eyes, and murmured with august satisfaction, 'Blessings on your attachment, my poor dear fellow!' Then he said aloud, 'Well, my dear Frederick, if you will only try, as we walk out, to show that you are alive to the occasion—that you think about it—'

'What would you advise me to think about it?' returned his submissive brother.

'Oh! my dear Frederick, how can I answer you? I can only say what, in leaving these good people, I think myself.'

'That's it!' cried his brother. 'That will help me.'

'I find that I think, my dear Frederick, and with mixed emotions in which a softened compassion predominates, What will they do without me!'

'True,' returned his brother. 'Yes, yes, yes, yes. I'll think that as we go, What will they do without my brother! Poor things! What will they do without him!'

Twelve o'clock having just struck, and the carriage being reported ready in the outer court-yard, the brothers proceeded down-stairs arm-in-arm. Edward Dorrit, Esquire (once Tip), and his sister Fanny followed, also arm-in-arm; Mr Plornish and Maggy, to whom had been entrusted the removal of such of the family effects as were considered worth removing, followed, bearing bundles and burdens to be packed in a cart.

In the yard, were the Collegians and turnkeys. In the yard, were Mr Pancks and Mr Rugg, come to see the last touch given to their work. In the yard, was Young John making a new epitaph for himself, on the occasion of his dying of a broken heart. In the yard, was the Patriarchal Casby, looking so tremendously benevolent that many enthusiastic Collegians grasped him fervently by the hand, and the wives and female relatives of many more Collegians kissed his hand, nothing doubting that he had done it all. In the yard, was the man with the shadowy grievance respecting the Fund which the Marshal embezzled, who had got up at five in the morning to complete the copying of a perfectly unintelligible history of that transaction, which he had committed to Mr Dorrit's care, as a document of the last importance, calculated to stun the Government and effect the Marshal's downfall. In the yard, was the insolvent whose utmost energies were always set on getting into debt, who broke into prison with as much pains as other men have broken out of it, and who was always being cleared and complimented;

while the insolvent at his elbow—a mere little, snivelling, striving tradesman, half dead of anxious efforts to keep out of debt—found it a hard matter, indeed, to get a Commissioner to release him with much reproof and reproach. In the yard, was the man of many children and many burdens, whose failure astonished everybody; in the yard, was the man of no children and large resources, whose failure astonished nobody. There, were the people who were always going out to-morrow, and always putting it off; there, were the people who had come in yesterday, and who were much more jealous and resentful of this freak of fortune than the seasoned birds. There, were some who, in pure meanness of spirit, cringed and bowed before the enriched Collegian and his family; there, were others who did so really because their eyes, accustomed to the gloom of their imprisonment and poverty, could not support the light of such bright sunshine. There, were many whose shillings had gone into his pocket to buy him meat and drink; but none who were now obtrusively Hail fellow well met! with him, on the strength of that assistance. It was rather to be remarked of the caged birds, that they were a little shy of the bird about to be so grandly free, and that they had a tendency to withdraw themselves towards the bars, and seem a little fluttered as he passed.

Through these spectators the little procession, headed by the two brothers, moved slowly to the gate. Mr Dorrit, yielding to the vast speculation how the poor creatures were to get on without him, was great, and sad, but not absorbed. He patted children on the head like Sir Roger de Coverley going to church, he spoke to people in the background by their Christian names, he condescended to all present, and seemed for their consolation to walk encircled by the legend in golden characters, 'Be comforted, my people! Bear it!'

At last three honest cheers announced that he had passed the gate, and that the Marshalsea was an orphan. Before they had ceased to ring in the echoes of the prison walls, the family had got into their carriage, and the attendant had the steps in his hand.

Then, and not before, 'Good Gracious!' cried Miss Fanny all at once, 'Where's Amy!'

Her father had thought she was with her sister. Her sister had thought she was 'somewhere or other.' They had all trusted to finding her, as they had always done, quietly in the right place at the right moment. This going away was perhaps the very first action of their joint lives that they had got through without her.

A minute might have been consumed in the ascertaining of these points, when Miss Fanny, who, from her seat in the carriage, commanded the long narrow passage leading to the Lodge, flushed indignantly.

'Now I do say, Pa,' cried she, 'that this is disgraceful!'

'What is disgraceful, Fanny?'

'I do say,' she repeated, 'this is perfectly infamous! Really almost enough, even at such a time as this, to make one wish one was dead! Here is that child Amy, in her ugly old shabby dress, which she was so obstinate about, Pa, which I over and over again begged and prayed her to change, and which she over and over again objected to, and promised to change to-day, saying she wished to wear it as long as ever she remained in there with you—which was absolutely romantic nonsense of the lowest kind—here is that child Amy disgracing us to the last moment and at the last moment, by being carried out in that dress after all. And by that Mr Clennam too!'

The offence was proved, as she delivered the indictment. Clennam appeared at the carriage-door, bearing the little insensible figure in his arms.

'She has been forgotten,' he said, in a tone of pity not free from reproach. 'I ran up to her room (which Mr Chivery showed me) and found the door open, and that she had fainted on the floor, dear child. She appeared to have gone to change her dress, and to have sunk down overpowered. It may have been the cheering, or it may have happened sooner. Take care of this poor cold hand, Miss Dorrit. Don't let it fall.'

'Thank you, sir,' returned Miss Dorrit, bursting into tears. 'I believe I know what to do, if you will give me leave. Dear Amy, open your eyes, that's a love! Oh, Amy, Amy, I really am so vexed and ashamed! Do rouse yourself, darling! Oh, why are they not driving on! Pray, Pa, do drive on!'

The attendant, getting between Clennam and the carriage-door, with a sharp 'By your leave, sir!' bundled up the steps, and they drove away.

BOOK THE SECOND: RICHES

CHAPTER 1. Fellow Travellers

In the autumn of the year, Darkness and Night were creeping up to the highest ridges of the Alps.

It was vintage time in the valleys on the Swiss side of the Pass of the Great Saint Bernard, and along the banks of the Lake of Geneva. The air there was charged with the scent of gathered grapes. Baskets, troughs, and tubs of grapes stood in the dim village doorways, stopped the steep and narrow village streets, and had been carrying all day along the roads and lanes. Grapes, split and crushed under foot, lay about everywhere. The child carried in a sling by the laden peasant woman toiling home, was quieted with picked-up grapes; the idiot sunning his big goitre under the leaves of the wooden chalet by the way to the Waterfall, sat munching grapes; the breath of the cows and goats was redolent of leaves and stalks of grapes; the company in every little cabaret were eating, drinking, talking grapes. A pity that no ripe touch of this generous abundance could be given to the thin, hard, stony wine, which after all was made from the grapes!

The air had been warm and transparent through the whole of the bright day. Shining metal spires and church-roofs, distant and rarely seen, had sparkled in the view; and the snowy mountain-tops had been so clear that unaccustomed eyes, cancelling the intervening country, and slighting their rugged heights for something fabulous, would have measured them as within a few hours easy reach. Mountain-peaks of great celebrity in the valleys, whence no trace of their existence was visible sometimes for months together, had been since morning plain and near in the blue sky. And now, when it was dark below, though they seemed solemnly to recede, like spectres who were going to vanish, as the red dye of the sunset faded out of them and left them coldly white, they were yet distinctly defined in their loneliness above the mists and shadows.

Seen from these solitudes, and from the Pass of the Great Saint Bernard, which was one of them, the ascending Night came up the mountain like a rising water. When it at last rose to the walls of the convent of the Great Saint Bernard, it was as if that weather-beaten structure were another Ark, and floated on the shadowy waves.

Darkness, outstripping some visitors on mules, had risen thus to the rough convent walls, when those travellers were yet climbing the mountain. As the heat of the glowing day when they had stopped to drink at the streams of melted ice and snow, was changed to the searching cold of the frosty rarefied night air at a great height, so the fresh beauty of the lower journey had yielded to barrenness and desolation. A craggy track, up which the mules in single file scrambled and turned from block to block, as though they were ascending the broken staircase of a gigantic ruin, was their way now. No trees were to be seen, nor any vegetable growth save a poor brown scrubby moss, freezing in the chinks of rock. Blackened skeleton arms of wood by the wayside pointed upward to the convent as if the ghosts of former travellers overwhelmed by the snow haunted the scene of their distress. Icicle-hung caves and cellars built for refuges from sudden storms, were like so many whispers of the perils of the place; never-resting wreaths and mazes of mist wandered about, hunted by a moaning wind; and snow, the besetting danger of the mountain, against which all its defences were taken, drifted sharply down.

The file of mules, jaded by their day's work, turned and wound slowly up the deep ascent; the foremost led by a guide on foot, in his broad-brimmed hat and round jacket, carrying a mountain staff or two upon his shoulder, with whom another guide conversed. There was no speaking among the string of riders. The sharp cold, the fatigue of the journey, and a new sensation of a catching in the breath, partly as if they had just emerged from very clear crisp water, and partly as if they had been sobbing, kept them silent.

At length, a light on the summit of the rocky staircase gleamed through the snow and mist. The guides called to the mules, the mules pricked up their drooping heads, the travellers' tongues were loosened, and in a sudden burst of slipping, climbing, jingling, clinking, and talking, they arrived at the convent door.

Other mules had arrived not long before, some with peasant riders and some with goods, and had trodden the snow about the door into a pool of mud. Riding-saddles and bridles, pack-saddles and strings of bells, mules and men, lanterns, torches, sacks, provender, barrels, cheeses, kegs of honey and butter, straw bundles and packages of many shapes, were crowded confusedly together in this thawed quagmire and about the steps. Up here in the clouds, everything was seen through cloud, and seemed dissolving into cloud. The breath of the men was cloud, the breath of the mules was cloud, the lights were encircled by cloud, speakers close at hand were not seen for cloud, though their voices and all other sounds were surprisingly clear. Of the cloudy line of mules hastily tied to rings in the wall, one would bite another, or kick another, and then the whole mist would be disturbed: with men diving into it, and cries of men and beasts coming out of it, and no bystander discerning what was wrong. In the midst of this, the great stable of the convent, occupying the basement story and entered by the basement door, outside which all the disorder was, poured forth its contribution of cloud, as if the whole rugged edifice were filled with nothing else, and would collapse as soon as it had emptied itself, leaving the snow to fall upon the bare mountain summit.

While all this noise and hurry were rife among the living travellers, there, too, silently assembled in a grated house half-a-dozen paces removed, with the same cloud enfolding them and the same snow flakes drifting in upon them, were the dead travellers found upon the mountain. The mother, storm-belated many winters ago, still standing in the corner with her baby at her breast; the man who had frozen with his arm raised to his mouth in fear or hunger, still pressing it with his dry lips after years and years. An awful company, mysteriously come together! A wild destiny for that mother to have foreseen! 'Surrounded by so many and such companions upon whom I never looked, and never shall look, I and my child will dwell together inseparable, on the Great Saint Bernard, outlasting generations who will come to see us, and will never know our name, or one word of our story but the end.'

The living travellers thought little or nothing of the dead just then. They thought much more of alighting at the convent door, and warming themselves at the convent fire. Disengaged from the turmoil, which was already calming down as the crowd of mules began to be bestowed in the stable, they hurried shivering up the steps and into the building. There was a smell within, coming up from the floor, of tethered beasts, like the smell of a menagerie of wild animals. There were strong arched galleries within, huge stone piers, great staircases, and thick walls pierced with small sunken windows—fortifications against the mountain storms, as if they had been human enemies. There were gloomy vaulted sleeping-rooms within, intensely cold, but clean and hospitably prepared for guests. Finally, there was a parlour for guests to sit in and sup in, where a table was already laid, and where a blazing fire shone red and high.

In this room, after having had their quarters for the night allotted to them by two young Fathers, the travellers presently drew round the hearth. They were in three parties; of whom the first, as the most numerous and important, was the slowest, and had been overtaken by one of the others on the way up. It consisted of an elderly lady, two grey-haired gentlemen, two young ladies, and their brother. These were attended (not to mention four guides), by a courier, two footmen, and two waiting-maids: which strong body of inconvenience was accommodated elsewhere under the same roof. The party that had overtaken them, and followed in their train, consisted of only three members: one lady and two gentlemen. The third party, which had ascended from the valley on the Italian side of the Pass, and had arrived first, were four in number: a plethoric, hungry, and silent German tutor in spectacles, on a tour with three young men, his pupils, all plethoric, hungry, and silent, and all in spectacles.

These three groups sat round the fire eyeing each other drily, and waiting for supper. Only one among them, one of the gentlemen belonging to the party of three, made advances towards conversation. Throwing out his lines for the Chief of the important tribe, while addressing himself to his own companions, he remarked, in a tone of voice which included all the company if they chose to be included, that it had been a long day, and that he felt for the ladies. That he feared one of the young ladies was not a strong or accustomed traveller, and had been over-fatigued two or three hours ago. That he had observed, from his station in the rear, that she sat her mule as if she were exhausted. That he had, twice or thrice afterwards, done himself the honour of inquiring of one of the guides, when he fell behind, how the lady did. That he had been enchanted to learn that she had recovered her spirits, and that it had been but a passing discomfort. That he trusted (by this time he had secured the eyes of the Chief, and addressed him) he might be permitted to express his hope that she was now none the worse, and that she would not regret having made the journey.

'My daughter, I am obliged to you, sir,' returned the Chief, 'is quite restored, and has been greatly interested.'

'New to mountains, perhaps?' said the insinuating traveller.

'New to—ha—to mountains,' said the Chief.

'But you are familiar with them, sir?' the insinuating traveller assumed.

'I am—hum—tolerably familiar. Not of late years. Not of late years,' replied the Chief, with a flourish of his hand.

The insinuating traveller, acknowledging the flourish with an inclination of his head, passed from the Chief to the second young lady, who had not yet been referred to otherwise than as one of the ladies in whose behalf he felt so sensitive an interest.

He hoped she was not incommoded by the fatigues of the day.

'Incommoded, certainly,' returned the young lady, 'but not tired.'

The insinuating traveller complimented her on the justice of the distinction. It was what he had meant to say. Every lady must doubtless be incommoded by having to do with that proverbially unaccommodating animal, the mule.

'We have had, of course,' said the young lady, who was rather reserved and haughty, 'to leave the carriages and fourgon at Martigny. And the impossibility of bringing anything that one wants to this inaccessible place, and the necessity of leaving every comfort behind, is not convenient.'

'A savage place indeed,' said the insinuating traveller.

The elderly lady, who was a model of accurate dressing, and whose manner was perfect, considered as a piece of machinery, here interposed a remark in a low soft voice.

'But, like other inconvenient places,' she observed, 'it must be seen. As a place much spoken of, it is necessary to see it.'

'O! I have not the least objection to seeing it, I assure you, Mrs General,' returned the other, carelessly.

'You, madam,' said the insinuating traveller, 'have visited this spot before?'

'Yes,' returned Mrs General. 'I have been here before. Let me commend you, my dear,' to the former young lady, 'to shade your face from the hot wood, after exposure to the mountain air and snow. You, too, my dear,' to the other and younger lady, who immediately did so; while the former merely said, 'Thank you, Mrs General, I am Perfectly comfortable, and prefer remaining as I am.'

The brother, who had left his chair to open a piano that stood in the room, and who had whistled into it and shut it up again, now came strolling back to the fire with his glass in his eye. He was dressed in the very fullest and completest travelling trim. The world seemed hardly large enough to yield him an amount of travel proportionate to his equipment.

'These fellows are an immense time with supper,' he drawled. 'I wonder what they'll give us! Has anybody any idea?'

'Not roast man, I believe,' replied the voice of the second gentleman of the party of three.

'I suppose not. What d'ye mean?' he inquired.

'That, as you are not to be served for the general supper, perhaps you will do us the favour of not cooking yourself at the general fire,' returned the other.

The young gentleman who was standing in an easy attitude on the hearth, cocking his glass at the company, with his back to the blaze and his coat tucked under his arms, something as if he were Of the Poultry species and were trussed for roasting, lost countenance at this reply; he seemed about to demand further explanation, when it was discovered—through all eyes turning on the speaker—that the lady with him, who was young and beautiful, had not heard what had passed through having fainted with her head upon his shoulder.

'I think,' said the gentleman in a subdued tone, 'I had best carry her straight to her room. Will you call to some one to bring a light?' addressing his companion, 'and to show the way? In this strange rambling place I don't know that I could find it.'

'Pray, let me call my maid,' cried the taller of the young ladies.

'Pray, let me put this water to her lips,' said the shorter, who had not spoken yet.

Each doing what she suggested, there was no want of assistance. Indeed, when the two maids came in (escorted by the courier, lest any one should strike them dumb by addressing a foreign language to them on the road), there was a prospect of too much assistance. Seeing this, and saying as much in a few words to the slighter and younger of the two ladies, the gentleman put his wife's arm over his shoulder, lifted her up, and carried her away.

His friend, being left alone with the other visitors, walked slowly up and down the room without coming to the fire again, pulling his black moustache in a contemplative manner, as if he felt himself committed to the late retort. While the subject of it was breathing injury in a corner, the Chief loftily addressed this gentleman.

'Your friend, sir,' said he, 'is—ha—is a little impatient; and, in his impatience, is not perhaps fully sensible of what he owes to—hum—to—but we will waive that, we will waive that. Your friend is a little impatient, sir.'

'It may be so, sir,' returned the other. 'But having had the honour of making that gentleman's acquaintance at the hotel at Geneva, where we and much good company met some time ago, and having had the honour of exchanging company and conversation with that gentleman on several subsequent excursions, I can hear nothing—no, not even from one of your appearance and station, sir—detrimental to that gentleman.'

'You are in no danger, sir, of hearing any such thing from me. In remarking that your friend has shown impatience, I say no such thing. I make that remark, because it is not to be doubted that my son, being by birth and by—ha—by education a—hum—a gentleman, would have readily adapted himself to any obligingly expressed wish on the subject of the fire being equally accessible to the whole of the present circle. Which, in principle, I—ha—for all are—hum—equal on these occasions—I consider right.'

'Good,' was the reply. 'And there it ends! I am your son's obedient servant. I beg your son to receive the assurance of my profound consideration. And now, sir, I may admit, freely admit, that my friend is sometimes of a sarcastic temper.'

'The lady is your friend's wife, sir?'

'The lady is my friend's wife, sir.'

'She is very handsome.'

'Sir, she is peerless. They are still in the first year of their marriage. They are still partly on a marriage, and partly on an artistic, tour.'

'Your friend is an artist, sir?'

The gentleman replied by kissing the fingers of his right hand, and wafting the kiss the length of his arm towards Heaven. As who should say, I devote him to the celestial Powers as an immortal artist!

'But he is a man of family,' he added. 'His connections are of the best. He is more than an artist: he is highly connected. He may, in effect, have repudiated his connections, proudly, impatiently, sarcastically (I make the concession of both words); but he has them. Sparks that have been struck out during our intercourse have shown me this.'

'Well! I hope,' said the lofty gentleman, with the air of finally disposing of the subject, 'that the lady's indisposition may be only temporary.'

'Sir, I hope so.'

'Mere fatigue, I dare say.'

'Not altogether mere fatigue, sir, for her mule stumbled to-day, and she fell from the saddle. She fell lightly, and was up again without assistance, and rode from us laughing; but she complained towards evening of a slight bruise in the side. She spoke of it more than once, as we followed your party up the mountain.'

The head of the large retinue, who was gracious but not familiar, appeared by this time to think that he had condescended more than enough. He said no more, and there was silence for some quarter of an hour until supper appeared.

With the supper came one of the young Fathers (there seemed to be no old Fathers) to take the head of the table. It was like the supper of an ordinary Swiss hotel, and good red wine grown by the convent in more genial air was not wanting. The artist traveller calmly came and took his place at table when the rest sat down, with no apparent sense upon him of his late skirmish with the completely dressed traveller.

'Pray,' he inquired of the host, over his soup, 'has your convent many of its famous dogs now?'

'Monsieur, it has three.'

'I saw three in the gallery below. Doubtless the three in question.'

The host, a slender, bright-eyed, dark young man of polite manners, whose garment was a black gown with strips of white crossed over it like braces, and who no more resembled the conventional breed of Saint Bernard monks than he resembled the conventional breed of Saint Bernard dogs, replied, doubtless those were the three in question.

'And I think,' said the artist traveller, 'I have seen one of them before.'

It was possible. He was a dog sufficiently well known. Monsieur might have easily seen him in the valley or somewhere on the lake, when he (the dog) had gone down with one of the order to solicit aid for the convent.

'Which is done in its regular season of the year, I think?'

Monsieur was right.

'And never without a dog. The dog is very important.'

Again Monsieur was right. The dog was very important. People were justly interested in the dog. As one of the dogs celebrated everywhere, Ma'amselle would observe.

Ma'amselle was a little slow to observe it, as though she were not yet well accustomed to the French tongue. Mrs General, however, observed it for her.

'Ask him if he has saved many lives?' said, in his native English, the young man who had been put out of countenance.

The host needed no translation of the question. He promptly replied in French, 'No. Not this one.'

'Why not?' the same gentleman asked.

'Pardon,' returned the host composedly, 'give him the opportunity and he will do it without doubt. For example, I am well convinced,' smiling sedately, as he cut up the dish of veal to be handed round, on the young man who had been put out of countenance, 'that if you, Monsieur, would give him the opportunity, he would hasten with great ardour to fulfil his duty.'

The artist traveller laughed. The insinuating traveller (who evinced a provident anxiety to get his full share of the supper), wiping some drops of wine from his moustache with a piece of bread, joined the conversation.

'It is becoming late in the year, my Father,' said he, 'for tourist-travellers, is it not?'

'Yes, it is late. Yet two or three weeks, at most, and we shall be left to the winter snows.'

'And then,' said the insinuating traveller, 'for the scratching dogs and the buried children, according to the pictures!'

'Pardon,' said the host, not quite understanding the allusion. 'How, then the scratching dogs and the buried children according to the pictures?'

The artist traveller struck in again before an answer could be given.

'Don't you know,' he coldly inquired across the table of his companion, 'that none but smugglers come this way in the winter or can have any possible business this way?'

'Holy blue! No; never heard of it.'

'So it is, I believe. And as they know the signs of the weather tolerably well, they don't give much employment to the dogs—who have consequently died out rather—though this house of entertainment is conveniently situated for themselves. Their young families, I am told, they usually leave at home. But it's a grand idea!' cried the artist traveller, unexpectedly rising into a tone of enthusiasm. 'It's a sublime idea. It's the finest idea in the world, and brings tears into a man's eyes, by Jupiter!' He then went on eating his veal with great composure.

There was enough of mocking inconsistency at the bottom of this speech to make it rather discordant, though the manner was refined and the person well-favoured, and though the depreciatory part of it was so skilfully thrown off as to be very difficult for one not perfectly acquainted with the English language to understand, or, even understanding, to take offence at: so simple and dispassionate was its tone. After finishing his veal in the midst of silence, the speaker again addressed his friend.

'Look,' said he, in his former tone, 'at this gentleman our host, not yet in the prime of life, who in so graceful a way and with such courtly urbanity and modesty presides over us! Manners fit for a crown! Dine with the Lord Mayor of London (if you can get an invitation) and observe the contrast. This dear fellow, with the finest cut face I ever saw, a face in perfect drawing, leaves some laborious life and comes up here I don't know how many feet above the level of the sea, for no other purpose on earth (except enjoying himself, I hope, in a capital refectory) than to keep an hotel for idle poor devils like you and me, and leave the bill to our consciences! Why, isn't it a beautiful sacrifice? What do we want more to touch us? Because rescued people of interesting appearance are not, for eight or nine months out of every twelve, holding on here round the necks of the most sagacious of dogs carrying wooden bottles, shall we disparage the place? No! Bless the place. It's a great place, a glorious place!'

The chest of the grey-haired gentleman who was the Chief of the important party, had swelled as if with a protest against his being numbered among poor devils. No sooner had the artist traveller ceased speaking than he himself spoke with great dignity, as having it incumbent on him to take the lead in most places, and having deserted that duty for a little while.

He weightily communicated his opinion to their host, that his life must be a very dreary life here in the winter.

The host allowed to Monsieur that it was a little monotonous. The air was difficult to breathe for a length of time consecutively. The cold was very severe. One needed youth and strength to bear it. However, having them and the blessing of Heaven—

Yes, that was very good. 'But the confinement,' said the grey-haired gentleman.

There were many days, even in bad weather, when it was possible to walk about outside. It was the custom to beat a little track, and take exercise there.

'But the space,' urged the grey-haired gentleman. 'So small. So—ha—very limited.'

Monsieur would recall to himself that there were the refuges to visit, and that tracks had to be made to them also.

Monsieur still urged, on the other hand, that the space was so—ha—hum—so very contracted. More than that, it was always the same, always the same.

With a deprecating smile, the host gently raised and gently lowered his shoulders. That was true, he remarked, but permit him to say that almost all objects had their various points of view. Monsieur and he did not see this poor life of his from the same point of view. Monsieur was not used to confinement.

'I—ha—yes, very true,' said the grey-haired gentleman. He seemed to receive quite a shock from the force of the argument.

Monsieur, as an English traveller, surrounded by all means of travelling pleasantly; doubtless possessing fortune, carriages, and servants—

'Perfectly, perfectly. Without doubt,' said the gentleman.

Monsieur could not easily place himself in the position of a person who had not the power to choose, I will go here to-morrow, or there next day; I will pass these barriers, I will enlarge those bounds. Monsieur could not realise, perhaps, how the mind accommodated itself in such things to the force of necessity.

'It is true,' said Monsieur. 'We will—ha—not pursue the subject. You are—hum—quite accurate, I have no doubt. We will say no more.'

The supper having come to a close, he drew his chair away as he spoke, and moved back to his former place by the fire. As it was very cold at the greater part of the table, the other guests also resumed their former seats by the fire, designing to toast themselves well before going to bed. The host, when they rose from the table, bowed to all present, wished them good night, and withdrew. But first the insinuating traveller had asked him if they could have some wine made hot; and as he had answered Yes, and had presently afterwards sent it in, that traveller, seated in the centre of the group, and in the full heat of the fire, was soon engaged in serving it out to the rest.

At this time, the younger of the two young ladies, who had been silently attentive in her dark corner (the fire-light was the chief light in the sombre room, the lamp being smoky and dull) to what had been said of the absent lady, glided out. She was at a loss which way to turn when she had softly closed the door; but, after a little hesitation among the sounding passages and the many ways, came to a room in a corner of the main gallery, where the servants were at their supper. From these she obtained a lamp, and a direction to the lady's room.

It was up the great staircase on the story above. Here and there, the bare white walls were broken by an iron grate, and she thought as she went along that the place was something like a prison. The arched door of the lady's room, or cell, was not quite shut. After knocking at it two or three times without receiving an answer, she pushed it gently open, and looked in.

The lady lay with closed eyes on the outside of the bed, protected from the cold by the blankets and wrappers with which she had been covered when she revived from her fainting fit. A dull light placed in the deep recess of the window, made little impression on the arched room. The visitor timidly stepped to the bed, and said, in a soft whisper, 'Are you better?'

The lady had fallen into a slumber, and the whisper was too low to awake her. Her visitor, standing quite still, looked at her attentively.

'She is very pretty,' she said to herself. 'I never saw so beautiful a face. O how unlike me!'

It was a curious thing to say, but it had some hidden meaning, for it filled her eyes with tears.

'I know I must be right. I know he spoke of her that evening. I could very easily be wrong on any other subject, but not on this, not on this!'

With a quiet and tender hand she put aside a straying fold of the sleeper's hair, and then touched the hand that lay outside the covering.

'I like to look at her,' she breathed to herself. 'I like to see what has affected him so much.'

She had not withdrawn her hand, when the sleeper opened her eyes and started.

'Pray don't be alarmed. I am only one of the travellers from down-stairs. I came to ask if you were better, and if I could do anything for you.'

'I think you have already been so kind as to send your servants to my assistance?'

'No, not I; that was my sister. Are you better?'

'Much better. It is only a slight bruise, and has been well looked to, and is almost easy now. It made me giddy and faint in a moment. It had hurt me before; but at last it overpowered me all at once.'

'May I stay with you until some one comes? Would you like it?'

'I should like it, for it is lonely here; but I am afraid you will feel the cold too much.'

'I don't mind cold. I am not delicate, if I look so.' She quickly moved one of the two rough chairs to the bedside, and sat down. The other as quickly moved a part of some travelling wrapper from herself, and drew it over her, so that her arm, in keeping it about her, rested on her shoulder.

'You have so much the air of a kind nurse,' said the lady, smiling on her, 'that you seem as if you had come to me from home.'

'I am very glad of it.'

'I was dreaming of home when I woke just now. Of my old home, I mean, before I was married.'

'And before you were so far away from it.'

'I have been much farther away from it than this; but then I took the best part of it with me, and missed nothing. I felt solitary as I dropped asleep here, and, missing it a little, wandered back to it.'

There was a sorrowfully affectionate and regretful sound in her voice, which made her visitor refrain from looking at her for the moment.

'It is a curious chance which at last brings us together, under this covering in which you have wrapped me,' said the visitor after a pause; 'for do you know, I think I have been looking for you some time.'

'Looking for me?'

'I believe I have a little note here, which I was to give to you whenever I found you. This is it. Unless I greatly mistake, it is addressed to you? Is it not?'

The lady took it, and said yes, and read it. Her visitor watched her as she did so. It was very short. She flushed a little as she put her lips to her visitor's cheek, and pressed her hand.

'The dear young friend to whom he presents me, may be a comfort to me at some time, he says. She is truly a comfort to me the first time I see her.'

'Perhaps you don't,' said the visitor, hesitating—'perhaps you don't know my story? Perhaps he never told you my story?'

'No.'

'Oh no, why should he! I have scarcely the right to tell it myself at present, because I have been entreated not to do so. There is not much in it, but it might account to you for my asking you not to say anything about the letter here. You saw my family with me, perhaps? Some of them—I only say this to you—are a little proud, a little prejudiced.'

'You shall take it back again,' said the other; 'and then my husband is sure not to see it. He might see it and speak of it, otherwise, by some accident. Will you put it in your bosom again, to be certain?'

She did so with great care. Her small, slight hand was still upon the letter, when they heard some one in the gallery outside.

'I promised,' said the visitor, rising, 'that I would write to him after seeing you (I could hardly fail to see you sooner or later), and tell him if you were well and happy. I had better say you were well and happy.'

'Yes, yes, yes! Say I was very well and very happy. And that I thanked him affectionately, and would never forget him.'

'I shall see you in the morning. After that we are sure to meet again before very long. Good night!'

'Good night. Thank you, thank you. Good night, my dear!'

Both of them were hurried and fluttered as they exchanged this parting, and as the visitor came out of the door. She had expected to meet the lady's husband approaching it; but the person in the gallery was not he: it was the traveller who had wiped the wine-drops from his moustache with the piece of bread. When he heard the step behind him, he turned round—for he was walking away in the dark.

His politeness, which was extreme, would not allow of the young lady's lighting herself down-stairs, or going down alone. He took her lamp, held it so as to throw the best light on the stone steps, and followed her all the way to the supper-room. She went down, not easily hiding how much she was inclined to shrink and tremble; for the appearance of this traveller was particularly disagreeable to her. She had sat in her quiet corner before supper imagining what he would have been in the scenes and places within her experience, until he inspired her with an aversion that made him little less than terrific.

He followed her down with his smiling politeness, followed her in, and resumed his seat in the best place in the hearth. There with the wood-fire, which was beginning to burn low, rising and falling upon him in the dark room, he sat with his legs thrust out to warm, drinking the hot wine down to the lees, with a monstrous shadow imitating him on the wall and ceiling.

The tired company had broken up, and all the rest were gone to bed except the young lady's father, who dozed in his chair by the fire. The traveller had been at the pains of going a long way up-stairs to his sleeping-room to fetch his pocket-flask of brandy. He told them so, as he poured its contents into what was left of the wine, and drank with a new relish.

'May I ask, sir, if you are on your way to Italy?'

The grey-haired gentleman had roused himself, and was preparing to withdraw. He answered in the affirmative.

'I also!' said the traveller. 'I shall hope to have the honour of offering my compliments in fairer scenes, and under softer circumstances, than on this dismal mountain.'

The gentleman bowed, distantly enough, and said he was obliged to him.

'We poor gentlemen, sir,' said the traveller, pulling his moustache dry with his hand, for he had dipped it in the wine and brandy; 'we poor gentlemen do not travel like princes, but the courtesies and graces of life are precious to us. To your health, sir!'

'Sir, I thank you.'

'To the health of your distinguished family—of the fair ladies, your daughters!'

'Sir, I thank you again, I wish you good night. My dear, are our—ha—our people in attendance?'

'They are close by, father.'

'Permit me!' said the traveller, rising and holding the door open, as the gentleman crossed the room towards it with his arm drawn through his daughter's. 'Good repose! To the pleasure of seeing you once more! To to-morrow!'

As he kissed his hand, with his best manner and his daintiest smile, the young lady drew a little nearer to her father, and passed him with a dread of touching him.

'Humph!' said the insinuating traveller, whose manner shrunk, and whose voice dropped when he was left alone. 'If they all go to bed, why I must go. They are in a devil of a hurry. One would think the night would be long enough, in this freezing silence and solitude, if one went to bed two hours hence.'

Throwing back his head in emptying his glass, he cast his eyes upon the travellers' book, which lay on the piano, open, with pens and ink beside it, as if the night's names had been registered when he was absent. Taking it in his hand, he read these entries.

William Dorrit, Esquire

Frederick Dorrit, Esquire

Edward Dorrit, Esquire

Miss Dorrit

Miss Amy Dorrit

Mrs General

and Suite.

From France to Italy.

Mr and Mrs Henry Gowan.

From France to Italy.

To which he added, in a small complicated hand, ending with a long lean flourish, not unlike a lasso thrown at all the rest of the names:

Blandois. Paris.

From France to Italy.

And then, with his nose coming down over his moustache and his moustache going up and under his nose, repaired to his allotted cell.

CHAPTER 2. Mrs General

It is indispensable to present the accomplished lady who was of sufficient importance in the suite of the Dorrit Family to have a line to herself in the Travellers' Book.

Mrs General was the daughter of a clerical dignitary in a cathedral town, where she had led the fashion until she was as near forty-five as a single lady can be. A stiff commissariat officer of sixty, famous as a martinet, had then become enamoured of the gravity with which she drove the proprieties four-in-hand through the cathedral town society, and had solicited to be taken beside her on the box of the cool coach of ceremony to which that team was harnessed. His proposal of marriage being accepted by the lady, the commissary took his seat behind the proprieties with great decorum, and Mrs General drove until the commissary died. In the course of their united journey, they ran over several people who came in the way of the proprieties; but always in a high style and with composure.

The commissary having been buried with all the decorations suitable to the service (the whole team of proprieties were harnessed to his hearse, and they all had feathers and black velvet housings with his coat of arms in the corner), Mrs General began to inquire what quantity of dust and ashes was deposited at the bankers'. It then transpired that the commissary had so far stolen a march on Mrs General as to have bought himself an annuity some years before his marriage, and to have reserved that circumstance in mentioning, at the period of his proposal, that his income was derived from the interest of his money. Mrs General consequently found her means so much diminished, that, but for the perfect regulation of her mind, she might have felt disposed to question the accuracy of that portion of the late service which had declared that

323

the commissary could take nothing away with him.

In this state of affairs it occurred to Mrs General, that she might 'form the mind,' and eke the manners of some young lady of distinction. Or, that she might harness the proprieties to the carriage of some rich young heiress or widow, and become at once the driver and guard of such vehicle through the social mazes. Mrs General's communication of this idea to her clerical and commissariat connection was so warmly applauded that, but for the lady's undoubted merit, it might have appeared as though they wanted to get rid of her. Testimonials representing Mrs General as a prodigy of piety, learning, virtue, and gentility, were lavishly contributed from influential quarters; and one venerable archdeacon even shed tears in recording his testimony to her perfections (described to him by persons on whom he could rely), though he had never had the honour and moral gratification of setting eyes on Mrs General in all his life.

Thus delegated on her mission, as it were by Church and State, Mrs General, who had always occupied high ground, felt in a condition to keep it, and began by putting herself up at a very high figure. An interval of some duration elapsed, in which there was no bid for Mrs General. At length a county-widower, with a daughter of fourteen, opened negotiations with the lady; and as it was a part either of the native dignity or of the artificial policy of Mrs General (but certainly one or the other) to comport herself as if she were much more sought than seeking, the widower pursued Mrs General until he prevailed upon her to form his daughter's mind and manners.

The execution of this trust occupied Mrs General about seven years, in the course of which time she made the tour of Europe, and saw most of that extensive miscellany of objects which it is essential that all persons of polite cultivation should see with other people's eyes, and never with their own. When her charge was at length formed, the marriage, not only of the young lady, but likewise of her father, the widower, was resolved on. The widower then finding Mrs General both inconvenient and expensive, became of a sudden almost as much affected by her merits as the archdeacon had been, and circulated such praises of her surpassing worth, in all quarters where he thought an opportunity might arise of transferring the blessing to somebody else, that Mrs General was a name more honourable than ever.

The phoenix was to let, on this elevated perch, when Mr Dorrit, who had lately succeeded to his property, mentioned to his bankers that he wished to discover a lady, well-bred, accomplished, well connected, well accustomed to good society, who was qualified at once to complete the education of his daughters, and to be their matron or chaperon. Mr Dorrit's bankers, as bankers of the county-widower, instantly said, 'Mrs General.'

Pursuing the light so fortunately hit upon, and finding the concurrent testimony of the whole of Mrs General's acquaintance to be of the pathetic nature already recorded, Mr Dorrit took the trouble of going down to the county of the county-widower to see Mrs General, in whom he found a lady of a quality superior to his highest expectations.

'Might I be excused,' said Mr Dorrit, 'if I inquired—ha—what remune—'

'Why, indeed,' returned Mrs General, stopping the word, 'it is a subject on which I prefer to avoid entering. I have never entered on it with my friends here; and I cannot overcome the delicacy, Mr Dorrit, with which I have always regarded it. I am not, as I hope you are aware, a governess—'

'O dear no!' said Mr Dorrit. 'Pray, madam, do not imagine for a moment that I think so.'

He really blushed to be suspected of it.

Mrs General gravely inclined her head. 'I cannot, therefore, put a price upon services which it is a pleasure to me to render if I can render them spontaneously, but which I could not render in mere return for any consideration. Neither do I know how, or where, to find a case parallel to my own. It is peculiar.'

No doubt. But how then (Mr Dorrit not unnaturally hinted) could the subject be approached?

'I cannot object,' said Mrs General—'though even that is disagreeable to me—to Mr Dorrit's inquiring, in confidence of my friends here, what amount they have been accustomed, at quarterly intervals, to pay to my credit at my bankers'.'

Mr Dorrit bowed his acknowledgements.

'Permit me to add,' said Mrs General, 'that beyond this, I can never resume the topic. Also that I can accept no second or inferior position. If the honour were proposed to me of becoming known to Mr Dorrit's family—I think two daughters were mentioned?—'

'Two daughters.'

'I could only accept it on terms of perfect equality, as a companion, protector, Mentor, and friend.'

Mr Dorrit, in spite of his sense of his importance, felt as if it would be quite a kindness in her to accept it on any conditions. He almost said as much.

'I think,' repeated Mrs General, 'two daughters were mentioned?'

'Two daughters,' said Mr Dorrit again.

'It would therefore,' said Mrs General, 'be necessary to add a third more to the payment (whatever its amount may prove to be), which my friends here have been accustomed to make to my bankers'.'

Mr Dorrit lost no time in referring the delicate question to the county-widower, and finding that he had been accustomed to pay three hundred pounds a-year to the credit of Mrs General, arrived, without any severe strain on his arithmetic, at the conclusion that he himself must pay four. Mrs General being an article of that lustrous surface which suggests that it is worth any money, he made a formal proposal to be allowed to have the honour and pleasure of regarding her as a member of his family. Mrs General conceded that high privilege, and here she was.

In person, Mrs General, including her skirts which had much to do with it, was of a dignified and imposing appearance; ample, rustling, gravely voluminous; always upright behind the proprieties. She might have been taken—had been taken—to the top of the Alps and the bottom of Herculaneum, without disarranging a fold in her dress, or displacing a pin. If her countenance and hair had rather a floury appearance, as though from living in some transcendently genteel Mill, it was rather because she was a chalky creation altogether, than because she mended her complexion with violet powder, or had turned grey. If her eyes had no expression, it was probably because they had nothing to express. If she had few wrinkles, it was because her mind had never traced its name or any other inscription on her face. A cool, waxy, blown-out woman, who had never lighted well.

Mrs General had no opinions. Her way of forming a mind was to prevent it from forming opinions. She had a little circular set of mental grooves or rails on which she started little trains of other people's opinions, which never overtook one another, and never got anywhere. Even her propriety could not dispute that there was impropriety in the world; but Mrs General's way of getting rid of it was to put it out of sight, and make believe that there was no such thing. This was another of her ways of forming a mind—to cram all articles of difficulty into cupboards, lock them up, and say they had no existence. It was the easiest way, and, beyond all comparison, the properest.

Mrs General was not to be told of anything shocking. Accidents, miseries, and offences, were never to be mentioned before her. Passion was to go to sleep in the presence of Mrs General, and blood was to change to milk and water. The little that was left in the world, when all these deductions were made, it was Mrs General's province to varnish. In that formation process of hers, she dipped the smallest of brushes into the largest of pots, and varnished the surface of every object that came under consideration. The more cracked it was, the more Mrs General varnished it.

There was varnish in Mrs General's voice, varnish in Mrs General's touch, an atmosphere of varnish round Mrs General's figure. Mrs General's dreams ought to have been varnished—if she had any—lying asleep in the arms of the good Saint Bernard, with the feathery snow falling on his house-top.

CHAPTER 3. On the Road

The bright morning sun dazzled the eyes, the snow had ceased, the mists had vanished, the mountain air was so clear and light that the new sensation of breathing it was like the having entered on a new existence. To help the delusion, the solid ground itself seemed gone, and the mountain, a shining waste of immense white heaps and masses, to be a region of cloud floating between the blue sky above and the earth far below.

Some dark specks in the snow, like knots upon a little thread, beginning at the convent door and winding away down the descent in broken lengths which were not yet pieced together, showed where the Brethren were at work in several places clearing the track. Already the snow had begun to be foot-thawed again about the door. Mules were busily brought out, tied to the rings in the wall, and laden; strings of bells were buckled on, burdens were adjusted, the voices of drivers and riders sounded musically. Some of the earliest had even already resumed their journey; and, both on the level summit by the dark water near the convent, and on the downward way of yesterday's ascent, little moving figures of men and mules, reduced to miniatures by the immensity around, went with a clear tinkling of bells and a pleasant harmony of tongues.

In the supper-room of last night, a new fire, piled upon the feathery ashes of the old one, shone upon a homely breakfast of loaves, butter, and milk. It also shone on the courier of the Dorrit family, making tea for his party from a supply he had brought up with him, together with several other small stores which were chiefly laid in for the use of the strong body of inconvenience. Mr Gowan and Blandois of Paris had already breakfasted, and were walking up and down by the lake, smoking their cigars.

'Gowan, eh?' muttered Tip, otherwise Edward Dorrit, Esquire, turning over the leaves of the book, when the courier had left them to breakfast. 'Then Gowan is the name of a puppy, that's all I have got to say! If it was worth my while, I'd pull his nose. But it isn't worth my while—fortunately for him. How's his wife, Amy? I suppose you know. You generally know things of that sort.'

'She is better, Edward. But they are not going to-day.'

'Oh! They are not going to-day! Fortunately for that fellow too,' said Tip, 'or he and I might have come into collision.'

'It is thought better here that she should lie quiet to-day, and not be fatigued and shaken by the ride down until to-morrow.'

'With all my heart. But you talk as if you had been nursing her. You haven't been relapsing into (Mrs General is not here) into old habits, have you, Amy?'

He asked her the question with a sly glance of observation at Miss Fanny, and at his father too.

'I have only been in to ask her if I could do anything for her, Tip,' said Little Dorrit.

'You needn't call me Tip, Amy child,' returned that young gentleman with a frown; 'because that's an old habit, and one you may as well lay aside.'

'I didn't mean to say so, Edward dear. I forgot. It was so natural once, that it seemed at the moment the right word.'

'Oh yes!' Miss Fanny struck in. 'Natural, and right word, and once, and all the rest of it! Nonsense, you little thing! I know perfectly well why you have been taking such an interest in this Mrs Gowan. You can't blind me.'

'I will not try to, Fanny. Don't be angry.'

'Oh! angry!' returned that young lady with a flounce. 'I have no patience' (which indeed was the truth).

'Pray, Fanny,' said Mr Dorrit, raising his eyebrows, 'what do you mean? Explain yourself.'

'Oh! Never mind, Pa,' replied Miss Fanny, 'it's no great matter. Amy will understand me. She knew, or knew of, this Mrs Gowan before yesterday, and she may as well admit that she did.'

'My child,' said Mr Dorrit, turning to his younger daughter, 'has your sister—any— ha—authority for this curious statement?'

'However meek we are,' Miss Fanny struck in before she could answer, 'we don't go creeping into people's rooms on the tops of cold mountains, and sitting perishing in the frost with people, unless we know something about them beforehand. It's not very hard to divine whose friend Mrs Gowan is.'

'Whose friend?' inquired her father.

'Pa, I am sorry to say,' returned Miss Fanny, who had by this time succeeded in goading herself into a state of much ill-usage and grievance, which she was often at great pains to do: 'that I believe her to be a friend of that very objectionable and unpleasant person, who, with a total absence of all delicacy, which our experience might have led us to expect from him, insulted us and outraged our feelings in so public and wilful a manner on an occasion to which it is understood among us that we will not more pointedly allude.'

'Amy, my child,' said Mr Dorrit, tempering a bland severity with a dignified affection, 'is this the case?'

Little Dorrit mildly answered, yes it was.

'Yes it is!' cried Miss Fanny. 'Of course! I said so! And now, Pa, I do declare once for all'—this young lady was in the habit of declaring the same thing once for all every day of her life, and even several times in a day—'that this is shameful! I do declare once for all that it ought to be put a stop to. Is it not enough that we have gone through what is only known to ourselves, but are we to have it thrown in our faces, perseveringly and systematically, by the very person who should spare our feelings most? Are we to be exposed to this unnatural conduct every moment of our lives? Are we never to be permitted to forget? I say again, it is absolutely infamous!'

'Well, Amy,' observed her brother, shaking his head, 'you know I stand by you whenever I can, and on most occasions. But I must say, that, upon my soul, I do consider it rather an unaccountable mode of showing your sisterly affection, that you should back up a man who treated me in the most ungentlemanly way in which one man can treat another. And who,' he added convincingly, 'must be a low-minded thief, you know, or he never could have conducted himself as he did.'

'And see,' said Miss Fanny, 'see what is involved in this! Can we ever hope to be respected by our servants? Never. Here are our two women, and Pa's valet, and a footman, and a courier, and all sorts of dependents, and yet in the midst of these, we are to have one of ourselves rushing about with tumblers of cold water, like a menial! Why, a policeman,' said Miss Fanny, 'if a beggar had a fit in the street, could but go plunging about with tumblers, as this very Amy did in this very room before our very eyes last night!'

'I don't so much mind that, once in a way,' remarked Mr Edward; 'but your Clennam, as he thinks proper to call himself, is another thing.'

'He is part of the same thing,' returned Miss Fanny, 'and of a piece with all the rest. He obtruded himself upon us in the first instance. We never wanted him. I always showed him, for one, that I could have dispensed with his company with the greatest pleasure. He then commits that gross outrage upon our feelings, which he never could or would have committed but for the delight he took in exposing us; and then we are to be demeaned for the service of his friends! Why, I don't wonder at this Mr Gowan's conduct towards you. What else was to be expected when he was enjoying our past misfortunes—gloating over them at the moment!'

'Father—Edward—no indeed!' pleaded Little Dorrit. 'Neither Mr nor Mrs Gowan had ever heard our name. They were, and they are, quite ignorant of our history.'

'So much the worse,' retorted Fanny, determined not to admit anything in extenuation, 'for then you have no excuse. If they had known about us, you might have felt yourself called upon to conciliate them. That would have been a weak and ridiculous mistake, but I can respect a mistake, whereas I can't respect a wilful and deliberate abasing of those who should be nearest and dearest to us. No. I can't respect that. I can do nothing but denounce that.'

'I never offend you wilfully, Fanny,' said Little Dorrit, 'though you are so hard with me.'

'Then you should be more careful, Amy,' returned her sister. 'If you do such things by accident, you should be more careful. If I happened to have been born in a peculiar place, and under peculiar circumstances that blunted my knowledge of propriety, I fancy I should think myself bound to consider at every step, "Am I going, ignorantly, to compromise any near and dear relations?" That is what I fancy I should do, if it was my case.'

Mr Dorrit now interposed, at once to stop these painful subjects by his authority, and to point their moral by his wisdom.

'My dear,' said he to his younger daughter, 'I beg you to—ha—to say no more. Your sister Fanny expresses herself strongly, but not without considerable reason. You have now a—hum—a great position to support. That great position is not occupied by yourself alone, but by—ha—by me, and—ha hum—by us. Us. Now, it is incumbent upon all people in an exalted position, but it is particularly so on this family, for reasons which I—ha—will not dwell upon, to make themselves respected. To be vigilant in making themselves respected. Dependants, to respect us, must be—ha—kept at a distance and—hum—kept down. Down. Therefore, your not exposing yourself to the remarks of our attendants by appearing to have at any time dispensed with their services and performed them for yourself, is—ha—highly important.'

'Why, who can doubt it?' cried Miss Fanny. 'It's the essence of everything.'

'Fanny,' returned her father, grandiloquently, 'give me leave, my dear. We then come to—ha—to Mr Clennam. I am free to say that I do not, Amy, share your sister's sentiments—that is to say altogether—hum— altogether—in reference to Mr Clennam. I am content to regard that individual in the light of—ha—generally—a well-behaved person. Hum. A well-behaved person. Nor will I inquire whether Mr Clennam did, at any time, obtrude himself on—ha—my society. He knew my society to be—hum—sought, and his plea might be that he regarded me in the light of a public character. But there were circumstances attending my—ha—slight knowledge of Mr Clennam (it was very slight), which,' here Mr Dorrit became extremely grave and impressive, 'would render it highly indelicate in Mr Clennam to—ha—to seek to renew communication with me or with any member of my family under existing circumstances. If Mr Clennam has sufficient delicacy to perceive the impropriety of any such attempt, I am bound as a responsible gentleman to—ha—defer to that delicacy on his part. If, on the other hand, Mr Clennam has not that delicacy, I cannot for a moment—ha—hold any correspondence with so—hum—coarse a mind. In either case, it would appear that Mr Clennam is put altogether out of the question, and that we have nothing to do with him or he with us. Ha—Mrs General!'

The entrance of the lady whom he announced, to take her place at the breakfast-table, terminated the discussion. Shortly afterwards, the courier announced that the valet, and the footman, and the two maids, and the four guides, and the fourteen mules, were in readiness; so the breakfast party went out to the convent door to join the cavalcade.

Mr Gowan stood aloof with his cigar and pencil, but Mr Blandois was on the spot to pay his respects to the ladies. When he gallantly pulled off his slouched hat to Little Dorrit, she thought he had even a more sinister look, standing swart and cloaked in the snow, than he had in the fire-light over-night. But, as both her father and her sister received his homage with some favour, she refrained from expressing any distrust of him, lest it should prove to be a new blemish derived from her prison birth.

Nevertheless, as they wound down the rugged way while the convent was yet in sight, she more than once looked round, and descried Mr Blandois, backed by the convent smoke which rose straight and high from the chimneys in a golden film, always standing on one jutting point looking down after them. Long after he was a mere black stick in the snow, she felt as though she could yet see that smile of his, that high nose, and those eyes that were too near it. And even after that, when the convent was gone and some light morning clouds veiled the pass below it, the ghastly skeleton arms by the wayside seemed to be all pointing up at him.

More treacherous than snow, perhaps, colder at heart, and harder to melt, Blandois of Paris by degrees passed out of her mind, as they came down into the softer regions. Again the sun was warm, again the streams descending from glaciers and snowy caverns were refreshing to drink at, again they came among the pine-trees, the rocky rivulets, the verdant heights and dales, the wooden chalets and rough zigzag fences of Swiss country. Sometimes the way so widened that she and her father could ride abreast. And then to look at him, handsomely clothed in his fur and broadcloths, rich, free, numerously served and attended, his eyes roving far away among the glories of the landscape, no miserable screen before them to darken his sight and cast its shadow on him, was enough.

Her uncle was so far rescued from that shadow of old, that he wore the clothes they gave him, and performed some ablutions as a sacrifice to the family credit, and went where he was taken, with a certain patient animal enjoyment, which seemed to express that the air and change did him good. In all other respects, save one, he shone with no light but such as was reflected from his brother. His brother's greatness, wealth, freedom, and grandeur, pleased him without any reference to himself. Silent and retiring, he had no use for speech when he could hear his brother speak; no desire to be waited on, so that the servants devoted themselves to his brother. The only noticeable change he originated in himself, was an alteration in his manner to his younger niece. Every day it refined more and more into a marked respect, very rarely shown by age to youth, and still more rarely susceptible, one would have said, of the fitness with which he invested it. On those occasions when Miss Fanny did declare once for all, he would take the next opportunity of baring his grey head before his younger niece, and of helping her to alight, or handing her to the carriage, or showing her any other attention, with the profoundest deference. Yet it never appeared misplaced or forced, being always heartily simple, spontaneous, and genuine. Neither would he ever consent, even at his brother's request, to be helped to any place before her, or to take precedence of her in anything. So jealous was he of her being respected, that, on this very journey down from the Great Saint Bernard, he took sudden and violent umbrage at the footman's being remiss to hold her stirrup, though standing near when she dismounted; and unspeakably astonished the whole retinue by charging at him on a hard-headed mule, riding him into a corner, and threatening to trample him to death.

They were a goodly company, and the Innkeepers all but worshipped them. Wherever they went, their importance preceded them in the person of the courier riding before, to see that the rooms of state were ready. He was the herald of the family procession. The great travelling-carriage came next: containing, inside, Mr Dorrit, Miss Dorrit, Miss Amy Dorrit, and Mrs General; outside, some of the retainers, and (in fine weather) Edward Dorrit, Esquire, for whom the box was reserved. Then came the chariot containing Frederick Dorrit, Esquire, and an empty place occupied by Edward Dorrit, Esquire, in wet weather. Then came the fourgon with the rest of the retainers, the heavy baggage, and as much as it could carry of the mud and dust which the other vehicles left behind.

These equipages adorned the yard of the hotel at Martigny, on the return of the family from their mountain excursion. Other vehicles were there, much company being on the road, from the patched Italian Vettura—like the body of a swing from an English fair put upon a wooden tray on wheels, and having another wooden tray without wheels put atop of it—to the trim English carriage. But there was another adornment of the hotel which Mr Dorrit had not bargained for. Two strange travellers embellished one of his rooms.

The Innkeeper, hat in hand in the yard, swore to the courier that he was blighted, that he was desolated, that he was profoundly afflicted, that he was the most miserable and unfortunate of beasts, that he had the head of a wooden pig. He ought never to have made the concession, he said, but the very genteel lady had so passionately prayed him for the accommodation of that room to dine in, only for a little half-hour, that he had been vanquished. The little half-hour was expired, the lady and gentleman were taking their little dessert and half-cup of coffee, the note was paid, the horses were ordered, they would depart immediately; but, owing to an unhappy destiny and the curse of Heaven, they were not yet gone.

Nothing could exceed Mr Dorrit's indignation, as he turned at the foot of the staircase on hearing these apologies. He felt that the family dignity was struck at by an assassin's hand. He had a sense of his dignity, which was of the most exquisite nature. He could detect a design upon it when nobody else had any perception of the fact. His life was made an agony by the number of fine scalpels that he felt to be incessantly engaged in dissecting his dignity.

'Is it possible, sir,' said Mr Dorrit, reddening excessively, 'that you have—ha—had the audacity to place one of my rooms at the disposition of any other person?'

Thousands of pardons! It was the host's profound misfortune to have been overcome by that too genteel lady. He besought Monseigneur not to enrage himself. He threw himself on Monseigneur for clemency. If Monseigneur would have the distinguished goodness to occupy the other salon especially reserved for him, for but five minutes, all would go well.

'No, sir,' said Mr Dorrit. 'I will not occupy any salon. I will leave your house without eating or drinking, or setting foot in it. How do you dare to act like this? Who am I that you—ha—separate me from other gentlemen?'

Alas! The host called all the universe to witness that Monseigneur was the most amiable of the whole body of nobility, the most important, the most estimable, the most honoured. If he separated Monseigneur from others, it was only because he was more distinguished, more cherished, more generous, more renowned.

'Don't tell me so, sir,' returned Mr Dorrit, in a mighty heat. 'You have affronted me. You have heaped insults upon me. How dare you? Explain yourself.'

Ah, just Heaven, then, how could the host explain himself when he had nothing more to explain; when he had only to apologise, and confide himself to the so well-known magnanimity of Monseigneur!

'I tell you, sir,' said Mr Dorrit, panting with anger, 'that you separate me—ha—from other gentlemen; that you make distinctions between me and other gentlemen of fortune and station. I demand of you, why? I wish to know on—ha—what authority, on whose authority. Reply sir. Explain. Answer why.'

Permit the landlord humbly to submit to Monsieur the Courier then, that Monseigneur, ordinarily so gracious, enraged himself without cause. There was no why. Monsieur the Courier would represent to Monseigneur, that he deceived himself in suspecting that there was any why, but the why his devoted servant had already had the honour to present to him. The very genteel lady—

'Silence!' cried Mr Dorrit. 'Hold your tongue! I will hear no more of the very genteel lady; I will hear no more of you. Look at this family—my family—a family more genteel than any lady. You have treated this family with disrespect; you have been insolent to this family. I'll ruin you. Ha—send for the horses, pack the carriages, I'll not set foot in this man's house again!'

No one had interfered in the dispute, which was beyond the French colloquial powers of Edward Dorrit, Esquire, and scarcely within the province of the ladies. Miss Fanny, however, now supported her father with great bitterness; declaring, in her native tongue, that it was quite clear there was something special in this man's impertinence; and that she considered it important that he should be, by some means, forced to give up his authority for making distinctions between that family and other wealthy families. What the reasons of his presumption could be, she was at a loss to imagine; but reasons he must have, and they ought to be torn from him.

All the guides, mule-drivers, and idlers in the yard, had made themselves parties to the angry conference, and were much impressed by the courier's now bestirring himself to get the carriages out. With the aid of some dozen people to each wheel, this was done at a great cost of noise; and then the loading was proceeded with, pending the arrival of the horses from the post-house.

But the very genteel lady's English chariot being already horsed and at the inn-door, the landlord had slipped up-stairs to represent his hard case. This was notified to the yard by his now coming down the staircase in attendance on the gentleman and the lady, and by his pointing out the offended majesty of Mr Dorrit to them with a significant motion of his hand.

'Beg your pardon,' said the gentleman, detaching himself from the lady, and coming forward. 'I am a man of few words and a bad hand at an explanation—but lady here is extremely anxious that there should be no Row. Lady—a mother of mine, in point of fact—wishes me to say that she hopes no Row.'

Mr Dorrit, still panting under his injury, saluted the gentleman, and saluted the lady, in a distant, final, and invincible manner.

'No, but really—here, old feller; you!' This was the gentleman's way of appealing to Edward Dorrit, Esquire, on whom he pounced as a great and providential relief. 'Let you and I try to make this all right. Lady so very much wishes no Row.'

Edward Dorrit, Esquire, led a little apart by the button, assumed a diplomatic expression of countenance in replying, 'Why you must confess, that when you bespeak a lot of rooms beforehand, and they belong to you, it's not pleasant to find other people in 'em.'

'No,' said the other, 'I know it isn't. I admit it. Still, let you and I try to make it all right, and avoid Row. The fault is not this chap's at all, but my mother's. Being a remarkably fine woman with no bigodd nonsense about her—well educated, too—she was too many for this chap. Regularly pocketed him.'

'If that's the case—' Edward Dorrit, Esquire, began.

'Assure you 'pon my soul 'tis the case. Consequently,' said the other gentleman, retiring on his main position, 'why Row?'

'Edmund,' said the lady from the doorway, 'I hope you have explained, or are explaining, to the satisfaction of this gentleman and his family that the civil landlord is not to blame?'

'Assure you, ma'am,' returned Edmund, 'perfectly paralysing myself with trying it on.' He then looked steadfastly at Edward Dorrit, Esquire, for some seconds, and suddenly added, in a burst of confidence, 'Old feller! Is it all right?'

'I don't know, after all,' said the lady, gracefully advancing a step or two towards Mr Dorrit, 'but that I had better say myself, at once, that I assured this good man I took all the consequences on myself of occupying one of a stranger's suite of rooms during his absence, for just as much (or as little) time as I could dine in. I had no idea the rightful owner would come back so soon, nor had I any idea that he had come back, or I should have hastened to make restoration of my ill-gotten chamber, and to have offered my explanation and apology. I trust in saying this—'

For a moment the lady, with a glass at her eye, stood transfixed and speechless before the two Miss Dorrits. At the same moment, Miss Fanny, in the foreground of a grand pictorial composition, formed by the family, the family equipages, and the family servants, held her sister tight under one arm to detain her on the spot, and with the other arm fanned herself with a distinguished air, and negligently surveyed the lady from head to foot.

The lady, recovering herself quickly—for it was Mrs Merdle and she was not easily dashed—went on to add that she trusted in saying this, she apologised for her boldness, and restored this well-behaved landlord to the favour that was so very valuable to him. Mr Dorrit, on the altar of whose dignity all this was incense, made a gracious reply; and said that his people should—ha—countermand his horses, and he would—hum—overlook what he had at first supposed to be an affront, but now regarded as an honour. Upon this the bosom bent to him; and its owner, with a wonderful command of feature, addressed a winning smile of adieu to the two sisters, as young ladies of fortune in whose favour she was much prepossessed, and whom she had never had the gratification of seeing before.

Not so, however, Mr Sparkler. This gentleman, becoming transfixed at the same moment as his lady-mother, could not by any means unfix himself again, but stood stiffly staring at the whole composition with Miss Fanny in the Foreground. On his mother saying, 'Edmund, we are quite ready; will you give me your arm?' he seemed, by the motion of his lips, to reply with some remark comprehending the form of words in which his shining talents found the most frequent utterance, but he relaxed no muscle. So fixed was his figure, that it would have been matter of some difficulty to bend him sufficiently to get him in the carriage-door, if he had not received the timely assistance of a maternal pull from within. He was no sooner within than the pad of the little window in the back of the chariot disappeared, and his eye usurped its place. There it remained as long as so small an object was discernible, and probably much longer, staring (as though something inexpressibly surprising should happen to a codfish) like an ill-executed eye in a large locket.

This encounter was so highly agreeable to Miss Fanny, and gave her so much to think of with triumph afterwards, that it softened her asperities exceedingly. When the procession was again in motion next day, she occupied her place in it with a new gaiety; and showed such a flow of spirits indeed, that Mrs General looked rather surprised.

Little Dorrit was glad to be found no fault with, and to see that Fanny was pleased; but her part in the procession was a musing part, and a quiet one. Sitting opposite her father in the travelling-carriage, and recalling the old Marshalsea room, her present existence was a dream. All that she saw was new and wonderful, but it was not real; it seemed to her as if those visions of mountains and picturesque countries might melt away at any moment, and the carriage, turning some abrupt corner, bring up with a jolt at the old Marshalsea gate.

To have no work to do was strange, but not half so strange as having glided into a corner where she had no one to think for, nothing to plan and contrive, no cares of others to load herself with. Strange as that was, it was far stranger yet to find a space between herself and her father, where others occupied themselves in taking care of him, and where she was never expected to be. At first, this was so much more unlike her old experience than even the mountains themselves, that she had been unable to resign herself to it, and had tried to retain her old place about him. But he had spoken to her alone, and had said that people—ha—people in an exalted position, my dear, must scrupulously exact respect from their dependents; and that for her, his daughter, Miss Amy Dorrit, of the sole remaining branch of the Dorrits of Dorsetshire, to be known to—hum—to occupy herself in fulfilling the functions of—ha hum—a valet, would be incompatible with that respect. Therefore, my dear, he—ha—he laid his parental injunctions upon her, to remember that she was a lady, who had now to conduct herself with—hum—a proper pride, and to preserve the rank of a lady; and consequently he requested her to abstain from doing what would occasion—ha—unpleasant and derogatory remarks. She had obeyed without a murmur. Thus it had been brought about that she now sat in her corner of the luxurious carriage with her little patient hands folded before her, quite displaced even from the last point of the old standing ground in life on which her feet had lingered.

It was from this position that all she saw appeared unreal; the more surprising the scenes, the more they resembled the unreality of her own inner life as she went through its vacant places all day long. The gorges of the Simplon, its enormous depths and thundering waterfalls, the wonderful road, the points of danger where a loose wheel or a faltering horse would have been destruction, the descent into Italy, the opening of that beautiful land as the rugged mountain-chasm widened and let them out from a gloomy and dark imprisonment— all a dream—only the old mean Marshalsea a reality. Nay, even the old mean Marshalsea was shaken to its foundations when she pictured it without her father. She could scarcely believe that the prisoners were still lingering in the close yard, that the mean rooms were still every one tenanted, and that the turnkey still stood in the Lodge letting people in and out, all just as she well knew it to be.

With a remembrance of her father's old life in prison hanging about her like the burden of a sorrowful tune, Little Dorrit would wake from a dream of her birth-place into a whole day's dream. The painted room in which she awoke, often a humbled state-chamber in a dilapidated palace, would begin it; with its wild red autumnal vine-leaves overhanging the glass, its orange-trees on the cracked white terrace outside the window, a group of monks and peasants in the little street below, misery and magnificence wrestling with each other upon every rood of ground in the prospect, no matter how widely diversified, and misery throwing magnificence with the strength of fate. To this would succeed a labyrinth of bare passages and pillared galleries, with the family procession already preparing in the quadrangle below, through the carriages and luggage being brought together by the servants for the day's journey. Then breakfast in another painted chamber, damp-stained and of desolate proportions; and then the departure, which, to her timidity and sense of not being grand enough for her place in the ceremonies, was always an uneasy thing. For then the courier (who himself would have been a foreign gentleman of high mark in the Marshalsea) would present himself to report that all was ready; and then her father's valet would pompously induct him into his travelling-cloak; and then Fanny's maid, and her own maid (who was a weight on Little Dorrit's mind—absolutely made her cry at first, she knew so little what to do with her), would be in attendance; and then her brother's man would complete his master's equipment; and then her father would give his arm to Mrs General, and her uncle would give his to her, and, escorted by the landlord and Inn servants, they would swoop down-stairs. There, a crowd would be collected to see them enter their carriages, which, amidst much bowing, and begging, and prancing, and lashing, and clattering, they would do; and so they would be driven madly through narrow unsavoury streets, and jerked out at the town gate.

Among the day's unrealities would be roads where the bright red vines were looped and garlanded together on trees for many miles; woods of olives; white villages and towns on hill-sides, lovely without, but frightful in their dirt and poverty within; crosses by the way; deep blue lakes with fairy islands, and clustering boats with awnings of bright colours and sails of beautiful forms; vast piles of building mouldering to dust; hanging-gardens where the weeds had grown so strong that their stems, like wedges driven home, had split the arch and rent the wall; stone-terraced lanes, with the lizards running into and out of every chink; beggars of all sorts everywhere: pitiful, picturesque, hungry, merry; children beggars and aged beggars. Often at posting-houses and other halting places, these miserable creatures would appear to her the only realities of the day; and many a time, when the money she had brought to give them was all given away, she would sit with her folded hands, thoughtfully looking after some diminutive girl leading her grey father, as if the sight reminded her of something in the days that were gone.

Again, there would be places where they stayed the week together in splendid rooms, had banquets every day, rode out among heaps of wonders, walked through miles of palaces, and rested in dark corners of great churches; where there were winking lamps of gold and silver among pillars and arches, kneeling figures dotted about at confessionals and on the pavements; where there was the mist and scent of incense; where there were pictures, fantastic images, gaudy altars, great heights and distances, all softly lighted through stained glass, and the massive curtains that hung in the doorways. From these cities they would go on again, by the roads of vines and olives, through squalid villages, where there was not a hovel without a gap in its filthy walls, not a window with a whole inch of glass or paper; where there seemed to be nothing to support life, nothing to eat, nothing to make, nothing to grow, nothing to hope, nothing to do but die.

Again they would come to whole towns of palaces, whose proper inmates were all banished, and which were all changed into barracks: troops of idle soldiers leaning out of the state windows, where their accoutrements hung drying on the marble architecture, and showing to the mind like hosts of rats who were (happily) eating away the props of the edifices that supported them, and must soon, with them, be smashed on the heads of the other swarms of soldiers and the swarms of priests, and the swarms of spies, who were all the ill-looking population left to be ruined, in the streets below.

Through such scenes, the family procession moved on to Venice. And here it dispersed for a time, as they were to live in Venice some few months in a palace (itself six times as big as the whole Marshalsea) on the Grand Canal.

In this crowning unreality, where all the streets were paved with water, and where the deathlike stillness of the days and nights was broken by no sound but the softened ringing of church-bells, the rippling of the current, and the cry of the gondoliers turning the corners of the flowing streets, Little Dorrit, quite lost by her task being done, sat down to muse. The family began a gay life, went here and there, and turned night into day; but she was timid of joining in their gaieties, and only asked leave to be left alone.

Sometimes she would step into one of the gondolas that were always kept in waiting, moored to painted posts at the door—when she could escape from the attendance of that oppressive maid, who was her mistress, and a very hard one—and would be taken all over the strange city. Social people in other gondolas began to ask each other who the little solitary girl was whom they passed, sitting in her boat with folded hands, looking so pensively and wonderingly about her. Never thinking that it would be worth anybody's while to notice her or her doings, Little Dorrit, in her quiet, scared, lost manner, went about the city none the less.

But her favourite station was the balcony of her own room, overhanging the canal, with other balconies below, and none above. It was of massive stone darkened by ages, built in a wild fancy which came from the East to that collection of wild fancies; and Little Dorrit was little indeed, leaning on the broad-cushioned ledge, and looking over. As she liked no place of an evening half so well, she soon began to be watched for, and many eyes in passing gondolas were raised, and many people said, There was the little figure of the English girl who was always alone.

Such people were not realities to the little figure of the English girl; such people were all unknown to her. She would watch the sunset, in its long low lines of purple and red, and its burning flush high up into the sky: so glowing on the buildings, and so lightening their structure, that it made them look as if their strong walls were transparent, and they shone from within. She would watch those glories expire; and then, after looking at the black gondolas underneath, taking guests to music and dancing, would raise her eyes to the shining stars. Was there no party of her own, in other times, on which the stars had shone? To think of that old gate now!

She would think of that old gate, and of herself sitting at it in the dead of the night, pillowing Maggy's head; and of other places and of other scenes associated with those different times. And then she would lean upon her balcony, and look over at the water, as though they all lay underneath it. When she got to that, she would musingly watch its running, as if, in the general vision, it might run dry, and show her the prison again, and herself, and the old room, and the old inmates, and the old visitors: all lasting realities that had never changed.

CHAPTER 4. A Letter from Little Dorrit

Dear Mr Clennam,

I write to you from my own room at Venice, thinking you will be glad to hear from me.

But I know you cannot be so glad to hear from me as I am to write to you; for everything about you is as you have been accustomed to see it, and you miss nothing—unless it should be me, which can only be for a very little while together and very seldom—while everything in my life is so strange, and I miss so much.

When we were in Switzerland, which appears to have been years ago, though it was only weeks, I met young Mrs Gowan, who was on a mountain excursion like ourselves. She told me she was very well and very happy. She sent you the message, by me, that she thanked you affectionately and would never forget you. She was quite confiding with me, and I loved her almost as soon as I spoke to her. But there is nothing singular in that; who could help loving so beautiful and winning a creature! I could not wonder at any one loving her. No indeed.

It will not make you uneasy on Mrs Gowan's account, I hope—for I remember that you said you had the interest of a true friend in her—if I tell you that I wish she could have married some one better suited to her. Mr Gowan seems fond of her, and of course she is very fond of him, but I thought he was not earnest enough—I don't mean in that respect—I mean in anything. I could not keep it out of my mind that if I was Mrs Gowan (what a change that would be, and how I must alter to become like her!) I should feel that I was rather lonely and lost, for the want of some one who was steadfast and firm in purpose. I even thought she felt this want a little, almost without knowing it. But mind you are not made uneasy by this, for she was 'very well and very happy.' And she looked most beautiful.

I expect to meet her again before long, and indeed have been expecting for some days past to see her here. I will ever be as good a friend to her as I can for your sake. Dear Mr Clennam, I dare say you think little of having been a friend to me when I had no other (not that I have any other now, for I have made no new friends), but I think much of it, and I never can forget it.

I wish I knew—but it is best for no one to write to me—how Mr and Mrs Plornish prosper in the business which my dear father bought for them, and that old Mr Nandy lives happily with them and his two grandchildren, and sings all his songs over and over again. I cannot quite keep back the tears from my eyes when I think of my poor Maggy, and of the blank she must have felt at first, however kind they all are to her, without her Little Mother. Will you go and tell her, as a strict secret, with my love, that she never can have regretted our separation more than I have regretted it? And will you tell them all that I have thought of them every day, and that my heart is faithful to them everywhere? O, if you could know how faithful, you would almost pity me for being so far away and being so grand!

You will be glad, I am sure, to know that my dear father is very well in health, and that all these changes are highly beneficial to him, and that he is very different indeed from what he used to be when you used to see him. There is an improvement in my uncle too, I think, though he never complained of old, and never exults now. Fanny is very graceful, quick, and clever. It is natural to her to be a lady; she has adapted herself to our new fortunes with wonderful ease.

This reminds me that I have not been able to do so, and that I sometimes almost despair of ever being able to do so. I find that I cannot learn. Mrs General is always with us, and we speak French and speak Italian, and she takes pains to form us in many ways. When I say we speak French and Italian, I mean they do. As for me, I am so slow that I scarcely get on at all.

As soon as I begin to plan, and think, and try, all my planning, thinking, and trying go in old directions, and I begin to feel careful again about the expenses of the day, and about my dear father, and about my work, and then I remember with a start that there are no such cares left, and that in itself is so new and improbable that it sets me wandering again. I should not have the courage to mention this to any one but you.

It is the same with all these new countries and wonderful sights. They are very beautiful, and they astonish me, but I am not collected enough—not familiar enough with myself, if you can quite understand what I mean—to have all the pleasure in them that I might have. What I knew before them, blends with them, too, so curiously. For instance, when we were among the mountains, I often felt (I hesitate to tell such an idle thing, dear Mr Clennam, even to you) as if the Marshalsea must be behind that great rock; or as if Mrs Clennam's room where I have worked so many days, and where I first saw you, must be just beyond that snow. Do you remember one night when I came with Maggy to your lodging in Covent Garden? That room I have often and often fancied I have seen before me, travelling along for miles by the side of our carriage, when I have looked out of the carriage-window after dark. We were shut out that night, and sat at the iron gate, and walked about till morning. I often look up at the stars, even from the balcony of this room, and believe that I am in the street again, shut out with Maggy. It is the same with people that I left in England.

When I go about here in a gondola, I surprise myself looking into other gondolas as if I hoped to see them. It would overcome me with joy to see them, but I don't think it would surprise me much, at first. In my fanciful times, I fancy that they might be anywhere; and I almost expect to see their dear faces on the bridges or the quays.

Another difficulty that I have will seem very strange to you. It must seem very strange to any one but me, and does even to me: I often feel the old sad pity for—I need not write the word—for him. Changed as he is, and inexpressibly blest and thankful as I always am to know it, the old sorrowful feeling of compassion comes upon me sometimes with such strength that I want to put my arms round his neck, tell him how I love him, and cry a little on his breast. I should be glad after that, and proud and happy. But I know that I must not do this; that he would not like it, that Fanny would be angry, that Mrs General would be amazed; and so I quiet myself. Yet in doing so, I struggle with the feeling that I have come to be at a distance from him; and that even in the midst of all the servants and attendants, he is deserted, and in want of me.

Dear Mr Clennam, I have written a great deal about myself, but I must write a little more still, or what I wanted most of all to say in this weak letter would be left out of it. In all these foolish thoughts of mine, which I have been so hardy as to confess to you because I know you will understand me if anybody can, and will make more allowance for me than anybody else would if you cannot—in all these thoughts, there is one thought scarcely ever—never—out of my memory, and that is that I hope you sometimes, in a quiet moment, have a thought for me. I must tell you that as to this, I have felt, ever since I have been away, an anxiety which I am very anxious to relieve. I have been afraid that you may think of me in a new light, or a new character. Don't do that, I could not bear that—it would make me more unhappy than you can suppose. It would break my heart to believe that you thought of me in any way that would make me stranger to you than I was when you were so good to me. What I have to pray and entreat of you is, that you will never think of me as the daughter of a rich person;

that you will never think of me as dressing any better, or living any better, than when you first knew me. That you will remember me only as the little shabby girl you protected with so much tenderness, from whose threadbare dress you have kept away the rain, and whose wet feet you have dried at your fire. That you will think of me (when you think of me at all), and of my true affection and devoted gratitude, always without change, as of

Your poor child,

LITTLE DORRIT.=

P.S.—Particularly remember that you are not to be uneasy about Mrs Gowan. Her words were, 'Very well and very happy.' And she looked most beautiful.

CHAPTER 5. Something Wrong Somewhere

The family had been a month or two at Venice, when Mr Dorrit, who was much among Counts and Marquises, and had but scant leisure, set an hour of one day apart, beforehand, for the purpose of holding some conference with Mrs General.

The time he had reserved in his mind arriving, he sent Mr Tinkler, his valet, to Mrs General's apartment (which would have absorbed about a third of the area of the Marshalsea), to present his compliments to that lady, and represent him as desiring the favour of an interview. It being that period of the forenoon when the various members of the family had coffee in their own chambers, some couple of hours before assembling at breakfast in a faded hall which had once been sumptuous, but was now the prey of watery vapours and a settled melancholy, Mrs General was accessible to the valet. That envoy found her on a little square of carpet, so extremely diminutive in reference to the size of her stone and marble floor that she looked as if she might have had it spread for the trying on of a ready-made pair of shoes; or as if she had come into possession of the enchanted piece of carpet, bought for forty purses by one of the three princes in the Arabian Nights, and had that moment been transported on it, at a wish, into a palatial saloon with which it had no connection.

Mrs General, replying to the envoy, as she set down her empty coffee-cup, that she was willing at once to proceed to Mr Dorrit's apartment, and spare him the trouble of coming to her (which, in his gallantry, he had proposed), the envoy threw open the door, and escorted Mrs General to the presence. It was quite a walk, by mysterious staircases and corridors, from Mrs General's apartment,—hoodwinked by a narrow side street with a low gloomy bridge in it, and dungeon-like opposite tenements, their walls besmeared with a thousand downward stains and streaks, as if every crazy aperture in them had been weeping tears of rust into the Adriatic for centuries—to Mr Dorrit's apartment: with a whole English house-front of window, a prospect of beautiful church-domes rising into the blue sky sheer out of the water which reflected them, and a hushed murmur of the Grand Canal laving the doorways below, where his gondolas and gondoliers attended his pleasure, drowsily swinging in a little forest of piles.

Mr Dorrit, in a resplendent dressing-gown and cap—the dormant grub that had so long bided its time among the Collegians had burst into a rare butterfly—rose to receive Mrs General. A chair to Mrs General. An easier chair, sir; what are you doing, what are you about, what do you mean? Now, leave us!

'Mrs General,' said Mr Dorrit, 'I took the liberty—'

'By no means,' Mrs General interposed. 'I was quite at your disposition. I had had my coffee.'

'—I took the liberty,' said Mr Dorrit again, with the magnificent placidity of one who was above correction, 'to solicit the favour of a little private conversation with you, because I feel rather worried respecting my—ha—my younger daughter. You will have observed a great difference of temperament, madam, between my two daughters?'

Said Mrs General in response, crossing her gloved hands (she was never without gloves, and they never creased and always fitted), 'There is a great difference.'

'May I ask to be favoured with your view of it?' said Mr Dorrit, with a deference not incompatible with majestic serenity.

'Fanny,' returned Mrs General, 'has force of character and self-reliance. Amy, none.'

None? O Mrs General, ask the Marshalsea stones and bars. O Mrs General, ask the milliner who taught her to work, and the dancing-master who taught her sister to dance. O Mrs General, Mrs General, ask me, her father, what I owe her; and hear my testimony touching the life of this slighted little creature from her childhood up!

No such adjuration entered Mr. Dorrit's head. He looked at Mrs General, seated in her usual erect attitude on her coach-box behind the proprieties, and he said in a thoughtful manner, 'True, madam.'

'I would not,' said Mrs General, 'be understood to say, observe, that there is nothing to improve in Fanny. But there is material there—perhaps, indeed, a little too much.'

'Will you be kind enough, madam,' said Mr Dorrit, 'to be—ha—more explicit? I do not quite understand my elder daughter's having—hum—too much material. What material?'

'Fanny,' returned Mrs General, 'at present forms too many opinions. Perfect breeding forms none, and is never demonstrative.'

Lest he himself should be found deficient in perfect breeding, Mr Dorrit hastened to reply, 'Unquestionably, madam, you are right.' Mrs General returned, in her emotionless and expressionless manner, 'I believe so.'

'But you are aware, my dear madam,' said Mr Dorrit, 'that my daughters had the misfortune to lose their lamented mother when they were very young; and that, in consequence of my not having been until lately the recognised heir to my property, they have lived with me as a comparatively poor, though always proud, gentleman, in—ha hum—retirement!'

'I do not,' said Mrs General, 'lose sight of the circumstance.'

'Madam,' pursued Mr Dorrit, 'of my daughter Fanny, under her present guidance and with such an example constantly before her—'

(Mrs General shut her eyes.)

—'I have no misgivings. There is adaptability of character in Fanny. But my younger daughter, Mrs General, rather worries and vexes my thoughts. I must inform you that she has always been my favourite.'

'There is no accounting,' said Mrs General, 'for these partialities.'

'Ha—no,' assented Mr Dorrit. 'No. Now, madam, I am troubled by noticing that Amy is not, so to speak, one of ourselves. She does not care to go about with us; she is lost in the society we have here; our tastes are evidently not her tastes. Which,' said Mr Dorrit, summing up with judicial gravity, 'is to say, in other words, that there is something wrong in—ha—Amy.'

'May we incline to the supposition,' said Mrs General, with a little touch of varnish, 'that something is referable to the novelty of the position?'

'Excuse me, madam,' observed Mr Dorrit, rather quickly. 'The daughter of a gentleman, though—ha—himself at one time comparatively far from affluent—comparatively—and herself reared in—hum—retirement, need not of necessity find this position so very novel.'

'True,' said Mrs General, 'true.'

'Therefore, madam,' said Mr Dorrit, 'I took the liberty' (he laid an emphasis on the phrase and repeated it, as though he stipulated, with urbane firmness, that he must not be contradicted again), 'I took the liberty of requesting this interview, in order that I might mention the topic to you, and inquire how you would advise me?'

'Mr Dorrit,' returned Mrs General, 'I have conversed with Amy several times since we have been residing here, on the general subject of the formation of a demeanour. She has expressed herself to me as wondering exceedingly at Venice. I have mentioned to her that it is better not to wonder. I have pointed out to her that the celebrated Mr Eustace, the classical tourist, did not think much of it; and that he compared the Rialto, greatly to its disadvantage, with Westminster and Blackfriars Bridges. I need not add, after what you have said, that I have not yet found my arguments successful. You do me the honour to ask me what to advise. It always appears to me (if this should prove to be a baseless assumption, I shall be pardoned), that Mr Dorrit has been accustomed to exercise influence over the minds of others.'

'Hum—madam,' said Mr Dorrit, 'I have been at the head of—ha of a considerable community. You are right in supposing that I am not unaccustomed to—an influential position.'

'I am happy,' returned Mrs General, 'to be so corroborated. I would therefore the more confidently recommend that Mr Dorrit should speak to Amy himself, and make his observations and wishes known to her. Being his favourite, besides, and no doubt attached to him, she is all the more likely to yield to his influence.'

'I had anticipated your suggestion, madam,' said Mr Dorrit, 'but—ha—was not sure that I might—hum—not encroach on—'

'On my province, Mr Dorrit?' said Mrs General, graciously. 'Do not mention it.'

'Then, with your leave, madam,' resumed Mr Dorrit, ringing his little bell to summon his valet, 'I will send for her at once.'

'Does Mr Dorrit wish me to remain?'

'Perhaps, if you have no other engagement, you would not object for a minute or two—'

'Not at all.'

So, Tinkler the valet was instructed to find Miss Amy's maid, and to request that subordinate to inform Miss Amy that Mr Dorrit wished to see her in his own room. In delivering this charge to Tinkler, Mr Dorrit looked severely at him, and also kept a jealous eye upon him until he went out at the door, mistrusting that he might have something in his mind prejudicial to the family dignity; that he might have even got wind of some Collegiate joke before he came into the service, and might be derisively reviving its remembrance at the present moment. If Tinkler had happened to smile, however faintly and innocently, nothing would have persuaded Mr Dorrit, to the hour of his death, but that this was the case. As Tinkler happened, however, very fortunately for himself, to be of a serious and composed countenance, he escaped the secret danger that threatened him. And as on his return—when Mr Dorrit eyed him again—he announced Miss Amy as if she had come to a funeral, he left a vague impression on Mr Dorrit's mind that he was a well-conducted young fellow, who had been brought up in the study of his Catechism by a widowed mother.

'Amy,' said Mr Dorrit, 'you have just now been the subject of some conversation between myself and Mrs General. We agree that you scarcely seem at home here. Ha—how is this?'

A pause.

'I think, father, I require a little time.'

'Papa is a preferable mode of address,' observed Mrs General. 'Father is rather vulgar, my dear. The word Papa, besides, gives a pretty form to the lips. Papa, potatoes, poultry, prunes, and prism are all very good words for the lips: especially prunes and prism. You will find it serviceable, in the formation of a demeanour, if you sometimes say to yourself in company—on entering a room, for instance—Papa, potatoes, poultry, prunes and prism, prunes and prism.'

'Pray, my child,' said Mr Dorrit, 'attend to the—hum—precepts of Mrs General.'

Poor Little Dorrit, with a rather forlorn glance at that eminent varnisher, promised to try.

'You say, Amy,' pursued Mr Dorrit, 'that you think you require time. Time for what?'

Another pause.

'To become accustomed to the novelty of my life, was all I meant,' said Little Dorrit, with her loving eyes upon her father; whom she had very nearly addressed as poultry, if not prunes and prism too, in her desire to submit herself to Mrs General and please him.

Mr Dorrit frowned, and looked anything but pleased. 'Amy,' he returned, 'it appears to me, I must say, that you have had abundance of time for that. Ha—you surprise me. You disappoint me. Fanny has conquered any such little difficulties, and—hum—why not you?'

'I hope I shall do better soon,' said Little Dorrit.

'I hope so,' returned her father. 'I—ha—I most devoutly hope so, Amy. I sent for you, in order that I might say—hum—impressively say, in the presence of Mrs General, to whom we are all so much indebted for obligingly being present among us, on—ha—on this or any other occasion,' Mrs General shut her eyes, 'that I—ha hum—am not pleased with you. You make Mrs General's a thankless task. You—ha—embarrass me very much. You have always (as I have informed Mrs General) been my favourite child; I have always made you a—hum—a friend and companion; in return, I beg—I—ha—I do beg, that you accommodate yourself better to—hum—circumstances, and dutifully do what becomes your—your station.'

Mr Dorrit was even a little more fragmentary than usual, being excited on the subject and anxious to make himself particularly emphatic.

'I do beg,' he repeated, 'that this may be attended to, and that you will seriously take pains and try to conduct yourself in a manner both becoming your position as—ha—Miss

Amy Dorrit, and satisfactory to myself and Mrs General.'

That lady shut her eyes again, on being again referred to; then, slowly opening them and rising, added these words:

'If Miss Amy Dorrit will direct her own attention to, and will accept of my poor assistance in, the formation of a surface, Mr. Dorrit will have no further cause of anxiety. May I take this opportunity of remarking, as an instance in point, that it is scarcely delicate to look at vagrants with the attention which I have seen bestowed upon them by a very dear young friend of mine? They should not be looked at. Nothing disagreeable should ever be looked at. Apart from such a habit standing in the way of that graceful equanimity of surface which is so expressive of good breeding, it hardly seems compatible with refinement of mind. A truly refined mind will seem to be ignorant of the existence of anything that is not perfectly proper, placid, and pleasant.' Having delivered this exalted sentiment, Mrs General made a sweeping obeisance, and retired with an expression of mouth indicative of Prunes and Prism.

Little Dorrit, whether speaking or silent, had preserved her quiet earnestness and her loving look. It had not been clouded, except for a passing moment, until now. But now that she was left alone with him the fingers of her lightly folded hands were agitated, and there was repressed emotion in her face.

Not for herself. She might feel a little wounded, but her care was not for herself. Her thoughts still turned, as they always had turned, to him. A faint misgiving, which had hung about her since their accession to fortune, that even now she could never see him as he used to be before the prison days, had gradually begun to assume form in her mind. She felt that, in what he had just now said to her and in his whole bearing towards her, there was the well-known shadow of the Marshalsea wall. It took a new shape, but it was the old sad shadow. She began with sorrowful unwillingness to acknowledge to herself that she was not strong enough to keep off the fear that no space in the life of man could overcome that quarter of a century behind the prison bars. She had no blame to bestow upon him, therefore: nothing to reproach him with, no emotions in her faithful heart but great compassion and unbounded tenderness.

This is why it was, that, even as he sat before her on his sofa, in the brilliant light of a bright Italian day, the wonderful city without and the splendours of an old palace within, she saw him at the moment in the long-familiar gloom of his Marshalsea lodging, and wished to take her seat beside him, and comfort him, and be again full of confidence with him, and of usefulness to him. If he divined what was in her thoughts, his own were not in tune with it. After some uneasy moving in his seat, he got up and walked about, looking very much dissatisfied.

'Is there anything else you wish to say to me, dear father?'

'No, no. Nothing else.'

'I am sorry you have not been pleased with me, dear. I hope you will not think of me with displeasure now. I am going to try, more than ever, to adapt myself as you wish to what surrounds me—for indeed I have tried all along, though I have failed, I know.'

'Amy,' he returned, turning short upon her. 'You—ha—habitually hurt me.'

'Hurt you, father! I!'

'There is a—hum—a topic,' said Mr Dorrit, looking all about the ceiling of the room, and never at the attentive, uncomplainingly shocked face, 'a painful topic, a series of events which I wish—ha—altogether to obliterate. This is understood by your sister, who has already remonstrated with you in my presence; it is understood by your brother; it is understood by—ha hum—by every one of delicacy and sensitiveness except yourself—ha—I am sorry to say, except yourself. You, Amy—hum—you alone and only you—constantly revive the topic, though not in words.'

She laid her hand on his arm. She did nothing more. She gently touched him. The trembling hand may have said, with some expression, 'Think of me, think how I have worked, think of my many cares!' But she said not a syllable herself.

There was a reproach in the touch so addressed to him that she had not foreseen, or she would have withheld her hand. He began to justify himself in a heated, stumbling, angry manner, which made nothing of it.

'I was there all those years. I was—ha—universally acknowledged as the head of the place. I—hum—I caused you to be respected there, Amy. I—ha hum—I gave my family a position there. I deserve a return. I claim a return. I say, sweep it off the face of the earth and begin afresh. Is that much? I ask, is that much?'

He did not once look at her, as he rambled on in this way; but gesticulated at, and appealed to, the empty air.

'I have suffered. Probably I know how much I have suffered better than any one—ha—I say than any one! If I can put that aside, if I can eradicate the marks of what I have endured, and can emerge before the world—a—ha—gentleman unspoiled, unspotted—is it a great deal to expect—I say again, is it a great deal to expect—that my children should—hum—do the same and sweep that accursed experience off the face of the earth?'

In spite of his flustered state, he made all these exclamations in a carefully suppressed voice, lest the valet should overhear anything.

'Accordingly, they do it. Your sister does it. Your brother does it. You alone, my favourite child, whom I made the friend and companion of my life when you were a mere—hum—Baby, do not do it. You alone say you can't do it. I provide you with valuable assistance to do it. I attach an accomplished and highly bred lady—ha—Mrs General, to you, for the purpose of doing it. Is it surprising that I should be displeased? Is it necessary that I should defend myself for expressing my displeasure? No!'

Notwithstanding which, he continued to defend himself, without any abatement of his flushed mood.

'I am careful to appeal to that lady for confirmation, before I express any displeasure at all. I—hum—I necessarily make that appeal within limited bounds, or I—ha—should render legible, by that lady, what I desire to be blotted out. Am I selfish? Do I complain for my own sake? No. No. Principally for—ha hum—your sake, Amy.'

This last consideration plainly appeared, from his manner of pursuing it, to have just that instant come into his head.

'I said I was hurt. So I am. So I—ha—am determined to be, whatever is advanced to the contrary. I am hurt that my daughter, seated in the—hum—lap of fortune, should mope and retire and proclaim herself unequal to her destiny. I am hurt that she should—ha—

systematically reproduce what the rest of us blot out; and seem—hum—I had almost said positively anxious—to announce to wealthy and distinguished society that she was born and bred in—ha hum—a place that I myself decline to name. But there is no inconsistency—ha—not the least, in my feeling hurt, and yet complaining principally for your sake, Amy. I do; I say again, I do. It is for your sake that I wish you, under the auspices of Mrs General, to form a—hum—a surface. It is for your sake that I wish you to have a—ha—truly refined mind, and (in the striking words of Mrs General) to be ignorant of everything that is not perfectly proper, placid, and pleasant.'

He had been running down by jerks, during his last speech, like a sort of ill-adjusted alarum. The touch was still upon his arm. He fell silent; and after looking about the ceiling again for a little while, looked down at her. Her head drooped, and he could not see her face; but her touch was tender and quiet, and in the expression of her dejected figure there was no blame—nothing but love. He began to whimper, just as he had done that night in the prison when she afterwards sat at his bedside till morning; exclaimed that he was a poor ruin and a poor wretch in the midst of his wealth; and clasped her in his arms. 'Hush, hush, my own dear! Kiss me!' was all she said to him. His tears were soon dried, much sooner than on the former occasion; and he was presently afterwards very high with his valet, as a way of righting himself for having shed any.

With one remarkable exception, to be recorded in its place, this was the only time, in his life of freedom and fortune, when he spoke to his daughter Amy of the old days.

But, now, the breakfast hour arrived; and with it Miss Fanny from her apartment, and Mr Edward from his apartment. Both these young persons of distinction were something the worse for late hours. As to Miss Fanny, she had become the victim of an insatiate mania for what she called 'going into society;' and would have gone into it head-foremost fifty times between sunset and sunrise, if so many opportunities had been at her disposal. As to Mr Edward, he, too, had a large acquaintance, and was generally engaged (for the most part, in diceing circles, or others of a kindred nature), during the greater part of every night. For this gentleman, when his fortunes changed, had stood at the great advantage of being already prepared for the highest associates, and having little to learn: so much was he indebted to the happy accidents which had made him acquainted with horse-dealing and billiard-marking.

At breakfast, Mr Frederick Dorrit likewise appeared. As the old gentleman inhabited the highest story of the palace, where he might have practised pistol-shooting without much chance of discovery by the other inmates, his younger niece had taken courage to propose the restoration to him of his clarionet, which Mr Dorrit had ordered to be confiscated, but which she had ventured to preserve. Notwithstanding some objections from Miss Fanny, that it was a low instrument, and that she detested the sound of it, the concession had been made. But it was then discovered that he had had enough of it, and never played it, now that it was no longer his means of getting bread. He had insensibly acquired a new habit of shuffling into the picture-galleries, always with his twisted paper of snuff in his hand (much to the indignation of Miss Fanny, who had proposed the purchase of a gold box for him that the family might not be discredited, which he had absolutely refused to carry when it was bought); and of passing hours and hours before the portraits of renowned Venetians. It was never made out what his dazed eyes saw in them; whether he had an interest in them merely as pictures, or whether he confusedly identified them with a glory that was departed, like the strength of his own mind. But he paid his court to them with great exactness, and clearly derived pleasure from the pursuit. After the first few days, Little Dorrit happened one morning to assist at these attentions. It so evidently heightened his gratification that she often accompanied him afterwards, and the greatest delight of which the old man had shown himself susceptible since his ruin, arose out of these excursions, when he would carry a chair about for her from picture to picture, and stand behind it, in spite of all her remonstrances, silently presenting her to the noble Venetians.

It fell out that, at this family breakfast, he referred to their having seen in a gallery, on the previous day, the lady and gentleman whom they had encountered on the Great Saint Bernard, 'I forget the name,' said he. 'I dare say you remember them, William? I dare say you do, Edward?'

'I remember 'em well enough,' said the latter.

'I should think so,' observed Miss Fanny, with a toss of her head and a glance at her sister. 'But they would not have been recalled to our remembrance, I suspect, if Uncle hadn't tumbled over the subject.'

'My dear, what a curious phrase,' said Mrs General. 'Would not inadvertently lighted upon, or accidentally referred to, be better?'

'Thank you very much, Mrs General,' returned the young lady, 'no, I think not. On the whole I prefer my own expression.'

This was always Miss Fanny's way of receiving a suggestion from Mrs General. But she always stored it up in her mind, and adopted it at another time.

'I should have mentioned our having met Mr and Mrs Gowan, Fanny,' said Little Dorrit, 'even if Uncle had not. I have scarcely seen you since, you know. I meant to have spoken of it at breakfast; because I should like to pay a visit to Mrs Gowan, and to become better acquainted with her, if Papa and Mrs General do not object.'

'Well, Amy,' said Fanny, 'I am sure I am glad to find you at last expressing a wish to become better acquainted with anybody in Venice. Though whether Mr and Mrs Gowan are desirable acquaintances, remains to be determined.'

'Mrs Gowan I spoke of, dear.'

'No doubt,' said Fanny. 'But you can't separate her from her husband, I believe, without an Act of Parliament.'

'Do you think, Papa,' inquired Little Dorrit, with diffidence and hesitation, 'there is any objection to my making this visit?'

'Really,' he replied, 'I—ha—what is Mrs General's view?'

Mrs General's view was, that not having the honour of any acquaintance with the lady and gentleman referred to, she was not in a position to varnish the present article. She could only remark, as a general principle observed in the varnishing trade, that much depended on the quarter from which the lady under consideration was accredited to a family so conspicuously niched in the social temple as the family of Dorrit.

At this remark the face of Mr Dorrit gloomed considerably. He was about (connecting the accrediting with an obtrusive person of the name of Clennam, whom he imperfectly remembered in some former state of existence) to black-ball the name of Gowan finally, when Edward Dorrit, Esquire, came into the conversation, with his glass in his eye, and the preliminary remark of 'I say—you there! Go out, will you!'—which was addressed to a couple of men who were handing the dishes round, as a courteous intimation that their services could be temporarily dispensed with.

Those menials having obeyed the mandate, Edward Dorrit, Esquire, proceeded.

'Perhaps it's a matter of policy to let you all know that these Gowans—in whose favour, or at least the gentleman's, I can't be supposed to be much prepossessed myself—are known to people of importance, if that makes any difference.'

'That, I would say,' observed the fair varnisher, 'Makes the greatest difference. The connection in question, being really people of importance and consideration—'

'As to that,' said Edward Dorrit, Esquire, 'I'll give you the means of judging for yourself. You are acquainted, perhaps, with the famous name of Merdle?'

'The great Merdle!' exclaimed Mrs General.

'The Merdle,' said Edward Dorrit, Esquire. 'They are known to him. Mrs Gowan—I mean the dowager, my polite friend's mother—is intimate with Mrs Merdle, and I know these two to be on their visiting list.'

'If so, a more undeniable guarantee could not be given,' said Mrs General to Mr Dorrit, raising her gloves and bowing her head, as if she were doing homage to some visible graven image.

'I beg to ask my son, from motives of—ah—curiosity,' Mr Dorrit observed, with a decided change in his manner, 'how he becomes possessed of this—hum—timely information?'

'It's not a long story, sir,' returned Edward Dorrit, Esquire, 'and you shall have it out of hand. To begin with, Mrs Merdle is the lady you had the parley with at what's-his-name place.'

'Martigny,' interposed Miss Fanny with an air of infinite languor.

'Martigny,' assented her brother, with a slight nod and a slight wink; in acknowledgment of which, Miss Fanny looked surprised, and laughed and reddened.

'How can that be, Edward?' said Mr Dorrit. 'You informed me that the name of the gentleman with whom you conferred was—ha—Sparkler. Indeed, you showed me his card. Hum. Sparkler.'

'No doubt of it, father; but it doesn't follow that his mother's name must be the same. Mrs Merdle was married before, and he is her son. She is in Rome now; where probably we shall know more of her, as you decide to winter there. Sparkler is just come here. I passed last evening in company with Sparkler. Sparkler is a very good fellow on the whole, though rather a bore on one subject, in consequence of being tremendously smitten with a certain young lady.' Here Edward Dorrit, Esquire, eyed Miss Fanny through his glass across the table. 'We happened last night to compare notes about our travels, and I had the information I have given you from Sparkler himself.' Here he ceased; continuing to eye Miss Fanny through his glass, with a face much twisted, and not ornamentally so, in part by the action of keeping his glass in his eye, and in part by the great subtlety of his smile.

'Under these circumstances,' said Mr Dorrit, 'I believe I express the sentiments of—ha—Mrs General, no less than my own, when I say that there is no objection, but—ha hum—quite the contrary—to your gratifying your desire, Amy. I trust I may—ha—hail—this desire,' said Mr Dorrit, in an encouraging and forgiving manner, 'as an auspicious omen. It is quite right to know these people. It is a very proper thing. Mr Merdle's is a name of—ha—world-wide repute. Mr Merdle's undertakings are immense. They bring him in such vast sums of money that they are regarded as—hum—national benefits. Mr Merdle is the man of this time. The name of Merdle is the name of the age. Pray do everything on my behalf that is civil to Mr and Mrs Gowan, for we will—ha—we will certainly notice them.'

This magnificent accordance of Mr Dorrit's recognition settled the matter. It was not observed that Uncle had pushed away his plate, and forgotten his breakfast; but he was not much observed at any time, except by Little Dorrit. The servants were recalled, and the meal proceeded to its conclusion. Mrs General rose and left the table. Little Dorrit rose and left the table. When Edward and Fanny remained whispering together across it, and when Mr Dorrit remained eating figs and reading a French newspaper, Uncle suddenly fixed the attention of all three by rising out of his chair, striking his hand upon the table, and saying, 'Brother! I protest against it!'

If he had made a proclamation in an unknown tongue, and given up the ghost immediately afterwards, he could not have astounded his audience more. The paper fell from Mr Dorrit's hand, and he sat petrified, with a fig half way to his mouth.

'Brother!' said the old man, conveying a surprising energy into his trembling voice, 'I protest against it! I love you; you know I love you dearly. In these many years I have never been untrue to you in a single thought. Weak as I am, I would at any time have struck any man who spoke ill of you. But, brother, brother, brother, I protest against it!'

It was extraordinary to see of what a burst of earnestness such a decrepit man was capable. His eyes became bright, his grey hair rose on his head, markings of purpose on his brow and face which had faded from them for five-and-twenty years, started out again, and there was an energy in his hand that made its action nervous once more.

'My dear Frederick!' exclaimed Mr Dorrit faintly. 'What is wrong? What is the matter?'

'How dare you,' said the old man, turning round on Fanny, 'how dare you do it? Have you no memory? Have you no heart?'

'Uncle?' cried Fanny, affrighted and bursting into tears, 'why do you attack me in this cruel manner? What have I done?'

'Done?' returned the old man, pointing to her sister's place, 'where's your affectionate invaluable friend? Where's your devoted guardian? Where's your more than mother? How dare you set up superiorities against all these characters combined in your sister? For shame, you false girl, for shame!'

'I love Amy,' cried Miss Fanny, sobbing and weeping, 'as well as I love my life—better than I love my life. I don't deserve to be so treated. I am as grateful to Amy, and as fond of Amy, as it's possible for any human being to be. I wish I was dead. I never was so wickedly wronged. And only because I am anxious for the family credit.'

'To the winds with the family credit!' cried the old man, with great scorn and indignation. 'Brother, I protest against pride. I protest against ingratitude. I protest against any one of us here who have known what we have known, and have seen what we have seen, setting up any pretension that puts Amy at a moment's disadvantage, or to the cost of a moment's pain. We may know that it's a base pretension by its having that effect. It ought to bring a judgment on us. Brother, I protest against it in the sight of God!'

As his hand went up above his head and came down on the table, it might have been a blacksmith's. After a few moments' silence, it had relaxed into its usual weak condition. He went round to his brother with his ordinary shuffling step, put the hand on his shoulder, and said, in a softened voice, 'William, my dear, I felt obliged to say it; forgive me, for I felt obliged to say it!' and then went, in his bowed way, out of the palace hall, just as he might have gone out of the Marshalsea room.

All this time Fanny had been sobbing and crying, and still continued to do so. Edward, beyond opening his mouth in amazement, had not opened his lips, and had done nothing but stare. Mr Dorrit also had been utterly discomfited, and quite unable to assert himself in any way. Fanny was now the first to speak.

'I never, never, never was so used!' she sobbed. 'There never was anything so harsh and unjustifiable, so disgracefully violent and cruel! Dear, kind, quiet little Amy, too, what would she feel if she could know that she had been innocently the means of exposing me to such treatment! But I'll never tell her! No, good darling, I'll never tell her!'

This helped Mr Dorrit to break his silence.

'My dear,' said he, 'I—ha—approve of your resolution. It will be—ha hum—much better not to speak of this to Amy. It might—hum—it might distress her. Ha. No doubt it would distress her greatly. It is considerate and right to avoid doing so. We will—ha—keep this to ourselves.'

'But the cruelty of Uncle!' cried Miss Fanny. 'O, I never can forgive the wanton cruelty of Uncle!'

'My dear,' said Mr Dorrit, recovering his tone, though he remained unusually pale, 'I must request you not to say so. You must remember that your uncle is—ha—not what he formerly was. You must remember that your uncle's state requires—hum—great forbearance from us, great forbearance.'

'I am sure,' cried Fanny, piteously, 'it is only charitable to suppose that there must be something wrong in him somewhere, or he never could have so attacked Me, of all the people in the world.'

'Fanny,' returned Mr Dorrit in a deeply fraternal tone, 'you know, with his innumerable good points, what a—hum—wreck your uncle is; and, I entreat you by the fondness that I have for him, and by the fidelity that you know I have always shown him, to—ha—to draw your own conclusions, and to spare my brotherly feelings.'

This ended the scene; Edward Dorrit, Esquire, saying nothing throughout, but looking, to the last, perplexed and doubtful. Miss Fanny awakened much affectionate uneasiness in her sister's mind that day by passing the greater part of it in violent fits of embracing her, and in alternately giving her brooches, and wishing herself dead.

CHAPTER 6. Something Right Somewhere

To be in the halting state of Mr Henry Gowan; to have left one of two powers in disgust; to want the necessary qualifications for finding promotion with another, and to be loitering moodily about on neutral ground, cursing both; is to be in a situation unwholesome for the mind, which time is not likely to improve. The worst class of sum worked in the every-day world is cyphered by the diseased arithmeticians who are always in the rule of Subtraction as to the merits and successes of others, and never in Addition as to their own.

The habit, too, of seeking some sort of recompense in the discontented boast of being disappointed, is a habit fraught with degeneracy. A certain idle carelessness and recklessness of consistency soon comes of it. To bring deserving things down by setting undeserving things up is one of its perverted delights; and there is no playing fast and loose with the truth, in any game, without growing the worse for it.

In his expressed opinions of all performances in the Art of painting that were completely destitute of merit, Gowan was the most liberal fellow on earth. He would declare such a man to have more power in his little finger (provided he had none), than such another had (provided he had much) in his whole mind and body. If the objection were taken that the thing commended was trash, he would reply, on behalf of his art, 'My good fellow, what do we all turn out but trash? I turn out nothing else, and I make you a present of the confession.'

To make a vaunt of being poor was another of the incidents of his splenetic state, though this may have had the design in it of showing that he ought to be rich; just as he would publicly laud and decry the Barnacles, lest it should be forgotten that he belonged to the family. Howbeit, these two subjects were very often on his lips; and he managed them so well that he might have praised himself by the month together, and not have made himself out half so important a man as he did by his light disparagement of his claims on anybody's consideration.

Out of this same airy talk of his, it always soon came to be understood, wherever he and his wife went, that he had married against the wishes of his exalted relations, and had had much ado to prevail on them to countenance her. He never made the representation, on the contrary seemed to laugh the idea to scorn; but it did happen that, with all his pains to depreciate himself, he was always in the superior position. From the days of their honeymoon, Minnie Gowan felt sensible of being usually regarded as the wife of a man who had made a descent in marrying her, but whose chivalrous love for her had cancelled that inequality.

To Venice they had been accompanied by Monsieur Blandois of Paris, and at Venice Monsieur Blandois of Paris was very much in the society of Gowan. When they had first met this gallant gentleman at Geneva, Gowan had been undecided whether to kick him or encourage him; and had remained for about four-and-twenty hours, so troubled to settle the point to his satisfaction, that he had thought of tossing up a five-franc piece on the terms, 'Tails, kick; heads, encourage,' and abiding by the voice of the oracle. It chanced, however, that his wife expressed a dislike to the engaging Blandois, and that the balance of feeling in the hotel was against him. Upon it, Gowan resolved to encourage him.

Why this perversity, if it were not in a generous fit?—which it was not. Why should Gowan, very much the superior of Blandois of Paris, and very well able to pull that prepossessing gentleman to pieces and find out the stuff he was made of, take up with such a man? In the first place, he opposed the first separate wish he observed in his wife, because her father had paid his debts and it was desirable to take an early opportunity of asserting his independence. In the second place, he opposed the prevalent feeling, because with many capacities of being otherwise, he was an ill-conditioned man. He found a pleasure in declaring that a courtier with the refined manners of Blandois ought to rise to the greatest distinction in any polished country. He found a pleasure in setting up Blandois as the type of elegance, and making him a satire upon others who piqued themselves on personal graces. He seriously protested that the bow of Blandois was perfect, that the address of Blandois was irresistible, and that the picturesque ease of Blandois would be cheaply purchased (if it were not a gift, and unpurchasable) for a hundred thousand francs. That exaggeration in the manner of the man which has been noticed as appertaining to him and to every such man, whatever his original breeding, as certainly as the sun belongs to this system, was acceptable to Gowan as a caricature, which he found it a humorous resource to have at hand for the ridiculing of numbers of people who necessarily did more or less of what Blandois overdid. Thus he had taken up with him; and thus, negligently strengthening these inclinations with habit, and idly deriving some amusement from his talk, he had glided into a way of having him for a companion. This, though he supposed him to live by his wits at play-tables and the like; though he suspected him to be a coward, while he himself was daring and courageous; though he thoroughly knew him to be disliked by Minnie; and though he cared so little for him, after all, that if he had given her any tangible personal cause to regard him with aversion, he would have had no compunction whatever in flinging him out of the highest window in Venice into the deepest water of the city.

Little Dorrit would have been glad to make her visit to Mrs Gowan, alone; but as Fanny, who had not yet recovered from her Uncle's protest, though it was four-and-twenty hours of age, pressingly offered her company, the two sisters stepped together into one of the gondolas under Mr Dorrit's window, and, with the courier in attendance, were taken in high state to Mrs Gowan's lodging. In truth, their state was rather too high for the lodging, which was, as Fanny complained, 'fearfully out of the way,' and which took them through a complexity of narrow streets of water, which the same lady disparaged as 'mere ditches.'

The house, on a little desert island, looked as if it had broken away from somewhere else, and had floated by chance into its present anchorage in company with a vine almost as much in want of training as the poor wretches who were lying under its leaves. The features of the surrounding picture were, a church with hoarding and scaffolding about it, which had been under suppositious repair so long that the means of repair looked a hundred years old, and had themselves fallen into decay; a quantity of washed linen, spread to dry in the sun; a number of houses at odds with one another and grotesquely out of the perpendicular, like rotten pre-Adamite cheeses cut into fantastic shapes and full of mites; and a feverish bewilderment of windows, with their lattice-blinds all hanging askew, and something draggled and dirty dangling out of most of them.

On the first-floor of the house was a Bank—a surprising experience for any gentleman of commercial pursuits bringing laws for all mankind from a British city—where two spare clerks, like dried dragoons, in green velvet caps adorned with golden tassels, stood, bearded, behind a small counter in a small room, containing no other visible objects than an empty iron-safe with the door open, a jug of water, and a papering of garland of roses; but who, on lawful requisition, by merely dipping their hands out of sight, could produce exhaustless mounds of five-franc pieces. Below the Bank was a suite of three or four rooms with barred windows, which had the appearance of a jail for criminal rats. Above the Bank was Mrs Gowan's residence.

Notwithstanding that its walls were blotched, as if missionary maps were bursting out of them to impart geographical knowledge; notwithstanding that its weird furniture was forlornly faded and musty, and that the prevailing Venetian odour of bilge water and an ebb tide on a weedy shore was very strong; the place was better within, than it promised. The door was opened by a smiling man like a reformed assassin—a temporary servant—who ushered them into the room where Mrs Gowan sat, with the announcement that two beautiful English ladies were come to see the mistress.

Mrs Gowan, who was engaged in needlework, put her work aside in a covered basket, and rose, a little hurriedly. Miss Fanny was excessively courteous to her, and said the usual nothings with the skill of a veteran.

'Papa was extremely sorry,' proceeded Fanny, 'to be engaged to-day (he is so much engaged here, our acquaintance being so wretchedly large!); and particularly requested me to bring his card for Mr Gowan. That I may be sure to acquit myself of a commission which he impressed upon me at least a dozen times, allow me to relieve my conscience by placing it on the table at once.'

Which she did with veteran ease.

'We have been,' said Fanny, 'charmed to understand that you know the Merdles. We hope it may be another means of bringing us together.'

'They are friends,' said Mrs Gowan, 'of Mr Gowan's family. I have not yet had the pleasure of a personal introduction to Mrs Merdle, but I suppose I shall be presented to her at Rome.'

'Indeed?' returned Fanny, with an appearance of amiably quenching her own superiority. 'I think you'll like her.'

'You know her very well?'

'Why, you see,' said Fanny, with a frank action of her pretty shoulders, 'in London one knows every one. We met her on our way here, and, to say the truth, papa was at first rather cross with her for taking one of the rooms that our people had ordered for us. However, of course, that soon blew over, and we were all good friends again.'

Although the visit had as yet given Little Dorrit no opportunity of conversing with Mrs Gowan, there was a silent understanding between them, which did as well. She looked at Mrs Gowan with keen and unabated interest; the sound of her voice was thrilling to her; nothing that was near her, or about her, or at all concerned her, escaped Little Dorrit. She was quicker to perceive the slightest matter here, than in any other case—but one.

'You have been quite well,' she now said, 'since that night?'

'Quite, my dear. And you?'

'Oh! I am always well,' said Little Dorrit, timidly. 'I—yes, thank you.'

There was no reason for her faltering and breaking off, other than that Mrs Gowan had touched her hand in speaking to her, and their looks had met. Something thoughtfully apprehensive in the large, soft eyes, had checked Little Dorrit in an instant.

'You don't know that you are a favourite of my husband's, and that I am almost bound to be jealous of you?' said Mrs Gowan.

Little Dorrit, blushing, shook her head.

'He will tell you, if he tells you what he tells me, that you are quieter and quicker of resource than any one he ever saw.'

'He speaks far too well of me,' said Little Dorrit.

'I doubt that; but I don't at all doubt that I must tell him you are here. I should never be forgiven, if I were to let you—and Miss Dorrit—go, without doing so. May I? You can excuse the disorder and discomfort of a painter's studio?'

The inquiries were addressed to Miss Fanny, who graciously replied that she would be beyond anything interested and enchanted. Mrs Gowan went to a door, looked in beyond it, and came back. 'Do Henry the favour to come in,' said she, 'I knew he would be pleased!'

The first object that confronted Little Dorrit, entering first, was Blandois of Paris in a great cloak and a furtive slouched hat, standing on a throne platform in a corner, as he had stood on the Great Saint Bernard, when the warning arms seemed to be all pointing up at him. She recoiled from this figure, as it smiled at her.

'Don't be alarmed,' said Gowan, coming from his easel behind the door. 'It's only Blandois. He is doing duty as a model to-day. I am making a study of him. It saves me money to turn him to some use. We poor painters have none to spare.'

Blandois of Paris pulled off his slouched hat, and saluted the ladies without coming out of his corner.

'A thousand pardons!' said he. 'But the Professore here is so inexorable with me, that I am afraid to stir.'

'Don't stir, then,' said Gowan coolly, as the sisters approached the easel. 'Let the ladies at least see the original of the daub, that they may know what it's meant for. There he stands, you see. A bravo waiting for his prey, a distinguished noble waiting to save his country, the common enemy waiting to do somebody a bad turn, an angelic messenger waiting to do somebody a good turn—whatever you think he looks most like!'

'Say, Professore Mio, a poor gentleman waiting to do homage to elegance and beauty,' remarked Blandois.

'Or say, Cattivo Soggetto Mio,' returned Gowan, touching the painted face with his brush in the part where the real face had moved, 'a murderer after the fact. Show that white hand of yours, Blandois. Put it outside the cloak. Keep it still.'

Blandois' hand was unsteady; but he laughed, and that would naturally shake it.

'He was formerly in some scuffle with another murderer, or with a victim, you observe,' said Gowan, putting in the markings of the hand with a quick, impatient, unskilful touch, 'and these are the tokens of it. Outside the cloak, man!—Corpo di San Marco, what are you thinking of?'

Blandois of Paris shook with a laugh again, so that his hand shook more; now he raised it to twist his moustache, which had a damp appearance; and now he stood in the required position, with a little new swagger.

His face was so directed in reference to the spot where Little Dorrit stood by the easel, that throughout he looked at her. Once attracted by his peculiar eyes, she could not remove her own, and they had looked at each other all the time. She trembled now; Gowan, feeling it, and supposing her to be alarmed by the large dog beside him, whose head she caressed in her hand,

and who had just uttered a low growl, glanced at her to say, 'He won't hurt you, Miss Dorrit.'

'I am not afraid of him,' she returned in the same breath; 'but will you look at him?'

In a moment Gowan had thrown down his brush, and seized the dog with both hands by the collar.

'Blandois! How can you be such a fool as to provoke him! By Heaven, and the other place too, he'll tear you to bits! Lie down! Lion! Do you hear my voice, you rebel!'

The great dog, regardless of being half-choked by his collar, was obdurately pulling with his dead weight against his master, resolved to get across the room. He had been crouching for a spring at the moment when his master caught him.

'Lion! Lion!' He was up on his hind legs, and it was a wrestle between master and dog. 'Get back! Down, Lion! Get out of his sight, Blandois! What devil have you conjured into the dog?'

'I have done nothing to him.'

'Get out of his sight or I can't hold the wild beast! Get out of the room! By my soul, he'll kill you!'

The dog, with a ferocious bark, made one other struggle as Blandois vanished; then, in the moment of the dog's submission, the master, little less angry than the dog, felled him with a blow on the head, and standing over him, struck him many times severely with the heel of his boot, so that his mouth was presently bloody.

'Now get you into that corner and lie down,' said Gowan, 'or I'll take you out and shoot you.'

Lion did as he was ordered, and lay down licking his mouth and chest. Lion's master stopped for a moment to take breath, and then, recovering his usual coolness of manner, turned to speak to his frightened wife and her visitors. Probably the whole occurrence had not occupied two minutes.

'Come, come, Minnie! You know he is always good-humoured and tractable. Blandois must have irritated him,—made faces at him. The dog has his likings and dislikings, and Blandois is no great favourite of his; but I am sure you will give him a character, Minnie, for never having been like this before.'

Minnie was too much disturbed to say anything connected in reply; Little Dorrit was already occupied in soothing her; Fanny, who had cried out twice or thrice, held Gowan's arm for protection; Lion, deeply ashamed of having caused them this alarm, came trailing himself along the ground to the feet of his mistress.

'You furious brute,' said Gowan, striking him with his foot again. 'You shall do penance for this.' And he struck him again, and yet again.

'O, pray don't punish him any more,' cried Little Dorrit. 'Don't hurt him. See how gentle he is!' At her entreaty, Gowan spared him; and he deserved her intercession, for truly he was as submissive, and as sorry, and as wretched as a dog could be.

It was not easy to recover this shock and make the visit unrestrained, even though Fanny had not been, under the best of circumstances, the least trifle in the way. In such further communication as passed among them before the sisters took their departure, Little Dorrit fancied it was revealed to her that Mr Gowan treated his wife, even in his very fondness, too much like a beautiful child. He seemed so unsuspicious of the depths of feeling which she knew must lie below that surface, that she doubted if there could be any such depths in himself. She wondered whether his want of earnestness might be the natural result of his want of such qualities, and whether it was with people as with ships, that, in too shallow and rocky waters, their anchors had no hold, and they drifted anywhere.

He attended them down the staircase, jocosely apologising for the poor quarters to which such poor fellows as himself were limited, and remarking that when the high and mighty Barnacles, his relatives, who would be dreadfully ashamed of them, presented him with better, he would live in better to oblige them. At the water's edge they were saluted by Blandois, who looked white enough after his late adventure, but who made very light of it notwithstanding,—laughing at the mention of Lion.

Leaving the two together under the scrap of vine upon the causeway, Gowan idly scattering the leaves from it into the water, and Blandois lighting a cigarette, the sisters were paddled away in state as they had come. They had not glided on for many minutes, when Little Dorrit became aware that Fanny was more showy in manner than the occasion appeared to require, and, looking about for the cause through the window and through the open door, saw another gondola evidently in waiting on them.

As this gondola attended their progress in various artful ways; sometimes shooting on a-head, and stopping to let them pass; sometimes, when the way was broad enough, skimming along side by side with them; and sometimes following close astern; and as Fanny gradually made no disguise that she was playing off graces upon somebody within it, of whom she at the same time feigned to be unconscious; Little Dorrit at length asked who it was?

To which Fanny made the short answer, 'That gaby.'

'Who?' said Little Dorrit.

'My dear child,' returned Fanny (in a tone suggesting that before her Uncle's protest she might have said, You little fool, instead), 'how slow you are! Young Sparkler.'

She lowered the window on her side, and, leaning back and resting her elbow on it negligently, fanned herself with a rich Spanish fan of black and gold. The attendant gondola, having skimmed forward again, with some swift trace of an eye in the window, Fanny laughed coquettishly and said, 'Did you ever see such a fool, my love?'

'Do you think he means to follow you all the way?' asked Little Dorrit.

'My precious child,' returned Fanny, 'I can't possibly answer for what an idiot in a state of desperation may do, but I should think it highly probable. It's not such an enormous distance. All Venice would scarcely be that, I imagine, if he's dying for a glimpse of me.'

'And is he?' asked Little Dorrit in perfect simplicity.

'Well, my love, that really is an awkward question for me to answer,' said her sister. 'I believe he is. You had better ask Edward. He tells Edward he is, I believe. I understand he makes a perfect spectacle of himself at the Casino, and that sort of places, by going on about me. But you had better ask Edward if you want to know.'

'I wonder he doesn't call,' said Little Dorrit after thinking a moment.

'My dear Amy, your wonder will soon cease, if I am rightly informed. I should not be at all surprised if he called to-day. The creature has only been waiting to get his courage up, I suspect.'

'Will you see him?'

'Indeed, my darling,' said Fanny, 'that's just as it may happen. Here he is again. Look at him. O, you simpleton!'

Mr Sparkler had, undeniably, a weak appearance; with his eye in the window like a knot in the glass, and no reason on earth for stopping his bark suddenly, except the real reason.

'When you asked me if I will see him, my dear,' said Fanny, almost as well composed in the graceful indifference of her attitude as Mrs Merdle herself, 'what do you mean?'

'I mean,' said Little Dorrit—'I think I rather mean what do you mean, dear Fanny?'

Fanny laughed again, in a manner at once condescending, arch, and affable; and said, putting her arm round her sister in a playfully affectionate way:

'Now tell me, my little pet. When we saw that woman at Martigny, how did you think she carried it off? Did you see what she decided on in a moment?'

'No, Fanny.'

'Then I'll tell you, Amy. She settled with herself, now I'll never refer to that meeting under such different circumstances, and I'll never pretend to have any idea that these are the same girls. That's her way out of a difficulty. What did I tell you when we came away from Harley Street that time? She is as insolent and false as any woman in the world. But in the first capacity, my love, she may find people who can match her.'

A significant turn of the Spanish fan towards Fanny's bosom, indicated with great expression where one of these people was to be found.

'Not only that,' pursued Fanny, 'but she gives the same charge to Young Sparkler; and doesn't let him come after me until she has got it thoroughly into his most ridiculous of all ridiculous noddles (for one really can't call it a head), that he is to pretend to have been first struck with me in that Inn Yard.'

'Why?' asked Little Dorrit.

'Why? Good gracious, my love!' (again very much in the tone of You stupid little creature) 'how can you ask? Don't you see that I may have become a rather desirable match for a noddle? And don't you see that she puts the deception upon us, and makes a pretence, while she shifts it from her own shoulders (very good shoulders they are too, I must say),' observed Miss Fanny, glancing complacently at herself, 'of considering our feelings?'

'But we can always go back to the plain truth.'

'Yes, but if you please we won't,' retorted Fanny. 'No; I am not going to have that done, Amy. The pretext is none of mine; it's hers, and she shall have enough of it.'

In the triumphant exaltation of her feelings, Miss Fanny, using her Spanish fan with one hand, squeezed her sister's waist with the other, as if she were crushing Mrs Merdle.

'No,' repeated Fanny. 'She shall find me go her way. She took it, and I'll follow it. And, with the blessing of fate and fortune, I'll go on improving that woman's acquaintance until I have given her maid, before her eyes, things from my dressmaker's ten times as handsome and expensive as she once gave me from hers!'

Little Dorrit was silent; sensible that she was not to be heard on any question affecting the family dignity, and unwilling to lose to no purpose her sister's newly and unexpectedly restored favour. She could not concur, but she was silent. Fanny well knew what she was thinking of; so well, that she soon asked her.

Her reply was, 'Do you mean to encourage Mr Sparkler, Fanny?'

'Encourage him, my dear?' said her sister, smiling contemptuously, 'that depends upon what you call encourage. No, I don't mean to encourage him. But I'll make a slave of him.'

Little Dorrit glanced seriously and doubtfully in her face, but Fanny was not to be so brought to a check. She furled her fan of black and gold, and used it to tap her sister's nose; with the air of a proud beauty and a great spirit, who toyed with and playfully instructed a homely companion.

'I shall make him fetch and carry, my dear, and I shall make him subject to me. And if I don't make his mother subject to me, too, it shall not be my fault.'

'Do you think—dear Fanny, don't be offended, we are so comfortable together now— that you can quite see the end of that course?'

'I can't say I have so much as looked for it yet, my dear,' answered Fanny, with supreme indifference; 'all in good time. Such are my intentions. And really they have taken me so long to develop, that here we are at home. And Young Sparkler at the door, inquiring who is within. By the merest accident, of course!'

In effect, the swain was standing up in his gondola, card-case in hand, affecting to put the question to a servant. This conjunction of circumstances led to his immediately afterwards presenting himself before the young ladies in a posture, which in ancient times would not have been considered one of favourable augury for his suit; since the gondoliers of the young ladies, having been put to some inconvenience by the chase, so neatly brought their own boat in the gentlest collision with the bark of Mr Sparkler, as to tip that gentleman over like a larger species of ninepin, and cause him to exhibit the soles of his shoes to the object of his dearest wishes: while the nobler portions of his anatomy struggled at the bottom of his boat in the arms of one of his men.

However, as Miss Fanny called out with much concern, Was the gentleman hurt, Mr Sparkler rose more restored than might have been expected, and stammered for himself with blushes, 'Not at all so.' Miss Fanny had no recollection of having ever seen him before, and was passing on, with a distant inclination of her head, when he announced himself by name. Even then she was in a difficulty from being unable to call it to mind, until he explained that he had had the honour of seeing her at Martigny. Then she remembered him, and hoped his lady-mother was well.

'Thank you,' stammered Mr Sparkler, 'she's uncommonly well—at least, poorly.'

'In Venice?' said Miss Fanny.

'In Rome,' Mr Sparkler answered. 'I am here by myself, myself. I came to call upon Mr Edward Dorrit myself. Indeed, upon Mr Dorrit likewise. In fact, upon the family.'

Turning graciously to the attendants, Miss Fanny inquired whether her papa or brother was within? The reply being that they were both within, Mr Sparkler humbly offered his arm. Miss Fanny accepting it, was squired up the great staircase by Mr Sparkler, who, if he still believed (which there is not any reason to doubt) that she had no nonsense about her, rather deceived himself.

Arrived in a mouldering reception-room, where the faded hangings, of a sad sea-green, had worn and withered until they looked as if they might have claimed kindred with the waifs of seaweed drifting under the windows, or clinging to the walls and weeping for their imprisoned relations, Miss Fanny despatched emissaries for her father and brother. Pending whose appearance, she showed to great advantage on a sofa, completing Mr Sparkler's conquest with some remarks upon Dante—known to that gentleman as an eccentric man in the nature of an Old File, who used to put leaves round his head, and sit upon a stool for some unaccountable purpose, outside the cathedral at Florence.

Mr Dorrit welcomed the visitor with the highest urbanity, and most courtly manners. He inquired particularly after Mrs Merdle. He inquired particularly after Mr Merdle. Mr Sparkler said, or rather twitched out of himself in small pieces by the shirt-collar, that Mrs Merdle having completely used up her place in the country, and also her house at Brighton, and being, of course, unable, don't you see, to remain in London when there wasn't a soul there, and not feeling herself this year quite up to visiting about at people's places, had resolved to have a touch at Rome, where a woman like herself, with a proverbially fine appearance, and with no nonsense about her, couldn't fail to be a great acquisition. As to Mr Merdle, he was so much wanted by the men in the City and the rest of those places, and was such a doosed extraordinary phenomenon in Buying and Banking and that, that Mr Sparkler doubted if the monetary system of the country would be able to spare him; though that his work was occasionally one too many for him, and that he would be all the better for a temporary shy at an entirely new scene and climate, Mr Sparkler did not conceal. As to himself, Mr Sparkler conveyed to the Dorrit family that he was going, on rather particular business, wherever they were going.

This immense conversational achievement required time, but was effected. Being effected, Mr Dorrit expressed his hope that Mr Sparkler would shortly dine with them. Mr Sparkler received the idea so kindly that Mr Dorrit asked what he was going to do that day, for instance? As he was going to do nothing that day (his usual occupation, and one for which he was particularly qualified), he was secured without postponement; being further bound over to accompany the ladies to the Opera in the evening.

At dinner-time Mr Sparkler rose out of the sea, like Venus's son taking after his mother, and made a splendid appearance ascending the great staircase. If Fanny had been charming in the morning, she was now thrice charming, very becomingly dressed in her most suitable colours, and with an air of negligence upon her that doubled Mr Sparkler's fetters, and riveted them.

'I hear you are acquainted, Mr Sparkler,' said his host at dinner, 'with—ha—Mr Gowan. Mr Henry Gowan?'

'Perfectly, sir,' returned Mr Sparkler. 'His mother and my mother are cronies in fact.'

'If I had thought of it, Amy,' said Mr Dorrit, with a patronage as magnificent as that of Lord Decimus himself, 'you should have despatched a note to them, asking them to dine to-day. Some of our people could have—ha—fetched them, and taken them home. We could have spared a—hum—gondola for that purpose. I am sorry to have forgotten this. Pray remind me of them to-morrow.'

Little Dorrit was not without doubts how Mr Henry Gowan might take their patronage; but she promised not to fail in the reminder.

'Pray, does Mr Henry Gowan paint—ha—Portraits?' inquired Mr Dorrit.

Mr Sparkler opined that he painted anything, if he could get the job.

'He has no particular walk?' said Mr Dorrit.

Mr Sparkler, stimulated by Love to brilliancy, replied that for a particular walk a man ought to have a particular pair of shoes; as, for example, shooting, shooting-shoes; cricket, cricket-shoes. Whereas, he believed that Henry Gowan had no particular pair of shoes.

'No speciality?' said Mr Dorrit.

This being a very long word for Mr Sparkler, and his mind being exhausted by his late effort, he replied, 'No, thank you. I seldom take it.'

'Well!' said Mr Dorrit. 'It would be very agreeable to me to present a gentleman so connected, with some—ha—Testimonial of my desire to further his interests, and develop the—hum—germs of his genius. I think I must engage Mr Gowan to paint my picture. If the result should be—ha—mutually satisfactory, I might afterwards engage him to try his hand upon my family.'

The exquisitely bold and original thought presented itself to Mr Sparkler, that there was an opening here for saying there were some of the family (emphasising 'some' in a marked manner) to whom no painter could render justice. But, for want of a form of words in which to express the idea, it returned to the skies.

This was the more to be regretted as Miss Fanny greatly applauded the notion of the portrait, and urged her papa to act upon it. She surmised, she said, that Mr Gowan had lost better and higher opportunities by marrying his pretty wife; and Love in a cottage, painting pictures for dinner, was so delightfully interesting, that she begged her papa to give him the commission whether he could paint a likeness or not: though indeed both she and Amy knew he could, from having seen a speaking likeness on his easel that day, and having had the opportunity of comparing it with the original. These remarks made Mr Sparkler (as perhaps they were intended to do) nearly distracted; for while on the one hand they expressed Miss Fanny's susceptibility of the tender passion, she herself showed such an innocent unconsciousness of his admiration that his eyes goggled in his head with jealousy of an unknown rival.

Descending into the sea again after dinner, and ascending out of it at the Opera staircase, preceded by one of their gondoliers, like an attendant Merman, with a great linen lantern, they entered their box, and Mr Sparkler entered on an evening of agony. The theatre being dark, and the box light, several visitors lounged in during the representation; in whom Fanny was so interested, and in conversation with whom she fell into such charming attitudes, as she had little confidences with them, and little disputes concerning the identity of people in distant boxes, that the wretched Sparkler hated all mankind. But he had two consolations at the close of the performance. She gave him her fan to hold while she adjusted her cloak, and it was his blessed privilege to give her his arm down-stairs again. These crumbs of encouragement, Mr Sparkler thought, would just keep him going; and it is not impossible that Miss Dorrit thought so too.

The Merman with his light was ready at the box-door, and other Mermen with other lights were ready at many of the doors. The Dorrit Merman held his lantern low, to show the steps, and Mr Sparkler put on another heavy set of fetters over his former set, as he watched her radiant feet twinkling down the stairs beside him. Among the loiterers here, was Blandois of Paris. He spoke, and moved forward beside Fanny.

Little Dorrit was in front with her brother and Mrs General (Mr Dorrit had remained at home), but on the brink of the quay they all came together. She started again to find Blandois close to her, handing Fanny into the boat.

'Gowan has had a loss,' he said, 'since he was made happy to-day by a visit from fair ladies.'

'A loss?' repeated Fanny, relinquished by the bereaved Sparkler, and taking her seat.

'A loss,' said Blandois. 'His dog Lion.'

Little Dorrit's hand was in his, as he spoke.

'He is dead,' said Blandois.

'Dead?' echoed Little Dorrit. 'That noble dog?'

'Faith, dear ladies!' said Blandois, smiling and shrugging his shoulders, 'somebody has poisoned that noble dog. He is as dead as the Doges!'

CHAPTER 7. Mostly, Prunes and Prism

Mrs General, always on her coach-box keeping the proprieties well together, took pains to form a surface on her very dear young friend, and Mrs General's very dear young friend tried hard to receive it. Hard as she had tried in her laborious life to attain many ends, she had never tried harder than she did now, to be varnished by Mrs General. It made her anxious and ill at ease to be operated upon by that smoothing hand, it is true; but she submitted herself to the family want in its greatness as she had submitted herself to the family want in its littleness, and yielded to her own inclinations in this thing no more than she had yielded to her hunger itself, in the days when she had saved her dinner that her father might have his supper.

One comfort that she had under the Ordeal by General was more sustaining to her, and made her more grateful than to a less devoted and affectionate spirit, not habituated to her struggles and sacrifices, might appear quite reasonable; and, indeed, it may often be observed in life, that spirits like Little Dorrit do not appear to reason half as carefully as the folks who get the better of them. The continued kindness of her sister was this comfort to Little Dorrit. It was nothing to her that the kindness took the form of tolerant patronage; she was used to that. It was nothing to her that it kept her in a tributary position, and showed her in attendance on the flaming car in which Miss Fanny sat on an elevated seat, exacting homage; she sought no better place. Always admiring Fanny's beauty, and grace, and readiness, and not now asking herself how much of her disposition to be strongly attached to Fanny was due to her own heart, and how much to Fanny's, she gave her all the sisterly fondness her great heart contained.

The wholesale amount of Prunes and Prism which Mrs General infused into the family life, combined with the perpetual plunges made by Fanny into society, left but a very small residue of any natural deposit at the bottom of the mixture. This rendered confidences with Fanny doubly precious to Little Dorrit, and heightened the relief they afforded her.

'Amy,' said Fanny to her one night when they were alone, after a day so tiring that Little Dorrit was quite worn out, though Fanny would have taken another dip into society with the greatest pleasure in life, 'I am going to put something into your little head. You won't guess what it is, I suspect.'

'I don't think that's likely, dear,' said Little Dorrit.

'Come, I'll give you a clue, child,' said Fanny. 'Mrs General.'

Prunes and Prism, in a thousand combinations, having been wearily in the ascendant all day—everything having been surface and varnish and show without substance—Little Dorrit looked as if she had hoped that Mrs General was safely tucked up in bed for some hours.

'Now, can you guess, Amy?' said Fanny.

'No, dear. Unless I have done anything,' said Little Dorrit, rather alarmed, and meaning anything calculated to crack varnish and ruffle surface.

Fanny was so very much amused by the misgiving, that she took up her favourite fan (being then seated at her dressing-table with her armoury of cruel instruments about her, most of them reeking from the heart of Sparkler), and tapped her sister frequently on the nose with it, laughing all the time.

'Oh, our Amy, our Amy!' said Fanny. 'What a timid little goose our Amy is! But this is nothing to laugh at. On the contrary, I am very cross, my dear.'

'As it is not with me, Fanny, I don't mind,' returned her sister, smiling.

'Ah! But I do mind,' said Fanny, 'and so will you, Pet, when I enlighten you. Amy, has it never struck you that somebody is monstrously polite to Mrs General?'

'Everybody is polite to Mrs General,' said Little Dorrit. 'Because—'

'Because she freezes them into it?' interrupted Fanny. 'I don't mean that; quite different from that. Come! Has it never struck you, Amy, that Pa is monstrously polite to Mrs General.'

Amy, murmuring 'No,' looked quite confounded.

'No; I dare say not. But he is,' said Fanny. 'He is, Amy. And remember my words. Mrs General has designs on Pa!'

'Dear Fanny, do you think it possible that Mrs General has designs on any one?'

'Do I think it possible?' retorted Fanny. 'My love, I know it. I tell you she has designs on Pa. And more than that, I tell you Pa considers her such a wonder, such a paragon of accomplishment, and such an acquisition to our family, that he is ready to get himself into a state of perfect infatuation with her at any moment. And that opens a pretty picture of things, I hope? Think of me with Mrs General for a Mama!'

Little Dorrit did not reply, 'Think of me with Mrs General for a Mama;' but she looked anxious, and seriously inquired what had led Fanny to these conclusions.

'Lord, my darling,' said Fanny, tartly. 'You might as well ask me how I know when a man is struck with myself! But, of course I do know. It happens pretty often: but I always know it.

I know this in much the same way, I suppose. At all events, I know it.'

'You never heard Papa say anything?'

'Say anything?' repeated Fanny. 'My dearest, darling child, what necessity has he had, yet awhile, to say anything?'

'And you have never heard Mrs General say anything?'

'My goodness me, Amy,' returned Fanny, 'is she the sort of woman to say anything? Isn't it perfectly plain and clear that she has nothing to do at present but to hold herself upright, keep her aggravating gloves on, and go sweeping about? Say anything! If she had the ace of trumps in her hand at whist, she wouldn't say anything, child. It would come out when she played it.'

'At least, you may be mistaken, Fanny. Now, may you not?'

'O yes, I may be,' said Fanny, 'but I am not. However, I am glad you can contemplate such an escape, my dear, and I am glad that you can take this for the present with sufficient coolness to think of such a chance. It makes me hope that you may be able to bear the connection. I should not be able to bear it, and I should not try. I'd marry young Sparkler first.'

'O, you would never marry him, Fanny, under any circumstances.'

'Upon my word, my dear,' rejoined that young lady with exceeding indifference, 'I wouldn't positively answer even for that. There's no knowing what might happen. Especially as I should have many opportunities, afterwards, of treating that woman, his mother, in her own style. Which I most decidedly should not be slow to avail myself of, Amy.'

No more passed between the sisters then; but what had passed gave the two subjects of Mrs General and Mr Sparkler great prominence in Little Dorrit's mind, and thenceforth she thought very much of both.

Mrs General, having long ago formed her own surface to such perfection that it hid whatever was below it (if anything), no observation was to be made in that quarter. Mr Dorrit was undeniably very polite to her and had a high opinion of her; but Fanny, impetuous at most times, might easily be wrong for all that. Whereas, the Sparkler question was on the different footing that any one could see what was going on there, and Little Dorrit saw it and pondered on it with many doubts and wonderings.

The devotion of Mr Sparkler was only to be equalled by the caprice and cruelty of his enslaver. Sometimes she would prefer him to such distinction of notice, that he would chuckle aloud with joy; next day, or next hour, she would overlook him so completely, and drop him into such an abyss of obscurity, that he would groan under a weak pretence of coughing. The constancy of his attendance never touched Fanny: though he was so inseparable from Edward, that, when that gentleman wished for a change of society, he was under the irksome necessity of gliding out like a conspirator in disguised boats and by secret doors and back ways; though he was so solicitous to know how Mr Dorrit was, that he called every other day to inquire, as if Mr Dorrit were the prey of an intermittent fever; though he was so constantly being paddled up and down before the principal windows, that he might have been supposed to have made a wager for a large stake to be paddled a thousand miles in a thousand hours; though whenever the gondola of his mistress left the gate, the gondola of Mr Sparkler shot out from some watery ambush and gave chase, as if she were a fair smuggler and he a custom-house officer. It was probably owing to this fortification of the natural strength of his constitution with so much exposure to the air, and the salt sea, that Mr Sparkler did not pine outwardly; but, whatever the cause, he was so far from having any prospect of moving his mistress by a languishing state of health, that he grew bluffer every day, and that peculiarity in his appearance of seeming rather a swelled boy than a young man, became developed to an extraordinary degree of ruddy puffiness.

Blandois calling to pay his respects, Mr Dorrit received him with affability as the friend of Mr Gowan, and mentioned to him his idea of commissioning Mr Gowan to transmit him to posterity. Blandois highly extolling it, it occurred to Mr Dorrit that it might be agreeable to Blandois to communicate to his friend the great opportunity reserved for him. Blandois accepted the commission with his own free elegance of manner, and swore he would discharge it before he was an hour older. On his imparting the news to Gowan, that Master gave Mr Dorrit to the Devil with great liberality some round dozen of times (for he resented patronage almost as much as he resented the want of it), and was inclined to quarrel with his friend for bringing him the message.

'It may be a defect in my mental vision, Blandois,' said he, 'but may I die if I see what you have to do with this.'

'Death of my life,' replied Blandois, 'nor I neither, except that I thought I was serving my friend.'

'By putting an upstart's hire in his pocket?' said Gowan, frowning. 'Do you mean that? Tell your other friend to get his head painted for the sign of some public-house, and to get it done by a sign-painter. Who am I, and who is he?'

'Professore,' returned the ambassador, 'and who is Blandois?'

Without appearing at all interested in the latter question, Gowan angrily whistled Mr Dorrit away. But, next day, he resumed the subject by saying in his off-hand manner and with a slighting laugh, 'Well, Blandois, when shall we go to this Maecenas of yours? We journeymen must take jobs when we can get them. When shall we go and look after this job?'

'When you will,' said the injured Blandois, 'as you please. What have I to do with it? What is it to me?'

'I can tell you what it is to me,' said Gowan. 'Bread and cheese. One must eat! So come along, my Blandois.'

Mr Dorrit received them in the presence of his daughters and of Mr Sparkler, who happened, by some surprising accident, to be calling there. 'How are you, Sparkler?' said Gowan carelessly. 'When you have to live by your mother wit, old boy, I hope you may get on better than I do.'

Mr Dorrit then mentioned his proposal. 'Sir,' said Gowan, laughing, after receiving it gracefully enough, 'I am new to the trade, and not expert at its mysteries. I believe I ought to look at you in various lights, tell you-you are a capital subject, and consider when I shall be sufficiently disengaged to devote myself with the necessary enthusiasm to the fine picture I mean to make of you. I assure you,' and he laughed again, 'I feel quite a traitor in the camp of those dear, gifted, good, noble fellows, my brother artists, by not doing the hocus-pocus better. But I have not been brought up to it, and it's too late to learn it. Now, the fact is, I am a very bad painter, but not much worse than the generality. If you are going to throw away a hundred guineas or so, I am as poor as a poor relation of great people usually is, and I shall be very much obliged to you, if you'll throw them away upon me. I'll do the best I can for the money; and if the best should be bad, why even then, you may probably have a bad picture with a small name to it, instead of a bad picture with a large name to it.'

This tone, though not what he had expected, on the whole suited Mr Dorrit remarkably well. It showed that the gentleman, highly connected, and not a mere workman, would be under an obligation to him. He expressed his satisfaction in placing himself in Mr Gowan's hands, and trusted that he would have the pleasure, in their characters of private gentlemen, of improving his acquaintance.

'You are very good,' said Gowan. 'I have not forsworn society since I joined the brotherhood of the brush (the most delightful fellows on the face of the earth), and am glad enough to smell the old fine gunpowder now and then, though it did blow me into mid-air and my present calling. You'll not think, Mr Dorrit,' and here he laughed again in the easiest way, 'that I am lapsing into the freemasonry of the craft—for it's not so; upon my life I can't help betraying it wherever I go, though, by Jupiter, I love and honour the craft with all my might—if I propose a stipulation as to time and place?'

Ha! Mr Dorrit could erect no—hum—suspicion of that kind on Mr Gowan's frankness.

'Again you are very good,' said Gowan. 'Mr Dorrit, I hear you are going to Rome. I am going to Rome, having friends there. Let me begin to do you the injustice I have conspired to do you, there—not here. We shall all be hurried during the rest of our stay here; and though there's not a poorer man with whole elbows in Venice, than myself, I have not quite got all the Amateur out of me yet—comprising the trade again, you see!—and can't fall on to order, in a hurry, for the mere sake of the sixpences.'

These remarks were not less favourably received by Mr Dorrit than their predecessors. They were the prelude to the first reception of Mr and Mrs Gowan at dinner, and they skilfully placed Gowan on his usual ground in the new family.

His wife, too, they placed on her usual ground. Miss Fanny understood, with particular distinctness, that Mrs Gowan's good looks had cost her husband very dear; that there had been a great disturbance about her in the Barnacle family; and that the Dowager Mrs Gowan, nearly heart-broken, had resolutely set her face against the marriage until overpowered by her maternal feelings. Mrs General likewise clearly understood that the attachment had occasioned much family grief and dissension. Of honest Mr Meagles no mention was made; except that it was natural enough that a person of that sort should wish to raise his daughter out of his own obscurity, and that no one could blame him for trying his best to do so.

Little Dorrit's interest in the fair subject of this easily accepted belief was too earnest and watchful to fail in accurate observation. She could see that it had its part in throwing upon Mrs Gowan the touch of a shadow under which she lived, and she even had an instinctive knowledge that there was not the least truth in it. But it had an influence in placing obstacles in the way of her association with Mrs Gowan by making the Prunes and Prism school excessively polite to her, but not very intimate with her; and Little Dorrit, as an enforced sizar of that college, was obliged to submit herself humbly to its ordinances.

Nevertheless, there was a sympathetic understanding already established between the two, which would have carried them over greater difficulties, and made a friendship out of a more restricted intercourse. As though accidents were determined to be favourable to it, they had a new assurance of congeniality in the aversion which each perceived that the other felt towards Blandois of Paris; an aversion amounting to the repugnance and horror of a natural antipathy towards an odious creature of the reptile kind.

And there was a passive congeniality between them, besides this active one. To both of them, Blandois behaved in exactly the same manner; and to both of them his manner had uniformly something in it, which they both knew to be different from his bearing towards others. The difference was too minute in its expression to be perceived by others, but they knew it to be there. A mere trick of his evil eyes, a mere turn of his smooth white hand, a mere hair's-breadth of addition to the fall of his nose and the rise of the moustache in the most frequent movement of his face, conveyed to both of them, equally, a swagger personal to themselves. It was as if he had said, 'I have a secret power in this quarter. I know what I know.'

This had never been felt by them both in so great a degree, and never by each so perfectly to the knowledge of the other, as on a day when he came to Mr Dorrit's to take his leave before quitting Venice. Mrs Gowan was herself there for the same purpose, and he came upon the two together; the rest of the family being out. The two had not been together five minutes, and the peculiar manner seemed to convey to them, 'You were going to talk about me. Ha! Behold me here to prevent it!'

'Gowan is coming here?' said Blandois, with a smile.

Mrs Gowan replied he was not coming.

'Not coming!' said Blandois. 'Permit your devoted servant, when you leave here, to escort you home.'

'Thank you: I am not going home.'

'Not going home!' said Blandois. 'Then I am forlorn.'

That he might be; but he was not so forlorn as to roam away and leave them together. He sat entertaining them with his finest compliments, and his choicest conversation; but he conveyed to them, all the time, 'No, no, no, dear ladies. Behold me here expressly to prevent it!'

He conveyed it to them with so much meaning, and he had such a diabolical persistency in him, that at length, Mrs Gowan rose to depart. On his offering his hand to Mrs Gowan to lead her down the staircase, she retained Little Dorrit's hand in hers, with a cautious pressure, and said, 'No, thank you. But, if you will please to see if my boatman is there, I shall be obliged to you.'

It left him no choice but to go down before them. As he did so, hat in hand, Mrs Gowan whispered:

'He killed the dog.'

'Does Mr Gowan know it?' Little Dorrit whispered.

'No one knows it. Don't look towards me; look towards him. He will turn his face in a moment. No one knows it, but I am sure he did. You are?'

'I—I think so,' Little Dorrit answered.

'Henry likes him, and he will not think ill of him; he is so generous and open himself. But you and I feel sure that we think of him as he deserves. He argued with Henry that the dog had been already poisoned when he changed so, and sprang at him. Henry believes it, but we do not. I see he is listening, but can't hear. Good-bye, my love! Good-bye!'

The last words were spoken aloud, as the vigilant Blandois stopped, turned his head, and looked at them from the bottom of the staircase. Assuredly he did look then, though he looked his politest, as if any real philanthropist could have desired no better employment than to lash a great stone to his neck, and drop him into the water flowing beyond the dark arched gateway in which he stood. No such benefactor to mankind being on the spot, he handed Mrs Gowan to her boat, and stood there until it had shot out of the narrow view; when he handed himself into his own boat and followed.

Little Dorrit had sometimes thought, and now thought again as she retraced her steps up the staircase, that he had made his way too easily into her father's house. But so many and such varieties of people did the same, through Mr Dorrit's participation in his elder daughter's society mania, that it was hardly an exceptional case. A perfect fury for making acquaintances on whom to impress their riches and importance, had seized the House of Dorrit.

It appeared on the whole, to Little Dorrit herself, that this same society in which they lived, greatly resembled a superior sort of Marshalsea. Numbers of people seemed to come abroad, pretty much as people had come into the prison; through debt, through idleness, relationship, curiosity, and general unfitness for getting on at home. They were brought into these foreign towns in the custody of couriers and local followers, just as the debtors had been brought into the prison. They prowled about the churches and picture-galleries, much in the old, dreary, prison-yard manner. They were usually going away again to-morrow or next week, and rarely knew their own minds, and seldom did what they said they would do, or went where they said they would go: in all this again, very like the prison debtors. They paid high for poor accommodation, and disparaged a place while they pretended to like it: which was exactly the Marshalsea custom. They were envied when they went away by people left behind, feigning not to want to go: and that again was the Marshalsea habit invariably. A certain set of words and phrases, as much belonging to tourists as the College and the Snuggery belonged to the jail, was always in their mouths. They had precisely the same incapacity for settling down to anything, as the prisoners used to have; they rather deteriorated one another, as the prisoners used to do; and they wore untidy dresses, and fell into a slouching way of life: still, always like the people in the Marshalsea.

The period of the family's stay at Venice came, in its course, to an end, and they moved, with their retinue, to Rome. Through a repetition of the former Italian scenes, growing more dirty and more haggard as they went on, and bringing them at length to where the very air was diseased, they passed to their destination. A fine residence had been taken for them on the Corso, and there they took up their abode, in a city where everything seemed to be trying to stand still for ever on the ruins of something else—except the water, which, following eternal laws, tumbled and rolled from its glorious multitude of fountains.

Here it seemed to Little Dorrit that a change came over the Marshalsea spirit of their society, and that Prunes and Prism got the upper hand. Everybody was walking about St Peter's and the Vatican on somebody else's cork legs, and straining every visible object through somebody else's sieve. Nobody said what anything was, but everybody said what the Mrs

Generals, Mr Eustace, or somebody else said it was. The whole body of travellers seemed to be a collection of voluntary human sacrifices, bound hand and foot, and delivered over to Mr Eustace and his attendants, to have the entrails of their intellects arranged according to the taste of that sacred priesthood. Through the rugged remains of temples and tombs and palaces and senate halls and theatres and amphitheatres of ancient days, hosts of tongue-tied and blindfolded moderns were carefully feeling their way, incessantly repeating Prunes and Prism in the endeavour to set their lips according to the received form. Mrs General was in her pure element. Nobody had an opinion. There was a formation of surface going on around her on an amazing scale, and it had not a flaw of courage or honest free speech in it.

Another modification of Prunes and Prism insinuated itself on Little Dorrit's notice very shortly after their arrival. They received an early visit from Mrs Merdle, who led that extensive department of life in the Eternal City that winter; and the skilful manner in which she and Fanny fenced with one another on the occasion, almost made her quiet sister wink, like the glittering of small-swords.

'So delighted,' said Mrs Merdle, 'to resume an acquaintance so inauspiciously begun at Martigny.'

'At Martigny, of course,' said Fanny. 'Charmed, I am sure!'

'I understand,' said Mrs Merdle, 'from my son Edmund Sparkler, that he has already improved that chance occasion. He has returned quite transported with Venice.'

'Indeed?' returned the careless Fanny. 'Was he there long?'

'I might refer that question to Mr Dorrit,' said Mrs Merdle, turning the bosom towards that gentleman; 'Edmund having been so much indebted to him for rendering his stay agreeable.'

'Oh, pray don't speak of it,' returned Fanny. 'I believe Papa had the pleasure of inviting Mr Sparkler twice or thrice,—but it was nothing. We had so many people about us, and kept such open house, that if he had that pleasure, it was less than nothing.'

'Except, my dear,' said Mr Dorrit, 'except—ha—as it afforded me unusual gratification to—hum—show by any means, however slight and worthless, the—ha, hum—high estimation in which, in—ha—common with the rest of the world, I hold so distinguished and princely a character as Mr Merdle's.'

The bosom received this tribute in its most engaging manner. 'Mr Merdle,' observed Fanny, as a means of dismissing Mr Sparkler into the background, 'is quite a theme of Papa's, you must know, Mrs Merdle.'

'I have been—ha—disappointed, madam,' said Mr Dorrit, 'to understand from Mr Sparkler that there is no great—hum—probability of Mr Merdle's coming abroad.'

'Why, indeed,' said Mrs Merdle, 'he is so much engaged and in such request, that I fear not. He has not been able to get abroad for years. You, Miss Dorrit, I believe have been almost continually abroad for a long time.'

'Oh dear yes,' drawled Fanny, with the greatest hardihood. 'An immense number of years.'

'So I should have inferred,' said Mrs Merdle.

'Exactly,' said Fanny.

'I trust, however,' resumed Mr Dorrit, 'that if I have not the—hum—great advantage of becoming known to Mr Merdle on this side of the Alps or Mediterranean, I shall have that honour on returning to England. It is an honour I particularly desire and shall particularly esteem.'

'Mr Merdle,' said Mrs Merdle, who had been looking admiringly at Fanny through her eye-glass, 'will esteem it, I am sure, no less.'

Little Dorrit, still habitually thoughtful and solitary though no longer alone, at first supposed this to be mere Prunes and Prism. But as her father when they had been to a brilliant reception at Mrs Merdle's, harped at their own family breakfast-table on his wish to know Mr Merdle, with the contingent view of benefiting by the advice of that wonderful man in the disposal of his fortune, she began to think it had a real meaning, and to entertain a curiosity on her own part to see the shining light of the time.

CHAPTER 8. The Dowager Mrs Gowan is reminded that 'It Never Does'

While the waters of Venice and the ruins of Rome were sunning themselves for the pleasure of the Dorrit family, and were daily being sketched out of all earthly proportion, lineament, and likeness, by travelling pencils innumerable, the firm of Doyce and Clennam hammered away in Bleeding Heart Yard, and the vigorous clink of iron upon iron was heard there through the working hours.

The younger partner had, by this time, brought the business into sound trim; and the elder, left free to follow his own ingenious devices, had done much to enhance the character of the factory. As an ingenious man, he had necessarily to encounter every discouragement that the ruling powers for a length of time had been able by any means to put in the way of this class of culprits; but that was only reasonable self-defence in the powers, since How to do it must obviously be regarded as the natural and mortal enemy of How not to do it. In this was to be found the basis of the wise system, by tooth and nail upheld by the Circumlocution Office, of warning every ingenious British subject to be ingenious at his peril: of harassing him, obstructing him, inviting robbers (by making his remedy uncertain, and expensive) to plunder him, and at the best of confiscating his property after a short term of enjoyment, as though invention were on a par with felony. The system had uniformly found great favour with the Barnacles, and that was only reasonable, too; for one who worthily invents must be in earnest, and the Barnacles abhorred and dreaded nothing half so much. That again was very reasonable; since in a country suffering under the affliction of a great amount of earnestness, there might, in an exceeding short space of time, be not a single Barnacle left sticking to a post.

Daniel Doyce faced his condition with its pains and penalties attached to it, and soberly worked on for the work's sake. Clennam cheering him with a hearty co-operation, was a moral support to him, besides doing good service in his business relation. The concern prospered, and the partners were fast friends.

But Daniel could not forget the old design of so many years. It was not in reason to be expected that he should; if he could have lightly forgotten it, he could never have conceived it, or had the patience and perseverance to work it out. So Clennam thought, when he sometimes observed him of an evening looking over the models and drawings, and consoling himself by muttering with a sigh as he put them away again, that the thing was as true as it ever was.

To show no sympathy with so much endeavour, and so much disappointment, would have been to fail in what Clennam regarded as among the implied obligations of his partnership. A revival of the passing interest in the subject which had been by chance awakened at the door of the Circumlocution Office, originated in this feeling. He asked his partner to explain the invention to him; 'having a lenient consideration,' he stipulated, 'for my being no workman, Doyce.'

'No workman?' said Doyce. 'You would have been a thorough workman if you had given yourself to it. You have as good a head for understanding such things as I have met with.'

'A totally uneducated one, I am sorry to add,' said Clennam.

'I don't know that,' returned Doyce, 'and I wouldn't have you say that. No man of sense who has been generally improved, and has improved himself, can be called quite uneducated as to anything. I don't particularly favour mysteries. I would as soon, on a fair and clear explanation, be judged by one class of man as another, provided he had the qualification I have named.'

'At all events,' said Clennam—'this sounds as if we were exchanging compliments, but we know we are not—I shall have the advantage of as plain an explanation as can be given.'

'Well!' said Daniel, in his steady even way, 'I'll try to make it so.'

He had the power, often to be found in union with such a character, of explaining what he himself perceived, and meant, with the direct force and distinctness with which it struck his own mind. His manner of demonstration was so orderly and neat and simple, that it was not easy to mistake him. There was something almost ludicrous in the complete irreconcilability of a vague conventional notion that he must be a visionary man, with the precise, sagacious travelling of his eye and thumb over the plans, their patient stoppages at particular points, their careful returns to other points whence little channels of explanation had to be traced up, and his steady manner of making everything good and everything sound at each important stage, before taking his hearer on a line's-breadth further. His dismissal of himself from his description, was hardly less remarkable. He never said, I discovered this adaptation or invented that combination; but showed the whole thing as if the Divine artificer had made it, and he had happened to find it; so modest he was about it, such a pleasant touch of respect was mingled with his quiet admiration of it, and so calmly convinced he was that it was established on irrefragable laws.

Not only that evening, but for several succeeding evenings, Clennam was quite charmed by this investigation. The more he pursued it, and the oftener he glanced at the grey head bending over it, and the shrewd eye kindling with pleasure in it and love of it—instrument for probing his heart though it had been made for twelve long years—the less he could reconcile it to his younger energy to let it go without one effort more. At length he said:

'Doyce, it came to this at last—that the business was to be sunk with Heaven knows how many more wrecks, or begun all over again?'

'Yes,' returned Doyce, 'that's what the noblemen and gentlemen made of it after a dozen years.'

'And pretty fellows too!' said Clennam, bitterly.

'The usual thing!' observed Doyce. 'I must not make a martyr of myself, when I am one of so large a company.'

'Relinquish it, or begin it all over again?' mused Clennam.

'That was exactly the long and the short of it,' said Doyce.

'Then, my friend,' cried Clennam, starting up and taking his work-roughened hand, 'it shall be begun all over again!'

Doyce looked alarmed, and replied in a hurry—for him, 'No, no. Better put it by. Far better put it by. It will be heard of, one day. I can put it by. You forget, my good Clennam; I have put it by. It's all at an end.'

'Yes, Doyce,' returned Clennam, 'at an end as far as your efforts and rebuffs are concerned, I admit, but not as far as mine are. I am younger than you: I have only once set foot in that precious office, and I am fresh game for them. Come! I'll try them. You shall do exactly as you have been doing since we have been together. I will add (as I easily can) to what I have been doing, the attempt to get public justice done to you; and, unless I have some success to report, you shall hear no more of it.'

Daniel Doyce was still reluctant to consent, and again and again urged that they had better put it by. But it was natural that he should gradually allow himself to be over-persuaded by Clennam, and should yield. Yield he did. So Arthur resumed the long and hopeless labour of striving to make way with the Circumlocution Office.

The waiting-rooms of that Department soon began to be familiar with his presence, and he was generally ushered into them by its janitors much as a pickpocket might be shown into a police-office; the principal difference being that the object of the latter class of public business is to keep the pickpocket, while the Circumlocution object was to get rid of Clennam. However, he was resolved to stick to the Great Department; and so the work of form-filling, corresponding, minuting, memorandum-making, signing, counter-signing, counter-counter-signing, referring backwards and forwards, and referring sideways, crosswise, and zig-zag, recommenced.

Here arises a feature of the Circumlocution Office, not previously mentioned in the present record. When that admirable Department got into trouble, and was, by some infuriated members of Parliament whom the smaller Barnacles almost suspected of labouring under diabolic possession, attacked on the merits of no individual case, but as an Institution wholly abominable and Bedlamite; then the noble or right honourable Barnacle who represented it in the House, would smite that member and cleave him asunder, with a statement of the quantity of business (for the prevention of business) done by the Circumlocution Office. Then would that noble or right honourable Barnacle hold in his hand a paper containing a few figures, to which, with the permission of the House, he would entreat its attention. Then would the inferior Barnacles exclaim, obeying orders, 'Hear, Hear, Hear!' and 'Read!' Then would the noble or right honourable Barnacle perceive, sir, from this little document, which he thought might carry conviction even to the perversest mind (Derisive laughter and cheering from the Barnacle fry), that within the short compass of the last financial half-year, this much-maligned Department (Cheers) had written and received fifteen thousand letters (Loud cheers), had written twenty-four thousand minutes (Louder cheers), and thirty-two thousand five hundred and seventeen memoranda (Vehement cheering). Nay, an ingenious gentleman connected with the Department, and himself a valuable public servant, had done him the favour to make a curious calculation of the amount of stationery consumed in it during the same period. It formed a part of this same short document; and he derived from it the remarkable fact that the sheets of foolscap paper it had devoted to the public service would pave the footways on both sides of Oxford Street from end to end, and leave nearly a quarter of a mile to spare for the park (Immense cheering and laughter); while of tape—red tape—it had used enough to stretch, in graceful festoons, from Hyde Park Corner to the General Post Office. Then, amidst a burst of official exultation, would the noble or right honourable Barnacle sit down, leaving the mutilated fragments of the Member on the field. No one, after that exemplary demolition of him, would have the hardihood to hint that the more the Circumlocution Office did, the less was done, and that the greatest blessing it could confer on an unhappy public would be to do nothing.

With sufficient occupation on his hands, now that he had this additional task—such a task had many and many a serviceable man died of before his day—Arthur Clennam led a life of slight variety. Regular visits to his mother's dull sick room, and visits scarcely less regular to Mr Meagles at Twickenham, were its only changes during many months.

He sadly and sorely missed Little Dorrit. He had been prepared to miss her very much, but not so much. He knew to the full extent only through experience, what a large place in his life was left blank when her familiar little figure went out of it. He felt, too, that he must relinquish the hope of its return, understanding the family character sufficiently well to be assured that he and she were divided by a broad ground of separation. The old interest he had had in her, and her old trusting reliance on him, were tinged with melancholy in his mind: so soon had change stolen over them, and so soon had they glided into the past with other secret tendernesses.

When he received her letter he was greatly moved, but did not the less sensibly feel that she was far divided from him by more than distance. It helped him to a clearer and keener perception of the place assigned him by the family. He saw that he was cherished in her grateful remembrance secretly, and that they resented him with the jail and the rest of its belongings.

Through all these meditations which every day of his life crowded about her, he thought of her otherwise in the old way. She was his innocent friend, his delicate child, his dear Little Dorrit. This very change of circumstances fitted curiously in with the habit, begun on the night when the roses floated away, of considering himself as a much older man than his years really made him. He regarded her from a point of view which in its remoteness, tender as it was, he little thought would have been unspeakable agony to her. He speculated about her future destiny, and about the husband she might have, with an affection for her which would have drained her heart of its dearest drop of hope, and broken it.

Everything about him tended to confirm him in the custom of looking on himself as an elderly man, from whom such aspirations as he had combated in the case of Minnie Gowan (though that was not so long ago either, reckoning by months and seasons), were finally departed. His relations with her father and mother were like those on which a widower son-in-law might have stood. If the twin sister who was dead had lived to pass away in the bloom of womanhood, and he had been her husband, the nature of his intercourse with Mr and Mrs Meagles would probably have been just what it was. This imperceptibly helped to render habitual the impression within him, that he had done with, and dismissed that part of life.

He invariably heard of Minnie from them, as telling them in her letters how happy she was, and how she loved her husband; but inseparable from that subject, he invariably saw the old cloud on Mr Meagles's face. Mr Meagles had never been quite so radiant since the marriage as before. He had never quite recovered the separation from Pet. He was the same good-humoured, open creature; but as if his face, from being much turned towards the pictures of his two children which could show him only one look, unconsciously adopted a characteristic from them, it always had now, through all its changes of expression, a look of loss in it.

One wintry Saturday when Clennam was at the cottage, the Dowager Mrs Gowan drove up, in the Hampton Court equipage which pretended to be the exclusive equipage of so many individual proprietors. She descended, in her shady ambuscade of green fan, to favour Mr and Mrs Meagles with a call.

'And how do you both do, Papa and Mama Meagles?' said she, encouraging her humble connections. 'And when did you last hear from or about my poor fellow?'

My poor fellow was her son; and this mode of speaking of him politely kept alive, without any offence in the world, the pretence that he had fallen a victim to the Meagles' wiles.

'And the dear pretty one?' said Mrs Gowan. 'Have you later news of her than I have?'

Which also delicately implied that her son had been captured by mere beauty, and under its fascination had forgone all sorts of worldly advantages.

'I am sure,' said Mrs Gowan, without straining her attention on the answers she received, 'it's an unspeakable comfort to know they continue happy. My poor fellow is of such a restless disposition, and has been so used to roving about, and to being inconstant and popular among all manner of people, that it's the greatest comfort in life. I suppose they're as poor as mice, Papa Meagles?'

Mr Meagles, fidgety under the question, replied, 'I hope not, ma'am. I hope they will manage their little income.'

'Oh! my dearest Meagles!' returned the lady, tapping him on the arm with the green fan and then adroitly interposing it between a yawn and the company, 'how can you, as a man of the world and one of the most business-like of human beings—for you know you are business-like, and a great deal too much for us who are not—'

(Which went to the former purpose, by making Mr Meagles out to be an artful schemer.)

'—How can you talk about their managing their little means? My poor dear fellow! The idea of his managing hundreds! And the sweet pretty creature too. The notion of her managing! Papa Meagles! Don't!'

'Well, ma'am,' said Mr Meagles, gravely, 'I am sorry to admit, then, that Henry certainly does anticipate his means.'

'My dear good man—I use no ceremony with you, because we are a kind of relations;— positively, Mama Meagles,' exclaimed Mrs Gowan cheerfully, as if the absurd coincidence then flashed upon her for the first time, 'a kind of relations! My dear good man, in this world none of us can have everything our own way.'

This again went to the former point, and showed Mr Meagles with all good breeding that, so far, he had been brilliantly successful in his deep designs. Mrs Gowan thought the hit so good a one, that she dwelt upon it; repeating 'Not everything. No, no; in this world we must not expect everything, Papa Meagles.'

'And may I ask, ma'am,' retorted Mr Meagles, a little heightened in colour, 'who does expect everything?'

'Oh, nobody, nobody!' said Mrs Gowan. 'I was going to say—but you put me out. You interrupting Papa, what was I going to say?'

Drooping her large green fan, she looked musingly at Mr Meagles while she thought about it; a performance not tending to the cooling of that gentleman's rather heated spirits.

'Ah! Yes, to be sure!' said Mrs Gowan. 'You must remember that my poor fellow has always been accustomed to expectations. They may have been realised, or they may not have been realised—'

'Let us say, then, may not have been realised,' observed Mr Meagles.

The Dowager for a moment gave him an angry look; but tossed it off with her head and her fan, and pursued the tenor of her way in her former manner.

'It makes no difference. My poor fellow has been accustomed to that sort of thing, and of course you knew it, and were prepared for the consequences. I myself always clearly foresaw the consequences, and am not surprised. And you must not be surprised. In fact, can't be surprised. Must have been prepared for it.'

Mr Meagles looked at his wife and at Clennam; bit his lip; and coughed.

'And now here's my poor fellow,' Mrs Gowan pursued, 'receiving notice that he is to hold himself in expectation of a baby, and all the expenses attendant on such an addition to his family! Poor Henry! But it can't be helped now; it's too late to help it now. Only don't talk of anticipating means, Papa Meagles, as a discovery; because that would be too much.'

'Too much, ma'am?' said Mr Meagles, as seeking an explanation.

'There, there!' said Mrs Gowan, putting him in his inferior place with an expressive action of her hand. 'Too much for my poor fellow's mother to bear at this time of day. They are fast married, and can't be unmarried. There, there! I know that! You needn't tell me that, Papa Meagles. I know it very well. What was it I said just now? That it was a great comfort they continued happy. It is to be hoped they will still continue happy. It is to be hoped Pretty One will do everything she can to make my poor fellow happy, and keep him contented. Papa and Mama Meagles, we had better say no more about it. We never did look at this subject from the same side, and we never shall. There, there! Now I am good.'

Truly, having by this time said everything she could say in maintenance of her wonderfully mythical position, and in admonition to Mr Meagles that he must not expect to bear his honours of alliance too cheaply, Mrs Gowan was disposed to forgo the rest. If Mr Meagles had submitted to a glance of entreaty from Mrs Meagles, and an expressive gesture from Clennam, he would have left her in the undisturbed enjoyment of this state of mind. But Pet was the darling and pride of his heart; and if he could ever have championed her more devotedly, or loved her better, than in the days when she was the sunlight of his house, it would have been now, when, as its daily grace and delight, she was lost to it.

'Mrs Gowan, ma'am,' said Mr Meagles, 'I have been a plain man all my life. If I was to try—no matter whether on myself, on somebody else, or both—any genteel mystifications, I should probably not succeed in them.'

'Papa Meagles,' returned the Dowager, with an affable smile, but with the bloom on her cheeks standing out a little more vividly than usual as the neighbouring surface became paler, 'probably not.'

'Therefore, my good madam,' said Mr Meagles, at great pains to restrain himself, 'I hope I may, without offence, ask to have no such mystification played off upon me.'

'Mama Meagles,' observed Mrs Gowan, 'your good man is incomprehensible.'

Her turning to that worthy lady was an artifice to bring her into the discussion, quarrel with her, and vanquish her. Mr Meagles interposed to prevent that consummation.

'Mother,' said he, 'you are inexpert, my dear, and it is not a fair match. Let me beg of you to remain quiet. Come, Mrs Gowan, come! Let us try to be sensible; let us try to be good-natured; let us try to be fair. Don't you pity Henry, and I won't pity Pet. And don't be one-sided, my dear madam; it's not considerate, it's not kind. Don't let us say that we hope Pet will make Henry happy, or even that we hope Henry will make Pet happy,' (Mr Meagles himself did not look happy as he spoke the words,) 'but let us hope they will make each other happy.'

'Yes, sure, and there leave it, father,' said Mrs Meagles the kind-hearted and comfortable.

'Why, mother, no,' returned Mr Meagles, 'not exactly there. I can't quite leave it there; I must say just half-a-dozen words more. Mrs Gowan, I hope I am not over-sensitive. I believe I don't look it.'

'Indeed you do not,' said Mrs Gowan, shaking her head and the great green fan together, for emphasis.

'Thank you, ma'am; that's well. Notwithstanding which, I feel a little—I don't want to use a strong word—now shall I say hurt?' asked Mr Meagles at once with frankness and moderation, and with a conciliatory appeal in his tone.

'Say what you like,' answered Mrs Gowan. 'It is perfectly indifferent to me.'

'No, no, don't say that,' urged Mr Meagles, 'because that's not responding amiably. I feel a little hurt when I hear references made to consequences having been foreseen, and to its being too late now, and so forth.'

'Do you, Papa Meagles?' said Mrs Gowan. 'I am not surprised.'

'Well, ma'am,' reasoned Mr Meagles, 'I was in hopes you would have been at least surprised, because to hurt me wilfully on so tender a subject is surely not generous.'

'I am not responsible,' said Mrs Gowan, 'for your conscience, you know.'

Poor Mr Meagles looked aghast with astonishment.

'If I am unluckily obliged to carry a cap about with me, which is yours and fits you,' pursued Mrs Gowan, 'don't blame me for its pattern, Papa Meagles, I beg!'

'Why, good Lord, ma'am!' Mr Meagles broke out, 'that's as much as to state—'

'Now, Papa Meagles, Papa Meagles,' said Mrs Gowan, who became extremely deliberate and prepossessing in manner whenever that gentleman became at all warm, 'perhaps to prevent confusion, I had better speak for myself than trouble your kindness to speak for me. It's as much as to state, you begin. If you please, I will finish the sentence. It is as much as to state—not that I wish to press it or even recall it, for it is of no use now, and my only wish is to make the best of existing circumstances—that from the first to the last I always objected to this match of yours, and at a very late period yielded a most unwilling consent to it.'

'Mother!' cried Mr Meagles. 'Do you hear this! Arthur! Do you hear this!'

'The room being of a convenient size,' said Mrs Gowan, looking about as she fanned herself, 'and quite charmingly adapted in all respects to conversation, I should imagine I am audible in any part of it.'

Some moments passed in silence, before Mr Meagles could hold himself in his chair with sufficient security to prevent his breaking out of it at the next word he spoke. At last he said: 'Ma'am, I am very unwilling to revive them, but I must remind you what my opinions and my course were, all along, on that unfortunate subject.'

'O, my dear sir!' said Mrs Gowan, smiling and shaking her head with accusatory intelligence, 'they were well understood by me, I assure you.'

'I never, ma'am,' said Mr Meagles, 'knew unhappiness before that time, I never knew anxiety before that time. It was a time of such distress to me that—' That Mr Meagles could really say no more about it, in short, but passed his handkerchief before his face.

'I understood the whole affair,' said Mrs Gowan, composedly looking over her fan. 'As you have appealed to Mr Clennam, I may appeal to Mr Clennam, too. He knows whether I did or not.'

'I am very unwilling,' said Clennam, looked to by all parties, 'to take any share in this discussion, more especially because I wish to preserve the best understanding and the clearest relations with Mr Henry Gowan. I have very strong reasons indeed, for entertaining that wish. Mrs Gowan attributed certain views of furthering the marriage to my friend here, in conversation with me before it took place; and I endeavoured to undeceive her. I represented that I knew him (as I did and do) to be strenuously opposed to it, both in opinion and action.'

'You see?' said Mrs Gowan, turning the palms of her hands towards Mr Meagles, as if she were Justice herself, representing to him that he had better confess, for he had not a leg to stand on. 'You see? Very good! Now Papa and Mama Meagles both!' here she rose; 'allow me to take the liberty of putting an end to this rather formidable controversy. I will not say another word upon its merits. I will only say that it is an additional proof of what one knows from all experience; that this kind of thing never answers—as my poor fellow himself would say, that it never pays—in one word, that it never does.'

Mr Meagles asked, What kind of thing?

'It is in vain,' said Mrs Gowan, 'for people to attempt to get on together who have such extremely different antecedents; who are jumbled against each other in this accidental, matrimonial sort of way; and who cannot look at the untoward circumstance which has shaken them together in the same light. It never does.'

Mr Meagles was beginning, 'Permit me to say, ma'am—'

'No, don't,' returned Mrs Gowan. 'Why should you! It is an ascertained fact. It never does. I will therefore, if you please, go my way, leaving you to yours. I shall at all times be happy to receive my poor fellow's pretty wife, and I shall always make a point of being on the most affectionate terms with her. But as to these terms, semi-family and semi-stranger, semi-goring and semi-boring, they form a state of things quite amusing in its impracticability. I assure you it never does.'

The Dowager here made a smiling obeisance, rather to the room than to any one in it, and therewith took a final farewell of Papa and Mama Meagles. Clennam stepped forward to hand her to the Pill-Box which was at the service of all the Pills in Hampton Court Palace; and she got into that vehicle with distinguished serenity, and was driven away.

Thenceforth the Dowager, with a light and careless humour, often recounted to her particular acquaintance how, after a hard trial, she had found it impossible to know those people who belonged to Henry's wife, and who had made that desperate set to catch him. Whether she had come to the conclusion beforehand, that to get rid of them would give her favourite pretence a better air, might save her some occasional inconvenience, and could risk no loss (the pretty creature being fast married, and her father devoted to her), was best known to herself. Though this history has its opinion on that point too, and decidedly in the affirmative.

CHAPTER 9. Appearance and Disappearance

'Arthur, my dear boy,' said Mr Meagles, on the evening of the following day, 'Mother and I have been talking this over, and we don't feel comfortable in remaining as we are. That elegant connection of ours—that dear lady who was here yesterday—'

'I understand,' said Arthur.

'Even that affable and condescending ornament of society,' pursued Mr Meagles, 'may misrepresent us, we are afraid. We could bear a great deal, Arthur, for her sake; but we think we would rather not bear that, if it was all the same to her.'

'Good,' said Arthur. 'Go on.'

'You see,' proceeded Mr Meagles 'it might put us wrong with our son-in-law, it might even put us wrong with our daughter, and it might lead to a great deal of domestic trouble. You see, don't you?'

'Yes, indeed,' returned Arthur, 'there is much reason in what you say.' He had glanced at Mrs Meagles, who was always on the good and sensible side; and a petition had shone out of her honest face that he would support Mr Meagles in his present inclinings.

'So we are very much disposed, are Mother and I,' said Mr Meagles, 'to pack up bags and baggage and go among the Allongers and Marshongers once more. I mean, we are very much disposed to be off, strike right through France into Italy, and see our Pet.'

'And I don't think,' replied Arthur, touched by the motherly anticipation in the bright face of Mrs Meagles (she must have been very like her daughter, once), 'that you could do better. And if you ask me for my advice, it is that you set off to-morrow.'

'Is it really, though?' said Mr Meagles. 'Mother, this is being backed in an idea!'

Mother, with a look which thanked Clennam in a manner very agreeable to him, answered that it was indeed.

'The fact is, besides, Arthur,' said Mr Meagles, the old cloud coming over his face, 'that my son-in-law is already in debt again, and that I suppose I must clear him again. It may be as well, even on this account, that I should step over there, and look him up in a friendly way. Then again, here's Mother foolishly anxious (and yet naturally too) about Pet's state of health, and that she should not be left to feel lonesome at the present time. It's undeniably a long way off, Arthur, and a strange place for the poor love under all the circumstances. Let her be as well cared for as any lady in that land, still it is a long way off. just as Home is Home though it's never so Homely, why you see,' said Mr Meagles, adding a new version to the proverb, 'Rome is Rome, though it's never so Romely.'

'All perfectly true,' observed Arthur, 'and all sufficient reasons for going.'

'I am glad you think so; it decides me. Mother, my dear, you may get ready. We have lost our pleasant interpreter (she spoke three foreign languages beautifully, Arthur; you have heard her many a time), and you must pull me through it, Mother, as well as you can. I require a deal of pulling through, Arthur,' said Mr Meagles, shaking his head, 'a deal of pulling through. I stick at everything beyond a noun-substantive—and I stick at him, if he's at all a tight one.'

'Now I think of it,' returned Clennam, 'there's Cavalletto. He shall go with you, if you like. I could not afford to lose him, but you will bring him safe back.'

'Well! I am much obliged to you, my boy,' said Mr Meagles, turning it over, 'but I think not. No, I think I'll be pulled through by Mother. Cavallooro (I stick at his very name to start with, and it sounds like the chorus to a comic song) is so necessary to you, that I don't like the thought of taking him away. More than that, there's no saying when we may come home again; and it would never do to take him away for an indefinite time. The cottage is not what it was. It only holds two little people less than it ever did, Pet, and her poor unfortunate maid Tattycoram; but it seems empty now. Once out of it, there's no knowing when we may come back to it. No, Arthur, I'll be pulled through by Mother.'

They would do best by themselves perhaps, after all, Clennam thought; therefore did not press his proposal.

'If you would come down and stay here for a change, when it wouldn't trouble you,' Mr Meagles resumed, 'I should be glad to think—and so would Mother too, I know—that you were brightening up the old place with a bit of life it was used to when it was full, and that the Babies on the wall there had a kind eye upon them sometimes. You so belong to the spot, and to them, Arthur, and we should every one of us have been so happy if it had fallen out—but, let us see—how's the weather for travelling now?' Mr Meagles broke off, cleared his throat, and got up to look out of the window.

They agreed that the weather was of high promise; and Clennam kept the talk in that safe direction until it had become easy again, when he gently diverted it to Henry Gowan and his quick sense and agreeable qualities when he was delicately dealt with; he likewise dwelt on the indisputable affection he entertained for his wife. Clennam did not fail of his effect upon good Mr Meagles, whom these commendations greatly cheered; and who took Mother to witness that the single and cordial desire of his heart in reference to their daughter's husband, was harmoniously to exchange friendship for friendship, and confidence for confidence. Within a few hours the cottage furniture began to be wrapped up for preservation in the family absence—or, as Mr Meagles expressed it, the house began to put its hair in papers—and within a few days Father and Mother were gone, Mrs Tickit and Dr Buchan were posted, as of yore, behind the parlour blind, and Arthur's solitary feet were rustling among the dry fallen leaves in the garden walks.

As he had a liking for the spot, he seldom let a week pass without paying a visit. Sometimes, he went down alone from Saturday to Monday; sometimes his partner accompanied him; sometimes, he merely strolled for an hour or two about the house and garden, saw that all was right, and returned to London again. At all times, and under all circumstances, Mrs Tickit, with her dark row of curls, and Dr Buchan, sat in the parlour window, looking out for the family return.

On one of his visits Mrs Tickit received him with the words, 'I have something to tell you, Mr Clennam, that will surprise you.' So surprising was the something in question, that it actually brought Mrs Tickit out of the parlour window and produced her in the garden walk, when Clennam went in at the gate on its being opened for him.

'What is it, Mrs Tickit?' said he.

'Sir,' returned that faithful housekeeper, having taken him into the parlour and closed the door; 'if ever I saw the led away and deluded child in my life, I saw her identically in the dusk of yesterday evening.'

'You don't mean Tatty—'

'Coram yes I do!' quoth Mrs Tickit, clearing the disclosure at a leap.

'Where?'

'Mr Clennam,' returned Mrs Tickit, 'I was a little heavy in my eyes, being that I was waiting longer than customary for my cup of tea which was then preparing by Mary Jane. I was not sleeping, nor what a person would term correctly, dozing. I was more what a person would strictly call watching with my eyes closed.'

Without entering upon an inquiry into this curious abnormal condition, Clennam said, 'Exactly. Well?'

'Well, sir,' proceeded Mrs Tickit, 'I was thinking of one thing and thinking of another, just as you yourself might. Just as anybody might.'

'Precisely so,' said Clennam. 'Well?'

'And when I do think of one thing and do think of another,' pursued Mrs Tickit, 'I hardly need to tell you, Mr Clennam, that I think of the family. Because, dear me! a person's thoughts,' Mrs Tickit said this with an argumentative and philosophic air, 'however they may stray, will go more or less on what is uppermost in their minds. They will do it, sir, and a person can't prevent them.'

Arthur subscribed to this discovery with a nod.

'You find it so yourself, sir, I'll be bold to say,' said Mrs Tickit, 'and we all find it so. It an't our stations in life that changes us, Mr Clennam; thoughts is free!—As I was saying, I was thinking of one thing and thinking of another, and thinking very much of the family. Not of the family in the present times only, but in the past times too. For when a person does begin thinking of one thing and thinking of another in that manner, as it's getting dark, what I say is, that all times seem to be present, and a person must get out of that state and consider before they can say which is which.'

He nodded again; afraid to utter a word, lest it should present any new opening to Mrs Tickit's conversational powers.

'In consequence of which,' said Mrs Tickit, 'when I quivered my eyes and saw her actual form and figure looking in at the gate, I let them close again without so much as starting, for that actual form and figure came so pat to the time when it belonged to the house as much as mine or your own, that I never thought at the moment of its having gone away. But, sir, when I quivered my eyes again, and saw that it wasn't there, then it all flooded upon me with a fright, and I jumped up.'

'You ran out directly?' said Clennam.

'I ran out,' assented Mrs Tickit, 'as fast as ever my feet would carry me; and if you'll credit it, Mr Clennam, there wasn't in the whole shining Heavens, no not so much as a finger of that young woman.'

Passing over the absence from the firmament of this novel constellation, Arthur inquired of Mrs Tickit if she herself went beyond the gate?

'Went to and fro, and high and low,' said Mrs Tickit, 'and saw no sign of her!'

He then asked Mrs Tickit how long a space of time she supposed there might have been between the two sets of ocular quiverings she had experienced? Mrs Tickit, though minutely circumstantial in her reply, had no settled opinion between five seconds and ten minutes. She was so plainly at sea on this part of the case, and had so clearly been startled out of slumber, that Clennam was much disposed to regard the appearance as a dream. Without hurting Mrs Tickit's feelings with that infidel solution of her mystery, he took it away from the cottage with him; and probably would have retained it ever afterwards if a circumstance had not soon happened to change his opinion.

He was passing at nightfall along the Strand, and the lamp-lighter was going on before him, under whose hand the street-lamps, blurred by the foggy air, burst out one after another, like so many blazing sunflowers coming into full-blow all at once,—when a stoppage on the pavement, caused by a train of coal-waggons toiling up from the wharves at the river-side, brought him to a stand-still. He had been walking quickly, and going with some current of thought, and the sudden check given to both operations caused him to look freshly about him, as people under such circumstances usually do.

Immediately, he saw in advance—a few people intervening, but still so near to him that he could have touched them by stretching out his arm—Tattycoram and a strange man of a remarkable appearance: a swaggering man, with a high nose, and a black moustache as false in its colour as his eyes were false in their expression, who wore his heavy cloak with the air of a foreigner. His dress and general appearance were those of a man on travel, and he seemed to have very recently joined the girl. In bending down (being much taller than she was), listening to whatever she said to him, he looked over his shoulder with the suspicious glance of one who was not unused to be mistrustful that his footsteps might be dogged. It was then that Clennam saw his face; as his eyes lowered on the people behind him in the aggregate, without particularly resting upon Clennam's face or any other.

He had scarcely turned his head about again, and it was still bent down, listening to the girl, when the stoppage ceased, and the obstructed stream of people flowed on. Still bending his head and listening to the girl, he went on at her side, and Clennam followed them, resolved to play this unexpected play out, and see where they went.

He had hardly made the determination (though he was not long about it), when he was again as suddenly brought up as he had been by the stoppage. They turned short into the Adelphi,—the girl evidently leading,—and went straight on, as if they were going to the Terrace which overhangs the river.

There is always, to this day, a sudden pause in that place to the roar of the great thoroughfare. The many sounds become so deadened that the change is like putting cotton in the ears, or having the head thickly muffled. At that time the contrast was far greater; there being no small steam-boats on the river, no landing places but slippery wooden stairs and foot-causeways, no railroad on the opposite bank, no hanging bridge or fish-market near at hand, no traffic on the nearest bridge of stone, nothing moving on the stream but watermen's wherries and coal-lighters. Long and broad black tiers of the latter, moored fast in the mud as if they were never to move again, made the shore funereal and silent after dark; and kept what little water-movement there was, far out towards mid-stream. At any hour later than sunset, and not least at that hour when most of the people who have anything to eat at home are going home to eat it, and when most of those who have nothing have hardly yet slunk out to beg or steal, it was a deserted place and looked on a deserted scene.

Such was the hour when Clennam stopped at the corner, observing the girl and the strange man as they went down the street. The man's footsteps were so noisy on the echoing stones that he was unwilling to add the sound of his own. But when they had passed the turning and were in the darkness of the dark corner leading to the terrace, he made after them with such indifferent appearance of being a casual passenger on his way, as he could assume.

When he rounded the dark corner, they were walking along the terrace towards a figure which was coming towards them. If he had seen it by itself, under such conditions of gas-lamp, mist, and distance, he might not have known it at first sight, but with the figure of the girl to prompt him, he at once recognised Miss Wade.

He stopped at the corner, seeming to look back expectantly up the street as if he had made an appointment with some one to meet him there; but he kept a careful eye on the three. When they came together, the man took off his hat, and made Miss Wade a bow. The girl appeared to say a few words as though she presented him, or accounted for his being late, or early, or what not; and then fell a pace or so behind, by herself. Miss Wade and the man then began to walk up and down; the man having the appearance of being extremely courteous and complimentary in manner; Miss Wade having the appearance of being extremely haughty.

When they came down to the corner and turned, she was saying, 'If I pinch myself for it, sir, that is my business. Confine yourself to yours, and ask me no question.'

'By Heaven, ma'am!' he replied, making her another bow. 'It was my profound respect for the strength of your character, and my admiration of your beauty.'

'I want neither the one nor the other from any one,' said she, 'and certainly not from you of all creatures. Go on with your report.'

'Am I pardoned?' he asked, with an air of half abashed gallantry.

'You are paid,' she said, 'and that is all you want.'

Whether the girl hung behind because she was not to hear the business, or as already knowing enough about it, Clennam could not determine. They turned and she turned. She looked away at the river, as she walked with her hands folded before her; and that was all he could make of her without showing his face. There happened, by good fortune, to be a lounger really waiting for some one; and he sometimes looked over the railing at the water, and sometimes came to the dark corner and looked up the street, rendering Arthur less conspicuous.

When Miss Wade and the man came back again, she was saying, 'You must wait until to-morrow.'

'A thousand pardons?' he returned. 'My faith! Then it's not convenient to-night?'

'No. I tell you I must get it before I can give it to you.'

She stopped in the roadway, as if to put an end to the conference. He of course stopped too. And the girl stopped.

'It's a little inconvenient,' said the man. 'A little. But, Holy Blue! that's nothing in such a service. I am without money to-night, by chance. I have a good banker in this city, but I would not wish to draw upon the house until the time when I shall draw for a round sum.'

'Harriet,' said Miss Wade, 'arrange with him—this gentleman here—for sending him some money to-morrow.' She said it with a slur of the word gentleman which was more contemptuous than any emphasis, and walked slowly on.

The man bent his head again, and the girl spoke to him as they both followed her. Clennam ventured to look at the girl as they moved away. He could note that her rich black eyes were fastened upon the man with a scrutinising expression, and that she kept at a little distance from him, as they walked side by side to the further end of the terrace.

A loud and altered clank upon the pavement warned him, before he could discern what was passing there, that the man was coming back alone. Clennam lounged into the road, towards the railing; and the man passed at a quick swing, with the end of his cloak thrown over his shoulder, singing a scrap of a French song.

The whole vista had no one in it now but himself. The lounger had lounged out of view, and Miss Wade and Tattycoram were gone. More than ever bent on seeing what became of them, and on having some information to give his good friend, Mr Meagles, he went out at the further end of the terrace, looking cautiously about him. He rightly judged that, at first at all events, they would go in a contrary direction from their late companion. He soon saw them in a neighbouring bye-street, which was not a thoroughfare, evidently allowing time for the man to get well out of their way. They walked leisurely arm-in-arm down one side of the street, and returned on the opposite side. When they came back to the street-corner, they changed their pace for the pace of people with an object and a distance before them, and walked steadily away. Clennam, no less steadily, kept them in sight.

They crossed the Strand, and passed through Covent Garden (under the windows of his old lodging where dear Little Dorrit had come that night), and slanted away north-east, until they passed the great building whence Tattycoram derived her name, and turned into the Gray's Inn Road. Clennam was quite at home here, in right of Flora, not to mention the Patriarch and Pancks, and kept them in view with ease. He was beginning to wonder where they might be going next, when that wonder was lost in the greater wonder with which he saw them turn into the Patriarchal street. That wonder was in its turn swallowed up on the greater wonder with which he saw them stop at the Patriarchal door. A low double knock at the bright brass knocker, a gleam of light into the road from the opened door, a brief pause for inquiry and answer and the door was shut, and they were housed.

After looking at the surrounding objects for assurance that he was not in an odd dream, and after pacing a little while before the house, Arthur knocked at the door. It was opened by the usual maid-servant, and she showed him up at once, with her usual alacrity, to Flora's sitting-room.

There was no one with Flora but Mr F.'s Aunt, which respectable gentlewoman, basking in a balmy atmosphere of tea and toast, was ensconced in an easy-chair by the fireside, with a little table at her elbow, and a clean white handkerchief spread over her lap on which two pieces of toast at that moment awaited consumption. Bending over a steaming vessel of tea, and looking through the steam, and breathing forth the steam, like a malignant Chinese enchantress engaged in the performance of unholy rites, Mr F.'s Aunt put down her great teacup and exclaimed, 'Drat him, if he an't come back again!'

It would seem from the foregoing exclamation that this uncompromising relative of the lamented Mr F., measuring time by the acuteness of her sensations and not by the clock, supposed Clennam to have lately gone away; whereas at least a quarter of a year had elapsed since he had had the temerity to present himself before her.

'My goodness Arthur!' cried Flora, rising to give him a cordial reception, 'Doyce and Clennam what a start and a surprise for though not far from the machinery and foundry business and surely might be taken sometimes if at no other time about mid-day when a glass of sherry and a humble sandwich of whatever cold meat in the larder might not come amiss nor taste the worse for being friendly for you know you buy it somewhere and wherever bought a profit must be made or they would never keep the place it stands to reason without a motive still never seen and learnt now not to be expected, for as Mr F. himself said if seeing is believing not seeing is believing too and when you don't see you may fully believe you're not remembered not that I expect you Arthur Doyce and Clennam to remember me why should I for the days are gone but bring another teacup here directly and tell her fresh toast and pray sit near the fire.'

Arthur was in the greatest anxiety to explain the object of his visit; but was put off for the moment, in spite of himself, by what he understood of the reproachful purport of these words, and by the genuine pleasure she testified in seeing him.

'And now pray tell me something all you know,' said Flora, drawing her chair near to his, 'about the good dear quiet little thing and all the changes of her fortunes carriage people now no doubt and horses without number most romantic, a coat of arms of course and wild beasts on their hind legs showing it as if it was a copy they had done with mouths from ear to ear good gracious, and has she her health which is the first consideration after all for what is wealth without it Mr F. himself so often saying when his twinges came that sixpence a day and find yourself and no gout so much preferable, not that he could have lived on anything like it being the last man or that the previous little thing though far too familiar an expression now had any tendency of that sort much too slight and small but looked so fragile bless her?'

Mr F.'s Aunt, who had eaten a piece of toast down to the crust, here solemnly handed the crust to Flora, who ate it for her as a matter of business. Mr F.'s Aunt then moistened her ten fingers in slow succession at her lips, and wiped them in exactly the same order on the white handkerchief; then took the other piece of toast, and fell to work upon it. While pursuing this routine, she looked at Clennam with an expression of such intense severity that he felt obliged to look at her in return, against his personal inclinations.

'She is in Italy, with all her family, Flora,' he said, when the dreaded lady was occupied again.

'In Italy is she really?' said Flora, 'with the grapes growing everywhere and lava necklaces and bracelets too that land of poetry with burning mountains picturesque beyond belief though if the organ-boys come away from the neighbourhood not to be scorched nobody can wonder being so young and bringing their white mice with them most humane, and is she really in that favoured land with nothing but blue about her and dying gladiators and Belvederes though Mr F. himself did not believe for his objection when in spirits was that the images could not be true there being no medium between expensive quantities of linen badly got up and all in creases and none whatever, which certainly does not seem probable though perhaps in consequence of the extremes of rich and poor which may account for it.'

Arthur tried to edge a word in, but Flora hurried on again.

'Venice Preserved too,' said she, 'I think you have been there is it well or ill preserved for people differ so and Maccaroni if they really eat it like the conjurors why not cut it shorter, you are acquainted Arthur—dear Doyce and Clennam at least not dear and most assuredly not Doyce for I have not the pleasure but pray excuse me—acquainted I believe with Mantua what has it got to do with Mantua-making for I never have been able to conceive?'

'I believe there is no connection, Flora, between the two,' Arthur was beginning, when she caught him up again.

'Upon your word no isn't there I never did but that's like me I run away with an idea and having none to spare I keep it, alas there was a time dear Arthur that is to say decidedly not dear nor Arthur neither but you understand me when one bright idea gilded the what's-his-name horizon of et cetera but it is darkly clouded now and all is over.'

Arthur's increasing wish to speak of something very different was by this time so plainly written on his face, that Flora stopped in a tender look, and asked him what it was?

'I have the greatest desire, Flora, to speak to some one who is now in this house—with Mr Casby no doubt. Some one whom I saw come in, and who, in a misguided and deplorable way, has deserted the house of a friend of mine.'

'Papa sees so many and such odd people,' said Flora, rising, 'that I shouldn't venture to go down for any one but you Arthur but for you I would willingly go down in a diving-bell much more a dining-room and will come back directly if you'll mind and at the same time not mind Mr F.'s Aunt while I'm gone.'

With those words and a parting glance, Flora bustled out, leaving Clennam under dreadful apprehension of this terrible charge.

The first variation which manifested itself in Mr F.'s Aunt's demeanour when she had finished her piece of toast, was a loud and prolonged sniff. Finding it impossible to avoid construing this demonstration into a defiance of himself, its gloomy significance being unmistakable, Clennam looked plaintively at the excellent though prejudiced lady from whom it emanated, in the hope that she might be disarmed by a meek submission.

'None of your eyes at me,' said Mr F.'s Aunt, shivering with hostility. 'Take that.'

'That' was the crust of the piece of toast. Clennam accepted the boon with a look of gratitude, and held it in his hand under the pressure of a little embarrassment, which was not relieved when Mr F.'s Aunt, elevating her voice into a cry of considerable power, exclaimed, 'He has a proud stomach, this chap! He's too proud a chap to eat it!' and, coming out of her chair, shook her venerable fist so very close to his nose as to tickle the surface. But for the timely return of Flora, to find him in this difficult situation, further consequences might have ensued. Flora, without the least discomposure or surprise, but congratulating the old lady in an approving manner on being 'very lively to-night', handed her back to her chair.

'He has a proud stomach, this chap,' said Mr F.'s relation, on being reseated. 'Give him a meal of chaff!'

'Oh! I don't think he would like that, aunt,' returned Flora.

'Give him a meal of chaff, I tell you,' said Mr F.'s Aunt, glaring round Flora on her enemy. 'It's the only thing for a proud stomach. Let him eat up every morsel. Drat him, give him a meal of chaff!'

Under a general pretence of helping him to this refreshment, Flora got him out on the staircase; Mr F.'s Aunt even then constantly reiterating, with inexpressible bitterness, that he was 'a chap,' and had a 'proud stomach,' and over and over again insisting on that equine provision being made for him which she had already so strongly prescribed.

'Such an inconvenient staircase and so many corner-stairs Arthur,' whispered Flora, 'would you object to putting your arm round me under my pelerine?'

With a sense of going down-stairs in a highly-ridiculous manner, Clennam descended in the required attitude, and only released his fair burden at the dining-room door; indeed, even there she was rather difficult to be got rid of, remaining in his embrace to murmur, 'Arthur, for mercy's sake, don't breathe it to papa!'

She accompanied Arthur into the room, where the Patriarch sat alone, with his list shoes on the fender, twirling his thumbs as if he had never left off. The youthful Patriarch, aged ten, looked out of his picture-frame above him with no calmer air than he. Both smooth heads were alike beaming, blundering, and bumpy.

'Mr Clennam, I am glad to see you. I hope you are well, sir, I hope you are well. Please to sit down, please to sit down.'

'I had hoped, sir,' said Clennam, doing so, and looking round with a face of blank disappointment, 'not to find you alone.'

'Ah, indeed?' said the Patriarch, sweetly. 'Ah, indeed?'

'I told you so you know papa,' cried Flora.

'Ah, to be sure!' returned the Patriarch. 'Yes, just so. Ah, to be sure!'

'Pray, sir,' demanded Clennam, anxiously, 'is Miss Wade gone?'

'Miss—? Oh, you call her Wade,' returned Mr Casby. 'Highly proper.'

Arthur quickly returned, 'What do you call her?'

'Wade,' said Mr Casby. 'Oh, always Wade.'

After looking at the philanthropic visage and the long silky white hair for a few seconds, during which Mr Casby twirled his thumbs, and smiled at the fire as if he were benevolently wishing it to burn him that he might forgive it, Arthur began:

'I beg your pardon, Mr Casby—'

'Not so, not so,' said the Patriarch, 'not so.'

'—But, Miss Wade had an attendant with her—a young woman brought up by friends of mine, over whom her influence is not considered very salutary, and to whom I should be glad to have the opportunity of giving the assurance that she has not yet forfeited the interest of those protectors.'

'Really, really?' returned the Patriarch.

'Will you therefore be so good as to give me the address of Miss Wade?'

'Dear, dear, dear!' said the Patriarch, 'how very unfortunate! If you had only sent in to me when they were here! I observed the young woman, Mr Clennam. A fine full-coloured young woman, Mr Clennam, with very dark hair and very dark eyes. If I mistake not, if I mistake not?'

Arthur assented, and said once more with new expression, 'If you would be so good as to give me the address.'

'Dear, dear, dear!' exclaimed the Patriarch in sweet regret. 'Tut, tut, tut! what a pity, what a pity! I have no address, sir. Miss Wade mostly lives abroad, Mr Clennam. She has done so for some years, and she is (if I may say so of a fellow-creature and a lady) fitful and uncertain to a fault, Mr Clennam. I may not see her again for a long, long time. I may never see her again. What a pity, what a pity!'

Clennam saw now, that he had as much hope of getting assistance out of the Portrait as out of the Patriarch; but he said nevertheless:

'Mr Casby, could you, for the satisfaction of the friends I have mentioned, and under any obligation of secrecy that you may consider it your duty to impose, give me any information at all touching Miss Wade? I have seen her abroad, and I have seen her at home, but I know nothing of her. Could you give me any account of her whatever?'

'None,' returned the Patriarch, shaking his big head with his utmost benevolence. 'None at all. Dear, dear, dear! What a real pity that she stayed so short a time, and you delayed! As confidential agency business, agency business, I have occasionally paid this lady money; but what satisfaction is it to you, sir, to know that?'

'Truly, none at all,' said Clennam.

'Truly,' assented the Patriarch, with a shining face as he philanthropically smiled at the fire, 'none at all, sir. You hit the wise answer, Mr Clennam. Truly, none at all, sir.'

His turning of his smooth thumbs over one another as he sat there, was so typical to Clennam of the way in which he would make the subject revolve if it were pursued, never showing any new part of it nor allowing it to make the smallest advance, that it did much to help to convince him of his labour having been in vain. He might have taken any time to think about it, for Mr Casby, well accustomed to get on anywhere by leaving everything to his bumps and his white hair, knew his strength to lie in silence. So there Casby sat, twirling and twirling, and making his polished head and forehead look largely benevolent in every knob.

With this spectacle before him, Arthur had risen to go, when from the inner Dock where the good ship Pancks was hove down when out in no cruising ground, the noise was heard of that steamer labouring towards him. It struck Arthur that the noise began demonstratively far off, as though Mr Pancks sought to impress on any one who might happen to think about it, that he was working on from out of hearing.

Mr Pancks and he shook hands, and the former brought his employer a letter or two to sign. Mr Pancks in shaking hands merely scratched his eyebrow with his left forefinger and snorted once, but Clennam, who understood him better now than of old, comprehended that he had almost done for the evening and wished to say a word to him outside. Therefore, when he had taken his leave of Mr Casby, and (which was a more difficult process) of Flora, he sauntered in the neighbourhood on Mr Pancks's line of road.

He had waited but a short time when Mr Pancks appeared. Mr Pancks shaking hands again with another expressive snort, and taking off his hat to put his hair up, Arthur thought he received his cue to speak to him as one who knew pretty well what had just now passed. Therefore he said, without any preface:

'I suppose they were really gone, Pancks?'

'Yes,' replied Pancks. 'They were really gone.'

'Does he know where to find that lady?'

'Can't say. I should think so.'

Mr Pancks did not? No, Mr Pancks did not. Did Mr Pancks know anything about her?

'I expect,' rejoined that worthy, 'I know as much about her as she knows about herself. She is somebody's child—anybody's, nobody's. Put her in a room in London here with any six people old enough to be her parents, and her parents may be there for anything she knows. They may be in any house she sees, they may be in any churchyard she passes, she may run against 'em in any street, she may make chance acquaintance of 'em at any time; and never know it. She knows nothing about 'em. She knows nothing about any relative whatever. Never did. Never will.'

'Mr Casby could enlighten her, perhaps?'

'May be,' said Pancks. 'I expect so, but don't know. He has long had money (not overmuch as I make out) in trust to dole out to her when she can't do without it. Sometimes she's proud and won't touch it for a length of time; sometimes she's so poor that she must have it. She writhes under her life. A woman more angry, passionate, reckless, and revengeful never lived. She came for money to-night. Said she had peculiar occasion for it.'

'I think,' observed Clennam musing, 'I by chance know what occasion—I mean into whose pocket the money is to go.'

'Indeed?' said Pancks. 'If it's a compact, I recommend that party to be exact in it. I wouldn't trust myself to that woman, young and handsome as she is, if I had wronged her; no, not for twice my proprietor's money! Unless,' Pancks added as a saving clause, 'I had a lingering illness on me, and wanted to get it over.'

Arthur, hurriedly reviewing his own observation of her, found it to tally pretty nearly with Mr Pancks's view.

'The wonder is to me,' pursued Pancks, 'that she has never done for my proprietor, as the only person connected with her story she can lay hold of. Mentioning that, I may tell you, between ourselves, that I am sometimes tempted to do for him myself.'

Arthur started and said, 'Dear me, Pancks, don't say that!'

'Understand me,' said Pancks, extending five cropped coaly finger-nails on Arthur's arm; 'I don't mean, cut his throat. But by all that's precious, if he goes too far, I'll cut his hair!'

Having exhibited himself in the new light of enunciating this tremendous threat, Mr Pancks, with a countenance of grave import, snorted several times and steamed away.

CHAPTER 10. The Dreams of Mrs Flintwinch thicken

The shady waiting-rooms of the Circumlocution Office, where he passed a good deal of time in company with various troublesome Convicts who were under sentence to be broken alive on that wheel, had afforded Arthur Clennam ample leisure, in three or four successive days, to exhaust the subject of his late glimpse of Miss Wade and Tattycoram. He had been able to make no more of it and no less of it, and in this unsatisfactory condition he was fain to leave it.

During this space he had not been to his mother's dismal old house. One of his customary evenings for repairing thither now coming round, he left his dwelling and his partner at nearly nine o'clock, and slowly walked in the direction of that grim home of his youth.

It always affected his imagination as wrathful, mysterious, and sad; and his imagination was sufficiently impressible to see the whole neighbourhood under some tinge of its dark shadow. As he went along, upon a dreary night, the dim streets by which he went, seemed all depositories of oppressive secrets. The deserted counting-houses, with their secrets of books and papers locked up in chests and safes; the banking-houses, with their secrets of strong rooms and wells, the keys of which were in a very few secret pockets and a very few secret breasts; the secrets of all the dispersed grinders in the vast mill, among whom there were doubtless plunderers, forgers, and trust-betrayers of many sorts, whom the light of any day that dawned might reveal; he could have fancied that these things, in hiding, imparted a heaviness to the air. The shadow thickening and thickening as he approached its source, he thought of the secrets of the lonely church-vaults, where the people who had hoarded and secreted in iron coffers were in their turn similarly hoarded, not yet at rest from doing harm; and then of the secrets of the river, as it rolled its turbid tide between two frowning wildernesses of secrets, extending, thick and dense, for many miles, and warding off the free air and the free country swept by winds and wings of birds.

The shadow still darkening as he drew near the house, the melancholy room which his father had once occupied, haunted by the appealing face he had himself seen fade away with him when there was no other watcher by the bed, arose before his mind. Its close air was secret. The gloom, and must, and dust of the whole tenement, were secret. At the heart of it his mother presided, inflexible of face, indomitable of will, firmly holding all the secrets of her own and his father's life, and austerely opposing herself, front to front, to the great final secret of all life.

He had turned into the narrow and steep street from which the court of enclosure wherein the house stood opened, when another footstep turned into it behind him, and so close upon his own that he was jostled to the wall. As his mind was teeming with these thoughts, the encounter took him altogether unprepared, so that the other passenger had had time to say, boisterously, 'Pardon! Not my fault!' and to pass on before the instant had elapsed which was requisite to his recovery of the realities about him.

When that moment had flashed away, he saw that the man striding on before him was the man who had been so much in his mind during the last few days. It was no casual resemblance, helped out by the force of the impression the man made upon him. It was the man; the man he had followed in company with the girl, and whom he had overheard talking to Miss Wade.

The street was a sharp descent and was crooked too, and the man (who although not drunk had the air of being flushed with some strong drink) went down it so fast that Clennam lost him as he looked at him. With no defined intention of following him, but with an impulse to keep the figure in view a little longer, Clennam quickened his pace to pass the twist in the street which hid him from his sight. On turning it, he saw the man no more.

Standing now, close to the gateway of his mother's house, he looked down the street: but it was empty. There was no projecting shadow large enough to obscure the man; there was no turning near that he could have taken; nor had there been any audible sound of the opening and closing of a door. Nevertheless, he concluded that the man must have had a key in his hand, and must have opened one of the many house-doors and gone in.

Ruminating on this strange chance and strange glimpse, he turned into the court-yard. As he looked, by mere habit, towards the feebly lighted windows of his mother's room, his eyes encountered the figure he had just lost, standing against the iron railings of the little waste enclosure looking up at those windows and laughing to himself. Some of the many vagrant cats who were always prowling about there by night, and who had taken fright at him, appeared to have stopped when he had stopped, and were looking at him with eyes by no means unlike his own from tops of walls and porches, and other safe points of pause. He had only halted for a moment to entertain himself thus; he immediately went forward, throwing the end of his cloak off his shoulder as he went, ascended the unevenly sunken steps, and knocked a sounding knock at the door.

Clennam's surprise was not so absorbing but that he took his resolution without any incertitude. He went up to the door too, and ascended the steps too. His friend looked at him with a braggart air, and sang to himself.

'Who passes by this road so late?

Compagnon de la Majolaine;

Who passes by this road so late?

Always gay!'

After which he knocked again.

'You are impatient, sir,' said Arthur.

'I am, sir. Death of my life, sir,' returned the stranger, 'it's my character to be impatient!'

The sound of Mistress Affery cautiously chaining the door before she opened it, caused them both to look that way. Affery opened it a very little, with a flaring candle in her hands and asked who was that, at that time of night, with that knock! 'Why, Arthur!' she added with astonishment, seeing him first. 'Not you sure? Ah, Lord save us! No,' she cried out, seeing the other. 'Him again!'

'It's true! Him again, dear Mrs Flintwinch,' cried the stranger. 'Open the door, and let me take my dear friend Jeremiah to my arms! Open the door, and let me hasten myself to embrace my Flintwinch!'

'He's not at home,' cried Affery.

'Fetch him!' cried the stranger. 'Fetch my Flintwinch! Tell him that it is his old Blandois, who comes from arriving in England; tell him that it is his little boy who is here, his cabbage, his well-beloved! Open the door, beautiful Mrs Flintwinch, and in the meantime let me to pass upstairs, to present my compliments—homage of Blandois—to my lady! My lady lives always? It is well. Open then!'

To Arthur's increased surprise, Mistress Affery, stretching her eyes wide at himself, as if in warning that this was not a gentleman for him to interfere with, drew back the chain, and opened the door. The stranger, without ceremony, walked into the hall, leaving Arthur to follow him.

'Despatch then! Achieve then! Bring my Flintwinch! Announce me to my lady!' cried the stranger, clanking about the stone floor.

'Pray tell me, Affery,' said Arthur aloud and sternly, as he surveyed him from head to foot with indignation; 'who is this gentleman?'

'Pray tell me, Affery,' the stranger repeated in his turn, 'who—ha, ha, ha!—who is this gentleman?'

The voice of Mrs Clennam opportunely called from her chamber above, 'Affery, let them both come up. Arthur, come straight to me!'

'Arthur?' exclaimed Blandois, taking off his hat at arm's length, and bringing his heels together from a great stride in making him a flourishing bow. 'The son of my lady? I am the all-devoted of the son of my lady!'

Arthur looked at him again in no more flattering manner than before, and, turning on his heel without acknowledgment, went up-stairs. The visitor followed him up-stairs. Mistress Affery took the key from behind the door, and deftly slipped out to fetch her lord.

A bystander, informed of the previous appearance of Monsieur Blandois in that room, would have observed a difference in Mrs Clennam's present reception of him. Her face was not one to betray it; and her suppressed manner, and her set voice, were equally under her control. It wholly consisted in her never taking her eyes off his face from the moment of his entrance, and in her twice or thrice, when he was becoming noisy, swaying herself a very little forward in the chair in which she sat upright, with her hands immovable upon its elbows; as if she gave him the assurance that he should be presently heard at any length he would. Arthur did not fail to observe this; though the difference between the present occasion and the former was not within his power of observation.

'Madame,' said Blandois, 'do me the honour to present me to Monsieur, your son. It appears to me, madame, that Monsieur, your son, is disposed to complain of me. He is not polite.'

'Sir,' said Arthur, striking in expeditiously, 'whoever you are, and however you come to be here, if I were the master of this house I would lose no time in placing you on the outside of it.'

'But you are not,' said his mother, without looking at him. 'Unfortunately for the gratification of your unreasonable temper, you are not the master, Arthur.'

'I make no claim to be, mother. If I object to this person's manner of conducting himself here, and object to it so much, that if I had any authority here I certainly would not suffer him to remain a minute, I object on your account.'

'In the case of objection being necessary,' she returned, 'I could object for myself. And of course I should.'

The subject of their dispute, who had seated himself, laughed aloud, and rapped his legs with his hand.

'You have no right,' said Mrs Clennam, always intent on Blandois, however directly she addressed her son, 'to speak to the prejudice of any gentleman (least of all a gentleman from another country), because he does not conform to your standard, or square his behaviour by your rules. It is possible that the gentleman may, on similar grounds, object to you.'

'I hope so,' returned Arthur.

'The gentleman,' pursued Mrs Clennam, 'on a former occasion brought a letter of recommendation to us from highly esteemed and responsible correspondents. I am perfectly unacquainted with the gentleman's object in coming here at present. I am entirely ignorant of it, and cannot be supposed likely to be able to form the remotest guess at its nature;' her habitual frown became stronger, as she very slowly and weightily emphasised those words; 'but, when the gentleman proceeds to explain his object, as I shall beg him to have the goodness to do to myself and Flintwinch, when Flintwinch returns, it will prove, no doubt, to be one more or less in the usual way of our business, which it will be both our business and our pleasure to advance. It can be nothing else.'

'We shall see, madame!' said the man of business.

'We shall see,' she assented. 'The gentleman is acquainted with Flintwinch; and when the gentleman was in London last, I remember to have heard that he and Flintwinch had some entertainment or good-fellowship together. I am not in the way of knowing much that passes outside this room, and the jingle of little worldly things beyond it does not much interest me; but I remember to have heard that.'

'Right, madame. It is true.' He laughed again, and whistled the burden of the tune he had sung at the door.

'Therefore, Arthur,' said his mother, 'the gentleman comes here as an acquaintance, and no stranger; and it is much to be regretted that your unreasonable temper should have found offence in him. I regret it. I say so to the gentleman. You will not say so, I know; therefore I say it for myself and Flintwinch, since with us two the gentleman's business lies.'

The key of the door below was now heard in the lock, and the door was heard to open and close. In due sequence Mr Flintwinch appeared; on whose entrance the visitor rose from his chair, laughing loud, and folded him in a close embrace.

'How goes it, my cherished friend!' said he. 'How goes the world, my Flintwinch? Rose-coloured? So much the better, so much the better! Ah, but you look charming! Ah, but you look young and fresh as the flowers of Spring! Ah, good little boy! Brave child, brave child!'

While heaping these compliments on Mr Flintwinch, he rolled him about with a hand on each of his shoulders, until the staggerings of that gentleman, who under the circumstances was dryer and more twisted than ever, were like those of a teetotum nearly spent.

'I had a presentiment, last time, that we should be better and more intimately acquainted. Is it coming on you, Flintwinch? Is it yet coming on?'

'Why, no, sir,' retorted Mr Flintwinch. 'Not unusually. Hadn't you better be seated? You have been calling for some more of that port, sir, I guess?'

'Ah, Little joker! Little pig!' cried the visitor. 'Ha ha ha ha!' And throwing Mr Flintwinch away, as a closing piece of raillery, he sat down again.

The amazement, suspicion, resentment, and shame, with which Arthur looked on at all this, struck him dumb. Mr Flintwinch, who had spun backward some two or three yards under the impetus last given to him, brought himself up with a face completely unchanged in its stolidity except as it was affected by shortness of breath, and looked hard at Arthur. Not a whit less reticent and wooden was Mr Flintwinch outwardly, than in the usual course of things: the only perceptible difference in him being that the knot of cravat which was generally under his ear, had worked round to the back of his head: where it formed an ornamental appendage not unlike a bagwig, and gave him something of a courtly appearance.

As Mrs Clennam never removed her eyes from Blandois (on whom they had some effect, as a steady look has on a lower sort of dog), so Jeremiah never removed his from Arthur. It was as if they had tacitly agreed to take their different provinces. Thus, in the ensuing silence, Jeremiah stood scraping his chin and looking at Arthur as though he were trying to screw his thoughts out of him with an instrument.

After a little, the visitor, as if he felt the silence irksome, rose, and impatiently put himself with his back to the sacred fire which had burned through so many years. Thereupon Mrs Clennam said, moving one of her hands for the first time, and moving it very slightly with an action of dismissal:

'Please to leave us to our business, Arthur.'

'Mother, I do so with reluctance.'

'Never mind with what,' she returned, 'or with what not. Please to leave us. Come back at any other time when you may consider it a duty to bury half an hour wearily here. Good night.'

She held up her muffled fingers that he might touch them with his, according to their usual custom, and he stood over her wheeled chair to touch her face with his lips. He thought, then, that her cheek was more strained than usual, and that it was colder. As he followed the direction of her eyes, in rising again, towards Mr Flintwinch's good friend, Mr Blandois, Mr Blandois snapped his finger and thumb with one loud contemptuous snap.

'I leave your—your business acquaintance in my mother's room, Mr Flintwinch,' said Clennam, 'with a great deal of surprise and a great deal of unwillingness.'

The person referred to snapped his finger and thumb again.

'Good night, mother.'

'Good night.'

'I had a friend once, my good comrade Flintwinch,' said Blandois, standing astride before the fire, and so evidently saying it to arrest Clennam's retreating steps, that he lingered near the door; 'I had a friend once, who had heard so much of the dark side of this city and its ways, that he wouldn't have confided himself alone by night with two people who had an interest in getting him under the ground—my faith! not even in a respectable house like this—unless he was bodily too strong for them. Bah! What a poltroon, my Flintwinch! Eh?'

'A cur, sir.'

'Agreed! A cur. But he wouldn't have done it, my Flintwinch, unless he had known them to have the will to silence him, without the power. He wouldn't have drunk from a glass of water under such circumstances—not even in a respectable house like this, my Flintwinch—unless he had seen one of them drink first, and swallow too!'

Disdaining to speak, and indeed not very well able, for he was half-choking, Clennam only glanced at the visitor as he passed out. The visitor saluted him with another parting snap, and his nose came down over his moustache and his moustache went up under his nose, in an ominous and ugly smile.

'For Heaven's sake, Affery,' whispered Clennam, as she opened the door for him in the dark hall, and he groped his way to the sight of the night-sky, 'what is going on here?'

Her own appearance was sufficiently ghastly, standing in the dark with her apron thrown over her head, and speaking behind it in a low, deadened voice.

'Don't ask me anything, Arthur. I've been in a dream for ever so long. Go away!'

He went out, and she shut the door upon him. He looked up at the windows of his mother's room, and the dim light, deadened by the yellow blinds, seemed to say a response after Affery, and to mutter, 'Don't ask me anything. Go away!'

CHAPTER 11. A Letter from Little Dorrit

Dear Mr Clennam,

As I said in my last that it was best for nobody to write to me, and as my sending you another little letter can therefore give you no other trouble than the trouble of reading it (perhaps you may not find leisure for even that, though I hope you will some day), I am now going to devote an hour to writing to you again. This time, I write from Rome.

We left Venice before Mr and Mrs Gowan did, but they were not so long upon the road as we were, and did not travel by the same way, and so when we arrived we found them in a lodging here, in a place called the Via Gregoriana. I dare say you know it.

Now I am going to tell you all I can about them, because I know that is what you most want to hear. Theirs is not a very comfortable lodging, but perhaps I thought it less so when I first saw it than you would have done, because you have been in many different countries and have seen many different customs. Of course it is a far, far better place—millions of times—than any I have ever been used to until lately; and I fancy I don't look at it with my own eyes, but with hers. For it would be easy to see that she has always been brought up in a tender and happy home, even if she had not told me so with great love for it.

Well, it is a rather bare lodging up a rather dark common staircase, and it is nearly all a large dull room, where Mr Gowan paints. The windows are blocked up where any one could look out, and the walls have been all drawn over with chalk and charcoal by others who have lived there before—oh,—I should think, for years! There is a curtain more dust-coloured than red, which divides it, and the part behind the curtain makes the private sitting-room. When I first saw her there she was alone, and her work had fallen out of her hand, and she was looking up at the sky shining through the tops of the windows. Pray do not be uneasy when I tell you, but it was not quite so airy, nor so bright, nor so cheerful, nor so happy and youthful altogether as I should have liked it to be.

On account of Mr Gowan's painting Papa's picture (which I am not quite convinced I should have known from the likeness if I had not seen him doing it), I have had more opportunities of being with her since then than I might have had without this fortunate chance. She is very much alone. Very much alone indeed.

Shall I tell you about the second time I saw her? I went one day, when it happened that I could run round by myself, at four or five o'clock in the afternoon. She was then dining alone, and her solitary dinner had been brought in from somewhere, over a kind of brazier with a fire in it, and she had no company or prospect of company, that I could see, but the old man who had brought it. He was telling her a long story (of robbers outside the walls being taken up by a stone statue of a Saint), to entertain her—as he said to me when I came out, 'because he had a daughter of his own, though she was not so pretty.'

I ought now to mention Mr Gowan, before I say what little more I have to say about her. He must admire her beauty, and he must be proud of her, for everybody praises it, and he must be fond of her, and I do not doubt that he is—but in his way. You know his way, and if it appears as careless and discontented in your eyes as it does in mine, I am not wrong in thinking that it might be better suited to her. If it does not seem so to you, I am quite sure I am wholly mistaken; for your unchanged poor child confides in your knowledge and goodness more than she could ever tell you if she was to try. But don't be frightened, I am not going to try.

Owing (as I think, if you think so too) to Mr Gowan's unsettled and dissatisfied way, he applies himself to his profession very little. He does nothing steadily or patiently; but equally takes things up and throws them down, and does them, or leaves them undone, without caring about them. When I have heard him talking to Papa during the sittings for the picture, I have sat wondering whether it could be that he has no belief in anybody else, because he has no belief in himself. Is it so? I wonder what you will say when you come to this! I know how you will look, and I can almost hear the voice in which you would tell me on the Iron Bridge.

Mr Gowan goes out a good deal among what is considered the best company here—though he does not look as if he enjoyed it or liked it when he is with it—and she sometimes accompanies him, but lately she has gone out very little. I think I have noticed that they have an inconsistent way of speaking about her, as if she had made some great self-interested success in marrying Mr Gowan, though, at the same time, the very same people, would not have dreamed of taking him for themselves or their daughters. Then he goes into the country besides, to think about making sketches; and in all places where there are visitors, he has a large acquaintance and is very well known. Besides all this, he has a friend who is much in his society both at home and away from home, though he treats this friend very coolly and is very uncertain in his behaviour to him. I am quite sure (because she has told me so), that she does not like this friend. He is so revolting to me, too, that his being away from here, at present, is quite a relief to my mind. How much more to hers!

But what I particularly want you to know, and why I have resolved to tell you so much while I am afraid it may make you a little uncomfortable without occasion, is this. She is so true and so devoted, and knows so completely that all her love and duty are his for ever, that you may be certain she will love him, admire him, praise him, and conceal all his faults, until she dies. I believe she conceals them, and always will conceal them, even from herself. She has given him a heart that can never be taken back; and however much he may try it, he will never wear out its affection. You know the truth of this, as you know everything, far far better than I; but I cannot help telling you what a nature she shows, and that you can never think too well of her.

I have not yet called her by her name in this letter, but we are such friends now that I do so when we are quietly together, and she speaks to me by my name—I mean, not my Christian name, but the name you gave me. When she began to call me Amy, I told her my short story, and that you had always called me Little Dorrit. I told her that the name was much dearer to me than any other, and so she calls me Little Dorrit too.

Perhaps you have not heard from her father or mother yet, and may not know that she has a baby son. He was born only two days ago, and just a week after they came. It has made them very happy. However, I must tell you, as I am to tell you all, that I fancy they are under a constraint with Mr Gowan, and that they feel as if his mocking way with them was sometimes a slight given to their love for her. It was but yesterday, when I was there, that I saw Mr Meagles change colour, and get up and go out, as if he was afraid that he might say so, unless he prevented himself by that means. Yet I am sure they are both so considerate, good-humoured, and reasonable, that he might spare them. It is hard in him not to think of them a little more.

I stopped at the last full stop to read all this over. It looked at first as if I was taking on myself to understand and explain so much, that I was half inclined not to send it. But when I thought it over a little, I felt more hopeful for your knowing at once that I had only been watchful for you, and had only noticed what I think I have noticed, because I was quickened by your interest in it. Indeed, you may be sure that is the truth.

And now I have done with the subject in the present letter, and have little left to say.

We are all quite well, and Fanny improves every day. You can hardly think how kind she is to me, and what pains she takes with me. She has a lover, who has followed her, first all the way from Switzerland, and then all the way from Venice, and who has just confided to me that he means to follow her everywhere. I was much confused by his speaking to me about it, but he would. I did not know what to say, but at last I told him that I thought he had better not. For Fanny (but I did not tell him this) is much too spirited and clever to suit him. Still, he said he would, all the same. I have no lover, of course.

If you should ever get so far as this in this long letter, you will perhaps say, Surely Little Dorrit will not leave off without telling me something about her travels, and surely it is time she did. I think it is indeed, but I don't know what to tell you. Since we left Venice we have been in a great many wonderful places, Genoa and Florence among them, and have seen so many wonderful sights, that I am almost giddy when I think what a crowd they make. But you can tell me so much more about them than I can tell you, that why should I tire you with my accounts and descriptions?

Dear Mr Clennam, as I had the courage to tell you what the familiar difficulties in my travelling mind were before, I will not be a coward now. One of my frequent thoughts is this:—Old as these cities are, their age itself is hardly so curious, to my reflections, as that they should have been in their places all through those days when I did not even know of the existence of more than two or three of them, and when I scarcely knew of anything outside our old walls. There is something melancholy in it, and I don't know why. When we went to see the famous leaning tower at Pisa, it was a bright sunny day, and it and the buildings near it looked so old, and the earth and the sky looked so young, and its shadow on the ground was so soft and retired! I could not at first think how beautiful it was, or how curious, but I thought, 'O how many times when the shadow of the wall was falling on our room, and when that weary tread of feet was going up and down the yard—O how many times this place was just as quiet and lovely as it is to-day!' It quite overpowered me. My heart was so full that tears burst out of my eyes, though I did what I could to restrain them. And I have the same feeling often—often.

Do you know that since the change in our fortunes, though I appear to myself to have dreamed more than before, I have always dreamed of myself as very young indeed! I am not very old, you may say. No, but that is not what I mean. I have always dreamed of myself as a child learning to do needlework. I have often dreamed of myself as back there, seeing faces in the yard little known, and which I should have thought I had quite forgotten; but, as often as not, I have been abroad here—in Switzerland, or France, or Italy—somewhere where we have been—yet always as that little child. I have dreamed of going down to Mrs General, with the patches on my clothes in which I can first remember myself. I have over and over again dreamed of taking my place at dinner at Venice when we have had a large company, in the mourning for my poor mother which I wore when I was eight years old, and wore long after it was threadbare and would mend no more. It has been a great distress to me to think how irreconcilable the company would consider it with my father's wealth, and how I should displease and disgrace him and Fanny and Edward by so plainly disclosing what they wished to keep secret. But I have not grown out of the little child in thinking of it; and at the self-same moment I have dreamed that I have sat with the heart-ache at table, calculating the expenses of the dinner, and quite distracting myself with thinking how they were ever to be made good. I have never dreamed of the change in our fortunes itself; I have never dreamed of your coming back with me that memorable morning to break it; I have never even dreamed of you.

Dear Mr Clennam, it is possible that I have thought of you—and others—so much by day, that I have no thoughts left to wander round you by night. For I must now confess to you that I suffer from home-sickness—that I long so ardently and earnestly for home, as sometimes, when no one sees me, to pine for it. I cannot bear to turn my face further away from it. My heart is a little lightened when we turn towards it, even for a few miles, and with the knowledge that we are soon to turn away again. So dearly do I love the scene of my poverty and your kindness. O so dearly, O so dearly!

Heaven knows when your poor child will see England again. We are all fond of the life here (except me), and there are no plans for our return. My dear father talks of a visit to London late in this next spring, on some affairs connected with the property, but I have no hope that he will bring me with him.

I have tried to get on a little better under Mrs General's instruction, and I hope I am not quite so dull as I used to be. I have begun to speak and understand, almost easily, the hard languages I told you about. I did not remember, at the moment when I wrote last, that you knew them both; but I remembered it afterwards, and it helped me on. God bless you, dear Mr Clennam. Do not forget

Your ever grateful and affectionate

LITTLE DORRIT.=

P.S.—Particularly remember that Minnie Gowan deserves the best remembrance in which you can hold her. You cannot think too generously or too highly of her. I forgot Mr Pancks last time. Please, if you should see him, give him your Little Dorrit's kind regard. He was very good to Little D.

CHAPTER 12. In which a Great Patriotic Conference is holden

The famous name of Merdle became, every day, more famous in the land. Nobody knew that the Merdle of such high renown had ever done any good to any one, alive or dead, or to any earthly thing; nobody knew that he had any capacity or utterance of any sort in him, which had ever thrown, for any creature, the feeblest farthing-candle ray of light on any path of duty or diversion, pain or pleasure, toil or rest, fact or fancy, among the multiplicity of paths in the labyrinth trodden by the sons of Adam; nobody had the smallest reason for supposing the clay of which this object of worship was made, to be other than the commonest clay, with as clogged a wick smouldering inside of it as ever kept an image of humanity from tumbling to pieces. All people knew (or thought they knew) that he had made himself immensely rich; and, for that reason alone, prostrated themselves before him, more degradedly and less excusably than the darkest savage creeps out of his hole in the ground to propitiate, in some log or reptile, the Deity of his benighted soul.

Nay, the high priests of this worship had the man before them as a protest against their meanness. The multitude worshipped on trust—though always distinctly knowing why—but the officiators at the altar had the man habitually in their view. They sat at his feasts, and he sat at theirs. There was a spectre always attendant on him, saying to these high priests, 'Are such the signs you trust, and love to honour; this head, these eyes, this mode of speech, the tone and manner of this man? You are the levers of the Circumlocution Office, and the rulers of men. When half-a-dozen of you fall out by the ears, it seems that mother earth can give birth to no other rulers. Does your qualification lie in the superior knowledge of men which accepts, courts, and puffs this man? Or, if you are competent to judge aright the signs I never fail to show you when he appears among you, is your superior honesty your qualification?' Two rather ugly questions these, always going about town with Mr Merdle; and there was a tacit agreement that they must be stifled.

In Mrs Merdle's absence abroad, Mr Merdle still kept the great house open for the passage through it of a stream Of visitors. A few of these took affable possession of the establishment. Three or four ladies of distinction and liveliness used to say to one another, 'Let us dine at our dear Merdle's next Thursday. Whom shall we have?' Our dear Merdle would then receive his instructions; and would sit heavily among the company at table and wander lumpishly about his drawing-rooms afterwards, only remarkable for appearing to have nothing to do with the entertainment beyond being in its way.

The Chief Butler, the Avenging Spirit of this great man's life, relaxed nothing of his severity. He looked on at these dinners when the bosom was not there, as he looked on at other dinners when the bosom was there; and his eye was a basilisk to Mr Merdle. He was a hard man, and would never bate an ounce of plate or a bottle of wine. He would not allow a dinner to be given, unless it was up to his mark. He set forth the table for his own dignity. If the guests chose to partake of what was served, he saw no objection; but it was served for the maintenance of his rank. As he stood by the sideboard he seemed to announce, 'I have accepted office to look at this which is now before me, and to look at nothing less than this.' If he missed the presiding bosom, it was as a part of his own state of which he was, from unavoidable circumstances, temporarily deprived, just as he might have missed a centre-piece, or a choice wine-cooler, which had been sent to the Banker's.

Mr Merdle issued invitations for a Barnacle dinner. Lord Decimus was to be there, Mr Tite Barnacle was to be there, the pleasant young Barnacle was to be there; and the Chorus of Parliamentary Barnacles who went about the provinces when the House was up, warbling the praises of their Chief, were to be represented there. It was understood to be a great occasion. Mr Merdle was going to take up the Barnacles. Some delicate little negotiations had occurred between him and the noble Decimus—the young Barnacle of engaging manners acting as negotiator—and Mr Merdle had decided to cast the weight of his great probity and great riches into the Barnacle scale. Jobbery was suspected by the malicious; perhaps because it was indisputable that if the adherence of the immortal Enemy of Mankind could have been secured by a job, the Barnacles would have jobbed him—for the good of the country, for the good of the country.

Mrs Merdle had written to this magnificent spouse of hers, whom it was heresy to regard as anything less than all the British Merchants since the days of Whittington rolled into one, and gilded three feet deep all over—had written to this spouse of hers, several letters from Rome, in quick succession, urging upon him with importunity that now or never was the time to provide for Edmund Sparkler. Mrs Merdle had shown him that the case of Edmund was urgent, and that infinite advantages might result from his having some good thing directly. In the grammar of Mrs Merdle's verbs on this momentous subject, there was only one mood, the Imperative; and that Mood had only one Tense, the Present. Mrs Merdle's verbs were so pressingly presented to Mr Merdle to conjugate, that his sluggish blood and his long coat-cuffs became quite agitated.

In which state of agitation, Mr Merdle, evasively rolling his eyes round the Chief Butler's shoes without raising them to the index of that stupendous creature's thoughts, had signified to him his intention of giving a special dinner: not a very large dinner, but a very special dinner. The Chief Butler had signified, in return, that he had no objection to look on at the most expensive thing in that way that could be done; and the day of the dinner was now come.

Mr Merdle stood in one of his drawing-rooms, with his back to the fire, waiting for the arrival of his important guests. He seldom or never took the liberty of standing with his back to the fire unless he was quite alone. In the presence of the Chief Butler, he could not have done such a deed. He would have clasped himself by the wrists in that constabulary manner of his, and have paced up and down the hearthrug, or gone creeping about among the rich objects of furniture, if his oppressive retainer had appeared in the room at that very moment. The sly shadows which seemed to dart out of hiding when the fire rose, and to dart back into it when the fire fell, were sufficient witnesses of his making himself so easy. They were even more than sufficient, if his uncomfortable glances at them might be taken to mean anything.

Mr Merdle's right hand was filled with the evening paper, and the evening paper was full of Mr Merdle. His wonderful enterprise, his wonderful wealth, his wonderful Bank, were the fattening food of the evening paper that night. The wonderful Bank, of which he was the chief projector, establisher, and manager, was the latest of the many Merdle wonders. So modest was Mr Merdle withal, in the midst of these splendid achievements, that he looked far more like a man in possession of his house under a distraint, than a commercial Colossus bestriding his own hearthrug, while the little ships were sailing into dinner.

Behold the vessels coming into port! The engaging young Barnacle was the first arrival; but Bar overtook him on the staircase. Bar, strengthened as usual with his double eye-glass and his little jury droop, was overjoyed to see the engaging young Barnacle; and opined that we were going to sit in Banco, as we lawyers called it, to take a special argument?

'Indeed,' said the sprightly young Barnacle, whose name was Ferdinand; 'how so?'

'Nay,' smiled Bar. 'If you don't know, how can I know? You are in the innermost sanctuary of the temple; I am one of the admiring concourse on the plain without.'

Bar could be light in hand, or heavy in hand, according to the customer he had to deal with. With Ferdinand Barnacle he was gossamer. Bar was likewise always modest and self-depreciatory—in his way. Bar was a man of great variety; but one leading thread ran through the woof of all his patterns. Every man with whom he had to do was in his eyes a jury-man; and he must get that jury-man over, if he could.

'Our illustrious host and friend,' said Bar; 'our shining mercantile star;—going into politics?'

'Going? He has been in Parliament some time, you know,' returned the engaging young Barnacle.

'True,' said Bar, with his light-comedy laugh for special jury-men, which was a very different thing from his low-comedy laugh for comic tradesmen on common juries: 'he has been in Parliament for some time. Yet hitherto our star has been a vacillating and wavering star? Humph?'

An average witness would have been seduced by the Humph? into an affirmative answer, But Ferdinand Barnacle looked knowingly at Bar as he strolled up-stairs, and gave him no answer at all.

'Just so, just so,' said Bar, nodding his head, for he was not to be put off in that way, 'and therefore I spoke of our sitting in Banco to take a special argument—meaning this to be a high and solemn occasion, when, as Captain Macheath says, "the judges are met: a terrible show!" We lawyers are sufficiently liberal, you see, to quote the Captain, though the Captain is severe upon us. Nevertheless, I think I could put in evidence an admission of the Captain's,' said Bar, with a little jocose roll of his head; for, in his legal current of speech, he always assumed the air of rallying himself with the best grace in the world; 'an admission of the Captain's that Law, in the gross, is at least intended to be impartial. For what says the Captain, if I quote him correctly—and if not,' with a light-comedy touch of his double eye-glass on his companion's shoulder, 'my learned friend will set me right:

"Since laws were made for every degree,

To curb vice in others as well as in me,

I wonder we ha'n't better company

Upon Tyburn Tree!"'

These words brought them to the drawing-room, where Mr Merdle stood before the fire. So immensely astounded was Mr Merdle by the entrance of Bar with such a reference in his mouth, that Bar explained himself to have been quoting Gay. 'Assuredly not one of our Westminster Hall authorities,' said he, 'but still no despicable one to a man possessing the largely-practical Mr Merdle's knowledge of the world.'

Mr Merdle looked as if he thought he would say something, but subsequently looked as if he thought he wouldn't. The interval afforded time for Bishop to be announced.

Bishop came in with meekness, and yet with a strong and rapid step as if he wanted to get his seven-league dress-shoes on, and go round the world to see that everybody was in a satisfactory state. Bishop had no idea that there was anything significant in the occasion. That was the most remarkable trait in his demeanour. He was crisp, fresh, cheerful, affable, bland; but so surprisingly innocent.

Bar sidled up to prefer his politest inquiries in reference to the health of Mrs Bishop. Mrs Bishop had been a little unfortunate in the article of taking cold at a Confirmation, but otherwise was well. Young Mr Bishop was also well. He was down, with his young wife and little family, at his Cure of Souls.

The representatives of the Barnacle Chorus dropped in next, and Mr Merdle's physician dropped in next. Bar, who had a bit of one eye and a bit of his double eye-glass for every one who came in at the door, no matter with whom he was conversing or what he was talking about, got among them all by some skilful means, without being seen to get at them, and touched each individual gentleman of the jury on his own individual favourite spot. With some of the Chorus, he laughed about the sleepy member who had gone out into the lobby the other night, and voted the wrong way: with others, he deplored that innovating spirit in the time which could not even be prevented from taking an unnatural interest in the public service and the public money: with the physician he had a word to say about the general health; he had also a little information to ask him for, concerning a professional man of unquestioned erudition and polished manners—but those credentials in their highest development he believed were the possession of other professors of the healing art (jury droop)—whom he had happened to have in the witness-box the day before yesterday, and from whom he had elicited in cross-examination that he claimed to be one of the exponents of this new mode of treatment which appeared to Bar to—eh?—well, Bar thought so; Bar had thought, and hoped, Physician would tell him so. Without presuming to decide where doctors disagreed, it did appear to Bar, viewing it as a question of common sense and not of so-called legal penetration, that this new system was—might be, in the presence of so great an authority—say, Humbug? Ah! Fortified by such encouragement, he could venture to say Humbug; and now Bar's mind was relieved.

Mr Tite Barnacle, who, like Dr Johnson's celebrated acquaintance, had only one idea in his head and that was a wrong one, had appeared by this time. This eminent gentleman and Mr Merdle, seated diverse ways and with ruminating aspects on a yellow ottoman in the light of the fire, holding no verbal communication with each other, bore a strong general resemblance to the two cows in the Cuyp picture over against them.

But now, Lord Decimus arrived. The Chief Butler, who up to this time had limited himself to a branch of his usual function by looking at the company as they entered (and that, with more of defiance than favour), put himself so far out of his way as to come up-stairs with him and announce him. Lord Decimus being an overpowering peer, a bashful young member of the Lower House who was the last fish but one caught by the Barnacles, and who had been invited on this occasion to commemorate his capture, shut his eyes when his Lordship came in.

Lord Decimus, nevertheless, was glad to see the Member. He was also glad to see Mr Merdle, glad to see Bishop, glad to see Bar, glad to see Physician, glad to see Tite Barnacle, glad to see Chorus, glad to see Ferdinand his private secretary. Lord Decimus, though one of the greatest of the earth, was not remarkable for ingratiatory manners, and Ferdinand had coached him up to the point of noticing all the fellows he might find there, and saying he was glad to see them. When he had achieved this rush of vivacity and condescension, his Lordship composed himself into the picture after Cuyp, and made a third cow in the group.

Bar, who felt that he had got all the rest of the jury and must now lay hold of the Foreman, soon came sidling up, double eye-glass in hand. Bar tendered the weather, as a subject neatly aloof from official reserve, for the Foreman's consideration. Bar said that he was told (as everybody always is told, though who tells them, and why, will ever remain a mystery), that there was to be no wall-fruit this year. Lord Decimus had not heard anything amiss of his peaches, but rather believed, if his people were correct, he was to have no apples. No apples? Bar was lost in astonishment and concern. It would have been all one to him, in reality, if there had not been a pippin on the surface of the earth, but his show of interest in this apple question was positively painful. Now, to what, Lord Decimus—for we troublesome lawyers loved to gather information, and could never tell how useful it might prove to us—to what, Lord Decimus, was this to be attributed? Lord Decimus could not undertake to propound any theory about it. This might have stopped another man; but Bar, sticking to him fresh as ever, said, 'As to pears, now?'

Long after Bar got made Attorney-General, this was told of him as a master-stroke. Lord Decimus had a reminiscence about a pear-tree formerly growing in a garden near the back of his dame's house at Eton, upon which pear-tree the only joke of his life perennially bloomed. It was a joke of a compact and portable nature, turning on the difference between Eton pears and Parliamentary pairs; but it was a joke, a refined relish of which would seem to have appeared to Lord Decimus impossible to be had without a thorough and intimate acquaintance with the tree. Therefore, the story at first had no idea of such a tree, sir, then gradually found it in winter, carried it through the changing season, saw it bud, saw it blossom, saw it bear fruit, saw the fruit ripen; in short, cultivated the tree in that diligent and minute manner before it got out of the bed-room window to steal the fruit, that many thanks had been offered up by belated listeners for the trees having been planted and grafted prior to Lord Decimus's time. Bar's interest in apples was so overtopped by the wrapt suspense in which he pursued the changes of these pears, from the moment when Lord Decimus solemnly opened with 'Your mentioning pears recalls to my remembrance a pear-tree,' down to the rich conclusion, 'And so we pass, through the various changes of life, from Eton pears to Parliamentary pairs,' that he had to go down-stairs with Lord Decimus, and even then to be seated next to him at table in order that he might hear the anecdote out. By that time, Bar felt that he had secured the Foreman, and might go to dinner with a good appetite.

It was a dinner to provoke an appetite, though he had not had one. The rarest dishes, sumptuously cooked and sumptuously served; the choicest fruits; the most exquisite wines; marvels of workmanship in gold and silver, china and glass; innumerable things delicious to the senses of taste, smell, and sight, were insinuated into its composition. O, what a wonderful man this Merdle, what a great man, what a master man, how blessedly and enviably endowed— in one word, what a rich man!

He took his usual poor eighteenpennyworth of food in his usual indigestive way, and had as little to say for himself as ever a wonderful man had. Fortunately Lord Decimus was one of those sublimities who have no occasion to be talked to, for they can be at any time sufficiently occupied with the contemplation of their own greatness. This enabled the bashful young Member to keep his eyes open long enough at a time to see his dinner. But, whenever Lord Decimus spoke, he shut them again.

The agreeable young Barnacle, and Bar, were the talkers of the party. Bishop would have been exceedingly agreeable also, but that his innocence stood in his way. He was so soon left behind. When there was any little hint of anything being in the wind, he got lost directly. Worldly affairs were too much for him; he couldn't make them out at all.

This was observable when Bar said, incidentally, that he was happy to have heard that we were soon to have the advantage of enlisting on the good side, the sound and plain sagacity— not demonstrative or ostentatious, but thoroughly sound and practical—of our friend Mr Sparkler.

Ferdinand Barnacle laughed, and said oh yes, he believed so. A vote was a vote, and always acceptable.

Bar was sorry to miss our good friend Mr Sparkler to-day, Mr Merdle.

'He is away with Mrs Merdle,' returned that gentleman, slowly coming out of a long abstraction, in the course of which he had been fitting a tablespoon up his sleeve. 'It is not indispensable for him to be on the spot.'

'The magic name of Merdle,' said Bar, with the jury droop, 'no doubt will suffice for all.'

'Why—yes—I believe so,' assented Mr Merdle, putting the spoon aside, and clumsily hiding each of his hands in the coat-cuff of the other hand. 'I believe the people in my interest down there will not make any difficulty.'

'Model people!' said Bar.

'I am glad you approve of them,' said Mr Merdle.

'And the people of those other two places, now,' pursued Bar, with a bright twinkle in his keen eye, as it slightly turned in the direction of his magnificent neighbour; 'we lawyers are always curious, always inquisitive, always picking up odds and ends for our patchwork minds, since there is no knowing when and where they may fit into some corner;—the people of those other two places now? Do they yield so laudably to the vast and cumulative influence of such enterprise and such renown; do those little rills become absorbed so quietly and easily, and, as it were by the influence of natural laws, so beautifully, in the swoop of the majestic stream as it flows upon its wondrous way enriching the surrounding lands; that their course is perfectly to be calculated, and distinctly to be predicated?'

Mr Merdle, a little troubled by Bar's eloquence, looked fitfully about the nearest salt-cellar for some moments, and then said hesitating:

'They are perfectly aware, sir, of their duty to Society. They will return anybody I send to them for that purpose.'

'Cheering to know,' said Bar. 'Cheering to know.'

The three places in question were three little rotten holes in this Island, containing three little ignorant, drunken, guzzling, dirty, out-of-the-way constituencies, that had reeled into Mr Merdle's pocket. Ferdinand Barnacle laughed in his easy way, and airily said they were a nice set of fellows. Bishop, mentally perambulating among paths of peace, was altogether swallowed up in absence of mind.

'Pray,' asked Lord Decimus, casting his eyes around the table, 'what is this story I have heard of a gentleman long confined in a debtors' prison proving to be of a wealthy family, and having come into the inheritance of a large sum of money? I have met with a variety of allusions to it. Do you know anything of it, Ferdinand?'

'I only know this much,' said Ferdinand, 'that he has given the Department with which I have the honour to be associated;' this sparkling young Barnacle threw off the phrase sportively, as who should say, We know all about these forms of speech, but we must keep it up, we must keep the game alive; 'no end of trouble, and has put us into innumerable fixes.'

'Fixes?' repeated Lord Decimus, with a majestic pausing and pondering on the word that made the bashful Member shut his eyes quite tight. 'Fixes?'

'A very perplexing business indeed,' observed Mr Tite Barnacle, with an air of grave resentment.

'What,' said Lord Decimus, 'was the character of his business; what was the nature of these—a—Fixes, Ferdinand?'

'Oh, it's a good story, as a story,' returned that gentleman; 'as good a thing of its kind as need be. This Mr Dorrit (his name is Dorrit) had incurred a responsibility to us, ages before the fairy came out of the Bank and gave him his fortune, under a bond he had signed for the performance of a contract which was not at all performed. He was a partner in a house in some large way—spirits, or buttons, or wine, or blacking, or oatmeal, or woollen, or pork, or hooks and eyes, or iron, or treacle, or shoes, or something or other that was wanted for troops, or seamen, or somebody—and the house burst, and we being among the creditors, detainees were lodged on the part of the Crown in a scientific manner, and all the rest of it. When the fairy had appeared and he wanted to pay us off, Egad we had got into such an exemplary state of checking and counter-checking, signing and counter-signing, that it was six months before we knew how to take the money, or how to give a receipt for it. It was a triumph of public business,' said this handsome young Barnacle, laughing heartily, 'You never saw such a lot of forms in your life. "Why," the attorney said to me one day, "if I wanted this office to give me two or three thousand pounds instead of take it, I couldn't have more trouble about it." "You are right, old fellow," I told him, "and in future you'll know that we have something to do here."' The pleasant young Barnacle finished by once more laughing heartily. He was a very easy, pleasant fellow indeed, and his manners were exceedingly winning.

Mr Tite Barnacle's view of the business was of a less airy character. He took it ill that Mr Dorrit had troubled the Department by wanting to pay the money, and considered it a grossly informal thing to do after so many years. But Mr Tite Barnacle was a buttoned-up man, and consequently a weighty one. All buttoned-up men are weighty. All buttoned-up men are believed in. Whether or no the reserved and never-exercised power of unbuttoning, fascinates mankind; whether or no wisdom is supposed to condense and augment when buttoned up, and to evaporate when unbuttoned; it is certain that the man to whom importance is accorded is the buttoned-up man. Mr Tite Barnacle never would have passed for half his current value, unless his coat had been always buttoned-up to his white cravat.

'May I ask,' said Lord Decimus, 'if Mr Darrit—or Dorrit—has any family?'

Nobody else replying, the host said, 'He has two daughters, my lord.'

'Oh! you are acquainted with him?' asked Lord Decimus.

'Mrs Merdle is. Mr Sparkler is, too. In fact,' said Mr Merdle, 'I rather believe that one of the young ladies has made an impression on Edmund Sparkler. He is susceptible, and—I—think—the conquest—' Here Mr Merdle stopped, and looked at the table-cloth, as he usually did when he found himself observed or listened to.

Bar was uncommonly pleased to find that the Merdle family, and this family, had already been brought into contact. He submitted, in a low voice across the table to Bishop, that it was a kind of analogical illustration of those physical laws, in virtue of which Like flies to Like. He regarded this power of attraction in wealth to draw wealth to it, as something remarkably interesting and curious—something indefinably allied to the loadstone and gravitation. Bishop, who had ambled back to earth again when the present theme was broached, acquiesced. He said it was indeed highly important to Society that one in the trying situation of unexpectedly finding himself invested with a power for good or for evil in Society, should become, as it were, merged in the superior power of a more legitimate and more gigantic growth, the influence of which (as in the case of our friend at whose board we sat) was habitually exercised in harmony with the best interests of Society. Thus, instead of two rival and contending flames, a larger and a lesser, each burning with a lurid and uncertain glare, we had a blended and a softened light whose genial ray diffused an equable warmth throughout the land. Bishop seemed to like his own way of putting the case very much, and rather dwelt upon it; Bar, meanwhile (not to throw away a jury-man), making a show of sitting at his feet and feeding on his precepts.

The dinner and dessert being three hours long, the bashful Member cooled in the shadow of Lord Decimus faster than he warmed with food and drink, and had but a chilly time of it. Lord Decimus, like a tall tower in a flat country, seemed to project himself across the table-cloth, hide the light from the honourable Member, cool the honourable Member's marrow, and give him a woeful idea of distance. When he asked this unfortunate traveller to take wine, he encompassed his faltering steps with the gloomiest of shades; and when he said, 'Your health sir!' all around him was barrenness and desolation.

At length Lord Decimus, with a coffee-cup in his hand, began to hover about among the pictures, and to cause an interesting speculation to arise in all minds as to the probabilities of his ceasing to hover, and enabling the smaller birds to flutter up-stairs; which could not be done until he had urged his noble pinions in that direction. After some delay, and several stretches of his wings which came to nothing, he soared to the drawing-rooms.

And here a difficulty arose, which always does arise when two people are specially brought together at a dinner to confer with one another. Everybody (except Bishop, who had no suspicion of it) knew perfectly well that this dinner had been eaten and drunk, specifically to the end that Lord Decimus and Mr Merdle should have five minutes' conversation together. The opportunity so elaborately prepared was now arrived, and it seemed from that moment that no mere human ingenuity could so much as get the two chieftains into the same room. Mr Merdle and his noble guest persisted in prowling about at opposite ends of the perspective. It was in vain for the engaging Ferdinand to bring Lord Decimus to look at the bronze horses near Mr Merdle. Then Mr Merdle evaded, and wandered away. It was in vain for him to bring Mr Merdle to Lord Decimus to tell him the history of the unique Dresden vases. Then Lord Decimus evaded and wandered away, while he was getting his man up to the mark.

'Did you ever see such a thing as this?' said Ferdinand to Bar when he had been baffled twenty times.

'Often,' returned Bar.

'Unless I butt one of them into an appointed corner, and you butt the other,' said Ferdinand, 'it will not come off after all.'

'Very good,' said Bar. 'I'll butt Merdle, if you like; but not my lord.'

Ferdinand laughed, in the midst of his vexation. 'Confound them both!' said he, looking at his watch. 'I want to get away. Why the deuce can't they come together! They both know what they want and mean to do. Look at them!'

They were still looming at opposite ends of the perspective, each with an absurd pretence of not having the other on his mind, which could not have been more transparently ridiculous though his real mind had been chalked on his back. Bishop, who had just now made a third with Bar and Ferdinand, but whose innocence had again cut him out of the subject and washed him in sweet oil, was seen to approach Lord Decimus and glide into conversation.

'I must get Merdle's doctor to catch and secure him, I suppose,' said Ferdinand; 'and then I must lay hold of my illustrious kinsman, and decoy him if I can—drag him if I can't—to the conference.'

'Since you do me the honour,' said Bar, with his slyest smile, to ask for my poor aid, it shall be yours with the greatest pleasure. I don't think this is to be done by one man. But if you will undertake to pen my lord into that furthest drawing-room where he is now so profoundly engaged, I will undertake to bring our dear Merdle into the presence, without the possibility of getting away.'

'Done!' said Ferdinand. 'Done!' said Bar.

Bar was a sight wondrous to behold, and full of matter, when, jauntily waving his double eye-glass by its ribbon, and jauntily drooping to an Universe of Jurymen, he, in the most accidental manner ever seen, found himself at Mr Merdle's shoulder, and embraced that opportunity of mentioning a little point to him, on which he particularly wished to be guided by the light of his practical knowledge. (Here he took Mr Merdle's arm and walked him gently away.) A banker, whom we would call A. B., advanced a considerable sum of money, which we would call fifteen thousand pounds, to a client or customer of his, whom he would call P. Q. (Here, as they were getting towards Lord Decimus, he held Mr Merdle tight.) As a security for the repayment of this advance to P. Q. whom we would call a widow lady, there were placed in A. B.'s hands the title-deeds of a freehold estate, which we would call Blinkiter Doddles. Now, the point was this. A limited right of felling and lopping in the woods of Blinkiter Doddles, lay in the son of P. Q. then past his majority, and whom we would call X. Y.—but really this was too bad! In the presence of Lord Decimus, to detain the host with chopping our dry chaff of law, was really too bad! Another time! Bar was truly repentant, and would not say another syllable. Would Bishop favour him with half-a-dozen words? (He had now set Mr Merdle down on a couch, side by side with Lord Decimus, and to it they must go, now or never.)

And now the rest of the company, highly excited and interested, always excepting Bishop, who had not the slightest idea that anything was going on, formed in one group round the fire in the next drawing-room, and pretended to be chatting easily on the infinite variety of small topics, while everybody's thoughts and eyes were secretly straying towards the secluded pair. The Chorus were excessively nervous, perhaps as labouring under the dreadful apprehension that some good thing was going to be diverted from them! Bishop alone talked steadily and evenly. He conversed with the great Physician on that relaxation of the throat with which young curates were too frequently afflicted, and on the means of lessening the great prevalence of that disorder in the church. Physician, as a general rule, was of opinion that the best way to avoid it was to know how to read, before you made a profession of reading. Bishop said dubiously, did he really think so? And Physician said, decidedly, yes he did.

Ferdinand, meanwhile, was the only one of the party who skirmished on the outside of the circle; he kept about mid-way between it and the two, as if some sort of surgical operation were being performed by Lord Decimus on Mr Merdle, or by Mr Merdle on Lord Decimus, and his services might at any moment be required as Dresser. In fact, within a quarter of an hour Lord Decimus called to him 'Ferdinand!' and he went, and took his place in the conference for some five minutes more. Then a half-suppressed gasp broke out among the Chorus; for Lord Decimus rose to take his leave. Again coached up by Ferdinand to the point of making himself popular, he shook hands in the most brilliant manner with the whole company, and even said to Bar, 'I hope you were not bored by my pears?' To which Bar retorted, 'Eton, my lord, or Parliamentary?' neatly showing that he had mastered the joke, and delicately insinuating that he could never forget it while his life remained.

All the grave importance that was buttoned up in Mr Tite Barnacle, took itself away next; and Ferdinand took himself away next, to the opera. Some of the rest lingered a little, marrying golden liqueur glasses to Buhl tables with sticky rings; on the desperate chance of Mr Merdle's saying something. But Merdle, as usual, oozed sluggishly and muddily about his drawing-room, saying never a word.

In a day or two it was announced to all the town, that Edmund Sparkler, Esquire, son-in-law of the eminent Mr Merdle of worldwide renown, was made one of the Lords of the Circumlocution Office; and proclamation was issued, to all true believers, that this admirable appointment was to be hailed as a graceful and gracious mark of homage, rendered by the graceful and gracious Decimus, to that commercial interest which must ever in a great commercial country—and all the rest of it, with blast of trumpet. So, bolstered by this mark of Government homage, the wonderful Bank and all the other wonderful undertakings went on and went up; and gapers came to Harley Street, Cavendish Square, only to look at the house where the golden wonder lived.

And when they saw the Chief Butler looking out at the hall-door in his moments of condescension, the gapers said how rich he looked, and wondered how much money he had in the wonderful Bank. But, if they had known that respectable Nemesis better, they would not have wondered about it, and might have stated the amount with the utmost precision.

CHAPTER 13. The Progress of an Epidemic

That it is at least as difficult to stay a moral infection as a physical one; that such a disease will spread with the malignity and rapidity of the Plague; that the contagion, when it has once made head, will spare no pursuit or condition, but will lay hold on people in the soundest health, and become developed in the most unlikely constitutions: is a fact as firmly established by experience as that we human creatures breathe an atmosphere. A blessing beyond appreciation would be conferred upon mankind, if the tainted, in whose weakness or wickedness these virulent disorders are bred, could be instantly seized and placed in close confinement (not to say summarily smothered) before the poison is communicable.

As a vast fire will fill the air to a great distance with its roar, so the sacred flame which the mighty Barnacles had fanned caused the air to resound more and more with the name of Merdle. It was deposited on every lip, and carried into every ear. There never was, there never had been, there never again should be, such a man as Mr Merdle. Nobody, as aforesaid, knew what he had done; but everybody knew him to be the greatest that had appeared.

Down in Bleeding Heart Yard, where there was not one unappropriated halfpenny, as lively an interest was taken in this paragon of men as on the Stock Exchange. Mrs Plornish, now established in the small grocery and general trade in a snug little shop at the crack end of the Yard, at the top of the steps, with her little old father and Maggy acting as assistants, habitually held forth about him over the counter in conversation with her customers. Mr Plornish, who had a small share in a small builder's business in the neighbourhood, said, trowel in hand, on the tops of scaffolds and on the tiles of houses, that people did tell him as Mr Merdle was the one, mind you, to put us all to rights in respects of that which all on us looked to, and to bring us all safe home as much as we needed, mind you, fur toe be brought. Mr Baptist, sole lodger of Mr and Mrs Plornish was reputed in whispers to lay by the savings which were the result of his simple and moderate life, for investment in one of Mr Merdle's certain enterprises. The female Bleeding Hearts, when they came for ounces of tea, and hundredweights of talk, gave Mrs Plornish to understand, That how, ma'am, they had heard from their cousin Mary Anne, which worked in the line, that his lady's dresses would fill three waggons. That how she was as handsome a lady, ma'am, as lived, no matter wheres, and a busk like marble itself. That how, according to what they was told, ma'am, it was her son by a former husband as was took into the Government; and a General he had been, and armies he had marched again and victory crowned, if all you heard was to be believed. That how it was reported that Mr Merdle's words had been, that if they could have made it worth his while to take the whole Government he would have took it without a profit, but that take it he could not and stand a loss. That how it was not to be expected, ma'am, that he should lose by it, his ways being, as you might say and utter no falsehood, paved with gold; but that how it was much to be regretted that something handsome hadn't been got up to make it worth his while; for it was such and only such that knowed the heighth to which the bread and butchers' meat had rose, and it was such and only such that both could and would bring that heighth down.

So rife and potent was the fever in Bleeding Heart Yard, that Mr Pancks's rent-days caused no interval in the patients. The disease took the singular form, on those occasions, of causing the infected to find an unfathomable excuse and consolation in allusions to the magic name.

'Now, then!' Mr Pancks would say, to a defaulting lodger. 'Pay up! Come on!'

'I haven't got it, Mr Pancks,' Defaulter would reply. 'I tell you the truth, sir, when I say I haven't got so much as a single sixpence of it to bless myself with.'

'This won't do, you know,' Mr Pancks would retort. 'You don't expect it will do; do you?'

Defaulter would admit, with a low-spirited 'No, sir,' having no such expectation.

'My proprietor isn't going to stand this, you know,' Mr Pancks would proceed. 'He don't send me here for this. Pay up! Come!'

The Defaulter would make answer, 'Ah, Mr Pancks. If I was the rich gentleman whose name is in everybody's mouth—if my name was Merdle, sir—I'd soon pay up, and be glad to do it.'

Dialogues on the rent-question usually took place at the house-doors or in the entries, and in the presence of several deeply interested Bleeding Hearts. They always received a reference of this kind with a low murmur of response, as if it were convincing; and the Defaulter, however black and discomfited before, always cheered up a little in making it.

'If I was Mr Merdle, sir, you wouldn't have cause to complain of me then. No, believe me!' the Defaulter would proceed with a shake of the head. 'I'd pay up so quick then, Mr Pancks, that you shouldn't have to ask me.'

The response would be heard again here, implying that it was impossible to say anything fairer, and that this was the next thing to paying the money down.

Mr Pancks would be now reduced to saying as he booked the case, 'Well! You'll have the broker in, and be turned out; that's what'll happen to you. It's no use talking to me about Mr Merdle. You are not Mr Merdle, any more than I am.'

'No, sir,' the Defaulter would reply. 'I only wish you were him, sir.'

The response would take this up quickly; replying with great feeling, 'Only wish you were him, sir.'

'You'd be easier with us if you were Mr Merdle, sir,' the Defaulter would go on with rising spirits, 'and it would be better for all parties. Better for our sakes, and better for yours, too. You wouldn't have to worry no one, then, sir. You wouldn't have to worry us, and you wouldn't have to worry yourself. You'd be easier in your own mind, sir, and you'd leave others easier, too, you would, if you were Mr Merdle.'

Mr Pancks, in whom these impersonal compliments produced an irresistible sheepishness, never rallied after such a charge. He could only bite his nails and puff away to the next Defaulter. The responsive Bleeding Hearts would then gather round the Defaulter whom he had just abandoned, and the most extravagant rumours would circulate among them, to their great comfort, touching the amount of Mr Merdle's ready money.

From one of the many such defeats of one of many rent-days, Mr Pancks, having finished his day's collection, repaired with his note-book under his arm to Mrs Plornish's corner. Mr Pancks's object was not professional, but social. He had had a trying day, and wanted a little brightening. By this time he was on friendly terms with the Plornish family, having often looked in upon them at similar seasons, and borne his part in recollections of Miss Dorrit.

Mrs Plornish's shop-parlour had been decorated under her own eye, and presented, on the side towards the shop, a little fiction in which Mrs Plornish unspeakably rejoiced. This poetical heightening of the parlour consisted in the wall being painted to represent the exterior of a thatched cottage; the artist having introduced (in as effective a manner as he found compatible with their highly disproportionate dimensions) the real door and window. The modest sunflower and hollyhock were depicted as flourishing with great luxuriance on this rustic dwelling, while a quantity of dense smoke issuing from the chimney indicated good cheer within, and also, perhaps, that it had not been lately swept. A faithful dog was represented as flying at the legs of the friendly visitor, from the threshold; and a circular pigeon-house, enveloped in a cloud of pigeons, arose from behind the garden-paling. On the door (when it was shut), appeared the semblance of a brass-plate, presenting the inscription, Happy Cottage, T. and M. Plornish; the partnership expressing man and wife. No Poetry and no Art ever charmed the imagination more than the union of the two in this counterfeit cottage charmed Mrs Plornish. It was nothing to her that Plornish had a habit of leaning against it as he smoked his pipe after work, when his hat blotted out the pigeon-house and all the pigeons, when his back swallowed up the dwelling, when his hands in his pockets uprooted the blooming garden and laid waste the adjacent country. To Mrs Plornish, it was still a most beautiful cottage, a most wonderful deception; and it made no difference that Mr Plornish's eye was some inches above the level of the gable bed-room in the thatch. To come out into the shop after it was shut, and hear her father sing a song inside this cottage, was a perfect Pastoral to Mrs Plornish, the Golden Age revived. And truly if that famous period had been revived, or had ever been at all, it may be doubted whether it would have produced many more heartily admiring daughters than the poor woman.

Warned of a visitor by the tinkling bell at the shop-door, Mrs Plornish came out of Happy Cottage to see who it might be. 'I guessed it was you, Mr Pancks,' said she, 'for it's quite your regular night; ain't it? Here's father, you see, come out to serve at the sound of the bell, like a brisk young shopman. Ain't he looking well? Father's more pleased to see you than if you was a customer, for he dearly loves a gossip; and when it turns upon Miss Dorrit, he loves it all the more. You never heard father in such voice as he is at present,' said Mrs Plornish, her own voice quavering, she was so proud and pleased. 'He gave us Strephon last night to that degree that Plornish gets up and makes him this speech across the table. "John Edward Nandy," says Plornish to father, "I never heard you come the warbles as I have heard you come the warbles this night." An't it gratifying, Mr Pancks, though; really?'

Mr Pancks, who had snorted at the old man in his friendliest manner, replied in the affirmative, and casually asked whether that lively Altro chap had come in yet? Mrs Plornish answered no, not yet, though he had gone to the West-End with some work, and had said he should be back by tea-time. Mr Pancks was then hospitably pressed into Happy Cottage, where he encountered the elder Master Plornish just come home from school. Examining that young student, lightly, on the educational proceedings of the day, he found that the more advanced pupils who were in the large text and the letter M, had been set the copy 'Merdle, Millions.'

'And how are you getting on, Mrs Plornish,' said Pancks, 'since we're mentioning millions?'

'Very steady, indeed, sir,' returned Mrs Plornish. 'Father, dear, would you go into the shop and tidy the window a little bit before tea, your taste being so beautiful?'

John Edward Nandy trotted away, much gratified, to comply with his daughter's request. Mrs Plornish, who was always in mortal terror of mentioning pecuniary affairs before the old gentleman, lest any disclosure she made might rouse his spirit and induce him to run away to the workhouse, was thus left free to be confidential with Mr Pancks.

'It's quite true that the business is very steady indeed,' said Mrs Plornish, lowering her voice; 'and has a excellent connection. The only thing that stands in its way, sir, is the Credit.'

This drawback, rather severely felt by most people who engaged in commercial transactions with the inhabitants of Bleeding Heart Yard, was a large stumbling-block in Mrs Plornish's trade. When Mr Dorrit had established her in the business, the Bleeding Hearts had shown an amount of emotion and a determination to support her in it, that did honour to human nature. Recognising her claim upon their generous feelings as one who had long been a member of their community, they pledged themselves, with great feeling, to deal with Mrs Plornish, come what would and bestow their patronage on no other establishment. Influenced by these noble sentiments, they had even gone out of their way to purchase little luxuries in the grocery and butter line to which they were unaccustomed; saying to one another, that if they did stretch a point, was it not for a neighbour and a friend, and for whom ought a point to be stretched if not for such? So stimulated, the business was extremely brisk, and the articles in stock went off with the greatest celerity. In short, if the

Bleeding Hearts had but paid, the undertaking would have been a complete success; whereas, by reason of their exclusively confining themselves to owing, the profits actually realised had not yet begun to appear in the books.

Mr Pancks was making a very porcupine of himself by sticking his hair up in the contemplation of this state of accounts, when old Mr Nandy, re-entering the cottage with an air of mystery, entreated them to come and look at the strange behaviour of Mr Baptist, who seemed to have met with something that had scared him. All three going into the shop, and watching through the window, then saw Mr Baptist, pale and agitated, go through the following extraordinary performances. First, he was observed hiding at the top of the steps leading down into the Yard, and peeping up and down the street with his head cautiously thrust out close to the side of the shop-door. After very anxious scrutiny, he came out of his retreat, and went briskly down the street as if he were going away altogether; then, suddenly turned about, and went, at the same pace, and with the same feint, up the street. He had gone no further up the street than he had gone down, when he crossed the road and disappeared. The object of this last manoeuvre was only apparent, when his entering the shop with a sudden twist, from the steps again, explained that he had made a wide and obscure circuit round to the other, or Doyce and Clennam, end of the Yard, and had come through the Yard and bolted in. He was out of breath by that time, as he might well be, and his heart seemed to jerk faster than the little shop-bell, as it quivered and jingled behind him with his hasty shutting of the door.

'Hallo, old chap!' said Mr Pancks. 'Altro, old boy! What's the matter?'

Mr Baptist, or Signor Cavalletto, understood English now almost as well as Mr Pancks himself, and could speak it very well too. Nevertheless, Mrs Plornish, with a pardonable vanity in that accomplishment of hers which made her all but Italian, stepped in as interpreter.

'E ask know,' said Mrs Plornish, 'what go wrong?'

'Come into the happy little cottage, Padrona,' returned Mr Baptist, imparting great stealthiness to his flurried back-handed shake of his right forefinger. 'Come there!'

Mrs Plornish was proud of the title Padrona, which she regarded as signifying: not so much Mistress of the house, as Mistress of the Italian tongue. She immediately complied with Mr Baptist's request, and they all went into the cottage.

'E ope you no fright,' said Mrs Plornish then, interpreting Mr Pancks in a new way with her usual fertility of resource. 'What appen? Peaka Padrona!'

'I have seen some one,' returned Baptist. 'I have rincontrato him.'

'Im? Oo him?' asked Mrs Plornish.

'A bad man. A baddest man. I have hoped that I should never see him again.'

'Ow you know him bad?' asked Mrs Plornish.

'It does not matter, Padrona. I know it too well.'

'E see you?' asked Mrs Plornish.

'No. I hope not. I believe not.'

'He says,' Mrs Plornish then interpreted, addressing her father and Pancks with mild condescension, 'that he has met a bad man, but he hopes the bad man didn't see him—Why,' inquired Mrs Plornish, reverting to the Italian language, 'why ope bad man no see?'

'Padrona, dearest,' returned the little foreigner whom she so considerately protected, 'do not ask, I pray. Once again I say it matters not. I have fear of this man. I do not wish to see him, I do not wish to be known of him—never again! Enough, most beautiful. Leave it.'

The topic was so disagreeable to him, and so put his usual liveliness to the rout, that Mrs Plornish forbore to press him further: the rather as the tea had been drawing for some time on the hob. But she was not the less surprised and curious for asking no more questions; neither was Mr Pancks, whose expressive breathing had been labouring hard since the entrance of the little man, like a locomotive engine with a great load getting up a steep incline. Maggy, now better dressed than of yore, though still faithful to the monstrous character of her cap, had

410

been in the background from the first with open mouth and eyes, which staring and gaping features were not diminished in breadth by the untimely suppression of the subject. However, no more was said about it, though much appeared to be thought on all sides: by no means excepting the two young Plornishes, who partook of the evening meal as if their eating the bread and butter were rendered almost superfluous by the painful probability of the worst of men shortly presenting himself for the purpose of eating them. Mr Baptist, by degrees began to chirp a little; but never stirred from the seat he had taken behind the door and close to the window, though it was not his usual place. As often as the little bell rang, he started and peeped out secretly, with the end of the little curtain in his hand and the rest before his face; evidently not at all satisfied but that the man he dreaded had tracked him through all his doublings and turnings, with the certainty of a terrible bloodhound.

The entrance, at various times, of two or three customers and of Mr Plornish, gave Mr Baptist just enough of this employment to keep the attention of the company fixed upon him. Tea was over, and the children were abed, and Mrs Plornish was feeling her way to the dutiful proposal that her father should favour them with Chloe, when the bell rang again, and Mr Clennam came in.

Clennam had been poring late over his books and letters; for the waiting-rooms of the Circumlocution Office ravaged his time sorely. Over and above that, he was depressed and made uneasy by the late occurrence at his mother's. He looked worn and solitary. He felt so, too; but, nevertheless, was returning home from his counting-house by that end of the Yard to give them the intelligence that he had received another letter from Miss Dorrit.

The news made a sensation in the cottage which drew off the general attention from Mr Baptist. Maggy, who pushed her way into the foreground immediately, would have seemed to draw in the tidings of her Little Mother equally at her ears, nose, mouth, and eyes, but that the last were obstructed by tears. She was particularly delighted when Clennam assured her that there were hospitals, and very kindly conducted hospitals, in Rome. Mr Pancks rose into new distinction in virtue of being specially remembered in the letter. Everybody was pleased and interested, and Clennam was well repaid for his trouble.

'But you are tired, sir. Let me make you a cup of tea,' said Mrs Plornish, 'if you'd condescend to take such a thing in the cottage; and many thanks to you, too, I am sure, for bearing us in mind so kindly.'

Mr Plornish deeming it incumbent on him, as host, to add his personal acknowledgments, tendered them in the form which always expressed his highest ideal of a combination of ceremony with sincerity.

'John Edward Nandy,' said Mr Plornish, addressing the old gentleman. 'Sir. It's not too often that you see unpretending actions without a spark of pride, and therefore when you see them give grateful honour unto the same, being that if you don't, and live to want 'em, it follows serve you right.'

To which Mr Nandy replied:

'I am heartily of your opinion, Thomas, and which your opinion is the same as mine, and therefore no more words and not being backwards with that opinion, which opinion giving it as yes, Thomas, yes, is the opinion in which yourself and me must ever be unanimously jined by all, and where there is not difference of opinion there can be none but one opinion, which fully no, Thomas, Thomas, no!'

Arthur, with less formality, expressed himself gratified by their high appreciation of so very slight an attention on his part; and explained as to the tea that he had not yet dined, and was going straight home to refresh after a long day's labour, or he would have readily accepted the hospitable offer. As Mr Pancks was somewhat noisily getting his steam up for departure, he concluded by asking that gentleman if he would walk with him? Mr Pancks said he desired no better engagement, and the two took leave of Happy Cottage.

'If you will come home with me, Pancks,' said Arthur, when they got into the street, 'and will share what dinner or supper there is, it will be next door to an act of charity; for I am weary and out of sorts to-night.'

'Ask me to do a greater thing than that,' said Pancks, 'when you want it done, and I'll do it.'

Between this eccentric personage and Clennam, a tacit understanding and accord had been always improving since Mr Pancks flew over Mr Rugg's back in the Marshalsea Yard. When the carriage drove away on the memorable day of the family's departure, these two had looked after it together, and had walked slowly away together. When the first letter came from little Dorrit, nobody was more interested in hearing of her than Mr Pancks. The second letter, at that moment in Clennam's breast-pocket, particularly remembered him by name. Though he had never before made any profession or protestation to Clennam, and though what he had just said was little enough as to the words in which it was expressed, Clennam had long had a growing belief that Mr Pancks, in his own odd way, was becoming attached to him. All these strings intertwining made Pancks a very cable of anchorage that night.

'I am quite alone,' Arthur explained as they walked on. 'My partner is away, busily engaged at a distance on his branch of our business, and you shall do just as you like.'

'Thank you. You didn't take particular notice of little Altro just now; did you?' said Pancks.

'No. Why?'

'He's a bright fellow, and I like him,' said Pancks. 'Something has gone amiss with him to-day. Have you any idea of any cause that can have overset him?'

'You surprise me! None whatever.'

Mr Pancks gave his reasons for the inquiry. Arthur was quite unprepared for them, and quite unable to suggest an explanation of them.

'Perhaps you'll ask him,' said Pancks, 'as he's a stranger?'

'Ask him what?' returned Clennam.

'What he has on his mind.'

'I ought first to see for myself that he has something on his mind, I think,' said Clennam. 'I have found him in every way so diligent, so grateful (for little enough), and so trustworthy, that it might look like suspecting him. And that would be very unjust.'

'True,' said Pancks. 'But, I say! You oughtn't to be anybody's proprietor, Mr Clennam. You're much too delicate.'

'For the matter of that,' returned Clennam laughing, 'I have not a large proprietary share in Cavalletto. His carving is his livelihood. He keeps the keys of the Factory, watches it every alternate night, and acts as a sort of housekeeper to it generally; but we have little work in the way of his ingenuity, though we give him what we have. No! I am rather his adviser than his proprietor. To call me his standing counsel and his banker would be nearer the fact. Speaking of being his banker, is it not curious, Pancks, that the ventures which run just now in so many people's heads, should run even in little Cavalletto's?'

'Ventures?' retorted Pancks, with a snort. 'What ventures?'

'These Merdle enterprises.'

'Oh! Investments,' said Pancks. 'Ay, ay! I didn't know you were speaking of investments.'

His quick way of replying caused Clennam to look at him, with a doubt whether he meant more than he said. As it was accompanied, however, with a quickening of his pace and a corresponding increase in the labouring of his machinery, Arthur did not pursue the matter, and they soon arrived at his house.

A dinner of soup and a pigeon-pie, served on a little round table before the fire, and flavoured with a bottle of good wine, oiled Mr Pancks's works in a highly effective manner; so that when Clennam produced his Eastern pipe, and handed Mr Pancks another Eastern pipe, the latter gentleman was perfectly comfortable.

They puffed for a while in silence, Mr Pancks like a steam-vessel with wind, tide, calm water, and all other sea-going conditions in her favour. He was the first to speak, and he spoke thus:

'Yes. Investments is the word.'

Clennam, with his former look, said 'Ah!'

'I am going back to it, you see,' said Pancks.

'Yes. I see you are going back to it,' returned Clennam, wondering why.

'Wasn't it a curious thing that they should run in little Altro's head? Eh?' said Pancks as he smoked. 'Wasn't that how you put it?'

'That was what I said.'

'Ay! But think of the whole Yard having got it. Think of their all meeting me with it, on my collecting days, here and there and everywhere. Whether they pay, or whether they don't pay. Merdle, Merdle, Merdle. Always Merdle.'

'Very strange how these runs on an infatuation prevail,' said Arthur.

'An't it?' returned Pancks. After smoking for a minute or so, more drily than comported with his recent oiling, he added: 'Because you see these people don't understand the subject.'

'Not a bit,' assented Clennam.

'Not a bit,' cried Pancks. 'Know nothing of figures. Know nothing of money questions. Never made a calculation. Never worked it, sir!'

'If they had—' Clennam was going on to say; when Mr Pancks, without change of countenance, produced a sound so far surpassing all his usual efforts, nasal or bronchial, that he stopped.

'If they had?' repeated Pancks in an inquiring tone.

'I thought you—spoke,' said Arthur, hesitating what name to give the interruption.

'Not at all,' said Pancks. 'Not yet. I may in a minute. If they had?'

'If they had,' observed Clennam, who was a little at a loss how to take his friend, 'why, I suppose they would have known better.'

'How so, Mr Clennam?' Pancks asked quickly, and with an odd effect of having been from the commencement of the conversation loaded with the heavy charge he now fired off. 'They're right, you know. They don't mean to be, but they're right.'

'Right in sharing Cavalletto's inclination to speculate with Mr Merdle?'

'Per-fectly, sir,' said Pancks. 'I've gone into it. I've made the calculations. I've worked it. They're safe and genuine.' Relieved by having got to this, Mr Pancks took as long a pull as his lungs would permit at his Eastern pipe, and looked sagaciously and steadily at Clennam while inhaling and exhaling too.

In those moments, Mr Pancks began to give out the dangerous infection with which he was laden. It is the manner of communicating these diseases; it is the subtle way in which they go about.

'Do you mean, my good Pancks,' asked Clennam emphatically, 'that you would put that thousand pounds of yours, let us say, for instance, out at this kind of interest?'

'Certainly,' said Pancks. 'Already done it, sir.'

Mr Pancks took another long inhalation, another long exhalation, another long sagacious look at Clennam.

'I tell you, Mr Clennam, I've gone into it,' said Pancks. 'He's a man of immense resources—enormous capital—government influence. They're the best schemes afloat. They're safe. They're certain.'

'Well!' returned Clennam, looking first at him gravely and then at the fire gravely. 'You surprise me!'

'Bah!' Pancks retorted. 'Don't say that, sir. It's what you ought to do yourself! Why don't you do as I do?'

Of whom Mr Pancks had taken the prevalent disease, he could no more have told than if he had unconsciously taken a fever. Bred at first, as many physical diseases are, in the wickedness of men, and then disseminated in their ignorance, these epidemics, after a period, get communicated to many sufferers who are neither ignorant nor wicked. Mr Pancks might, or might not, have caught the illness himself from a subject of this class; but in this category he appeared before Clennam, and the infection he threw off was all the more virulent.

'And you have really invested,' Clennam had already passed to that word, 'your thousand pounds, Pancks?'

'To be sure, sir!' replied Pancks boldly, with a puff of smoke. 'And only wish it ten!'

Now, Clennam had two subjects lying heavy on his lonely mind that night; the one, his partner's long-deferred hope; the other, what he had seen and heard at his mother's. In the relief of having this companion, and of feeling that he could trust him, he passed on to both, and both brought him round again, with an increase and acceleration of force, to his point of departure.

It came about in the simplest manner. Quitting the investment subject, after an interval of silent looking at the fire through the smoke of his pipe, he told Pancks how and why he was occupied with the great National Department. 'A hard case it has been, and a hard case it is on Doyce,' he finished by saying, with all the honest feeling the topic roused in him.

'Hard indeed,' Pancks acquiesced. 'But you manage for him, Mr Clennam?'

'How do you mean?'

'Manage the money part of the business?'

'Yes. As well as I can.'

'Manage it better, sir,' said Pancks. 'Recompense him for his toils and disappointments. Give him the chances of the time. He'll never benefit himself in that way, patient and preoccupied workman. He looks to you, sir.'

'I do my best, Pancks,' returned Clennam, uneasily. 'As to duly weighing and considering these new enterprises of which I have had no experience, I doubt if I am fit for it, I am growing old.'

'Growing old?' cried Pancks. 'Ha, ha!'

There was something so indubitably genuine in the wonderful laugh, and series of snorts and puffs, engendered in Mr Pancks's astonishment at, and utter rejection of, the idea, that his being quite in earnest could not be questioned.

'Growing old?' cried Pancks. 'Hear, hear, hear! Old? Hear him, hear him!'

The positive refusal expressed in Mr Pancks's continued snorts, no less than in these exclamations, to entertain the sentiment for a single instant, drove Arthur away from it. Indeed, he was fearful of something happening to Mr Pancks in the violent conflict that took place between the breath he jerked out of himself and the smoke he jerked into himself. This abandonment of the second topic threw him on the third.

'Young, old, or middle-aged, Pancks,' he said, when there was a favourable pause, 'I am in a very anxious and uncertain state; a state that even leads me to doubt whether anything now seeming to belong to me, may be really mine. Shall I tell you how this is? Shall I put a great trust in you?'

'You shall, sir,' said Pancks, 'if you believe me worthy of it.'

'I do.'

'You may!' Mr Pancks's short and sharp rejoinder, confirmed by the sudden outstretching of his coaly hand, was most expressive and convincing. Arthur shook the hand warmly.

He then, softening the nature of his old apprehensions as much as was possible consistently with their being made intelligible and never alluding to his mother by name, but speaking vaguely of a relation of his, confided to Mr Pancks a broad outline of the misgivings he entertained, and of the interview he had witnessed. Mr Pancks listened with such interest that, regardless of the charms of the Eastern pipe, he put it in the grate among the fire-irons, and occupied his hands during the whole recital in so erecting the loops and hooks of hair all over his head, that he looked, when it came to a conclusion, like a journeyman Hamlet in conversation with his father's spirit.

'Brings me back, sir,' was his exclamation then, with a startling touch on Clennam's knee, 'brings me back, sir, to the Investments! I don't say anything of your making yourself poor to repair a wrong you never committed. That's you. A man must be himself. But I say this, fearing you may want money to save your own blood from exposure and disgrace—make as much as you can!'

Arthur shook his head, but looked at him thoughtfully too.

'Be as rich as you can, sir,' Pancks adjured him with a powerful concentration of all his energies on the advice. 'Be as rich as you honestly can. It's your duty. Not for your sake, but for the sake of others. Take time by the forelock. Poor Mr Doyce (who really is growing old) depends upon you. Your relative depends upon you. You don't know what depends upon you.'

'Well, well, well!' returned Arthur. 'Enough for to-night.'

'One word more, Mr Clennam,' retorted Pancks, 'and then enough for to-night. Why should you leave all the gains to the gluttons, knaves, and impostors? Why should you leave all the gains that are to be got to my proprietor and the like of him? Yet you're always doing it. When I say you, I mean such men as you. You know you are. Why, I see it every day of my life. I see nothing else. It's my business to see it. Therefore I say,' urged Pancks, 'Go in and win!'

'But what of Go in and lose?' said Arthur.

'Can't be done, sir,' returned Pancks. 'I have looked into it. Name up everywhere—immense resources—enormous capital—great position—high connection—government influence. Can't be done!'

Gradually, after this closing exposition, Mr Pancks subsided; allowed his hair to droop as much as it ever would droop on the utmost persuasion; reclaimed the pipe from the fire-irons, filled it anew, and smoked it out. They said little more; but were company to one another in silently pursuing the same subjects, and did not part until midnight. On taking his leave, Mr Pancks, when he had shaken hands with Clennam, worked completely round him before he steamed out at the door. This, Arthur received as an assurance that he might implicitly rely on Pancks, if he ever should come to need assistance; either in any of the matters of which they had spoken that night, or any other subject that could in any way affect himself.

At intervals all next day, and even while his attention was fixed on other things, he thought of Mr Pancks's investment of his thousand pounds, and of his having 'looked into it.' He thought of Mr Pancks's being so sanguine in this matter, and of his not being usually of a sanguine character. He thought of the great National Department, and of the delight it would be to him to see Doyce better off. He thought of the darkly threatening place that went by the name of Home in his remembrance, and of the gathering shadows which made it yet more darkly threatening than of old. He observed anew that wherever he went, he saw, or heard, or touched, the celebrated name of Merdle; he found it difficult even to remain at his desk a couple of hours, without having it presented to one of his bodily senses through some agency or other. He began to think it was curious too that it should be everywhere, and that nobody but he should seem to have any mistrust of it. Though indeed he began to remember, when he got to this, even he did not mistrust it; he had only happened to keep aloof from it.

Such symptoms, when a disease of the kind is rife, are usually the signs of sickening.

CHAPTER 14. Taking Advice

When it became known to the Britons on the shore of the yellow Tiber that their intelligent compatriot, Mr Sparkler, was made one of the Lords of their Circumlocution Office, they took it as a piece of news with which they had no nearer concern than with any other piece of news—any other Accident or Offence—in the English papers. Some laughed; some said, by way of complete excuse, that the post was virtually a sinecure, and any fool who could spell his name was good enough for it; some, and these the more solemn political oracles, said that Decimus did wisely to strengthen himself, and that the sole constitutional purpose of all places within the gift of Decimus, was, that Decimus should strengthen himself. A few bilious Britons there were who would not subscribe to this article of faith; but their objection was purely theoretical. In a practical point of view, they listlessly abandoned the matter, as being the business of some other Britons unknown, somewhere, or nowhere. In like manner, at home, great numbers of Britons maintained, for as long as four-and-twenty consecutive hours, that those invisible and anonymous Britons 'ought to take it up;' and that if they quietly acquiesced in it, they deserved it. But of what class the remiss Britons were composed, and where the unlucky creatures hid themselves, and why they hid themselves, and how it constantly happened that they neglected their interests, when so many other Britons were quite at a loss to account for their not looking after those interests, was not, either upon the shore of the yellow Tiber or the shore of the black Thames, made apparent to men.

Mrs Merdle circulated the news, as she received congratulations on it, with a careless grace that displayed it to advantage, as the setting displays the jewel. Yes, she said, Edmund had taken the place. Mr Merdle wished him to take it, and he had taken it. She hoped Edmund might like it, but really she didn't know. It would keep him in town a good deal, and he preferred the country. Still, it was not a disagreeable position—and it was a position. There was no denying that the thing was a compliment to Mr Merdle, and was not a bad thing for Edmund if he liked it. It was just as well that he should have something to do, and it was just as well that he should have something for doing it. Whether it would be more agreeable to Edmund than the army, remained to be seen.

Thus the Bosom; accomplished in the art of seeming to make things of small account, and really enhancing them in the process. While Henry Gowan, whom Decimus had thrown away, went through the whole round of his acquaintance between the Gate of the People and the town of Albano, vowing, almost (but not quite) with tears in his eyes, that Sparkler was the sweetest-tempered, simplest-hearted, altogether most lovable jackass that ever grazed on the public common; and that only one circumstance could have delighted him (Gowan) more, than his (the beloved jackass's) getting this post, and that would have been his (Gowan's) getting it himself. He said it was the very thing for Sparkler. There was nothing to do, and he would do it charmingly; there was a handsome salary to draw, and he would draw it charmingly; it was a delightful, appropriate, capital appointment; and he almost forgave the donor his slight of himself, in his joy that the dear donkey for whom he had so great an affection was so admirably stabled. Nor did his benevolence stop here. He took pains, on all social occasions, to draw Mr Sparkler out, and make him conspicuous before the company; and, although the considerate action always resulted in that young gentleman's making a dreary and forlorn mental spectacle of himself, the friendly intention was not to be doubted.

Unless, indeed, it chanced to be doubted by the object of Mr Sparkler's affections. Miss

Fanny was now in the difficult situation of being universally known in that light, and of not having dismissed Mr Sparkler, however capriciously she used him. Hence, she was sufficiently identified with the gentleman to feel compromised by his being more than usually ridiculous; and hence, being by no means deficient in quickness, she sometimes came to his rescue against Gowan, and did him very good service. But, while doing this, she was ashamed of him, undetermined whether to get rid of him or more decidedly encourage him, distracted with apprehensions that she was every day becoming more and more immeshed in her uncertainties, and tortured by misgivings that Mrs Merdle triumphed in her distress. With this tumult in her mind, it is no subject for surprise that Miss Fanny came home one night in a state of agitation from a concert and ball at Mrs Merdle's house, and on her sister affectionately trying to soothe her, pushed that sister away from the toilette-table at which she sat angrily trying to cry, and declared with a heaving bosom that she detested everybody, and she wished she was dead.

'Dear Fanny, what is the matter? Tell me.'

'Matter, you little Mole,' said Fanny. 'If you were not the blindest of the blind, you would have no occasion to ask me. The idea of daring to pretend to assert that you have eyes in your head, and yet ask me what's the matter!'

'Is it Mr Sparkler, dear?'

'Mis-ter Spark-ler!' repeated Fanny, with unbounded scorn, as if he were the last subject in the Solar system that could possibly be near her mind. 'No, Miss Bat, it is not.'

Immediately afterwards, she became remorseful for having called her sister names; declaring with sobs that she knew she made herself hateful, but that everybody drove her to it.

'I don't think you are well to-night, dear Fanny.'

'Stuff and nonsense!' replied the young lady, turning angry again; 'I am as well as you are. Perhaps I might say better, and yet make no boast of it.'

Poor Little Dorrit, not seeing her way to the offering of any soothing words that would escape repudiation, deemed it best to remain quiet. At first, Fanny took this ill, too; protesting to her looking-glass, that of all the trying sisters a girl could have, she did think the most trying sister was a flat sister. That she knew she was at times a wretched temper; that she knew she made herself hateful; that when she made herself hateful, nothing would do her half the good as being told so; but that, being afflicted with a flat sister, she never was told so, and the consequence resulted that she was absolutely tempted and goaded into making herself disagreeable. Besides (she angrily told her looking-glass), she didn't want to be forgiven. It was not a right example, that she should be constantly stooping to be forgiven by a younger sister. And this was the Art of it—that she was always being placed in the position of being forgiven, whether she liked it or not. Finally she burst into violent weeping, and, when her sister came and sat close at her side to comfort her, said, 'Amy, you're an Angel!'

'But, I tell you what, my Pet,' said Fanny, when her sister's gentleness had calmed her, 'it now comes to this; that things cannot and shall not go on as they are at present going on, and that there must be an end of this, one way or another.'

As the announcement was vague, though very peremptory, Little Dorrit returned, 'Let us talk about it.'

'Quite so, my dear,' assented Fanny, as she dried her eyes. 'Let us talk about it. I am rational again now, and you shall advise me. Will you advise me, my sweet child?'

Even Amy smiled at this notion, but she said, 'I will, Fanny, as well as I can.'

'Thank you, dearest Amy,' returned Fanny, kissing her. 'You are my anchor.'

Having embraced her Anchor with great affection, Fanny took a bottle of sweet toilette water from the table, and called to her maid for a fine handkerchief. She then dismissed that attendant for the night, and went on to be advised; dabbing her eyes and forehead from time to time to cool them.

'My love,' Fanny began, 'our characters and points of view are sufficiently different (kiss me again, my darling), to make it very probable that I shall surprise you by what I am going to say. What I am going to say, my dear, is, that notwithstanding our property, we labour, socially speaking, under disadvantages. You don't quite understand what I mean, Amy?'

'I have no doubt I shall,' said Amy, mildly, 'after a few words more.'

'Well, my dear, what I mean is, that we are, after all, newcomers into fashionable life.'

'I am sure, Fanny,' Little Dorrit interposed in her zealous admiration, 'no one need find that out in you.'

'Well, my dear child, perhaps not,' said Fanny, 'though it's most kind and most affectionate in you, you precious girl, to say so.' Here she dabbed her sister's forehead, and blew upon it a little. 'But you are,' resumed Fanny, 'as is well known, the dearest little thing that ever was! To resume, my child. Pa is extremely gentlemanly and extremely well informed, but he is, in some trifling respects, a little different from other gentlemen of his fortune: partly on account of what he has gone through, poor dear: partly, I fancy, on account of its often running in his mind that other people are thinking about that, while he is talking to them. Uncle, my love, is altogether unpresentable. Though a dear creature to whom I am tenderly attached, he is, socially speaking, shocking. Edward is frightfully expensive and dissipated. I don't mean that there is anything ungenteel in that itself—far from it—but I do mean that he doesn't do it well, and that he doesn't, if I may so express myself, get the money's-worth in the sort of dissipated reputation that attaches to him.'

'Poor Edward!' sighed Little Dorrit, with the whole family history in the sigh.

'Yes. And poor you and me, too,' returned Fanny, rather sharply. 'Very true! Then, my dear, we have no mother, and we have a Mrs General. And I tell you again, darling, that Mrs General, if I may reverse a common proverb and adapt it to her, is a cat in gloves who will catch mice. That woman, I am quite sure and confident, will be our mother-in-law.'

'I can hardly think, Fanny—' Fanny stopped her.

'Now, don't argue with me about it, Amy,' said she, 'because I know better.' Feeling that she had been sharp again, she dabbed her sister's forehead again, and blew upon it again. 'To resume once more, my dear. It then becomes a question with me (I am proud and spirited, Amy, as you very well know: too much so, I dare say) whether I shall make up my mind to take it upon myself to carry the family through.'

'How?' asked her sister, anxiously.

'I will not,' said Fanny, without answering the question, 'submit to be mother-in-lawed by Mrs General; and I will not submit to be, in any respect whatever, either patronised or tormented by Mrs Merdle.'

Little Dorrit laid her hand upon the hand that held the bottle of sweet water, with a still more anxious look. Fanny, quite punishing her own forehead with the vehement dabs she now began to give it, fitfully went on.

'That he has somehow or other, and how is of no consequence, attained a very good position, no one can deny. That it is a very good connection, no one can deny. And as to the question of clever or not clever, I doubt very much whether a clever husband would be suitable to me. I cannot submit. I should not be able to defer to him enough.'

'O, my dear Fanny!' expostulated Little Dorrit, upon whom a kind of terror had been stealing as she perceived what her sister meant. 'If you loved any one, all this feeling would change. If you loved any one, you would no more be yourself, but you would quite lose and forget yourself in your devotion to him. If you loved him, Fanny—' Fanny had stopped the dabbing hand, and was looking at her fixedly.

'O, indeed!' cried Fanny. 'Really? Bless me, how much some people know of some subjects! They say every one has a subject, and I certainly seem to have hit upon yours, Amy. There, you little thing, I was only in fun,' dabbing her sister's forehead; 'but don't you be a silly puss, and don't you think flightily and eloquently about degenerate impossibilities. There! Now, I'll go back to myself.'

'Dear Fanny, let me say first, that I would far rather we worked for a scanty living again than I would see you rich and married to Mr Sparkler.'

'Let you say, my dear?' retorted Fanny. 'Why, of course, I will let you say anything. There is no constraint upon you, I hope. We are together to talk it over. And as to marrying Mr Sparkler, I have not the slightest intention of doing so to-night, my dear, or to-morrow morning either.'

'But at some time?'

'At no time, for anything I know at present,' answered Fanny, with indifference. Then, suddenly changing her indifference into a burning restlessness, she added, 'You talk about the clever men, you little thing! It's all very fine and easy to talk about the clever men; but where are they? I don't see them anywhere near me!'

'My dear Fanny, so short a time—'

'Short time or long time,' interrupted Fanny. 'I am impatient of our situation. I don't like our situation, and very little would induce me to change it. Other girls, differently reared and differently circumstanced altogether, might wonder at what I say or may do. Let them. They are driven by their lives and characters; I am driven by mine.'

'Fanny, my dear Fanny, you know that you have qualities to make you the wife of one very superior to Mr Sparkler.'

'Amy, my dear Amy,' retorted Fanny, parodying her words, 'I know that I wish to have a more defined and distinct position, in which I can assert myself with greater effect against that insolent woman.'

'Would you therefore—forgive my asking, Fanny—therefore marry her son?'

'Why, perhaps,' said Fanny, with a triumphant smile. 'There may be many less promising ways of arriving at an end than that, my dear. That piece of insolence may think, now, that it would be a great success to get her son off upon me, and shelve me. But, perhaps, she little thinks how I would retort upon her if I married her son. I would oppose her in everything, and compete with her. I would make it the business of my life.'

Fanny set down the bottle when she came to this, and walked about the room; always stopping and standing still while she spoke.

'One thing I could certainly do, my child: I could make her older. And I would!'

This was followed by another walk.

'I would talk of her as an old woman. I would pretend to know—if I didn't, but I should from her son—all about her age. And she should hear me say, Amy: affectionately, quite dutifully and affectionately: how well she looked, considering her time of life. I could make her seem older at once, by being myself so much younger. I may not be as handsome as she is; I am not a fair judge of that question, I suppose; but I know I am handsome enough to be a thorn in her side. And I would be!'

'My dear sister, would you condemn yourself to an unhappy life for this?'

'It wouldn't be an unhappy life, Amy. It would be the life I am fitted for. Whether by disposition, or whether by circumstances, is no matter; I am better fitted for such a life than for almost any other.'

There was something of a desolate tone in those words; but, with a short proud laugh she took another walk, and after passing a great looking-glass came to another stop.

'Figure! Figure, Amy! Well. The woman has a good figure. I will give her her due, and not deny it. But is it so far beyond all others that it is altogether unapproachable? Upon my word, I am not so sure of it. Give some much younger woman the latitude as to dress that she has, being married; and we would see about that, my dear!'

Something in the thought that was agreeable and flattering, brought her back to her seat in a gayer temper. She took her sister's hands in hers, and clapped all four hands above her head as she looked in her sister's face laughing:

'And the dancer, Amy, that she has quite forgotten—the dancer who bore no sort of resemblance to me, and of whom I never remind her, oh dear no!—should dance through her life, and dance in her way, to such a tune as would disturb her insolent placidity a little. Just a little, my dear Amy, just a little!'

Meeting an earnest and imploring look in Amy's face, she brought the four hands down, and laid only one on Amy's lips.

'Now, don't argue with me, child,' she said in a sterner way, 'because it is of no use. I understand these subjects much better than you do. I have not nearly made up my mind, but it may be. Now we have talked this over comfortably, and may go to bed. You best and dearest little mouse, Good night!' With those words Fanny weighed her Anchor, and—having taken so much advice—left off being advised for that occasion.

Thenceforward, Amy observed Mr Sparkler's treatment by his enslaver, with new reasons for attaching importance to all that passed between them. There were times when Fanny appeared quite unable to endure his mental feebleness, and when she became so sharply impatient of it that she would all but dismiss him for good. There were other times when she got on much better with him; when he amused her, and when her sense of superiority seemed to counterbalance that opposite side of the scale. If Mr Sparkler had been other than the faithfullest and most submissive of swains, he was sufficiently hard pressed to have fled from the scene of his trials, and have set at least the whole distance from Rome to London between himself and his enchantress. But he had no greater will of his own than a boat has when it is towed by a steam-ship; and he followed his cruel mistress through rough and smooth, on equally strong compulsion.

Mrs Merdle, during these passages, said little to Fanny, but said more about her. She was, as it were, forced to look at her through her eye-glass, and in general conversation to allow commendations of her beauty to be wrung from her by its irresistible demands. The defiant character it assumed when Fanny heard these extollings (as it generally happened that she did), was not expressive of concessions to the impartial bosom; but the utmost revenge the bosom took was, to say audibly, 'A spoilt beauty—but with that face and shape, who could wonder?'

It might have been about a month or six weeks after the night of the new advice, when Little Dorrit began to think she detected some new understanding between Mr Sparkler and Fanny. Mr Sparkler, as if in attendance to some compact, scarcely ever spoke without first looking towards Fanny for leave. That young lady was too discreet ever to look back again; but, if Mr Sparkler had permission to speak, she remained silent; if he had not, she herself spoke. Moreover, it became plain whenever Henry Gowan attempted to perform the friendly office of drawing him out, that he was not to be drawn. And not only that, but Fanny would presently, without any pointed application in the world, chance to say something with such a sting in it that Gowan would draw back as if he had put his hand into a bee-hive.

There was yet another circumstance which went a long way to confirm Little Dorrit in her fears, though it was not a great circumstance in itself. Mr Sparkler's demeanour towards herself changed. It became fraternal. Sometimes, when she was in the outer circle of assemblies—at their own residence, at Mrs Merdle's, or elsewhere—she would find herself stealthily supported round the waist by Mr Sparkler's arm. Mr Sparkler never offered the slightest explanation of this attention; but merely smiled with an air of blundering, contented, good-natured proprietorship, which, in so heavy a gentleman, was ominously expressive.

Little Dorrit was at home one day, thinking about Fanny with a heavy heart. They had a room at one end of their drawing-room suite, nearly all irregular bay-window, projecting over the street, and commanding all the picturesque life and variety of the Corso, both up and down. At three or four o'clock in the afternoon, English time, the view from this window was very bright and peculiar; and Little Dorrit used to sit and muse here, much as she had been used to while away the time in her balcony at Venice. Seated thus one day, she was softly touched on the shoulder, and Fanny said, 'Well, Amy dear,' and took her seat at her side. Their seat was a part of the window; when there was anything in the way of a procession going on, they used to have bright draperies hung out of the window, and used to kneel or sit on this seat, and look out at it, leaning on the brilliant colour. But there was no procession that day, and Little Dorrit was rather surprised by Fanny's being at home at that hour, as she was generally out on horseback then.

'Well, Amy,' said Fanny, 'what are you thinking of, little one?'

'I was thinking of you, Fanny.'

'No? What a coincidence! I declare here's some one else. You were not thinking of this some one else too; were you, Amy?'

Amy had been thinking of this some one else too; for it was Mr Sparkler. She did not say so, however, as she gave him her hand. Mr Sparkler came and sat down on the other side of her, and she felt the fraternal railing come behind her, and apparently stretch on to include Fanny.

'Well, my little sister,' said Fanny with a sigh, 'I suppose you know what this means?'

'She's as beautiful as she's doated on,' stammered Mr Sparkler—'and there's no nonsense about her—it's arranged—'

'You needn't explain, Edmund,' said Fanny.

'No, my love,' said Mr Sparkler.

'In short, pet,' proceeded Fanny, 'on the whole, we are engaged. We must tell papa about it either to-night or to-morrow, according to the opportunities. Then it's done, and very little more need be said.'

'My dear Fanny,' said Mr Sparkler, with deference, 'I should like to say a word to Amy.'

'Well, well! Say it for goodness' sake,' returned the young lady.

'I am convinced, my dear Amy,' said Mr Sparkler, 'that if ever there was a girl, next to your highly endowed and beautiful sister, who had no nonsense about her—'

'We know all about that, Edmund,' interposed Miss Fanny. 'Never mind that. Pray go on to something else besides our having no nonsense about us.'

'Yes, my love,' said Mr Sparkler. 'And I assure you, Amy, that nothing can be a greater happiness to myself, myself—next to the happiness of being so highly honoured with the choice of a glorious girl who hasn't an atom of—'

'Pray, Edmund, pray!' interrupted Fanny, with a slight pat of her pretty foot upon the floor.

'My love, you're quite right,' said Mr Sparkler, 'and I know I have a habit of it. What I wished to declare was, that nothing can be a greater happiness to myself, myself-next to the happiness of being united to pre-eminently the most glorious of girls—than to have the happiness of cultivating the affectionate acquaintance of Amy. I may not myself,' said Mr Sparkler manfully, 'be up to the mark on some other subjects at a short notice, and I am aware that if you were to poll Society the general opinion would be that I am not; but on the subject of Amy I AM up to the mark!'

Mr Sparkler kissed her, in witness thereof.

'A knife and fork and an apartment,' proceeded Mr Sparkler, growing, in comparison with his oratorical antecedents, quite diffuse, 'will ever be at Amy's disposal. My Governor, I am sure, will always be proud to entertain one whom I so much esteem. And regarding my mother,' said Mr Sparkler, 'who is a remarkably fine woman, with—'

'Edmund, Edmund!' cried Miss Fanny, as before.

'With submission, my soul,' pleaded Mr Sparkler. 'I know I have a habit of it, and I thank you very much, my adorable girl, for taking the trouble to correct it; but my mother is admitted on all sides to be a remarkably fine woman, and she really hasn't any.'

'That may be, or may not be,' returned Fanny, 'but pray don't mention it any more.'

'I will not, my love,' said Mr Sparkler.

'Then, in fact, you have nothing more to say, Edmund; have you?' inquired Fanny.

'So far from it, my adorable girl,' answered Mr Sparkler, 'I apologise for having said so much.'

Mr Sparkler perceived, by a kind of inspiration, that the question implied had he not better go? He therefore withdrew the fraternal railing, and neatly said that he thought he would, with submission, take his leave. He did not go without being congratulated by Amy, as well as she could discharge that office in the flutter and distress of her spirits.

When he was gone, she said, 'O Fanny, Fanny!' and turned to her sister in the bright window, and fell upon her bosom and cried there. Fanny laughed at first; but soon laid her face against her sister's and cried too—a little. It was the last time Fanny ever showed that there was any hidden, suppressed, or conquered feeling in her on the matter. From that hour the way she had chosen lay before her, and she trod it with her own imperious self-willed step.

CHAPTER 15. No just Cause or Impediment why these Two Persons

should not be joined together

Mr Dorrit, on being informed by his elder daughter that she had accepted matrimonial overtures from Mr Sparkler, to whom she had plighted her troth, received the communication at once with great dignity and with a large display of parental pride; his dignity dilating with the widened prospect of advantageous ground from which to make acquaintances, and his parental pride being developed by Miss Fanny's ready sympathy with that great object of his existence. He gave her to understand that her noble ambition found harmonious echoes in his heart; and bestowed his blessing on her, as a child brimful of duty and good principle, self-devoted to the aggrandisement of the family name.

To Mr Sparkler, when Miss Fanny permitted him to appear, Mr Dorrit said, he would not disguise that the alliance Mr Sparkler did him the honour to propose was highly congenial to his feelings; both as being in unison with the spontaneous affections of his daughter Fanny, and as opening a family connection of a gratifying nature with Mr Merdle, the master spirit of the age. Mrs Merdle also, as a leading lady rich in distinction, elegance, grace, and beauty, he mentioned in very laudatory terms. He felt it his duty to remark (he was sure a gentleman of Mr Sparkler's fine sense would interpret him with all delicacy), that he could not consider this proposal definitely determined on, until he should have had the privilege of holding some correspondence with Mr Merdle; and of ascertaining it to be so far accordant with the views of that eminent gentleman as that his (Mr Dorrit's) daughter would be received on that footing which her station in life and her dowry and expectations warranted him in requiring that she should maintain in what he trusted he might be allowed, without the appearance of being mercenary, to call the Eye of the Great World. While saying this, which his character as a gentleman of some little station, and his character as a father, equally demanded of him, he would not be so diplomatic as to conceal that the proposal remained in hopeful abeyance and under conditional acceptance, and that he thanked Mr Sparkler for the compliment rendered to himself and to his family. He concluded with some further and more general observations on the—ha—character of an independent gentleman, and the—hum—character of a possibly too partial and admiring parent. To sum the whole up shortly, he received Mr Sparkler's offer very much as he would have received three or four half-crowns from him in the days that were gone.

Mr Sparkler, finding himself stunned by the words thus heaped upon his inoffensive head, made a brief though pertinent rejoinder; the same being neither more nor less than that he had long perceived Miss Fanny to have no nonsense about her, and that he had no doubt of its being all right with his Governor. At that point the object of his affections shut him up like a box with a spring lid, and sent him away.

Proceeding shortly afterwards to pay his respects to the Bosom, Mr Dorrit was received by it with great consideration. Mrs Merdle had heard of this affair from Edmund. She had been surprised at first, because she had not thought Edmund a marrying man. Society had not thought Edmund a marrying man. Still, of course she had seen, as a woman (we women did instinctively see these things, Mr Dorrit!), that Edmund had been immensely captivated by Miss Dorrit, and she had openly said that Mr Dorrit had much to answer for in bringing so charming a girl abroad to turn the heads of his countrymen.

'Have I the honour to conclude, madam,' said Mr Dorrit, 'that the direction which Mr Sparkler's affections have taken, is—ha-approved of by you?'

'I assure you, Mr Dorrit,' returned the lady, 'that, personally, I am charmed.'

That was very gratifying to Mr Dorrit.

'Personally,' repeated Mrs Merdle, 'charmed.'

This casual repetition of the word 'personally,' moved Mr Dorrit to express his hope that Mr Merdle's approval, too, would not be wanting?

'I cannot,' said Mrs Merdle, 'take upon myself to answer positively for Mr Merdle; gentlemen, especially gentlemen who are what Society calls capitalists, having their own ideas of these matters. But I should think—merely giving an opinion, Mr Dorrit—I should think Mr Merdle would be upon the whole,' here she held a review of herself before adding at her leisure, 'quite charmed.'

At the mention of gentlemen whom Society called capitalists, Mr Dorrit had coughed, as if some internal demur were breaking out of him. Mrs Merdle had observed it, and went on to take up the cue.

'Though, indeed, Mr Dorrit, it is scarcely necessary for me to make that remark, except in the mere openness of saying what is uppermost to one whom I so highly regard, and with whom I hope I may have the pleasure of being brought into still more agreeable relations. For one cannot but see the great probability of your considering such things from Mr Merdle's own point of view, except indeed that circumstances have made it Mr Merdle's accidental fortune, or misfortune, to be engaged in business transactions, and that they, however vast, may a little cramp his horizons. I am a very child as to having any notion of business,' said Mrs Merdle; 'but I am afraid, Mr Dorrit, it may have that tendency.'

This skilful see-saw of Mr Dorrit and Mrs Merdle, so that each of them sent the other up, and each of them sent the other down, and neither had the advantage, acted as a sedative on

Mr Dorrit's cough. He remarked with his utmost politeness, that he must beg to protest against its being supposed, even by Mrs Merdle, the accomplished and graceful (to which compliment she bent herself), that such enterprises as Mr Merdle's, apart as they were from the puny undertakings of the rest of men, had any lower tendency than to enlarge and expand the genius in which they were conceived. 'You are generosity itself,' said Mrs Merdle in return, smiling her best smile; 'let us hope so. But I confess I am almost superstitious in my ideas about business.'

Mr Dorrit threw in another compliment here, to the effect that business, like the time which was precious in it, was made for slaves; and that it was not for Mrs Merdle, who ruled all hearts at her supreme pleasure, to have anything to do with it. Mrs Merdle laughed, and conveyed to Mr Dorrit an idea that the Bosom flushed—which was one of her best effects.

'I say so much,' she then explained, 'merely because Mr Merdle has always taken the greatest interest in Edmund, and has always expressed the strongest desire to advance his prospects. Edmund's public position, I think you know. His private position rests solely with Mr Merdle. In my foolish incapacity for business, I assure you I know no more.'

Mr Dorrit again expressed, in his own way, the sentiment that business was below the ken of enslavers and enchantresses. He then mentioned his intention, as a gentleman and a parent, of writing to Mr Merdle. Mrs Merdle concurred with all her heart—or with all her art, which was exactly the same thing—and herself despatched a preparatory letter by the next post to the eighth wonder of the world.

In his epistolary communication, as in his dialogues and discourses on the great question to which it related, Mr Dorrit surrounded the subject with flourishes, as writing-masters embellish copy-books and ciphering-books: where the titles of the elementary rules of arithmetic diverge into swans, eagles, griffins, and other calligraphic recreations, and where the capital letters go out of their minds and bodies into ecstasies of pen and ink. Nevertheless, he did render the purport of his letter sufficiently clear, to enable Mr Merdle to make a decent pretence of having learnt it from that source. Mr Merdle replied to it accordingly. Mr Dorrit replied to Mr Merdle; Mr Merdle replied to Mr Dorrit; and it was soon announced that the corresponding powers had come to a satisfactory understanding.

Now, and not before, Miss Fanny burst upon the scene, completely arrayed for her new part. Now and not before, she wholly absorbed Mr Sparkler in her light, and shone for both, and twenty more. No longer feeling that want of a defined place and character which had caused her so much trouble, this fair ship began to steer steadily on a shaped course, and to swim with a weight and balance that developed her sailing qualities.

'The preliminaries being so satisfactorily arranged, I think I will now, my dear,' said Mr Dorrit, 'announce—ha—formally, to Mrs General—'

'Papa,' returned Fanny, taking him up short upon that name, 'I don't see what Mrs General has got to do with it.'

'My dear,' said Mr Dorrit, 'it will be an act of courtesy to—hum—a lady, well bred and refined—'

'Oh! I am sick of Mrs General's good breeding and refinement, papa,' said Fanny. 'I am tired of Mrs General.'

'Tired,' repeated Mr Dorrit in reproachful astonishment, 'of—ha—Mrs General.'

'Quite disgusted with her, papa,' said Fanny. 'I really don't see what she has to do with my marriage. Let her keep to her own matrimonial projects—if she has any.'

'Fanny,' returned Mr Dorrit, with a grave and weighty slowness upon him, contrasting strongly with his daughter's levity: 'I beg the favour of your explaining—ha—what it is you mean.'

'I mean, papa,' said Fanny, 'that if Mrs General should happen to have any matrimonial projects of her own, I dare say they are quite enough to occupy her spare time. And that if she has not, so much the better; but still I don't wish to have the honour of making announcements to her.'

'Permit me to ask you, Fanny,' said Mr Dorrit, 'why not?'

'Because she can find my engagement out for herself, papa,' retorted Fanny. 'She is watchful enough, I dare say. I think I have seen her so. Let her find it out for herself. If she should not find it out for herself, she will know it when I am married. And I hope you will not consider me wanting in affection for you, papa, if I say it strikes me that will be quite enough for Mrs General.'

'Fanny,' returned Mr Dorrit, 'I am amazed, I am displeased by this—hum—this capricious and unintelligible display of animosity towards—ha—Mrs General.'

'Do not, if you please, papa,' urged Fanny, 'call it animosity, because I assure you I do not consider Mrs General worth my animosity.'

At this, Mr Dorrit rose from his chair with a fixed look of severe reproof, and remained standing in his dignity before his daughter. His daughter, turning the bracelet on her arm, and now looking at him, and now looking from him, said, 'Very well, papa. I am truly sorry if you don't like it; but I can't help it. I am not a child, and I am not Amy, and I must speak.'

'Fanny,' gasped Mr Dorrit, after a majestic silence, 'if I request you to remain here, while I formally announce to Mrs General, as an exemplary lady, who is—hum—a trusted member of this family, the—ha—the change that is contemplated among us; if I—ha—not only request it, but—hum—insist upon it—'

'Oh, papa,' Fanny broke in with pointed significance, 'if you make so much of it as that, I have in duty nothing to do but comply. I hope I may have my thoughts upon the subject, however, for I really cannot help it under the circumstances.' So, Fanny sat down with a meekness which, in the junction of extremes, became defiance; and her father, either not deigning to answer, or not knowing what to answer, summoned Mr Tinkler into his presence.

'Mrs General.'

Mr Tinkler, unused to receive such short orders in connection with the fair varnisher, paused. Mr Dorrit, seeing the whole Marshalsea and all its testimonials in the pause, instantly flew at him with, 'How dare you, sir? What do you mean?'

'I beg your pardon, sir,' pleaded Mr Tinkler, 'I was wishful to know—'

'You wished to know nothing, sir,' cried Mr Dorrit, highly flushed. 'Don't tell me you did. Ha. You didn't. You are guilty of mockery, sir.'

'I assure you, sir—' Mr Tinkler began.

'Don't assure me!' said Mr Dorrit. 'I will not be assured by a domestic. You are guilty of mockery. You shall leave me—hum—the whole establishment shall leave me. What are you waiting for?'

'Only for my orders, sir.'

'It's false,' said Mr Dorrit, 'you have your orders. Ha—hum. My compliments to Mrs General, and I beg the favour of her coming to me, if quite convenient, for a few minutes. Those are your orders.'

In his execution of this mission, Mr Tinkler perhaps expressed that Mr Dorrit was in a raging fume. However that was, Mrs General's skirts were very speedily heard outside, coming along—one might almost have said bouncing along—with unusual expedition. Albeit, they settled down at the door and swept into the room with their customary coolness.

'Mrs General,' said Mr Dorrit, 'take a chair.'

Mrs General, with a graceful curve of acknowledgment, descended into the chair which Mr Dorrit offered.

'Madam,' pursued that gentleman, 'as you have had the kindness to undertake the—hum—formation of my daughters, and as I am persuaded that nothing nearly affecting them can—ha—be indifferent to you—'

'Wholly impossible,' said Mrs General in the calmest of ways.

'—I therefore wish to announce to you, madam, that my daughter now present—'

Mrs General made a slight inclination of her head to Fanny, who made a very low inclination of her head to Mrs General, and came loftily upright again.

'—That my daughter Fanny is—ha—contracted to be married to Mr Sparkler, with whom you are acquainted. Hence, madam, you will be relieved of half your difficult charge—ha—difficult charge.' Mr Dorrit repeated it with his angry eye on Fanny. 'But not, I hope, to the—hum—diminution of any other portion, direct or indirect, of the footing you have at present the kindness to occupy in my family.'

'Mr Dorrit,' returned Mrs General, with her gloved hands resting on one another in exemplary repose, 'is ever considerate, and ever but too appreciative of my friendly services.'

(Miss Fanny coughed, as much as to say, 'You are right.')

'Miss Dorrit has no doubt exercised the soundest discretion of which the circumstances admitted, and I trust will allow me to offer her my sincere congratulations. When free from the trammels of passion,' Mrs General closed her eyes at the word, as if she could not utter it, and see anybody; 'when occurring with the approbation of near relatives; and when cementing the proud structure of a family edifice; these are usually auspicious events. I trust Miss Dorrit will allow me to offer her my best congratulations.'

Here Mrs General stopped, and added internally, for the setting of her face, 'Papa, potatoes, poultry, Prunes, and prism.'

'Mr Dorrit,' she superadded aloud, 'is ever most obliging; and for the attention, and I will add distinction, of having this confidence imparted to me by himself and Miss Dorrit at this early time, I beg to offer the tribute of my thanks. My thanks, and my congratulations, are equally the meed of Mr Dorrit and of Miss Dorrit.'

'To me,' observed Miss Fanny, 'they are excessively gratifying—inexpressibly so. The relief of finding that you have no objection to make, Mrs General, quite takes a load off my mind, I am sure. I hardly know what I should have done,' said Fanny, 'if you had interposed any objection, Mrs General.'

Mrs General changed her gloves, as to the right glove being uppermost and the left undermost, with a Prunes and Prism smile.

'To preserve your approbation, Mrs General,' said Fanny, returning the smile with one in which there was no trace of those ingredients, 'will of course be the highest object of my married life; to lose it, would of course be perfect wretchedness. I am sure your great kindness will not object, and I hope papa will not object, to my correcting a small mistake you have made, however. The best of us are so liable to mistakes, that even you, Mrs General, have fallen into a little error. The attention and distinction you have so impressively mentioned, Mrs General, as attaching to this confidence, are, I have no doubt, of the most complimentary and gratifying description; but they don't at all proceed from me. The merit of having consulted you on the subject would have been so great in me, that I feel I must not lay claim to it when it really is not mine. It is wholly papa's. I am deeply obliged to you for your encouragement and patronage, but it was papa who asked for it. I have to thank you, Mrs General, for relieving my breast of a great weight by so handsomely giving your consent to my engagement, but you have really nothing to thank me for. I hope you will always approve of my proceedings after I have left home and that my sister also may long remain the favoured object of your condescension, Mrs General.'

With this address, which was delivered in her politest manner, Fanny left the room with an elegant and cheerful air—to tear up-stairs with a flushed face as soon as she was out of hearing, pounce in upon her sister, call her a little Dormouse, shake her for the better opening of her eyes, tell her what had passed below, and ask her what she thought of Pa now?

Towards Mrs Merdle, the young lady comported herself with great independence and self-possession; but not as yet with any more decided opening of hostilities. Occasionally they had a slight skirmish, as when Fanny considered herself patted on the back by that lady, or as when Mrs Merdle looked particularly young and well; but Mrs Merdle always soon terminated those passages of arms by sinking among her cushions with the gracefullest indifference, and finding her attention otherwise engaged. Society (for that mysterious creature sat upon the Seven Hills too) found Miss Fanny vastly improved by her engagement. She was much more accessible, much more free and engaging, much less exacting; insomuch that she now entertained a host of followers and admirers, to the bitter indignation of ladies with daughters to marry, who were to be regarded as Having revolted from Society on the Miss Dorrit grievance, and erected a rebellious standard. Enjoying the flutter she caused. Miss Dorrit not only haughtily moved through it in her own proper person, but haughtily, even Ostentatiously, led Mr Sparkler through it too: seeming to say to them all, 'If I think proper to march among you in triumphal procession attended by this weak captive in bonds, rather than a stronger one, that is my business. Enough that I choose to do it!' Mr Sparkler for his part, questioned nothing; but went wherever he was taken, did whatever he was told, felt that for his bride-elect to be distinguished was for him to be distinguished on the easiest terms, and was truly grateful for being so openly acknowledged.

The winter passing on towards the spring while this condition of affairs prevailed, it became necessary for Mr Sparkler to repair to England, and take his appointed part in the expression and direction of its genius, learning, commerce, spirit, and sense. The land of Shakespeare, Milton, Bacon, Newton, Watt, the land of a host of past and present abstract philosophers, natural philosophers, and subduers of Nature and Art in their myriad forms, called to Mr Sparkler to come and take care of it, lest it should perish. Mr Sparkler, unable to resist the agonised cry from the depths of his country's soul, declared that he must go.

It followed that the question was rendered pressing when, where, and how Mr Sparkler should be married to the foremost girl in all this world with no nonsense about her. Its solution, after some little mystery and secrecy, Miss Fanny herself announced to her sister.

'Now, my child,' said she, seeking her out one day, 'I am going to tell you something. It is only this moment broached; and naturally I hurry to you the moment it is broached.'

'Your marriage, Fanny?'

'My precious child,' said Fanny, 'don't anticipate me. Let me impart my confidence to you, you flurried little thing, in my own way. As to your guess, if I answered it literally, I should answer no. For really it is not my marriage that is in question, half as much as it is Edmund's.'

Little Dorrit looked, and perhaps not altogether without cause, somewhat at a loss to understand this fine distinction.

'I am in no difficulty,' exclaimed Fanny, 'and in no hurry. I am not wanted at any public office, or to give any vote anywhere else. But Edmund is. And Edmund is deeply dejected at the idea of going away by himself, and, indeed, I don't like that he should be trusted by himself. For, if it's possible—and it generally is—to do a foolish thing, he is sure to do it.'

As she concluded this impartial summary of the reliance that might be safely placed upon her future husband, she took off, with an air of business, the bonnet she wore, and dangled it by its strings upon the ground.

'It is far more Edmund's question, therefore, than mine. However, we need say no more about that. That is self-evident on the face of it. Well, my dearest Amy! The point arising, is he to go by himself, or is he not to go by himself, this other point arises, are we to be married here and shortly, or are we to be married at home months hence?'

'I see I am going to lose you, Fanny.'

'What a little thing you are,' cried Fanny, half tolerant and half impatient, 'for anticipating one! Pray, my darling, hear me out. That woman,' she spoke of Mrs Merdle, of course, 'remains here until after Easter; so, in the case of my being married here and going to London with Edmund, I should have the start of her. That is something. Further, Amy. That woman being out of the way, I don't know that I greatly object to Mr Merdle's proposal to Pa that Edmund and I should take up our abode in that house—you know—where you once went with a dancer, my dear, until our own house can be chosen and fitted up. Further still, Amy. Papa having always intended to go to town himself, in the spring,—you see, if Edmund and I were married here, we might go off to Florence, where papa might join us, and we might all three travel home together. Mr Merdle has entreated Pa to stay with him in that same mansion I have mentioned, and I suppose he will. But he is master of his own actions; and upon that point (which is not at all material) I can't speak positively.'

The difference between papa's being master of his own actions and Mr Sparkler's being nothing of the sort, was forcibly expressed by Fanny in her manner of stating the case. Not that her sister noticed it; for she was divided between regret at the coming separation, and a lingering wish that she had been included in the plans for visiting England.

'And these are the arrangements, Fanny dear?'

'Arrangements!' repeated Fanny. 'Now, really, child, you are a little trying. You know I particularly guarded myself against laying my words open to any such construction. What I said was, that certain questions present themselves; and these are the questions.'

Little Dorrit's thoughtful eyes met hers, tenderly and quietly.

'Now, my own sweet girl,' said Fanny, weighing her bonnet by the strings with considerable impatience, 'it's no use staring. A little owl could stare. I look to you for advice, Amy. What do you advise me to do?'

'Do you think,' asked Little Dorrit, persuasively, after a short hesitation, 'do you think, Fanny, that if you were to put it off for a few months, it might be, considering all things, best?'

'No, little Tortoise,' retorted Fanny, with exceeding sharpness. 'I don't think anything of the kind.'

Here, she threw her bonnet from her altogether, and flounced into a chair. But, becoming affectionate almost immediately, she flounced out of it again, and kneeled down on the floor to take her sister, chair and all, in her arms.

'Don't suppose I am hasty or unkind, darling, because I really am not. But you are such a little oddity! You make one bite your head off, when one wants to be soothing beyond everything. Didn't I tell you, you dearest baby, that Edmund can't be trusted by himself? And don't you know that he can't?'

'Yes, yes, Fanny. You said so, I know.'

'And you know it, I know,' retorted Fanny. 'Well, my precious child! If he is not to be trusted by himself, it follows, I suppose, that I should go with him?'

'It—seems so, love,' said Little Dorrit.

'Therefore, having heard the arrangements that are feasible to carry out that object, am I to understand, dearest Amy, that on the whole you advise me to make them?'

'It—seems so, love,' said Little Dorrit again.

'Very well,' cried Fanny with an air of resignation, 'then I suppose it must be done! I came to you, my sweet, the moment I saw the doubt, and the necessity of deciding. I have now decided. So let it be.'

After yielding herself up, in this pattern manner, to sisterly advice and the force of circumstances, Fanny became quite benignant: as one who had laid her own inclinations at the feet of her dearest friend, and felt a glow of conscience in having made the sacrifice. 'After all, my Amy,' she said to her sister, 'you are the best of small creatures, and full of good sense; and I don't know what I shall ever do without you!'

With which words she folded her in a closer embrace, and a really fond one.

'Not that I contemplate doing without You, Amy, by any means, for I hope we shall ever be next to inseparable. And now, my pet, I am going to give you a word of advice. When you are left alone here with Mrs General—'

'I am to be left alone here with Mrs General?' said Little Dorrit, quietly.

'Why, of course, my precious, till papa comes back! Unless you call Edward company, which he certainly is not, even when he is here, and still more certainly is not when he is away at Naples or in Sicily. I was going to say—but you are such a beloved little Marplot for putting one out—when you are left alone here with Mrs General, Amy, don't you let her slide into any sort of artful understanding with you that she is looking after Pa, or that Pa is looking after her. She will if she can. I know her sly manner of feeling her way with those gloves of hers. But don't you comprehend her on any account. And if Pa should tell you when he comes back, that he has it in contemplation to make Mrs General your mama (which is not the less likely because I am going away), my advice to you is, that you say at once, "Papa, I beg to object most strongly. Fanny cautioned me about this, and she objected, and I object." I don't mean to say that any objection from you, Amy, is likely to be of the smallest effect, or that I think you likely to make it with any degree of firmness. But there is a principle involved—a filial principle—and I implore you not to submit to be mother-in-lawed by Mrs General, without asserting it in making every one about you as uncomfortable as possible. I don't expect you to stand by it—indeed, I know you won't, Pa being concerned—but I wish to rouse you to a sense of duty. As to any help from me, or as to any opposition that I can offer to such a match, you shall not be left in the lurch, my love. Whatever weight I may derive from my position as a married girl not wholly devoid of attractions—used, as that position always shall be, to oppose that woman—I will bring to bear, you May depend upon it, on the head and false hair (for I am confident it's not all real, ugly as it is and unlikely as it appears that any One in their Senses would go to the expense of buying it) of Mrs General!'

Little Dorrit received this counsel without venturing to oppose it but without giving Fanny any reason to believe that she intended to act upon it. Having now, as it were, formally wound up her single life and arranged her worldly affairs, Fanny proceeded with characteristic ardour to prepare for the serious change in her condition.

The preparation consisted in the despatch of her maid to Paris under the protection of the Courier, for the purchase of that outfit for a bride on which it would be extremely low, in the present narrative, to bestow an English name, but to which (on a vulgar principle it observes of adhering to the language in which it professes to be written) it declines to give a French one. The rich and beautiful wardrobe purchased by these agents, in the course of a few weeks made its way through the intervening country, bristling with custom-houses, garrisoned by an immense army of shabby mendicants in uniform who incessantly repeated the Beggar's Petition over it, as if every individual warrior among them were the ancient Belisarius: and of whom there were so many Legions, that unless the Courier had expended just one bushel and a half of silver money relieving their distresses, they would have worn the wardrobe out before it got to Rome, by turning it over and over. Through all such dangers, however, it was triumphantly brought, inch by inch, and arrived at its journey's end in fine condition.

There it was exhibited to select companies of female viewers, in whose gentle bosoms it awakened implacable feelings. Concurrently, active preparations were made for the day on which some of its treasures were to be publicly displayed. Cards of breakfast-invitation were sent out to half the English in the city of Romulus; the other half made arrangements to be under arms, as criticising volunteers, at various outer points of the solemnity. The most high and illustrious English Signor Edgardo Dorrit, came post through the deep mud and ruts (from forming a surface under the improving Neapolitan nobility), to grace the occasion. The best hotel and all its culinary myrmidons, were set to work to prepare the feast. The drafts of Mr Dorrit almost constituted a run on the Torlonia Bank. The British Consul hadn't had such a marriage in the whole of his Consularity.

The day came, and the She-Wolf in the Capitol might have snarled with envy to see how the Island Savages contrived these things now-a-days. The murderous-headed statues of the wicked Emperors of the Soldiery, whom sculptors had not been able to flatter out of their villainous hideousness, might have come off their pedestals to run away with the Bride. The choked old fountain, where erst the gladiators washed, might have leaped into life again to honour the ceremony. The Temple of Vesta might have sprung up anew from its ruins, expressly to lend its countenance to the occasion. Might have done; but did not. Like sentient things—even like the lords and ladies of creation sometimes—might have done much, but did nothing. The celebration went off with admirable pomp; monks in black robes, white robes, and russet robes stopped to look after the carriages; wandering peasants in fleeces of sheep, begged and piped under the house-windows; the English volunteers defiled; the day wore on to the hour of vespers; the festival wore away; the thousand churches rang their bells without any reference to it; and St Peter denied that he had anything to do with it.

But by that time the Bride was near the end of the first day's journey towards Florence. It was the peculiarity of the nuptials that they were all Bride. Nobody noticed the Bridegroom. Nobody noticed the first Bridesmaid. Few could have seen Little Dorrit (who held that post) for the glare, even supposing many to have sought her. So, the Bride had mounted into her handsome chariot, incidentally accompanied by the Bridegroom; and after rolling for a few minutes smoothly over a fair pavement, had begun to jolt through a Slough of Despond, and through a long, long avenue of wrack and ruin. Other nuptial carriages are said to have gone the same road, before and since.

If Little Dorrit found herself left a little lonely and a little low that night, nothing would have done so much against her feeling of depression as the being able to sit at work by her father, as in the old time, and help him to his supper and his rest. But that was not to be thought of now, when they sat in the state-equipage with Mrs General on the coach-box. And as to supper! If Mr Dorrit had wanted supper, there was an Italian cook and there was a Swiss confectioner, who must have put on caps as high as the Pope's Mitre, and have performed the mysteries of Alchemists in a copper-saucepaned laboratory below, before he could have got it.

He was sententious and didactic that night. If he had been simply loving, he would have done Little Dorrit more good; but she accepted him as he was—when had she not accepted him as he was!—and made the most and best of him. Mrs General at length retired. Her retirement for the night was always her frostiest ceremony, as if she felt it necessary that the human imagination should be chilled into stone to prevent its following her. When she had gone through her rigid preliminaries, amounting to a sort of genteel platoon-exercise, she withdrew. Little Dorrit then put her arm round her father's neck, to bid him good night.

'Amy, my dear,' said Mr Dorrit, taking her by the hand, 'this is the close of a day, that has—ha—greatly impressed and gratified me.'

'A little tired you, dear, too?'

'No,' said Mr Dorrit, 'no: I am not sensible of fatigue when it arises from an occasion so—hum—replete with gratification of the purest kind.'

Little Dorrit was glad to find him in such heart, and smiled from her own heart.

'My dear,' he continued, 'this is an occasion—ha—teeming with a good example. With a good example, my favourite and attached child—hum—to you.'

Little Dorrit, fluttered by his words, did not know what to say, though he stopped as if he expected her to say something.

'Amy,' he resumed; 'your dear sister, our Fanny, has contracted ha hum—a marriage, eminently calculated to extend the basis of our—ha—connection, and to—hum—consolidate our social relations. My love, I trust that the time is not far distant when some—ha—eligible partner may be found for you.'

'Oh no! Let me stay with you. I beg and pray that I may stay with you! I want nothing but to stay and take care of you!'

She said it like one in sudden alarm.

'Nay, Amy, Amy,' said Mr Dorrit. 'This is weak and foolish, weak and foolish. You have a—ha—responsibility imposed upon you by your position. It is to develop that position, and be—hum—worthy of that position. As to taking care of me; I can—ha—take care of myself. Or,' he added after a moment, 'if I should need to be taken care of, I—hum—can, with the—ha—blessing of Providence, be taken care of, I—ha hum—I cannot, my dear child, think of engrossing, and—ha—as it were, sacrificing you.'

O what a time of day at which to begin that profession of self-denial; at which to make it, with an air of taking credit for it; at which to believe it, if such a thing could be!

'Don't speak, Amy. I positively say I cannot do it. I—ha—must not do it. My—hum—conscience would not allow it. I therefore, my love, take the opportunity afforded by this gratifying and impressive occasion of—ha—solemnly remarking, that it is now a cherished wish and purpose of mine to see you—ha—eligibly (I repeat eligibly) married.'

'Oh no, dear! Pray!'

'Amy,' said Mr Dorrit, 'I am well persuaded that if the topic were referred to any person of superior social knowledge, of superior delicacy and sense—let us say, for instance, to—ha—Mrs General—that there would not be two opinions as to the—hum—affectionate character and propriety of my sentiments. But, as I know your loving and dutiful nature from—hum—from experience, I am quite satisfied that it is necessary to say no more. I have—hum—no husband to propose at present, my dear: I have not even one in view. I merely wish that we should—ha—understand each other. Hum. Good night, my dear and sole remaining daughter. Good night. God bless you!'

If the thought ever entered Little Dorrit's head that night, that he could give her up lightly now in his prosperity, and when he had it in his mind to replace her with a second wife, she drove it away. Faithful to him still, as in the worst times through which she had borne him single-handed, she drove the thought away; and entertained no harder reflection, in her tearful unrest, than that he now saw everything through their wealth, and through the care he always had upon him that they should continue rich, and grow richer.

They sat in their equipage of state, with Mrs General on the box, for three weeks longer, and then he started for Florence to join Fanny. Little Dorrit would have been glad to bear him company so far, only for the sake of her own love, and then to have turned back alone, thinking of dear England. But, though the Courier had gone on with the Bride, the Valet was next in the line; and the succession would not have come to her, as long as any one could be got for money.

Mrs General took life easily—as easily, that is, as she could take anything—when the Roman establishment remained in their sole occupation; and Little Dorrit would often ride out in a hired carriage that was left them, and alight alone and wander among the ruins of old Rome. The ruins of the vast old Amphitheatre, of the old Temples, of the old commemorative Arches, of the old trodden highways, of the old tombs, besides being what they were, to her were ruins of the old Marshalsea—ruins of her own old life—ruins of the faces and forms that of old peopled it—ruins of its loves, hopes, cares, and joys. Two ruined spheres of action and suffering were before the solitary girl often sitting on some broken fragment; and in the lonely places, under the blue sky, she saw them both together.

Up, then, would come Mrs General; taking all the colour out of everything, as Nature and Art had taken it out of herself; writing Prunes and Prism, in Mr Eustace's text, wherever she could lay a hand; looking everywhere for Mr Eustace and company, and seeing nothing else; scratching up the driest little bones of antiquity, and bolting them whole without any human visitings—like a Ghoule in gloves.

CHAPTER 16. Getting on

The newly married pair, on their arrival in Harley Street, Cavendish Square, London, were received by the Chief Butler. That great man was not interested in them, but on the whole endured them. People must continue to be married and given in marriage, or Chief Butlers would not be wanted. As nations are made to be taxed, so families are made to be butlered. The Chief Butler, no doubt, reflected that the course of nature required the wealthy population to be kept up, on his account.

He therefore condescended to look at the carriage from the Hall-door without frowning at it, and said, in a very handsome way, to one of his men, 'Thomas, help with the luggage.' He even escorted the Bride up-stairs into Mr Merdle's presence; but this must be considered as an act of homage to the sex (of which he was an admirer, being notoriously captivated by the charms of a certain Duchess), and not as a committal of himself with the family.

Mr Merdle was slinking about the hearthrug, waiting to welcome Mrs Sparkler. His hand seemed to retreat up his sleeve as he advanced to do so, and he gave her such a superfluity of coat-cuff that it was like being received by the popular conception of Guy Fawkes. When he put his lips to hers, besides, he took himself into custody by the wrists, and backed himself among the ottomans and chairs and tables as if he were his own Police officer, saying to himself, 'Now, none of that! Come! I've got you, you know, and you go quietly along with me!'

Mrs Sparkler, installed in the rooms of state—the innermost sanctuary of down, silk, chintz, and fine linen—felt that so far her triumph was good, and her way made, step by step. On the day before her marriage, she had bestowed on Mrs Merdle's maid with an air of gracious indifference, in Mrs Merdle's presence, a trifling little keepsake (bracelet, bonnet, and two dresses, all new) about four times as valuable as the present formerly made by Mrs Merdle to her. She was now established in Mrs Merdle's own rooms, to which some extra touches had been given to render them more worthy of her occupation. In her mind's eye, as she lounged there, surrounded by every luxurious accessory that wealth could obtain or invention devise, she saw the fair bosom that beat in unison with the exultation of her thoughts, competing with the bosom that had been famous so long, outshining it, and deposing it. Happy? Fanny must have been happy. No more wishing one's self dead now.

The Courier had not approved of Mr Dorrit's staying in the house of a friend, and had preferred to take him to an hotel in Brook Street, Grosvenor Square. Mr Merdle ordered his carriage to be ready early in the morning that he might wait upon Mr Dorrit immediately after breakfast.

Bright the carriage looked, sleek the horses looked, gleaming the harness looked, luscious and lasting the liveries looked. A rich, responsible turn-out. An equipage for a Merdle. Early people looked after it as it rattled along the streets, and said, with awe in their breath, 'There he goes!'

There he went, until Brook Street stopped him. Then, forth from its magnificent case came the jewel; not lustrous in itself, but quite the contrary.

Commotion in the office of the hotel. Merdle! The landlord, though a gentleman of a haughty spirit who had just driven a pair of thorough-bred horses into town, turned out to show him up-stairs. The clerks and servants cut him off by back-passages, and were found accidentally hovering in doorways and angles, that they might look upon him. Merdle! O ye sun, moon, and stars, the great man! The rich man, who had in a manner revised the New Testament, and already entered into the kingdom of Heaven. The man who could have any one he chose to dine with him, and who had made the money! As he went up the stairs, people were already posted on the lower stairs, that his shadow might fall upon them when he came down. So were the sick brought out and laid in the track of the Apostle—who had not got into the good society, and had not made the money.

Mr Dorrit, dressing-gowned and newspapered, was at his breakfast. The Courier, with agitation in his voice, announced 'Miss Mairdale!' Mr Dorrit's overwrought heart bounded as he leaped up.

'Mr Merdle, this is—ha—indeed an honour. Permit me to express the—hum—sense, the high sense, I entertain of this—ha hum—highly gratifying act of attention. I am well aware, sir, of the many demands upon your time, and its—ha—enormous value,' Mr Dorrit could not say enormous roundly enough for his own satisfaction. 'That you should—ha—at this early hour, bestow any of your priceless time upon me, is—ha—a compliment that I acknowledge with the greatest esteem.' Mr Dorrit positively trembled in addressing the great man.

Mr Merdle uttered, in his subdued, inward, hesitating voice, a few sounds that were to no purpose whatever; and finally said, 'I am glad to see you, sir.'

'You are very kind,' said Mr Dorrit. 'Truly kind.' By this time the visitor was seated, and was passing his great hand over his exhausted forehead. 'You are well, I hope, Mr Merdle?'

'I am as well as I—yes, I am as well as I usually am,' said Mr Merdle.

'Your occupations must be immense.'

'Tolerably so. But—Oh dear no, there's not much the matter with me,' said Mr Merdle, looking round the room.

'A little dyspeptic?' Mr Dorrit hinted.

'Very likely. But I—Oh, I am well enough,' said Mr Merdle.

There were black traces on his lips where they met, as if a little train of gunpowder had been fired there; and he looked like a man who, if his natural temperament had been quicker, would have been very feverish that morning. This, and his heavy way of passing his hand over his forehead, had prompted Mr Dorrit's solicitous inquiries.

'Mrs Merdle,' Mr Dorrit insinuatingly pursued, 'I left, as you will be prepared to hear, the—ha—observed of all observers, the—hum—admired of all admirers, the leading fascination and charm of Society in Rome. She was looking wonderfully well when I quitted it.'

'Mrs Merdle,' said Mr Merdle, 'is generally considered a very attractive woman. And she is, no doubt. I am sensible of her being so.'

'Who can be otherwise?' responded Mr Dorrit.

Mr Merdle turned his tongue in his closed mouth—it seemed rather a stiff and unmanageable tongue—moistened his lips, passed his hand over his forehead again, and looked all round the room again, principally under the chairs.

'But,' he said, looking Mr Dorrit in the face for the first time, and immediately afterwards dropping his eyes to the buttons of Mr Dorrit's waistcoat; 'if we speak of attractions, your daughter ought to be the subject of our conversation. She is extremely beautiful. Both in face and figure, she is quite uncommon. When the young people arrived last night, I was really surprised to see such charms.'

Mr Dorrit's gratification was such that he said—ha—he could not refrain from telling Mr Merdle verbally, as he had already done by letter, what honour and happiness he felt in this union of their families. And he offered his hand. Mr Merdle looked at the hand for a little while, took it on his for a moment as if his were a yellow salver or fish-slice, and then returned it to Mr Dorrit.

'I thought I would drive round the first thing,' said Mr Merdle, 'to offer my services, in case I can do anything for you; and to say that I hope you will at least do me the honour of dining with me to-day, and every day when you are not better engaged during your stay in town.'

Mr Dorrit was enraptured by these attentions.

'Do you stay long, sir?'

'I have not at present the intention,' said Mr Dorrit, 'of—ha—exceeding a fortnight.'

'That's a very short stay, after so long a journey,' returned Mr Merdle.

'Hum. Yes,' said Mr Dorrit. 'But the truth is—ha—my dear Mr Merdle, that I find a foreign life so well suited to my health and taste, that I—hum—have but two objects in my present visit to London. First, the—ha—the distinguished happiness and—ha—privilege which I now enjoy and appreciate; secondly, the arrangement—hum—the laying out, that is to say, in the best way, of—ha, hum—my money.'

'Well, sir,' said Mr Merdle, after turning his tongue again, 'if I can be of any use to you in that respect, you may command me.'

Mr Dorrit's speech had had more hesitation in it than usual, as he approached the ticklish topic, for he was not perfectly clear how so exalted a potentate might take it. He had doubts whether reference to any individual capital, or fortune, might not seem a wretchedly retail affair to so wholesale a dealer. Greatly relieved by Mr Merdle's affable offer of assistance, he caught at it directly, and heaped acknowledgments upon him.

'I scarcely—ha—dared,' said Mr Dorrit, 'I assure you, to hope for so—hum—vast an advantage as your direct advice and assistance. Though of course I should, under any circumstances, like the—ha, hum—rest of the civilised world, have followed in Mr Merdle's train.'

'You know we may almost say we are related, sir,' said Mr Merdle, curiously interested in the pattern of the carpet, 'and, therefore, you may consider me at your service.'

'Ha. Very handsome, indeed!' cried Mr Dorrit. 'Ha. Most handsome!'

'It would not,' said Mr Merdle, 'be at the present moment easy for what I may call a mere outsider to come into any of the good things—of course I speak of my own good things—'

'Of course, of course!' cried Mr Dorrit, in a tone implying that there were no other good things.

'—Unless at a high price. At what we are accustomed to term a very long figure.'

Mr Dorrit laughed in the buoyancy of his spirit. Ha, ha, ha! Long figure. Good. Ha. Very expressive to be sure!

'However,' said Mr Merdle, 'I do generally retain in my own hands the power of exercising some preference—people in general would be pleased to call it favour—as a sort of compliment for my care and trouble.'

'And public spirit and genius,' Mr Dorrit suggested.

Mr Merdle, with a dry, swallowing action, seemed to dispose of those qualities like a bolus; then added, 'As a sort of return for it. I will see, if you please, how I can exert this limited power (for people are jealous, and it is limited), to your advantage.'

'You are very good,' replied Mr Dorrit. 'You are very good.'

'Of course,' said Mr Merdle, 'there must be the strictest integrity and uprightness in these transactions; there must be the purest faith between man and man; there must be unimpeached and unimpeachable confidence; or business could not be carried on.'

Mr Dorrit hailed these generous sentiments with fervour.

'Therefore,' said Mr Merdle, 'I can only give you a preference to a certain extent.'

'I perceive. To a defined extent,' observed Mr Dorrit.

'Defined extent. And perfectly above-board. As to my advice, however,' said Mr Merdle, 'that is another matter. That, such as it is—'

Oh! Such as it was! (Mr Dorrit could not bear the faintest appearance of its being depreciated, even by Mr Merdle himself.)

'—That, there is nothing in the bonds of spotless honour between myself and my fellow-man to prevent my parting with, if I choose. And that,' said Mr Merdle, now deeply intent upon a dust-cart that was passing the windows, 'shall be at your command whenever you think proper.'

New acknowledgments from Mr Dorrit. New passages of Mr Merdle's hand over his forehead. Calm and silence. Contemplation of Mr Dorrit's waistcoat buttons by Mr Merdle.

'My time being rather precious,' said Mr Merdle, suddenly getting up, as if he had been waiting in the interval for his legs and they had just come, 'I must be moving towards the City. Can I take you anywhere, sir? I shall be happy to set you down, or send you on. My carriage is at your disposal.'

Mr Dorrit bethought himself that he had business at his banker's. His banker's was in the City. That was fortunate; Mr Merdle would take him into the City. But, surely, he might not detain Mr Merdle while he assumed his coat? Yes, he might and must; Mr Merdle insisted on it. So Mr Dorrit, retiring into the next room, put himself under the hands of his valet, and in five minutes came back glorious.

Then said Mr Merdle, 'Allow me, sir. Take my arm!' Then leaning on Mr Merdle's arm, did Mr Dorrit descend the staircase, seeing the worshippers on the steps, and feeling that the light of Mr Merdle shone by reflection in himself. Then the carriage, and the ride into the City; and the people who looked at them; and the hats that flew off grey heads; and the general bowing and crouching before this wonderful mortal the like of which prostration of spirit was not to be seen—no, by high Heaven, no! It may be worth thinking of by Fawners of all denominations—in Westminster Abbey and Saint Paul's Cathedral put together, on any Sunday in the year. It was a rapturous dream to Mr Dorrit to find himself set aloft in this public car of triumph, making a magnificent progress to that befitting destination, the golden Street of the Lombards.

There Mr Merdle insisted on alighting and going his way a-foot, and leaving his poor equipage at Mr Dorrit's disposition. So the dream increased in rapture when Mr Dorrit came out of the bank alone, and people looked at him in default of Mr Merdle, and when, with the ears of his mind, he heard the frequent exclamation as he rolled glibly along, 'A wonderful man to be Mr Merdle's friend!'

At dinner that day, although the occasion was not foreseen and provided for, a brilliant company of such as are not made of the dust of the earth, but of some superior article for the present unknown, shed their lustrous benediction upon Mr Dorrit's daughter's marriage. And Mr Dorrit's daughter that day began, in earnest, her competition with that woman not present; and began it so well that Mr Dorrit could all but have taken his affidavit, if required, that Mrs Sparkler had all her life been lying at full length in the lap of luxury, and had never heard of such a rough word in the English tongue as Marshalsea.

Next day, and the day after, and every day, all graced by more dinner company, cards descended on Mr Dorrit like theatrical snow. As the friend and relative by marriage of the illustrious Merdle, Bar, Bishop, Treasury, Chorus, Everybody, wanted to make or improve Mr Dorrit's acquaintance. In Mr Merdle's heap of offices in the City, when Mr Dorrit appeared at any of them on his business taking him Eastward (which it frequently did, for it throve amazingly), the name of Dorrit was always a passport to the great presence of Merdle. So the dream increased in rapture every hour, as Mr Dorrit felt increasingly sensible that this connection had brought him forward indeed.

Only one thing sat otherwise than auriferously, and at the same time lightly, on Mr Dorrit's mind. It was the Chief Butler. That stupendous character looked at him, in the course of his official looking at the dinners, in a manner that Mr Dorrit considered questionable. He looked at him, as he passed through the hall and up the staircase, going to dinner, with a glazed fixedness that Mr Dorrit did not like. Seated at table in the act of drinking, Mr Dorrit still saw him through his wine-glass, regarding him with a cold and ghostly eye. It misgave him that the Chief Butler must have known a Collegian, and must have seen him in the College—perhaps had been presented to him. He looked as closely at the Chief Butler as such a man could be looked at, and yet he did not recall that he had ever seen him elsewhere. Ultimately he was inclined to think that there was no reverence in the man, no sentiment in the great creature. But he was not relieved by that; for, let him think what he would, the Chief Butler had him in his supercilious eye, even when that eye was on the plate and other table-garniture; and he never let him out of it. To hint to him that this confinement in his eye was disagreeable, or to ask him what he meant, was an act too daring to venture upon; his severity with his employers and their visitors being terrific, and he never permitting himself to be approached with the slightest liberty.

CHAPTER 17. Missing

The term of Mr Dorrit's visit was within two days of being out, and he was about to dress for another inspection by the Chief Butler (whose victims were always dressed expressly for him), when one of the servants of the hotel presented himself bearing a card. Mr Dorrit, taking it, read:

'Mrs Finching.'

The servant waited in speechless deference.

'Man, man,' said Mr Dorrit, turning upon him with grievous indignation, 'explain your motive in bringing me this ridiculous name. I am wholly unacquainted with it. Finching, sir?' said Mr Dorrit, perhaps avenging himself on the Chief Butler by Substitute. 'Ha! What do you mean by Finching?'

The man, man, seemed to mean Flinching as much as anything else, for he backed away from Mr Dorrit's severe regard, as he replied, 'A lady, sir.'

'I know no such lady, sir,' said Mr Dorrit. 'Take this card away. I know no Finching of either sex.'

'Ask your pardon, sir. The lady said she was aware she might be unknown by name. But she begged me to say, sir, that she had formerly the honour of being acquainted with Miss Dorrit. The lady said, sir, the youngest Miss Dorrit.'

Mr Dorrit knitted his brows and rejoined, after a moment or two, 'Inform Mrs Finching, sir,' emphasising the name as if the innocent man were solely responsible for it, 'that she can come up.'

He had reflected, in his momentary pause, that unless she were admitted she might leave some message, or might say something below, having a disgraceful reference to that former state of existence. Hence the concession, and hence the appearance of Flora, piloted in by the man, man.

'I have not the pleasure,' said Mr Dorrit, standing with the card in his hand, and with an air which imported that it would scarcely have been a first-class pleasure if he had had it, 'of knowing either this name, or yourself, madam. Place a chair, sir.'

The responsible man, with a start, obeyed, and went out on tiptoe. Flora, putting aside her veil with a bashful tremor upon her, proceeded to introduce herself. At the same time a singular combination of perfumes was diffused through the room, as if some brandy had been put by mistake in a lavender-water bottle, or as if some lavender-water had been put by mistake in a brandy-bottle.

'I beg Mr Dorrit to offer a thousand apologies and indeed they would be far too few for such an intrusion which I know must appear extremely bold in a lady and alone too, but I thought it best upon the whole however difficult and even apparently improper though Mr F.'s Aunt would have willingly accompanied me and as a character of great force and spirit would probably have struck one possessed of such a knowledge of life as no doubt with so many changes must have been acquired, for Mr F. himself said frequently that although well educated in the neighbourhood of Blackheath at as high as eighty guineas which is a good deal for parents and the plate kept back too on going away but that is more a meanness than its value that he had learnt more in his first years as a commercial traveller with a large commission on the sale of an article that nobody would hear of much less buy which preceded the wine trade a long time than in the whole six years in that academy conducted by a college Bachelor, though why a Bachelor more clever than a married man I do not see and never did but pray excuse me that is not the point.'

Mr Dorrit stood rooted to the carpet, a statue of mystification.

'I must openly admit that I have no pretensions,' said Flora, 'but having known the dear little thing which under altered circumstances appears a liberty but is not so intended and Goodness knows there was no favour in half-a-crown a-day to such a needle as herself but quite the other way and as to anything lowering in it far from it the labourer is worthy of his hire and I am sure I only wish he got it oftener and more animal food and less rheumatism in the back and legs poor soul.'

'Madam,' said Mr Dorrit, recovering his breath by a great effort, as the relict of the late Mr Finching stopped to take hers; 'madam,' said Mr Dorrit, very red in the face, 'if I understand you to refer to—ha—to anything in the antecedents of—hum—a daughter of mine, involving—ha hum—daily compensation, madam, I beg to observe that the—ha—fact, assuming it—ha—to be fact, never was within my knowledge. Hum. I should not have permitted it. Ha. Never! Never!'

'Unnecessary to pursue the subject,' returned Flora, 'and would not have mentioned it on any account except as supposing it a favourable and only letter of introduction but as to being fact no doubt whatever and you may set your mind at rest for the very dress I have on now can prove it and sweetly made though there is no denying that it would tell better on a better figure for my own is much too fat though how to bring it down I know not, pray excuse me I am roving off again.'

Mr Dorrit backed to his chair in a stony way, and seated himself, as Flora gave him a softening look and played with her parasol.

'The dear little thing,' said Flora, 'having gone off perfectly limp and white and cold in my own house or at least papa's for though not a freehold still a long lease at a peppercorn on the morning when Arthur—foolish habit of our youthful days and Mr Clennam far more adapted to existing circumstances particularly addressing a stranger and that stranger a gentleman in an elevated station—communicated the glad tidings imparted by a person of name of Pancks emboldens me.'

At the mention of these two names, Mr Dorrit frowned, stared, frowned again, hesitated with his fingers at his lips, as he had hesitated long ago, and said, 'Do me the favour to—ha—state your pleasure, madam.'

'Mr Dorrit,' said Flora, 'you are very kind in giving me permission and highly natural it seems to me that you should be kind for though more stately I perceive a likeness filled out of course but a likeness still, the object of my intruding is my own without the slightest consultation with any human being and most decidedly not with Arthur—pray excuse me Doyce and Clennam I don't know what I am saying Mr Clennam solus—for to put that individual linked by a golden chain to a purple time when all was ethereal out of any anxiety would be worth to me the ransom of a monarch not that I have the least idea how much that would come to but using it as the total of all I have in the world and more.'

Mr Dorrit, without greatly regarding the earnestness of these latter words, repeated, 'State your pleasure, madam.'

'It's not likely I well know,' said Flora, 'but it's possible and being possible when I had the gratification of reading in the papers that you had arrived from Italy and were going back I made up my mind to try it for you might come across him or hear something of him and if so what a blessing and relief to all!'

'Allow me to ask, madam,' said Mr Dorrit, with his ideas in wild confusion, 'to whom—ha—TO WHOM,' he repeated it with a raised voice in mere desperation, 'you at present allude?'

'To the foreigner from Italy who disappeared in the City as no doubt you have read in the papers equally with myself,' said Flora, 'not referring to private sources by the name of Pancks from which one gathers what dreadfully ill-natured things some people are wicked enough to whisper most likely judging others by themselves and what the uneasiness and indignation of Arthur—quite unable to overcome it Doyce and Clennam—cannot fail to be.'

It happened, fortunately for the elucidation of any intelligible result, that Mr Dorrit had heard or read nothing about the matter. This caused Mrs Finching, with many apologies for being in great practical difficulties as to finding the way to her pocket among the stripes of her dress at length to produce a police handbill, setting forth that a foreign gentleman of the name of Blandois, last from Venice, had unaccountably disappeared on such a night in such a part of the city of London; that he was known to have entered such a house, at such an hour; that he was stated by the inmates of that house to have left it, about so many minutes before midnight; and that he had never been beheld since. This, with exact particulars of time and locality, and with a good detailed description of the foreign gentleman who had so mysteriously vanished, Mr Dorrit read at large.

'Blandois!' said Mr Dorrit. 'Venice! And this description! I know this gentleman. He has been in my house. He is intimately acquainted with a gentleman of good family (but in indifferent circumstances), of whom I am a—hum—patron.'

'Then my humble and pressing entreaty is the more,' said Flora, 'that in travelling back you will have the kindness to look for this foreign gentleman along all the roads and up and down all the turnings and to make inquiries for him at all the hotels and orange-trees and vineyards and volcanoes and places for he must be somewhere and why doesn't he come forward and say he's there and clear all parties up?'

'Pray, madam,' said Mr Dorrit, referring to the handbill again, 'who is Clennam and Co.? Ha. I see the name mentioned here, in connection with the occupation of the house which Monsieur Blandois was seen to enter: who is Clennam and Co.? Is it the individual of whom I had formerly—hum—some—ha—slight transitory knowledge, and to whom I believe you have referred? Is it—ha—that person?'

'It's a very different person indeed,' replied Flora, 'with no limbs and wheels instead and the grimmest of women though his mother.'

'Clennam and Co. a—hum—a mother!' exclaimed Mr Dorrit.

'And an old man besides,' said Flora.

Mr Dorrit looked as if he must immediately be driven out of his mind by this account. Neither was it rendered more favourable to sanity by Flora's dashing into a rapid analysis of Mr Flintwinch's cravat, and describing him, without the lightest boundary line of separation between his identity and Mrs Clennam's, as a rusty screw in gaiters. Which compound of man and woman, no limbs, wheels, rusty screw, grimness, and gaiters, so completely stupefied Mr Dorrit, that he was a spectacle to be pitied.

'But I would not detain you one moment longer,' said Flora, upon whom his condition wrought its effect, though she was quite unconscious of having produced it, 'if you would have the goodness to give your promise as a gentleman that both in going back to Italy and in Italy too you would look for this Mr Blandois high and low and if you found or heard of him make him come forward for the clearing of all parties.'

By that time Mr Dorrit had so far recovered from his bewilderment, as to be able to say, in a tolerably connected manner, that he should consider that his duty. Flora was delighted with her success, and rose to take her leave.

'With a million thanks,' said she, 'and my address upon my card in case of anything to be communicated personally, I will not send my love to the dear little thing for it might not be acceptable, and indeed there is no dear little thing left in the transformation so why do it but both myself and Mr F.'s Aunt ever wish her well and lay no claim to any favour on our side you may be sure of that but quite the other way for what she undertook to do she did and that is more than a great many of us do, not to say anything of her doing it as well as it could be done and I myself am one of them for I have said ever since I began to recover the blow of Mr F's death that I would learn the Organ of which I am extremely fond but of which I am ashamed to say I do not yet know a note, good evening!'

When Mr Dorrit, who attended her to the room-door, had had a little time to collect his senses, he found that the interview had summoned back discarded reminiscences which jarred with the Merdle dinner-table. He wrote and sent off a brief note excusing himself for that day, and ordered dinner presently in his own rooms at the hotel. He had another reason for this.

His time in London was very nearly out, and was anticipated by engagements; his plans were made for returning; and he thought it behoved his importance to pursue some direct inquiry into the Blandois disappearance, and be in a condition to carry back to Mr Henry Gowan the result of his own personal investigation. He therefore resolved that he would take advantage of that evening's freedom to go down to Clennam and Co.'s, easily to be found by the direction set forth in the handbill; and see the place, and ask a question or two there himself.

Having dined as plainly as the establishment and the Courier would let him, and having taken a short sleep by the fire for his better recovery from Mrs Finching, he set out in a hackney-cabriolet alone. The deep bell of St Paul's was striking nine as he passed under the shadow of Temple Bar, headless and forlorn in these degenerate days.

As he approached his destination through the by-streets and water-side ways, that part of London seemed to him an uglier spot at such an hour than he had ever supposed it to be. Many long years had passed since he had seen it; he had never known much of it; and it wore a mysterious and dismal aspect in his eyes. So powerfully was his imagination impressed by it, that when his driver stopped, after having asked the way more than once, and said to the best of his belief this was the gateway they wanted, Mr Dorrit stood hesitating, with the coach-door in his hand, half afraid of the dark look of the place.

Truly, it looked as gloomy that night as even it had ever looked. Two of the handbills were posted on the entrance wall, one on either side, and as the lamp flickered in the night air, shadows passed over them, not unlike the shadows of fingers following the lines. A watch was evidently kept upon the place. As Mr Dorrit paused, a man passed in from over the way, and another man passed out from some dark corner within; and both looked at him in passing, and both remained standing about.

As there was only one house in the enclosure, there was no room for uncertainty, so he went up the steps of that house and knocked. There was a dim light in two windows on the first-floor. The door gave back a dreary, vacant sound, as though the house were empty; but it was not, for a light was visible, and a step was audible, almost directly. They both came to the door, and a chain grated, and a woman with her apron thrown over her face and head stood in the aperture.

'Who is it?' said the woman.

Mr Dorrit, much amazed by this appearance, replied that he was from Italy, and that he wished to ask a question relative to the missing person, whom he knew.

'Hi!' cried the woman, raising a cracked voice. 'Jeremiah!'

Upon this, a dry old man appeared, whom Mr Dorrit thought he identified by his gaiters, as the rusty screw. The woman was under apprehensions of the dry old man, for she whisked her apron away as he approached, and disclosed a pale affrighted face. 'Open the door, you fool,' said the old man; 'and let the gentleman in.'

Mr Dorrit, not without a glance over his shoulder towards his driver and the cabriolet, walked into the dim hall. 'Now, sir,' said Mr Flintwinch, 'you can ask anything here you think proper; there are no secrets here, sir.'

Before a reply could be made, a strong stern voice, though a woman's, called from above, 'Who is it?'

'Who is it?' returned Jeremiah. 'More inquiries. A gentleman from Italy.'

'Bring him up here!'

Mr Flintwinch muttered, as if he deemed that unnecessary; but, turning to Mr Dorrit, said, 'Mrs Clennam. She will do as she likes. I'll show you the way.' He then preceded Mr Dorrit up the blackened staircase; that gentleman, not unnaturally looking behind him on the road, saw the woman following, with her apron thrown over her head again in her former ghastly manner.

Mrs Clennam had her books open on her little table. 'Oh!' said she abruptly, as she eyed her visitor with a steady look. 'You are from Italy, sir, are you. Well?'

Mr Dorrit was at a loss for any more distinct rejoinder at the moment than 'Ha—well?'

'Where is this missing man? Have you come to give us information where he is? I hope you have?'

'So far from it, I—hum—have come to seek information.'

'Unfortunately for us, there is none to be got here. Flintwinch, show the gentleman the handbill. Give him several to take away. Hold the light for him to read it.'

Mr Flintwinch did as he was directed, and Mr Dorrit read it through, as if he had not previously seen it; glad enough of the opportunity of collecting his presence of mind, which the air of the house and of the people in it had a little disturbed. While his eyes were on the paper, he felt that the eyes of Mr Flintwinch and of Mrs Clennam were on him. He found, when he looked up, that this sensation was not a fanciful one.

'Now you know as much,' said Mrs Clennam, 'as we know, sir. Is Mr Blandois a friend of yours?'

'No—a—hum—an acquaintance,' answered Mr Dorrit.

'You have no commission from him, perhaps?'

'I? Ha. Certainly not.'

The searching look turned gradually to the floor, after taking Mr Flintwinch's face in its way. Mr Dorrit, discomfited by finding that he was the questioned instead of the questioner, applied himself to the reversal of that unexpected order of things.

'I am—ha—a gentleman of property, at present residing in Italy with my family, my servants, and—hum—my rather large establishment. Being in London for a short time on affairs connected with—ha—my estate, and hearing of this strange disappearance, I wished to make myself acquainted with the circumstances at first-hand, because there is—ha hum—an English gentleman in Italy whom I shall no doubt see on my return, who has been in habits of close and daily intimacy with Monsieur Blandois. Mr Henry Gowan. You may know the name.'

'Never heard of it.'

Mrs Clennam said it, and Mr Flintwinch echoed it.

'Wishing to—ha—make the narrative coherent and consecutive to him,' said Mr Dorrit, 'may I ask—say, three questions?'

'Thirty, if you choose.'

'Have you known Monsieur Blandois long?'

'Not a twelvemonth. Mr Flintwinch here, will refer to the books and tell you when, and by whom at Paris he was introduced to us. If that,' Mrs Clennam added, 'should be any satisfaction to you. It is poor satisfaction to us.'

'Have you seen him often?'

'No. Twice. Once before, and—'

'That once,' suggested Mr Flintwinch.

'And that once.'

'Pray, madam,' said Mr Dorrit, with a growing fancy upon him as he recovered his importance, that he was in some superior way in the Commission of the Peace; 'pray, madam, may I inquire, for the greater satisfaction of the gentleman whom I have the honour to—ha—retain, or protect or let me say to—hum—know—to know—Was Monsieur Blandois here on business on the night indicated in this present sheet?'

'On what he called business,' returned Mrs Clennam.

'Is—ha—excuse me—is its nature to be communicated?'

'No.'

It was evidently impracticable to pass the barrier of that reply.

'The question has been asked before,' said Mrs Clennam, 'and the answer has been, No. We don't choose to publish our transactions, however unimportant, to all the town. We say, No.'

'I mean, he took away no money with him, for example,' said Mr Dorrit.

'He took away none of ours, sir, and got none here.'

'I suppose,' observed Mr Dorrit, glancing from Mrs Clennam to Mr Flintwinch, and from Mr Flintwinch to Mrs Clennam, 'you have no way of accounting to yourself for this mystery?'

'Why do you suppose so?' rejoined Mrs Clennam.

Disconcerted by the cold and hard inquiry, Mr Dorrit was unable to assign any reason for his supposing so.

'I account for it, sir,' she pursued after an awkward silence on Mr Dorrit's part, 'by having no doubt that he is travelling somewhere, or hiding somewhere.'

'Do you know—ha—why he should hide anywhere?'

'No.'

It was exactly the same No as before, and put another barrier up.

'You asked me if I accounted for the disappearance to myself,' Mrs Clennam sternly reminded him, 'not if I accounted for it to you. I do not pretend to account for it to you, sir. I understand it to be no more my business to do that, than it is yours to require that.'

Mr Dorrit answered with an apologetic bend of his head. As he stepped back, preparatory to saying he had no more to ask, he could not but observe how gloomily and fixedly she sat with her eyes fastened on the ground, and a certain air upon her of resolute waiting; also, how exactly the self-same expression was reflected in Mr Flintwinch, standing at a little distance from her chair, with his eyes also on the ground, and his right hand softly rubbing his chin.

At that moment, Mistress Affery (of course, the woman with the apron) dropped the candlestick she held, and cried out, 'There! O good Lord! there it is again. Hark, Jeremiah! Now!'

If there were any sound at all, it was so slight that she must have fallen into a confirmed habit of listening for sounds; but Mr Dorrit believed he did hear a something, like the falling of dry leaves. The woman's terror, for a very short space, seemed to touch the three; and they all listened.

Mr Flintwinch was the first to stir. 'Affery, my woman,' said he, sidling at her with his fists clenched, and his elbows quivering with impatience to shake her, 'you are at your old tricks. You'll be walking in your sleep next, my woman, and playing the whole round of your distempered antics. You must have some physic. When I have shown this gentleman out, I'll make you up such a comfortable dose, my woman; such a comfortable dose!'

It did not appear altogether comfortable in expectation to Mistress Affery; but Jeremiah, without further reference to his healing medicine, took another candle from Mrs Clennam's table, and said, 'Now, sir; shall I light you down?'

Mr Dorrit professed himself obliged, and went down. Mr Flintwinch shut him out, and chained him out, without a moment's loss of time. He was again passed by the two men, one going out and the other coming in; got into the vehicle he had left waiting, and was driven away.

Before he had gone far, the driver stopped to let him know that he had given his name, number, and address to the two men, on their joint requisition; and also the address at which he had taken Mr Dorrit up, the hour at which he had been called from his stand and the way by which he had come. This did not make the night's adventure run any less hotly in Mr Dorrit's mind, either when he sat down by his fire again, or when he went to bed. All night he haunted the dismal house, saw the two people resolutely waiting, heard the woman with her apron over her face cry out about the noise, and found the body of the missing Blandois, now buried in the cellar, and now bricked up in a wall.

CHAPTER 18. A Castle in the Air

Manifold are the cares of wealth and state. Mr Dorrit's satisfaction in remembering that it had not been necessary for him to announce himself to Clennam and Co., or to make an allusion to his having had any knowledge of the intrusive person of that name, had been damped over-night, while it was still fresh, by a debate that arose within him whether or no he should take the Marshalsea in his way back, and look at the old gate. He had decided not to do so; and had astonished the coachman by being very fierce with him for proposing to go over London Bridge and recross the river by Waterloo Bridge—a course which would have taken him almost within sight of his old quarters. Still, for all that, the question had raised a conflict in his breast; and, for some odd reason or no reason, he was vaguely dissatisfied. Even at the Merdle dinner-table next day, he was so out of sorts about it that he continued at intervals to turn it over and over, in a manner frightfully inconsistent with the good society surrounding him. It made him hot to think what the Chief Butler's opinion of him would have been, if that illustrious personage could have plumbed with that heavy eye of his the stream of his meditations.

The farewell banquet was of a gorgeous nature, and wound up his visit in a most brilliant manner. Fanny combined with the attractions of her youth and beauty, a certain weight of self-sustainment as if she had been married twenty years. He felt that he could leave her with a quiet mind to tread the paths of distinction, and wished—but without abatement of patronage, and without prejudice to the retiring virtues of his favourite child—that he had such another daughter.

'My dear,' he told her at parting, 'our family looks to you to—ha—assert its dignity and—hum—maintain its importance. I know you will never disappoint it.'

'No, papa,' said Fanny, 'you may rely upon that, I think. My best love to dearest Amy, and I will write to her very soon.'

'Shall I convey any message to—ha—anybody else?' asked Mr Dorrit, in an insinuating manner.

'Papa,' said Fanny, before whom Mrs General instantly loomed, 'no, I thank you. You are very kind, Pa, but I must beg to be excused. There is no other message to send, I thank you, dear papa, that it would be at all agreeable to you to take.'

They parted in an outer drawing-room, where only Mr Sparkler waited on his lady, and dutifully bided his time for shaking hands. When Mr Sparkler was admitted to this closing audience, Mr Merdle came creeping in with not much more appearance of arms in his sleeves than if he had been the twin brother of Miss Biffin, and insisted on escorting Mr Dorrit downstairs. All Mr Dorrit's protestations being in vain, he enjoyed the honour of being accompanied to the hall-door by this distinguished man, who (as Mr Dorrit told him in shaking hands on the step) had really overwhelmed him with attentions and services during this memorable visit. Thus they parted; Mr Dorrit entering his carriage with a swelling breast, not at all sorry that his Courier, who had come to take leave in the lower regions, should have an opportunity of beholding the grandeur of his departure.

The aforesaid grandeur was yet full upon Mr Dorrit when he alighted at his hotel. Helped out by the Courier and some half-dozen of the hotel servants, he was passing through the hall with a serene magnificence, when lo! a sight presented itself that struck him dumb and motionless. John Chivery, in his best clothes, with his tall hat under his arm, his ivory-handled cane genteelly embarrassing his deportment, and a bundle of cigars in his hand!

'Now, young man,' said the porter. 'This is the gentleman. This young man has persisted in waiting, sir, saying you would be glad to see him.'

Mr Dorrit glared on the young man, choked, and said, in the mildest of tones, 'Ah! Young John! It is Young John, I think; is it not?'

'Yes, sir,' returned Young John.

'I—ha—thought it was Young John!' said Mr Dorrit. 'The young man may come up,' turning to the attendants, as he passed on: 'oh yes, he may come up. Let Young John follow. I will speak to him above.'

Young John followed, smiling and much gratified. Mr Dorrit's rooms were reached.

Candles were lighted. The attendants withdrew.

'Now, sir,' said Mr Dorrit, turning round upon him and seizing him by the collar when they were safely alone. 'What do you mean by this?'

The amazement and horror depicted in the unfortunate John's face—for he had rather expected to be embraced next—were of that powerfully expressive nature that Mr Dorrit withdrew his hand and merely glared at him.

'How dare you do this?' said Mr Dorrit. 'How do you presume to come here? How dare you insult me?'

'I insult you, sir?' cried Young John. 'Oh!'

'Yes, sir,' returned Mr Dorrit. 'Insult me. Your coming here is an affront, an impertinence, an audacity. You are not wanted here. Who sent you here? What—ha—the Devil do you do here?'

'I thought, sir,' said Young John, with as pale and shocked a face as ever had been turned to Mr Dorrit's in his life—even in his College life: 'I thought, sir, you mightn't object to have the goodness to accept a bundle—'

'Damn your bundle, sir!' cried Mr Dorrit, in irrepressible rage. 'I—hum—don't smoke.'

'I humbly beg your pardon, sir. You used to.'

'Tell me that again,' cried Mr Dorrit, quite beside himself, 'and I'll take the poker to you!'

John Chivery backed to the door.

'Stop, sir!' cried Mr Dorrit. 'Stop! Sit down. Confound you sit down!'

John Chivery dropped into the chair nearest the door, and Mr Dorrit walked up and down the room; rapidly at first; then, more slowly. Once, he went to the window, and stood there with his forehead against the glass. All of a sudden, he turned and said:

'What else did you come for, Sir?'

'Nothing else in the world, sir. Oh dear me! Only to say, Sir, that I hoped you was well, and only to ask if Miss Amy was Well?'

'What's that to you, sir?' retorted Mr Dorrit.

'It's nothing to me, sir, by rights. I never thought of lessening the distance betwixt us, I am sure. I know it's a liberty, sir, but I never thought you'd have taken it ill. Upon my word and honour, sir,' said Young John, with emotion, 'in my poor way, I am too proud to have come, I assure you, if I had thought so.'

Mr Dorrit was ashamed. He went back to the window, and leaned his forehead against the glass for some time. When he turned, he had his handkerchief in his hand, and he had been wiping his eyes with it, and he looked tired and ill.

'Young John, I am very sorry to have been hasty with you, but—ha—some remembrances are not happy remembrances, and—hum—you shouldn't have come.'

'I feel that now, sir,' returned John Chivery; 'but I didn't before, and Heaven knows I meant no harm, sir.'

'No. No,' said Mr Dorrit. 'I am—hum—sure of that. Ha. Give me your hand, Young

John, give me your hand.'

Young John gave it; but Mr Dorrit had driven his heart out of it, and nothing could change his face now, from its white, shocked look.

'There!' said Mr Dorrit, slowly shaking hands with him. 'Sit down again, Young John.'

'Thank you, sir—but I'd rather stand.'

Mr Dorrit sat down instead. After painfully holding his head a little while, he turned it to his visitor, and said, with an effort to be easy:

'And how is your father, Young John? How—ha—how are they all, Young John?'

'Thank you, sir, They're all pretty well, sir. They're not any ways complaining.'

'Hum. You are in your—ha—old business I see, John?' said Mr Dorrit, with a glance at the offending bundle he had anathematised.

'Partly, sir. I am in my'—John hesitated a little—'father's business likewise.'

'Oh indeed!' said Mr Dorrit. 'Do you—ha hum—go upon the ha—'

'Lock, sir? Yes, sir.'

'Much to do, John?'

'Yes, sir; we're pretty heavy at present. I don't know how it is, but we generally are pretty heavy.'

'At this time of the year, Young John?'

'Mostly at all times of the year, sir. I don't know the time that makes much difference to us. I wish you good night, sir.'

'Stay a moment, John—ha—stay a moment. Hum. Leave me the cigars, John, I—ha—beg.'

'Certainly, sir.' John put them, with a trembling hand, on the table.

'Stay a moment, Young John; stay another moment. It would be a—ha—a gratification to me to send a little—hum—Testimonial, by such a trusty messenger, to be divided among—ha hum—them—them—according to their wants. Would you object to take it, John?'

'Not in any ways, sir. There's many of them, I'm sure, that would be the better for it.'

'Thank you, John. I—ha—I'll write it, John.'

His hand shook so that he was a long time writing it, and wrote it in a tremulous scrawl at last. It was a cheque for one hundred pounds. He folded it up, put it in Young John's hand, and pressed the hand in his.

'I hope you'll—ha—overlook—hum—what has passed, John.'

'Don't speak of it, sir, on any accounts. I don't in any ways bear malice, I'm sure.'

But nothing while John was there could change John's face to its natural colour and expression, or restore John's natural manner.

'And, John,' said Mr Dorrit, giving his hand a final pressure, and releasing it, 'I hope we—ha—agree that we have spoken together in confidence; and that you will abstain, in going out, from saying anything to any one that might—hum—suggest that—ha—once I—'

'Oh! I assure you, sir,' returned John Chivery, 'in my poor humble way, sir, I'm too proud and honourable to do it, sir.'

Mr Dorrit was not too proud and honourable to listen at the door that he might ascertain for himself whether John really went straight out, or lingered to have any talk with any one. There was no doubt that he went direct out at the door, and away down the street with a quick step. After remaining alone for an hour, Mr Dorrit rang for the Courier, who found him with his chair on the hearth-rug, sitting with his back towards him and his face to the fire. 'You can take that bundle of cigars to smoke on the journey, if you like,' said Mr Dorrit, with a careless wave of his hand. 'Ha—brought by—hum—little offering from—ha—son of old tenant of mine.'

Next morning's sun saw Mr Dorrit's equipage upon the Dover road, where every red-jacketed postilion was the sign of a cruel house, established for the unmerciful plundering of travellers. The whole business of the human race, between London and Dover, being spoliation, Mr Dorrit was waylaid at Dartford, pillaged at Gravesend, rifled at Rochester, fleeced at Sittingbourne, and sacked at Canterbury. However, it being the Courier's business to get him out of the hands of the banditti, the Courier brought him off at every stage; and so the red-jackets went gleaming merrily along the spring landscape, rising and falling to a regular measure, between Mr Dorrit in his snug corner and the next chalky rise in the dusty highway.

Another day's sun saw him at Calais. And having now got the Channel between himself and John Chivery, he began to feel safe, and to find that the foreign air was lighter to breathe than the air of England.

On again by the heavy French roads for Paris. Having now quite recovered his equanimity, Mr Dorrit, in his snug corner, fell to castle-building as he rode along. It was evident that he had a very large castle in hand. All day long he was running towers up, taking towers down, adding a wing here, putting on a battlement there, looking to the walls, strengthening the defences, giving ornamental touches to the interior, making in all respects a superb castle of it. His preoccupied face so clearly denoted the pursuit in which he was engaged, that every cripple at the post-houses, not blind, who shoved his little battered tin-box in at the carriage window for Charity in the name of Heaven, Charity in the name of our Lady, Charity in the name of all the Saints, knew as well what work he was at, as their countryman Le Brun could have known it himself, though he had made that English traveller the subject of a special physiognomical treatise.

Arrived at Paris, and resting there three days, Mr Dorrit strolled much about the streets alone, looking in at the shop-windows, and particularly the jewellers' windows. Ultimately, he went into the most famous jeweller's, and said he wanted to buy a little gift for a lady.

It was a charming little woman to whom he said it—a sprightly little woman, dressed in perfect taste, who came out of a green velvet bower to attend upon him, from posting up some dainty little books of account which one could hardly suppose to be ruled for the entry of any articles more commercial than kisses, at a dainty little shining desk which looked in itself like a sweetmeat.

For example, then, said the little woman, what species of gift did Monsieur desire? A love-gift?

Mr Dorrit smiled, and said, Eh, well! Perhaps. What did he know? It was always possible;

the sex being so charming. Would she show him some?

Most willingly, said the little woman. Flattered and enchanted to show him many. But pardon! To begin with, he would have the great goodness to observe that there were love-gifts, and there were nuptial gifts. For example, these ravishing ear-rings and this necklace so superb to correspond, were what one called a love-gift. These brooches and these rings, of a beauty so gracious and celestial, were what one called, with the permission of Monsieur, nuptial gifts.

Perhaps it would be a good arrangement, Mr Dorrit hinted, smiling, to purchase both, and to present the love-gift first, and to finish with the nuptial offering?

Ah Heaven! said the little woman, laying the tips of the fingers of her two little hands against each other, that would be generous indeed, that would be a special gallantry! And without doubt the lady so crushed with gifts would find them irresistible.

Mr Dorrit was not sure of that. But, for example, the sprightly little woman was very sure of it, she said. So Mr Dorrit bought a gift of each sort, and paid handsomely for it. As he strolled back to his hotel afterwards, he carried his head high: having plainly got up his castle now to a much loftier altitude than the two square towers of Notre Dame.

Building away with all his might, but reserving the plans of his castle exclusively for his own eye, Mr Dorrit posted away for Marseilles. Building on, building on, busily, busily, from morning to night. Falling asleep, and leaving great blocks of building materials dangling in the air; waking again, to resume work and get them into their places. What time the Courier in the rumble, smoking Young John's best cigars, left a little thread of thin light smoke behind—perhaps as he built a castle or two with stray pieces of Mr Dorrit's money.

Not a fortified town that they passed in all their journey was as strong, not a Cathedral summit was as high, as Mr Dorrit's castle. Neither the Saone nor the Rhone sped with the swiftness of that peerless building; nor was the Mediterranean deeper than its foundations; nor were the distant landscapes on the Cornice road, nor the hills and bay of Genoa the Superb, more beautiful. Mr Dorrit and his matchless castle were disembarked among the dirty white houses and dirtier felons of Civita Vecchia, and thence scrambled on to Rome as they could, through the filth that festered on the way.

CHAPTER 19. The Storming of the Castle in the Air

The sun had gone down full four hours, and it was later than most travellers would like it to be for finding themselves outside the walls of Rome, when Mr Dorrit's carriage, still on its last wearisome stage, rattled over the solitary Campagna. The savage herdsmen and the fierce-looking peasants who had chequered the way while the light lasted, had all gone down with the sun, and left the wilderness blank. At some turns of the road, a pale flare on the horizon, like an exhalation from the ruin-sown land, showed that the city was yet far off; but this poor relief was rare and short-lived. The carriage dipped down again into a hollow of the black dry sea, and for a long time there was nothing visible save its petrified swell and the gloomy sky.

Mr Dorrit, though he had his castle-building to engage his mind, could not be quite easy in that desolate place. He was far more curious, in every swerve of the carriage, and every cry of the postilions, than he had been since he quitted London. The valet on the box evidently quaked. The Courier in the rumble was not altogether comfortable in his mind. As often as Mr Dorrit let down the glass and looked back at him (which was very often), he saw him smoking John Chivery out, it is true, but still generally standing up the while and looking about him, like a man who had his suspicions, and kept upon his guard. Then would Mr Dorrit, pulling up the glass again, reflect that those postilions were cut-throat looking fellows, and that he would have done better to have slept at Civita Vecchia, and have started betimes in the morning. But, for all this, he worked at his castle in the intervals.

And now, fragments of ruinous enclosure, yawning window-gap and crazy wall, deserted houses, leaking wells, broken water-tanks, spectral cypress-trees, patches of tangled vine, and the changing of the track to a long, irregular, disordered lane where everything was crumbling away, from the unsightly buildings to the jolting road—now, these objects showed that they were nearing Rome. And now, a sudden twist and stoppage of the carriage inspired Mr Dorrit with the mistrust that the brigand moment was come for twisting him into a ditch and robbing him; until, letting down the glass again and looking out, he perceived himself assailed by nothing worse than a funeral procession, which came mechanically chaunting by, with an indistinct show of dirty vestments, lurid torches, swinging censers, and a great cross borne before a priest. He was an ugly priest by torchlight; of a lowering aspect, with an overhanging brow; and as his eyes met those of Mr Dorrit, looking bareheaded out of the carriage, his lips, moving as they chaunted, seemed to threaten that important traveller; likewise the action of his hand, which was in fact his manner of returning the traveller's salutation, seemed to come in aid of that menace. So thought Mr Dorrit, made fanciful by the weariness of building and travelling, as the priest drifted past him, and the procession straggled away, taking its dead along with it. Upon their so-different way went Mr Dorrit's company too; and soon, with their coach load of luxuries from the two great capitals of Europe, they were (like the Goths reversed) beating at the gates of Rome.

Mr Dorrit was not expected by his own people that night. He had been; but they had given him up until to-morrow, not doubting that it was later than he would care, in those parts, to be out. Thus, when his equipage stopped at his own gate, no one but the porter appeared to receive him. Was Miss Dorrit from home? he asked. No. She was within. Good, said Mr Dorrit to the assembling servants; let them keep where they were; let them help to unload the carriage; he would find Miss Dorrit for himself.

So he went up his grand staircase, slowly, and tired, and looked into various chambers which were empty, until he saw a light in a small ante-room. It was a curtained nook, like a tent, within two other rooms; and it looked warm and bright in colour, as he approached it through the dark avenue they made.

There was a draped doorway, but no door; and as he stopped here, looking in unseen, he felt a pang. Surely not like jealousy? For why like jealousy? There was only his daughter and his brother there: he, with his chair drawn to the hearth, enjoying the warmth of the evening wood fire; she seated at a little table, busied with some embroidery work. Allowing for the great difference in the still-life of the picture, the figures were much the same as of old; his brother being sufficiently like himself to represent himself, for a moment, in the composition. So had he sat many a night, over a coal fire far away; so had she sat, devoted to him. Yet surely there was nothing to be jealous of in the old miserable poverty. Whence, then, the pang in his heart?

'Do you know, uncle, I think you are growing young again?'

Her uncle shook his head and said, 'Since when, my dear; since when?'

'I think,' returned Little Dorrit, plying her needle, 'that you have been growing younger for weeks past. So cheerful, uncle, and so ready, and so interested.'

'My dear child—all you.'

'All me, uncle!'

'Yes, yes. You have done me a world of good. You have been so considerate of me, and so tender with me, and so delicate in trying to hide your attentions from me, that I—well, well, well! It's treasured up, my darling, treasured up.'

'There is nothing in it but your own fresh fancy, uncle,' said Little Dorrit, cheerfully.

'Well, well, well!' murmured the old man. 'Thank God!'

She paused for an instant in her work to look at him, and her look revived that former pain in her father's breast; in his poor weak breast, so full of contradictions, vacillations, inconsistencies, the little peevish perplexities of this ignorant life, mists which the morning without a night only can clear away.

'I have been freer with you, you see, my dove,' said the old man, 'since we have been alone. I say, alone, for I don't count Mrs General; I don't care for her; she has nothing to do with me. But I know Fanny was impatient of me. And I don't wonder at it, or complain of it, for I am sensible that I must be in the way, though I try to keep out of it as well as I can. I know I am not fit company for our company. My brother William,' said the old man admiringly, 'is fit company for monarchs; but not so your uncle, my dear. Frederick Dorrit is no credit to William Dorrit, and he knows it quite well. Ah! Why, here's your father, Amy! My dear William, welcome back! My beloved brother, I am rejoiced to see you!'

(Turning his head in speaking, he had caught sight of him as he stood in the doorway.)

Little Dorrit with a cry of pleasure put her arms about her father's neck, and kissed him again and again. Her father was a little impatient, and a little querulous. 'I am glad to find you at last, Amy,' he said. 'Ha. Really I am glad to find—hum—any one to receive me at last. I appear to have been—ha—so little expected, that upon my word I began—ha hum—to think it might be right to offer an apology for—ha—taking the liberty of coming back at all.'

'It was so late, my dear William,' said his brother, 'that we had given you up for to-night.'

'I am stronger than you, dear Frederick,' returned his brother with an elaboration of fraternity in which there was severity; 'and I hope I can travel without detriment at—ha—any hour I choose.'

'Surely, surely,' returned the other, with a misgiving that he had given offence. 'Surely, William.'

'Thank you, Amy,' pursued Mr Dorrit, as she helped him to put off his wrappers. 'I can do it without assistance. I—ha—need not trouble you, Amy. Could I have a morsel of bread and a glass of wine, or—hum—would it cause too much inconvenience?'

'Dear father, you shall have supper in a very few minutes.'

'Thank you, my love,' said Mr Dorrit, with a reproachful frost upon him; 'I—ha—am afraid I am causing inconvenience. Hum. Mrs General pretty well?'

'Mrs General complained of a headache, and of being fatigued; and so, when we gave you up, she went to bed, dear.'

Perhaps Mr Dorrit thought that Mrs General had done well in being overcome by the disappointment of his not arriving. At any rate, his face relaxed, and he said with obvious satisfaction, 'Extremely sorry to hear that Mrs General is not well.'

During this short dialogue, his daughter had been observant of him, with something more than her usual interest. It would seem as though he had a changed or worn appearance in her eyes, and he perceived and resented it; for he said with renewed peevishness, when he had divested himself of his travelling-cloak, and had come to the fire:

'Amy, what are you looking at? What do you see in me that causes you to—ha—concentrate your solicitude on me in that—hum—very particular manner?'

'I did not know it, father; I beg your pardon. It gladdens my eyes to see you again; that's all.'

'Don't say that's all, because—ha—that's not all. You—hum—you think,' said Mr Dorrit, with an accusatory emphasis, 'that I am not looking well.'

'I thought you looked a little tired, love.'

'Then you are mistaken,' said Mr Dorrit. 'Ha, I am not tired. Ha, hum. I am very much fresher than I was when I went away.'

He was so inclined to be angry that she said nothing more in her justification, but remained quietly beside him embracing his arm. As he stood thus, with his brother on the other side, he fell into a heavy doze, of not a minute's duration, and awoke with a start.

'Frederick,' he said, turning to his brother: 'I recommend you to go to bed immediately.'

'No, William. I'll wait and see you sup.'

'Frederick,' he retorted, 'I beg you to go to bed. I—ha—make it a personal request that you go to bed. You ought to have been in bed long ago. You are very feeble.'

'Hah!' said the old man, who had no wish but to please him. 'Well, well, well! I dare say I am.'

'My dear Frederick,' returned Mr Dorrit, with an astonishing superiority to his brother's failing powers, 'there can be no doubt of it. It is painful to me to see you so weak. Ha. It distresses me. Hum. I don't find you looking at all well. You are not fit for this sort of thing. You should be more careful, you should be very careful.'

'Shall I go to bed?' asked Frederick.

'Dear Frederick,' said Mr Dorrit, 'do, I adjure you! Good night, brother. I hope you will be stronger to-morrow. I am not at all pleased with your looks. Good night, dear fellow.' After dismissing his brother in this gracious way, he fell into a doze again before the old man was well out of the room: and he would have stumbled forward upon the logs, but for his daughter's restraining hold.

'Your uncle wanders very much, Amy,' he said, when he was thus roused. 'He is less—ha—coherent, and his conversation is more—hum—broken, than I have—ha, hum—ever known. Has he had any illness since I have been gone?'

'No, father.'

'You—ha—see a great change in him, Amy?'

'I have not observed it, dear.'

'Greatly broken,' said Mr Dorrit. 'Greatly broken. My poor, affectionate, failing Frederick! Ha. Even taking into account what he was before, he is—hum—sadly broken!'

His supper, which was brought to him there, and spread upon the little table where he had seen her working, diverted his attention. She sat at his side as in the days that were gone, for the first time since those days ended. They were alone, and she helped him to his meat and poured out his drink for him, as she had been used to do in the prison. All this happened now, for the first time since their accession to wealth. She was afraid to look at him much, after the offence he had taken; but she noticed two occasions in the course of his meal, when he all of a sudden looked at her, and looked about him, as if the association were so strong that he needed assurance from his sense of sight that they were not in the old prison-room. Both times, he put his hand to his head as if he missed his old black cap—though it had been ignominiously given away in the Marshalsea, and had never got free to that hour, but still hovered about the yards on the head of his successor.

He took very little supper, but was a long time over it, and often reverted to his brother's declining state. Though he expressed the greatest pity for him, he was almost bitter upon him. He said that poor Frederick—ha hum—drivelled. There was no other word to express it; drivelled. Poor fellow! It was melancholy to reflect what Amy must have undergone from the excessive tediousness of his Society—wandering and babbling on, poor dear estimable creature, wandering and babbling on—if it had not been for the relief she had had in Mrs General. Extremely sorry, he then repeated with his former satisfaction, that that—ha—superior woman was poorly.

Little Dorrit, in her watchful love, would have remembered the lightest thing he said or did that night, though she had had no subsequent reason to recall that night. She always remembered that, when he looked about him under the strong influence of the old association, he tried to keep it out of her mind, and perhaps out of his own too, by immediately expatiating on the great riches and great company that had encompassed him in his absence, and on the lofty position he and his family had to sustain. Nor did she fail to recall that there were two under-currents, side by side, pervading all his discourse and all his manner; one showing her how well he had got on without her, and how independent he was of her; the other, in a fitful and unintelligible way almost complaining of her, as if it had been possible that she had neglected him while he was away.

His telling her of the glorious state that Mr Merdle kept, and of the court that bowed before him, naturally brought him to Mrs Merdle. So naturally indeed, that although there was an unusual want of sequence in the greater part of his remarks, he passed to her at once, and asked how she was.

'She is very well. She is going away next week.'

'Home?' asked Mr Dorrit.

'After a few weeks' stay upon the road.'

'She will be a vast loss here,' said Mr Dorrit. 'A vast—ha—acquisition at home. To Fanny, and to—hum—the rest of the—ha—great world.'

Little Dorrit thought of the competition that was to be entered upon, and assented very softly.

'Mrs Merdle is going to have a great farewell Assembly, dear, and a dinner before it. She has been expressing her anxiety that you should return in time. She has invited both you and me to her dinner.'

'She is—ha—very kind. When is the day?'

'The day after to-morrow.'

'Write round in the morning, and say that I have returned, and shall—hum—be delighted.'

'May I walk with you up the stairs to your room, dear?'

'No!' he answered, looking angrily round; for he was moving away, as if forgetful of leave-taking. 'You may not, Amy. I want no help. I am your father, not your infirm uncle!' He checked himself, as abruptly as he had broken into this reply, and said, 'You have not kissed me, Amy. Good night, my dear! We must marry—ha—we must marry you, now.' With that he went, more slowly and more tired, up the staircase to his rooms, and, almost as soon as he got there, dismissed his valet. His next care was to look about him for his Paris purchases, and, after opening their cases and carefully surveying them, to put them away under lock and key. After that, what with dozing and what with castle-building, he lost himself for a long time, so that there was a touch of morning on the eastward rim of the desolate Campagna when he crept to bed.

Mrs General sent up her compliments in good time next day, and hoped he had rested well after this fatiguing journey. He sent down his compliments, and begged to inform Mrs General that he had rested very well indeed, and was in high condition. Nevertheless, he did not come forth from his own rooms until late in the afternoon; and, although he then caused himself to be magnificently arrayed for a drive with Mrs General and his daughter, his appearance was scarcely up to his description of himself.

As the family had no visitors that day, its four members dined alone together. He conducted Mrs General to the seat at his right hand with immense ceremony; and Little Dorrit could not but notice as she followed with her uncle, both that he was again elaborately dressed, and that his manner towards Mrs General was very particular. The perfect formation of that accomplished lady's surface rendered it difficult to displace an atom of its genteel glaze, but Little Dorrit thought she descried a slight thaw of triumph in a corner of her frosty eye.

Notwithstanding what may be called in these pages the Pruney and Prismatic nature of the family banquet, Mr Dorrit several times fell asleep while it was in progress. His fits of dozing were as sudden as they had been overnight, and were as short and profound. When the first of these slumberings seized him, Mrs General looked almost amazed: but, on each recurrence of the symptoms, she told her polite beads, Papa, Potatoes, Poultry, Prunes, and Prism; and, by dint of going through that infallible performance very slowly, appeared to finish her rosary at about the same time as Mr Dorrit started from his sleep.

He was again painfully aware of a somnolent tendency in Frederick (which had no existence out of his own imagination), and after dinner, when Frederick had withdrawn, privately apologised to Mrs General for the poor man. 'The most estimable and affectionate of brothers,' he said, 'but—ha, hum—broken up altogether. Unhappily, declining fast.'

'Mr Frederick, sir,' quoth Mrs General, 'is habitually absent and drooping, but let us hope it is not so bad as that.'

Mr Dorrit, however, was determined not to let him off. 'Fast declining, madam. A wreck. A ruin. Mouldering away before our eyes. Hum. Good Frederick!'

'You left Mrs Sparkler quite well and happy, I trust?' said Mrs General, after heaving a cool sigh for Frederick.

'Surrounded,' replied Mr Dorrit, 'by—ha—all that can charm the taste, and—hum— elevate the mind. Happy, my dear madam, in a—hum—husband.'

Mrs General was a little fluttered; seeming delicately to put the word away with her gloves, as if there were no knowing what it might lead to.

'Fanny,' Mr Dorrit continued. 'Fanny, Mrs General, has high qualities. Ha. Ambition— hum—purpose, consciousness of—ha—position, determination to support that position— ha, hum—grace, beauty, and native nobility.'

'No doubt,' said Mrs General (with a little extra stiffness).

'Combined with these qualities, madam,' said Mr Dorrit, 'Fanny has—ha—manifested one blemish which has made me—hum—made me uneasy, and—ha—I must add, angry; but which I trust may now be considered at an end, even as to herself, and which is undoubtedly at an end as to—ha—others.'

'To what, Mr Dorrit,' returned Mrs General, with her gloves again somewhat excited, 'can you allude? I am at a loss to—'

'Do not say that, my dear madam,' interrupted Mr Dorrit.

Mrs General's voice, as it died away, pronounced the words, 'at a loss to imagine.'

After which Mr Dorrit was seized with a doze for about a minute, out of which he sprang with spasmodic nimbleness.

'I refer, Mrs General, to that—ha—strong spirit of opposition, or—hum—I might say—ha—jealousy in Fanny, which has occasionally risen against the—ha—sense I entertain of—hum—the claims of—ha—the lady with whom I have now the honour of communing.'

'Mr Dorrit,' returned Mrs General, 'is ever but too obliging, ever but too appreciative. If there have been moments when I have imagined that Miss Dorrit has indeed resented the favourable opinion Mr Dorrit has formed of my services, I have found, in that only too high opinion, my consolation and recompense.'

'Opinion of your services, madam?' said Mr Dorrit.

'Of,' Mrs General repeated, in an elegantly impressive manner, 'my services.'

'Of your services alone, dear madam?' said Mr Dorrit.

'I presume,' retorted Mrs General, in her former impressive manner, 'of my services alone. For, to what else,' said Mrs General, with a slightly interrogative action of her gloves, 'could I impute—'

'To—ha—yourself, Mrs General. Ha, hum. To yourself and your merits,' was Mr Dorrit's rejoinder.

'Mr Dorrit will pardon me,' said Mrs General, 'if I remark that this is not a time or place for the pursuit of the present conversation. Mr Dorrit will excuse me if I remind him that Miss Dorrit is in the adjoining room, and is visible to myself while I utter her name. Mr Dorrit will forgive me if I observe that I am agitated, and that I find there are moments when weaknesses I supposed myself to have subdued, return with redoubled power. Mr Dorrit will allow me to withdraw.'

'Hum. Perhaps we may resume this—ha—interesting conversation,' said Mr Dorrit, 'at another time; unless it should be, what I hope it is not—hum—in any way disagreeable to— ah—Mrs General.'

'Mr Dorrit,' said Mrs General, casting down her eyes as she rose with a bend, 'must ever claim my homage and obedience.'

Mrs General then took herself off in a stately way, and not with that amount of trepidation upon her which might have been expected in a less remarkable woman. Mr Dorrit, who had conducted his part of the dialogue with a certain majestic and admiring condescension— much as some people may be seen to conduct themselves in Church, and to perform their part in the service—appeared, on the whole, very well satisfied with himself and with Mrs General too. On the return of that lady to tea, she had touched herself up with a little powder and pomatum, and was not without moral enchantment likewise: the latter showing itself in much sweet patronage of manner towards Miss Dorrit, and in an air of as tender interest in Mr Dorrit as was consistent with rigid propriety. At the close of the evening, when she rose to retire, Mr Dorrit took her by the hand as if he were going to lead her out into the Piazza of the people to walk a minuet by moonlight, and with great solemnity conducted her to the room door, where he raised her knuckles to his lips. Having parted from her with what may be conjectured to have been a rather bony kiss of a cosmetic flavour, he gave his daughter his blessing, graciously. And having thus hinted that there was something remarkable in the wind, he again went to bed.

He remained in the seclusion of his own chamber next morning; but, early in the afternoon, sent down his best compliments to Mrs General, by Mr Tinkler, and begged she would accompany Miss Dorrit on an airing without him. His daughter was dressed for Mrs Merdle's dinner before he appeared. He then presented himself in a refulgent condition as to his attire, but looking indefinably shrunken and old. However, as he was plainly determined to be angry with her if she so much as asked him how he was, she only ventured to kiss his cheek, before accompanying him to Mrs Merdle's with an anxious heart.

The distance that they had to go was very short, but he was at his building work again before the carriage had half traversed it. Mrs Merdle received him with great distinction; the bosom was in admirable preservation, and on the best terms with itself; the dinner was very choice; and the company was very select.

It was principally English; saving that it comprised the usual French Count and the usual Italian Marchese—decorative social milestones, always to be found in certain places, and varying very little in appearance. The table was long, and the dinner was long; and Little Dorrit, overshadowed by a large pair of black whiskers and a large white cravat, lost sight of her father altogether, until a servant put a scrap of paper in her hand, with a whispered request from Mrs Merdle that she would read it directly. Mrs Merdle had written on it in pencil, 'Pray come and speak to Mr Dorrit, I doubt if he is well.'

She was hurrying to him, unobserved, when he got up out of his chair, and leaning over the table called to her, supposing her to be still in her place:

'Amy, Amy, my child!'

The action was so unusual, to say nothing of his strange eager appearance and strange eager voice, that it instantaneously caused a profound silence.

'Amy, my dear,' he repeated. 'Will you go and see if Bob is on the lock?'

She was at his side, and touching him, but he still perversely supposed her to be in her seat, and called out, still leaning over the table, 'Amy, Amy. I don't feel quite myself. Ha. I don't know what's the matter with me. I particularly wish to see Bob. Ha. Of all the turnkeys, he's as much my friend as yours. See if Bob is in the lodge, and beg him to come to me.'

All the guests were now in consternation, and everybody rose.

'Dear father, I am not there; I am here, by you.'

'Oh! You are here, Amy! Good. Hum. Good. Ha. Call Bob. If he has been relieved, and is not on the lock, tell Mrs Bangham to go and fetch him.'

She was gently trying to get him away; but he resisted, and would not go.

'I tell you, child,' he said petulantly, 'I can't be got up the narrow stairs without Bob. Ha. Send for Bob. Hum. Send for Bob—best of all the turnkeys—send for Bob!'

He looked confusedly about him, and, becoming conscious of the number of faces by which he was surrounded, addressed them:

'Ladies and gentlemen, the duty—ha—devolves upon me of—hum—welcoming you to the Marshalsea! Welcome to the Marshalsea! The space is—ha—limited—limited—the parade might be wider; but you will find it apparently grow larger after a time—a time, ladies and gentlemen—and the air is, all things considered, very good. It blows over the—ha—Surrey hills. Blows over the Surrey hills. This is the Snuggery. Hum. Supported by a small subscription of the—ha—Collegiate body. In return for which—hot water—general kitchen—and little domestic advantages. Those who are habituated to the—ha—Marshalsea, are pleased to call me its father. I am accustomed to be complimented by strangers as the—ha—Father of the Marshalsea. Certainly, if years of residence may establish a claim to so—ha—honourable a title, I may accept the—hum—conferred distinction. My child, ladies and gentlemen. My daughter. Born here!'

She was not ashamed of it, or ashamed of him. She was pale and frightened; but she had no other care than to soothe him and get him away, for his own dear sake. She was between him and the wondering faces, turned round upon his breast with her own face raised to his. He held her clasped in his left arm, and between whiles her low voice was heard tenderly imploring him to go away with her.

'Born here,' he repeated, shedding tears. 'Bred here. Ladies and gentlemen, my daughter. Child of an unfortunate father, but—ha—always a gentleman. Poor, no doubt, but—hum—proud. Always proud. It has become a—hum—not infrequent custom for my—ha—personal admirers—personal admirers solely—to be pleased to express their desire to acknowledge my semi-official position here, by offering—ha—little tributes, which usually take the form of—ha—voluntary recognitions of my humble endeavours to—hum—to uphold a Tone here—a Tone—I beg it to be understood that I do not consider myself compromised. Ha. Not compromised. Ha. Not a beggar. No; I repudiate the title! At the same time far be it from me to—hum—to put upon the fine feelings by which my partial friends are actuated, the slight of scrupling to admit that those offerings are—hum—highly acceptable. On the contrary, they are most acceptable. In my child's name, if not in my own, I make the admission in the fullest manner, at the same time reserving—ha—shall I say my personal dignity? Ladies and gentlemen, God bless you all!'

By this time, the exceeding mortification undergone by the Bosom had occasioned the withdrawal of the greater part of the company into other rooms. The few who had lingered thus long followed the rest, and Little Dorrit and her father were left to the servants and themselves. Dearest and most precious to her, he would come with her now, would he not? He replied to her fervid entreaties, that he would never be able to get up the narrow stairs without Bob; where was Bob, would nobody fetch Bob? Under pretence of looking for Bob, she got him out against the stream of gay company now pouring in for the evening assembly, and got him into a coach that had just set down its load, and got him home.

The broad stairs of his Roman palace were contracted in his failing sight to the narrow stairs of his London prison; and he would suffer no one but her to touch him, his brother excepted. They got him up to his room without help, and laid him down on his bed. And from that hour his poor maimed spirit, only remembering the place where it had broken its wings, cancelled the dream through which it had since groped, and knew of nothing beyond the Marshalsea. When he heard footsteps in the street, he took them for the old weary tread in the yards. When the hour came for locking up, he supposed all strangers to be excluded for the night. When the time for opening came again, he was so anxious to see Bob, that they were fain to patch up a narrative how that Bob—many a year dead then, gentle turnkey—had taken cold, but hoped to be out to-morrow, or the next day, or the next at furthest.

He fell away into a weakness so extreme that he could not raise his hand. But he still protected his brother according to his long usage; and would say with some complacency, fifty times a day, when he saw him standing by his bed, 'My good Frederick, sit down. You are very feeble indeed.'

They tried him with Mrs General, but he had not the faintest knowledge of her. Some injurious suspicion lodged itself in his brain, that she wanted to supplant Mrs Bangham, and that she was given to drinking. He charged her with it in no measured terms; and was so urgent with his daughter to go round to the Marshal and entreat him to turn her out, that she was never reproduced after the first failure.

Saving that he once asked 'if Tip had gone outside?' the remembrance of his two children not present seemed to have departed from him. But the child who had done so much for him and had been so poorly repaid, was never out of his mind. Not that he spared her, or was fearful of her being spent by watching and fatigue; he was not more troubled on that score than he had usually been. No; he loved her in his old way. They were in the jail again, and she tended him, and he had constant need of her, and could not turn without her; and he even told her, sometimes, that he was content to have undergone a great deal for her sake. As to her, she bent over his bed with her quiet face against his, and would have laid down her own life to restore him.

When he had been sinking in this painless way for two or three days, she observed him to be troubled by the ticking of his watch—a pompous gold watch that made as great a to-do about its going as if nothing else went but itself and Time. She suffered it to run down; but he was still uneasy, and showed that was not what he wanted. At length he roused himself to explain that he wanted money to be raised on this watch. He was quite pleased when she pretended to take it away for the purpose, and afterwards had a relish for his little tastes of wine and jelly, that he had not had before.

He soon made it plain that this was so; for, in another day or two he sent off his sleeve-buttons and finger-rings. He had an amazing satisfaction in entrusting her with these errands, and appeared to consider it equivalent to making the most methodical and provident arrangements. After his trinkets, or such of them as he had been able to see about him, were gone, his clothes engaged his attention; and it is as likely as not that he was kept alive for some days by the satisfaction of sending them, piece by piece, to an imaginary pawnbroker's.

Thus for ten days Little Dorrit bent over his pillow, laying her cheek against his. Sometimes she was so worn out that for a few minutes they would slumber together. Then she would awake; to recollect with fast-flowing silent tears what it was that touched her face, and to see, stealing over the cherished face upon the pillow, a deeper shadow than the shadow of the Marshalsea Wall.

Quietly, quietly, all the lines of the plan of the great Castle melted one after another. Quietly, quietly, the ruled and cross-ruled countenance on which they were traced, became fair and blank. Quietly, quietly, the reflected marks of the prison bars and of the zig-zag iron on the wall-top, faded away. Quietly, quietly, the face subsided into a far younger likeness of her own than she had ever seen under the grey hair, and sank to rest.

At first her uncle was stark distracted. 'O my brother! O William, William! You to go before me; you to go alone; you to go, and I to remain! You, so far superior, so distinguished, so noble; I, a poor useless creature fit for nothing, and whom no one would have missed!'

It did her, for the time, the good of having him to think of and to succour.

'Uncle, dear uncle, spare yourself, spare me!'

The old man was not deaf to the last words. When he did begin to restrain himself, it was that he might spare her. He had no care for himself; but, with all the remaining power of the honest heart, stunned so long and now awaking to be broken, he honoured and blessed her.

'O God,' he cried, before they left the room, with his wrinkled hands clasped over her. 'Thou seest this daughter of my dear dead brother! All that I have looked upon, with my half-blind and sinful eyes, Thou hast discerned clearly, brightly. Not a hair of her head shall be harmed before Thee. Thou wilt uphold her here to her last hour. And I know Thou wilt reward her hereafter!'

They remained in a dim room near, until it was almost midnight, quiet and sad together. At times his grief would seek relief in a burst like that in which it had found its earliest expression; but, besides that his little strength would soon have been unequal to such strains, he never failed to recall her words, and to reproach himself and calm himself. The only utterance with which he indulged his sorrow, was the frequent exclamation that his brother was gone, alone; that they had been together in the outset of their lives, that they had fallen into misfortune together, that they had kept together through their many years of poverty, that they had remained together to that day; and that his brother was gone alone, alone!

They parted, heavy and sorrowful. She would not consent to leave him anywhere but in his own room, and she saw him lie down in his clothes upon his bed, and covered him with her own hands. Then she sank upon her own bed, and fell into a deep sleep: the sleep of exhaustion and rest, though not of complete release from a pervading consciousness of affliction. Sleep, good Little Dorrit. Sleep through the night!

It was a moonlight night; but the moon rose late, being long past the full. When it was high in the peaceful firmament, it shone through half-closed lattice blinds into the solemn room where the stumblings and wanderings of a life had so lately ended. Two quiet figures were within the room; two figures, equally still and impassive, equally removed by an untraversable distance from the teeming earth and all that it contains, though soon to lie in it.

One figure reposed upon the bed. The other, kneeling on the floor, drooped over it; the arms easily and peacefully resting on the coverlet; the face bowed down, so that the lips touched the hand over which with its last breath it had bent. The two brothers were before their Father; far beyond the twilight judgment of this world; high above its mists and obscurities.

CHAPTER 20. Introduces the next

The passengers were landing from the packet on the pier at Calais. A low-lying place and a low-spirited place Calais was, with the tide ebbing out towards low water-mark. There had been no more water on the bar than had sufficed to float the packet in; and now the bar itself, with a shallow break of sea over it, looked like a lazy marine monster just risen to the surface, whose form was indistinctly shown as it lay asleep. The meagre lighthouse all in white, haunting the seaboard as if it were the ghost of an edifice that had once had colour and rotundity, dropped melancholy tears after its late buffeting by the waves. The long rows of gaunt black piles, slimy and wet and weather-worn, with funeral garlands of seaweed twisted about them by the late tide, might have represented an unsightly marine cemetery. Every wave-dashed, storm-beaten object, was so low and so little, under the broad grey sky, in the noise of the wind and sea, and before the curling lines of surf, making at it ferociously, that the wonder was there was any Calais left, and that its low gates and low wall and low roofs and low ditches and low sand-hills and low ramparts and flat streets, had not yielded long ago to the undermining and besieging sea, like the fortifications children make on the sea-shore.

After slipping among oozy piles and planks, stumbling up wet steps and encountering many salt difficulties, the passengers entered on their comfortless peregrination along the pier; where all the French vagabonds and English outlaws in the town (half the population) attended to prevent their recovery from bewilderment. After being minutely inspected by all the English, and claimed and reclaimed and counter-claimed as prizes by all the French in a hand-to-hand scuffle three quarters of a mile long, they were at last free to enter the streets, and to make off in their various directions, hotly pursued.

Clennam, harassed by more anxieties than one, was among this devoted band. Having rescued the most defenceless of his compatriots from situations of great extremity, he now went his way alone, or as nearly alone as he could be, with a native gentleman in a suit of grease and a cap of the same material, giving chase at a distance of some fifty yards, and continually calling after him, 'Hi! Ice-say! You! Seer! Ice-say! Nice Oatel!'

Even this hospitable person, however, was left behind at last, and Clennam pursued his way, unmolested. There was a tranquil air in the town after the turbulence of the Channel and the beach, and its dulness in that comparison was agreeable. He met new groups of his countrymen, who had all a straggling air of having at one time overblown themselves, like certain uncomfortable kinds of flowers, and of being now mere weeds. They had all an air, too, of lounging out a limited round, day after day, which strongly reminded him of the Marshalsea. But, taking no further note of them than was sufficient to give birth to the reflection, he sought out a certain street and number which he kept in his mind.

'So Pancks said,' he murmured to himself, as he stopped before a dull house answering to the address. 'I suppose his information to be correct and his discovery, among Mr Casby's loose papers, indisputable; but, without it, I should hardly have supposed this to be a likely place.'

A dead sort of house, with a dead wall over the way and a dead gateway at the side, where a pendant bell-handle produced two dead tinkles, and a knocker produced a dead, flat, surface-tapping, that seemed not to have depth enough in it to penetrate even the cracked door. However, the door jarred open on a dead sort of spring; and he closed it behind him as he entered a dull yard, soon brought to a close by another dead wall, where an attempt had been made to train some creeping shrubs, which were dead; and to make a little fountain in a grotto, which was dry; and to decorate that with a little statue, which was gone.

The entry to the house was on the left, and it was garnished as the outer gateway was, with two printed bills in French and English, announcing Furnished Apartments to let, with immediate possession. A strong cheerful peasant woman, all stocking, petticoat, white cap, and ear-ring, stood here in a dark doorway, and said with a pleasant show of teeth, 'Ice-say! Seer! Who?'

Clennam, replying in French, said the English lady; he wished to see the English lady. 'Enter then and ascend, if you please,' returned the peasant woman, in French likewise. He did both, and followed her up a dark bare staircase to a back room on the first-floor. Hence, there was a gloomy view of the yard that was dull, and of the shrubs that were dead, and of the fountain that was dry, and of the pedestal of the statue that was gone.

'Monsieur Blandois,' said Clennam.

'With pleasure, Monsieur.'

Thereupon the woman withdrew and left him to look at the room. It was the pattern of room always to be found in such a house. Cool, dull, and dark. Waxed floor very slippery. A room not large enough to skate in; nor adapted to the easy pursuit of any other occupation. Red and white curtained windows, little straw mat, little round table with a tumultuous assemblage of legs underneath, clumsy rush-bottomed chairs, two great red velvet arm-chairs affording plenty of space to be uncomfortable in, bureau, chimney-glass in several pieces pretending to be in one piece, pair of gaudy vases of very artificial flowers; between them a Greek warrior with his helmet off, sacrificing a clock to the Genius of France.

After some pause, a door of communication with another room was opened, and a lady entered. She manifested great surprise on seeing Clennam, and her glance went round the room in search of some one else.

'Pardon me, Miss Wade. I am alone.'

'It was not your name that was brought to me.'

'No; I know that. Excuse me. I have already had experience that my name does not predispose you to an interview; and I ventured to mention the name of one I am in search of.'

'Pray,' she returned, motioning him to a chair so coldly that he remained standing, 'what name was it that you gave?'

'I mentioned the name of Blandois.'

'Blandois?'

'A name you are acquainted with.'

'It is strange,' she said, frowning, 'that you should still press an undesired interest in me and my acquaintances, in me and my affairs, Mr Clennam. I don't know what you mean.'

'Pardon me. You know the name?'

'What can you have to do with the name? What can I have to do with the name? What can you have to do with my knowing or not knowing any name? I know many names and I have forgotten many more. This may be in the one class, or it may be in the other, or I may never have heard it. I am acquainted with no reason for examining myself, or for being examined, about it.'

'If you will allow me,' said Clennam, 'I will tell you my reason for pressing the subject. I admit that I do press it, and I must beg you to forgive me if I do so, very earnestly. The reason is all mine, I do not insinuate that it is in any way yours.'

'Well, sir,' she returned, repeating a little less haughtily than before her former invitation to him to be seated: to which he now deferred, as she seated herself. 'I am at least glad to know that this is not another bondswoman of some friend of yours, who is bereft of free choice, and whom I have spirited away. I will hear your reason, if you please.'

'First, to identify the person of whom we speak,' said Clennam, 'let me observe that it is the person you met in London some time back. You will remember meeting him near the river—in the Adelphi!'

'You mix yourself most unaccountably with my business,' she replied, looking full at him with stern displeasure. 'How do you know that?'

'I entreat you not to take it ill. By mere accident.'

'What accident?'

'Solely the accident of coming upon you in the street and seeing the meeting.'

'Do you speak of yourself, or of some one else?'

'Of myself. I saw it.'

'To be sure it was in the open street,' she observed, after a few moments of less and less angry reflection. 'Fifty people might have seen it. It would have signified nothing if they had.'

'Nor do I make my having seen it of any moment, nor (otherwise than as an explanation of my coming here) do I connect my visit with it or the favour that I have to ask.'

'Oh! You have to ask a favour! It occurred to me,' and the handsome face looked bitterly at him, 'that your manner was softened, Mr Clennam.'

He was content to protest against this by a slight action without contesting it in words. He then referred to Blandois' disappearance, of which it was probable she had heard? However probable it was to him, she had heard of no such thing. Let him look round him (she said) and judge for himself what general intelligence was likely to reach the ears of a woman who had been shut up there while it was rife, devouring her own heart. When she had uttered this denial, which he believed to be true, she asked him what he meant by disappearance? That led to his narrating the circumstances in detail, and expressing something of his anxiety to discover what had really become of the man, and to repel the dark suspicions that clouded about his mother's house. She heard him with evident surprise, and with more marks of suppressed interest than he had seen in her; still they did not overcome her distant, proud, and self-secluded manner. When he had finished, she said nothing but these words:

'You have not yet told me, sir, what I have to do with it, or what the favour is? Will you be so good as come to that?'

'I assume,' said Arthur, persevering, in his endeavour to soften her scornful demeanour, 'that being in communication—may I say, confidential communication?—with this person—'

'You may say, of course, whatever you like,' she remarked; 'but I do not subscribe to your assumptions, Mr Clennam, or to any one's.'

'—that being, at least in personal communication with him,' said Clennam, changing the form of his position in the hope of making it unobjectionable, 'you can tell me something of his antecedents, pursuits, habits, usual place of residence. Can give me some little clue by which to seek him out in the likeliest manner, and either produce him, or establish what has become of him. This is the favour I ask, and I ask it in a distress of mind for which I hope you will feel some consideration. If you should have any reason for imposing conditions upon me, I will respect it without asking what it is.'

'You chanced to see me in the street with the man,' she observed, after being, to his mortification, evidently more occupied with her own reflections on the matter than with his appeal. 'Then you knew the man before?'

'Not before; afterwards. I never saw him before, but I saw him again on this very night of his disappearance. In my mother's room, in fact. I left him there. You will read in this paper all that is known of him.'

He handed her one of the printed bills, which she read with a steady and attentive face.

'This is more than I knew of him,' she said, giving it back. Clennam's looks expressed his heavy disappointment, perhaps his incredulity; for she added in the same unsympathetic tone: 'You don't believe it. Still, it is so. As to personal communication: it seems that there was personal communication between him and your mother. And yet you say you believe her declaration that she knows no more of him!'

A sufficiently expressive hint of suspicion was conveyed in these words, and in the smile by which they were accompanied, to bring the blood into Clennam's cheeks.

'Come, sir,' she said, with a cruel pleasure in repeating the stab, 'I will be as open with you as you can desire. I will confess that if I cared for my credit (which I do not), or had a good name to preserve (which I have not, for I am utterly indifferent to its being considered good or bad), I should regard myself as heavily compromised by having had anything to do with this fellow. Yet he never passed in at my door—never sat in colloquy with me until midnight.'

She took her revenge for her old grudge in thus turning his subject against him. Hers was not the nature to spare him, and she had no compunction.

'That he is a low, mercenary wretch; that I first saw him prowling about Italy (where I was, not long ago), and that I hired him there, as the suitable instrument of a purpose I happened to have; I have no objection to tell you. In short, it was worth my while, for my own pleasure—the gratification of a strong feeling—to pay a spy who would fetch and carry for money. I paid this creature. And I dare say that if I had wanted to make such a bargain, and if I could have paid him enough, and if he could have done it in the dark, free from all risk, he would have taken any life with as little scruple as he took my money. That, at least, is my opinion of him; and I see it is not very far removed from yours. Your mother's opinion of him, I am to assume (following your example of assuming this and that), was vastly different.'

'My mother, let me remind you,' said Clennam, 'was first brought into communication with him in the unlucky course of business.'

'It appears to have been an unlucky course of business that last brought her into communication with him,' returned Miss Wade; 'and business hours on that occasion were late.'

'You imply,' said Arthur, smarting under these cool-handed thrusts, of which he had deeply felt the force already, 'that there was something—'

'Mr Clennam,' she composedly interrupted, 'recollect that I do not speak by implication about the man. He is, I say again without disguise, a low mercenary wretch. I suppose such a creature goes where there is occasion for him. If I had not had occasion for him, you would not have seen him and me together.'

Wrung by her persistence in keeping that dark side of the case before him, of which there was a half-hidden shadow in his own breast, Clennam was silent.

'I have spoken of him as still living,' she added, 'but he may have been put out of the way for anything I know. For anything I care, also. I have no further occasion for him.'

With a heavy sigh and a despondent air, Arthur Clennam slowly rose. She did not rise also, but said, having looked at him in the meanwhile with a fixed look of suspicion, and lips angrily compressed:

'He was the chosen associate of your dear friend, Mr Gowan, was he not? Why don't you ask your dear friend to help you?'

The denial that he was a dear friend rose to Arthur's lips; but he repressed it, remembering his old struggles and resolutions, and said:

'Further than that he has never seen Blandois since Blandois set out for England, Mr Gowan knows nothing additional about him. He was a chance acquaintance, made abroad.'

'A chance acquaintance made abroad!' she repeated. 'Yes. Your dear friend has need to divert himself with all the acquaintances he can make, seeing what a wife he has. I hate his wife, sir.'

The anger with which she said it, the more remarkable for being so much under her restraint, fixed Clennam's attention, and kept him on the spot. It flashed out of her dark eyes as they regarded him, quivered in her nostrils, and fired the very breath she exhaled; but her face was otherwise composed into a disdainful serenity; and her attitude was as calmly and haughtily graceful as if she had been in a mood of complete indifference.

'All I will say is, Miss Wade,' he remarked, 'that you can have received no provocation to a feeling in which I believe you have no sharer.'

'You may ask your dear friend, if you choose,' she returned, 'for his opinion upon that subject.'

'I am scarcely on those intimate terms with my dear friend,' said Arthur, in spite of his resolutions, 'that would render my approaching the subject very probable, Miss Wade.'

'I hate him,' she returned. 'Worse than his wife, because I was once dupe enough, and false enough to myself, almost to love him. You have seen me, sir, only on common-place occasions, when I dare say you have thought me a common-place woman, a little more self-willed than the generality. You don't know what I mean by hating, if you know me no better than that; you can't know, without knowing with what care I have studied myself and people about me. For this reason I have for some time inclined to tell you what my life has been—not to propitiate your opinion, for I set no value on it; but that you may comprehend, when you think of your dear friend and his dear wife, what I mean by hating. Shall I give you something I have written and put by for your perusal, or shall I hold my hand?'

Arthur begged her to give it to him. She went to the bureau, unlocked it, and took from an inner drawer a few folded sheets of paper. Without any conciliation of him, scarcely addressing him, rather speaking as if she were speaking to her own looking-glass for the justification of her own stubbornness, she said, as she gave them to him:

'Now you may know what I mean by hating! No more of that. Sir, whether you find me temporarily and cheaply lodging in an empty London house, or in a Calais apartment, you find Harriet with me. You may like to see her before you leave. Harriet, come in!' She called Harriet again. The second call produced Harriet, once Tattycoram.

'Here is Mr Clennam,' said Miss Wade; 'not come for you; he has given you up,—I suppose you have, by this time?'

'Having no authority, or influence—yes,' assented Clennam.

'Not come in search of you, you see; but still seeking some one. He wants that Blandois man.'

'With whom I saw you in the Strand in London,' hinted Arthur.

'If you know anything of him, Harriet, except that he came from Venice—which we all know—tell it to Mr Clennam freely.'

'I know nothing more about him,' said the girl.

'Are you satisfied?' Miss Wade inquired of Arthur.

He had no reason to disbelieve them; the girl's manner being so natural as to be almost convincing, if he had had any previous doubts. He replied, 'I must seek for intelligence elsewhere.'

He was not going in the same breath; but he had risen before the girl entered, and she evidently thought he was. She looked quickly at him, and said:

'Are they well, sir?'

'Who?'

She stopped herself in saying what would have been 'all of them;' glanced at Miss Wade; and said 'Mr and Mrs Meagles.'

'They were, when I last heard of them. They are not at home. By the way, let me ask you. Is it true that you were seen there?'

'Where? Where does any one say I was seen?' returned the girl, sullenly casting down her eyes.

'Looking in at the garden gate of the cottage.'

'No,' said Miss Wade. 'She has never been near it.'

'You are wrong, then,' said the girl. 'I went down there the last time we were in London. I went one afternoon when you left me alone. And I did look in.'

'You poor-spirited girl,' returned Miss Wade with infinite contempt; 'does all our companionship, do all our conversations, do all your old complainings, tell for so little as that?'

'There was no harm in looking in at the gate for an instant,' said the girl. 'I saw by the windows that the family were not there.'

'Why should you go near the place?'

'Because I wanted to see it. Because I felt that I should like to look at it again.'

As each of the two handsome faces looked at the other, Clennam felt how each of the two natures must be constantly tearing the other to pieces.

'Oh!' said Miss Wade, coldly subduing and removing her glance; 'if you had any desire to see the place where you led the life from which I rescued you because you had found out what it was, that is another thing. But is that your truth to me? Is that your fidelity to me? Is that the common cause I make with you? You are not worth the confidence I have placed in you. You are not worth the favour I have shown you. You are no higher than a spaniel, and had better go back to the people who did worse than whip you.'

'If you speak so of them with any one else by to hear, you'll provoke me to take their part,' said the girl.

'Go back to them,' Miss Wade retorted. 'Go back to them.'

'You know very well,' retorted Harriet in her turn, 'that I won't go back to them. You know very well that I have thrown them off, and never can, never shall, never will, go back to them. Let them alone, then, Miss Wade.'

'You prefer their plenty to your less fat living here,' she rejoined. 'You exalt them, and slight me. What else should I have expected? I ought to have known it.'

'It's not so,' said the girl, flushing high, 'and you don't say what you mean. I know what you mean. You are reproaching me, underhanded, with having nobody but you to look to. And because I have nobody but you to look to, you think you are to make me do, or not do, everything you please, and are to put any affront upon me. You are as bad as they were, every bit. But I will not be quite tamed, and made submissive. I will say again that I went to look at the house, because I had often thought that I should like to see it once more. I will ask again how they are, because I once liked them and at times thought they were kind to me.'

Hereupon Clennam said that he was sure they would still receive her kindly, if she should ever desire to return.

'Never!' said the girl passionately. 'I shall never do that. Nobody knows that better than Miss Wade, though she taunts me because she has made me her dependent. And I know I am so; and I know she is overjoyed when she can bring it to my mind.'

'A good pretence!' said Miss Wade, with no less anger, haughtiness, and bitterness; 'but too threadbare to cover what I plainly see in this. My poverty will not bear competition with their money. Better go back at once, better go back at once, and have done with it!'

Arthur Clennam looked at them, standing a little distance asunder in the dull confined room, each proudly cherishing her own anger; each, with a fixed determination, torturing her own breast, and torturing the other's. He said a word or two of leave-taking; but Miss Wade barely inclined her head, and Harriet, with the assumed humiliation of an abject dependent and serf (but not without defiance for all that), made as if she were too low to notice or to be noticed.

He came down the dark winding stairs into the yard with an increased sense upon him of the gloom of the wall that was dead, and of the shrubs that were dead, and of the fountain that was dry, and of the statue that was gone. Pondering much on what he had seen and heard in that house, as well as on the failure of all his efforts to trace the suspicious character who was lost, he returned to London and to England by the packet that had taken him over. On the way he unfolded the sheets of paper, and read in them what is reproduced in the next chapter.

CHAPTER 21. The History of a Self-Tormentor

I have the misfortune of not being a fool. From a very early age I have detected what those about me thought they hid from me. If I could have been habitually imposed upon, instead of habitually discerning the truth, I might have lived as smoothly as most fools do.

My childhood was passed with a grandmother; that is to say, with a lady who represented that relative to me, and who took that title on herself. She had no claim to it, but I—being to that extent a little fool—had no suspicion of her. She had some children of her own family in her house, and some children of other people. All girls; ten in number, including me. We all lived together and were educated together.

I must have been about twelve years old when I began to see how determinedly those girls patronised me. I was told I was an orphan. There was no other orphan among us; and I perceived (here was the first disadvantage of not being a fool) that they conciliated me in an insolent pity, and in a sense of superiority. I did not set this down as a discovery, rashly. I tried them often. I could hardly make them quarrel with me. When I succeeded with any of them, they were sure to come after an hour or two, and begin a reconciliation. I tried them over and over again, and I never knew them wait for me to begin. They were always forgiving me, in their vanity and condescension. Little images of grown people!

One of them was my chosen friend. I loved that stupid mite in a passionate way that she could no more deserve than I can remember without feeling ashamed of, though I was but a child. She had what they called an amiable temper, an affectionate temper. She could distribute, and did distribute pretty looks and smiles to every one among them. I believe there was not a soul in the place, except myself, who knew that she did it purposely to wound and gall me!

Nevertheless, I so loved that unworthy girl that my life was made stormy by my fondness for her. I was constantly lectured and disgraced for what was called 'trying her;' in other words charging her with her little perfidy and throwing her into tears by showing her that I read her heart. However, I loved her faithfully; and one time I went home with her for the holidays.

She was worse at home than she had been at school. She had a crowd of cousins and acquaintances, and we had dances at her house, and went out to dances at other houses, and, both at home and out, she tormented my love beyond endurance. Her plan was, to make them all fond of her—and so drive me wild with jealousy. To be familiar and endearing with them all—and so make me mad with envying them. When we were left alone in our bedroom at night, I would reproach her with my perfect knowledge of her baseness; and then she would cry and cry and say I was cruel, and then I would hold her in my arms till morning: loving her as much as ever, and often feeling as if, rather than suffer so, I could so hold her in my arms and plunge to the bottom of a river—where I would still hold her after we were both dead.

It came to an end, and I was relieved. In the family there was an aunt who was not fond of me. I doubt if any of the family liked me much; but I never wanted them to like me, being altogether bound up in the one girl. The aunt was a young woman, and she had a serious way with her eyes of watching me. She was an audacious woman, and openly looked compassionately at me. After one of the nights that I have spoken of, I came down into a greenhouse before breakfast. Charlotte (the name of my false young friend) had gone down before me, and I heard this aunt speaking to her about me as I entered. I stopped where I was, among the leaves, and listened.

The aunt said, 'Charlotte, Miss Wade is wearing you to death, and this must not continue.' I repeat the very words I heard.

Now, what did she answer? Did she say, 'It is I who am wearing her to death, I who am keeping her on a rack and am the executioner, yet she tells me every night that she loves me devotedly, though she knows what I make her undergo?' No; my first memorable experience was true to what I knew her to be, and to all my experience. She began sobbing and weeping (to secure the aunt's sympathy to herself), and said, 'Dear aunt, she has an unhappy temper; other girls at school, besides I, try hard to make it better; we all try hard.'

Upon that the aunt fondled her, as if she had said something noble instead of despicable and false, and kept up the infamous pretence by replying, 'But there are reasonable limits, my dear love, to everything, and I see that this poor miserable girl causes you more constant and useless distress than even so good an effort justifies.'

The poor miserable girl came out of her concealment, as you may be prepared to hear, and said, 'Send me home.' I never said another word to either of them, or to any of them, but 'Send me home, or I will walk home alone, night and day!' When I got home, I told my supposed grandmother that, unless I was sent away to finish my education somewhere else before that girl came back, or before any one of them came back, I would burn my sight away

471

by throwing myself into the fire, rather than I would endure to look at their plotting faces.

I went among young women next, and I found them no better. Fair words and fair pretences; but I penetrated below those assertions of themselves and depreciations of me, and they were no better. Before I left them, I learned that I had no grandmother and no recognised relation. I carried the light of that information both into my past and into my future. It showed me many new occasions on which people triumphed over me, when they made a pretence of treating me with consideration, or doing me a service.

A man of business had a small property in trust for me. I was to be a governess; I became a governess; and went into the family of a poor nobleman, where there were two daughters— little children, but the parents wished them to grow up, if possible, under one instructress. The mother was young and pretty. From the first, she made a show of behaving to me with great delicacy. I kept my resentment to myself; but I knew very well that it was her way of petting the knowledge that she was my Mistress, and might have behaved differently to her servant if it had been her fancy.

I say I did not resent it, nor did I; but I showed her, by not gratifying her, that I understood her. When she pressed me to take wine, I took water. If there happened to be anything choice at table, she always sent it to me: but I always declined it, and ate of the rejected dishes. These disappointments of her patronage were a sharp retort, and made me feel independent.

I liked the children. They were timid, but on the whole disposed to attach themselves to me. There was a nurse, however, in the house, a rosy-faced woman always making an obtrusive pretence of being gay and good-humoured, who had nursed them both, and who had secured their affections before I saw them. I could almost have settled down to my fate but for this woman. Her artful devices for keeping herself before the children in constant competition with me, might have blinded many in my place; but I saw through them from the first. On the pretext of arranging my rooms and waiting on me and taking care of my wardrobe (all of which she did busily), she was never absent. The most crafty of her many subtleties was her feint of seeking to make the children fonder of me. She would lead them to me and coax them to me. 'Come to good Miss Wade, come to dear Miss Wade, come to pretty Miss Wade. She loves you very much. Miss Wade is a clever lady, who has read heaps of books, and can tell you far better and more interesting stories than I know. Come and hear Miss Wade!' How could I engage their attentions, when my heart was burning against these ignorant designs? How could I wonder, when I saw their innocent faces shrinking away, and their arms twining round her neck, instead of mine? Then she would look up at me, shaking their curls from her face, and say, 'They'll come round soon, Miss Wade; they're very simple and loving, ma'am; don't be at all cast down about it, ma'am'—exulting over me!

There was another thing the woman did. At times, when she saw that she had safely plunged me into a black despondent brooding by these means, she would call the attention of the children to it, and would show them the difference between herself and me. 'Hush! Poor Miss Wade is not well. Don't make a noise, my dears, her head aches. Come and comfort her. Come and ask her if she is better; come and ask her to lie down. I hope you have nothing on your mind, ma'am. Don't take on, ma'am, and be sorry!'

It became intolerable. Her ladyship, my Mistress, coming in one day when I was alone, and at the height of feeling that I could support it no longer, I told her I must go. I could not bear the presence of that woman Dawes.

'Miss Wade! Poor Dawes is devoted to you; would do anything for you!'

I knew beforehand she would say so; I was quite prepared for it; I only answered, it was not for me to contradict my Mistress; I must go.

'I hope, Miss Wade,' she returned, instantly assuming the tone of superiority she had always so thinly concealed, 'that nothing I have ever said or done since we have been together, has justified your use of that disagreeable word, "Mistress." It must have been wholly inadvertent on my part. Pray tell me what it is.'

I replied that I had no complaint to make, either of my Mistress or to my Mistress; but I must go.

She hesitated a moment, and then sat down beside me, and laid her hand on mine. As if that honour would obliterate any remembrance!

'Miss Wade, I fear you are unhappy, through causes over which I have no influence.'

I smiled, thinking of the experience the word awakened, and said, 'I have an unhappy temper, I suppose.'

'I did not say that.'

'It is an easy way of accounting for anything,' said I.

'It may be; but I did not say so. What I wish to approach is something very different. My husband and I have exchanged some remarks upon the subject, when we have observed with pain that you have not been easy with us.'

'Easy? Oh! You are such great people, my lady,' said I.

'I am unfortunate in using a word which may convey a meaning—and evidently does— quite opposite to my intention.' (She had not expected my reply, and it shamed her.) 'I only mean, not happy with us. It is a difficult topic to enter on; but, from one young woman to another, perhaps—in short, we have been apprehensive that you may allow some family circumstances of which no one can be more innocent than yourself, to prey upon your spirits. If so, let us entreat you not to make them a cause of grief. My husband himself, as is well known, formerly had a very dear sister who was not in law his sister, but who was universally beloved and respected—'

I saw directly that they had taken me in for the sake of the dead woman, whoever she was, and to have that boast of me and advantage of me; I saw, in the nurse's knowledge of it, an encouragement to goad me as she had done; and I saw, in the children's shrinking away, a vague impression, that I was not like other people. I left that house that night.

After one or two short and very similar experiences, which are not to the present purpose, I entered another family where I had but one pupil: a girl of fifteen, who was the only daughter. The parents here were elderly people: people of station, and rich. A nephew whom they had brought up was a frequent visitor at the house, among many other visitors; and he began to pay me attention. I was resolute in repulsing him; for I had determined when I went there, that no one should pity me or condescend to me. But he wrote me a letter. It led to our being engaged to be married.

He was a year younger than I, and young-looking even when that allowance was made.

He was on absence from India, where he had a post that was soon to grow into a very good one. In six months we were to be married, and were to go to India. I was to stay in the house, and was to be married from the house. Nobody objected to any part of the plan.

I cannot avoid saying he admired me; but, if I could, I would. Vanity has nothing to do with the declaration, for his admiration worried me. He took no pains to hide it; and caused me to feel among the rich people as if he had bought me for my looks, and made a show of his purchase to justify himself. They appraised me in their own minds, I saw, and were curious to ascertain what my full value was. I resolved that they should not know. I was immovable and silent before them; and would have suffered any one of them to kill me sooner than I would have laid myself out to bespeak their approval.

He told me I did not do myself justice. I told him I did, and it was because I did and meant to do so to the last, that I would not stoop to propitiate any of them. He was concerned and even shocked, when I added that I wished he would not parade his attachment before them; but he said he would sacrifice even the honest impulses of his affection to my peace.

Under that pretence he began to retort upon me. By the hour together, he would keep at a distance from me, talking to any one rather than to me. I have sat alone and unnoticed, half an evening, while he conversed with his young cousin, my pupil. I have seen all the while, in people's eyes, that they thought the two looked nearer on an equality than he and I. I have sat, divining their thoughts, until I have felt that his young appearance made me ridiculous, and have raged against myself for ever loving him.

For I did love him once. Undeserving as he was, and little as he thought of all these agonies that it cost me—agonies which should have made him wholly and gratefully mine to his life's end—I loved him. I bore with his cousin's praising him to my face, and with her pretending to think that it pleased me, but full well knowing that it rankled in my breast; for his sake. While I have sat in his presence recalling all my slights and wrongs, and deliberating whether I should not fly from the house at once and never see him again—I have loved him.

His aunt (my Mistress you will please to remember) deliberately, wilfully, added to my trials and vexations. It was her delight to expatiate on the style in which we were to live in India, and on the establishment we should keep, and the company we should entertain when he got his advancement. My pride rose against this barefaced way of pointing out the contrast my married life was to present to my then dependent and inferior position. I suppressed my indignation; but I showed her that her intention was not lost upon me, and I repaid her annoyance by affecting humility. What she described would surely be a great deal too much honour for me, I would tell her. I was afraid I might not be able to support so great a change. Think of a mere governess, her daughter's governess, coming to that high distinction! It made her uneasy, and made them all uneasy, when I answered in this way. They knew that I fully understood her.

It was at the time when my troubles were at their highest, and when I was most incensed against my lover for his ingratitude in caring as little as he did for the innumerable distresses and mortifications I underwent on his account, that your dear friend, Mr Gowan, appeared at the house. He had been intimate there for a long time, but had been abroad. He understood the state of things at a glance, and he understood me.

He was the first person I had ever seen in my life who had understood me. He was not in the house three times before I knew that he accompanied every movement of my mind. In his coldly easy way with all of them, and with me, and with the whole subject, I saw it clearly. In his light protestations of admiration of my future husband, in his enthusiasm regarding our engagement and our prospects, in his hopeful congratulations on our future wealth and his despondent references to his own poverty—all equally hollow, and jesting, and full of mockery—I saw it clearly. He made me feel more and more resentful, and more and more contemptible, by always presenting to me everything that surrounded me with some new hateful light upon it, while he pretended to exhibit it in its best aspect for my admiration and his own. He was like the dressed-up Death in the Dutch series; whatever figure he took upon his arm, whether it was youth or age, beauty or ugliness, whether he danced with it, sang with it, played with it, or prayed with it, he made it ghastly.

You will understand, then, that when your dear friend complimented me, he really condoled with me; that when he soothed me under my vexations, he laid bare every smarting wound I had; that when he declared my 'faithful swain' to be 'the most loving young fellow in the world, with the tenderest heart that ever beat,' he touched my old misgiving that I was made ridiculous. These were not great services, you may say. They were acceptable to me, because they echoed my own mind, and confirmed my own knowledge. I soon began to like the society of your dear friend better than any other.

When I perceived (which I did, almost as soon) that jealousy was growing out of this, I liked this society still better. Had I not been subject to jealousy, and were the endurances to be all mine? No. Let him know what it was! I was delighted that he should know it; I was delighted that he should feel keenly, and I hoped he did. More than that. He was tame in comparison with Mr Gowan, who knew how to address me on equal terms, and how to anatomise the wretched people around us.

This went on, until the aunt, my Mistress, took it upon herself to speak to me. It was scarcely worth alluding to; she knew I meant nothing; but she suggested from herself, knowing it was only necessary to suggest, that it might be better if I were a little less companionable with Mr Gowan.

I asked her how she could answer for what I meant? She could always answer, she replied, for my meaning nothing wrong. I thanked her, but said I would prefer to answer for myself and to myself. Her other servants would probably be grateful for good characters, but I wanted none.

Other conversation followed, and induced me to ask her how she knew that it was only necessary for her to make a suggestion to me, to have it obeyed? Did she presume on my birth, or on my hire? I was not bought, body and soul. She seemed to think that her distinguished nephew had gone into a slave-market and purchased a wife.

It would probably have come, sooner or later, to the end to which it did come, but she brought it to its issue at once. She told me, with assumed commiseration, that I had an unhappy temper. On this repetition of the old wicked injury, I withheld no longer, but exposed to her all I had known of her and seen in her, and all I had undergone within myself since I had occupied the despicable position of being engaged to her nephew. I told her that Mr Gowan was the only relief I had had in my degradation; that I had borne it too long, and that I shook it off too late; but that I would see none of them more. And I never did.

Your dear friend followed me to my retreat, and was very droll on the severance of the connection; though he was sorry, too, for the excellent people (in their way the best he had ever met), and deplored the necessity of breaking mere house-flies on the wheel. He protested before long, and far more truly than I then supposed, that he was not worth acceptance by a woman of such endowments, and such power of character; but—well, well—!

Your dear friend amused me and amused himself as long as it suited his inclinations; and then reminded me that we were both people of the world, that we both understood mankind, that we both knew there was no such thing as romance, that we were both prepared for going different ways to seek our fortunes like people of sense, and that we both foresaw that whenever we encountered one another again we should meet as the best friends on earth. So he said, and I did not contradict him.

It was not very long before I found that he was courting his present wife, and that she had been taken away to be out of his reach. I hated her then, quite as much as I hate her now; and naturally, therefore, could desire nothing better than that she should marry him. But I was restlessly curious to look at her—so curious that I felt it to be one of the few sources of entertainment left to me. I travelled a little: travelled until I found myself in her society, and in yours. Your dear friend, I think, was not known to you then, and had not given you any of those signal marks of his friendship which he has bestowed upon you.

In that company I found a girl, in various circumstances of whose position there was a singular likeness to my own, and in whose character I was interested and pleased to see much of the rising against swollen patronage and selfishness, calling themselves kindness, protection, benevolence, and other fine names, which I have described as inherent in my nature. I often heard it said, too, that she had 'an unhappy temper.' Well understanding what was meant by the convenient phrase, and wanting a companion with a knowledge of what I knew, I thought I would try to release the girl from her bondage and sense of injustice. I have no occasion to relate that I succeeded.

We have been together ever since, sharing my small means.

CHAPTER 22. Who passes by this Road so late?

Arthur Clennam had made his unavailing expedition to Calais in the midst of a great pressure of business. A certain barbaric Power with valuable possessions on the map of the world, had occasion for the services of one or two engineers, quick in invention and determined in execution: practical men, who could make the men and means their ingenuity perceived to be wanted out of the best materials they could find at hand; and who were as bold and fertile in the adaptation of such materials to their purpose, as in the conception of their purpose itself. This Power, being a barbaric one, had no idea of stowing away a great national object in a Circumlocution Office, as strong wine is hidden from the light in a cellar until its fire and youth are gone, and the labourers who worked in the vineyard and pressed the grapes are dust. With characteristic ignorance, it acted on the most decided and energetic notions of How to do it; and never showed the least respect for, or gave any quarter to, the great political science, How not to do it. Indeed it had a barbarous way of striking the latter art and mystery dead, in the person of any enlightened subject who practised it.

Accordingly, the men who were wanted were sought out and found; which was in itself a most uncivilised and irregular way of proceeding. Being found, they were treated with great confidence and honour (which again showed dense political ignorance), and were invited to come at once and do what they had to do. In short, they were regarded as men who meant to do it, engaging with other men who meant it to be done.

Daniel Doyce was one of the chosen. There was no foreseeing at that time whether he would be absent months or years. The preparations for his departure, and the conscientious arrangement for him of all the details and results of their joint business, had necessitated labour within a short compass of time, which had occupied Clennam day and night. He had slipped across the water in his first leisure, and had slipped as quickly back again for his farewell interview with Doyce.

Him Arthur now showed, with pains and care, the state of their gains and losses, responsibilities and prospects. Daniel went through it all in his patient manner, and admired it all exceedingly. He audited the accounts, as if they were a far more ingenious piece of mechanism than he had ever constructed, and afterwards stood looking at them, weighing his hat over his head by the brims, as if he were absorbed in the contemplation of some wonderful engine.

'It's all beautiful, Clennam, in its regularity and order. Nothing can be plainer. Nothing can be better.'

'I am glad you approve, Doyce. Now, as to the management of your capital while you are away, and as to the conversion of so much of it as the business may need from time to time—' His partner stopped him.

'As to that, and as to everything else of that kind, all rests with you. You will continue in all such matters to act for both of us, as you have done hitherto, and to lighten my mind of a load it is much relieved from.'

'Though, as I often tell you,' returned Clennam, 'you unreasonably depreciate your business qualities.'

'Perhaps so,' said Doyce, smiling. 'And perhaps not. Anyhow, I have a calling that I have studied more than such matters, and that I am better fitted for. I have perfect confidence in my partner, and I am satisfied that he will do what is best. If I have a prejudice connected with money and money figures,' continued Doyce, laying that plastic workman's thumb of his on the lapel of his partner's coat, 'it is against speculating. I don't think I have any other. I dare say I entertain that prejudice, only because I have never given my mind fully to the subject.'

'But you shouldn't call it a prejudice,' said Clennam. 'My dear Doyce, it is the soundest sense.'

'I am glad you think so,' returned Doyce, with his grey eye looking kind and bright.

'It so happens,' said Clennam, 'that just now, not half an hour before you came down, I was saying the same thing to Pancks, who looked in here. We both agreed that to travel out of safe investments is one of the most dangerous, as it is one of the most common, of those follies which often deserve the name of vices.'

'Pancks?' said Doyce, tilting up his hat at the back, and nodding with an air of confidence. 'Aye, aye, aye! That's a cautious fellow.'

'He is a very cautious fellow indeed,' returned Arthur. 'Quite a specimen of caution.'

They both appeared to derive a larger amount of satisfaction from the cautious character of Mr Pancks, than was quite intelligible, judged by the surface of their conversation.

'And now,' said Daniel, looking at his watch, 'as time and tide wait for no man, my trusty partner, and as I am ready for starting, bag and baggage, at the gate below, let me say a last word. I want you to grant a request of mine.'

'Any request you can make—Except,' Clennam was quick with his exception, for his partner's face was quick in suggesting it, 'except that I will abandon your invention.'

'That's the request, and you know it is,' said Doyce.

'I say, No, then. I say positively, No. Now that I have begun, I will have some definite reason, some responsible statement, something in the nature of a real answer, from those people.'

'You will not,' returned Doyce, shaking his head. 'Take my word for it, you never will.'

'At least, I'll try,' said Clennam. 'It will do me no harm to try.'

'I am not certain of that,' rejoined Doyce, laying his hand persuasively on his shoulder. 'It has done me harm, my friend. It has aged me, tired me, vexed me, disappointed me. It does no man any good to have his patience worn out, and to think himself ill-used. I fancy, even already, that unavailing attendance on delays and evasions has made you something less elastic than you used to be.'

'Private anxieties may have done that for the moment,' said Clennam, 'but not official harrying. Not yet. I am not hurt yet.'

'Then you won't grant my request?'

'Decidedly, No,' said Clennam. 'I should be ashamed if I submitted to be so soon driven out of the field, where a much older and a much more sensitively interested man contended with fortitude so long.'

As there was no moving him, Daniel Doyce returned the grasp of his hand, and, casting a farewell look round the counting-house, went down-stairs with him. Doyce was to go to Southampton to join the small staff of his fellow-travellers; and a coach was at the gate, well furnished and packed, and ready to take him there. The workmen were at the gate to see him off, and were mightily proud of him. 'Good luck to you, Mr Doyce!' said one of the number. 'Wherever you go, they'll find as they've got a man among 'em, a man as knows his tools and as his tools knows, a man as is willing and a man as is able, and if that's not a man, where is a man!' This oration from a gruff volunteer in the back-ground, not previously suspected of any powers in that way, was received with three loud cheers; and the speaker became a distinguished character for ever afterwards. In the midst of the three loud cheers, Daniel gave them all a hearty 'Good Bye, Men!' and the coach disappeared from sight, as if the concussion of the air had blown it out of Bleeding Heart Yard.

Mr Baptist, as a grateful little fellow in a position of trust, was among the workmen, and had done as much towards the cheering as a mere foreigner could. In truth, no men on earth can cheer like Englishmen, who do so rally one another's blood and spirit when they cheer in earnest, that the stir is like the rush of their whole history, with all its standards waving at once, from Saxon Alfred's downwards. Mr Baptist had been in a manner whirled away before the onset, and was taking his breath in quite a scared condition when Clennam beckoned him to follow up-stairs, and return the books and papers to their places.

In the lull consequent on the departure—in that first vacuity which ensues on every separation, foreshadowing the great separation that is always overhanging all mankind—Arthur stood at his desk, looking dreamily out at a gleam of sun. But his liberated attention soon reverted to the theme that was foremost in his thoughts, and began, for the hundredth time, to dwell upon every circumstance that had impressed itself upon his mind on the mysterious night when he had seen the man at his mother's. Again the man jostled him in the crooked street, again he followed the man and lost him, again he came upon the man in the court-yard looking at the house, again he followed the man and stood beside him on the door-steps.

'Who passes by this road so late?

Compagnon de la Majolaine;

Who passes by this road so late?

Always gay!'

It was not the first time, by many, that he had recalled the song of the child's game, of which the fellow had hummed this verse while they stood side by side; but he was so unconscious of having repeated it audibly, that he started to hear the next verse.

'Of all the king's knights 'tis the flower,

Compagnon de la Majolaine;

Of all the king's knights 'tis the flower,

Always gay!'

Cavalletto had deferentially suggested the words and tune, supposing him to have stopped short for want of more.

'Ah! You know the song, Cavalletto?'

'By Bacchus, yes, sir! They all know it in France. I have heard it many times, sung by the little children. The last time when it I have heard,' said Mr Baptist, formerly Cavalletto, who usually went back to his native construction of sentences when his memory went near home, 'is from a sweet little voice. A little voice, very pretty, very innocent. Altro!'

'The last time I heard it,' returned Arthur, 'was in a voice quite the reverse of pretty, and quite the reverse of innocent.' He said it more to himself than to his companion, and added to himself, repeating the man's next words. 'Death of my life, sir, it's my character to be impatient!'

'EH!' cried Cavalletto, astounded, and with all his colour gone in a moment.

'What is the matter?'

'Sir! You know where I have heard that song the last time?'

With his rapid native action, his hands made the outline of a high hook nose, pushed his eyes near together, dishevelled his hair, puffed out his upper lip to represent a thick moustache, and threw the heavy end of an ideal cloak over his shoulder. While doing this, with a swiftness incredible to one who has not watched an Italian peasant, he indicated a very remarkable and sinister smile. The whole change passed over him like a flash of light, and he stood in the same instant, pale and astonished, before his patron.

'In the name of Fate and wonder,' said Clennam, 'what do you mean? Do you know a man of the name of Blandois?'

'No!' said Mr Baptist, shaking his head.

'You have just now described a man who was by when you heard that song; have you not?'

'Yes!' said Mr Baptist, nodding fifty times.

'And was he not called Blandois?'

'No!' said Mr Baptist. 'Altro, Altro, Altro, Altro!' He could not reject the name sufficiently, with his head and his right forefinger going at once.

'Stay!' cried Clennam, spreading out the handbill on his desk. 'Was this the man? You can understand what I read aloud?'

'Altogether. Perfectly.'

'But look at it, too. Come here and look over me, while I read.'

Mr Baptist approached, followed every word with his quick eyes, saw and heard it all out with the greatest impatience, then clapped his two hands flat upon the bill as if he had fiercely caught some noxious creature, and cried, looking eagerly at Clennam, 'It is the man! Behold him!'

'This is of far greater moment to me' said Clennam, in great agitation, 'than you can imagine. Tell me where you knew the man.'

Mr Baptist, releasing the paper very slowly and with much discomfiture, and drawing himself back two or three paces, and making as though he dusted his hands, returned, very much against his will:

'At Marsiglia—Marseilles.'

'What was he?'

'A prisoner, and—Altro! I believe yes!—an,' Mr Baptist crept closer again to whisper it, 'Assassin!'

Clennam fell back as if the word had struck him a blow: so terrible did it make his mother's communication with the man appear. Cavalletto dropped on one knee, and implored him, with a redundancy of gesticulation, to hear what had brought himself into such foul company.

He told with perfect truth how it had come of a little contraband trading, and how he had in time been released from prison, and how he had gone away from those antecedents. How, at the house of entertainment called the Break of Day at Chalons on the Saone, he had been awakened in his bed at night by the same assassin, then assuming the name of Lagnier, though his name had formerly been Rigaud; how the assassin had proposed that they should join their fortunes together; how he held the assassin in such dread and aversion that he had fled from him at daylight, and how he had ever since been haunted by the fear of seeing the assassin again and being claimed by him as an acquaintance. When he had related this, with an emphasis and poise on the word, 'assassin,' peculiarly belonging to his own language, and which did not serve to render it less terrible to Clennam, he suddenly sprang to his feet, pounced upon the bill again, and with a vehemence that would have been absolute madness in any man of Northern origin, cried 'Behold the same assassin! Here he is!'

In his passionate raptures, he at first forgot the fact that he had lately seen the assassin in London. On his remembering it, it suggested hope to Clennam that the recognition might be of later date than the night of the visit at his mother's; but Cavalletto was too exact and clear about time and place, to leave any opening for doubt that it had preceded that occasion.

'Listen,' said Arthur, very seriously. 'This man, as we have read here, has wholly disappeared.'

'Of it I am well content!' said Cavalletto, raising his eyes piously. 'A thousand thanks to Heaven! Accursed assassin!'

'Not so,' returned Clennam; 'for until something more is heard of him, I can never know an hour's peace.'

'Enough, Benefactor; that is quite another thing. A million of excuses!'

'Now, Cavalletto,' said Clennam, gently turning him by the arm, so that they looked into each other's eyes. 'I am certain that for the little I have been able to do for you, you are the most sincerely grateful of men.'

'I swear it!' cried the other.

'I know it. If you could find this man, or discover what has become of him, or gain any later intelligence whatever of him, you would render me a service above any other service I could receive in the world, and would make me (with far greater reason) as grateful to you as you are to me.'

'I know not where to look,' cried the little man, kissing Arthur's hand in a transport. 'I know not where to begin. I know not where to go. But, courage! Enough! It matters not! I go, in this instant of time!'

'Not a word to any one but me, Cavalletto.'

'Al-tro!' cried Cavalletto. And was gone with great speed.

CHAPTER 23. Mistress Affery makes a Conditional Promise,

respecting her Dreams

Left alone, with the expressive looks and gestures of Mr Baptist, otherwise Giovanni Baptista Cavalletto, vividly before him, Clennam entered on a weary day. It was in vain that he tried to control his attention by directing it to any business occupation or train of thought; it rode at anchor by the haunting topic, and would hold to no other idea. As though a criminal should be chained in a stationary boat on a deep clear river, condemned, whatever countless leagues of water flowed past him, always to see the body of the fellow-creature he had drowned lying at the bottom, immovable, and unchangeable, except as the eddies made it broad or long, now expanding, now contracting its terrible lineaments; so Arthur, below the shifting current of transparent thoughts and fancies which were gone and succeeded by others as soon as come, saw, steady and dark, and not to be stirred from its place, the one subject that he endeavoured with all his might to rid himself of, and that he could not fly from.

The assurance he now had, that Blandois, whatever his right name, was one of the worst of characters, greatly augmented the burden of his anxieties. Though the disappearance should be accounted for to-morrow, the fact that his mother had been in communication with such a man, would remain unalterable. That the communication had been of a secret kind, and that she had been submissive to him and afraid of him, he hoped might be known to no one beyond himself; yet, knowing it, how could he separate it from his old vague fears, and how believe that there was nothing evil in such relations?

Her resolution not to enter on the question with him, and his knowledge of her indomitable character, enhanced his sense of helplessness. It was like the oppression of a dream to believe that shame and exposure were impending over her and his father's memory, and to be shut out, as by a brazen wall, from the possibility of coming to their aid. The purpose he had brought home to his native country, and had ever since kept in view, was, with her greatest determination, defeated by his mother herself, at the time of all others when he feared that it pressed most. His advice, energy, activity, money, credit, all his resources whatsoever, were all made useless. If she had been possessed of the old fabled influence, and had turned those who looked upon her into stone, she could not have rendered him more completely powerless (so it seemed to him in his distress of mind) than she did, when she turned her unyielding face to his in her gloomy room.

But the light of that day's discovery, shining on these considerations, roused him to take a more decided course of action. Confident in the rectitude of his purpose, and impelled by a sense of overhanging danger closing in around, he resolved, if his mother would still admit of no approach, to make a desperate appeal to Affery. If she could be brought to become communicative, and to do what lay in her to break the spell of secrecy that enshrouded the house, he might shake off the paralysis of which every hour that passed over his head made him more acutely sensible. This was the result of his day's anxiety, and this was the decision he put in practice when the day closed in.

His first disappointment, on arriving at the house, was to find the door open, and Mr Flintwinch smoking a pipe on the steps. If circumstances had been commonly favourable, Mistress Affery would have opened the door to his knock. Circumstances being uncommonly unfavourable, the door stood open, and Mr Flintwinch was smoking his pipe on the steps.

'Good evening,' said Arthur.

'Good evening,' said Mr Flintwinch.

The smoke came crookedly out of Mr Flintwinch's mouth, as if it circulated through the whole of his wry figure and came back by his wry throat, before coming forth to mingle with the smoke from the crooked chimneys and the mists from the crooked river.

'Have you any news?' said Arthur.

'We have no news,' said Jeremiah.

'I mean of the foreign man,' Arthur explained.

'I mean of the foreign man,' said Jeremiah.

He looked so grim, as he stood askew, with the knot of his cravat under his ear, that the thought passed into Clennam's mind, and not for the first time by many, could Flintwinch for a purpose of his own have got rid of Blandois? Could it have been his secret, and his safety, that were at issue? He was small and bent, and perhaps not actively strong; yet he was as tough as an old yew-tree, and as crusty as an old jackdaw. Such a man, coming behind a much younger and more vigorous man, and having the will to put an end to him and no relenting, might do it pretty surely in that solitary place at a late hour.

While, in the morbid condition of his thoughts, these thoughts drifted over the main one that was always in Clennam's mind, Mr Flintwinch, regarding the opposite house over the gateway with his neck twisted and one eye shut up, stood smoking with a vicious expression upon him; more as if he were trying to bite off the stem of his pipe, than as if he were enjoying it. Yet he was enjoying it in his own way.

'You'll be able to take my likeness, the next time you call, Arthur, I should think,' said Mr Flintwinch, drily, as he stooped to knock the ashes out.

Rather conscious and confused, Arthur asked his pardon, if he had stared at him unpolitely. 'But my mind runs so much upon this matter,' he said, 'that I lose myself.'

'Hah! Yet I don't see,' returned Mr Flintwinch, quite at his leisure, 'why it should trouble you, Arthur.'

'No?'

'No,' said Mr Flintwinch, very shortly and decidedly: much as if he were of the canine race, and snapped at Arthur's hand.

'Is it nothing to see those placards about? Is it nothing to me to see my mother's name and residence hawked up and down in such an association?'

'I don't see,' returned Mr Flintwinch, scraping his horny cheek, 'that it need signify much to you. But I'll tell you what I do see, Arthur,' glancing up at the windows; 'I see the light of fire and candle in your mother's room!'

'And what has that to do with it?'

'Why, sir, I read by it,' said Mr Flintwinch, screwing himself at him, 'that if it's advisable (as the proverb says it is) to let sleeping dogs lie, it's just as advisable, perhaps, to let missing dogs lie. Let 'em be. They generally turn up soon enough.'

Mr Flintwinch turned short round when he had made this remark, and went into the dark hall. Clennam stood there, following him with his eyes, as he dipped for a light in the phosphorus-box in the little room at the side, got one after three or four dips, and lighted the dim lamp against the wall. All the while, Clennam was pursuing the probabilities—rather as if they were being shown to him by an invisible hand than as if he himself were conjuring them up—of Mr Flintwinch's ways and means of doing that darker deed, and removing its traces by any of the black avenues of shadow that lay around them.

'Now, sir,' said the testy Jeremiah; 'will it be agreeable to walk up-stairs?'

'My mother is alone, I suppose?'

'Not alone,' said Mr Flintwinch. 'Mr Casby and his daughter are with her. They came in while I was smoking, and I stayed behind to have my smoke out.'

This was the second disappointment. Arthur made no remark upon it, and repaired to his mother's room, where Mr Casby and Flora had been taking tea, anchovy paste, and hot buttered toast. The relics of those delicacies were not yet removed, either from the table or from the scorched countenance of Affery, who, with the kitchen toasting-fork still in her hand, looked like a sort of allegorical personage; except that she had a considerable advantage over the general run of such personages in point of significant emblematical purpose.

Flora had spread her bonnet and shawl upon the bed, with a care indicative of an intention to stay some time. Mr Casby, too, was beaming near the hob, with his benevolent knobs shining as if the warm butter of the toast were exuding through the patriarchal skull, and with his face as ruddy as if the colouring matter of the anchovy paste were mantling in the patriarchal visage. Seeing this, as he exchanged the usual salutations, Clennam decided to speak to his mother without postponement.

It had long been customary, as she never changed her room, for those who had anything to say to her apart, to wheel her to her desk; where she sat, usually with the back of her chair turned towards the rest of the room, and the person who talked with her seated in a corner, on a stool which was always set in that place for that purpose. Except that it was long since the mother and son had spoken together without the intervention of a third person, it was an ordinary matter of course within the experience of visitors for Mrs Clennam to be asked, with a word of apology for the interruption, if she could be spoken with on a matter of business, and, on her replying in the affirmative, to be wheeled into the position described.

Therefore, when Arthur now made such an apology, and such a request, and moved her to her desk and seated himself on the stool, Mrs Finching merely began to talk louder and faster, as a delicate hint that she could overhear nothing, and Mr Casby stroked his long white locks with sleepy calmness.

'Mother, I have heard something to-day which I feel persuaded you don't know, and which I think you should know, of the antecedents of that man I saw here.'

'I know nothing of the antecedents of the man you saw here, Arthur.'

She spoke aloud. He had lowered his own voice; but she rejected that advance towards confidence as she rejected every other, and spoke in her usual key and in her usual stern voice.

'I have received it on no circuitous information; it has come to me direct.'

She asked him, exactly as before, if he were there to tell her what it was?

'I thought it right that you should know it.'

'And what is it?'

'He has been a prisoner in a French gaol.'

She answered with composure, 'I should think that very likely.'

'But in a gaol for criminals, mother. On an accusation of murder.'

She started at the word, and her looks expressed her natural horror. Yet she still spoke aloud, when she demanded:—

'Who told you so?'

'A man who was his fellow-prisoner.'

'That man's antecedents, I suppose, were not known to you, before he told you?'

'No.'

'Though the man himself was?'

'Yes.'

'My case and Flintwinch's, in respect of this other man! I dare say the resemblance is not so exact, though, as that your informant became known to you through a letter from a correspondent with whom he had deposited money? How does that part of the parallel stand?'

Arthur had no choice but to say that his informant had not become known to him through the agency of any such credentials, or indeed of any credentials at all. Mrs Clennam's attentive frown expanded by degrees into a severe look of triumph, and she retorted with emphasis, 'Take care how you judge others, then. I say to you, Arthur, for your good, take care how you judge!'

Her emphasis had been derived from her eyes quite as much as from the stress she laid upon her words. She continued to look at him; and if, when he entered the house, he had had any latent hope of prevailing in the least with her, she now looked it out of his heart.

'Mother, shall I do nothing to assist you?'

'Nothing.'

'Will you entrust me with no confidence, no charge, no explanation? Will you take no counsel with me? Will you not let me come near you?'

'How can you ask me? You separated yourself from my affairs. It was not my act; it was yours. How can you consistently ask me such a question? You know that you left me to Flintwinch, and that he occupies your place.'

Glancing at Jeremiah, Clennam saw in his very gaiters that his attention was closely directed to them, though he stood leaning against the wall scraping his jaw, and pretended to listen to Flora as she held forth in a most distracting manner on a chaos of subjects, in which mackerel, and Mr F.'s Aunt in a swing, had become entangled with cockchafers and the wine trade.

'A prisoner, in a French gaol, on an accusation of murder,' repeated Mrs Clennam, steadily going over what her son had said. 'That is all you know of him from the fellow-prisoner?'

'In substance, all.'

'And was the fellow-prisoner his accomplice and a murderer, too? But, of course, he gives a better account of himself than of his friend; it is needless to ask. This will supply the rest of them here with something new to talk about. Casby, Arthur tells me—'

'Stay, mother! Stay, stay!' He interrupted her hastily, for it had not entered his imagination that she would openly proclaim what he had told her.

'What now?' she said with displeasure. 'What more?'

'I beg you to excuse me, Mr Casby—and you, too, Mrs Finching—for one other moment with my mother—'

He had laid his hand upon her chair, or she would otherwise have wheeled it round with the touch of her foot upon the ground. They were still face to face. She looked at him, as he ran over the possibilities of some result he had not intended, and could not foresee, being influenced by Cavalletto's disclosure becoming a matter of notoriety, and hurriedly arrived at the conclusion that it had best not be talked about; though perhaps he was guided by no more distinct reason than that he had taken it for granted that his mother would reserve it to herself and her partner.

'What now?' she said again, impatiently. 'What is it?'

'I did not mean, mother, that you should repeat what I have communicated. I think you had better not repeat it.'

'Do you make that a condition with me?'

'Well! Yes.'

'Observe, then! It is you who make this a secret,' said she, holding up her hand, 'and not I. It is you, Arthur, who bring here doubts and suspicions and entreaties for explanations, and it is you, Arthur, who bring secrets here. What is it to me, do you think, where the man has been, or what he has been? What can it be to me? The whole world may know it, if they care to know it; it is nothing to me. Now, let me go.'

He yielded to her imperious but elated look, and turned her chair back to the place from which he had wheeled it. In doing so he saw elation in the face of Mr Flintwinch, which most assuredly was not inspired by Flora. This turning of his intelligence and of his whole attempt and design against himself, did even more than his mother's fixedness and firmness to convince him that his efforts with her were idle. Nothing remained but the appeal to his old friend Affery.

But even to get the very doubtful and preliminary stage of making the appeal, seemed one of the least promising of human undertakings. She was so completely under the thrall of the two clever ones, was so systematically kept in sight by one or other of them, and was so afraid to go about the house besides, that every opportunity of speaking to her alone appeared to be forestalled. Over and above that, Mistress Affery, by some means (it was not very difficult to guess, through the sharp arguments of her liege lord), had acquired such a lively conviction of the hazard of saying anything under any circumstances, that she had remained all this time in a corner guarding herself from approach with that symbolical instrument of hers; so that, when a word or two had been addressed to her by Flora, or even by the bottle-green patriarch himself, she had warded off conversation with the toasting-fork like a dumb woman.

After several abortive attempts to get Affery to look at him while she cleared the table and washed the tea-service, Arthur thought of an expedient which Flora might originate. To whom he therefore whispered, 'Could you say you would like to go through the house?'

Now, poor Flora, being always in fluctuating expectation of the time when Clennam would renew his boyhood and be madly in love with her again, received the whisper with the utmost delight; not only as rendered precious by its mysterious character, but as preparing the way for a tender interview in which he would declare the state of his affections. She immediately began to work out the hint.

'Ah dear me the poor old room,' said Flora, glancing round, 'looks just as ever Mrs Clennam I am touched to see except for being smokier which was to be expected with time and which we must all expect and reconcile ourselves to being whether we like it or not as I am sure I have had to do myself if not exactly smokier dreadfully stouter which is the same or worse, to think of the days when papa used to bring me here the least of girls a perfect mass of chilblains to be stuck upon a chair with my feet on the rails and stare at Arthur—pray excuse me—Mr Clennam—the least of boys in the frightfullest of frills and jackets ere yet Mr F. appeared a misty shadow on the horizon paying attentions like the well-known spectre of some place in Germany beginning with a B is a moral lesson inculcating that all the paths in life are similar to the paths down in the North of England where they get the coals and make the iron and things gravelled with ashes!'

Having paid the tribute of a sigh to the instability of human existence, Flora hurried on with her purpose.

'Not that at any time,' she proceeded, 'its worst enemy could have said it was a cheerful house for that it was never made to be but always highly impressive, fond memory recalls an occasion in youth ere yet the judgment was mature when Arthur—confirmed habit—Mr Clennam—took me down into an unused kitchen eminent for mouldiness and proposed to secrete me there for life and feed me on what he could hide from his meals when he was not at home for the holidays and on dry bread in disgrace which at that halcyon period too frequently occurred, would it be inconvenient or asking too much to beg to be permitted to revive those scenes and walk through the house?'

Mrs Clennam, who responded with a constrained grace to Mrs Finching's good nature in being there at all, though her visit (before Arthur's unexpected arrival) was undoubtedly an act of pure good nature and no self-gratification, intimated that all the house was open to her. Flora rose and looked to Arthur for his escort. 'Certainly,' said he, aloud; 'and Affery will light us, I dare say.'

Affery was excusing herself with 'Don't ask nothing of me, Arthur!' when Mr Flintwinch stopped her with 'Why not? Affery, what's the matter with you, woman? Why not, jade!' Thus expostulated with, she came unwillingly out of her corner, resigned the toasting-fork into one of her husband's hands, and took the candlestick he offered from the other.

'Go before, you fool!' said Jeremiah. 'Are you going up, or down, Mrs Finching?'

Flora answered, 'Down.'

'Then go before, and down, you Affery,' said Jeremiah. 'And do it properly, or I'll come rolling down the banisters, and tumbling over you!'

Affery headed the exploring party; Jeremiah closed it. He had no intention of leaving them. Clennam looking back, and seeing him following three stairs behind, in the coolest and most methodical manner exclaimed in a low voice, 'Is there no getting rid of him!' Flora reassured his mind by replying promptly, 'Why though not exactly proper Arthur and a thing I couldn't think of before a younger man or a stranger still I don't mind him if you so particularly wish it and provided you'll have the goodness not to take me too tight.'

Wanting the heart to explain that this was not at all what he meant, Arthur extended his supporting arm round Flora's figure. 'Oh my goodness me,' said she. 'You are very obedient indeed really and it's extremely honourable and gentlemanly in you I am sure but still at the same time if you would like to be a little tighter than that I shouldn't consider it intruding.'

In this preposterous attitude, unspeakably at variance with his anxious mind, Clennam descended to the basement of the house; finding that wherever it became darker than elsewhere, Flora became heavier, and that when the house was lightest she was too. Returning from the dismal kitchen regions, which were as dreary as they could be, Mistress Affery passed with the light into his father's old room, and then into the old dining-room; always passing on before like a phantom that was not to be overtaken, and neither turning nor answering when he whispered, 'Affery! I want to speak to you!'

In the dining-room, a sentimental desire came over Flora to look into the dragon closet which had so often swallowed Arthur in the days of his boyhood—not improbably because, as a very dark closet, it was a likely place to be heavy in. Arthur, fast subsiding into despair, had opened it, when a knock was heard at the outer door.

Mistress Affery, with a suppressed cry, threw her apron over her head.

'What? You want another dose!' said Mr Flintwinch. 'You shall have it, my woman, you shall have a good one! Oh! You shall have a sneezer, you shall have a teaser!'

'In the meantime is anybody going to the door?' said Arthur.

'In the meantime, I am going to the door, sir,' returned the old man so savagely, as to render it clear that in a choice of difficulties he felt he must go, though he would have preferred not to go. 'Stay here the while, all! Affery, my woman, move an inch, or speak a word in your foolishness, and I'll treble your dose!'

The moment he was gone, Arthur released Mrs Finching: with some difficulty, by reason of that lady misunderstanding his intentions, and making arrangements with a view to tightening instead of slackening.

'Affery, speak to me now!'

'Don't touch me, Arthur!' she cried, shrinking from him. 'Don't come near me. He'll see you. Jeremiah will. Don't.'

'He can't see me,' returned Arthur, suiting the action to the word, 'if I blow the candle out.'

'He'll hear you,' cried Affery.

'He can't hear me,' returned Arthur, suiting the action to the words again, 'if I draw you into this black closet, and speak here. Why do you hide your face?'

'Because I am afraid of seeing something.'

'You can't be afraid of seeing anything in this darkness, Affery.'

'Yes I am. Much more than if it was light.'

'Why are you afraid?'

'Because the house is full of mysteries and secrets; because it's full of whisperings and counsellings; because it's full of noises. There never was such a house for noises. I shall die of 'em, if Jeremiah don't strangle me first. As I expect he will.'

'I have never heard any noises here, worth speaking of.'

'Ah! But you would, though, if you lived in the house, and was obliged to go about it as I am,' said Affery; 'and you'd feel that they was so well worth speaking of, that you'd feel you was nigh bursting through not being allowed to speak of 'em. Here's Jeremiah! You'll get me killed.'

'My good Affery, I solemnly declare to you that I can see the light of the open door on the pavement of the hall, and so could you if you would uncover your face and look.'

'I durstn't do it,' said Affery, 'I durstn't never, Arthur. I'm always blind-folded when

Jeremiah an't a looking, and sometimes even when he is.'

'He cannot shut the door without my seeing him,' said Arthur. 'You are as safe with me as if he was fifty miles away.'

('I wish he was!' cried Affery.)

'Affery, I want to know what is amiss here; I want some light thrown on the secrets of this house.'

'I tell you, Arthur,' she interrupted, 'noises is the secrets, rustlings and stealings about, tremblings, treads overhead and treads underneath.'

'But those are not all the secrets.'

'I don't know,' said Affery. 'Don't ask me no more. Your old sweetheart an't far off, and she's a blabber.'

His old sweetheart, being in fact so near at hand that she was then reclining against him in a flutter, a very substantial angle of forty-five degrees, here interposed to assure Mistress Affery with greater earnestness than directness of asseveration, that what she heard should go no further, but should be kept inviolate, 'if on no other account on Arthur's—sensible of intruding in being too familiar Doyce and Clennam's.'

'I make an imploring appeal to you, Affery, to you, one of the few agreeable early remembrances I have, for my mother's sake, for your husband's sake, for my own, for all our sakes. I am sure you can tell me something connected with the coming here of this man, if you will.'

'Why, then I'll tell you, Arthur,' returned Affery—'Jeremiah's coming!'

'No, indeed he is not. The door is open, and he is standing outside, talking.'

'I'll tell you then,' said Affery, after listening, 'that the first time he ever come he heard the noises his own self. "What's that?" he said to me. "I don't know what it is," I says to him, catching hold of him, "but I have heard it over and over again." While I says it, he stands a looking at me, all of a shake, he do.'

'Has he been here often?'

'Only that night, and the last night.'

'What did you see of him on the last night, after I was gone?'

'Them two clever ones had him all alone to themselves. Jeremiah come a dancing at me sideways, after I had let you out (he always comes a dancing at me sideways when he's going to hurt me), and he said to me, "Now, Affery," he said, "I am a coming behind you, my woman, and a going to run you up." So he took and squeezed the back of my neck in his hand, till it made me open my mouth, and then he pushed me before him to bed, squeezing all the way. That's what he calls running me up, he do. Oh, he's a wicked one!'

'And did you hear or see no more, Affery?'

'Don't I tell you I was sent to bed, Arthur! Here he is!'

'I assure you he is still at the door. Those whisperings and counsellings, Affery, that you have spoken of. What are they?'

'How should I know? Don't ask me nothing about 'em, Arthur. Get away!'

'But my dear Affery; unless I can gain some insight into these hidden things, in spite of your husband and in spite of my mother, ruin will come of it.'

'Don't ask me nothing,' repeated Affery. 'I have been in a dream for ever so long. Go away, go away!'

'You said that before,' returned Arthur. 'You used the same expression that night, at the door, when I asked you what was going on here. What do you mean by being in a dream?'

'I an't a going to tell you. Get away! I shouldn't tell you, if you was by yourself; much less with your old sweetheart here.'

It was equally vain for Arthur to entreat, and for Flora to protest. Affery, who had been trembling and struggling the whole time, turned a deaf ear to all adjuration, and was bent on forcing herself out of the closet.

'I'd sooner scream to Jeremiah than say another word! I'll call out to him, Arthur, if you don't give over speaking to me. Now here's the very last word I'll say afore I call to him—If ever you begin to get the better of them two clever ones your own self (you ought to it, as I told you when you first come home, for you haven't been a living here long years, to be made afeared of your life as I have), then do you get the better of 'em afore my face; and then do you say to me, Affery tell your dreams! Maybe, then I'll tell 'em!'

The shutting of the door stopped Arthur from replying. They glided into the places where Jeremiah had left them; and Clennam, stepping forward as that old gentleman returned, informed him that he had accidentally extinguished the candle. Mr Flintwinch looked on as he re-lighted it at the lamp in the hall, and preserved a profound taciturnity respecting the person who had been holding him in conversation. Perhaps his irascibility demanded compensation for some tediousness that the visitor had expended on him; however that was, he took such umbrage at seeing his wife with her apron over her head, that he charged at her, and taking her veiled nose between his thumb and finger, appeared to throw the whole screw-power of his person into the wring he gave it.

Flora, now permanently heavy, did not release Arthur from the survey of the house, until it had extended even to his old garret bedchamber. His thoughts were otherwise occupied than with the tour of inspection; yet he took particular notice at the time, as he afterwards had occasion to remember, of the airlessness and closeness of the house; that they left the track of their footsteps in the dust on the upper floors; and that there was a resistance to the opening of one room door, which occasioned Affery to cry out that somebody was hiding inside, and to continue to believe so, though somebody was sought and not discovered. When they at last returned to his mother's room, they found her shading her face with her muffled hand, and talking in a low voice to the Patriarch as he stood before the fire, whose blue eyes, polished head, and silken locks, turning towards them as they came in, imparted an inestimable value and inexhaustible love of his species to his remark:

'So you have been seeing the premises, seeing the premises—premises— seeing the premises!'

It was not in itself a jewel of benevolence or wisdom, yet he made it an exemplar of both that one would have liked to have a copy of.

CHAPTER 24. The Evening of a Long Day

That illustrious man and great national ornament, Mr Merdle, continued his shining course. It began to be widely understood that one who had done society the admirable service of making so much money out of it, could not be suffered to remain a commoner. A baronetcy was spoken of with confidence; a peerage was frequently mentioned. Rumour had it that Mr Merdle had set his golden face against a baronetcy; that he had plainly intimated to Lord Decimus that a baronetcy was not enough for him; that he had said, 'No—a Peerage, or plain Merdle.' This was reported to have plunged Lord Decimus as nigh to his noble chin in a slough of doubts as so lofty a person could be sunk. For the Barnacles, as a group of themselves in creation, had an idea that such distinctions belonged to them; and that when a soldier, sailor, or lawyer became ennobled, they let him in, as it were, by an act of condescension, at the family door, and immediately shut it again. Not only (said Rumour) had the troubled Decimus his own hereditary part in this impression, but he also knew of several Barnacle claims already on the file, which came into collision with that of the master spirit. Right or wrong, Rumour was very busy; and Lord Decimus, while he was, or was supposed to be, in stately excogitation of the difficulty, lent her some countenance by taking, on several public occasions, one of those elephantine trots of his through a jungle of overgrown sentences, waving Mr Merdle about on his trunk as Gigantic Enterprise, The Wealth of England, Elasticity, Credit, Capital, Prosperity, and all manner of blessings.

So quietly did the mowing of the old scythe go on, that fully three months had passed unnoticed since the two English brothers had been laid in one tomb in the strangers' cemetery at Rome. Mr and Mrs Sparkler were established in their own house: a little mansion, rather of the Tite Barnacle class, quite a triumph of inconvenience, with a perpetual smell in it of the day before yesterday's soup and coach-horses, but extremely dear, as being exactly in the centre of the habitable globe. In this enviable abode (and envied it really was by many people), Mrs Sparkler had intended to proceed at once to the demolition of the Bosom, when active hostilities had been suspended by the arrival of the Courier with his tidings of death. Mrs Sparkler, who was not unfeeling, had received them with a violent burst of grief, which had lasted twelve hours; after which, she had arisen to see about her mourning, and to take every precaution that could ensure its being as becoming as Mrs Merdle's. A gloom was then cast over more than one distinguished family (according to the politest sources of intelligence), and the Courier went back again.

Mr and Mrs Sparkler had been dining alone, with their gloom cast over them, and Mrs Sparkler reclined on a drawing-room sofa. It was a hot summer Sunday evening. The residence in the centre of the habitable globe, at all times stuffed and close as if it had an incurable cold in its head, was that evening particularly stifling. The bells of the churches had done their worst in the way of clanging among the unmelodious echoes of the streets, and the lighted windows of the churches had ceased to be yellow in the grey dusk, and had died out opaque black. Mrs Sparkler, lying on her sofa, looking through an open window at the opposite side of a narrow street over boxes of mignonette and flowers, was tired of the view. Mrs Sparkler, looking at another window where her husband stood in the balcony, was tired of that view. Mrs Sparkler, looking at herself in her mourning, was even tired of that view: though, naturally, not so tired of that as of the other two.

'It's like lying in a well,' said Mrs Sparkler, changing her position fretfully. 'Dear me,

Edmund, if you have anything to say, why don't you say it?'

Mr Sparkler might have replied with ingenuousness, 'My life, I have nothing to say.' But, as the repartee did not occur to him, he contented himself with coming in from the balcony and standing at the side of his wife's couch.

'Good gracious, Edmund!' said Mrs Sparkler more fretfully still, 'you are absolutely putting mignonette up your nose! Pray don't!'

Mr Sparkler, in absence of mind—perhaps in a more literal absence of mind than is usually understood by the phrase—had smelt so hard at a sprig in his hand as to be on the verge of the offence in question. He smiled, said, 'I ask your pardon, my dear,' and threw it out of window.

'You make my head ache by remaining in that position, Edmund,' said Mrs Sparkler, raising her eyes to him after another minute; 'you look so aggravatingly large by this light. Do sit down.'

'Certainly, my dear,' said Mr Sparkler, and took a chair on the same spot.

'If I didn't know that the longest day was past,' said Fanny, yawning in a dreary manner, 'I should have felt certain this was the longest day. I never did experience such a day.'

'Is that your fan, my love?' asked Mr Sparkler, picking up one and presenting it.

'Edmund,' returned his wife, more wearily yet, 'don't ask weak questions, I entreat you not. Whose can it be but mine?'

'Yes, I thought it was yours,' said Mr Sparkler.

'Then you shouldn't ask,' retorted Fanny. After a little while she turned on her sofa and exclaimed, 'Dear me, dear me, there never was such a long day as this!' After another little while, she got up slowly, walked about, and came back again.

'My dear,' said Mr Sparkler, flashing with an original conception, 'I think you must have got the fidgets.'

'Oh, Fidgets!' repeated Mrs Sparkler. 'Don't.'

'My adorable girl,' urged Mr Sparkler, 'try your aromatic vinegar. I have often seen my mother try it, and it seemingly refreshed her.

And she is, as I believe you are aware, a remarkably fine woman, with no non—'

'Good Gracious!' exclaimed Fanny, starting up again. 'It's beyond all patience! This is the most wearisome day that ever did dawn upon the world, I am certain.'

Mr Sparkler looked meekly after her as she lounged about the room, and he appeared to be a little frightened. When she had tossed a few trifles about, and had looked down into the darkening street out of all the three windows, she returned to her sofa, and threw herself among its pillows.

'Now Edmund, come here! Come a little nearer, because I want to be able to touch you with my fan, that I may impress you very much with what I am going to say. That will do. Quite close enough. Oh, you do look so big!'

Mr Sparkler apologised for the circumstance, pleaded that he couldn't help it, and said that 'our fellows,' without more particularly indicating whose fellows, used to call him by the name of Quinbus Flestrin, Junior, or the Young Man Mountain.

'You ought to have told me so before,' Fanny complained.

'My dear,' returned Mr Sparkler, rather gratified, 'I didn't know It would interest you, or I would have made a point of telling you.'

'There! For goodness sake, don't talk,' said Fanny; 'I want to talk, myself. Edmund, we must not be alone any more. I must take such precautions as will prevent my being ever again reduced to the state of dreadful depression in which I am this evening.'

'My dear,' answered Mr Sparkler; 'being as you are well known to be, a remarkably fine woman with no—'

'Oh, good GRACIOUS!' cried Fanny.

Mr Sparkler was so discomposed by the energy of this exclamation, accompanied with a flouncing up from the sofa and a flouncing down again, that a minute or two elapsed before he felt himself equal to saying in explanation:

'I mean, my dear, that everybody knows you are calculated to shine in society.'

'Calculated to shine in society,' retorted Fanny with great irritability; 'yes, indeed! And then what happens? I no sooner recover, in a visiting point of view, the shock of poor dear papa's death, and my poor uncle's—though I do not disguise from myself that the last was a happy release, for, if you are not presentable you had much better die—'

'You are not referring to me, my love, I hope?' Mr Sparkler humbly interrupted.

'Edmund, Edmund, you would wear out a Saint. Am I not expressly speaking of my poor uncle?'

'You looked with so much expression at myself, my dear girl,' said Mr Sparkler, 'that I felt a little uncomfortable. Thank you, my love.'

'Now you have put me out,' observed Fanny with a resigned toss of her fan, 'and I had better go to bed.'

'Don't do that, my love,' urged Mr Sparkler. 'Take time.'

Fanny took a good deal of time: lying back with her eyes shut, and her eyebrows raised with a hopeless expression as if she had utterly given up all terrestrial affairs. At length, without the slightest notice, she opened her eyes again, and recommenced in a short, sharp manner:

'What happens then, I ask! What happens? Why, I find myself at the very period when I might shine most in society, and should most like for very momentous reasons to shine in society—I find myself in a situation which to a certain extent disqualifies me for going into society. It's too bad, really!'

'My dear,' said Mr Sparkler. 'I don't think it need keep you at home.'

'Edmund, you ridiculous creature,' returned Fanny, with great indignation; 'do you suppose that a woman in the bloom of youth and not wholly devoid of personal attractions, can put herself, at such a time, in competition as to figure with a woman in every other way her inferior? If you do suppose such a thing, your folly is boundless.'

Mr Sparkler submitted that he had thought 'it might be got over.'

'Got over!' repeated Fanny, with immeasurable scorn.

'For a time,' Mr Sparkler submitted.

Honouring the last feeble suggestion with no notice, Mrs Sparkler declared with bitterness that it really was too bad, and that positively it was enough to make one wish one was dead!

'However,' she said, when she had in some measure recovered from her sense of personal ill-usage; 'provoking as it is, and cruel as it seems, I suppose it must be submitted to.'

'Especially as it was to be expected,' said Mr Sparkler.

'Edmund,' returned his wife, 'if you have nothing more becoming to do than to attempt to insult the woman who has honoured you with her hand, when she finds herself in adversity, I think you had better go to bed!'

Mr Sparkler was much afflicted by the charge, and offered a most tender and earnest apology. His apology was accepted; but Mrs Sparkler requested him to go round to the other side of the sofa and sit in the window-curtain, to tone himself down.

'Now, Edmund,' she said, stretching out her fan, and touching him with it at arm's length, 'what I was going to say to you when you began as usual to prose and worry, is, that I shall guard against our being alone any more, and that when circumstances prevent my going out to my own satisfaction, I must arrange to have some people or other always here; for I really cannot, and will not, have another such day as this has been.'

Mr Sparkler's sentiments as to the plan were, in brief, that it had no nonsense about it. He added, 'And besides, you know it's likely that you'll soon have your sister—'

'Dearest Amy, yes!' cried Mrs Sparkler with a sigh of affection. 'Darling little thing! Not, however, that Amy would do here alone.'

Mr Sparkler was going to say 'No?' interrogatively, but he saw his danger and said it assentingly, 'No, Oh dear no; she wouldn't do here alone.'

'No, Edmund. For not only are the virtues of the precious child of that still character that they require a contrast—require life and movement around them to bring them out in their right colours and make one love them of all things; but she will require to be roused, on more accounts than one.'

'That's it,' said Mr Sparkler. 'Roused.'

'Pray don't, Edmund! Your habit of interrupting without having the least thing in the world to say, distracts one. You must be broken of it. Speaking of Amy;—my poor little pet was devotedly attached to poor papa, and no doubt will have lamented his loss exceedingly, and grieved very much. I have done so myself. I have felt it dreadfully. But Amy will no doubt have felt it even more, from having been on the spot the whole time, and having been with poor dear papa at the last; which I unhappily was not.'

Here Fanny stopped to weep, and to say, 'Dear, dear, beloved papa! How truly gentlemanly he was! What a contrast to poor uncle!'

'From the effects of that trying time,' she pursued, 'my good little Mouse will have to be roused. Also, from the effects of this long attendance upon Edward in his illness; an attendance which is not yet over, which may even go on for some time longer, and which in the meanwhile unsettles us all by keeping poor dear papa's affairs from being wound up. Fortunately, however, the papers with his agents here being all sealed up and locked up, as he left them when he providentially came to England, the affairs are in that state of order that they can wait until my brother Edward recovers his health in Sicily, sufficiently to come over, and administer, or execute, or whatever it may be that will have to be done.'

'He couldn't have a better nurse to bring him round,' Mr Sparkler made bold to opine.

'For a wonder, I can agree with you,' returned his wife, languidly turning her eyelids a little in his direction (she held forth, in general, as if to the drawing-room furniture), 'and can adopt your words. He couldn't have a better nurse to bring him round. There are times when my dear child is a little wearing to an active mind; but, as a nurse, she is Perfection. Best of Amys!'

Mr Sparkler, growing rash on his late success, observed that Edward had had, biggodd, a long bout of it, my dear girl.

'If Bout, Edmund,' returned Mrs Sparkler, 'is the slang term for indisposition, he has. If it is not, I am unable to give an opinion on the barbarous language you address to Edward's sister. That he contracted Malaria Fever somewhere, either by travelling day and night to Rome, where, after all, he arrived too late to see poor dear papa before his death—or under some other unwholesome circumstances—is indubitable, if that is what you mean. Likewise that his extremely careless life has made him a very bad subject for it indeed.'

Mr Sparkler considered it a parallel case to that of some of our fellows in the West Indies with Yellow Jack. Mrs Sparkler closed her eyes again, and refused to have any consciousness of our fellows of the West Indies, or of Yellow Jack.

'So, Amy,' she pursued, when she reopened her eyelids, 'will require to be roused from the effects of many tedious and anxious weeks. And lastly, she will require to be roused from a low tendency which I know very well to be at the bottom of her heart. Don't ask me what it is, Edmund, because I must decline to tell you.'

'I am not going to, my dear,' said Mr Sparkler.

'I shall thus have much improvement to effect in my sweet child,' Mrs Sparkler continued, 'and cannot have her near me too soon. Amiable and dear little Twoshoes! As to the settlement of poor papa's affairs, my interest in that is not very selfish. Papa behaved very generously to me when I was married, and I have little or nothing to expect. Provided he had made no will that can come into force, leaving a legacy to Mrs General, I am contented. Dear papa, dear papa.'

She wept again, but Mrs General was the best of restoratives. The name soon stimulated her to dry her eyes and say:

'It is a highly encouraging circumstance in Edward's illness, I am thankful to think, and gives one the greatest confidence in his sense not being impaired, or his proper spirit weakened—down to the time of poor dear papa's death at all events—that he paid off Mrs General instantly, and sent her out of the house. I applaud him for it. I could forgive him a great deal for doing, with such promptitude, so exactly what I would have done myself!'

Mrs Sparkler was in the full glow of her gratification, when a double knock was heard at the door. A very odd knock. Low, as if to avoid making a noise and attracting attention. Long, as if the person knocking were preoccupied in mind, and forgot to leave off.

'Halloa!' said Mr Sparkler. 'Who's this?'

'Not Amy and Edward without notice and without a carriage!' said Mrs Sparkler. 'Look out.'

The room was dark, but the street was lighter, because of its lamps. Mr Sparkler's head peeping over the balcony looked so very bulky and heavy that it seemed on the point of overbalancing him and flattening the unknown below.

'It's one fellow,' said Mr Sparkler. 'I can't see who—stop though!'

On this second thought he went out into the balcony again and had another look. He came back as the door was opened, and announced that he believed he had identified 'his governor's tile.' He was not mistaken, for his governor, with his tile in his hand, was introduced immediately afterwards.

'Candles!' said Mrs Sparkler, with a word of excuse for the darkness.

'It's light enough for me,' said Mr Merdle.

When the candles were brought in, Mr Merdle was discovered standing behind the door, picking his lips. 'I thought I'd give you a call,' he said. 'I am rather particularly occupied just now; and, as I happened to be out for a stroll, I thought I'd give you a call.'

As he was in dinner dress, Fanny asked him where he had been dining?

'Well,' said Mr Merdle, 'I haven't been dining anywhere, particularly.'

'Of course you have dined?' said Fanny.

'Why—no, I haven't exactly dined,' said Mr Merdle.

He had passed his hand over his yellow forehead and considered, as if he were not sure about it. Something to eat was proposed. 'No, thank you,' said Mr Merdle, 'I don't feel inclined for it. I was to have dined out along with Mrs Merdle. But as I didn't feel inclined for dinner, I let Mrs Merdle go by herself just as we were getting into the carriage, and thought I'd take a stroll instead.'

Would he have tea or coffee? 'No, thank you,' said Mr Merdle. 'I looked in at the Club, and got a bottle of wine.'

At this period of his visit, Mr Merdle took the chair which Edmund Sparkler had offered him, and which he had hitherto been pushing slowly about before him, like a dull man with a pair of skates on for the first time, who could not make up his mind to start. He now put his hat upon another chair beside him, and, looking down into it as if it were some twenty feet deep, said again: 'You see I thought I'd give you a call.'

'Flattering to us,' said Fanny, 'for you are not a calling man.'

'No—no,' returned Mr Merdle, who was by this time taking himself into custody under both coat-sleeves. 'No, I am not a calling man.'

'You have too much to do for that,' said Fanny. 'Having so much to do, Mr Merdle, loss of appetite is a serious thing with you, and you must have it seen to. You must not be ill.'

'Oh! I am very well,' replied Mr Merdle, after deliberating about it. 'I am as well as I usually am. I am well enough. I am as well as I want to be.'

The master-mind of the age, true to its characteristic of being at all times a mind that had as little as possible to say for itself and great difficulty in saying it, became mute again. Mrs

Sparkler began to wonder how long the master-mind meant to stay.

'I was speaking of poor papa when you came in, sir.'

'Aye! Quite a coincidence,' said Mr Merdle.

Fanny did not see that; but felt it incumbent on her to continue talking. 'I was saying,' she pursued, 'that my brother's illness has occasioned a delay in examining and arranging papa's property.'

'Yes,' said Mr Merdle; 'yes. There has been a delay.'

'Not that it is of consequence,' said Fanny.

'Not,' assented Mr Merdle, after having examined the cornice of all that part of the room which was within his range: 'not that it is of any consequence.'

'My only anxiety is,' said Fanny, 'that Mrs General should not get anything.'

'She won't get anything,' said Mr Merdle.

Fanny was delighted to hear him express the opinion. Mr Merdle, after taking another gaze into the depths of his hat as if he thought he saw something at the bottom, rubbed his hair and slowly appended to his last remark the confirmatory words, 'Oh dear no. No. Not she. Not likely.'

As the topic seemed exhausted, and Mr Merdle too, Fanny inquired if he were going to take up Mrs Merdle and the carriage in his way home?

'No,' he answered; 'I shall go by the shortest way, and leave Mrs Merdle to—' here he looked all over the palms of both his hands as if he were telling his own fortune—'to take care of herself. I dare say she'll manage to do it.'

'Probably,' said Fanny.

There was then a long silence; during which, Mrs Sparkler, lying back on her sofa again, shut her eyes and raised her eyebrows in her former retirement from mundane affairs.

'But, however,' said Mr Merdle, 'I am equally detaining you and myself. I thought I'd give you a call, you know.'

'Charmed, I am sure,' said Fanny.

'So I am off,' added Mr Merdle, getting up. 'Could you lend me a penknife?'

It was an odd thing, Fanny smilingly observed, for her who could seldom prevail upon herself even to write a letter, to lend to a man of such vast business as Mr Merdle. 'Isn't it?' Mr Merdle acquiesced; 'but I want one; and I know you have got several little wedding keepsakes about, with scissors and tweezers and such things in them. You shall have it back to-morrow.'

'Edmund,' said Mrs Sparkler, 'open (now, very carefully, I beg and beseech, for you are so very awkward) the mother of pearl box on my little table there, and give Mr Merdle the mother of pearl penknife.'

'Thank you,' said Mr Merdle; 'but if you have got one with a darker handle, I think I should prefer one with a darker handle.'

'Tortoise-shell?'

'Thank you,' said Mr Merdle; 'yes. I think I should prefer tortoise-shell.'

Edmund accordingly received instructions to open the tortoise-shell box, and give Mr Merdle the tortoise-shell knife. On his doing so, his wife said to the master-spirit graciously:

'I will forgive you, if you ink it.'

'I'll undertake not to ink it,' said Mr Merdle.

The illustrious visitor then put out his coat-cuff, and for a moment entombed Mrs Sparkler's hand: wrist, bracelet, and all. Where his own hand had shrunk to, was not made manifest, but it was as remote from Mrs Sparkler's sense of touch as if he had been a highly meritorious Chelsea Veteran or Greenwich Pensioner.

Thoroughly convinced, as he went out of the room, that it was the longest day that ever did come to an end at last, and that there never was a woman, not wholly devoid of personal attractions, so worn out by idiotic and lumpish people, Fanny passed into the balcony for a breath of air. Waters of vexation filled her eyes; and they had the effect of making the famous Mr Merdle, in going down the street, appear to leap, and waltz, and gyrate, as if he were possessed of several Devils.

CHAPTER 25. The Chief Butler Resigns the Seals of Office

The dinner-party was at the great Physician's. Bar was there, and in full force. Ferdinand Barnacle was there, and in his most engaging state. Few ways of life were hidden from Physician, and he was oftener in its darkest places than even Bishop. There were brilliant ladies about London who perfectly doted on him, my dear, as the most charming creature and the most delightful person, who would have been shocked to find themselves so close to him if they could have known on what sights those thoughtful eyes of his had rested within an hour or two, and near to whose beds, and under what roofs, his composed figure had stood. But Physician was a composed man, who performed neither on his own trumpet, nor on the trumpets of other people. Many wonderful things did he see and hear, and much irreconcilable moral contradiction did he pass his life among; yet his equality of compassion was no more disturbed than the Divine Master's of all healing was. He went, like the rain, among the just and unjust, doing all the good he could, and neither proclaiming it in the synagogues nor at the corner of streets.

As no man of large experience of humanity, however quietly carried it may be, can fail to be invested with an interest peculiar to the possession of such knowledge, Physician was an attractive man. Even the daintier gentlemen and ladies who had no idea of his secret, and who would have been startled out of more wits than they had, by the monstrous impropriety of his proposing to them 'Come and see what I see!' confessed his attraction. Where he was, something real was. And half a grain of reality, like the smallest portion of some other scarce natural productions, will flavour an enormous quantity of diluent.

It came to pass, therefore, that Physician's little dinners always presented people in their least conventional lights. The guests said to themselves, whether they were conscious of it or no, 'Here is a man who really has an acquaintance with us as we are, who is admitted to some of us every day with our wigs and paint off, who hears the wanderings of our minds, and sees the undisguised expression of our faces, when both are past our control; we may as well make an approach to reality with him, for the man has got the better of us and is too strong for us.' Therefore, Physician's guests came out so surprisingly at his round table that they were almost natural.

Bar's knowledge of that agglomeration of jurymen which is called humanity was as sharp as a razor; yet a razor is not a generally convenient instrument, and Physician's plain bright scalpel, though far less keen, was adaptable to far wider purposes. Bar knew all about the gullibility and knavery of people; but Physician could have given him a better insight into their tendernesses and affections, in one week of his rounds, than Westminster Hall and all the circuits put together, in threescore years and ten. Bar always had a suspicion of this, and perhaps was glad to encourage it (for, if the world were really a great Law Court, one would think that the last day of Term could not too soon arrive); and so he liked and respected Physician quite as much as any other kind of man did.

Mr Merdle's default left a Banquo's chair at the table; but, if he had been there, he would have merely made the difference of Banquo in it, and consequently he was no loss. Bar, who picked up all sorts of odds and ends about Westminster Hall, much as a raven would have done if he had passed as much of his time there, had been picking up a great many straws lately and tossing them about, to try which way the Merdle wind blew. He now had a little talk on the subject with Mrs Merdle herself; sidling up to that lady, of course, with his double eye-glass and his jury droop.

'A certain bird,' said Bar; and he looked as if it could have been no other bird than a magpie; 'has been whispering among us lawyers lately, that there is to be an addition to the titled personages of this realm.'

'Really?' said Mrs Merdle.

'Yes,' said Bar. 'Has not the bird been whispering in very different ears from ours—in lovely ears?' He looked expressively at Mrs Merdle's nearest ear-ring.

'Do you mean mine?' asked Mrs Merdle.

'When I say lovely,' said Bar, 'I always mean you.'

'You never mean anything, I think,' returned Mrs Merdle (not displeased).

'Oh, cruelly unjust!' said Bar. 'But, the bird.'

'I am the last person in the world to hear news,' observed Mrs Merdle, carelessly arranging her stronghold. 'Who is it?'

'What an admirable witness you would make!' said Bar. 'No jury (unless we could empanel one of blind men) could resist you, if you were ever so bad a one; but you would be such a good one!'

'Why, you ridiculous man?' asked Mrs Merdle, laughing.

Bar waved his double eye-glass three or four times between himself and the Bosom, as a rallying answer, and inquired in his most insinuating accents:

'What am I to call the most elegant, accomplished and charming of women, a few weeks, or it may be a few days, hence?'

'Didn't your bird tell you what to call her?' answered Mrs Merdle. 'Do ask it to-morrow, and tell me the next time you see me what it says.'

This led to further passages of similar pleasantry between the two; but Bar, with all his sharpness, got nothing out of them. Physician, on the other hand, taking Mrs Merdle down to her carriage and attending on her as she put on her cloak, inquired into the symptoms with his usual calm directness.

'May I ask,' he said, 'is this true about Merdle?'

'My dear doctor,' she returned, 'you ask me the very question that I was half disposed to ask you.'

'To ask me! Why me?'

'Upon my honour, I think Mr Merdle reposes greater confidence in you than in any one.'

'On the contrary, he tells me absolutely nothing, even professionally. You have heard the talk, of course?'

'Of course I have. But you know what Mr Merdle is; you know how taciturn and reserved he is. I assure you I have no idea what foundation for it there may be. I should like it to be true; why should I deny that to you? You would know better, if I did!'

'Just so,' said Physician.

'But whether it is all true, or partly true, or entirely false, I am wholly unable to say. It is a most provoking situation, a most absurd situation; but you know Mr Merdle, and are not surprised.'

Physician was not surprised, handed her into her carriage, and bade her Good Night. He stood for a moment at his own hall door, looking sedately at the elegant equipage as it rattled away. On his return up-stairs, the rest of the guests soon dispersed, and he was left alone. Being a great reader of all kinds of literature (and never at all apologetic for that weakness), he sat down comfortably to read.

The clock upon his study table pointed to a few minutes short of twelve, when his attention was called to it by a ringing at the door bell. A man of plain habits, he had sent his servants to bed and must needs go down to open the door. He went down, and there found a man without hat or coat, whose shirt sleeves were rolled up tight to his shoulders. For a moment, he thought the man had been fighting: the rather, as he was much agitated and out of breath. A second look, however, showed him that the man was particularly clean, and not otherwise discomposed as to his dress than as it answered this description.

'I come from the warm-baths, sir, round in the neighbouring street.'

'And what is the matter at the warm-baths?'

'Would you please to come directly, sir. We found that, lying on the table.'

He put into the physician's hand a scrap of paper. Physician looked at it, and read his own name and address written in pencil; nothing more. He looked closer at the writing, looked at the man, took his hat from its peg, put the key of his door in his pocket, and they hurried away together.

When they came to the warm-baths, all the other people belonging to that establishment were looking out for them at the door, and running up and down the passages. 'Request everybody else to keep back, if you please,' said the physician aloud to the master; 'and do you take me straight to the place, my friend,' to the messenger.

The messenger hurried before him, along a grove of little rooms, and turning into one at the end of the grove, looked round the door. Physician was close upon him, and looked round the door too.

There was a bath in that corner, from which the water had been hastily drained off. Lying in it, as in a grave or sarcophagus, with a hurried drapery of sheet and blanket thrown across it, was the body of a heavily-made man, with an obtuse head, and coarse, mean, common features. A sky-light had been opened to release the steam with which the room had been filled; but it hung, condensed into water-drops, heavily upon the walls, and heavily upon the face and figure in the bath. The room was still hot, and the marble of the bath still warm; but the face and figure were clammy to the touch. The white marble at the bottom of the bath was veined with a dreadful red. On the ledge at the side, were an empty laudanum-bottle and a tortoise-shell handled penknife—soiled, but not with ink.

'Separation of jugular vein—death rapid—been dead at least half an hour.' This echo of the physician's words ran through the passages and little rooms, and through the house while he was yet straightening himself from having bent down to reach to the bottom of the bath, and while he was yet dabbling his hands in water; redly veining it as the marble was veined, before it mingled into one tint.

He turned his eyes to the dress upon the sofa, and to the watch, money, and pocket-book on the table. A folded note half buckled up in the pocket-book, and half protruding from it, caught his observant glance. He looked at it, touched it, pulled it a little further out from among the leaves, said quietly, 'This is addressed to me,' and opened and read it.

There were no directions for him to give. The people of the house knew what to do; the proper authorities were soon brought; and they took an equable business-like possession of the deceased, and of what had been his property, with no greater disturbance of manner or countenance than usually attends the winding-up of a clock. Physician was glad to walk out into the night air—was even glad, in spite of his great experience, to sit down upon a door-step for a little while: feeling sick and faint.

Bar was a near neighbour of his, and, when he came to the house, he saw a light in the room where he knew his friend often sat late getting up his work. As the light was never there when Bar was not, it gave him assurance that Bar was not yet in bed. In fact, this busy bee had a verdict to get to-morrow, against evidence, and was improving the shining hours in setting snares for the gentlemen of the jury.

Physician's knock astonished Bar; but, as he immediately suspected that somebody had come to tell him that somebody else was robbing him, or otherwise trying to get the better of him, he came down promptly and softly. He had been clearing his head with a lotion of cold water, as a good preparative to providing hot water for the heads of the jury, and had been reading with the neck of his shirt thrown wide open that he might the more freely choke the opposite witnesses. In consequence, he came down, looking rather wild. Seeing Physician, the least expected of men, he looked wilder and said, 'What's the matter?'

'You asked me once what Merdle's complaint was.'

'Extraordinary answer! I know I did.'

'I told you I had not found out.'

'Yes. I know you did.'

'I have found it out.'

'My God!' said Bar, starting back, and clapping his hand upon the other's breast. 'And so have I! I see it in your face.'

They went into the nearest room, where Physician gave him the letter to read. He read it through half-a-dozen times. There was not much in it as to quantity; but it made a great demand on his close and continuous attention. He could not sufficiently give utterance to his regret that he had not himself found a clue to this. The smallest clue, he said, would have made him master of the case, and what a case it would have been to have got to the bottom of!

Physician had engaged to break the intelligence in Harley Street. Bar could not at once return to his inveiglements of the most enlightened and remarkable jury he had ever seen in that box, with whom, he could tell his learned friend, no shallow sophistry would go down, and no unhappily abused professional tact and skill prevail (this was the way he meant to begin with them); so he said he would go too, and would loiter to and fro near the house while his friend was inside. They walked there, the better to recover self-possession in the air; and the wings of day were fluttering the night when Physician knocked at the door.

A footman of rainbow hues, in the public eye, was sitting up for his master—that is to say, was fast asleep in the kitchen over a couple of candles and a newspaper, demonstrating the great accumulation of mathematical odds against the probabilities of a house being set on fire by accident When this serving man was roused, Physician had still to await the rousing of the Chief Butler. At last that noble creature came into the dining-room in a flannel gown and list shoes; but with his cravat on, and a Chief Butler all over. It was morning now. Physician had opened the shutters of one window while waiting, that he might see the light.

'Mrs Merdle's maid must be called, and told to get Mrs Merdle up, and prepare her as gently as she can to see me. I have dreadful news to break to her.'

Thus Physician to the Chief Butler. The latter, who had a candle in his hand, called his man to take it away. Then he approached the window with dignity; looking on at Physician's news exactly as he had looked on at the dinners in that very room.

'Mr Merdle is dead.'

'I should wish,' said the Chief Butler, 'to give a month's notice.'

'Mr Merdle has destroyed himself.'

'Sir,' said the Chief Butler, 'that is very unpleasant to the feelings of one in my position, as calculated to awaken prejudice; and I should wish to leave immediately.'

'If you are not shocked, are you not surprised, man?' demanded the Physician, warmly.

The Chief Butler, erect and calm, replied in these memorable words. 'Sir, Mr Merdle never was the gentleman, and no ungentlemanly act on Mr Merdle's part would surprise me. Is there anybody else I can send to you, or any other directions I can give before I leave, respecting what you would wish to be done?'

When Physician, after discharging himself of his trust up-stairs, rejoined Bar in the street, he said no more of his interview with Mrs Merdle than that he had not yet told her all, but that what he had told her she had borne pretty well. Bar had devoted his leisure in the street to the construction of a most ingenious man-trap for catching the whole of his jury at a blow; having got that matter settled in his mind, it was lucid on the late catastrophe, and they walked home slowly, discussing it in every bearing. Before parting at the Physician's door, they both looked up at the sunny morning sky, into which the smoke of a few early fires and the breath and voices of a few early stirrers were peacefully rising, and then looked round upon the immense city, and said, if all those hundreds and thousands of beggared people who were yet asleep could only know, as they two spoke, the ruin that impended over them, what a fearful cry against one miserable soul would go up to Heaven!

The report that the great man was dead, got about with astonishing rapidity. At first, he was dead of all the diseases that ever were known, and of several bran-new maladies invented with the speed of Light to meet the demand of the occasion. He had concealed a dropsy from infancy, he had inherited a large estate of water on the chest from his grandfather, he had had an operation performed upon him every morning of his life for eighteen years, he had been subject to the explosion of important veins in his body after the manner of fireworks, he had had something the matter with his lungs, he had had something the matter with his heart, he had had something the matter with his brain. Five hundred people who sat down to breakfast entirely uninformed on the whole subject, believed before they had done breakfast, that they privately and personally knew Physician to have said to Mr Merdle, 'You must expect to go out, some day, like the snuff of a candle;' and that they knew Mr Merdle to have said to Physician, 'A man can die but once.' By about eleven o'clock in the forenoon, something the matter with the brain, became the favourite theory against the field; and by twelve the something had been distinctly ascertained to be 'Pressure.'

Pressure was so entirely satisfactory to the public mind, and seemed to make everybody so comfortable, that it might have lasted all day but for Bar's having taken the real state of the case into Court at half-past nine. This led to its beginning to be currently whispered all over London by about one, that Mr Merdle had killed himself. Pressure, however, so far from being overthrown by the discovery, became a greater favourite than ever. There was a general moralising upon Pressure, in every street. All the people who had tried to make money and had not been able to do it, said, There you were! You no sooner began to devote yourself to the pursuit of wealth than you got Pressure. The idle people improved the occasion in a similar manner. See, said they, what you brought yourself to by work, work, work! You persisted in working, you overdid it. Pressure came on, and you were done for! This consideration was very potent in many quarters, but nowhere more so than among the young clerks and partners who had never been in the slightest danger of overdoing it. These, one and all, declared, quite piously, that they hoped they would never forget the warning as long as they lived, and that their conduct might be so regulated as to keep off Pressure, and preserve them, a comfort to their friends, for many years.

But, at about the time of High 'Change, Pressure began to wane, and appalling whispers to circulate, east, west, north, and south. At first they were faint, and went no further than a doubt whether Mr Merdle's wealth would be found to be as vast as had been supposed; whether there might not be a temporary difficulty in 'realising' it; whether there might not even be a temporary suspension (say a month or so), on the part of the wonderful Bank. As the whispers became louder, which they did from that time every minute, they became more threatening. He had sprung from nothing, by no natural growth or process that any one could account for; he had been, after all, a low, ignorant fellow; he had been a down-looking man, and no one had ever been able to catch his eye; he had been taken up by all sorts of people in quite an unaccountable manner; he had never had any money of his own, his ventures had been utterly reckless, and his expenditure had been most enormous. In steady progression, as the day declined, the talk rose in sound and purpose. He had left a letter at the Baths addressed to his physician, and his physician had got the letter, and the letter would be produced at the Inquest on the morrow, and it would fall like a thunderbolt upon the multitude he had deluded. Numbers of men in every profession and trade would be blighted by his insolvency; old people who had been in easy circumstances all their lives would have no place of repentance for their trust in him but the workhouse; legions of women and children would have their whole future desolated by the hand of this mighty scoundrel. Every partaker of his magnificent feasts would be seen to have been a sharer in the plunder of innumerable homes; every servile worshipper of riches who had helped to set him on his pedestal, would have done better to worship the Devil point-blank. So, the talk, lashed louder and higher by confirmation on confirmation, and by edition after edition of the evening papers, swelled into such a roar when night came, as might have brought one to believe that a solitary watcher on the gallery above the Dome of St Paul's would have perceived the night air to be laden with a heavy muttering of the name of Merdle, coupled with every form of execration.

For by that time it was known that the late Mr Merdle's complaint had been simply Forgery and Robbery. He, the uncouth object of such wide-spread adulation, the sitter at great men's feasts, the roc's egg of great ladies' assemblies, the subduer of exclusiveness, the leveller of pride, the patron of patrons, the bargain-driver with a Minister for Lordships of the Circumlocution Office, the recipient of more acknowledgment within some ten or fifteen years, at most, than had been bestowed in England upon all peaceful public benefactors, and upon all the leaders of all the Arts and Sciences, with all their works to testify for them, during two centuries at least—he, the shining wonder, the new constellation to be followed by the wise men bringing gifts, until it stopped over a certain carrion at the bottom of a bath and disappeared—was simply the greatest Forger and the greatest Thief that ever cheated the gallows.

CHAPTER 26. Reaping the Whirlwind

With a precursory sound of hurried breath and hurried feet, Mr Pancks rushed into Arthur Clennam's Counting-house. The Inquest was over, the letter was public, the Bank was broken, the other model structures of straw had taken fire and were turned to smoke. The admired piratical ship had blown up, in the midst of a vast fleet of ships of all rates, and boats of all sizes; and on the deep was nothing but ruin; nothing but burning hulls, bursting magazines, great guns self-exploded tearing friends and neighbours to pieces, drowning men clinging to unseaworthy spars and going down every minute, spent swimmers, floating dead, and sharks.

The usual diligence and order of the Counting-house at the Works were overthrown. Unopened letters and unsorted papers lay strewn about the desk. In the midst of these tokens of prostrated energy and dismissed hope, the master of the Counting-house stood idle in his usual place, with his arms crossed on the desk, and his head bowed down upon them.

Mr Pancks rushed in and saw him, and stood still. In another minute, Mr Pancks's arms were on the desk, and Mr Pancks's head was bowed down upon them; and for some time they remained in these attitudes, idle and silent, with the width of the little room between them.

Mr Pancks was the first to lift up his head and speak.

'I persuaded you to it, Mr Clennam. I know it. Say what you will. You can't say more to me than I say to myself. You can't say more than I deserve.'

'O, Pancks, Pancks!' returned Clennam, 'don't speak of deserving. What do I myself deserve!'

'Better luck,' said Pancks.

'I,' pursued Clennam, without attending to him, 'who have ruined my partner! Pancks, Pancks, I have ruined Doyce! The honest, self-helpful, indefatigable old man who has worked his way all through his life; the man who has contended against so much disappointment, and who has brought out of it such a good and hopeful nature; the man I have felt so much for, and meant to be so true and useful to; I have ruined him—brought him to shame and disgrace—ruined him, ruined him!'

The agony into which the reflection wrought his mind was so distressing to see, that Mr Pancks took hold of himself by the hair of his head, and tore it in desperation at the spectacle.

'Reproach me!' cried Pancks. 'Reproach me, sir, or I'll do myself an injury. Say,—You fool, you villain. Say,—Ass, how could you do it; Beast, what did you mean by it! Catch hold of me somewhere. Say something abusive to me!' All the time, Mr Pancks was tearing at his tough hair in a most pitiless and cruel manner.

'If you had never yielded to this fatal mania, Pancks,' said Clennam, more in commiseration than retaliation, 'it would have been how much better for you, and how much better for me!'

'At me again, sir!' cried Pancks, grinding his teeth in remorse. 'At me again!'

'If you had never gone into those accursed calculations, and brought out your results with such abominable clearness,' groaned Clennam, 'it would have been how much better for you, Pancks, and how much better for me!'

'At me again, sir!' exclaimed Pancks, loosening his hold of his hair; 'at me again, and again!'

Clennam, however, finding him already beginning to be pacified, had said all he wanted to say, and more. He wrung his hand, only adding, 'Blind leaders of the blind, Pancks! Blind leaders of the blind! But Doyce, Doyce, Doyce; my injured partner!' That brought his head down on the desk once more.

Their former attitudes and their former silence were once more first encroached upon by Pancks.

'Not been to bed, sir, since it began to get about. Been high and low, on the chance of finding some hope of saving any cinders from the fire. All in vain. All gone. All vanished.'

'I know it,' returned Clennam, 'too well.'

Mr Pancks filled up a pause with a groan that came out of the very depths of his soul.

'Only yesterday, Pancks,' said Arthur; 'only yesterday, Monday, I had the fixed intention of selling, realising, and making an end of it.'

'I can't say as much for myself, sir,' returned Pancks. 'Though it's wonderful how many people I've heard of, who were going to realise yesterday, of all days in the three hundred and sixty-five, if it hadn't been too late!'

His steam-like breathings, usually droll in their effect, were more tragic than so many groans: while from head to foot, he was in that begrimed, besmeared, neglected state, that he might have been an authentic portrait of Misfortune which could scarcely be discerned through its want of cleaning.

'Mr Clennam, had you laid out—everything?' He got over the break before the last word, and also brought out the last word itself with great difficulty.

'Everything.'

Mr Pancks took hold of his tough hair again, and gave it such a wrench that he pulled out several prongs of it. After looking at these with an eye of wild hatred, he put them in his pocket.

'My course,' said Clennam, brushing away some tears that had been silently dropping down his face, 'must be taken at once. What wretched amends I can make must be made. I must clear my unfortunate partner's reputation. I must retain nothing for myself. I must resign to our creditors the power of management I have so much abused, and I must work out as much of my fault—or crime—as is susceptible of being worked out in the rest of my days.'

'Is it impossible, sir, to tide over the present?'

'Out of the question. Nothing can be tided over now, Pancks. The sooner the business can pass out of my hands, the better for it. There are engagements to be met, this week, which would bring the catastrophe before many days were over, even if I would postpone it for a single day by going on for that space, secretly knowing what I know. All last night I thought of what I would do; what remains is to do it.'

'Not entirely of yourself?' said Pancks, whose face was as damp as if his steam were turning into water as fast as he dismally blew it off. 'Have some legal help.'

'Perhaps I had better.'

'Have Rugg.'

'There is not much to do. He will do it as well as another.'

'Shall I fetch Rugg, Mr Clennam?'

'If you could spare the time, I should be much obliged to you.'

Mr Pancks put on his hat that moment, and steamed away to Pentonville. While he was gone Arthur never raised his head from the desk, but remained in that one position.

Mr Pancks brought his friend and professional adviser, Mr Rugg, back with him. Mr Rugg had had such ample experience, on the road, of Mr Pancks's being at that present in an irrational state of mind, that he opened his professional mediation by requesting that gentleman to take himself out of the way. Mr Pancks, crushed and submissive, obeyed.

'He is not unlike what my daughter was, sir, when we began the Breach of Promise action of Rugg and Bawkins, in which she was Plaintiff,' said Mr Rugg. 'He takes too strong and direct an interest in the case. His feelings are worked upon. There is no getting on, in our

506

profession, with feelings worked upon, sir.'

As he pulled off his gloves and put them in his hat, he saw, in a side glance or two, that a great change had come over his client.

'I am sorry to perceive, sir,' said Mr Rugg, 'that you have been allowing your own feelings to be worked upon. Now, pray don't, pray don't. These losses are much to be deplored, sir, but we must look 'em in the face.'

'If the money I have sacrificed had been all my own, Mr Rugg,' sighed Mr Clennam, 'I should have cared far less.'

'Indeed, sir?' said Mr Rugg, rubbing his hands with a cheerful air. 'You surprise me. That's singular, sir. I have generally found, in my experience, that it's their own money people are most particular about. I have seen people get rid of a good deal of other people's money, and bear it very well: very well indeed.'

With these comforting remarks, Mr Rugg seated himself on an office-stool at the desk and proceeded to business.

'Now, Mr Clennam, by your leave, let us go into the matter. Let us see the state of the case. The question is simple. The question is the usual plain, straightforward, common-sense question. What can we do for ourself? What can we do for ourself?'

'This is not the question with me, Mr Rugg,' said Arthur. 'You mistake it in the beginning. It is, what can I do for my partner, how can I best make reparation to him?'

'I am afraid, sir, do you know,' argued Mr Rugg persuasively, 'that you are still allowing your feeling to be worked upon. I don't like the term "reparation," sir, except as a lever in the hands of counsel. Will you excuse my saying that I feel it my duty to offer you the caution, that you really must not allow your feelings to be worked upon?'

'Mr Rugg,' said Clennam, nerving himself to go through with what he had resolved upon, and surprising that gentleman by appearing, in his despondency, to have a settled determination of purpose; 'you give me the impression that you will not be much disposed to adopt the course I have made up my mind to take. If your disapproval of it should render you unwilling to discharge such business as it necessitates, I am sorry for it, and must seek other aid. But I will represent to you at once, that to argue against it with me is useless.'

'Good, sir,' answered Mr Rugg, shrugging his shoulders. 'Good, sir. Since the business is to be done by some hands, let it be done by mine. Such was my principle in the case of Rugg and Bawkins. Such is my principle in most cases.'

Clennam then proceeded to state to Mr Rugg his fixed resolution. He told Mr Rugg that his partner was a man of great simplicity and integrity, and that in all he meant to do, he was guided above all things by a knowledge of his partner's character, and a respect for his feelings. He explained that his partner was then absent on an enterprise of importance, and that it particularly behoved himself publicly to accept the blame of what he had rashly done, and publicly to exonerate his partner from all participation in the responsibility of it, lest the successful conduct of that enterprise should be endangered by the slightest suspicion wrongly attaching to his partner's honour and credit in another country. He told Mr Rugg that to clear his partner morally, to the fullest extent, and publicly and unreservedly to declare that he, Arthur Clennam, of that Firm, had of his own sole act, and even expressly against his partner's caution, embarked its resources in the swindles that had lately perished, was the only real atonement within his power; was a better atonement to the particular man than it would be to many men; and was therefore the atonement he had first to make. With this view, his intention was to print a declaration to the foregoing effect, which he had already drawn up; and, besides circulating it among all who had dealings with the House, to advertise it in the public papers. Concurrently with this measure (the description of which cost Mr Rugg innumerable wry faces and great uneasiness in his limbs), he would address a letter to all the creditors, exonerating his partner in a solemn manner, informing them of the stoppage of the House until their pleasure could be known and his partner communicated with, and humbly submitting himself to their direction. If, through their consideration for his partner's innocence, the affairs could ever be got into such train as that the business could be profitably resumed, and its present downfall overcome, then his own share in it should revert to his partner, as the only reparation he could make to him in money value for the distress and loss he had unhappily brought upon him, and he himself, at as small a salary as he could live upon, would ask to be allowed to serve the business as a faithful clerk.

Though Mr Rugg saw plainly there was no preventing this from being done, still the wryness of his face and the uneasiness of his limbs so sorely required the propitiation of a Protest, that he made one. 'I offer no objection, sir,' said he, 'I argue no point with you. I will carry out your views, sir; but, under protest.' Mr Rugg then stated, not without prolixity, the heads of his protest. These were, in effect, because the whole town, or he might say the whole country, was in the first madness of the late discovery, and the resentment against the victims would be very strong: those who had not been deluded being certain to wax exceedingly wroth with them for not having been as wise as they were: and those who had been deluded being certain to find excuses and reasons for themselves, of which they were equally certain to see that other sufferers were wholly devoid: not to mention the great probability of every individual sufferer persuading himself, to his violent indignation, that but for the example of all the other sufferers he never would have put himself in the way of suffering. Because such a declaration as Clennam's, made at such a time, would certainly draw down upon him a storm of animosity, rendering it impossible to calculate on forbearance in the creditors, or on unanimity among them; and exposing him a solitary target to a straggling cross-fire, which might bring him down from half-a-dozen quarters at once.

To all this Clennam merely replied that, granting the whole protest, nothing in it lessened the force, or could lessen the force, of the voluntary and public exoneration of his partner. He therefore, once and for all, requested Mr Rugg's immediate aid in getting the business despatched. Upon that, Mr Rugg fell to work; and Arthur, retaining no property to himself but his clothes and books, and a little loose money, placed his small private banker's-account with the papers of the business.

The disclosure was made, and the storm raged fearfully. Thousands of people were wildly staring about for somebody alive to heap reproaches on; and this notable case, courting publicity, set the living somebody so much wanted, on a scaffold. When people who had nothing to do with the case were so sensible of its flagrancy, people who lost money by it could scarcely be expected to deal mildly with it. Letters of reproach and invective showered in from the creditors; and Mr Rugg, who sat upon the high stool every day and read them all, informed his client within a week that he feared there were writs out.

'I must take the consequences of what I have done,' said Clennam. 'The writs will find me here.'

On the very next morning, as he was turning in Bleeding Heart Yard by Mrs Plornish's corner, Mrs Plornish stood at the door waiting for him, and mysteriously besought him to step into Happy Cottage. There he found Mr Rugg.

'I thought I'd wait for you here. I wouldn't go on to the Counting-house this morning if I was you, sir.'

'Why not, Mr Rugg?'

'There are as many as five out, to my knowledge.'

'It cannot be too soon over,' said Clennam. 'Let them take me at once.'

'Yes, but,' said Mr Rugg, getting between him and the door, 'hear reason, hear reason. They'll take you soon enough, Mr Clennam, I don't doubt; but, hear reason. It almost always happens, in these cases, that some insignificant matter pushes itself in front and makes much of itself. Now, I find there's a little one out—a mere Palace Court jurisdiction—and I have reason to believe that a caption may be made upon that. I wouldn't be taken upon that.'

'Why not?' asked Clennam.

'I'd be taken on a full-grown one, sir,' said Mr Rugg. 'It's as well to keep up appearances. As your professional adviser, I should prefer your being taken on a writ from one of the Superior Courts, if you have no objection to do me that favour. It looks better.'

'Mr Rugg,' said Arthur, in his dejection, 'my only wish is, that it should be over. I will go on, and take my chance.'

'Another word of reason, sir!' cried Mr Rugg. 'Now, this is reason. The other may be taste; but this is reason. If you should be taken on a little one, sir, you would go to the Marshalsea. Now, you know what the Marshalsea is. Very close. Excessively confined. Whereas in the King's Bench—' Mr Rugg waved his right hand freely, as expressing abundance of space.

'I would rather,' said Clennam, 'be taken to the Marshalsea than to any other prison.'

'Do you say so indeed, sir?' returned Mr Rugg. 'Then this is taste, too, and we may be walking.'

He was a little offended at first, but he soon overlooked it. They walked through the Yard to the other end. The Bleeding Hearts were more interested in Arthur since his reverses than formerly; now regarding him as one who was true to the place and had taken up his freedom. Many of them came out to look after him, and to observe to one another, with great unctuousness, that he was 'pulled down by it.' Mrs Plornish and her father stood at the top of the steps at their own end, much depressed and shaking their heads.

There was nobody visibly in waiting when Arthur and Mr Rugg arrived at the Counting-house. But an elderly member of the Jewish persuasion, preserved in rum, followed them close, and looked in at the glass before Mr Rugg had opened one of the day's letters. 'Oh!' said Mr Rugg, looking up. 'How do you do? Step in—Mr Clennam, I think this is the gentleman I was mentioning.'

This gentleman explained the object of his visit to be 'a tyfling madder ob bithznithz,' and executed his legal function.

'Shall I accompany you, Mr Clennam?' asked Mr Rugg politely, rubbing his hands.

'I would rather go alone, thank you. Be so good as send me my clothes.' Mr Rugg in a light airy way replied in the affirmative, and shook hands with him. He and his attendant then went down-stairs, got into the first conveyance they found, and drove to the old gates.

'Where I little thought, Heaven forgive me,' said Clennam to himself, 'that I should ever enter thus!'

Mr Chivery was on the Lock, and Young John was in the Lodge: either newly released from it, or waiting to take his own spell of duty. Both were more astonished on seeing who the prisoner was, than one might have thought turnkeys would have been. The elder Mr Chivery shook hands with him in a shame-faced kind of way, and said, 'I don't call to mind, sir, as I was ever less glad to see you.' The younger Mr Chivery, more distant, did not shake hands with him at all; he stood looking at him in a state of indecision so observable that it even came within the observation of Clennam with his heavy eyes and heavy heart. Presently afterwards, Young John disappeared into the jail.

As Clennam knew enough of the place to know that he was required to remain in the Lodge a certain time, he took a seat in a corner, and feigned to be occupied with the perusal of letters from his pocket. They did not so engross his attention, but that he saw, with gratitude, how the elder Mr Chivery kept the Lodge clear of prisoners; how he signed to some, with his keys, not to come in, how he nudged others with his elbows to go out, and how he made his misery as easy to him as he could.

Arthur was sitting with his eyes fixed on the floor, recalling the past, brooding over the present, and not attending to either, when he felt himself touched upon the shoulder. It was by Young John; and he said, 'You can come now.'

He got up and followed Young John. When they had gone a step or two within the inner iron-gate, Young John turned and said to him:

'You want a room. I have got you one.'

'I thank you heartily.'

Young John turned again, and took him in at the old doorway, up the old staircase, into the old room. Arthur stretched out his hand. Young John looked at it, looked at him—sternly—swelled, choked, and said:

'I don't know as I can. No, I find I can't. But I thought you'd like the room, and here it is for you.'

Surprise at this inconsistent behaviour yielded when he was gone (he went away directly) to the feelings which the empty room awakened in Clennam's wounded breast, and to the crowding associations with the one good and gentle creature who had sanctified it. Her absence in his altered fortunes made it, and him in it, so very desolate and so much in need of such a face of love and truth, that he turned against the wall to weep, sobbing out, as his heart relieved itself, 'O my Little Dorrit!'

CHAPTER 27. The Pupil of the Marshalsea

The day was sunny, and the Marshalsea, with the hot noon striking upon it, was unwontedly quiet. Arthur Clennam dropped into a solitary arm-chair, itself as faded as any debtor in the jail, and yielded himself to his thoughts.

In the unnatural peace of having gone through the dreaded arrest, and got there,—the first change of feeling which the prison most commonly induced, and from which dangerous resting-place so many men had slipped down to the depths of degradation and disgrace by so many ways,—he could think of some passages in his life, almost as if he were removed from them into another state of existence. Taking into account where he was, the interest that had first brought him there when he had been free to keep away, and the gentle presence that was equally inseparable from the walls and bars about him and from the impalpable remembrances of his later life which no walls or bars could imprison, it was not remarkable that everything his memory turned upon should bring him round again to Little Dorrit. Yet it was remarkable to him; not because of the fact itself, but because of the reminder it brought with it, how much the dear little creature had influenced his better resolutions.

None of us clearly know to whom or to what we are indebted in this wise, until some marked stop in the whirling wheel of life brings the right perception with it. It comes with sickness, it comes with sorrow, it comes with the loss of the dearly loved, it is one of the most frequent uses of adversity. It came to Clennam in his adversity, strongly and tenderly. 'When I first gathered myself together,' he thought, 'and set something like purpose before my jaded eyes, whom had I before me, toiling on, for a good object's sake, without encouragement, without notice, against ignoble obstacles that would have turned an army of received heroes and heroines? One weak girl! When I tried to conquer my misplaced love, and to be generous to the man who was more fortunate than I, though he should never know it or repay me with a gracious word, in whom had I watched patience, self-denial, self-subdual, charitable construction, the noblest generosity of the affections? In the same poor girl! If I, a man, with a man's advantages and means and energies, had slighted the whisper in my heart, that if my father had erred, it was my first duty to conceal the fault and to repair it, what youthful figure with tender feet going almost bare on the damp ground, with spare hands ever working, with its slight shape but half protected from the sharp weather, would have stood before me to put me to shame? Little Dorrit's.' So always as he sat alone in the faded chair, thinking. Always, Little Dorrit. Until it seemed to him as if he met the reward of having wandered away from her, and suffered anything to pass between him and his remembrance of her virtues.

His door was opened, and the head of the elder Chivery was put in a very little way, without being turned towards him.

'I am off the Lock, Mr Clennam, and going out. Can I do anything for you?'

'Many thanks. Nothing.'

'You'll excuse me opening the door,' said Mr Chivery; 'but I couldn't make you hear.'

'Did you knock?' 'Half-a-dozen times.'

Rousing himself, Clennam observed that the prison had awakened from its noontide doze, that the inmates were loitering about the shady yard, and that it was late in the afternoon. He had been thinking for hours.

'Your things is come,' said Mr Chivery, 'and my son is going to carry 'em up. I should have sent 'em up but for his wishing to carry 'em himself. Indeed he would have 'em himself, and so I couldn't send 'em up. Mr Clennam, could I say a word to you?'

'Pray come in,' said Arthur; for Mr Chivery's head was still put in at the door a very little way, and Mr Chivery had but one ear upon him, instead of both eyes. This was native delicacy in Mr Chivery—true politeness; though his exterior had very much of a turnkey about it, and not the least of a gentleman.

'Thank you, sir,' said Mr Chivery, without advancing; 'it's no odds me coming in. Mr Clennam, don't you take no notice of my son (if you'll be so good) in case you find him cut up anyways difficult. My son has a 'art, and my son's 'art is in the right place. Me and his mother knows where to find it, and we find it sitiwated correct.'

With this mysterious speech, Mr Chivery took his ear away and shut the door. He might have been gone ten minutes, when his son succeeded him.

'Here's your portmanteau,' he said to Arthur, putting it carefully down.

'It's very kind of you. I am ashamed that you should have the trouble.'

He was gone before it came to that; but soon returned, saying exactly as before, 'Here's your black box:' which he also put down with care.

'I am very sensible of this attention. I hope we may shake hands now, Mr John.'

Young John, however, drew back, turning his right wrist in a socket made of his left thumb and middle-finger and said as he had said at first, 'I don't know as I can. No; I find I can't!' He then stood regarding the prisoner sternly, though with a swelling humour in his eyes that looked like pity.

'Why are you angry with me,' said Clennam, 'and yet so ready to do me these kind services? There must be some mistake between us. If I have done anything to occasion it I am sorry.'

'No mistake, sir,' returned John, turning the wrist backwards and forwards in the socket, for which it was rather tight. 'No mistake, sir, in the feelings with which my eyes behold you at the present moment! If I was at all fairly equal to your weight, Mr Clennam—which I am not; and if you weren't under a cloud—which you are; and if it wasn't against all rules of the Marshalsea—which it is; those feelings are such, that they would stimulate me, more to having it out with you in a Round on the present spot than to anything else I could name.'

Arthur looked at him for a moment in some wonder, and some little anger. 'Well, well!' he said. 'A mistake, a mistake!' Turning away, he sat down with a heavy sigh in the faded chair again.

Young John followed him with his eyes, and, after a short pause, cried out, 'I beg your pardon!'

'Freely granted,' said Clennam, waving his hand without raising his sunken head. 'Say no more. I am not worth it.'

'This furniture, sir,' said Young John in a voice of mild and soft explanation, 'belongs to me. I am in the habit of letting it out to parties without furniture, that have the room. It an't much, but it's at your service. Free, I mean. I could not think of letting you have it on any other terms. You're welcome to it for nothing.'

Arthur raised his head again to thank him, and to say he could not accept the favour. John was still turning his wrist, and still contending with himself in his former divided manner.

512

'What is the matter between us?' said Arthur.

'I decline to name it, sir,' returned Young John, suddenly turning loud and sharp. 'Nothing's the matter.'

Arthur looked at him again, in vain, for an explanation of his behaviour. After a while, Arthur turned away his head again. Young John said, presently afterwards, with the utmost mildness:

'The little round table, sir, that's nigh your elbow, was—you know whose—I needn't mention him—he died a great gentleman. I bought it of an individual that he gave it to, and that lived here after him. But the individual wasn't any ways equal to him. Most individuals would find it hard to come up to his level.'

Arthur drew the little table nearer, rested his arm upon it, and kept it there.

'Perhaps you may not be aware, sir,' said Young John, 'that I intruded upon him when he was over here in London. On the whole he was of opinion that it was an intrusion, though he was so good as to ask me to sit down and to inquire after father and all other old friends. Leastways humblest acquaintances. He looked, to me, a good deal changed, and I said so when I came back. I asked him if Miss Amy was well—'

'And she was?'

'I should have thought you would have known without putting the question to such as me,' returned Young John, after appearing to take a large invisible pill. 'Since you do put me the question, I am sorry I can't answer it. But the truth is, he looked upon the inquiry as a liberty, and said, "What was that to me?" It was then I became quite aware I was intruding: of which I had been fearful before. However, he spoke very handsome afterwards; very handsome.'

They were both silent for several minutes: except that Young John remarked, at about the middle of the pause, 'He both spoke and acted very handsome.'

It was again Young John who broke the silence by inquiring:

'If it's not a liberty, how long may it be your intentions, sir, to go without eating and drinking?'

'I have not felt the want of anything yet,' returned Clennam. 'I have no appetite just now.'

'The more reason why you should take some support, sir,' urged Young John. 'If you find yourself going on sitting here for hours and hours partaking of no refreshment because you have no appetite, why then you should and must partake of refreshment without an appetite. I'm going to have tea in my own apartment. If it's not a liberty, please to come and take a cup. Or I can bring a tray here in two minutes.'

Feeling that Young John would impose that trouble on himself if he refused, and also feeling anxious to show that he bore in mind both the elder Mr Chivery's entreaty, and the younger Mr Chivery's apology, Arthur rose and expressed his willingness to take a cup of tea in Mr John's apartment. Young John locked his door for him as they went out, slided the key into his pocket with great dexterity, and led the way to his own residence.

It was at the top of the house nearest to the gateway. It was the room to which Clennam had hurried on the day when the enriched family had left the prison for ever, and where he had lifted her insensible from the floor. He foresaw where they were going as soon as their feet touched the staircase. The room was so far changed that it was papered now, and had been repainted, and was far more comfortably furnished; but he could recall it just as he had seen it in that single glance, when he raised her from the ground and carried her down to the carriage.

Young John looked hard at him, biting his fingers.

'I see you recollect the room, Mr Clennam?'

'I recollect it well, Heaven bless her!'

Oblivious of the tea, Young John continued to bite his fingers and to look at his visitor, as long as his visitor continued to glance about the room. Finally, he made a start at the teapot, gustily rattled a quantity of tea into it from a canister, and set off for the common kitchen to fill it with hot water.

The room was so eloquent to Clennam in the changed circumstances of his return to the miserable Marshalsea; it spoke to him so mournfully of her, and of his loss of her; that it would have gone hard with him to resist it, even though he had not been alone. Alone, he did not try. He had his hand on the insensible wall as tenderly as if it had been herself that he touched, and pronounced her name in a low voice. He stood at the window, looking over the prison-parapet with its grim spiked border, and breathed a benediction through the summer haze towards the distant land where she was rich and prosperous.

Young John was some time absent, and, when he came back, showed that he had been outside by bringing with him fresh butter in a cabbage leaf, some thin slices of boiled ham in another cabbage leaf, and a little basket of water-cresses and salad herbs. When these were arranged upon the table to his satisfaction, they sat down to tea.

Clennam tried to do honour to the meal, but unavailingly. The ham sickened him, the bread seemed to turn to sand in his mouth. He could force nothing upon himself but a cup of tea.

'Try a little something green,' said Young John, handing him the basket.

He took a sprig or so of water-cress, and tried again; but the bread turned to a heavier sand than before, and the ham (though it was good enough of itself) seemed to blow a faint simoom of ham through the whole Marshalsea.

'Try a little more something green, sir,' said Young John; and again handed the basket.

It was so like handing green meat into the cage of a dull imprisoned bird, and John had so evidently brought the little basket as a handful of fresh relief from the stale hot paving-stones and bricks of the jail, that Clennam said, with a smile, 'It was very kind of you to think of putting this between the wires; but I cannot even get this down to-day.'

As if the difficulty were contagious, Young John soon pushed away his own plate, and fell to folding the cabbage-leaf that had contained the ham. When he had folded it into a number of layers, one over another, so that it was small in the palm of his hand, he began to flatten it between both his hands, and to eye Clennam attentively.

'I wonder,' he at length said, compressing his green packet with some force, 'that if it's not worth your while to take care of yourself for your own sake, it's not worth doing for some one else's.'

'Truly,' returned Arthur, with a sigh and a smile, 'I don't know for whose.'

'Mr Clennam,' said John, warmly, 'I am surprised that a gentleman who is capable of the straightforwardness that you are capable of, should be capable of the mean action of making me such an answer. Mr Clennam, I am surprised that a gentleman who is capable of having a heart of his own, should be capable of the heartlessness of treating mine in that way. I am astonished at it, sir. Really and truly I am astonished!'

Having got upon his feet to emphasise his concluding words, Young John sat down again, and fell to rolling his green packet on his right leg; never taking his eyes off Clennam, but surveying him with a fixed look of indignant reproach.

'I had got over it, sir,' said John. 'I had conquered it, knowing that it must be conquered, and had come to the resolution to think no more about it. I shouldn't have given my mind to it again, I hope, if to this prison you had not been brought, and in an hour unfortunate for me, this day!' (In his agitation Young John adopted his mother's powerful construction of sentences.) 'When you first came upon me, sir, in the Lodge, this day, more as if a Upas tree had been made a capture of than a private defendant, such mingled streams of feelings broke loose again within me, that everything was for the first few minutes swept away before them, and I was going round and round in a vortex. I got out of it. I struggled, and got out of it. If it was the last word I had to speak, against that vortex with my utmost powers I strove, and out of it I came. I argued that if I had been rude, apologies was due, and those apologies without a question of demeaning, I did make. And now, when I've been so wishful to show that one thought is next to being a holy one with me and goes before all others—now, after all, you dodge me when I ever so gently hint at it, and throw me back upon myself. For, do not, sir,' said Young John, 'do not be so base as to deny that dodge you do, and thrown me back upon myself you have!'

All amazement, Arthur gazed at him like one lost, only saying, 'What is it? What do you mean, John?' But, John, being in that state of mind in which nothing would seem to be more impossible to a certain class of people than the giving of an answer, went ahead blindly.

'I hadn't,' John declared, 'no, I hadn't, and I never had the audaciousness to think, I am sure, that all was anything but lost. I hadn't, no, why should I say I hadn't if I ever had, any hope that it was possible to be so blest, not after the words that passed, not even if barriers insurmountable had not been raised! But is that a reason why I am to have no memory, why I am to have no thoughts, why I am to have no sacred spots, nor anything?'

'What can you mean?' cried Arthur.

'It's all very well to trample on it, sir,' John went on, scouring a very prairie of wild words, 'if a person can make up his mind to be guilty of the action. It's all very well to trample on it, but it's there. It may be that it couldn't be trampled upon if it wasn't there. But that doesn't make it gentlemanly, that doesn't make it honourable, that doesn't justify throwing a person back upon himself after he has struggled and strived out of himself like a butterfly. The world may sneer at a turnkey, but he's a man—when he isn't a woman, which among female criminals he's expected to be.'

Ridiculous as the incoherence of his talk was, there was yet a truthfulness in Young John's simple, sentimental character, and a sense of being wounded in some very tender respect, expressed in his burning face and in the agitation of his voice and manner, which Arthur must have been cruel to disregard. He turned his thoughts back to the starting-point of this unknown injury; and in the meantime Young John, having rolled his green packet pretty round, cut it carefully into three pieces, and laid it on a plate as if it were some particular delicacy.

'It seems to me just possible,' said Arthur, when he had retraced the conversation to the water-cresses and back again, 'that you have made some reference to Miss Dorrit.'

'It is just possible, sir,' returned John Chivery.

'I don't understand it. I hope I may not be so unlucky as to make you think I mean to offend you again, for I never have meant to offend you yet, when I say I don't understand it.'

'Sir,' said Young John, 'will you have the perfidy to deny that you know and long have known that I felt towards Miss Dorrit, call it not the presumption of love, but adoration and sacrifice?'

'Indeed, John, I will not have any perfidy if I know it; why you should suspect me of it I am at a loss to think. Did you ever hear from Mrs Chivery, your mother, that I went to see her once?'

'No, sir,' returned John, shortly. 'Never heard of such a thing.'

'But I did. Can you imagine why?'

'No, sir,' returned John, shortly. 'I can't imagine why.'

'I will tell you. I was solicitous to promote Miss Dorrit's happiness; and if I could have supposed that Miss Dorrit returned your affection—'

Poor John Chivery turned crimson to the tips of his ears. 'Miss Dorrit never did, sir. I wish to be honourable and true, so far as in my humble way I can, and I would scorn to pretend for a moment that she ever did, or that she ever led me to believe she did; no, nor even that it was ever to be expected in any cool reason that she would or could. She was far above me in all respects at all times. As likewise,' added John, 'similarly was her gen-teel family.'

His chivalrous feeling towards all that belonged to her made him so very respectable, in spite of his small stature and his rather weak legs, and his very weak hair, and his poetical temperament, that a Goliath might have sat in his place demanding less consideration at Arthur's hands.

'You speak, John,' he said, with cordial admiration, 'like a Man.'

'Well, sir,' returned John, brushing his hand across his eyes, 'then I wish you'd do the same.'

He was quick with this unexpected retort, and it again made Arthur regard him with a wondering expression of face.

'Leastways,' said John, stretching his hand across the tea-tray, 'if too strong a remark, withdrawn! But, why not, why not? When I say to you, Mr Clennam, take care of yourself for some one else's sake, why not be open, though a turnkey? Why did I get you the room which I knew you'd like best? Why did I carry up your things? Not that I found 'em heavy; I don't mention 'em on that accounts; far from it. Why have I cultivated you in the manner I have done since the morning? On the ground of your own merits? No. They're very great, I've no doubt at all; but not on the ground of them. Another's merits have had their weight, and have had far more weight with Me. Then why not speak free?'

'Unaffectedly, John,' said Clennam, 'you are so good a fellow and I have so true a respect for your character, that if I have appeared to be less sensible than I really am of the fact that the kind services you have rendered me to-day are attributable to my having been trusted by Miss Dorrit as her friend—I confess it to be a fault, and I ask your forgiveness.'

'Oh! why not,' John repeated with returning scorn, 'why not speak free!'

'I declare to you,' returned Arthur, 'that I do not understand you. Look at me. Consider the trouble I have been in. Is it likely that I would wilfully add to my other self-reproaches, that of being ungrateful or treacherous to you. I do not understand you.'

John's incredulous face slowly softened into a face of doubt. He rose, backed into the garret-window of the room, beckoned Arthur to come there, and stood looking at him thoughtfully.

'Mr Clennam, do you mean to say that you don't know?'

'What, John?'

'Lord,' said Young John, appealing with a gasp to the spikes on the wall. 'He says, What!'

Clennam looked at the spikes, and looked at John; and looked at the spikes, and looked at John.

'He says What! And what is more,' exclaimed Young John, surveying him in a doleful maze, 'he appears to mean it! Do you see this window, sir?'

'Of course I see this window.'

'See this room?'

'Why, of course I see this room.'

'That wall opposite, and that yard down below? They have all been witnesses of it, from day to day, from night to night, from week to week, from month to month. For how often have I seen Miss Dorrit here when she has not seen me!'

'Witnesses of what?' said Clennam.

'Of Miss Dorrit's love.'

'For whom?'

'You,' said John. And touched him with the back of his hand upon the breast, and backed to his chair, and sat down on it with a pale face, holding the arms, and shaking his head at him.

If he had dealt Clennam a heavy blow, instead of laying that light touch upon him, its effect could not have been to shake him more. He stood amazed; his eyes looking at John; his lips parted, and seeming now and then to form the word 'Me!' without uttering it; his hands dropped at his sides; his whole appearance that of a man who has been awakened from sleep, and stupefied by intelligence beyond his full comprehension.

'Me!' he at length said aloud.

'Ah!' groaned Young John. 'You!'

He did what he could to muster a smile, and returned, 'Your fancy. You are completely mistaken.'

'I mistaken, sir!' said Young John. 'I completely mistaken on that subject! No, Mr

Clennam, don't tell me so. On any other, if you like, for I don't set up to be a penetrating character, and am well aware of my own deficiencies. But, I mistaken on a point that has caused me more smart in my breast than a flight of savages' arrows could have done! I mistaken on a point that almost sent me into my grave, as I sometimes wished it would, if the grave could only have been made compatible with the tobacco-business and father and mother's feelings! I mistaken on a point that, even at the present moment, makes me take out my pocket-handkerchief like a great girl, as people say: though I am sure I don't know why a great girl should be a term of reproach, for every rightly constituted male mind loves 'em great and small. Don't tell me so, don't tell me so!'

Still highly respectable at bottom, though absurd enough upon the surface, Young John took out his pocket-handkerchief with a genuine absence both of display and concealment, which is only to be seen in a man with a great deal of good in him, when he takes out his pocket-handkerchief for the purpose of wiping his eyes. Having dried them, and indulged in the harmless luxury of a sob and a sniff, he put it up again.

The touch was still in its influence so like a blow that Arthur could not get many words together to close the subject with. He assured John Chivery when he had returned his handkerchief to his pocket, that he did all honour to his disinterestedness and to the fidelity of his remembrance of Miss Dorrit. As to the impression on his mind, of which he had just relieved it—here John interposed, and said, 'No impression! Certainty!'—as to that, they might perhaps speak of it at another time, but would say no more now. Feeling low-spirited and weary, he would go back to his room, with John's leave, and come out no more that night. John assented, and he crept back in the shadow of the wall to his own lodging.

The feeling of the blow was still so strong upon him that, when the dirty old woman was gone whom he found sitting on the stairs outside his door, waiting to make his bed, and who gave him to understand while doing it, that she had received her instructions from Mr Chivery, 'not the old 'un but the young 'un,' he sat down in the faded arm-chair, pressing his head between his hands, as if he had been stunned. Little Dorrit love him! More bewildering to him than his misery, far.

Consider the improbability. He had been accustomed to call her his child, and his dear child, and to invite her confidence by dwelling upon the difference in their respective ages, and to speak of himself as one who was turning old. Yet she might not have thought him old. Something reminded him that he had not thought himself so, until the roses had floated away upon the river.

He had her two letters among other papers in his box, and he took them out and read them. There seemed to be a sound in them like the sound of her sweet voice. It fell upon his ear with many tones of tenderness, that were not insusceptible of the new meaning. Now it was that the quiet desolation of her answer, 'No, No, No,' made to him that night in that very room—that night when he had been shown the dawn of her altered fortune, and when other words had passed between them which he had been destined to remember in humiliation and a prisoner, rushed into his mind.

Consider the improbability.

But it had a preponderating tendency, when considered, to become fainter. There was another and a curious inquiry of his own heart's that concurrently became stronger. In the reluctance he had felt to believe that she loved any one; in his desire to set that question at rest; in a half-formed consciousness he had had that there would be a kind of nobleness in his helping her love for any one, was there no suppressed something on his own side that he had hushed as it arose? Had he ever whispered to himself that he must not think of such a thing as her loving him, that he must not take advantage of her gratitude, that he must keep his experience in remembrance as a warning and reproof; that he must regard such youthful hopes as having passed away, as his friend's dead daughter had passed away; that he must be steady in saying to himself that the time had gone by him, and he was too saddened and old?

He had kissed her when he raised her from the ground on the day when she had been so consistently and expressively forgotten. Quite as he might have kissed her, if she had been conscious? No difference?

The darkness found him occupied with these thoughts. The darkness also found Mr and Mrs Plornish knocking at his door. They brought with them a basket, filled with choice selections from that stock in trade which met with such a quick sale and produced such a slow return. Mrs Plornish was affected to tears. Mr Plornish amiably growled, in his philosophical but not lucid manner, that there was ups you see, and there was downs. It was in vain to ask why ups, why downs; there they was, you know. He had heerd it given for a truth that accordin' as the world went round, which round it did rewolve undoubted, even the best of gentlemen must take his turn of standing with his ed upside down and all his air a flying the wrong way into what you might call Space. Wery well then. What Mr Plornish said was, wery well then. That gentleman's ed would come up-ards when his turn come, that gentleman's air would be a pleasure to look upon being all smooth again, and wery well then!

It has been already stated that Mrs Plornish, not being philosophical, wept. It further happened that Mrs Plornish, not being philosophical, was intelligible. It may have arisen out of her softened state of mind, out of her sex's wit, out of a woman's quick association of ideas, or out of a woman's no association of ideas, but it further happened somehow that Mrs Plornish's intelligibility displayed itself upon the very subject of Arthur's meditations.

'The way father has been talking about you, Mr Clennam,' said Mrs Plornish, 'you hardly would believe. It's made him quite poorly. As to his voice, this misfortune has took it away. You know what a sweet singer father is; but he couldn't get a note out for the children at tea, if you'll credit what I tell you.'

While speaking, Mrs Plornish shook her head, and wiped her eyes, and looked retrospectively about the room.

'As to Mr Baptist,' pursued Mrs Plornish, 'whatever he'll do when he comes to know of it, I can't conceive nor yet imagine. He'd have been here before now, you may be sure, but that he's away on confidential business of your own. The persevering manner in which he follows up that business, and gives himself no rest from it—it really do,' said Mrs Plornish, winding up in the Italian manner, 'as I say to him, Mooshattonisha padrona.'

Though not conceited, Mrs Plornish felt that she had turned this Tuscan sentence with peculiar elegance. Mr Plornish could not conceal his exultation in her accomplishments as a linguist.

'But what I say is, Mr Clennam,' the good woman went on, 'there's always something to be thankful for, as I am sure you will yourself admit. Speaking in this room, it's not hard to think what the present something is. It's a thing to be thankful for, indeed, that Miss Dorrit is not here to know it.'

Arthur thought she looked at him with particular expression.

'It's a thing,' reiterated Mrs Plornish, 'to be thankful for, indeed, that Miss Dorrit is far away. It's to be hoped she is not likely to hear of it. If she had been here to see it, sir, it's not to be doubted that the sight of you,' Mrs Plornish repeated those words—'not to be doubted, that the sight of you—in misfortune and trouble, would have been almost too much for her affectionate heart. There's nothing I can think of, that would have touched Miss Dorrit so bad as that.'

Of a certainty Mrs Plornish did look at him now, with a sort of quivering defiance in her friendly emotion.

'Yes!' said she. 'And it shows what notice father takes, though at his time of life, that he says to me this afternoon, which Happy Cottage knows I neither make it up nor any ways enlarge, "Mary, it's much to be rejoiced in that Miss Dorrit is not on the spot to behold it." Those were father's words. Father's own words was, "Much to be rejoiced in, Mary, that Miss Dorrit is not on the spot to behold it." I says to father then, I says to him, "Father, you are right!" That,' Mrs Plornish concluded, with the air of a very precise legal witness, 'is what passed betwixt father and me. And I tell you nothing but what did pass betwixt me and father.'

Mr Plornish, as being of a more laconic temperament, embraced this opportunity of interposing with the suggestion that she should now leave Mr Clennam to himself. 'For, you see,' said Mr Plornish, gravely, 'I know what it is, old gal;' repeating that valuable remark several times, as if it appeared to him to include some great moral secret. Finally, the worthy couple went away arm in arm.

Little Dorrit, Little Dorrit. Again, for hours. Always Little Dorrit!

Happily, if it ever had been so, it was over, and better over. Granted that she had loved him, and he had known it and had suffered himself to love her, what a road to have led her away upon—the road that would have brought her back to this miserable place! He ought to be much comforted by the reflection that she was quit of it forever; that she was, or would soon be, married (vague rumours of her father's projects in that direction had reached Bleeding Heart Yard, with the news of her sister's marriage); and that the Marshalsea gate had shut for ever on all those perplexed possibilities of a time that was gone.

Dear Little Dorrit.

Looking back upon his own poor story, she was its vanishing-point. Every thing in its perspective led to her innocent figure. He had travelled thousands of miles towards it; previous unquiet hopes and doubts had worked themselves out before it; it was the centre of the interest of his life; it was the termination of everything that was good and pleasant in it; beyond, there was nothing but mere waste and darkened sky.

As ill at ease as on the first night of his lying down to sleep within those dreary walls, he wore the night out with such thoughts. What time Young John lay wrapt in peaceful slumber, after composing and arranging the following monumental inscription on his pillow—

STRANGER!

RESPECT THE TOMB OF

JOHN CHIVERY, JUNIOR,

WHO DIED AT AN ADVANCED AGE

NOT NECESSARY TO MENTION.

HE ENCOUNTERED HIS RIVAL IN A DISTRESSED STATE,

AND FELT INCLINED

TO HAVE A ROUND WITH HIM;

BUT, FOR THE SAKE OF THE LOVED ONE,

CONQUERED THOSE FEELINGS OF BITTERNESS, AND BECAME

MAGNANIMOUS.

CHAPTER 28. An Appearance in the Marshalsea

The opinion of the community outside the prison gates bore hard on Clennam as time went on, and he made no friends among the community within. Too depressed to associate with the herd in the yard, who got together to forget their cares; too retiring and too unhappy to join in the poor socialities of the tavern; he kept his own room, and was held in distrust. Some said he was proud; some objected that he was sullen and reserved; some were contemptuous of him, for that he was a poor-spirited dog who pined under his debts. The whole population were shy of him on these various counts of indictment, but especially the last, which involved a species of domestic treason; and he soon became so confirmed in his seclusion, that his only time for walking up and down was when the evening Club were assembled at their songs and toasts and sentiments, and when the yard was nearly left to the women and children.

Imprisonment began to tell upon him. He knew that he idled and moped. After what he had known of the influences of imprisonment within the four small walls of the very room he occupied, this consciousness made him afraid of himself. Shrinking from the observation of other men, and shrinking from his own, he began to change very sensibly. Anybody might see that the shadow of the wall was dark upon him.

One day when he might have been some ten or twelve weeks in jail, and when he had been trying to read and had not been able to release even the imaginary people of the book from the Marshalsea, a footstep stopped at his door, and a hand tapped at it. He arose and opened it, and an agreeable voice accosted him with 'How do you do, Mr Clennam? I hope I am not unwelcome in calling to see you.'

It was the sprightly young Barnacle, Ferdinand. He looked very good-natured and prepossessing, though overpoweringly gay and free, in contrast with the squalid prison.

'You are surprised to see me, Mr Clennam,' he said, taking the seat which Clennam offered him.

'I must confess to being much surprised.'

'Not disagreeably, I hope?'

'By no means.'

'Thank you. Frankly,' said the engaging young Barnacle, 'I have been excessively sorry to hear that you were under the necessity of a temporary retirement here, and I hope (of course as between two private gentlemen) that our place has had nothing to do with it?'

'Your office?'

'Our Circumlocution place.'

'I cannot charge any part of my reverses upon that remarkable establishment.'

'Upon my life,' said the vivacious young Barnacle, 'I am heartily glad to know it. It is quite a relief to me to hear you say it. I should have so exceedingly regretted our place having had anything to do with your difficulties.'

Clennam again assured him that he absolved it of the responsibility.

'That's right,' said Ferdinand. 'I am very happy to hear it. I was rather afraid in my own mind that we might have helped to floor you, because there is no doubt that it is our misfortune to do that kind of thing now and then. We don't want to do it; but if men will be gravelled, why—we can't help it.'

'Without giving an unqualified assent to what you say,' returned Arthur, gloomily, 'I am much obliged to you for your interest in me.'

'No, but really! Our place is,' said the easy young Barnacle, 'the most inoffensive place possible. You'll say we are a humbug. I won't say we are not; but all that sort of thing is intended to be, and must be. Don't you see?'

'I do not,' said Clennam.

'You don't regard it from the right point of view. It is the point of view that is the essential thing. Regard our place from the point of view that we only ask you to leave us alone, and we are as capital a Department as you'll find anywhere.'

'Is your place there to be left alone?' asked Clennam.

'You exactly hit it,' returned Ferdinand. 'It is there with the express intention that everything shall be left alone. That is what it means. That is what it's for. No doubt there's a certain form to be kept up that it's for something else, but it's only a form. Why, good Heaven, we are nothing but forms! Think what a lot of our forms you have gone through. And you have never got any nearer to an end?'

'Never,' said Clennam.

'Look at it from the right point of view, and there you have us—official and effectual. It's like a limited game of cricket. A field of outsiders are always going in to bowl at the Public Service, and we block the balls.'

Clennam asked what became of the bowlers? The airy young Barnacle replied that they grew tired, got dead beat, got lamed, got their backs broken, died off, gave it up, went in for other games.

'And this occasions me to congratulate myself again,' he pursued, 'on the circumstance that our place has had nothing to do with your temporary retirement. It very easily might have had a hand in it; because it is undeniable that we are sometimes a most unlucky place, in our effects upon people who will not leave us alone. Mr Clennam, I am quite unreserved with you. As between yourself and myself, I know I may be. I was so, when I first saw you making the mistake of not leaving us alone; because I perceived that you were inexperienced and sanguine, and had—I hope you'll not object to my saying—some simplicity?'

'Not at all.'

'Some simplicity. Therefore I felt what a pity it was, and I went out of my way to hint to you (which really was not official, but I never am official when I can help it) something to the effect that if I were you, I wouldn't bother myself. However, you did bother yourself, and you have since bothered yourself. Now, don't do it any more.'

'I am not likely to have the opportunity,' said Clennam.

'Oh yes, you are! You'll leave here. Everybody leaves here. There are no ends of ways of leaving here. Now, don't come back to us. That entreaty is the second object of my call. Pray, don't come back to us. Upon my honour,' said Ferdinand in a very friendly and confiding way, 'I shall be greatly vexed if you don't take warning by the past and keep away from us.'

'And the invention?' said Clennam.

'My good fellow,' returned Ferdinand, 'if you'll excuse the freedom of that form of address, nobody wants to know of the invention, and nobody cares twopence-halfpenny about it.'

'Nobody in the Office, that is to say?'

'Nor out of it. Everybody is ready to dislike and ridicule any invention. You have no idea how many people want to be left alone. You have no idea how the Genius of the country (overlook the Parliamentary nature of the phrase, and don't be bored by it) tends to being left alone. Believe me, Mr Clennam,' said the sprightly young Barnacle in his pleasantest manner, 'our place is not a wicked Giant to be charged at full tilt; but only a windmill showing you, as it grinds immense quantities of chaff, which way the country wind blows.'

'If I could believe that,' said Clennam, 'it would be a dismal prospect for all of us.'

'Oh! Don't say so!' returned Ferdinand. 'It's all right. We must have humbug, we all like humbug, we couldn't get on without humbug. A little humbug, and a groove, and everything goes on admirably, if you leave it alone.'

With this hopeful confession of his faith as the head of the rising Barnacles who were born of woman, to be followed under a variety of watchwords which they utterly repudiated and disbelieved, Ferdinand rose. Nothing could be more agreeable than his frank and courteous bearing, or adapted with a more gentlemanly instinct to the circumstances of his visit.

'Is it fair to ask,' he said, as Clennam gave him his hand with a real feeling of thankfulness for his candour and good-humour, 'whether it is true that our late lamented Merdle is the cause of this passing inconvenience?'

'I am one of the many he has ruined. Yes.'

'He must have been an exceedingly clever fellow,' said Ferdinand Barnacle.

Arthur, not being in the mood to extol the memory of the deceased, was silent.

'A consummate rascal, of course,' said Ferdinand, 'but remarkably clever! One cannot help admiring the fellow. Must have been such a master of humbug. Knew people so well—got over them so completely—did so much with them!'

In his easy way, he was really moved to genuine admiration.

'I hope,' said Arthur, 'that he and his dupes may be a warning to people not to have so much done with them again.'

'My dear Mr Clennam,' returned Ferdinand, laughing, 'have you really such a verdant hope? The next man who has as large a capacity and as genuine a taste for swindling, will succeed as well. Pardon me, but I think you really have no idea how the human bees will swarm to the beating of any old tin kettle; in that fact lies the complete manual of governing them. When they can be got to believe that the kettle is made of the precious metals, in that fact lies the whole power of men like our late lamented. No doubt there are here and there,' said Ferdinand politely, 'exceptional cases, where people have been taken in for what appeared to them to be much better reasons; and I need not go far to find such a case; but they don't invalidate the rule. Good day! I hope that when I have the pleasure of seeing you, next, this passing cloud will have given place to sunshine. Don't come a step beyond the door. I know the way out perfectly. Good day!'

With those words, the best and brightest of the Barnacles went down-stairs, hummed his way through the Lodge, mounted his horse in the front court-yard, and rode off to keep an appointment with his noble kinsman, who wanted a little coaching before he could triumphantly answer certain infidel Snobs who were going to question the Nobs about their statesmanship.

He must have passed Mr Rugg on his way out, for, a minute or two afterwards, that ruddy-headed gentleman shone in at the door, like an elderly Phoebus.

'How do you do to-day, sir?' said Mr Rugg. 'Is there any little thing I can do for you to-day, sir?'

'No, I thank you.'

Mr Rugg's enjoyment of embarrassed affairs was like a housekeeper's enjoyment in pickling and preserving, or a washerwoman's enjoyment of a heavy wash, or a dustman's enjoyment of an overflowing dust-bin, or any other professional enjoyment of a mess in the way of business.

'I still look round, from time to time, sir,' said Mr Rugg, cheerfully, 'to see whether any lingering Detainers are accumulating at the gate. They have fallen in pretty thick, sir; as thick as we could have expected.'

He remarked upon the circumstance as if it were matter of congratulation: rubbing his hands briskly, and rolling his head a little.

'As thick,' repeated Mr Rugg, 'as we could reasonably have expected. Quite a shower-bath of 'em. I don't often intrude upon you now, when I look round, because I know you are not inclined for company, and that if you wished to see me, you would leave word in the Lodge. But I am here pretty well every day, sir. Would this be an unseasonable time, sir,' asked Mr Rugg, coaxingly, 'for me to offer an observation?'

'As seasonable a time as any other.'

'Hum! Public opinion, sir,' said Mr Rugg, 'has been busy with you.'

'I don't doubt it.'

'Might it not be advisable, sir,' said Mr Rugg, more coaxingly yet, 'now to make, at last

524

and after all, a trifling concession to public opinion? We all do it in one way or another. The fact is, we must do it.'

'I cannot set myself right with it, Mr Rugg, and have no business to expect that I ever shall.'

'Don't say that, sir, don't say that. The cost of being moved to the Bench is almost insignificant, and if the general feeling is strong that you ought to be there, why—really—'

'I thought you had settled, Mr Rugg,' said Arthur, 'that my determination to remain here was a matter of taste.'

'Well, sir, well! But is it good taste, is it good taste? That's the Question.' Mr Rugg was so soothingly persuasive as to be quite pathetic. 'I was almost going to say, is it good feeling? This is an extensive affair of yours; and your remaining here where a man can come for a pound or two, is remarked upon as not in keeping. It is not in keeping. I can't tell you, sir, in how many quarters I heard it mentioned. I heard comments made upon it last night in a Parlour frequented by what I should call, if I did not look in there now and then myself, the best legal company—I heard, there, comments on it that I was sorry to hear. They hurt me on your account. Again, only this morning at breakfast. My daughter (but a woman, you'll say: yet still with a feeling for these things, and even with some little personal experience, as the plaintiff in Rugg and Bawkins) was expressing her great surprise; her great surprise. Now under these circumstances, and considering that none of us can quite set ourselves above public opinion, wouldn't a trifling concession to that opinion be—Come, sir,' said Rugg, 'I will put it on the lowest ground of argument, and say, Amiable?'

Arthur's thoughts had once more wandered away to Little Dorrit, and the question remained unanswered.

'As to myself, sir,' said Mr Rugg, hoping that his eloquence had reduced him to a state of indecision, 'it is a principle of mine not to consider myself when a client's inclinations are in the scale. But, knowing your considerate character and general wish to oblige, I will repeat that I should prefer your being in the Bench. Your case has made a noise; it is a creditable case to be professionally concerned in; I should feel on a better standing with my connection, if you went to the Bench. Don't let that influence you, sir. I merely state the fact.'

So errant had the prisoner's attention already grown in solitude and dejection, and so accustomed had it become to commune with only one silent figure within the ever-frowning walls, that Clennam had to shake off a kind of stupor before he could look at Mr Rugg, recall the thread of his talk, and hurriedly say, 'I am unchanged, and unchangeable, in my decision. Pray, let it be; let it be!' Mr Rugg, without concealing that he was nettled and mortified, replied:

'Oh! Beyond a doubt, sir. I have travelled out of the record, sir, I am aware, in putting the point to you. But really, when I hear it remarked in several companies, and in very good company, that however worthy of a foreigner, it is not worthy of the spirit of an Englishman to remain in the Marshalsea when the glorious liberties of his island home admit of his removal to the Bench, I thought I would depart from the narrow professional line marked out to me, and mention it. Personally,' said Mr Rugg, 'I have no opinion on the topic.'

'That's well,' returned Arthur.

'Oh! None at all, sir!' said Mr Rugg. 'If I had, I should have been unwilling, some minutes ago, to see a client of mine visited in this place by a gentleman of a high family riding a saddle-horse. But it was not my business. If I had, I might have wished to be now empowered to mention to another gentleman, a gentleman of military exterior at present waiting in the Lodge, that my client had never intended to remain here, and was on the eve of removal to a superior abode. But my course as a professional machine is clear; I have nothing to do with it. Is it your good pleasure to see the gentleman, sir?'

'Who is waiting to see me, did you say?'

'I did take that unprofessional liberty, sir. Hearing that I was your professional adviser, he declined to interpose before my very limited function was performed. Happily,' said Mr Rugg, with sarcasm, 'I did not so far travel out of the record as to ask the gentleman for his name.'

'I suppose I have no resource but to see him,' sighed Clennam, wearily.

'Then it is your good pleasure, sir?' retorted Rugg. 'Am I honoured by your instructions to mention as much to the gentleman, as I pass out? I am? Thank you, sir. I take my leave.' His leave he took accordingly, in dudgeon.

The gentleman of military exterior had so imperfectly awakened Clennam's curiosity, in the existing state of his mind, that a half-forgetfulness of such a visitor's having been referred to, was already creeping over it as a part of the sombre veil which almost always dimmed it now, when a heavy footstep on the stairs aroused him. It appeared to ascend them, not very promptly or spontaneously, yet with a display of stride and clatter meant to be insulting. As it paused for a moment on the landing outside his door, he could not recall his association with the peculiarity of its sound, though he thought he had one. Only a moment was given him for consideration. His door was immediately swung open by a thump, and in the doorway stood the missing Blandois, the cause of many anxieties.

'Salve, fellow jail-bird!' said he. 'You want me, it seems. Here I am!'

Before Arthur could speak to him in his indignant wonder, Cavalletto followed him into the room. Mr Pancks followed Cavalletto. Neither of the two had been there since its present occupant had had possession of it. Mr Pancks, breathing hard, sidled near the window, put his hat on the ground, stirred his hair up with both hands, and folded his arms, like a man who had come to a pause in a hard day's work. Mr Baptist, never taking his eyes from his dreaded chum of old, softly sat down on the floor with his back against the door and one of his ankles in each hand: resuming the attitude (except that it was now expressive of unwinking watchfulness) in which he had sat before the same man in the deeper shade of another prison, one hot morning at Marseilles.

'I have it on the witnessing of these two madmen,' said Monsieur Blandois, otherwise Lagnier, otherwise Rigaud, 'that you want me, brother-bird. Here I am!'

Glancing round contemptuously at the bedstead, which was turned up by day, he leaned his back against it as a resting-place, without removing his hat from his head, and stood defiantly lounging with his hands in his pockets.

'You villain of ill-omen!' said Arthur. 'You have purposely cast a dreadful suspicion upon my mother's house. Why have you done it? What prompted you to the devilish invention?'

Monsieur Rigaud, after frowning at him for a moment, laughed. 'Hear this noble gentleman! Listen, all the world, to this creature of Virtue! But take care, take care. It is possible, my friend, that your ardour is a little compromising. Holy Blue! It is possible.'

'Signore!' interposed Cavalletto, also addressing Arthur: 'for to commence, hear me! I received your instructions to find him, Rigaud; is it not?'

'It is the truth.'

'I go, consequentementally,'—it would have given Mrs Plornish great concern if she could have been persuaded that his occasional lengthening of an adverb in this way, was the chief fault of his English,—'first among my countrymen. I ask them what news in Londra, of foreigners arrived. Then I go among the French. Then I go among the Germans. They all tell me. The great part of us know well the other, and they all tell me. But!—no person can tell me nothing of him, Rigaud. Fifteen times,' said Cavalletto, thrice throwing out his left hand with all its fingers spread, and doing it so rapidly that the sense of sight could hardly follow the action, 'I ask of him in every place where go the foreigners; and fifteen times,' repeating the same swift performance, 'they know nothing. But!—'

At this significant Italian rest on the word 'But,' his backhanded shake of his right forefinger came into play; a very little, and very cautiously.

'But!—After a long time when I have not been able to find that he is here in Londra, some one tells me of a soldier with white hair—hey?—not hair like this that he carries—white—who lives retired secrettementally, in a certain place. But!—' with another rest upon the word, 'who sometimes in the after-dinner, walks, and smokes. It is necessary, as they say in Italy (and as they know, poor people), to have patience. I have patience. I ask where is this certain place. One. believes it is here, one believes it is there. Eh well! It is not here, it is not there. I wait patientissamentally. At last I find it. Then I watch; then I hide, until he walks and smokes. He is a soldier with grey hair—But!—' a very decided rest indeed, and a very vigorous play from side to side of the back-handed forefinger—'he is also this man that you see.'

It was noticeable, that, in his old habit of submission to one who had been at the trouble of asserting superiority over him, he even then bestowed upon Rigaud a confused bend of his head, after thus pointing him out.

'Eh well, Signore!' he cried in conclusion, addressing Arthur again. 'I waited for a good opportunity. I writed some words to Signor Panco,' an air of novelty came over Mr Pancks with this designation, 'to come and help. I showed him, Rigaud, at his window, to Signor Panco, who was often the spy in the day. I slept at night near the door of the house. At last we entered, only this to-day, and now you see him! As he would not come up in presence of the illustrious Advocate,' such was Mr Baptist's honourable mention of Mr Rugg, 'we waited down below there, together, and Signor Panco guarded the street.'

At the close of this recital, Arthur turned his eyes upon the impudent and wicked face. As it met his, the nose came down over the moustache and the moustache went up under the nose. When nose and moustache had settled into their places again, Monsieur Rigaud loudly snapped his fingers half-a-dozen times; bending forward to jerk the snaps at Arthur, as if they were palpable missiles which he jerked into his face.

'Now, Philosopher!' said Rigaud. 'What do you want with me?'

'I want to know,' returned Arthur, without disguising his abhorrence, 'how you dare direct a suspicion of murder against my mother's house?'

'Dare!' cried Rigaud. 'Ho, ho! Hear him! Dare? Is it dare? By Heaven, my small boy, but you are a little imprudent!'

'I want that suspicion to be cleared away,' said Arthur. 'You shall be taken there, and be publicly seen. I want to know, moreover, what business you had there when I had a burning desire to fling you down-stairs. Don't frown at me, man! I have seen enough of you to know that you are a bully and coward. I need no revival of my spirits from the effects of this wretched place to tell you so plain a fact, and one that you know so well.'

White to the lips, Rigaud stroked his moustache, muttering, 'By Heaven, my small boy, but you are a little compromising of my lady, your respectable mother'—and seemed for a minute undecided how to act. His indecision was soon gone. He sat himself down with a threatening swagger, and said:

'Give me a bottle of wine. You can buy wine here. Send one of your madmen to get me a bottle of wine. I won't talk to you without wine. Come! Yes or no?'

'Fetch him what he wants, Cavalletto,' said Arthur, scornfully, producing the money.

'Contraband beast,' added Rigaud, 'bring Port wine! I'll drink nothing but Porto-Porto.'

The contraband beast, however, assuring all present, with his significant finger, that he peremptorily declined to leave his post at the door, Signor Panco offered his services. He soon returned with the bottle of wine: which, according to the custom of the place, originating in a scarcity of corkscrews among the Collegians (in common with a scarcity of much else), was already opened for use.

'Madman! A large glass,' said Rigaud.

Signor Panco put a tumbler before him; not without a visible conflict of feeling on the question of throwing it at his head.

'Haha!' boasted Rigaud. 'Once a gentleman, and always a gentleman. A gentleman from the beginning, and a gentleman to the end. What the Devil! A gentleman must be waited on, I hope? It's a part of my character to be waited on!'

He half filled the tumbler as he said it, and drank off the contents when he had done saying it.

'Hah!' smacking his lips. 'Not a very old prisoner that! I judge by your looks, brave sir, that imprisonment will subdue your blood much sooner than it softens this hot wine. You are mellowing—losing body and colour already. I salute you!'

He tossed off another half glass: holding it up both before and afterwards, so as to display his small, white hand.

'To business,' he then continued. 'To conversation. You have shown yourself more free of speech than body, sir.'

'I have used the freedom of telling you what you know yourself to be. You know yourself, as we all know you, to be far worse than that.'

'Add, always a gentleman, and it's no matter. Except in that regard, we are all alike. For example: you couldn't for your life be a gentleman; I couldn't for my life be otherwise. How great the difference! Let us go on. Words, sir, never influence the course of the cards, or the course of the dice. Do you know that? You do? I also play a game, and words are without power over it.'

Now that he was confronted with Cavalletto, and knew that his story was known—whatever thin disguise he had worn, he dropped; and faced it out, with a bare face, as the infamous wretch he was.

'No, my son,' he resumed, with a snap of his fingers. 'I play my game to the end in spite of words; and Death of my Body and Death of my Soul! I'll win it. You want to know why I played this little trick that you have interrupted? Know then that I had, and that I have—do you understand me? have—a commodity to sell to my lady your respectable mother. I described my precious commodity, and fixed my price. Touching the bargain, your admirable mother was a little too calm, too stolid, too immovable and statue-like. In fine, your admirable mother vexed me. To make variety in my position, and to amuse myself—what! a gentleman must be amused at somebody's expense!—I conceived the happy idea of disappearing. An idea, see you, that your characteristic mother and my Flintwinch would have been well enough pleased to execute. Ah! Bah, bah, bah, don't look as from high to low at me! I repeat it. Well enough pleased, excessively enchanted, and with all their hearts ravished. How strongly will you have it?'

He threw out the lees of his glass on the ground, so that they nearly spattered Cavalletto. This seemed to draw his attention to him anew. He set down his glass and said:

'I'll not fill it. What! I am born to be served. Come then, you Cavalletto, and fill!'

The little man looked at Clennam, whose eyes were occupied with Rigaud, and, seeing no prohibition, got up from the ground, and poured out from the bottle into the glass. The blending, as he did so, of his old submission with a sense of something humorous; the striving of that with a certain smouldering ferocity, which might have flashed fire in an instant (as the born gentleman seemed to think, for he had a wary eye upon him); and the easy yielding of all to a good-natured, careless, predominant propensity to sit down on the ground again: formed a very remarkable combination of character.

'This happy idea, brave sir,' Rigaud resumed after drinking, 'was a happy idea for several reasons. It amused me, it worried your dear mama and my Flintwinch, it caused you agonies (my terms for a lesson in politeness towards a gentleman), and it suggested to all the amiable persons interested that your entirely devoted is a man to fear. By Heaven, he is a man to fear! Beyond this; it might have restored her wit to my lady your mother—might, under the pressing little suspicion your wisdom has recognised, have persuaded her at last to announce, covertly, in the journals, that the difficulties of a certain contract would be removed by the appearance of a certain important party to it. Perhaps yes, perhaps no. But that, you have interrupted. Now, what is it you say? What is it you want?'

Never had Clennam felt more acutely that he was a prisoner in bonds, than when he saw this man before him, and could not accompany him to his mother's house. All the undiscernible difficulties and dangers he had ever feared were closing in, when he could not stir hand or foot.

'Perhaps, my friend, philosopher, man of virtue, Imbecile, what you will; perhaps,' said Rigaud, pausing in his drink to look out of his glass with his horrible smile, 'you would have done better to leave me alone?'

'No! At least,' said Clennam, 'you are known to be alive and unharmed. At least you cannot escape from these two witnesses; and they can produce you before any public authorities, or before hundreds of people!'

'But will not produce me before one,' said Rigaud, snapping his fingers again with an air of triumphant menace. 'To the Devil with your witnesses! To the Devil with your produced! To the Devil with yourself! What! Do I know what I know, for that? Have I my commodity on sale, for that? Bah, poor debtor! You have interrupted my little project. Let it pass. How then? What remains? To you, nothing; to me, all. Produce me! Is that what you want? I will produce myself, only too quickly. Contrabandist! Give me pen, ink, and paper.'

Cavalletto got up again as before, and laid them before him in his former manner. Rigaud, after some villainous thinking and smiling, wrote, and read aloud, as follows:

'To MRS CLENNAM.

'Wait answer.

'Prison of the Marshalsea. 'At the apartment of your son.

'Dear Madam, 'I am in despair to be informed to-day by our prisoner here (who has had the goodness to employ spies to seek me, living for politic reasons in retirement), that you have had fears for my safety.

'Reassure yourself, dear madam. I am well, I am strong and constant.

'With the greatest impatience I should fly to your house, but that I foresee it to be possible, under the circumstances, that you will not yet have quite definitively arranged the little proposition I have had the honour to submit to you. I name one week from this day, for a last final visit on my part; when you will unconditionally accept it or reject it, with its train of consequences.

'I suppress my ardour to embrace you and achieve this interesting business, in order that you may have leisure to adjust its details to our perfect mutual satisfaction.

'In the meanwhile, it is not too much to propose (our prisoner having deranged my housekeeping), that my expenses of lodging and nourishment at an hotel shall be paid by you.

'Receive, dear madam, the assurance of my highest and most distinguished consideration,

RIGAUD BLANDOIS.

'A thousand friendships to that dear Flintwinch.

'I kiss the hands of Madame F.'

When he had finished this epistle, Rigaud folded it and tossed it with a flourish at Clennam's feet. 'Hola you! Apropos of producing, let somebody produce that at its address, and produce the answer here.'

'Cavalletto,' said Arthur. 'Will you take this fellow's letter?'

But, Cavalletto's significant finger again expressing that his post was at the door to keep watch over Rigaud, now he had found him with so much trouble, and that the duty of his post was to sit on the floor backed up by the door, looking at Rigaud and holding his own ankles,—Signor Panco once more volunteered. His services being accepted, Cavalletto suffered the door to open barely wide enough to admit of his squeezing himself out, and immediately shut it on him.

'Touch me with a finger, touch me with an epithet, question my superiority as I sit here drinking my wine at my pleasure,' said Rigaud, 'and I follow the letter and cancel my week's grace. You wanted me? You have got me! How do you like me?'

'You know,' returned Clennam, with a bitter sense of his helplessness, 'that when I sought you, I was not a prisoner.'

'To the Devil with you and your prison,' retorted Rigaud, leisurely, as he took from his pocket a case containing the materials for making cigarettes, and employed his facile hands in folding a few for present use; 'I care for neither of you. Contrabandist! A light.'

Again Cavalletto got up, and gave him what he wanted. There had been something dreadful in the noiseless skill of his cold, white hands, with the fingers lithely twisting about and twining one over another like serpents. Clennam could not prevent himself from shuddering inwardly, as if he had been looking on at a nest of those creatures.

'Hola, Pig!' cried Rigaud, with a noisy stimulating cry, as if Cavalletto were an Italian horse or mule. 'What! The infernal old jail was a respectable one to this. There was dignity in the bars and stones of that place. It was a prison for men. But this? Bah! A hospital for imbeciles!'

He smoked his cigarette out, with his ugly smile so fixed upon his face that he looked as though he were smoking with his drooping beak of a nose, rather than with his mouth; like a fancy in a weird picture. When he had lighted a second cigarette at the still burning end of the first, he said to Clennam:

'One must pass the time in the madman's absence. One must talk. One can't drink strong wine all day long, or I would have another bottle. She's handsome, sir. Though not exactly to my taste, still, by the Thunder and the Lightning! handsome. I felicitate you on your admiration.'

'I neither know nor ask,' said Clennam, 'of whom you speak.'

'Della bella Gowana, sir, as they say in Italy. Of the Gowan, the fair Gowan.'

'Of whose husband you were the—follower, I think?'

'Sir? Follower? You are insolent. The friend.'

'Do you sell all your friends?'

Rigaud took his cigarette from his mouth, and eyed him with a momentary revelation of surprise. But he put it between his lips again, as he answered with coolness:

'I sell anything that commands a price. How do your lawyers live, your politicians, your intriguers, your men of the Exchange? How do you live? How do you come here? Have you sold no friend? Lady of mine! I rather think, yes!'

Clennam turned away from him towards the window, and sat looking out at the wall.

'Effectively, sir,' said Rigaud, 'Society sells itself and sells me: and I sell Society. I perceive you have acquaintance with another lady. Also handsome. A strong spirit. Let us see. How do they call her? Wade.'

He received no answer, but could easily discern that he had hit the mark.

'Yes,' he went on, 'that handsome lady and strong spirit addresses me in the street, and I am not insensible. I respond. That handsome lady and strong spirit does me the favour to remark, in full confidence, "I have my curiosity, and I have my chagrins. You are not more than ordinarily honourable, perhaps?" I announce myself, "Madame, a gentleman from the birth, and a gentleman to the death; but not more than ordinarily honourable. I despise such a weak fantasy." Thereupon she is pleased to compliment. "The difference between you and the rest is," she answers, "that you say so." For she knows Society. I accept her congratulations with gallantry and politeness. Politeness and little gallantries are inseparable from my character. She then makes a proposition, which is, in effect, that she has seen us much together; that it appears to her that I am for the passing time the cat of the house, the friend of the family; that her curiosity and her chagrins awaken the fancy to be acquainted with their movements, to know the manner of their life, how the fair Gowana is beloved, how the fair Gowana is cherished, and so on. She is not rich, but offers such and such little recompenses for the little cares and derangements of such services; and I graciously—to do everything graciously is a part of my character—consent to accept them. O yes! So goes the world. It is the mode.'

Though Clennam's back was turned while he spoke, and thenceforth to the end of the interview, he kept those glittering eyes of his that were too near together, upon him, and evidently saw in the very carriage of the head, as he passed with his braggart recklessness from clause to clause of what he said, that he was saying nothing which Clennam did not already know.

'Whoof! The fair Gowana!' he said, lighting a third cigarette with a sound as if his lightest breath could blow her away. 'Charming, but imprudent! For it was not well of the fair Gowana to make mysteries of letters from old lovers, in her bedchamber on the mountain, that her husband might not see them. No, no. That was not well. Whoof! The Gowana was mistaken there.'

'I earnestly hope,' cried Arthur aloud, 'that Pancks may not be long gone, for this man's presence pollutes the room.'

'Ah! But he'll flourish here, and everywhere,' said Rigaud, with an exulting look and snap of his fingers. 'He always has; he always will!' Stretching his body out on the only three chairs in the room besides that on which Clennam sat, he sang, smiting himself on the breast as the gallant personage of the song.

'*Who passes by this road so late?*

Compagnon de la Majolaine!

Who passes by this road so late?

Always gay!

'Sing the Refrain, pig! You could sing it once, in another jail. Sing it! Or, by every Saint who was stoned to death, I'll be affronted and compromising; and then some people who are not dead yet, had better have been stoned along with them!'

'*Of all the king's knights 'tis the flower,*

Compagnon de la Majolaine!

Of all the king's knights 'tis the flower,

Always gay!'

Partly in his old habit of submission, partly because his not doing it might injure his benefactor, and partly because he would as soon do it as anything else, Cavalletto took up the Refrain this time. Rigaud laughed, and fell to smoking with his eyes shut.

Possibly another quarter of an hour elapsed before Mr Pancks's step was heard upon the stairs, but the interval seemed to Clennam insupportably long. His step was attended by another step; and when Cavalletto opened the door, he admitted Mr Pancks and Mr Flintwinch. The latter was no sooner visible, than Rigaud rushed at him and embraced him boisterously.

'How do you find yourself, sir?' said Mr Flintwinch, as soon as he could disengage himself, which he struggled to do with very little ceremony. 'Thank you, no; I don't want any more.' This was in reference to another menace of attention from his recovered friend. 'Well, Arthur. You remember what I said to you about sleeping dogs and missing ones. It's come true, you see.'

He was as imperturbable as ever, to all appearance, and nodded his head in a moralising way as he looked round the room.

'And this is the Marshalsea prison for debt!' said Mr Flintwinch. 'Hah! you have brought your pigs to a very indifferent market, Arthur.'

If Arthur had patience, Rigaud had not. He took his little Flintwinch, with fierce playfulness, by the two lapels of his coat, and cried:

'To the Devil with the Market, to the Devil with the Pigs, and to the Devil with the Pig-Driver! Now! Give me the answer to my letter.'

'If you can make it convenient to let go a moment, sir,' returned Mr Flintwinch, 'I'll first hand Mr Arthur a little note that I have for him.'

He did so. It was in his mother's maimed writing, on a slip of paper, and contained only these words:

'I hope it is enough that you have ruined yourself. Rest contented without more ruin. Jeremiah Flintwinch is my messenger and representative. Your affectionate M. C.'

Clennam read this twice, in silence, and then tore it to pieces. Rigaud in the meanwhile stepped into a chair, and sat himself on the back with his feet upon the seat.

'Now, Beau Flintwinch,' he said, when he had closely watched the note to its destruction, 'the answer to my letter?'

'Mrs Clennam did not write, Mr Blandois, her hands being cramped, and she thinking it as well to send it verbally by me.' Mr Flintwinch screwed this out of himself, unwillingly and rustily. 'She sends her compliments, and says she doesn't on the whole wish to term you unreasonable, and that she agrees. But without prejudicing the appointment that stands for this day week.'

Monsieur Rigaud, after indulging in a fit of laughter, descended from his throne, saying, 'Good! I go to seek an hotel!' But, there his eyes encountered Cavalletto, who was still at his post.

'Come, Pig,' he added, 'I have had you for a follower against my will; now, I'll have you against yours. I tell you, my little reptiles, I am born to be served. I demand the service of this contrabandist as my domestic until this day week.'

In answer to Cavalletto's look of inquiry, Clennam made him a sign to go; but he added aloud, 'unless you are afraid of him.' Cavalletto replied with a very emphatic finger-negative.'No, master, I am not afraid of him, when I no more keep it secrettementally that he was once my comrade.' Rigaud took no notice of either remark until he had lighted his last cigarette and was quite ready for walking.

'Afraid of him,' he said then, looking round upon them all. 'Whoof! My children, my babies, my little dolls, you are all afraid of him. You give him his bottle of wine here; you give him meat, drink, and lodging there; you dare not touch him with a finger or an epithet. No. It is his character to triumph! Whoof!

'Of all the king's knights he's the flower,

And he's always gay!'

With this adaptation of the Refrain to himself, he stalked out of the room closely followed by Cavalletto, whom perhaps he had pressed into his service because he tolerably well knew it would not be easy to get rid of him. Mr Flintwinch, after scraping his chin, and looking about with caustic disparagement of the Pig-Market, nodded to Arthur, and followed. Mr Pancks, still penitent and depressed, followed too; after receiving with great attention a secret word or two of instructions from Arthur, and whispering back that he would see this affair out, and stand by it to the end. The prisoner, with the feeling that he was more despised, more scorned and repudiated, more helpless, altogether more miserable and fallen than before, was left alone again.

CHAPTER 29. A Plea in the Marshalsea

Haggard anxiety and remorse are bad companions to be barred up with. Brooding all day, and resting very little indeed at night, will not arm a man against misery. Next morning, Clennam felt that his health was sinking, as his spirits had already sunk and that the weight under which he bent was bearing him down.

Night after night he had risen from his bed of wretchedness at twelve or one o'clock, and had sat at his window watching the sickly lamps in the yard, and looking upward for the first wan trace of day, hours before it was possible that the sky could show it to him. Now when the night came, he could not even persuade himself to undress.

For a burning restlessness set in, an agonised impatience of the prison, and a conviction that he was going to break his heart and die there, which caused him indescribable suffering. His dread and hatred of the place became so intense that he felt it a labour to draw his breath in it. The sensation of being stifled sometimes so overpowered him, that he would stand at the window holding his throat and gasping. At the same time a longing for other air, and a yearning to be beyond the blind blank wall, made him feel as if he must go mad with the ardour of the desire.

Many other prisoners had had experience of this condition before him, and its violence and continuity had worn themselves out in their cases, as they did in his. Two nights and a day exhausted it. It came back by fits, but those grew fainter and returned at lengthening intervals. A desolate calm succeeded; and the middle of the week found him settled down in the despondency of low, slow fever.

With Cavalletto and Pancks away, he had no visitors to fear but Mr and Mrs Plornish. His anxiety, in reference to that worthy pair, was that they should not come near him; for, in the morbid state of his nerves, he sought to be left alone, and spared the being seen so subdued and weak. He wrote a note to Mrs Plornish representing himself as occupied with his affairs, and bound by the necessity of devoting himself to them, to remain for a time even without the pleasant interruption of a sight of her kind face. As to Young John, who looked in daily at a certain hour, when the turnkeys were relieved, to ask if he could do anything for him; he always made a pretence of being engaged in writing, and to answer cheerfully in the negative. The subject of their only long conversation had never been revived between them. Through all these changes of unhappiness, however, it had never lost its hold on Clennam's mind.

The sixth day of the appointed week was a moist, hot, misty day. It seemed as though the prison's poverty, and shabbiness, and dirt, were growing in the sultry atmosphere. With an aching head and a weary heart, Clennam had watched the miserable night out, listening to the fall of rain on the yard pavement, thinking of its softer fall upon the country earth. A blurred circle of yellow haze had risen up in the sky in lieu of sun, and he had watched the patch it put upon his wall, like a bit of the prison's raggedness. He had heard the gates open; and the badly shod feet that waited outside shuffle in; and the sweeping, and pumping, and moving about, begin, which commenced the prison morning. So ill and faint that he was obliged to rest many times in the process of getting himself washed, he had at length crept to his chair by the open window. In it he sat dozing, while the old woman who arranged his room went through her morning's work.

Light of head with want of sleep and want of food (his appetite, and even his sense of taste, having forsaken him), he had been two or three times conscious, in the night, of going astray. He had heard fragments of tunes and songs in the warm wind, which he knew had no existence. Now that he began to doze in exhaustion, he heard them again; and voices seemed to address him, and he answered, and started.

Dozing and dreaming, without the power of reckoning time, so that a minute might have been an hour and an hour a minute, some abiding impression of a garden stole over him—a garden of flowers, with a damp warm wind gently stirring their scents. It required such a painful effort to lift his head for the purpose of inquiring into this, or inquiring into anything, that the impression appeared to have become quite an old and importunate one when he looked round. Beside the tea-cup on his table he saw, then, a blooming nosegay: a wonderful handful of the choicest and most lovely flowers.

Nothing had ever appeared so beautiful in his sight. He took them up and inhaled their fragrance, and he lifted them to his hot head, and he put them down and opened his parched hands to them, as cold hands are opened to receive the cheering of a fire. It was not until he had delighted in them for some time, that he wondered who had sent them; and opened his door to ask the woman who must have put them there, how they had come into her hands. But she was gone, and seemed to have been long gone; for the tea she had left for him on the table was cold. He tried to drink some, but could not bear the odour of it: so he crept back to his chair by the open window, and put the flowers on the little round table of old.

When the first faintness consequent on having moved about had left him, he subsided into his former state. One of the night-tunes was playing in the wind, when the door of his room seemed to open to a light touch, and, after a moment's pause, a quiet figure seemed to stand there, with a black mantle on it. It seemed to draw the mantle off and drop it on the ground, and then it seemed to be his Little Dorrit in her old, worn dress. It seemed to tremble, and to clasp its hands, and to smile, and to burst into tears.

He roused himself, and cried out. And then he saw, in the loving, pitying, sorrowing, dear face, as in a mirror, how changed he was; and she came towards him; and with her hands laid on his breast to keep him in his chair, and with her knees upon the floor at his feet, and with her lips raised up to kiss him, and with her tears dropping on him as the rain from Heaven had dropped upon the flowers, Little Dorrit, a living presence, called him by his name.

'O, my best friend! Dear Mr Clennam, don't let me see you weep! Unless you weep with pleasure to see me. I hope you do. Your own poor child come back!'

So faithful, tender, and unspoiled by Fortune. In the sound of her voice, in the light of her eyes, in the touch of her hands, so Angelically comforting and true!

As he embraced her, she said to him, 'They never told me you were ill,' and drawing an arm softly round his neck, laid his head upon her bosom, put a hand upon his head, and resting her cheek upon that hand, nursed him as lovingly, and GOD knows as innocently, as she had nursed her father in that room when she had been but a baby, needing all the care from others that she took of them.

When he could speak, he said, 'Is it possible that you have come to me? And in this dress?'

'I hoped you would like me better in this dress than any other. I have always kept it by me, to remind me: though I wanted no reminding. I am not alone, you see. I have brought an old friend with me.'

Looking round, he saw Maggy in her big cap which had been long abandoned, with a basket on her arm as in the bygone days, chuckling rapturously.

'It was only yesterday evening that I came to London with my brother. I sent round to Mrs Plornish almost as soon as we arrived, that I might hear of you and let you know I had come. Then I heard that you were here. Did you happen to think of me in the night? I almost believe you must have thought of me a little. I thought of you so anxiously, and it appeared so long to morning.'

'I have thought of you—' he hesitated what to call her. She perceived it in an instant.

'You have not spoken to me by my right name yet. You know what my right name always is with you.'

'I have thought of you, Little Dorrit, every day, every hour, every minute, since I have been here.'

'Have you? Have you?'

He saw the bright delight of her face, and the flush that kindled in it, with a feeling of shame. He, a broken, bankrupt, sick, dishonoured prisoner.

'I was here before the gates were opened, but I was afraid to come straight to you. I should have done you more harm than good, at first; for the prison was so familiar and yet so strange, and it brought back so many remembrances of my poor father, and of you too, that at first it overpowered me. But we went to Mr Chivery before we came to the gate, and he brought us in, and got John's room for us—my poor old room, you know—and we waited there a little. I brought the flowers to the door, but you didn't hear me.'

She looked something more womanly than when she had gone away, and the ripening touch of the Italian sun was visible upon her face. But, otherwise, she was quite unchanged. The same deep, timid earnestness that he had always seen in her, and never without emotion, he saw still. If it had a new meaning that smote him to the heart, the change was in his perception, not in her.

She took off her old bonnet, hung it in the old place, and noiselessly began, with Maggy's help, to make his room as fresh and neat as it could be made, and to sprinkle it with a pleasant-smelling water. When that was done, the basket, which was filled with grapes and other fruit, was unpacked, and all its contents were quietly put away. When that was done, a moment's whisper despatched Maggy to despatch somebody else to fill the basket again; which soon came back replenished with new stores, from which a present provision of cooling drink and jelly, and a prospective supply of roast chicken and wine and water, were the first extracts. These various arrangements completed, she took out her old needle-case to make him a curtain for his window; and thus, with a quiet reigning in the room, that seemed to diffuse itself through the else noisy prison, he found himself composed in his chair, with Little Dorrit working at his side.

To see the modest head again bent down over its task, and the nimble fingers busy at their old work—though she was not so absorbed in it, but that her compassionate eyes were often raised to his face, and, when they drooped again had tears in them—to be so consoled and comforted, and to believe that all the devotion of this great nature was turned to him in his adversity to pour out its inexhaustible wealth of goodness upon him, did not steady Clennam's trembling voice or hand, or strengthen him in his weakness. Yet it inspired him with an inward fortitude, that rose with his love. And how dearly he loved her now, what words can tell!

As they sat side by side in the shadow of the wall, the shadow fell like light upon him. She would not let him speak much, and he lay back in his chair, looking at her. Now and again she would rise and give him the glass that he might drink, or would smooth the resting-place of his head; then she would gently resume her seat by him, and bend over her work again.

The shadow moved with the sun, but she never moved from his side, except to wait upon him. The sun went down and she was still there. She had done her work now, and her hand, faltering on the arm of his chair since its last tending of him, was hesitating there yet. He laid his hand upon it, and it clasped him with a trembling supplication.

'Dear Mr Clennam, I must say something to you before I go. I have put it off from hour to hour, but I must say it.'

'I too, dear Little Dorrit. I have put off what I must say.'

She nervously moved her hand towards his lips as if to stop him; then it dropped, trembling, into its former place.

'I am not going abroad again. My brother is, but I am not. He was always attached to me, and he is so grateful to me now—so much too grateful, for it is only because I happened to be with him in his illness—that he says I shall be free to stay where I like best, and to do what I like best. He only wishes me to be happy, he says.'

There was one bright star shining in the sky. She looked up at it while she spoke, as if it were the fervent purpose of her own heart shining above her.

'You will understand, I dare say, without my telling you, that my brother has come home to find my dear father's will, and to take possession of his property. He says, if there is a will, he is sure I shall be left rich; and if there is none, that he will make me so.'

He would have spoken; but she put up her trembling hand again, and he stopped.

'I have no use for money, I have no wish for it. It would be of no value at all to me but for your sake. I could not be rich, and you here. I must always be much worse than poor, with you distressed. Will you let me lend you all I have? Will you let me give it you? Will you let me show you that I have never forgotten, that I never can forget, your protection of me when this was my home? Dear Mr Clennam, make me of all the world the happiest, by saying Yes? Make me as happy as I can be in leaving you here, by saying nothing to-night, and letting me go away with the hope that you will think of it kindly; and that for my sake—not for yours, for mine, for nobody's but mine!—you will give me the greatest joy I can experience on earth, the joy of knowing that I have been serviceable to you, and that I have paid some little of the great debt of my affection and gratitude. I can't say what I wish to say. I can't visit you here where I have lived so long, I can't think of you here where I have seen so much, and be as calm and comforting as I ought. My tears will make their way. I cannot keep them back. But pray, pray, pray, do not turn from your Little Dorrit, now, in your affliction! Pray, pray, pray, I beg you and implore you with all my grieving heart, my friend—my dear!—take all I have, and make it a Blessing to me!'

The star had shone on her face until now, when her face sank upon his hand and her own.

It had grown darker when he raised her in his encircling arm, and softly answered her.

'No, darling Little Dorrit. No, my child. I must not hear of such a sacrifice. Liberty and hope would be so dear, bought at such a price, that I could never support their weight, never bear the reproach of possessing them. But with what ardent thankfulness and love I say this, I may call Heaven to witness!'

'And yet you will not let me be faithful to you in your affliction?'

'Say, dearest Little Dorrit, and yet I will try to be faithful to you. If, in the bygone days when this was your home and when this was your dress, I had understood myself (I speak only of myself) better, and had read the secrets of my own breast more distinctly; if, through my reserve and self-mistrust, I had discerned a light that I see brightly now when it has passed far away, and my weak footsteps can never overtake it; if I had then known, and told you that I loved and honoured you, not as the poor child I used to call you, but as a woman whose true hand would raise me high above myself and make me a far happier and better man; if I had so used the opportunity there is no recalling—as I wish I had, O I wish I had!—and if something had kept us apart then, when I was moderately thriving, and when you were poor; I might have met your noble offer of your fortune, dearest girl, with other words than these, and still have

538

blushed to touch it. But, as it is, I must never touch it, never!'

She besought him, more pathetically and earnestly, with her little supplicatory hand, than she could have done in any words.

'I am disgraced enough, my Little Dorrit. I must not descend so low as that, and carry you—so dear, so generous, so good—down with me. GOD bless you, GOD reward you! It is past.'

He took her in his arms, as if she had been his daughter.

'Always so much older, so much rougher, and so much less worthy, even what I was must be dismissed by both of us, and you must see me only as I am. I put this parting kiss upon your cheek, my child—who might have been more near to me, who never could have been more dear—a ruined man far removed from you, for ever separated from you, whose course is run while yours is but beginning. I have not the courage to ask to be forgotten by you in my humiliation; but I ask to be remembered only as I am.'

The bell began to ring, warning visitors to depart. He took her mantle from the wall, and tenderly wrapped it round her.

'One other word, my Little Dorrit. A hard one to me, but it is a necessary one. The time when you and this prison had anything in common has long gone by. Do you understand?'

'O! you will never say to me,' she cried, weeping bitterly, and holding up her clasped hands in entreaty, 'that I am not to come back any more! You will surely not desert me so!'

'I would say it, if I could; but I have not the courage quite to shut out this dear face, and abandon all hope of its return. But do not come soon, do not come often! This is now a tainted place, and I well know the taint of it clings to me. You belong to much brighter and better scenes. You are not to look back here, my Little Dorrit; you are to look away to very different and much happier paths. Again, GOD bless you in them! GOD reward you!'

Maggy, who had fallen into very low spirits, here cried, 'Oh get him into a hospital; do get him into a hospital, Mother! He'll never look like hisself again, if he an't got into a hospital. And then the little woman as was always a spinning at her wheel, she can go to the cupboard with the Princess, and say, what do you keep the Chicking there for? and then they can take it out and give it to him, and then all be happy!'

The interruption was seasonable, for the bell had nearly rung itself out. Again tenderly wrapping her mantle about her, and taking her on his arm (though, but for her visit, he was almost too weak to walk), Arthur led Little Dorrit down-stairs. She was the last visitor to pass out at the Lodge, and the gate jarred heavily and hopelessly upon her.

With the funeral clang that it sounded into Arthur's heart, his sense of weakness returned. It was a toilsome journey up-stairs to his room, and he re-entered its dark solitary precincts in unutterable misery.

When it was almost midnight, and the prison had long been quiet, a cautious creak came up the stairs, and a cautious tap of a key was given at his door. It was Young John. He glided in, in his stockings, and held the door closed, while he spoke in a whisper.

'It's against all rules, but I don't mind. I was determined to come through, and come to you.'

'What is the matter?'

'Nothing's the matter, sir. I was waiting in the court-yard for Miss Dorrit when she came out. I thought you'd like some one to see that she was safe.'

'Thank you, thank you! You took her home, John?'

'I saw her to her hotel. The same that Mr Dorrit was at. Miss Dorrit walked all the way, and talked to me so kind, it quite knocked me over. Why do you think she walked instead of riding?'

'I don't know, John.'

'To talk about you. She said to me, "John, you was always honourable, and if you'll promise me that you will take care of him, and never let him want for help and comfort when I am not there, my mind will be at rest so far." I promised her. And I'll stand by you,' said John Chivery, 'for ever!'

Clennam, much affected, stretched out his hand to this honest spirit.

'Before I take it,' said John, looking at it, without coming from the door, 'guess what message Miss Dorrit gave me.'

Clennam shook his head.

'"Tell him,"' repeated John, in a distinct, though quavering voice, '"that his Little Dorrit sent him her undying love." Now it's delivered. Have I been honourable, sir?'

'Very, very!'

'Will you tell Miss Dorrit I've been honourable, sir?'

'I will indeed.'

'There's my hand, sir,' said John, 'and I'll stand by you forever!'

After a hearty squeeze, he disappeared with the same cautious creak upon the stair, crept shoeless over the pavement of the yard, and, locking the gates behind him, passed out into the front where he had left his shoes. If the same way had been paved with burning ploughshares, it is not at all improbable that John would have traversed it with the same devotion, for the same purpose.

CHAPTER 30. Closing in

The last day of the appointed week touched the bars of the Marshalsea gate. Black, all night, since the gate had clashed upon Little Dorrit, its iron stripes were turned by the early-glowing sun into stripes of gold. Far aslant across the city, over its jumbled roofs, and through the open tracery of its church towers, struck the long bright rays, bars of the prison of this lower world.

Throughout the day the old house within the gateway remained untroubled by any visitors. But, when the sun was low, three men turned in at the gateway and made for the dilapidated house.

Rigaud was the first, and walked by himself smoking. Mr Baptist was the second, and jogged close after him, looking at no other object. Mr Pancks was the third, and carried his hat under his arm for the liberation of his restive hair; the weather being extremely hot. They all came together at the door-steps.

'You pair of madmen!' said Rigaud, facing about. 'Don't go yet!'

'We don't mean to,' said Mr Pancks.

Giving him a dark glance in acknowledgment of his answer, Rigaud knocked loudly. He had charged himself with drink, for the playing out of his game, and was impatient to begin. He had hardly finished one long resounding knock, when he turned to the knocker again and began another. That was not yet finished when Jeremiah Flintwinch opened the door, and they all clanked into the stone hall. Rigaud, thrusting Mr Flintwinch aside, proceeded straight up-stairs. His two attendants followed him, Mr Flintwinch followed them, and they all came trooping into Mrs Clennam's quiet room. It was in its usual state; except that one of the windows was wide open, and Affery sat on its old-fashioned window-seat, mending a stocking. The usual articles were on the little table; the usual deadened fire was in the grate; the bed had its usual pall upon it; and the mistress of all sat on her black bier-like sofa, propped up by her black angular bolster that was like the headsman's block.

Yet there was a nameless air of preparation in the room, as if it were strung up for an occasion. From what the room derived it—every one of its small variety of objects being in the fixed spot it had occupied for years—no one could have said without looking attentively at its mistress, and that, too, with a previous knowledge of her face. Although her unchanging black dress was in every plait precisely as of old, and her unchanging attitude was rigidly preserved, a very slight additional setting of her features and contraction of her gloomy forehead was so powerfully marked, that it marked everything about her.

'Who are these?' she said, wonderingly, as the two attendants entered. 'What do these people want here?'

'Who are these, dear madame, is it?' returned Rigaud. 'Faith, they are friends of your son the prisoner. And what do they want here, is it? Death, madame, I don't know. You will do well to ask them.'

'You know you told us at the door, not to go yet,' said Pancks.

'And you know you told me at the door, you didn't mean to go,' retorted Rigaud. 'In a word, madame, permit me to present two spies of the prisoner's—madmen, but spies. If you wish them to remain here during our little conversation, say the word. It is nothing to me.'

'Why should I wish them to remain here?' said Mrs Clennam. 'What have I to do with them?'

'Then, dearest madame,' said Rigaud, throwing himself into an arm-chair so heavily that the old room trembled, 'you will do well to dismiss them. It is your affair. They are not my spies, not my rascals.'

'Hark! You Pancks,' said Mrs Clennam, bending her brows upon him angrily, 'you Casby's clerk! Attend to your employer's business and your own. Go. And take that other man with you.'

'Thank you, ma'am,' returned Mr Pancks, 'I am glad to say I see no objection to our both retiring. We have done all we undertook to do for Mr Clennam. His constant anxiety has been (and it grew worse upon him when he became a prisoner), that this agreeable gentleman should be brought back here to the place from which he slipped away. Here he is—brought back. And I will say,' added Mr Pancks, 'to his ill-looking face, that in my opinion the world would be no worse for his slipping out of it altogether.'

'Your opinion is not asked,' answered Mrs Clennam. 'Go.'

'I am sorry not to leave you in better company, ma'am,' said Pancks; 'and sorry, too, that Mr Clennam can't be present. It's my fault, that is.'

'You mean his own,' she returned.

'No, I mean mine, ma'am,' said Pancks, 'for it was my misfortune to lead him into a ruinous investment.' (Mr Pancks still clung to that word, and never said speculation.) 'Though I can prove by figures,' added Mr Pancks, with an anxious countenance, 'that it ought to have been a good investment. I have gone over it since it failed, every day of my life, and it comes out—regarded as a question of figures—triumphant. The present is not a time or place,' Mr Pancks pursued, with a longing glance into his hat, where he kept his calculations, 'for entering upon the figures; but the figures are not to be disputed. Mr Clennam ought to have been at this moment in his carriage and pair, and I ought to have been worth from three to five thousand pound.'

Mr Pancks put his hair erect with a general aspect of confidence that could hardly have been surpassed, if he had had the amount in his pocket. These incontrovertible figures had been the occupation of every moment of his leisure since he had lost his money, and were destined to afford him consolation to the end of his days.

'However,' said Mr Pancks, 'enough of that. Altro, old boy, you have seen the figures, and you know how they come out.' Mr Baptist, who had not the slightest arithmetical power of compensating himself in this way, nodded, with a fine display of bright teeth.

At whom Mr Flintwinch had been looking, and to whom he then said:

'Oh! it's you, is it? I thought I remembered your face, but I wasn't certain till I saw your teeth. Ah! yes, to be sure. It was this officious refugee,' said Jeremiah to Mrs Clennam, 'who came knocking at the door on the night when Arthur and Chatterbox were here, and who asked me a whole Catechism of questions about Mr Blandois.'

'It is true,' Mr Baptist cheerfully admitted. 'And behold him, padrone! I have found him consequentementally.'

'I shouldn't have objected,' returned Mr Flintwinch, 'to your having broken your neck consequentementally.'

'And now,' said Mr Pancks, whose eye had often stealthily wandered to the window-seat and the stocking that was being mended there, 'I've only one other word to say before I go. If Mr Clennam was here—but unfortunately, though he has so far got the better of this fine gentleman as to return him to this place against his will, he is ill and in prison—ill and in prison, poor fellow—if he was here,' said Mr Pancks, taking one step aside towards the window-seat, and laying his right hand upon the stocking; 'he would say, "Affery, tell your dreams!"'

Mr Pancks held up his right forefinger between his nose and the stocking with a ghostly air of warning, turned, steamed out and towed Mr Baptist after him. The house-door was heard to close upon them, their steps were heard passing over the dull pavement of the echoing court-yard, and still nobody had added a word. Mrs Clennam and Jeremiah had exchanged a look; and had then looked, and looked still, at Affery, who sat mending the stocking with great assiduity.

'Come!' said Mr Flintwinch at length, screwing himself a curve or two in the direction of the window-seat, and rubbing the palms of his hands on his coat-tail as if he were preparing them to do something: 'Whatever has to be said among us had better be begun to be said without more loss of time.—So, Affery, my woman, take yourself away!'

In a moment Affery had thrown the stocking down, started up, caught hold of the windowsill with her right hand, lodged herself upon the window-seat with her right knee, and was flourishing her left hand, beating expected assailants off.

'No, I won't, Jeremiah—no, I won't—no, I won't! I won't go! I'll stay here. I'll hear all I don't know, and say all I know. I will, at last, if I die for it. I will, I will, I will, I will!'

Mr Flintwinch, stiffening with indignation and amazement, moistened the fingers of one hand at his lips, softly described a circle with them in the palm of the other hand, and continued with a menacing grin to screw himself in the direction of his wife; gasping some remark as he advanced, of which, in his choking anger, only the words, 'Such a dose!' were audible.

'Not a bit nearer, Jeremiah!' cried Affery, never ceasing to beat the air. 'Don't come a bit nearer to me, or I'll rouse the neighbourhood! I'll throw myself out of window. I'll scream Fire and Murder! I'll wake the dead! Stop where you are, or I'll make shrieks enough to wake the dead!'

The determined voice of Mrs Clennam echoed 'Stop!' Jeremiah had stopped already.

'It is closing in, Flintwinch. Let her alone. Affery, do you turn against me after these many years?'

'I do, if it's turning against you to hear what I don't know, and say what I know. I have broke out now, and I can't go back. I am determined to do it. I will do it, I will, I will, I will! If that's turning against you, yes, I turn against both of you two clever ones. I told Arthur when he first come home to stand up against you. I told him it was no reason, because I was afeard of my life of you, that he should be. All manner of things have been a-going on since then, and I won't be run up by Jeremiah, nor yet I won't be dazed and scared, nor made a party to I don't know what, no more. I won't, I won't, I won't! I'll up for Arthur when he has nothing left, and is ill, and in prison, and can't up for himself. I will, I will, I will, I will!'

'How do you know, you heap of confusion,' asked Mrs Clennam sternly, 'that in doing what you are doing now, you are even serving Arthur?'

'I don't know nothing rightly about anything,' said Affery; 'and if ever you said a true word in your life, it's when you call me a heap of confusion, for you two clever ones have done your most to make me such. You married me whether I liked it or not, and you've led me, pretty well ever since, such a life of dreaming and frightening as never was known, and what do you expect me to be but a heap of confusion? You wanted to make me such, and I am such; but I won't submit no longer; no, I won't, I won't, I won't, I won't!' She was still beating the air against all comers.

After gazing at her in silence, Mrs Clennam turned to Rigaud. 'You see and hear this foolish creature. Do you object to such a piece of distraction remaining where she is?'

'I, madame,' he replied, 'do I? That's a question for you.'

'I do not,' she said, gloomily. 'There is little left to choose now. Flintwinch, it is closing in.'

Mr Flintwinch replied by directing a look of red vengeance at his wife, and then, as if to pinion himself from falling upon her, screwed his crossed arms into the breast of his waistcoat, and with his chin very near one of his elbows stood in a corner, watching Rigaud in the oddest attitude. Rigaud, for his part, arose from his chair, and seated himself on the table with his legs dangling. In this easy attitude, he met Mrs Clennam's set face, with his moustache going up and his nose coming down.

'Madame, I am a gentleman—'

'Of whom,' she interrupted in her steady tones, 'I have heard disparagement, in connection with a French jail and an accusation of murder.'

He kissed his hand to her with his exaggerated gallantry.

'Perfectly. Exactly. Of a lady too! What absurdity! How incredible! I had the honour of making a great success then; I hope to have the honour of making a great success now. I kiss your hands. Madame, I am a gentleman (I was going to observe), who when he says, "I will definitely finish this or that affair at the present sitting," does definitely finish it. I announce to you that we are arrived at our last sitting on our little business. You do me the favour to follow, and to comprehend?'

She kept her eyes fixed upon him with a frown. 'Yes.'

'Further, I am a gentleman to whom mere mercenary trade-bargains are unknown, but to whom money is always acceptable as the means of pursuing his pleasures. You do me the favour to follow, and to comprehend?'

'Scarcely necessary to ask, one would say. Yes.'

'Further, I am a gentleman of the softest and sweetest disposition, but who, if trifled with, becomes enraged. Noble natures under such circumstances become enraged. I possess a noble nature. When the lion is awakened—that is to say, when I enrage—the satisfaction of my animosity is as acceptable to me as money. You always do me the favour to follow, and to comprehend?'

'Yes,' she answered, somewhat louder than before.

'Do not let me derange you; pray be tranquil. I have said we are now arrived at our last sitting. Allow me to recall the two sittings we have held.'

'It is not necessary.'

'Death, madame,' he burst out, 'it's my fancy! Besides, it clears the way. The first sitting was limited. I had the honour of making your acquaintance—of presenting my letter; I am a Knight of Industry, at your service, madame, but my polished manners had won me so much of success, as a master of languages, among your compatriots who are as stiff as their own starch is to one another, but are ready to relax to a foreign gentleman of polished manners— and of observing one or two little things,' he glanced around the room and smiled, 'about this honourable house, to know which was necessary to assure me, and to convince me that I had the distinguished pleasure of making the acquaintance of the lady I sought. I achieved this. I gave my word of honour to our dear Flintwinch that I would return. I gracefully departed.'

Her face neither acquiesced nor demurred. The same when he paused, and when he spoke, it as yet showed him always the one attentive frown, and the dark revelation before mentioned of her being nerved for the occasion.

'I say, gracefully departed, because it was graceful to retire without alarming a lady. To be morally graceful, not less than physically, is a part of the character of Rigaud Blandois. It was also politic, as leaving you with something overhanging you, to expect me again with a little anxiety on a day not named. But your slave is politic. By Heaven, madame, politic! Let us return. On the day not named, I have again the honour to render myself at your house. I intimate that I have something to sell, which, if not bought, will compromise madame whom I highly esteem. I explain myself generally. I demand—I think it was a thousand pounds. Will you correct me?'

Thus forced to speak, she replied with constraint, 'You demanded as much as a thousand pounds.'

'I demand at present, Two. Such are the evils of delay. But to return once more. We are not accordant; we differ on that occasion. I am playful; playfulness is a part of my amiable character. Playfully, I become as one slain and hidden. For, it may alone be worth half the sum to madame, to be freed from the suspicions that my droll idea awakens. Accident and spies intermix themselves against my playfulness, and spoil the fruit, perhaps—who knows? only you and Flintwinch—when it is just ripe. Thus, madame, I am here for the last time. Listen! Definitely the last.'

As he struck his straggling boot-heels against the flap of the table, meeting her frown with an insolent gaze, he began to change his tone for a fierce one.

'Bah! Stop an instant! Let us advance by steps. Here is my Hotel-note to be paid, according to contract. Five minutes hence we may be at daggers' points. I'll not leave it till then, or you'll cheat me. Pay it! Count me the money!'

'Take it from his hand and pay it, Flintwinch,' said Mrs Clennam.

He spirted it into Mr Flintwinch's face when the old man advanced to take it, and held forth his hand, repeating noisily, 'Pay it! Count it out! Good money!' Jeremiah picked the bill up, looked at the total with a bloodshot eye, took a small canvas bag from his pocket, and told the amount into his hand.

Rigaud chinked the money, weighed it in his hand, threw it up a little way and caught it, chinked it again.

'The sound of it, to the bold Rigaud Blandois, is like the taste of fresh meat to the tiger. Say, then, madame. How much?'

He turned upon her suddenly with a menacing gesture of the weighted hand that clenched the money, as if he were going to strike her with it.

'I tell you again, as I told you before, that we are not rich here, as you suppose us to be, and that your demand is excessive. I have not the present means of complying with such a demand, if I had ever so great an inclination.'

'If!' cried Rigaud. 'Hear this lady with her If! Will you say that you have not the inclination?'

'I will say what presents itself to me, and not what presents itself to you.'

'Say it then. As to the inclination. Quick! Come to the inclination, and I know what to do.'

She was no quicker, and no slower, in her reply. 'It would seem that you have obtained possession of a paper—or of papers—which I assuredly have the inclination to recover.'

Rigaud, with a loud laugh, drummed his heels against the table, and chinked his money. 'I think so! I believe you there!'

'The paper might be worth, to me, a sum of money. I cannot say how much, or how little.'

'What the Devil!' he asked savagely. 'Not after a week's grace to consider?'

'No! I will not out of my scanty means—for I tell you again, we are poor here, and not rich—I will not offer any price for a power that I do not know the worst and the fullest extent of. This is the third time of your hinting and threatening. You must speak explicitly, or you may go where you will, and do what you will. It is better to be torn to pieces at a spring, than to be a mouse at the caprice of such a cat.'

He looked at her so hard with those eyes too near together that the sinister sight of each, crossing that of the other, seemed to make the bridge of his hooked nose crooked. After a long survey, he said, with the further setting off of his internal smile:

'You are a bold woman!'

'I am a resolved woman.'

'You always were. What? She always was; is it not so, my little Flintwinch?'

'Flintwinch, say nothing to him. It is for him to say, here and now, all he can; or to go hence, and do all he can. You know this to be our determination. Leave him to his action on it.'

She did not shrink under his evil leer, or avoid it. He turned it upon her again, but she remained steady at the point to which she had fixed herself. He got off the table, placed a chair near the sofa, sat down in it, and leaned an arm upon the sofa close to her own, which he touched with his hand. Her face was ever frowning, attentive, and settled.

'It is your pleasure then, madame, that I shall relate a morsel of family history in this little family society,' said Rigaud, with a warning play of his lithe fingers on her arm. 'I am something of a doctor. Let me touch your pulse.'

She suffered him to take her wrist in his hand. Holding it, he proceeded to say:

'A history of a strange marriage, and a strange mother, and a revenge, and a suppression.— Aye, aye, aye? this pulse is beating curiously! It appears to me that it doubles while I touch it. Are these the usual changes of your malady, madame?'

There was a struggle in her maimed arm as she twisted it away, but there was none in her face. On his face there was his own smile.

'I have lived an adventurous life. I am an adventurous character. I have known many adventurers; interesting spirits—amiable society! To one of them I owe my knowledge and my proofs—I repeat it, estimable lady—proofs—of the ravishing little family history I go to commence. You will be charmed with it. But, bah! I forget. One should name a history. Shall I name it the history of a house? But, bah, again. There are so many houses. Shall I name it the history of this house?'

Leaning over the sofa, poised on two legs of his chair and his left elbow; that hand often tapping her arm to beat his words home; his legs crossed; his right hand sometimes arranging his hair, sometimes smoothing his moustache, sometimes striking his nose, always threatening her whatever it did; coarse, insolent, rapacious, cruel, and powerful, he pursued his narrative at his ease.

'In fine, then, I name it the history of this house. I commence it. There live here, let us suppose, an uncle and nephew. The uncle, a rigid old gentleman of strong force of character; the nephew, habitually timid, repressed, and under constraint.'

Mistress Affery, fixedly attentive in the window-seat, biting the rolled up end of her apron, and trembling from head to foot, here cried out, 'Jeremiah, keep off from me! I've heerd, in my dreams, of Arthur's father and his uncle. He's a talking of them. It was before my time here; but I've heerd in my dreams that Arthur's father was a poor, irresolute, frightened chap, who had had everything but his orphan life scared out of him when he was young, and that he had no voice in the choice of his wife even, but his uncle chose her. There she sits! I heerd it in my dreams, and you said it to her own self.'

As Mr Flintwinch shook his fist at her, and as Mrs Clennam gazed upon her, Rigaud kissed his hand to her.

'Perfectly right, dear Madame Flintwinch. You have a genius for dreaming.'

'I don't want none of your praises,' returned Affery. 'I don't want to have nothing at all to say to you. But Jeremiah said they was dreams, and I'll tell 'em as such!' Here she put her apron in her mouth again, as if she were stopping somebody else's mouth—perhaps Jeremiah's, which was chattering with threats as if he were grimly cold.

'Our beloved Madame Flintwinch,' said Rigaud, 'developing all of a sudden a fine susceptibility and spirituality, is right to a marvel. Yes. So runs the history. Monsieur, the uncle, commands the nephew to marry. Monsieur says to him in effect, "My nephew, I introduce to you a lady of strong force of character, like myself—a resolved lady, a stern lady, a lady who has a will that can break the weak to powder: a lady without pity, without love, implacable, revengeful, cold as the stone, but raging as the fire." Ah! what fortitude! Ah, what superiority of intellectual strength! Truly, a proud and noble character that I describe in the supposed words of Monsieur, the uncle. Ha, ha, ha! Death of my soul, I love the sweet lady!'

Mrs Clennam's face had changed. There was a remarkable darkness of colour on it, and the brow was more contracted. 'Madame, madame,' said Rigaud, tapping her on the arm, as if his cruel hand were sounding a musical instrument, 'I perceive I interest you. I perceive I awaken your sympathy. Let us go on.'

The drooping nose and the ascending moustache had, however, to be hidden for a moment with the white hand, before he could go on; he enjoyed the effect he made so much.

'The nephew, being, as the lucid Madame Flintwinch has remarked, a poor devil who has had everything but his orphan life frightened and famished out of him—the nephew abases his head, and makes response: "My uncle, it is to you to command. Do as you will!" Monsieur, the uncle, does as he will. It is what he always does. The auspicious nuptials take place; the newly married come home to this charming mansion; the lady is received, let us suppose, by Flintwinch. Hey, old intriguer?'

Jeremiah, with his eyes upon his mistress, made no reply. Rigaud looked from one to the other, struck his ugly nose, and made a clucking with his tongue.

'Soon the lady makes a singular and exciting discovery. Thereupon, full of anger, full of jealousy, full of vengeance, she forms—see you, madame!—a scheme of retribution, the weight of which she ingeniously forces her crushed husband to bear himself, as well as execute upon her enemy. What superior intelligence!'

'Keep off, Jeremiah!' cried the palpitating Affery, taking her apron from her mouth again. 'But it was one of my dreams, that you told her, when you quarrelled with her one winter evening at dusk—there she sits and you looking at her—that she oughtn't to have let Arthur when he come home, suspect his father only; that she had always had the strength and the power; and that she ought to have stood up more to Arthur, for his father. It was in the same dream where you said to her that she was not—not something, but I don't know what, for she burst out tremendous and stopped you. You know the dream as well as I do. When you come down-stairs into the kitchen with the candle in your hand, and hitched my apron off my head. When you told me I had been dreaming. When you wouldn't believe the noises.' After this explosion Affery put her apron into her mouth again; always keeping her hand on the window-sill and her knee on the window-seat, ready to cry out or jump out if her lord and master approached.

Rigaud had not lost a word of this.

'Haha!' he cried, lifting his eyebrows, folding his arms, and leaning back in his chair. 'Assuredly, Madame Flintwinch is an oracle! How shall we interpret the oracle, you and I and the old intriguer? He said that you were not—? And you burst out and stopped him! What was it you were not? What is it you are not? Say then, madame!'

Under this ferocious banter, she sat breathing harder, and her mouth was disturbed. Her lips quivered and opened, in spite of her utmost efforts to keep them still.

'Come then, madame! Speak, then! Our old intriguer said that you were not—and you stopped him. He was going to say that you were not—what? I know already, but I want a little confidence from you. How, then? You are not what?'

She tried again to repress herself, but broke out vehemently, 'Not Arthur's mother!'

'Good,' said Rigaud. 'You are amenable.'

With the set expression of her face all torn away by the explosion of her passion, and with a bursting, from every rent feature, of the smouldering fire so long pent up, she cried out: 'I will tell it myself! I will not hear it from your lips, and with the taint of your wickedness upon it. Since it must be seen, I will have it seen by the light I stood in. Not another word. Hear me!'

'Unless you are a more obstinate and more persisting woman than even I know you to be,' Mr Flintwinch interposed, 'you had better leave Mr Rigaud, Mr Blandois, Mr Beelzebub, to tell it in his own way. What does it signify when he knows all about it?'

'He does not know all about it.'

'He knows all he cares about it,' Mr Flintwinch testily urged.

'He does not know me.'

'What do you suppose he cares for you, you conceited woman?' said Mr Flintwinch.

'I tell you, Flintwinch, I will speak. I tell you when it has come to this, I will tell it with my own lips, and will express myself throughout it. What! Have I suffered nothing in this room, no deprivation, no imprisonment, that I should condescend at last to contemplate myself in such a glass as that. Can you see him? Can you hear him? If your wife were a hundred times the ingrate that she is, and if I were a thousand times more hopeless than I am of inducing her to be silent if this man is silenced, I would tell it myself, before I would bear the torment of the hearing it from him.'

Rigaud pushed his chair a little back; pushed his legs out straight before him; and sat with his arms folded over against her.

'You do not know what it is,' she went on addressing him, 'to be brought up strictly and straitly. I was so brought up. Mine was no light youth of sinful gaiety and pleasure. Mine were days of wholesome repression, punishment, and fear. The corruption of our hearts, the evil of our ways, the curse that is upon us, the terrors that surround us—these were the themes of my childhood. They formed my character, and filled me with an abhorrence of evil-doers. When old Mr Gilbert Clennam proposed his orphan nephew to my father for my husband, my father impressed upon me that his bringing-up had been, like mine, one of severe restraint. He told me, that besides the discipline his spirit had undergone, he had lived in a starved house, where rioting and gaiety were unknown, and where every day was a day of toil and trial like the last. He told me that he had been a man in years long before his uncle had acknowledged him as one; and that from his school-days to that hour, his uncle's roof has been a sanctuary to him from the contagion of the irreligious and dissolute. When, within a twelvemonth of our marriage, I found my husband, at that time when my father spoke of him, to have sinned against the Lord and outraged me by holding a guilty creature in my place, was I to doubt that it had been appointed to me to make the discovery, and that it was appointed to me to lay the hand of punishment upon that creature of perdition? Was I to dismiss in a moment—not my own wrongs—what was I! but all the rejection of sin, and all the war against it, in which I had been bred?'

She laid her wrathful hand upon the watch on the table.

'No! "Do not forget." The initials of those words are within here now, and were within here then. I was appointed to find the old letter that referred to them, and that told me what they meant, and whose work they were, and why they were worked, lying with this watch in his secret drawer. But for that appointment there would have been no discovery. "Do not forget." It spoke to me like a voice from an angry cloud. Do not forget the deadly sin, do not forget the appointed discovery, do not forget the appointed suffering. I did not forget. Was it my own wrong I remembered? Mine! I was but a servant and a minister. What power could I have over them, but that they were bound in the bonds of their sin, and delivered to me!'

More than forty years had passed over the grey head of this determined woman, since the time she recalled. More than forty years of strife and struggle with the whisper that, by whatever name she called her vindictive pride and rage, nothing through all eternity could change their nature. Yet, gone those more than forty years, and come this Nemesis now looking her in the face, she still abided by her old impiety—still reversed the order of Creation, and breathed her own breath into a clay image of her Creator. Verily, verily, travellers have seen many monstrous idols in many countries; but no human eyes have ever seen more daring, gross, and shocking images of the Divine nature than we creatures of the dust make in our own likenesses, of our own bad passions.

'When I forced him to give her up to me, by her name and place of abode,' she went on in her torrent of indignation and defence; 'when I accused her, and she fell hiding her face at my feet, was it my injury that I asserted, were they my reproaches that I poured upon her? Those who were appointed of old to go to wicked kings and accuse them—were they not ministers and servants? And had not I, unworthy and far-removed from them, sin to denounce? When she pleaded to me her youth, and his wretched and hard life (that was her phrase for the virtuous training he had belied), and the desecrated ceremony of marriage there had secretly been between them, and the terrors of want and shame that had overwhelmed them both when I was first appointed to be the instrument of their punishment, and the love (for she said the word to me, down at my feet) in which she had abandoned him and left him to me, was it my enemy that became my footstool, were they the words of my wrath that made her shrink and quiver! Not unto me the strength be ascribed; not unto me the wringing of the expiation!'

Many years had come and gone since she had had the free use even of her fingers; but it was noticeable that she had already more than once struck her clenched hand vigorously upon the table, and that when she said these words she raised her whole arm in the air, as though it had been a common action with her.

'And what was the repentance that was extorted from the hardness of her heart and the blackness of her depravity? I, vindictive and implacable? It may be so, to such as you who know no righteousness, and no appointment except Satan's. Laugh; but I will be known as I know myself, and as Flintwinch knows me, though it is only to you and this half-witted woman.'

'Add, to yourself, madame,' said Rigaud. 'I have my little suspicions that madame is rather solicitous to be justified to herself.'

'It is false. It is not so. I have no need to be,' she said, with great energy and anger.

'Truly?' retorted Rigaud. 'Hah!'

'I ask, what was the penitence, in works, that was demanded of her? "You have a child; I have none. You love that child. Give him to me. He shall believe himself to be my son, and he shall be believed by every one to be my son. To save you from exposure, his father shall swear never to see or communicate with you more; equally to save him from being stripped by his uncle, and to save your child from being a beggar, you shall swear never to see or communicate with either of them more. That done, and your present means, derived from my husband, renounced, I charge myself with your support. You may, with your place of retreat unknown, then leave, if you please, uncontradicted by me, the lie that when you passed out of all knowledge but mine, you merited a good name." That was all. She had to sacrifice her sinful and shameful affections; no more. She was then free to bear her load of guilt in secret, and to break her heart in secret; and through such present misery (light enough for her, I think!) to purchase her redemption from endless misery, if she could. If, in this, I punished her here, did I not open to her a way hereafter? If she knew herself to be surrounded by insatiable vengeance and unquenchable fires, were they mine? If I threatened her, then and afterwards, with the terrors that encompassed her, did I hold them in my right hand?'

She turned the watch upon the table, and opened it, and, with an unsoftening face, looked at the worked letters within.

'They did not forget. It is appointed against such offences that the offenders shall not be able to forget. If the presence of Arthur was a daily reproach to his father, and if the absence of Arthur was a daily agony to his mother, that was the just dispensation of Jehovah. As well might it be charged upon me, that the stings of an awakened conscience drove her mad, and that it was the will of the Disposer of all things that she should live so, many years. I devoted myself to reclaim the otherwise predestined and lost boy; to give him the reputation of an honest origin; to bring him up in fear and trembling, and in a life of practical contrition for the sins that were heavy on his head before his entrance into this condemned world. Was that a cruelty? Was I, too, not visited with consequences of the original offence in which I had no complicity? Arthur's father and I lived no further apart, with half the globe between us, than when we were together in this house. He died, and sent this watch back to me, with its Do not forget. I do NOT forget, though I do not read it as he did. I read in it, that I was appointed to do these things. I have so read these three letters since I have had them lying on this table, and I did so read them, with equal distinctness, when they were thousands of miles away.'

As she took the watch-case in her hand, with that new freedom in the use of her hand of which she showed no consciousness whatever, bending her eyes upon it as if she were defying it to move her, Rigaud cried with a loud and contemptuous snapping of his fingers. 'Come, madame! Time runs out. Come, lady of piety, it must be! You can tell nothing I don't know. Come to the money stolen, or I will! Death of my soul, I have had enough of your other jargon. Come straight to the stolen money!'

'Wretch that you are,' she answered, and now her hands clasped her head: 'through what fatal error of Flintwinch's, through what incompleteness on his part, who was the only other person helping in these things and trusted with them, through whose and what bringing together of the ashes of a burnt paper, you have become possessed of that codicil, I know no more than how you acquired the rest of your power here—'

'And yet,' interrupted Rigaud, 'it is my odd fortune to have by me, in a convenient place that I know of, that same short little addition to the will of Monsieur Gilbert Clennam, written by a lady and witnessed by the same lady and our old intriguer! Ah, bah, old intriguer, crooked little puppet! Madame, let us go on. Time presses. You or I to finish?'

'I!' she answered, with increased determination, if it were possible. 'I, because I will not endure to be shown myself, and have myself shown to any one, with your horrible distortion upon me. You, with your practices of infamous foreign prisons and galleys would make it the money that impelled me. It was not the money.'

'Bah, bah, bah! I repudiate, for the moment, my politeness, and say, Lies, lies, lies. You know you suppressed the deed and kept the money.'

'Not for the money's sake, wretch!' She made a struggle as if she were starting up; even as if, in her vehemence, she had almost risen on her disabled feet. 'If Gilbert Clennam, reduced to imbecility, at the point of death, and labouring under the delusion of some imaginary relenting towards a girl of whom he had heard that his nephew had once had a fancy for her which he had crushed out of him, and that she afterwards drooped away into melancholy and withdrawal from all who knew her—if, in that state of weakness, he dictated to me, whose life she had darkened with her sin, and who had been appointed to know her wickedness from her own hand and her own lips, a bequest meant as a recompense to her for supposed unmerited suffering; was there no difference between my spurning that injustice, and coveting mere money—a thing which you, and your comrades in the prisons, may steal from anyone?'

'Time presses, madame. Take care!'

'If this house was blazing from the roof to the ground,' she returned, 'I would stay in it to justify myself against my righteous motives being classed with those of stabbers and thieves.'

Rigaud snapped his fingers tauntingly in her face. 'One thousand guineas to the little beauty you slowly hunted to death. One thousand guineas to the youngest daughter her patron might have at fifty, or (if he had none) brother's youngest daughter, on her coming of age, "as the remembrance his disinterestedness may like best, of his protection of a friendless young orphan girl." Two thousand guineas. What! You will never come to the money?'

'That patron,' she was vehemently proceeding, when he checked her.

'Names! Call him Mr Frederick Dorrit. No more evasions.'

'That Frederick Dorrit was the beginning of it all. If he had not been a player of music, and had not kept, in those days of his youth and prosperity, an idle house where singers, and players, and such-like children of Evil turned their backs on the Light and their faces to the Darkness, she might have remained in her lowly station, and might not have been raised out of it to be cast down. But, no. Satan entered into that Frederick Dorrit, and counselled him that he was a man of innocent and laudable tastes who did kind actions, and that here was a poor girl with a voice for singing music with. Then he is to have her taught. Then Arthur's father, who has all along been secretly pining in the ways of virtuous ruggedness for those accursed snares which are called the Arts, becomes acquainted with her. And so, a graceless orphan, training to be a singing girl, carries it, by that Frederick Dorrit's agency, against me, and I am humbled and deceived!—Not I, that is to say,' she added quickly, as colour flushed into her face; 'a greater than I. What am I?'

Jeremiah Flintwinch, who had been gradually screwing himself towards her, and who was now very near her elbow without her knowing it, made a specially wry face of objection when she said these words, and moreover twitched his gaiters, as if such pretensions were equivalent to little barbs in his legs.

'Lastly,' she continued, 'for I am at the end of these things, and I will say no more of them, and you shall say no more of them, and all that remains will be to determine whether the knowledge of them can be kept among us who are here present; lastly, when I suppressed that paper, with the knowledge of Arthur's father—'

'But not with his consent, you know,' said Mr Flintwinch.

'Who said with his consent?' She started to find Jeremiah so near her, and drew back her head, looking at him with some rising distrust. 'You were often enough between us when he would have had me produce it and I would not, to have contradicted me if I had said, with his consent. I say, when I suppressed that paper, I made no effort to destroy it, but kept it by me, here in this house, many years. The rest of the Gilbert property being left to Arthur's father, I could at any time, without unsettling more than the two sums, have made a pretence of finding it. But, besides that I must have supported such pretence by a direct falsehood (a great responsibility), I have seen no new reason, in all the time I have been tried here, to bring it to light. It was a rewarding of sin; the wrong result of a delusion. I did what I was appointed to do, and I have undergone, within these four walls, what I was appointed to undergo. When the paper was at last destroyed—as I thought—in my presence, she had long been dead, and her patron, Frederick Dorrit, had long been deservedly ruined and imbecile. He had no daughter. I had found the niece before then; and what I did for her, was better for her far than the money of which she would have had no good.' She added, after a moment, as though she addressed the watch: 'She herself was innocent, and I might not have forgotten to relinquish it to her at my death:' and sat looking at it.

'Shall I recall something to you, worthy madame?' said Rigaud. 'The little paper was in this house on the night when our friend the prisoner—jail-comrade of my soul—came home from foreign countries. Shall I recall yet something more to you? The little singing-bird that never was fledged, was long kept in a cage by a guardian of your appointing, well enough known to our old intriguer here. Shall we coax our old intriguer to tell us when he saw him last?'

'I'll tell you!' cried Affery, unstopping her mouth. 'I dreamed it, first of all my dreams. Jeremiah, if you come a-nigh me now, I'll scream to be heard at St Paul's! The person as this man has spoken of, was Jeremiah's own twin brother; and he was here in the dead of the night, on the night when Arthur come home, and Jeremiah with his own hands give him this paper, along with I don't know what more, and he took it away in an iron box—Help! Murder! Save me from Jere-mi-ah!'

Mr Flintwinch had made a run at her, but Rigaud had caught him in his arms midway. After a moment's wrestle with him, Flintwinch gave up, and put his hands in his pockets.

'What!' cried Rigaud, rallying him as he poked and jerked him back with his elbows, 'assault a lady with such a genius for dreaming! Ha, ha, ha! Why, she'll be a fortune to you as an exhibition. All that she dreams comes true. Ha, ha, ha! You're so like him, Little Flintwinch. So like him, as I knew him (when I first spoke English for him to the host) in the Cabaret of the Three Billiard Tables, in the little street of the high roofs, by the wharf at Antwerp! Ah, but he was a brave boy to drink. Ah, but he was a brave boy to smoke! Ah, but he lived in a sweet bachelor-apartment—furnished, on the fifth floor, above the wood and charcoal merchant's, and the dress-maker's, and the chair-maker's, and the maker of tubs—where I knew him too, and wherewith his cognac and tobacco, he had twelve sleeps a day and one fit, until he had a fit too much, and ascended to the skies. Ha, ha, ha! What does it matter how I took possession of the papers in his iron box? Perhaps he confided it to my hands for you, perhaps it was locked and my curiosity was piqued, perhaps I suppressed it. Ha, ha, ha! What does it matter, so that I have it safe? We are not particular here; hey, Flintwinch? We are not particular here; is it not so, madame?'

Retiring before him with vicious counter-jerks of his own elbows, Mr Flintwinch had got back into his corner, where he now stood with his hands in his pockets, taking breath, and returning Mrs Clennam's stare. 'Ha, ha, ha! But what's this?' cried Rigaud. 'It appears as if you don't know, one the other. Permit me, Madame Clennam who suppresses, to present Monsieur Flintwinch who intrigues.'

Mr Flintwinch, unpocketing one of his hands to scrape his jaw, advanced a step or so in that attitude, still returning Mrs Clennam's look, and thus addressed her:

'Now, I know what you mean by opening your eyes so wide at me, but you needn't take the trouble, because I don't care for it. I've been telling you for how many years that you're one of the most opinionated and obstinate of women. That's what you are. You call yourself humble and sinful, but you are the most Bumptious of your sex. That's what you are. I have told you, over and over again when we have had a tiff, that you wanted to make everything go down before you, but I wouldn't go down before you—that you wanted to swallow up everybody alive, but I wouldn't be swallowed up alive. Why didn't you destroy the paper when you first laid hands upon it? I advised you to; but no, it's not your way to take advice. You must keep it forsooth. Perhaps you may carry it out at some other time, forsooth. As if I didn't know better than that! I think I see your pride carrying it out, with a chance of being suspected of having kept it by you. But that's the way you cheat yourself. Just as you cheat yourself into making out that you didn't do all this business because you were a rigorous woman, all slight, and spite, and power, and unforgiveness, but because you were a servant and a minister, and were appointed to do it. Who are you, that you should be appointed to do it? That may be your religion, but it's my gammon. And to tell you all the truth while I am about it,' said Mr Flintwinch, crossing his arms, and becoming the express image of irascible doggedness, 'I have been rasped—rasped these forty years—by your taking such high ground even with me, who knows better; the effect of it being coolly to put me on low ground. I admire you very much; you are a woman of strong head and great talent; but the strongest head, and the greatest talent, can't rasp a man for forty years without making him sore. So I don't care for your present eyes. Now, I am coming to the paper, and mark what I say. You put it away somewhere, and you kept your own counsel where. You're an active woman at that time, and if you want to get that paper, you can get it. But, mark. There comes a time when you are struck into what you are now, and then if you want to get that paper, you can't get it. So it lies, long years, in its hiding-place. At last, when we are expecting Arthur home every day, and when any day may bring him home, and it's impossible to say what rummaging he may make about the house, I recommend you five thousand times, if you can't get at it, to let me get at it, that it may be put in the fire. But no—no one but you knows where it is, and that's power; and, call yourself whatever humble names you will, I call you a female Lucifer in appetite for power! On a Sunday night, Arthur comes home. He has not been in this room ten minutes, when he speaks of his father's watch. You know very well that the Do Not Forget, at the time when his father sent that watch to you, could only mean, the rest of the story being then all dead and over, Do Not Forget the suppression. Make restitution! Arthur's ways have frightened you a bit, and the paper shall be burnt after all. So, before that jumping jade and Jezebel,' Mr Flintwinch grinned at his wife, 'has got you into bed, you at last tell me where you have put the paper, among the old ledgers in the cellars, where Arthur himself went prowling the very next morning. But it's not to be burnt on a Sunday night. No; you are strict, you are; we must wait over twelve o'clock, and get into Monday. Now, all this is a swallowing of me up alive that rasps me; so, feeling a little out of temper, and not being as strict as yourself, I take a look at the document before twelve o'clock to refresh my memory as to its appearance—fold up one of the many yellow old papers

554

in the cellars like it—and afterwards, when we have got into Monday morning, and I have, by the light of your lamp, to walk from you, lying on that bed, to this grate, make a little exchange like the conjuror, and burn accordingly. My brother Ephraim, the lunatic-keeper (I wish he had had himself to keep in a strait-waistcoat), had had many jobs since the close of the long job he got from you, but had not done well. His wife died (not that that was much; mine might have died instead, and welcome), he speculated unsuccessfully in lunatics, he got into difficulty about over-roasting a patient to bring him to reason, and he got into debt. He was going out of the way, on what he had been able to scrape up, and a trifle from me. He was here that early Monday morning, waiting for the tide; in short, he was going to Antwerp, where (I am afraid you'll be shocked at my saying, And be damned to him!) he made the acquaintance of this gentleman. He had come a long way, and, I thought then, was only sleepy; but, I suppose now, was drunk. When Arthur's mother had been under the care of him and his wife, she had been always writing, incessantly writing,—mostly letters of confession to you, and Prayers for forgiveness. My brother had handed, from time to time, lots of these sheets to me. I thought I might as well keep them to myself as have them swallowed up alive too; so I kept them in a box, looking over them when I felt in the humour. Convinced that it was advisable to get the paper out of the place, with Arthur coming about it, I put it into this same box, and I locked the whole up with two locks, and I trusted it to my brother to take away and keep, till I should write about it. I did write about it, and never got an answer. I didn't know what to make of it, till this gentleman favoured us with his first visit. Of course, I began to suspect how it was, then; and I don't want his word for it now to understand how he gets his knowledge from my papers, and your paper, and my brother's cognac and tobacco talk (I wish he'd had to gag himself). Now, I have only one thing more to say, you hammer-headed woman, and that is, that I haven't altogether made up my mind whether I might, or might not, have ever given you any trouble about the codicil. I think not; and that I should have been quite satisfied with knowing I had got the better of you, and that I held the power over you. In the present state of circumstances, I have no more explanation to give you till this time to-morrow night. So you may as well,' said Mr Flintwinch, terminating his oration with a screw, 'keep your eyes open at somebody else, for it's no use keeping 'em open at me.'

She slowly withdrew them when he had ceased, and dropped her forehead on her hand. Her other hand pressed hard upon the table, and again the curious stir was observable in her, as if she were going to rise.

'This box can never bring, elsewhere, the price it will bring here. This knowledge can never be of the same profit to you, sold to any other person, as sold to me. But I have not the present means of raising the sum you have demanded. I have not prospered. What will you take now, and what at another time, and how am I to be assured of your silence?'

'My angel,' said Rigaud, 'I have said what I will take, and time presses. Before coming here, I placed copies of the most important of these papers in another hand. Put off the time till the Marshalsea gate shall be shut for the night, and it will be too late to treat. The prisoner will have read them.'

She put her two hands to her head again, uttered a loud exclamation, and started to her feet. She staggered for a moment, as if she would have fallen; then stood firm.

'Say what you mean. Say what you mean, man!'

Before her ghostly figure, so long unused to its erect attitude, and so stiffened in it, Rigaud fell back and dropped his voice. It was, to all the three, almost as if a dead woman had risen.

'Miss Dorrit,' answered Rigaud, 'the little niece of Monsieur Frederick, whom I have known across the water, is attached to the prisoner. Miss Dorrit, little niece of Monsieur Frederick, watches at this moment over the prisoner, who is ill. For her I with my own hands left a packet at the prison, on my way here, with a letter of instructions, "for his sake"—she will do anything for his sake—to keep it without breaking the seal, in case of its being reclaimed before the hour of shutting up to-night—if it should not be reclaimed before the ringing of the prison bell, to give it to him; and it encloses a second copy for herself, which he must give to her. What! I don't trust myself among you, now we have got so far, without giving my secret a second life. And as to its not bringing me, elsewhere, the price it will bring here, say then, madame, have you limited and settled the price the little niece will give—for his sake—to hush it up? Once more I say, time presses. The packet not reclaimed before the ringing of the bell to-night, you cannot buy. I sell, then, to the little girl!'

Once more the stir and struggle in her, and she ran to a closet, tore the door open, took down a hood or shawl, and wrapped it over her head. Affery, who had watched her in terror, darted to her in the middle of the room, caught hold of her dress, and went on her knees to her.

'Don't, don't, don't! What are you doing? Where are you going? You're a fearful woman, but I don't bear you no ill-will. I can do poor Arthur no good now, that I see; and you needn't be afraid of me. I'll keep your secret. Don't go out, you'll fall dead in the street. Only promise me, that, if it's the poor thing that's kept here secretly, you'll let me take charge of her and be her nurse. Only promise me that, and never be afraid of me.'

Mrs Clennam stood still for an instant, at the height of her rapid haste, saying in stern amazement:

'Kept here? She has been dead a score of years or more. Ask Flintwinch—ask him. They can both tell you that she died when Arthur went abroad.'

'So much the worse,' said Affery, with a shiver, 'for she haunts the house, then. Who else rustles about it, making signals by dropping dust so softly? Who else comes and goes, and marks the walls with long crooked touches when we are all a-bed? Who else holds the door sometimes? But don't go out—don't go out! Mistress, you'll die in the street!'

Her mistress only disengaged her dress from the beseeching hands, said to Rigaud, 'Wait here till I come back!' and ran out of the room. They saw her, from the window, run wildly through the court-yard and out at the gateway.

For a few moments they stood motionless. Affery was the first to move, and she, wringing her hands, pursued her mistress. Next, Jeremiah Flintwinch, slowly backing to the door, with one hand in a pocket, and the other rubbing his chin, twisted himself out in his reticent way, speechlessly. Rigaud, left alone, composed himself upon the window-seat of the open window, in the old Marseilles-jail attitude. He laid his cigarettes and fire-box ready to his hand, and fell to smoking.

'Whoof! Almost as dull as the infernal old jail. Warmer, but almost as dismal. Wait till she comes back? Yes, certainly; but where is she gone, and how long will she be gone? No matter! Rigaud Lagnier Blandois, my amiable subject, you will get your money. You will enrich yourself. You have lived a gentleman; you will die a gentleman. You triumph, my little boy; but it is your character to triumph. Whoof!'

In the hour of his triumph, his moustache went up and his nose came down, as he ogled a great beam over his head with particular satisfaction.

CHAPTER 31. Closed

The sun had set, and the streets were dim in the dusty twilight, when the figure so long unused to them hurried on its way. In the immediate neighbourhood of the old house it attracted little attention, for there were only a few straggling people to notice it; but, ascending from the river by the crooked ways that led to London Bridge, and passing into the great main road, it became surrounded by astonishment.

Resolute and wild of look, rapid of foot and yet weak and uncertain, conspicuously dressed in its black garments and with its hurried head-covering, gaunt and of an unearthly paleness, it pressed forward, taking no more heed of the throng than a sleep-walker. More remarkable by being so removed from the crowd it was among than if it had been lifted on a pedestal to be seen, the figure attracted all eyes. Saunterers pricked up their attention to observe it; busy people, crossing it, slackened their pace and turned their heads; companions pausing and standing aside, whispered one another to look at this spectral woman who was coming by; and the sweep of the figure as it passed seemed to create a vortex, drawing the most idle and most curious after it.

Made giddy by the turbulent irruption of this multitude of staring faces into her cell of years, by the confusing sensation of being in the air, and the yet more confusing sensation of being afoot, by the unexpected changes in half-remembered objects, and the want of likeness between the controllable pictures her imagination had often drawn of the life from which she was secluded and the overwhelming rush of the reality, she held her way as if she were environed by distracting thoughts, rather than by external humanity and observation. But, having crossed the bridge and gone some distance straight onward, she remembered that she must ask for a direction; and it was only then, when she stopped and turned to look about her for a promising place of inquiry, that she found herself surrounded by an eager glare of faces.

'Why are you encircling me?' she asked, trembling.

None of those who were nearest answered; but from the outer ring there arose a shrill cry of ''Cause you're mad!'

'I am sure as sane as any one here. I want to find the Marshalsea prison.'

The shrill outer circle again retorted, 'Then that 'ud show you was mad if nothing else did, 'cause it's right opposite!'

A short, mild, quiet-looking young man made his way through to her, as a whooping ensued on this reply, and said: 'Was it the Marshalsea you wanted? I'm going on duty there. Come across with me.'

She laid her hand upon his arm, and he took her over the way; the crowd, rather injured by the near prospect of losing her, pressing before and behind and on either side, and recommending an adjournment to Bedlam. After a momentary whirl in the outer court-yard, the prison-door opened, and shut upon them. In the Lodge, which seemed by contrast with the outer noise a place of refuge and peace, a yellow lamp was already striving with the prison shadows.

'Why, John!' said the turnkey who admitted them. 'What is it?'

'Nothing, father; only this lady not knowing her way, and being badgered by the boys. Who did you want, ma'am?'

'Miss Dorrit. Is she here?'

The young man became more interested. 'Yes, she is here. What might your name be?'

'Mrs Clennam.'

'Mr Clennam's mother?' asked the young man.

She pressed her lips together, and hesitated. 'Yes. She had better be told it is his mother.'

'You see,' said the young man, 'the Marshal's family living in the country at present, the Marshal has given Miss Dorrit one of the rooms in his house to use when she likes. Don't you think you had better come up there, and let me bring Miss Dorrit?'

She signified her assent, and he unlocked a door and conducted her up a side staircase into a dwelling-house above. He showed her into a darkening room, and left her. The room looked down into the darkening prison-yard, with its inmates strolling here and there, leaning out of windows communing as much apart as they could with friends who were going away, and generally wearing out their imprisonment as they best might that summer evening. The air was heavy and hot; the closeness of the place, oppressive; and from without there arose a rush of free sounds, like the jarring memory of such things in a headache and heartache. She stood at the window, bewildered, looking down into this prison as it were out of her own different prison, when a soft word or two of surprise made her start, and Little Dorrit stood before her.

'Is it possible, Mrs Clennam, that you are so happily recovered as—'

Little Dorrit stopped, for there was neither happiness nor health in the face that turned to her.

'This is not recovery; it is not strength; I don't know what it is.' With an agitated wave of her hand, she put all that aside. 'You have a packet left with you which you were to give to Arthur, if it was not reclaimed before this place closed to-night.'

'Yes.'

'I reclaim it.'

Little Dorrit took it from her bosom, and gave it into her hand, which remained stretched out after receiving it.

'Have you any idea of its contents?'

Frightened by her being there with that new power Of Movement in her, which, as she said herself, was not strength, and which was unreal to look upon, as though a picture or statue had been animated, Little Dorrit answered 'No.'

'Read them.'

Little Dorrit took the packet from the still outstretched hand, and broke the seal. Mrs

558

Clennam then gave her the inner packet that was addressed to herself, and held the other. The shadow of the wall and of the prison buildings, which made the room sombre at noon, made it too dark to read there, with the dusk deepening apace, save in the window. In the window, where a little of the bright summer evening sky could shine upon her, Little Dorrit stood, and read. After a broken exclamation or so of wonder and of terror, she read in silence. When she had finished, she looked round, and her old mistress bowed herself before her.

'You know, now, what I have done.'

'I think so. I am afraid so; though my mind is so hurried, and so sorry, and has so much to pity that it has not been able to follow all I have read,' said Little Dorrit tremulously.

'I will restore to you what I have withheld from you. Forgive me. Can you forgive me?'

'I can, and Heaven knows I do! Do not kiss my dress and kneel to me; you are too old to kneel to me; I forgive you freely without that.'

'I have more yet to ask.'

'Not in that posture,' said Little Dorrit. 'It is unnatural to see your grey hair lower than mine. Pray rise; let me help you.' With that she raised her up, and stood rather shrinking from her, but looking at her earnestly.

'The great petition that I make to you (there is another which grows out of it), the great supplication that I address to your merciful and gentle heart, is, that you will not disclose this to Arthur until I am dead. If you think, when you have had time for consideration, that it can do him any good to know it while I am yet alive, then tell him. But you will not think that; and in such case, will you promise me to spare me until I am dead?'

'I am so sorry, and what I have read has so confused my thoughts,' returned Little Dorrit, 'that I can scarcely give you a steady answer. If I should be quite sure that to be acquainted with it will do Mr Clennam no good—'

'I know you are attached to him, and will make him the first consideration. It is right that he should be the first consideration. I ask that. But, having regarded him, and still finding that you may spare me for the little time I shall remain on earth, will you do it?'

'I will.'

'GOD bless you!'

She stood in the shadow so that she was only a veiled form to Little Dorrit in the light; but the sound of her voice, in saying those three grateful words, was at once fervent and broken—broken by emotion as unfamiliar to her frozen eyes as action to her frozen limbs.

'You will wonder, perhaps,' she said in a stronger tone, 'that I can better bear to be known to you whom I have wronged, than to the son of my enemy who wronged me.—For she did wrong me! She not only sinned grievously against the Lord, but she wronged me. What Arthur's father was to me, she made him. From our marriage day I was his dread, and that she made me. I was the scourge of both, and that is referable to her. You love Arthur (I can see the blush upon your face; may it be the dawn of happier days to both of you!), and you will have thought already that he is as merciful and kind as you, and why do I not trust myself to him as soon as to you. Have you not thought so?'

'No thought,' said Little Dorrit, 'can be quite a stranger to my heart, that springs out of the knowledge that Mr Clennam is always to be relied upon for being kind and generous and good.'

'I do not doubt it. Yet Arthur is, of the whole world, the one person from whom I would conceal this, while I am in it. I kept over him as a child, in the days of his first remembrance, my restraining and correcting hand. I was stern with him, knowing that the transgressions of the parents are visited on their offspring, and that there was an angry mark upon him at his birth. I have sat with him and his father, seeing the weakness of his father yearning to unbend to him; and forcing it back, that the child might work out his release in bondage and hardship. I have seen him, with his mother's face, looking up at me in awe from his little books, and trying to soften me with his mother's ways that hardened me.'

The shrinking of her auditress stopped her for a moment in her flow of words, delivered in a retrospective gloomy voice.

'For his good. Not for the satisfaction of my injury. What was I, and what was the worth of that, before the curse of Heaven! I have seen that child grow up; not to be pious in a chosen way (his mother's influence lay too heavy on him for that), but still to be just and upright, and to be submissive to me. He never loved me, as I once half-hoped he might—so frail we are, and so do the corrupt affections of the flesh war with our trusts and tasks; but he always respected me and ordered himself dutifully to me. He does to this hour. With an empty place in his heart that he has never known the meaning of, he has turned away from me and gone his separate road; but even that he has done considerately and with deference. These have been his relations towards me. Yours have been of a much slighter kind, spread over a much shorter time. When you have sat at your needle in my room, you have been in fear of me, but you have supposed me to have been doing you a kindness; you are better informed now, and know me to have done you an injury. Your misconstruction and misunderstanding of the cause in which, and the motives with which, I have worked out this work, is lighter to endure than his would be. I would not, for any worldly recompense I can imagine, have him in a moment, however blindly, throw me down from the station I have held before him all his life, and change me altogether into something he would cast out of his respect, and think detected and exposed. Let him do it, if it must be done, when I am not here to see it. Let me never feel, while I am still alive, that I die before his face, and utterly perish away from him, like one consumed by lightning and swallowed by an earthquake.'

Her pride was very strong in her, the pain of it and of her old passions was very sharp with her, when she thus expressed herself. Not less so, when she added:

'Even now, I see you shrink from me, as if I had been cruel.'

Little Dorrit could not gainsay it. She tried not to show it, but she recoiled with dread from the state of mind that had burnt so fiercely and lasted so long. It presented itself to her, with no sophistry upon it, in its own plain nature.

'I have done,' said Mrs Clennam, 'what it was given to me to do. I have set myself against evil; not against good. I have been an instrument of severity against sin. Have not mere sinners like myself been commissioned to lay it low in all time?'

'In all time?' repeated Little Dorrit.

'Even if my own wrong had prevailed with me, and my own vengeance had moved me, could I have found no justification? None in the old days when the innocent perished with the guilty, a thousand to one? When the wrath of the hater of the unrighteous was not slaked even in blood, and yet found favour?'

'O, Mrs Clennam, Mrs Clennam,' said Little Dorrit, 'angry feelings and unforgiving deeds are no comfort and no guide to you and me. My life has been passed in this poor prison, and my teaching has been very defective; but let me implore you to remember later and better days. Be guided only by the healer of the sick, the raiser of the dead, the friend of all who were afflicted and forlorn, the patient Master who shed tears of compassion for our infirmities. We cannot but be right if we put all the rest away, and do everything in remembrance of Him. There is no vengeance and no infliction of suffering in His life, I am sure. There can be no confusion in following Him, and seeking for no other footsteps, I am certain.'

In the softened light of the window, looking from the scene of her early trials to the shining sky, she was not in stronger opposition to the black figure in the shade than the life and doctrine on which she rested were to that figure's history. It bent its head low again, and said not a word. It remained thus, until the first warning bell began to ring.

'Hark!' cried Mrs Clennam starting, 'I said I had another petition. It is one that does not admit of delay. The man who brought you this packet and possesses these proofs, is now waiting at my house to be bought off. I can keep this from Arthur, only by buying him off. He asks a large sum; more than I can get together to pay him without having time. He refuses to make any abatement, because his threat is, that if he fails with me, he will come to you. Will you return with me and show him that you already know it? Will you return with me and try to prevail with him? Will you come and help me with him? Do not refuse what I ask in Arthur's name, though I dare not ask it for Arthur's sake!'

Little Dorrit yielded willingly. She glided away into the prison for a few moments, returned, and said she was ready to go. They went out by another staircase, avoiding the lodge; and coming into the front court-yard, now all quiet and deserted, gained the street.

It was one of those summer evenings when there is no greater darkness than a long twilight. The vista of street and bridge was plain to see, and the sky was serene and beautiful. People stood and sat at their doors, playing with children and enjoying the evening; numbers were walking for air; the worry of the day had almost worried itself out, and few but themselves were hurried. As they crossed the bridge, the clear steeples of the many churches looked as if they had advanced out of the murk that usually enshrouded them, and come much nearer. The smoke that rose into the sky had lost its dingy hue and taken a brightness upon it. The beauties of the sunset had not faded from the long light films of cloud that lay at peace in the horizon. From a radiant centre, over the whole length and breadth of the tranquil firmament, great shoots of light streamed among the early stars, like signs of the blessed later covenant of peace and hope that changed the crown of thorns into a glory.

Less remarkable, now that she was not alone and it was darker, Mrs Clennam hurried on at Little Dorrit's side, unmolested. They left the great thoroughfare at the turning by which she had entered it, and wound their way down among the silent, empty, cross-streets. Their feet were at the gateway, when there was a sudden noise like thunder.

'What was that! Let us make haste in,' cried Mrs Clennam.

They were in the gateway. Little Dorrit, with a piercing cry, held her back.

In one swift instant the old house was before them, with the man lying smoking in the window; another thundering sound, and it heaved, surged outward, opened asunder in fifty places, collapsed, and fell. Deafened by the noise, stifled, choked, and blinded by the dust, they hid their faces and stood rooted to the spot. The dust storm, driving between them and the placid sky, parted for a moment and showed them the stars. As they looked up, wildly crying for help, the great pile of chimneys, which was then alone left standing like a tower in a whirlwind, rocked, broke, and hailed itself down upon the heap of ruin, as if every tumbling fragment were intent on burying the crushed wretch deeper.

So blackened by the flying particles of rubbish as to be unrecognisable, they ran back from the gateway into the street, crying and shrieking. There, Mrs Clennam dropped upon the stones; and she never from that hour moved so much as a finger again, or had the power to speak one word. For upwards of three years she reclined in a wheeled chair, looking attentively at those about her and appearing to understand what they said; but the rigid silence she had so long held was evermore enforced upon her, and except that she could move her eyes and faintly express a negative and affirmative with her head, she lived and died a statue.

Affery had been looking for them at the prison, and had caught sight of them at a distance on the bridge. She came up to receive her old mistress in her arms, to help to carry her into a neighbouring house, and to be faithful to her. The mystery of the noises was out now; Affery, like greater people, had always been right in her facts, and always wrong in the theories she deduced from them.

When the storm of dust had cleared away and the summer night was calm again, numbers of people choked up every avenue of access, and parties of diggers were formed to relieve one another in digging among the ruins. There had been a hundred people in the house at the time of its fall, there had been fifty, there had been fifteen, there had been two. Rumour finally settled the number at two; the foreigner and Mr Flintwinch.

The diggers dug all through the short night by flaring pipes of gas, and on a level with the early sun, and deeper and deeper below it as it rose into its zenith, and aslant of it as it declined, and on a level with it again as it departed. Sturdy digging, and shovelling, and carrying away, in carts, barrows, and baskets, went on without intermission, by night and by day; but it was night for the second time when they found the dirty heap of rubbish that had been the foreigner before his head had been shivered to atoms, like so much glass, by the great beam that lay upon him, crushing him.

Still, they had not come upon Flintwinch yet; so the sturdy digging and shovelling and carrying away went on without intermission by night and by day. It got about that the old house had had famous cellarage (which indeed was true), and that Flintwinch had been in a cellar at the moment, or had had time to escape into one, and that he was safe under its strong arch, and even that he had been heard to cry, in hollow, subterranean, suffocated notes, 'Here I am!' At the opposite extremity of the town it was even known that the excavators had been able to open a communication with him through a pipe, and that he had received both soup and brandy by that channel, and that he had said with admirable fortitude that he was All right, my lads, with the exception of his collar-bone. But the digging and shovelling and carrying away went on without intermission, until the ruins were all dug out, and the cellars opened to the light; and still no Flintwinch, living or dead, all right or all wrong, had been turned up by pick or spade.

It began then to be perceived that Flintwinch had not been there at the time of the fall; and it began then to be perceived that he had been rather busy elsewhere, converting securities into as much money as could be got for them on the shortest notice, and turning to his own exclusive account his authority to act for the Firm. Affery, remembering that the clever one had said he would explain himself further in four-and-twenty hours' time, determined for her part that his taking himself off within that period with all he could get, was the final satisfactory sum and substance of his promised explanation; but she held her peace, devoutly thankful to be quit of him. As it seemed reasonable to conclude that a man who had never been buried could not be unburied, the diggers gave him up when their task was done, and did not dig down for him into the depths of the earth.

This was taken in ill part by a great many people, who persisted in believing that Flintwinch was lying somewhere among the London geological formation. Nor was their belief much shaken by repeated intelligence which came over in course of time, that an old man who wore the tie of his neckcloth under one ear, and who was very well known to be an Englishman, consorted with the Dutchmen on the quaint banks of the canals of the Hague and in the drinking-shops of Amsterdam, under the style and designation of Mynheer von Flyntevynge.

CHAPTER 32. Going

Arthur continuing to lie very ill in the Marshalsea, and Mr Rugg descrying no break in the legal sky affording a hope of his enlargement, Mr Pancks suffered desperately from self-reproaches. If it had not been for those infallible figures which proved that Arthur, instead of pining in imprisonment, ought to be promenading in a carriage and pair, and that Mr Pancks, instead of being restricted to his clerkly wages, ought to have from three to five thousand pounds of his own at his immediate disposal, that unhappy arithmetician would probably have taken to his bed, and there have made one of the many obscure persons who turned their faces to the wall and died, as a last sacrifice to the late Mr Merdle's greatness. Solely supported by his unimpugnable calculations, Mr Pancks led an unhappy and restless life; constantly carrying his figures about with him in his hat, and not only going over them himself on every possible occasion, but entreating every human being he could lay hold of to go over them with him, and observe what a clear case it was. Down in Bleeding Heart Yard there was scarcely an inhabitant of note to whom Mr Pancks had not imparted his demonstration, and, as figures are catching, a kind of cyphering measles broke out in that locality, under the influence of which the whole Yard was light-headed.

The more restless Mr Pancks grew in his mind, the more impatient he became of the Patriarch. In their later conferences his snorting assumed an irritable sound which boded the Patriarch no good; likewise, Mr Pancks had on several occasions looked harder at the Patriarchal bumps than was quite reconcilable with the fact of his not being a painter, or a peruke-maker in search of the living model.

However, he steamed in and out of his little back Dock according as he was wanted or not wanted in the Patriarchal presence, and business had gone on in its customary course. Bleeding Heart Yard had been harrowed by Mr Pancks, and cropped by Mr Casby, at the regular seasons; Mr Pancks had taken all the drudgery and all the dirt of the business as his share; Mr Casby had taken all the profits, all the ethereal vapour, and all the moonshine, as his share; and, in the form of words which that benevolent beamer generally employed on Saturday evenings, when he twirled his fat thumbs after striking the week's balance, 'everything had been satisfactory to all parties—all parties—satisfactory, sir, to all parties.'

The Dock of the Steam-Tug, Pancks, had a leaden roof, which, frying in the very hot sunshine, may have heated the vessel. Be that as it may, one glowing Saturday evening, on being hailed by the lumbering bottle-green ship, the Tug instantly came working out of the Dock in a highly heated condition.

'Mr Pancks,' was the Patriarchal remark, 'you have been remiss, you have been remiss, sir.'

'What do you mean by that?' was the short rejoinder.

The Patriarchal state, always a state of calmness and composure, was so particularly serene that evening as to be provoking. Everybody else within the bills of mortality was hot; but the Patriarch was perfectly cool. Everybody was thirsty, and the Patriarch was drinking. There was a fragrance of limes or lemons about him; and he made a drink of golden sherry, which shone in a large tumbler as if he were drinking the evening sunshine. This was bad, but not the worst. The worst was, that with his big blue eyes, and his polished head, and his long white hair, and his bottle-green legs stretched out before him, terminating in his easy shoes easily crossed at the instep, he had a radiant appearance of having in his extensive benevolence made the drink for the human species, while he himself wanted nothing but his own milk of human kindness.

Wherefore, Mr Pancks said, 'What do you mean by that?' and put his hair up with both hands, in a highly portentous manner.

'I mean, Mr Pancks, that you must be sharper with the people, sharper with the people, much sharper with the people, sir. You don't squeeze them. You don't squeeze them. Your receipts are not up to the mark. You must squeeze them, sir, or our connection will not continue to be as satisfactory as I could wish it to be to all parties. All parties.'

'Don't I squeeze 'em?' retorted Mr Pancks. 'What else am I made for?'

'You are made for nothing else, Mr Pancks. You are made to do your duty, but you don't do your duty. You are paid to squeeze, and you must squeeze to pay.' The Patriarch so much surprised himself by this brilliant turn, after Dr Johnson, which he had not in the least expected or intended, that he laughed aloud; and repeated with great satisfaction, as he twirled his thumbs and nodded at his youthful portrait, 'Paid to squeeze, sir, and must squeeze to pay.'

'Oh,' said Pancks. 'Anything more?'

'Yes, sir, yes, sir. Something more. You will please, Mr Pancks, to squeeze the Yard again, the first thing on Monday morning.'

'Oh!' said Pancks. 'Ain't that too soon? I squeezed it dry to-day.'

'Nonsense, sir. Not near the mark, not near the mark.'

'Oh!' said Pancks, watching him as he benevolently gulped down a good draught of his mixture. 'Anything more?'

'Yes, sir, yes, sir, something more. I am not at all pleased, Mr Pancks, with my daughter; not at all pleased. Besides calling much too often to inquire for Mrs Clennam, Mrs Clennam, who is not just now in circumstances that are by any means calculated to—to be satisfactory to all parties, she goes, Mr Pancks, unless I am much deceived, to inquire for Mr Clennam in jail. In jail.'

'He's laid up, you know,' said Pancks. 'Perhaps it's kind.'

'Pooh, pooh, Mr Pancks. She has nothing to do with that, nothing to do with that. I can't allow it. Let him pay his debts and come out, come out; pay his debts, and come out.'

Although Mr Pancks's hair was standing up like strong wire, he gave it another double-handed impulse in the perpendicular direction, and smiled at his proprietor in a most hideous manner.

'You will please to mention to my daughter, Mr Pancks, that I can't allow it, can't allow it,' said the Patriarch blandly.

'Oh!' said Pancks. 'You couldn't mention it yourself?'

'No, sir, no; you are paid to mention it,' the blundering old booby could not resist the temptation of trying it again, 'and you must mention it to pay, mention it to pay.'

'Oh!' said Pancks. 'Anything more?'

'Yes, sir. It appears to me, Mr Pancks, that you yourself are too often and too much in that direction, that direction. I recommend you, Mr Pancks, to dismiss from your attention both your own losses and other people's losses, and to mind your business, mind your business.'

Mr Pancks acknowledged this recommendation with such an extraordinarily abrupt, short, and loud utterance of the monosyllable 'Oh!' that even the unwieldy Patriarch moved his blue eyes in something of a hurry, to look at him. Mr Pancks, with a sniff of corresponding intensity, then added, 'Anything more?'

'Not at present, sir, not at present. I am going,' said the Patriarch, finishing his mixture, and rising with an amiable air, 'to take a little stroll, a little stroll. Perhaps I shall find you here when I come back. If not, sir, duty, duty; squeeze, squeeze, squeeze, on Monday; squeeze on Monday!'

Mr Pancks, after another stiffening of his hair, looked on at the Patriarchal assumption of the broad-brimmed hat, with a momentary appearance of indecision contending with a sense of injury. He was also hotter than at first, and breathed harder. But he suffered Mr Casby to go out, without offering any further remark, and then took a peep at him over the little green window-blinds. 'I thought so,' he observed. 'I knew where you were bound to. Good!' He then steamed back to his Dock, put it carefully in order, took down his hat, looked round the Dock, said 'Good-bye!' and puffed away on his own account. He steered straight for Mrs Plornish's end of Bleeding Heart Yard, and arrived there, at the top of the steps, hotter than ever.

At the top of the steps, resisting Mrs Plornish's invitations to come and sit along with father in Happy Cottage—which to his relief were not so numerous as they would have been on any other night than Saturday, when the connection who so gallantly supported the business with everything but money gave their orders freely—at the top of the steps Mr Pancks remained until he beheld the Patriarch, who always entered the Yard at the other end, slowly advancing, beaming, and surrounded by suitors. Then Mr Pancks descended and bore down upon him, with his utmost pressure of steam on.

The Patriarch, approaching with his usual benignity, was surprised to see Mr Pancks, but supposed him to have been stimulated to an immediate squeeze instead of postponing that operation until Monday. The population of the Yard were astonished at the meeting, for the two powers had never been seen there together, within the memory of the oldest Bleeding Heart. But they were overcome by unutterable amazement when Mr Pancks, going close up to the most venerable of men and halting in front of the bottle-green waistcoat, made a trigger of his right thumb and forefinger, applied the same to the brim of the broad-brimmed hat, and, with singular smartness and precision, shot it off the polished head as if it had been a large marble.

Having taken this little liberty with the Patriarchal person, Mr Pancks further astounded and attracted the Bleeding Hearts by saying in an audible voice, 'Now, you sugary swindler, I mean to have it out with you!'

Mr Pancks and the Patriarch were instantly the centre of a press, all eyes and ears; windows were thrown open, and door-steps were thronged.

'What do you pretend to be?' said Mr Pancks. 'What's your moral game? What do you go in for? Benevolence, an't it? You benevolent!' Here Mr Pancks, apparently without the intention of hitting him, but merely to relieve his mind and expend his superfluous power in wholesome exercise, aimed a blow at the bumpy head, which the bumpy head ducked to avoid. This singular performance was repeated, to the ever-increasing admiration of the spectators, at the end of every succeeding article of Mr Pancks's oration.

'I have discharged myself from your service,' said Pancks, 'that I may tell you what you are. You're one of a lot of impostors that are the worst lot of all the lots to be met with. Speaking as a sufferer by both, I don't know that I wouldn't as soon have the Merdle lot as your lot. You're a driver in disguise, a screwer by deputy, a wringer, and squeezer, and shaver by substitute. You're a philanthropic sneak. You're a shabby deceiver!'

(The repetition of the performance at this point was received with a burst of laughter.)

'Ask these good people who's the hard man here. They'll tell you Pancks, I believe.'

This was confirmed with cries of 'Certainly,' and 'Hear!'

'But I tell you, good people—Casby! This mound of meekness, this lump of love, this bottle-green smiler, this is your driver!' said Pancks. 'If you want to see the man who would flay you alive—here he is! Don't look for him in me, at thirty shillings a week, but look for him in Casby, at I don't know how much a year!'

'Good!' cried several voices. 'Hear Mr Pancks!'

'Hear Mr Pancks?' cried that gentleman (after repeating the popular performance). 'Yes, I should think so! It's almost time to hear Mr Pancks. Mr Pancks has come down into the Yard to-night on purpose that you should hear him. Pancks is only the Works; but here's the Winder!'

The audience would have gone over to Mr Pancks, as one man, woman, and child, but for the long, grey, silken locks, and the broad-brimmed hat.

'Here's the Stop,' said Pancks, 'that sets the tune to be ground. And there is but one tune, and its name is Grind, Grind, Grind! Here's the Proprietor, and here's his Grubber. Why, good people, when he comes smoothly spinning through the Yard to-night, like a slow-going benevolent Humming-Top, and when you come about him with your complaints of the Grubber, you don't know what a cheat the Proprietor is! What do you think of his showing himself to-night, that I may have all the blame on Monday? What do you think of his having had me over the coals this very evening, because I don't squeeze you enough? What do you think of my being, at the present moment, under special orders to squeeze you dry on Monday?'

The reply was given in a murmur of 'Shame!' and 'Shabby!'

'Shabby?' snorted Pancks. 'Yes, I should think so! The lot that your Casby belongs to, is the shabbiest of all the lots. Setting their Grubbers on, at a wretched pittance, to do what they're ashamed and afraid to do and pretend not to do, but what they will have done, or give a man no rest! Imposing on you to give their Grubbers nothing but blame, and to give them nothing but credit! Why, the worst-looking cheat in all this town who gets the value of eighteenpence under false pretences, an't half such a cheat as this sign-post of The Casby's Head here!'

Cries of 'That's true!' and 'No more he an't!'

'And see what you get of these fellows, besides,' said Pancks. 'See what more you get of these precious Humming-Tops, revolving among you with such smoothness that you've no idea of the pattern painted on 'em, or the little window in 'em. I wish to call your attention to myself for a moment. I an't an agreeable style of chap, I know that very well.'

The auditory were divided on this point; its more uncompromising members crying, 'No, you are not,' and its politer materials, 'Yes, you are.'

'I am, in general,' said Mr Pancks, 'a dry, uncomfortable, dreary Plodder and Grubber. That's your humble servant. There's his full-length portrait, painted by himself and presented to you, warranted a likeness! But what's a man to be, with such a man as this for his Proprietor? What can be expected of him? Did anybody ever find boiled mutton and caper-sauce growing in a cocoa-nut?'

None of the Bleeding Hearts ever had, it was clear from the alacrity of their response.

'Well,' said Mr Pancks, 'and neither will you find in Grubbers like myself, under Proprietors like this, pleasant qualities. I've been a Grubber from a boy. What has my life been? Fag and grind, fag and grind, turn the wheel, turn the wheel! I haven't been agreeable to myself, and I haven't been likely to be agreeable to anybody else. If I was a shilling a week less useful in ten years' time, this impostor would give me a shilling a week less; if as useful a man could be got at sixpence cheaper, he would be taken in my place at sixpence cheaper. Bargain and sale, bless you! Fixed principles! It's a mighty fine sign-post, is The Casby's Head,' said Mr Pancks, surveying it with anything rather than admiration; 'but the real name of the House is the Sham's Arms. Its motto is, Keep the Grubber always at it. Is any gentleman present,' said Mr Pancks, breaking off and looking round, 'acquainted with the English Grammar?'

Bleeding Heart Yard was shy of claiming that acquaintance.

'It's no matter,' said Mr Pancks, 'I merely wish to remark that the task this Proprietor has set me, has been never to leave off conjugating the Imperative Mood Present Tense of the verb To keep always at it. Keep thou always at it. Let him keep always at it. Keep we or do we keep always at it. Keep ye or do ye or you keep always at it. Let them keep always at it. Here is your benevolent Patriarch of a Casby, and there is his golden rule. He is uncommonly improving to look at, and I am not at all so. He is as sweet as honey, and I am as dull as ditch-water. He provides the pitch, and I handle it, and it sticks to me. Now,' said Mr Pancks, closing upon his late Proprietor again, from whom he had withdrawn a little for the better display of him to the Yard; 'as I am not accustomed to speak in public, and as I have made a rather lengthy speech, all circumstances considered, I shall bring my observations to a close by requesting you to get out of this.'

The Last of the Patriarchs had been so seized by assault, and required so much room to catch an idea in, an so much more room to turn it in, that he had not a word to offer in reply. He appeared to be meditating some Patriarchal way out of his delicate position, when Mr Pancks, once more suddenly applying the trigger to his hat, shot it off again with his former dexterity. On the preceding occasion, one or two of the Bleeding Heart Yarders had obsequiously picked it up and handed it to its owner; but Mr Pancks had now so far impressed his audience, that the Patriarch had to turn and stoop for it himself.

Quick as lightning, Mr Pancks, who, for some moments, had had his right hand in his coat pocket, whipped out a pair of shears, swooped upon the Patriarch behind, and snipped off short the sacred locks that flowed upon his shoulders. In a paroxysm of animosity and rapidity, Mr Pancks then caught the broad-brimmed hat out of the astounded Patriarch's hand, cut it down into a mere stewpan, and fixed it on the Patriarch's head.

Before the frightful results of this desperate action, Mr Pancks himself recoiled in consternation. A bare-polled, goggle-eyed, big-headed lumbering personage stood staring at him, not in the least impressive, not in the least venerable, who seemed to have started out of the earth to ask what was become of Casby. After staring at this phantom in return, in silent awe, Mr Pancks threw down his shears, and fled for a place of hiding, where he might lie sheltered from the consequences of his crime. Mr Pancks deemed it prudent to use all possible despatch in making off, though he was pursued by nothing but the sound of laughter in Bleeding Heart Yard, rippling through the air and making it ring again.

CHAPTER 33. Going!

The changes of a fevered room are slow and fluctuating; but the changes of the fevered world are rapid and irrevocable.

It was Little Dorrit's lot to wait upon both kinds of change. The Marshalsea walls, during a portion of every day, again embraced her in their shadows as their child, while she thought for Clennam, worked for him, watched him, and only left him, still to devote her utmost love and care to him. Her part in the life outside the gate urged its pressing claims upon her too, and her patience untiringly responded to them. Here was Fanny, proud, fitful, whimsical, further advanced in that disqualified state for going into society which had so much fretted her on the evening of the tortoise-shell knife, resolved always to want comfort, resolved not to be comforted, resolved to be deeply wronged, and resolved that nobody should have the audacity to think her so. Here was her brother, a weak, proud, tipsy, young old man, shaking from head to foot, talking as indistinctly as if some of the money he plumed himself upon had got into his mouth and couldn't be got out, unable to walk alone in any act of his life, and patronising the sister whom he selfishly loved (he always had that negative merit, ill-starred and ill-launched Tip!) because he suffered her to lead him. Here was Mrs Merdle in gauzy mourning—the original cap whereof had possibly been rent to pieces in a fit of grief, but had certainly yielded to a highly becoming article from the Parisian market—warring with Fanny foot to foot, and breasting her with her desolate bosom every hour in the day. Here was poor Mr Sparkler, not knowing how to keep the peace between them, but humbly inclining to the opinion that they could do no better than agree that they were both remarkably fine women, and that there was no nonsense about either of them—for which gentle recommendation they united in falling upon him frightfully. Then, too, here was Mrs General, got home from foreign parts, sending a Prune and a Prism by post every other day, demanding a new Testimonial by way of recommendation to some vacant appointment or other. Of which remarkable gentlewoman it may be finally observed, that there surely never was a gentlewoman of whose transcendent fitness for any vacant appointment on the face of this earth, so many people were (as the warmth of her Testimonials evinced) so perfectly satisfied—or who was so very unfortunate in having a large circle of ardent and distinguished admirers, who never themselves happened to want her in any capacity.

On the first crash of the eminent Mr Merdle's decease, many important persons had been unable to determine whether they should cut Mrs Merdle, or comfort her. As it seemed, however, essential to the strength of their own case that they should admit her to have been cruelly deceived, they graciously made the admission, and continued to know her. It followed that Mrs Merdle, as a woman of fashion and good breeding who had been sacrificed to the wiles of a vulgar barbarian (for Mr Merdle was found out from the crown of his head to the sole of his foot, the moment he was found out in his pocket), must be actively championed by her order for her order's sake. She returned this fealty by causing it to be understood that she was even more incensed against the felonious shade of the deceased than anybody else was; thus, on the whole, she came out of her furnace like a wise woman, and did exceedingly well.

Mr Sparkler's lordship was fortunately one of those shelves on which a gentleman is considered to be put away for life, unless there should be reasons for hoisting him up with the Barnacle crane to a more lucrative height. That patriotic servant accordingly stuck to his colours (the Standard of four Quarterings), and was a perfect Nelson in respect of nailing them to the mast. On the profits of his intrepidity, Mrs Sparkler and Mrs Merdle, inhabiting different floors of the genteel little temple of inconvenience to which the smell of the day before yesterday's soup and coach-horses was as constant as Death to man, arrayed themselves to fight it out in the lists of Society, sworn rivals. And Little Dorrit, seeing all these things as they developed themselves, could not but wonder, anxiously, into what back corner of the genteel establishment Fanny's children would be poked by-and-by, and who would take care of those unborn little victims.

Arthur being far too ill to be spoken with on subjects of emotion or anxiety, and his recovery greatly depending on the repose into which his weakness could be hushed, Little Dorrit's sole reliance during this heavy period was on Mr Meagles. He was still abroad; but she had written to him through his daughter, immediately after first seeing Arthur in the Marshalsea and since, confiding her uneasiness to him on the points on which she was most anxious, but especially on one. To that one, the continued absence of Mr Meagles abroad, instead of his comforting presence in the Marshalsea, was referable.

Without disclosing the precise nature of the documents that had fallen into Rigaud's hands, Little Dorrit had confided the general outline of that story to Mr Meagles, to whom she had also recounted his fate. The old cautious habits of the scales and scoop at once showed

Mr Meagles the importance of recovering the original papers; wherefore he wrote back to Little Dorrit, strongly confirming her in the solicitude she expressed on that head, and adding that he would not come over to England 'without making some attempt to trace them out.'

By this time Mr Henry Gowan had made up his mind that it would be agreeable to him not to know the Meagleses. He was so considerate as to lay no injunctions on his wife in that particular; but he mentioned to Mr Meagles that personally they did not appear to him to get on together, and that he thought it would be a good thing if—politely, and without any scene, or anything of that sort—they agreed that they were the best fellows in the world, but were best apart. Poor Mr Meagles, who was already sensible that he did not advance his daughter's happiness by being constantly slighted in her presence, said 'Good, Henry! You are my Pet's husband; you have displaced me, in the course of nature; if you wish it, good!' This arrangement involved the contingent advantage, which perhaps Henry Gowan had not foreseen, that both Mr and Mrs Meagles were more liberal than before to their daughter, when their communication was only with her and her young child: and that his high spirit found itself better provided with money, without being under the degrading necessity of knowing whence it came.

Mr Meagles, at such a period, naturally seized an occupation with great ardour. He knew from his daughter the various towns which Rigaud had been haunting, and the various hotels at which he had been living for some time back. The occupation he set himself was to visit these with all discretion and speed, and, in the event of finding anywhere that he had left a bill unpaid, and a box or parcel behind, to pay such bill, and bring away such box or parcel.

With no other attendant than Mother, Mr Meagles went upon his pilgrimage, and encountered a number of adventures. Not the least of his difficulties was, that he never knew what was said to him, and that he pursued his inquiries among people who never knew what he said to them. Still, with an unshaken confidence that the English tongue was somehow the mother tongue of the whole world, only the people were too stupid to know it, Mr Meagles harangued innkeepers in the most voluble manner, entered into loud explanations of the most complicated sort, and utterly renounced replies in the native language of the respondents, on the ground that they were 'all bosh.' Sometimes interpreters were called in; whom Mr Meagles addressed in such idiomatic terms of speech, as instantly to extinguish and shut up—which made the matter worse. On a balance of the account, however, it may be doubted whether he lost much; for, although he found no property, he found so many debts and various associations of discredit with the proper name, which was the only word he made intelligible, that he was almost everywhere overwhelmed with injurious accusations. On no fewer than four occasions the police were called in to receive denunciations of Mr Meagles as a Knight of Industry, a good-for-nothing, and a thief, all of which opprobrious language he bore with the best temper (having no idea what it meant), and was in the most ignominious manner escorted to steam-boats and public carriages, to be got rid of, talking all the while, like a cheerful and fluent Briton as he was, with Mother under his arm.

But, in his own tongue, and in his own head, Mr Meagles was a clear, shrewd, persevering man. When he had 'worked round,' as he called it, to Paris in his pilgrimage, and had wholly failed in it so far, he was not disheartened. 'The nearer to England I follow him, you see, Mother,' argued Mr Meagles, 'the nearer I am likely to come to the papers, whether they turn up or no. Because it is only reasonable to conclude that he would deposit them somewhere

where they would be safe from people over in England, and where they would yet be accessible to himself, don't you see?'

At Paris Mr Meagles found a letter from Little Dorrit, lying waiting for him; in which she mentioned that she had been able to talk for a minute or two with Mr Clennam about this man who was no more; and that when she told Mr Clennam that his friend Mr Meagles, who was on his way to see him, had an interest in ascertaining something about the man if he could, he had asked her to tell Mr Meagles that he had been known to Miss Wade, then living in such a street at Calais. 'Oho!' said Mr Meagles.

As soon afterwards as might be in those Diligence days, Mr Meagles rang the cracked bell at the cracked gate, and it jarred open, and the peasant-woman stood in the dark doorway, saying, 'Ice-say! Seer! Who?' In acknowledgment of whose address, Mr Meagles murmured to himself that there was some sense about these Calais people, who really did know something of what you and themselves were up to; and returned, 'Miss Wade, my dear.' He was then shown into the presence of Miss Wade.

'It's some time since we met,' said Mr Meagles, clearing his throat; 'I hope you have been pretty well, Miss Wade?'

Without hoping that he or anybody else had been pretty well, Miss Wade asked him to what she was indebted for the honour of seeing him again? Mr Meagles, in the meanwhile, glanced all round the room without observing anything in the shape of a box.

'Why, the truth is, Miss Wade,' said Mr Meagles, in a comfortable, managing, not to say coaxing voice, 'it is possible that you may be able to throw a light upon a little something that is at present dark. Any unpleasant bygones between us are bygones, I hope. Can't be helped now. You recollect my daughter? Time changes so! A mother!'

In his innocence, Mr Meagles could not have struck a worse key-note. He paused for any expression of interest, but paused in vain.

'That is not the subject you wished to enter on?' she said, after a cold silence.

'No, no,' returned Mr Meagles. 'No. I thought your good nature might—'

'I thought you knew,' she interrupted, with a smile, 'that my good nature is not to be calculated upon?'

'Don't say so,' said Mr Meagles; 'you do yourself an injustice. However, to come to the point.' For he was sensible of having gained nothing by approaching it in a roundabout way. 'I have heard from my friend Clennam, who, you will be sorry to hear, has been and still is very ill—'

He paused again, and again she was silent.

'—that you had some knowledge of one Blandois, lately killed in London by a violent accident. Now, don't mistake me! I know it was a slight knowledge,' said Mr Meagles, dexterously forestalling an angry interruption which he saw about to break. 'I am fully aware of that. It was a slight knowledge, I know. But the question is,' Mr Meagles's voice here became comfortable again, 'did he, on his way to England last time, leave a box of papers, or a bundle of papers, or some papers or other in some receptacle or other—any papers—with you: begging you to allow him to leave them here for a short time, until he wanted them?'

'The question is?' she repeated. 'Whose question is?'

'Mine,' said Mr Meagles. 'And not only mine but Clennam's question, and other people's question. Now, I am sure,' continued Mr Meagles, whose heart was overflowing with Pet, 'that you can't have any unkind feeling towards my daughter; it's impossible. Well! It's her question, too; being one in which a particular friend of hers is nearly interested. So here I am, frankly to say that is the question, and to ask, Now, did he?'

'Upon my word,' she returned, 'I seem to be a mark for everybody who knew anything of a man I once in my life hired, and paid, and dismissed, to aim their questions at!'

'Now, don't,' remonstrated Mr Meagles, 'don't! Don't take offence, because it's the plainest question in the world, and might be asked of any one. The documents I refer to were not his own, were wrongfully obtained, might at some time or other be troublesome to an innocent person to have in keeping, and are sought by the people to whom they really belong. He passed through Calais going to London, and there were reasons why he should not take them with him then, why he should wish to be able to put his hand upon them readily, and why he should distrust leaving them with people of his own sort. Did he leave them here? I declare if I knew how to avoid giving you offence, I would take any pains to do it. I put the question personally, but there's nothing personal in it. I might put it to any one; I have put it already to many people. Did he leave them here? Did he leave anything here?'

'No.'

'Then unfortunately, Miss Wade, you know nothing about them?'

'I know nothing about them. I have now answered your unaccountable question. He did not leave them here, and I know nothing about them.'

'There!' said Mr Meagles rising. 'I am sorry for it; that's over; and I hope there is not much harm done.—Tattycoram well, Miss Wade?'

'Harriet well? O yes!'

'I have put my foot in it again,' said Mr Meagles, thus corrected. 'I can't keep my foot out of it here, it seems. Perhaps, if I had thought twice about it, I might never have given her the jingling name. But, when one means to be good-natured and sportive with young people, one doesn't think twice. Her old friend leaves a kind word for her, Miss Wade, if you should think proper to deliver it.'

She said nothing as to that; and Mr Meagles, taking his honest face out of the dull room, where it shone like a sun, took it to the Hotel where he had left Mrs Meagles, and where he made the Report: 'Beaten, Mother; no effects!' He took it next to the London Steam Packet, which sailed in the night; and next to the Marshalsea.

The faithful John was on duty when Father and Mother Meagles presented themselves at the wicket towards nightfall. Miss Dorrit was not there then, he said; but she had been there in the morning, and invariably came in the evening. Mr Clennam was slowly mending; and Maggy and Mrs Plornish and Mr Baptist took care of him by turns. Miss Dorrit was sure to come back that evening before the bell rang. There was the room the Marshal had lent her, up-stairs, in which they could wait for her, if they pleased. Mistrustful that it might be hazardous to Arthur to see him without preparation, Mr Meagles accepted the offer; and they were left shut up in the room, looking down through its barred window into the jail.

The cramped area of the prison had such an effect on Mrs Meagles that she began to weep, and such an effect on Mr Meagles that he began to gasp for air. He was walking up and down the room, panting, and making himself worse by laboriously fanning himself with her handkerchief, when he turned towards the opening door.

'Eh? Good gracious!' said Mr Meagles, 'this is not Miss Dorrit! Why, Mother, look! Tattycoram!'

No other. And in Tattycoram's arms was an iron box some two feet square. Such a box had Affery Flintwinch seen, in the first of her dreams, going out of the old house in the dead of the night under Double's arm. This, Tattycoram put on the ground at her old master's feet: this, Tattycoram fell on her knees by, and beat her hands upon, crying half in exultation and half in despair, half in laughter and half in tears, 'Pardon, dear Master; take me back, dear Mistress; here it is!'

'Tatty!' exclaimed Mr Meagles.

'What you wanted!' said Tattycoram. 'Here it is! I was put in the next room not to see you. I heard you ask her about it, I heard her say she hadn't got it, I was there when he left it, and I took it at bedtime and brought it away. Here it is!'

'Why, my girl,' cried Mr Meagles, more breathless than before, 'how did you come over?'

'I came in the boat with you. I was sitting wrapped up at the other end. When you took a coach at the wharf, I took another coach and followed you here. She never would have given it up after what you had said to her about its being wanted; she would sooner have sunk it in the sea, or burnt it. But, here it is!'

The glow and rapture that the girl was in, with her 'Here it is!'

'She never wanted it to be left, I must say that for her; but he left it, and I knew well that after what you said, and after her denying it, she never would have given it up. But here it is! Dear Master, dear Mistress, take me back again, and give me back the dear old name! Let this intercede for me. Here it is!'

Father and Mother Meagles never deserved their names better than when they took the headstrong foundling-girl into their protection again.

'Oh! I have been so wretched,' cried Tattycoram, weeping much more, 'always so unhappy, and so repentant! I was afraid of her from the first time I saw her. I knew she had got a power over me through understanding what was bad in me so well. It was a madness in me, and she could raise it whenever she liked. I used to think, when I got into that state, that people were all against me because of my first beginning; and the kinder they were to me, the worse fault I found in them. I made it out that they triumphed above me, and that they wanted to make me envy them, when I know—when I even knew then—that they never thought of such a thing. And my beautiful young mistress not so happy as she ought to have been, and I gone away from her! Such a brute and a wretch as she must think me! But you'll say a word to her for me, and ask her to be as forgiving as you two are? For I am not so bad as I was,' pleaded Tattycoram; 'I am bad enough, but not so bad as I was, indeed. I have had Miss Wade before me all this time, as if it was my own self grown ripe—turning everything the wrong way, and twisting all good into evil. I have had her before me all this time, finding no pleasure in anything but keeping me as miserable, suspicious, and tormenting as herself. Not that she had much to do, to do that,' cried Tattycoram, in a closing great burst of distress, 'for I was as bad as bad could be. I only mean to say, that, after what I have gone through, I hope I shall never be quite so bad again, and that I shall get better by very slow degrees. I'll try very hard. I won't stop at five-and-twenty, sir, I'll count five-and-twenty hundred, five-and-twenty thousand!'

Another opening of the door, and Tattycoram subsided, and Little Dorrit came in, and Mr Meagles with pride and joy produced the box, and her gentle face was lighted up with grateful happiness and joy. The secret was safe now! She could keep her own part of it from him; he should never know of her loss; in time to come he should know all that was of import to himself; but he should never know what concerned her only. That was all passed, all forgiven, all forgotten.

'Now, my dear Miss Dorrit,' said Mr Meagles; 'I am a man of business—or at least was—and I am going to take my measures promptly, in that character. Had I better see Arthur to-night?'

'I think not to-night. I will go to his room and ascertain how he is. But I think it will be better not to see him to-night.'

'I am much of your opinion, my dear,' said Mr Meagles, 'and therefore I have not been any nearer to him than this dismal room. Then I shall probably not see him for some little time to come. But I'll explain what I mean when you come back.'

She left the room. Mr Meagles, looking through the bars of the window, saw her pass out of the Lodge below him into the prison-yard. He said gently, 'Tattycoram, come to me a moment, my good girl.'

She went up to the window.

'You see that young lady who was here just now—that little, quiet, fragile figure passing along there, Tatty? Look. The people stand out of the way to let her go by. The men—see the poor, shabby fellows—pull off their hats to her quite politely, and now she glides in at that doorway. See her, Tattycoram?'

'Yes, sir.'

'I have heard tell, Tatty, that she was once regularly called the child of this place. She was born here, and lived here many years. I can't breathe here. A doleful place to be born and bred in, Tattycoram?'

'Yes indeed, sir!'

'If she had constantly thought of herself, and settled with herself that everybody visited this place upon her, turned it against her, and cast it at her, she would have led an irritable and probably an useless existence. Yet I have heard tell, Tattycoram, that her young life has been one of active resignation, goodness, and noble service. Shall I tell you what I consider those eyes of hers, that were here just now, to have always looked at, to get that expression?'

'Yes, if you please, sir.'

'Duty, Tattycoram. Begin it early, and do it well; and there is no antecedent to it, in any origin or station, that will tell against us with the Almighty, or with ourselves.'

They remained at the window, Mother joining them and pitying the prisoners, until she was seen coming back. She was soon in the room, and recommended that Arthur, whom she had left calm and composed, should not be visited that night.

'Good!' said Mr Meagles, cheerily. 'I have not a doubt that's best. I shall trust my remembrances then, my sweet nurse, in your hands, and I well know they couldn't be in better. I am off again to-morrow morning.'

Little Dorrit, surprised, asked him where?

'My dear,' said Mr Meagles, 'I can't live without breathing. This place has taken my breath away, and I shall never get it back again until Arthur is out of this place.'

'How is that a reason for going off again to-morrow morning?'

'You shall understand,' said Mr Meagles. 'To-night we three will put up at a City Hotel. To-morrow morning, Mother and Tattycoram will go down to Twickenham, where Mrs Tickit, sitting attended by Dr Buchan in the parlour-window, will think them a couple of ghosts; and I shall go abroad again for Doyce. We must have Dan here. Now, I tell you, my love, it's of no use writing and planning and conditionally speculating upon this and that and the other, at uncertain intervals and distances; we must have Doyce here. I devote myself at daybreak to-morrow morning, to bringing Doyce here. It's nothing to me to go and find him. I'm an old traveller, and all foreign languages and customs are alike to me—I never understand anything about any of 'em. Therefore I can't be put to any inconvenience. Go at once I must, it stands to reason; because I can't live without breathing freely; and I can't breathe freely until Arthur is out of this Marshalsea. I am stifled at the present moment, and have scarcely breath enough to say this much, and to carry this precious box down-stairs for you.'

They got into the street as the bell began to ring, Mr Meagles carrying the box. Little Dorrit had no conveyance there: which rather surprised him. He called a coach for her and she got into it, and he placed the box beside her when she was seated. In her joy and gratitude she kissed his hand.

'I don't like that, my dear,' said Mr Meagles. 'It goes against my feeling of what's right, that you should do homage to me—at the Marshalsea Gate.'

She bent forward, and kissed his cheek.

'You remind me of the days,' said Mr Meagles, suddenly drooping—'but she's very fond of him, and hides his faults, and thinks that no one sees them—and he certainly is well connected and of a very good family!'

It was the only comfort he had in the loss of his daughter, and if he made the most of it, who could blame him?

CHAPTER 34. Gone

On a healthy autumn day, the Marshalsea prisoner, weak but otherwise restored, sat listening to a voice that read to him. On a healthy autumn day; when the golden fields had been reaped and ploughed again, when the summer fruits had ripened and waned, when the green perspectives of hops had been laid low by the busy pickers, when the apples clustering in the orchards were russet, and the berries of the mountain ash were crimson among the yellowing foliage. Already in the woods, glimpses of the hardy winter that was coming were to be caught through unaccustomed openings among the boughs where the prospect shone defined and clear, free from the bloom of the drowsy summer weather, which had rested on it as the bloom lies on the plum. So, from the seashore the ocean was no longer to be seen lying asleep in the heat, but its thousand sparkling eyes were open, and its whole breadth was in joyful animation, from the cool sand on the beach to the little sails on the horizon, drifting away like autumn-tinted leaves that had drifted from the trees.

Changeless and barren, looking ignorantly at all the seasons with its fixed, pinched face of poverty and care, the prison had not a touch of any of these beauties on it. Blossom what would, its bricks and bars bore uniformly the same dead crop. Yet Clennam, listening to the voice as it read to him, heard in it all that great Nature was doing, heard in it all the soothing songs she sings to man. At no Mother's knee but hers had he ever dwelt in his youth on hopeful promises, on playful fancies, on the harvests of tenderness and humility that lie hidden in the early-fostered seeds of the imagination; on the oaks of retreat from blighting winds, that have the germs of their strong roots in nursery acorns. But, in the tones of the voice that read to him, there were memories of an old feeling of such things, and echoes of every merciful and loving whisper that had ever stolen to him in his life.

When the voice stopped, he put his hand over his eyes, murmuring that the light was strong upon them.

Little Dorrit put the book by, and presently arose quietly to shade the window. Maggy sat at her needlework in her old place. The light softened, Little Dorrit brought her chair closer to his side.

'This will soon be over now, dear Mr Clennam. Not only are Mr Doyce's letters to you so full of friendship and encouragement, but Mr Rugg says his letters to him are so full of help, and that everybody (now a little anger is past) is so considerate, and speaks so well of you, that it will soon be over now.'

'Dear girl. Dear heart. Good angel!'

'You praise me far too much. And yet it is such an exquisite pleasure to me to hear you speak so feelingly, and to—and to see,' said Little Dorrit, raising her eyes to his, 'how deeply you mean it, that I cannot say Don't.'

He lifted her hand to his lips.

'You have been here many, many times, when I have not seen you, Little Dorrit?'

'Yes, I have been here sometimes when I have not come into the room.'

'Very often?'

'Rather often,' said Little Dorrit, timidly.

'Every day?'

'I think,' said Little Dorrit, after hesitating, 'that I have been here at least twice every day.'

He might have released the little light hand after fervently kissing it again; but that, with a very gentle lingering where it was, it seemed to court being retained. He took it in both of his, and it lay softly on his breast.

'Dear Little Dorrit, it is not my imprisonment only that will soon be over. This sacrifice of you must be ended. We must learn to part again, and to take our different ways so wide asunder. You have not forgotten what we said together, when you came back?'

'O no, I have not forgotten it. But something has been—You feel quite strong to-day, don't you?'

'Quite strong.'

The hand he held crept up a little nearer his face.

'Do you feel quite strong enough to know what a great fortune I have got?'

'I shall be very glad to be told. No fortune can be too great or good for Little Dorrit.'

'I have been anxiously waiting to tell you. I have been longing and longing to tell you. You are sure you will not take it?'

'Never!'

'You are quite sure you will not take half of it?'

'Never, dear Little Dorrit!'

As she looked at him silently, there was something in her affectionate face that he did not quite comprehend: something that could have broken into tears in a moment, and yet that was happy and proud.

'You will be sorry to hear what I have to tell you about Fanny. Poor Fanny has lost everything. She has nothing left but her husband's income. All that papa gave her when she married was lost as your money was lost. It was in the same hands, and it is all gone.'

Arthur was more shocked than surprised to hear it. 'I had hoped it might not be so bad,' he said: 'but I had feared a heavy loss there, knowing the connection between her husband and the defaulter.'

'Yes. It is all gone. I am very sorry for Fanny; very, very, very sorry for poor Fanny. My poor brother too!'

'Had he property in the same hands?'

'Yes! And it's all gone.—How much do you think my own great fortune is?'

As Arthur looked at her inquiringly, with a new apprehension on him, she withdrew her hand, and laid her face down on the spot where it had rested.

'I have nothing in the world. I am as poor as when I lived here. When papa came over to England, he confided everything he had to the same hands, and it is all swept away. O my dearest and best, are you quite sure you will not share my fortune with me now?'

Locked in his arms, held to his heart, with his manly tears upon her own cheek, she drew the slight hand round his neck, and clasped it in its fellow-hand.

'Never to part, my dearest Arthur; never any more, until the last! I never was rich before, I never was proud before, I never was happy before, I am rich in being taken by you, I am proud in having been resigned by you, I am happy in being with you in this prison, as I should be happy in coming back to it with you, if it should be the will of GOD, and comforting and serving you with all my love and truth. I am yours anywhere, everywhere! I love you dearly! I would rather pass my life here with you, and go out daily, working for our bread, than I would have the greatest fortune that ever was told, and be the greatest lady that ever was honoured. O, if poor papa may only know how blest at last my heart is, in this room where he suffered for so many years!'

Maggy had of course been staring from the first, and had of course been crying her eyes out long before this. Maggy was now so overjoyed that, after hugging her little mother with all her might, she went down-stairs like a clog-hornpipe to find somebody or other to whom to impart her gladness. Whom should Maggy meet but Flora and Mr F.'s Aunt opportunely coming in? And whom else, as a consequence of that meeting, should Little Dorrit find waiting for herself, when, a good two or three hours afterwards, she went out?

Flora's eyes were a little red, and she seemed rather out of spirits. Mr F.'s Aunt was so stiffened that she had the appearance of being past bending by any means short of powerful mechanical pressure. Her bonnet was cocked up behind in a terrific manner; and her stony reticule was as rigid as if it had been petrified by the Gorgon's head, and had got it at that moment inside. With these imposing attributes, Mr F.'s Aunt, publicly seated on the steps of the Marshal's official residence, had been for the two or three hours in question a great boon to the younger inhabitants of the Borough, whose sallies of humour she had considerably flushed herself by resenting at the point of her umbrella, from time to time.

'Painfully aware, Miss Dorrit, I am sure,' said Flora, 'that to propose an adjournment to any place to one so far removed by fortune and so courted and caressed by the best society must ever appear intruding even if not a pie-shop far below your present sphere and a back-parlour though a civil man but if for the sake of Arthur—cannot overcome it more improper now than ever late Doyce and Clennam—one last remark I might wish to make one last explanation I might wish to offer perhaps your good nature might excuse under pretence of three kidney ones the humble place of conversation.'

Rightly interpreting this rather obscure speech, Little Dorrit returned that she was quite at Flora's disposition. Flora accordingly led the way across the road to the pie-shop in question: Mr F.'s Aunt stalking across in the rear, and putting herself in the way of being run over, with a perseverance worthy of a better cause.

When the 'three kidney ones,' which were to be a blind to the conversation, were set before them on three little tin platters, each kidney one ornamented with a hole at the top, into which the civil man poured hot gravy out of a spouted can as if he were feeding three lamps, Flora took out her pocket-handkerchief.

'If Fancy's fair dreams,' she began, 'have ever pictured that when Arthur—cannot overcome it pray excuse me—was restored to freedom even a pie as far from flaky as the present and so deficient in kidney as to be in that respect like a minced nutmeg might not prove unacceptable if offered by the hand of true regard such visions have for ever fled and all is cancelled but being aware that tender relations are in contemplation beg to state that I heartily wish well to both and find no fault with either not the least, it may be withering to know that ere the hand of Time had made me much less slim than formerly and dreadfully red on the slightest exertion particularly after eating I well know when it takes the form of a rash, it might have been and was not through the interruption of parents and mental torpor succeeded until the mysterious clue was held by Mr F. still I would not be ungenerous to either and I heartily wish well to both.'

Little Dorrit took her hand, and thanked her for all her old kindness.

'Call it not kindness,' returned Flora, giving her an honest kiss, 'for you always were the best and dearest little thing that ever was if I may take the liberty and even in a money point of view a saving being Conscience itself though I must add much more agreeable than mine ever was to me for though not I hope more burdened than other people's yet I have always found it far readier to make one uncomfortable than comfortable and evidently taking a greater pleasure in doing it but I am wandering, one hope I wish to express ere yet the closing scene draws in and it is that I do trust for the sake of old times and old sincerity that Arthur will know that I didn't desert him in his misfortunes but that I came backwards and forwards constantly to ask if I could do anything for him and that I sat in the pie-shop where they very civilly fetched something warm in a tumbler from the hotel and really very nice hours after hours to keep him company over the way without his knowing it.'

Flora really had tears in her eyes now, and they showed her to great advantage.

'Over and above which,' said Flora, 'I earnestly beg you as the dearest thing that ever was if you'll still excuse the familiarity from one who moves in very different circles to let Arthur understand that I don't know after all whether it wasn't all nonsense between us though pleasant at the time and trying too and certainly Mr F. did work a change and the spell being broken nothing could be expected to take place without weaving it afresh which various circumstances have combined to prevent of which perhaps not the least powerful was that it was not to be, I am not prepared to say that if it had been agreeable to Arthur and had brought itself about naturally in the first instance I should not have been very glad being of a lively disposition and moped at home where papa undoubtedly is the most aggravating of his sex and not improved since having been cut down by the hand of the Incendiary into something of which I never saw the counterpart in all my life but jealousy is not my character nor ill-will though many faults.'

Without having been able closely to follow Mrs Finching through this labyrinth, Little Dorrit understood its purpose, and cordially accepted the trust.

'The withered chaplet my dear,' said Flora, with great enjoyment, 'is then perished the column is crumbled and the pyramid is standing upside down upon its what's-his-name call it not giddiness call it not weakness call it not folly I must now retire into privacy and look upon the ashes of departed joys no more but taking a further liberty of paying for the pastry which has formed the humble pretext of our interview will for ever say Adieu!'

Mr F.'s Aunt, who had eaten her pie with great solemnity, and who had been elaborating some grievous scheme of injury in her mind since her first assumption of that public position on the Marshal's steps, took the present opportunity of addressing the following Sibyllic apostrophe to the relict of her late nephew.

'Bring him for'ard, and I'll chuck him out o' winder!'

Flora tried in vain to soothe the excellent woman by explaining that they were going home to dinner. Mr F.'s Aunt persisted in replying, 'Bring him for'ard and I'll chuck him out o' winder!' Having reiterated this demand an immense number of times, with a sustained glare of defiance at Little Dorrit, Mr F.'s Aunt folded her arms, and sat down in the corner of the pie-shop parlour; steadfastly refusing to budge until such time as 'he' should have been 'brought for'ard,' and the chucking portion of his destiny accomplished.

In this condition of things, Flora confided to Little Dorrit that she had not seen Mr F.'s Aunt so full of life and character for weeks; that she would find it necessary to remain there 'hours perhaps,' until the inexorable old lady could be softened; and that she could manage her best alone. They parted, therefore, in the friendliest manner, and with the kindest feeling on both sides.

Mr F.'s Aunt holding out like a grim fortress, and Flora becoming in need of refreshment, a messenger was despatched to the hotel for the tumbler already glanced at, which was afterwards replenished. With the aid of its content, a newspaper, and some skimming of the cream of the pie-stock, Flora got through the remainder of the day in perfect good humour; though occasionally embarrassed by the consequences of an idle rumour which circulated among the credulous infants of the neighbourhood, to the effect that an old lady had sold herself to the pie-shop to be made up, and was then sitting in the pie-shop parlour, declining to complete her contract. This attracted so many young persons of both sexes, and, when the shades of evening began to fall, occasioned so much interruption to the business, that the merchant became very pressing in his proposals that Mr F.'s Aunt should be removed. A conveyance was accordingly brought to the door, which, by the joint efforts of the merchant and Flora, this remarkable woman was at last induced to enter; though not without even then putting her head out of the window, and demanding to have him 'brought for'ard' for the purpose originally mentioned. As she was observed at this time to direct baleful glances towards the Marshalsea, it has been supposed that this admirably consistent female intended by 'him,' Arthur Clennam. This, however, is mere speculation; who the person was, who, for the satisfaction of Mr F.'s Aunt's mind, ought to have been brought forward and never was brought forward, will never be positively known.

The autumn days went on, and Little Dorrit never came to the Marshalsea now and went away without seeing him. No, no, no.

One morning, as Arthur listened for the light feet that every morning ascended winged to his heart, bringing the heavenly brightness of a new love into the room where the old love had wrought so hard and been so true; one morning, as he listened, he heard her coming, not alone.

'Dear Arthur,' said her delighted voice outside the door, 'I have some one here. May I bring some one in?'

He had thought from the tread there were two with her. He answered 'Yes,' and she came in with Mr Meagles. Sun-browned and jolly Mr Meagles looked, and he opened his arms and folded Arthur in them, like a sun-browned and jolly father.

'Now I am all right,' said Mr Meagles, after a minute or so. 'Now it's over. Arthur, my dear fellow, confess at once that you expected me before.'

'I did,' said Arthur; 'but Amy told me—'

'Little Dorrit. Never any other name.' (It was she who whispered it.)

'—But my Little Dorrit told me that, without asking for any further explanation, I was not to expect you until I saw you.'

'And now you see me, my boy,' said Mr Meagles, shaking him by the hand stoutly; 'and now you shall have any explanation and every explanation. The fact is, I was here—came straight to you from the Allongers and Marshongers, or I should be ashamed to look you in the face this day,—but you were not in company trim at the moment, and I had to start off again to catch Doyce.'

'Poor Doyce!' sighed Arthur.

'Don't call him names that he don't deserve,' said Mr Meagles. 'He's not poor; he's doing well enough. Doyce is a wonderful fellow over there. I assure you he is making out his case like a house a-fire. He has fallen on his legs, has Dan. Where they don't want things done and find a man to do 'em, that man's off his legs; but where they do want things done and find a man to do 'em, that man's on his legs. You won't have occasion to trouble the Circumlocution Office any more. Let me tell you, Dan has done without 'em!'

'What a load you take from my mind!' cried Arthur. 'What happiness you give me!'

'Happiness?' retorted Mr Meagles. 'Don't talk about happiness till you see Dan. I assure you Dan is directing works and executing labours over yonder, that it would make your hair stand on end to look at. He's no public offender, bless you, now! He's medalled and ribboned, and starred and crossed, and I don't-know-what all'd, like a born nobleman. But we mustn't talk about that over here.'

'Why not?'

'Oh, egad!' said Mr Meagles, shaking his head very seriously, 'he must hide all those things under lock and key when he comes over here. They won't do over here. In that particular, Britannia is a Britannia in the Manger—won't give her children such distinctions herself, and won't allow them to be seen when they are given by other countries. No, no, Dan!' said Mr Meagles, shaking his head again. 'That won't do here!'

'If you had brought me (except for Doyce's sake) twice what I have lost,' cried Arthur, 'you would not have given me the pleasure that you give me in this news.'

'Why, of course, of course,' assented Mr Meagles. 'Of course I know that, my good fellow, and therefore I come out with it in the first burst. Now, to go back, about catching Doyce. I caught Doyce. Ran against him among a lot of those dirty brown dogs in women's nightcaps a great deal too big for 'em, calling themselves Arabs and all sorts of incoherent races. You know 'em! Well! He was coming straight to me, and I was going to him, and so we came back together.'

'Doyce in England!' exclaimed Arthur.

'There!' said Mr Meagles, throwing open his arms. 'I am the worst man in the world to manage a thing of this sort. I don't know what I should have done if I had been in the diplomatic line—right, perhaps! The long and short of it is, Arthur, we have both been in England this fortnight. And if you go on to ask where Doyce is at the present moment, why, my plain answer is—here he is! And now I can breathe again at last!'

Doyce darted in from behind the door, caught Arthur by both hands, and said the rest for himself.

'There are only three branches of my subject, my dear Clennam,' said Doyce, proceeding to mould them severally, with his plastic thumb, on the palm of his hand, 'and they're soon disposed of. First, not a word more from you about the past. There was an error in your calculations. I know what that is. It affects the whole machine, and failure is the consequence. You will profit by the failure, and will avoid it another time. I have done a similar thing myself, in construction, often. Every failure teaches a man something, if he will learn; and you are too sensible a man not to learn from this failure. So much for firstly. Secondly. I was sorry you should have taken it so heavily to heart, and reproached yourself so severely; I was travelling home night and day to put matters right, with the assistance of our friend, when I fell in with our friend as he has informed you. Thirdly. We two agreed, that, after what you had undergone, after your distress of mind, and after your illness, it would be a pleasant surprise if we could so far keep quiet as to get things perfectly arranged without your knowledge, and then come and say that all the affairs were smooth, that everything was right, that the business stood in greater want of you than ever it did, and that a new and prosperous career was opened before you and me as partners. That's thirdly. But you know we always make an allowance for friction, and so I have reserved space to close in. My dear Clennam, I thoroughly confide in you; you have it in your power to be quite as useful to me as I have, or have had, it in my power to be useful to you; your old place awaits you, and wants you very much; there is nothing to detain you here one half-hour longer.'

There was silence, which was not broken until Arthur had stood for some time at the window with his back towards them, and until his little wife that was to be had gone to him and stayed by him.

'I made a remark a little while ago,' said Daniel Doyce then, 'which I am inclined to think was an incorrect one. I said there was nothing to detain you here, Clennam, half an hour longer. Am I mistaken in supposing that you would rather not leave here till to-morrow morning? Do I know, without being very wise, where you would like to go, direct from these walls and from this room?'

'You do,' returned Arthur. 'It has been our cherished purpose.'

'Very well!' said Doyce. 'Then, if this young lady will do me the honour of regarding me for four-and-twenty hours in the light of a father, and will take a ride with me now towards Saint Paul's Churchyard, I dare say I know what we want to get there.'

Little Dorrit and he went out together soon afterwards, and Mr Meagles lingered behind to say a word to his friend.

'I think, Arthur, you will not want Mother and me in the morning and we will keep away. It might set Mother thinking about Pet; she's a soft-hearted woman. She's best at the Cottage, and I'll stay there and keep her company.'

With that they parted for the time. And the day ended, and the night ended, and the morning came, and Little Dorrit, simply dressed as usual and having no one with her but Maggy, came into the prison with the sunshine. The poor room was a happy room that morning. Where in the world was there a room so full of quiet joy!

'My dear love,' said Arthur. 'Why does Maggy light the fire? We shall be gone directly.'

'I asked her to do it. I have taken such an odd fancy. I want you to burn something for me.'

'What?'

'Only this folded paper. If you will put it in the fire with your own hand, just as it is, my fancy will be gratified.'

'Superstitious, darling Little Dorrit? Is it a charm?'

'It is anything you like best, my own,' she answered, laughing with glistening eyes and standing on tiptoe to kiss him, 'if you will only humour me when the fire burns up.'

So they stood before the fire, waiting: Clennam with his arm about her waist, and the fire shining, as fire in that same place had often shone, in Little Dorrit's eyes. 'Is it bright enough now?' said Arthur. 'Quite bright enough now,' said Little Dorrit. 'Does the charm want any words to be said?' asked Arthur, as he held the paper over the flame. 'You can say (if you don't mind) "I love you!"' answered Little Dorrit. So he said it, and the paper burned away.

They passed very quietly along the yard; for no one was there, though many heads were stealthily peeping from the windows. Only one face, familiar of old, was in the Lodge. When they had both accosted it, and spoken many kind words, Little Dorrit turned back one last time with her hand stretched out, saying, 'Good-bye, good John! I hope you will live very happy, dear!'

Then they went up the steps of the neighbouring Saint George's Church, and went up to the altar, where Daniel Doyce was waiting in his paternal character. And there was Little Dorrit's old friend who had given her the Burial Register for a pillow; full of admiration that she should come back to them to be married, after all.

And they were married with the sun shining on them through the painted figure of Our Saviour on the window. And they went into the very room where Little Dorrit had slumbered after her party, to sign the Marriage Register. And there, Mr Pancks, (destined to be chief clerk to Doyce and Clennam, and afterwards partner in the house), sinking the Incendiary in the peaceful friend, looked in at the door to see it done, with Flora gallantly supported on one arm and Maggy on the other, and a back-ground of John Chivery and father and other turnkeys who had run round for the moment, deserting the parent Marshalsea for its happy child. Nor had Flora the least signs of seclusion upon her, notwithstanding her recent declaration; but, on the contrary, was wonderfully smart, and enjoyed the ceremonies mightily, though in a fluttered way.

Little Dorrit's old friend held the inkstand as she signed her name, and the clerk paused in taking off the good clergyman's surplice, and all the witnesses looked on with special interest. 'For, you see,' said Little Dorrit's old friend, 'this young lady is one of our curiosities, and has come now to the third volume of our Registers. Her birth is in what I call the first volume; she lay asleep, on this very floor, with her pretty head on what I call the second volume; and she's now a-writing her little name as a bride in what I call the third volume.'

They all gave place when the signing was done, and Little Dorrit and her husband walked out of the church alone. They paused for a moment on the steps of the portico, looking at the fresh perspective of the street in the autumn morning sun's bright rays, and then went down.

Went down into a modest life of usefulness and happiness. Went down to give a mother's care, in the fulness of time, to Fanny's neglected children no less than to their own, and to leave that lady going into Society for ever and a day. Went down to give a tender nurse and friend to Tip for some few years, who was never vexed by the great exactions he made of her in return for the riches he might have given her if he had ever had them, and who lovingly closed his eyes upon the Marshalsea and all its blighted fruits. They went quietly down into the roaring streets, inseparable and blessed; and as they passed along in sunshine and shade, the noisy and the eager, and the arrogant and the froward and the vain, fretted and chafed, and made their usual uproar.

OLIVER TWIST; OR, THE PARISH BOY'S PROGRESS

CHAPTER I. TREATS OF THE PLACE WHERE OLIVER TWIST WAS BORN AND OF THE CIRCUMSTANCES ATTENDING HIS BIRTH

Among other public buildings in a certain town, which for many reasons it will be prudent to refrain from mentioning, and to which I will assign no fictitious name, there is one anciently common to most towns, great or small: to wit, a workhouse; and in this workhouse was born; on a day and date which I need not trouble myself to repeat, inasmuch as it can be of no possible consequence to the reader, in this stage of the business at all events; the item of mortality whose name is prefixed to the head of this chapter.

For a long time after it was ushered into this world of sorrow and trouble, by the parish surgeon, it remained a matter of considerable doubt whether the child would survive to bear any name at all; in which case it is somewhat more than probable that these memoirs would never have appeared; or, if they had, that being comprised within a couple of pages, they would have possessed the inestimable merit of being the most concise and faithful specimen of biography, extant in the literature of any age or country.

Although I am not disposed to maintain that the being born in a workhouse, is in itself the most fortunate and enviable circumstance that can possibly befall a human being, I do mean to say that in this particular instance, it was the best thing for Oliver Twist that could by possibility have occurred. The fact is, that there was considerable difficulty in inducing Oliver to take upon himself the office of respiration,—a troublesome practice, but one which custom has rendered necessary to our easy existence; and for some time he lay gasping on a little flock mattress, rather unequally poised between this world and the next: the balance being decidedly in favour of the latter. Now, if, during this brief period, Oliver had been surrounded by careful grandmothers, anxious aunts, experienced nurses, and doctors of profound wisdom, he would most inevitably and indubitably have been killed in no time. There being nobody by, however, but a pauper old woman, who was rendered rather misty by an unwonted allowance of beer; and a parish surgeon who did such matters by contract; Oliver and Nature fought out the point between them. The result was, that, after a few struggles, Oliver breathed, sneezed, and proceeded to advertise to the inmates of the workhouse the fact of a new burden having been imposed upon the parish, by setting up as loud a cry as could reasonably have been expected from a male infant who had not been possessed of that very useful appendage, a voice, for a much longer space of time than three minutes and a quarter.

As Oliver gave this first proof of the free and proper action of his lungs, the patchwork coverlet which was carelessly flung over the iron bedstead, rustled; the pale face of a young woman was raised feebly from the pillow; and a faint voice imperfectly articulated the words, 'Let me see the child, and die.'

The surgeon had been sitting with his face turned towards the fire: giving the palms of his hands a warm and a rub alternately. As the young woman spoke, he rose, and advancing to the bed's head, said, with more kindness than might have been expected of him:

'Oh, you must not talk about dying yet.'

'Lor bless her dear heart, no!' interposed the nurse, hastily depositing in her pocket a green glass bottle, the contents of which she had been tasting in a corner with evident satisfaction.

'Lor bless her dear heart, when she has lived as long as I have, sir, and had thirteen children of her own, and all on 'em dead except two, and them in the wurkus with me, she'll know better than to take on in that way, bless her dear heart! Think what it is to be a mother, there's a dear young lamb do.'

Apparently this consolatory perspective of a mother's prospects failed in producing its due effect. The patient shook her head, and stretched out her hand towards the child.

The surgeon deposited it in her arms. She imprinted her cold white lips passionately on its forehead; passed her hands over her face; gazed wildly round; shuddered; fell back—and died. They chafed her breast, hands, and temples; but the blood had stopped forever. They talked of hope and comfort. They had been strangers too long.

'It's all over, Mrs. Thingummy!' said the surgeon at last.

'Ah, poor dear, so it is!' said the nurse, picking up the cork of the green bottle, which had fallen out on the pillow, as she stooped to take up the child. 'Poor dear!'

'You needn't mind sending up to me, if the child cries, nurse,' said the surgeon, putting on his gloves with great deliberation. 'It's very likely it will be troublesome. Give it a little gruel if it is.' He put on his hat, and, pausing by the bed-side on his way to the door, added, 'She was a good-looking girl, too; where did she come from?'

'She was brought here last night,' replied the old woman, 'by the overseer's order. She was found lying in the street. She had walked some distance, for her shoes were worn to pieces; but where she came from, or where she was going to, nobody knows.'

The surgeon leaned over the body, and raised the left hand. 'The old story,' he said, shaking his head: 'no wedding-ring, I see. Ah! Good-night!'

The medical gentleman walked away to dinner; and the nurse, having once more applied herself to the green bottle, sat down on a low chair before the fire, and proceeded to dress the infant.

What an excellent example of the power of dress, young Oliver Twist was! Wrapped in the blanket which had hitherto formed his only covering, he might have been the child of a nobleman or a beggar; it would have been hard for the haughtiest stranger to have assigned him his proper station in society. But now that he was enveloped in the old calico robes which had grown yellow in the same service, he was badged and ticketed, and fell into his place at once—a parish child—the orphan of a workhouse—the humble, half-starved drudge—to be cuffed and buffeted through the world—despised by all, and pitied by none.

Oliver cried lustily. If he could have known that he was an orphan, left to the tender mercies of church-wardens and overseers, perhaps he would have cried the louder.

CHAPTER II. TREATS OF OLIVER TWIST'S GROWTH, EDUCATION, AND BOARD

586

For the next eight or ten months, Oliver was the victim of a systematic course of treachery and deception. He was brought up by hand. The hungry and destitute situation of the infant orphan was duly reported by the workhouse authorities to the parish authorities. The parish authorities inquired with dignity of the workhouse authorities, whether there was no female then domiciled in 'the house' who was in a situation to impart to Oliver Twist, the consolation and nourishment of which he stood in need. The workhouse authorities replied with humility, that there was not. Upon this, the parish authorities magnanimously and humanely resolved, that Oliver should be 'farmed,' or, in other words, that he should be dispatched to a branch-workhouse some three miles off, where twenty or thirty other juvenile offenders against the poor-laws, rolled about the floor all day, without the inconvenience of too much food or too much clothing, under the parental superintendence of an elderly female, who received the culprits at and for the consideration of sevenpence-halfpenny per small head per week. Sevenpence-halfpenny's worth per week is a good round diet for a child; a great deal may be got for sevenpence-halfpenny, quite enough to overload its stomach, and make it uncomfortable. The elderly female was a woman of wisdom and experience; she knew what was good for children; and she had a very accurate perception of what was good for herself. So, she appropriated the greater part of the weekly stipend to her own use, and consigned the rising parochial generation to even a shorter allowance than was originally provided for them. Thereby finding in the lowest depth a deeper still; and proving herself a very great experimental philosopher.

Everybody knows the story of another experimental philosopher who had a great theory about a horse being able to live without eating, and who demonstrated it so well, that he had got his own horse down to a straw a day, and would unquestionably have rendered him a very spirited and rampacious animal on nothing at all, if he had not died, four-and-twenty hours before he was to have had his first comfortable bait of air. Unfortunately for, the experimental philosophy of the female to whose protecting care Oliver Twist was delivered over, a similar result usually attended the operation of her system; for at the very moment when the child had contrived to exist upon the smallest possible portion of the weakest possible food, it did perversely happen in eight and a half cases out of ten, either that it sickened from want and cold, or fell into the fire from neglect, or got half-smothered by accident; in any one of which cases, the miserable little being was usually summoned into another world, and there gathered to the fathers it had never known in this.

Occasionally, when there was some more than usually interesting inquest upon a parish child who had been overlooked in turning up a bedstead, or inadvertently scalded to death when there happened to be a washing—though the latter accident was very scarce, anything approaching to a washing being of rare occurrence in the farm—the jury would take it into their heads to ask troublesome questions, or the parishioners would rebelliously affix their signatures to a remonstrance. But these impertinences were speedily checked by the evidence of the surgeon, and the testimony of the beadle; the former of whom had always opened the body and found nothing inside (which was very probable indeed), and the latter of whom invariably swore whatever the parish wanted; which was very self-devotional. Besides, the board made periodical pilgrimages to the farm, and always sent the beadle the day before, to say they were going. The children were neat and clean to behold, when they went; and what more would the people have!

It cannot be expected that this system of farming would produce any very extraordinary or luxuriant crop. Oliver Twist's ninth birthday found him a pale thin child, somewhat diminutive in stature, and decidedly small in circumference. But nature or inheritance had implanted a good sturdy spirit in Oliver's breast. It had had plenty of room to expand, thanks to the spare diet of the establishment; and perhaps to this circumstance may be attributed his having any ninth birth-day at all. Be this as it may, however, it was his ninth birthday; and he was keeping it in the coal-cellar with a select party of two other young gentleman, who, after participating with him in a sound thrashing, had been locked up for atrociously presuming to be hungry, when Mrs. Mann, the good lady of the house, was unexpectedly startled by the apparition of Mr. Bumble, the beadle, striving to undo the wicket of the garden-gate.

'Goodness gracious! Is that you, Mr. Bumble, sir?' said Mrs. Mann, thrusting her head out of the window in well-affected ecstasies of joy. '(Susan, take Oliver and them two brats upstairs, and wash 'em directly.)—My heart alive! Mr. Bumble, how glad I am to see you, sure-ly!'

Now, Mr. Bumble was a fat man, and a choleric; so, instead of responding to this open-hearted salutation in a kindred spirit, he gave the little wicket a tremendous shake, and then bestowed upon it a kick which could have emanated from no leg but a beadle's.

'Lor, only think,' said Mrs. Mann, running out,—for the three boys had been removed by this time,—'only think of that! That I should have forgotten that the gate was bolted on the inside, on account of them dear children! Walk in sir; walk in, pray, Mr. Bumble, do, sir.'

Although this invitation was accompanied with a curtsey that might have softened the heart of a church-warden, it by no means mollified the beadle.

'Do you think this respectful or proper conduct, Mrs. Mann,' inquired Mr. Bumble, grasping his cane, 'to keep the parish officers a waiting at your garden-gate, when they come here upon porochial business with the porochial orphans? Are you aweer, Mrs. Mann, that you are, as I may say, a porochial delegate, and a stipendiary?'

'I'm sure Mr. Bumble, that I was only a telling one or two of the dear children as is so fond of you, that it was you a coming,' replied Mrs. Mann with great humility.

Mr. Bumble had a great idea of his oratorical powers and his importance. He had displayed the one, and vindicated the other. He relaxed.

'Well, well, Mrs. Mann,' he replied in a calmer tone; 'it may be as you say; it may be. Lead the way in, Mrs. Mann, for I come on business, and have something to say.'

Mrs. Mann ushered the beadle into a small parlour with a brick floor; placed a seat for him; and officiously deposited his cocked hat and cane on the table before him. Mr. Bumble wiped from his forehead the perspiration which his walk had engendered, glanced complacently at the cocked hat, and smiled. Yes, he smiled. Beadles are but men: and Mr. Bumble smiled.

'Now don't you be offended at what I'm a going to say,' observed Mrs. Mann, with captivating sweetness. 'You've had a long walk, you know, or I wouldn't mention it. Now, will you take a little drop of somethink, Mr. Bumble?'

'Not a drop. Nor a drop,' said Mr. Bumble, waving his right hand in a dignified, but placid manner.

'I think you will,' said Mrs. Mann, who had noticed the tone of the refusal, and the gesture that had accompanied it. 'Just a leetle drop, with a little cold water, and a lump of sugar.'

Mr. Bumble coughed.

'Now, just a leetle drop,' said Mrs. Mann persuasively.

'What is it?' inquired the beadle.

'Why, it's what I'm obliged to keep a little of in the house, to put into the blessed infants' Daffy, when they ain't well, Mr. Bumble,' replied Mrs. Mann as she opened a corner cupboard, and took down a bottle and glass. 'It's gin. I'll not deceive you, Mr. B. It's gin.'

'Do you give the children Daffy, Mrs. Mann?' inquired Bumble, following with his eyes the interesting process of mixing.

'Ah, bless 'em, that I do, dear as it is,' replied the nurse. 'I couldn't see 'em suffer before my very eyes, you know sir.'

'No'; said Mr. Bumble approvingly; 'no, you could not. You are a humane woman, Mrs. Mann.' (Here she set down the glass.) 'I shall take a early opportunity of mentioning it to the board, Mrs. Mann.' (He drew it towards him.) 'You feel as a mother, Mrs. Mann.' (He stirred the gin-and-water.) 'I—I drink your health with cheerfulness, Mrs. Mann'; and he swallowed half of it.

'And now about business,' said the beadle, taking out a leathern pocket-book. 'The child that was half-baptized Oliver Twist, is nine year old to-day.'

'Bless him!' interposed Mrs. Mann, inflaming her left eye with the corner of her apron.

'And notwithstanding a offered reward of ten pound, which was afterwards increased to twenty pound. Notwithstanding the most superlative, and, I may say, supernat'ral exertions on the part of this parish,' said Bumble, 'we have never been able to discover who is his father, or what was his mother's settlement, name, or condition.'

Mrs. Mann raised her hands in astonishment; but added, after a moment's reflection, 'How comes he to have any name at all, then?'

The beadle drew himself up with great pride, and said, 'I inwented it.'

'You, Mr. Bumble!'

'I, Mrs. Mann. We name our fondlings in alphabetical order. The last was a S,—Swubble, I named him. This was a T,—Twist, I named him. The next one comes will be Unwin, and the next Vilkins. I have got names ready made to the end of the alphabet, and all the way through it again, when we come to Z.'

'Why, you're quite a literary character, sir!' said Mrs. Mann.

'Well, well,' said the beadle, evidently gratified with the compliment; 'perhaps I may be. Perhaps I may be, Mrs. Mann.' He finished the gin-and-water, and added, 'Oliver being now too old to remain here, the board have determined to have him back into the house. I have come out myself to take him there. So let me see him at once.'

'I'll fetch him directly,' said Mrs. Mann, leaving the room for that purpose. Oliver, having had by this time as much of the outer coat of dirt which encrusted his face and hands, removed, as could be scrubbed off in one washing, was led into the room by his benevolent protectress.

'Make a bow to the gentleman, Oliver,' said Mrs. Mann.

Oliver made a bow, which was divided between the beadle on the chair, and the cocked hat on the table.

'Will you go along with me, Oliver?' said Mr. Bumble, in a majestic voice.

Oliver was about to say that he would go along with anybody with great readiness, when, glancing upward, he caught sight of Mrs. Mann, who had got behind the beadle's chair, and was shaking her fist at him with a furious countenance. He took the hint at once, for the fist had been too often impressed upon his body not to be deeply impressed upon his recollection.

'Will she go with me?' inquired poor Oliver.

'No, she can't,' replied Mr. Bumble. 'But she'll come and see you sometimes.'

This was no very great consolation to the child. Young as he was, however, he had sense enough to make a feint of feeling great regret at going away. It was no very difficult matter for the boy to call tears into his eyes. Hunger and recent ill-usage are great assistants if you want to cry; and Oliver cried very naturally indeed. Mrs. Mann gave him a thousand embraces, and what Oliver wanted a great deal more, a piece of bread and butter, less he should seem too hungry when he got to the workhouse. With the slice of bread in his hand, and the little brown-cloth parish cap on his head, Oliver was then led away by Mr. Bumble from the wretched home where one kind word or look had never lighted the gloom of his infant years. And yet he burst into an agony of childish grief, as the cottage-gate closed after him. Wretched as were the little companions in misery he was leaving behind, they were the only friends he had ever known; and a sense of his loneliness in the great wide world, sank into the child's heart for the first time.

Mr. Bumble walked on with long strides; little Oliver, firmly grasping his gold-laced cuff, trotted beside him, inquiring at the end of every quarter of a mile whether they were 'nearly there.' To these interrogations Mr. Bumble returned very brief and snappish replies; for the temporary blandness which gin-and-water awakens in some bosoms had by this time evaporated; and he was once again a beadle.

Oliver had not been within the walls of the workhouse a quarter of an hour, and had scarcely completed the demolition of a second slice of bread, when Mr. Bumble, who had handed him over to the care of an old woman, returned; and, telling him it was a board night, informed him that the board had said he was to appear before it forthwith.

Not having a very clearly defined notion of what a live board was, Oliver was rather astounded by this intelligence, and was not quite certain whether he ought to laugh or cry. He had no time to think about the matter, however; for Mr. Bumble gave him a tap on the head, with his cane, to wake him up: and another on the back to make him lively: and bidding him to follow, conducted him into a large white-washed room, where eight or ten fat gentlemen were sitting round a table. At the top of the table, seated in an arm-chair rather higher than the rest, was a particularly fat gentleman with a very round, red face.

'Bow to the board,' said Bumble. Oliver brushed away two or three tears that were lingering in his eyes; and seeing no board but the table, fortunately bowed to that.

'What's your name, boy?' said the gentleman in the high chair.

Oliver was frightened at the sight of so many gentlemen, which made him tremble: and the beadle gave him another tap behind, which made him cry. These two causes made him answer in a very low and hesitating voice; whereupon a gentleman in a white waistcoat said he was a fool. Which was a capital way of raising his spirits, and putting him quite at his ease.

'Boy,' said the gentleman in the high chair, 'listen to me. You know you're an orphan, I suppose?'

'What's that, sir?' inquired poor Oliver.

'The boy is a fool—I thought he was,' said the gentleman in the white waistcoat.

'Hush!' said the gentleman who had spoken first. 'You know you've got no father or mother, and that you were brought up by the parish, don't you?'

'Yes, sir,' replied Oliver, weeping bitterly.

'What are you crying for?' inquired the gentleman in the white waistcoat. And to be sure it was very extraordinary. What could the boy be crying for?

'I hope you say your prayers every night,' said another gentleman in a gruff voice; 'and pray for the people who feed you, and take care of you—like a Christian.'

'Yes, sir,' stammered the boy. The gentleman who spoke last was unconsciously right. It would have been very like a Christian, and a marvellously good Christian too, if Oliver had prayed for the people who fed and took care of him. But he hadn't, because nobody had taught him.

'Well! You have come here to be educated, and taught a useful trade,' said the red-faced gentleman in the high chair.

'So you'll begin to pick oakum to-morrow morning at six o'clock,' added the surly one in the white waistcoat.

For the combination of both these blessings in the one simple process of picking oakum, Oliver bowed low by the direction of the beadle, and was then hurried away to a large ward; where, on a rough, hard bed, he sobbed himself to sleep. What a novel illustration of the tender laws of England! They let the paupers go to sleep!

Poor Oliver! He little thought, as he lay sleeping in happy unconsciousness of all around him, that the board had that very day arrived at a decision which would exercise the most material influence over all his future fortunes. But they had. And this was it:

The members of this board were very sage, deep, philosophical men; and when they came to turn their attention to the workhouse, they found out at once, what ordinary folks would never have discovered—the poor people liked it! It was a regular place of public entertainment for the poorer classes; a tavern where there was nothing to pay; a public breakfast, dinner, tea, and supper all the year round; a brick and mortar elysium, where it was all play and no work. 'Oho!' said the board, looking very knowing; 'we are the fellows to set this to rights; we'll stop it all, in no time.' So, they established the rule, that all poor people should have the alternative (for they would compel nobody, not they), of being starved by a gradual process in the house, or by a quick one out of it. With this view, they contracted with the water-works to lay on an unlimited supply of water; and with a corn-factor to supply periodically small quantities of oatmeal; and issued three meals of thin gruel a day, with an onion twice a week, and half a roll of Sundays. They made a great many other wise and humane regulations, having reference to the ladies, which it is not necessary to repeat; kindly undertook to divorce poor married people, in consequence of the great expense of a suit in Doctors' Commons; and, instead of compelling a man to support his family, as they had theretofore done, took his family away from him, and made him a bachelor! There is no saying how many applicants for relief, under these last two heads, might have started up in all classes of society, if it had not been coupled with the workhouse; but the board were long-headed men, and had provided for this difficulty. The relief was inseparable from the workhouse and the gruel; and that frightened people.

For the first six months after Oliver Twist was removed, the system was in full operation. It was rather expensive at first, in consequence of the increase in the undertaker's bill, and the necessity of taking in the clothes of all the paupers, which fluttered loosely on their wasted, shrunken forms, after a week or two's gruel. But the number of workhouse inmates got thin as well as the paupers; and the board were in ecstasies.

The room in which the boys were fed, was a large stone hall, with a copper at one end: out of which the master, dressed in an apron for the purpose, and assisted by one or two women, ladled the gruel at mealtimes. Of this festive composition each boy had one porringer, and no more—except on occasions of great public rejoicing, when he had two ounces and a quarter of bread besides.

The bowls never wanted washing. The boys polished them with their spoons till they shone again; and when they had performed this operation (which never took very long, the spoons being nearly as large as the bowls), they would sit staring at the copper, with such eager eyes, as if they could have devoured the very bricks of which it was composed; employing themselves, meanwhile, in sucking their fingers most assiduously, with the view of catching up any stray splashes of gruel that might have been cast thereon. Boys have generally excellent appetites. Oliver Twist and his companions suffered the tortures of slow starvation for three months: at last they got so voracious and wild with hunger, that one boy, who was tall for his age, and hadn't been used to that sort of thing (for his father had kept a small cook-shop), hinted darkly to his companions, that unless he had another basin of gruel per diem, he was afraid he might some night happen to eat the boy who slept next him, who happened to be a weakly youth of tender age. He had a wild, hungry eye; and they implicitly believed him. A council was held; lots were cast who should walk up to the master after supper that evening, and ask for more; and it fell to Oliver Twist.

The evening arrived; the boys took their places. The master, in his cook's uniform, stationed himself at the copper; his pauper assistants ranged themselves behind him; the gruel was served out; and a long grace was said over the short commons. The gruel disappeared; the boys whispered each other, and winked at Oliver; while his next neighbors nudged him. Child as he was, he was desperate with hunger, and reckless with misery. He rose from the table; and advancing to the master, basin and spoon in hand, said: somewhat alarmed at his own temerity:

'Please, sir, I want some more.'

The master was a fat, healthy man; but he turned very pale. He gazed in stupefied astonishment on the small rebel for some seconds, and then clung for support to the copper. The assistants were paralysed with wonder; the boys with fear.

'What!' said the master at length, in a faint voice.

'Please, sir,' replied Oliver, 'I want some more.'

The master aimed a blow at Oliver's head with the ladle; pinioned him in his arm; and shrieked aloud for the beadle.

The board were sitting in solemn conclave, when Mr. Bumble rushed into the room in great excitement, and addressing the gentleman in the high chair, said,

'Mr. Limbkins, I beg your pardon, sir! Oliver Twist has asked for more!'

There was a general start. Horror was depicted on every countenance.

'For more!' said Mr. Limbkins. 'Compose yourself, Bumble, and answer me distinctly. Do I understand that he asked for more, after he had eaten the supper allotted by the dietary?'

'He did, sir,' replied Bumble.

'That boy will be hung,' said the gentleman in the white waistcoat. 'I know that boy will be hung.'

Nobody controverted the prophetic gentleman's opinion. An animated discussion took place. Oliver was ordered into instant confinement; and a bill was next morning pasted on the outside of the gate, offering a reward of five pounds to anybody who would take Oliver Twist off the hands of the parish. In other words, five pounds and Oliver Twist were offered to any man or woman who wanted an apprentice to any trade, business, or calling.

'I never was more convinced of anything in my life,' said the gentleman in the white waistcoat, as he knocked at the gate and read the bill next morning: 'I never was more convinced of anything in my life, than I am that that boy will come to be hung.'

As I purpose to show in the sequel whether the white waistcoated gentleman was right or not, I should perhaps mar the interest of this narrative (supposing it to possess any at all), if I ventured to hint just yet, whether the life of Oliver Twist had this violent termination or no.

CHAPTER III. RELATES HOW OLIVER TWIST WAS VERY NEAR GETTING A PLACE WHICH WOULD NOT HAVE BEEN A SINECURE

For a week after the commission of the impious and profane offence of asking for more, Oliver remained a close prisoner in the dark and solitary room to which he had been consigned by the wisdom and mercy of the board. It appears, at first sight not unreasonable to suppose, that, if he had entertained a becoming feeling of respect for the prediction of the gentleman in the white waistcoat, he would have established that sage individual's prophetic character, once and for ever, by tying one end of his pocket-handkerchief to a hook in the wall, and attaching himself to the other. To the performance of this feat, however, there was one obstacle: namely, that pocket-handkerchiefs being decided articles of luxury, had been, for all future times and ages, removed from the noses of paupers by the express order of the board, in council assembled: solemnly given and pronounced under their hands and seals. There was a still greater obstacle in Oliver's youth and childishness. He only cried bitterly all day; and, when the long, dismal night came on, spread his little hands before his eyes to shut out the darkness, and crouching in the corner, tried to sleep: ever and anon waking with a start and tremble, and drawing himself closer and closer to the wall, as if to feel even its cold hard surface were a protection in the gloom and loneliness which surrounded him.

Let it not be supposed by the enemies of 'the system,' that, during the period of his solitary incarceration, Oliver was denied the benefit of exercise, the pleasure of society, or the advantages of religious consolation. As for exercise, it was nice cold weather, and he was allowed to perform his ablutions every morning under the pump, in a stone yard, in the presence of Mr. Bumble, who prevented his catching cold, and caused a tingling sensation to pervade his frame, by repeated applications of the cane. As for society, he was carried every other day into the hall where the boys dined, and there sociably flogged as a public warning and example. And so far from being denied the advantages of religious consolation, he was kicked into the same apartment every evening at prayer-time, and there permitted to listen to, and console his mind with, a general supplication of the boys, containing a special clause, therein inserted by authority of the board, in which they entreated to be made good, virtuous, contented, and obedient, and to be guarded from the sins and vices of Oliver Twist: whom the supplication distinctly set forth to be under the exclusive patronage and protection of the powers of wickedness, and an article direct from the manufactory of the very Devil himself.

It chanced one morning, while Oliver's affairs were in this auspicious and comfortable state, that Mr. Gamfield, chimney-sweep, went his way down the High Street, deeply cogitating in his mind his ways and means of paying certain arrears of rent, for which his landlord had become rather pressing. Mr. Gamfield's most sanguine estimate of his finances could not raise them within full five pounds of the desired amount; and, in a species of arithmetical desperation, he was alternately cudgelling his brains and his donkey, when passing the workhouse, his eyes encountered the bill on the gate.

'Wo—o!' said Mr. Gamfield to the donkey.

The donkey was in a state of profound abstraction: wondering, probably, whether he was destined to be regaled with a cabbage-stalk or two when he had disposed of the two sacks of soot with which the little cart was laden; so, without noticing the word of command, he jogged onward.

Mr. Gamfield growled a fierce imprecation on the donkey generally, but more particularly on his eyes; and, running after him, bestowed a blow on his head, which would inevitably have beaten in any skull but a donkey's. Then, catching hold of the bridle, he gave his jaw a sharp wrench, by way of gentle reminder that he was not his own master; and by these means turned him round. He then gave him another blow on the head, just to stun him till he came back again. Having completed these arrangements, he walked up to the gate, to read the bill.

The gentleman with the white waistcoat was standing at the gate with his hands behind him, after having delivered himself of some profound sentiments in the board-room. Having witnessed the little dispute between Mr. Gamfield and the donkey, he smiled joyously when that person came up to read the bill, for he saw at once that Mr. Gamfield was exactly the sort of master Oliver Twist wanted. Mr. Gamfield smiled, too, as he perused the document; for five pounds was just the sum he had been wishing for; and, as to the boy with which it was encumbered, Mr. Gamfield, knowing what the dietary of the workhouse was, well knew he would be a nice small pattern, just the very thing for register stoves. So, he spelt the bill through again, from beginning to end; and then, touching his fur cap in token of humility, accosted the gentleman in the white waistcoat.

'This here boy, sir, wot the parish wants to 'prentis,' said Mr. Gamfield.

'Ay, my man,' said the gentleman in the white waistcoat, with a condescending smile. 'What of him?'

'If the parish vould like him to learn a right pleasant trade, in a good 'spectable chimbley-sweepin' bisness,' said Mr. Gamfield, 'I wants a 'prentis, and I am ready to take him.'

'Walk in,' said the gentleman in the white waistcoat. Mr. Gamfield having lingered behind, to give the donkey another blow on the head, and another wrench of the jaw, as a caution not to run away in his absence, followed the gentleman with the white waistcoat into the room where Oliver had first seen him.

'It's a nasty trade,' said Mr. Limbkins, when Gamfield had again stated his wish.

'Young boys have been smothered in chimneys before now,' said another gentleman.

'That's acause they damped the straw afore they lit it in the chimbley to make 'em come down again,' said Gamfield; 'that's all smoke, and no blaze; vereas smoke ain't o' no use at all in making a boy come down, for it only sinds him to sleep, and that's wot he likes. Boys is wery obstinit, and wery lazy, Gen'l'men, and there's nothink like a good hot blaze to make 'em come down vith a run. It's humane too, gen'l'men, acause, even if they've stuck in the chimbley, roasting their feet makes 'em struggle to hextricate theirselves.'

The gentleman in the white waistcoat appeared very much amused by this explanation; but his mirth was speedily checked by a look from Mr. Limbkins. The board then proceeded to converse among themselves for a few minutes, but in so low a tone, that the words 'saving of expenditure,' 'looked well in the accounts,' 'have a printed report published,' were alone audible. These only chanced to be heard, indeed, or account of their being very frequently repeated with great emphasis.

At length the whispering ceased; and the members of the board, having resumed their seats and their solemnity, Mr. Limbkins said:

'We have considered your proposition, and we don't approve of it.'

'Not at all,' said the gentleman in the white waistcoat.

'Decidedly not,' added the other members.

As Mr. Gamfield did happen to labour under the slight imputation of having bruised three or four boys to death already, it occurred to him that the board had, perhaps, in some unaccountable freak, taken it into their heads that this extraneous circumstance ought to influence their proceedings. It was very unlike their general mode of doing business, if they had; but still, as he had no particular wish to revive the rumour, he twisted his cap in his hands, and walked slowly from the table.

'So you won't let me have him, gen'l'men?' said Mr. Gamfield, pausing near the door.

'No,' replied Mr. Limbkins; 'at least, as it's a nasty business, we think you ought to take something less than the premium we offered.'

Mr. Gamfield's countenance brightened, as, with a quick step, he returned to the table, and said,

'What'll you give, gen'l'men? Come! Don't be too hard on a poor man. What'll you give?'

'I should say, three pound ten was plenty,' said Mr. Limbkins.

'Ten shillings too much,' said the gentleman in the white waistcoat.

'Come!' said Gamfield; 'say four pound, gen'l'men. Say four pound, and you've got rid of him for good and all. There!'

'Three pound ten,' repeated Mr. Limbkins, firmly.

'Come! I'll split the diff'erence, gen'l'men,' urged Gamfield. 'Three pound fifteen.'

'Not a farthing more,' was the firm reply of Mr. Limbkins.

'You're desperate hard upon me, gen'l'men,' said Gamfield, wavering.

'Pooh! pooh! nonsense!' said the gentleman in the white waistcoat. 'He'd be cheap with nothing at all, as a premium. Take him, you silly fellow! He's just the boy for you. He wants the stick, now and then: it'll do him good; and his board needn't come very expensive, for he hasn't been overfed since he was born. Ha! ha! ha!'

Mr. Gamfield gave an arch look at the faces round the table, and, observing a smile on all of them, gradually broke into a smile himself. The bargain was made. Mr. Bumble, was at once instructed that Oliver Twist and his indentures were to be conveyed before the magistrate, for signature and approval, that very afternoon.

In pursuance of this determination, little Oliver, to his excessive astonishment, was released from bondage, and ordered to put himself into a clean shirt. He had hardly achieved this very unusual gymnastic performance, when Mr. Bumble brought him, with his own hands, a basin of gruel, and the holiday allowance of two ounces and a quarter of bread. At this tremendous sight, Oliver began to cry very piteously: thinking, not unnaturally, that the board must have determined to kill him for some useful purpose, or they never would have begun to fatten him up in that way.

'Don't make your eyes red, Oliver, but eat your food and be thankful,' said Mr. Bumble, in a tone of impressive pomposity. 'You're a going to be made a 'prentice of, Oliver.'

'A prentice, sir!' said the child, trembling.

'Yes, Oliver,' said Mr. Bumble. 'The kind and blessed gentleman which is so many parents to you, Oliver, when you have none of your own: are a going to 'prentice' you: and to set you up in life, and make a man of you: although the expense to the parish is three pound ten!—three pound ten, Oliver!—seventy shillins—one hundred and forty sixpences!—and all for a naughty orphan which nobody can't love.'

As Mr. Bumble paused to take breath, after delivering this address in an awful voice, the tears rolled down the poor child's face, and he sobbed bitterly.

'Come,' said Mr. Bumble, somewhat less pompously, for it was gratifying to his feelings to observe the effect his eloquence had produced; 'Come, Oliver! Wipe your eyes with the cuffs of your jacket, and don't cry into your gruel; that's a very foolish action, Oliver.' It certainly was, for there was quite enough water in it already.

On their way to the magistrate, Mr. Bumble instructed Oliver that all he would have to do, would be to look very happy, and say, when the gentleman asked him if he wanted to be apprenticed, that he should like it very much indeed; both of which injunctions Oliver promised to obey: the rather as Mr. Bumble threw in a gentle hint, that if he failed in either particular, there was no telling what would be done to him. When they arrived at the office, he was shut up in a little room by himself, and admonished by Mr. Bumble to stay there, until he came back to fetch him.

There the boy remained, with a palpitating heart, for half an hour. At the expiration of which time Mr. Bumble thrust in his head, unadorned with the cocked hat, and said aloud:

'Now, Oliver, my dear, come to the gentleman.' As Mr. Bumble said this, he put on a grim and threatening look, and added, in a low voice, 'Mind what I told you, you young rascal!'

Oliver stared innocently in Mr. Bumble's face at this somewhat contradictory style of address; but that gentleman prevented his offering any remark thereupon, by leading him at once into an adjoining room: the door of which was open. It was a large room, with a great window. Behind a desk, sat two old gentleman with powdered heads: one of whom was reading the newspaper; while the other was perusing, with the aid of a pair of tortoise-shell spectacles, a small piece of parchment which lay before him. Mr. Limbkins was standing in front of the desk on one side; and Mr. Gamfield, with a partially washed face, on the other; while two or three bluff-looking men, in top-boots, were lounging about.

The old gentleman with the spectacles gradually dozed off, over the little bit of parchment; and there was a short pause, after Oliver had been stationed by Mr. Bumble in front of the desk.

'This is the boy, your worship,' said Mr. Bumble.

The old gentleman who was reading the newspaper raised his head for a moment, and pulled the other old gentleman by the sleeve; whereupon, the last-mentioned old gentleman woke up.

'Oh, is this the boy?' said the old gentleman.

'This is him, sir,' replied Mr. Bumble. 'Bow to the magistrate, my dear.'

Oliver roused himself, and made his best obeisance. He had been wondering, with his eyes fixed on the magistrates' powder, whether all boards were born with that white stuff on their heads, and were boards from thenceforth on that account.

'Well,' said the old gentleman, 'I suppose he's fond of chimney-sweeping?'

'He doats on it, your worship,' replied Bumble; giving Oliver a sly pinch, to intimate that he had better not say he didn't.

'And he will be a sweep, will he?' inquired the old gentleman.

'If we was to bind him to any other trade to-morrow, he'd run away simultaneous, your worship,' replied Bumble.

'And this man that's to be his master—you, sir—you'll treat him well, and feed him, and do all that sort of thing, will you?' said the old gentleman.

'When I says I will, I means I will,' replied Mr. Gamfield doggedly.

'You're a rough speaker, my friend, but you look an honest, open-hearted man,' said the old gentleman: turning his spectacles in the direction of the candidate for Oliver's premium, whose villainous countenance was a regular stamped receipt for cruelty. But the magistrate was half blind and half childish, so he couldn't reasonably be expected to discern what other people did.

'I hope I am, sir,' said Mr. Gamfield, with an ugly leer.

'I have no doubt you are, my friend,' replied the old gentleman: fixing his spectacles more firmly on his nose, and looking about him for the inkstand.

It was the critical moment of Oliver's fate. If the inkstand had been where the old gentleman thought it was, he would have dipped his pen into it, and signed the indentures, and Oliver would have been straightway hurried off. But, as it chanced to be immediately under his nose, it followed, as a matter of course, that he looked all over his desk for it, without finding it; and happening in the course of his search to look straight before him, his gaze encountered the pale and terrified face of Oliver Twist: who, despite all the admonitory looks and pinches of Bumble, was regarding the repulsive countenance of his future master, with a mingled expression of horror and fear, too palpable to be mistaken, even by a half-blind magistrate.

The old gentleman stopped, laid down his pen, and looked from Oliver to Mr. Limbkins; who attempted to take snuff with a cheerful and unconcerned aspect.

'My boy!' said the old gentleman, 'you look pale and alarmed. What is the matter?'

'Stand a little away from him, Beadle,' said the other magistrate: laying aside the paper, and leaning forward with an expression of interest. 'Now, boy, tell us what's the matter: don't be afraid.'

Oliver fell on his knees, and clasping his hands together, prayed that they would order him back to the dark room—that they would starve him—beat him—kill him if they pleased—rather than send him away with that dreadful man.

'Well!' said Mr. Bumble, raising his hands and eyes with most impressive solemnity. 'Well! of all the artful and designing orphans that ever I see, Oliver, you are one of the most bare-facedest.'

'Hold your tongue, Beadle,' said the second old gentleman, when Mr. Bumble had given vent to this compound adjective.

'I beg your worship's pardon,' said Mr. Bumble, incredulous of having heard aright. 'Did your worship speak to me?'

'Yes. Hold your tongue.'

Mr. Bumble was stupefied with astonishment. A beadle ordered to hold his tongue! A moral revolution!

The old gentleman in the tortoise-shell spectacles looked at his companion, he nodded significantly.

'We refuse to sanction these indentures,' said the old gentleman: tossing aside the piece of parchment as he spoke.

'I hope,' stammered Mr. Limbkins: 'I hope the magistrates will not form the opinion that the authorities have been guilty of any improper conduct, on the unsupported testimony of a child.'

'The magistrates are not called upon to pronounce any opinion on the matter,' said the second old gentleman sharply. 'Take the boy back to the workhouse, and treat him kindly. He seems to want it.'

That same evening, the gentleman in the white waistcoat most positively and decidedly affirmed, not only that Oliver would be hung, but that he would be drawn and quartered into the bargain. Mr. Bumble shook his head with gloomy mystery, and said he wished he might come to good; whereunto Mr. Gamfield replied, that he wished he might come to him; which, although he agreed with the beadle in most matters, would seem to be a wish of a totally opposite description.

The next morning, the public were once informed that Oliver Twist was again To Let, and that five pounds would be paid to anybody who would take possession of him.

CHAPTER IV. OLIVER, BEING OFFERED ANOTHER PLACE, MAKES HIS FIRST ENTRY INTO PUBLIC LIFE

In great families, when an advantageous place cannot be obtained, either in possession, reversion, remainder, or expectancy, for the young man who is growing up, it is a very general custom to send him to sea. The board, in imitation of so wise and salutary an example, took counsel together on the expediency of shipping off Oliver Twist, in some small trading vessel bound to a good unhealthy port. This suggested itself as the very best thing that could possibly be done with him: the probability being, that the skipper would flog him to death, in a playful mood, some day after dinner, or would knock his brains out with an iron bar; both pastimes being, as is pretty generally known, very favourite and common recreations among gentleman of that class. The more the case presented itself to the board, in this point of view, the more manifold the advantages of the step appeared; so, they came to the conclusion that the only way of providing for Oliver effectually, was to send him to sea without delay.

Mr. Bumble had been despatched to make various preliminary inquiries, with the view of finding out some captain or other who wanted a cabin-boy without any friends; and was returning to the workhouse to communicate the result of his mission; when he encountered at the gate, no less a person than Mr. Sowerberry, the parochial undertaker.

Mr. Sowerberry was a tall gaunt, large-jointed man, attired in a suit of threadbare black, with darned cotton stockings of the same colour, and shoes to answer. His features were not naturally intended to wear a smiling aspect, but he was in general rather given to professional jocosity. His step was elastic, and his face betokened inward pleasantry, as he advanced to Mr. Bumble, and shook him cordially by the hand.

'I have taken the measure of the two women that died last night, Mr. Bumble,' said the undertaker.

'You'll make your fortune, Mr. Sowerberry,' said the beadle, as he thrust his thumb and forefinger into the proffered snuff-box of the undertaker: which was an ingenious little model of a patent coffin. 'I say you'll make your fortune, Mr. Sowerberry,' repeated Mr. Bumble, tapping the undertaker on the shoulder, in a friendly manner, with his cane.

'Think so?' said the undertaker in a tone which half admitted and half disputed the probability of the event. 'The prices allowed by the board are very small, Mr. Bumble.'

'So are the coffins,' replied the beadle: with precisely as near an approach to a laugh as a great official ought to indulge in.

Mr. Sowerberry was much tickled at this: as of course he ought to be; and laughed a long time without cessation. 'Well, well, Mr. Bumble,' he said at length, 'there's no denying that, since the new system of feeding has come in, the coffins are something narrower and more shallow than they used to be; but we must have some profit, Mr. Bumble. Well-seasoned timber is an expensive article, sir; and all the iron handles come, by canal, from Birmingham.'

'Well, well,' said Mr. Bumble, 'every trade has its drawbacks. A fair profit is, of course, allowable.'

'Of course, of course,' replied the undertaker; 'and if I don't get a profit upon this or that particular article, why, I make it up in the long-run, you see—he! he! he!'

'Just so,' said Mr. Bumble.

'Though I must say,' continued the undertaker, resuming the current of observations which the beadle had interrupted: 'though I must say, Mr. Bumble, that I have to contend against one very great disadvantage: which is, that all the stout people go off the quickest. The people who have been better off, and have paid rates for many years, are the first to sink when they come into the house; and let me tell you, Mr. Bumble, that three or four inches over one's calculation makes a great hole in one's profits: especially when one has a family to provide for, sir.'

As Mr. Sowerberry said this, with the becoming indignation of an ill-used man; and as Mr. Bumble felt that it rather tended to convey a reflection on the honour of the parish; the latter gentleman thought it advisable to change the subject. Oliver Twist being uppermost in his mind, he made him his theme.

'By the bye,' said Mr. Bumble, 'you don't know anybody who wants a boy, do you? A porochial 'prentis, who is at present a dead-weight; a millstone, as I may say, round the porochial throat? Liberal terms, Mr. Sowerberry, liberal terms?' As Mr. Bumble spoke, he raised his cane to the bill above him, and gave three distinct raps upon the words 'five pounds': which were printed thereon in Roman capitals of gigantic size.

'Gadso!' said the undertaker: taking Mr. Bumble by the gilt-edged lappel of his official coat; 'that's just the very thing I wanted to speak to you about. You know—dear me, what a very elegant button this is, Mr. Bumble! I never noticed it before.'

'Yes, I think it rather pretty,' said the beadle, glancing proudly downwards at the large brass buttons which embellished his coat. 'The die is the same as the porochial seal—the Good Samaritan healing the sick and bruised man. The board presented it to me on Newyear's morning, Mr. Sowerberry. I put it on, I remember, for the first time, to attend the inquest on that reduced tradesman, who died in a doorway at midnight.'

'I recollect,' said the undertaker. 'The jury brought it in, "Died from exposure to the cold, and want of the common necessaries of life," didn't they?'

Mr. Bumble nodded.

'And they made it a special verdict, I think,' said the undertaker, 'by adding some words to the effect, that if the relieving officer had—'

'Tush! Foolery!' interposed the beadle. 'If the board attended to all the nonsense that ignorant jurymen talk, they'd have enough to do.'

'Very true,' said the undertaker; 'they would indeed.'

'Juries,' said Mr. Bumble, grasping his cane tightly, as was his wont when working into a passion: 'juries is ineddicated, vulgar, grovelling wretches.'

'So they are,' said the undertaker.

'They haven't no more philosophy nor political economy about 'em than that,' said the beadle, snapping his fingers contemptuously.

'No more they have,' acquiesced the undertaker.

'I despise 'em,' said the beadle, growing very red in the face.

'So do I,' rejoined the undertaker.

'And I only wish we'd a jury of the independent sort, in the house for a week or two,' said the beadle; 'the rules and regulations of the board would soon bring their spirit down for 'em.'

'Let 'em alone for that,' replied the undertaker. So saying, he smiled, approvingly: to calm the rising wrath of the indignant parish officer.

Mr Bumble lifted off his cocked hat; took a handkerchief from the inside of the crown; wiped from his forehead the perspiration which his rage had engendered; fixed the cocked hat on again; and, turning to the undertaker, said in a calmer voice:

'Well; what about the boy?'

'Oh!' replied the undertaker; 'why, you know, Mr. Bumble, I pay a good deal towards the poor's rates.'

'Hem!' said Mr. Bumble. 'Well?'

'Well,' replied the undertaker, 'I was thinking that if I pay so much towards 'em, I've a right to get as much out of 'em as I can, Mr. Bumble; and so—I think I'll take the boy myself.'

Mr. Bumble grasped the undertaker by the arm, and led him into the building. Mr. Sowerberry was closeted with the board for five minutes; and it was arranged that Oliver should go to him that evening 'upon liking'—a phrase which means, in the case of a parish apprentice, that if the master find, upon a short trial, that he can get enough work out of a boy without putting too much food into him, he shall have him for a term of years, to do what he likes with.

When little Oliver was taken before 'the gentlemen' that evening; and informed that he was to go, that night, as general house-lad to a coffin-maker's; and that if he complained of his situation, or ever came back to the parish again, he would be sent to sea, there to be drowned, or knocked on the head, as the case might be, he evinced so little emotion, that they by common consent pronounced him a hardened young rascal, and ordered Mr. Bumble to remove him forthwith.

Now, although it was very natural that the board, of all people in the world, should feel in a great state of virtuous astonishment and horror at the smallest tokens of want of feeling on the part of anybody, they were rather out, in this particular instance. The simple fact was, that Oliver, instead of possessing too little feeling, possessed rather too much; and was in a fair way of being reduced, for life, to a state of brutal stupidity and sullenness by the ill usage he had received. He heard the news of his destination, in perfect silence; and, having had his luggage put into his hand—which was not very difficult to carry, inasmuch as it was all comprised within the limits of a brown paper parcel, about half a foot square by three inches deep—he pulled his cap over his eyes; and once more attaching himself to Mr. Bumble's coat cuff, was led away by that dignitary to a new scene of suffering.

For some time, Mr. Bumble drew Oliver along, without notice or remark; for the beadle carried his head very erect, as a beadle always should: and, it being a windy day, little Oliver was completely enshrouded by the skirts of Mr. Bumble's coat as they blew open, and disclosed to great advantage his flapped waistcoat and drab plush knee-breeches. As they drew near to their destination, however, Mr. Bumble thought it expedient to look down, and see that the boy was in good order for inspection by his new master: which he accordingly did, with a fit and becoming air of gracious patronage.

'Oliver!' said Mr. Bumble.

'Yes, sir,' replied Oliver, in a low, tremulous voice.

'Pull that cap off your eyes, and hold up your head, sir.'

Although Oliver did as he was desired, at once; and passed the back of his unoccupied hand briskly across his eyes, he left a tear in them when he looked up at his conductor. As Mr. Bumble gazed sternly upon him, it rolled down his cheek. It was followed by another, and another. The child made a strong effort, but it was an unsuccessful one. Withdrawing his other hand from Mr. Bumble's he covered his face with both; and wept until the tears sprung out from between his chin and bony fingers.

'Well!' exclaimed Mr. Bumble, stopping short, and darting at his little charge a look of intense malignity. 'Well! Of all the ungratefullest, and worst-disposed boys as ever I see, Oliver, you are the—'

'No, no, sir,' sobbed Oliver, clinging to the hand which held the well-known cane; 'no, no, sir; I will be good indeed; indeed, indeed I will, sir! I am a very little boy, sir; and it is so—so—'

'So what?' inquired Mr. Bumble in amazement.

'So lonely, sir! So very lonely!' cried the child. 'Everybody hates me. Oh! sir, don't, don't pray be cross to me!' The child beat his hand upon his heart; and looked in his companion's face, with tears of real agony.

Mr. Bumble regarded Oliver's piteous and helpless look, with some astonishment, for a few seconds; hemmed three or four times in a husky manner; and after muttering something about 'that troublesome cough,' bade Oliver dry his eyes and be a good boy. Then once more taking his hand, he walked on with him in silence.

The undertaker, who had just put up the shutters of his shop, was making some entries in his day-book by the light of a most appropriate dismal candle, when Mr. Bumble entered.

'Aha!' said the undertaker; looking up from the book, and pausing in the middle of a word; 'is that you, Bumble?'

'No one else, Mr. Sowerberry,' replied the beadle. 'Here! I've brought the boy.' Oliver made a bow.

'Oh! that's the boy, is it?' said the undertaker: raising the candle above his head, to get a better view of Oliver. 'Mrs. Sowerberry, will you have the goodness to come here a moment, my dear?'

Mrs. Sowerberry emerged from a little room behind the shop, and presented the form of a short, then, squeezed-up woman, with a vixenish countenance.

'My dear,' said Mr. Sowerberry, deferentially, 'this is the boy from the workhouse that I told you of.' Oliver bowed again.

'Dear me!' said the undertaker's wife, 'he's very small.'

'Why, he is rather small,' replied Mr. Bumble: looking at Oliver as if it were his fault that he was no bigger; 'he is small. There's no denying it. But he'll grow, Mrs. Sowerberry—he'll grow.'

'Ah! I dare say he will,' replied the lady pettishly, 'on our victuals and our drink. I see no saving in parish children, not I; for they always cost more to keep, than they're worth. However, men always think they know best. There! Get downstairs, little bag o' bones.' With this, the undertaker's wife opened a side door, and pushed Oliver down a steep flight of stairs into a stone cell, damp and dark: forming the ante-room to the coal-cellar, and denominated 'kitchen'; wherein sat a slatternly girl, in shoes down at heel, and blue worsted stockings very much out of repair.

'Here, Charlotte,' said Mr. Sowerberry, who had followed Oliver down, 'give this boy some of the cold bits that were put by for Trip. He hasn't come home since the morning, so he may go without 'em. I dare say the boy isn't too dainty to eat 'em—are you, boy?'

Oliver, whose eyes had glistened at the mention of meat, and who was trembling with eagerness to devour it, replied in the negative; and a plateful of coarse broken victuals was set before him.

I wish some well-fed philosopher, whose meat and drink turn to gall within him; whose blood is ice, whose heart is iron; could have seen Oliver Twist clutching at the dainty viands that the dog had neglected. I wish he could have witnessed the horrible avidity with which Oliver tore the bits asunder with all the ferocity of famine. There is only one thing I should like better; and that would be to see the Philosopher making the same sort of meal himself, with the same relish.

'Well,' said the undertaker's wife, when Oliver had finished his supper: which she had regarded in silent horror, and with fearful auguries of his future appetite: 'have you done?'

There being nothing eatable within his reach, Oliver replied in the affirmative.

'Then come with me,' said Mrs. Sowerberry: taking up a dim and dirty lamp, and leading the way upstairs; 'your bed's under the counter. You don't mind sleeping among the coffins, I suppose? But it doesn't much matter whether you do or don't, for you can't sleep anywhere else. Come; don't keep me here all night!'

Oliver lingered no longer, but meekly followed his new mistress.

CHAPTER V. OLIVER MINGLES WITH NEW ASSOCIATES. GOING TO A FUNERAL FOR THE FIRST TIME, HE FORMS AN UNFAVOURABLE NOTION OF HIS MASTER'S BUSINESS

Oliver, being left to himself in the undertaker's shop, set the lamp down on a workman's bench, and gazed timidly about him with a feeling of awe and dread, which many people a good deal older than he will be at no loss to understand. An unfinished coffin on black tressels, which stood in the middle of the shop, looked so gloomy and death-like that a cold tremble came over him, every time his eyes wandered in the direction of the dismal object: from which he almost expected to see some frightful form slowly rear its head, to drive him mad with terror. Against the wall were ranged, in regular array, a long row of elm boards cut in the same shape: looking in the dim light, like high-shouldered ghosts with their hands in their breeches pockets. Coffin-plates, elm-chips, bright-headed nails, and shreds of black cloth, lay scattered on the floor; and the wall behind the counter was ornamented with a lively representation of two mutes in very stiff neckcloths, on duty at a large private door, with a hearse drawn by four black steeds, approaching in the distance. The shop was close and hot. The atmosphere seemed tainted with the smell of coffins. The recess beneath the counter in which his flock mattress was thrust, looked like a grave.

Nor were these the only dismal feelings which depressed Oliver. He was alone in a strange place; and we all know how chilled and desolate the best of us will sometimes feel in such a situation. The boy had no friends to care for, or to care for him. The regret of no recent separation was fresh in his mind; the absence of no loved and well-remembered face sank heavily into his heart.

But his heart was heavy, notwithstanding; and he wished, as he crept into his narrow bed, that that were his coffin, and that he could be lain in a calm and lasting sleep in the churchyard ground, with the tall grass waving gently above his head, and the sound of the old deep bell to soothe him in his sleep.

Oliver was awakened in the morning, by a loud kicking at the outside of the shop-door: which, before he could huddle on his clothes, was repeated, in an angry and impetuous manner, about twenty-five times. When he began to undo the chain, the legs desisted, and a voice began.

'Open the door, will yer?' cried the voice which belonged to the legs which had kicked at the door.

'I will, directly, sir,' replied Oliver: undoing the chain, and turning the key.

'I suppose yer the new boy, ain't yer?' said the voice through the key-hole.

'Yes, sir,' replied Oliver.

'How old are yer?' inquired the voice.

'Ten, sir,' replied Oliver.

'Then I'll whop yer when I get in,' said the voice; 'you just see if I don't, that's all, my work'us brat!' and having made this obliging promise, the voice began to whistle.

Oliver had been too often subjected to the process to which the very expressive monosyllable just recorded bears reference, to entertain the smallest doubt that the owner of the voice, whoever he might be, would redeem his pledge, most honourably. He drew back the bolts with a trembling hand, and opened the door.

For a second or two, Oliver glanced up the street, and down the street, and over the way: impressed with the belief that the unknown, who had addressed him through the key-hole, had walked a few paces off, to warm himself; for nobody did he see but a big charity-boy, sitting on a post in front of the house, eating a slice of bread and butter: which he cut into wedges, the size of his mouth, with a clasp-knife, and then consumed with great dexterity.

'I beg your pardon, sir,' said Oliver at length: seeing that no other visitor made his appearance; 'did you knock?'

'I kicked,' replied the charity-boy.

'Did you want a coffin, sir?' inquired Oliver, innocently.

At this, the charity-boy looked monstrous fierce; and said that Oliver would want one before long, if he cut jokes with his superiors in that way.

'Yer don't know who I am, I suppose, Work'us?' said the charity-boy, in continuation: descending from the top of the post, meanwhile, with edifying gravity.

'No, sir,' rejoined Oliver.

'I'm Mister Noah Claypole,' said the charity-boy, 'and you're under me. Take down the shutters, yer idle young ruffian!' With this, Mr. Claypole administered a kick to Oliver, and entered the shop with a dignified air, which did him great credit. It is difficult for a large-headed, small-eyed youth, of lumbering make and heavy countenance, to look dignified under any circumstances; but it is more especially so, when superadded to these personal attractions are a red nose and yellow smalls.

Oliver, having taken down the shutters, and broken a pane of glass in his effort to stagger away beneath the weight of the first one to a small court at the side of the house in which they were kept during the day, was graciously assisted by Noah: who having consoled him with the assurance that 'he'd catch it,' condescended to help him. Mr. Sowerberry came down soon after. Shortly afterwards, Mrs. Sowerberry appeared. Oliver having 'caught it,' in fulfilment of Noah's prediction, followed that young gentleman down the stairs to breakfast.

'Come near the fire, Noah,' said Charlotte. 'I saved a nice little bit of bacon for you from master's breakfast. Oliver, shut that door at Mister Noah's back, and take them bits that I've put out on the cover of the bread-pan. There's your tea; take it away to that box, and drink it there, and make haste, for they'll want you to mind the shop. D'ye hear?'

'D'ye hear, Work'us?' said Noah Claypole.

'Lor, Noah!' said Charlotte, 'what a rum creature you are! Why don't you let the boy alone?'

'Let him alone!' said Noah. 'Why everybody lets him alone enough, for the matter of that. Neither his father nor his mother will ever interfere with him. All his relations let him have his own way pretty well. Eh, Charlotte? He! he! he!'

'Oh, you queer soul!' said Charlotte, bursting into a hearty laugh, in which she was joined by Noah; after which they both looked scornfully at poor Oliver Twist, as he sat shivering on the box in the coldest corner of the room, and ate the stale pieces which had been specially reserved for him.

Noah was a charity-boy, but not a workhouse orphan. No chance-child was he, for he could trace his genealogy all the way back to his parents, who lived hard by; his mother being a washerwoman, and his father a drunken soldier, discharged with a wooden leg, and a diurnal pension of twopence-halfpenny and an unstateable fraction. The shop-boys in the neighbourhood had long been in the habit of branding Noah in the public streets, with the ignominious epithets of 'leathers,' 'charity,' and the like; and Noah had bourne them without reply. But, now that fortune had cast in his way a nameless orphan, at whom even the meanest could point the finger of scorn, he retorted on him with interest. This affords charming food for contemplation. It shows us what a beautiful thing human nature may be made to be; and how impartially the same amiable qualities are developed in the finest lord and the dirtiest charity-boy.

Oliver had been sojourning at the undertaker's some three weeks or a month. Mr. and Mrs. Sowerberry—the shop being shut up—were taking their supper in the little back-parlour, when Mr. Sowerberry, after several deferential glances at his wife, said,

'My dear—' He was going to say more; but, Mrs. Sowerberry looking up, with a peculiarly unpropitious aspect, he stopped short.

'Well,' said Mrs. Sowerberry, sharply.

'Nothing, my dear, nothing,' said Mr. Sowerberry.

'Ugh, you brute!' said Mrs. Sowerberry.

'Not at all, my dear,' said Mr. Sowerberry humbly. 'I thought you didn't want to hear, my dear. I was only going to say—'

'Oh, don't tell me what you were going to say,' interposed Mrs. Sowerberry. 'I am nobody; don't consult me, pray. I don't want to intrude upon your secrets.' As Mrs. Sowerberry said this, she gave an hysterical laugh, which threatened violent consequences.

'But, my dear,' said Sowerberry, 'I want to ask your advice.'

'No, no, don't ask mine,' replied Mrs. Sowerberry, in an affecting manner: 'ask somebody else's.' Here, there was another hysterical laugh, which frightened Mr. Sowerberry very much. This is a very common and much-approved matrimonial course of treatment, which is often very effective. It at once reduced Mr. Sowerberry to begging, as a special favour, to be allowed to say what Mrs. Sowerberry was most curious to hear. After a short duration, the permission was most graciously conceded.

'It's only about young Twist, my dear,' said Mr. Sowerberry. 'A very good-looking boy, that, my dear.'

'He need be, for he eats enough,' observed the lady.

'There's an expression of melancholy in his face, my dear,' resumed Mr. Sowerberry, 'which is very interesting. He would make a delightful mute, my love.'

Mrs. Sowerberry looked up with an expression of considerable wonderment. Mr. Sowerberry remarked it and, without allowing time for any observation on the good lady's part, proceeded.

'I don't mean a regular mute to attend grown-up people, my dear, but only for children's practice. It would be very new to have a mute in proportion, my dear. You may depend upon it, it would have a superb effect.'

Mrs. Sowerberry, who had a good deal of taste in the undertaking way, was much struck by the novelty of this idea; but, as it would have been compromising her dignity to have said so, under existing circumstances, she merely inquired, with much sharpness, why such an obvious suggestion had not presented itself to her husband's mind before? Mr. Sowerberry rightly construed this, as an acquiescence in his proposition; it was speedily determined, therefore, that Oliver should be at once initiated into the mysteries of the trade; and, with this view, that he should accompany his master on the very next occasion of his services being required.

The occasion was not long in coming. Half an hour after breakfast next morning, Mr. Bumble entered the shop; and supporting his cane against the counter, drew forth his large leathern pocket-book: from which he selected a small scrap of paper, which he handed over to Sowerberry.

'Aha!' said the undertaker, glancing over it with a lively countenance; 'an order for a coffin, eh?'

'For a coffin first, and a porochial funeral afterwards,' replied Mr. Bumble, fastening the strap of the leathern pocket-book: which, like himself, was very corpulent.

'Bayton,' said the undertaker, looking from the scrap of paper to Mr. Bumble. 'I never heard the name before.'

Bumble shook his head, as he replied, 'Obstinate people, Mr. Sowerberry; very obstinate. Proud, too, I'm afraid, sir.'

'Proud, eh?' exclaimed Mr. Sowerberry with a sneer. 'Come, that's too much.'

'Oh, it's sickening,' replied the beadle. 'Antimonial, Mr. Sowerberry!'

'So it is,' acquiesced the undertaker.

'We only heard of the family the night before last,' said the beadle; 'and we shouldn't have known anything about them, then, only a woman who lodges in the same house made an application to the porochial committee for them to send the porochial surgeon to see a woman as was very bad. He had gone out to dinner; but his 'prentice (which is a very clever lad) sent 'em some medicine in a blacking-bottle, offhand.'

'Ah, there's promptness,' said the undertaker.

'Promptness, indeed!' replied the beadle. 'But what's the consequence; what's the ungrateful behaviour of these rebels, sir? Why, the husband sends back word that the medicine won't suit his wife's complaint, and so she shan't take it—says she shan't take it, sir! Good, strong, wholesome medicine, as was given with great success to two Irish labourers and a coalheaver, only a week before—sent 'em for nothing, with a blackin'-bottle in,—and he sends back word that she shan't take it, sir!'

As the atrocity presented itself to Mr. Bumble's mind in full force, he struck the counter sharply with his cane, and became flushed with indignation.

'Well,' said the undertaker, 'I ne—ver—did—'

'Never did, sir!' ejaculated the beadle. 'No, nor nobody never did; but now she's dead, we've got to bury her; and that's the direction; and the sooner it's done, the better.'

Thus saying, Mr. Bumble put on his cocked hat wrong side first, in a fever of parochial excitement; and flounced out of the shop.

'Why, he was so angry, Oliver, that he forgot even to ask after you!' said Mr. Sowerberry, looking after the beadle as he strode down the street.

'Yes, sir,' replied Oliver, who had carefully kept himself out of sight, during the interview; and who was shaking from head to foot at the mere recollection of the sound of Mr. Bumble's voice.

He needn't haven taken the trouble to shrink from Mr. Bumble's glance, however; for that functionary, on whom the prediction of the gentleman in the white waistcoat had made a very strong impression, thought that now the undertaker had got Oliver upon trial the subject was better avoided, until such time as he should be firmly bound for seven years, and all danger of his being returned upon the hands of the parish should be thus effectually and legally overcome.

'Well,' said Mr. Sowerberry, taking up his hat, 'the sooner this job is done, the better. Noah, look after the shop. Oliver, put on your cap, and come with me.' Oliver obeyed, and followed his master on his professional mission.

They walked on, for some time, through the most crowded and densely inhabited part of the town; and then, striking down a narrow street more dirty and miserable than any they had yet passed through, paused to look for the house which was the object of their search. The houses on either side were high and large, but very old, and tenanted by people of the poorest class: as their neglected appearance would have sufficiently denoted, without the concurrent testimony afforded by the squalid looks of the few men and women who, with folded arms and bodies half doubled, occasionally skulked along. A great many of the tenements had shop-fronts; but these were fast closed, and mouldering away; only the upper rooms being inhabited. Some houses which had become insecure from age and decay, were prevented from falling into the street, by huge beams of wood reared against the walls, and firmly planted in the road; but even these crazy dens seemed to have been selected as the nightly haunts of some houseless wretches, for many of the rough boards which supplied the place of door and window, were wrenched from their positions, to afford an aperture wide enough for the passage of a human body. The kennel was stagnant and filthy. The very rats, which here and there lay putrefying in its rottenness, were hideous with famine.

There was neither knocker nor bell-handle at the open door where Oliver and his master stopped; so, groping his way cautiously through the dark passage, and bidding Oliver keep close to him and not be afraid the undertaker mounted to the top of the first flight of stairs. Stumbling against a door on the landing, he rapped at it with his knuckles.

It was opened by a young girl of thirteen or fourteen. The undertaker at once saw enough of what the room contained, to know it was the apartment to which he had been directed. He stepped in; Oliver followed him.

There was no fire in the room; but a man was crouching, mechanically, over the empty stove. An old woman, too, had drawn a low stool to the cold hearth, and was sitting beside him. There were some ragged children in another corner; and in a small recess, opposite the door, there lay upon the ground, something covered with an old blanket. Oliver shuddered as he cast his eyes toward the place, and crept involuntarily closer to his master; for though it was covered up, the boy felt that it was a corpse.

The man's face was thin and very pale; his hair and beard were grizzly; his eyes were bloodshot. The old woman's face was wrinkled; her two remaining teeth protruded over her under lip; and her eyes were bright and piercing. Oliver was afraid to look at either her or the man. They seemed so like the rats he had seen outside.

'Nobody shall go near her,' said the man, starting fiercely up, as the undertaker approached the recess. 'Keep back! Damn you, keep back, if you've a life to lose!'

'Nonsense, my good man,' said the undertaker, who was pretty well used to misery in all its shapes. 'Nonsense!'

'I tell you,' said the man: clenching his hands, and stamping furiously on the floor,—'I tell you I won't have her put into the ground. She couldn't rest there. The worms would worry her—not eat her—she is so worn away.'

The undertaker offered no reply to this raving; but producing a tape from his pocket, knelt down for a moment by the side of the body.

'Ah!' said the man: bursting into tears, and sinking on his knees at the feet of the dead woman; 'kneel down, kneel down—kneel round her, every one of you, and mark my words! I say she was starved to death. I never knew how bad she was, till the fever came upon her; and then her bones were starting through the skin. There was neither fire nor candle; she died in the dark—in the dark! She couldn't even see her children's faces, though we heard her gasping out their names. I begged for her in the streets: and they sent me to prison. When I came back, she was dying; and all the blood in my heart has dried up, for they starved her to death. I swear it before the God that saw it! They starved her!' He twined his hands in his hair; and, with a loud scream, rolled grovelling upon the floor: his eyes fixed, and the foam covering his lips.

The terrified children cried bitterly; but the old woman, who had hitherto remained as quiet as if she had been wholly deaf to all that passed, menaced them into silence. Having unloosened the cravat of the man who still remained extended on the ground, she tottered towards the undertaker.

'She was my daughter,' said the old woman, nodding her head in the direction of the corpse; and speaking with an idiotic leer, more ghastly than even the presence of death in such a place. 'Lord, Lord! Well, it is strange that I who gave birth to her, and was a woman then, should be alive and merry now, and she lying there: so cold and stiff! Lord, Lord!—to think of it; it's as good as a play—as good as a play!'

As the wretched creature mumbled and chuckled in her hideous merriment, the undertaker turned to go away.

'Stop, stop!' said the old woman in a loud whisper. 'Will she be buried to-morrow, or next day, or to-night? I laid her out; and I must walk, you know. Send me a large cloak: a good warm one: for it is bitter cold. We should have cake and wine, too, before we go! Never mind; send some bread—only a loaf of bread and a cup of water. Shall we have some bread, dear?' she said eagerly: catching at the undertaker's coat, as he once more moved towards the door.

'Yes, yes,' said the undertaker,'of course. Anything you like!' He disengaged himself from the old woman's grasp; and, drawing Oliver after him, hurried away.

The next day, (the family having been meanwhile relieved with a half-quartern loaf and a piece of cheese, left with them by Mr. Bumble himself,) Oliver and his master returned to the miserable abode; where Mr. Bumble had already arrived, accompanied by four men from the workhouse, who were to act as bearers. An old black cloak had been thrown over the rags of the old woman and the man; and the bare coffin having been screwed down, was hoisted on the shoulders of the bearers, and carried into the street.

'Now, you must put your best leg foremost, old lady!' whispered Sowerberry in the old woman's ear; 'we are rather late; and it won't do, to keep the clergyman waiting. Move on, my men,—as quick as you like!'

Thus directed, the bearers trotted on under their light burden; and the two mourners kept as near them, as they could. Mr. Bumble and Sowerberry walked at a good smart pace in front; and Oliver, whose legs were not so long as his master's, ran by the side.

There was not so great a necessity for hurrying as Mr. Sowerberry had anticipated, however; for when they reached the obscure corner of the churchyard in which the nettles grew, and where the parish graves were made, the clergyman had not arrived; and the clerk, who was sitting by the vestry-room fire, seemed to think it by no means improbable that it might be an hour or so, before he came. So, they put the bier on the brink of the grave; and the two mourners waited patiently in the damp clay, with a cold rain drizzling down, while the ragged boys whom the spectacle had attracted into the churchyard played a noisy game at hide-and-seek among the tombstones, or varied their amusements by jumping backwards and forwards over the coffin. Mr. Sowerberry and Bumble, being personal friends of the clerk, sat by the fire with him, and read the paper.

At length, after a lapse of something more than an hour, Mr. Bumble, and Sowerberry, and the clerk, were seen running towards the grave. Immediately afterwards, the clergyman appeared: putting on his surplice as he came along. Mr. Bumble then thrashed a boy or two, to keep up appearances; and the reverend gentleman, having read as much of the burial service as could be compressed into four minutes, gave his surplice to the clerk, and walked away again.

'Now, Bill!' said Sowerberry to the grave-digger. 'Fill up!'

It was no very difficult task, for the grave was so full, that the uppermost coffin was within a few feet of the surface. The grave-digger shovelled in the earth; stamped it loosely down with his feet: shouldered his spade; and walked off, followed by the boys, who murmured very loud complaints at the fun being over so soon.

'Come, my good fellow!' said Bumble, tapping the man on the back. 'They want to shut up the yard.'

The man who had never once moved, since he had taken his station by the grave side, started, raised his head, stared at the person who had addressed him, walked forward for a few paces; and fell down in a swoon. The crazy old woman was too much occupied in bewailing the loss of her cloak (which the undertaker had taken off), to pay him any attention; so they threw a can of cold water over him; and when he came to, saw him safely out of the churchyard, locked the gate, and departed on their different ways.

'Well, Oliver,' said Sowerberry, as they walked home, 'how do you like it?'

'Pretty well, thank you, sir' replied Oliver, with considerable hesitation. 'Not very much, sir.'

'Ah, you'll get used to it in time, Oliver,' said Sowerberry. 'Nothing when you are used to it, my boy.'

Oliver wondered, in his own mind, whether it had taken a very long time to get Mr. Sowerberry used to it. But he thought it better not to ask the question; and walked back to the shop: thinking over all he had seen and heard.

610

CHAPTER VI. OLIVER, BEING GOADED BY THE TAUNTS OF NOAH, ROUSES INTO ACTION, AND RATHER ASTONISHES HIM

The month's trial over, Oliver was formally apprenticed. It was a nice sickly season just at this time. In commercial phrase, coffins were looking up; and, in the course of a few weeks, Oliver acquired a great deal of experience. The success of Mr. Sowerberry's ingenious speculation, exceeded even his most sanguine hopes. The oldest inhabitants recollected no period at which measles had been so prevalent, or so fatal to infant existence; and many were the mournful processions which little Oliver headed, in a hat-band reaching down to his knees, to the indescribable admiration and emotion of all the mothers in the town. As Oliver accompanied his master in most of his adult expeditions too, in order that he might acquire that equanimity of demeanour and full command of nerve which was essential to a finished undertaker, he had many opportunities of observing the beautiful resignation and fortitude with which some strong-minded people bear their trials and losses.

For instance; when Sowerberry had an order for the burial of some rich old lady or gentleman, who was surrounded by a great number of nephews and nieces, who had been perfectly inconsolable during the previous illness, and whose grief had been wholly irrepressible even on the most public occasions, they would be as happy among themselves as need be— quite cheerful and contented—conversing together with as much freedom and gaiety, as if nothing whatever had happened to disturb them. Husbands, too, bore the loss of their wives with the most heroic calmness. Wives, again, put on weeds for their husbands, as if, so far from grieving in the garb of sorrow, they had made up their minds to render it as becoming and attractive as possible. It was observable, too, that ladies and gentlemen who were in passions of anguish during the ceremony of interment, recovered almost as soon as they reached home, and became quite composed before the tea-drinking was over. All this was very pleasant and improving to see; and Oliver beheld it with great admiration.

That Oliver Twist was moved to resignation by the example of these good people, I cannot, although I am his biographer, undertake to affirm with any degree of confidence; but I can most distinctly say, that for many months he continued meekly to submit to the domination and ill-treatment of Noah Claypole: who used him far worse than before, now that his jealousy was roused by seeing the new boy promoted to the black stick and hatband, while he, the old one, remained stationary in the muffin-cap and leathers. Charlotte treated him ill, because Noah did; and Mrs. Sowerberry was his decided enemy, because Mr. Sowerberry was disposed to be his friend; so, between these three on one side, and a glut of funerals on the other, Oliver was not altogether as comfortable as the hungry pig was, when he was shut up, by mistake, in the grain department of a brewery.

And now, I come to a very important passage in Oliver's history; for I have to record an act, slight and unimportant perhaps in appearance, but which indirectly produced a material change in all his future prospects and proceedings.

One day, Oliver and Noah had descended into the kitchen at the usual dinner-hour, to banquet upon a small joint of mutton—a pound and a half of the worst end of the neck— when Charlotte being called out of the way, there ensued a brief interval of time, which Noah Claypole, being hungry and vicious, considered he could not possibly devote to a worthier purpose than aggravating and tantalising young Oliver Twist.

Intent upon this innocent amusement, Noah put his feet on the table-cloth; and pulled Oliver's hair; and twitched his ears; and expressed his opinion that he was a 'sneak'; and furthermore announced his intention of coming to see him hanged, whenever that desirable event should take place; and entered upon various topics of petty annoyance, like a malicious and ill-conditioned charity-boy as he was. But, making Oliver cry, Noah attempted to be more facetious still; and in his attempt, did what many sometimes do to this day, when they want to be funny. He got rather personal.

'Work'us,' said Noah, 'how's your mother?'

'She's dead,' replied Oliver; 'don't you say anything about her to me!'

Oliver's colour rose as he said this; he breathed quickly; and there was a curious working of the mouth and nostrils, which Mr. Claypole thought must be the immediate precursor of a violent fit of crying. Under this impression he returned to the charge.

'What did she die of, Work'us?' said Noah.

'Of a broken heart, some of our old nurses told me,' replied Oliver: more as if he were talking to himself, than answering Noah. 'I think I know what it must be to die of that!'

'Tol de rol lol lol, right fol lairy, Work'us,' said Noah, as a tear rolled down Oliver's cheek. 'What's set you a snivelling now?'

'Not you,' replied Oliver, sharply. 'There; that's enough. Don't say anything more to me about her; you'd better not!'

'Better not!' exclaimed Noah. 'Well! Better not! Work'us, don't be impudent. Your mother, too! She was a nice 'un she was. Oh, Lor!' And here, Noah nodded his head expressively; and curled up as much of his small red nose as muscular action could collect together, for the occasion.

'Yer know, Work'us,' continued Noah, emboldened by Oliver's silence, and speaking in a jeering tone of affected pity: of all tones the most annoying: 'Yer know, Work'us, it can't be helped now; and of course yer couldn't help it then; and I am very sorry for it; and I'm sure we all are, and pity yer very much. But yer must know, Work'us, yer mother was a regular right-down bad 'un.'

'What did you say?' inquired Oliver, looking up very quickly.

'A regular right-down bad 'un, Work'us,' replied Noah, coolly. 'And it's a great deal better, Work'us, that she died when she did, or else she'd have been hard labouring in Bridewell, or transported, or hung; which is more likely than either, isn't it?'

Crimson with fury, Oliver started up; overthrew the chair and table; seized Noah by the throat; shook him, in the violence of his rage, till his teeth chattered in his head; and collecting his whole force into one heavy blow, felled him to the ground.

A minute ago, the boy had looked the quiet child, mild, dejected creature that harsh treatment had made him. But his spirit was roused at last; the cruel insult to his dead mother had set his blood on fire. His breast heaved; his attitude was erect; his eye bright and vivid; his whole person changed, as he stood glaring over the cowardly tormentor who now lay crouching at his feet; and defied him with an energy he had never known before.

'He'll murder me!' blubbered Noah. 'Charlotte! missis! Here's the new boy a murdering of me! Help! help! Oliver's gone mad! Char—lotte!'

Noah's shouts were responded to, by a loud scream from Charlotte, and a louder from Mrs. Sowerberry; the former of whom rushed into the kitchen by a side-door, while the latter paused on the staircase till she was quite certain that it was consistent with the preservation of human life, to come further down.

'Oh, you little wretch!' screamed Charlotte: seizing Oliver with her utmost force, which was about equal to that of a moderately strong man in particularly good training. 'Oh, you little un-grate-ful, mur-de-rous, hor-rid villain!' And between every syllable, Charlotte gave Oliver a blow with all her might: accompanying it with a scream, for the benefit of society.

Charlotte's fist was by no means a light one; but, lest it should not be effectual in calming Oliver's wrath, Mrs. Sowerberry plunged into the kitchen, and assisted to hold him with one hand, while she scratched his face with the other. In this favourable position of affairs, Noah rose from the ground, and pommelled him behind.

This was rather too violent exercise to last long. When they were all wearied out, and could tear and beat no longer, they dragged Oliver, struggling and shouting, but nothing daunted, into the dust-cellar, and there locked him up. This being done, Mrs. Sowerberry sunk into a chair, and burst into tears.

'Bless her, she's going off!' said Charlotte. 'A glass of water, Noah, dear. Make haste!'

'Oh! Charlotte,' said Mrs. Sowerberry: speaking as well as she could, through a deficiency of breath, and a sufficiency of cold water, which Noah had poured over her head and shoulders. 'Oh! Charlotte, what a mercy we have not all been murdered in our beds!'

'Ah! mercy indeed, ma'am,' was the reply. I only hope this'll teach master not to have any more of these dreadful creatures, that are born to be murderers and robbers from their very cradle. Poor Noah! He was all but killed, ma'am, when I come in.'

'Poor fellow!' said Mrs. Sowerberry: looking piteously on the charity-boy.

Noah, whose top waistcoat-button might have been somewhere on a level with the crown of Oliver's head, rubbed his eyes with the inside of his wrists while this commiseration was bestowed upon him, and performed some affecting tears and sniffs.

'What's to be done!' exclaimed Mrs. Sowerberry. 'Your master's not at home; there's not a man in the house, and he'll kick that door down in ten minutes.' Oliver's vigorous plunges against the bit of timber in question, rendered this occurance highly probable.

'Dear, dear! I don't know, ma'am,' said Charlotte, 'unless we send for the police-officers.'

'Or the millingtary,' suggested Mr. Claypole.

'No, no,' said Mrs. Sowerberry: bethinking herself of Oliver's old friend. 'Run to Mr. Bumble, Noah, and tell him to come here directly, and not to lose a minute; never mind your cap! Make haste! You can hold a knife to that black eye, as you run along. It'll keep the swelling down.'

Noah stopped to make no reply, but started off at his fullest speed; and very much it astonished the people who were out walking, to see a charity-boy tearing through the streets pell-mell, with no cap on his head, and a clasp-knife at his eye.

CHAPTER VII. OLIVER CONTINUES REFRACTORY

Noah Claypole ran along the streets at his swiftest pace, and paused not once for breath, until he reached the workhouse-gate. Having rested here, for a minute or so, to collect a good burst of sobs and an imposing show of tears and terror, he knocked loudly at the wicket; and presented such a rueful face to the aged pauper who opened it, that even he, who saw nothing but rueful faces about him at the best of times, started back in astonishment.

'Why, what's the matter with the boy!' said the old pauper.

'Mr. Bumble! Mr. Bumble!' cried Noah, with well-affected dismay: and in tones so loud and agitated, that they not only caught the ear of Mr. Bumble himself, who happened to be hard by, but alarmed him so much that he rushed into the yard without his cocked hat,—which is a very curious and remarkable circumstance: as showing that even a beadle, acted upon a sudden and powerful impulse, may be afflicted with a momentary visitation of loss of self-possession, and forgetfulness of personal dignity.

'Oh, Mr. Bumble, sir!' said Noah: 'Oliver, sir,—Oliver has—'

'What? What?' interposed Mr. Bumble: with a gleam of pleasure in his metallic eyes. 'Not run away; he hasn't run away, has he, Noah?'

'No, sir, no. Not run away, sir, but he's turned wicious,' replied Noah. 'He tried to murder me, sir; and then he tried to murder Charlotte; and then missis. Oh! what dreadful pain it is!

Such agony, please, sir!' And here, Noah writhed and twisted his body into an extensive variety of eel-like positions; thereby giving Mr. Bumble to understand that, from the violent and sanguinary onset of Oliver Twist, he had sustained severe internal injury and damage, from which he was at that moment suffering the acutest torture.

When Noah saw that the intelligence he communicated perfectly paralysed Mr. Bumble, he imparted additional effect thereunto, by bewailing his dreadful wounds ten times louder than before; and when he observed a gentleman in a white waistcoat crossing the yard, he was more tragic in his lamentations than ever: rightly conceiving it highly expedient to attract the notice, and rouse the indignation, of the gentleman aforesaid.

The gentleman's notice was very soon attracted; for he had not walked three paces, when he turned angrily round, and inquired what that young cur was howling for, and why Mr. Bumble did not favour him with something which would render the series of vocular exclamations so designated, an involuntary process?

'It's a poor boy from the free-school, sir,' replied Mr. Bumble, 'who has been nearly murdered—all but murdered, sir,—by young Twist.'

'By Jove!' exclaimed the gentleman in the white waistcoat, stopping short. 'I knew it! I felt a strange presentiment from the very first, that that audacious young savage would come to be hung!'

'He has likewise attempted, sir, to murder the female servant,' said Mr. Bumble, with a face of ashy paleness.

'And his missis,' interposed Mr. Claypole.

'And his master, too, I think you said, Noah?' added Mr. Bumble.

'No! he's out, or he would have murdered him,' replied Noah. 'He said he wanted to.'

'Ah! Said he wanted to, did he, my boy?' inquired the gentleman in the white waistcoat.

'Yes, sir,' replied Noah. 'And please, sir, missis wants to know whether Mr. Bumble can spare time to step up there, directly, and flog him—'cause master's out.'

'Certainly, my boy; certainly,' said the gentleman in the white waistcoat: smiling benignly, and patting Noah's head, which was about three inches higher than his own. 'You're a good boy—a very good boy. Here's a penny for you. Bumble, just step up to Sowerberry's with your cane, and see what's best to be done. Don't spare him, Bumble.'

'No, I will not, sir,' replied the beadle. And the cocked hat and cane having been, by this time, adjusted to their owner's satisfaction, Mr. Bumble and Noah Claypole betook themselves with all speed to the undertaker's shop.

Here the position of affairs had not at all improved. Sowerberry had not yet returned, and Oliver continued to kick, with undiminished vigour, at the cellar-door. The accounts of his ferocity as related by Mrs. Sowerberry and Charlotte, were of so startling a nature, that Mr. Bumble judged it prudent to parley, before opening the door. With this view he gave a kick at the outside, by way of prelude; and, then, applying his mouth to the keyhole, said, in a deep and impressive tone:

'Oliver!'

'Come; you let me out!' replied Oliver, from the inside.

'Do you know this here voice, Oliver?' said Mr. Bumble.

'Yes,' replied Oliver.

'Ain't you afraid of it, sir? Ain't you a-trembling while I speak, sir?' said Mr. Bumble.

'No!' replied Oliver, boldly.

An answer so different from the one he had expected to elicit, and was in the habit of receiving, staggered Mr. Bumble not a little. He stepped back from the keyhole; drew himself up to his full height; and looked from one to another of the three bystanders, in mute astonishment.

'Oh, you know, Mr. Bumble, he must be mad,' said Mrs. Sowerberry.

'No boy in half his senses could venture to speak so to you.'

'It's not Madness, ma'am,' replied Mr. Bumble, after a few moments of deep meditation. 'It's Meat.'

'What?' exclaimed Mrs. Sowerberry.

'Meat, ma'am, meat,' replied Bumble, with stern emphasis. 'You've over-fed him, ma'am. You've raised a artificial soul and spirit in him, ma'am unbecoming a person of his condition: as the board, Mrs. Sowerberry, who are practical philosophers, will tell you. What have paupers to do with soul or spirit? It's quite enough that we let 'em have live bodies. If you had kept the boy on gruel, ma'am, this would never have happened.'

'Dear, dear!' ejaculated Mrs. Sowerberry, piously raising her eyes to the kitchen ceiling: 'this comes of being liberal!'

The liberality of Mrs. Sowerberry to Oliver, had consisted of a profuse bestowal upon him of all the dirty odds and ends which nobody else would eat; so there was a great deal of meekness and self-devotion in her voluntarily remaining under Mr. Bumble's heavy accusation. Of which, to do her justice, she was wholly innocent, in thought, word, or deed.

'Ah!' said Mr. Bumble, when the lady brought her eyes down to earth again; 'the only thing that can be done now, that I know of, is to leave him in the cellar for a day or so, till he's a little starved down; and then to take him out, and keep him on gruel all through the apprenticeship. He comes of a bad family. Excitable natures, Mrs. Sowerberry! Both the nurse and doctor said, that that mother of his made her way here, against difficulties and pain that would have killed any well-disposed woman, weeks before.'

At this point of Mr. Bumble's discourse, Oliver, just hearing enough to know that some allusion was being made to his mother, recommenced kicking, with a violence that rendered every other sound inaudible. Sowerberry returned at this juncture. Oliver's offence having been explained to him, with such exaggerations as the ladies thought best calculated to rouse his ire, he unlocked the cellar-door in a twinkling, and dragged his rebellious apprentice out, by the collar.

Oliver's clothes had been torn in the beating he had received; his face was bruised and scratched; and his hair scattered over his forehead. The angry flush had not disappeared, however; and when he was pulled out of his prison, he scowled boldly on Noah, and looked quite undismayed.

'Now, you are a nice young fellow, ain't you?' said Sowerberry; giving Oliver a shake, and a box on the ear.

'He called my mother names,' replied Oliver.

'Well, and what if he did, you little ungrateful wretch?' said Mrs. Sowerberry. 'She deserved what he said, and worse.'

'She didn't' said Oliver.

'She did,' said Mrs. Sowerberry.

'It's a lie!' said Oliver.

Mrs. Sowerberry burst into a flood of tears.

This flood of tears left Mr. Sowerberry no alternative. If he had hesitated for one instant to punish Oliver most severely, it must be quite clear to every experienced reader that he would have been, according to all precedents in disputes of matrimony established, a brute, an unnatural husband, an insulting creature, a base imitation of a man, and various other agreeable characters too numerous for recital within the limits of this chapter. To do him justice, he was, as far as his power went—it was not very extensive—kindly disposed towards the boy; perhaps, because it was his interest to be so; perhaps, because his wife disliked him. The flood of tears, however, left him no resource; so he at once gave him a drubbing, which satisfied even Mrs. Sowerberry herself, and rendered Mr. Bumble's subsequent application of the parochial cane, rather unnecessary. For the rest of the day, he was shut up in the back kitchen, in company with a pump and a slice of bread; and at night, Mrs. Sowerberry, after making various remarks outside the door, by no means complimentary to the memory of his mother, looked into the room, and, amidst the jeers and pointings of Noah and Charlotte, ordered him upstairs to his dismal bed.

It was not until he was left alone in the silence and stillness of the gloomy workshop of the undertaker, that Oliver gave way to the feelings which the day's treatment may be supposed likely to have awakened in a mere child. He had listened to their taunts with a look of contempt; he had borne the lash without a cry: for he felt that pride swelling in his heart which would have kept down a shriek to the last, though they had roasted him alive. But now, when there were none to see or hear him, he fell upon his knees on the floor; and, hiding his face in his hands, wept such tears as, God send for the credit of our nature, few so young may ever have cause to pour out before him!

For a long time, Oliver remained motionless in this attitude. The candle was burning low in the socket when he rose to his feet. Having gazed cautiously round him, and listened intently, he gently undid the fastenings of the door, and looked abroad.

It was a cold, dark night. The stars seemed, to the boy's eyes, farther from the earth than he had ever seen them before; there was no wind; and the sombre shadows thrown by the trees upon the ground, looked sepulchral and death-like, from being so still. He softly reclosed the door. Having availed himself of the expiring light of the candle to tie up in a handkerchief the few articles of wearing apparel he had, sat himself down upon a bench, to wait for morning.

With the first ray of light that struggled through the crevices in the shutters, Oliver arose, and again unbarred the door. One timid look around—one moment's pause of hesitation—he had closed it behind him, and was in the open street.

He looked to the right and to the left, uncertain whither to fly.

He remembered to have seen the waggons, as they went out, toiling up the hill. He took the same route; and arriving at a footpath across the fields: which he knew, after some distance, led out again into the road; struck into it, and walked quickly on.

Along this same footpath, Oliver well-remembered he had trotted beside Mr. Bumble, when he first carried him to the workhouse from the farm. His way lay directly in front of the cottage. His heart beat quickly when he bethought himself of this; and he half resolved to turn back. He had come a long way though, and should lose a great deal of time by doing so. Besides, it was so early that there was very little fear of his being seen; so he walked on.

He reached the house. There was no appearance of its inmates stirring at that early hour. Oliver stopped, and peeped into the garden. A child was weeding one of the little beds; as he stopped, he raised his pale face and disclosed the features of one of his former companions. Oliver felt glad to see him, before he went; for, though younger than himself, he had been his little friend and playmate. They had been beaten, and starved, and shut up together, many and many a time.

'Hush, Dick!' said Oliver, as the boy ran to the gate, and thrust his thin arm between the rails to greet him. 'Is any one up?'

'Nobody but me,' replied the child.

'You musn't say you saw me, Dick,' said Oliver. 'I am running away. They beat and ill-use me, Dick; and I am going to seek my fortune, some long way off. I don't know where. How pale you are!'

'I heard the doctor tell them I was dying,' replied the child with a faint smile. 'I am very glad to see you, dear; but don't stop, don't stop!'

'Yes, yes, I will, to say good-b'ye to you,' replied Oliver. 'I shall see you again, Dick. I know I shall! You will be well and happy!'

'I hope so,' replied the child. 'After I am dead, but not before. I know the doctor must be right, Oliver, because I dream so much of Heaven, and Angels, and kind faces that I never see when I am awake. Kiss me,' said the child, climbing up the low gate, and flinging his little arms round Oliver's neck. 'Good-b'ye, dear! God bless you!'

The blessing was from a young child's lips, but it was the first that Oliver had ever heard invoked upon his head; and through the struggles and sufferings, and troubles and changes, of his after life, he never once forgot it.

CHAPTER VIII. OLIVER WALKS TO LONDON. HE ENCOUNTERS ON THE ROAD A STRANGE SORT OF YOUNG GENTLEMAN

Oliver reached the stile at which the by-path terminated; and once more gained the high-road. It was eight o'clock now. Though he was nearly five miles away from the town, he ran, and hid behind the hedges, by turns, till noon: fearing that he might be pursued and overtaken. Then he sat down to rest by the side of the milestone, and began to think, for the first time, where he had better go and try to live.

The stone by which he was seated, bore, in large characters, an intimation that it was just seventy miles from that spot to London. The name awakened a new train of ideas in the boy's mind.

London!—that great place!—nobody—not even Mr. Bumble—could ever find him there! He had often heard the old men in the workhouse, too, say that no lad of spirit need want in London; and that there were ways of living in that vast city, which those who had been bred up in country parts had no idea of. It was the very place for a homeless boy, who must die in the streets unless some one helped him. As these things passed through his thoughts, he jumped upon his feet, and again walked forward.

He had diminished the distance between himself and London by full four miles more, before he recollected how much he must undergo ere he could hope to reach his place of destination. As this consideration forced itself upon him, he slackened his pace a little, and meditated upon his means of getting there. He had a crust of bread, a coarse shirt, and two pairs of stockings, in his bundle. He had a penny too—a gift of Sowerberry's after some funeral in which he had acquitted himself more than ordinarily well—in his pocket. 'A clean shirt,' thought Oliver, 'is a very comfortable thing; and so are two pairs of darned stockings; and so is a penny; but they are small helps to a sixty-five miles' walk in winter time.' But Oliver's thoughts, like those of most other people, although they were extremely ready and active to point out his difficulties, were wholly at a loss to suggest any feasible mode of surmounting them; so, after a good deal of thinking to no particular purpose, he changed his little bundle over to the other shoulder, and trudged on.

Oliver walked twenty miles that day; and all that time tasted nothing but the crust of dry bread, and a few draughts of water, which he begged at the cottage-doors by the road-side. When the night came, he turned into a meadow; and, creeping close under a hay-rick, determined to lie there, till morning. He felt frightened at first, for the wind moaned dismally over the empty fields: and he was cold and hungry, and more alone than he had ever felt before. Being very tired with his walk, however, he soon fell asleep and forgot his troubles.

He felt cold and stiff, when he got up next morning, and so hungry that he was obliged to exchange the penny for a small loaf, in the very first village through which he passed. He had walked no more than twelve miles, when night closed in again. His feet were sore, and his legs so weak that they trembled beneath him. Another night passed in the bleak damp air, made him worse; when he set forward on his journey next morning he could hardly crawl along.

He waited at the bottom of a steep hill till a stage-coach came up, and then begged of the outside passengers; but there were very few who took any notice of him: and even those told him to wait till they got to the top of the hill, and then let them see how far he could run for a halfpenny. Poor Oliver tried to keep up with the coach a little way, but was unable to do it, by reason of his fatigue and sore feet. When the outsides saw this, they put their halfpence back into their pockets again, declaring that he was an idle young dog, and didn't deserve anything; and the coach rattled away and left only a cloud of dust behind.

In some villages, large painted boards were fixed up: warning all persons who begged within the district, that they would be sent to jail. This frightened Oliver very much, and made him glad to get out of those villages with all possible expedition. In others, he would stand about the inn-yards, and look mournfully at every one who passed: a proceeding which generally terminated in the landlady's ordering one of the post-boys who were lounging about, to drive that strange boy out of the place, for she was sure he had come to steal something. If he begged at a farmer's house, ten to one but they threatened to set the dog on him; and when he showed his nose in a shop, they talked about the beadle—which brought Oliver's heart into his mouth,—very often the only thing he had there, for many hours together.

In fact, if it had not been for a good-hearted turnpike-man, and a benevolent old lady, Oliver's troubles would have been shortened by the very same process which had put an end to his mother's; in other words, he would most assuredly have fallen dead upon the king's highway. But the turnpike-man gave him a meal of bread and cheese; and the old lady, who had a shipwrecked grandson wandering barefoot in some distant part of the earth, took pity upon the poor orphan, and gave him what little she could afford—and more—with such kind and gentle words, and such tears of sympathy and compassion, that they sank deeper into Oliver's soul, than all the sufferings he had ever undergone.

Early on the seventh morning after he had left his native place, Oliver limped slowly into the little town of Barnet. The window-shutters were closed; the street was empty; not a soul had awakened to the business of the day. The sun was rising in all its splendid beauty; but the light only served to show the boy his own lonesomeness and desolation, as he sat, with bleeding feet and covered with dust, upon a door-step.

By degrees, the shutters were opened; the window-blinds were drawn up; and people began passing to and fro. Some few stopped to gaze at Oliver for a moment or two, or turned round to stare at him as they hurried by; but none relieved him, or troubled themselves to inquire how he came there. He had no heart to beg. And there he sat.

He had been crouching on the step for some time: wondering at the great number of public-houses (every other house in Barnet was a tavern, large or small), gazing listlessly at the coaches as they passed through, and thinking how strange it seemed that they could do, with ease, in a few hours, what it had taken him a whole week of courage and determination beyond his years to accomplish: when he was roused by observing that a boy, who had passed him carelessly some minutes before, had returned, and was now surveying him most earnestly from the opposite side of the way. He took little heed of this at first; but the boy remained in the same attitude of close observation so long, that Oliver raised his head, and returned his steady look. Upon this, the boy crossed over; and walking close up to Oliver, said,

'Hullo, my covey! What's the row?'

The boy who addressed this inquiry to the young wayfarer, was about his own age: but one of the queerest looking boys that Oliver had even seen. He was a snub-nosed, flat-browed, common-faced boy enough; and as dirty a juvenile as one would wish to see; but he had about him all the airs and manners of a man. He was short of his age: with rather bow-legs, and little, sharp, ugly eyes. His hat was stuck on the top of his head so lightly, that it threatened to fall off every moment—and would have done so, very often, if the wearer had not had a knack of every now and then giving his head a sudden twitch, which brought it back to its old place again. He wore a man's coat, which reached nearly to his heels. He had turned the cuffs back, half-way up his arm, to get his hands out of the sleeves: apparently with the ultimate view of thrusting them into the pockets of his corduroy trousers; for there he kept them. He was, altogether, as roystering and swaggering a young gentleman as ever stood four feet six, or something less, in the bluchers.

'Hullo, my covey! What's the row?' said this strange young gentleman to Oliver.

'I am very hungry and tired,' replied Oliver: the tears standing in his eyes as he spoke. 'I have walked a long way. I have been walking these seven days.'

'Walking for sivin days!' said the young gentleman. 'Oh, I see. Beak's order, eh? But,' he added, noticing Oliver's look of surprise, 'I suppose you don't know what a beak is, my flash com-pan-i-on.'

Oliver mildly replied, that he had always heard a bird's mouth described by the term in question.

'My eyes, how green!' exclaimed the young gentleman. 'Why, a beak's a madgst'rate; and when you walk by a beak's order, it's not straight forerd, but always agoing up, and niver a coming down agin. Was you never on the mill?'

'What mill?' inquired Oliver.

'What mill! Why, the mill—the mill as takes up so little room that it'll work inside a Stone Jug; and always goes better when the wind's low with people, than when it's high; acos then they can't get workmen. But come,' said the young gentleman; 'you want grub, and you shall have it. I'm at low-water-mark myself—only one bob and a magpie; but, as far as it goes, I'll fork out and stump. Up with you on your pins. There! Now then! 'Morrice!'

Assisting Oliver to rise, the young gentleman took him to an adjacent chandler's shop, where he purchased a sufficiency of ready-dressed ham and a half-quartern loaf, or, as he himself expressed it, 'a fourpenny bran!' the ham being kept clean and preserved from dust, by the ingenious expedient of making a hole in the loaf by pulling out a portion of the crumb, and stuffing it therein. Taking the bread under his arm, the young gentlman turned into a small public-house, and led the way to a tap-room in the rear of the premises. Here, a pot of beer was brought in, by direction of the mysterious youth; and Oliver, falling to, at his new friend's bidding, made a long and hearty meal, during the progress of which the strange boy eyed him from time to time with great attention.

'Going to London?' said the strange boy, when Oliver had at length concluded.

'Yes.'

'Got any lodgings?'

'No.'

'Money?'

'No.'

The strange boy whistled; and put his arms into his pockets, as far as the big coat-sleeves would let them go.

'Do you live in London?' inquired Oliver.

'Yes. I do, when I'm at home,' replied the boy. 'I suppose you want some place to sleep in to-night, don't you?'

'I do, indeed,' answered Oliver. 'I have not slept under a roof since I left the country.'

'Don't fret your eyelids on that score,' said the young gentleman. 'I've got to be in London to-night; and I know a 'spectable old gentleman as lives there, wot'll give you lodgings for nothink, and never ask for the change—that is, if any genelman he knows interduces you. And don't he know me? Oh, no! Not in the least! By no means. Certainly not!'

The young gentleman smiled, as if to intimate that the latter fragments of discourse were playfully ironical; and finished the beer as he did so.

This unexpected offer of shelter was too tempting to be resisted; especially as it was immediately followed up, by the assurance that the old gentleman referred to, would doubtless provide Oliver with a comfortable place, without loss of time. This led to a more friendly and confidential dialogue; from which Oliver discovered that his friend's name was Jack Dawkins, and that he was a peculiar pet and protege of the elderly gentleman before mentioned.

Mr. Dawkin's appearance did not say a vast deal in favour of the comforts which his patron's interest obtained for those whom he took under his protection; but, as he had a rather flighty and dissolute mode of conversing, and furthermore avowed that among his intimate friends he was better known by the sobriquet of 'The Artful Dodger,' Oliver concluded that, being of a dissipated and careless turn, the moral precepts of his benefactor had hitherto been thrown away upon him. Under this impression, he secretly resolved to cultivate the good opinion of the old gentleman as quickly as possible; and, if he found the Dodger incorrigible, as he more than half suspected he should, to decline the honour of his farther acquaintance.

As John Dawkins objected to their entering London before nightfall, it was nearly eleven o'clock when they reached the turnpike at Islington. They crossed from the Angel into St. John's Road; struck down the small street which terminates at Sadler's Wells Theatre; through Exmouth Street and Coppice Row; down the little court by the side of the workhouse; across the classic ground which once bore the name of Hockley-in-the-Hole; thence into Little Saffron Hill; and so into Saffron Hill the Great: along which the Dodger scudded at a rapid pace, directing Oliver to follow close at his heels.

Although Oliver had enough to occupy his attention in keeping sight of his leader, he could not help bestowing a few hasty glances on either side of the way, as he passed along. A dirtier or more wretched place he had never seen. The street was very narrow and muddy, and the air was impregnated with filthy odours.

There were a good many small shops; but the only stock in trade appeared to be heaps of children, who, even at that time of night, were crawling in and out at the doors, or screaming from the inside. The sole places that seemed to prosper amid the general blight of the place, were the public-houses; and in them, the lowest orders of Irish were wrangling with might and main. Covered ways and yards, which here and there diverged from the main street, disclosed little knots of houses, where drunken men and women were positively wallowing in filth; and from several of the door-ways, great ill-looking fellows were cautiously emerging, bound, to all appearance, on no very well-disposed or harmless errands.

Oliver was just considering whether he hadn't better run away, when they reached the bottom of the hill. His conductor, catching him by the arm, pushed open the door of a house near Field Lane; and drawing him into the passage, closed it behind them.

'Now, then!' cried a voice from below, in reply to a whistle from the Dodger.

'Plummy and slam!' was the reply.

This seemed to be some watchword or signal that all was right; for the light of a feeble candle gleamed on the wall at the remote end of the passage; and a man's face peeped out, from where a balustrade of the old kitchen staircase had been broken away.

'There's two on you,' said the man, thrusting the candle farther out, and shielding his eyes with his hand. 'Who's the t'other one?'

'A new pal,' replied Jack Dawkins, pulling Oliver forward.

'Where did he come from?'

'Greenland. Is Fagin upstairs?'

'Yes, he's a sortin' the wipes. Up with you!' The candle was drawn back, and the face disappeared.

Oliver, groping his way with one hand, and having the other firmly grasped by his companion, ascended with much difficulty the dark and broken stairs: which his conductor mounted with an ease and expedition that showed he was well acquainted with them.

He threw open the door of a back-room, and drew Oliver in after him.

The walls and ceiling of the room were perfectly black with age and dirt. There was a deal table before the fire: upon which were a candle, stuck in a ginger-beer bottle, two or three pewter pots, a loaf and butter, and a plate. In a frying-pan, which was on the fire, and which was secured to the mantelshelf by a string, some sausages were cooking; and standing over them, with a toasting-fork in his hand, was a very old shrivelled Jew, whose villainous-looking and repulsive face was obscured by a quantity of matted red hair. He was dressed in a greasy flannel gown, with his throat bare; and seemed to be dividing his attention between the frying-pan and the clothes-horse, over which a great number of silk handkerchiefs were hanging. Several rough beds made of old sacks, were huddled side by side on the floor. Seated round the table were four or five boys, none older than the Dodger, smoking long clay pipes, and drinking spirits with the air of middle-aged men. These all crowded about their associate as he whispered a few words to the Jew; and then turned round and grinned at Oliver. So did the Jew himself, toasting-fork in hand.

'This is him, Fagin,' said Jack Dawkins;'my friend Oliver Twist.'

The Jew grinned; and, making a low obeisance to Oliver, took him by the hand, and hoped he should have the honour of his intimate acquaintance. Upon this, the young gentleman with the pipes came round him, and shook both his hands very hard—especially the one in which he held his little bundle. One young gentleman was very anxious to hang up his cap for him; and another was so obliging as to put his hands in his pockets, in order that, as he was very tired, he might not have the trouble of emptying them, himself, when he went to bed. These civilities would probably be extended much farther, but for a liberal exercise of the Jew's toasting-fork on the heads and shoulders of the affectionate youths who offered them.

'We are very glad to see you, Oliver, very,' said the Jew. 'Dodger, take off the sausages; and draw a tub near the fire for Oliver. Ah, you're a-staring at the pocket-handkerchiefs! eh, my dear. There are a good many of 'em, ain't there? We've just looked 'em out, ready for the wash; that's all, Oliver; that's all. Ha! ha! ha!'

The latter part of this speech, was hailed by a boisterous shout from all the hopeful pupils of the merry old gentleman. In the midst of which they went to supper.

Oliver ate his share, and the Jew then mixed him a glass of hot gin-and-water: telling him he must drink it off directly, because another gentleman wanted the tumbler. Oliver did as he was desired. Immediately afterwards he felt himself gently lifted on to one of the sacks; and then he sunk into a deep sleep.

CHAPTER IX. CONTAINING FURTHER PARTICULARS CONCERNING THE PLEASANT OLD GENTLEMAN, AND HIS HOPEFUL PUPILS

It was late next morning when Oliver awoke, from a sound, long sleep. There was no other person in the room but the old Jew, who was boiling some coffee in a saucepan for breakfast, and whistling softly to himself as he stirred it round and round, with an iron spoon. He would stop every now and then to listen when there was the least noise below: and when he had satisfied himself, he would go on whistling and stirring again, as before.

Although Oliver had roused himself from sleep, he was not thoroughly awake. There is a drowsy state, between sleeping and waking, when you dream more in five minutes with your eyes half open, and yourself half conscious of everything that is passing around you, than you would in five nights with your eyes fast closed, and your senses wrapt in perfect unconsciousness. At such time, a mortal knows just enough of what his mind is doing, to form some glimmering conception of its mighty powers, its bounding from earth and spurning time and space, when freed from the restraint of its corporeal associate.

Oliver was precisely in this condition. He saw the Jew with his half-closed eyes; heard his low whistling; and recognised the sound of the spoon grating against the saucepan's sides: and yet the self-same senses were mentally engaged, at the same time, in busy action with almost everybody he had ever known.

When the coffee was done, the Jew drew the saucepan to the hob. Standing, then in an irresolute attitude for a few minutes, as if he did not well know how to employ himself, he turned round and looked at Oliver, and called him by his name. He did not answer, and was to all appearances asleep.

After satisfying himself upon this head, the Jew stepped gently to the door: which he fastened. He then drew forth: as it seemed to Oliver, from some trap in the floor: a small box, which he placed carefully on the table. His eyes glistened as he raised the lid, and looked in. Dragging an old chair to the table, he sat down; and took from it a magnificent gold watch, sparkling with jewels.

'Aha!' said the Jew, shrugging up his shoulders, and distorting every feature with a hideous grin. 'Clever dogs! Clever dogs! Staunch to the last! Never told the old parson where they were. Never poached upon old Fagin! And why should they? It wouldn't have loosened the knot, or kept the drop up, a minute longer. No, no, no! Fine fellows! Fine fellows!'

With these, and other muttered reflections of the like nature, the Jew once more deposited the watch in its place of safety. At least half a dozen more were severally drawn forth from the same box, and surveyed with equal pleasure; besides rings, brooches, bracelets, and other articles of jewellery, of such magnificent materials, and costly workmanship, that Oliver had no idea, even of their names.

Having replaced these trinkets, the Jew took out another: so small that it lay in the palm of his hand. There seemed to be some very minute inscription on it; for the Jew laid it flat upon the table, and shading it with his hand, pored over it, long and earnestly. At length he put it down, as if despairing of success; and, leaning back in his chair, muttered:

'What a fine thing capital punishment is! Dead men never repent; dead men never bring awkward stories to light. Ah, it's a fine thing for the trade! Five of 'em strung up in a row, and none left to play booty, or turn white-livered!'

As the Jew uttered these words, his bright dark eyes, which had been staring vacantly before him, fell on Oliver's face; the boy's eyes were fixed on his in mute curiosity; and although the recognition was only for an instant—for the briefest space of time that can possibly be conceived—it was enough to show the old man that he had been observed.

He closed the lid of the box with a loud crash; and, laying his hand on a bread knife which was on the table, started furiously up. He trembled very much though; for, even in his terror, Oliver could see that the knife quivered in the air.

'What's that?' said the Jew. 'What do you watch me for? Why are you awake? What have you seen? Speak out, boy! Quick—quick! for your life.

'I wasn't able to sleep any longer, sir,' replied Oliver, meekly. 'I am very sorry if I have disturbed you, sir.'

'You were not awake an hour ago?' said the Jew, scowling fiercely on the boy.

'No! No, indeed!' replied Oliver.

'Are you sure?' cried the Jew: with a still fiercer look than before: and a threatening attitude.

'Upon my word I was not, sir,' replied Oliver, earnestly. 'I was not, indeed, sir.'

'Tush, tush, my dear!' said the Jew, abruptly resuming his old manner, and playing with the knife a little, before he laid it down; as if to induce the belief that he had caught it up, in mere sport. 'Of course I know that, my dear. I only tried to frighten you. You're a brave boy. Ha! ha! you're a brave boy, Oliver.' The Jew rubbed his hands with a chuckle, but glanced uneasily at the box, notwithstanding.

'Did you see any of these pretty things, my dear?' said the Jew, laying his hand upon it after a short pause.

'Yes, sir,' replied Oliver.

'Ah!' said the Jew, turning rather pale. 'They—they're mine, Oliver; my little property. All I have to live upon, in my old age. The folks call me a miser, my dear. Only a miser; that's all.'

Oliver thought the old gentleman must be a decided miser to live in such a dirty place, with so many watches; but, thinking that perhaps his fondness for the Dodger and the other boys, cost him a good deal of money, he only cast a deferential look at the Jew, and asked if he might get up.

'Certainly, my dear, certainly,' replied the old gentleman. 'Stay. There's a pitcher of water in the corner by the door. Bring it here; and I'll give you a basin to wash in, my dear.'

Oliver got up; walked across the room; and stooped for an instant to raise the pitcher. When he turned his head, the box was gone.

He had scarcely washed himself, and made everything tidy, by emptying the basin out of the window, agreeably to the Jew's directions, when the Dodger returned: accompanied by a very sprightly young friend, whom Oliver had seen smoking on the previous night, and who was now formally introduced to him as Charley Bates. The four sat down, to breakfast, on the coffee, and some hot rolls and ham which the Dodger had brought home in the crown of his hat.

'Well,' said the Jew, glancing slyly at Oliver, and addressing himself to the Dodger, 'I hope you've been at work this morning, my dears?'

'Hard,' replied the Dodger.

'As nails,' added Charley Bates.

'Good boys, good boys!' said the Jew. 'What have you got, Dodger?'

'A couple of pocket-books,' replied that young gentlman.

'Lined?' inquired the Jew, with eagerness.

'Pretty well,' replied the Dodger, producing two pocket-books; one green, and the other red.

'Not so heavy as they might be,' said the Jew, after looking at the insides carefully; 'but very neat and nicely made. Ingenious workman, ain't he, Oliver?'

'Very indeed, sir,' said Oliver. At which Mr. Charles Bates laughed uproariously; very much to the amazement of Oliver, who saw nothing to laugh at, in anything that had passed.

'And what have you got, my dear?' said Fagin to Charley Bates.

'Wipes,' replied Master Bates; at the same time producing four pocket-handkerchiefs.

'Well,' said the Jew, inspecting them closely; 'they're very good ones, very. You haven't marked them well, though, Charley; so the marks shall be picked out with a needle, and we'll teach Oliver how to do it. Shall us, Oliver, eh? Ha! ha! ha!'

'If you please, sir,' said Oliver.

'You'd like to be able to make pocket-handkerchiefs as easy as Charley Bates, wouldn't you, my dear?' said the Jew.

'Very much, indeed, if you'll teach me, sir,' replied Oliver.

Master Bates saw something so exquisitely ludicrous in this reply, that he burst into another laugh; which laugh, meeting the coffee he was drinking, and carrying it down some wrong channel, very nearly terminated in his premature suffocation.

'He is so jolly green!' said Charley when he recovered, as an apology to the company for his unpolite behaviour.

The Dodger said nothing, but he smoothed Oliver's hair over his eyes, and said he'd know better, by and by; upon which the old gentleman, observing Oliver's colour mounting, changed the subject by asking whether there had been much of a crowd at the execution that morning? This made him wonder more and more; for it was plain from the replies of the two boys that they had both been there; and Oliver naturally wondered how they could possibly have found time to be so very industrious.

When the breakfast was cleared away; the merry old gentlman and the two boys played at a very curious and uncommon game, which was performed in this way. The merry old gentleman, placing a snuff-box in one pocket of his trousers, a note-case in the other, and a watch in his waistcoat pocket, with a guard-chain round his neck, and sticking a mock diamond pin in his shirt: buttoned his coat tight round him, and putting his spectacle-case and handkerchief in his pockets, trotted up and down the room with a stick, in imitation of the manner in which old gentlemen walk about the streets any hour in the day. Sometimes he stopped at the fire-place, and sometimes at the door, making believe that he was staring with all his might into shop-windows. At such times, he would look constantly round him, for fear of thieves, and would keep slapping all his pockets in turn, to see that he hadn't lost anything, in such a very funny and natural manner, that Oliver laughed till the tears ran down his face. All this time, the two boys followed him closely about: getting out of his sight, so nimbly, every time he turned round, that it was impossible to follow their motions. At last, the Dodger trod upon his toes, or ran upon his boot accidently, while Charley Bates stumbled up against him behind; and in that one moment they took from him, with the most extraordinary rapidity, snuff-box, note-case, watch-guard, chain, shirt-pin, pocket-handkerchief, even the spectacle-case. If the old gentlman felt a hand in any one of his pockets, he cried out where it was; and then the game began all over again.

When this game had been played a great many times, a couple of young ladies called to see the young gentleman; one of whom was named Bet, and the other Nancy. They wore a good deal of hair, not very neatly turned up behind, and were rather untidy about the shoes and stockings. They were not exactly pretty, perhaps; but they had a great deal of colour in their faces, and looked quite stout and hearty. Being remarkably free and agreeable in their manners, Oliver thought them very nice girls indeed. As there is no doubt they were.

The visitors stopped a long time. Spirits were produced, in consequence of one of the young ladies complaining of a coldness in her inside; and the conversation took a very convivial and improving turn. At length, Charley Bates expressed his opinion that it was time to pad the hoof. This, it occurred to Oliver, must be French for going out; for directly afterwards, the Dodger, and Charley, and the two young ladies, went away together, having been kindly furnished by the amiable old Jew with money to spend.

'There, my dear,' said Fagin. 'That's a pleasant life, isn't it? They have gone out for the day.'

'Have they done work, sir?' inquired Oliver.

'Yes,' said the Jew; 'that is, unless they should unexpectedly come across any, when they are out; and they won't neglect it, if they do, my dear, depend upon it. Make 'em your models, my dear. Make 'em your models,' tapping the fire-shovel on the hearth to add force to his words; 'do everything they bid you, and take their advice in all matters—especially the Dodger's, my dear. He'll be a great man himself, and will make you one too, if you take pattern by him.—Is my handkerchief hanging out of my pocket, my dear?' said the Jew, stopping short.

'Yes, sir,' said Oliver.

'See if you can take it out, without my feeling it; as you saw them do, when we were at play this morning.'

Oliver held up the bottom of the pocket with one hand, as he had seen the Dodger hold it, and drew the handkerchief lightly out of it with the other.

'Is it gone?' cried the Jew.

'Here it is, sir,' said Oliver, showing it in his hand.

'You're a clever boy, my dear,' said the playful old gentleman, patting Oliver on the head approvingly. 'I never saw a sharper lad. Here's a shilling for you. If you go on, in this way, you'll be the greatest man of the time. And now come here, and I'll show you how to take the marks out of the handkerchiefs.'

Oliver wondered what picking the old gentleman's pocket in play, had to do with his chances of being a great man. But, thinking that the Jew, being so much his senior, must know best, he followed him quietly to the table, and was soon deeply involved in his new study.

CHAPTER X. OLIVER BECOMES BETTER ACQUAINTED WITH THE CHARACTERS OF HIS NEW ASSOCIATES; AND PURCHASES EXPERIENCE AT A HIGH PRICE. BEING A SHORT, BUT VERY IMPORTANT CHAPTER, IN THIS HISTORY

For many days, Oliver remained in the Jew's room, picking the marks out of the pocket-handkerchief, (of which a great number were brought home,) and sometimes taking part in the game already described: which the two boys and the Jew played, regularly, every morning. At length, he began to languish for fresh air, and took many occasions of earnestly entreating the old gentleman to allow him to go out to work with his two companions.

Oliver was rendered the more anxious to be actively employed, by what he had seen of the stern morality of the old gentleman's character. Whenever the Dodger or Charley Bates came home at night, empty-handed, he would expatiate with great vehemence on the misery of idle and lazy habits; and would enforce upon them the necessity of an active life, by sending them supperless to bed. On one occasion, indeed, he even went so far as to knock them both down a flight of stairs; but this was carrying out his virtuous precepts to an unusual extent.

At length, one morning, Oliver obtained the permission he had so eagerly sought. There had been no handkerchiefs to work upon, for two or three days, and the dinners had been rather meagre. Perhaps these were reasons for the old gentleman's giving his assent; but, whether they were or no, he told Oliver he might go, and placed him under the joint guardianship of Charley Bates, and his friend the Dodger.

The three boys sallied out; the Dodger with his coat-sleeves tucked up, and his hat cocked, as usual; Master Bates sauntering along with his hands in his pockets; and Oliver between them, wondering where they were going, and what branch of manufacture he would be instructed in, first.

The pace at which they went, was such a very lazy, ill-looking saunter, that Oliver soon began to think his companions were going to deceive the old gentleman, by not going to work at all. The Dodger had a vicious propensity, too, of pulling the caps from the heads of small boys and tossing them down areas; while Charley Bates exhibited some very loose notions concerning the rights of property, by pilfering divers apples and onions from the stalls at the kennel sides, and thrusting them into pockets which were so surprisingly capacious, that they seemed to undermine his whole suit of clothes in every direction. These things looked so bad, that Oliver was on the point of declaring his intention of seeking his way back, in the best way he could; when his thoughts were suddenly directed into another channel, by a very mysterious change of behaviour on the part of the Dodger.

They were just emerging from a narrow court not far from the open square in Clerkenwell, which is yet called, by some strange perversion of terms, 'The Green': when the Dodger made a sudden stop; and, laying his finger on his lip, drew his companions back again, with the greatest caution and circumspection.

'What's the matter?' demanded Oliver.

'Hush!' replied the Dodger. 'Do you see that old cove at the book-stall?'

'The old gentleman over the way?' said Oliver. 'Yes, I see him.'

'He'll do,' said the Dodger.

'A prime plant,' observed Master Charley Bates.

Oliver looked from one to the other, with the greatest surprise; but he was not permitted to make any inquiries; for the two boys walked stealthily across the road, and slunk close behind the old gentleman towards whom his attention had been directed. Oliver walked a few paces after them; and, not knowing whether to advance or retire, stood looking on in silent amazement.

The old gentleman was a very respectable-looking personage, with a powdered head and gold spectacles. He was dressed in a bottle-green coat with a black velvet collar; wore white trousers; and carried a smart bamboo cane under his arm. He had taken up a book from the stall, and there he stood, reading away, as hard as if he were in his elbow-chair, in his own study. It is very possible that he fancied himself there, indeed; for it was plain, from his abstraction, that he saw not the book-stall, nor the street, nor the boys, nor, in short, anything but the book itself: which he was reading straight through: turning over the leaf when he got to the bottom of a page, beginning at the top line of the next one, and going regularly on, with the greatest interest and eagerness.

What was Oliver's horror and alarm as he stood a few paces off, looking on with his eyelids as wide open as they would possibly go, to see the Dodger plunge his hand into the old gentleman's pocket, and draw from thence a handkerchief! To see him hand the same to Charley Bates; and finally to behold them, both running away round the corner at full speed!

In an instant the whole mystery of the hankerchiefs, and the watches, and the jewels, and the Jew, rushed upon the boy's mind.

He stood, for a moment, with the blood so tingling through all his veins from terror, that he felt as if he were in a burning fire; then, confused and frightened, he took to his heels; and, not knowing what he did, made off as fast as he could lay his feet to the ground.

This was all done in a minute's space. In the very instant when Oliver began to run, the old gentleman, putting his hand to his pocket, and missing his handkerchief, turned sharp round. Seeing the boy scudding away at such a rapid pace, he very naturally concluded him to be the depredator; and shouting 'Stop thief!' with all his might, made off after him, book in hand.

But the old gentleman was not the only person who raised the hue-and-cry. The Dodger and Master Bates, unwilling to attract public attention by running down the open street, had merely retired into the very first doorway round the corner. They no sooner heard the cry, and saw Oliver running, than, guessing exactly how the matter stood, they issued forth with great promptitude; and, shouting 'Stop thief!' too, joined in the pursuit like good citizens.

Although Oliver had been brought up by philosophers, he was not theoretically acquainted with the beautiful axiom that self-preservation is the first law of nature. If he had been, perhaps he would have been prepared for this. Not being prepared, however, it alarmed him the more; so away he went like the wind, with the old gentleman and the two boys roaring and shouting behind him.

'Stop thief! Stop thief!' There is a magic in the sound. The tradesman leaves his counter, and the car-man his waggon; the butcher throws down his tray; the baker his basket; the milkman his pail; the errand-boy his parcels; the school-boy his marbles; the paviour his pickaxe; the child his battledore. Away they run, pell-mell, helter-skelter, slap-dash: tearing, yelling, screaming, knocking down the passengers as they turn the corners, rousing up the dogs, and astonishing the fowls: and streets, squares, and courts, re-echo with the sound.

'Stop thief! Stop thief!' The cry is taken up by a hundred voices, and the crowd accumulate at every turning. Away they fly, splashing through the mud, and rattling along the pavements: up go the windows, out run the people, onward bear the mob, a whole audience desert Punch in the very thickest of the plot, and, joining the rushing throng, swell the shout, and lend fresh vigour to the cry, 'Stop thief! Stop thief!'

'Stop thief! Stop thief!' There is a passion FOR hunting something deeply implanted in the human breast. One wretched breathless child, panting with exhaustion; terror in his looks; agony in his eyes; large drops of perspiration streaming down his face; strains every nerve to make head upon his pursuers; and as they follow on his track, and gain upon him every instant, they hail his decreasing strength with joy. 'Stop thief!' Ay, stop him for God's sake, were it only in mercy!

Stopped at last! A clever blow. He is down upon the pavement; and the crowd eagerly gather round him: each new comer, jostling and struggling with the others to catch a glimpse. 'Stand aside!' 'Give him a little air!' 'Nonsense! he don't deserve it.' 'Where's the gentleman?' 'Here his is, coming down the street.' 'Make room there for the gentleman!' 'Is this the boy, sir!' 'Yes.'

Oliver lay, covered with mud and dust, and bleeding from the mouth, looking wildly round upon the heap of faces that surrounded him, when the old gentleman was officiously dragged and pushed into the circle by the foremost of the pursuers.

'Yes,' said the gentleman, 'I am afraid it is the boy.'

'Afraid!' murmured the crowd. 'That's a good 'un!'

'Poor fellow!' said the gentleman, 'he has hurt himself.'

'I did that, sir,' said a great lubberly fellow, stepping forward; 'and preciously I cut my knuckle agin' his mouth. I stopped him, sir.'

The fellow touched his hat with a grin, expecting something for his pains; but, the old gentleman, eyeing him with an expression of dislike, look anxiously round, as if he contemplated running away himself: which it is very possible he might have attempted to do, and thus have afforded another chase, had not a police officer (who is generally the last person to arrive in such cases) at that moment made his way through the crowd, and seized Oliver by the collar.

'Come, get up,' said the man, roughly.

'It wasn't me indeed, sir. Indeed, indeed, it was two other boys,' said Oliver, clasping his hands passionately, and looking round. 'They are here somewhere.'

'Oh no, they ain't,' said the officer. He meant this to be ironical, but it was true besides; for the Dodger and Charley Bates had filed off down the first convenient court they came to.

'Come, get up!'

'Don't hurt him,' said the old gentleman, compassionately.

'Oh no, I won't hurt him,' replied the officer, tearing his jacket half off his back, in proof thereof. 'Come, I know you; it won't do. Will you stand upon your legs, you young devil?'

Oliver, who could hardly stand, made a shift to raise himself on his feet, and was at once lugged along the streets by the jacket-collar, at a rapid pace. The gentleman walked on with them by the officer's side; and as many of the crowd as could achieve the feat, got a little ahead, and stared back at Oliver from time to time. The boys shouted in triumph; and on they went.

CHAPTER XI. TREATS OF MR. FANG THE POLICE MAGISTRATE; AND FURNISHES A SLIGHT SPECIMEN OF HIS MODE OF ADMINISTERING JUSTICE

The offence had been committed within the district, and indeed in the immediate neighborhood of, a very notorious metropolitan police office. The crowd had only the satisfaction of accompanying Oliver through two or three streets, and down a place called Mutton Hill, when he was led beneath a low archway, and up a dirty court, into this dispensary of summary justice, by the back way. It was a small paved yard into which they turned; and here they encountered a stout man with a bunch of whiskers on his face, and a bunch of keys in his hand.

'What's the matter now?' said the man carelessly.

'A young fogle-hunter,' replied the man who had Oliver in charge.

'Are you the party that's been robbed, sir?' inquired the man with the keys.

'Yes, I am,' replied the old gentleman; 'but I am not sure that this boy actually took the handkerchief. I—I would rather not press the case.'

'Must go before the magistrate now, sir,' replied the man. 'His worship will be disengaged in half a minute. Now, young gallows!'

This was an invitation for Oliver to enter through a door which he unlocked as he spoke, and which led into a stone cell. Here he was searched; and nothing being found upon him, locked up.

This cell was in shape and size something like an area cellar, only not so light. It was most intolerably dirty; for it was Monday morning; and it had been tenanted by six drunken people, who had been locked up, elsewhere, since Saturday night. But this is little. In our station-houses, men and women are every night confined on the most trivial charges—the word is worth noting—in dungeons, compared with which, those in Newgate, occupied by the most atrocious felons, tried, found guilty, and under sentence of death, are palaces. Let any one who doubts this, compare the two.

The old gentleman looked almost as rueful as Oliver when the key grated in the lock. He turned with a sigh to the book, which had been the innocent cause of all this disturbance.

'There is something in that boy's face,' said the old gentleman to himself as he walked slowly away, tapping his chin with the cover of the book, in a thoughtful manner; 'something that touches and interests me. Can he be innocent? He looked like—Bye the bye,' exclaimed the old gentleman, halting very abruptly, and staring up into the sky, 'Bless my soul!—where have I seen something like that look before?'

After musing for some minutes, the old gentleman walked, with the same meditative face, into a back anteroom opening from the yard; and there, retiring into a corner, called up before his mind's eye a vast amphitheatre of faces over which a dusky curtain had hung for many years. 'No,' said the old gentleman, shaking his head; 'it must be imagination.'

He wandered over them again. He had called them into view, and it was not easy to replace the shroud that had so long concealed them. There were the faces of friends, and foes, and of many that had been almost strangers peering intrusively from the crowd; there were the faces of young and blooming girls that were now old women; there were faces that the grave had changed and closed upon, but which the mind, superior to its power, still dressed in their old freshness and beauty, calling back the lustre of the eyes, the brightness of the smile, the beaming of the soul through its mask of clay, and whispering of beauty beyond the tomb, changed but to be heightened, and taken from earth only to be set up as a light, to shed a soft and gentle glow upon the path to Heaven.

But the old gentleman could recall no one countenance of which Oliver's features bore a trace. So, he heaved a sigh over the recollections he awakened; and being, happily for himself, an absent old gentleman, buried them again in the pages of the musty book.

He was roused by a touch on the shoulder, and a request from the man with the keys to follow him into the office. He closed his book hastily; and was at once ushered into the imposing presence of the renowned Mr. Fang.

The office was a front parlour, with a panelled wall. Mr. Fang sat behind a bar, at the upper end; and on one side the door was a sort of wooden pen in which poor little Oliver was already deposited; trembling very much at the awfulness of the scene.

Mr. Fang was a lean, long-backed, stiff-necked, middle-sized man, with no great quantity of hair, and what he had, growing on the back and sides of his head. His face was stern, and much flushed. If he were really not in the habit of drinking rather more than was exactly good for him, he might have brought action against his countenance for libel, and have recovered heavy damages.

The old gentleman bowed respectfully; and advancing to the magistrate's desk, said, suiting the action to the word, 'That is my name and address, sir.' He then withdrew a pace or two; and, with another polite and gentlemanly inclination of the head, waited to be questioned.

Now, it so happened that Mr. Fang was at that moment perusing a leading article in a newspaper of the morning, adverting to some recent decision of his, and commending him, for the three hundred and fiftieth time, to the special and particular notice of the Secretary of State for the Home Department. He was out of temper; and he looked up with an angry scowl.

'Who are you?' said Mr. Fang.

The old gentleman pointed, with some surprise, to his card.

'Officer!' said Mr. Fang, tossing the card contemptuously away with the newspaper. 'Who is this fellow?'

'My name, sir,' said the old gentleman, speaking like a gentleman, 'my name, sir, is Brownlow. Permit me to inquire the name of the magistrate who offers a gratuitous and unprovoked insult to a respectable person, under the protection of the bench.' Saying this, Mr. Brownlow looked around the office as if in search of some person who would afford him the required information.

'Officer!' said Mr. Fang, throwing the paper on one side, 'what's this fellow charged with?'

'He's not charged at all, your worship,' replied the officer. 'He appears against this boy, your worship.'

His worship knew this perfectly well; but it was a good annoyance, and a safe one.

'Appears against the boy, does he?' said Mr. Fang, surveying Mr. Brownlow contemptuously from head to foot. 'Swear him!'

'Before I am sworn, I must beg to say one word,' said Mr. Brownlow; 'and that is, that I really never, without actual experience, could have believed—'

'Hold your tongue, sir!' said Mr. Fang, peremptorily.

'I will not, sir!' replied the old gentleman.

'Hold your tongue this instant, or I'll have you turned out of the office!' said Mr. Fang. 'You're an insolent impertinent fellow. How dare you bully a magistrate!'

'What!' exclaimed the old gentleman, reddening.

'Swear this person!' said Fang to the clerk. 'I'll not hear another word. Swear him.'

Mr. Brownlow's indignation was greatly roused; but reflecting perhaps, that he might only injure the boy by giving vent to it, he suppressed his feelings and submitted to be sworn at once.

'Now,' said Fang, 'what's the charge against this boy? What have you got to say, sir?'

'I was standing at a bookstall—' Mr. Brownlow began.

'Hold your tongue, sir,' said Mr. Fang. 'Policeman! Where's the policeman? Here, swear this policeman. Now, policeman, what is this?'

The policeman, with becoming humility, related how he had taken the charge; how he had searched Oliver, and found nothing on his person; and how that was all he knew about it.

'Are there any witnesses?' inquired Mr. Fang.

'None, your worship,' replied the policeman.

Mr. Fang sat silent for some minutes, and then, turning round to the prosecutor, said in a towering passion.

'Do you mean to state what your complaint against this boy is, man, or do you not? You have been sworn. Now, if you stand there, refusing to give evidence, I'll punish you for disrespect to the bench; I will, by—'

By what, or by whom, nobody knows, for the clerk and jailor coughed very loud, just at the right moment; and the former dropped a heavy book upon the floor, thus preventing the word from being heard—accidently, of course.

With many interruptions, and repeated insults, Mr. Brownlow contrived to state his case; observing that, in the surprise of the moment, he had run after the boy because he had saw him running away; and expressing his hope that, if the magistrate should believe him, although not actually the thief, to be connected with the thieves, he would deal as leniently with him as justice would allow.

'He has been hurt already,' said the old gentleman in conclusion. 'And I fear,' he added, with great energy, looking towards the bar, 'I really fear that he is ill.'

'Oh! yes, I dare say!' said Mr. Fang, with a sneer. 'Come, none of your tricks here, you young vagabond; they won't do. What's your name?'

Oliver tried to reply but his tongue failed him. He was deadly pale; and the whole place seemed turning round and round.

'What's your name, you hardened scoundrel?' demanded Mr. Fang. 'Officer, what's his name?'

This was addressed to a bluff old fellow, in a striped waistcoat, who was standing by the bar. He bent over Oliver, and repeated the inquiry; but finding him really incapable of understanding the question; and knowing that his not replying would only infuriate the magistrate the more, and add to the severity of his sentence; he hazarded a guess.

'He says his name's Tom White, your worship,' said the kind-hearted thief-taker.

'Oh, he won't speak out, won't he?' said Fang. 'Very well, very well. Where does he live?'

'Where he can, your worship,' replied the officer; again pretending to receive Oliver's answer.

'Has he any parents?' inquired Mr. Fang.

'He says they died in his infancy, your worship,' replied the officer: hazarding the usual reply.

At this point of the inquiry, Oliver raised his head; and, looking round with imploring eyes, murmured a feeble prayer for a draught of water.

'Stuff and nonsense!' said Mr. Fang: 'don't try to make a fool of me.'

'I think he really is ill, your worship,' remonstrated the officer.

'I know better,' said Mr. Fang.

'Take care of him, officer,' said the old gentleman, raising his hands instinctively; 'he'll fall down.'

'Stand away, officer,' cried Fang; 'let him, if he likes.'

Oliver availed himself of the kind permission, and fell to the floor in a fainting fit. The men in the office looked at each other, but no one dared to stir.

'I knew he was shamming,' said Fang, as if this were incontestable proof of the fact. 'Let him lie there; he'll soon be tired of that.'

'How do you propose to deal with the case, sir?' inquired the clerk in a low voice.

'Summarily,' replied Mr. Fang. 'He stands committed for three months—hard labour of course. Clear the office.'

The door was opened for this purpose, and a couple of men were preparing to carry the insensible boy to his cell; when an elderly man of decent but poor appearance, clad in an old suit of black, rushed hastily into the office, and advanced towards the bench.

'Stop, stop! don't take him away! For Heaven's sake stop a moment!' cried the new comer, breathless with haste.

Although the presiding Genii in such an office as this, exercise a summary and arbitrary power over the liberties, the good name, the character, almost the lives, of Her Majesty's subjects, especially of the poorer class; and although, within such walls, enough fantastic tricks are daily played to make the angels blind with weeping; they are closed to the public, save through the medium of the daily press.[Footnote: Or were virtually, then.] Mr. Fang was consequently not a little indignant to see an unbidden guest enter in such irreverent disorder.

'What is this? Who is this? Turn this man out. Clear the office!' cried Mr. Fang.

'I will speak,' cried the man; 'I will not be turned out. I saw it all. I keep the book-stall. I demand to be sworn. I will not be put down. Mr. Fang, you must hear me. You must not refuse, sir.'

The man was right. His manner was determined; and the matter was growing rather too serious to be hushed up.

'Swear the man,' growled Mr. Fang, with a very ill grace. 'Now, man, what have you got to say?'

'This,' said the man: 'I saw three boys: two others and the prisoner here: loitering on the opposite side of the way, when this gentleman was reading. The robbery was committed by another boy. I saw it done; and I saw that this boy was perfectly amazed and stupified by it.' Having by this time recovered a little breath, the worthy book-stall keeper proceeded to relate, in a more coherent manner the exact circumstances of the robbery.

'Why didn't you come here before?' said Fang, after a pause.

'I hadn't a soul to mind the shop,' replied the man. 'Everybody who could have helped me, had joined in the pursuit. I could get nobody till five minutes ago; and I've run here all the way.'

'The prosecutor was reading, was he?' inquired Fang, after another pause.

'Yes,' replied the man. 'The very book he has in his hand.'

'Oh, that book, eh?' said Fang. 'Is it paid for?'

'No, it is not,' replied the man, with a smile.

'Dear me, I forgot all about it!' exclaimed the absent old gentleman, innocently.

'A nice person to prefer a charge against a poor boy!' said Fang, with a comical effort to look humane. 'I consider, sir, that you have obtained possession of that book, under very suspicious and disreputable circumstances; and you may think yourself very fortunate that the owner of the property declines to prosecute. Let this be a lesson to you, my man, or the law will overtake you yet. The boy is discharged. Clear the office!'

'D—n me!' cried the old gentleman, bursting out with the rage he had kept down so long, 'd—n me! I'll—'

'Clear the office!' said the magistrate. 'Officers, do you hear? Clear the office!'

The mandate was obeyed; and the indignant Mr. Brownlow was conveyed out, with the book in one hand, and the bamboo cane in the other: in a perfect phrenzy of rage and defiance. He reached the yard; and his passion vanished in a moment. Little Oliver Twist lay on his back on the pavement, with his shirt unbuttoned, and his temples bathed with water; his face a deadly white; and a cold tremble convulsing his whole frame.

'Poor boy, poor boy!' said Mr. Brownlow, bending over him. 'Call a coach, somebody, pray. Directly!'

A coach was obtained, and Oliver having been carefully laid on the seat, the old gentleman got in and sat himself on the other.

'May I accompany you?' said the book-stall keeper, looking in.

'Bless me, yes, my dear sir,' said Mr. Brownlow quickly. 'I forgot you. Dear, dear! I have this unhappy book still! Jump in. Poor fellow! There's no time to lose.'

The book-stall keeper got into the coach; and away they drove.

CHAPTER XII. IN WHICH OLIVER IS TAKEN BETTER CARE OF THAN HE EVER WAS BEFORE. AND IN WHICH THE NARRATIVE REVERTS TO THE MERRY OLD GENTLEMAN AND HIS YOUTHFUL FRIENDS.

The coach rattled away, over nearly the same ground as that which Oliver had traversed when he first entered London in company with the Dodger; and, turning a different way when it reached the Angel at Islington, stopped at length before a neat house, in a quiet shady street near Pentonville. Here, a bed was prepared, without loss of time, in which Mr. Brownlow saw his young charge carefully and comfortably deposited; and here, he was tended with a kindness and solicitude that knew no bounds.

But, for many days, Oliver remained insensible to all the goodness of his new friends. The sun rose and sank, and rose and sank again, and many times after that; and still the boy lay stretched on his uneasy bed, dwindling away beneath the dry and wasting heat of fever. The worm does not work more surely on the dead body, than does this slow creeping fire upon the living frame.

Weak, and thin, and pallid, he awoke at last from what seemed to have been a long and troubled dream. Feebly raising himself in the bed, with his head resting on his trembling arm, he looked anxiously around.

'What room is this? Where have I been brought to?' said Oliver. 'This is not the place I went to sleep in.'

He uttered these words in a feeble voice, being very faint and weak; but they were overheard at once. The curtain at the bed's head was hastily drawn back, and a motherly old lady, very neatly and precisely dressed, rose as she undrew it, from an arm-chair close by, in which she had been sitting at needle-work.

'Hush, my dear,' said the old lady softly. 'You must be very quiet, or you will be ill again; and you have been very bad,—as bad as bad could be, pretty nigh. Lie down again; there's a dear!' With those words, the old lady very gently placed Oliver's head upon the pillow; and, smoothing back his hair from his forehead, looked so kindly and loving in his face, that he could not help placing his little withered hand in hers, and drawing it round his neck.

'Save us!' said the old lady, with tears in her eyes. 'What a grateful little dear it is. Pretty creetur! What would his mother feel if she had sat by him as I have, and could see him now!'

'Perhaps she does see me,' whispered Oliver, folding his hands together; 'perhaps she has sat by me. I almost feel as if she had.'

'That was the fever, my dear,' said the old lady mildly.

'I suppose it was,' replied Oliver, 'because heaven is a long way off; and they are too happy there, to come down to the bedside of a poor boy. But if she knew I was ill, she must have pitied me, even there; for she was very ill herself before she died. She can't know anything about me though,' added Oliver after a moment's silence. 'If she had seen me hurt, it would have made her sorrowful; and her face has always looked sweet and happy, when I have dreamed of her.'

The old lady made no reply to this; but wiping her eyes first, and her spectacles, which lay on the counterpane, afterwards, as if they were part and parcel of those features, brought some cool stuff for Oliver to drink; and then, patting him on the cheek, told him he must lie very quiet, or he would be ill again.

So, Oliver kept very still; partly because he was anxious to obey the kind old lady in all things; and partly, to tell the truth, because he was completely exhausted with what he had already said. He soon fell into a gentle doze, from which he was awakened by the light of a candle: which, being brought near the bed, showed him a gentleman with a very large and loud-ticking gold watch in his hand, who felt his pulse, and said he was a great deal better.

'You are a great deal better, are you not, my dear?' said the gentleman.

'Yes, thank you, sir,' replied Oliver.

'Yes, I know you are,' said the gentleman: 'You're hungry too, an't you?'

'No, sir,' answered Oliver.

'Hem!' said the gentleman. 'No, I know you're not. He is not hungry, Mrs. Bedwin,' said the gentleman: looking very wise.

The old lady made a respectful inclination of the head, which seemed to say that she thought the doctor was a very clever man. The doctor appeared much of the same opinion himself.

'You feel sleepy, don't you, my dear?' said the doctor.

'No, sir,' replied Oliver.

'No,' said the doctor, with a very shrewd and satisfied look. 'You're not sleepy. Nor thirsty. Are you?'

'Yes, sir, rather thirsty,' answered Oliver.

'Just as I expected, Mrs. Bedwin,' said the doctor. 'It's very natural that he should be thirsty. You may give him a little tea, ma'am, and some dry toast without any butter. Don't keep him too warm, ma'am; but be careful that you don't let him be too cold; will you have the goodness?'

The old lady dropped a curtsey. The doctor, after tasting the cool stuff, and expressing a qualified approval of it, hurried away: his boots creaking in a very important and wealthy manner as he went downstairs.

Oliver dozed off again, soon after this; when he awoke, it was nearly twelve o'clock. The old lady tenderly bade him good-night shortly afterwards, and left him in charge of a fat old woman who had just come: bringing with her, in a little bundle, a small Prayer Book and a large nightcap. Putting the latter on her head and the former on the table, the old woman, after telling Oliver that she had come to sit up with him, drew her chair close to the fire and went off into a series of short naps, chequered at frequent intervals with sundry tumblings forward, and divers moans and chokings. These, however, had no worse effect than causing her to rub her nose very hard, and then fall asleep again.

And thus the night crept slowly on. Oliver lay awake for some time, counting the little circles of light which the reflection of the rushlight-shade threw upon the ceiling; or tracing with his languid eyes the intricate pattern of the paper on the wall. The darkness and the deep stillness of the room were very solemn; as they brought into the boy's mind the thought that death had been hovering there, for many days and nights, and might yet fill it with the gloom and dread of his awful presence, he turned his face upon the pillow, and fervently prayed to Heaven.

Gradually, he fell into that deep tranquil sleep which ease from recent suffering alone imparts; that calm and peaceful rest which it is pain to wake from. Who, if this were death, would be roused again to all the struggles and turmoils of life; to all its cares for the present; its anxieties for the future; more than all, its weary recollections of the past!

It had been bright day, for hours, when Oliver opened his eyes; he felt cheerful and happy. The crisis of the disease was safely past. He belonged to the world again.

In three days' time he was able to sit in an easy-chair, well propped up with pillows; and, as he was still too weak to walk, Mrs. Bedwin had him carried downstairs into the little housekeeper's room, which belonged to her. Having him set, here, by the fire-side, the good old lady sat herself down too; and, being in a state of considerable delight at seeing him so much better, forthwith began to cry most violently.

'Never mind me, my dear,' said the old lady; 'I'm only having a regular good cry. There; it's all over now; and I'm quite comfortable.'

'You're very, very kind to me, ma'am,' said Oliver.

'Well, never you mind that, my dear,' said the old lady; 'that's got nothing to do with your broth; and it's full time you had it; for the doctor says Mr. Brownlow may come in to see you this morning; and we must get up our best looks, because the better we look, the more he'll be pleased.' And with this, the old lady applied herself to warming up, in a little saucepan, a basin full of broth: strong enough, Oliver thought, to furnish an ample dinner, when reduced to the regulation strength, for three hundred and fifty paupers, at the lowest computation.

'Are you fond of pictures, dear?' inquired the old lady, seeing that Oliver had fixed his eyes, most intently, on a portrait which hung against the wall; just opposite his chair.

'I don't quite know, ma'am,' said Oliver, without taking his eyes from the canvas; 'I have seen so few that I hardly know. What a beautiful, mild face that lady's is!'

'Ah!' said the old lady, 'painters always make ladies out prettier than they are, or they wouldn't get any custom, child. The man that invented the machine for taking likenesses might have known that would never succeed; it's a deal too honest. A deal,' said the old lady, laughing very heartily at her own acuteness.

'Is—is that a likeness, ma'am?' said Oliver.

'Yes,' said the old lady, looking up for a moment from the broth; 'that's a portrait.'

'Whose, ma'am?' asked Oliver.

'Why, really, my dear, I don't know,' answered the old lady in a good-humoured manner. 'It's not a likeness of anybody that you or I know, I expect. It seems to strike your fancy, dear.'

'It is so pretty,' replied Oliver.

'Why, sure you're not afraid of it?' said the old lady: observing in great surprise, the look of awe with which the child regarded the painting.

'Oh no, no,' returned Oliver quickly; 'but the eyes look so sorrowful; and where I sit, they seem fixed upon me. It makes my heart beat,' added Oliver in a low voice, 'as if it was alive, and wanted to speak to me, but couldn't.'

'Lord save us!' exclaimed the old lady, starting; 'don't talk in that way, child. You're weak and nervous after your illness. Let me wheel your chair round to the other side; and then you won't see it. There!' said the old lady, suiting the action to the word; 'you don't see it now, at all events.'

Oliver did see it in his mind's eye as distinctly as if he had not altered his position; but he thought it better not to worry the kind old lady; so he smiled gently when she looked at him; and Mrs. Bedwin, satisfied that he felt more comfortable, salted and broke bits of toasted bread into the broth, with all the bustle befitting so solemn a preparation. Oliver got through it with extraordinary expedition. He had scarcely swallowed the last spoonful, when there came a soft rap at the door. 'Come in,' said the old lady; and in walked Mr. Brownlow.

Now, the old gentleman came in as brisk as need be; but, he had no sooner raised his spectacles on his forehead, and thrust his hands behind the skirts of his dressing-gown to take a good long look at Oliver, than his countenance underwent a very great variety of odd contortions. Oliver looked very worn and shadowy from sickness, and made an ineffectual attempt to stand up, out of respect to his benefactor, which terminated in his sinking back into the chair again; and the fact is, if the truth must be told, that Mr. Brownlow's heart, being large enough for any six ordinary old gentlemen of humane disposition, forced a supply of tears into his eyes, by some hydraulic process which we are not sufficiently philosophical to be in a condition to explain.

'Poor boy, poor boy!' said Mr. Brownlow, clearing his throat. 'I'm rather hoarse this morning, Mrs. Bedwin. I'm afraid I have caught cold.'

'I hope not, sir,' said Mrs. Bedwin. 'Everything you have had, has been well aired, sir.'

'I don't know, Bedwin. I don't know,' said Mr. Brownlow; 'I rather think I had a damp napkin at dinner-time yesterday; but never mind that. How do you feel, my dear?'

'Very happy, sir,' replied Oliver. 'And very grateful indeed, sir, for your goodness to me.'

'Good by,' said Mr. Brownlow, stoutly. 'Have you given him any nourishment, Bedwin? Any slops, eh?'

'He has just had a basin of beautiful strong broth, sir,' replied Mrs. Bedwin: drawing herself up slightly, and laying strong emphasis on the last word: to intimate that between slops, and broth will compounded, there existed no affinity or connection whatsoever.

'Ugh!' said Mr. Brownlow, with a slight shudder; 'a couple of glasses of port wine would have done him a great deal more good. Wouldn't they, Tom White, eh?'

'My name is Oliver, sir,' replied the little invalid: with a look of great astonishment.

'Oliver,' said Mr. Brownlow; 'Oliver what? Oliver White, eh?'

'No, sir, Twist, Oliver Twist.'

'Queer name!' said the old gentleman. 'What made you tell the magistrate your name was White?'

'I never told him so, sir,' returned Oliver in amazement.

This sounded so like a falsehood, that the old gentleman looked somewhat sternly in

Oliver's face. It was impossible to doubt him; there was truth in every one of its thin and sharpened lineaments.

'Some mistake,' said Mr. Brownlow. But, although his motive for looking steadily at Oliver no longer existed, the old idea of the resemblance between his features and some familiar face came upon him so strongly, that he could not withdraw his gaze.

'I hope you are not angry with me, sir?' said Oliver, raising his eyes beseechingly.

'No, no,' replied the old gentleman. 'Why! what's this? Bedwin, look there!'

As he spoke, he pointed hastily to the picture over Oliver's head, and then to the boy's face. There was its living copy. The eyes, the head, the mouth; every feature was the same. The expression was, for the instant, so precisely alike, that the minutest line seemed copied with startling accuracy!

Oliver knew not the cause of this sudden exclamation; for, not being strong enough to bear the start it gave him, he fainted away. A weakness on his part, which affords the narrative an opportunity of relieving the reader from suspense, in behalf of the two young pupils of the Merry Old Gentleman; and of recording—

That when the Dodger, and his accomplished friend Master Bates, joined in the hue-and-cry which was raised at Oliver's heels, in consequence of their executing an illegal conveyance of Mr. Brownlow's personal property, as has been already described, they were actuated by a very laudable and becoming regard for themselves; and forasmuch as the freedom of the subject and the liberty of the individual are among the first and proudest boasts of a true-hearted Englishman, so, I need hardly beg the reader to observe, that this action should tend to exalt them in the opinion of all public and patriotic men, in almost as great a degree as this strong proof of their anxiety for their own preservation and safety goes to corroborate and confirm the little code of laws which certain profound and sound-judging philosophers have laid down as the main-springs of all Nature's deeds and actions: the said philosophers very wisely reducing the good lady's proceedings to matters of maxim and theory: and, by a very neat and pretty compliment to her exalted wisdom and understanding, putting entirely out of sight any considerations of heart, or generous impulse and feeling. For, these are matters totally beneath a female who is acknowledged by universal admission to be far above the numerous little foibles and weaknesses of her sex.

If I wanted any further proof of the strictly philosophical nature of the conduct of these young gentlemen in their very delicate predicament, I should at once find it in the fact (also recorded in a foregoing part of this narrative), of their quitting the pursuit, when the general attention was fixed upon Oliver; and making immediately for their home by the shortest possible cut. Although I do not mean to assert that it is usually the practice of renowned and learned sages, to shorten the road to any great conclusion (their course indeed being rather to lengthen the distance, by various circumlocutions and discursive staggerings, like unto those in which drunken men under the pressure of a too mighty flow of ideas, are prone to indulge); still, I do mean to say, and do say distinctly, that it is the invariable practice of many mighty philosophers, in carrying out their theories, to evince great wisdom and foresight in providing against every possible contingency which can be supposed at all likely to affect themselves. Thus, to do a great right, you may do a little wrong; and you may take any means which the end to be attained, will justify; the amount of the right, or the amount of the wrong, or indeed the distinction between the two, being left entirely to the philosopher concerned, to be settled and determined by his clear, comprehensive, and impartial view of his own particular case.

It was not until the two boys had scoured, with great rapidity, through a most intricate maze of narrow streets and courts, that they ventured to halt beneath a low and dark archway. Having remained silent here, just long enough to recover breath to speak, Master Bates uttered an exclamation of amusement and delight; and, bursting into an uncontrollable fit of laughter, flung himself upon a doorstep, and rolled thereon in a transport of mirth.

'What's the matter?' inquired the Dodger.

'Ha! ha! ha!' roared Charley Bates.

'Hold your noise,' remonstrated the Dodger, looking cautiously round. 'Do you want to be grabbed, stupid?'

'I can't help it,' said Charley, 'I can't help it! To see him splitting away at that pace, and cutting round the corners, and knocking up again' the posts, and starting on again as if he was made of iron as well as them, and me with the wipe in my pocket, singing out arter him—oh, my eye!' The vivid imagination of Master Bates presented the scene before him in too strong colours. As he arrived at this apostrophe, he again rolled upon the door-step, and laughed louder than before.

'What'll Fagin say?' inquired the Dodger; taking advantage of the next interval of breathlessness on the part of his friend to propound the question.

'What?' repeated Charley Bates.

'Ah, what?' said the Dodger.

'Why, what should he say?' inquired Charley: stopping rather suddenly in his merriment; for the Dodger's manner was impressive. 'What should he say?'

Mr. Dawkins whistled for a couple of minutes; then, taking off his hat, scratched his head, and nodded thrice.

'What do you mean?' said Charley.

'Toor rul lol loo, gammon and spinnage, the frog he wouldn't, and high cockolorum,' said the Dodger: with a slight sneer on his intellectual countenance.

This was explanatory, but not satisfactory. Master Bates felt it so; and again said, 'What do you mean?'

The Dodger made no reply; but putting his hat on again, and gathering the skirts of his long-tailed coat under his arm, thrust his tongue into his cheek, slapped the bridge of his nose some half-dozen times in a familiar but expressive manner, and turning on his heel, slunk down the court. Master Bates followed, with a thoughtful countenance.

The noise of footsteps on the creaking stairs, a few minutes after the occurrence of this conversation, roused the merry old gentleman as he sat over the fire with a saveloy and a small loaf in his hand; a pocket-knife in his right; and a pewter pot on the trivet. There was a rascally smile on his white face as he turned round, and looking sharply out from under his thick red eyebrows, bent his ear towards the door, and listened.

'Why, how's this?' muttered the Jew: changing countenance; 'only two of 'em? Where's the third? They can't have got into trouble. Hark!'

The footsteps approached nearer; they reached the landing. The door was slowly opened; and the Dodger and Charley Bates entered, closing it behind them.

CHAPTER XIII. SOME NEW ACQUAINTANCES ARE INTRODUCED TO THE INTELLIGENT READER, CONNECTED WITH WHOM VARIOUS PLEASANT MATTERS ARE RELATED, APPERTAINING TO THIS HISTORY

'Where's Oliver?' said the Jew, rising with a menacing look. 'Where's the boy?'

The young thieves eyed their preceptor as if they were alarmed at his violence; and looked uneasily at each other. But they made no reply.

'What's become of the boy?' said the Jew, seizing the Dodger tightly by the collar, and threatening him with horrid imprecations. 'Speak out, or I'll throttle you!'

Mr. Fagin looked so very much in earnest, that Charley Bates, who deemed it prudent in all cases to be on the safe side, and who conceived it by no means improbable that it might be his turn to be throttled second, dropped upon his knees, and raised a loud, well-sustained, and continuous roar—something between a mad bull and a speaking trumpet.

'Will you speak?' thundered the Jew: shaking the Dodger so much that his keeping in the big coat at all, seemed perfectly miraculous.

'Why, the traps have got him, and that's all about it,' said the Dodger, sullenly. 'Come, let go o' me, will you!' And, swinging himself, at one jerk, clean out of the big coat, which he left in the Jew's hands, the Dodger snatched up the toasting fork, and made a pass at the merry old gentleman's waistcoat; which, if it had taken effect, would have let a little more merriment out than could have been easily replaced.

The Jew stepped back in this emergency, with more agility than could have been anticipated in a man of his apparent decrepitude; and, seizing up the pot, prepared to hurl it at his assailant's head. But Charley Bates, at this moment, calling his attention by a perfectly terrific howl, he suddenly altered its destination, and flung it full at that young gentleman.

'Why, what the blazes is in the wind now!' growled a deep voice. 'Who pitched that 'ere at me? It's well it's the beer, and not the pot, as hit me, or I'd have settled somebody. I might have know'd, as nobody but an infernal, rich, plundering, thundering old Jew could afford to throw away any drink but water—and not that, unless he done the River Company every quarter. Wot's it all about, Fagin? D—me, if my neck-handkercher an't lined with beer! Come in, you sneaking warmint; wot are you stopping outside for, as if you was ashamed of your master! Come in!'

The man who growled out these words, was a stoutly-built fellow of about five-and-thirty, in a black velveteen coat, very soiled drab breeches, lace-up half boots, and grey cotton stockings which inclosed a bulky pair of legs, with large swelling calves;—the kind of legs, which in such costume, always look in an unfinished and incomplete state without a set of fetters to garnish them. He had a brown hat on his head, and a dirty belcher handkerchief round his neck: with the long frayed ends of which he smeared the beer from his face as he spoke. He disclosed, when he had done so, a broad heavy countenance with a beard of three days' growth, and two scowling eyes; one of which displayed various parti-coloured symptoms of having been recently damaged by a blow.

'Come in, d'ye hear?' growled this engaging ruffian.

A white shaggy dog, with his face scratched and torn in twenty different places, skulked into the room.

'Why didn't you come in afore?' said the man. 'You're getting too proud to own me afore company, are you? Lie down!'

This command was accompanied with a kick, which sent the animal to the other end of the room. He appeared well used to it, however; for he coiled himself up in a corner very quietly, without uttering a sound, and winking his very ill-looking eyes twenty times in a minute, appeared to occupy himself in taking a survey of the apartment.

'What are you up to? Ill-treating the boys, you covetous, avaricious, in-sa-ti-a-ble old fence?' said the man, seating himself deliberately. 'I wonder they don't murder you! I would if I was them. If I'd been your 'prentice, I'd have done it long ago, and—no, I couldn't have sold you afterwards, for you're fit for nothing but keeping as a curiosity of ugliness in a glass bottle, and I suppose they don't blow glass bottles large enough.'

'Hush! hush! Mr. Sikes,' said the Jew, trembling; 'don't speak so loud!'

'None of your mistering,' replied the ruffian; 'you always mean mischief when you come that. You know my name: out with it! I shan't disgrace it when the time comes.'

'Well, well, then—Bill Sikes,' said the Jew, with abject humility. 'You seem out of humour, Bill.'

'Perhaps I am,' replied Sikes; 'I should think you was rather out of sorts too, unless you mean as little harm when you throw pewter pots about, as you do when you blab and—'

'Are you mad?' said the Jew, catching the man by the sleeve, and pointing towards the boys.

Mr. Sikes contented himself with tying an imaginary knot under his left ear, and jerking his head over on the right shoulder; a piece of dumb show which the Jew appeared to understand perfectly. He then, in cant terms, with which his whole conversation was plentifully besprinkled, but which would be quite unintelligible if they were recorded here, demanded a glass of liquor.

'And mind you don't poison it,' said Mr. Sikes, laying his hat upon the table.

This was said in jest; but if the speaker could have seen the evil leer with which the Jew bit his pale lip as he turned round to the cupboard, he might have thought the caution not wholly unnecessary, or the wish (at all events) to improve upon the distiller's ingenuity not very far from the old gentleman's merry heart.

After swallowing two of three glasses of spirits, Mr. Sikes condescended to take some notice of the young gentlemen; which gracious act led to a conversation, in which the cause and manner of Oliver's capture were circumstantially detailed, with such alterations and improvements on the truth, as to the Dodger appeared most advisable under the circumstances.

'I'm afraid,' said the Jew, 'that he may say something which will get us into trouble.'

'That's very likely,' returned Sikes with a malicious grin. 'You're blowed upon, Fagin.'

'And I'm afraid, you see,' added the Jew, speaking as if he had not noticed the interruption; and regarding the other closely as he did so,—'I'm afraid that, if the game was up with us, it might be up with a good many more, and that it would come out rather worse for you than it would for me, my dear.'

The man started, and turned round upon the Jew. But the old gentleman's shoulders were shrugged up to his ears; and his eyes were vacantly staring on the opposite wall.

There was a long pause. Every member of the respectable coterie appeared plunged in his own reflections; not excepting the dog, who by a certain malicious licking of his lips seemed to be meditating an attack upon the legs of the first gentleman or lady he might encounter in the streets when he went out.

'Somebody must find out wot's been done at the office,' said Mr. Sikes in a much lower tone than he had taken since he came in.

The Jew nodded assent.

'If he hasn't peached, and is committed, there's no fear till he comes out again,' said Mr. Sikes, 'and then he must be taken care on. You must get hold of him somehow.'

Again the Jew nodded.

The prudence of this line of action, indeed, was obvious; but, unfortunately, there was one very strong objection to its being adopted. This was, that the Dodger, and Charley Bates, and Fagin, and Mr. William Sikes, happened, one and all, to entertain a violent and deeply-rooted antipathy to going near a police-office on any ground or pretext whatever.

How long they might have sat and looked at each other, in a state of uncertainty not the most pleasant of its kind, it is difficult to guess. It is not necessary to make any guesses on the subject, however; for the sudden entrance of the two young ladies whom Oliver had seen on a former occasion, caused the conversation to flow afresh.

'The very thing!' said the Jew. 'Bet will go; won't you, my dear?'

'Wheres?' inquired the young lady.

'Only just up to the office, my dear,' said the Jew coaxingly.

It is due to the young lady to say that she did not positively affirm that she would not, but that she merely expressed an emphatic and earnest desire to be 'blessed' if she would; a polite and delicate evasion of the request, which shows the young lady to have been possessed of that natural good breeding which cannot bear to inflict upon a fellow-creature, the pain of a direct and pointed refusal.

The Jew's countenance fell. He turned from this young lady, who was gaily, not to say gorgeously attired, in a red gown, green boots, and yellow curl-papers, to the other female.

'Nancy, my dear,' said the Jew in a soothing manner, 'what do YOU say?'

'That it won't do; so it's no use a-trying it on, Fagin,' replied Nancy.

'What do you mean by that?' said Mr. Sikes, looking up in a surly manner.

'What I say, Bill,' replied the lady collectedly.

'Why, you're just the very person for it,' reasoned Mr. Sikes: 'nobody about here knows anything of you.'

'And as I don't want 'em to, neither,' replied Nancy in the same composed manner, 'it's rather more no than yes with me, Bill.'

'She'll go, Fagin,' said Sikes.

'No, she won't, Fagin,' said Nancy.

'Yes, she will, Fagin,' said Sikes.

And Mr. Sikes was right. By dint of alternate threats, promises, and bribes, the lady in question was ultimately prevailed upon to undertake the commission. She was not, indeed, withheld by the same considerations as her agreeable friend; for, having recently removed into the neighborhood of Field Lane from the remote but genteel suburb of Ratcliffe, she was not under the same apprehension of being recognised by any of her numerous acquaintants.

Accordingly, with a clean white apron tied over her gown, and her curl-papers tucked up under a straw bonnet,—both articles of dress being provided from the Jew's inexhaustible stock,—Miss Nancy prepared to issue forth on her errand.

'Stop a minute, my dear,' said the Jew, producing, a little covered basket. 'Carry that in one hand. It looks more respectable, my dear.'

'Give her a door-key to carry in her t'other one, Fagin,' said Sikes; 'it looks real and genivine like.'

'Yes, yes, my dear, so it does,' said the Jew, hanging a large street-door key on the forefinger of the young lady's right hand.

'There; very good! Very good indeed, my dear!' said the Jew, rubbing his hands.

'Oh, my brother! My poor, dear, sweet, innocent little brother!' exclaimed Nancy, bursting into tears, and wringing the little basket and the street-door key in an agony of distress. 'What has become of him! Where have they taken him to! Oh, do have pity, and tell me what's been done with the dear boy, gentlemen; do, gentlemen, if you please, gentlemen!'

Having uttered those words in a most lamentable and heart-broken tone: to the immeasurable delight of her hearers: Miss Nancy paused, winked to the company, nodded smilingly round, and disappeared.

'Ah, she's a clever girl, my dears,' said the Jew, turning round to his young friends, and shaking his head gravely, as if in mute admonition to them to follow the bright example they had just beheld.

'She's a honour to her sex,' said Mr. Sikes, filling his glass, and smiting the table with his enormous fist. 'Here's her health, and wishing they was all like her!'

While these, and many other encomiums, were being passed on the accomplished Nancy, that young lady made the best of her way to the police-office; whither, notwithstanding a little natural timidity consequent upon walking through the streets alone and unprotected, she arrived in perfect safety shortly afterwards.

Entering by the back way, she tapped softly with the key at one of the cell-doors, and listened. There was no sound within: so she coughed and listened again. Still there was no reply: so she spoke.

'Nolly, dear?' murmured Nancy in a gentle voice; 'Nolly?'

There was nobody inside but a miserable shoeless criminal, who had been taken up for playing the flute, and who, the offence against society having been clearly proved, had been very properly committed by Mr. Fang to the House of Correction for one month; with the appropriate and amusing remark that since he had so much breath to spare, it would be more wholesomely expended on the treadmill than in a musical instrument. He made no answer: being occupied mentally bewailing the loss of the flute, which had been confiscated for the use of the county: so Nancy passed on to the next cell, and knocked there.

'Well!' cried a faint and feeble voice.

'Is there a little boy here?' inquired Nancy, with a preliminary sob.

'No,' replied the voice; 'God forbid.'

This was a vagrant of sixty-five, who was going to prison for not playing the flute; or, in other words, for begging in the streets, and doing nothing for his livelihood. In the next cell was another man, who was going to the same prison for hawking tin saucepans without license; thereby doing something for his living, in defiance of the Stamp-office.

But, as neither of these criminals answered to the name of Oliver, or knew anything about him, Nancy made straight up to the bluff officer in the striped waistcoat; and with the most piteous wailings and lamentations, rendered more piteous by a prompt and efficient use of the street-door key and the little basket, demanded her own dear brother.

'I haven't got him, my dear,' said the old man.

'Where is he?' screamed Nancy, in a distracted manner.

'Why, the gentleman's got him,' replied the officer.

'What gentleman! Oh, gracious heavens! What gentleman?' exclaimed Nancy.

In reply to this incoherent questioning, the old man informed the deeply affected sister that Oliver had been taken ill in the office, and discharged in consequence of a witness having proved the robbery to have been committed by another boy, not in custody; and that the prosecutor had carried him away, in an insensible condition, to his own residence: of and concerning which, all the informant knew was, that it was somewhere in Pentonville, he having heard that word mentioned in the directions to the coachman.

In a dreadful state of doubt and uncertainty, the agonised young woman staggered to the gate, and then, exchanging her faltering walk for a swift run, returned by the most devious and complicated route she could think of, to the domicile of the Jew.

Mr. Bill Sikes no sooner heard the account of the expedition delivered, than he very hastily called up the white dog, and, putting on his hat, expeditiously departed: without devoting any time to the formality of wishing the company good-morning.

'We must know where he is, my dears; he must be found,' said the Jew greatly excited. 'Charley, do nothing but skulk about, till you bring home some news of him! Nancy, my dear, I must have him found. I trust to you, my dear,—to you and the Artful for everything! Stay, stay,' added the Jew, unlocking a drawer with a shaking hand; 'there's money, my dears. I shall shut up this shop to-night. You'll know where to find me! Don't stop here a minute. Not an instant, my dears!'

With these words, he pushed them from the room: and carefully double-locking and barring the door behind them, drew from its place of concealment the box which he had unintentionally disclosed to Oliver. Then, he hastily proceeded to dispose the watches and jewellery beneath his clothing.

A rap at the door startled him in this occupation. 'Who's there?' he cried in a shrill tone.

'Me!' replied the voice of the Dodger, through the key-hole.

'What now?' cried the Jew impatiently.

'Is he to be kidnapped to the other ken, Nancy says?' inquired the Dodger.

'Yes,' replied the Jew, 'wherever she lays hands on him. Find him, find him out, that's all. I shall know what to do next; never fear.'

The boy murmured a reply of intelligence: and hurried downstairs after his companions.

'He has not peached so far,' said the Jew as he pursued his occupation. 'If he means to blab us among his new friends, we may stop his mouth yet.'

CHAPTER XIV. COMPRISING FURTHER PARTICULARS OF OLIVER'S STAY AT MR. BROWNLOW'S, WITH THE REMARKABLE PREDICTION WHICH ONE MR. GRIMWIG UTTERED CONCERNING HIM, WHEN HE WENT OUT ON AN ERRAND

Oliver soon recovering from the fainting-fit into which Mr. Brownlow's abrupt exclamation had thrown him, the subject of the picture was carefully avoided, both by the old gentleman and Mrs. Bedwin, in the conversation that ensued: which indeed bore no reference to Oliver's history or prospects, but was confined to such topics as might amuse without exciting him. He was still too weak to get up to breakfast; but, when he came down into the housekeeper's room next day, his first act was to cast an eager glance at the wall, in the hope of again looking on the face of the beautiful lady. His expectations were disappointed, however, for the picture had been removed.

'Ah!' said the housekeeper, watching the direction of Oliver's eyes. 'It is gone, you see.'

'I see it is ma'am,' replied Oliver. 'Why have they taken it away?'

'It has been taken down, child, because Mr. Brownlow said, that as it seemed to worry you, perhaps it might prevent your getting well, you know,' rejoined the old lady.

'Oh, no, indeed. It didn't worry me, ma'am,' said Oliver. 'I liked to see it. I quite loved it.'

'Well, well!' said the old lady, good-humouredly; 'you get well as fast as ever you can, dear, and it shall be hung up again. There! I promise you that! Now, let us talk about something else.'

This was all the information Oliver could obtain about the picture at that time. As the old lady had been so kind to him in his illness, he endeavoured to think no more of the subject just then; so he listened attentively to a great many stories she told him, about an amiable and handsome daughter of hers, who was married to an amiable and handsome man, and lived in the country; and about a son, who was clerk to a merchant in the West Indies; and who was, also, such a good young man, and wrote such dutiful letters home four times a-year, that it brought the tears into her eyes to talk about them. When the old lady had expatiated, a long time, on the excellences of her children, and the merits of her kind good husband besides, who had been dead and gone, poor dear soul! just six-and-twenty years, it was time to have tea. After tea she began to teach Oliver cribbage: which he learnt as quickly as she could teach: and at which game they played, with great interest and gravity, until it was time for the invalid to have some warm wine and water, with a slice of dry toast, and then to go cosily to bed.

They were happy days, those of Oliver's recovery. Everything was so quiet, and neat, and orderly; everybody so kind and gentle; that after the noise and turbulence in the midst of which he had always lived, it seemed like Heaven itself. He was no sooner strong enough to put his clothes on, properly, than Mr. Brownlow caused a complete new suit, and a new cap, and a new pair of shoes, to be provided for him. As Oliver was told that he might do what he liked with the old clothes, he gave them to a servant who had been very kind to him, and asked her to sell them to a Jew, and keep the money for herself. This she very readily did; and, as Oliver looked out of the parlour window, and saw the Jew roll them up in his bag and walk away, he felt quite delighted to think that they were safely gone, and that there was now no possible danger of his ever being able to wear them again. They were sad rags, to tell the truth; and Oliver had never had a new suit before.

One evening, about a week after the affair of the picture, as he was sitting talking to Mrs. Bedwin, there came a message down from Mr. Brownlow, that if Oliver Twist felt pretty well, he should like to see him in his study, and talk to him a little while.

'Bless us, and save us! Wash your hands, and let me part your hair nicely for you, child,' said Mrs. Bedwin. 'Dear heart alive! If we had known he would have asked for you, we would have put you a clean collar on, and made you as smart as sixpence!'

Oliver did as the old lady bade him; and, although she lamented grievously, meanwhile, that there was not even time to crimp the little frill that bordered his shirt-collar; he looked so delicate and handsome, despite that important personal advantage, that she went so far as to say: looking at him with great complacency from head to foot, that she really didn't think it would have been possible, on the longest notice, to have made much difference in him for the better.

Thus encouraged, Oliver tapped at the study door. On Mr. Brownlow calling to him to come in, he found himself in a little back room, quite full of books, with a window, looking into some pleasant little gardens. There was a table drawn up before the window, at which Mr. Brownlow was seated reading. When he saw Oliver, he pushed the book away from him, and told him to come near the table, and sit down. Oliver complied; marvelling where the people could be found to read such a great number of books as seemed to be written to make the world wiser. Which is still a marvel to more experienced people than Oliver Twist, every day of their lives.

'There are a good many books, are there not, my boy?' said Mr. Brownlow, observing the curiosity with which Oliver surveyed the shelves that reached from the floor to the ceiling.

'A great number, sir,' replied Oliver. 'I never saw so many.'

'You shall read them, if you behave well,' said the old gentleman kindly; 'and you will like that, better than looking at the outsides,—that is, some cases; because there are books of which the backs and covers are by far the best parts.'

'I suppose they are those heavy ones, sir,' said Oliver, pointing to some large quartos, with a good deal of gilding about the binding.

'Not always those,' said the old gentleman, patting Oliver on the head, and smiling as he did so; 'there are other equally heavy ones, though of a much smaller size. How should you like to grow up a clever man, and write books, eh?'

'I think I would rather read them, sir,' replied Oliver.

'What! wouldn't you like to be a book-writer?' said the old gentleman.

Oliver considered a little while; and at last said, he should think it would be a much better thing to be a book-seller; upon which the old gentleman laughed heartily, and declared he had said a very good thing. Which Oliver felt glad to have done, though he by no means knew what it was.

'Well, well,' said the old gentleman, composing his features. 'Don't be afraid! We won't make an author of you, while there's an honest trade to be learnt, or brick-making to turn to.'

'Thank you, sir,' said Oliver. At the earnest manner of his reply, the old gentleman laughed again; and said something about a curious instinct, which Oliver, not understanding, paid no very great attention to.

'Now,' said Mr. Brownlow, speaking if possible in a kinder, but at the same time in a much more serious manner, than Oliver had ever known him assume yet, 'I want you to pay great attention, my boy, to what I am going to say. I shall talk to you without any reserve; because I am sure you are well able to understand me, as many older persons would be.'

'Oh, don't tell you are going to send me away, sir, pray!' exclaimed Oliver, alarmed at the serious tone of the old gentleman's commencement! 'Don't turn me out of doors to wander in the streets again. Let me stay here, and be a servant. Don't send me back to the wretched place I came from. Have mercy upon a poor boy, sir!'

'My dear child,' said the old gentleman, moved by the warmth of Oliver's sudden appeal; 'you need not be afraid of my deserting you, unless you give me cause.'

'I never, never will, sir,' interposed Oliver.

'I hope not,' rejoined the old gentleman. 'I do not think you ever will. I have been deceived, before, in the objects whom I have endeavoured to benefit; but I feel strongly disposed to trust you, nevertheless; and I am more interested in your behalf than I can well account for, even to myself. The persons on whom I have bestowed my dearest love, lie deep in their graves; but, although the happiness and delight of my life lie buried there too, I have not made a coffin of my heart, and sealed it up, forever, on my best affections. Deep affliction has but strengthened and refined them.'

As the old gentleman said this in a low voice: more to himself than to his companion: and as he remained silent for a short time afterwards: Oliver sat quite still.

'Well, well!' said the old gentleman at length, in a more cheerful tone, 'I only say this, because you have a young heart; and knowing that I have suffered great pain and sorrow, you will be more careful, perhaps, not to wound me again. You say you are an orphan, without a friend in the world; all the inquiries I have been able to make, confirm the statement. Let me hear your story; where you come from; who brought you up; and how you got into the company in which I found you. Speak the truth, and you shall not be friendless while I live.'

Oliver's sobs checked his utterance for some minutes; when he was on the point of beginning to relate how he had been brought up at the farm, and carried to the workhouse by Mr. Bumble, a peculiarly impatient little double-knock was heard at the street-door: and the servant, running upstairs, announced Mr. Grimwig.

'Is he coming up?' inquired Mr. Brownlow.

'Yes, sir,' replied the servant. 'He asked if there were any muffins in the house; and, when I told him yes, he said he had come to tea.'

Mr. Brownlow smiled; and, turning to Oliver, said that Mr. Grimwig was an old friend of his, and he must not mind his being a little rough in his manners; for he was a worthy creature at bottom, as he had reason to know.

'Shall I go downstairs, sir?' inquired Oliver.

'No,' replied Mr. Brownlow, 'I would rather you remained here.'

At this moment, there walked into the room: supporting himself by a thick stick: a stout old gentleman, rather lame in one leg, who was dressed in a blue coat, striped waistcoat, nankeen breeches and gaiters, and a broad-brimmed white hat, with the sides turned up with green. A very small-plaited shirt frill stuck out from his waistcoat; and a very long steel watch-chain, with nothing but a key at the end, dangled loosely below it. The ends of his white neckerchief were twisted into a ball about the size of an orange; the variety of shapes into which his countenance was twisted, defy description. He had a manner of screwing his head on one side when he spoke; and of looking out of the corners of his eyes at the same time: which irresistibly reminded the beholder of a parrot. In this attitude, he fixed himself, the moment he made his appearance; and, holding out a small piece of orange-peel at arm's length, exclaimed, in a growling, discontented voice.

'Look here! do you see this! Isn't it a most wonderful and extraordinary thing that I can't call at a man's house but I find a piece of this poor surgeon's friend on the staircase? I've been lamed with orange-peel once, and I know orange-peel will be my death, or I'll be content to eat my own head, sir!'

This was the handsome offer with which Mr. Grimwig backed and confirmed nearly every assertion he made; and it was the more singular in his case, because, even admitting for the sake of argument, the possibility of scientific improvements being brought to that pass which will enable a gentleman to eat his own head in the event of his being so disposed, Mr. Grimwig's head was such a particularly large one, that the most sanguine man alive could hardly entertain a hope of being able to get through it at a sitting—to put entirely out of the question, a very thick coating of powder.

'I'll eat my head, sir,' repeated Mr. Grimwig, striking his stick upon the ground. 'Hallo! what's that!' looking at Oliver, and retreating a pace or two.

'This is young Oliver Twist, whom we were speaking about,' said Mr. Brownlow.

Oliver bowed.

'You don't mean to say that's the boy who had the fever, I hope?' said Mr. Grimwig, recoiling a little more. 'Wait a minute! Don't speak! Stop—' continued Mr. Grimwig, abruptly, losing all dread of the fever in his triumph at the discovery; 'that's the boy who had the orange! If that's not the boy, sir, who had the orange, and threw this bit of peel upon the staircase, I'll eat my head, and his too.'

'No, no, he has not had one,' said Mr. Brownlow, laughing. 'Come! Put down your hat; and speak to my young friend.'

'I feel strongly on this subject, sir,' said the irritable old gentleman, drawing off his gloves. 'There's always more or less orange-peel on the pavement in our street; and I know it's put there by the surgeon's boy at the corner. A young woman stumbled over a bit last night, and fell against my garden-railings; directly she got up I saw her look towards his infernal red lamp with the pantomime-light. "Don't go to him," I called out of the window, "he's an assassin! A man-trap!" So he is. If he is not—' Here the irascible old gentleman gave a great knock on the ground with his stick; which was always understood, by his friends, to imply the customary offer, whenever it was not expressed in words. Then, still keeping his stick in his hand, he sat down; and, opening a double eye-glass, which he wore attached to a broad black riband, took a view of Oliver: who, seeing that he was the object of inspection, coloured, and bowed again.

'That's the boy, is it?' said Mr. Grimwig, at length.

'That's the boy,' replied Mr. Brownlow.

'How are you, boy?' said Mr. Grimwig.

'A great deal better, thank you, sir,' replied Oliver.

Mr. Brownlow, seeming to apprehend that his singular friend was about to say something disagreeable, asked Oliver to step downstairs and tell Mrs. Bedwin they were ready for tea; which, as he did not half like the visitor's manner, he was very happy to do.

'He is a nice-looking boy, is he not?' inquired Mr. Brownlow.

'I don't know,' replied Mr. Grimwig, pettishly.

'Don't know?'

'No. I don't know. I never see any difference in boys. I only knew two sort of boys. Mealy boys, and beef-faced boys.'

'And which is Oliver?'

'Mealy. I know a friend who has a beef-faced boy; a fine boy, they call him; with a round head, and red cheeks, and glaring eyes; a horrid boy; with a body and limbs that appear to be swelling out of the seams of his blue clothes; with the voice of a pilot, and the appetite of a wolf. I know him! The wretch!'

'Come,' said Mr. Brownlow, 'these are not the characteristics of young Oliver Twist; so he needn't excite your wrath.'

'They are not,' replied Mr. Grimwig. 'He may have worse.'

Here, Mr. Brownlow coughed impatiently; which appeared to afford Mr. Grimwig the most exquisite delight.

'He may have worse, I say,' repeated Mr. Grimwig. 'Where does he come from! Who is he? What is he? He has had a fever. What of that? Fevers are not peculiar to good people; are they? Bad people have fevers sometimes; haven't they, eh? I knew a man who was hung in

Jamaica for murdering his master. He had had a fever six times; he wasn't recommended to mercy on that account. Pooh! nonsense!'

Now, the fact was, that in the inmost recesses of his own heart, Mr. Grimwig was strongly disposed to admit that Oliver's appearance and manner were unusually prepossessing; but he had a strong appetite for contradiction, sharpened on this occasion by the finding of the orange-peel; and, inwardly determining that no man should dictate to him whether a boy was well-looking or not, he had resolved, from the first, to oppose his friend. When Mr. Brownlow admitted that on no one point of inquiry could he yet return a satisfactory answer; and that he had postponed any investigation into Oliver's previous history until he thought the boy was strong enough to hear it; Mr. Grimwig chuckled maliciously. And he demanded, with a sneer, whether the housekeeper was in the habit of counting the plate at night; because if she didn't find a table-spoon or two missing some sunshiny morning, why, he would be content to—and so forth.

All this, Mr. Brownlow, although himself somewhat of an impetuous gentleman: knowing his friend's peculiarities, bore with great good humour; as Mr. Grimwig, at tea, was graciously pleased to express his entire approval of the muffins, matters went on very smoothly; and Oliver, who made one of the party, began to feel more at his ease than he had yet done in the fierce old gentleman's presence.

'And when are you going to hear a full, true, and particular account of the life and adventures of Oliver Twist?' asked Grimwig of Mr. Brownlow, at the conclusion of the meal; looking sideways at Oliver, as he resumed his subject.

'To-morrow morning,' replied Mr. Brownlow. 'I would rather he was alone with me at the time. Come up to me to-morrow morning at ten o'clock, my dear.'

'Yes, sir,' replied Oliver. He answered with some hesitation, because he was confused by Mr. Grimwig's looking so hard at him.

'I'll tell you what,' whispered that gentleman to Mr. Brownlow; 'he won't come up to you to-morrow morning. I saw him hesitate. He is deceiving you, my good friend.'

'I'll swear he is not,' replied Mr. Brownlow, warmly.

'If he is not,' said Mr. Grimwig, 'I'll—' and down went the stick.

'I'll answer for that boy's truth with my life!' said Mr. Brownlow, knocking the table.

'And I for his falsehood with my head!' rejoined Mr. Grimwig, knocking the table also.

'We shall see,' said Mr. Brownlow, checking his rising anger.

'We will,' replied Mr. Grimwig, with a provoking smile; 'we will.'

As fate would have it, Mrs. Bedwin chanced to bring in, at this moment, a small parcel of books, which Mr. Brownlow had that morning purchased of the identical bookstall-keeper, who has already figured in this history; having laid them on the table, she prepared to leave the room.

'Stop the boy, Mrs. Bedwin!' said Mr. Brownlow; 'there is something to go back.'

'He has gone, sir,' replied Mrs. Bedwin.

'Call after him,' said Mr. Brownlow; 'it's particular. He is a poor man, and they are not paid for. There are some books to be taken back, too.'

The street-door was opened. Oliver ran one way; and the girl ran another; and Mrs. Bedwin stood on the step and screamed for the boy; but there was no boy in sight. Oliver and the girl returned, in a breathless state, to report that there were no tidings of him.

'Dear me, I am very sorry for that,' exclaimed Mr. Brownlow; 'I particularly wished those books to be returned to-night.'

'Send Oliver with them,' said Mr. Grimwig, with an ironical smile; 'he will be sure to deliver them safely, you know.'

'Yes; do let me take them, if you please, sir,' said Oliver. 'I'll run all the way, sir.'

The old gentleman was just going to say that Oliver should not go out on any account; when a most malicious cough from Mr. Grimwig determined him that he should; and that, by his prompt discharge of the commission, he should prove to him the injustice of his suspicions: on this head at least: at once.

'You shall go, my dear,' said the old gentleman. 'The books are on a chair by my table. Fetch them down.'

Oliver, delighted to be of use, brought down the books under his arm in a great bustle; and waited, cap in hand, to hear what message he was to take.

'You are to say,' said Mr. Brownlow, glancing steadily at Grimwig; 'you are to say that you have brought those books back; and that you have come to pay the four pound ten I owe him. This is a five-pound note, so you will have to bring me back, ten shillings change.'

'I won't be ten minutes, sir,' said Oliver, eagerly. Having buttoned up the bank-note in his jacket pocket, and placed the books carefully under his arm, he made a respectful bow, and left the room. Mrs. Bedwin followed him to the street-door, giving him many directions about the nearest way, and the name of the bookseller, and the name of the street: all of which Oliver said he clearly understood. Having superadded many injunctions to be sure and not take cold, the old lady at length permitted him to depart.

'Bless his sweet face!' said the old lady, looking after him. 'I can't bear, somehow, to let him go out of my sight.'

At this moment, Oliver looked gaily round, and nodded before he turned the corner. The old lady smilingly returned his salutation, and, closing the door, went back to her own room.

'Let me see; he'll be back in twenty minutes, at the longest,' said Mr. Brownlow, pulling out his watch, and placing it on the table. 'It will be dark by that time.'

'Oh! you really expect him to come back, do you?' inquired Mr. Grimwig.

'Don't you?' asked Mr. Brownlow, smiling.

The spirit of contradiction was strong in Mr. Grimwig's breast, at the moment; and it was rendered stronger by his friend's confident smile.

'No,' he said, smiting the table with his fist, 'I do not. The boy has a new suit of clothes on his back, a set of valuable books under his arm, and a five-pound note in his pocket. He'll join his old friends the thieves, and laugh at you. If ever that boy returns to this house, sir, I'll eat my head.'

With these words he drew his chair closer to the table; and there the two friends sat, in silent expectation, with the watch between them.

It is worthy of remark, as illustrating the importance we attach to our own judgments, and the pride with which we put forth our most rash and hasty conclusions, that, although Mr. Grimwig was not by any means a bad-hearted man, and though he would have been unfeignedly sorry to see his respected friend duped and deceived, he really did most earnestly and strongly hope at that moment, that Oliver Twist might not come back.

It grew so dark, that the figures on the dial-plate were scarcely discernible; but there the two old gentlemen continued to sit, in silence, with the watch between them.

CHAPTER XV. SHOWING HOW VERY FOND OF OLIVER TWIST, THE MERRY OLD JEW AND MISS NANCY WERE

In the obscure parlour of a low public-house, in the filthiest part of Little Saffron Hill; a dark and gloomy den, where a flaring gas-light burnt all day in the winter-time; and where no ray of sun ever shone in the summer: there sat, brooding over a little pewter measure and a small glass, strongly impregnated with the smell of liquor, a man in a velveteen coat, drab shorts, half-boots and stockings, whom even by that dim light no experienced agent of the police would have hesitated to recognise as Mr. William Sikes. At his feet, sat a white-coated, red-eyed dog; who occupied himself, alternately, in winking at his master with both eyes at the same time; and in licking a large, fresh cut on one side of his mouth, which appeared to be the result of some recent conflict.

'Keep quiet, you warmint! Keep quiet!' said Mr. Sikes, suddenly breaking silence. Whether his meditations were so intense as to be disturbed by the dog's winking, or whether his feelings were so wrought upon by his reflections that they required all the relief derivable from kicking an unoffending animal to allay them, is matter for argument and consideration. Whatever was the cause, the effect was a kick and a curse, bestowed upon the dog simultaneously.

Dogs are not generally apt to revenge injuries inflicted upon them by their masters; but Mr. Sikes's dog, having faults of temper in common with his owner, and labouring, perhaps, at this moment, under a powerful sense of injury, made no more ado but at once fixed his teeth in one of the half-boots. Having given in a hearty shake, he retired, growling, under a form; just escaping the pewter measure which Mr. Sikes levelled at his head.

'You would, would you?' said Sikes, seizing the poker in one hand, and deliberately opening with the other a large clasp-knife, which he drew from his pocket. 'Come here, you born devil! Come here! D'ye hear?'

The dog no doubt heard; because Mr. Sikes spoke in the very harshest key of a very harsh voice; but, appearing to entertain some unaccountable objection to having his throat cut, he remained where he was, and growled more fiercely than before: at the same time grasping the end of the poker between his teeth, and biting at it like a wild beast.

This resistance only infuriated Mr. Sikes the more; who, dropping on his knees, began to assail the animal most furiously. The dog jumped from right to left, and from left to right; snapping, growling, and barking; the man thrust and swore, and struck and blasphemed; and the struggle was reaching a most critical point for one or other; when, the door suddenly opening, the dog darted out: leaving Bill Sikes with the poker and the clasp-knife in his hands.

There must always be two parties to a quarrel, says the old adage. Mr. Sikes, being disappointed of the dog's participation, at once transferred his share in the quarrel to the new comer.

'What the devil do you come in between me and my dog for?' said Sikes, with a fierce gesture.

'I didn't know, my dear, I didn't know,' replied Fagin, humbly; for the Jew was the new comer.

'Didn't know, you white-livered thief!' growled Sikes. 'Couldn't you hear the noise?'

'Not a sound of it, as I'm a living man, Bill,' replied the Jew.

'Oh no! You hear nothing, you don't,' retorted Sikes with a fierce sneer. 'Sneaking in and out, so as nobody hears how you come or go! I wish you had been the dog, Fagin, half a minute ago.'

'Why?' inquired the Jew with a forced smile.

''Cause the government, as cares for the lives of such men as you, as haven't half the pluck of curs, lets a man kill a dog how he likes,' replied Sikes, shutting up the knife with a very expressive look; 'that's why.'

The Jew rubbed his hands; and, sitting down at the table, affected to laugh at the pleasantry of his friend. He was obviously very ill at ease, however.

'Grin away,' said Sikes, replacing the poker, and surveying him with savage contempt; 'grin away. You'll never have the laugh at me, though, unless it's behind a nightcap. I've got the upper hand over you, Fagin; and, d—me, I'll keep it. There! If I go, you go; so take care of me.'

'Well, well, my dear,' said the Jew, 'I know all that; we—we—have a mutual interest, Bill,—a mutual interest.'

'Humph,' said Sikes, as if he thought the interest lay rather more on the Jew's side than on his. 'Well, what have you got to say to me?'

'It's all passed safe through the melting-pot,' replied Fagin, 'and this is your share. It's rather more than it ought to be, my dear; but as I know you'll do me a good turn another time, and—'

'Stow that gammon,' interposed the robber, impatiently. 'Where is it? Hand over!'

'Yes, yes, Bill; give me time, give me time,' replied the Jew, soothingly. 'Here it is! All safe!' As he spoke, he drew forth an old cotton handkerchief from his breast; and untying a large knot in one corner, produced a small brown-paper packet. Sikes, snatching it from him, hastily opened it; and proceeded to count the sovereigns it contained.

'This is all, is it?' inquired Sikes.

'All,' replied the Jew.

'You haven't opened the parcel and swallowed one or two as you come along, have you?' inquired Sikes, suspiciously. 'Don't put on an injured look at the question; you've done it many a time. Jerk the tinkler.'

These words, in plain English, conveyed an injunction to ring the bell. It was answered by another Jew: younger than Fagin, but nearly as vile and repulsive in appearance.

Bill Sikes merely pointed to the empty measure. The Jew, perfectly understanding the hint, retired to fill it: previously exchanging a remarkable look with Fagin, who raised his eyes for an instant, as if in expectation of it, and shook his head in reply; so slightly that the action would have been almost imperceptible to an observant third person. It was lost upon Sikes, who was stooping at the moment to tie the boot-lace which the dog had torn. Possibly, if he had observed the brief interchange of signals, he might have thought that it boded no good to him.

'Is anybody here, Barney?' inquired Fagin; speaking, now that that Sikes was looking on, without raising his eyes from the ground.

'Dot a shoul,' replied Barney; whose words: whether they came from the heart or not: made their way through the nose.

'Nobody?' inquired Fagin, in a tone of surprise: which perhaps might mean that Barney was at liberty to tell the truth.

'Dobody but Biss Dadsy,' replied Barney.

'Nancy!' exclaimed Sikes. 'Where? Strike me blind, if I don't honour that 'ere girl, for her native talents.'

'She's bid havid a plate of boiled beef id the bar,' replied Barney.

'Send her here,' said Sikes, pouring out a glass of liquor. 'Send her here.'

Barney looked timidly at Fagin, as if for permission; the Jew remaining silent, and not lifting his eyes from the ground, he retired; and presently returned, ushering in Nancy; who was decorated with the bonnet, apron, basket, and street-door key, complete.

'You are on the scent, are you, Nancy?' inquired Sikes, proffering the glass.

'Yes, I am, Bill,' replied the young lady, disposing of its contents; 'and tired enough of it I am, too. The young brat's been ill and confined to the crib; and—'

'Ah, Nancy, dear!' said Fagin, looking up.

Now, whether a peculiar contraction of the Jew's red eye-brows, and a half closing of his deeply-set eyes, warned Miss Nancy that she was disposed to be too communicative, is not a matter of much importance. The fact is all we need care for here; and the fact is, that she suddenly checked herself, and with several gracious smiles upon Mr. Sikes, turned the conversation to other matters. In about ten minutes' time, Mr. Fagin was seized with a fit of coughing; upon which Nancy pulled her shawl over her shoulders, and declared it was time to go. Mr. Sikes, finding that he was walking a short part of her way himself, expressed his intention of accompanying her; they went away together, followed, at a little distant, by the dog, who slunk out of a back-yard as soon as his master was out of sight.

The Jew thrust his head out of the room door when Sikes had left it; looked after him as he walked up the dark passage; shook his clenched fist; muttered a deep curse; and then, with a horrible grin, reseated himself at the table; where he was soon deeply absorbed in the interesting pages of the Hue-and-Cry.

Meanwhile, Oliver Twist, little dreaming that he was within so very short a distance of the merry old gentleman, was on his way to the book-stall. When he got into Clerkenwell, he accidently turned down a by-street which was not exactly in his way; but not discovering his mistake until he had got half-way down it, and knowing it must lead in the right direction, he did not think it worth while to turn back; and so marched on, as quickly as he could, with the books under his arm.

He was walking along, thinking how happy and contented he ought to feel; and how much he would give for only one look at poor little Dick, who, starved and beaten, might be weeping bitterly at that very moment; when he was startled by a young woman screaming out very loud. 'Oh, my dear brother!' And he had hardly looked up, to see what the matter was, when he was stopped by having a pair of arms thrown tight round his neck.

'Don't,' cried Oliver, struggling. 'Let go of me. Who is it? What are you stopping me for?'

The only reply to this, was a great number of loud lamentations from the young woman who had embraced him; and who had a little basket and a street-door key in her hand.

'Oh my gracious!' said the young woman, 'I have found him! Oh! Oliver! Oliver! Oh you naughty boy, to make me suffer such distress on your account! Come home, dear, come. Oh, I've found him. Thank gracious goodness heavins, I've found him!' With these incoherent exclamations, the young woman burst into another fit of crying, and got so dreadfully hysterical, that a couple of women who came up at the moment asked a butcher's boy with a shiny head of hair anointed with suet, who was also looking on, whether he didn't think he had better run for the doctor. To which, the butcher's boy: who appeared of a lounging, not to say indolent disposition: replied, that he thought not.

'Oh, no, no, never mind,' said the young woman, grasping Oliver's hand; 'I'm better now. Come home directly, you cruel boy! Come!'

'Oh, ma'am,' replied the young woman, 'he ran away, near a month ago, from his parents, who are hard-working and respectable people; and went and joined a set of thieves and bad characters; and almost broke his mother's heart.'

'Young wretch!' said one woman.

'Go home, do, you little brute,' said the other.

'I am not,' replied Oliver, greatly alarmed. 'I don't know her. I haven't any sister, or father and mother either. I'm an orphan; I live at Pentonville.'

'Only hear him, how he braves it out!' cried the young woman.

'Why, it's Nancy!' exclaimed Oliver; who now saw her face for the first time; and started back, in irrepressible astonishment.

'You see he knows me!' cried Nancy, appealing to the bystanders. 'He can't help himself. Make him come home, there's good people, or he'll kill his dear mother and father, and break my heart!'

'What the devil's this?' said a man, bursting out of a beer-shop, with a white dog at his heels; 'young Oliver! Come home to your poor mother, you young dog! Come home directly.'

'I don't belong to them. I don't know them. Help! help!' cried Oliver, struggling in the man's powerful grasp.

'Help!' repeated the man. 'Yes; I'll help you, you young rascal!'

What books are these? You've been a stealing 'em, have you? Give 'em here.' With these words, the man tore the volumes from his grasp, and struck him on the head.

'That's right!' cried a looker-on, from a garret-window. 'That's the only way of bringing him to his senses!'

'To be sure!' cried a sleepy-faced carpenter, casting an approving look at the garret-window.

'It'll do him good!' said the two women.

'And he shall have it, too!' rejoined the man, administering another blow, and seizing Oliver by the collar. 'Come on, you young villain! Here, Bull's-eye, mind him, boy! Mind him!'

Weak with recent illness; stupified by the blows and the suddenness of the attack; terrified by the fierce growling of the dog, and the brutality of the man; overpowered by the conviction of the bystanders that he really was the hardened little wretch he was described to be; what could one poor child do! Darkness had set in; it was a low neighborhood; no help was near; resistance was useless. In another moment he was dragged into a labyrinth of dark narrow courts, and was forced along them at a pace which rendered the few cries he dared to give utterance to, unintelligible. It was of little moment, indeed, whether they were intelligible or no; for there was nobody to care for them, had they been ever so plain.

The gas-lamps were lighted; Mrs. Bedwin was waiting anxiously at the open door; the servant had run up the street twenty times to see if there were any traces of Oliver; and still the two old gentlemen sat, perseveringly, in the dark parlour, with the watch between them.

CHAPTER XVI. RELATES WHAT BECAME OF OLIVER TWIST, AFTER HE HAD BEEN CLAIMED BY NANCY

The narrow streets and courts, at length, terminated in a large open space; scattered about which, were pens for beasts, and other indications of a cattle-market. Sikes slackened his pace when they reached this spot: the girl being quite unable to support any longer, the rapid rate at which they had hitherto walked. Turning to Oliver, he roughly commanded him to take hold of Nancy's hand.

'Do you hear?' growled Sikes, as Oliver hesitated, and looked round.

They were in a dark corner, quite out of the track of passengers.

Oliver saw, but too plainly, that resistance would be of no avail. He held out his hand, which Nancy clasped tight in hers.

'Give me the other,' said Sikes, seizing Oliver's unoccupied hand. 'Here, Bull's-Eye!'

The dog looked up, and growled.

'See here, boy!' said Sikes, putting his other hand to Oliver's throat; 'if he speaks ever so soft a word, hold him! D'ye mind!'

The dog growled again; and licking his lips, eyed Oliver as if he were anxious to attach himself to his windpipe without delay.

'He's as willing as a Christian, strike me blind if he isn't!' said Sikes, regarding the animal with a kind of grim and ferocious approval. 'Now, you know what you've got to expect, master, so call away as quick as you like; the dog will soon stop that game. Get on, young'un!'

Bull's-eye wagged his tail in acknowledgment of this unusually endearing form of speech; and, giving vent to another admonitory growl for the benefit of Oliver, led the way onward.

It was Smithfield that they were crossing, although it might have been Grosvenor Square, for anything Oliver knew to the contrary. The night was dark and foggy. The lights in the shops could scarcely struggle through the heavy mist, which thickened every moment and shrouded the streets and houses in gloom; rendering the strange place still stranger in Oliver's eyes; and making his uncertainty the more dismal and depressing.

They had hurried on a few paces, when a deep church-bell struck the hour. With its first stroke, his two conductors stopped, and turned their heads in the direction whence the sound proceeded.

'Eight o' clock, Bill,' said Nancy, when the bell ceased.

'What's the good of telling me that; I can hear it, can't I!' replied Sikes.

'I wonder whether THEY can hear it,' said Nancy.

'Of course they can,' replied Sikes. 'It was Bartlemy time when I was shopped; and there warn't a penny trumpet in the fair, as I couldn't hear the squeaking on. Arter I was locked up for the night, the row and din outside made the thundering old jail so silent, that I could almost have beat my brains out against the iron plates of the door.'

'Poor fellow!' said Nancy, who still had her face turned towards the quarter in which the bell had sounded. 'Oh, Bill, such fine young chaps as them!'

'Yes; that's all you women think of,' answered Sikes. 'Fine young chaps! Well, they're as good as dead, so it don't much matter.'

With this consolation, Mr. Sikes appeared to repress a rising tendency to jealousy, and, clasping Oliver's wrist more firmly, told him to step out again.

'Wait a minute!' said the girl: 'I wouldn't hurry by, if it was you that was coming out to be hung, the next time eight o'clock struck, Bill. I'd walk round and round the place till I dropped, if the snow was on the ground, and I hadn't a shawl to cover me.'

'And what good would that do?' inquired the unsentimental Mr. Sikes. 'Unless you could pitch over a file and twenty yards of good stout rope, you might as well be walking fifty mile off, or not walking at all, for all the good it would do me. Come on, and don't stand preaching there.'

The girl burst into a laugh; drew her shawl more closely round her; and they walked away. But Oliver felt her hand tremble, and, looking up in her face as they passed a gas-lamp, saw that it had turned a deadly white.

They walked on, by little-frequented and dirty ways, for a full half-hour: meeting very few people, and those appearing from their looks to hold much the same position in society as Mr. Sikes himself. At length they turned into a very filthy narrow street, nearly full of old-clothes shops; the dog running forward, as if conscious that there was no further occasion for his keeping on guard, stopped before the door of a shop that was closed and apparently untenanted; the house was in a ruinous condition, and on the door was nailed a board, intimating that it was to let: which looked as if it had hung there for many years.

'All right,' cried Sikes, glancing cautiously about.

Nancy stooped below the shutters, and Oliver heard the sound of a bell. They crossed to the opposite side of the street, and stood for a few moments under a lamp. A noise, as if a sash window were gently raised, was heard; and soon afterwards the door softly opened. Mr. Sikes then seized the terrified boy by the collar with very little ceremony; and all three were quickly inside the house.

The passage was perfectly dark. They waited, while the person who had let them in, chained and barred the door.

'Anybody here?' inquired Sikes.

'No,' replied a voice, which Oliver thought he had heard before.

'Is the old 'un here?' asked the robber.

'Yes,' replied the voice, 'and precious down in the mouth he has been. Won't he be glad to see you? Oh, no!'

The style of this reply, as well as the voice which delivered it, seemed familiar to Oliver's ears: but it was impossible to distinguish even the form of the speaker in the darkness.

'Let's have a glim,' said Sikes, 'or we shall go breaking our necks, or treading on the dog. Look after your legs if you do!'

'Stand still a moment, and I'll get you one,' replied the voice. The receding footsteps of the speaker were heard; and, in another minute, the form of Mr. John Dawkins, otherwise the Artful Dodger, appeared. He bore in his right hand a tallow candle stuck in the end of a cleft stick.

The young gentleman did not stop to bestow any other mark of recognition upon Oliver than a humourous grin; but, turning away, beckoned the visitors to follow him down a flight of stairs. They crossed an empty kitchen; and, opening the door of a low earthy-smelling room, which seemed to have been built in a small back-yard, were received with a shout of laughter.

'Oh, my wig, my wig!' cried Master Charles Bates, from whose lungs the laughter had proceeded: 'here he is! oh, cry, here he is! Oh, Fagin, look at him! Fagin, do look at him! I can't bear it; it is such a jolly game, I cant' bear it. Hold me, somebody, while I laugh it out.'

With this irrepressible ebullition of mirth, Master Bates laid himself flat on the floor: and kicked convulsively for five minutes, in an ectasy of facetious joy. Then jumping to his feet, he snatched the cleft stick from the Dodger; and, advancing to Oliver, viewed him round and round; while the Jew, taking off his nightcap, made a great number of low bows to the bewildered boy. The Artful, meantime, who was of a rather saturnine disposition, and seldom gave way to merriment when it interfered with business, rifled Oliver's pockets with steady assiduity.

'Look at his togs, Fagin!' said Charley, putting the light so close to his new jacket as nearly to set him on fire. 'Look at his togs! Superfine cloth, and the heavy swell cut! Oh, my eye, what a game! And his books, too! Nothing but a gentleman, Fagin!'

'Delighted to see you looking so well, my dear,' said the Jew, bowing with mock humility. 'The Artful shall give you another suit, my dear, for fear you should spoil that Sunday one. Why didn't you write, my dear, and say you were coming? We'd have got something warm for supper.'

At his, Master Bates roared again: so loud, that Fagin himself relaxed, and even the Dodger smiled; but as the Artful drew forth the five-pound note at that instant, it is doubtful whether the sally of the discovery awakened his merriment.

'Hallo, what's that?' inquired Sikes, stepping forward as the Jew seized the note. 'That's mine, Fagin.'

'No, no, my dear,' said the Jew. 'Mine, Bill, mine. You shall have the books.'

'If that ain't mine!' said Bill Sikes, putting on his hat with a determined air; 'mine and Nancy's that is; I'll take the boy back again.'

The Jew started. Oliver started too, though from a very different cause; for he hoped that the dispute might really end in his being taken back.

'Come! Hand over, will you?' said Sikes.

'This is hardly fair, Bill; hardly fair, is it, Nancy?' inquired the Jew.

'Fair, or not fair,' retorted Sikes, 'hand over, I tell you! Do you think Nancy and me has got nothing else to do with our precious time but to spend it in scouting arter, and kidnapping, every young boy as gets grabbed through you? Give it here, you avaricious old skeleton, give it here!'

With this gentle remonstrance, Mr. Sikes plucked the note from between the Jew's finger and thumb; and looking the old man coolly in the face, folded it up small, and tied it in his neckerchief.

'That's for our share of the trouble,' said Sikes; 'and not half enough, neither. You may keep the books, if you're fond of reading. If you ain't, sell 'em.'

'They're very pretty,' said Charley Bates: who, with sundry grimaces, had been affecting to read one of the volumes in question; 'beautiful writing, isn't is, Oliver?' At sight of the dismayed look with which Oliver regarded his tormentors, Master Bates, who was blessed with a lively sense of the ludicrous, fell into another ectasy, more boisterous than the first.

'They belong to the old gentleman,' said Oliver, wringing his hands; 'to the good, kind, old gentleman who took me into his house, and had me nursed, when I was near dying of the fever. Oh, pray send them back; send him back the books and money. Keep me here all my life long; but pray, pray send them back. He'll think I stole them; the old lady: all of them who were so kind to me: will think I stole them. Oh, do have mercy upon me, and send them back!'

With these words, which were uttered with all the energy of passionate grief, Oliver fell upon his knees at the Jew's feet; and beat his hands together, in perfect desperation.

'The boy's right,' remarked Fagin, looking covertly round, and knitting his shaggy eyebrows into a hard knot. 'You're right, Oliver, you're right; they WILL think you have stolen 'em. Ha! ha!' chuckled the Jew, rubbing his hands, 'it couldn't have happened better, if we had chosen our time!'

'Of course it couldn't,' replied Sikes; 'I know'd that, directly I see him coming through Clerkenwell, with the books under his arm. It's all right enough. They're soft-hearted psalm-singers, or they wouldn't have taken him in at all; and they'll ask no questions after him, fear they should be obliged to prosecute, and so get him lagged. He's safe enough.'

Oliver had looked from one to the other, while these words were being spoken, as if he were bewildered, and could scarcely understand what passed; but when Bill Sikes concluded, he jumped suddenly to his feet, and tore wildly from the room: uttering shrieks for help, which made the bare old house echo to the roof.

'Keep back the dog, Bill!' cried Nancy, springing before the door, and closing it, as the Jew and his two pupils darted out in pursuit. 'Keep back the dog; he'll tear the boy to pieces.'

'Serve him right!' cried Sikes, struggling to disengage himself from the girl's grasp. 'Stand off from me, or I'll split your head against the wall.'

'I don't care for that, Bill, I don't care for that,' screamed the girl, struggling violently with the man, 'the child shan't be torn down by the dog, unless you kill me first.'

'Shan't he!' said Sikes, setting his teeth. 'I'll soon do that, if you don't keep off.'

The housebreaker flung the girl from him to the further end of the room, just as the Jew and the two boys returned, dragging Oliver among them.

'What's the matter here!' said Fagin, looking round.

'The girl's gone mad, I think,' replied Sikes, savagely.

'No, she hasn't,' said Nancy, pale and breathless from the scuffle; 'no, she hasn't, Fagin; don't think it.'

'Then keep quiet, will you?' said the Jew, with a threatening look.

'No, I won't do that, neither,' replied Nancy, speaking very loud. 'Come! What do you think of that?'

Mr. Fagin was sufficiently well acquainted with the manners and customs of that particular species of humanity to which Nancy belonged, to feel tolerably certain that it would be rather unsafe to prolong any conversation with her, at present. With the view of diverting the attention of the company, he turned to Oliver.

'So you wanted to get away, my dear, did you?' said the Jew, taking up a jagged and knotted club which law in a corner of the fireplace; 'eh?'

Oliver made no reply. But he watched the Jew's motions, and breathed quickly.

'Wanted to get assistance; called for the police; did you?' sneered the Jew, catching the boy by the arm. 'We'll cure you of that, my young master.'

The Jew inflicted a smart blow on Oliver's shoulders with the club; and was raising it for a second, when the girl, rushing forward, wrested it from his hand. She flung it into the fire, with a force that brought some of the glowing coals whirling out into the room.

'I won't stand by and see it done, Fagin,' cried the girl. 'You've got the boy, and what more would you have?—Let him be—let him be—or I shall put that mark on some of you, that will bring me to the gallows before my time.'

The girl stamped her foot violently on the floor as she vented this threat; and with her lips compressed, and her hands clenched, looked alternately at the Jew and the other robber: her face quite colourless from the passion of rage into which she had gradually worked herself.

'Why, Nancy!' said the Jew, in a soothing tone; after a pause, during which he and Mr. Sikes had stared at one another in a disconcerted manner; 'you,—you're more clever than ever to-night. Ha! ha! my dear, you are acting beautifully.'

'Am I!' said the girl. 'Take care I don't overdo it. You will be the worse for it, Fagin, if I do; and so I tell you in good time to keep clear of me.'

There is something about a roused woman: especially if she add to all her other strong passions, the fierce impulses of recklessness and despair; which few men like to provoke. The Jew saw that it would be hopeless to affect any further mistake regarding the reality of Miss Nancy's rage; and, shrinking involuntarily back a few paces, cast a glance, half imploring and half cowardly, at Sikes: as if to hint that he was the fittest person to pursue the dialogue.

Mr. Sikes, thus mutely appealed to; and possibly feeling his personal pride and influence interested in the immediate reduction of Miss Nancy to reason; gave utterance to about a couple of score of curses and threats, the rapid production of which reflected great credit on the fertility of his invention. As they produced no visible effect on the object against whom they were discharged, however, he resorted to more tangible arguments.

'What do you mean by this?' said Sikes; backing the inquiry with a very common imprecation concerning the most beautiful of human features: which, if it were heard above, only once out of every fifty thousand times that it is uttered below, would render blindness as common a disorder as measles: 'what do you mean by it? Burn my body! Do you know who you are, and what you are?'

'Oh, yes, I know all about it,' replied the girl, laughing hysterically; and shaking her head from side to side, with a poor assumption of indifference.

'Well, then, keep quiet,' rejoined Sikes, with a growl like that he was accustomed to use when addressing his dog, 'or I'll quiet you for a good long time to come.'

The girl laughed again: even less composedly than before; and, darting a hasty look at Sikes, turned her face aside, and bit her lip till the blood came.

'You're a nice one,' added Sikes, as he surveyed her with a contemptuous air, 'to take up the humane and gen—teel side! A pretty subject for the child, as you call him, to make a friend of!'

'God Almighty help me, I am!' cried the girl passionately; 'and I wish I had been struck dead in the street, or had changed places with them we passed so near to-night, before I had lent a hand in bringing him here. He's a thief, a liar, a devil, all that's bad, from this night forth. Isn't that enough for the old wretch, without blows?'

'Come, come, Sikes,' said the Jew appealing to him in a remonstratory tone, and motioning towards the boys, who were eagerly attentive to all that passed; 'we must have civil words; civil words, Bill.'

'Civil words!' cried the girl, whose passion was frightful to see. 'Civil words, you villain! Yes, you deserve 'em from me. I thieved for you when I was a child not half as old as this!' pointing to Oliver. 'I have been in the same trade, and in the same service, for twelve years since. Don't you know it? Speak out! Don't you know it?'

'Well, well,' replied the Jew, with an attempt at pacification; 'and, if you have, it's your living!'

'Aye, it is!' returned the girl; not speaking, but pouring out the words in one continuous and vehement scream. 'It is my living; and the cold, wet, dirty streets are my home; and you're the wretch that drove me to them long ago, and that'll keep me there, day and night, day and night, till I die!'

'I shall do you a mischief!' interposed the Jew, goaded by these reproaches; 'a mischief worse than that, if you say much more!'

The girl said nothing more; but, tearing her hair and dress in a transport of passion, made such a rush at the Jew as would probably have left signal marks of her revenge upon him, had not her wrists been seized by Sikes at the right moment; upon which, she made a few ineffectual struggles, and fainted.

'She's all right now,' said Sikes, laying her down in a corner. 'She's uncommon strong in the arms, when she's up in this way.'

The Jew wiped his forehead: and smiled, as if it were a relief to have the disturbance over; but neither he, nor Sikes, nor the dog, nor the boys, seemed to consider it in any other light than a common occurance incidental to business.

'It's the worst of having to do with women,' said the Jew, replacing his club; 'but they're clever, and we can't get on, in our line, without 'em. Charley, show Oliver to bed.'

'I suppose he'd better not wear his best clothes tomorrow, Fagin, had he?' inquired Charley Bates.

'Certainly not,' replied the Jew, reciprocating the grin with which Charley put the question.

Master Bates, apparently much delighted with his commission, took the cleft stick: and led Oliver into an adjacent kitchen, where there were two or three of the beds on which he had slept before; and here, with many uncontrollable bursts of laughter, he produced the identical old suit of clothes which Oliver had so much congratulated himself upon leaving off at Mr. Brownlow's; and the accidental display of which, to Fagin, by the Jew who purchased them, had been the very first clue received, of his whereabout.

'Put off the smart ones,' said Charley, 'and I'll give 'em to Fagin to take care of. What fun it is!'

Poor Oliver unwillingly complied. Master Bates rolling up the new clothes under his arm, departed from the room, leaving Oliver in the dark, and locking the door behind him.

The noise of Charley's laughter, and the voice of Miss Betsy, who opportunely arrived to throw water over her friend, and perform other feminine offices for the promotion of her recovery, might have kept many people awake under more happy circumstances than those in which Oliver was placed. But he was sick and weary; and he soon fell sound asleep.

CHAPTER XVII. OLIVER'S DESTINY CONTINUING UNPROPITIOUS, BRINGS A GREAT MAN TO LONDON TO INJURE HIS REPUTATION

It is the custom on the stage, in all good murderous melodramas, to present the tragic and the comic scenes, in as regular alternation, as the layers of red and white in a side of streaky bacon. The hero sinks upon his straw bed, weighed down by fetters and misfortunes; in the next scene, his faithful but unconscious squire regales the audience with a comic song. We behold, with throbbing bosoms, the heroine in the grasp of a proud and ruthless baron: her virtue and her life alike in danger, drawing forth her dagger to preserve the one at the cost of the other; and just as our expectations are wrought up to the highest pitch, a whistle is heard, and we are straightway transported to the great hall of the castle; where a grey-headed seneschal sings a funny chorus with a funnier body of vassals, who are free of all sorts of places, from church vaults to palaces, and roam about in company, carolling perpetually.

Such changes appear absurd; but they are not so unnatural as they would seem at first sight. The transitions in real life from well-spread boards to death-beds, and from mourning-weeds to holiday garments, are not a whit less startling; only, there, we are busy actors, instead of passive lookers-on, which makes a vast difference. The actors in the mimic life of the theatre, are blind to violent transitions and abrupt impulses of passion or feeling, which, presented before the eyes of mere spectators, are at once condemned as outrageous and preposterous.

As sudden shiftings of the scene, and rapid changes of time and place, are not only sanctioned in books by long usage, but are by many considered as the great art of authorship: an author's skill in his craft being, by such critics, chiefly estimated with relation to the dilemmas in which he leaves his characters at the end of every chapter: this brief introduction to the present one may perhaps be deemed unnecessary. If so, let it be considered a delicate intimation on the part of the historian that he is going back to the town in which Oliver Twist was born; the reader taking it for granted that there are good and substantial reasons for making the journey, or he would not be invited to proceed upon such an expedition.

Mr. Bumble emerged at early morning from the workhouse-gate, and walked with portly carriage and commanding steps, up the High Street. He was in the full bloom and pride of beadlehood; his cocked hat and coat were dazzling in the morning sun; he clutched his cane with the vigorous tenacity of health and power. Mr. Bumble always carried his head high; but this morning it was higher than usual. There was an abstraction in his eye, an elevation in his air, which might have warned an observant stranger that thoughts were passing in the beadle's mind, too great for utterance.

Mr. Bumble stopped not to converse with the small shopkeepers and others who spoke to him, deferentially, as he passed along. He merely returned their salutations with a wave of his hand, and relaxed not in his dignified pace, until he reached the farm where Mrs. Mann tended the infant paupers with parochial care.

'Drat that beadle!' said Mrs. Mann, hearing the well-known shaking at the garden-gate. 'If it isn't him at this time in the morning! Lauk, Mr. Bumble, only think of its being you! Well, dear me, it IS a pleasure, this is! Come into the parlour, sir, please.'

The first sentence was addressed to Susan; and the exclamations of delight were uttered to Mr. Bumble: as the good lady unlocked the garden-gate: and showed him, with great attention and respect, into the house.

'Mrs. Mann,' said Mr. Bumble; not sitting upon, or dropping himself into a seat, as any common jackanapes would: but letting himself gradually and slowly down into a chair; 'Mrs. Mann, ma'am, good morning.'

'Well, and good morning to you, sir,' replied Mrs. Mann, with many smiles; 'and hoping you find yourself well, sir!'

'So-so, Mrs. Mann,' replied the beadle. 'A porochial life is not a bed of roses, Mrs. Mann.'

'Ah, that it isn't indeed, Mr. Bumble,' rejoined the lady. And all the infant paupers might have chorussed the rejoinder with great propriety, if they had heard it.

'A porochial life, ma'am,' continued Mr. Bumble, striking the table with his cane, 'is a life of worrit, and vexation, and hardihood; but all public characters, as I may say, must suffer prosecution.'

Mrs. Mann, not very well knowing what the beadle meant, raised her hands with a look of sympathy, and sighed.

'Ah! You may well sigh, Mrs. Mann!' said the beadle.

Finding she had done right, Mrs. Mann sighed again: evidently to the satisfaction of the public character: who, repressing a complacent smile by looking sternly at his cocked hat, said,

'Mrs. Mann, I am going to London.'

'Lauk, Mr. Bumble!' cried Mrs. Mann, starting back.

'To London, ma'am,' resumed the inflexible beadle, 'by coach. I and two paupers, Mrs. Mann! A legal action is a coming on, about a settlement; and the board has appointed me—me, Mrs. Mann—to dispose to the matter before the quarter-sessions at Clerkinwell.

And I very much question,' added Mr. Bumble, drawing himself up, 'whether the Clerkinwell Sessions will not find themselves in the wrong box before they have done with me.'

'Oh! you mustn't be too hard upon them, sir,' said Mrs. Mann, coaxingly.

'The Clerkinwell Sessions have brought it upon themselves, ma'am,' replied Mr. Bumble; 'and if the Clerkinwell Sessions find that they come off rather worse than they expected, the Clerkinwell Sessions have only themselves to thank.'

There was so much determination and depth of purpose about the menacing manner in which Mr. Bumble delivered himself of these words, that Mrs. Mann appeared quite awed by them. At length she said,

'You're going by coach, sir? I thought it was always usual to send them paupers in carts.'

'That's when they're ill, Mrs. Mann,' said the beadle. 'We put the sick paupers into open carts in the rainy weather, to prevent their taking cold.'

'Oh!' said Mrs. Mann.

'The opposition coach contracts for these two; and takes them cheap,' said Mr. Bumble. 'They are both in a very low state, and we find it would come two pound cheaper to move 'em than to bury 'em—that is, if we can throw 'em upon another parish, which I think we shall be able to do, if they don't die upon the road to spite us. Ha! ha! ha!'

When Mr. Bumble had laughed a little while, his eyes again encountered the cocked hat; and he became grave.

'We are forgetting business, ma'am,' said the beadle; 'here is your porochial stipend for the month.'

Mr. Bumble produced some silver money rolled up in paper, from his pocket-book; and requested a receipt: which Mrs. Mann wrote.

'It's very much blotted, sir,' said the farmer of infants; 'but it's formal enough, I dare say.

Thank you, Mr. Bumble, sir, I am very much obliged to you, I'm sure.'

Mr. Bumble nodded, blandly, in acknowledgment of Mrs. Mann's curtsey; and inquired how the children were.

'Bless their dear little hearts!' said Mrs. Mann with emotion, 'they're as well as can be, the dears! Of course, except the two that died last week. And little Dick.'

'Isn't that boy no better?' inquired Mr. Bumble.

Mrs. Mann shook her head.

'He's a ill-conditioned, wicious, bad-disposed porochial child that,' said Mr. Bumble angrily. 'Where is he?'

'I'll bring him to you in one minute, sir,' replied Mrs. Mann. 'Here, you Dick!'

After some calling, Dick was discovered. Having had his face put under the pump, and dried upon Mrs. Mann's gown, he was led into the awful presence of Mr. Bumble, the beadle.

The child was pale and thin; his cheeks were sunken; and his eyes large and bright. The scanty parish dress, the livery of his misery, hung loosely on his feeble body; and his young limbs had wasted away, like those of an old man.

Such was the little being who stood trembling beneath Mr. Bumble's glance; not daring to lift his eyes from the floor; and dreading even to hear the beadle's voice.

'Can't you look at the gentleman, you obstinate boy?' said Mrs. Mann.

The child meekly raised his eyes, and encountered those of Mr. Bumble.

'What's the matter with you, porochial Dick?' inquired Mr. Bumble, with well-timed jocularity.

'Nothing, sir,' replied the child faintly.

'I should think not,' said Mrs. Mann, who had of course laughed very much at Mr. Bumble's humour.

'You want for nothing, I'm sure.'

'I should like—' faltered the child.

'Hey-day!' interposed Mr. Mann, 'I suppose you're going to say that you DO want for something, now? Why, you little wretch—'

'Stop, Mrs. Mann, stop!' said the beadle, raising his hand with a show of authority. 'Like what, sir, eh?'

'I should like,' faltered the child, 'if somebody that can write, would put a few words down for me on a piece of paper, and fold it up and seal it, and keep it for me, after I am laid in the ground.'

'Why, what does the boy mean?' exclaimed Mr. Bumble, on whom the earnest manner and wan aspect of the child had made some impression: accustomed as he was to such things. 'What do you mean, sir?'

'I should like,' said the child, 'to leave my dear love to poor Oliver Twist; and to let him know how often I have sat by myself and cried to think of his wandering about in the dark nights with nobody to help him. And I should like to tell him,' said the child pressing his small hands together, and speaking with great fervour, 'that I was glad to die when I was very young; for, perhaps, if I had lived to be a man, and had grown old, my little sister who is in Heaven, might forget me, or be unlike me; and it would be so much happier if we were both children there together.'

Mr. Bumble surveyed the little speaker, from head to foot, with indescribable astonishment; and, turning to his companion, said, 'They're all in one story, Mrs. Mann. That out-dacious Oliver had demogalized them all!'

'I couldn't have believed it, sir' said Mrs Mann, holding up her hands, and looking malignantly at Dick. 'I never see such a hardened little wretch!'

'Take him away, ma'am!' said Mr. Bumble imperiously. 'This must be stated to the board, Mrs. Mann.

'I hope the gentleman will understand that it isn't my fault, sir?' said Mrs. Mann, whimpering pathetically.

'They shall understand that, ma'am; they shall be acquainted with the true state of the case,' said Mr. Bumble. 'There; take him away, I can't bear the sight on him.'

Dick was immediately taken away, and locked up in the coal-cellar. Mr. Bumble shortly afterwards took himself off, to prepare for his journey.

At six o'clock next morning, Mr. Bumble: having exchanged his cocked hat for a round one, and encased his person in a blue great-coat with a cape to it: took his place on the outside of the coach, accompanied by the criminals whose settlement was disputed; with whom, in due course of time, he arrived in London.

He experienced no other crosses on the way, than those which originated in the perverse behaviour of the two paupers, who persisted in shivering, and complaining of the cold, in a manner which, Mr. Bumble declared, caused his teeth to chatter in his head, and made him feel quite uncomfortable; although he had a great-coat on.

Having disposed of these evil-minded persons for the night, Mr. Bumble sat himself down in the house at which the coach stopped; and took a temperate dinner of steaks, oyster sauce, and porter. Putting a glass of hot gin-and-water on the chimney-piece, he drew his chair to the fire; and, with sundry moral reflections on the too-prevalent sin of discontent and complaining, composed himself to read the paper.

The very first paragraph upon which Mr. Bumble's eye rested, was the following advertisement.

'FIVE GUINEAS REWARD

'Whereas a young boy, named Oliver Twist, absconded, or was enticed, on Thursday evening last, from his home, at Pentonville; and has not since been heard of. The above reward will be paid to any person who will give such information as will lead to the discovery of the said Oliver Twist, or tend to throw any light upon his previous history, in which the advertiser is, for many reasons, warmly interested.'

And then followed a full description of Oliver's dress, person, appearance, and disappearance: with the name and address of Mr. Brownlow at full length.

Mr. Bumble opened his eyes; read the advertisement, slowly and carefully, three several times; and in something more than five minutes was on his way to Pentonville: having actually, in his excitement, left the glass of hot gin-and-water, untasted.

'Is Mr. Brownlow at home?' inquired Mr. Bumble of the girl who opened the door.

To this inquiry the girl returned the not uncommon, but rather evasive reply of 'I don't know; where do you come from?'

Mr. Bumble no sooner uttered Oliver's name, in explanation of his errand, than Mrs. Bedwin, who had been listening at the parlour door, hastened into the passage in a breathless state.

'Come in, come in,' said the old lady: 'I knew we should hear of him. Poor dear! I knew we should! I was certain of it. Bless his heart! I said so all along.'

Having heard this, the worthy old lady hurried back into the parlour again; and seating herself on a sofa, burst into tears. The girl, who was not quite so susceptible, had run upstairs meanwhile; and now returned with a request that Mr. Bumble would follow her immediately: which he did.

He was shown into the little back study, where sat Mr. Brownlow and his friend Mr. Grimwig, with decanters and glasses before them. The latter gentleman at once burst into the exclamation:

'A beadle. A parish beadle, or I'll eat my head.'

'Pray don't interrupt just now,' said Mr. Brownlow. 'Take a seat, will you?'

Mr. Bumble sat himself down; quite confounded by the oddity of Mr. Grimwig's manner. Mr. Brownlow moved the lamp, so as to obtain an uninterrupted view of the beadle's countenance; and said, with a little impatience,

'Now, sir, you come in consequence of having seen the advertisement?'

'Yes, sir,' said Mr. Bumble.

'And you ARE a beadle, are you not?' inquired Mr. Grimwig.

'I am a porochial beadle, gentlemen,' rejoined Mr. Bumble proudly.

'Of course,' observed Mr. Grimwig aside to his friend, 'I knew he was. A beadle all over!'

Mr. Brownlow gently shook his head to impose silence on his friend, and resumed:

'Do you know where this poor boy is now?'

'No more than nobody,' replied Mr. Bumble.

'Well, what DO you know of him?' inquired the old gentleman. 'Speak out, my friend, if you have anything to say. What DO you know of him?'

'You don't happen to know any good of him, do you?' said Mr. Grimwig, caustically; after an attentive perusal of Mr. Bumble's features.

Mr. Bumble, catching at the inquiry very quickly, shook his head with portentous solemnity.

'You see?' said Mr. Grimwig, looking triumphantly at Mr. Brownlow.

Mr. Brownlow looked apprehensively at Mr. Bumble's pursed-up countenance; and requested him to communicate what he knew regarding Oliver, in as few words as possible.

Mr. Bumble put down his hat; unbuttoned his coat; folded his arms; inclined his head in a retrospective manner; and, after a few moments' reflection, commenced his story.

It would be tedious if given in the beadle's words: occupying, as it did, some twenty minutes in the telling; but the sum and substance of it was, that Oliver was a foundling, born of low and vicious parents. That he had, from his birth, displayed no better qualities than treachery, ingratitude, and malice. That he had terminated his brief career in the place of his birth, by making a sanguinary and cowardly attack on an unoffending lad, and running away in the night-time from his master's house. In proof of his really being the person he represented himself, Mr. Bumble laid upon the table the papers he had brought to town. Folding his arms again, he then awaited Mr. Brownlow's observations.

'I fear it is all too true,' said the old gentleman sorrowfully, after looking over the papers. 'This is not much for your intelligence; but I would gladly have given you treble the money, if it had been favourable to the boy.'

It is not improbable that if Mr. Bumble had been possessed of this information at an earlier period of the interview, he might have imparted a very different colouring to his little history. It was too late to do it now, however; so he shook his head gravely, and, pocketing the five guineas, withdrew.

Mr. Brownlow paced the room to and fro for some minutes; evidently so much disturbed by the beadle's tale, that even Mr. Grimwig forbore to vex him further.

At length he stopped, and rang the bell violently.

'Mrs. Bedwin,' said Mr. Brownlow, when the housekeeper appeared; 'that boy, Oliver, is an imposter.'

'It can't be, sir. It cannot be,' said the old lady energetically.

'I tell you he is,' retorted the old gentleman. 'What do you mean by can't be? We have just heard a full account of him from his birth; and he has been a thorough-paced little villain, all his life.'

'I never will believe it, sir,' replied the old lady, firmly. 'Never!'

'You old women never believe anything but quack-doctors, and lying story-books,' growled Mr. Grimwig. 'I knew it all along. Why didn't you take my advise in the beginning; you would if he hadn't had a fever, I suppose, eh? He was interesting, wasn't he? Interesting! Bah!' And Mr. Grimwig poked the fire with a flourish.

'He was a dear, grateful, gentle child, sir,' retorted Mrs. Bedwin, indignantly. 'I know what children are, sir; and have done these forty years; and people who can't say the same, shouldn't say anything about them. That's my opinion!'

This was a hard hit at Mr. Grimwig, who was a bachelor. As it extorted nothing from that gentleman but a smile, the old lady tossed her head, and smoothed down her apron preparatory to another speech, when she was stopped by Mr. Brownlow.

'Silence!' said the old gentleman, feigning an anger he was far from feeling. 'Never let me hear the boy's name again. I rang to tell you that. Never. Never, on any pretence, mind! You may leave the room, Mrs. Bedwin. Remember! I am in earnest.'

There were sad hearts at Mr. Brownlow's that night.

Oliver's heart sank within him, when he thought of his good friends; it was well for him that he could not know what they had heard, or it might have broken outright.

CHAPTER XVIII. HOW OLIVER PASSED HIS TIME IN THE IMPROVING SOCIETY OF HIS REPUTABLE FRIENDS

About noon next day, when the Dodger and Master Bates had gone out to pursue their customary avocations, Mr. Fagin took the opportunity of reading Oliver a long lecture on the crying sin of ingratitude; of which he clearly demonstrated he had been guilty, to no ordinary extent, in wilfully absenting himself from the society of his anxious friends; and, still more, in endeavouring to escape from them after so much trouble and expense had been incurred in his recovery. Mr. Fagin laid great stress on the fact of his having taken Oliver in, and cherished him, when, without his timely aid, he might have perished with hunger; and he related the dismal and affecting history of a young lad whom, in his philanthropy, he had succoured under parallel circumstances, but who, proving unworthy of his confidence and evincing a desire to communicate with the police, had unfortunately come to be hanged at the Old Bailey one morning. Mr. Fagin did not seek to conceal his share in the catastrophe, but lamented with tears in his eyes that the wrong-headed and treacherous behaviour of the young person in question, had rendered it necessary that he should become the victim of certain evidence for the crown: which, if it were not precisely true, was indispensably necessary for the safety of him (Mr. Fagin) and a few select friends. Mr. Fagin concluded by drawing a rather disagreeable picture of the discomforts of hanging; and, with great friendliness and politeness of manner, expressed his anxious hopes that he might never be obliged to submit Oliver Twist to that unpleasant operation.

Little Oliver's blood ran cold, as he listened to the Jew's words, and imperfectly comprehended the dark threats conveyed in them. That it was possible even for justice itself to confound the innocent with the guilty when they were in accidental companionship, he knew already; and that deeply-laid plans for the destruction of inconveniently knowing or over-communicative persons, had been really devised and carried out by the Jew on more occasions than one, he thought by no means unlikely, when he recollected the general nature of the altercations between that gentleman and Mr. Sikes: which seemed to bear reference to some foregone conspiracy of the kind. As he glanced timidly up, and met the Jew's searching look, he felt that his pale face and trembling limbs were neither unnoticed nor unrelished by that wary old gentleman.

The Jew, smiling hideously, patted Oliver on the head, and said, that if he kept himself quiet, and applied himself to business, he saw they would be very good friends yet. Then, taking his hat, and covering himself with an old patched great-coat, he went out, and locked the room-door behind him.

And so Oliver remained all that day, and for the greater part of many subsequent days, seeing nobody, between early morning and midnight, and left during the long hours to commune with his own thoughts. Which, never failing to revert to his kind friends, and the opinion they must long ago have formed of him, were sad indeed.

After the lapse of a week or so, the Jew left the room-door unlocked; and he was at liberty to wander about the house.

It was a very dirty place. The rooms upstairs had great high wooden chimney-pieces and large doors, with panelled walls and cornices to the ceiling; which, although they were black with neglect and dust, were ornamented in various ways. From all of these tokens Oliver concluded that a long time ago, before the old Jew was born, it had belonged to better people, and had perhaps been quite gay and handsome: dismal and dreary as it looked now.

Spiders had built their webs in the angles of the walls and ceilings; and sometimes, when Oliver walked softly into a room, the mice would scamper across the floor, and run back terrified to their holes. With these exceptions, there was neither sight nor sound of any living thing; and often, when it grew dark, and he was tired of wandering from room to room, he would crouch in the corner of the passage by the street-door, to be as near living people as he could; and would remain there, listening and counting the hours, until the Jew or the boys returned.

In all the rooms, the mouldering shutters were fast closed: the bars which held them were screwed tight into the wood; the only light which was admitted, stealing its way through round holes at the top: which made the rooms more gloomy, and filled them with strange shadows. There was a back-garret window with rusty bars outside, which had no shutter; and out of this, Oliver often gazed with a melancholy face for hours together; but nothing was to be descried from it but a confused and crowded mass of housetops, blackened chimneys, and gable-ends. Sometimes, indeed, a grizzly head might be seen, peering over the parapet-wall of a distant house; but it was quickly withdrawn again; and as the window of Oliver's observatory was nailed down, and dimmed with the rain and smoke of years, it was as much as he could do to make out the forms of the different objects beyond, without making any attempt to be seen or heard,—which he had as much chance of being, as if he had lived inside the ball of St. Paul's Cathedral.

One afternoon, the Dodger and Master Bates being engaged out that evening, the first-named young gentleman took it into his head to evince some anxiety regarding the decoration of his person (to do him justice, this was by no means an habitual weakness with him); and, with this end and aim, he condescendingly commanded Oliver to assist him in his toilet, straightway.

Oliver was but too glad to make himself useful; too happy to have some faces, however bad, to look upon; too desirous to conciliate those about him when he could honestly do so; to throw any objection in the way of this proposal. So he at once expressed his readiness; and, kneeling on the floor, while the Dodger sat upon the table so that he could take his foot in his laps, he applied himself to a process which Mr. Dawkins designated as 'japanning his trotter-cases.' The phrase, rendered into plain English, signifieth, cleaning his boots.

Whether it was the sense of freedom and independence which a rational animal may be supposed to feel when he sits on a table in an easy attitude smoking a pipe, swinging one leg carelessly to and fro, and having his boots cleaned all the time, without even the past trouble of having taken them off, or the prospective misery of putting them on, to disturb his reflections; or whether it was the goodness of the tobacco that soothed the feelings of the Dodger, or the mildness of the beer that mollified his thoughts; he was evidently tinctured, for the nonce, with a spice of romance and enthusiasm, foreign to his general nature. He looked down on Oliver, with a thoughtful countenance, for a brief space; and then, raising his head, and heaving a gentle sign, said, half in abstraction, and half to Master Bates:

'What a pity it is he isn't a prig!'

'Ah!' said Master Charles Bates; 'he don't know what's good for him.'

The Dodger sighed again, and resumed his pipe: as did Charley Bates. They both smoked, for some seconds, in silence.

'I suppose you don't even know what a prig is?' said the Dodger mournfully.

'I think I know that,' replied Oliver, looking up. 'It's a the—; you're one, are you not?' inquired Oliver, checking himself.

'I am,' replied the Dodger. 'I'd scorn to be anything else.' Mr. Dawkins gave his hat a ferocious cock, after delivering this sentiment, and looked at Master Bates, as if to denote that he would feel obliged by his saying anything to the contrary.

'I am,' repeated the Dodger. 'So's Charley. So's Fagin. So's Sikes. So's Nancy. So's Bet. So we all are, down to the dog. And he's the downiest one of the lot!'

'And the least given to peaching,' added Charley Bates.

'He wouldn't so much as bark in a witness-box, for fear of committing himself; no, not if you tied him up in one, and left him there without wittles for a fortnight,' said the Dodger.

'Not a bit of it,' observed Charley.

'He's a rum dog. Don't he look fierce at any strange cove that laughs or sings when he's in company!' pursued the Dodger. 'Won't he growl at all, when he hears a fiddle playing! And don't he hate other dogs as ain't of his breed! Oh, no!'

'He's an out-and-out Christian,' said Charley.

This was merely intended as a tribute to the animal's abilities, but it was an appropriate remark in another sense, if Master Bates had only known it; for there are a good many ladies and gentlemen, claiming to be out-and-out Christians, between whom, and Mr. Sikes' dog, there exist strong and singular points of resemblance.

'Well, well,' said the Dodger, recurring to the point from which they had strayed: with that mindfulness of his profession which influenced all his proceedings. 'This hasn't go anything to do with young Green here.'

'No more it has,' said Charley. 'Why don't you put yourself under Fagin, Oliver?'

'And make your fortun' out of hand?' added the Dodger, with a grin.

'And so be able to retire on your property, and do the gen-teel: as I mean to, in the very next leap-year but four that ever comes, and the forty-second Tuesday in Trinity-week,' said Charley Bates.

'I don't like it,' rejoined Oliver, timidly; 'I wish they would let me go. I—I—would rather go.'

'And Fagin would RATHER not!' rejoined Charley.

Oliver knew this too well; but thinking it might be dangerous to express his feelings more openly, he only sighed, and went on with his boot-cleaning.

'Go!' exclaimed the Dodger. 'Why, where's your spirit? Don't you take any pride out of yourself? Would you go and be dependent on your friends?'

'Oh, blow that!' said Master Bates: drawing two or three silk handkerchiefs from his pocket, and tossing them into a cupboard, 'that's too mean; that is.'

'I couldn't do it,' said the Dodger, with an air of haughty disgust.

'You can leave your friends, though,' said Oliver with a half smile; 'and let them be punished for what you did.'

'That,' rejoined the Dodger, with a wave of his pipe, 'That was all out of consideration for Fagin, 'cause the traps know that we work together, and he might have got into trouble if we hadn't made our lucky; that was the move, wasn't it, Charley?'

Master Bates nodded assent, and would have spoken, but the recollection of Oliver's flight came so suddenly upon him, that the smoke he was inhaling got entangled with a laugh, and went up into his head, and down into his throat: and brought on a fit of coughing and stamping, about five minutes long.

'Look here!' said the Dodger, drawing forth a handful of shillings and halfpence. 'Here's a jolly life! What's the odds where it comes from? Here, catch hold; there's plenty more where they were took from. You won't, won't you? Oh, you precious flat!'

'It's naughty, ain't it, Oliver?' inquired Charley Bates. 'He'll come to be scragged, won't he?'

'I don't know what that means,' replied Oliver.

'Something in this way, old feller,' said Charly. As he said it, Master Bates caught up an end of his neckerchief; and, holding it erect in the air, dropped his head on his shoulder, and jerked a curious sound through his teeth; thereby indicating, by a lively pantomimic representation, that scragging and hanging were one and the same thing.

'That's what it means,' said Charley. 'Look how he stares, Jack!

I never did see such prime company as that 'ere boy; he'll be the death of me, I know he will.' Master Charley Bates, having laughed heartily again, resumed his pipe with tears in his eyes.

'You've been brought up bad,' said the Dodger, surveying his boots with much satisfaction when Oliver had polished them. 'Fagin will make something of you, though, or you'll be the first he ever had that turned out unprofitable. You'd better begin at once; for you'll come to the trade long before you think of it; and you're only losing time, Oliver.'

Master Bates backed this advice with sundry moral admonitions of his own: which, being exhausted, he and his friend Mr. Dawkins launched into a glowing description of the numerous pleasures incidental to the life they led, interspersed with a variety of hints to Oliver that the best thing he could do, would be to secure Fagin's favour without more delay, by the means which they themselves had employed to gain it.

'And always put this in your pipe, Nolly,' said the Dodger, as the Jew was heard unlocking the door above, 'if you don't take fogels and tickers—'

'What's the good of talking in that way?' interposed Master Bates; 'he don't know what you mean.'

674

'If you don't take pocket-handkechers and watches,' said the Dodger, reducing his conversation to the level of Oliver's capacity, 'some other cove will; so that the coves that lose 'em will be all the worse, and you'll be all the worse, too, and nobody half a ha'p'orth the better, except the chaps wot gets them—and you've just as good a right to them as they have.'

'To be sure, to be sure!' said the Jew, who had entered unseen by Oliver. 'It all lies in a nutshell my dear; in a nutshell, take the Dodger's word for it. Ha! ha! ha! He understands the catechism of his trade.'

The old man rubbed his hands gleefully together, as he corroborated the Dodger's reasoning in these terms; and chuckled with delight at his pupil's proficiency.

The conversation proceeded no farther at this time, for the Jew had returned home accompanied by Miss Betsy, and a gentleman whom Oliver had never seen before, but who was accosted by the Dodger as Tom Chitling; and who, having lingered on the stairs to exchange a few gallantries with the lady, now made his appearance.

Mr. Chitling was older in years than the Dodger: having perhaps numbered eighteen winters; but there was a degree of deference in his deportment towards that young gentleman which seemed to indicate that he felt himself conscious of a slight inferiority in point of genius and professional aquirements. He had small twinkling eyes, and a pock-marked face; wore a fur cap, a dark corduroy jacket, greasy fustian trousers, and an apron. His wardrobe was, in truth, rather out of repair; but he excused himself to the company by stating that his 'time' was only out an hour before; and that, in consequence of having worn the regimentals for six weeks past, he had not been able to bestow any attention on his private clothes. Mr. Chitling added, with strong marks of irritation, that the new way of fumigating clothes up yonder was infernal unconstitutional, for it burnt holes in them, and there was no remedy against the County. The same remark he considered to apply to the regulation mode of cutting the hair: which he held to be decidedly unlawful. Mr. Chitling wound up his observations by stating that he had not touched a drop of anything for forty-two moral long hard-working days; and that he 'wished he might be busted if he warn't as dry as a lime-basket.'

'Where do you think the gentleman has come from, Oliver?' inquired the Jew, with a grin, as the other boys put a bottle of spirits on the table.

'I—I—don't know, sir,' replied Oliver.

'Who's that?' inquired Tom Chitling, casting a contemptuous look at Oliver.

'A young friend of mine, my dear,' replied the Jew.

'He's in luck, then,' said the young man, with a meaning look at Fagin. 'Never mind where I came from, young 'un; you'll find your way there, soon enough, I'll bet a crown!'

At this sally, the boys laughed. After some more jokes on the same subject, they exchanged a few short whispers with Fagin; and withdrew.

After some words apart between the last comer and Fagin, they drew their chairs towards the fire; and the Jew, telling Oliver to come and sit by him, led the conversation to the topics most calculated to interest his hearers. These were, the great advantages of the trade, the proficiency of the Dodger, the amiability of Charley Bates, and the liberality of the Jew himself. At length these subjects displayed signs of being thoroughly exhausted; and Mr. Chitling did the same: for the house of correction becomes fatiguing after a week or two. Miss

Betsy accordingly withdrew; and left the party to their repose.

From this day, Oliver was seldom left alone; but was placed in almost constant communication with the two boys, who played the old game with the Jew every day: whether for their own improvement or Oliver's, Mr. Fagin best knew. At other times the old man would tell them stories of robberies he had committed in his younger days: mixed up with so much that was droll and curious, that Oliver could not help laughing heartily, and showing that he was amused in spite of all his better feelings.

In short, the wily old Jew had the boy in his toils. Having prepared his mind, by solitude and gloom, to prefer any society to the companionship of his own sad thoughts in such a dreary place, he was now slowly instilling into his soul the poison which he hoped would blacken it, and change its hue for ever.

CHAPTER XIX. IN WHICH A NOTABLE PLAN IS DISCUSSED AND DETERMINED ON

It was a chill, damp, windy night, when the Jew: buttoning his great-coat tight round his shrivelled body, and pulling the collar up over his ears so as completely to obscure the lower part of his face: emerged from his den. He paused on the step as the door was locked and chained behind him; and having listened while the boys made all secure, and until their retreating footsteps were no longer audible, slunk down the street as quickly as he could.

The house to which Oliver had been conveyed, was in the neighborhood of Whitechapel. The Jew stopped for an instant at the corner of the street; and, glancing suspiciously round, crossed the road, and struck off in the direction of the Spitalfields.

The mud lay thick upon the stones, and a black mist hung over the streets; the rain fell sluggishly down, and everything felt cold and clammy to the touch. It seemed just the night when it befitted such a being as the Jew to be abroad. As he glided stealthily along, creeping beneath the shelter of the walls and doorways, the hideous old man seemed like some loathsome reptile, engendered in the slime and darkness through which he moved: crawling forth, by night, in search of some rich offal for a meal.

He kept on his course, through many winding and narrow ways, until he reached Bethnal Green; then, turning suddenly off to the left, he soon became involved in a maze of the mean and dirty streets which abound in that close and densely-populated quarter.

The Jew was evidently too familiar with the ground he traversed to be at all bewildered, either by the darkness of the night, or the intricacies of the way. He hurried through several alleys and streets, and at length turned into one, lighted only by a single lamp at the farther end. At the door of a house in this street, he knocked; having exchanged a few muttered words with the person who opened it, he walked upstairs.

A dog growled as he touched the handle of a room-door; and a man's voice demanded who was there.

'Only me, Bill; only me, my dear,' said the Jew looking in.

'Bring in your body then,' said Sikes. 'Lie down, you stupid brute! Don't you know the devil when he's got a great-coat on?'

Apparently, the dog had been somewhat deceived by Mr. Fagin's outer garment; for as the

Jew unbuttoned it, and threw it over the back of a chair, he retired to the corner from which he had risen: wagging his tail as he went, to show that he was as well satisfied as it was in his nature to be.

'Well!' said Sikes.

'Well, my dear,' replied the Jew.—'Ah! Nancy.'

The latter recognition was uttered with just enough of embarrassment to imply a doubt of its reception; for Mr. Fagin and his young friend had not met, since she had interfered in behalf of Oliver. All doubts upon the subject, if he had any, were speedily removed by the young lady's behaviour. She took her feet off the fender, pushed back her chair, and bade Fagin draw up his, without saying more about it: for it was a cold night, and no mistake.

'It is cold, Nancy dear,' said the Jew, as he warmed his skinny hands over the fire. 'It seems to go right through one,' added the old man, touching his side.

'It must be a piercer, if it finds its way through your heart,' said Mr. Sikes. 'Give him something to drink, Nancy. Burn my body, make haste! It's enough to turn a man ill, to see his lean old carcase shivering in that way, like a ugly ghost just rose from the grave.'

Nancy quickly brought a bottle from a cupboard, in which there were many: which, to judge from the diversity of their appearance, were filled with several kinds of liquids. Sikes pouring out a glass of brandy, bade the Jew drink it off.

'Quite enough, quite, thankye, Bill,' replied the Jew, putting down the glass after just setting his lips to it.

'What! You're afraid of our getting the better of you, are you?' inquired Sikes, fixing his eyes on the Jew. 'Ugh!'

With a hoarse grunt of contempt, Mr. Sikes seized the glass, and threw the remainder of its contents into the ashes: as a preparatory ceremony to filling it again for himself: which he did at once.

The Jew glanced round the room, as his companion tossed down the second glassful; not in curiosity, for he had seen it often before; but in a restless and suspicious manner habitual to him. It was a meanly furnished apartment, with nothing but the contents of the closet to induce the belief that its occupier was anything but a working man; and with no more suspicious articles displayed to view than two or three heavy bludgeons which stood in a corner, and a 'life-preserver' that hung over the chimney-piece.

'There,' said Sikes, smacking his lips. 'Now I'm ready.'

'For business?' inquired the Jew.

'For business,' replied Sikes; 'so say what you've got to say.'

'About the crib at Chertsey, Bill?' said the Jew, drawing his chair forward, and speaking in a very low voice.

'Yes. Wot about it?' inquired Sikes.

'Ah! you know what I mean, my dear,' said the Jew. 'He knows what I mean, Nancy; don't he?'

'No, he don't,' sneered Mr. Sikes. 'Or he won't, and that's the same thing. Speak out, and call things by their right names; don't sit there, winking and blinking, and talking to me in hints, as if you warn't the very first that thought about the robbery. Wot d'ye mean?'

'Hush, Bill, hush!' said the Jew, who had in vain attempted to stop this burst of indignation; 'somebody will hear us, my dear. Somebody will hear us.'

'Let 'em hear!' said Sikes; 'I don't care.' But as Mr. Sikes DID care, on reflection, he dropped his voice as he said the words, and grew calmer.

'There, there,' said the Jew, coaxingly. 'It was only my caution, nothing more. Now, my dear, about that crib at Chertsey; when is it to be done, Bill, eh? When is it to be done? Such plate, my dear, such plate!' said the Jew: rubbing his hands, and elevating his eyebrows in a rapture of anticipation.

'Not at all,' replied Sikes coldly.

'Not to be done at all!' echoed the Jew, leaning back in his chair.

'No, not at all,' rejoined Sikes. 'At least it can't be a put-up job, as we expected.'

'Then it hasn't been properly gone about,' said the Jew, turning pale with anger. 'Don't tell me!'

'But I will tell you,' retorted Sikes. 'Who are you that's not to be told? I tell you that Toby Crackit has been hanging about the place for a fortnight, and he can't get one of the servants in line.'

'Do you mean to tell me, Bill,' said the Jew: softening as the other grew heated: 'that neither of the two men in the house can be got over?'

'Yes, I do mean to tell you so,' replied Sikes. 'The old lady has had 'em these twenty years; and if you were to give 'em five hundred pound, they wouldn't be in it.'

'But do you mean to say, my dear,' remonstrated the Jew, 'that the women can't be got over?'

'Not a bit of it,' replied Sikes.

'Not by flash Toby Crackit?' said the Jew incredulously. 'Think what women are, Bill,'

'No; not even by flash Toby Crackit,' replied Sikes. 'He says he's worn sham whiskers, and a canary waistcoat, the whole blessed time he's been loitering down there, and it's all of no use.'

'He should have tried mustachios and a pair of military trousers, my dear,' said the Jew.

'So he did,' rejoined Sikes, 'and they warn't of no more use than the other plant.'

The Jew looked blank at this information. After ruminating for some minutes with his chin sunk on his breast, he raised his head and said, with a deep sigh, that if flash Toby Crackit reported aright, he feared the game was up.

'And yet,' said the old man, dropping his hands on his knees, 'it's a sad thing, my dear, to lose so much when we had set our hearts upon it.'

'So it is,' said Mr. Sikes. 'Worse luck!'

A long silence ensued; during which the Jew was plunged in deep thought, with his face wrinkled into an expression of villainy perfectly demoniacal. Sikes eyed him furtively from time to time. Nancy, apparently fearful of irritating the housebreaker, sat with her eyes fixed upon the fire, as if she had been deaf to all that passed.

'Fagin,' said Sikes, abruptly breaking the stillness that prevailed; 'is it worth fifty shiners extra, if it's safely done from the outside?'

'Yes,' said the Jew, as suddenly rousing himself.

'Is it a bargain?' inquired Sikes.

'Yes, my dear, yes,' rejoined the Jew; his eyes glistening, and every muscle in his face working, with the excitement that the inquiry had awakened.

'Then,' said Sikes, thrusting aside the Jew's hand, with some disdain, 'let it come off as soon as you like. Toby and me were over the garden-wall the night afore last, sounding the panels of the door and shutters. The crib's barred up at night like a jail; but there's one part we can crack, safe and softly.'

'Which is that, Bill?' asked the Jew eagerly.

'Why,' whispered Sikes, 'as you cross the lawn—'

'Yes?' said the Jew, bending his head forward, with his eyes almost starting out of it.

'Umph!' cried Sikes, stopping short, as the girl, scarcely moving her head, looked suddenly round, and pointed for an instant to the Jew's face. 'Never mind which part it is. You can't do it without me, I know; but it's best to be on the safe side when one deals with you.'

'As you like, my dear, as you like' replied the Jew. 'Is there no help wanted, but yours and Toby's?'

'None,' said Sikes. ''Cept a centre-bit and a boy. The first we've both got; the second you must find us.'

'A boy!' exclaimed the Jew. 'Oh! then it's a panel, eh?'

'Never mind wot it is!' replied Sikes. 'I want a boy, and he musn't be a big 'un. Lord!' said Mr. Sikes, reflectively, 'if I'd only got that young boy of Ned, the chimbley-sweeper's! He kept him small on purpose, and let him out by the job. But the father gets lagged; and then the Juvenile Delinquent Society comes, and takes the boy away from a trade where he was earning money, teaches him to read and write, and in time makes a 'prentice of him. And so they go on,' said Mr. Sikes, his wrath rising with the recollection of his wrongs, 'so they go on; and, if they'd got money enough (which it's a Providence they haven't,) we shouldn't have half a dozen boys left in the whole trade, in a year or two.'

'No more we should,' acquiesced the Jew, who had been considering during this speech, and had only caught the last sentence. 'Bill!'

'What now?' inquired Sikes.

The Jew nodded his head towards Nancy, who was still gazing at the fire; and intimated, by a sign, that he would have her told to leave the room. Sikes shrugged his shoulders impatiently, as if he thought the precaution unnecessary; but complied, nevertheless, by requesting Miss Nancy to fetch him a jug of beer.

'You don't want any beer,' said Nancy, folding her arms, and retaining her seat very composedly.

'I tell you I do!' replied Sikes.

'Nonsense,' rejoined the girl coolly, 'Go on, Fagin. I know what he's going to say, Bill; he needn't mind me.'

The Jew still hesitated. Sikes looked from one to the other in some surprise.

'Why, you don't mind the old girl, do you, Fagin?' he asked at length. 'You've known her long enough to trust her, or the Devil's in it. She ain't one to blab. Are you Nancy?'

'I should think not!' replied the young lady: drawing her chair up to the table, and putting her elbows upon it.

'No, no, my dear, I know you're not,' said the Jew; 'but—' and again the old man paused.

'But wot?' inquired Sikes.

'I didn't know whether she mightn't p'r'aps be out of sorts, you know, my dear, as she was the other night,' replied the Jew.

At this confession, Miss Nancy burst into a loud laugh; and, swallowing a glass of brandy, shook her head with an air of defiance, and burst into sundry exclamations of 'Keep the game a-going!' 'Never say die!' and the like. These seemed to have the effect of re-assuring both gentlemen; for the Jew nodded his head with a satisfied air, and resumed his seat: as did Mr. Sikes likewise.

'Now, Fagin,' said Nancy with a laugh. 'Tell Bill at once, about Oliver!'

'Ha! you're a clever one, my dear: the sharpest girl I ever saw!' said the Jew, patting her on the neck. 'It WAS about Oliver I was going to speak, sure enough. Ha! ha! ha!'

'What about him?' demanded Sikes.

'He's the boy for you, my dear,' replied the Jew in a hoarse whisper; laying his finger on the side of his nose, and grinning frightfully.

'He!' exclaimed Sikes.

'Have him, Bill!' said Nancy. 'I would, if I was in your place. He mayn't be so much up, as any of the others; but that's not what you want, if he's only to open a door for you. Depend upon it he's a safe one, Bill.'

'I know he is,' rejoined Fagin. 'He's been in good training these last few weeks, and it's time he began to work for his bread. Besides, the others are all too big.'

'Well, he is just the size I want,' said Mr. Sikes, ruminating.

'And will do everything you want, Bill, my dear,' interposed the Jew; 'he can't help himself. That is, if you frighten him enough.'

'Frighten him!' echoed Sikes. 'It'll be no sham frightening, mind you. If there's anything queer about him when we once get into the work; in for a penny, in for a pound. You won't see him alive again, Fagin. Think of that, before you send him. Mark my words!' said the robber, poising a crowbar, which he had drawn from under the bedstead.

'I've thought of it all,' said the Jew with energy. 'I've—I've had my eye upon him, my dears, close—close. Once let him feel that he is one of us; once fill his mind with the idea that he has been a thief; and he's ours! Ours for his life. Oho! It couldn't have come about better!

The old man crossed his arms upon his breast; and, drawing his head and shoulders into a heap, literally hugged himself for joy.

'Ours!' said Sikes. 'Yours, you mean.'

'Perhaps I do, my dear,' said the Jew, with a shrill chuckle. 'Mine, if you like, Bill.'

'And wot,' said Sikes, scowling fiercely on his agreeable friend, 'wot makes you take so much pains about one chalk-faced kid, when you know there are fifty boys snoozing about Common Garden every night, as you might pick and choose from?'

'Because they're of no use to me, my dear,' replied the Jew, with some confusion, 'not worth the taking. Their looks convict 'em when they get into trouble, and I lose 'em all. With this boy, properly managed, my dears, I could do what I couldn't with twenty of them. Besides,' said the Jew, recovering his self-possession, 'he has us now if he could only give us leg-bail again; and he must be in the same boat with us. Never mind how he came there; it's quite enough for my power over him that he was in a robbery; that's all I want. Now, how much better this is, than being obliged to put the poor leetle boy out of the way—which would be dangerous, and we should lose by it besides.'

'When is it to be done?' asked Nancy, stopping some turbulent exclamation on the part of Mr. Sikes, expressive of the disgust with which he received Fagin's affectation of humanity.

'Ah, to be sure,' said the Jew; 'when is it to be done, Bill?'

'I planned with Toby, the night arter to-morrow,' rejoined Sikes in a surly voice, 'if he heerd nothing from me to the contrairy.'

'Good,' said the Jew; 'there's no moon.'

'No,' rejoined Sikes.

'It's all arranged about bringing off the swag, is it?' asked the Jew.

Sikes nodded.

'And about—'

'Oh, ah, it's all planned,' rejoined Sikes, interrupting him. 'Never mind particulars. You'd better bring the boy here to-morrow night. I shall get off the stone an hour arter daybreak. Then you hold your tongue, and keep the melting-pot ready, and that's all you'll have to do.'

After some discussion, in which all three took an active part, it was decided that Nancy should repair to the Jew's next evening when the night had set in, and bring Oliver away with her; Fagin craftily observing, that, if he evinced any disinclination to the task, he would be more willing to accompany the girl who had so recently interfered in his behalf, than anybody else. It was also solemnly arranged that poor Oliver should, for the purposes of the contemplated expedition, be unreservedly consigned to the care and custody of Mr. William Sikes; and further, that the said Sikes should deal with him as he thought fit; and should not be held responsible by the Jew for any mischance or evil that might be necessary to visit him: it being understood that, to render the compact in this respect binding, any representations made by Mr. Sikes on his return should be required to be confirmed and corroborated, in all important particulars, by the testimony of flash Toby Crackit.

These preliminaries adjusted, Mr. Sikes proceeded to drink brandy at a furious rate, and to flourish the crowbar in an alarming manner; yelling forth, at the same time, most unmusical snatches of song, mingled with wild execrations. At length, in a fit of professional enthusiasm, he insisted upon producing his box of housebreaking tools: which he had no sooner stumbled in with, and opened for the purpose of explaining the nature and properties of the various implements it contained, and the peculiar beauties of their construction, than he fell over the box upon the floor, and went to sleep where he fell.

'Good-night, Nancy,' said the Jew, muffling himself up as before.

'Good-night.'

Their eyes met, and the Jew scrutinised her, narrowly. There was no flinching about the girl. She was as true and earnest in the matter as Toby Crackit himself could be.

The Jew again bade her good-night, and, bestowing a sly kick upon the prostrate form of Mr. Sikes while her back was turned, groped downstairs.

'Always the way!' muttered the Jew to himself as he turned homeward. 'The worst of these women is, that a very little thing serves to call up some long-forgotten feeling; and, the best of them is, that it never lasts. Ha! ha! The man against the child, for a bag of gold!'

Beguiling the time with these pleasant reflections, Mr. Fagin wended his way, through mud and mire, to his gloomy abode: where the Dodger was sitting up, impatiently awaiting his return.

'Is Oliver a-bed? I want to speak to him,' was his first remark as they descended the stairs.

'Hours ago,' replied the Dodger, throwing open a door. 'Here he is!'

The boy was lying, fast asleep, on a rude bed upon the floor; so pale with anxiety, and sadness, and the closeness of his prison, that he looked like death; not death as it shows in shroud and coffin, but in the guise it wears when life has just departed; when a young and gentle spirit has, but an instant, fled to Heaven, and the gross air of the world has not had time to breathe upon the changing dust it hallowed.

'Not now,' said the Jew, turning softly away. 'To-morrow. To-morrow.'

CHAPTER XX. WHEREIN OLIVER IS DELIVERED OVER TO MR. WILLIAM SIKES

When Oliver awoke in the morning, he was a good deal surprised to find that a new pair of shoes, with strong thick soles, had been placed at his bedside; and that his old shoes had been removed. At first, he was pleased with the discovery: hoping that it might be the forerunner of his release; but such thoughts were quickly dispelled, on his sitting down to breakfast along with the Jew, who told him, in a tone and manner which increased his alarm, that he was to be taken to the residence of Bill Sikes that night.

'To—to—stop there, sir?' asked Oliver, anxiously.

'No, no, my dear. Not to stop there,' replied the Jew. 'We shouldn't like to lose you. Don't be afraid, Oliver, you shall come back to us again. Ha! ha! ha! We won't be so cruel as to send you away, my dear. Oh no, no!'

The old man, who was stooping over the fire toasting a piece of bread, looked round as he bantered Oliver thus; and chuckled as if to show that he knew he would still be very glad to get away if he could.

'I suppose,' said the Jew, fixing his eyes on Oliver, 'you want to know what you're going to Bill's for—-eh, my dear?'

Oliver coloured, involuntarily, to find that the old thief had been reading his thoughts; but boldly said, Yes, he did want to know.

'Why, do you think?' inquired Fagin, parrying the question.

'Indeed I don't know, sir,' replied Oliver.

'Bah!' said the Jew, turning away with a disappointed countenance from a close perusal of the boy's face. 'Wait till Bill tells you, then.'

The Jew seemed much vexed by Oliver's not expressing any greater curiosity on the subject; but the truth is, that, although Oliver felt very anxious, he was too much confused by the earnest cunning of Fagin's looks, and his own speculations, to make any further inquiries just then. He had no other opportunity: for the Jew remained very surly and silent till night: when he prepared to go abroad.

'You may burn a candle,' said the Jew, putting one upon the table. 'And here's a book for you to read, till they come to fetch you. Good-night!'

'Good-night!' replied Oliver, softly.

The Jew walked to the door: looking over his shoulder at the boy as he went. Suddenly stopping, he called him by his name.

Oliver looked up; the Jew, pointing to the candle, motioned him to light it. He did so; and, as he placed the candlestick upon the table, saw that the Jew was gazing fixedly at him, with lowering and contracted brows, from the dark end of the room.

'Take heed, Oliver! take heed!' said the old man, shaking his right hand before him in a warning manner. 'He's a rough man, and thinks nothing of blood when his own is up. Whatever falls out, say nothing; and do what he bids you. Mind!' Placing a strong emphasis on the last word, he suffered his features gradually to resolve themselves into a ghastly grin, and, nodding his head, left the room.

Oliver leaned his head upon his hand when the old man disappeared, and pondered, with a trembling heart, on the words he had just heard. The more he thought of the Jew's admonition, the more he was at a loss to divine its real purpose and meaning.

He could think of no bad object to be attained by sending him to Sikes, which would not be equally well answered by his remaining with Fagin; and after meditating for a long time, concluded that he had been selected to perform some ordinary menial offices for the housebreaker, until another boy, better suited for his purpose could be engaged. He was too well accustomed to suffering, and had suffered too much where he was, to bewail the prospect of change very severely. He remained lost in thought for some minutes; and then, with a heavy sigh, snuffed the candle, and, taking up the book which the Jew had left with him, began to read.

He turned over the leaves. Carelessly at first; but, lighting on a passage which attracted his attention, he soon became intent upon the volume. It was a history of the lives and trials of great criminals; and the pages were soiled and thumbed with use. Here, he read of dreadful crimes that made the blood run cold; of secret murders that had been committed by the lonely wayside; of bodies hidden from the eye of man in deep pits and wells: which would not keep them down, deep as they were, but had yielded them up at last, after many years, and so maddened the murderers with the sight, that in their horror they had confessed their guilt, and yelled for the gibbet to end their agony. Here, too, he read of men who, lying in their beds at dead of night, had been tempted (so they said) and led on, by their own bad thoughts, to such dreadful bloodshed as it made the flesh creep, and the limbs quail, to think of. The terrible descriptions were so real and vivid, that the sallow pages seemed to turn red with gore; and the words upon them, to be sounded in his ears, as if they were whispered, in hollow murmurs, by the spirits of the dead.

In a paroxysm of fear, the boy closed the book, and thrust it from him. Then, falling upon his knees, he prayed Heaven to spare him from such deeds; and rather to will that he should die at once, than be reserved for crimes, so fearful and appalling. By degrees, he grew more calm, and besought, in a low and broken voice, that he might be rescued from his present dangers; and that if any aid were to be raised up for a poor outcast boy who had never known the love of friends or kindred, it might come to him now, when, desolate and deserted, he stood alone in the midst of wickedness and guilt.

He had concluded his prayer, but still remained with his head buried in his hands, when a rustling noise aroused him.

'What's that!' he cried, starting up, and catching sight of a figure standing by the door. 'Who's there?'

'Me. Only me,' replied a tremulous voice.

Oliver raised the candle above his head: and looked towards the door. It was Nancy.

'Put down the light,' said the girl, turning away her head. 'It hurts my eyes.'

Oliver saw that she was very pale, and gently inquired if she were ill. The girl threw herself into a chair, with her back towards him: and wrung her hands; but made no reply.

'God forgive me!' she cried after a while, 'I never thought of this.'

'Has anything happened?' asked Oliver. 'Can I help you? I will if I can. I will, indeed.'

She rocked herself to and fro; caught her throat; and, uttering a gurgling sound, gasped for breath.

'Nancy!' cried Oliver, 'What is it?'

The girl beat her hands upon her knees, and her feet upon the ground; and, suddenly stopping, drew her shawl close round her: and shivered with cold.

Oliver stirred the fire. Drawing her chair close to it, she sat there, for a little time, without speaking; but at length she raised her head, and looked round.

'I don't know what comes over me sometimes,' said she, affecting to busy herself in arranging her dress; 'it's this damp dirty room, I think. Now, Nolly, dear, are you ready?'

'Am I to go with you?' asked Oliver.

'Yes. I have come from Bill,' replied the girl. 'You are to go with me.'

'What for?' asked Oliver, recoiling.

'What for?' echoed the girl, raising her eyes, and averting them again, the moment they encountered the boy's face. 'Oh! For no harm.'

'I don't believe it,' said Oliver: who had watched her closely.

'Have it your own way,' rejoined the girl, affecting to laugh. 'For no good, then.'

Oliver could see that he had some power over the girl's better feelings, and, for an instant, thought of appealing to her compassion for his helpless state. But, then, the thought darted across his mind that it was barely eleven o'clock; and that many people were still in the streets: of whom surely some might be found to give credence to his tale. As the reflection occured to him, he stepped forward: and said, somewhat hastily, that he was ready.

Neither his brief consideration, nor its purport, was lost on his companion. She eyed him narrowly, while he spoke; and cast upon him a look of intelligence which sufficiently showed that she guessed what had been passing in his thoughts.

'Hush!' said the girl, stooping over him, and pointing to the door as she looked cautiously round. 'You can't help yourself. I have tried hard for you, but all to no purpose. You are hedged round and round. If ever you are to get loose from here, this is not the time.'

Struck by the energy of her manner, Oliver looked up in her face with great surprise. She seemed to speak the truth; her countenance was white and agitated; and she trembled with very earnestness.

'I have saved you from being ill-used once, and I will again, and I do now,' continued the girl aloud; 'for those who would have fetched you, if I had not, would have been far more rough than me. I have promised for your being quiet and silent; if you are not, you will only do harm to yourself and me too, and perhaps be my death. See here! I have borne all this for you already, as true as God sees me show it.'

She pointed, hastily, to some livid bruises on her neck and arms; and continued, with great rapidity:

'Remember this! And don't let me suffer more for you, just now. If I could help you, I would; but I have not the power. They don't mean to harm you; whatever they make you do, is no fault of yours. Hush! Every word from you is a blow for me. Give me your hand. Make haste! Your hand!'

She caught the hand which Oliver instinctively placed in hers, and, blowing out the light, drew him after her up the stairs. The door was opened, quickly, by some one shrouded in the darkness, and was as quickly closed, when they had passed out. A hackney-cabriolet was in waiting; with the same vehemence which she had exhibited in addressing Oliver, the girl pulled him in with her, and drew the curtains close. The driver wanted no directions, but lashed his horse into full speed, without the delay of an instant.

The girl still held Oliver fast by the hand, and continued to pour into his ear, the warnings and assurances she had already imparted. All was so quick and hurried, that he had scarcely time to recollect where he was, or how he came there, when the carriage stopped at the house to which the Jew's steps had been directed on the previous evening.

For one brief moment, Oliver cast a hurried glance along the empty street, and a cry for help hung upon his lips. But the girl's voice was in his ear, beseeching him in such tones of agony to remember her, that he had not the heart to utter it. While he hesitated, the opportunity was gone; he was already in the house, and the door was shut.

'This way,' said the girl, releasing her hold for the first time. 'Bill!'

'Hallo!' replied Sikes: appearing at the head of the stairs, with a candle. 'Oh! That's the time of day. Come on!'

This was a very strong expression of approbation, an uncommonly hearty welcome, from a person of Mr. Sikes' temperament. Nancy, appearing much gratified thereby, saluted him cordially.

'Bull's-eye's gone home with Tom,' observed Sikes, as he lighted them up. 'He'd have been in the way.'

'That's right,' rejoined Nancy.

'So you've got the kid,' said Sikes when they had all reached the room: closing the door as he spoke.

'Yes, here he is,' replied Nancy.

'Did he come quiet?' inquired Sikes.

'Like a lamb,' rejoined Nancy.

'I'm glad to hear it,' said Sikes, looking grimly at Oliver; 'for the sake of his young carcase: as would otherways have suffered for it. Come here, young 'un; and let me read you a lectur', which is as well got over at once.'

Thus addressing his new pupil, Mr. Sikes pulled off Oliver's cap and threw it into a corner; and then, taking him by the shoulder, sat himself down by the table, and stood the boy in front of him.

'Now, first: do you know wot this is?' inquired Sikes, taking up a pocket-pistol which lay on the table.

Oliver replied in the affirmative.

'Well, then, look here,' continued Sikes. 'This is powder; that 'ere's a bullet; and this is a little bit of a old hat for waddin'.'

Oliver murmured his comprehension of the different bodies referred to; and Mr. Sikes proceeded to load the pistol, with great nicety and deliberation.

'Now it's loaded,' said Mr. Sikes, when he had finished.

'Yes, I see it is, sir,' replied Oliver.

'Well,' said the robber, grasping Oliver's wrist, and putting the barrel so close to his temple that they touched; at which moment the boy could not repress a start; 'if you speak a word when you're out o'doors with me, except when I speak to you, that loading will be in your head without notice. So, if you do make up your mind to speak without leave, say your prayers first.'

Having bestowed a scowl upon the object of this warning, to increase its effect, Mr. Sikes continued.

'As near as I know, there isn't anybody as would be asking very partickler arter you, if you was disposed of; so I needn't take this devil-and-all of trouble to explain matters to you, if it warn't for your own good. D'ye hear me?'

'The short and the long of what you mean,' said Nancy: speaking very emphatically, and slightly frowning at Oliver as if to bespeak his serious attention to her words: 'is, that if you're crossed by him in this job you have on hand, you'll prevent his ever telling tales afterwards, by shooting him through the head, and will take your chance of swinging for it, as you do for a great many other things in the way of business, every month of your life.'

'That's it!' observed Mr. Sikes, approvingly; 'women can always put things in fewest words.—Except when it's blowing up; and then they lengthens it out. And now that he's thoroughly up to it, let's have some supper, and get a snooze before starting.'

In pursuance of this request, Nancy quickly laid the cloth; disappearing for a few minutes, she presently returned with a pot of porter and a dish of sheep's heads: which gave occasion to several pleasant witticisms on the part of Mr. Sikes, founded upon the singular coincidence of 'jemmies' being a can name, common to them, and also to an ingenious implement much used in his profession. Indeed, the worthy gentleman, stimulated perhaps by the immediate prospect of being on active service, was in great spirits and good humour; in proof whereof, it may be here remarked, that he humourously drank all the beer at a draught, and did not utter, on a rough calculation, more than four-score oaths during the whole progress of the meal.

Supper being ended—it may be easily conceived that Oliver had no great appetite for it—Mr. Sikes disposed of a couple of glasses of spirits and water, and threw himself on the bed; ordering Nancy, with many imprecations in case of failure, to call him at five precisely. Oliver stretched himself in his clothes, by command of the same authority, on a mattress upon the floor; and the girl, mending the fire, sat before it, in readiness to rouse them at the appointed time.

For a long time Oliver lay awake, thinking it not impossible that Nancy might seek that opportunity of whispering some further advice; but the girl sat brooding over the fire, without moving, save now and then to trim the light. Weary with watching and anxiety, he at length fell asleep.

When he awoke, the table was covered with tea-things, and Sikes was thrusting various articles into the pockets of his great-coat, which hung over the back of a chair. Nancy was busily engaged in preparing breakfast. It was not yet daylight; for the candle was still burning, and it was quite dark outside. A sharp rain, too, was beating against the window-panes; and the sky looked black and cloudy.

'Now, then!' growled Sikes, as Oliver started up; 'half-past five! Look sharp, or you'll get no breakfast; for it's late as it is.'

Oliver was not long in making his toilet; having taken some breakfast, he replied to a surly inquiry from Sikes, by saying that he was quite ready.

Nancy, scarcely looking at the boy, threw him a handkerchief to tie round his throat; Sikes gave him a large rough cape to button over his shoulders. Thus attired, he gave his hand to the robber, who, merely pausing to show him with a menacing gesture that he had that same pistol in a side-pocket of his great-coat, clasped it firmly in his, and, exchanging a farewell with Nancy, led him away.

Oliver turned, for an instant, when they reached the door, in the hope of meeting a look from the girl. But she had resumed her old seat in front of the fire, and sat, perfectly motionless before it.

CHAPTER XXI. THE EXPEDITION

It was a cheerless morning when they got into the street; blowing and raining hard; and the clouds looking dull and stormy. The night had been very wet: large pools of water had collected in the road: and the kennels were overflowing. There was a faint glimmering of the coming day in the sky; but it rather aggravated than relieved the gloom of the scene: the sombre light only serving to pale that which the street lamps afforded, without shedding any warmer or brighter tints upon the wet house-tops, and dreary streets. There appeared to be nobody stirring in that quarter of the town; the windows of the houses were all closely shut; and the streets through which they passed, were noiseless and empty.

By the time they had turned into the Bethnal Green Road, the day had fairly begun to break. Many of the lamps were already extinguished; a few country waggons were slowly toiling on, towards London; now and then, a stage-coach, covered with mud, rattled briskly by: the driver bestowing, as he passed, an admonitory lash upon the heavy waggoner who, by keeping on the wrong side of the road, had endangered his arriving at the office, a quarter of a minute after his time. The public-houses, with gas-lights burning inside, were already open. By degrees, other shops began to be unclosed, and a few scattered people were met with. Then, came straggling groups of labourers going to their work; then, men and women with fish-baskets on their heads; donkey-carts laden with vegetables; chaise-carts filled with live-stock or whole carcasses of meat; milk-women with pails; an unbroken concourse of people, trudging out with various supplies to the eastern suburbs of the town. As they approached the City, the noise and traffic gradually increased; when they threaded the streets between Shoreditch and Smithfield, it had swelled into a roar of sound and bustle. It was as light as it was likely to be, till night came on again, and the busy morning of half the London population had begun.

Turning down Sun Street and Crown Street, and crossing Finsbury square, Mr. Sikes struck, by way of Chiswell Street, into Barbican: thence into Long Lane, and so into Smithfield; from which latter place arose a tumult of discordant sounds that filled Oliver Twist with amazement.

It was market-morning. The ground was covered, nearly ankle-deep, with filth and mire; a thick steam, perpetually rising from the reeking bodies of the cattle, and mingling with the fog, which seemed to rest upon the chimney-tops, hung heavily above. All the pens in the centre of the large area, and as many temporary pens as could be crowded into the vacant space, were filled with sheep; tied up to posts by the gutter side were long lines of beasts and oxen, three or four deep. Countrymen, butchers, drovers, hawkers, boys, thieves, idlers, and vagabonds of every low grade, were mingled together in a mass; the whistling of drovers, the barking dogs, the bellowing and plunging of the oxen, the bleating of sheep, the grunting and squeaking of pigs, the cries of hawkers, the shouts, oaths, and quarrelling on all sides; the ringing of bells and roar of voices, that issued from every public-house; the crowding, pushing, driving, beating, whooping and yelling; the hideous and discordant dim that resounded from every corner of the market; and the unwashed, unshaven, squalid, and dirty figures constantly running to and fro, and bursting in and out of the throng; rendered it a stunning and bewildering scene, which quite confounded the senses.

Mr. Sikes, dragging Oliver after him, elbowed his way through the thickest of the crowd, and bestowed very little attention on the numerous sights and sounds, which so astonished the boy. He nodded, twice or thrice, to a passing friend; and, resisting as many invitations to take a morning dram, pressed steadily onward, until they were clear of the turmoil, and had made their way through Hosier Lane into Holborn.

'Now, young 'un!' said Sikes, looking up at the clock of St. Andrew's Church, 'hard upon seven! you must step out. Come, don't lag behind already, Lazy-legs!'

Mr. Sikes accompanied this speech with a jerk at his little companion's wrist; Oliver, quickening his pace into a kind of trot between a fast walk and a run, kept up with the rapid strides of the house-breaker as well as he could.

They held their course at this rate, until they had passed Hyde Park corner, and were on their way to Kensington: when Sikes relaxed his pace, until an empty cart which was at some little distance behind, came up. Seeing 'Hounslow' written on it, he asked the driver with as much civility as he could assume, if he would give them a lift as far as Isleworth.

'Jump up,' said the man. 'Is that your boy?'

'Yes; he's my boy,' replied Sikes, looking hard at Oliver, and putting his hand abstractedly into the pocket where the pistol was.

'Your father walks rather too quick for you, don't he, my man?' inquired the driver: seeing that Oliver was out of breath.

'Not a bit of it,' replied Sikes, interposing. 'He's used to it.

Here, take hold of my hand, Ned. In with you!'

Thus addressing Oliver, he helped him into the cart; and the driver, pointing to a heap of sacks, told him to lie down there, and rest himself.

As they passed the different mile-stones, Oliver wondered, more and more, where his companion meant to take him. Kensington, Hammersmith, Chiswick, Kew Bridge, Brentford, were all passed; and yet they went on as steadily as if they had only just begun their journey. At length, they came to a public-house called the Coach and Horses; a little way beyond which, another road appeared to run off. And here, the cart stopped.

Sikes dismounted with great precipitation, holding Oliver by the hand all the while; and lifting him down directly, bestowed a furious look upon him, and rapped the side-pocket with his fist, in a significant manner.

'Good-bye, boy,' said the man.

'He's sulky,' replied Sikes, giving him a shake; 'he's sulky. A young dog! Don't mind him.'

'Not I!' rejoined the other, getting into his cart. 'It's a fine day, after all.' And he drove away.

Sikes waited until he had fairly gone; and then, telling Oliver he might look about him if he wanted, once again led him onward on his journey.

They turned round to the left, a short way past the public-house; and then, taking a right-hand road, walked on for a long time: passing many large gardens and gentlemen's houses on both sides of the way, and stopping for nothing but a little beer, until they reached a town. Here against the wall of a house, Oliver saw written up in pretty large letters, 'Hampton.' They lingered about, in the fields, for some hours. At length they came back into the town; and, turning into an old public-house with a defaced sign-board, ordered some dinner by the kitchen fire.

The kitchen was an old, low-roofed room; with a great beam across the middle of the ceiling, and benches, with high backs to them, by the fire; on which were seated several rough men in smock-frocks, drinking and smoking. They took no notice of Oliver; and very little of Sikes; and, as Sikes took very little notice of them, he and his young comrade sat in a corner by themselves, without being much troubled by their company.

They had some cold meat for dinner, and sat so long after it, while Mr. Sikes indulged himself with three or four pipes, that Oliver began to feel quite certain they were not going any further. Being much tired with the walk, and getting up so early, he dozed a little at first; then, quite overpowered by fatigue and the fumes of the tobacco, fell asleep.

It was quite dark when he was awakened by a push from Sikes. Rousing himself sufficiently to sit up and look about him, he found that worthy in close fellowship and communication with a labouring man, over a pint of ale.

'So, you're going on to Lower Halliford, are you?' inquired Sikes.

'Yes, I am,' replied the man, who seemed a little the worse—or better, as the case might be—for drinking; 'and not slow about it neither. My horse hasn't got a load behind him going back, as he had coming up in the mornin'; and he won't be long a-doing of it. Here's luck to him. Ecod! he's a good 'un!'

'Could you give my boy and me a lift as far as there?' demanded Sikes, pushing the ale towards his new friend.

'If you're going directly, I can,' replied the man, looking out of the pot. 'Are you going to Halliford?'

'Going on to Shepperton,' replied Sikes.

'I'm your man, as far as I go,' replied the other. 'Is all paid, Becky?'

'Yes, the other gentleman's paid,' replied the girl.

'I say!' said the man, with tipsy gravity; 'that won't do, you know.'

'Why not?' rejoined Sikes. 'You're a-going to accommodate us, and wot's to prevent my standing treat for a pint or so, in return?'

The stranger reflected upon this argument, with a very profound face; having done so, he seized Sikes by the hand: and declared he was a real good fellow. To which Mr. Sikes replied, he was joking; as, if he had been sober, there would have been strong reason to suppose he was.

After the exchange of a few more compliments, they bade the company good-night, and went out; the girl gathering up the pots and glasses as they did so, and lounging out to the door, with her hands full, to see the party start.

The horse, whose health had been drunk in his absence, was standing outside: ready harnessed to the cart. Oliver and Sikes got in without any further ceremony; and the man to whom he belonged, having lingered for a minute or two 'to bear him up,' and to defy the hostler and the world to produce his equal, mounted also. Then, the hostler was told to give the horse his head; and, his head being given him, he made a very unpleasant use of it: tossing it into the air with great disdain, and running into the parlour windows over the way; after performing those feats, and supporting himself for a short time on his hind-legs, he started off at great speed, and rattled out of the town right gallantly.

The night was very dark. A damp mist rose from the river, and the marshy ground about; and spread itself over the dreary fields. It was piercing cold, too; all was gloomy and black. Not a word was spoken; for the driver had grown sleepy; and Sikes was in no mood to lead him into conversation. Oliver sat huddled together, in a corner of the cart; bewildered with alarm and apprehension; and figuring strange objects in the gaunt trees, whose branches waved grimly to and fro, as if in some fantastic joy at the desolation of the scene.

As they passed Sunbury Church, the clock struck seven. There was a light in the ferry-house window opposite: which streamed across the road, and threw into more sombre shadow a dark yew-tree with graves beneath it. There was a dull sound of falling water not far off; and the leaves of the old tree stirred gently in the night wind. It seemed like quiet music for the repose of the dead.

Sunbury was passed through, and they came again into the lonely road. Two or three miles more, and the cart stopped. Sikes alighted, took Oliver by the hand, and they once again walked on.

They turned into no house at Shepperton, as the weary boy had expected; but still kept walking on, in mud and darkness, through gloomy lanes and over cold open wastes, until they came within sight of the lights of a town at no great distance. On looking intently forward, Oliver saw that the water was just below them, and that they were coming to the foot of a bridge.

Sikes kept straight on, until they were close upon the bridge; then turned suddenly down a bank upon the left.

'The water!' thought Oliver, turning sick with fear. 'He has brought me to this lonely place to murder me!'

He was about to throw himself on the ground, and make one struggle for his young life, when he saw that they stood before a solitary house: all ruinous and decayed. There was a window on each side of the dilapidated entrance; and one story above; but no light was visible. The house was dark, dismantled: and the all appearance, uninhabited.

Sikes, with Oliver's hand still in his, softly approached the low porch, and raised the latch. The door yielded to the pressure, and they passed in together.

CHAPTER XXII. THE BURGLARY

'Hallo!' cried a loud, hoarse voice, as soon as they set foot in the passage.

'Don't make such a row,' said Sikes, bolting the door. 'Show a glim, Toby.'

'Aha! my pal!' cried the same voice. 'A glim, Barney, a glim! Show the gentleman in, Barney; wake up first, if convenient.'

The speaker appeared to throw a boot-jack, or some such article, at the person he addressed, to rouse him from his slumbers: for the noise of a wooden body, falling violently, was heard; and then an indistinct muttering, as of a man between sleep and awake.

'Do you hear?' cried the same voice. 'There's Bill Sikes in the passage with nobody to do the civil to him; and you sleeping there, as if you took laudanum with your meals, and nothing stronger. Are you any fresher now, or do you want the iron candlestick to wake you thoroughly?'

A pair of slipshod feet shuffled, hastily, across the bare floor of the room, as this interrogatory was put; and there issued, from a door on the right hand; first, a feeble candle: and next, the form of the same individual who has been heretofore described as labouring under the infirmity of speaking through his nose, and officiating as waiter at the public-house on Saffron Hill.

'Bister Sikes!' exclaimed Barney, with real or counterfeit joy; 'cub id, sir; cub id.'

'Here! you get on first,' said Sikes, putting Oliver in front of him. 'Quicker! or I shall tread upon your heels.'

Muttering a curse upon his tardiness, Sikes pushed Oliver before him; and they entered a low dark room with a smoky fire, two or three broken chairs, a table, and a very old couch: on which, with his legs much higher than his head, a man was reposing at full length, smoking a long clay pipe. He was dressed in a smartly-cut snuff-coloured coat, with large brass buttons; an orange neckerchief; a coarse, staring, shawl-pattern waistcoat; and drab breeches. Mr. Crackit (for he it was) had no very great quantity of hair, either upon his head or face; but what he had, was of a reddish dye, and tortured into long corkscrew curls, through which he occasionally thrust some very dirty fingers, ornamented with large common rings. He was a trifle above the middle size, and apparently rather weak in the legs; but this circumstance by no means detracted from his own admiration of his top-boots, which he contemplated, in their elevated situation, with lively satisfaction.

'Bill, my boy!' said this figure, turning his head towards the door, 'I'm glad to see you. I was almost afraid you'd given it up: in which case I should have made a personal wentur. Hallo!'

Uttering this exclamation in a tone of great surprise, as his eyes rested on Oliver, Mr. Toby Crackit brought himself into a sitting posture, and demanded who that was.

'The boy. Only the boy!' replied Sikes, drawing a chair towards the fire.

'Wud of Bister Fagid's lads,' exclaimed Barney, with a grin.

'Fagin's, eh!' exclaimed Toby, looking at Oliver. 'Wot an inwalable boy that'll make, for the old ladies' pockets in chapels! His mug is a fortin' to him.'

'There—there's enough of that,' interposed Sikes, impatiently; and stooping over his recumbant friend, he whispered a few words in his ear: at which Mr. Crackit laughed immensely, and honoured Oliver with a long stare of astonishment.

'Now,' said Sikes, as he resumed his seat, 'if you'll give us something to eat and drink while we're waiting, you'll put some heart in us; or in me, at all events. Sit down by the fire, younker, and rest yourself; for you'll have to go out with us again to-night, though not very far off.'

Oliver looked at Sikes, in mute and timid wonder; and drawing a stool to the fire, sat with his aching head upon his hands, scarcely knowing where he was, or what was passing around him.

'Here,' said Toby, as the young Jew placed some fragments of food, and a bottle upon the table, 'Success to the crack!' He rose to honour the toast; and, carefully depositing his empty pipe in a corner, advanced to the table, filled a glass with spirits, and drank off its contents. Mr. Sikes did the same.

'A drain for the boy,' said Toby, half-filling a wine-glass. 'Down with it, innocence.'

'Indeed,' said Oliver, looking piteously up into the man's face; 'indeed, I—'

'Down with it!' echoed Toby. 'Do you think I don't know what's good for you? Tell him to drink it, Bill.'

'He had better!' said Sikes clapping his hand upon his pocket. 'Burn my body, if he isn't more trouble than a whole family of Dodgers. Drink it, you perwerse imp; drink it!'

Frightened by the menacing gestures of the two men, Oliver hastily swallowed the contents of the glass, and immediately fell into a violent fit of coughing: which delighted Toby Crackit and Barney, and even drew a smile from the surly Mr. Sikes.

This done, and Sikes having satisfied his appetite (Oliver could eat nothing but a small crust of bread which they made him swallow), the two men laid themselves down on chairs for a short nap. Oliver retained his stool by the fire; Barney wrapped in a blanket, stretched himself on the floor: close outside the fender.

They slept, or appeared to sleep, for some time; nobody stirring but Barney, who rose once or twice to throw coals on the fire. Oliver fell into a heavy doze: imagining himself straying along the gloomy lanes, or wandering about the dark churchyard, or retracing some one or other of the scenes of the past day: when he was roused by Toby Crackit jumping up and declaring it was half-past one.

In an instant, the other two were on their legs, and all were actively engaged in busy preparation. Sikes and his companion enveloped their necks and chins in large dark shawls, and drew on their great-coats; Barney, opening a cupboard, brought forth several articles, which he hastily crammed into the pockets.

'Barkers for me, Barney,' said Toby Crackit.

'Here they are,' replied Barney, producing a pair of pistols. 'You loaded them yourself.'

'All right!' replied Toby, stowing them away. 'The persuaders?'

'I've got 'em,' replied Sikes.

'Crape, keys, centre-bits, darkies—nothing forgotten?' inquired Toby: fastening a small crowbar to a loop inside the skirt of his coat.

'All right,' rejoined his companion. 'Bring them bits of timber, Barney. That's the time of day.'

With these words, he took a thick stick from Barney's hands, who, having delivered another to Toby, busied himself in fastening on Oliver's cape.

'Now then!' said Sikes, holding out his hand.

Oliver: who was completely stupified by the unwonted exercise, and the air, and the drink which had been forced upon him: put his hand mechanically into that which Sikes extended for the purpose.

'Take his other hand, Toby,' said Sikes. 'Look out, Barney.'

The man went to the door, and returned to announce that all was quiet. The two robbers issued forth with Oliver between them. Barney, having made all fast, rolled himself up as before, and was soon asleep again.

It was now intensely dark. The fog was much heavier than it had been in the early part of the night; and the atmosphere was so damp, that, although no rain fell, Oliver's hair and eyebrows, within a few minutes after leaving the house, had become stiff with the half-frozen moisture that was floating about. They crossed the bridge, and kept on towards the lights which he had seen before. They were at no great distance off; and, as they walked pretty briskly, they soon arrived at Chertsey.

'Slap through the town,' whispered Sikes; 'there'll be nobody in the way, to-night, to see us.'

Toby acquiesced; and they hurried through the main street of the little town, which at that late hour was wholly deserted. A dim light shone at intervals from some bed-room window; and the hoarse barking of dogs occasionally broke the silence of the night. But there was nobody abroad. They had cleared the town, as the church-bell struck two.

Quickening their pace, they turned up a road upon the left hand. After walking about a quarter of a mile, they stopped before a detached house surrounded by a wall: to the top of which, Toby Crackit, scarcely pausing to take breath, climbed in a twinkling.

'The boy next,' said Toby. 'Hoist him up; I'll catch hold of him.'

Before Oliver had time to look round, Sikes had caught him under the arms; and in three or four seconds he and Toby were lying on the grass on the other side. Sikes followed directly. And they stole cautiously towards the house.

And now, for the first time, Oliver, well-nigh mad with grief and terror, saw that housebreaking and robbery, if not murder, were the objects of the expedition. He clasped his hands together, and involuntarily uttered a subdued exclamation of horror. A mist came before his eyes; the cold sweat stood upon his ashy face; his limbs failed him; and he sank upon his knees.

'Get up!' murmured Sikes, trembling with rage, and drawing the pistol from his pocket; 'Get up, or I'll strew your brains upon the grass.'

'Oh! for God's sake let me go!' cried Oliver; 'let me run away and die in the fields. I will never come near London; never, never! Oh! pray have mercy on me, and do not make me steal. For the love of all the bright Angels that rest in Heaven, have mercy upon me!'

The man to whom this appeal was made, swore a dreadful oath, and had cocked the pistol, when Toby, striking it from his grasp, placed his hand upon the boy's mouth, and dragged him to the house.

'Hush!' cried the man; 'it won't answer here. Say another word, and I'll do your business myself with a crack on the head. That makes no noise, and is quite as certain, and more genteel. Here, Bill, wrench the shutter open. He's game enough now, I'll engage. I've seen older hands of his age took the same way, for a minute or two, on a cold night.'

Sikes, invoking terrific imprecations upon Fagin's head for sending Oliver on such an errand, plied the crowbar vigorously, but with little noise. After some delay, and some assistance from Toby, the shutter to which he had referred, swung open on its hinges.

It was a little lattice window, about five feet and a half above the ground, at the back of the house: which belonged to a scullery, or small brewing-place, at the end of the passage. The aperture was so small, that the inmates had probably not thought it worth while to defend it more securely; but it was large enough to admit a boy of Oliver's size, nevertheless. A very brief exercise of Mr. Sike's art, sufficed to overcome the fastening of the lattice; and it soon stood wide open also.

'Now listen, you young limb,' whispered Sikes, drawing a dark lantern from his pocket, and throwing the glare full on Oliver's face; 'I'm a going to put you through there. Take this light; go softly up the steps straight afore you, and along the little hall, to the street door; unfasten it, and let us in.'

'There's a bolt at the top, you won't be able to reach,' interposed Toby. 'Stand upon one of the hall chairs. There are three there, Bill, with a jolly large blue unicorn and gold pitchfork on 'em: which is the old lady's arms.'

'Keep quiet, can't you?' replied Sikes, with a threatening look. 'The room-door is open, is it?'

'Wide,' replied Toby, after peeping in to satisfy himself. 'The game of that is, that they always leave it open with a catch, so that the dog, who's got a bed in here, may walk up and down the passage when he feels wakeful. Ha! ha! Barney 'ticed him away to-night. So neat!'

Although Mr. Crackit spoke in a scarcely audible whisper, and laughed without noise, Sikes imperiously commanded him to be silent, and to get to work. Toby complied, by first producing his lantern, and placing it on the ground; then by planting himself firmly with his head against the wall beneath the window, and his hands upon his knees, so as to make a step of his back. This was no sooner done, than Sikes, mounting upon him, put Oliver gently through the window with his feet first; and, without leaving hold of his collar, planted him safely on the floor inside.

'Take this lantern,' said Sikes, looking into the room. 'You see the stairs afore you?'

Oliver, more dead than alive, gasped out, 'Yes.' Sikes, pointing to the street-door with the pistol-barrel, briefly advised him to take notice that he was within shot all the way; and that if he faltered, he would fall dead that instant.

'It's done in a minute,' said Sikes, in the same low whisper. 'Directly I leave go of you, do your work. Hark!'

'What's that?' whispered the other man.

They listened intently.

'Nothing,' said Sikes, releasing his hold of Oliver. 'Now!'

In the short time he had had to collect his senses, the boy had firmly resolved that, whether he died in the attempt or not, he would make one effort to dart upstairs from the hall, and alarm the family. Filled with this idea, he advanced at once, but stealthily.

'Come back!' suddenly cried Sikes aloud. 'Back! back!'

Scared by the sudden breaking of the dead stillness of the place, and by a loud cry which followed it, Oliver let his lantern fall, and knew not whether to advance or fly.

The cry was repeated—a light appeared—a vision of two terrified half-dressed men at the top of the stairs swam before his eyes—a flash—a loud noise—a smoke—a crash somewhere, but where he knew not,—and he staggered back.

Sikes had disappeared for an instant; but he was up again, and had him by the collar before the smoke had cleared away. He fired his own pistol after the men, who were already retreating; and dragged the boy up.

'Clasp your arm tighter,' said Sikes, as he drew him through the window. 'Give me a shawl here. They've hit him. Quick! How the boy bleeds!'

Then came the loud ringing of a bell, mingled with the noise of fire-arms, and the shouts of men, and the sensation of being carried over uneven ground at a rapid pace. And then, the noises grew confused in the distance; and a cold deadly feeling crept over the boy's heart; and he saw or heard no more.

CHAPTER XXIII. WHICH CONTAINS THE SUBSTANCE OF A PLEASANT CONVERSATION BETWEEN MR. BUMBLE AND A LADY; AND SHOWS THAT EVEN A BEADLE MAY BE SUSCEPTIBLE ON SOME POINTS

The night was bitter cold. The snow lay on the ground, frozen into a hard thick crust, so that only the heaps that had drifted into byways and corners were affected by the sharp wind that howled abroad: which, as if expending increased fury on such prey as it found, caught it savagely up in clouds, and, whirling it into a thousand misty eddies, scattered it in air. Bleak, dark, and piercing cold, it was a night for the well-housed and fed to draw round the bright fire and thank God they were at home; and for the homeless, starving wretch to lay him down and die. Many hunger-worn outcasts close their eyes in our bare streets, at such times, who, let their crimes have been what they may, can hardly open them in a more bitter world.

Such was the aspect of out-of-doors affairs, when Mrs. Corney, the matron of the workhouse to which our readers have been already introduced as the birthplace of Oliver Twist, sat herself down before a cheerful fire in her own little room, and glanced, with no small degree of complacency, at a small round table: on which stood a tray of corresponding size, furnished with all necessary materials for the most grateful meal that matrons enjoy. In fact, Mrs. Corney was about to solace herself with a cup of tea. As she glanced from the table to the fireplace, where the smallest of all possible kettles was singing a small song in a small voice, her inward satisfaction evidently increased,—so much so, indeed, that Mrs. Corney smiled.

'Well!' said the matron, leaning her elbow on the table, and looking reflectively at the fire; 'I'm sure we have all on us a great deal to be grateful for! A great deal, if we did but know it. Ah!'

Mrs. Corney shook her head mournfully, as if deploring the mental blindness of those paupers who did not know it; and thrusting a silver spoon (private property) into the inmost recesses of a two-ounce tin tea-caddy, proceeded to make the tea.

How slight a thing will disturb the equanimity of our frail minds! The black teapot, being very small and easily filled, ran over while Mrs. Corney was moralising; and the water slightly scalded Mrs. Corney's hand.

'Drat the pot!' said the worthy matron, setting it down very hastily on the hob; 'a little stupid thing, that only holds a couple of cups! What use is it of, to anybody! Except,' said Mrs. Corney, pausing, 'except to a poor desolate creature like me. Oh dear!'

With these words, the matron dropped into her chair, and, once more resting her elbow on the table, thought of her solitary fate. The small teapot, and the single cup, had awakened in her mind sad recollections of Mr. Corney (who had not been dead more than five-and-twenty years); and she was overpowered.

'I shall never get another!' said Mrs. Corney, pettishly; 'I shall never get another—like him.'

Whether this remark bore reference to the husband, or the teapot, is uncertain. It might have been the latter; for Mrs. Corney looked at it as she spoke; and took it up afterwards. She had just tasted her first cup, when she was disturbed by a soft tap at the room-door.

'Oh, come in with you!' said Mrs. Corney, sharply. 'Some of the old women dying, I suppose. They always die when I'm at meals. Don't stand there, letting the cold air in, don't. What's amiss now, eh?'

'Nothing, ma'am, nothing,' replied a man's voice.

'Dear me!' exclaimed the matron, in a much sweeter tone, 'is that Mr. Bumble?'

'At your service, ma'am,' said Mr. Bumble, who had been stopping outside to rub his shoes clean, and to shake the snow off his coat; and who now made his appearance, bearing the cocked hat in one hand and a bundle in the other. 'Shall I shut the door, ma'am?'

The lady modestly hesitated to reply, lest there should be any impropriety in holding an interview with Mr. Bumble, with closed doors. Mr. Bumble taking advantage of the hesitation, and being very cold himself, shut it without permission.

'Hard weather, Mr. Bumble,' said the matron.

'Hard, indeed, ma'am,' replied the beadle. 'Anti-porochial weather this, ma'am. We have given away, Mrs. Corney, we have given away a matter of twenty quartern loaves and a cheese and a half, this very blessed afternoon; and yet them paupers are not contented.'

'Of course not. When would they be, Mr. Bumble?' said the matron, sipping her tea.

'When, indeed, ma'am!' rejoined Mr. Bumble. 'Why here's one man that, in consideration of his wife and large family, has a quartern loaf and a good pound of cheese, full weight. Is he grateful, ma'am? Is he grateful? Not a copper farthing's worth of it! What does he do, ma'am, but ask for a few coals; if it's only a pocket handkerchief full, he says! Coals! What would he do with coals? Toast his cheese with 'em and then come back for more. That's the way with these people, ma'am; give 'em a apron full of coals to-day, and they'll come back for another, the day after to-morrow, as brazen as alabaster.'

The matron expressed her entire concurrence in this intelligible simile; and the beadle went on.

'I never,' said Mr. Bumble, 'see anything like the pitch it's got to. The day afore yesterday, a man—you have been a married woman, ma'am, and I may mention it to you—a man, with hardly a rag upon his back (here Mrs. Corney looked at the floor), goes to our overseer's door when he has got company coming to dinner; and says, he must be relieved, Mrs. Corney. As he wouldn't go away, and shocked the company very much, our overseer sent him out a pound of potatoes and half a pint of oatmeal. "My heart!" says the ungrateful villain, "what's the use of this to me? You might as well give me a pair of iron spectacles!" "Very good," says our overseer, taking 'em away again, "you won't get anything else here." "Then I'll die in the streets!" says the vagrant. "Oh no, you won't," says our overseer.'

'Ha! ha! That was very good! So like Mr. Grannett, wasn't it?' interposed the matron. 'Well, Mr. Bumble?'

'Well, ma'am,' rejoined the beadle, 'he went away; and he did die in the streets. There's a obstinate pauper for you!'

'It beats anything I could have believed,' observed the matron emphatically. 'But don't you think out-of-door relief a very bad thing, any way, Mr. Bumble? You're a gentleman of experience, and ought to know. Come.'

'Mrs. Corney,' said the beadle, smiling as men smile who are conscious of superior information, 'out-of-door relief, properly managed: properly managed, ma'am: is the porochial safeguard. The great principle of out-of-door relief is, to give the paupers exactly what they don't want; and then they get tired of coming.'

'Dear me!' exclaimed Mrs. Corney. 'Well, that is a good one, too!'

'Yes. Betwixt you and me, ma'am,' returned Mr. Bumble, 'that's the great principle; and that's the reason why, if you look at any cases that get into them owdacious newspapers, you'll always observe that sick families have been relieved with slices of cheese. That's the rule now, Mrs. Corney, all over the country. But, however,' said the beadle, stopping to unpack his bundle, 'these are official secrets, ma'am; not to be spoken of; except, as I may say, among the porochial officers, such as ourselves. This is the port wine, ma'am, that the board ordered for the infirmary; real, fresh, genuine port wine; only out of the cask this forenoon; clear as a bell, and no sediment!'

Having held the first bottle up to the light, and shaken it well to test its excellence, Mr. Bumble placed them both on top of a chest of drawers; folded the handkerchief in which they had been wrapped; put it carefully in his pocket; and took up his hat, as if to go.

'You'll have a very cold walk, Mr. Bumble,' said the matron.

'It blows, ma'am,' replied Mr. Bumble, turning up his coat-collar, 'enough to cut one's ears off.'

The matron looked, from the little kettle, to the beadle, who was moving towards the door; and as the beadle coughed, preparatory to bidding her good-night, bashfully inquired whether—whether he wouldn't take a cup of tea?

Mr. Bumble instantaneously turned back his collar again; laid his hat and stick upon a chair; and drew another chair up to the table. As he slowly seated himself, he looked at the lady. She fixed her eyes upon the little teapot. Mr. Bumble coughed again, and slightly smiled.

Mrs. Corney rose to get another cup and saucer from the closet. As she sat down, her eyes once again encountered those of the gallant beadle; she coloured, and applied herself to the task of making his tea. Again Mr. Bumble coughed—louder this time than he had coughed yet.

'Sweet? Mr. Bumble?' inquired the matron, taking up the sugar-basin.

'Very sweet, indeed, ma'am,' replied Mr. Bumble. He fixed his eyes on Mrs. Corney as he said this; and if ever a beadle looked tender, Mr. Bumble was that beadle at that moment.

The tea was made, and handed in silence. Mr. Bumble, having spread a handkerchief over his knees to prevent the crumbs from sullying the splendour of his shorts, began to eat and drink; varying these amusements, occasionally, by fetching a deep sigh; which, however, had no injurious effect upon his appetite, but, on the contrary, rather seemed to facilitate his operations in the tea and toast department.

'You have a cat, ma'am, I see,' said Mr. Bumble, glancing at one who, in the centre of her family, was basking before the fire; 'and kittens too, I declare!'

'I am so fond of them, Mr. Bumble, you can't think,' replied the matron. 'They're so happy, so frolicsome, and so cheerful, that they are quite companions for me.'

'Very nice animals, ma'am,' replied Mr. Bumble, approvingly; 'so very domestic.'

'Oh, yes!' rejoined the matron with enthusiasm; 'so fond of their home too, that it's quite a pleasure, I'm sure.'

'Mrs. Corney, ma'am,' said Mr. Bumble, slowly, and marking the time with his teaspoon, 'I mean to say this, ma'am; that any cat, or kitten, that could live with you, ma'am, and not be fond of its home, must be a ass, ma'am.'

'Oh, Mr. Bumble!' remonstrated Mrs. Corney.

'It's of no use disguising facts, ma'am,' said Mr. Bumble, slowly flourishing the teaspoon with a kind of amorous dignity which made him doubly impressive; 'I would drown it myself, with pleasure.'

'Then you're a cruel man,' said the matron vivaciously, as she held out her hand for the beadle's cup; 'and a very hard-hearted man besides.'

'Hard-hearted, ma'am?' said Mr. Bumble. 'Hard?' Mr. Bumble resigned his cup without another word; squeezed Mrs. Corney's little finger as she took it; and inflicting two open-handed slaps upon his laced waistcoat, gave a mighty sigh, and hitched his chair a very little morsel farther from the fire.

It was a round table; and as Mrs. Corney and Mr. Bumble had been sitting opposite each other, with no great space between them, and fronting the fire, it will be seen that Mr. Bumble, in receding from the fire, and still keeping at the table, increased the distance between himself and Mrs. Corney; which proceeding, some prudent readers will doubtless be disposed to admire, and to consider an act of great heroism on Mr. Bumble's part: he being in some sort tempted by time, place, and opportunity, to give utterance to certain soft nothings, which however well they may become the lips of the light and thoughtless, do seem immeasurably beneath the dignity of judges of the land, members of parliament, ministers of state, lord mayors, and other great public functionaries, but more particularly beneath the stateliness and gravity of a beadle: who (as is well known) should be the sternest and most inflexible among them all.

Whatever were Mr. Bumble's intentions, however (and no doubt they were of the best): it unfortunately happened, as has been twice before remarked, that the table was a round one; consequently Mr. Bumble, moving his chair by little and little, soon began to diminish the distance between himself and the matron; and, continuing to travel round the outer edge of the circle, brought his chair, in time, close to that in which the matron was seated.

Indeed, the two chairs touched; and when they did so, Mr. Bumble stopped.

Now, if the matron had moved her chair to the right, she would have been scorched by the fire; and if to the left, she must have fallen into Mr. Bumble's arms; so (being a discreet matron, and no doubt foreseeing these consequences at a glance) she remained where she was, and handed Mr. Bumble another cup of tea.

'Hard-hearted, Mrs. Corney?' said Mr. Bumble, stirring his tea, and looking up into the matron's face; 'are you hard-hearted, Mrs. Corney?'

'Dear me!' exclaimed the matron, 'what a very curious question from a single man. What can you want to know for, Mr. Bumble?'

The beadle drank his tea to the last drop; finished a piece of toast; whisked the crumbs off his knees; wiped his lips; and deliberately kissed the matron.

'Mr. Bumble!' cried that discreet lady in a whisper; for the fright was so great, that she had quite lost her voice, 'Mr. Bumble, I shall scream!' Mr. Bumble made no reply; but in a slow and dignified manner, put his arm round the matron's waist.

As the lady had stated her intention of screaming, of course she would have screamed at this additional boldness, but that the exertion was rendered unnecessary by a hasty knocking at the door: which was no sooner heard, than Mr. Bumble darted, with much agility, to the wine bottles, and began dusting them with great violence: while the matron sharply demanded who was there.

It is worthy of remark, as a curious physical instance of the efficacy of a sudden surprise in counteracting the effects of extreme fear, that her voice had quite recovered all its official asperity.

'If you please, mistress,' said a withered old female pauper, hideously ugly: putting her head in at the door, 'Old Sally is a-going fast.'

'Well, what's that to me?' angrily demanded the matron. 'I can't keep her alive, can I?'

'No, no, mistress,' replied the old woman, 'nobody can; she's far beyond the reach of help. I've seen a many people die; little babes and great strong men; and I know when death's a-coming, well enough. But she's troubled in her mind: and when the fits are not on her,—and that's not often, for she is dying very hard,—she says she has got something to tell, which you must hear. She'll never die quiet till you come, mistress.'

At this intelligence, the worthy Mrs. Corney muttered a variety of invectives against old women who couldn't even die without purposely annoying their betters; and, muffling herself in a thick shawl which she hastily caught up, briefly requested Mr. Bumble to stay till she came back, lest anything particular should occur. Bidding the messenger walk fast, and not be all night hobbling up the stairs, she followed her from the room with a very ill grace, scolding all the way.

Mr. Bumble's conduct on being left to himself, was rather inexplicable. He opened the closet, counted the teaspoons, weighed the sugar-tongs, closely inspected a silver milk-pot to ascertain that it was of the genuine metal, and, having satisfied his curiosity on these points, put on his cocked hat corner-wise, and danced with much gravity four distinct times round the table.

Having gone through this very extraordinary performance, he took off the cocked hat again, and, spreading himself before the fire with his back towards it, seemed to be mentally engaged in taking an exact inventory of the furniture.

CHAPTER XXIV. TREATS ON A VERY POOR SUBJECT. BUT IS A SHORT ONE, AND MAY BE FOUND OF IMPORTANCE IN THIS HISTORY

It was no unfit messenger of death, who had disturbed the quiet of the matron's room. Her body was bent by age; her limbs trembled with palsy; her face, distorted into a mumbling leer, resembled more the grotesque shaping of some wild pencil, than the work of Nature's hand.

Alas! How few of Nature's faces are left alone to gladden us with their beauty! The cares, and sorrows, and hungerings, of the world, change them as they change hearts; and it is only when those passions sleep, and have lost their hold for ever, that the troubled clouds pass off, and leave Heaven's surface clear. It is a common thing for the countenances of the dead, even in that fixed and rigid state, to subside into the long-forgotten expression of sleeping infancy, and settle into the very look of early life; so calm, so peaceful, do they grow again, that those who knew them in their happy childhood, kneel by the coffin's side in awe, and see the Angel even upon earth.

The old crone tottered along the passages, and up the stairs, muttering some indistinct answers to the chidings of her companion; being at length compelled to pause for breath, she gave the light into her hand, and remained behind to follow as she might: while the more nimble superior made her way to the room where the sick woman lay.

It was a bare garret-room, with a dim light burning at the farther end. There was another old woman watching by the bed; the parish apothecary's apprentice was standing by the fire, making a toothpick out of a quill.

'Cold night, Mrs. Corney,' said this young gentleman, as the matron entered.

'Very cold, indeed, sir,' replied the mistress, in her most civil tones, and dropping a curtsey as she spoke.

'You should get better coals out of your contractors,' said the apothecary's deputy, breaking a lump on the top of the fire with the rusty poker; 'these are not at all the sort of thing for a cold night.'

'They're the board's choosing, sir,' returned the matron. 'The least they could do, would be to keep us pretty warm: for our places are hard enough.'

The conversation was here interrupted by a moan from the sick woman.

'Oh!' said the young mag, turning his face towards the bed, as if he had previously quite forgotten the patient, 'it's all U.P. there, Mrs. Corney.'

'It is, is it, sir?' asked the matron.

'If she lasts a couple of hours, I shall be surprised,' said the apothecary's apprentice, intent upon the toothpick's point. 'It's a break-up of the system altogether. Is she dozing, old lady?'

The attendant stooped over the bed, to ascertain; and nodded in the affirmative.

'Then perhaps she'll go off in that way, if you don't make a row,' said the young man. 'Put the light on the floor. She won't see it there.'

The attendant did as she was told: shaking her head meanwhile, to intimate that the woman would not die so easily; having done so, she resumed her seat by the side of the other nurse, who had by this time returned. The mistress, with an expression of impatience, wrapped herself in her shawl, and sat at the foot of the bed.

The apothecary's apprentice, having completed the manufacture of the toothpick, planted himself in front of the fire and made good use of it for ten minutes or so: when apparently growing rather dull, he wished Mrs. Corney joy of her job, and took himself off on tiptoe.

When they had sat in silence for some time, the two old women rose from the bed, and crouching over the fire, held out their withered hands to catch the heat. The flame threw a ghastly light on their shrivelled faces, and made their ugliness appear terrible, as, in this position, they began to converse in a low voice.

'Did she say any more, Anny dear, while I was gone?' inquired the messenger.

'Not a word,' replied the other. 'She plucked and tore at her arms for a little time; but I held her hands, and she soon dropped off. She hasn't much strength in her, so I easily kept her quiet. I ain't so weak for an old woman, although I am on parish allowance; no, no!'

'Did she drink the hot wine the doctor said she was to have?' demanded the first.

'I tried to get it down,' rejoined the other. 'But her teeth were tight set, and she clenched the mug so hard that it was as much as I could do to get it back again. So I drank it; and it did me good!'

Looking cautiously round, to ascertain that they were not overheard, the two hags cowered nearer to the fire, and chuckled heartily.

'I mind the time,' said the first speaker, 'when she would have done the same, and made rare fun of it afterwards.'

'Ay, that she would,' rejoined the other; 'she had a merry heart. 'A many, many, beautiful corpses she laid out, as nice and neat as waxwork. My old eyes have seen them—ay, and those old hands touched them too; for I have helped her, scores of times.'

Stretching forth her trembling fingers as she spoke, the old creature shook them exultingly before her face, and fumbling in her pocket, brought out an old time-discoloured tin snuff-box, from which she shook a few grains into the outstretched palm of her companion, and a few more into her own. While they were thus employed, the matron, who had been impatiently watching until the dying woman should awaken from her stupor, joined them by the fire, and sharply asked how long she was to wait?

'Not long, mistress,' replied the second woman, looking up into her face. 'We have none of us long to wait for Death. Patience, patience! He'll be here soon enough for us all.'

'Hold your tongue, you doting idiot!' said the matron sternly. 'You, Martha, tell me; has she been in this way before?'

'Often,' answered the first woman.

'But will never be again,' added the second one; 'that is, she'll never wake again but once—and mind, mistress, that won't be for long!'

'Long or short,' said the matron, snappishly, 'she won't find me here when she does wake; take care, both of you, how you worry me again for nothing. It's no part of my duty to see all the old women in the house die, and I won't—that's more. Mind that, you impudent old harridans. If you make a fool of me again, I'll soon cure you, I warrant you!'

She was bouncing away, when a cry from the two women, who had turned towards the bed, caused her to look round. The patient had raised herself upright, and was stretching her arms towards them.

'Who's that?' she cried, in a hollow voice.

'Hush, hush!' said one of the women, stooping over her. 'Lie down, lie down!'

'I'll never lie down again alive!' said the woman, struggling. 'I will tell her! Come here! Nearer! Let me whisper in your ear.'

She clutched the matron by the arm, and forcing her into a chair by the bedside, was about to speak, when looking round, she caught sight of the two old women bending forward in the attitude of eager listeners.

'Turn them away,' said the woman, drowsily; 'make haste! make haste!'

The two old crones, chiming in together, began pouring out many piteous lamentations that the poor dear was too far gone to know her best friends; and were uttering sundry protestations that they would never leave her, when the superior pushed them from the room, closed the door, and returned to the bedside. On being excluded, the old ladies changed their tone, and cried through the keyhole that old Sally was drunk; which, indeed, was not unlikely; since, in addition to a moderate dose of opium prescribed by the apothecary, she was labouring under the effects of a final taste of gin-and-water which had been privily administered, in the openness of their hearts, by the worthy old ladies themselves.

'Now listen to me,' said the dying woman aloud, as if making a great effort to revive one latent spark of energy. 'In this very room—in this very bed—I once nursed a pretty young creetur', that was brought into the house with her feet cut and bruised with walking, and all soiled with dust and blood. She gave birth to a boy, and died. Let me think—what was the year again!'

'Never mind the year,' said the impatient auditor; 'what about her?'

'Ay,' murmured the sick woman, relapsing into her former drowsy state, 'what about her?—what about—I know!' she cried, jumping fiercely up: her face flushed, and her eyes starting from her head—'I robbed her, so I did! She wasn't cold—I tell you she wasn't cold, when I stole it!'

'Stole what, for God's sake?' cried the matron, with a gesture as if she would call for help.

'It!' replied the woman, laying her hand over the other's mouth. 'The only thing she had. She wanted clothes to keep her warm, and food to eat; but she had kept it safe, and had it in her bosom. It was gold, I tell you! Rich gold, that might have saved her life!'

'Gold!' echoed the matron, bending eagerly over the woman as she fell back. 'Go on, go on—yes—what of it? Who was the mother? When was it?'

'She charged me to keep it safe,' replied the woman with a groan, 'and trusted me as the only woman about her. I stole it in my heart when she first showed it me hanging round her neck; and the child's death, perhaps, is on me besides! They would have treated him better, if they had known it all!'

'Known what?' asked the other. 'Speak!'

'The boy grew so like his mother,' said the woman, rambling on, and not heeding the question, 'that I could never forget it when I saw his face. Poor girl! poor girl! She was so young, too! Such a gentle lamb! Wait; there's more to tell. I have not told you all, have I?'

'No, no,' replied the matron, inclining her head to catch the words, as they came more faintly from the dying woman. 'Be quick, or it may be too late!'

'The mother,' said the woman, making a more violent effort than before; 'the mother, when the pains of death first came upon her, whispered in my ear that if her baby was born alive, and thrived, the day might come when it would not feel so much disgraced to hear its poor young mother named. "And oh, kind Heaven!" she said, folding her thin hands together, "whether it be boy or girl, raise up some friends for it in this troubled world, and take pity upon a lonely desolate child, abandoned to its mercy!"'

'The boy's name?' demanded the matron.

'They called him Oliver,' replied the woman, feebly. 'The gold I stole was—'

'Yes, yes—what?' cried the other.

She was bending eagerly over the woman to hear her reply; but drew back, instinctively, as she once again rose, slowly and stiffly, into a sitting posture; then, clutching the coverlid with both hands, muttered some indistinct sounds in her throat, and fell lifeless on the bed.

'Stone dead!' said one of the old women, hurrying in as soon as the door was opened.

'And nothing to tell, after all,' rejoined the matron, walking carelessly away.

The two crones, to all appearance, too busily occupied in the preparations for their dreadful duties to make any reply, were left alone, hovering about the body.

CHAPTER XXV. WHEREIN THIS HISTORY REVERTS TO MR. FAGIN AND COMPANY

While these things were passing in the country workhouse, Mr. Fagin sat in the old den—the same from which Oliver had been removed by the girl—brooding over a dull, smoky fire. He held a pair of bellows upon his knee, with which he had apparently been endeavouring to rouse it into more cheerful action; but he had fallen into deep thought; and with his arms folded on them, and his chin resting on his thumbs, fixed his eyes, abstractedly, on the rusty bars.

At a table behind him sat the Artful Dodger, Master Charles Bates, and Mr. Chitling: all intent upon a game of whist; the Artful taking dummy against Master Bates and Mr. Chitling. The countenance of the first-named gentleman, peculiarly intelligent at all times, acquired great additional interest from his close observance of the game, and his attentive perusal of Mr. Chitling's hand; upon which, from time to time, as occasion served, he bestowed a variety of earnest glances: wisely regulating his own play by the result of his observations upon his neighbour's cards. It being a cold night, the Dodger wore his hat, as, indeed, was often his custom within doors. He also sustained a clay pipe between his teeth, which he only removed for a brief space when he deemed it necessary to apply for refreshment to a quart pot upon the table, which stood ready filled with gin-and-water for the accommodation of the company.

Master Bates was also attentive to the play; but being of a more excitable nature than his accomplished friend, it was observable that he more frequently applied himself to the gin-and-water, and moreover indulged in many jests and irrelevant remarks, all highly unbecoming a scientific rubber. Indeed, the Artful, presuming upon their close attachment, more than once took occasion to reason gravely with his companion upon these improprieties; all of which remonstrances, Master Bates received in extremely good part; merely requesting his friend to be 'blowed,' or to insert his head in a sack, or replying with some other neatly-turned witticism of a similar kind, the happy application of which, excited considerable admiration in the mind of Mr. Chitling. It was remarkable that the latter gentleman and his partner invariably lost; and that the circumstance, so far from angering Master Bates, appeared to afford him the highest amusement, inasmuch as he laughed most uproariously at the end of every deal, and protested that he had never seen such a jolly game in all his born days.

'That's two doubles and the rub,' said Mr. Chitling, with a very long face, as he drew half-a-crown from his waistcoat-pocket. 'I never see such a feller as you, Jack; you win everything. Even when we've good cards, Charley and I can't make nothing of 'em.'

Either the master or the manner of this remark, which was made very ruefully, delighted Charley Bates so much, that his consequent shout of laughter roused the Jew from his reverie, and induced him to inquire what was the matter.

'Matter, Fagin!' cried Charley. 'I wish you had watched the play. Tommy Chitling hasn't won a point; and I went partners with him against the Artfull and dumb.'

'Ay, ay!' said the Jew, with a grin, which sufficiently demonstrated that he was at no loss to understand the reason. 'Try 'em again, Tom; try 'em again.'

'No more of it for me, thank 'ee, Fagin,' replied Mr. Chitling; 'I've had enough. That 'ere Dodger has such a run of luck that there's no standing again' him.'

'Ha! ha! my dear,' replied the Jew, 'you must get up very early in the morning, to win against the Dodger.'

'Morning!' said Charley Bates; 'you must put your boots on over-night, and have a telescope at each eye, and a opera-glass between your shoulders, if you want to come over him.'

Mr. Dawkins received these handsome compliments with much philosophy, and offered to cut any gentleman in company, for the first picture-card, at a shilling at a time. Nobody accepting the challenge, and his pipe being by this time smoked out, he proceeded to amuse himself by sketching a ground-plan of Newgate on the table with the piece of chalk which had served him in lieu of counters; whistling, meantime, with peculiar shrillness.

'How precious dull you are, Tommy!' said the Dodger, stopping short when there had been a long silence; and addressing Mr. Chitling. 'What do you think he's thinking of, Fagin?'

'How should I know, my dear?' replied the Jew, looking round as he plied the bellows. 'About his losses, maybe; or the little retirement in the country that he's just left, eh? Ha! ha! Is that it, my dear?'

'Not a bit of it,' replied the Dodger, stopping the subject of discourse as Mr. Chitling was about to reply. 'What do you say, Charley?'

'I should say,' replied Master Bates, with a grin, 'that he was uncommon sweet upon Betsy. See how he's a-blushing! Oh, my eye! here's a merry-go-rounder! Tommy Chitling's in love! Oh, Fagin, Fagin! what a spree!'

Thoroughly overpowered with the notion of Mr. Chitling being the victim of the tender passion, Master Bates threw himself back in his chair with such violence, that he lost his balance, and pitched over upon the floor; where (the accident abating nothing of his merriment) he lay at full length until his laugh was over, when he resumed his former position, and began another laugh.

'Never mind him, my dear,' said the Jew, winking at Mr. Dawkins, and giving Master Bates a reproving tap with the nozzle of the bellows. 'Betsy's a fine girl. Stick up to her, Tom. Stick up to her.'

'What I mean to say, Fagin,' replied Mr. Chitling, very red in the face, 'is, that that isn't anything to anybody here.'

'No more it is,' replied the Jew; 'Charley will talk. Don't mind him, my dear; don't mind him. Betsy's a fine girl. Do as she bids you, Tom, and you will make your fortune.'

'So I do do as she bids me,' replied Mr. Chitling; 'I shouldn't have been milled, if it hadn't been for her advice. But it turned out a good job for you; didn't it, Fagin! And what's six weeks of it? It must come, some time or another, and why not in the winter time when you don't want to go out a-walking so much; eh, Fagin?'

'Ah, to be sure, my dear,' replied the Jew.

'You wouldn't mind it again, Tom, would you,' asked the Dodger, winking upon Charley and the Jew, 'if Bet was all right?'

'I mean to say that I shouldn't,' replied Tom, angrily. 'There, now. Ah! Who'll say as much as that, I should like to know; eh, Fagin?'

'Nobody, my dear,' replied the Jew; 'not a soul, Tom. I don't know one of 'em that would do it besides you; not one of 'em, my dear.'

'I might have got clear off, if I'd split upon her; mightn't I, Fagin?' angrily pursued the poor half-witted dupe. 'A word from me would have done it; wouldn't it, Fagin?'

'To be sure it would, my dear,' replied the Jew.

'But I didn't blab it; did I, Fagin?' demanded Tom, pouring question upon question with great volubility.

'No, no, to be sure,' replied the Jew; 'you were too stout-hearted for that. A deal too stout, my dear!'

'Perhaps I was,' rejoined Tom, looking round; 'and if I was, what's to laugh at, in that; eh, Fagin?'

The Jew, perceiving that Mr. Chitling was considerably roused, hastened to assure him that nobody was laughing; and to prove the gravity of the company, appealed to Master Bates, the principal offender. But, unfortunately, Charley, in opening his mouth to reply that he was never more serious in his life, was unable to prevent the escape of such a violent roar, that the abused Mr. Chitling, without any preliminary ceremonies, rushed across the room and aimed a blow at the offender; who, being skilful in evading pursuit, ducked to avoid it, and chose his time so well that it lighted on the chest of the merry old gentleman, and caused him to stagger to the wall, where he stood panting for breath, while Mr. Chitling looked on in intense dismay.

'Hark!' cried the Dodger at this moment, 'I heard the tinkler.' Catching up the light, he crept softly upstairs.

The bell was rung again, with some impatience, while the party were in darkness. After a short pause, the Dodger reappeared, and whispered Fagin mysteriously.

'What!' cried the Jew, 'alone?'

The Dodger nodded in the affirmative, and, shading the flame of the candle with his hand, gave Charley Bates a private intimation, in dumb show, that he had better not be funny just then. Having performed this friendly office, he fixed his eyes on the Jew's face, and awaited his directions.

The old man bit his yellow fingers, and meditated for some seconds; his face working with agitation the while, as if he dreaded something, and feared to know the worst. At length he raised his head.

'Where is he?' he asked.

The Dodger pointed to the floor above, and made a gesture, as if to leave the room.

'Yes,' said the Jew, answering the mute inquiry; 'bring him down. Hush! Quiet, Charley! Gently, Tom! Scarce, scarce!'

This brief direction to Charley Bates, and his recent antagonist, was softly and immediately obeyed. There was no sound of their whereabout, when the Dodger descended the stairs, bearing the light in his hand, and followed by a man in a coarse smock-frock; who, after casting a hurried glance round the room, pulled off a large wrapper which had concealed the lower portion of his face, and disclosed: all haggard, unwashed, and unshorn: the features of flash Toby Crackit.

'How are you, Faguey?' said this worthy, nodding to the Jew. 'Pop that shawl away in my castor, Dodger, so that I may know where to find it when I cut; that's the time of day! You'll be a fine young cracksman afore the old file now.'

With these words he pulled up the smock-frock; and, winding it round his middle, drew a chair to the fire, and placed his feet upon the hob.

'See there, Faguey,' he said, pointing disconsolately to his top boots; 'not a drop of Day and Martin since you know when; not a bubble of blacking, by Jove! But don't look at me in that way, man. All in good time. I can't talk about business till I've eat and drank; so produce the sustainance, and let's have a quiet fill-out for the first time these three days!'

The Jew motioned to the Dodger to place what eatables there were, upon the table; and, seating himself opposite the housebreaker, waited his leisure.

To judge from appearances, Toby was by no means in a hurry to open the conversation. At first, the Jew contented himself with patiently watching his countenance, as if to gain from its expression some clue to the intelligence he brought; but in vain.

He looked tired and worn, but there was the same complacent repose upon his features that they always wore: and through dirt, and beard, and whisker, there still shone, unimpaired, the self-satisfied smirk of flash Toby Crackit. Then the Jew, in an agony of impatience, watched every morsel he put into his mouth; pacing up and down the room, meanwhile, in irrepressible excitement. It was all of no use. Toby continued to eat with the utmost outward indifference, until he could eat no more; then, ordering the Dodger out, he closed the door, mixed a glass of spirits and water, and composed himself for talking.

'First and foremost, Faguey,' said Toby.

'Yes, yes!' interposed the Jew, drawing up his chair.

Mr. Crackit stopped to take a draught of spirits and water, and to declare that the gin was excellent; then placing his feet against the low mantelpiece, so as to bring his boots to about the level of his eye, he quietly resumed.

'First and foremost, Faguey,' said the housebreaker, 'how's Bill?'

'What!' screamed the Jew, starting from his seat.

'Why, you don't mean to say—' began Toby, turning pale.

'Mean!' cried the Jew, stamping furiously on the ground. 'Where are they? Sikes and the boy! Where are they? Where have they been? Where are they hiding? Why have they not been here?'

'The crack failed,' said Toby faintly.

'I know it,' replied the Jew, tearing a newspaper from his pocket and pointing to it. 'What more?'

'They fired and hit the boy. We cut over the fields at the back, with him between us— straight as the crow flies—through hedge and ditch. They gave chase. Damme! the whole country was awake, and the dogs upon us.'

'The boy!'

'Bill had him on his back, and scudded like the wind. We stopped to take him between us; his head hung down, and he was cold. They were close upon our heels; every man for himself, and each from the gallows! We parted company, and left the youngster lying in a ditch. Alive or dead, that's all I know about him.'

The Jew stopped to hear no more; but uttering a loud yell, and twining his hands in his hair, rushed from the room, and from the house.

CHAPTER XXVI. IN WHICH A MYSTERIOUS CHARACTER APPEARS UPON THE SCENE; AND MANY THINGS, INSEPARABLE FROM THIS HISTORY, ARE DONE AND PERFORMED

The old man had gained the street corner, before he began to recover the effect of Toby Crackit's intelligence. He had relaxed nothing of his unusual speed; but was still pressing onward, in the same wild and disordered manner, when the sudden dashing past of a carriage:

and a boisterous cry from the foot passengers, who saw his danger: drove him back upon the pavement. Avoiding, as much as was possible, all the main streets, and skulking only through the by-ways and alleys, he at length emerged on Snow Hill. Here he walked even faster than before; nor did he linger until he had again turned into a court; when, as if conscious that he was now in his proper element, he fell into his usual shuffling pace, and seemed to breathe more freely.

Near to the spot on which Snow Hill and Holborn Hill meet, opens, upon the right hand as you come out of the City, a narrow and dismal alley, leading to Saffron Hill. In its filthy shops are exposed for sale huge bunches of second-hand silk handkerchiefs, of all sizes and patterns; for here reside the traders who purchase them from pick-pockets. Hundreds of these handkerchiefs hang dangling from pegs outside the windows or flaunting from the door-posts; and the shelves, within, are piled with them. Confined as the limits of Field Lane are, it has its barber, its coffee-shop, its beer-shop, and its fried-fish warehouse. It is a commercial colony of itself: the emporium of petty larceny: visited at early morning, and setting-in of dusk, by silent merchants, who traffic in dark back-parlours, and who go as strangely as they come. Here, the clothesman, the shoe-vamper, and the rag-merchant, display their goods, as sign-boards to the petty thief; here, stores of old iron and bones, and heaps of mildewy fragments of woollen-stuff and linen, rust and rot in the grimy cellars.

It was into this place that the Jew turned. He was well known to the sallow denizens of the lane; for such of them as were on the look-out to buy or sell, nodded, familiarly, as he passed along. He replied to their salutations in the same way; but bestowed no closer recognition until he reached the further end of the alley; when he stopped, to address a salesman of small stature, who had squeezed as much of his person into a child's chair as the chair would hold, and was smoking a pipe at his warehouse door.

'Why, the sight of you, Mr. Fagin, would cure the hoptalmy!' said this respectable trader, in acknowledgment of the Jew's inquiry after his health.

'The neighbourhood was a little too hot, Lively,' said Fagin, elevating his eyebrows, and crossing his hands upon his shoulders.

'Well, I've heerd that complaint of it, once or twice before,' replied the trader; 'but it soon cools down again; don't you find it so?'

Fagin nodded in the affirmative. Pointing in the direction of Saffron Hill, he inquired whether any one was up yonder to-night.

'At the Cripples?' inquired the man.

The Jew nodded.

'Let me see,' pursued the merchant, reflecting.

'Yes, there's some half-dozen of 'em gone in, that I knows. I don't think your friend's there.'

'Sikes is not, I suppose?' inquired the Jew, with a disappointed countenance.

'Non istwentus, as the lawyers say,' replied the little man, shaking his head, and looking amazingly sly. 'Have you got anything in my line to-night?'

'Nothing to-night,' said the Jew, turning away.

'Are you going up to the Cripples, Fagin?' cried the little man, calling after him. 'Stop! I don't mind if I have a drop there with you!'

But as the Jew, looking back, waved his hand to intimate that he preferred being alone; and, moreover, as the little man could not very easily disengage himself from the chair; the sign of the Cripples was, for a time, bereft of the advantage of Mr. Lively's presence. By the time he had got upon his legs, the Jew had disappeared; so Mr. Lively, after ineffectually standing on tiptoe, in the hope of catching sight of him, again forced himself into the little chair, and, exchanging a shake of the head with a lady in the opposite shop, in which doubt and mistrust were plainly mingled, resumed his pipe with a grave demeanour.

The Three Cripples, or rather the Cripples; which was the sign by which the establishment was familiarly known to its patrons: was the public-house in which Mr. Sikes and his dog have already figured. Merely making a sign to a man at the bar, Fagin walked straight upstairs, and opening the door of a room, and softly insinuating himself into the chamber, looked anxiously about: shading his eyes with his hand, as if in search of some particular person.

The room was illuminated by two gas-lights; the glare of which was prevented by the barred shutters, and closely-drawn curtains of faded red, from being visible outside. The ceiling was blackened, to prevent its colour from being injured by the flaring of the lamps; and the place was so full of dense tobacco smoke, that at first it was scarcely possible to discern anything more. By degrees, however, as some of it cleared away through the open door, an assemblage of heads, as confused as the noises that greeted the ear, might be made out; and as the eye grew more accustomed to the scene, the spectator gradually became aware of the presence of a numerous company, male and female, crowded round a long table: at the upper end of which, sat a chairman with a hammer of office in his hand; while a professional gentleman with a bluish nose, and his face tied up for the benefit of a toothache, presided at a jingling piano in a remote corner.

As Fagin stepped softly in, the professional gentleman, running over the keys by way of prelude, occasioned a general cry of order for a song; which having subsided, a young lady proceeded to entertain the company with a ballad in four verses, between each of which the accompanyist played the melody all through, as loud as he could. When this was over, the chairman gave a sentiment, after which, the professional gentleman on the chairman's right and left volunteered a duet, and sang it, with great applause.

It was curious to observe some faces which stood out prominently from among the group. There was the chairman himself, (the landlord of the house,) a coarse, rough, heavy built fellow, who, while the songs were proceeding, rolled his eyes hither and thither, and, seeming to give himself up to joviality, had an eye for everything that was done, and an ear for everything that was said—and sharp ones, too. Near him were the singers: receiving, with professional indifference, the compliments of the company, and applying themselves, in turn, to a dozen proffered glasses of spirits and water, tendered by their more boisterous admirers; whose countenances, expressive of almost every vice in almost every grade, irresistibly attracted the attention, by their very repulsiveness. Cunning, ferocity, and drunkeness in all its stages, were there, in their strongest aspect; and women: some with the last lingering tinge of their early freshness almost fading as you looked: others with every mark and stamp of their sex utterly beaten out, and presenting but one loathsome blank of profligacy and crime; some mere girls, others but young women, and none past the prime of life; formed the darkest and saddest portion of this dreary picture.

Fagin, troubled by no grave emotions, looked eagerly from face to face while these proceedings were in progress; but apparently without meeting that of which he was in search. Succeeding, at length, in catching the eye of the man who occupied the chair, he beckoned to him slightly, and left the room, as quietly as he had entered it.

'What can I do for you, Mr. Fagin?' inquired the man, as he followed him out to the landing. 'Won't you join us? They'll be delighted, every one of 'em.'

The Jew shook his head impatiently, and said in a whisper, 'Is he here?'

'No,' replied the man.

'And no news of Barney?' inquired Fagin.

'None,' replied the landlord of the Cripples; for it was he. 'He won't stir till it's all safe. Depend on it, they're on the scent down there; and that if he moved, he'd blow upon the thing at once. He's all right enough, Barney is, else I should have heard of him. I'll pound it, that Barney's managing properly. Let him alone for that.'

'Will he be here to-night?' asked the Jew, laying the same emphasis on the pronoun as before.

'Monks, do you mean?' inquired the landlord, hesitating.

'Hush!' said the Jew. 'Yes.'

'Certain,' replied the man, drawing a gold watch from his fob; 'I expected him here before now. If you'll wait ten minutes, he'll be—'

'No, no,' said the Jew, hastily; as though, however desirous he might be to see the person in question, he was nevertheless relieved by his absence. 'Tell him I came here to see him; and that he must come to me to-night. No, say to-morrow. As he is not here, to-morrow will be time enough.'

'Good!' said the man. 'Nothing more?'

'Not a word now,' said the Jew, descending the stairs.

'I say,' said the other, looking over the rails, and speaking in a hoarse whisper; 'what a time this would be for a sell! I've got Phil Barker here: so drunk, that a boy might take him!'

'Ah! But it's not Phil Barker's time,' said the Jew, looking up.

'Phil has something more to do, before we can afford to part with him; so go back to the company, my dear, and tell them to lead merry lives—while they last. Ha! ha! ha!'

The landlord reciprocated the old man's laugh; and returned to his guests. The Jew was no sooner alone, than his countenance resumed its former expression of anxiety and thought. After a brief reflection, he called a hack-cabriolet, and bade the man drive towards Bethnal Green. He dismissed him within some quarter of a mile of Mr. Sikes's residence, and performed the short remainder of the distance, on foot.

'Now,' muttered the Jew, as he knocked at the door, 'if there is any deep play here, I shall have it out of you, my girl, cunning as you are.'

She was in her room, the woman said. Fagin crept softly upstairs, and entered it without any previous ceremony. The girl was alone; lying with her head upon the table, and her hair straggling over it.

'She has been drinking,' thought the Jew, cooly, 'or perhaps she is only miserable.'

The old man turned to close the door, as he made this reflection; the noise thus occasioned, roused the girl. She eyed his crafty face narrowly, as she inquired to his recital of Toby Crackit's story. When it was concluded, she sank into her former attitude, but spoke not a word. She pushed the candle impatiently away; and once or twice as she feverishly changed her position, shuffled her feet upon the ground; but this was all.

During the silence, the Jew looked restlessly about the room, as if to assure himself that there were no appearances of Sikes having covertly returned. Apparently satisfied with his inspection, he coughed twice or thrice, and made as many efforts to open a conversation; but the girl heeded him no more than if he had been made of stone. At length he made another attempt; and rubbing his hands together, said, in his most conciliatory tone,

'And where should you think Bill was now, my dear?'

The girl moaned out some half intelligible reply, that she could not tell; and seemed, from the smothered noise that escaped her, to be crying.

'And the boy, too,' said the Jew, straining his eyes to catch a glimpse of her face. 'Poor leetle child! Left in a ditch, Nance; only think!'

'The child,' said the girl, suddenly looking up, 'is better where he is, than among us; and if no harm comes to Bill from it, I hope he lies dead in the ditch and that his young bones may rot there.'

'What!' cried the Jew, in amazement.

'Ay, I do,' returned the girl, meeting his gaze. 'I shall be glad to have him away from my eyes, and to know that the worst is over. I can't bear to have him about me. The sight of him turns me against myself, and all of you.'

'Pooh!' said the Jew, scornfully. 'You're drunk.'

'Am I?' cried the girl bitterly. 'It's no fault of yours, if I am not! You'd never have me anything else, if you had your will, except now;—the humour doesn't suit you, doesn't it?'

'No!' rejoined the Jew, furiously. 'It does not.'

'Change it, then!' responded the girl, with a laugh.

'Change it!' exclaimed the Jew, exasperated beyond all bounds by his companion's unexpected obstinacy, and the vexation of the night, 'I will change it! Listen to me, you drab. Listen to me, who with six words, can strangle Sikes as surely as if I had his bull's throat between my fingers now. If he comes back, and leaves the boy behind him; if he gets off free, and dead or alive, fails to restore him to me; murder him yourself if you would have him escape Jack Ketch. And do it the moment he sets foot in this room, or mind me, it will be too late!'

'What is all this?' cried the girl involuntarily.

'What is it?' pursued Fagin, mad with rage. 'When the boy's worth hundreds of pounds to me, am I to lose what chance threw me in the way of getting safely, through the whims of a drunken gang that I could whistle away the lives of! And me bound, too, to a born devil that

712

only wants the will, and has the power to, to—'

Panting for breath, the old man stammered for a word; and in that instant checked the torrent of his wrath, and changed his whole demeanour. A moment before, his clenched hands had grasped the air; his eyes had dilated; and his face grown livid with passion; but now, he shrunk into a chair, and, cowering together, trembled with the apprehension of having himself disclosed some hidden villainy. After a short silence, he ventured to look round at his companion. He appeared somewhat reassured, on beholding her in the same listless attitude from which he had first roused her.

'Nancy, dear!' croaked the Jew, in his usual voice. 'Did you mind me, dear?'

'Don't worry me now, Fagin!' replied the girl, raising her head languidly. 'If Bill has not done it this time, he will another. He has done many a good job for you, and will do many more when he can; and when he can't he won't; so no more about that.'

'Regarding this boy, my dear?' said the Jew, rubbing the palms of his hands nervously together.

'The boy must take his chance with the rest,' interrupted Nancy, hastily; 'and I say again, I hope he is dead, and out of harm's way, and out of yours,—that is, if Bill comes to no harm. And if Toby got clear off, Bill's pretty sure to be safe; for Bill's worth two of Toby any time.'

'And about what I was saying, my dear?' observed the Jew, keeping his glistening eye steadily upon her.

'You must say it all over again, if it's anything you want me to do,' rejoined Nancy; 'and if it is, you had better wait till to-morrow. You put me up for a minute; but now I'm stupid again.'

Fagin put several other questions: all with the same drift of ascertaining whether the girl had profited by his unguarded hints; but, she answered them so readily, and was withal so utterly unmoved by his searching looks, that his original impression of her being more than a trifle in liquor, was confirmed. Nancy, indeed, was not exempt from a failing which was very common among the Jew's female pupils; and in which, in their tenderer years, they were rather encouraged than checked. Her disordered appearance, and a wholesale perfume of Geneva which pervaded the apartment, afforded strong confirmatory evidence of the justice of the Jew's supposition; and when, after indulging in the temporary display of violence above described, she subsided, first into dullness, and afterwards into a compound of feelings: under the influence of which she shed tears one minute, and in the next gave utterance to various exclamations of 'Never say die!' and divers calculations as to what might be the amount of the odds so long as a lady or gentleman was happy, Mr. Fagin, who had had considerable experience of such matters in his time, saw, with great satisfaction, that she was very far gone indeed.

Having eased his mind by this discovery; and having accomplished his twofold object of imparting to the girl what he had, that night, heard, and of ascertaining, with his own eyes, that Sikes had not returned, Mr. Fagin again turned his face homeward: leaving his young friend asleep, with her head upon the table.

It was within an hour of midnight. The weather being dark, and piercing cold, he had no great temptation to loiter. The sharp wind that scoured the streets, seemed to have cleared them of passengers, as of dust and mud, for few people were abroad, and they were to all appearance hastening fast home. It blew from the right quarter for the Jew, however, and straight before it he went: trembling, and shivering, as every fresh gust drove him rudely on his way.

He had reached the corner of his own street, and was already fumbling in his pocket for the door-key, when a dark figure emerged from a projecting entrance which lay in deep shadow, and, crossing the road, glided up to him unperceived.

'Fagin!' whispered a voice close to his ear.

'Ah!' said the Jew, turning quickly round, 'is that—'

'Yes!' interrupted the stranger. 'I have been lingering here these two hours. Where the devil have you been?'

'On your business, my dear,' replied the Jew, glancing uneasily at his companion, and slackening his pace as he spoke. 'On your business all night.'

'Oh, of course!' said the stranger, with a sneer. 'Well; and what's come of it?'

'Nothing good,' said the Jew.

'Nothing bad, I hope?' said the stranger, stopping short, and turning a startled look on his companion.

The Jew shook his head, and was about to reply, when the stranger, interrupting him, motioned to the house, before which they had by this time arrived: remarking, that he had better say what he had got to say, under cover: for his blood was chilled with standing about so long, and the wind blew through him.

Fagin looked as if he could have willingly excused himself from taking home a visitor at that unseasonable hour; and, indeed, muttered something about having no fire; but his companion repeating his request in a peremptory manner, he unlocked the door, and requested him to close it softly, while he got a light.

'It's as dark as the grave,' said the man, groping forward a few steps. 'Make haste!'

'Shut the door,' whispered Fagin from the end of the passage. As he spoke, it closed with a loud noise.

'That wasn't my doing,' said the other man, feeling his way. 'The wind blew it to, or it shut of its own accord: one or the other. Look sharp with the light, or I shall knock my brains out against something in this confounded hole.'

Fagin stealthily descended the kitchen stairs. After a short absence, he returned with a lighted candle, and the intelligence that Toby Crackit was asleep in the back room below, and that the boys were in the front one. Beckoning the man to follow him, he led the way upstairs.

'We can say the few words we've got to say in here, my dear,' said the Jew, throwing open a door on the first floor; 'and as there are holes in the shutters, and we never show lights to our neighbours, we'll set the candle on the stairs. There!'

With those words, the Jew, stooping down, placed the candle on an upper flight of stairs, exactly opposite to the room door. This done, he led the way into the apartment; which was destitute of all movables save a broken arm-chair, and an old couch or sofa without covering, which stood behind the door. Upon this piece of furniture, the stranger sat himself with the air of a weary man; and the Jew, drawing up the arm-chair opposite, they sat face to face. It was not quite dark; the door was partially open; and the candle outside, threw a feeble reflection on the opposite wall.

They conversed for some time in whispers. Though nothing of the conversation was distinguishable beyond a few disjointed words here and there, a listener might easily have perceived that Fagin appeared to be defending himself against some remarks of the stranger; and that the latter was in a state of considerable irritation. They might have been talking, thus, for a quarter of an hour or more, when Monks—by which name the Jew had designated the strange man several times in the course of their colloquy—said, raising his voice a little,

'I tell you again, it was badly planned. Why not have kept him here among the rest, and made a sneaking, snivelling pickpocket of him at once?'

'Only hear him!' exclaimed the Jew, shrugging his shoulders.

'Why, do you mean to say you couldn't have done it, if you had chosen?' demanded Monks, sternly. 'Haven't you done it, with other boys, scores of times? If you had had patience for a twelvemonth, at most, couldn't you have got him convicted, and sent safely out of the kingdom; perhaps for life?'

'Whose turn would that have served, my dear?' inquired the Jew humbly.

'Mine,' replied Monks.

'But not mine,' said the Jew, submissively. 'He might have become of use to me. When there are two parties to a bargain, it is only reasonable that the interests of both should be consulted; is it, my good friend?'

'What then?' demanded Monks.

'I saw it was not easy to train him to the business,' replied the Jew; 'he was not like other boys in the same circumstances.'

'Curse him, no!' muttered the man, 'or he would have been a thief, long ago.'

'I had no hold upon him to make him worse,' pursued the Jew, anxiously watching the countenance of his companion. 'His hand was not in. I had nothing to frighten him with; which we always must have in the beginning, or we labour in vain. What could I do? Send him out with the Dodger and Charley? We had enough of that, at first, my dear; I trembled for us all.'

'That was not my doing,' observed Monks.

'No, no, my dear!' renewed the Jew. 'And I don't quarrel with it now; because, if it had never happened, you might never have clapped eyes on the boy to notice him, and so led to the discovery that it was him you were looking for. Well! I got him back for you by means of the girl; and then she begins to favour him.'

'Throttle the girl!' said Monks, impatiently.

'Why, we can't afford to do that just now, my dear,' replied the Jew, smiling; 'and, besides, that sort of thing is not in our way; or, one of these days, I might be glad to have it done. I know what these girls are, Monks, well. As soon as the boy begins to harden, she'll care no more for him, than for a block of wood. You want him made a thief. If he is alive, I can make him one from this time; and, if—if—' said the Jew, drawing nearer to the other,—'it's not likely, mind,—but if the worst comes to the worst, and he is dead—'

'It's no fault of mine if he is!' interposed the other man, with a look of terror, and clasping the Jew's arm with trembling hands. 'Mind that. Fagin! I had no hand in it. Anything but his death, I told you from the first. I won't shed blood; it's always found out, and haunts a man besides. If they shot him dead, I was not the cause; do you hear me? Fire this infernal den! What's that?'

'What!' cried the Jew, grasping the coward round the body, with both arms, as he sprung to his feet. 'Where?'

'Yonder!' replied the man, glaring at the opposite wall. 'The shadow! I saw the shadow of a woman, in a cloak and bonnet, pass along the wainscot like a breath!'

The Jew released his hold, and they rushed tumultuously from the room. The candle, wasted by the draught, was standing where it had been placed. It showed them only the empty staircase, and their own white faces. They listened intently: a profound silence reigned throughout the house.

'It's your fancy,' said the Jew, taking up the light and turning to his companion.

'I'll swear I saw it!' replied Monks, trembling. 'It was bending forward when I saw it first; and when I spoke, it darted away.'

The Jew glanced contemptuously at the pale face of his associate, and, telling him he could follow, if he pleased, ascended the stairs. They looked into all the rooms; they were cold, bare, and empty. They descended into the passage, and thence into the cellars below. The green damp hung upon the low walls; the tracks of the snail and slug glistened in the light of the candle; but all was still as death.

'What do you think now?' said the Jew, when they had regained the passage. 'Besides ourselves, there's not a creature in the house except Toby and the boys; and they're safe enough. See here!'

As a proof of the fact, the Jew drew forth two keys from his pocket; and explained, that when he first went downstairs, he had locked them in, to prevent any intrusion on the conference.

This accumulated testimony effectually staggered Mr. Monks. His protestations had gradually become less and less vehement as they proceeded in their search without making any discovery; and, now, he gave vent to several very grim laughs, and confessed it could only have been his excited imagination. He declined any renewal of the conversation, however, for that night: suddenly remembering that it was past one o'clock. And so the amiable couple parted.

CHAPTER XXVII. ATONES FOR THE UNPOLITENESS OF A FORMER CHAPTER; WHICH DESERTED A LADY, MOST UNCEREMONIOUSLY

As it would be, by no means, seemly in a humble author to keep so mighty a personage as a beadle waiting, with his back to the fire, and the skirts of his coat gathered up under his arms, until such time as it might suit his pleasure to relieve him; and as it would still less become his station, or his gallantry to involve in the same neglect a lady on whom that beadle had looked with an eye of tenderness and affection, and in whose ear he had whispered sweet words, which, coming from such a quarter, might well thrill the bosom of maid or matron of whatsoever degree; the historian whose pen traces these words—trusting that he knows his place, and that he entertains a becoming reverence for those upon earth to whom high and important authority is delegated—hastens to pay them that respect which their position demands, and to treat them with all that duteous ceremony which their exalted rank, and (by consequence) great virtues, imperatively claim at his hands. Towards this end, indeed, he had purposed to introduce, in this place, a dissertation touching the divine right of beadles, and elucidative of the position, that a beadle can do no wrong: which could not fail to have been both pleasurable and profitable to the right-minded reader but which he is unfortunately compelled, by want of time and space, to postpone to some more convenient and fitting opportunity; on the arrival of which, he will be prepared to show, that a beadle properly constituted: that is to say, a parochial beadle, attached to a parochial workhouse, and attending in his official capacity the parochial church: is, in right and virtue of his office, possessed of all the excellences and best qualities of humanity; and that to none of those excellences, can mere companies' beadles, or court-of-law beadles, or even chapel-of-ease beadles (save the last, and they in a very lowly and inferior degree), lay the remotest sustainable claim.

Mr. Bumble had re-counted the teaspoons, re-weighed the sugar-tongs, made a closer inspection of the milk-pot, and ascertained to a nicety the exact condition of the furniture, down to the very horse-hair seats of the chairs; and had repeated each process full half a dozen times; before he began to think that it was time for Mrs. Corney to return. Thinking begets thinking; as there were no sounds of Mrs. Corney's approach, it occured to Mr. Bumble that it would be an innocent and virtuous way of spending the time, if he were further to allay his curiosity by a cursory glance at the interior of Mrs. Corney's chest of drawers.

Having listened at the keyhole, to assure himself that nobody was approaching the chamber, Mr. Bumble, beginning at the bottom, proceeded to make himself acquainted with the contents of the three long drawers: which, being filled with various garments of good fashion and texture, carefully preserved between two layers of old newspapers, speckled with dried lavender: seemed to yield him exceeding satisfaction. Arriving, in course of time, at the right-hand corner drawer (in which was the key), and beholding therein a small padlocked box, which, being shaken, gave forth a pleasant sound, as of the chinking of coin, Mr. Bumble returned with a stately walk to the fireplace; and, resuming his old attitude, said, with a grave and determined air, 'I'll do it!' He followed up this remarkable declaration, by shaking his head in a waggish manner for ten minutes, as though he were remonstrating with himself for being such a pleasant dog; and then, he took a view of his legs in profile, with much seeming pleasure and interest.

He was still placidly engaged in this latter survey, when Mrs. Corney, hurrying into the room, threw herself, in a breathless state, on a chair by the fireside, and covering her eyes with one hand, placed the other over her heart, and gasped for breath.

'Mrs. Corney,' said Mr. Bumble, stooping over the matron, 'what is this, ma'am? Has anything happened, ma'am? Pray answer me: I'm on—on—' Mr. Bumble, in his alarm, could not immediately think of the word 'tenterhooks,' so he said 'broken bottles.'

'Oh, Mr. Bumble!' cried the lady, 'I have been so dreadfully put out!'

'Put out, ma'am!' exclaimed Mr. Bumble; 'who has dared to—? I know!' said Mr. Bumble,

717

checking himself, with native majesty, 'this is them wicious paupers!'

'It's dreadful to think of!' said the lady, shuddering.

'Then don't think of it, ma'am,' rejoined Mr. Bumble.

'I can't help it,' whimpered the lady.

'Then take something, ma'am,' said Mr. Bumble soothingly. 'A little of the wine?'

'Not for the world!' replied Mrs. Corney. 'I couldn't,—oh! The top shelf in the right-hand corner—oh!' Uttering these words, the good lady pointed, distractedly, to the cupboard, and underwent a convulsion from internal spasms. Mr. Bumble rushed to the closet; and, snatching a pint green-glass bottle from the shelf thus incoherently indicated, filled a tea-cup with its contents, and held it to the lady's lips.

'I'm better now,' said Mrs. Corney, falling back, after drinking half of it.

Mr. Bumble raised his eyes piously to the ceiling in thankfulness; and, bringing them down again to the brim of the cup, lifted it to his nose.

'Peppermint,' exclaimed Mrs. Corney, in a faint voice, smiling gently on the beadle as she spoke. 'Try it! There's a little—a little something else in it.'

Mr. Bumble tasted the medicine with a doubtful look; smacked his lips; took another taste; and put the cup down empty.

'It's very comforting,' said Mrs. Corney.

'Very much so indeed, ma'am,' said the beadle. As he spoke, he drew a chair beside the matron, and tenderly inquired what had happened to distress her.

'Nothing,' replied Mrs. Corney. 'I am a foolish, excitable, weak creetur.'

'Not weak, ma'am,' retorted Mr. Bumble, drawing his chair a little closer. 'Are you a weak creetur, Mrs. Corney?'

'We are all weak creeturs,' said Mrs. Corney, laying down a general principle.

'So we are,' said the beadle.

Nothing was said on either side, for a minute or two afterwards. By the expiration of that time, Mr. Bumble had illustrated the position by removing his left arm from the back of Mrs. Corney's chair, where it had previously rested, to Mrs. Corney's apron-string, round which it gradually became entwined.

'We are all weak creeturs,' said Mr. Bumble.

Mrs. Corney sighed.

'Don't sigh, Mrs. Corney,' said Mr. Bumble.

'I can't help it,' said Mrs. Corney. And she sighed again.

'This is a very comfortable room, ma'am,' said Mr. Bumble looking round. 'Another room, and this, ma'am, would be a complete thing.'

'It would be too much for one,' murmured the lady.

'But not for two, ma'am,' rejoined Mr. Bumble, in soft accents. 'Eh, Mrs. Corney?'

Mrs. Corney drooped her head, when the beadle said this; the beadle drooped his, to get a view of Mrs. Corney's face. Mrs. Corney, with great propriety, turned her head away, and released her hand to get at her pocket-handkerchief; but insensibly replaced it in that of Mr. Bumble.

'The board allows you coals, don't they, Mrs. Corney?' inquired the beadle, affectionately pressing her hand.

'And candles,' replied Mrs. Corney, slightly returning the pressure.

'Coals, candles, and house-rent free,' said Mr. Bumble. 'Oh, Mrs. Corney, what an Angel you are!'

The lady was not proof against this burst of feeling. She sank into Mr. Bumble's arms; and that gentleman in his agitation, imprinted a passionate kiss upon her chaste nose.

'Such porochial perfection!' exclaimed Mr. Bumble, rapturously. 'You know that Mr. Slout is worse to-night, my fascinator?'

'Yes,' replied Mrs. Corney, bashfully.

'He can't live a week, the doctor says,' pursued Mr. Bumble. 'He is the master of this establishment; his death will cause a wacancy; that wacancy must be filled up. Oh, Mrs. Corney, what a prospect this opens! What a opportunity for a jining of hearts and housekeepings!'

Mrs. Corney sobbed.

'The little word?' said Mr. Bumble, bending over the bashful beauty. 'The one little, little, little word, my blessed Corney?'

'Ye—ye—yes!' sighed out the matron.

'One more,' pursued the beadle; 'compose your darling feelings for only one more. When is it to come off?'

Mrs. Corney twice essayed to speak: and twice failed. At length summoning up courage, she threw her arms around Mr. Bumble's neck, and said, it might be as soon as ever he pleased, and that he was 'a irresistible duck.'

Matters being thus amicably and satisfactorily arranged, the contract was solemnly ratified in another teacupful of the peppermint mixture; which was rendered the more necessary, by the flutter and agitation of the lady's spirits. While it was being disposed of, she acquainted Mr. Bumble with the old woman's decease.

'Very good,' said that gentleman, sipping his peppermint; 'I'll call at Sowerberry's as I go home, and tell him to send to-morrow morning. Was it that as frightened you, love?'

'It wasn't anything particular, dear,' said the lady evasively.

'It must have been something, love,' urged Mr. Bumble. 'Won't you tell your own B.?'

'Not now,' rejoined the lady; 'one of these days. After we're married, dear.'

'After we're married!' exclaimed Mr. Bumble. 'It wasn't any impudence from any of them male paupers as—'

'No, no, love!' interposed the lady, hastily.

'If I thought it was,' continued Mr. Bumble; 'if I thought as any one of 'em had dared to lift his wulgar eyes to that lovely countenance—'

'They wouldn't have dared to do it, love,' responded the lady.

'They had better not!' said Mr. Bumble, clenching his fist. 'Let me see any man, porochial or extra-porochial, as would presume to do it; and I can tell him that he wouldn't do it a second time!'

Unembellished by any violence of gesticulation, this might have seemed no very high compliment to the lady's charms; but, as Mr. Bumble accompanied the threat with many warlike gestures, she was much touched with this proof of his devotion, and protested, with great admiration, that he was indeed a dove.

The dove then turned up his coat-collar, and put on his cocked hat; and, having exchanged a long and affectionate embrace with his future partner, once again braved the cold wind of the night: merely pausing, for a few minutes, in the male paupers' ward, to abuse them a little, with the view of satisfying himself that he could fill the office of workhouse-master with needful acerbity. Assured of his qualifications, Mr. Bumble left the building with a light heart, and bright visions of his future promotion: which served to occupy his mind until he reached the shop of the undertaker.

Now, Mr. and Mrs. Sowerberry having gone out to tea and supper: and Noah Claypole not being at any time disposed to take upon himself a greater amount of physical exertion than is necessary to a convenient performance of the two functions of eating and drinking, the shop was not closed, although it was past the usual hour of shutting-up. Mr. Bumble tapped with his cane on the counter several times; but, attracting no attention, and beholding a light shining through the glass-window of the little parlour at the back of the shop, he made bold to peep in and see what was going forward; and when he saw what was going forward, he was not a little surprised.

The cloth was laid for supper; the table was covered with bread and butter, plates and glasses; a porter-pot and a wine-bottle. At the upper end of the table, Mr. Noah Claypole lolled negligently in an easy-chair, with his legs thrown over one of the arms: an open clasp-knife in one hand, and a mass of buttered bread in the other. Close beside him stood Charlotte, opening oysters from a barrel: which Mr. Claypole condescended to swallow, with remarkable avidity. A more than ordinary redness in the region of the young gentleman's nose, and a kind of fixed wink in his right eye, denoted that he was in a slight degree intoxicated; these symptoms were confirmed by the intense relish with which he took his oysters, for which nothing but a strong appreciation of their cooling properties, in cases of internal fever, could have sufficiently accounted.

'Here's a delicious fat one, Noah, dear!' said Charlotte; 'try him, do; only this one.'

'What a delicious thing is a oyster!' remarked Mr. Claypole, after he had swallowed it. 'What a pity it is, a number of 'em should ever make you feel uncomfortable; isn't it, Charlotte?'

'It's quite a cruelty,' said Charlotte.

'So it is,' acquiesced Mr. Claypole. 'An't yer fond of oysters?'

'Not overmuch,' replied Charlotte. 'I like to see you eat 'em, Noah dear, better than eating 'em myself.'

'Lor!' said Noah, reflectively; 'how queer!'

'Have another,' said Charlotte. 'Here's one with such a beautiful, delicate beard!'

'I can't manage any more,' said Noah. 'I'm very sorry. Come here, Charlotte, and I'll kiss yer.'

'What!' said Mr. Bumble, bursting into the room. 'Say that again, sir.'

Charlotte uttered a scream, and hid her face in her apron. Mr. Claypole, without making any further change in his position than suffering his legs to reach the ground, gazed at the beadle in drunken terror.

'Say it again, you wile, owdacious fellow!' said Mr. Bumble. 'How dare you mention such a thing, sir? And how dare you encourage him, you insolent minx? Kiss her!' exclaimed Mr. Bumble, in strong indignation. 'Faugh!'

'I didn't mean to do it!' said Noah, blubbering. 'She's always a-kissing of me, whether I like it, or not.'

'Oh, Noah,' cried Charlotte, reproachfully.

'Yer are; yer know yer are!' retorted Noah. 'She's always a-doin' of it, Mr. Bumble, sir; she chucks me under the chin, please, sir; and makes all manner of love!'

'Silence!' cried Mr. Bumble, sternly. 'Take yourself downstairs, ma'am. Noah, you shut up the shop; say another word till your master comes home, at your peril; and, when he does come home, tell him that Mr. Bumble said he was to send a old woman's shell after breakfast to-morrow morning. Do you hear sir? Kissing!' cried Mr. Bumble, holding up his hands. 'The sin and wickedness of the lower orders in this porochial district is frightful! If Parliament don't take their abominable courses under consideration, this country's ruined, and the character of the peasantry gone for ever!' With these words, the beadle strode, with a lofty and gloomy air, from the undertaker's premises.

And now that we have accompanied him so far on his road home, and have made all necessary preparations for the old woman's funeral, let us set on foot a few inquires after young Oliver Twist, and ascertain whether he be still lying in the ditch where Toby Crackit left him.

CHAPTER XXVIII. LOOKS AFTER OLIVER, AND PROCEEDS WITH HIS ADVENTURES

'Wolves tear your throats!' muttered Sikes, grinding his teeth. 'I wish I was among some of you; you'd howl the hoarser for it.'

As Sikes growled forth this imprecation, with the most desperate ferocity that his desperate nature was capable of, he rested the body of the wounded boy across his bended knee; and turned his head, for an instant, to look back at his pursuers.

There was little to be made out, in the mist and darkness; but the loud shouting of men vibrated through the air, and the barking of the neighbouring dogs, roused by the sound of the alarm bell, resounded in every direction.

'Stop, you white-livered hound!' cried the robber, shouting after Toby Crackit, who, making the best use of his long legs, was already ahead. 'Stop!'

The repetition of the word, brought Toby to a dead stand-still. For he was not quite satisfied that he was beyond the range of pistol-shot; and Sikes was in no mood to be played with.

'Bear a hand with the boy,' cried Sikes, beckoning furiously to his confederate. 'Come back!'

Toby made a show of returning; but ventured, in a low voice, broken for want of breath, to intimate considerable reluctance as he came slowly along.

'Quicker!' cried Sikes, laying the boy in a dry ditch at his feet, and drawing a pistol from his pocket. 'Don't play booty with me.'

At this moment the noise grew louder. Sikes, again looking round, could discern that the men who had given chase were already climbing the gate of the field in which he stood; and that a couple of dogs were some paces in advance of them.

'It's all up, Bill!' cried Toby; 'drop the kid, and show 'em your heels.' With this parting advice, Mr. Crackit, preferring the chance of being shot by his friend, to the certainty of being taken by his enemies, fairly turned tail, and darted off at full speed. Sikes clenched his teeth; took one look around; threw over the prostrate form of Oliver, the cape in which he had been hurriedly muffled; ran along the front of the hedge, as if to distract the attention of those behind, from the spot where the boy lay; paused, for a second, before another hedge which met it at right angles; and whirling his pistol high into the air, cleared it at a bound, and was gone.

'Ho, ho, there!' cried a tremulous voice in the rear. 'Pincher! Neptune! Come here, come here!'

The dogs, who, in common with their masters, seemed to have no particular relish for the sport in which they were engaged, readily answered to the command. Three men, who had by this time advanced some distance into the field, stopped to take counsel together.

'My advice, or, leastways, I should say, my orders, is,' said the fattest man of the party, 'that we 'mediately go home again.'

'I am agreeable to anything which is agreeable to Mr. Giles,' said a shorter man; who was by no means of a slim figure, and who was very pale in the face, and very polite: as frightened men frequently are.

'I shouldn't wish to appear ill-mannered, gentlemen,' said the third, who had called the dogs back, 'Mr. Giles ought to know.'

'Certainly,' replied the shorter man; 'and whatever Mr. Giles says, it isn't our place to contradict him. No, no, I know my sitiwation! Thank my stars, I know my sitiwation.' To tell the truth, the little man did seem to know his situation, and to know perfectly well that it was by no means a desirable one; for his teeth chattered in his head as he spoke.

'You are afraid, Brittles,' said Mr. Giles.

'I an't,' said Brittles.

'You are,' said Giles.

'You're a falsehood, Mr. Giles,' said Brittles.

'You're a lie, Brittles,' said Mr. Giles.

Now, these four retorts arose from Mr. Giles's taunt; and Mr. Giles's taunt had arisen from his indignation at having the responsibility of going home again, imposed upon himself under cover of a compliment. The third man brought the dispute to a close, most philosophically.

'I'll tell you what it is, gentlemen,' said he, 'we're all afraid.'

'Speak for yourself, sir,' said Mr. Giles, who was the palest of the party.

'So I do,' replied the man. 'It's natural and proper to be afraid, under such circumstances. I am.'

'So am I,' said Brittles; 'only there's no call to tell a man he is, so bounceably.'

These frank admissions softened Mr. Giles, who at once owned that he was afraid; upon which, they all three faced about, and ran back again with the completest unanimity, until Mr. Giles (who had the shortest wind of the party, as was encumbered with a pitchfork) most handsomely insisted on stopping, to make an apology for his hastiness of speech.

'But it's wonderful,' said Mr. Giles, when he had explained, 'what a man will do, when his blood is up. I should have committed murder—I know I should—if we'd caught one of them rascals.'

As the other two were impressed with a similar presentiment; and as their blood, like his, had all gone down again; some speculation ensued upon the cause of this sudden change in their temperament.

'I know what it was,' said Mr. Giles; 'it was the gate.'

'I shouldn't wonder if it was,' exclaimed Brittles, catching at the idea.

'You may depend upon it,' said Giles, 'that that gate stopped the flow of the excitement. I felt all mine suddenly going away, as I was climbing over it.'

By a remarkable coincidence, the other two had been visited with the same unpleasant sensation at that precise moment. It was quite obvious, therefore, that it was the gate; especially as there was no doubt regarding the time at which the change had taken place, because all three remembered that they had come in sight of the robbers at the instant of its occurance.

This dialogue was held between the two men who had surprised the burglars, and a travelling tinker who had been sleeping in an outhouse, and who had been roused, together with his two mongrel curs, to join in the pursuit. Mr. Giles acted in the double capacity of butler and steward to the old lady of the mansion; Brittles was a lad of all-work: who, having entered her service a mere child, was treated as a promising young boy still, though he was something past thirty.

Encouraging each other with such converse as this; but, keeping very close together, notwithstanding, and looking apprehensively round, whenever a fresh gust rattled through the boughs; the three men hurried back to a tree, behind which they had left their lantern, lest its light should inform the thieves in what direction to fire. Catching up the light, they made the best of their way home, at a good round trot; and long after their dusky forms had ceased to be discernible, the light might have been seen twinkling and dancing in the distance, like some exhalation of the damp and gloomy atmosphere through which it was swiftly borne.

The air grew colder, as day came slowly on; and the mist rolled along the ground like a dense cloud of smoke. The grass was wet; the pathways, and low places, were all mire and water; the damp breath of an unwholesome wind went languidly by, with a hollow moaning. Still, Oliver lay motionless and insensible on the spot where Sikes had left him.

Morning drew on apace. The air become more sharp and piercing, as its first dull hue—

the death of night, rather than the birth of day—glimmered faintly in the sky. The objects which had looked dim and terrible in the darkness, grew more and more defined, and gradually resolved into their familiar shapes. The rain came down, thick and fast, and pattered noisily among the leafless bushes. But, Oliver felt it not, as it beat against him; for he still lay stretched, helpless and unconscious, on his bed of clay.

At length, a low cry of pain broke the stillness that prevailed; and uttering it, the boy awoke. His left arm, rudely bandaged in a shawl, hung heavy and useless at his side; the bandage was saturated with blood. He was so weak, that he could scarcely raise himself into a sitting posture; when he had done so, he looked feebly round for help, and groaned with pain. Trembling in every joint, from cold and exhaustion, he made an effort to stand upright; but, shuddering from head to foot, fell prostrate on the ground.

After a short return of the stupor in which he had been so long plunged, Oliver: urged by a creeping sickness at his heart, which seemed to warn him that if he lay there, he must surely die: got upon his feet, and essayed to walk. His head was dizzy, and he staggered to and fro like a drunken man. But he kept up, nevertheless, and, with his head drooping languidly on his breast, went stumbling onward, he knew not whither.

And now, hosts of bewildering and confused ideas came crowding on his mind. He seemed to be still walking between Sikes and Crackit, who were angrily disputing—for the very words they said, sounded in his ears; and when he caught his own attention, as it were, by making some violent effort to save himself from falling, he found that he was talking to them. Then, he was alone with Sikes, plodding on as on the previous day; and as shadowy people passed them, he felt the robber's grasp upon his wrist. Suddenly, he started back at the report of firearms; there rose into the air, loud cries and shouts; lights gleamed before his eyes; all was noise and tumult, as some unseen hand bore him hurriedly away. Through all these rapid visions, there ran an undefined, uneasy consciousness of pain, which wearied and tormented him incessantly.

Thus he staggered on, creeping, almost mechanically, between the bars of gates, or through hedge-gaps as they came in his way, until he reached a road. Here the rain began to fall so heavily, that it roused him.

He looked about, and saw that at no great distance there was a house, which perhaps he could reach. Pitying his condition, they might have compassion on him; and if they did not, it would be better, he thought, to die near human beings, than in the lonely open fields. He summoned up all his strength for one last trial, and bent his faltering steps towards it.

As he drew nearer to this house, a feeling come over him that he had seen it before. He remembered nothing of its details; but the shape and aspect of the building seemed familiar to him.

That garden wall! On the grass inside, he had fallen on his knees last night, and prayed the two men's mercy. It was the very house they had attempted to rob.

Oliver felt such fear come over him when he recognised the place, that, for the instant, he forgot the agony of his wound, and thought only of flight. Flight! He could scarcely stand: and if he were in full possession of all the best powers of his slight and youthful frame, whither could he fly? He pushed against the garden-gate; it was unlocked, and swung open on its hinges. He tottered across the lawn; climbed the steps; knocked faintly at the door; and, his whole strength failing him, sunk down against one of the pillars of the little portico.

It happened that about this time, Mr. Giles, Brittles, and the tinker, were recruiting themselves, after the fatigues and terrors of the night, with tea and sundries, in the kitchen. Not that it was Mr. Giles's habit to admit to too great familiarity the humbler servants: towards whom it was rather his wont to deport himself with a lofty affability, which, while it gratified, could not fail to remind them of his superior position in society. But, death, fires, and burglary, make all men equals; so Mr. Giles sat with his legs stretched out before the kitchen fender, leaning his left arm on the table, while, with his right, he illustrated a circumstantial and minute account of the robbery, to which his bearers (but especially the cook and housemaid, who were of the party) listened with breathless interest.

'It was about half-past two,' said Mr. Giles, 'or I wouldn't swear that it mightn't have been a little nearer three, when I woke up, and, turning round in my bed, as it might be so, (here Mr. Giles turned round in his chair, and pulled the corner of the table-cloth over him to imitate bed-clothes,) I fancied I heerd a noise.'

At this point of the narrative the cook turned pale, and asked the housemaid to shut the door: who asked Brittles, who asked the tinker, who pretended not to hear.

'—Heerd a noise,' continued Mr. Giles. 'I says, at first, "This is illusion"; and was composing myself off to sleep, when I heerd the noise again, distinct.'

'What sort of a noise?' asked the cook.

'A kind of a busting noise,' replied Mr. Giles, looking round him.

'More like the noise of powdering a iron bar on a nutmeg-grater,' suggested Brittles.

'It was, when you heerd it, sir,' rejoined Mr. Giles; 'but, at this time, it had a busting sound. I turned down the clothes'; continued Giles, rolling back the table-cloth, 'sat up in bed; and listened.'

The cook and housemaid simultaneously ejaculated 'Lor!' and drew their chairs closer together.

'I heerd it now, quite apparent,' resumed Mr. Giles. '"Somebody," I says, "is forcing of a door, or window; what's to be done? I'll call up that poor lad, Brittles, and save him from being murdered in his bed; or his throat," I says, "may be cut from his right ear to his left, without his ever knowing it."'

Here, all eyes were turned upon Brittles, who fixed his upon the speaker, and stared at him, with his mouth wide open, and his face expressive of the most unmitigated horror.

'I tossed off the clothes,' said Giles, throwing away the table-cloth, and looking very hard at the cook and housemaid, 'got softly out of bed; drew on a pair of—'

'Ladies present, Mr. Giles,' murmured the tinker.

'—Of shoes, sir,' said Giles, turning upon him, and laying great emphasis on the word; 'seized the loaded pistol that always goes upstairs with the plate-basket; and walked on tiptoes to his room. "Brittles," I says, when I had woke him, "don't be frightened!"'

'So you did,' observed Brittles, in a low voice.

'"We're dead men, I think, Brittles," I says,' continued Giles; '"but don't be frightened."'

'Was he frightened?' asked the cook.

'Not a bit of it,' replied Mr. Giles. 'He was as firm—ah! pretty near as firm as I was.'

'I should have died at once, I'm sure, if it had been me,' observed the housemaid.

'You're a woman,' retorted Brittles, plucking up a little.

'Brittles is right,' said Mr. Giles, nodding his head, approvingly; 'from a woman, nothing else was to be expected. We, being men, took a dark lantern that was standing on Brittle's hob, and groped our way downstairs in the pitch dark,—as it might be so.'

Mr. Giles had risen from his seat, and taken two steps with his eyes shut, to accompany his description with appropriate action, when he started violently, in common with the rest of the company, and hurried back to his chair. The cook and housemaid screamed.

'It was a knock,' said Mr. Giles, assuming perfect serenity. 'Open the door, somebody.'

Nobody moved.

'It seems a strange sort of a thing, a knock coming at such a time in the morning,' said Mr. Giles, surveying the pale faces which surrounded him, and looking very blank himself; 'but the door must be opened. Do you hear, somebody?'

Mr. Giles, as he spoke, looked at Brittles; but that young man, being naturally modest, probably considered himself nobody, and so held that the inquiry could not have any application to him; at all events, he tendered no reply. Mr. Giles directed an appealing glance at the tinker; but he had suddenly fallen asleep. The women were out of the question.

'If Brittles would rather open the door, in the presence of witnesses,' said Mr. Giles, after a short silence, 'I am ready to make one.'

'So am I,' said the tinker, waking up, as suddenly as he had fallen asleep.

Brittles capitulated on these terms; and the party being somewhat re-assured by the discovery (made on throwing open the shutters) that it was now broad day, took their way upstairs; with the dogs in front. The two women, who were afraid to stay below, brought up the rear. By the advice of Mr. Giles, they all talked very loud, to warn any evil-disposed person outside, that they were strong in numbers; and by a master-stoke of policy, originating in the brain of the same ingenious gentleman, the dogs' tails were well pinched, in the hall, to make them bark savagely.

These precautions having been taken, Mr. Giles held on fast by the tinker's arm (to prevent his running away, as he pleasantly said), and gave the word of command to open the door. Brittles obeyed; the group, peeping timorously over each other's shoulders, beheld no more formidable object than poor little Oliver Twist, speechless and exhausted, who raised his heavy eyes, and mutely solicited their compassion.

'A boy!' exclaimed Mr. Giles, valiantly, pushing the tinker into the background. 'What's the matter with the—eh?—Why—Brittles—look here—don't you know?'

Brittles, who had got behind the door to open it, no sooner saw Oliver, than he uttered a loud cry. Mr. Giles, seizing the boy by one leg and one arm (fortunately not the broken limb) lugged him straight into the hall, and deposited him at full length on the floor thereof.

'Here he is!' bawled Giles, calling in a state of great excitement, up the staircase; 'here's one of the thieves, ma'am! Here's a thief, miss! Wounded, miss! I shot him, miss; and Brittles held the light.'

'—In a lantern, miss,' cried Brittles, applying one hand to the side of his mouth, so that his voice might travel the better.

The two women-servants ran upstairs to carry the intelligence that Mr. Giles had captured a robber; and the tinker busied himself in endeavouring to restore Oliver, lest he should die before he could be hanged. In the midst of all this noise and commotion, there was heard a sweet female voice, which quelled it in an instant.

'Giles!' whispered the voice from the stair-head.

'I'm here, miss,' replied Mr. Giles. 'Don't be frightened, miss; I ain't much injured. He didn't make a very desperate resistance, miss! I was soon too many for him.'

'Hush!' replied the young lady; 'you frighten my aunt as much as the thieves did. Is the poor creature much hurt?'

'Wounded desperate, miss,' replied Giles, with indescribable complacency.

'He looks as if he was a-going, miss,' bawled Brittles, in the same manner as before. 'Wouldn't you like to come and look at him, miss, in case he should?'

'Hush, pray; there's a good man!' rejoined the lady. 'Wait quietly only one instant, while I speak to aunt.'

With a footstep as soft and gentle as the voice, the speaker tripped away. She soon returned, with the direction that the wounded person was to be carried, carefully, upstairs to Mr. Giles's room; and that Brittles was to saddle the pony and betake himself instantly to Chertsey: from which place, he was to despatch, with all speed, a constable and doctor.

'But won't you take one look at him, first, miss?' asked Mr. Giles, with as much pride as if Oliver were some bird of rare plumage, that he had skilfully brought down. 'Not one little peep, miss?'

'Not now, for the world,' replied the young lady. 'Poor fellow! Oh! treat him kindly, Giles for my sake!'

The old servant looked up at the speaker, as she turned away, with a glance as proud and admiring as if she had been his own child. Then, bending over Oliver, he helped to carry him upstairs, with the care and solicitude of a woman.

CHAPTER XXIX. HAS AN INTRODUCTORY ACCOUNT OF THE INMATES OF THE HOUSE, TO WHICH OLIVER RESORTED

In a handsome room: though its furniture had rather the air of old-fashioned comfort, than of modern elegance: there sat two ladies at a well-spread breakfast-table. Mr. Giles, dressed with scrupulous care in a full suit of black, was in attendance upon them. He had taken his station some half-way between the side-board and the breakfast-table; and, with his body drawn up to its full height, his head thrown back, and inclined the merest trifle on one side, his left leg advanced, and his right hand thrust into his waist-coat, while his left hung down by his side, grasping a waiter, looked like one who laboured under a very agreeable sense of his own merits and importance.

Of the two ladies, one was well advanced in years; but the high-backed oaken chair in which she sat, was not more upright than she. Dressed with the utmost nicety and precision, in a quaint mixture of by-gone costume, with some slight concessions to the prevailing taste, which rather served to point the old style pleasantly than to impair its effect, she sat, in a stately manner, with her hands folded on the table before her. Her eyes (and age had dimmed but little of their brightness) were attentively upon her young companion.

The younger lady was in the lovely bloom and spring-time of womanhood; at that age, when, if ever angels be for God's good purposes enthroned in mortal forms, they may be, without impiety, supposed to abide in such as hers.

She was not past seventeen. Cast in so slight and exquisite a mould; so mild and gentle; so pure and beautiful; that earth seemed not her element, nor its rough creatures her fit companions. The very intelligence that shone in her deep blue eye, and was stamped upon her noble head, seemed scarcely of her age, or of the world; and yet the changing expression of sweetness and good humour, the thousand lights that played about the face, and left no shadow there; above all, the smile, the cheerful, happy smile, were made for Home, and fireside peace and happiness.

She was busily engaged in the little offices of the table. Chancing to raise her eyes as the elder lady was regarding her, she playfully put back her hair, which was simply braided on her forehead; and threw into her beaming look, such an expression of affection and artless loveliness, that blessed spirits might have smiled to look upon her.

'And Brittles has been gone upwards of an hour, has he?' asked the old lady, after a pause.

'An hour and twelve minutes, ma'am,' replied Mr. Giles, referring to a silver watch, which he drew forth by a black ribbon.

'He is always slow,' remarked the old lady.

'Brittles always was a slow boy, ma'am,' replied the attendant. And seeing, by the bye, that Brittles had been a slow boy for upwards of thirty years, there appeared no great probability of his ever being a fast one.

'He gets worse instead of better, I think,' said the elder lady.

'It is very inexcusable in him if he stops to play with any other boys,' said the young lady, smiling.

Mr. Giles was apparently considering the propriety of indulging in a respectful smile himself, when a gig drove up to the garden-gate: out of which there jumped a fat gentleman, who ran straight up to the door: and who, getting quickly into the house by some mysterious process, burst into the room, and nearly overturned Mr. Giles and the breakfast-table together.

'I never heard of such a thing!' exclaimed the fat gentleman. 'My dear Mrs. Maylie—bless my soul—in the silence of the night, too—I never heard of such a thing!'

With these expressions of condolence, the fat gentleman shook hands with both ladies, and drawing up a chair, inquired how they found themselves.

'You ought to be dead; positively dead with the fright,' said the fat gentleman. 'Why didn't you send? Bless me, my man should have come in a minute; and so would I; and my assistant would have been delighted; or anybody, I'm sure, under such circumstances. Dear,

dear! So unexpected! In the silence of the night, too!'

The doctor seemed especially troubled by the fact of the robbery having been unexpected, and attempted in the night-time; as if it were the established custom of gentlemen in the housebreaking way to transact business at noon, and to make an appointment, by post, a day or two previous.

'And you, Miss Rose,' said the doctor, turning to the young lady, 'I—'

'Oh! very much so, indeed,' said Rose, interrupting him; 'but there is a poor creature upstairs, whom aunt wishes you to see.'

'Ah! to be sure,' replied the doctor, 'so there is. That was your handiwork, Giles, I understand.'

Mr. Giles, who had been feverishly putting the tea-cups to rights, blushed very red, and said that he had had that honour.

'Honour, eh?' said the doctor; 'well, I don't know; perhaps it's as honourable to hit a thief in a back kitchen, as to hit your man at twelve paces. Fancy that he fired in the air, and you've fought a duel, Giles.'

Mr. Giles, who thought this light treatment of the matter an unjust attempt at diminishing his glory, answered respectfully, that it was not for the like of him to judge about that; but he rather thought it was no joke to the opposite party.

'Gad, that's true!' said the doctor. 'Where is he? Show me the way. I'll look in again, as I come down, Mrs. Maylie. That's the little window that he got in at, eh? Well, I couldn't have believed it!'

Talking all the way, he followed Mr. Giles upstairs; and while he is going upstairs, the reader may be informed, that Mr. Losberne, a surgeon in the neighbourhood, known through a circuit of ten miles round as 'the doctor,' had grown fat, more from good-humour than from good living: and was as kind and hearty, and withal as eccentric an old bachelor, as will be found in five times that space, by any explorer alive.

The doctor was absent, much longer than either he or the ladies had anticipated. A large flat box was fetched out of the gig; and a bedroom bell was rung very often; and the servants ran up and down stairs perpetually; from which tokens it was justly concluded that something important was going on above. At length he returned; and in reply to an anxious inquiry after his patient; looked very mysterious, and closed the door, carefully.

'This is a very extraordinary thing, Mrs. Maylie,' said the doctor, standing with his back to the door, as if to keep it shut.

'He is not in danger, I hope?' said the old lady.

'Why, that would not be an extraordinary thing, under the circumstances,' replied the doctor; 'though I don't think he is. Have you seen the thief?'

'No,' rejoined the old lady.

'Nor heard anything about him?'

'No.'

'I beg your pardon, ma'am, interposed Mr. Giles; 'but I was going to tell you about him when Doctor Losberne came in.'

The fact was, that Mr. Giles had not, at first, been able to bring his mind to the avowal, that he had only shot a boy. Such commendations had been bestowed upon his bravery, that he could not, for the life of him, help postponing the explanation for a few delicious minutes; during which he had flourished, in the very zenith of a brief reputation for undaunted courage.

'Rose wished to see the man,' said Mrs. Maylie, 'but I wouldn't hear of it.'

'Humph!' rejoined the doctor. 'There is nothing very alarming in his appearance. Have you any objection to see him in my presence?'

'If it be necessary,' replied the old lady, 'certainly not.'

'Then I think it is necessary,' said the doctor; 'at all events, I am quite sure that you would deeply regret not having done so, if you postponed it. He is perfectly quiet and comfortable now. Allow me—Miss Rose, will you permit me? Not the slightest fear, I pledge you my honour!'

CHAPTER XXX. RELATES WHAT OLIVER'S NEW VISITORS THOUGHT OF HIM

With many loquacious assurances that they would be agreeably surprised in the aspect of the criminal, the doctor drew the young lady's arm through one of his; and offering his disengaged hand to Mrs. Maylie, led them, with much ceremony and stateliness, upstairs.

'Now,' said the doctor, in a whisper, as he softly turned the handle of a bedroom-door, 'let us hear what you think of him. He has not been shaved very recently, but he don't look at all ferocious notwithstanding. Stop, though! Let me first see that he is in visiting order.'

Stepping before them, he looked into the room. Motioning them to advance, he closed the door when they had entered; and gently drew back the curtains of the bed. Upon it, in lieu of the dogged, black-visaged ruffian they had expected to behold, there lay a mere child: worn with pain and exhaustion, and sunk into a deep sleep. His wounded arm, bound and splintered up, was crossed upon his breast; his head reclined upon the other arm, which was half hidden by his long hair, as it streamed over the pillow.

The honest gentleman held the curtain in his hand, and looked on, for a minute or so, in silence. Whilst he was watching the patient thus, the younger lady glided softly past, and seating herself in a chair by the bedside, gathered Oliver's hair from his face. As she stooped over him, her tears fell upon his forehead.

The boy stirred, and smiled in his sleep, as though these marks of pity and compassion had awakened some pleasant dream of a love and affection he had never known. Thus, a strain of gentle music, or the rippling of water in a silent place, or the odour of a flower, or the mention of a familiar word, will sometimes call up sudden dim remembrances of scenes that never were, in this life; which vanish like a breath; which some brief memory of a happier existence, long gone by, would seem to have awakened; which no voluntary exertion of the mind can ever recall.

'What can this mean?' exclaimed the elder lady. 'This poor child can never have been the pupil of robbers!'

'Vice,' said the surgeon, replacing the curtain, 'takes up her abode in many temples; and who can say that a fair outside shell not enshrine her?'

'But at so early an age!' urged Rose.

'My dear young lady,' rejoined the surgeon, mournfully shaking his head; 'crime, like death, is not confined to the old and withered alone. The youngest and fairest are too often its chosen victims.'

'But, can you—oh! can you really believe that this delicate boy has been the voluntary associate of the worst outcasts of society?' said Rose.

The surgeon shook his head, in a manner which intimated that he feared it was very possible; and observing that they might disturb the patient, led the way into an adjoining apartment.

'But even if he has been wicked,' pursued Rose, 'think how young he is; think that he may never have known a mother's love, or the comfort of a home; that ill-usage and blows, or the want of bread, may have driven him to herd with men who have forced him to guilt. Aunt, dear aunt, for mercy's sake, think of this, before you let them drag this sick child to a prison, which in any case must be the grave of all his chances of amendment. Oh! as you love me, and know that I have never felt the want of parents in your goodness and affection, but that I might have done so, and might have been equally helpless and unprotected with this poor child, have pity upon him before it is too late!'

'My dear love,' said the elder lady, as she folded the weeping girl to her bosom, 'do you think I would harm a hair of his head?'

'Oh, no!' replied Rose, eagerly.

'No, surely,' said the old lady; 'my days are drawing to their close: and may mercy be shown to me as I show it to others! What can I do to save him, sir?'

'Let me think, ma'am,' said the doctor; 'let me think.'

Mr. Losberne thrust his hands into his pockets, and took several turns up and down the room; often stopping, and balancing himself on his toes, and frowning frightfully. After various exclamations of 'I've got it now' and 'no, I haven't,' and as many renewals of the walking and frowning, he at length made a dead halt, and spoke as follows:

'I think if you give me a full and unlimited commission to bully Giles, and that little boy, Brittles, I can manage it. Giles is a faithful fellow and an old servant, I know; but you can make it up to him in a thousand ways, and reward him for being such a good shot besides. You don't object to that?'

'Unless there is some other way of preserving the child,' replied Mrs. Maylie.

'There is no other,' said the doctor. 'No other, take my word for it.'

'Then my aunt invests you with full power,' said Rose, smiling through her tears; 'but pray don't be harder upon the poor fellows than is indispensably necessary.'

'You seem to think,' retorted the doctor, 'that everybody is disposed to be hard-hearted to-day, except yourself, Miss Rose. I only hope, for the sake of the rising male sex generally, that you may be found in as vulnerable and soft-hearted a mood by the first eligible young fellow who appeals to your compassion; and I wish I were a young fellow, that I might avail myself, on the spot, of such a favourable opportunity for doing so, as the present.'

'You are as great a boy as poor Brittles himself,' returned Rose, blushing.

'Well,' said the doctor, laughing heartily, 'that is no very difficult matter. But to return to this boy. The great point of our agreement is yet to come. He will wake in an hour or so, I dare say; and although I have told that thick-headed constable-fellow downstairs that he musn't be moved or spoken to, on peril of his life, I think we may converse with him without danger. Now I make this stipulation—that I shall examine him in your presence, and that, if, from what he says, we judge, and I can show to the satisfaction of your cool reason, that he is a real and thorough bad one (which is more than possible), he shall be left to his fate, without any farther interference on my part, at all events.'

'Oh no, aunt!' entreated Rose.

'Oh yes, aunt!' said the doctor. 'Is is a bargain?'

'He cannot be hardened in vice,' said Rose; 'It is impossible.'

'Very good,' retorted the doctor; 'then so much the more reason for acceding to my proposition.'

Finally the treaty was entered into; and the parties thereunto sat down to wait, with some impatience, until Oliver should awake.

The patience of the two ladies was destined to undergo a longer trial than Mr. Losberne had led them to expect; for hour after hour passed on, and still Oliver slumbered heavily. It was evening, indeed, before the kind-hearted doctor brought them the intelligence, that he was at length sufficiently restored to be spoken to. The boy was very ill, he said, and weak from the loss of blood; but his mind was so troubled with anxiety to disclose something, that he deemed it better to give him the opportunity, than to insist upon his remaining quiet until next morning: which he should otherwise have done.

The conference was a long one. Oliver told them all his simple history, and was often compelled to stop, by pain and want of strength. It was a solemn thing, to hear, in the darkened room, the feeble voice of the sick child recounting a weary catalogue of evils and calamities which hard men had brought upon him. Oh! if when we oppress and grind our fellow-creatures, we bestowed but one thought on the dark evidences of human error, which, like dense and heavy clouds, are rising, slowly it is true, but not less surely, to Heaven, to pour their after-vengeance on our heads; if we heard but one instant, in imagination, the deep testimony of dead men's voices, which no power can stifle, and no pride shut out; where would be the injury and injustice, the suffering, misery, cruelty, and wrong, that each day's life brings with it!

Oliver's pillow was smoothed by gentle hands that night; and loveliness and virtue watched him as he slept. He felt calm and happy, and could have died without a murmur.

The momentous interview was no sooner concluded, and Oliver composed to rest again, than the doctor, after wiping his eyes, and condemning them for being weak all at once, betook himself downstairs to open upon Mr. Giles. And finding nobody about the parlours, it occurred to him, that he could perhaps originate the proceedings with better effect in the kitchen; so into the kitchen he went.

There were assembled, in that lower house of the domestic parliament, the women-servants, Mr. Brittles, Mr. Giles, the tinker (who had received a special invitation to regale himself for the remainder of the day, in consideration of his services), and the constable. The latter gentleman had a large staff, a large head, large features, and large half-boots; and he looked as if he had been taking a proportionate allowance of ale—as indeed he had.

The adventures of the previous night were still under discussion; for Mr. Giles was expatiating upon his presence of mind, when the doctor entered; Mr. Brittles, with a mug of ale in his hand, was corroborating everything, before his superior said it.

'Sit still!' said the doctor, waving his hand.

'Thank you, sir,' said Mr. Giles. 'Misses wished some ale to be given out, sir; and as I felt no ways inclined for my own little room, sir, and was disposed for company, I am taking mine among 'em here.'

Brittles headed a low murmur, by which the ladies and gentlemen generally were understood to express the gratification they derived from Mr. Giles's condescension. Mr. Giles looked round with a patronising air, as much as to say that so long as they behaved properly, he would never desert them.

'How is the patient to-night, sir?' asked Giles.

'So-so'; returned the doctor. 'I am afraid you have got yourself into a scrape there, Mr. Giles.'

'I hope you don't mean to say, sir,' said Mr. Giles, trembling, 'that he's going to die. If I thought it, I should never be happy again. I wouldn't cut a boy off: no, not even Brittles here; not for all the plate in the county, sir.'

'That's not the point,' said the doctor, mysteriously. 'Mr. Giles, are you a Protestant?'

'Yes, sir, I hope so,' faltered Mr. Giles, who had turned very pale.

'And what are you, boy?' said the doctor, turning sharply upon Brittles.

'Lord bless me, sir!' replied Brittles, starting violently; 'I'm the same as Mr. Giles, sir.'

'Then tell me this,' said the doctor, 'both of you, both of you! Are you going to take upon yourselves to swear, that that boy upstairs is the boy that was put through the little window last night? Out with it! Come! We are prepared for you!'

The doctor, who was universally considered one of the best-tempered creatures on earth, made this demand in such a dreadful tone of anger, that Giles and Brittles, who were considerably muddled by ale and excitement, stared at each other in a state of stupefaction.

'Pay attention to the reply, constable, will you?' said the doctor, shaking his forefinger with great solemnity of manner, and tapping the bridge of his nose with it, to bespeak the exercise of that worthy's utmost acuteness. 'Something may come of this before long.'

The constable looked as wise as he could, and took up his staff of office: which had been reclining indolently in the chimney-corner.

'It's a simple question of identity, you will observe,' said the doctor.

'That's what it is, sir,' replied the constable, coughing with great violence; for he had finished his ale in a hurry, and some of it had gone the wrong way.

'Here's the house broken into,' said the doctor, 'and a couple of men catch one moment's glimpse of a boy, in the midst of gunpowder smoke, and in all the distraction of alarm and darkness. Here's a boy comes to that very same house, next morning, and because he happens to have his arm tied up, these men lay violent hands upon him—by doing which, they place his life in great danger—and swear he is the thief. Now, the question is, whether these men are justified by the fact; if not, in what situation do they place themselves?'

The constable nodded profoundly. He said, if that wasn't law, he would be glad to know what was.

'I ask you again,' thundered the doctor, 'are you, on your solemn oaths, able to identify that boy?'

Brittles looked doubtfully at Mr. Giles; Mr. Giles looked doubtfully at Brittles; the constable put his hand behind his ear, to catch the reply; the two women and the tinker leaned forward to listen; the doctor glanced keenly round; when a ring was heard at the gate, and at the same moment, the sound of wheels.

'It's the runners!' cried Brittles, to all appearance much relieved.

'The what?' exclaimed the doctor, aghast in his turn.

'The Bow Street officers, sir,' replied Brittles, taking up a candle; 'me and Mr. Giles sent for 'em this morning.'

'What?' cried the doctor.

'Yes,' replied Brittles; 'I sent a message up by the coachman, and I only wonder they weren't here before, sir.'

'You did, did you? Then confound your—slow coaches down here; that's all,' said the doctor, walking away.

CHAPTER XXXI. INVOLVES A CRITICAL POSITION

'Who's that?' inquired Brittles, opening the door a little way, with the chain up, and peeping out, shading the candle with his hand.

'Open the door,' replied a man outside; 'it's the officers from Bow Street, as was sent to to-day.'

Much comforted by this assurance, Brittles opened the door to its full width, and confronted a portly man in a great-coat; who walked in, without saying anything more, and wiped his shoes on the mat, as coolly as if he lived there.

'Just send somebody out to relieve my mate, will you, young man?' said the officer; 'he's in the gig, a-minding the prad. Have you got a coach 'us here, that you could put it up in, for five or ten minutes?'

Brittles replying in the affirmative, and pointing out the building, the portly man stepped back to the garden-gate, and helped his companion to put up the gig: while Brittles lighted them, in a state of great admiration. This done, they returned to the house, and, being shown into a parlour, took off their great-coats and hats, and showed like what they were.

The man who had knocked at the door, was a stout personage of middle height, aged about fifty: with shiny black hair, cropped pretty close; half-whiskers, a round face, and sharp eyes. The other was a red-headed, bony man, in top-boots; with a rather ill-favoured countenance, and a turned-up sinister-looking nose.

'Tell your governor that Blathers and Duff is here, will you?' said the stouter man, smoothing down his hair, and laying a pair of handcuffs on the table. 'Oh! Good-evening, master. Can I have a word or two with you in private, if you please?'

This was addressed to Mr. Losberne, who now made his appearance; that gentleman, motioning Brittles to retire, brought in the two ladies, and shut the door.

'This is the lady of the house,' said Mr. Losberne, motioning towards Mrs. Maylie.

Mr. Blathers made a bow. Being desired to sit down, he put his hat on the floor, and taking a chair, motioned to Duff to do the same. The latter gentleman, who did not appear quite so much accustomed to good society, or quite so much at his ease in it—one of the two—seated himself, after undergoing several muscular affections of the limbs, and the head of his stick into his mouth, with some embarrassment.

'Now, with regard to this here robbery, master,' said Blathers. 'What are the circumstances?'

Mr. Losberne, who appeared desirous of gaining time, recounted them at great length, and with much circumlocution. Messrs. Blathers and Duff looked very knowing meanwhile, and occasionally exchanged a nod.

'I can't say, for certain, till I see the work, of course,' said Blathers; 'but my opinion at once is,—I don't mind committing myself to that extent,—that this wasn't done by a yokel; eh, Duff?'

'Certainly not,' replied Duff.

'And, translating the word yokel for the benefit of the ladies, I apprehend your meaning to be, that this attempt was not made by a countryman?' said Mr. Losberne, with a smile.

'That's it, master,' replied Blathers. 'This is all about the robbery, is it?'

'All,' replied the doctor.

'Now, what is this, about this here boy that the servants are a-talking on?' said Blathers.

'Nothing at all,' replied the doctor. 'One of the frightened servants chose to take it into his head, that he had something to do with this attempt to break into the house; but it's nonsense: sheer absurdity.'

'Wery easy disposed of, if it is,' remarked Duff.

'What he says is quite correct,' observed Blathers, nodding his head in a confirmatory way, and playing carelessly with the handcuffs, as if they were a pair of castanets. 'Who is the boy? What account does he give of himself? Where did he come from? He didn't drop out of the clouds, did he, master?'

'Of course not,' replied the doctor, with a nervous glance at the two ladies. 'I know his whole history: but we can talk about that presently. You would like, first, to see the place where the thieves made their attempt, I suppose?'

'Certainly,' rejoined Mr. Blathers. 'We had better inspect the premises first, and examine the servants afterwards. That's the usual way of doing business.'

Lights were then procured; and Messrs. Blathers and Duff, attended by the native constable, Brittles, Giles, and everybody else in short, went into the little room at the end of the passage and looked out at the window; and afterwards went round by way of the lawn, and looked in at the window; and after that, had a candle handed out to inspect the shutter with; and after that, a lantern to trace the footsteps with; and after that, a pitchfork to poke the bushes with. This done, amidst the breathless interest of all beholders, they came in again; and Mr. Giles and Brittles were put through a melodramatic representation of their share in the previous night's adventures: which they performed some six times over: contradicting each other, in not more than one important respect, the first time, and in not more than a dozen the last. This consummation being arrived at, Blathers and Duff cleared the room, and held a long council together, compared with which, for secrecy and solemnity, a consultation of great doctors on the knottiest point in medicine, would be mere child's play.

Meanwhile, the doctor walked up and down the next room in a very uneasy state; and Mrs. Maylie and Rose looked on, with anxious faces.

'Upon my word,' he said, making a halt, after a great number of very rapid turns, 'I hardly know what to do.'

'Surely,' said Rose, 'the poor child's story, faithfully repeated to these men, will be sufficient to exonerate him.'

'I doubt it, my dear young lady,' said the doctor, shaking his head. 'I don't think it would exonerate him, either with them, or with legal functionaries of a higher grade. What is he, after all, they would say? A runaway. Judged by mere worldly considerations and probabilities, his story is a very doubtful one.'

'You believe it, surely?' interrupted Rose.

'I believe it, strange as it is; and perhaps I may be an old fool for doing so,' rejoined the doctor; 'but I don't think it is exactly the tale for a practical police-officer, nevertheless.'

'Why not?' demanded Rose.

'Because, my pretty cross-examiner,' replied the doctor: 'because, viewed with their eyes, there are many ugly points about it; he can only prove the parts that look ill, and none of those that look well. Confound the fellows, they will have the why and the wherefore, and will take nothing for granted. On his own showing, you see, he has been the companion of thieves for some time past; he has been carried to a police-officer, on a charge of picking a gentleman's pocket; he has been taken away, forcibly, from that gentleman's house, to a place which he cannot describe or point out, and of the situation of which he has not the remotest idea. He is brought down to Chertsey, by men who seem to have taken a violent fancy to him, whether he will or no; and is put through a window to rob a house; and then, just at the very moment when he is going to alarm the inmates, and so do the very thing that would set him all to rights, there rushes into the way, a blundering dog of a half-bred butler, and shoots him! As if on purpose to prevent his doing any good for himself! Don't you see all this?'

'I see it, of course,' replied Rose, smiling at the doctor's impetuosity; 'but still I do not see anything in it, to criminate the poor child.'

'No,' replied the doctor; 'of course not! Bless the bright eyes of your sex! They never see, whether for good or bad, more than one side of any question; and that is, always, the one which first presents itself to them.'

Having given vent to this result of experience, the doctor put his hands into his pockets, and walked up and down the room with even greater rapidity than before.

'The more I think of it,' said the doctor, 'the more I see that it will occasion endless trouble and difficulty if we put these men in possession of the boy's real story. I am certain it will not be believed; and even if they can do nothing to him in the end, still the dragging it forward, and giving publicity to all the doubts that will be cast upon it, must interfere, materially, with your benevolent plan of rescuing him from misery.'

'Oh! what is to be done?' cried Rose. 'Dear, dear! why did they send for these people?'

'Why, indeed!' exclaimed Mrs. Maylie. 'I would not have had them here, for the world.'

'All I know is,' said Mr. Losberne, at last: sitting down with a kind of desperate calmness, 'that we must try and carry it off with a bold face. The object is a good one, and that must be our excuse. The boy has strong symptoms of fever upon him, and is in no condition to be talked to any more; that's one comfort. We must make the best of it; and if bad be the best, it is no fault of ours. Come in!'

'Well, master,' said Blathers, entering the room followed by his colleague, and making the door fast, before he said any more. 'This warn't a put-up thing.'

'And what the devil's a put-up thing?' demanded the doctor, impatiently.

'We call it a put-up robbery, ladies,' said Blathers, turning to them, as if he pitied their ignorance, but had a contempt for the doctor's, 'when the servants is in it.'

'Nobody suspected them, in this case,' said Mrs. Maylie.

'Wery likely not, ma'am,' replied Blathers; 'but they might have been in it, for all that.'

'More likely on that wery account,' said Duff.

'We find it was a town hand,' said Blathers, continuing his report; 'for the style of work is first-rate.'

'Wery pretty indeed it is,' remarked Duff, in an undertone.

'There was two of 'em in it,' continued Blathers; 'and they had a boy with 'em; that's plain from the size of the window. That's all to be said at present. We'll see this lad that you've got upstairs at once, if you please.'

'Perhaps they will take something to drink first, Mrs. Maylie?' said the doctor: his face brightening, as if some new thought had occurred to him.

'Oh! to be sure!' exclaimed Rose, eagerly. 'You shall have it immediately, if you will.'

'Why, thank you, miss!' said Blathers, drawing his coat-sleeve across his mouth; 'it's dry work, this sort of duty. Anythink that's handy, miss; don't put yourself out of the way, on our accounts.'

'What shall it be?' asked the doctor, following the young lady to the sideboard.

'A little drop of spirits, master, if it's all the same,' replied Blathers. 'It's a cold ride from London, ma'am; and I always find that spirits comes home warmer to the feelings.'

This interesting communication was addressed to Mrs. Maylie, who received it very graciously. While it was being conveyed to her, the doctor slipped out of the room.

'Ah!' said Mr. Blathers: not holding his wine-glass by the stem, but grasping the bottom between the thumb and forefinger of his left hand: and placing it in front of his chest; 'I have seen a good many pieces of business like this, in my time, ladies.'

'That crack down in the back lane at Edmonton, Blathers,' said Mr. Duff, assisting his colleague's memory.

'That was something in this way, warn't it?' rejoined Mr. Blathers; 'that was done by Conkey Chickweed, that was.'

'You always gave that to him' replied Duff. 'It was the Family Pet, I tell you. Conkey hadn't any more to do with it than I had.'

'Get out!' retorted Mr. Blathers; 'I know better. Do you mind that time when Conkey was robbed of his money, though? What a start that was! Better than any novel-book I ever see!'

'What was that?' inquired Rose: anxious to encourage any symptoms of good-humour in the unwelcome visitors.

'It was a robbery, miss, that hardly anybody would have been down upon,' said Blathers. 'This here Conkey Chickweed—'

'Conkey means Nosey, ma'am,' interposed Duff.

'Of course the lady knows that, don't she?' demanded Mr. Blathers. 'Always interrupting, you are, partner! This here Conkey Chickweed, miss, kept a public-house over Battlebridge way, and he had a cellar, where a good many young lords went to see cock-fighting, and badger-drawing, and that; and a wery intellectual manner the sports was conducted in, for I've seen 'em off en. He warn't one of the family, at that time; and one night he was robbed of three hundred and twenty-seven guineas in a canvas bag, that was stole out of his bedroom in the dead of night, by a tall man with a black patch over his eye, who had concealed himself under the bed, and after committing the robbery, jumped slap out of window: which was only a story high. He was wery quick about it. But Conkey was quick, too; for he fired a blunderbuss arter him, and roused the neighbourhood. They set up a hue-and-cry, directly, and when they came to look about 'em, found that Conkey had hit the robber; for there was traces of blood, all the way to some palings a good distance off; and there they lost 'em. However, he had made off with the blunt; and, consequently, the name of Mr. Chickweed, licensed witler, appeared in the Gazette among the other bankrupts; and all manner of benefits and subscriptions, and I don't know what all, was got up for the poor man, who was in a wery low state of mind about his loss, and went up and down the streets, for three or four days, a pulling his hair off in such a desperate manner that many people was afraid he might be going to make away with himself. One day he came up to the office, all in a hurry, and had a private interview with the magistrate, who, after a deal of talk, rings the bell, and orders Jem Spyers in (Jem was a active officer), and tells him to go and assist Mr. Chickweed in apprehending the man as robbed his house. "I see him, Spyers," said Chickweed, "pass my house yesterday morning," "Why didn't you up, and collar him!" says Spyers. "I was so struck all of a heap, that you might have fractured my skull with a toothpick," says the poor man; "but we're sure to have him; for between ten and eleven o'clock at night he passed again." Spyers no sooner heard this, than he put some clean linen and a comb, in his pocket, in case he should have to stop a day or two; and away he goes, and sets himself down at one of the public-house windows behind the little red curtain, with his hat on, all ready to bolt out, at a moment's notice. He was smoking his pipe here, late at night, when all of a sudden Chickweed roars out, "Here he is! Stop thief! Murder!" Jem Spyers dashes out; and there he sees Chickweed, a-tearing down the street full cry. Away goes Spyers; on goes Chickweed; round turns the people; everybody roars out, "Thieves!" and Chickweed himself keeps on shouting, all the time, like mad. Spyers loses sight of him a minute as he turns a corner; shoots round; sees a little crowd; dives in; "Which is the man?" "D—me!" says Chickweed, "I've lost him again!" It was a remarkable occurrence, but he warn't to be seen nowhere, so they went back to the public-house. Next morning, Spyers took his old place, and looked out, from behind the curtain, for a tall man with a black patch over his eye, till his own two eyes ached again. At last, he couldn't help shutting 'em, to ease 'em a minute; and the very moment he did so, he hears Chickweed a-roaring out, "Here he is!" Off he starts once more, with Chickweed half-way down the street ahead of him; and after twice as long a run as the yesterday's one, the man's lost again! This was done, once or twice more, till one-half the neighbours gave out that Mr. Chickweed had been robbed by the devil, who was playing tricks with him arterwards; and the other half, that poor Mr. Chickweed had gone mad with grief.'

'What did Jem Spyers say?' inquired the doctor; who had returned to the room shortly after the commencement of the story.

'Jem Spyers,' resumed the officer, 'for a long time said nothing at all, and listened to everything without seeming to, which showed he understood his business. But, one morning, he walked into the bar, and taking out his snuffbox, says "Chickweed, I've found out who done this here robbery." "Have you?" said Chickweed. "Oh, my dear Spyers, only let me have wengeance, and I shall die contented! Oh, my dear Spyers, where is the villain!" "Come!" said Spyers, offering him a pinch of snuff, "none of that gammon! You did it yourself." So he had; and a good bit of money he had made by it, too; and nobody would never have found it out, if he hadn't been so precious anxious to keep up appearances!' said Mr. Blathers, putting down his wine-glass, and clinking the handcuffs together.

'Very curious, indeed,' observed the doctor. 'Now, if you please, you can walk upstairs.'

'If you please, sir,' returned Mr. Blathers. Closely following Mr. Losberne, the two officers ascended to Oliver's bedroom; Mr. Giles preceding the party, with a lighted candle.

Oliver had been dozing; but looked worse, and was more feverish than he had appeared yet. Being assisted by the doctor, he managed to sit up in bed for a minute or so; and looked at the strangers without at all understanding what was going forward—in fact, without seeming to recollect where he was, or what had been passing.

'This,' said Mr. Losberne, speaking softly, but with great vehemence notwithstanding, 'this is the lad, who, being accidently wounded by a spring-gun in some boyish trespass on Mr. What-d' ye-call-him's grounds, at the back here, comes to the house for assistance this morning, and is immediately laid hold of and maltreated, by that ingenious gentleman with the candle in his hand: who has placed his life in considerable danger, as I can professionally certify.'

Messrs. Blathers and Duff looked at Mr. Giles, as he was thus recommended to their notice. The bewildered butler gazed from them towards Oliver, and from Oliver towards Mr. Losberne, with a most ludicrous mixture of fear and perplexity.

'You don't mean to deny that, I suppose?' said the doctor, laying Oliver gently down again.

'It was all done for the—for the best, sir,' answered Giles. 'I am sure I thought it was the boy, or I wouldn't have meddled with him. I am not of an inhuman disposition, sir.'

'Thought it was what boy?' inquired the senior officer.

'The housebreaker's boy, sir!' replied Giles. 'They—they certainly had a boy.'

'Well? Do you think so now?' inquired Blathers.

'Think what, now?' replied Giles, looking vacantly at his questioner.

'Think it's the same boy, Stupid-head?' rejoined Blathers, impatiently.

'I don't know; I really don't know,' said Giles, with a rueful countenance. 'I couldn't swear to him.'

'What do you think?' asked Mr. Blathers.

'I don't know what to think,' replied poor Giles. 'I don't think it is the boy; indeed, I'm almost certain that it isn't. You know it can't be.'

'Has this man been a-drinking, sir?' inquired Blathers, turning to the doctor.

'What a precious muddle-headed chap you are!' said Duff, addressing Mr. Giles, with supreme contempt.

Mr. Losberne had been feeling the patient's pulse during this short dialogue; but he now rose from the chair by the bedside, and remarked, that if the officers had any doubts upon the subject, they would perhaps like to step into the next room, and have Brittles before them.

Acting upon this suggestion, they adjourned to a neighbouring apartment, where Mr. Brittles, being called in, involved himself and his respected superior in such a wonderful maze of fresh contradictions and impossibilities, as tended to throw no particular light on anything, but the fact of his own strong mystification; except, indeed, his declarations that he shouldn't know the real boy, if he were put before him that instant; that he had only taken Oliver to be he, because Mr. Giles had said he was; and that Mr. Giles had, five minutes previously, admitted in the kitchen, that he began to be very much afraid he had been a little too hasty.

Among other ingenious surmises, the question was then raised, whether Mr. Giles had really hit anybody; and upon examination of the fellow pistol to that which he had fired, it turned out to have no more destructive loading than gunpowder and brown paper: a discovery which made a considerable impression on everybody but the doctor, who had drawn the ball about ten minutes before. Upon no one, however, did it make a greater impression than on Mr. Giles himself; who, after labouring, for some hours, under the fear of having mortally wounded a fellow-creature, eagerly caught at this new idea, and favoured it to the utmost. Finally, the officers, without troubling themselves very much about Oliver, left the Chertsey constable in the house, and took up their rest for that night in the town; promising to return the next morning.

With the next morning, there came a rumour, that two men and a boy were in the cage at Kingston, who had been apprehended over night under suspicious circumstances; and to Kingston Messrs. Blathers and Duff journeyed accordingly. The suspicious circumstances, however, resolving themselves, on investigation, into the one fact, that they had been discovered sleeping under a haystack; which, although a great crime, is only punishable by imprisonment, and is, in the merciful eye of the English law, and its comprehensive love of all the King's subjects, held to be no satisfactory proof, in the absence of all other evidence, that the sleeper, or sleepers, have committed burglary accompanied with violence, and have therefore rendered themselves liable to the punishment of death; Messrs. Blathers and Duff came back again, as wise as they went.

In short, after some more examination, and a great deal more conversation, a neighbouring magistrate was readily induced to take the joint bail of Mrs. Maylie and Mr. Losberne for Oliver's appearance if he should ever be called upon; and Blathers and Duff, being rewarded with a couple of guineas, returned to town with divided opinions on the subject of their expedition: the latter gentleman on a mature consideration of all the circumstances, inclining to the belief that the burglarious attempt had originated with the Family Pet; and the former being equally disposed to concede the full merit of it to the great Mr. Conkey Chickweed.

Meanwhile, Oliver gradually throve and prospered under the united care of Mrs. Maylie, Rose, and the kind-hearted Mr. Losberne. If fervent prayers, gushing from hearts overcharged with gratitude, be heard in heaven—and if they be not, what prayers are!—the blessings which the orphan child called down upon them, sunk into their souls, diffusing peace and happiness.

CHAPTER XXXII. OF THE HAPPY LIFE OLIVER BEGAN TO LEAD WITH HIS KIND FRIENDS

Oliver's ailings were neither slight nor few. In addition to the pain and delay attendant on a broken limb, his exposure to the wet and cold had brought on fever and ague: which hung about him for many weeks, and reduced him sadly. But, at length, he began, by slow degrees, to get better, and to be able to say sometimes, in a few tearful words, how deeply he felt the goodness of the two sweet ladies, and how ardently he hoped that when he grew strong and well again, he could do something to show his gratitude; only something, which would let them see the love and duty with which his breast was full; something, however slight, which would prove to them that their gentle kindness had not been cast away; but that the poor boy whom their charity had rescued from misery, or death, was eager to serve them with his whole heart and soul.

'Poor fellow!' said Rose, when Oliver had been one day feebly endeavouring to utter the words of thankfulness that rose to his pale lips; 'you shall have many opportunities of serving us, if you will. We are going into the country, and my aunt intends that you shall accompany us. The quiet place, the pure air, and all the pleasure and beauties of spring, will restore you in a few days. We will employ you in a hundred ways, when you can bear the trouble.'

'The trouble!' cried Oliver. 'Oh! dear lady, if I could but work for you; if I could only give you pleasure by watering your flowers, or watching your birds, or running up and down the whole day long, to make you happy; what would I give to do it!'

'You shall give nothing at all,' said Miss Maylie, smiling; 'for, as I told you before, we shall employ you in a hundred ways; and if you only take half the trouble to please us, that you promise now, you will make me very happy indeed.'

'Happy, ma'am!' cried Oliver; 'how kind of you to say so!'

'You will make me happier than I can tell you,' replied the young lady. 'To think that my dear good aunt should have been the means of rescuing any one from such sad misery as you have described to us, would be an unspeakable pleasure to me; but to know that the object of her goodness and compassion was sincerely grateful and attached, in consequence, would delight me, more than you can well imagine. Do you understand me?' she inquired, watching Oliver's thoughtful face.

'Oh yes, ma'am, yes!' replied Oliver eagerly; 'but I was thinking that I am ungrateful now.'

'To whom?' inquired the young lady.

'To the kind gentleman, and the dear old nurse, who took so much care of me before,' rejoined Oliver. 'If they knew how happy I am, they would be pleased, I am sure.'

'I am sure they would,' rejoined Oliver's benefactress; 'and Mr. Losberne has already been kind enough to promise that when you are well enough to bear the journey, he will carry you to see them.'

'Has he, ma'am?' cried Oliver, his face brightening with pleasure. 'I don't know what I shall do for joy when I see their kind faces once again!'

In a short time Oliver was sufficiently recovered to undergo the fatigue of this expedition. One morning he and Mr. Losberne set out, accordingly, in a little carriage which belonged to Mrs. Maylie. When they came to Chertsey Bridge, Oliver turned very pale, and uttered a loud exclamation.

'What's the matter with the boy?' cried the doctor, as usual, all in a bustle. 'Do you see anything—hear anything—feel anything—eh?'

'That, sir,' cried Oliver, pointing out of the carriage window. 'That house!'

'Yes; well, what of it? Stop coachman. Pull up here,' cried the doctor. 'What of the house, my man; eh?'

'The thieves—the house they took me to!' whispered Oliver.

'The devil it is!' cried the doctor. 'Hallo, there! let me out!'

But, before the coachman could dismount from his box, he had tumbled out of the coach, by some means or other; and, running down to the deserted tenement, began kicking at the door like a madman.

'Halloa?' said a little ugly hump-backed man: opening the door so suddenly, that the doctor, from the very impetus of his last kick, nearly fell forward into the passage. 'What's the matter here?'

'Matter!' exclaimed the other, collaring him, without a moment's reflection. 'A good deal. Robbery is the matter.'

'There'll be Murder the matter, too,' replied the hump-backed man, coolly, 'if you don't take your hands off. Do you hear me?'

'I hear you,' said the doctor, giving his captive a hearty shake.

'Where's—confound the fellow, what's his rascally name—Sikes; that's it. Where's Sikes, you thief?'

The hump-backed man stared, as if in excess of amazement and indignation; then, twisting himself, dexterously, from the doctor's grasp, growled forth a volley of horrid oaths, and retired into the house. Before he could shut the door, however, the doctor had passed into the parlour, without a word of parley.

He looked anxiously round; not an article of furniture; not a vestige of anything, animate or inanimate; not even the position of the cupboards; answered Oliver's description!

'Now!' said the hump-backed man, who had watched him keenly, 'what do you mean by coming into my house, in this violent way? Do you want to rob me, or to murder me? Which is it?'

'Did you ever know a man come out to do either, in a chariot and pair, you ridiculous old vampire?' said the irritable doctor.

'What do you want, then?' demanded the hunchback. 'Will you take yourself off, before I do you a mischief? Curse you!'

'As soon as I think proper,' said Mr. Losberne, looking into the other parlour; which, like the first, bore no resemblance whatever to Oliver's account of it. 'I shall find you out, some day, my friend.'

'Will you?' sneered the ill-favoured cripple. 'If you ever want me, I'm here. I haven't lived here mad and all alone, for five-and-twenty years, to be scared by you. You shall pay for this; you shall pay for this.' And so saying, the mis-shapen little demon set up a yell, and danced upon the ground, as if wild with rage.

'Stupid enough, this,' muttered the doctor to himself; 'the boy must have made a mistake. Here! Put that in your pocket, and shut yourself up again.' With these words he flung the hunchback a piece of money, and returned to the carriage.

The man followed to the chariot door, uttering the wildest imprecations and curses all the way; but as Mr. Losberne turned to speak to the driver, he looked into the carriage, and eyed Oliver for an instant with a glance so sharp and fierce and at the same time so furious and vindictive, that, waking or sleeping, he could not forget it for months afterwards. He continued to utter the most fearful imprecations, until the driver had resumed his seat; and when they were once more on their way, they could see him some distance behind: beating his feet upon the ground, and tearing his hair, in transports of real or pretended rage.

'I am an ass!' said the doctor, after a long silence. 'Did you know that before, Oliver?'

'No, sir.'

'Then don't forget it another time.'

'An ass,' said the doctor again, after a further silence of some minutes. 'Even if it had been the right place, and the right fellows had been there, what could I have done, single-handed? And if I had had assistance, I see no good that I should have done, except leading to my own exposure, and an unavoidable statement of the manner in which I have hushed up this business. That would have served me right, though. I am always involving myself in some scrape or other, by acting on impulse. It might have done me good.'

Now, the fact was that the excellent doctor had never acted upon anything but impulse all through his life, and it was no bad compliment to the nature of the impulses which governed him, that so far from being involved in any peculiar troubles or misfortunes, he had the warmest respect and esteem of all who knew him. If the truth must be told, he was a little out of temper, for a minute or two, at being disappointed in procuring corroborative evidence of Oliver's story on the very first occasion on which he had a chance of obtaining any. He soon came round again, however; and finding that Oliver's replies to his questions, were still as straightforward and consistent, and still delivered with as much apparent sincerity and truth, as they had ever been, he made up his mind to attach full credence to them, from that time forth.

As Oliver knew the name of the street in which Mr. Brownlow resided, they were enabled to drive straight thither. When the coach turned into it, his heart beat so violently, that he could scarcely draw his breath.

'Now, my boy, which house is it?' inquired Mr. Losberne.

'That! That!' replied Oliver, pointing eagerly out of the window. 'The white house. Oh! make haste! Pray make haste! I feel as if I should die: it makes me tremble so.'

'Come, come!' said the good doctor, patting him on the shoulder. 'You will see them directly, and they will be overjoyed to find you safe and well.'

'Oh! I hope so!' cried Oliver. 'They were so good to me; so very, very good to me.'

The coach rolled on. It stopped. No; that was the wrong house; the next door. It went on a few paces, and stopped again. Oliver looked up at the windows, with tears of happy expectation coursing down his face.

Alas! the white house was empty, and there was a bill in the window. 'To Let.'

'Knock at the next door,' cried Mr. Losberne, taking Oliver's arm in his. 'What has become of Mr. Brownlow, who used to live in the adjoining house, do you know?'

The servant did not know; but would go and inquire. She presently returned, and said, that Mr. Brownlow had sold off his goods, and gone to the West Indies, six weeks before. Oliver clasped his hands, and sank feebly backward.

'Has his housekeeper gone too?' inquired Mr. Losberne, after a moment's pause.

'Yes, sir'; replied the servant. 'The old gentleman, the housekeeper, and a gentleman who was a friend of Mr. Brownlow's, all went together.'

'Then turn towards home again,' said Mr. Losberne to the driver; 'and don't stop to bait the horses, till you get out of this confounded London!'

'The book-stall keeper, sir?' said Oliver. 'I know the way there. See him, pray, sir! Do see him!'

'My poor boy, this is disappointment enough for one day,' said the doctor. 'Quite enough for both of us. If we go to the book-stall keeper's, we shall certainly find that he is dead, or has set his house on fire, or run away. No; home again straight!' And in obedience to the doctor's impulse, home they went.

This bitter disappointment caused Oliver much sorrow and grief, even in the midst of his happiness; for he had pleased himself, many times during his illness, with thinking of all that Mr. Brownlow and Mrs. Bedwin would say to him: and what delight it would be to tell them how many long days and nights he had passed in reflecting on what they had done for him, and in bewailing his cruel separation from them. The hope of eventually clearing himself with them, too, and explaining how he had been forced away, had buoyed him up, and sustained him, under many of his recent trials; and now, the idea that they should have gone so far, and carried with them the belief that he was an impostor and a robber—a belief which might remain uncontradicted to his dying day—was almost more than he could bear.

The circumstance occasioned no alteration, however, in the behaviour of his benefactors. After another fortnight, when the fine warm weather had fairly begun, and every tree and flower was putting forth its young leaves and rich blossoms, they made preparations for quitting the house at Chertsey, for some months.

Sending the plate, which had so excited Fagin's cupidity, to the banker's; and leaving Giles and another servant in care of the house, they departed to a cottage at some distance in the country, and took Oliver with them.

Who can describe the pleasure and delight, the peace of mind and soft tranquillity, the sickly boy felt in the balmy air, and among the green hills and rich woods, of an inland village! Who can tell how scenes of peace and quietude sink into the minds of pain-worn dwellers in close and noisy places, and carry their own freshness, deep into their jaded hearts! Men who have lived in crowded, pent-up streets, through lives of toil, and who have never wished for change; men, to whom custom has indeed been second nature, and who have come almost to love each brick and stone that formed the narrow boundaries of their daily walks; even they, with the hand of death upon them, have been known to yearn at last for one short glimpse of Nature's face; and, carried far from the scenes of their old pains and pleasures, have seemed to pass at once into a new state of being. Crawling forth, from day to day, to some green sunny spot, they have had such memories wakened up within them by the sight of the sky, and hill and plain, and glistening water, that a foretaste of heaven itself has soothed their quick decline, and they have sunk into their tombs, as peacefully as the sun whose setting they watched from their lonely chamber window but a few hours before, faded from their dim and feeble sight! The memories which peaceful country scenes call up, are not of this world, nor of its thoughts and hopes. Their gentle influence may teach us how to weave fresh garlands for the graves of those we loved: may purify our thoughts, and bear down before it old enmity and hatred; but beneath all this, there lingers, in the least reflective mind, a vague and half-formed consciousness of having held such feelings long before, in some remote and distant time, which calls up solemn thoughts of distant times to come, and bends down pride and worldliness beneath it.

It was a lovely spot to which they repaired. Oliver, whose days had been spent among squalid crowds, and in the midst of noise and brawling, seemed to enter on a new existence there. The rose and honeysuckle clung to the cottage walls; the ivy crept round the trunks of the trees; and the garden-flowers perfumed the air with delicious odours. Hard by, was a little churchyard; not crowded with tall unsightly gravestones, but full of humble mounds, covered with fresh turf and moss: beneath which, the old people of the village lay at rest. Oliver often wandered here; and, thinking of the wretched grave in which his mother lay, would sometimes sit him down and sob unseen; but, when he raised his eyes to the deep sky overhead, he would cease to think of her as lying in the ground, and would weep for her, sadly, but without pain.

It was a happy time. The days were peaceful and serene; the nights brought with them neither fear nor care; no languishing in a wretched prison, or associating with wretched men;

nothing but pleasant and happy thoughts. Every morning he went to a white-headed old gentleman, who lived near the little church: who taught him to read better, and to write: and who spoke so kindly, and took such pains, that Oliver could never try enough to please him. Then, he would walk with Mrs. Maylie and Rose, and hear them talk of books; or perhaps sit near them, in some shady place, and listen whilst the young lady read: which he could have done, until it grew too dark to see the letters. Then, he had his own lesson for the next day to prepare; and at this, he would work hard, in a little room which looked into the garden, till evening came slowly on, when the ladies would walk out again, and he with them: listening with such pleasure to all they said: and so happy if they wanted a flower that he could climb to reach, or had forgotten anything he could run to fetch: that he could never be quick enough about it. When it became quite dark, and they returned home, the young lady would sit down to the piano, and play some pleasant air, or sing, in a low and gentle voice, some old song which it pleased her aunt to hear. There would be no candles lighted at such times as these; and Oliver would sit by one of the windows, listening to the sweet music, in a perfect rapture.

And when Sunday came, how differently the day was spent, from any way in which he had ever spent it yet! and how happily too; like all the other days in that most happy time! There was the little church, in the morning, with the green leaves fluttering at the windows: the birds singing without: and the sweet-smelling air stealing in at the low porch, and filling the homely building with its fragrance. The poor people were so neat and clean, and knelt so reverently in prayer, that it seemed a pleasure, not a tedious duty, their assembling there together; and though the singing might be rude, it was real, and sounded more musical (to Oliver's ears at least) than any he had ever heard in church before. Then, there were the walks as usual, and many calls at the clean houses of the labouring men; and at night, Oliver read a chapter or two from the Bible, which he had been studying all the week, and in the performance of which duty he felt more proud and pleased, than if he had been the clergyman himself.

In the morning, Oliver would be a-foot by six o'clock, roaming the fields, and plundering the hedges, far and wide, for nosegays of wild flowers, with which he would return laden, home; and which it took great care and consideration to arrange, to the best advantage, for the embellishment of the breakfast-table. There was fresh groundsel, too, for Miss Maylie's birds, with which Oliver, who had been studying the subject under the able tuition of the village clerk, would decorate the cages, in the most approved taste. When the birds were made all spruce and smart for the day, there was usually some little commission of charity to execute in the village; or, failing that, there was rare cricket-playing, sometimes, on the green; or, failing that, there was always something to do in the garden, or about the plants, to which Oliver (who had studied this science also, under the same master, who was a gardener by trade,) applied himself with hearty good-will, until Miss Rose made her appearance: when there were a thousand commendations to be bestowed on all he had done.

So three months glided away; three months which, in the life of the most blessed and favoured of mortals, might have been unmingled happiness, and which, in Oliver's were true felicity. With the purest and most amiable generosity on one side; and the truest, warmest, soul-felt gratitude on the other; it is no wonder that, by the end of that short time, Oliver Twist had become completely domesticated with the old lady and her niece, and that the fervent attachment of his young and sensitive heart, was repaid by their pride in, and attachment to, himself.

CHAPTER XXXIII. WHEREIN THE HAPPINESS OF OLIVER AND HIS FRIENDS, EXPERIENCES A SUDDEN CHECK

Spring flew swiftly by, and summer came. If the village had been beautiful at first it was now in the full glow and luxuriance of its richness. The great trees, which had looked shrunken and bare in the earlier months, had now burst into strong life and health; and stretching forth their green arms over the thirsty ground, converted open and naked spots into choice nooks, where was a deep and pleasant shade from which to look upon the wide prospect, steeped in sunshine, which lay stretched beyond. The earth had donned her mantle of brightest green; and shed her richest perfumes abroad. It was the prime and vigour of the year; all things were glad and flourishing.

Still, the same quiet life went on at the little cottage, and the same cheerful serenity prevailed among its inmates. Oliver had long since grown stout and healthy; but health or sickness made no difference in his warm feelings of a great many people. He was still the same gentle, attached, affectionate creature that he had been when pain and suffering had wasted his strength, and when he was dependent for every slight attention, and comfort on those who tended him.

One beautiful night, when they had taken a longer walk than was customary with them: for the day had been unusually warm, and there was a brilliant moon, and a light wind had sprung up, which was unusually refreshing. Rose had been in high spirits, too, and they had walked on, in merry conversation, until they had far exceeded their ordinary bounds. Mrs. Maylie being fatigued, they returned more slowly home. The young lady merely throwing off her simple bonnet, sat down to the piano as usual. After running abstractedly over the keys for a few minutes, she fell into a low and very solemn air; and as she played it, they heard a sound as if she were weeping.

'Rose, my dear!' said the elder lady.

Rose made no reply, but played a little quicker, as though the words had roused her from some painful thoughts.

'Rose, my love!' cried Mrs. Maylie, rising hastily, and bending over her. 'What is this? In tears! My dear child, what distresses you?'

'Nothing, aunt; nothing,' replied the young lady. 'I don't know what it is; I can't describe it; but I feel—'

'Not ill, my love?' interposed Mrs. Maylie.

'No, no! Oh, not ill!' replied Rose: shuddering as though some deadly chillness were passing over her, while she spoke; 'I shall be better presently. Close the window, pray!'

Oliver hastened to comply with her request. The young lady, making an effort to recover her cheerfulness, strove to play some livelier tune; but her fingers dropped powerless over the keys. Covering her face with her hands, she sank upon a sofa, and gave vent to the tears which she was now unable to repress.

'My child!' said the elderly lady, folding her arms about her, 'I never saw you so before.'

'I would not alarm you if I could avoid it,' rejoined Rose; 'but indeed I have tried very hard, and cannot help this. I fear I am ill, aunt.'

She was, indeed; for, when candles were brought, they saw that in the very short time which had elapsed since their return home, the hue of her countenance had changed to a marble whiteness. Its expression had lost nothing of its beauty; but it was changed; and there was an anxious haggard look about the gentle face, which it had never worn before. Another minute, and it was suffused with a crimson flush: and a heavy wildness came over the soft blue eye. Again this disappeared, like the shadow thrown by a passing cloud; and she was once more deadly pale.

Oliver, who watched the old lady anxiously, observed that she was alarmed by these appearances; and so in truth, was he; but seeing that she affected to make light of them, he endeavoured to do the same, and they so far succeeded, that when Rose was persuaded by her aunt to retire for the night, she was in better spirits; and appeared even in better health: assuring them that she felt certain she should rise in the morning, quite well.

'I hope,' said Oliver, when Mrs. Maylie returned, 'that nothing is the matter? She don't look well to-night, but—'

The old lady motioned to him not to speak; and sitting herself down in a dark corner of the room, remained silent for some time. At length, she said, in a trembling voice:

'I hope not, Oliver. I have been very happy with her for some years: too happy, perhaps. It may be time that I should meet with some misfortune; but I hope it is not this.'

'What?' inquired Oliver.

'The heavy blow,' said the old lady, 'of losing the dear girl who has so long been my comfort and happiness.'

'Oh! God forbid!' exclaimed Oliver, hastily.

'Amen to that, my child!' said the old lady, wringing her hands.

'Surely there is no danger of anything so dreadful?' said Oliver. 'Two hours ago, she was quite well.'

'She is very ill now,' rejoined Mrs. Maylies; 'and will be worse, I am sure. My dear, dear Rose! Oh, what shall I do without her!'

She gave way to such great grief, that Oliver, suppressing his own emotion, ventured to remonstrate with her; and to beg, earnestly, that, for the sake of the dear young lady herself, she would be more calm.

'And consider, ma'am,' said Oliver, as the tears forced themselves into his eyes, despite of his efforts to the contrary. 'Oh! consider how young and good she is, and what pleasure and comfort she gives to all about her. I am sure—certain—quite certain—that, for your sake, who are so good yourself; and for her own; and for the sake of all she makes so happy; she will not die. Heaven will never let her die so young.'

'Hush!' said Mrs. Maylie, laying her hand on Oliver's head. 'You think like a child, poor boy. But you teach me my duty, notwithstanding. I had forgotten it for a moment, Oliver, but I hope I may be pardoned, for I am old, and have seen enough of illness and death to know the agony of separation from the objects of our love. I have seen enough, too, to know that it is not always the youngest and best who are spared to those that love them; but this should give us comfort in our sorrow; for Heaven is just; and such things teach us, impressively, that there is a brighter world than this; and that the passage to it is speedy. God's will be done! I love her; and He knows how well!'

Oliver was surprised to see that as Mrs. Maylie said these words, she checked her lamentations as though by one effort; and drawing herself up as she spoke, became composed and firm. He was still more astonished to find that this firmness lasted; and that, under all the care and watching which ensued, Mrs. Maylie was ever ready and collected: performing all the duties which had devolved upon her, steadily, and, to all external appearances, even cheerfully. But he was young, and did not know what strong minds are capable of, under trying circumstances. How should he, when their possessors so seldom know themselves?

An anxious night ensued. When morning came, Mrs. Maylie's predictions were but too well verified. Rose was in the first stage of a high and dangerous fever.

'We must be active, Oliver, and not give way to useless grief,' said Mrs. Maylie, laying her finger on her lip, as she looked steadily into his face; 'this letter must be sent, with all possible expedition, to Mr. Losberne. It must be carried to the market-town: which is not more than four miles off, by the footpath across the field: and thence dispatched, by an express on horseback, straight to Chertsey. The people at the inn will undertake to do this: and I can trust to you to see it done, I know.'

Oliver could make no reply, but looked his anxiety to be gone at once.

'Here is another letter,' said Mrs. Maylie, pausing to reflect; 'but whether to send it now, or wait until I see how Rose goes on, I scarcely know. I would not forward it, unless I feared the worst.'

'Is it for Chertsey, too, ma'am?' inquired Oliver; impatient to execute his commission, and holding out his trembling hand for the letter.

'No,' replied the old lady, giving it to him mechanically. Oliver glanced at it, and saw that it was directed to Harry Maylie, Esquire, at some great lord's house in the country; where, he could not make out.

'Shall it go, ma'am?' asked Oliver, looking up, impatiently.

'I think not,' replied Mrs. Maylie, taking it back. 'I will wait until to-morrow.'

With these words, she gave Oliver her purse, and he started off, without more delay, at the greatest speed he could muster.

Swiftly he ran across the fields, and down the little lanes which sometimes divided them: now almost hidden by the high corn on either side, and now emerging on an open field, where the mowers and haymakers were busy at their work: nor did he stop once, save now and then, for a few seconds, to recover breath, until he came, in a great heat, and covered with dust, on the little market-place of the market-town.

Here he paused, and looked about for the inn. There were a white bank, and a red brewery, and a yellow town-hall; and in one corner there was a large house, with all the wood about it painted green: before which was the sign of 'The George.' To this he hastened, as soon as it caught his eye.

He spoke to a postboy who was dozing under the gateway; and who, after hearing what he wanted, referred him to the ostler; who after hearing all he had to say again, referred him to the landlord; who was a tall gentleman in a blue neckcloth, a white hat, drab breeches, and boots with tops to match, leaning against a pump by the stable-door, picking his teeth with a silver toothpick.

This gentleman walked with much deliberation into the bar to make out the bill: which took a long time making out: and after it was ready, and paid, a horse had to be saddled, and a man to be dressed, which took up ten good minutes more. Meanwhile Oliver was in such a desperate state of impatience and anxiety, that he felt as if he could have jumped upon the horse himself, and galloped away, full tear, to the next stage. At length, all was ready; and the little parcel having been handed up, with many injunctions and entreaties for its speedy delivery, the man set spurs to his horse, and rattling over the uneven paving of the market-place, was out of the town, and galloping along the turnpike-road, in a couple of minutes.

As it was something to feel certain that assistance was sent for, and that no time had been lost, Oliver hurried up the inn-yard, with a somewhat lighter heart. He was turning out of the gateway when he accidently stumbled against a tall man wrapped in a cloak, who was at that moment coming out of the inn door.

'Hah!' cried the man, fixing his eyes on Oliver, and suddenly recoiling. 'What the devil's this?'

'I beg your pardon, sir,' said Oliver; 'I was in a great hurry to get home, and didn't see you were coming.'

'Death!' muttered the man to himself, glaring at the boy with his large dark eyes. 'Who would have thought it! Grind him to ashes! He'd start up from a stone coffin, to come in my way!'

'I am sorry,' stammered Oliver, confused by the strange man's wild look. 'I hope I have not hurt you!'

'Rot you!' murmured the man, in a horrible passion; between his clenched teeth; 'if I had only had the courage to say the word, I might have been free of you in a night. Curses on your head, and black death on your heart, you imp! What are you doing here?'

The man shook his fist, as he uttered these words incoherently. He advanced towards Oliver, as if with the intention of aiming a blow at him, but fell violently on the ground: writhing and foaming, in a fit.

Oliver gazed, for a moment, at the struggles of the madman (for such he supposed him to be); and then darted into the house for help. Having seen him safely carried into the hotel, he turned his face homewards, running as fast as he could, to make up for lost time: and recalling with a great deal of astonishment and some fear, the extraordinary behaviour of the person from whom he had just parted.

The circumstance did not dwell in his recollection long, however: for when he reached the cottage, there was enough to occupy his mind, and to drive all considerations of self completely from his memory.

Rose Maylie had rapidly grown worse; before mid-night she was delirious. A medical practitioner, who resided on the spot, was in constant attendance upon her; and after first seeing the patient, he had taken Mrs. Maylie aside, and pronounced her disorder to be one of a most alarming nature. 'In fact,' he said, 'it would be little short of a miracle, if she recovered.'

How often did Oliver start from his bed that night, and stealing out, with noiseless footstep, to the staircase, listen for the slightest sound from the sick chamber! How often did a tremble shake his frame, and cold drops of terror start upon his brow, when a sudden trampling of feet caused him to fear that something too dreadful to think of, had even then occurred! And what had been the fervency of all the prayers he had ever muttered, compared with those he poured forth, now, in the agony and passion of his supplication for the life and health of the gentle creature, who was tottering on the deep grave's verge!

Oh! the suspense, the fearful, acute suspense, of standing idly by while the life of one we dearly love, is trembling in the balance! Oh! the racking thoughts that crowd upon the mind, and make the heart beat violently, and the breath come thick, by the force of the images they conjure up before it; the desperate anxiety to be doing something to relieve the pain, or lessen the danger, which we have no power to alleviate; the sinking of soul and spirit, which the sad remembrance of our helplessness produces; what tortures can equal these; what reflections or endeavours can, in the full tide and fever of the time, allay them!

Morning came; and the little cottage was lonely and still. People spoke in whispers; anxious faces appeared at the gate, from time to time; women and children went away in tears. All the livelong day, and for hours after it had grown dark, Oliver paced softly up and down the garden, raising his eyes every instant to the sick chamber, and shuddering to see the darkened window, looking as if death lay stretched inside. Late that night, Mr. Losberne arrived. 'It is hard,' said the good doctor, turning away as he spoke; 'so young; so much beloved; but there is very little hope.'

Another morning. The sun shone brightly; as brightly as if it looked upon no misery or care; and, with every leaf and flower in full bloom about her; with life, and health, and sounds and sights of joy, surrounding her on every side: the fair young creature lay, wasting fast. Oliver crept away to the old churchyard, and sitting down on one of the green mounds, wept and prayed for her, in silence.

There was such peace and beauty in the scene; so much of brightness and mirth in the sunny landscape; such blithesome music in the songs of the summer birds; such freedom in the rapid flight of the rook, careering overhead; so much of life and joyousness in all; that, when the boy raised his aching eyes, and looked about, the thought instinctively occurred to him, that this was not a time for death; that Rose could surely never die when humbler things were all so glad and gay; that graves were for cold and cheerless winter: not for sunlight and fragrance. He almost thought that shrouds were for the old and shrunken; and that they never wrapped the young and graceful form in their ghastly folds.

A knell from the church bell broke harshly on these youthful thoughts. Another! Again! It was tolling for the funeral service. A group of humble mourners entered the gate: wearing white favours; for the corpse was young. They stood uncovered by a grave; and there was a mother—a mother once—among the weeping train. But the sun shone brightly, and the birds sang on.

Oliver turned homeward, thinking on the many kindnesses he had received from the young lady, and wishing that the time could come again, that he might never cease showing her how grateful and attached he was. He had no cause for self-reproach on the score of neglect, or want of thought, for he had been devoted to her service; and yet a hundred little occasions rose up before him, on which he fancied he might have been more zealous, and more earnest, and wished he had been. We need be careful how we deal with those about us, when every death carries to some small circle of survivors, thoughts of so much omitted, and so little done—of so many things forgotten, and so many more which might have been repaired! There is no remorse so deep as that which is unavailing; if we would be spared its tortures, let us remember this, in time.

When he reached home Mrs. Maylie was sitting in the little parlour. Oliver's heart sank at sight of her; for she had never left the bedside of her niece; and he trembled to think what change could have driven her away. He learnt that she had fallen into a deep sleep, from which she would waken, either to recovery and life, or to bid them farewell, and die.

They sat, listening, and afraid to speak, for hours. The untasted meal was removed, with looks which showed that their thoughts were elsewhere, they watched the sun as he sank lower and lower, and, at length, cast over sky and earth those brilliant hues which herald his departure. Their quick ears caught the sound of an approaching footstep. They both involuntarily darted to the door, as Mr. Losberne entered.

'What of Rose?' cried the old lady. 'Tell me at once! I can bear it; anything but suspense! Oh, tell me! in the name of Heaven!'

'You must compose yourself,' said the doctor supporting her. 'Be calm, my dear ma'am, pray.'

'Let me go, in God's name! My dear child! She is dead! She is dying!'

'No!' cried the doctor, passionately. 'As He is good and merciful, she will live to bless us all, for years to come.'

The lady fell upon her knees, and tried to fold her hands together; but the energy which had supported her so long, fled up to Heaven with her first thanksgiving; and she sank into the friendly arms which were extended to receive her.

CHAPTER XXXIV. CONTAINS SOME INTRODUCTORY PARTICULARS RELATIVE TO A YOUNG GENTLEMAN WHO NOW ARRIVES UPON THE SCENE; AND A NEW ADVENTURE WHICH HAPPENED TO OLIVER

It was almost too much happiness to bear. Oliver felt stunned and stupefied by the unexpected intelligence; he could not weep, or speak, or rest. He had scarcely the power of understanding anything that had passed, until, after a long ramble in the quiet evening air, a burst of tears came to his relief, and he seemed to awaken, all at once, to a full sense of the joyful change that had occurred, and the almost insupportable load of anguish which had been taken from his breast.

The night was fast closing in, when he returned homeward: laden with flowers which he had culled, with peculiar care, for the adornment of the sick chamber. As he walked briskly along the road, he heard behind him, the noise of some vehicle, approaching at a furious pace. Looking round, he saw that it was a post-chaise, driven at great speed; and as the horses were galloping, and the road was narrow, he stood leaning against a gate until it should have passed him.

As it dashed on, Oliver caught a glimpse of a man in a white nightcap, whose face seemed familiar to him, although his view was so brief that he could not identify the person. In another second or two, the nightcap was thrust out of the chaise-window, and a stentorian voice bellowed to the driver to stop: which he did, as soon as he could pull up his horses. Then, the nightcap once again appeared: and the same voice called Oliver by his name.

'Here!' cried the voice. 'Oliver, what's the news? Miss Rose! Master O-li-ver!'

'Is it you, Giles?' cried Oliver, running up to the chaise-door.

Giles popped out his nightcap again, preparatory to making some reply, when he was suddenly pulled back by a young gentleman who occupied the other corner of the chaise, and who eagerly demanded what was the news.

'In a word!' cried the gentleman, 'Better or worse?'

'Better—much better!' replied Oliver, hastily.

'Thank Heaven!' exclaimed the gentleman. 'You are sure?'

'Quite, sir,' replied Oliver. 'The change took place only a few hours ago; and Mr. Losberne says, that all danger is at an end.'

The gentleman said not another word, but, opening the chaise-door, leaped out, and taking Oliver hurriedly by the arm, led him aside.

'You are quite certain? There is no possibility of any mistake on your part, my boy, is there?' demanded the gentleman in a tremulous voice. 'Do not deceive me, by awakening hopes that are not to be fulfilled.'

'I would not for the world, sir,' replied Oliver. 'Indeed you may believe me. Mr. Losberne's words were, that she would live to bless us all for many years to come. I heard him say so.'

The tears stood in Oliver's eyes as he recalled the scene which was the beginning of so much happiness; and the gentleman turned his face away, and remained silent, for some minutes. Oliver thought he heard him sob, more than once; but he feared to interrupt him by any fresh remark—for he could well guess what his feelings were—and so stood apart, feigning to be occupied with his nosegay.

All this time, Mr. Giles, with the white nightcap on, had been sitting on the steps of the chaise, supporting an elbow on each knee, and wiping his eyes with a blue cotton pocket-handkerchief dotted with white spots. That the honest fellow had not been feigning emotion, was abundantly demonstrated by the very red eyes with which he regarded the young gentleman, when he turned round and addressed him.

'I think you had better go on to my mother's in the chaise, Giles,' said he. 'I would rather walk slowly on, so as to gain a little time before I see her. You can say I am coming.'

'I beg your pardon, Mr. Harry,' said Giles: giving a final polish to his ruffled countenance with the handkerchief; 'but if you would leave the postboy to say that, I should be very much obliged to you. It wouldn't be proper for the maids to see me in this state, sir; I should never have any more authority with them if they did.'

'Well,' rejoined Harry Maylie, smiling, 'you can do as you like. Let him go on with the luggage, if you wish it, and do you follow with us. Only first exchange that nightcap for some more appropriate covering, or we shall be taken for madmen.'

Mr. Giles, reminded of his unbecoming costume, snatched off and pocketed his nightcap; and substituted a hat, of grave and sober shape, which he took out of the chaise. This done, the postboy drove off; Giles, Mr. Maylie, and Oliver, followed at their leisure.

As they walked along, Oliver glanced from time to time with much interest and curiosity at the new comer. He seemed about five-and-twenty years of age, and was of the middle height; his countenance was frank and handsome; and his demeanor easy and prepossessing. Notwithstanding the difference between youth and age, he bore so strong a likeness to the old lady, that Oliver would have had no great difficulty in imagining their relationship, if he had not already spoken of her as his mother.

Mrs. Maylie was anxiously waiting to receive her son when he reached the cottage. The meeting did not take place without great emotion on both sides.

'Mother!' whispered the young man; 'why did you not write before?'

'I did,' replied Mrs. Maylie; 'but, on reflection, I determined to keep back the letter until I had heard Mr. Losberne's opinion.'

'But why,' said the young man, 'why run the chance of that occurring which so nearly happened? If Rose had—I cannot utter that word now—if this illness had terminated differently, how could you ever have forgiven yourself! How could I ever have know happiness again!'

'If that had been the case, Harry,' said Mrs. Maylie, 'I fear your happiness would have been effectually blighted, and that your arrival here, a day sooner or a day later, would have been of very, very little import.'

'And who can wonder if it be so, mother?' rejoined the young man; 'or why should I say, if?—It is—it is—you know it, mother—you must know it!'

'I know that she deserves the best and purest love the heart of man can offer,' said Mrs. Maylie; 'I know that the devotion and affection of her nature require no ordinary return, but one that shall be deep and lasting. If I did not feel this, and know, besides, that a changed behaviour in one she loved would break her heart, I should not feel my task so difficult of performance, or have to encounter so many struggles in my own bosom, when I take what seems to me to be the strict line of duty.'

'This is unkind, mother,' said Harry. 'Do you still suppose that I am a boy ignorant of my own mind, and mistaking the impulses of my own soul?'

'I think, my dear son,' returned Mrs. Maylie, laying her hand upon his shoulder, 'that youth has many generous impulses which do not last; and that among them are some, which, being gratified, become only the more fleeting. Above all, I think' said the lady, fixing her eyes on her son's face, 'that if an enthusiastic, ardent, and ambitious man marry a wife on whose name there is a stain, which, though it originate in no fault of hers, may be visited by cold and sordid people upon her, and upon his children also: and, in exact proportion to his success in the world, be cast in his teeth, and made the subject of sneers against him: he may, no matter how generous and good his nature, one day repent of the connection he formed in early life. And she may have the pain of knowing that he does so.'

'Mother,' said the young man, impatiently, 'he would be a selfish brute, unworthy alike of the name of man and of the woman you describe, who acted thus.'

'You think so now, Harry,' replied his mother.

'And ever will!' said the young man. 'The mental agony I have suffered, during the last two days, wrings from me the avowal to you of a passion which, as you well know, is not one of yesterday, nor one I have lightly formed. On Rose, sweet, gentle girl! my heart is set, as firmly as ever heart of man was set on woman. I have no thought, no view, no hope in life, beyond her; and if you oppose me in this great stake, you take my peace and happiness in your hands, and cast them to the wind. Mother, think better of this, and of me, and do not disregard the happiness of which you seem to think so little.'

'Harry,' said Mrs. Maylie, 'it is because I think so much of warm and sensitive hearts, that I would spare them from being wounded. But we have said enough, and more than enough, on this matter, just now.'

'Let it rest with Rose, then,' interposed Harry. 'You will not press these overstrained opinions of yours, so far, as to throw any obstacle in my way?'

'I will not,' rejoined Mrs. Maylie; 'but I would have you consider—'

'I have considered!' was the impatient reply; 'Mother, I have considered, years and years. I have considered, ever since I have been capable of serious reflection. My feelings remain unchanged, as they ever will; and why should I suffer the pain of a delay in giving them vent, which can be productive of no earthly good? No! Before I leave this place, Rose shall hear me.'

'She shall,' said Mrs. Maylie.

'There is something in your manner, which would almost imply that she will hear me coldly, mother,' said the young man.

'Not coldly,' rejoined the old lady; 'far from it.'

'How then?' urged the young man. 'She has formed no other attachment?'

'No, indeed,' replied his mother; 'you have, or I mistake, too strong a hold on her affections already. What I would say,' resumed the old lady, stopping her son as he was about to speak, 'is this. Before you stake your all on this chance; before you suffer yourself to be carried to the highest point of hope; reflect for a few moments, my dear child, on Rose's history, and consider what effect the knowledge of her doubtful birth may have on her decision: devoted as she is to us, with all the intensity of her noble mind, and with that perfect sacrifice of self which, in all matters, great or trifling, has always been her characteristic.'

'What do you mean?'

'That I leave you to discover,' replied Mrs. Maylie. 'I must go back to her. God bless you!'

'I shall see you again to-night?' said the young man, eagerly.

'By and by,' replied the lady; 'when I leave Rose.'

'You will tell her I am here?' said Harry.

'Of course,' replied Mrs. Maylie.

'And say how anxious I have been, and how much I have suffered, and how I long to see her. You will not refuse to do this, mother?'

'No,' said the old lady; 'I will tell her all.' And pressing her son's hand, affectionately, she hastened from the room.

Mr. Losberne and Oliver had remained at another end of the apartment while this hurried conversation was proceeding. The former now held out his hand to Harry Maylie; and hearty salutations were exchanged between them. The doctor then communicated, in reply to multifarious questions from his young friend, a precise account of his patient's situation; which was quite as consolatory and full of promise, as Oliver's statement had encouraged him to hope; and to the whole of which, Mr. Giles, who affected to be busy about the luggage, listened with greedy ears.

'Have you shot anything particular, lately, Giles?' inquired the doctor, when he had concluded.

'Nothing particular, sir,' replied Mr. Giles, colouring up to the eyes.

'Nor catching any thieves, nor identifying any house-breakers?' said the doctor.

'None at all, sir,' replied Mr. Giles, with much gravity.

'Well,' said the doctor, 'I am sorry to hear it, because you do that sort of thing admirably. Pray, how is Brittles?'

'The boy is very well, sir,' said Mr. Giles, recovering his usual tone of patronage; 'and sends his respectful duty, sir.'

'That's well,' said the doctor. 'Seeing you here, reminds me, Mr. Giles, that on the day before that on which I was called away so hurriedly, I executed, at the request of your good mistress, a small commission in your favour. Just step into this corner a moment, will you?'

Mr. Giles walked into the corner with much importance, and some wonder, and was honoured with a short whispering conference with the doctor, on the termination of which, he made a great many bows, and retired with steps of unusual stateliness. The subject matter of this conference was not disclosed in the parlour, but the kitchen was speedily enlightened concerning it; for Mr. Giles walked straight thither, and having called for a mug of ale, announced, with an air of majesty, which was highly effective, that it had pleased his mistress, in consideration of his gallant behaviour on the occasion of that attempted robbery, to deposit, in the local savings-bank, the sum of five-and-twenty pounds, for his sole use and benefit. At this, the two women-servants lifted up their hands and eyes, and supposed that Mr. Giles, pulling out his shirt-frill, replied, 'No, no'; and that if they observed that he was at all haughty to his inferiors, he would thank them to tell him so. And then he made a great many other remarks, no less illustrative of his humility, which were received with equal favour and applause, and were, withal, as original and as much to the purpose, as the remarks of great men commonly are.

Above stairs, the remainder of the evening passed cheerfully away; for the doctor was in high spirits; and however fatigued or thoughtful Harry Maylie might have been at first, he was not proof against the worthy gentleman's good humour, which displayed itself in a great variety of sallies and professional recollections, and an abundance of small jokes, which struck Oliver as being the drollest things he had ever heard, and caused him to laugh proportionately; to the evident satisfaction of the doctor, who laughed immoderately at himself, and made Harry laugh almost as heartily, by the very force of sympathy. So, they were as pleasant a party as, under the circumstances, they could well have been; and it was late before they retired, with light and thankful hearts, to take that rest of which, after the doubt and suspense they had recently undergone, they stood much in need.

Oliver rose next morning, in better heart, and went about his usual occupations, with more hope and pleasure than he had known for many days. The birds were once more hung out, to sing, in their old places; and the sweetest wild flowers that could be found, were once more gathered to gladden Rose with their beauty. The melancholy which had seemed to the sad eyes of the anxious boy to hang, for days past, over every object, beautiful as all were, was dispelled by magic. The dew seemed to sparkle more brightly on the green leaves; the air to rustle among them with a sweeter music; and the sky itself to look more blue and bright. Such is the influence which the condition of our own thoughts, exercise, even over the appearance of external objects. Men who look on nature, and their fellow-men, and cry that all is dark and gloomy, are in the right; but the sombre colours are reflections from their own jaundiced eyes and hearts. The real hues are delicate, and need a clearer vision.

It is worthy of remark, and Oliver did not fail to note it at the time, that his morning expeditions were no longer made alone. Harry Maylie, after the very first morning when he met Oliver coming laden home, was seized with such a passion for flowers, and displayed such a taste in their arrangement, as left his young companion far behind. If Oliver were behindhand in these respects, he knew where the best were to be found; and morning after morning they scoured the country together, and brought home the fairest that blossomed. The window of the young lady's chamber was opened now; for she loved to feel the rich summer air stream in, and revive her with its freshness; but there always stood in water, just inside the lattice, one particular little bunch, which was made up with great care, every morning. Oliver could not help noticing that the withered flowers were never thrown away, although the little vase was regularly replenished; nor, could he help observing, that whenever the doctor came into the garden, he invariably cast his eyes up to that particular corner, and nodded his head most expressively, as he set forth on his morning's walk. Pending these observations, the days were flying by; and Rose was rapidly recovering.

Nor did Oliver's time hang heavy on his hands, although the young lady had not yet left her chamber, and there were no evening walks, save now and then, for a short distance, with Mrs. Maylie. He applied himself, with redoubled assiduity, to the instructions of the white-headed old gentleman, and laboured so hard that his quick progress surprised even himself. It was while he was engaged in this pursuit, that he was greatly startled and distressed by a most unexpected occurrence.

The little room in which he was accustomed to sit, when busy at his books, was on the ground-floor, at the back of the house. It was quite a cottage-room, with a lattice-window: around which were clusters of jessamine and honeysuckle, that crept over the casement, and filled the place with their delicious perfume. It looked into a garden, whence a wicket-gate opened into a small paddock; all beyond, was fine meadow-land and wood. There was no other dwelling near, in that direction; and the prospect it commanded was very extensive.

One beautiful evening, when the first shades of twilight were beginning to settle upon the earth, Oliver sat at this window, intent upon his books. He had been poring over them for some time; and, as the day had been uncommonly sultry, and he had exerted himself a great deal, it is no disparagement to the authors, whoever they may have been, to say, that gradually and by slow degrees, he fell asleep.

There is a kind of sleep that steals upon us sometimes, which, while it holds the body prisoner, does not free the mind from a sense of things about it, and enable it to ramble at its pleasure. So far as an overpowering heaviness, a prostration of strength, and an utter inability to control our thoughts or power of motion, can be called sleep, this is it; and yet, we have a consciousness of all that is going on about us, and, if we dream at such a time, words which are really spoken, or sounds which really exist at the moment, accommodate themselves with surprising readiness to our visions, until reality and imagination become so strangely blended that it is afterwards almost matter of impossibility to separate the two. Nor is this, the most striking phenomenon incidental to such a state. It is an undoubted fact, that although our senses of touch and sight be for the time dead, yet our sleeping thoughts, and the visionary scenes that pass before us, will be influenced and materially influenced, by the mere silent presence of some external object; which may not have been near us when we closed our eyes: and of whose vicinity we have had no waking consciousness.

Oliver knew, perfectly well, that he was in his own little room; that his books were lying on the table before him; that the sweet air was stirring among the creeping plants outside. And yet he was asleep. Suddenly, the scene changed; the air became close and confined; and he thought, with a glow of terror, that he was in the Jew's house again. There sat the hideous old man, in his accustomed corner, pointing at him, and whispering to another man, with his face averted, who sat beside him.

'Hush, my dear!' he thought he heard the Jew say; 'it is he, sure enough. Come away.'

'He!' the other man seemed to answer; 'could I mistake him, think you? If a crowd of ghosts were to put themselves into his exact shape, and he stood amongst them, there is something that would tell me how to point him out. If you buried him fifty feet deep, and took me across his grave, I fancy I should know, if there wasn't a mark above it, that he lay buried there?'

The man seemed to say this, with such dreadful hatred, that Oliver awoke with the fear, and started up.

Good Heaven! what was that, which sent the blood tingling to his heart, and deprived him of his voice, and of power to move! There—there—at the window—close before him—so close, that he could have almost touched him before he started back: with his eyes peering into the room, and meeting his: there stood the Jew! And beside him, white with rage or fear, or both, were the scowling features of the man who had accosted him in the inn-yard.

It was but an instant, a glance, a flash, before his eyes; and they were gone. But they had recognised him, and he them; and their look was as firmly impressed upon his memory, as if it had been deeply carved in stone, and set before him from his birth. He stood transfixed for a moment; then, leaping from the window into the garden, called loudly for help.

CHAPTER XXXV. CONTAINING THE UNSATISFACTORY RESULT OF OLIVER'S ADVENTURE; AND A CONVERSATION OF SOME IMPORTANCE BETWEEN HARRY MAYLIE AND ROSE

When the inmates of the house, attracted by Oliver's cries, hurried to the spot from which they proceeded, they found him, pale and agitated, pointing in the direction of the meadows behind the house, and scarcely able to articulate the words, 'The Jew! the Jew!'

Mr. Giles was at a loss to comprehend what this outcry meant; but Harry Maylie, whose perceptions were something quicker, and who had heard Oliver's history from his mother, understood it at once.

'What direction did he take?' he asked, catching up a heavy stick which was standing in a corner.

'That,' replied Oliver, pointing out the course the man had taken; 'I missed them in an instant.'

'Then, they are in the ditch!' said Harry. 'Follow! And keep as near me, as you can.' So saying, he sprang over the hedge, and darted off with a speed which rendered it matter of exceeding difficulty for the others to keep near him.

Giles followed as well as he could; and Oliver followed too; and in the course of a minute or two, Mr. Losberne, who had been out walking, and just then returned, tumbled over the hedge after them, and picking himself up with more agility than he could have been supposed to possess, struck into the same course at no contemptible speed, shouting all the while, most prodigiously, to know what was the matter.

On they all went; nor stopped they once to breathe, until the leader, striking off into an angle of the field indicated by Oliver, began to search, narrowly, the ditch and hedge adjoining; which afforded time for the remainder of the party to come up; and for Oliver to communicate to Mr. Losberne the circumstances that had led to so vigorous a pursuit.

The search was all in vain. There were not even the traces of recent footsteps, to be seen. They stood now, on the summit of a little hill, commanding the open fields in every direction for three or four miles. There was the village in the hollow on the left; but, in order to gain that, after pursuing the track Oliver had pointed out, the men must have made a circuit of open ground, which it was impossible they could have accomplished in so short a time. A thick wood skirted the meadow-land in another direction; but they could not have gained that covert for the same reason.

'It must have been a dream, Oliver,' said Harry Maylie.

'Oh no, indeed, sir,' replied Oliver, shuddering at the very recollection of the old wretch's countenance; 'I saw him too plainly for that. I saw them both, as plainly as I see you now.'

'Who was the other?' inquired Harry and Mr. Losberne, together.

'The very same man I told you of, who came so suddenly upon me at the inn,' said Oliver. 'We had our eyes fixed full upon each other; and I could swear to him.'

'They took this way?' demanded Harry: 'are you sure?'

'As I am that the men were at the window,' replied Oliver, pointing down, as he spoke, to the hedge which divided the cottage-garden from the meadow. 'The tall man leaped over, just there; and the Jew, running a few paces to the right, crept through that gap.'

The two gentlemen watched Oliver's earnest face, as he spoke, and looking from him to each other, seemed to feel satisfied of the accuracy of what he said. Still, in no direction were there any appearances of the trampling of men in hurried flight. The grass was long; but it was trodden down nowhere, save where their own feet had crushed it. The sides and brinks of the ditches were of damp clay; but in no one place could they discern the print of men's shoes, or the slightest mark which would indicate that any feet had pressed the ground for hours before.

'This is strange!' said Harry.

'Strange?' echoed the doctor. 'Blathers and Duff, themselves, could make nothing of it.'

Notwithstanding the evidently useless nature of their search, they did not desist until the coming on of night rendered its further prosecution hopeless; and even then, they gave it up with reluctance. Giles was dispatched to the different ale-houses in the village, furnished with the best description Oliver could give of the appearance and dress of the strangers. Of these, the Jew was, at all events, sufficiently remarkable to be remembered, supposing he had been seen drinking, or loitering about; but Giles returned without any intelligence, calculated to dispel or lessen the mystery.

On the next day, fresh search was made, and the inquiries renewed; but with no better success. On the day following, Oliver and Mr. Maylie repaired to the market-town, in the hope of seeing or hearing something of the men there; but this effort was equally fruitless. After a few days, the affair began to be forgotten, as most affairs are, when wonder, having no fresh food to support it, dies away of itself.

Meanwhile, Rose was rapidly recovering. She had left her room: was able to go out; and mixing once more with the family, carried joy into the hearts of all.

But, although this happy change had a visible effect on the little circle; and although cheerful voices and merry laughter were once more heard in the cottage; there was at times, an unwonted restraint upon some there: even upon Rose herself: which Oliver could not fail to remark. Mrs. Maylie and her son were often closeted together for a long time; and more than once Rose appeared with traces of tears upon her face. After Mr. Losberne had fixed a day for his departure to Chertsey, these symptoms increased; and it became evident that something was in progress which affected the peace of the young lady, and of somebody else besides.

At length, one morning, when Rose was alone in the breakfast-parlour, Harry Maylie entered; and, with some hesitation, begged permission to speak with her for a few moments.

'A few—a very few—will suffice, Rose,' said the young man, drawing his chair towards her. 'What I shall have to say, has already presented itself to your mind; the most cherished hopes of my heart are not unknown to you, though from my lips you have not heard them stated.'

Rose had been very pale from the moment of his entrance; but that might have been the effect of her recent illness. She merely bowed; and bending over some plants that stood near, waited in silence for him to proceed.

'I—I—ought to have left here, before,' said Harry.

'You should, indeed,' replied Rose. 'Forgive me for saying so, but I wish you had.'

'I was brought here, by the most dreadful and agonising of all apprehensions,' said the young man; 'the fear of losing the one dear being on whom my every wish and hope are fixed. You had been dying; trembling between earth and heaven. We know that when the young, the beautiful, and good, are visited with sickness, their pure spirits insensibly turn towards their bright home of lasting rest; we know, Heaven help us! that the best and fairest of our kind, too often fade in blooming.'

There were tears in the eyes of the gentle girl, as these words were spoken; and when one fell upon the flower over which she bent, and glistened brightly in its cup, making it more beautiful, it seemed as though the outpouring of her fresh young heart, claimed kindred naturally, with the loveliest things in nature.

'A creature,' continued the young man, passionately, 'a creature as fair and innocent of guile as one of God's own angels, fluttered between life and death. Oh! who could hope, when the distant world to which she was akin, half opened to her view, that she would return to the sorrow and calamity of this! Rose, Rose, to know that you were passing away like some soft shadow, which a light from above, casts upon the earth; to have no hope that you would be spared to those who linger here; hardly to know a reason why you should be; to feel that you belonged to that bright sphere whither so many of the fairest and the best have winged their early flight; and yet to pray, amid all these consolations, that you might be restored to those who loved you—these were distractions almost too great to bear. They were mine, by day and night; and with them, came such a rushing torrent of fears, and apprehensions, and selfish regrets, lest you should die, and never know how devotedly I loved you, as almost bore down sense and reason in its course. You recovered. Day by day, and almost hour by hour, some drop of health came back, and mingling with the spent and feeble stream of life which circulated languidly within you, swelled it again to a high and rushing tide. I have watched you change almost from death, to life, with eyes that turned blind with their eagerness and deep affection. Do not tell me that you wish I had lost this; for it has softened my heart to all mankind.'

'I did not mean that,' said Rose, weeping; 'I only wish you had left here, that you might have turned to high and noble pursuits again; to pursuits well worthy of you.'

'There is no pursuit more worthy of me: more worthy of the highest nature that exists: than the struggle to win such a heart as yours,' said the young man, taking her hand. 'Rose, my own dear Rose! For years—for years—I have loved you; hoping to win my way to fame, and then come proudly home and tell you it had been pursued only for you to share; thinking, in my daydreams, how I would remind you, in that happy moment, of the many silent tokens I had given of a boy's attachment, and claim your hand, as in redemption of some old mute contract that had been sealed between us! That time has not arrived; but here, with not fame won, and no young vision realised, I offer you the heart so long your own, and stake my all upon the words with which you greet the offer.'

'Your behaviour has ever been kind and noble.' said Rose, mastering the emotions by which she was agitated. 'As you believe that I am not insensible or ungrateful, so hear my answer.'

'It is, that I may endeavour to deserve you; it is, dear Rose?'

'It is,' replied Rose, 'that you must endeavour to forget me; not as your old and dearly-attached companion, for that would wound me deeply; but, as the object of your love. Look into the world; think how many hearts you would be proud to gain, are there. Confide some other passion to me, if you will; I will be the truest, warmest, and most faithful friend you have.'

There was a pause, during which, Rose, who had covered her face with one hand, gave free vent to her tears. Harry still retained the other.

'And your reasons, Rose,' he said, at length, in a low voice; 'your reasons for this decision?'

'You have a right to know them,' rejoined Rose. 'You can say nothing to alter my resolution. It is a duty that I must perform. I owe it, alike to others, and to myself.'

'To yourself?'

'Yes, Harry. I owe it to myself, that I, a friendless, portionless, girl, with a blight upon my name, should not give your friends reason to suspect that I had sordidly yielded to your first passion, and fastened myself, a clog, on all your hopes and projects. I owe it to you and yours, to prevent you from opposing, in the warmth of your generous nature, this great obstacle to your progress in the world.'

'If your inclinations chime with your sense of duty—' Harry began.

'They do not,' replied Rose, colouring deeply.

'Then you return my love?' said Harry. 'Say but that, dear Rose; say but that; and soften the bitterness of this hard disappointment!'

'If I could have done so, without doing heavy wrong to him I loved,' rejoined Rose, 'I could have—'

'Have received this declaration very differently?' said Harry. 'Do not conceal that from me, at least, Rose.'

'I could,' said Rose. 'Stay!' she added, disengaging her hand, 'why should we prolong this painful interview? Most painful to me, and yet productive of lasting happiness, notwithstanding; for it will be happiness to know that I once held the high place in your regard which I now occupy, and every triumph you achieve in life will animate me with new fortitude and firmness. Farewell, Harry! As we have met to-day, we meet no more; but in other relations than those in which this conversation have placed us, we may be long and happily entwined; and may every blessing that the prayers of a true and earnest heart can call down from the source of all truth and sincerity, cheer and prosper you!'

'Another word, Rose,' said Harry. 'Your reason in your own words. From your own lips, let me hear it!'

'The prospect before you,' answered Rose, firmly, 'is a brilliant one. All the honours to which great talents and powerful connections can help men in public life, are in store for you. But those connections are proud; and I will neither mingle with such as may hold in scorn the mother who gave me life; nor bring disgrace or failure on the son of her who has so well supplied that mother's place. In a word,' said the young lady, turning away, as her temporary firmness forsook her, 'there is a stain upon my name, which the world visits on innocent heads. I will carry it into no blood but my own; and the reproach shall rest alone on me.'

'One word more, Rose. Dearest Rose! one more!' cried Harry, throwing himself before her. 'If I had been less—less fortunate, the world would call it—if some obscure and peaceful life had been my destiny—if I had been poor, sick, helpless—would you have turned from me then? Or has my probable advancement to riches and honour, given this scruple birth?'

'Do not press me to reply,' answered Rose. 'The question does not arise, and never will. It is unfair, almost unkind, to urge it.'

'If your answer be what I almost dare to hope it is,' retorted Harry, 'it will shed a gleam of happiness upon my lonely way, and light the path before me. It is not an idle thing to do so much, by the utterance of a few brief words, for one who loves you beyond all else. Oh, Rose: in the name of my ardent and enduring attachment; in the name of all I have suffered for you, and all you doom me to undergo; answer me this one question!'

'Then, if your lot had been differently cast,' rejoined Rose; 'if you had been even a little, but not so far, above me; if I could have been a help and comfort to you in any humble scene of peace and retirement, and not a blot and drawback in ambitious and distinguished crowds; I should have been spared this trial. I have every reason to be happy, very happy, now; but then, Harry, I own I should have been happier.'

Busy recollections of old hopes, cherished as a girl, long ago, crowded into the mind of Rose, while making this avowal; but they brought tears with them, as old hopes will when they come back withered; and they relieved her.

'I cannot help this weakness, and it makes my purpose stronger,' said Rose, extending her hand. 'I must leave you now, indeed.'

'I ask one promise,' said Harry. 'Once, and only once more,—say within a year, but it may be much sooner,—I may speak to you again on this subject, for the last time.'

'Not to press me to alter my right determination,' replied Rose, with a melancholy smile; 'it will be useless.'

'No,' said Harry; 'to hear you repeat it, if you will—finally repeat it! I will lay at your feet, whatever of station of fortune I may possess; and if you still adhere to your present resolution, will not seek, by word or act, to change it.'

'Then let it be so,' rejoined Rose; 'it is but one pang the more, and by that time I may be enabled to bear it better.'

She extended her hand again. But the young man caught her to his bosom; and imprinting one kiss on her beautiful forehead, hurried from the room.

CHAPTER XXXVI. IS A VERY SHORT ONE, AND MAY APPEAR OF NO GREAT IMPORTANCE IN ITS PLACE, BUT IT SHOULD BE READ NOTWITHSTANDING, AS A SEQUEL TO THE LAST, AND A KEY TO ONE THAT WILL FOLLOW WHEN ITS TIME ARRIVES

'And so you are resolved to be my travelling companion this morning; eh?' said the doctor, as Harry Maylie joined him and Oliver at the breakfast-table. 'Why, you are not in the same mind or intention two half-hours together!'

'You will tell me a different tale one of these days,' said Harry, colouring without any perceptible reason.

'I hope I may have good cause to do so,' replied Mr. Losberne; 'though I confess I don't think I shall. But yesterday morning you had made up your mind, in a great hurry, to stay here, and to accompany your mother, like a dutiful son, to the sea-side. Before noon, you announce that you are going to do me the honour of accompanying me as far as I go, on your road to London. And at night, you urge me, with great mystery, to start before the ladies are stirring; the consequence of which is, that young Oliver here is pinned down to his breakfast when he ought to be ranging the meadows after botanical phenomena of all kinds. Too bad, isn't it, Oliver?'

'I should have been very sorry not to have been at home when you and Mr. Maylie went away, sir,' rejoined Oliver.

'That's a fine fellow,' said the doctor; 'you shall come and see me when you return. But, to speak seriously, Harry; has any communication from the great nobs produced this sudden anxiety on your part to be gone?'

'The great nobs,' replied Harry, 'under which designation, I presume, you include my most stately uncle, have not communicated with me at all, since I have been here; nor, at this time of the year, is it likely that anything would occur to render necessary my immediate attendance among them.'

'Well,' said the doctor, 'you are a queer fellow. But of course they will get you into parliament at the election before Christmas, and these sudden shiftings and changes are no bad preparation for political life. There's something in that. Good training is always desirable, whether the race be for place, cup, or sweepstakes.'

Harry Maylie looked as if he could have followed up this short dialogue by one or two remarks that would have staggered the doctor not a little; but he contented himself with saying, 'We shall see,' and pursued the subject no farther. The post-chaise drove up to the door shortly afterwards; and Giles coming in for the luggage, the good doctor bustled out, to see it packed.

'Oliver,' said Harry Maylie, in a low voice, 'let me speak a word with you.'

Oliver walked into the window-recess to which Mr. Maylie beckoned him; much surprised at the mixture of sadness and boisterous spirits, which his whole behaviour displayed.

'You can write well now?' said Harry, laying his hand upon his arm.

'I hope so, sir,' replied Oliver.

'I shall not be at home again, perhaps for some time; I wish you would write to me—say once a fort-night: every alternate Monday: to the General Post Office in London. Will you?'

'Oh! certainly, sir; I shall be proud to do it,' exclaimed Oliver, greatly delighted with the commission.

'I should like to know how—how my mother and Miss Maylie are,' said the young man; 'and you can fill up a sheet by telling me what walks you take, and what you talk about, and whether she—they, I mean—seem happy and quite well. You understand me?'

'Oh! quite, sir, quite,' replied Oliver.

'I would rather you did not mention it to them,' said Harry, hurrying over his words; 'because it might make my mother anxious to write to me oftener, and it is a trouble and worry to her. Let it be a secret between you and me; and mind you tell me everything! I depend upon you.'

Oliver, quite elated and honoured by a sense of his importance, faithfully promised to be secret and explicit in his communications. Mr. Maylie took leave of him, with many assurances of his regard and protection.

The doctor was in the chaise; Giles (who, it had been arranged, should be left behind) held the door open in his hand; and the women-servants were in the garden, looking on. Harry cast one slight glance at the latticed window, and jumped into the carriage.

'Drive on!' he cried, 'hard, fast, full gallop! Nothing short of flying will keep pace with me, to-day.'

'Halloa!' cried the doctor, letting down the front glass in a great hurry, and shouting to the postillion; 'something very short of flying will keep pace with me. Do you hear?'

Jingling and clattering, till distance rendered its noise inaudible, and its rapid progress only perceptible to the eye, the vehicle wound its way along the road, almost hidden in a cloud of dust: now wholly disappearing, and now becoming visible again, as intervening objects, or the intricacies of the way, permitted. It was not until even the dusty cloud was no longer to be seen, that the gazers dispersed.

And there was one looker-on, who remained with eyes fixed upon the spot where the carriage had disappeared, long after it was many miles away; for, behind the white curtain which had shrouded her from view when Harry raised his eyes towards the window, sat Rose herself.

'He seems in high spirits and happy,' she said, at length. 'I feared for a time he might be otherwise. I was mistaken. I am very, very glad.'

Tears are signs of gladness as well as grief; but those which coursed down Rose's face, as she sat pensively at the window, still gazing in the same direction, seemed to tell more of sorrow than of joy.

CHAPTER XXXVII. IN WHICH THE READER MAY PERCEIVE A CONTRAST, NOT UNCOMMON IN MATRIMONIAL CASES

Mr. Bumble sat in the workhouse parlour, with his eyes moodily fixed on the cheerless grate, whence, as it was summer time, no brighter gleam proceeded, than the reflection of certain sickly rays of the sun, which were sent back from its cold and shining surface. A paper fly-cage dangled from the ceiling, to which he occasionally raised his eyes in gloomy thought; and, as the heedless insects hovered round the gaudy net-work, Mr. Bumble would heave a deep sigh, while a more gloomy shadow overspread his countenance. Mr. Bumble was meditating; it might be that the insects brought to mind, some painful passage in his own past life.

Nor was Mr. Bumble's gloom the only thing calculated to awaken a pleasing melancholy in the bosom of a spectator. There were not wanting other appearances, and those closely connected with his own person, which announced that a great change had taken place in the position of his affairs. The laced coat, and the cocked hat; where were they? He still wore knee-breeches, and dark cotton stockings on his nether limbs; but they were not the breeches. The coat was wide-skirted; and in that respect like the coat, but, oh how different! The mighty cocked hat was replaced by a modest round one. Mr. Bumble was no longer a beadle.

There are some promotions in life, which, independent of the more substantial rewards they offer, require peculiar value and dignity from the coats and waistcoats connected with them. A field-marshal has his uniform; a bishop his silk apron; a counsellor his silk gown; a beadle his cocked hat. Strip the bishop of his apron, or the beadle of his hat and lace; what are they? Men. Mere men. Dignity, and even holiness too, sometimes, are more questions of coat and waistcoat than some people imagine.

Mr. Bumble had married Mrs. Corney, and was master of the workhouse. Another beadle had come into power. On him the cocked hat, gold-laced coat, and staff, had all three descended.

'And to-morrow two months it was done!' said Mr. Bumble, with a sigh. 'It seems a age.'

Mr. Bumble might have meant that he had concentrated a whole existence of happiness into the short space of eight weeks; but the sigh—there was a vast deal of meaning in the sigh.

'I sold myself,' said Mr. Bumble, pursuing the same train of relection, 'for six teaspoons, a pair of sugar-tongs, and a milk-pot; with a small quantity of second-hand furniture, and twenty pound in money. I went very reasonable. Cheap, dirt cheap!'

'Cheap!' cried a shrill voice in Mr. Bumble's ear: 'you would have been dear at any price; and dear enough I paid for you, Lord above knows that!'

Mr. Bumble turned, and encountered the face of his interesting consort, who, imperfectly comprehending the few words she had overheard of his complaint, had hazarded the foregoing remark at a venture.

'Mrs. Bumble, ma'am!' said Mr. Bumble, with a sentimental sternness.

'Well!' cried the lady.

'Have the goodness to look at me,' said Mr. Bumble, fixing his eyes upon her. ('If she stands such a eye as that,' said Mr. Bumble to himself, 'she can stand anything. It is a eye I never knew to fail with paupers. If it fails with her, my power is gone.')

Whether an exceedingly small expansion of eye be sufficient to quell paupers, who, being lightly fed, are in no very high condition; or whether the late Mrs. Corney was particularly proof against eagle glances; are matters of opinion. The matter of fact, is, that the matron was in no way overpowered by Mr. Bumble's scowl, but, on the contrary, treated it with great disdain, and even raised a laugh thereat, which sounded as though it were genuine.

On hearing this most unexpected sound, Mr. Bumble looked, first incredulous, and afterwards amazed. He then relapsed into his former state; nor did he rouse himself until his attention was again awakened by the voice of his partner.

'Are you going to sit snoring there, all day?' inquired Mrs. Bumble.

'I am going to sit here, as long as I think proper, ma'am,' rejoined Mr. Bumble; 'and although I was not snoring, I shall snore, gape, sneeze, laugh, or cry, as the humour strikes me; such being my prerogative.'

'Your prerogative!' sneered Mrs. Bumble, with ineffable contempt.

'I said the word, ma'am,' said Mr. Bumble. 'The prerogative of a man is to command.'

'And what's the prerogative of a woman, in the name of Goodness?' cried the relict of Mr. Corney deceased.

'To obey, ma'am,' thundered Mr. Bumble. 'Your late unfortunate husband should have taught it you; and then, perhaps, he might have been alive now. I wish he was, poor man!'

Mrs. Bumble, seeing at a glance, that the decisive moment had now arrived, and that a blow struck for the mastership on one side or other, must necessarily be final and conclusive, no sooner heard this allusion to the dead and gone, than she dropped into a chair, and with a loud scream that Mr. Bumble was a hard-hearted brute, fell into a paroxysm of tears.

But, tears were not the things to find their way to Mr. Bumble's soul; his heart was waterproof. Like washable beaver hats that improve with rain, his nerves were rendered stouter and more vigorous, by showers of tears, which, being tokens of weakness, and so far tacit admissions of his own power, pleased and exalted him. He eyed his good lady with looks of great satisfaction, and begged, in an encouraging manner, that she should cry her hardest: the exercise being looked upon, by the faculty, as strongly conducive to health.

'It opens the lungs, washes the countenance, exercises the eyes, and softens down the temper,' said Mr. Bumble. 'So cry away.'

As he discharged himself of this pleasantry, Mr. Bumble took his hat from a peg, and putting it on, rather rakishly, on one side, as a man might, who felt he had asserted his superiority in a becoming manner, thrust his hands into his pockets, and sauntered towards the door, with much ease and waggishness depicted in his whole appearance.

Now, Mrs. Corney that was, had tried the tears, because they were less troublesome than a manual assault; but, she was quite prepared to make trial of the latter mode of proceeding, as Mr. Bumble was not long in discovering.

The first proof he experienced of the fact, was conveyed in a hollow sound, immediately succeeded by the sudden flying off of his hat to the opposite end of the room. This preliminary proceeding laying bare his head, the expert lady, clasping him tightly round the throat with one hand, inflicted a shower of blows (dealt with singular vigour and dexterity) upon it with the other. This done, she created a little variety by scratching his face, and tearing his hair; and, having, by this time, inflicted as much punishment as she deemed necessary for the offence, she pushed him over a chair, which was luckily well situated for the purpose: and defied him to talk about his prerogative again, if he dared.

'Get up!' said Mrs. Bumble, in a voice of command. 'And take yourself away from here, unless you want me to do something desperate.'

Mr. Bumble rose with a very rueful countenance: wondering much what something desperate might be. Picking up his hat, he looked towards the door.

'Are you going?' demanded Mrs. Bumble.

'Certainly, my dear, certainly,' rejoined Mr. Bumble, making a quicker motion towards the door. 'I didn't intend to—I'm going, my dear! You are so very violent, that really I—'

At this instant, Mrs. Bumble stepped hastily forward to replace the carpet, which had been kicked up in the scuffle. Mr. Bumble immediately darted out of the room, without bestowing another thought on his unfinished sentence: leaving the late Mrs. Corney in full possession of the field.

Mr. Bumble was fairly taken by surprise, and fairly beaten. He had a decided propensity for bullying: derived no inconsiderable pleasure from the exercise of petty cruelty; and, consequently, was (it is needless to say) a coward. This is by no means a disparagement to his character; for many official personages, who are held in high respect and admiration, are the victims of similar infirmities. The remark is made, indeed, rather in his favour than otherwise, and with a view of impressing the reader with a just sense of his qualifications for office.

But, the measure of his degradation was not yet full. After making a tour of the house, and thinking, for the first time, that the poor-laws really were too hard on people; and that men who ran away from their wives, leaving them chargeable to the parish, ought, in justice to be visited with no punishment at all, but rather rewarded as meritorious individuals who had suffered much; Mr. Bumble came to a room where some of the female paupers were usually employed in washing the parish linen: when the sound of voices in conversation, now proceeded.

'Hem!' said Mr. Bumble, summoning up all his native dignity. 'These women at least shall continue to respect the prerogative. Hallo! hallo there! What do you mean by this noise, you hussies?'

With these words, Mr. Bumble opened the door, and walked in with a very fierce and angry manner: which was at once exchanged for a most humiliated and cowering air, as his eyes unexpectedly rested on the form of his lady wife.

'My dear,' said Mr. Bumble, 'I didn't know you were here.'

'Didn't know I was here!' repeated Mrs. Bumble. 'What do you do here?'

'I thought they were talking rather too much to be doing their work properly, my dear,' replied Mr. Bumble: glancing distractedly at a couple of old women at the wash-tub, who were comparing notes of admiration at the workhouse-master's humility.

'You thought they were talking too much?' said Mrs. Bumble. 'What business is it of yours?'

'Why, my dear—' urged Mr. Bumble submissively.

'What business is it of yours?' demanded Mrs. Bumble, again.

'It's very true, you're matron here, my dear,' submitted Mr. Bumble; 'but I thought you mightn't be in the way just then.'

'I'll tell you what, Mr. Bumble,' returned his lady. 'We don't want any of your interference. You're a great deal too fond of poking your nose into things that don't concern you, making everybody in the house laugh, the moment your back is turned, and making yourself look like a fool every hour in the day. Be off; come!'

Mr. Bumble, seeing with excruciating feelings, the delight of the two old paupers, who were tittering together most rapturously, hesitated for an instant. Mrs. Bumble, whose patience brooked no delay, caught up a bowl of soap-suds, and motioning him towards the door, ordered him instantly to depart, on pain of receiving the contents upon his portly person.

What could Mr. Bumble do? He looked dejectedly round, and slunk away; and, as he reached the door, the titterings of the paupers broke into a shrill chuckle of irrepressible delight. It wanted but this. He was degraded in their eyes; he had lost caste and station before the very paupers; he had fallen from all the height and pomp of beadleship, to the lowest depth of the most snubbed hen-peckery.

'All in two months!' said Mr. Bumble, filled with dismal thoughts. 'Two months! No more than two months ago, I was not only my own master, but everybody else's, so far as the porochial workhouse was concerned, and now!—'

It was too much. Mr. Bumble boxed the ears of the boy who opened the gate for him (for he had reached the portal in his reverie); and walked, distractedly, into the street.

He walked up one street, and down another, until exercise had abated the first passion of his grief; and then the revulsion of feeling made him thirsty. He passed a great many public-houses; but, at length paused before one in a by-way, whose parlour, as he gathered from a hasty peep over the blinds, was deserted, save by one solitary customer. It began to rain, heavily, at the moment. This determined him. Mr. Bumble stepped in; and ordering something to drink, as he passed the bar, entered the apartment into which he had looked from the street.

The man who was seated there, was tall and dark, and wore a large cloak. He had the air of a stranger; and seemed, by a certain haggardness in his look, as well as by the dusty soils on his dress, to have travelled some distance. He eyed Bumble askance, as he entered, but scarcely deigned to nod his head in acknowledgment of his salutation.

Mr. Bumble had quite dignity enough for two; supposing even that the stranger had been more familiar: so he drank his gin-and-water in silence, and read the paper with great show of pomp and circumstance.

It so happened, however: as it will happen very often, when men fall into company under such circumstances: that Mr. Bumble felt, every now and then, a powerful inducement, which he could not resist, to steal a look at the stranger: and that whenever he did so, he withdrew his eyes, in some confusion, to find that the stranger was at that moment stealing a look at him. Mr. Bumble's awkwardness was enhanced by the very remarkable expression of the stranger's eye, which was keen and bright, but shadowed by a scowl of distrust and suspicion, unlike anything he had ever observed before, and repulsive to behold.

When they had encountered each other's glance several times in this way, the stranger, in a harsh, deep voice, broke silence.

'Were you looking for me,' he said, 'when you peered in at the window?'

'Not that I am aware of, unless you're Mr.—' Here Mr. Bumble stopped short; for he was curious to know the stranger's name, and thought in his impatience, he might supply the blank.

'I see you were not,' said the stranger; an expression of quiet sarcasm playing about his mouth; 'or you have known my name. You don't know it. I would recommend you not to ask for it.'

'I meant no harm, young man,' observed Mr. Bumble, majestically.

'And have done none,' said the stranger.

Another silence succeeded this short dialogue: which was again broken by the stranger.

'I have seen you before, I think?' said he. 'You were differently dressed at that time, and I only passed you in the street, but I should know you again. You were beadle here, once; were you not?'

'I was,' said Mr. Bumble, in some surprise; 'porochial beadle.'

'Just so,' rejoined the other, nodding his head. 'It was in that character I saw you. What are you now?'

'Master of the workhouse,' rejoined Mr. Bumble, slowly and impressively, to check any undue familiarity the stranger might otherwise assume. 'Master of the workhouse, young man!'

'You have the same eye to your own interest, that you always had, I doubt not?' resumed the stranger, looking keenly into Mr. Bumble's eyes, as he raised them in astonishment at the question.

'Don't scruple to answer freely, man. I know you pretty well, you see.'

'I suppose, a married man,' replied Mr. Bumble, shading his eyes with his hand, and surveying the stranger, from head to foot, in evident perplexity, 'is not more averse to turning an honest penny when he can, than a single one. Porochial officers are not so well paid that they can afford to refuse any little extra fee, when it comes to them in a civil and proper manner.'

The stranger smiled, and nodded his head again: as much to say, he had not mistaken his man; then rang the bell.

'Fill this glass again,' he said, handing Mr. Bumble's empty tumbler to the landlord. 'Let it be strong and hot. You like it so, I suppose?'

'Not too strong,' replied Mr. Bumble, with a delicate cough.

'You understand what that means, landlord!' said the stranger, drily.

The host smiled, disappeared, and shortly afterwards returned with a steaming jorum: of which, the first gulp brought the water into Mr. Bumble's eyes.

'Now listen to me,' said the stranger, after closing the door and window. 'I came down to this place, to-day, to find you out; and, by one of those chances which the devil throws in the way of his friends sometimes, you walked into the very room I was sitting in, while you were uppermost in my mind. I want some information from you. I don't ask you to give it for nothing, slight as it is. Put up that, to begin with.'

As he spoke, he pushed a couple of sovereigns across the table to his companion, carefully, as though unwilling that the chinking of money should be heard without. When Mr. Bumble had scrupulously examined the coins, to see that they were genuine, and had put them up, with much satisfaction, in his waistcoat-pocket, he went on:

'Carry your memory back—let me see—twelve years, last winter.'

'It's a long time,' said Mr. Bumble. 'Very good. I've done it.'

'The scene, the workhouse.'

'Good!'

'And the time, night.'

'Yes.'

'And the place, the crazy hole, wherever it was, in which miserable drabs brought forth the life and health so often denied to themselves—gave birth to puling children for the parish to rear; and hid their shame, rot 'em in the grave!'

'The lying-in room, I suppose?' said Mr. Bumble, not quite following the stranger's excited description.

'Yes,' said the stranger. 'A boy was born there.'

'A many boys,' observed Mr. Bumble, shaking his head, despondingly.

'A murrain on the young devils!' cried the stranger; 'I speak of one; a meek-looking, pale-faced boy, who was apprenticed down here, to a coffin-maker—I wish he had made his coffin, and screwed his body in it—and who afterwards ran away to London, as it was supposed.'

'Why, you mean Oliver! Young Twist!' said Mr. Bumble; 'I remember him, of course. There wasn't a obstinater young rascal—'

'It's not of him I want to hear; I've heard enough of him,' said the stranger, stopping Mr. Bumble in the outset of a tirade on the subject of poor Oliver's vices. 'It's of a woman; the hag that nursed his mother. Where is she?'

'Where is she?' said Mr. Bumble, whom the gin-and-water had rendered facetious. 'It would be hard to tell. There's no midwifery there, whichever place she's gone to; so I suppose she's out of employment, anyway.'

'What do you mean?' demanded the stranger, sternly.

'That she died last winter,' rejoined Mr. Bumble.

The man looked fixedly at him when he had given this information, and although he did not withdraw his eyes for some time afterwards, his gaze gradually became vacant and abstracted, and he seemed lost in thought. For some time, he appeared doubtful whether he ought to be relieved or disappointed by the intelligence; but at length he breathed more freely; and withdrawing his eyes, observed that it was no great matter. With that he rose, as if to depart.

But Mr. Bumble was cunning enough; and he at once saw that an opportunity was opened, for the lucrative disposal of some secret in the possession of his better half. He well remembered the night of old Sally's death, which the occurrences of that day had given him good reason to recollect, as the occasion on which he had proposed to Mrs. Corney; and although that lady had never confided to him the disclosure of which she had been the solitary witness, he had heard enough to know that it related to something that had occurred in the old woman's attendance, as workhouse nurse, upon the young mother of Oliver Twist. Hastily calling this circumstance to mind, he informed the stranger, with an air of mystery, that one woman had been closeted with the old harridan shortly before she died; and that she could, as he had reason to believe, throw some light on the subject of his inquiry.

'How can I find her?' said the stranger, thrown off his guard; and plainly showing that all his fears (whatever they were) were aroused afresh by the intelligence.

'Only through me,' rejoined Mr. Bumble.

'When?' cried the stranger, hastily.

'To-morrow,' rejoined Bumble.

'At nine in the evening,' said the stranger, producing a scrap of paper, and writing down upon it, an obscure address by the water-side, in characters that betrayed his agitation; 'at nine in the evening, bring her to me there. I needn't tell you to be secret. It's your interest.'

With these words, he led the way to the door, after stopping to pay for the liquor that had been drunk. Shortly remarking that their roads were different, he departed, without more ceremony than an emphatic repetition of the hour of appointment for the following night.

On glancing at the address, the parochial functionary observed that it contained no name. The stranger had not gone far, so he made after him to ask it.

'What do you want?' cried the man, turning quickly round, as Bumble touched him on the arm. 'Following me?'

'Only to ask a question,' said the other, pointing to the scrap of paper. 'What name am I to ask for?'

'Monks!' rejoined the man; and strode hastily, away.

CHAPTER XXXVIII. CONTAINING AN ACCOUNT OF WHAT PASSED BETWEEN MR. AND MRS. BUMBLE, AND MR. MONKS, AT THEIR NOCTURNAL INTERVIEW

It was a dull, close, overcast summer evening. The clouds, which had been threatening all day, spread out in a dense and sluggish mass of vapour, already yielded large drops of rain, and seemed to presage a violent thunder-storm, when Mr. and Mrs. Bumble, turning out of the main street of the town, directed their course towards a scattered little colony of ruinous houses, distant from it some mile and a-half, or thereabouts, and erected on a low unwholesome swamp, bordering upon the river.

They were both wrapped in old and shabby outer garments, which might, perhaps, serve the double purpose of protecting their persons from the rain, and sheltering them from observation. The husband carried a lantern, from which, however, no light yet shone; and trudged on, a few paces in front, as though—the way being dirty—to give his wife the benefit of treading in his heavy footprints. They went on, in profound silence; every now and then, Mr. Bumble relaxed his pace, and turned his head as if to make sure that his helpmate was following; then, discovering that she was close at his heels, he mended his rate of walking, and proceeded, at a considerable increase of speed, towards their place of destination.

This was far from being a place of doubtful character; for it had long been known as the residence of none but low ruffians, who, under various pretences of living by their labour, subsisted chiefly on plunder and crime. It was a collection of mere hovels: some, hastily built with loose bricks: others, of old worm-eaten ship-timber: jumbled together without any attempt at order or arrangement, and planted, for the most part, within a few feet of the river's bank. A few leaky boats drawn up on the mud, and made fast to the dwarf wall which skirted it: and here and there an oar or coil of rope: appeared, at first, to indicate that the inhabitants of these miserable cottages pursued some avocation on the river; but a glance at the shattered and useless condition of the articles thus displayed, would have led a passer-by, without much difficulty, to the conjecture that they were disposed there, rather for the preservation of appearances, than with any view to their being actually employed.

In the heart of this cluster of huts; and skirting the river, which its upper stories overhung; stood a large building, formerly used as a manufactory of some kind. It had, in its day, probably furnished employment to the inhabitants of the surrounding tenements. But it had long since gone to ruin. The rat, the worm, and the action of the damp, had weakened and rotted the piles on which it stood; and a considerable portion of the building had already sunk down into the water; while the remainder, tottering and bending over the dark stream, seemed to wait a favourable opportunity of following its old companion, and involving itself in the same fate.

It was before this ruinous building that the worthy couple paused, as the first peal of distant thunder reverberated in the air, and the rain commenced pouring violently down.

'The place should be somewhere here,' said Bumble, consulting a scrap of paper he held in his hand.

'Halloa there!' cried a voice from above.

Following the sound, Mr. Bumble raised his head and descried a man looking out of a door, breast-high, on the second story.

'Stand still, a minute,' cried the voice; 'I'll be with you directly.' With which the head disappeared, and the door closed.

'Is that the man?' asked Mr. Bumble's good lady.

Mr. Bumble nodded in the affirmative.

'Then, mind what I told you,' said the matron: 'and be careful to say as little as you can, or you'll betray us at once.'

Mr. Bumble, who had eyed the building with very rueful looks, was apparently about to express some doubts relative to the advisability of proceeding any further with the enterprise just then, when he was prevented by the appearance of Monks: who opened a small door, near which they stood, and beckoned them inwards.

'Come in!' he cried impatiently, stamping his foot upon the ground. 'Don't keep me here!'

The woman, who had hesitated at first, walked boldly in, without any other invitation. Mr. Bumble, who was ashamed or afraid to lag behind, followed: obviously very ill at ease and with scarcely any of that remarkable dignity which was usually his chief characteristic.

'What the devil made you stand lingering there, in the wet?' said Monks, turning round, and addressing Bumble, after he had bolted the door behind them.

'We—we were only cooling ourselves,' stammered Bumble, looking apprehensively about him.

'Cooling yourselves!' retorted Monks. 'Not all the rain that ever fell, or ever will fall, will put as much of hell's fire out, as a man can carry about with him. You won't cool yourself so easily; don't think it!'

With this agreeable speech, Monks turned short upon the matron, and bent his gaze upon her, till even she, who was not easily cowed, was fain to withdraw her eyes, and turn them towards the ground.

'This is the woman, is it?' demanded Monks.

'Hem! That is the woman,' replied Mr. Bumble, mindful of his wife's caution.

'You think women never can keep secrets, I suppose?' said the matron, interposing, and returning, as she spoke, the searching look of Monks.

'I know they will always keep one till it's found out,' said Monks.

'And what may that be?' asked the matron.

'The loss of their own good name,' replied Monks. 'So, by the same rule, if a woman's a party to a secret that might hang or transport her, I'm not afraid of her telling it to anybody;

not I! Do you understand, mistress?'

'No,' rejoined the matron, slightly colouring as she spoke.

'Of course you don't!' said Monks. 'How should you?'

Bestowing something half-way between a smile and a frown upon his two companions, and again beckoning them to follow him, the man hastened across the apartment, which was of considerable extent, but low in the roof. He was preparing to ascend a steep staircase, or rather ladder, leading to another floor of warehouses above: when a bright flash of lightning streamed down the aperture, and a peal of thunder followed, which shook the crazy building to its centre.

'Hear it!' he cried, shrinking back. 'Hear it! Rolling and crashing on as if it echoed through a thousand caverns where the devils were hiding from it. I hate the sound!'

He remained silent for a few moments; and then, removing his hands suddenly from his face, showed, to the unspeakable discomposure of Mr. Bumble, that it was much distorted and discoloured.

'These fits come over me, now and then,' said Monks, observing his alarm; 'and thunder sometimes brings them on. Don't mind me now; it's all over for this once.'

Thus speaking, he led the way up the ladder; and hastily closing the window-shutter of the room into which it led, lowered a lantern which hung at the end of a rope and pulley passed through one of the heavy beams in the ceiling: and which cast a dim light upon an old table and three chairs that were placed beneath it.

'Now,' said Monks, when they had all three seated themselves, 'the sooner we come to our business, the better for all. The woman know what it is, does she?'

The question was addressed to Bumble; but his wife anticipated the reply, by intimating that she was perfectly acquainted with it.

'He is right in saying that you were with this hag the night she died; and that she told you something—'

'About the mother of the boy you named,' replied the matron interrupting him. 'Yes.'

'The first question is, of what nature was her communication?' said Monks.

'That's the second,' observed the woman with much deliberation. 'The first is, what may the communication be worth?'

'Who the devil can tell that, without knowing of what kind it is?' asked Monks.

'Nobody better than you, I am persuaded,' answered Mrs. Bumble: who did not want for spirit, as her yoke-fellow could abundantly testify.

'Humph!' said Monks significantly, and with a look of eager inquiry; 'there may be money's worth to get, eh?'

'Perhaps there may,' was the composed reply.

'Something that was taken from her,' said Monks. 'Something that she wore. Something that—'

'You had better bid,' interrupted Mrs. Bumble. 'I have heard enough, already, to assure me that you are the man I ought to talk to.'

Mr. Bumble, who had not yet been admitted by his better half into any greater share of the secret than he had originally possessed, listened to this dialogue with outstretched neck and distended eyes: which he directed towards his wife and Monks, by turns, in undisguised astonishment; increased, if possible, when the latter sternly demanded, what sum was required for the disclosure.

'What's it worth to you?' asked the woman, as collectedly as before.

'It may be nothing; it may be twenty pounds,' replied Monks. 'Speak out, and let me know which.'

'Add five pounds to the sum you have named; give me five-and-twenty pounds in gold,' said the woman; 'and I'll tell you all I know. Not before.'

'Five-and-twenty pounds!' exclaimed Monks, drawing back.

'I spoke as plainly as I could,' replied Mrs. Bumble. 'It's not a large sum, either.'

'Not a large sum for a paltry secret, that may be nothing when it's told!' cried Monks impatiently; 'and which has been lying dead for twelve years past or more!'

'Such matters keep well, and, like good wine, often double their value in course of time,' answered the matron, still preserving the resolute indifference she had assumed. 'As to lying dead, there are those who will lie dead for twelve thousand years to come, or twelve million, for anything you or I know, who will tell strange tales at last!'

'What if I pay it for nothing?' asked Monks, hesitating.

'You can easily take it away again,' replied the matron. 'I am but a woman; alone here; and unprotected.'

'Not alone, my dear, nor unprotected, neither,' submitted Mr. Bumble, in a voice tremulous with fear: 'I am here, my dear. And besides,' said Mr. Bumble, his teeth chattering as he spoke, 'Mr. Monks is too much of a gentleman to attempt any violence on porochial persons. Mr. Monks is aware that I am not a young man, my dear, and also that I am a little run to seed, as I may say; bu he has heerd: I say I have no doubt Mr. Monks has heerd, my dear: that I am a very determined officer, with very uncommon strength, if I'm once roused. I only want a little rousing; that's all.'

As Mr. Bumble spoke, he made a melancholy feint of grasping his lantern with fierce determination; and plainly showed, by the alarmed expression of every feature, that he did want a little rousing, and not a little, prior to making any very warlike demonstration: unless, indeed, against paupers, or other person or persons trained down for the purpose.

'You are a fool,' said Mrs. Bumble, in reply; 'and had better hold your tongue.'

'He had better have cut it out, before he came, if he can't speak in a lower tone,' said Monks, grimly. 'So! He's your husband, eh?'

'He my husband!' tittered the matron, parrying the question.

'I thought as much, when you came in,' rejoined Monks, marking the angry glance which the lady darted at her spouse as she spoke. 'So much the better; I have less hesitation in dealing with two people, when I find that there's only one will between them. I'm in earnest.

See here!'

He thrust his hand into a side-pocket; and producing a canvas bag, told out twenty-five sovereigns on the table, and pushed them over to the woman.

'Now,' he said, 'gather them up; and when this cursed peal of thunder, which I feel is coming up to break over the house-top, is gone, let's hear your story.'

The thunder, which seemed in fact much nearer, and to shiver and break almost over their heads, having subsided, Monks, raising his face from the table, bent forward to listen to what the woman should say. The faces of the three nearly touched, as the two men leant over the small table in their eagerness to hear, and the woman also leant forward to render her whisper audible. The sickly rays of the suspended lantern falling directly upon them, aggravated the paleness and anxiety of their countenances: which, encircled by the deepest gloom and darkness, looked ghastly in the extreme.

'When this woman, that we called old Sally, died,' the matron began, 'she and I were alone.'

'Was there no one by?' asked Monks, in the same hollow whisper; 'No sick wretch or idiot in some other bed? No one who could hear, and might, by possibility, understand?'

'Not a soul,' replied the woman; 'we were alone. I stood alone beside the body when death came over it.'

'Good,' said Monks, regarding her attentively. 'Go on.'

'She spoke of a young creature,' resumed the matron, 'who had brought a child into the world some years before; not merely in the same room, but in the same bed, in which she then lay dying.'

'Ay?' said Monks, with quivering lip, and glancing over his shoulder, 'Blood! How things come about!'

'The child was the one you named to him last night,' said the matron, nodding carelessly towards her husband; 'the mother this nurse had robbed.'

'In life?' asked Monks.

'In death,' replied the woman, with something like a shudder. 'She stole from the corpse, when it had hardly turned to one, that which the dead mother had prayed her, with her last breath, to keep for the infant's sake.'

'She sold it,' cried Monks, with desperate eagerness; 'did she sell it? Where? When? To whom? How long before?'

'As she told me, with great difficulty, that she had done this,' said the matron, 'she fell back and died.'

'Without saying more?' cried Monks, in a voice which, from its very suppression, seemed only the more furious. 'It's a lie! I'll not be played with. She said more. I'll tear the life out of you both, but I'll know what it was.'

'She didn't utter another word,' said the woman, to all appearance unmoved (as Mr. Bumble was very far from being) by the strange man's violence; 'but she clutched my gown, violently, with one hand, which was partly closed; and when I saw that she was dead, and so removed the hand by force, I found it clasped a scrap of dirty paper.'

'Which contained—' interposed Monks, stretching forward.

'Nothing,' replied the woman; 'it was a pawnbroker's duplicate.'

'For what?' demanded Monks.

'In good time I'll tell you.' said the woman. 'I judge that she had kept the trinket, for some time, in the hope of turning it to better account; and then had pawned it; and had saved or scraped together money to pay the pawnbroker's interest year by year, and prevent its running out; so that if anything came of it, it could still be redeemed. Nothing had come of it; and, as I tell you, she died with the scrap of paper, all worn and tattered, in her hand. The time was out in two days; I thought something might one day come of it too; and so redeemed the pledge.'

'Where is it now?' asked Monks quickly.

'There,' replied the woman. And, as if glad to be relieved of it, she hastily threw upon the table a small kid bag scarcely large enough for a French watch, which Monks pouncing upon, tore open with trembling hands. It contained a little gold locket: in which were two locks of hair, and a plain gold wedding-ring.

'It has the word "Agnes" engraved on the inside,' said the woman.

'There is a blank left for the surname; and then follows the date; which is within a year before the child was born. I found out that.'

'And this is all?' said Monks, after a close and eager scrutiny of the contents of the little packet.

'All,' replied the woman.

Mr. Bumble drew a long breath, as if he were glad to find that the story was over, and no mention made of taking the five-and-twenty pounds back again; and now he took courage to wipe the perspiration which had been trickling over his nose, unchecked, during the whole of the previous dialogue.

'I know nothing of the story, beyond what I can guess at,' said his wife addressing Monks, after a short silence; 'and I want to know nothing; for it's safer not. But I may ask you two questions, may I?'

'You may ask,' said Monks, with some show of surprise; 'but whether I answer or not is another question.'

'—Which makes three,' observed Mr. Bumble, essaying a stroke of facetiousness.

'Is that what you expected to get from me?' demanded the matron.

'It is,' replied Monks. 'The other question?'

'What do you propose to do with it? Can it be used against me?'

'Never,' rejoined Monks; 'nor against me either. See here! But don't move a step forward, or your life is not worth a bulrush.'

With these words, he suddenly wheeled the table aside, and pulling an iron ring in the boarding, threw back a large trap-door which opened close at Mr. Bumble's feet, and caused that gentleman to retire several paces backward, with great precipitation.

'Look down,' said Monks, lowering the lantern into the gulf. 'Don't fear me. I could have let you down, quietly enough, when you were seated over it, if that had been my game.'

Thus encouraged, the matron drew near to the brink; and even Mr. Bumble himself, impelled by curiosity, ventured to do the same. The turbid water, swollen by the heavy rain, was rushing rapidly on below; and all other sounds were lost in the noise of its plashing and eddying against the green and slimy piles. There had once been a water-mill beneath; the tide foaming and chafing round the few rotten stakes, and fragments of machinery that yet remained, seemed to dart onward, with a new impulse, when freed from the obstacles which had unavailingly attempted to stem its headlong course.

'If you flung a man's body down there, where would it be to-morrow morning?' said Monks, swinging the lantern to and fro in the dark well.

'Twelve miles down the river, and cut to pieces besides,' replied Bumble, recoiling at the thought.

Monks drew the little packet from his breast, where he had hurriedly thrust it; and tying it to a leaden weight, which had formed a part of some pulley, and was lying on the floor, dropped it into the stream. It fell straight, and true as a die; clove the water with a scarcely audible splash; and was gone.

The three looking into each other's faces, seemed to breathe more freely.

'There!' said Monks, closing the trap-door, which fell heavily back into its former position. 'If the sea ever gives up its dead, as books say it will, it will keep its gold and silver to itself, and that trash among it. We have nothing more to say, and may break up our pleasant party.'

'By all means,' observed Mr. Bumble, with great alacrity.

'You'll keep a quiet tongue in your head, will you?' said Monks, with a threatening look. 'I am not afraid of your wife.'

'You may depend upon me, young man,' answered Mr. Bumble, bowing himself gradually towards the ladder, with excessive politeness. 'On everybody's account, young man; on my own, you know, Mr. Monks.'

'I am glad, for your sake, to hear it,' remarked Monks. 'Light your lantern! And get away from here as fast as you can.'

It was fortunate that the conversation terminated at this point, or Mr. Bumble, who had bowed himself to within six inches of the ladder, would infallibly have pitched headlong into the room below. He lighted his lantern from that which Monks had detached from the rope, and now carried in his hand; and making no effort to prolong the discourse, descended in silence, followed by his wife. Monks brought up the rear, after pausing on the steps to satisfy himself that there were no other sounds to be heard than the beating of the rain without, and the rushing of the water.

They traversed the lower room, slowly, and with caution; for Monks started at every shadow; and Mr. Bumble, holding his lantern a foot above the ground, walked not only with remarkable care, but with a marvellously light step for a gentleman of his figure: looking nervously about him for hidden trap-doors. The gate at which they had entered, was softly unfastened and opened by Monks; merely exchanging a nod with their mysterious acquaintance, the married couple emerged into the wet and darkness outside.

They were no sooner gone, than Monks, who appeared to entertain an invincible repugnance to being left alone, called to a boy who had been hidden somewhere below. Bidding him go first, and bear the light, he returned to the chamber he had just quitted.

CHAPTER XXXIX. INTRODUCES SOME RESPECTABLE CHARACTERS WITH WHOM THE READER IS ALREADY ACQUAINTED, AND SHOWS HOW MONKS AND THE JEW LAID THEIR WORTHY HEADS TOGETHER

On the evening following that upon which the three worthies mentioned in the last chapter, disposed of their little matter of business as therein narrated, Mr. William Sikes, awakening from a nap, drowsily growled forth an inquiry what time of night it was.

The room in which Mr. Sikes propounded this question, was not one of those he had tenanted, previous to the Chertsey expedition, although it was in the same quarter of the town, and was situated at no great distance from his former lodgings. It was not, in appearance, so desirable a habitation as his old quarters: being a mean and badly-furnished apartment, of very limited size; lighted only by one small window in the shelving roof, and abutting on a close and dirty lane. Nor were there wanting other indications of the good gentleman's having gone down in the world of late: for a great scarcity of furniture, and total absence of comfort, together with the disappearance of all such small moveables as spare clothes and linen, bespoke a state of extreme poverty; while the meagre and attenuated condition of Mr. Sikes himself would have fully confirmed these symptoms, if they had stood in any need of corroboration.

The housebreaker was lying on the bed, wrapped in his white great-coat, by way of dressing-gown, and displaying a set of features in no degree improved by the cadaverous hue of illness, and the addition of a soiled nightcap, and a stiff, black beard of a week's growth. The dog sat at the bedside: now eyeing his master with a wistful look, and now pricking his ears, and uttering a low growl as some noise in the street, or in the lower part of the house, attracted his attention. Seated by the window, busily engaged in patching an old waistcoat which formed a portion of the robber's ordinary dress, was a female: so pale and reduced with watching and privation, that there would have been considerable difficulty in recognising her as the same Nancy who has already figured in this tale, but for the voice in which she replied to Mr. Sikes's question.

'Not long gone seven,' said the girl. 'How do you feel to-night, Bill?'

'As weak as water,' replied Mr. Sikes, with an imprecation on his eyes and limbs. 'Here; lend us a hand, and let me get off this thundering bed anyhow.'

Illness had not improved Mr. Sikes's temper; for, as the girl raised him up and led him to a chair, he muttered various curses on her awkwardness, and struck her.

'Whining are you?' said Sikes. 'Come! Don't stand snivelling there. If you can't do anything better than that, cut off altogether. D'ye hear me?'

'I hear you,' replied the girl, turning her face aside, and forcing a laugh. 'What fancy have you got in your head now?'

'Oh! you've thought better of it, have you?' growled Sikes, marking the tear which trembled in her eye. 'All the better for you, you have.'

'Why, you don't mean to say, you'd be hard upon me to-night, Bill,' said the girl, laying her hand upon his shoulder.

'No!' cried Mr. Sikes. 'Why not?'

'Such a number of nights,' said the girl, with a touch of woman's tenderness, which communicated something like sweetness of tone, even to her voice: 'such a number of nights as I've been patient with you, nursing and caring for you, as if you had been a child: and this the first that I've seen you like yourself; you wouldn't have served me as you did just now, if you'd thought of that, would you? Come, come; say you wouldn't.'

'Well, then,' rejoined Mr. Sikes, 'I wouldn't. Why, damme, now, the girls's whining again!'

'It's nothing,' said the girl, throwing herself into a chair. 'Don't you seem to mind me. It'll soon be over.'

'What'll be over?' demanded Mr. Sikes in a savage voice. 'What foolery are you up to, now, again? Get up and bustle about, and don't come over me with your woman's nonsense.'

At any other time, this remonstrance, and the tone in which it was delivered, would have had the desired effect; but the girl being really weak and exhausted, dropped her head over the back of the chair, and fainted, before Mr. Sikes could get out a few of the appropriate oaths with which, on similar occasions, he was accustomed to garnish his threats. Not knowing, very well, what to do, in this uncommon emergency; for Miss Nancy's hysterics were usually of that violent kind which the patient fights and struggles out of, without much assistance; Mr. Sikes tried a little blasphemy: and finding that mode of treatment wholly ineffectual, called for assistance.

'What's the matter here, my dear?' said Fagin, looking in.

'Lend a hand to the girl, can't you?' replied Sikes impatiently. 'Don't stand chattering and grinning at me!'

With an exclamation of surprise, Fagin hastened to the girl's assistance, while Mr. John Dawkins (otherwise the Artful Dodger), who had followed his venerable friend into the room, hastily deposited on the floor a bundle with which he was laden; and snatching a bottle from the grasp of Master Charles Bates who came close at his heels, uncorked it in a twinkling with his teeth, and poured a portion of its contents down the patient's throat: previously taking a taste, himself, to prevent mistakes.

'Give her a whiff of fresh air with the bellows, Charley,' said Mr. Dawkins; 'and you slap her hands, Fagin, while Bill undoes the petticuts.'

These united restoratives, administered with great energy: especially that department consigned to Master Bates, who appeared to consider his share in the proceedings, a piece of unexampled pleasantry: were not long in producing the desired effect. The girl gradually recovered her senses; and, staggering to a chair by the bedside, hid her face upon the pillow: leaving Mr. Sikes to confront the new comers, in some astonishment at their unlooked-for appearance.

'Why, what evil wind has blowed you here?' he asked Fagin.

'No evil wind at all, my dear, for evil winds blow nobody any good; and I've brought something good with me, that you'll be glad to see. Dodger, my dear, open the bundle; and give Bill the little trifles that we spent all our money on, this morning.'

In compliance with Mr. Fagin's request, the Artful untied this bundle, which was of large size, and formed of an old table-cloth; and handed the articles it contained, one by one, to Charley Bates: who placed them on the table, with various encomiums on their rarity and excellence.

'Sitch a rabbit pie, Bill,' exclaimed that young gentleman, disclosing to view a huge pasty; 'sitch delicate creeturs, with sitch tender limbs, Bill, that the wery bones melt in your mouth, and there's no occasion to pick 'em; half a pound of seven and six-penny green, so precious strong that if you mix it with biling water, it'll go nigh to blow the lid of the tea-pot off; a pound and a half of moist sugar that the niggers didn't work at all at, afore they got it up to sitch a pitch of goodness,—oh no! Two half-quartern brans; pound of best fresh; piece of double Glo'ster; and, to wind up all, some of the richest sort you ever lushed!'

Uttering this last panegyric, Master Bates produced, from one of his extensive pockets, a full-sized wine-bottle, carefully corked; while Mr. Dawkins, at the same instant, poured out a wine-glassful of raw spirits from the bottle he carried: which the invalid tossed down his throat without a moment's hesitation.

'Ah!' said Fagin, rubbing his hands with great satisfaction. 'You'll do, Bill; you'll do now.'

'Do!' exclaimed Mr. Sikes; 'I might have been done for, twenty times over, afore you'd have done anything to help me. What do you mean by leaving a man in this state, three weeks and more, you false-hearted wagabond?'

'Only hear him, boys!' said Fagin, shrugging his shoulders. 'And us come to bring him all these beau-ti-ful things.'

'The things is well enough in their way,' observed Mr. Sikes: a little soothed as he glanced over the table; 'but what have you got to say for yourself, why you should leave me here, down in the mouth, health, blunt, and everything else; and take no more notice of me, all this mortal time, than if I was that 'ere dog.—Drive him down, Charley!'

'I never see such a jolly dog as that,' cried Master Bates, doing as he was desired. 'Smelling the grub like a old lady a going to market! He'd make his fortun' on the stage that dog would, and rewive the drayma besides.'

'Hold your din,' cried Sikes, as the dog retreated under the bed: still growling angrily. 'What have you got to say for yourself, you withered old fence, eh?'

'I was away from London, a week and more, my dear, on a plant,' replied the Jew.

'And what about the other fortnight?' demanded Sikes. 'What about the other fortnight that you've left me lying here, like a sick rat in his hole?'

'I couldn't help it, Bill. I can't go into a long explanation before company; but I couldn't help it, upon my honour.'

'Upon your what?' growled Sikes, with excessive disgust. 'Here! Cut me off a piece of that pie, one of you boys, to take the taste of that out of my mouth, or it'll choke me dead.'

'Don't be out of temper, my dear,' urged Fagin, submissively. 'I have never forgot you, Bill; never once.'

'No! I'll pound it that you han't,' replied Sikes, with a bitter grin. 'You've been scheming and plotting away, every hour that I have laid shivering and burning here; and Bill was to do this; and Bill was to do that; and Bill was to do it all, dirt cheap, as soon as he got well: and was quite poor enough for your work. If it hadn't been for the girl, I might have died.'

'There now, Bill,' remonstrated Fagin, eagerly catching at the word. 'If it hadn't been for the girl! Who but poor ould Fagin was the means of your having such a handy girl about you?'

'He says true enough there!' said Nancy, coming hastily forward. 'Let him be; let him be.'

Nancy's appearance gave a new turn to the conversation; for the boys, receiving a sly wink from the wary old Jew, began to ply her with liquor: of which, however, she took very sparingly; while Fagin, assuming an unusual flow of spirits, gradually brought Mr. Sikes into a better temper, by affecting to regard his threats as a little pleasant banter; and, moreover, by laughing very heartily at one or two rough jokes, which, after repeated applications to the spirit-bottle, he condescended to make.

'It's all very well,' said Mr. Sikes; 'but I must have some blunt from you to-night.'

'I haven't a piece of coin about me,' replied the Jew.

'Then you've got lots at home,' retorted Sikes; 'and I must have some from there.'

'Lots!' cried Fagin, holding up is hands. 'I haven't so much as would—'

'I don't know how much you've got, and I dare say you hardly know yourself, as it would take a pretty long time to count it,' said Sikes; 'but I must have some to-night; and that's flat.'

'Well, well,' said Fagin, with a sigh, 'I'll send the Artful round presently.'

'You won't do nothing of the kind,' rejoined Mr. Sikes. 'The Artful's a deal too artful, and would forget to come, or lose his way, or get dodged by traps and so be perwented, or anything for an excuse, if you put him up to it. Nancy shall go to the ken and fetch it, to make all sure; and I'll lie down and have a snooze while she's gone.'

After a great deal of haggling and squabbling, Fagin beat down the amount of the required advance from five pounds to three pounds four and sixpence: protesting with many solemn asseverations that that would only leave him eighteen-pence to keep house with; Mr. Sikes sullenly remarking that if he couldn't get any more he must accompany him home; with the Dodger and Master Bates put the eatables in the cupboard. The Jew then, taking leave of his affectionate friend, returned homeward, attended by Nancy and the boys: Mr. Sikes, meanwhile, flinging himself on the bed, and composing himself to sleep away the time until the young lady's return.

In due course, they arrived at Fagin's abode, where they found Toby Crackit and Mr. Chitling intent upon their fifteenth game at cribbage, which it is scarcely necessary to say the latter gentleman lost, and with it, his fifteenth and last sixpence: much to the amusement of his young friends. Mr. Crackit, apparently somewhat ashamed at being found relaxing himself with a gentleman so much his inferior in station and mental endowments, yawned, and inquiring after Sikes, took up his hat to go.

'Has nobody been, Toby?' asked Fagin.

'Not a living leg,' answered Mr. Crackit, pulling up his collar; 'it's been as dull as swipes. You ought to stand something handsome, Fagin, to recompense me for keeping house so long. Damme, I'm as flat as a juryman; and should have gone to sleep, as fast as Newgate, if I hadn't had the good natur' to amuse this youngster. Horrid dull, I'm blessed if I an't!'

With these and other ejaculations of the same kind, Mr. Toby Crackit swept up his winnings, and crammed them into his waistcoat pocket with a haughty air, as though such small pieces of silver were wholly beneath the consideration of a man of his figure; this done, he swaggered out of the room, with so much elegance and gentility, that Mr. Chitling, bestowing numerous admiring glances on his legs and boots till they were out of sight, assured the company that he considered his acquaintance cheap at fifteen sixpences an interview, and that he didn't value his losses the snap of his little finger.

'Wot a rum chap you are, Tom!' said Master Bates, highly amused by this declaration.

'Not a bit of it,' replied Mr. Chitling. 'Am I, Fagin?'

'A very clever fellow, my dear,' said Fagin, patting him on the shoulder, and winking to his other pupils.

'And Mr. Crackit is a heavy swell; an't he, Fagin?' asked Tom.

'No doubt at all of that, my dear.'

'And it is a creditable thing to have his acquaintance; an't it, Fagin?' pursued Tom.

'Very much so, indeed, my dear. They're only jealous, Tom, because he won't give it to them.'

'Ah!' cried Tom, triumphantly, 'that's where it is! He has cleaned me out. But I can go and earn some more, when I like; can't I, Fagin?'

'To be sure you can, and the sooner you go the better, Tom; so make up your loss at once, and don't lose any more time. Dodger! Charley! It's time you were on the lay. Come! It's near ten, and nothing done yet.'

In obedience to this hint, the boys, nodding to Nancy, took up their hats, and left the room; the Dodger and his vivacious friend indulging, as they went, in many witticisms at the expense of Mr. Chitling; in whose conduct, it is but justice to say, there was nothing very conspicuous or peculiar: inasmuch as there are a great number of spirited young bloods upon town, who pay a much higher price than Mr. Chitling for being seen in good society: and a great number of fine gentlemen (composing the good society aforesaid) who established their reputation upon very much the same footing as flash Toby Crackit.

'Now,' said Fagin, when they had left the room, 'I'll go and get you that cash, Nancy. This is only the key of a little cupboard where I keep a few odd things the boys get, my dear. I never lock up my money, for I've got none to lock up, my dear—ha! ha! ha!—none to lock up. It's a poor trade, Nancy, and no thanks; but I'm fond of seeing the young people about me; and I bear it all, I bear it all. Hush!' he said, hastily concealing the key in his breast; 'who's that? Listen!'

The girl, who was sitting at the table with her arms folded, appeared in no way interested in the arrival: or to care whether the person, whoever he was, came or went: until the murmur of a man's voice reached her ears. The instant she caught the sound, she tore off her bonnet and shawl, with the rapidity of lightning, and thrust them under the table. The Jew, turning round immediately afterwards, she muttered a complaint of the heat: in a tone of languor that contrasted, very remarkably, with the extreme haste and violence of this action: which, however, had been unobserved by Fagin, who had his back towards her at the time.

'Bah!' he whispered, as though nettled by the interruption; 'it's the man I expected before; he's coming downstairs. Not a word about the money while he's here, Nance. He won't stop long. Not ten minutes, my dear.'

Laying his skinny forefinger upon his lip, the Jew carried a candle to the door, as a man's step was heard upon the stairs without. He reached it, at the same moment as the visitor, who, coming hastily into the room, was close upon the girl before he observed her.

It was Monks.

'Only one of my young people,' said Fagin, observing that Monks drew back, on beholding a stranger. 'Don't move, Nancy.'

The girl drew closer to the table, and glancing at Monks with an air of careless levity, withdrew her eyes; but as he turned towards Fagin, she stole another look; so keen and searching, and full of purpose, that if there had been any bystander to observe the change, he could hardly have believed the two looks to have proceeded from the same person.

'Any news?' inquired Fagin.

'Great.'

'And—and—good?' asked Fagin, hesitating as though he feared to vex the other man by being too sanguine.

'Not bad, any way,' replied Monks with a smile. 'I have been prompt enough this time. Let me have a word with you.'

The girl drew closer to the table, and made no offer to leave the room, although she could see that Monks was pointing to her. The Jew: perhaps fearing she might say something aloud about the money, if he endeavoured to get rid of her: pointed upward, and took Monks out of the room.

'Not that infernal hole we were in before,' she could hear the man say as they went upstairs. Fagin laughed; and making some reply which did not reach her, seemed, by the creaking of the boards, to lead his companion to the second story.

Before the sound of their footsteps had ceased to echo through the house, the girl had slipped off her shoes; and drawing her gown loosely over her head, and muffling her arms in it, stood at the door, listening with breathless interest. The moment the noise ceased, she glided from the room; ascended the stairs with incredible softness and silence; and was lost in the gloom above.

The room remained deserted for a quarter of an hour or more; the girl glided back with the same unearthly tread; and, immediately afterwards, the two men were heard descending. Monks went at once into the street; and the Jew crawled upstairs again for the money. When he returned, the girl was adjusting her shawl and bonnet, as if preparing to be gone.

'Why, Nance!' exclaimed the Jew, starting back as he put down the candle, 'how pale you are!'

784

'Pale!' echoed the girl, shading her eyes with her hands, as if to look steadily at him.

'Quite horrible. What have you been doing to yourself?'

'Nothing that I know of, except sitting in this close place for I don't know how long and all,' replied the girl carelessly. 'Come! Let me get back; that's a dear.'

With a sigh for every piece of money, Fagin told the amount into her hand. They parted without more conversation, merely interchanging a 'good-night.'

When the girl got into the open street, she sat down upon a doorstep; and seemed, for a few moments, wholly bewildered and unable to pursue her way. Suddenly she arose; and hurrying on, in a direction quite opposite to that in which Sikes was awaiting her returned, quickened her pace, until it gradually resolved into a violent run. After completely exhausting herself, she stopped to take breath: and, as if suddenly recollecting herself, and deploring her inability to do something she was bent upon, wrung her hands, and burst into tears.

It might be that her tears relieved her, or that she felt the full hopelessness of her condition; but she turned back; and hurrying with nearly as great rapidity in the contrary direction; partly to recover lost time, and partly to keep pace with the violent current of her own thoughts: soon reached the dwelling where she had left the housebreaker.

If she betrayed any agitation, when she presented herself to Mr. Sikes, he did not observe it; for merely inquiring if she had brought the money, and receiving a reply in the affirmative, he uttered a growl of satisfaction, and replacing his head upon the pillow, resumed the slumbers which her arrival had interrupted.

It was fortunate for her that the possession of money occasioned him so much employment next day in the way of eating and drinking; and withal had so beneficial an effect in smoothing down the asperities of his temper; that he had neither time nor inclination to be very critical upon her behaviour and deportment. That she had all the abstracted and nervous manner of one who is on the eve of some bold and hazardous step, which it has required no common struggle to resolve upon, would have been obvious to the lynx-eyed Fagin, who would most probably have taken the alarm at once; but Mr. Sikes lacking the niceties of discrimination, and being troubled with no more subtle misgivings than those which resolve themselves into a dogged roughness of behaviour towards everybody; and being, furthermore, in an unusually amiable condition, as has been already observed; saw nothing unusual in her demeanor, and indeed, troubled himself so little about her, that, had her agitation been far more perceptible than it was, it would have been very unlikely to have awakened his suspicions.

As that day closed in, the girl's excitement increased; and, when night came on, and she sat by, watching until the housebreaker should drink himself asleep, there was an unusual paleness in her cheek, and a fire in her eye, that even Sikes observed with astonishment.

Mr. Sikes being weak from the fever, was lying in bed, taking hot water with his gin to render it less inflammatory; and had pushed his glass towards Nancy to be replenished for the third or fourth time, when these symptoms first struck him.

'Why, burn my body!' said the man, raising himself on his hands as he stared the girl in the face. 'You look like a corpse come to life again. What's the matter?'

'Matter!' replied the girl. 'Nothing. What do you look at me so hard for?'

'What foolery is this?' demanded Sikes, grasping her by the arm, and shaking her roughly.

'What is it? What do you mean? What are you thinking of?'

'Of many things, Bill,' replied the girl, shivering, and as she did so, pressing her hands upon her eyes. 'But, Lord! What odds in that?'

The tone of forced gaiety in which the last words were spoken, seemed to produce a deeper impression on Sikes than the wild and rigid look which had preceded them.

'I tell you wot it is,' said Sikes; 'if you haven't caught the fever, and got it comin' on, now, there's something more than usual in the wind, and something dangerous too. You're not a-going to—. No, damme! you wouldn't do that!'

'Do what?' asked the girl.

'There ain't,' said Sikes, fixing his eyes upon her, and muttering the words to himself; 'there ain't a stauncher-hearted gal going, or I'd have cut her throat three months ago. She's got the fever coming on; that's it.'

Fortifying himself with this assurance, Sikes drained the glass to the bottom, and then, with many grumbling oaths, called for his physic. The girl jumped up, with great alacrity; poured it quickly out, but with her back towards him; and held the vessel to his lips, while he drank off the contents.

'Now,' said the robber, 'come and sit aside of me, and put on your own face; or I'll alter it so, that you won't know it agin when you do want it.'

The girl obeyed. Sikes, locking her hand in his, fell back upon the pillow: turning his eyes upon her face. They closed; opened again; closed once more; again opened. He shifted his position restlessly; and, after dozing again, and again, for two or three minutes, and as often springing up with a look of terror, and gazing vacantly about him, was suddenly stricken, as it were, while in the very attitude of rising, into a deep and heavy sleep. The grasp of his hand relaxed; the upraised arm fell languidly by his side; and he lay like one in a profound trance.

'The laudanum has taken effect at last,' murmured the girl, as she rose from the bedside. 'I may be too late, even now.'

She hastily dressed herself in her bonnet and shawl: looking fearfully round, from time to time, as if, despite the sleeping draught, she expected every moment to feel the pressure of Sikes's heavy hand upon her shoulder; then, stooping softly over the bed, she kissed the robber's lips; and then opening and closing the room-door with noiseless touch, hurried from the house.

A watchman was crying half-past nine, down a dark passage through which she had to pass, in gaining the main thoroughfare.

'Has it long gone the half-hour?' asked the girl.

'It'll strike the hour in another quarter,' said the man: raising his lantern to her face.

'And I cannot get there in less than an hour or more,' muttered Nancy: brushing swiftly past him, and gliding rapidly down the street.

Many of the shops were already closing in the back lanes and avenues through which she tracked her way, in making from Spitalfields towards the West-End of London. The clock struck ten, increasing her impatience. She tore along the narrow pavement: elbowing the passengers from side to side; and darting almost under the horses' heads, crossed crowded streets, where clusters of persons were eagerly watching their opportunity to do the like.

'The woman is mad!' said the people, turning to look after her as she rushed away.

When she reached the more wealthy quarter of the town, the streets were comparatively deserted; and here her headlong progress excited a still greater curiosity in the stragglers whom she hurried past. Some quickened their pace behind, as though to see whither she was hastening at such an unusual rate; and a few made head upon her, and looked back, surprised at her undiminished speed; but they fell off one by one; and when she neared her place of destination, she was alone.

It was a family hotel in a quiet but handsome street near Hyde Park. As the brilliant light of the lamp which burnt before its door, guided her to the spot, the clock struck eleven. She had loitered for a few paces as though irresolute, and making up her mind to advance; but the sound determined her, and she stepped into the hall. The porter's seat was vacant. She looked round with an air of incertitude, and advanced towards the stairs.

'Now, young woman!' said a smartly-dressed female, looking out from a door behind her, 'who do you want here?'

'A lady who is stopping in this house,' answered the girl.

'A lady!' was the reply, accompanied with a scornful look. 'What lady?'

'Miss Maylie,' said Nancy.

The young woman, who had by this time, noted her appearance, replied only by a look of virtuous disdain; and summoned a man to answer her. To him, Nancy repeated her request.

'What name am I to say?' asked the waiter.

'It's of no use saying any,' replied Nancy.

'Nor business?' said the man.

'No, nor that neither,' rejoined the girl. 'I must see the lady.'

'Come!' said the man, pushing her towards the door. 'None of this. Take yourself off.'

'I shall be carried out if I go!' said the girl violently; 'and I can make that a job that two of you won't like to do. Isn't there anybody here,' she said, looking round, 'that will see a simple message carried for a poor wretch like me?'

This appeal produced an effect on a good-tempered-faced man-cook, who with some of the other servants was looking on, and who stepped forward to interfere.

'Take it up for her, Joe; can't you?' said this person.

'What's the good?' replied the man. 'You don't suppose the young lady will see such as her; do you?'

This allusion to Nancy's doubtful character, raised a vast quantity of chaste wrath in the bosoms of four housemaids, who remarked, with great fervour, that the creature was a disgrace to her sex; and strongly advocated her being thrown, ruthlessly, into the kennel.

'Do what you like with me,' said the girl, turning to the men again; 'but do what I ask you first, and I ask you to give this message for God Almighty's sake.'

The soft-hearted cook added his intercession, and the result was that the man who had first appeared undertook its delivery.

'What's it to be?' said the man, with one foot on the stairs.

'That a young woman earnestly asks to speak to Miss Maylie alone,' said Nancy; 'and that if the lady will only hear the first word she has to say, she will know whether to hear her business, or to have her turned out of doors as an impostor.'

'I say,' said the man, 'you're coming it strong!'

'You give the message,' said the girl firmly; 'and let me hear the answer.'

The man ran upstairs. Nancy remained, pale and almost breathless, listening with quivering lip to the very audible expressions of scorn, of which the chaste housemaids were very prolific; and of which they became still more so, when the man returned, and said the young woman was to walk upstairs.

'It's no good being proper in this world,' said the first housemaid.

'Brass can do better than the gold what has stood the fire,' said the second.

The third contented herself with wondering 'what ladies was made of'; and the fourth took the first in a quartette of 'Shameful!' with which the Dianas concluded.

Regardless of all this: for she had weightier matters at heart: Nancy followed the man, with trembling limbs, to a small ante-chamber, lighted by a lamp from the ceiling. Here he left her, and retired.

CHAPTER XL. A STRANGE INTERVIEW, WHICH IS A SEQUEL TO THE LAST CHAMBER

The girl's life had been squandered in the streets, and among the most noisome of the stews and dens of London, but there was something of the woman's original nature left in her still; and when she heard a light step approaching the door opposite to that by which she had entered, and thought of the wide contrast which the small room would in another moment contain, she felt burdened with the sense of her own deep shame, and shrunk as though she could scarcely bear the presence of her with whom she had sought this interview.

But struggling with these better feelings was pride,—the vice of the lowest and most debased creatures no less than of the high and self-assured. The miserable companion of thieves and ruffians, the fallen outcast of low haunts, the associate of the scourings of the jails and hulks, living within the shadow of the gallows itself,—even this degraded being felt too proud to betray a feeble gleam of the womanly feeling which she thought a weakness, but which alone connected her with that humanity, of which her wasting life had obliterated so many, many traces when a very child.

She raised her eyes sufficiently to observe that the figure which presented itself was that of a slight and beautiful girl; then, bending them on the ground, she tossed her head with affected carelessness as she said:

'It's a hard matter to get to see you, lady. If I had taken offence, and gone away, as many would have done, you'd have been sorry for it one day, and not without reason either.'

'I am very sorry if any one has behaved harshly to you,' replied Rose. 'Do not think of that. Tell me why you wished to see me. I am the person you inquired for.'

The kind tone of this answer, the sweet voice, the gentle manner, the absence of any accent of haughtiness or displeasure, took the girl completely by surprise, and she burst into tears.

'Oh, lady, lady!' she said, clasping her hands passionately before her face, 'if there was more like you, there would be fewer like me,—there would—there would!'

'Sit down,' said Rose, earnestly. 'If you are in poverty or affliction I shall be truly glad to relieve you if I can,—I shall indeed. Sit down.'

'Let me stand, lady,' said the girl, still weeping, 'and do not speak to me so kindly till you know me better. It is growing late. Is—is—that door shut?'

'Yes,' said Rose, recoiling a few steps, as if to be nearer assistance in case she should require it. 'Why?'

'Because,' said the girl, 'I am about to put my life and the lives of others in your hands. I am the girl that dragged little Oliver back to old Fagin's on the night he went out from the house in Pentonville.'

'You!' said Rose Maylie.

'I, lady!' replied the girl. 'I am the infamous creature you have heard of, that lives among the thieves, and that never from the first moment I can recollect my eyes and senses opening on London streets have known any better life, or kinder words than they have given me, so help me God! Do not mind shrinking openly from me, lady. I am younger than you would think, to look at me, but I am well used to it. The poorest women fall back, as I make my way along the crowded pavement.'

'What dreadful things are these!' said Rose, involuntarily falling from her strange companion.

'Thank Heaven upon your knees, dear lady,' cried the girl, 'that you had friends to care for and keep you in your childhood, and that you were never in the midst of cold and hunger, and riot and drunkenness, and—and—something worse than all—as I have been from my cradle. I may use the word, for the alley and the gutter were mine, as they will be my deathbed.'

'I pity you!' said Rose, in a broken voice. 'It wrings my heart to hear you!'

'Heaven bless you for your goodness!' rejoined the girl. 'If you knew what I am sometimes, you would pity me, indeed. But I have stolen away from those who would surely murder me, if they knew I had been here, to tell you what I have overheard. Do you know a man named Monks?'

'No,' said Rose.

'He knows you,' replied the girl; 'and knew you were here, for it was by hearing him tell the place that I found you out.'

'I never heard the name,' said Rose.

'Then he goes by some other amongst us,' rejoined the girl, 'which I more than thought before. Some time ago, and soon after Oliver was put into your house on the night of the robbery, I—suspecting this man—listened to a conversation held between him and Fagin in the dark. I found out, from what I heard, that Monks—the man I asked you about, you know—'

'Yes,' said Rose, 'I understand.'

'—That Monks,' pursued the girl, 'had seen him accidently with two of our boys on the day we first lost him, and had known him directly to be the same child that he was watching for, though I couldn't make out why. A bargain was struck with Fagin, that if Oliver was got back he should have a certain sum; and he was to have more for making him a thief, which this Monks wanted for some purpose of his own.'

'For what purpose?' asked Rose.

'He caught sight of my shadow on the wall as I listened, in the hope of finding out,' said the girl; 'and there are not many people besides me that could have got out of their way in time to escape discovery. But I did; and I saw him no more till last night.'

'And what occurred then?'

'I'll tell you, lady. Last night he came again. Again they went upstairs, and I, wrapping myself up so that my shadow would not betray me, again listened at the door. The first words I heard Monks say were these: "So the only proofs of the boy's identity lie at the bottom of the river, and the old hag that received them from the mother is rotting in her coffin." They laughed, and talked of his success in doing this; and Monks, talking on about the boy, and getting very wild, said that though he had got the young devil's money safely now, he'd rather have had it the other way; for, what a game it would have been to have brought down the boast of the father's will, by driving him through every jail in town, and then hauling him up for some capital felony which Fagin could easily manage, after having made a good profit of him besides.'

'What is all this!' said Rose.

'The truth, lady, though it comes from my lips,' replied the girl. 'Then, he said, with oaths common enough in my ears, but strange to yours, that if he could gratify his hatred by taking the boy's life without bringing his own neck in danger, he would; but, as he couldn't, he'd be upon the watch to meet him at every turn in life; and if he took advantage of his birth and history, he might harm him yet. "In short, Fagin," he says, "Jew as you are, you never laid such snares as I'll contrive for my young brother, Oliver."'

'His brother!' exclaimed Rose.

'Those were his words,' said Nancy, glancing uneasily round, as she had scarcely ceased to do, since she began to speak, for a vision of Sikes haunted her perpetually. 'And more. When he spoke of you and the other lady, and said it seemed contrived by Heaven, or the devil, against him, that Oliver should come into your hands, he laughed, and said there was some comfort in that too, for how many thousands and hundreds of thousands of pounds would you not give, if you had them, to know who your two-legged spaniel was.'

'You do not mean,' said Rose, turning very pale, 'to tell me that this was said in earnest?'

'He spoke in hard and angry earnest, if a man ever did,' replied the girl, shaking her head. 'He is an earnest man when his hatred is up. I know many who do worse things; but I'd rather listen to them all a dozen times, than to that Monks once. It is growing late, and I have to reach home without suspicion of having been on such an errand as this. I must get back quickly.'

'But what can I do?' said Rose. 'To what use can I turn this communication without you? Back! Why do you wish to return to companions you paint in such terrible colors? If you repeat this information to a gentleman whom I can summon in an instant from the next room, you can be consigned to some place of safety without half an hour's delay.'

'I wish to go back,' said the girl. 'I must go back, because—how can I tell such things to an innocent lady like you?—because among the men I have told you of, there is one: the most desperate among them all; that I can't leave: no, not even to be saved from the life I am leading now.'

'Your having interfered in this dear boy's behalf before,' said Rose; 'your coming here, at so great a risk, to tell me what you have heard; your manner, which convinces me of the truth of what you say; your evident contrition, and sense of shame; all lead me to believe that you might yet be reclaimed. Oh!' said the earnest girl, folding her hands as the tears coursed down her face, 'do not turn a deaf ear to the entreaties of one of your own sex; the first—the first, I do believe, who ever appealed to you in the voice of pity and compassion. Do hear my words, and let me save you yet, for better things.'

'Lady,' cried the girl, sinking on her knees, 'dear, sweet, angel lady, you are the first that ever blessed me with such words as these, and if I had heard them years ago, they might have turned me from a life of sin and sorrow; but it is too late, it is too late!'

'It is never too late,' said Rose, 'for penitence and atonement.'

'It is,' cried the girl, writhing in agony of her mind; 'I cannot leave him now! I could not be his death.'

'Why should you be?' asked Rose.

'Nothing could save him,' cried the girl. 'If I told others what I have told you, and led to their being taken, he would be sure to die. He is the boldest, and has been so cruel!'

'Is it possible,' cried Rose, 'that for such a man as this, you can resign every future hope, and the certainty of immediate rescue? It is madness.'

'I don't know what it is,' answered the girl; 'I only know that it is so, and not with me alone, but with hundreds of others as bad and wretched as myself. I must go back. Whether it is God's wrath for the wrong I have done, I do not know; but I am drawn back to him through every suffering and ill usage; and I should be, I believe, if I knew that I was to die by his hand at last.'

'What am I to do?' said Rose. 'I should not let you depart from me thus.'

'You should, lady, and I know you will,' rejoined the girl, rising. 'You will not stop my going because I have trusted in your goodness, and forced no promise from you, as I might have done.'

'Of what use, then, is the communication you have made?' said Rose. 'This mystery must be investigated, or how will its disclosure to me, benefit Oliver, whom you are anxious to serve?'

'You must have some kind gentleman about you that will hear it as a secret, and advise you what to do,' rejoined the girl.

'But where can I find you again when it is necessary?' asked Rose. 'I do not seek to know where these dreadful people live, but where will you be walking or passing at any settled period from this time?'

'Will you promise me that you will have my secret strictly kept, and come alone, or with the only other person that knows it; and that I shall not be watched or followed?' asked the girl.

'I promise you solemnly,' answered Rose.

'Every Sunday night, from eleven until the clock strikes twelve,' said the girl without hesitation, 'I will walk on London Bridge if I am alive.'

'Stay another moment,' interposed Rose, as the girl moved hurriedly towards the door. 'Think once again on your own condition, and the opportunity you have of escaping from it. You have a claim on me: not only as the voluntary bearer of this intelligence, but as a woman lost almost beyond redemption. Will you return to this gang of robbers, and to this man, when a word can save you? What fascination is it that can take you back, and make you cling to wickedness and misery? Oh! is there no chord in your heart that I can touch! Is there nothing left, to which I can appeal against this terrible infatuation!'

'When ladies as young, and good, and beautiful as you are,' replied the girl steadily, 'give away your hearts, love will carry you all lengths—even such as you, who have home, friends, other admirers, everything, to fill them. When such as I, who have no certain roof but the coffinlid, and no friend in sickness or death but the hospital nurse, set our rotten hearts on any man, and let him fill the place that has been a blank through all our wretched lives, who can hope to cure us? Pity us, lady—pity us for having only one feeling of the woman left, and for having that turned, by a heavy judgment, from a comfort and a pride, into a new means of violence and suffering.'

'You will,' said Rose, after a pause, 'take some money from me, which may enable you to live without dishonesty—at all events until we meet again?'

'Not a penny,' replied the girl, waving her hand.

'Do not close your heart against all my efforts to help you,' said Rose, stepping gently forward. 'I wish to serve you indeed.'

'You would serve me best, lady,' replied the girl, wringing her hands, 'if you could take my life at once; for I have felt more grief to think of what I am, to-night, than I ever did before, and it would be something not to die in the hell in which I have lived. God bless you, sweet lady, and send as much happiness on your head as I have brought shame on mine!'

Thus speaking, and sobbing aloud, the unhappy creature turned away; while Rose Maylie, overpowered by this extraordinary interview, which had more the semblance of a rapid dream than an actual occurrence, sank into a chair, and endeavoured to collect her wandering thoughts.

CHAPTER XLI. CONTAINING FRESH DISCOVERIES, AND SHOWING THAT SUPRISES, LIKE MISFORTUNES, SELDOM COME ALONE

Her situation was, indeed, one of no common trial and difficulty. While she felt the most eager and burning desire to penetrate the mystery in which Oliver's history was enveloped, she could not but hold sacred the confidence which the miserable woman with whom she had just conversed, had reposed in her, as a young and guileless girl. Her words and manner had touched Rose Maylie's heart; and, mingled with her love for her young charge, and scarcely less intense in its truth and fervour, was her fond wish to win the outcast back to repentance and hope.

They purposed remaining in London only three days, prior to departing for some weeks to a distant part of the coast. It was now midnight of the first day. What course of action could she determine upon, which could be adopted in eight-and-forty hours? Or how could she postpone the journey without exciting suspicion?

Mr. Losberne was with them, and would be for the next two days; but Rose was too well acquainted with the excellent gentleman's impetuosity, and foresaw too clearly the wrath with which, in the first explosion of his indignation, he would regard the instrument of Oliver's recapture, to trust him with the secret, when her representations in the girl's behalf could be seconded by no experienced person. These were all reasons for the greatest caution and most circumspect behaviour in communicating it to Mrs. Maylie, whose first impulse would infallibly be to hold a conference with the worthy doctor on the subject. As to resorting to any legal adviser, even if she had known how to do so, it was scarcely to be thought of, for the same reason. Once the thought occurred to her of seeking assistance from Harry; but this awakened the recollection of their last parting, and it seemed unworthy of her to call him back, when— the tears rose to her eyes as she pursued this train of reflection—he might have by this time learnt to forget her, and to be happier away.

Disturbed by these different reflections; inclining now to one course and then to another, and again recoiling from all, as each successive consideration presented itself to her mind; Rose passed a sleepless and anxious night. After more communing with herself next day, she arrived at the desperate conclusion of consulting Harry.

'If it be painful to him,' she thought, 'to come back here, how painful it will be to me! But perhaps he will not come; he may write, or he may come himself, and studiously abstain from meeting me—he did when he went away. I hardly thought he would; but it was better for us both.' And here Rose dropped the pen, and turned away, as though the very paper which was to be her messenger should not see her weep.

She had taken up the same pen, and laid it down again fifty times, and had considered and reconsidered the first line of her letter without writing the first word, when Oliver, who had been walking in the streets, with Mr. Giles for a body-guard, entered the room in such breathless haste and violent agitation, as seemed to betoken some new cause of alarm.

'What makes you look so flurried?' asked Rose, advancing to meet him.

'I hardly know how; I feel as if I should be choked,' replied the boy. 'Oh dear! To think that I should see him at last, and you should be able to know that I have told you the truth!'

'I never thought you had told us anything but the truth,' said Rose, soothing him. 'But what is this?—of whom do you speak?'

'I have seen the gentleman,' replied Oliver, scarcely able to articulate, 'the gentleman who was so good to me—Mr. Brownlow, that we have so often talked about.'

'Where?' asked Rose.

'Getting out of a coach,' replied Oliver, shedding tears of delight, 'and going into a house. I didn't speak to him—I couldn't speak to him, for he didn't see me, and I trembled so, that I was not able to go up to him. But Giles asked, for me, whether he lived there, and they said he did. Look here,' said Oliver, opening a scrap of paper, 'here it is; here's where he lives—I'm going there directly! Oh, dear me, dear me! What shall I do when I come to see him and hear him speak again!'

With her attention not a little distracted by these and a great many other incoherent exclamations of joy, Rose read the address, which was Craven Street, in the Strand. She very soon determined upon turning the discovery to account.

'Quick!' she said. 'Tell them to fetch a hackney-coach, and be ready to go with me. I will take you there directly, without a minute's loss of time. I will only tell my aunt that we are going out for an hour, and be ready as soon as you are.'

Oliver needed no prompting to despatch, and in little more than five minutes they were on their way to Craven Street. When they arrived there, Rose left Oliver in the coach, under pretence of preparing the old gentleman to receive him; and sending up her card by the servant, requested to see Mr. Brownlow on very pressing business. The servant soon returned, to beg that she would walk upstairs; and following him into an upper room, Miss Maylie was presented to an elderly gentleman of benevolent appearance, in a bottle-green coat. At no great distance from whom, was seated another old gentleman, in nankeen breeches and gaiters; who did not look particularly benevolent, and who was sitting with his hands clasped on the top of a thick stick, and his chin propped thereupon.

'Dear me,' said the gentleman, in the bottle-green coat, hastily rising with great politeness, 'I beg your pardon, young lady—I imagined it was some importunate person who—I beg you will excuse me. Be seated, pray.'

'Mr. Brownlow, I believe, sir?' said Rose, glancing from the other gentleman to the one who had spoken.

'That is my name,' said the old gentleman. 'This is my friend, Mr. Grimwig. Grimwig, will you leave us for a few minutes?'

'I believe,' interposed Miss Maylie, 'that at this period of our interview, I need not give that gentleman the trouble of going away. If I am correctly informed, he is cognizant of the business on which I wish to speak to you.'

Mr. Brownlow inclined his head. Mr. Grimwig, who had made one very stiff bow, and risen from his chair, made another very stiff bow, and dropped into it again.

'I shall surprise you very much, I have no doubt,' said Rose, naturally embarrassed; 'but you once showed great benevolence and goodness to a very dear young friend of mine, and I am sure you will take an interest in hearing of him again.'

'Indeed!' said Mr. Brownlow.

'Oliver Twist you knew him as,' replied Rose.

The words no sooner escaped her lips, than Mr. Grimwig, who had been affecting to dip into a large book that lay on the table, upset it with a great crash, and falling back in his chair, discharged from his features every expression but one of unmitigated wonder, and indulged in a prolonged and vacant stare; then, as if ashamed of having betrayed so much emotion, he jerked himself, as it were, by a convulsion into his former attitude, and looking out straight before him emitted a long deep whistle, which seemed, at last, not to be discharged on empty air, but to die away in the innermost recesses of his stomach.

Mr. Browlow was no less surprised, although his astonishment was not expressed in the same eccentric manner. He drew his chair nearer to Miss Maylie's, and said,

'Do me the favour, my dear young lady, to leave entirely out of the question that goodness and benevolence of which you speak, and of which nobody else knows anything; and if you have it in your power to produce any evidence which will alter the unfavourable opinion I was once induced to entertain of that poor child, in Heaven's name put me in possession of it.'

'A bad one! I'll eat my head if he is not a bad one,' growled Mr. Grimwig, speaking by some ventriloquial power, without moving a muscle of his face.

'He is a child of a noble nature and a warm heart,' said Rose, colouring; 'and that Power which has thought fit to try him beyond his years, has planted in his breast affections and feelings which would do honour to many who have numbered his days six times over.'

'I'm only sixty-one,' said Mr. Grimwig, with the same rigid face. 'And, as the devil's in it if this Oliver is not twelve years old at least, I don't see the application of that remark.'

'Do not heed my friend, Miss Maylie,' said Mr. Brownlow; 'he does not mean what he says.'

'Yes, he does,' growled Mr. Grimwig.

'No, he does not,' said Mr. Brownlow, obviously rising in wrath as he spoke.

'He'll eat his head, if he doesn't,' growled Mr. Grimwig.

'He would deserve to have it knocked off, if he does,' said Mr. Brownlow.

'And he'd uncommonly like to see any man offer to do it,' responded Mr. Grimwig, knocking his stick upon the floor.

Having gone thus far, the two old gentlemen severally took snuff, and afterwards shook hands, according to their invariable custom.

'Now, Miss Maylie,' said Mr. Brownlow, 'to return to the subject in which your humanity is so much interested. Will you let me know what intelligence you have of this poor child: allowing me to promise that I exhausted every means in my power of discovering him, and that since I have been absent from this country, my first impression that he had imposed upon me, and had been persuaded by his former associates to rob me, has been considerably shaken.'

Rose, who had had time to collect her thoughts, at once related, in a few natural words, all that had befallen Oliver since he left Mr. Brownlow's house; reserving Nancy's information for that gentleman's private ear, and concluding with the assurance that his only sorrow, for some months past, had been not being able to meet with his former benefactor and friend.

'Thank God!' said the old gentleman. 'This is great happiness to me, great happiness. But you have not told me where he is now, Miss Maylie. You must pardon my finding fault with you,—but why not have brought him?'

'He is waiting in a coach at the door,' replied Rose.

'At this door!' cried the old gentleman. With which he hurried out of the room, down the stairs, up the coachsteps, and into the coach, without another word.

When the room-door closed behind him, Mr. Grimwig lifted up his head, and converting one of the hind legs of his chair into a pivot, described three distinct circles with the assistance of his stick and the table; sitting in it all the time. After performing this evolution, he rose and limped as fast as he could up and down the room at least a dozen times, and then stopping suddenly before Rose, kissed her without the slightest preface.

'Hush!' he said, as the young lady rose in some alarm at this unusual proceeding. 'Don't be afraid. I'm old enough to be your grandfather. You're a sweet girl. I like you. Here they are!'

In fact, as he threw himself at one dexterous dive into his former seat, Mr. Brownlow returned, accompanied by Oliver, whom Mr. Grimwig received very graciously; and if the gratification of that moment had been the only reward for all her anxiety and care in Oliver's behalf, Rose Maylie would have been well repaid.

'There is somebody else who should not be forgotten, by the bye,' said Mr. Brownlow, ringing the bell. 'Send Mrs. Bedwin here, if you please.'

The old housekeeper answered the summons with all dispatch; and dropping a curtsey at the door, waited for orders.

'Why, you get blinder every day, Bedwin,' said Mr. Brownlow, rather testily.

'Well, that I do, sir,' replied the old lady. 'People's eyes, at my time of life, don't improve with age, sir.'

'I could have told you that,' rejoined Mr. Brownlow; 'but put on your glasses, and see if you can't find out what you were wanted for, will you?'

The old lady began to rummage in her pocket for her spectacles. But Oliver's patience was not proof against this new trial; and yielding to his first impulse, he sprang into her arms.

'God be good to me!' cried the old lady, embracing him; 'it is my innocent boy!'

'My dear old nurse!' cried Oliver.

'He would come back—I knew he would,' said the old lady, holding him in her arms. 'How well he looks, and how like a gentleman's son he is dressed again! Where have you been, this long, long while? Ah! the same sweet face, but not so pale; the same soft eye, but not so sad. I have never forgotten them or his quiet smile, but have seen them every day, side by side with those of my own dear children, dead and gone since I was a lightsome young creature.' Running on thus, and now holding Oliver from her to mark how he had grown, now clasping him to her and passing her fingers fondly through his hair, the good soul laughed and wept upon his neck by turns.

Leaving her and Oliver to compare notes at leisure, Mr. Brownlow led the way into another room; and there, heard from Rose a full narration of her interview with Nancy, which occasioned him no little surprise and perplexity. Rose also explained her reasons for not confiding in her friend Mr. Losberne in the first instance. The old gentleman considered that she had acted prudently, and readily undertook to hold solemn conference with the worthy doctor himself. To afford him an early opportunity for the execution of this design, it was arranged that he should call at the hotel at eight o'clock that evening, and that in the meantime Mrs. Maylie should be cautiously informed of all that had occurred. These preliminaries adjusted, Rose and Oliver returned home.

Rose had by no means overrated the measure of the good doctor's wrath. Nancy's history was no sooner unfolded to him, than he poured forth a shower of mingled threats and execrations; threatened to make her the first victim of the combined ingenuity of Messrs. Blathers and Duff; and actually put on his hat preparatory to sallying forth to obtain the assistance of those worthies. And, doubtless, he would, in this first outbreak, have carried the intention into effect without a moment's consideration of the consequences, if he had not been restrained, in part, by corresponding violence on the side of Mr. Brownlow, who was himself of an irascible temperament, and party by such arguments and representations as seemed best calculated to dissuade him from his hotbrained purpose.

'Then what the devil is to be done?' said the impetuous doctor, when they had rejoined the two ladies. 'Are we to pass a vote of thanks to all these vagabonds, male and female, and beg them to accept a hundred pounds, or so, apiece, as a trifling mark of our esteem, and some slight acknowledgment of their kindness to Oliver?'

'Not exactly that,' rejoined Mr. Brownlow, laughing; 'but we must proceed gently and with great care.'

'Gentleness and care,' exclaimed the doctor. 'I'd send them one and all to—'

'Never mind where,' interposed Mr. Brownlow. 'But reflect whether sending them anywhere is likely to attain the object we have in view.'

'What object?' asked the doctor.

'Simply, the discovery of Oliver's parentage, and regaining for him the inheritance of which, if this story be true, he has been fraudulently deprived.'

'Ah!' said Mr. Losberne, cooling himself with his pocket-handkerchief; 'I almost forgot that.'

'You see,' pursued Mr. Brownlow; 'placing this poor girl entirely out of the question, and supposing it were possible to bring these scoundrels to justice without compromising her safety, what good should we bring about?'

'Hanging a few of them at least, in all probability,' suggested the doctor, 'and transporting the rest.'

'Very good,' replied Mr. Brownlow, smiling; 'but no doubt they will bring that about for themselves in the fulness of time, and if we step in to forestall them, it seems to me that we shall be performing a very Quixotic act, in direct opposition to our own interest—or at least to Oliver's, which is the same thing.'

'How?' inquired the doctor.

'Thus. It is quite clear that we shall have extreme difficulty in getting to the bottom of this mystery, unless we can bring this man, Monks, upon his knees. That can only be done by stratagem, and by catching him when he is not surrounded by these people. For, suppose he were apprehended, we have no proof against him. He is not even (so far as we know, or as the facts appear to us) concerned with the gang in any of their robberies. If he were not discharged, it is very unlikely that he could receive any further punishment than being committed to prison as a rogue and vagabond; and of course ever afterwards his mouth would be so obstinately closed that he might as well, for our purposes, be deaf, dumb, blind, and an idiot.'

'Then,' said the doctor impetuously, 'I put it to you again, whether you think it reasonable that this promise to the girl should be considered binding; a promise made with the best and kindest intentions, but really—'

'Do not discuss the point, my dear young lady, pray,' said Mr. Brownlow, interrupting Rose as she was about to speak. 'The promise shall be kept. I don't think it will, in the slightest degree, interfere with our proceedings. But, before we can resolve upon any precise course of action, it will be necessary to see the girl; to ascertain from her whether she will point out this Monks, on the understanding that he is to be dealt with by us, and not by the law; or, if she will not, or cannot do that, to procure from her such an account of his haunts and description of his person, as will enable us to identify him. She cannot be seen until next Sunday night; this is Tuesday. I would suggest that in the meantime, we remain perfectly quiet, and keep these matters secret even from Oliver himself.'

Although Mr. Losberne received with many wry faces a proposal involving a delay of five whole days, he was fain to admit that no better course occurred to him just then; and as both Rose and Mrs. Maylie sided very strongly with Mr. Brownlow, that gentleman's proposition was carried unanimously.

'I should like,' he said, 'to call in the aid of my friend Grimwig. He is a strange creature, but a shrewd one, and might prove of material assistance to us; I should say that he was bred a lawyer, and quitted the Bar in disgust because he had only one brief and a motion of course, in twenty years, though whether that is recommendation or not, you must determine for yourselves.'

'I have no objection to your calling in your friend if I may call in mine,' said the doctor.

'We must put it to the vote,' replied Mr. Brownlow, 'who may he be?'

'That lady's son, and this young lady's—very old friend,' said the doctor, motioning towards Mrs. Maylie, and concluding with an expressive glance at her niece.

Rose blushed deeply, but she did not make any audible objection to this motion (possibly she felt in a hopeless minority); and Harry Maylie and Mr. Grimwig were accordingly added to the committee.

'We stay in town, of course,' said Mrs. Maylie, 'while there remains the slightest prospect of prosecuting this inquiry with a chance of success. I will spare neither trouble nor expense in behalf of the object in which we are all so deeply interested, and I am content to remain here, if it be for twelve months, so long as you assure me that any hope remains.'

'Good!' rejoined Mr. Brownlow. 'And as I see on the faces about me, a disposition to inquire how it happened that I was not in the way to corroborate Oliver's tale, and had so suddenly left the kingdom, let me stipulate that I shall be asked no questions until such time as I may deem it expedient to forestall them by telling my own story. Believe me, I make this request with good reason, for I might otherwise excite hopes destined never to be realised, and only increase difficulties and disappointments already quite numerous enough. Come! Supper has been announced, and young Oliver, who is all alone in the next room, will have begun to think, by this time, that we have wearied of his company, and entered into some dark conspiracy to thrust him forth upon the world.'

With these words, the old gentleman gave his hand to Mrs. Maylie, and escorted her into the supper-room. Mr. Losberne followed, leading Rose; and the council was, for the present, effectually broken up.

CHAPTER XLII. AN OLD ACQUAINTANCE OF OLIVER'S, EXHIBITING DECIDED MARKS OF GENIUS, BECOMES A PUBLIC CHARACTER IN THE METROPOLIS

Upon the night when Nancy, having lulled Mr. Sikes to sleep, hurried on her self-imposed mission to Rose Maylie, there advanced towards London, by the Great North Road, two persons, upon whom it is expedient that this history should bestow some attention.

They were a man and woman; or perhaps they would be better described as a male and female: for the former was one of those long-limbed, knock-kneed, shambling, bony people, to whom it is difficult to assign any precise age,—looking as they do, when they are yet boys, like undergrown men, and when they are almost men, like overgrown boys. The woman was young, but of a robust and hardy make, as she need have been to bear the weight of the heavy bundle which was strapped to her back. Her companion was not encumbered with much luggage, as there merely dangled from a stick which he carried over his shoulder, a small parcel wrapped in a common handkerchief, and apparently light enough. This circumstance, added to the length of his legs, which were of unusual extent, enabled him with much ease to keep some half-dozen paces in advance of his companion, to whom he occasionally turned with an impatient jerk of the head: as if reproaching her tardiness, and urging her to greater exertion.

Thus, they had toiled along the dusty road, taking little heed of any object within sight, save when they stepped aside to allow a wider passage for the mail-coaches which were whirling out of town, until they passed through Highgate archway; when the foremost traveller stopped and called impatiently to his companion,

'Come on, can't yer? What a lazybones yer are, Charlotte.'

'It's a heavy load, I can tell you,' said the female, coming up, almost breathless with fatigue.

'Heavy! What are yer talking about? What are yer made for?' rejoined the male traveller, changing his own little bundle as he spoke, to the other shoulder. 'Oh, there yer are, resting again! Well, if yer ain't enough to tire anybody's patience out, I don't know what is!'

'Is it much farther?' asked the woman, resting herself against a bank, and looking up with the perspiration streaming from her face.

'Much farther! Yer as good as there,' said the long-legged tramper, pointing out before him. 'Look there! Those are the lights of London.'

'They're a good two mile off, at least,' said the woman despondingly.

'Never mind whether they're two mile off, or twenty,' said Noah Claypole; for he it was; 'but get up and come on, or I'll kick yer, and so I give yer notice.'

As Noah's red nose grew redder with anger, and as he crossed the road while speaking, as if fully prepared to put his threat into execution, the woman rose without any further remark, and trudged onward by his side.

'Where do you mean to stop for the night, Noah?' she asked, after they had walked a few hundred yards.

'How should I know?' replied Noah, whose temper had been considerably impaired by walking.

'Near, I hope,' said Charlotte.

'No, not near,' replied Mr. Claypole. 'There! Not near; so don't think it.'

'Why not?'

'When I tell yer that I don't mean to do a thing, that's enough, without any why or because either,' replied Mr. Claypole with dignity.

'Well, you needn't be so cross,' said his companion.

'A pretty thing it would be, wouldn't it to go and stop at the very first public-house outside the town, so that Sowerberry, if he come up after us, might poke in his old nose, and have us taken back in a cart with handcuffs on,' said Mr. Claypole in a jeering tone. 'No! I shall go and lose myself among the narrowest streets I can find, and not stop till we come to the very out-of-the-wayest house I can set eyes on. 'Cod, yer may thanks yer stars I've got a head; for if we hadn't gone, at first, the wrong road a purpose, and come back across country, yer'd have been locked up hard and fast a week ago, my lady. And serve yer right for being a fool.'

'I know I ain't as cunning as you are,' replied Charlotte; 'but don't put all the blame on me, and say I should have been locked up. You would have been if I had been, any way.'

'Yer took the money from the till, yer know yer did,' said Mr. Claypole.

'I took it for you, Noah, dear,' rejoined Charlotte.

'Did I keep it?' asked Mr. Claypole.

'No; you trusted in me, and let me carry it like a dear, and so you are,' said the lady, chucking him under the chin, and drawing her arm through his.

This was indeed the case; but as it was not Mr. Claypole's habit to repose a blind and foolish confidence in anybody, it should be observed, in justice to that gentleman, that he had trusted Charlotte to this extent, in order that, if they were pursued, the money might be found on her: which would leave him an opportunity of asserting his innocence of any theft, and would greatly facilitate his chances of escape. Of course, he entered at this juncture, into no explanation of his motives, and they walked on very lovingly together.

In pursuance of this cautious plan, Mr. Claypole went on, without halting, until he arrived at the Angel at Islington, where he wisely judged, from the crowd of passengers and numbers of vehicles, that London began in earnest. Just pausing to observe which appeared the most crowded streets, and consequently the most to be avoided, he crossed into Saint John's Road, and was soon deep in the obscurity of the intricate and dirty ways, which, lying between Gray's Inn Lane and Smithfield, render that part of the town one of the lowest and worst that improvement has left in the midst of London.

Through these streets, Noah Claypole walked, dragging Charlotte after him; now stepping into the kennel to embrace at a glance the whole external character of some small public-house; now jogging on again, as some fancied appearance induced him to believe it too public for his purpose. At length, he stopped in front of one, more humble in appearance and more dirty than any he had yet seen; and, having crossed over and surveyed it from the opposite pavement, graciously announced his intention of putting up there, for the night.

'So give us the bundle,' said Noah, unstrapping it from the woman's shoulders, and slinging it over his own; 'and don't yer speak, except when yer spoke to. What's the name of the house—t-h-r—three what?'

'Cripples,' said Charlotte.

'Three Cripples,' repeated Noah, 'and a very good sign too. Now, then! Keep close at my heels, and come along.' With these injunctions, he pushed the rattling door with his shoulder, and entered the house, followed by his companion.

There was nobody in the bar but a young Jew, who, with his two elbows on the counter, was reading a dirty newspaper. He stared very hard at Noah, and Noah stared very hard at him.

If Noah had been attired in his charity-boy's dress, there might have been some reason for the Jew opening his eyes so wide; but as he had discarded the coat and badge, and wore a short smock-frock over his leathers, there seemed no particular reason for his appearance exciting so much attention in a public-house.

'Is this the Three Cripples?' asked Noah.

'That is the dabe of this 'ouse,' replied the Jew.

'A gentleman we met on the road, coming up from the country, recommended us here,' said Noah, nudging Charlotte, perhaps to call her attention to this most ingenious device for attracting respect, and perhaps to warn her to betray no surprise. 'We want to sleep here to-night.'

'I'b dot certaid you cad,' said Barney, who was the attendant sprite; 'but I'll idquire.'

'Show us the tap, and give us a bit of cold meat and a drop of beer while yer inquiring, will yer?' said Noah.

Barney complied by ushering them into a small back-room, and setting the required viands before them; having done which, he informed the travellers that they could be lodged that night, and left the amiable couple to their refreshment.

Now, this back-room was immediately behind the bar, and some steps lower, so that any person connected with the house, undrawing a small curtain which concealed a single pane of glass fixed in the wall of the last-named apartment, about five feet from its flooring, could not only look down upon any guests in the back-room without any great hazard of being observed (the glass being in a dark angle of the wall, between which and a large upright beam the observer had to thrust himself), but could, by applying his ear to the partition, ascertain with tolerable distinctness, their subject of conversation. The landlord of the house had not withdrawn his eye from this place of espial for five minutes, and Barney had only just returned from making the communication above related, when Fagin, in the course of his evening's business, came into the bar to inquire after some of his young pupils.

'Hush!' said Barney: 'stradegers id the next roob.'

'Strangers!' repeated the old man in a whisper.

'Ah! Ad rub uds too,' added Barney. 'Frob the cuttry, but subthig in your way, or I'b bistaked.'

Fagin appeared to receive this communication with great interest.

Mounting a stool, he cautiously applied his eye to the pane of glass, from which secret post he could see Mr. Claypole taking cold beef from the dish, and porter from the pot, and administering homeopathic doses of both to Charlotte, who sat patiently by, eating and drinking at his pleasure.

'Aha!' he whispered, looking round to Barney, 'I like that fellow's looks. He'd be of use to us; he knows how to train the girl already. Don't make as much noise as a mouse, my dear, and let me hear 'em talk—let me hear 'em.'

He again applied his eye to the glass, and turning his ear to the partition, listened attentively: with a subtle and eager look upon his face, that might have appertained to some old goblin.

'So I mean to be a gentleman,' said Mr. Claypole, kicking out his legs, and continuing a conversation, the commencement of which Fagin had arrived too late to hear. 'No more jolly old coffins, Charlotte, but a gentleman's life for me: and, if yer like, yer shall be a lady.'

'I should like that well enough, dear,' replied Charlotte; 'but tills ain't to be emptied every day, and people to get clear off after it.'

'Tills be blowed!' said Mr. Claypole; 'there's more things besides tills to be emptied.'

'What do you mean?' asked his companion.

'Pockets, women's ridicules, houses, mail-coaches, banks!' said Mr. Claypole, rising with the porter.

'But you can't do all that, dear,' said Charlotte.

'I shall look out to get into company with them as can,' replied Noah. 'They'll be able to make us useful some way or another. Why, you yourself are worth fifty women; I never see such a precious sly and deceitful creetur as yer can be when I let yer.'

'Lor, how nice it is to hear yer say so!' exclaimed Charlotte, imprinting a kiss upon his ugly face.

'There, that'll do: don't yer be too affectionate, in case I'm cross with yer,' said Noah, disengaging himself with great gravity. 'I should like to be the captain of some band, and have the whopping of 'em, and follering 'em about, unbeknown to themselves. That would suit me, if there was good profit; and if we could only get in with some gentleman of this sort, I say it would be cheap at that twenty-pound note you've got,—especially as we don't very well know how to get rid of it ourselves.'

After expressing this opinion, Mr. Claypole looked into the porter-pot with an aspect of deep wisdom; and having well shaken its contents, nodded condescendingly to Charlotte, and took a draught, wherewith he appeared greatly refreshed. He was meditating another, when the sudden opening of the door, and the appearance of a stranger, interrupted him.

The stranger was Mr. Fagin. And very amiable he looked, and a very low bow he made, as he advanced, and setting himself down at the nearest table, ordered something to drink of the grinning Barney.

'A pleasant night, sir, but cool for the time of year,' said Fagin, rubbing his hands. 'From the country, I see, sir?'

'How do yer see that?' asked Noah Claypole.

'We have not so much dust as that in London,' replied Fagin, pointing from Noah's shoes to those of his companion, and from them to the two bundles.

'Yer a sharp feller,' said Noah. 'Ha! ha! only hear that, Charlotte!'

'Why, one need be sharp in this town, my dear,' replied the Jew, sinking his voice to a confidential whisper; 'and that's the truth.'

Fagin followed up this remark by striking the side of his nose with his right forefinger,—a gesture which Noah attempted to imitate, though not with complete success, in consequence of his own nose not being large enough for the purpose. However, Mr. Fagin seemed to interpret the endeavour as expressing a perfect coincidence with his opinion, and put about the liquor which Barney reappeared with, in a very friendly manner.

'Good stuff that,' observed Mr. Claypole, smacking his lips.

'Dear!' said Fagin. 'A man need be always emptying a till, or a pocket, or a woman's reticule, or a house, or a mail-coach, or a bank, if he drinks it regularly.'

Mr. Claypole no sooner heard this extract from his own remarks than he fell back in his chair, and looked from the Jew to Charlotte with a countenance of ashy paleness and excessive terror.

'Don't mind me, my dear,' said Fagin, drawing his chair closer. 'Ha! ha! it was lucky it was only me that heard you by chance. It was very lucky it was only me.'

'I didn't take it,' stammered Noah, no longer stretching out his legs like an independent gentleman, but coiling them up as well as he could under his chair; 'it was all her doing; yer've got it now, Charlotte, yer know yer have.'

'No matter who's got it, or who did it, my dear,' replied Fagin, glancing, nevertheless, with a hawk's eye at the girl and the two bundles. 'I'm in that way myself, and I like you for it.'

'In what way?' asked Mr. Claypole, a little recovering.

'In that way of business,' rejoined Fagin; 'and so are the people of the house. You've hit the right nail upon the head, and are as safe here as you could be. There is not a safer place in all this town than is the Cripples; that is, when I like to make it so. And I have taken a fancy to you and the young woman; so I've said the word, and you may make your minds easy.'

Noah Claypole's mind might have been at ease after this assurance, but his body certainly was not; for he shuffled and writhed about, into various uncouth positions: eyeing his new friend meanwhile with mingled fear and suspicion.

'I'll tell you more,' said Fagin, after he had reassured the girl, by dint of friendly nods and muttered encouragements. 'I have got a friend that I think can gratify your darling wish, and put you in the right way, where you can take whatever department of the business you think will suit you best at first, and be taught all the others.'

'Yer speak as if yer were in earnest,' replied Noah.

'What advantage would it be to me to be anything else?' inquired Fagin, shrugging his shoulders. 'Here! Let me have a word with you outside.'

'There's no occasion to trouble ourselves to move,' said Noah, getting his legs by gradual degrees abroad again. 'She'll take the luggage upstairs the while. Charlotte, see to them bundles.'

This mandate, which had been delivered with great majesty, was obeyed without the slightest demur; and Charlotte made the best of her way off with the packages while Noah held the door open and watched her out.

'She's kept tolerably well under, ain't she?' he asked as he resumed his seat: in the tone of a keeper who had tamed some wild animal.

'Quite perfect,' rejoined Fagin, clapping him on the shoulder. 'You're a genius, my dear.'

'Why, I suppose if I wasn't, I shouldn't be here,' replied Noah. 'But, I say, she'll be back if yer lose time.'

'Now, what do you think?' said Fagin. 'If you was to like my friend, could you do better than join him?'

'Is he in a good way of business; that's where it is!' responded Noah, winking one of his little eyes.

'The top of the tree; employs a power of hands; has the very best society in the profession.'

'Regular town-maders?' asked Mr. Claypole.

'Not a countryman among 'em; and I don't think he'd take you, even on my recommendation, if he didn't run rather short of assistants just now,' replied Fagin.

'Should I have to hand over?' said Noah, slapping his breeches-pocket.

'It couldn't possibly be done without,' replied Fagin, in a most decided manner.

'Twenty pound, though—it's a lot of money!'

'Not when it's in a note you can't get rid of,' retorted Fagin. 'Number and date taken, I suppose? Payment stopped at the Bank? Ah! It's not worth much to him. It'll have to go abroad, and he couldn't sell it for a great deal in the market.'

'When could I see him?' asked Noah doubtfully.

'To-morrow morning.'

'Where?'

'Here.'

'Um!' said Noah. 'What's the wages?'

'Live like a gentleman—board and lodging, pipes and spirits free—half of all you earn, and half of all the young woman earns,' replied Mr. Fagin.

Whether Noah Claypole, whose rapacity was none of the least comprehensive, would have acceded even to these glowing terms, had he been a perfectly free agent, is very doubtful; but as he recollected that, in the event of his refusal, it was in the power of his new acquaintance to give him up to justice immediately (and more unlikely things had come to pass), he gradually relented, and said he thought that would suit him.

'But, yer see,' observed Noah, 'as she will be able to do a good deal, I should like to take something very light.'

'A little fancy work?' suggested Fagin.

'Ah! something of that sort,' replied Noah. 'What do you think would suit me now? Something not too trying for the strength, and not very dangerous, you know. That's the sort of thing!'

'I heard you talk of something in the spy way upon the others, my dear,' said Fagin. 'My friend wants somebody who would do that well, very much.'

'Why, I did mention that, and I shouldn't mind turning my hand to it sometimes,' rejoined Mr. Claypole slowly; 'but it wouldn't pay by itself, you know.'

'That's true!' observed the Jew, ruminating or pretending to ruminate. 'No, it might not.'

'What do you think, then?' asked Noah, anxiously regarding him. 'Something in the sneaking way, where it was pretty sure work, and not much more risk than being at home.'

'What do you think of the old ladies?' asked Fagin. 'There's a good deal of money made in snatching their bags and parcels, and running round the corner.'

'Don't they holler out a good deal, and scratch sometimes?' asked Noah, shaking his head. 'I don't think that would answer my purpose. Ain't there any other line open?'

'Stop!' said Fagin, laying his hand on Noah's knee. 'The kinchin lay.'

'What's that?' demanded Mr. Claypole.

'The kinchins, my dear,' said Fagin, 'is the young children that's sent on errands by their mothers, with sixpences and shillings; and the lay is just to take their money away—they've always got it ready in their hands,—then knock 'em into the kennel, and walk off very slow, as if there were nothing else the matter but a child fallen down and hurt itself. Ha! ha! ha!'

'Ha! ha!' roared Mr. Claypole, kicking up his legs in an ecstasy. 'Lord, that's the very thing!'

'To be sure it is,' replied Fagin; 'and you can have a few good beats chalked out in Camden Town, and Battle Bridge, and neighborhoods like that, where they're always going errands; and you can upset as many kinchins as you want, any hour in the day. Ha! ha! ha!'

With this, Fagin poked Mr. Claypole in the side, and they joined in a burst of laughter both long and loud.

'Well, that's all right!' said Noah, when he had recovered himself, and Charlotte had returned. 'What time to-morrow shall we say?'

'Will ten do?' asked Fagin, adding, as Mr. Claypole nodded assent, 'What name shall I tell my good friend.'

'Mr. Bolter,' replied Noah, who had prepared himself for such emergency. 'Mr. Morris Bolter. This is Mrs. Bolter.'

'Mrs. Bolter's humble servant,' said Fagin, bowing with grotesque politeness. 'I hope I shall know her better very shortly.'

'Do you hear the gentleman, Charlotte?' thundered Mr. Claypole.

'Yes, Noah, dear!' replied Mrs. Bolter, extending her hand.

'She calls me Noah, as a sort of fond way of talking,' said Mr. Morris Bolter, late Claypole, turning to Fagin. 'You understand?'

'Oh yes, I understand—perfectly,' replied Fagin, telling the truth for once. 'Good-night! Good-night!'

With many adieus and good wishes, Mr. Fagin went his way. Noah Claypole, bespeaking his good lady's attention, proceeded to enlighten her relative to the arrangement he had made, with all that haughtiness and air of superiority, becoming, not only a member of the sterner sex, but a gentleman who appreciated the dignity of a special appointment on the kinchin lay, in London and its vicinity.

CHAPTER XLIII. WHEREIN IS SHOWN HOW THE ARTFUL DODGER GOT INTO TROUBLE

'And so it was you that was your own friend, was it?' asked Mr. Claypole, otherwise Bolter, when, by virtue of the compact entered into between them, he had removed next day to Fagin's house. ''Cod, I thought as much last night!'

'Every man's his own friend, my dear,' replied Fagin, with his most insinuating grin. 'He hasn't as good a one as himself anywhere.'

'Except sometimes,' replied Morris Bolter, assuming the air of a man of the world. 'Some people are nobody's enemies but their own, yer know.'

'Don't believe that,' said Fagin. 'When a man's his own enemy, it's only because he's too much his own friend; not because he's careful for everybody but himself. Pooh! pooh! There ain't such a thing in nature.'

'There oughn't to be, if there is,' replied Mr. Bolter.

'That stands to reason. Some conjurers say that number three is the magic number, and some say number seven. It's neither, my friend, neither. It's number one.'

'Ha! ha!' cried Mr. Bolter. 'Number one for ever.'

'In a little community like ours, my dear,' said Fagin, who felt it necessary to qualify this position, 'we have a general number one, without considering me too as the same, and all the other young people.'

'Oh, the devil!' exclaimed Mr. Bolter.

'You see,' pursued Fagin, affecting to disregard this interruption, 'we are so mixed up together, and identified in our interests, that it must be so. For instance, it's your object to take care of number one—meaning yourself.'

'Certainly,' replied Mr. Bolter. 'Yer about right there.'

'Well! You can't take care of yourself, number one, without taking care of me, number one.'

'Number two, you mean,' said Mr. Bolter, who was largely endowed with the quality of selfishness.

'No, I don't!' retorted Fagin. 'I'm of the same importance to you, as you are to yourself.'

'I say,' interrupted Mr. Bolter, 'yer a very nice man, and I'm very fond of yer; but we ain't quite so thick together, as all that comes to.'

'Only think,' said Fagin, shrugging his shoulders, and stretching out his hands; 'only consider. You've done what's a very pretty thing, and what I love you for doing; but what at the same time would put the cravat round your throat, that's so very easily tied and so very difficult to unloose—in plain English, the halter!'

Mr. Bolter put his hand to his neckerchief, as if he felt it inconveniently tight; and murmured an assent, qualified in tone but not in substance.

'The gallows,' continued Fagin, 'the gallows, my dear, is an ugly finger-post, which points out a very short and sharp turning that has stopped many a bold fellow's career on the broad highway. To keep in the easy road, and keep it at a distance, is object number one with you.'

'Of course it is,' replied Mr. Bolter. 'What do yer talk about such things for?'

'Only to show you my meaning clearly,' said the Jew, raising his eyebrows. 'To be able to do that, you depend upon me. To keep my little business all snug, I depend upon you. The first is your number one, the second my number one. The more you value your number one, the more careful you must be of mine; so we come at last to what I told you at first—that a regard for number one holds us all together, and must do so, unless we would all go to pieces in company.'

'That's true,' rejoined Mr. Bolter, thoughtfully. 'Oh! yer a cunning old codger!'

Mr. Fagin saw, with delight, that this tribute to his powers was no mere compliment, but that he had really impressed his recruit with a sense of his wily genius, which it was most important that he should entertain in the outset of their acquaintance. To strengthen an impression so desirable and useful, he followed up the blow by acquainting him, in some detail, with the magnitude and extent of his operations; blending truth and fiction together, as best served his purpose; and bringing both to bear, with so much art, that Mr. Bolter's respect visibly increased, and became tempered, at the same time, with a degree of wholesome fear, which it was highly desirable to awaken.

'It's this mutual trust we have in each other that consoles me under heavy losses,' said Fagin. 'My best hand was taken from me, yesterday morning.'

'You don't mean to say he died?' cried Mr. Bolter.

'No, no,' replied Fagin, 'not so bad as that. Not quite so bad.'

'What, I suppose he was—'

'Wanted,' interposed Fagin. 'Yes, he was wanted.'

'Very particular?' inquired Mr. Bolter.

'No,' replied Fagin, 'not very. He was charged with attempting to pick a pocket, and they found a silver snuff-box on him,—his own, my dear, his own, for he took snuff himself, and was very fond of it. They remanded him till to-day, for they thought they knew the owner. Ah! he was worth fifty boxes, and I'd give the price of as many to have him back. You should have known the Dodger, my dear; you should have known the Dodger.'

'Well, but I shall know him, I hope; don't yer think so?' said Mr. Bolter.

'I'm doubtful about it,' replied Fagin, with a sigh. 'If they don't get any fresh evidence, it'll only be a summary conviction, and we shall have him back again after six weeks or so; but, if they do, it's a case of lagging. They know what a clever lad he is; he'll be a lifer. They'll make the Artful nothing less than a lifer.'

'What do you mean by lagging and a lifer?' demanded Mr. Bolter. 'What's the good of talking in that way to me; why don't yer speak so as I can understand yer?'

Fagin was about to translate these mysterious expressions into the vulgar tongue; and, being interpreted, Mr. Bolter would have been informed that they represented that combination of words, 'transportation for life,' when the dialogue was cut short by the entry of Master Bates, with his hands in his breeches-pockets, and his face twisted into a look of semi-comical woe.

'It's all up, Fagin,' said Charley, when he and his new companion had been made known to each other.

'What do you mean?'

'They've found the gentleman as owns the box; two or three more's a coming to 'dentify him; and the Artful's booked for a passage out,' replied Master Bates. 'I must have a full suit of mourning, Fagin, and a hatband, to wisit him in, afore he sets out upon his travels. To think of Jack Dawkins—lummy Jack—the Dodger—the Artful Dodger—going abroad for a common twopenny-halfpenny sneeze-box! I never thought he'd a done it under a gold watch, chain, and seals, at the lowest. Oh, why didn't he rob some rich old gentleman of all his walables, and go out as a gentleman, and not like a common prig, without no honour nor glory!'

With this expression of feeling for his unfortunate friend, Master Bates sat himself on the nearest chair with an aspect of chagrin and despondency.

'What do you talk about his having neither honour nor glory for!' exclaimed Fagin, darting an angry look at his pupil. 'Wasn't he always the top-sawyer among you all! Is there one of you that could touch him or come near him on any scent! Eh?'

'Not one,' replied Master Bates, in a voice rendered husky by regret; 'not one.'

'Then what do you talk of?' replied Fagin angrily; 'what are you blubbering for?'

''Cause it isn't on the rec-ord, is it?' said Charley, chafed into perfect defiance of his venerable friend by the current of his regrets; ''cause it can't come out in the 'dictment; 'cause nobody will never know half of what he was. How will he stand in the Newgate Calendar? P'raps not be there at all. Oh, my eye, my eye, wot a blow it is!'

'Ha! ha!' cried Fagin, extending his right hand, and turning to Mr. Bolter in a fit of chuckling which shook him as though he had the palsy; 'see what a pride they take in their profession, my dear. Ain't it beautiful?'

Mr. Bolter nodded assent, and Fagin, after contemplating the grief of Charley Bates for some seconds with evident satisfaction, stepped up to that young gentleman and patted him on the shoulder.

'Never mind, Charley,' said Fagin soothingly; 'it'll come out, it'll be sure to come out. They'll all know what a clever fellow he was; he'll show it himself, and not disgrace his old pals and teachers. Think how young he is too! What a distinction, Charley, to be lagged at his time of life!'

'Well, it is a honour that is!' said Charley, a little consoled.

'He shall have all he wants,' continued the Jew. 'He shall be kept in the Stone Jug, Charley, like a gentleman. Like a gentleman! With his beer every day, and money in his pocket to pitch and toss with, if he can't spend it.'

'No, shall he though?' cried Charley Bates.

'Ay, that he shall,' replied Fagin, 'and we'll have a big-wig, Charley: one that's got the greatest gift of the gab: to carry on his defence; and he shall make a speech for himself too, if he likes; and we'll read it all in the papers—"Artful Dodger—shrieks of laughter—here the court was convulsed"—eh, Charley, eh?'

'Ha! ha!' laughed Master Bates, 'what a lark that would be, wouldn't it, Fagin? I say, how the Artful would bother 'em wouldn't he?'

'Would!' cried Fagin. 'He shall—he will!'

'Ah, to be sure, so he will,' repeated Charley, rubbing his hands.

'I think I see him now,' cried the Jew, bending his eyes upon his pupil.

'So do I,' cried Charley Bates. 'Ha! ha! ha! so do I. I see it all afore me, upon my soul I do, Fagin. What a game! What a regular game! All the big-wigs trying to look solemn, and Jack Dawkins addressing of 'em as intimate and comfortable as if he was the judge's own son making a speech arter dinner—ha! ha! ha!'

In fact, Mr. Fagin had so well humoured his young friend's eccentric disposition, that Master Bates, who had at first been disposed to consider the imprisoned Dodger rather in the light of a victim, now looked upon him as the chief actor in a scene of most uncommon and exquisite humour, and felt quite impatient for the arrival of the time when his old companion should have so favourable an opportunity of displaying his abilities.

'We must know how he gets on to-day, by some handy means or other,' said Fagin. 'Let me think.'

'Shall I go?' asked Charley.

'Not for the world,' replied Fagin. 'Are you mad, my dear, stark mad, that you'd walk into the very place where—No, Charley, no. One is enough to lose at a time.'

'You don't mean to go yourself, I suppose?' said Charley with a humorous leer.

'That wouldn't quite fit,' replied Fagin shaking his head.

'Then why don't you send this new cove?' asked Master Bates, laying his hand on Noah's arm. 'Nobody knows him.'

'Why, if he didn't mind—' observed Fagin.

'Mind!' interposed Charley. 'What should he have to mind?'

'Really nothing, my dear,' said Fagin, turning to Mr. Bolter, 'really nothing.'

'Oh, I dare say about that, yer know,' observed Noah, backing towards the door, and shaking his head with a kind of sober alarm. 'No, no—none of that. It's not in my department, that ain't.'

'Wot department has he got, Fagin?' inquired Master Bates, surveying Noah's lank form with much disgust. 'The cutting away when there's anything wrong, and the eating all the wittles when there's everything right; is that his branch?'

'Never mind,' retorted Mr. Bolter; 'and don't yer take liberties with yer superiors, little boy, or yer'll find yerself in the wrong shop.'

Master Bates laughed so vehemently at this magnificent threat, that it was some time before Fagin could interpose, and represent to Mr. Bolter that he incurred no possible danger in visiting the police-office; that, inasmuch as no account of the little affair in which he had engaged, nor any description of his person, had yet been forwarded to the metropolis, it was very probable that he was not even suspected of having resorted to it for shelter; and that, if he were properly disguised, it would be as safe a spot for him to visit as any in London, inasmuch as it would be, of all places, the very last, to which he could be supposed likely to resort of his own free will.

Persuaded, in part, by these representations, but overborne in a much greater degree by his fear of Fagin, Mr. Bolter at length consented, with a very bad grace, to undertake the expedition. By Fagin's directions, he immediately substituted for his own attire, a waggoner's frock, velveteen breeches, and leather leggings: all of which articles the Jew had at hand. He was likewise furnished with a felt hat well garnished with turnpike tickets; and a carter's whip. Thus equipped, he was to saunter into the office, as some country fellow from Covent Garden market might be supposed to do for the gratification of his curiousity; and as he was as awkward, ungainly, and raw-boned a fellow as need be, Mr. Fagin had no fear but that he would look the part to perfection.

These arrangements completed, he was informed of the necessary signs and tokens by which to recognise the Artful Dodger, and was conveyed by Master Bates through dark and winding ways to within a very short distance of Bow Street. Having described the precise situation of the office, and accompanied it with copious directions how he was to walk straight up the passage, and when he got into the side, and pull off his hat as he went into the room, Charley Bates bade him hurry on alone, and promised to bide his return on the spot of their parting.

Noah Claypole, or Morris Bolter as the reader pleases, punctually followed the directions he had received, which—Master Bates being pretty well acquainted with the locality—were so exact that he was enabled to gain the magisterial presence without asking any question, or meeting with any interruption by the way.

He found himself jostled among a crowd of people, chiefly women, who were huddled together in a dirty frowsy room, at the upper end of which was a raised platform railed off from the rest, with a dock for the prisoners on the left hand against the wall, a box for the witnesses in the middle, and a desk for the magistrates on the right; the awful locality last named, being screened off by a partition which concealed the bench from the common gaze, and left the vulgar to imagine (if they could) the full majesty of justice.

There were only a couple of women in the dock, who were nodding to their admiring friends, while the clerk read some depositions to a couple of policemen and a man in plain clothes who leant over the table. A jailer stood reclining against the dock-rail, tapping his nose listlessly with a large key, except when he repressed an undue tendency to conversation among the idlers, by proclaiming silence; or looked sternly up to bid some woman 'Take that baby out,' when the gravity of justice was disturbed by feeble cries, half-smothered in the mother's shawl, from some meagre infant. The room smelt close and unwholesome; the walls were dirt-discoloured; and the ceiling blackened. There was an old smoky bust over the mantel-shelf, and a dusty clock above the dock—the only thing present, that seemed to go on as it ought; for depravity, or poverty, or an habitual acquaintance with both, had left a taint on all the animate matter, hardly less unpleasant than the thick greasy scum on every inanimate object that frowned upon it.

Noah looked eagerly about him for the Dodger; but although there were several women who would have done very well for that distinguished character's mother or sister, and more than one man who might be supposed to bear a strong resemblance to his father, nobody at all answering the description given him of Mr. Dawkins was to be seen. He waited in a state of much suspense and uncertainty until the women, being committed for trial, went flaunting out; and then was quickly relieved by the appearance of another prisoner who he felt at once could be no other than the object of his visit.

It was indeed Mr. Dawkins, who, shuffling into the office with the big coat sleeves tucked up as usual, his left hand in his pocket, and his hat in his right hand, preceded the jailer, with a rolling gait altogether indescribable, and, taking his place in the dock, requested in an audible voice to know what he was placed in that 'ere disgraceful sitivation for.

'Hold your tongue, will you?' said the jailer.

'I'm an Englishman, ain't I?' rejoined the Dodger. 'Where are my priwileges?'

'You'll get your privileges soon enough,' retorted the jailer, 'and pepper with 'em.'

'We'll see wot the Secretary of State for the Home Affairs has got to say to the beaks, if I don't,' replied Mr. Dawkins. 'Now then! Wot is this here business? I shall thank the madg'strates to dispose of this here little affair, and not to keep me while they read the paper, for I've got an appointment with a genelman in the City, and as I am a man of my word and wery punctual in business matters, he'll go away if I ain't there to my time, and then pr'aps ther won't be an action for damage against them as kep me away. Oh no, certainly not!'

At this point, the Dodger, with a show of being very particular with a view to proceedings to be had thereafter, desired the jailer to communicate 'the names of them two files as was on the bench.' Which so tickled the spectators, that they laughed almost as heartily as Master Bates could have done if he had heard the request.

'Silence there!' cried the jailer.

'What is this?' inquired one of the magistrates.

'A pick-pocketing case, your worship.'

'Has the boy ever been here before?'

'He ought to have been, a many times,' replied the jailer. 'He has been pretty well everywhere else. I know him well, your worship.'

'Oh! you know me, do you?' cried the Artful, making a note of the statement. 'Wery good. That's a case of deformation of character, any way.'

Here there was another laugh, and another cry of silence.

'Now then, where are the witnesses?' said the clerk.

'Ah! that's right,' added the Dodger. 'Where are they? I should like to see 'em.'

This wish was immediately gratified, for a policeman stepped forward who had seen the prisoner attempt the pocket of an unknown gentleman in a crowd, and indeed take a handkerchief therefrom, which, being a very old one, he deliberately put back again, after trying it on his own countenance. For this reason, he took the Dodger into custody as soon as he could get near him, and the said Dodger, being searched, had upon his person a silver snuff-box, with the owner's name engraved upon the lid. This gentleman had been discovered on reference to the Court Guide, and being then and there present, swore that the snuff-box was his, and that he had missed it on the previous day, the moment he had disengaged himself from the crowd before referred to. He had also remarked a young gentleman in the throng, particularly active in making his way about, and that young gentleman was the prisoner before him.

'Have you anything to ask this witness, boy?' said the magistrate.

'I wouldn't abase myself by descending to hold no conversation with him,' replied the Dodger.

'Have you anything to say at all?'

'Do you hear his worship ask if you've anything to say?' inquired the jailer, nudging the silent Dodger with his elbow.

'I beg your pardon,' said the Dodger, looking up with an air of abstraction. 'Did you redress yourself to me, my man?'

'I never see such an out-and-out young wagabond, your worship,' observed the officer with a grin. 'Do you mean to say anything, you young shaver?'

'No,' replied the Dodger, 'not here, for this ain't the shop for justice: besides which, my attorney is a-breakfasting this morning with the Wice President of the House of Commons; but I shall have something to say elsewhere, and so will he, and so will a wery numerous and 'spectable circle of acquaintance as'll make them beaks wish they'd never been born, or that they'd got their footmen to hang 'em up to their own hat-pegs, afore they let 'em come out this morning to try it on upon me. I'll—'

'There! He's fully committed!' interposed the clerk. 'Take him away.'

'Come on,' said the jailer.

'Oh ah! I'll come on,' replied the Dodger, brushing his hat with the palm of his hand. 'Ah! (to the Bench) it's no use your looking frightened; I won't show you no mercy, not a ha'porth of it. You'll pay for this, my fine fellers. I wouldn't be you for something! I wouldn't go free, now, if you was to fall down on your knees and ask me. Here, carry me off to prison! Take me away!'

With these last words, the Dodger suffered himself to be led off by the collar; threatening, till he got into the yard, to make a parliamentary business of it; and then grinning in the officer's face, with great glee and self-approval.

Having seen him locked up by himself in a little cell, Noah made the best of his way back to where he had left Master Bates. After waiting here some time, he was joined by that young gentleman, who had prudently abstained from showing himself until he had looked carefully abroad from a snug retreat, and ascertained that his new friend had not been followed by any impertinent person.

The two hastened back together, to bear to Mr. Fagin the animating news that the Dodger was doing full justice to his bringing-up, and establishing for himself a glorious reputation.

CHAPTER XLIV. THE TIME ARRIVES FOR NANCY TO REDEEM HER PLEDGE TO ROSE MAYLIE. SHE FAILS.

Adept as she was, in all the arts of cunning and dissimulation, the girl Nancy could not wholly conceal the effect which the knowledge of the step she had taken, wrought upon her mind. She remembered that both the crafty Jew and the brutal Sikes had confided to her schemes, which had been hidden from all others: in the full confidence that she was trustworthy and beyond the reach of their suspicion. Vile as those schemes were, desperate as were their originators, and bitter as were her feelings towards Fagin, who had led her, step by step, deeper and deeper down into an abyss of crime and misery, whence was no escape; still, there were times when, even towards him, she felt some relenting, lest her disclosure should bring him within the iron grasp he had so long eluded, and he should fall at last—richly as he merited such a fate—by her hand.

But, these were the mere wanderings of a mind unable wholly to detach itself from old companions and associations, though enabled to fix itself steadily on one object, and resolved not to be turned aside by any consideration. Her fears for Sikes would have been more powerful inducements to recoil while there was yet time; but she had stipulated that her secret should be rigidly kept, she had dropped no clue which could lead to his discovery, she had refused, even for his sake, a refuge from all the guilt and wretchedness that encompasses her—and what more could she do! She was resolved.

Though all her mental struggles terminated in this conclusion, they forced themselves upon her, again and again, and left their traces too. She grew pale and thin, even within a few days. At times, she took no heed of what was passing before her, or no part in conversations where once, she would have been the loudest. At other times, she laughed without merriment, and was noisy without a moment afterwards—she sat silent and dejected, brooding with her head upon her hands, while the very effort by which she roused herself, told, more forcibly than even these indications, that she was ill at ease, and that her thoughts were occupied with matters very different and distant from those in the course of discussion by her companions.

It was Sunday night, and the bell of the nearest church struck the hour. Sikes and the Jew were talking, but they paused to listen. The girl looked up from the low seat on which she crouched, and listened too. Eleven.

'An hour this side of midnight,' said Sikes, raising the blind to look out and returning to his seat. 'Dark and heavy it is too. A good night for business this.'

'Ah!' replied Fagin. 'What a pity, Bill, my dear, that there's none quite ready to be done.'

'You're right for once,' replied Sikes gruffly. 'It is a pity, for I'm in the humour too.'

Fagin sighed, and shook his head despondingly.

'We must make up for lost time when we've got things into a good train. That's all I know,' said Sikes.

'That's the way to talk, my dear,' replied Fagin, venturing to pat him on the shoulder. 'It does me good to hear you.'

'Does you good, does it!' cried Sikes. 'Well, so be it.'

'Ha! ha! ha!' laughed Fagin, as if he were relieved by even this concession. 'You're like yourself to-night, Bill. Quite like yourself.'

'I don't feel like myself when you lay that withered old claw on my shoulder, so take it away,' said Sikes, casting off the Jew's hand.

'It make you nervous, Bill,—reminds you of being nabbed, does it?' said Fagin, determined not to be offended.

'Reminds me of being nabbed by the devil,' returned Sikes. 'There never was another man with such a face as yours, unless it was your father, and I suppose he is singeing his grizzled red beard by this time, unless you came straight from the old 'un without any father at all betwixt you; which I shouldn't wonder at, a bit.'

Fagin offered no reply to this compliment: but, pulling Sikes by the sleeve, pointed his finger towards Nancy, who had taken advantage of the foregoing conversation to put on her bonnet, and was now leaving the room.

'Hallo!' cried Sikes. 'Nance. Where's the gal going to at this time of night?'

'Not far.'

'What answer's that?' retorted Sikes. 'Do you hear me?'

'I don't know where,' replied the girl.

'Then I do,' said Sikes, more in the spirit of obstinacy than because he had any real objection to the girl going where she listed. 'Nowhere. Sit down.'

'I'm not well. I told you that before,' rejoined the girl. 'I want a breath of air.'

'Put your head out of the winder,' replied Sikes.

'There's not enough there,' said the girl. 'I want it in the street.'

'Then you won't have it,' replied Sikes. With which assurance he rose, locked the door, took the key out, and pulling her bonnet from her head, flung it up to the top of an old press. 'There,' said the robber. 'Now stop quietly where you are, will you?'

'It's not such a matter as a bonnet would keep me,' said the girl turning very pale. 'What do you mean, Bill? Do you know what you're doing?'

'Know what I'm—Oh!' cried Sikes, turning to Fagin, 'she's out of her senses, you know, or she daren't talk to me in that way.'

'You'll drive me on the something desperate,' muttered the girl placing both hands upon her breast, as though to keep down by force some violent outbreak. 'Let me go, will you,—this minute—this instant.'

'No!' said Sikes.

'Tell him to let me go, Fagin. He had better. It'll be better for him. Do you hear me?' cried Nancy stamping her foot upon the ground.

'Hear you!' repeated Sikes turning round in his chair to confront her. 'Aye! And if I hear you for half a minute longer, the dog shall have such a grip on your throat as'll tear some of that screaming voice out. Wot has come over you, you jade! Wot is it?'

'Let me go,' said the girl with great earnestness; then sitting herself down on the floor, before the door, she said, 'Bill, let me go; you don't know what you are doing. You don't, indeed. For only one hour—do—do!'

'Cut my limbs off one by one!' cried Sikes, seizing her roughly by the arm, 'If I don't think the gal's stark raving mad. Get up.'

'Not till you let me go—not till you let me go—Never—never!' screamed the girl. Sikes looked on, for a minute, watching his opportunity, and suddenly pinioning her hands dragged her, struggling and wrestling with him by the way, into a small room adjoining, where he sat himself on a bench, and thrusting her into a chair, held her down by force. She struggled and implored by turns until twelve o'clock had struck, and then, wearied and exhausted, ceased to contest the point any further. With a caution, backed by many oaths, to make no more efforts to go out that night, Sikes left her to recover at leisure and rejoined Fagin.

'Whew!' said the housebreaker wiping the perspiration from his face. 'Wot a precious strange gal that is!'

'You may say that, Bill,' replied Fagin thoughtfully. 'You may say that.'

'Wot did she take it into her head to go out to-night for, do you think?' asked Sikes. 'Come; you should know her better than me. Wot does it mean?'

'Obstinacy; woman's obstinacy, I suppose, my dear.'

'Well, I suppose it is,' growled Sikes. 'I thought I had tamed her, but she's as bad as ever.'

'Worse,' said Fagin thoughtfully. 'I never knew her like this, for such a little cause.'

'Nor I,' said Sikes. 'I think she's got a touch of that fever in her blood yet, and it won't come out—eh?'

'Like enough.'

'I'll let her a little blood, without troubling the doctor, if she's took that way again,' said Sikes.

Fagin nodded an expressive approval of this mode of treatment.

'She was hanging about me all day, and night too, when I was stretched on my back; and you, like a blackhearted wolf as you are, kept yourself aloof,' said Sikes. 'We was poor too, all the time, and I think, one way or other, it's worried and fretted her; and that being shut up here so long has made her restless—eh?'

'That's it, my dear,' replied the Jew in a whisper. 'Hush!'

As he uttered these words, the girl herself appeared and resumed her former seat. Her eyes were swollen and red; she rocked herself to and fro; tossed her head; and, after a little time, burst out laughing.

'Why, now she's on the other tack!' exclaimed Sikes, turning a look of excessive surprise on his companion.

Fagin nodded to him to take no further notice just then; and, in a few minutes, the girl subsided into her accustomed demeanour. Whispering Sikes that there was no fear of her relapsing, Fagin took up his hat and bade him good-night. He paused when he reached the room-door, and looking round, asked if somebody would light him down the dark stairs.

'Light him down,' said Sikes, who was filling his pipe. 'It's a pity he should break his neck himself, and disappoint the sight-seers. Show him a light.'

Nancy followed the old man downstairs, with a candle. When they reached the passage, he laid his finger on his lip, and drawing close to the girl, said, in a whisper.

'What is it, Nancy, dear?'

'What do you mean?' replied the girl, in the same tone.

'The reason of all this,' replied Fagin. 'If he'—he pointed with his skinny fore-finger up the stairs—'is so hard with you (he's a brute, Nance, a brute-beast), why don't you—'

'Well?' said the girl, as Fagin paused, with his mouth almost touching her ear, and his eyes looking into hers.

'No matter just now. We'll talk of this again. You have a friend in me, Nance; a staunch friend. I have the means at hand, quiet and close. If you want revenge on those that treat you like a dog—like a dog! worse than his dog, for he humours him sometimes—come to me. I say, come to me. He is the mere hound of a day, but you know me of old, Nance.'

'I know you well,' replied the girl, without manifesting the least emotion. 'Good-night.'

She shrank back, as Fagin offered to lay his hand on hers, but said good-night again, in a steady voice, and, answering his parting look with a nod of intelligence, closed the door between them.

Fagin walked towards his home, intent upon the thoughts that were working within his brain. He had conceived the idea—not from what had just passed though that had tended to confirm him, but slowly and by degrees—that Nancy, wearied of the housebreaker's brutality, had conceived an attachment for some new friend. Her altered manner, her repeated absences from home alone, her comparative indifference to the interests of the gang for which she had once been so zealous, and, added to these, her desperate impatience to leave home that night at a particular hour, all favoured the supposition, and rendered it, to him at least, almost matter of certainty. The object of this new liking was not among his myrmidons. He would be a valuable acquisition with such an assistant as Nancy, and must (thus Fagin argued) be secured without delay.

There was another, and a darker object, to be gained. Sikes knew too much, and his ruffian taunts had not galled Fagin the less, because the wounds were hidden. The girl must know, well, that if she shook him off, she could never be safe from his fury, and that it would be surely wreaked—to the maiming of limbs, or perhaps the loss of life—on the object of her more recent fancy.

'With a little persuasion,' thought Fagin, 'what more likely than that she would consent to poison him? Women have done such things, and worse, to secure the same object before now. There would be the dangerous villain: the man I hate: gone; another secured in his place; and my influence over the girl, with a knowledge of this crime to back it, unlimited.'

These things passed through the mind of Fagin, during the short time he sat alone, in the housebreaker's room; and with them uppermost in his thoughts, he had taken the opportunity afterwards afforded him, of sounding the girl in the broken hints he threw out at parting. There was no expression of surprise, no assumption of an inability to understand his meaning. The girl clearly comprehended it. Her glance at parting showed that.

But perhaps she would recoil from a plot to take the life of Sikes, and that was one of the chief ends to be attained. 'How,' thought Fagin, as he crept homeward, 'can I increase my influence with her? What new power can I acquire?'

Such brains are fertile in expedients. If, without extracting a confession from herself, he laid a watch, discovered the object of her altered regard, and threatened to reveal the whole history to Sikes (of whom she stood in no common fear) unless she entered into his designs, could he not secure her compliance?

'I can,' said Fagin, almost aloud. 'She durst not refuse me then. Not for her life, not for her life! I have it all. The means are ready, and shall be set to work. I shall have you yet!'

He cast back a dark look, and a threatening motion of the hand, towards the spot where he had left the bolder villain; and went on his way: busying his bony hands in the folds of his tattered garment, which he wrenched tightly in his grasp, as though there were a hated enemy crushed with every motion of his fingers.

CHAPTER XLV. NOAH CLAYPOLE IS EMPLOYED BY FAGIN ON A SECRET MISSION

The old man was up, betimes, next morning, and waited impatiently for the appearance of his new associate, who after a delay that seemed interminable, at length presented himself, and commenced a voracious assault on the breakfast.

'Bolter,' said Fagin, drawing up a chair and seating himself opposite Morris Bolter.

'Well, here I am,' returned Noah. 'What's the matter? Don't yer ask me to do anything till I have done eating. That's a great fault in this place. Yer never get time enough over yer meals.'

'You can talk as you eat, can't you?' said Fagin, cursing his dear young friend's greediness from the very bottom of his heart.

'Oh yes, I can talk. I get on better when I talk,' said Noah, cutting a monstrous slice of bread. 'Where's Charlotte?'

'Out,' said Fagin. 'I sent her out this morning with the other young woman, because I wanted us to be alone.'

'Oh!' said Noah. 'I wish yer'd ordered her to make some buttered toast first. Well. Talk away. Yer won't interrupt me.'

There seemed, indeed, no great fear of anything interrupting him, as he had evidently sat down with a determination to do a great deal of business.

'You did well yesterday, my dear,' said Fagin. 'Beautiful! Six shillings and ninepence halfpenny on the very first day! The kinchin lay will be a fortune to you.'

'Don't you forget to add three pint-pots and a milk-can,' said Mr. Bolter.

'No, no, my dear. The pint-pots were great strokes of genius: but the milk-can was a perfect masterpiece.'

'Pretty well, I think, for a beginner,' remarked Mr. Bolter complacently. 'The pots I took off airy railings, and the milk-can was standing by itself outside a public-house. I thought it might get rusty with the rain, or catch cold, yer know. Eh? Ha! ha! ha!'

Fagin affected to laugh very heartily; and Mr. Bolter having had his laugh out, took a series of large bites, which finished his first hunk of bread and butter, and assisted himself to a second.

'I want you, Bolter,' said Fagin, leaning over the table, 'to do a piece of work for me, my dear, that needs great care and caution.'

'I say,' rejoined Bolter, 'don't yer go shoving me into danger, or sending me any more o' yer police-offices. That don't suit me, that don't; and so I tell yer.'

'That's not the smallest danger in it—not the very smallest,' said the Jew; 'it's only to dodge a woman.'

'An old woman?' demanded Mr. Bolter.

'A young one,' replied Fagin.

'I can do that pretty well, I know,' said Bolter. 'I was a regular cunning sneak when I was at school. What am I to dodge her for? Not to—'

'Not to do anything, but to tell me where she goes, who she sees, and, if possible, what she says; to remember the street, if it is a street, or the house, if it is a house; and to bring me back all the information you can.'

'What'll yer give me?' asked Noah, setting down his cup, and looking his employer, eagerly, in the face.

'If you do it well, a pound, my dear. One pound,' said Fagin, wishing to interest him in the scent as much as possible. 'And that's what I never gave yet, for any job of work where there wasn't valuable consideration to be gained.'

'Who is she?' inquired Noah.

'One of us.'

'Oh Lor!' cried Noah, curling up his nose. 'Yer doubtful of her, are yer?'

'She has found out some new friends, my dear, and I must know who they are,' replied Fagin.

'I see,' said Noah. 'Just to have the pleasure of knowing them, if they're respectable people, eh? Ha! ha! ha! I'm your man.'

'I knew you would be,' cried Fagin, elated by the success of his proposal.

'Of course, of course,' replied Noah. 'Where is she? Where am I to wait for her? Where am I to go?'

'All that, my dear, you shall hear from me. I'll point her out at the proper time,' said Fagin. 'You keep ready, and leave the rest to me.'

That night, and the next, and the next again, the spy sat booted and equipped in his carter's dress: ready to turn out at a word from Fagin. Six nights passed—six long weary nights—and on each, Fagin came home with a disappointed face, and briefly intimated that it was not yet time. On the seventh, he returned earlier, and with an exultation he could not conceal. It was Sunday.

'She goes abroad to-night,' said Fagin, 'and on the right errand, I'm sure; for she has been alone all day, and the man she is afraid of will not be back much before daybreak. Come with

818

me. Quick!'

Noah started up without saying a word; for the Jew was in a state of such intense excitement that it infected him. They left the house stealthily, and hurrying through a labyrinth of streets, arrived at length before a public-house, which Noah recognised as the same in which he had slept, on the night of his arrival in London.

It was past eleven o'clock, and the door was closed. It opened softly on its hinges as Fagin gave a low whistle. They entered, without noise; and the door was closed behind them.

Scarcely venturing to whisper, but substituting dumb show for words, Fagin, and the young Jew who had admitted them, pointed out the pane of glass to Noah, and signed to him to climb up and observe the person in the adjoining room.

'Is that the woman?' he asked, scarcely above his breath.

Fagin nodded yes.

'I can't see her face well,' whispered Noah. 'She is looking down, and the candle is behind her.'

'Stay there,' whispered Fagin. He signed to Barney, who withdrew. In an instant, the lad entered the room adjoining, and, under pretence of snuffing the candle, moved it in the required position, and, speaking to the girl, caused her to raise her face.

'I see her now,' cried the spy.

'Plainly?'

'I should know her among a thousand.'

He hastily descended, as the room-door opened, and the girl came out. Fagin drew him behind a small partition which was curtained off, and they held their breaths as she passed within a few feet of their place of concealment, and emerged by the door at which they had entered.

'Hist!' cried the lad who held the door. 'Dow.'

Noah exchanged a look with Fagin, and darted out.

'To the left,' whispered the lad; 'take the left had, and keep od the other side.'

He did so; and, by the light of the lamps, saw the girl's retreating figure, already at some distance before him. He advanced as near as he considered prudent, and kept on the opposite side of the street, the better to observe her motions. She looked nervously round, twice or thrice, and once stopped to let two men who were following close behind her, pass on. She seemed to gather courage as she advanced, and to walk with a steadier and firmer step. The spy preserved the same relative distance between them, and followed: with his eye upon her.

CHAPTER XLVI. THE APPOINTMENT KEPT

The church clocks chimed three quarters past eleven, as two figures emerged on London Bridge. One, which advanced with a swift and rapid step, was that of a woman who looked eagerly about her as though in quest of some expected object; the other figure was that of a man, who slunk along in the deepest shadow he could find, and, at some distance, accommodated his pace to hers: stopping when she stopped: and as she moved again, creeping stealthily on:

but never allowing himself, in the ardour of his pursuit, to gain upon her footsteps. Thus, they crossed the bridge, from the Middlesex to the Surrey shore, when the woman, apparently disappointed in her anxious scrutiny of the foot-passengers, turned back. The movement was sudden; but he who watched her, was not thrown off his guard by it; for, shrinking into one of the recesses which surmount the piers of the bridge, and leaning over the parapet the better to conceal his figure, he suffered her to pass on the opposite pavement. When she was about the same distance in advance as she had been before, he slipped quietly down, and followed her again. At nearly the centre of the bridge, she stopped. The man stopped too.

It was a very dark night. The day had been unfavourable, and at that hour and place there were few people stirring. Such as there were, hurried quickly past: very possibly without seeing, but certainly without noticing, either the woman, or the man who kept her in view. Their appearance was not calculated to attract the importunate regards of such of London's destitute population, as chanced to take their way over the bridge that night in search of some cold arch or doorless hovel wherein to lay their heads; they stood there in silence: neither speaking nor spoken to, by any one who passed.

A mist hung over the river, deepening the red glare of the fires that burnt upon the small craft moored off the different wharfs, and rendering darker and more indistinct the murky buildings on the banks. The old smoke-stained storehouses on either side, rose heavy and dull from the dense mass of roofs and gables, and frowned sternly upon water too black to reflect even their lumbering shapes. The tower of old Saint Saviour's Church, and the spire of Saint Magnus, so long the giant-warders of the ancient bridge, were visible in the gloom; but the forest of shipping below bridge, and the thickly scattered spires of churches above, were nearly all hidden from sight.

The girl had taken a few restless turns to and fro—closely watched meanwhile by her hidden observer—when the heavy bell of St. Paul's tolled for the death of another day. Midnight had come upon the crowded city. The palace, the night-cellar, the jail, the madhouse: the chambers of birth and death, of health and sickness, the rigid face of the corpse and the calm sleep of the child: midnight was upon them all.

The hour had not struck two minutes, when a young lady, accompanied by a grey-haired gentleman, alighted from a hackney-carriage within a short distance of the bridge, and, having dismissed the vehicle, walked straight towards it. They had scarcely set foot upon its pavement, when the girl started, and immediately made towards them.

They walked onward, looking about them with the air of persons who entertained some very slight expectation which had little chance of being realised, when they were suddenly joined by this new associate. They halted with an exclamation of surprise, but suppressed it immediately; for a man in the garments of a countryman came close up—brushed against them, indeed—at that precise moment.

'Not here,' said Nancy hurriedly, 'I am afraid to speak to you here. Come away—out of the public road—down the steps yonder!'

As she uttered these words, and indicated, with her hand, the direction in which she wished them to proceed, the countryman looked round, and roughly asking what they took up the whole pavement for, passed on.

The steps to which the girl had pointed, were those which, on the Surrey bank, and on the same side of the bridge as Saint Saviour's Church, form a landing-stairs from the river. To this spot, the man bearing the appearance of a countryman, hastened unobserved; and after a moment's survey of the place, he began to descend.

These stairs are a part of the bridge; they consist of three flights. Just below the end of the second, going down, the stone wall on the left terminates in an ornamental pilaster facing towards the Thames. At this point the lower steps widen: so that a person turning that angle of the wall, is necessarily unseen by any others on the stairs who chance to be above him, if only a step. The countryman looked hastily round, when he reached this point; and as there seemed no better place of concealment, and, the tide being out, there was plenty of room, he slipped aside, with his back to the pilaster, and there waited: pretty certain that they would come no lower, and that even if he could not hear what was said, he could follow them again, with safety.

So tardily stole the time in this lonely place, and so eager was the spy to penetrate the motives of an interview so different from what he had been led to expect, that he more than once gave the matter up for lost, and persuaded himself, either that they had stopped far above, or had resorted to some entirely different spot to hold their mysterious conversation. He was on the point of emerging from his hiding-place, and regaining the road above, when he heard the sound of footsteps, and directly afterwards of voices almost close at his ear.

He drew himself straight upright against the wall, and, scarcely breathing, listened attentively.

'This is far enough,' said a voice, which was evidently that of the gentleman. 'I will not suffer the young lady to go any farther. Many people would have distrusted you too much to have come even so far, but you see I am willing to humour you.'

'To humour me!' cried the voice of the girl whom he had followed. 'You're considerate, indeed, sir. To humour me! Well, well, it's no matter.'

'Why, for what,' said the gentleman in a kinder tone, 'for what purpose can you have brought us to this strange place? Why not have let me speak to you, above there, where it is light, and there is something stirring, instead of bringing us to this dark and dismal hole?'

'I told you before,' replied Nancy, 'that I was afraid to speak to you there. I don't know why it is,' said the girl, shuddering, 'but I have such a fear and dread upon me to-night that I can hardly stand.'

'A fear of what?' asked the gentleman, who seemed to pity her.

'I scarcely know of what,' replied the girl. 'I wish I did. Horrible thoughts of death, and shrouds with blood upon them, and a fear that has made me burn as if I was on fire, have been upon me all day. I was reading a book to-night, to wile the time away, and the same things came into the print.'

'Imagination,' said the gentleman, soothing her.

'No imagination,' replied the girl in a hoarse voice. 'I'll swear I saw "coffin" written in every page of the book in large black letters,—aye, and they carried one close to me, in the streets to-night.'

'There is nothing unusual in that,' said the gentleman. 'They have passed me often.'

'Real ones,' rejoined the girl. 'This was not.'

There was something so uncommon in her manner, that the flesh of the concealed listener crept as he heard the girl utter these words, and the blood chilled within him. He had never experienced a greater relief than in hearing the sweet voice of the young lady as she begged her to be calm, and not allow herself to become the prey of such fearful fancies.

'Speak to her kindly,' said the young lady to her companion. 'Poor creature! She seems to need it.'

'Your haughty religious people would have held their heads up to see me as I am to-night, and preached of flames and vengeance,' cried the girl. 'Oh, dear lady, why ar'n't those who claim to be God's own folks as gentle and as kind to us poor wretches as you, who, having youth, and beauty, and all that they have lost, might be a little proud instead of so much humbler?'

'Ah!' said the gentleman. 'A Turk turns his face, after washing it well, to the East, when he says his prayers; these good people, after giving their faces such a rub against the World as to take the smiles off, turn with no less regularity, to the darkest side of Heaven. Between the Mussulman and the Pharisee, commend me to the first!'

These words appeared to be addressed to the young lady, and were perhaps uttered with the view of affording Nancy time to recover herself. The gentleman, shortly afterwards, addressed himself to her.

'You were not here last Sunday night,' he said.

'I couldn't come,' replied Nancy; 'I was kept by force.'

'By whom?'

'Him that I told the young lady of before.'

'You were not suspected of holding any communication with anybody on the subject which has brought us here to-night, I hope?' asked the old gentleman.

'No,' replied the girl, shaking her head. 'It's not very easy for me to leave him unless he knows why; I couldn't give him a drink of laudanum before I came away.'

'Did he awake before you returned?' inquired the gentleman.

'No; and neither he nor any of them suspect me.'

'Good,' said the gentleman. 'Now listen to me.'

'I am ready,' replied the girl, as he paused for a moment.

'This young lady,' the gentleman began, 'has communicated to me, and to some other friends who can be safely trusted, what you told her nearly a fortnight since. I confess to you that I had doubts, at first, whether you were to be implicitly relied upon, but now I firmly believe you are.'

'I am,' said the girl earnestly.

'I repeat that I firmly believe it. To prove to you that I am disposed to trust you, I tell you without reserve, that we propose to extort the secret, whatever it may be, from the fear of this man Monks. But if—if—' said the gentleman, 'he cannot be secured, or, if secured, cannot be acted upon as we wish, you must deliver up the Jew.'

'Fagin,' cried the girl, recoiling.

'That man must be delivered up by you,' said the gentleman.

'I will not do it! I will never do it!' replied the girl. 'Devil that he is, and worse than devil as he has been to me, I will never do that.'

'You will not?' said the gentleman, who seemed fully prepared for this answer.

'Never!' returned the girl.

'Tell me why?'

'For one reason,' rejoined the girl firmly, 'for one reason, that the lady knows and will stand by me in, I know she will, for I have her promise: and for this other reason, besides, that, bad life as he has led, I have led a bad life too; there are many of us who have kept the same courses together, and I'll not turn upon them, who might—any of them—have turned upon me, but didn't, bad as they are.'

'Then,' said the gentleman, quickly, as if this had been the point he had been aiming to attain; 'put Monks into my hands, and leave him to me to deal with.'

'What if he turns against the others?'

'I promise you that in that case, if the truth is forced from him, there the matter will rest; there must be circumstances in Oliver's little history which it would be painful to drag before the public eye, and if the truth is once elicited, they shall go scot free.'

'And if it is not?' suggested the girl.

'Then,' pursued the gentleman, 'this Fagin shall not be brought to justice without your consent. In such a case I could show you reasons, I think, which would induce you to yield it.'

'Have I the lady's promise for that?' asked the girl.

'You have,' replied Rose. 'My true and faithful pledge.'

'Monks would never learn how you knew what you do?' said the girl, after a short pause.

'Never,' replied the gentleman. 'The intelligence should be brought to bear upon him, that he could never even guess.'

'I have been a liar, and among liars from a little child,' said the girl after another interval of silence, 'but I will take your words.'

After receiving an assurance from both, that she might safely do so, she proceeded in a voice so low that it was often difficult for the listener to discover even the purport of what she said, to describe, by name and situation, the public-house whence she had been followed that night. From the manner in which she occasionally paused, it appeared as if the gentleman were making some hasty notes of the information she communicated. When she had thoroughly explained the localities of the place, the best position from which to watch it without exciting observation, and the night and hour on which Monks was most in the habit of frequenting it, she seemed to consider for a few moments, for the purpose of recalling his features and appearances more forcibly to her recollection.

'He is tall,' said the girl, 'and a strongly made man, but not stout; he has a lurking walk; and as he walks, constantly looks over his shoulder, first on one side, and then on the other. Don't forget that, for his eyes are sunk in his head so much deeper than any other man's, that you might almost tell him by that alone. His face is dark, like his hair and eyes; and, although he can't be more than six or eight and twenty, withered and haggard. His lips are often discoloured and disfigured with the marks of teeth; for he has desperate fits, and sometimes even bites his hands and covers them with wounds—why did you start?' said the girl, stopping suddenly.

The gentleman replied, in a hurried manner, that he was not conscious of having done so, and begged her to proceed.

'Part of this,' said the girl, 'I have drawn out from other people at the house I tell you of, for I have only seen him twice, and both times he was covered up in a large cloak. I think that's all I can give you to know him by. Stay though,' she added. 'Upon his throat: so high that you can see a part of it below his neckerchief when he turns his face: there is—'

'A broad red mark, like a burn or scald?' cried the gentleman.

'How's this?' said the girl. 'You know him!'

The young lady uttered a cry of surprise, and for a few moments they were so still that the listener could distinctly hear them breathe.

'I think I do,' said the gentleman, breaking silence. 'I should by your description. We shall see. Many people are singularly like each other. It may not be the same.'

As he expressed himself to this effect, with assumed carelessness, he took a step or two nearer the concealed spy, as the latter could tell from the distinctness with which he heard him mutter, 'It must be he!'

'Now,' he said, returning: so it seemed by the sound: to the spot where he had stood before, 'you have given us most valuable assistance, young woman, and I wish you to be the better for it. What can I do to serve you?'

'Nothing,' replied Nancy.

'You will not persist in saying that,' rejoined the gentleman, with a voice and emphasis of kindness that might have touched a much harder and more obdurate heart. 'Think now. Tell me.'

'Nothing, sir,' rejoined the girl, weeping. 'You can do nothing to help me. I am past all hope, indeed.'

'You put yourself beyond its pale,' said the gentleman. 'The past has been a dreary waste with you, of youthful energies mis-spent, and such priceless treasures lavished, as the Creator bestows but once and never grants again, but, for the future, you may hope. I do not say that it is in our power to offer you peace of heart and mind, for that must come as you seek it; but a quiet asylum, either in England, or, if you fear to remain here, in some foreign country, it is not only within the compass of our ability but our most anxious wish to secure you. Before the dawn of morning, before this river wakes to the first glimpse of day-light, you shall be placed as entirely beyond the reach of your former associates, and leave as utter an absence of all trace behind you, as if you were to disappear from the earth this moment. Come! I would not have you go back to exchange one word with any old companion, or take one look at any old haunt, or breathe the very air which is pestilence and death to you. Quit them all, while there is time and opportunity!'

'She will be persuaded now,' cried the young lady. 'She hesitates, I am sure.'

'I fear not, my dear,' said the gentleman.

'No sir, I do not,' replied the girl, after a short struggle. 'I am chained to my old life. I loathe and hate it now, but I cannot leave it. I must have gone too far to turn back,—and yet I don't know, for if you had spoken to me so, some time ago, I should have laughed it off. But,' she said, looking hastily round, 'this fear comes over me again. I must go home.'

'Home!' repeated the young lady, with great stress upon the word.

'Home, lady,' rejoined the girl. 'To such a home as I have raised for myself with the work of my whole life. Let us part. I shall be watched or seen. Go! Go! If I have done you any service all I ask is, that you leave me, and let me go my way alone.'

'It is useless,' said the gentleman, with a sigh. 'We compromise her safety, perhaps, by staying here. We may have detained her longer than she expected already.'

'Yes, yes,' urged the girl. 'You have.'

'What,' cried the young lady, 'can be the end of this poor creature's life!'

'What!' repeated the girl. 'Look before you, lady. Look at that dark water. How many times do you read of such as I who spring into the tide, and leave no living thing, to care for, or bewail them. It may be years hence, or it may be only months, but I shall come to that at last.'

'Do not speak thus, pray,' returned the young lady, sobbing.

'It will never reach your ears, dear lady, and God forbid such horrors should!' replied the girl. 'Good-night, good-night!'

The gentleman turned away.

'This purse,' cried the young lady. 'Take it for my sake, that you may have some resource in an hour of need and trouble.'

'No!' replied the girl. 'I have not done this for money. Let me have that to think of. And yet—give me something that you have worn: I should like to have something—no, no, not a ring—your gloves or handkerchief—anything that I can keep, as having belonged to you, sweet lady. There. Bless you! God bless you. Good-night, good-night!'

The violent agitation of the girl, and the apprehension of some discovery which would subject her to ill-usage and violence, seemed to determine the gentleman to leave her, as she requested.

The sound of retreating footsteps were audible and the voices ceased.

The two figures of the young lady and her companion soon afterwards appeared upon the bridge. They stopped at the summit of the stairs.

'Hark!' cried the young lady, listening. 'Did she call! I thought I heard her voice.'

'No, my love,' replied Mr. Brownlow, looking sadly back. 'She has not moved, and will not till we are gone.'

Rose Maylie lingered, but the old gentleman drew her arm through his, and led her, with gentle force, away. As they disappeared, the girl sunk down nearly at her full length upon one of the stone stairs, and vented the anguish of her heart in bitter tears.

After a time she arose, and with feeble and tottering steps ascended the street. The astonished listener remained motionless on his post for some minutes afterwards, and having ascertained, with many cautious glances round him, that he was again alone, crept slowly from his hiding-place, and returned, stealthily and in the shade of the wall, in the same manner as he had descended.

Peeping out, more than once, when he reached the top, to make sure that he was unobserved, Noah Claypole darted away at his utmost speed, and made for the Jew's house as fast as his legs would carry him.

CHAPTER XLVII. FATAL CONSEQUENCES

It was nearly two hours before day-break; that time which in the autumn of the year, may be truly called the dead of night; when the streets are silent and deserted; when even sounds appear to slumber, and profligacy and riot have staggered home to dream; it was at this still and silent hour, that Fagin sat watching in his old lair, with face so distorted and pale, and eyes so red and blood-shot, that he looked less like a man, than like some hideous phantom, moist from the grave, and worried by an evil spirit.

He sat crouching over a cold hearth, wrapped in an old torn coverlet, with his face turned towards a wasting candle that stood upon a table by his side. His right hand was raised to his lips, and as, absorbed in thought, he hit his long black nails, he disclosed among his toothless gums a few such fangs as should have been a dog's or rat's.

Stretched upon a mattress on the floor, lay Noah Claypole, fast asleep. Towards him the old man sometimes directed his eyes for an instant, and then brought them back again to the candle; which with a long-burnt wick drooping almost double, and hot grease falling down in clots upon the table, plainly showed that his thoughts were busy elsewhere.

Indeed they were. Mortification at the overthrow of his notable scheme; hatred of the girl who had dared to palter with strangers; and utter distrust of the sincerity of her refusal to yield him up; bitter disappointment at the loss of his revenge on Sikes; the fear of detection, and ruin, and death; and a fierce and deadly rage kindled by all; these were the passionate considerations which, following close upon each other with rapid and ceaseless whirl, shot through the brain of Fagin, as every evil thought and blackest purpose lay working at his heart.

He sat without changing his attitude in the least, or appearing to take the smallest heed of time, until his quick ear seemed to be attracted by a footstep in the street.

'At last,' he muttered, wiping his dry and fevered mouth. 'At last!'

The bell rang gently as he spoke. He crept upstairs to the door, and presently returned accompanied by a man muffled to the chin, who carried a bundle under one arm. Sitting down and throwing back his outer coat, the man displayed the burly frame of Sikes.

'There!' he said, laying the bundle on the table. 'Take care of that, and do the most you can with it. It's been trouble enough to get; I thought I should have been here, three hours ago.'

Fagin laid his hand upon the bundle, and locking it in the cupboard, sat down again without speaking. But he did not take his eyes off the robber, for an instant, during this action; and now that they sat over against each other, face to face, he looked fixedly at him, with his lips quivering so violently, and his face so altered by the emotions which had mastered him, that the housebreaker involuntarily drew back his chair, and surveyed him with a look of real affright.

'Wot now?' cried Sikes. 'Wot do you look at a man so for?'

Fagin raised his right hand, and shook his trembling forefinger in the air; but his passion was so great, that the power of speech was for the moment gone.

'Damme!' said Sikes, feeling in his breast with a look of alarm. 'He's gone mad. I must look to myself here.'

'No, no,' rejoined Fagin, finding his voice. 'It's not—you're not the person, Bill. I've no—no fault to find with you.'

'Oh, you haven't, haven't you?' said Sikes, looking sternly at him, and ostentatiously passing a pistol into a more convenient pocket. 'That's lucky—for one of us. Which one that is, don't matter.'

'I've got that to tell you, Bill,' said Fagin, drawing his chair nearer, 'will make you worse than me.'

'Aye?' returned the robber with an incredulous air. 'Tell away! Look sharp, or Nance will think I'm lost.'

'Lost!' cried Fagin. 'She has pretty well settled that, in her own mind, already.'

Sikes looked with an aspect of great perplexity into the Jew's face, and reading no satisfactory explanation of the riddle there, clenched his coat collar in his huge hand and shook him soundly.

'Speak, will you!' he said; 'or if you don't, it shall be for want of breath. Open your mouth and say wot you've got to say in plain words. Out with it, you thundering old cur, out with it!'

'Suppose that lad that's laying there—' Fagin began.

Sikes turned round to where Noah was sleeping, as if he had not previously observed him. 'Well!' he said, resuming his former position.

'Suppose that lad,' pursued Fagin, 'was to peach—to blow upon us all—first seeking out the right folks for the purpose, and then having a meeting with 'em in the street to paint our likenesses, describe every mark that they might know us by, and the crib where we might be most easily taken. Suppose he was to do all this, and besides to blow upon a plant we've all been in, more or less—of his own fancy; not grabbed, trapped, tried, earwigged by the parson and brought to it on bread and water,—but of his own fancy; to please his own taste; stealing out at nights to find those most interested against us, and peaching to them. Do you hear me?' cried the Jew, his eyes flashing with rage. 'Suppose he did all this, what then?'

'What then!' replied Sikes; with a tremendous oath. 'If he was left alive till I came, I'd grind his skull under the iron heel of my boot into as many grains as there are hairs upon his head.'

'What if I did it!' cried Fagin almost in a yell. 'I, that knows so much, and could hang so many besides myself!'

'I don't know,' replied Sikes, clenching his teeth and turning white at the mere suggestion. 'I'd do something in the jail that 'ud get me put in irons; and if I was tried along with you, I'd fall upon you with them in the open court, and beat your brains out afore the people. I should have such strength,' muttered the robber, poising his brawny arm, 'that I could smash your head as if a loaded waggon had gone over it.'

'You would?'

'Would I!' said the housebreaker. 'Try me.'

'If it was Charley, or the Dodger, or Bet, or—'

'I don't care who,' replied Sikes impatiently. 'Whoever it was, I'd serve them the same.'

Fagin looked hard at the robber; and, motioning him to be silent, stooped over the bed upon the floor, and shook the sleeper to rouse him. Sikes leant forward in his chair: looking on with his hands upon his knees, as if wondering much what all this questioning and preparation was to end in.

'Bolter, Bolter! Poor lad!' said Fagin, looking up with an expression of devilish anticipation, and speaking slowly and with marked emphasis. 'He's tired—tired with watching for her so long,—watching for her, Bill.'

'Wot d'ye mean?' asked Sikes, drawing back.

Fagin made no answer, but bending over the sleeper again, hauled him into a sitting posture. When his assumed name had been repeated several times, Noah rubbed his eyes, and, giving a heavy yawn, looked sleepily about him.

'Tell me that again—once again, just for him to hear,' said the Jew, pointing to Sikes as he spoke.

'Tell yer what?' asked the sleepy Noah, shaking himself pettishly.

'That about— Nancy,' said Fagin, clutching Sikes by the wrist, as if to prevent his leaving the house before he had heard enough. 'You followed her?'

'Yes.'

'To London Bridge?'

'Yes.'

'Where she met two people.'

'So she did.'

'A gentleman and a lady that she had gone to of her own accord before, who asked her to give up all her pals, and Monks first, which she did—and to describe him, which she did—and to tell her what house it was that we meet at, and go to, which she did—and where it could be best watched from, which she did—and what time the people went there, which she did. She did all this. She told it all every word without a threat, without a murmur—she did—did she not?' cried Fagin, half mad with fury.

'All right,' replied Noah, scratching his head. 'That's just what it was!'

'What did they say, about last Sunday?'

'About last Sunday!' replied Noah, considering. 'Why I told yer that before.'

'Again. Tell it again!' cried Fagin, tightening his grasp on Sikes, and brandishing his other hand aloft, as the foam flew from his lips.

'They asked her,' said Noah, who, as he grew more wakeful, seemed to have a dawning perception who Sikes was, 'they asked her why she didn't come, last Sunday, as she promised. She said she couldn't.'

'Why—why? Tell him that.'

'Because she was forcibly kept at home by Bill, the man she had told them of before,' replied Noah.

'What more of him?' cried Fagin. 'What more of the man she had told them of before? Tell him that, tell him that.'

'Why, that she couldn't very easily get out of doors unless he knew where she was going to,' said Noah; 'and so the first time she went to see the lady, she—ha! ha! ha! it made me laugh when she said it, that it did—she gave him a drink of laudanum.'

'Hell's fire!' cried Sikes, breaking fiercely from the Jew. 'Let me go!'

Flinging the old man from him, he rushed from the room, and darted, wildly and furiously, up the stairs.

'Bill, Bill!' cried Fagin, following him hastily. 'A word. Only a word.'

The word would not have been exchanged, but that the housebreaker was unable to open the door: on which he was expending fruitless oaths and violence, when the Jew came panting up.

'Let me out,' said Sikes. 'Don't speak to me; it's not safe. Let me out, I say!'

'Hear me speak a word,' rejoined Fagin, laying his hand upon the lock. 'You won't be—'

'Well,' replied the other.

'You won't be—too—violent, Bill?'

The day was breaking, and there was light enough for the men to see each other's faces. They exchanged one brief glance; there was a fire in the eyes of both, which could not be mistaken.

'I mean,' said Fagin, showing that he felt all disguise was now useless, 'not too violent for safety. Be crafty, Bill, and not too bold.'

Sikes made no reply; but, pulling open the door, of which Fagin had turned the lock, dashed into the silent streets.

Without one pause, or moment's consideration; without once turning his head to the right or left, or raising his eyes to the sky, or lowering them to the ground, but looking straight before him with savage resolution: his teeth so tightly compressed that the strained jaw seemed starting through his skin; the robber held on his headlong course, nor muttered a word, nor relaxed a muscle, until he reached his own door. He opened it, softly, with a key; strode lightly up the stairs; and entering his own room, double-locked the door, and lifting a heavy table against it, drew back the curtain of the bed.

The girl was lying, half-dressed, upon it. He had roused her from her sleep, for she raised herself with a hurried and startled look.

'Get up!' said the man.

'It is you, Bill!' said the girl, with an expression of pleasure at his return.

'It is,' was the reply. 'Get up.'

There was a candle burning, but the man hastily drew it from the candlestick, and hurled it under the grate. Seeing the faint light of early day without, the girl rose to undraw the curtain.

'Let it be,' said Sikes, thrusting his hand before her. 'There's enough light for wot I've got to do.'

'Bill,' said the girl, in the low voice of alarm, 'why do you look like that at me!'

The robber sat regarding her, for a few seconds, with dilated nostrils and heaving breast; and then, grasping her by the head and throat, dragged her into the middle of the room, and looking once towards the door, placed his heavy hand upon her mouth.

'Bill, Bill!' gasped the girl, wrestling with the strength of mortal fear,—'I—I won't scream or cry—not once—hear me—speak to me—tell me what I have done!'

'You know, you she devil!' returned the robber, suppressing his breath. 'You were watched to-night; every word you said was heard.'

'Then spare my life for the love of Heaven, as I spared yours,' rejoined the girl, clinging to him. 'Bill, dear Bill, you cannot have the heart to kill me. Oh! think of all I have given up, only this one night, for you. You shall have time to think, and save yourself this crime; I will not loose my hold, you cannot throw me off. Bill, Bill, for dear God's sake, for your own, for mine, stop before you spill my blood! I have been true to you, upon my guilty soul I have!'

The man struggled violently, to release his arms; but those of the girl were clasped round his, and tear her as he would, he could not tear them away.

'Bill,' cried the girl, striving to lay her head upon his breast, 'the gentleman and that dear lady, told me to-night of a home in some foreign country where I could end my days in solitude and peace. Let me see them again, and beg them, on my knees, to show the same mercy and goodness to you; and let us both leave this dreadful place, and far apart lead better lives, and forget how we have lived, except in prayers, and never see each other more. It is never too late to repent. They told me so—I feel it now—but we must have time—a little, little time!'

The housebreaker freed one arm, and grasped his pistol. The certainty of immediate detection if he fired, flashed across his mind even in the midst of his fury; and he beat it twice with all the force he could summon, upon the upturned face that almost touched his own.

She staggered and fell: nearly blinded with the blood that rained down from a deep gash in her forehead; but raising herself, with difficulty, on her knees, drew from her bosom a white handkerchief—Rose Maylie's own—and holding it up, in her folded hands, as high towards Heaven as her feeble strength would allow, breathed one prayer for mercy to her Maker.

It was a ghastly figure to look upon. The murderer staggering backward to the wall, and shutting out the sight with his hand, seized a heavy club and struck her down.

CHAPTER XLVIII. THE FLIGHT OF SIKES

Of all bad deeds that, under cover of the darkness, had been committed within wide London's bounds since night hung over it, that was the worst. Of all the horrors that rose with an ill scent upon the morning air, that was the foulest and most cruel.

The sun—the bright sun, that brings back, not light alone, but new life, and hope, and freshness to man—burst upon the crowded city in clear and radiant glory. Through costly-coloured glass and paper-mended window, through cathedral dome and rotten crevice, it shed its equal ray. It lighted up the room where the murdered woman lay. It did. He tried to shut it out, but it would stream in. If the sight had been a ghastly one in the dull morning, what was it, now, in all that brilliant light!

He had not moved; he had been afraid to stir. There had been a moan and motion of the hand; and, with terror added to rage, he had struck and struck again. Once he threw a rug over it; but it was worse to fancy the eyes, and imagine them moving towards him, than to see them glaring upward, as if watching the reflection of the pool of gore that quivered and danced in the sunlight on the ceiling. He had plucked it off again. And there was the body—mere flesh and blood, no more—but such flesh, and so much blood!

He struck a light, kindled a fire, and thrust the club into it. There was hair upon the end, which blazed and shrunk into a light cinder, and, caught by the air, whirled up the chimney. Even that frightened him, sturdy as he was; but he held the weapon till it broke, and then piled it on the coals to burn away, and smoulder into ashes. He washed himself, and rubbed his clothes; there were spots that would not be removed, but he cut the pieces out, and burnt them. How those stains were dispersed about the room! The very feet of the dog were bloody.

All this time he had, never once, turned his back upon the corpse; no, not for a moment. Such preparations completed, he moved, backward, towards the door: dragging the dog with him, lest he should soil his feet anew and carry out new evidence of the crime into the streets. He shut the door softly, locked it, took the key, and left the house.

He crossed over, and glanced up at the window, to be sure that nothing was visible from the outside. There was the curtain still drawn, which she would have opened to admit the light she never saw again. It lay nearly under there. He knew that. God, how the sun poured down upon the very spot!

The glance was instantaneous. It was a relief to have got free of the room. He whistled on the dog, and walked rapidly away.

He went through Islington; strode up the hill at Highgate on which stands the stone in honour of Whittington; turned down to Highgate Hill, unsteady of purpose, and uncertain where to go; struck off to the right again, almost as soon as he began to descend it; and taking the foot-path across the fields, skirted Caen Wood, and so came on Hampstead Heath. Traversing the hollow by the Vale of Heath, he mounted the opposite bank, and crossing the road which joins the villages of Hampstead and Highgate, made along the remaining portion of the heath to the fields at North End, in one of which he laid himself down under a hedge, and slept.

Soon he was up again, and away,—not far into the country, but back towards London by the high-road—then back again—then over another part of the same ground as he already traversed—then wandering up and down in fields, and lying on ditches' brinks to rest, and starting up to make for some other spot, and do the same, and ramble on again.

Where could he go, that was near and not too public, to get some meat and drink? Hendon. That was a good place, not far off, and out of most people's way. Thither he directed his steps,—running sometimes, and sometimes, with a strange perversity, loitering at a snail's pace, or stopping altogether and idly breaking the hedges with a stick. But when he got there, all the people he met—the very children at the doors—seemed to view him with suspicion. Back he turned again, without the courage to purchase bit or drop, though he had tasted no food for many hours; and once more he lingered on the Heath, uncertain where to go.

He wandered over miles and miles of ground, and still came back to the old place. Morning and noon had passed, and the day was on the wane, and still he rambled to and fro, and up and down, and round and round, and still lingered about the same spot. At last he got away, and shaped his course for Hatfield.

It was nine o'clock at night, when the man, quite tired out, and the dog, limping and lame from the unaccustomed exercise, turned down the hill by the church of the quiet village, and plodding along the little street, crept into a small public-house, whose scanty light had guided them to the spot. There was a fire in the tap-room, and some country-labourers were drinking before it.

They made room for the stranger, but he sat down in the furthest corner, and ate and drank alone, or rather with his dog: to whom he cast a morsel of food from time to time.

The conversation of the men assembled here, turned upon the neighbouring land, and farmers; and when those topics were exhausted, upon the age of some old man who had been buried on the previous Sunday; the young men present considering him very old, and the old men present declaring him to have been quite young—not older, one white-haired grandfather said, than he was—with ten or fifteen year of life in him at least—if he had taken care; if he had taken care.

There was nothing to attract attention, or excite alarm in this. The robber, after paying his reckoning, sat silent and unnoticed in his corner, and had almost dropped asleep, when he was half wakened by the noisy entrance of a new comer.

This was an antic fellow, half pedlar and half mountebank, who travelled about the country on foot to vend hones, strops, razors, washballs, harness-paste, medicine for dogs and horses, cheap perfumery, cosmetics, and such-like wares, which he carried in a case slung to his back. His entrance was the signal for various homely jokes with the countrymen, which slackened not until he had made his supper, and opened his box of treasures, when he ingeniously contrived to unite business with amusement.

'And what be that stoof? Good to eat, Harry?' asked a grinning countryman, pointing to some composition-cakes in one corner.

'This,' said the fellow, producing one, 'this is the infallible and invaluable composition for removing all sorts of stain, rust, dirt, mildew, spick, speck, spot, or spatter, from silk, satin, linen, cambric, cloth, crape, stuff, carpet, merino, muslin, bombazeen, or woollen stuff. Wine-stains, fruit-stains, beer-stains, water-stains, paint-stains, pitch-stains, any stains, all come out at one rub with the infallible and invaluable composition. If a lady stains her honour, she has only need to swallow one cake and she's cured at once—for it's poison. If a gentleman wants to prove this, he has only need to bolt one little square, and he has put it beyond question—for it's quite as satisfactory as a pistol-bullet, and a great deal nastier in the flavour, consequently the more credit in taking it. One penny a square. With all these virtues, one penny a square!'

There were two buyers directly, and more of the listeners plainly hesitated. The vendor observing this, increased in loquacity.

'It's all bought up as fast as it can be made,' said the fellow. 'There are fourteen water-mills, six steam-engines, and a galvanic battery, always a-working upon it, and they can't make it fast enough, though the men work so hard that they die off, and the widows is pensioned directly, with twenty pound a-year for each of the children, and a premium of fifty for twins. One penny a square! Two half-pence is all the same, and four farthings is received with joy. One penny a square! Wine-stains, fruit-stains, beer-stains, water-stains, paint-stains, pitch-stains, mud-stains, blood-stains! Here is a stain upon the hat of a gentleman in company, that I'll take clean out, before he can order me a pint of ale.'

'Hah!' cried Sikes starting up. 'Give that back.'

'I'll take it clean out, sir,' replied the man, winking to the company, 'before you can come across the room to get it. Gentlemen all, observe the dark stain upon this gentleman's hat, no wider than a shilling, but thicker than a half-crown. Whether it is a wine-stain, fruit-stain, beer-stain, water-stain, paint-stain, pitch-stain, mud-stain, or blood-stain—'

The man got no further, for Sikes with a hideous imprecation overthrew the table, and tearing the hat from him, burst out of the house.

With the same perversity of feeling and irresolution that had fastened upon him, despite himself, all day, the murderer, finding that he was not followed, and that they most probably considered him some drunken sullen fellow, turned back up the town, and getting out of the glare of the lamps of a stage-coach that was standing in the street, was walking past, when he recognised the mail from London, and saw that it was standing at the little post-office. He almost knew what was to come; but he crossed over, and listened.

The guard was standing at the door, waiting for the letter-bag. A man, dressed like a game-keeper, came up at the moment, and he handed him a basket which lay ready on the pavement.

'That's for your people,' said the guard. 'Now, look alive in there, will you. Damn that 'ere bag, it warn't ready night afore last; this won't do, you know!'

'Anything new up in town, Ben?' asked the game-keeper, drawing back to the window-shutters, the better to admire the horses.

'No, nothing that I knows on,' replied the man, pulling on his gloves. 'Corn's up a little. I heerd talk of a murder, too, down Spitalfields way, but I don't reckon much upon it.'

'Oh, that's quite true,' said a gentleman inside, who was looking out of the window. 'And a dreadful murder it was.'

'Was it, sir?' rejoined the guard, touching his hat. 'Man or woman, pray, sir?'

'A woman,' replied the gentleman. 'It is supposed—'

'Now, Ben,' replied the coachman impatiently.

'Damn that 'ere bag,' said the guard; 'are you gone to sleep in there?'

'Coming!' cried the office keeper, running out.

'Coming,' growled the guard. 'Ah, and so's the young 'ooman of property that's going to take a fancy to me, but I don't know when. Here, give hold. All ri—ight!'

The horn sounded a few cheerful notes, and the coach was gone.

Sikes remained standing in the street, apparently unmoved by what he had just heard, and agitated by no stronger feeling than a doubt where to go. At length he went back again, and took the road which leads from Hatfield to St. Albans.

He went on doggedly; but as he left the town behind him, and plunged into the solitude and darkness of the road, he felt a dread and awe creeping upon him which shook him to the core. Every object before him, substance or shadow, still or moving, took the semblance of some fearful thing; but these fears were nothing compared to the sense that haunted him of that morning's ghastly figure following at his heels. He could trace its shadow in the gloom, supply the smallest item of the outline, and note how stiff and solemn it seemed to stalk along. He could hear its garments rustling in the leaves, and every breath of wind came laden with that last low cry. If he stopped it did the same. If he ran, it followed—not running too: that would have been a relief: but like a corpse endowed with the mere machinery of life, and borne on one slow melancholy wind that never rose or fell.

At times, he turned, with desperate determination, resolved to beat this phantom off, though it should look him dead; but the hair rose on his head, and his blood stood still, for it had turned with him and was behind him then. He had kept it before him that morning, but it was behind now—always. He leaned his back against a bank, and felt that it stood above him, visibly out against the cold night-sky. He threw himself upon the road—on his back upon the road. At his head it stood, silent, erect, and still—a living grave-stone, with its epitaph in blood.

Let no man talk of murderers escaping justice, and hint that Providence must sleep. There were twenty score of violent deaths in one long minute of that agony of fear.

There was a shed in a field he passed, that offered shelter for the night. Before the door, were three tall poplar trees, which made it very dark within; and the wind moaned through them with a dismal wail. He could not walk on, till daylight came again; and here he stretched himself close to the wall—to undergo new torture.

For now, a vision came before him, as constant and more terrible than that from which he had escaped. Those widely staring eyes, so lustreless and so glassy, that he had better borne to see them than think upon them, appeared in the midst of the darkness: light in themselves, but giving light to nothing. There were but two, but they were everywhere. If he shut out the sight, there came the room with every well-known object—some, indeed, that he would have forgotten, if he had gone over its contents from memory—each in its accustomed place. The body was in its place, and its eyes were as he saw them when he stole away. He got up, and rushed into the field without. The figure was behind him. He re-entered the shed, and shrunk down once more. The eyes were there, before he had laid himself along.

And here he remained in such terror as none but he can know, trembling in every limb, and the cold sweat starting from every pore, when suddenly there arose upon the night-wind the noise of distant shouting, and the roar of voices mingled in alarm and wonder. Any sound of men in that lonely place, even though it conveyed a real cause of alarm, was something to him. He regained his strength and energy at the prospect of personal danger; and springing to his feet, rushed into the open air.

The broad sky seemed on fire. Rising into the air with showers of sparks, and rolling one above the other, were sheets of flame, lighting the atmosphere for miles round, and driving clouds of smoke in the direction where he stood. The shouts grew louder as new voices swelled the roar, and he could hear the cry of Fire! mingled with the ringing of an alarm-bell, the fall of heavy bodies, and the crackling of flames as they twined round some new obstacle, and shot aloft as though refreshed by food. The noise increased as he looked. There were people there— men and women—light, bustle. It was like new life to him. He darted onward—straight, headlong—dashing through brier and brake, and leaping gate and fence as madly as his dog, who careered with loud and sounding bark before him.

He came upon the spot. There were half-dressed figures tearing to and fro, some endeavouring to drag the frightened horses from the stables, others driving the cattle from the yard and out-houses, and others coming laden from the burning pile, amidst a shower of falling sparks, and the tumbling down of red-hot beams. The apertures, where doors and windows stood an hour ago, disclosed a mass of raging fire; walls rocked and crumbled into the burning well; the molten lead and iron poured down, white hot, upon the ground. Women and children shrieked, and men encouraged each other with noisy shouts and cheers. The clanking of the engine-pumps, and the spirting and hissing of the water as it fell upon the blazing wood, added to the tremendous roar. He shouted, too, till he was hoarse; and flying from memory and himself, plunged into the thickest of the throng. Hither and thither he dived that night: now working at the pumps, and now hurrying through the smoke and flame, but never ceasing to engage himself wherever noise and men were thickest. Up and down the ladders, upon the roofs of buildings, over floors that quaked and trembled with his weight, under the lee of falling bricks and stones, in every part of that great fire was he; but he bore a charmed life, and had neither scratch nor bruise, nor weariness nor thought, till morning dawned again, and only smoke and blackened ruins remained.

This mad excitement over, there returned, with ten-fold force, the dreadful consciousness of his crime. He looked suspiciously about him, for the men were conversing in groups, and he feared to be the subject of their talk. The dog obeyed the significant beck of his finger, and they drew off, stealthily, together. He passed near an engine where some men were seated, and they called to him to share in their refreshment. He took some bread and meat; and as he drank a draught of beer, heard the firemen, who were from London, talking about the murder. 'He has gone to Birmingham, they say,' said one: 'but they'll have him yet, for the scouts are out, and by to-morrow night there'll be a cry all through the country.'

He hurried off, and walked till he almost dropped upon the ground; then lay down in a lane, and had a long, but broken and uneasy sleep. He wandered on again, irresolute and undecided, and oppressed with the fear of another solitary night.

Suddenly, he took the desperate resolution to going back to London.

'There's somebody to speak to there, at all event,' he thought. 'A good hiding-place, too. They'll never expect to nab me there, after this country scent. Why can't I lie by for a week or so, and, forcing blunt from Fagin, get abroad to France? Damme, I'll risk it.'

He acted upon this impulse without delay, and choosing the least frequented roads began his journey back, resolved to lie concealed within a short distance of the metropolis, and, entering it at dusk by a circuitous route, to proceed straight to that part of it which he had fixed on for his destination.

The dog, though. If any description of him were out, it would not be forgotten that the dog was missing, and had probably gone with him. This might lead to his apprehension as he passed along the streets. He resolved to drown him, and walked on, looking about for a pond: picking up a heavy stone and tying it to his handkerchief as he went.

The animal looked up into his master's face while these preparations were making; whether his instinct apprehended something of their purpose, or the robber's sidelong look at him was sterner than ordinary, he skulked a little farther in the rear than usual, and cowered as he came more slowly along. When his master halted at the brink of a pool, and looked round to call him, he stopped outright.

'Do you hear me call? Come here!' cried Sikes.

The animal came up from the very force of habit; but as Sikes stooped to attach the handkerchief to his throat, he uttered a low growl and started back.

'Come back!' said the robber.

The dog wagged his tail, but moved not. Sikes made a running noose and called him again.

The dog advanced, retreated, paused an instant, and scoured away at his hardest speed.

The man whistled again and again, and sat down and waited in the expectation that he would return. But no dog appeared, and at length he resumed his journey.

CHAPTER XLIX. MONKS AND MR. BROWNLOW AT LENGTH MEET. THEIR CONVERSATION, AND THE INTELLIGENCE THAT INTERRUPTS IT

The twilight was beginning to close in, when Mr. Brownlow

alighted from a hackney-coach at his own door, and knocked softly. The door being opened, a sturdy man got out of the coach and stationed himself on one side of the steps, while another man, who had been seated on the box, dismounted too, and stood upon the other side. At a sign from Mr. Brownlow, they helped out a third man, and taking him between them, hurried him into the house. This man was Monks.

They walked in the same manner up the stairs without speaking, and Mr. Brownlow, preceding them, led the way into a back-room. At the door of this apartment, Monks, who had ascended with evident reluctance, stopped. The two men looked at the old gentleman as if for instructions.

'He knows the alternative,' said Mr. Browlow. 'If he hesitates or moves a finger but as you bid him, drag him into the street, call for the aid of the police, and impeach him as a felon in my name.'

'How dare you say this of me?' asked Monks.

'How dare you urge me to it, young man?' replied Mr. Brownlow, confronting him with a steady look. 'Are you mad enough to leave this house? Unhand him. There, sir. You are free to go, and we to follow. But I warn you, by all I hold most solemn and most sacred, that instant will have you apprehended on a charge of fraud and robbery. I am resolute and immoveable. If you are determined to be the same, your blood be upon your own head!'

'By what authority am I kidnapped in the street, and brought here by these dogs?' asked

Monks, looking from one to the other of the men who stood beside him.

'By mine,' replied Mr. Brownlow. 'Those persons are indemnified by me. If you complain of being deprived of your liberty—you had power and opportunity to retrieve it as you came along, but you deemed it advisable to remain quiet—I say again, throw yourself for protection on the law. I will appeal to the law too; but when you have gone too far to recede, do not sue to me for leniency, when the power will have passed into other hands; and do not say I plunged you down the gulf into which you rushed, yourself.'

Monks was plainly disconcerted, and alarmed besides. He hesitated.

'You will decide quickly,' said Mr. Brownlow, with perfect firmness and composure. 'If you wish me to prefer my charges publicly, and consign you to a punishment the extent of which, although I can, with a shudder, foresee, I cannot control, once more, I say, for you know the way. If not, and you appeal to my forbearance, and the mercy of those you have deeply injured, seat yourself, without a word, in that chair. It has waited for you two whole days.'

Monks muttered some unintelligible words, but wavered still.

'You will be prompt,' said Mr. Brownlow. 'A word from me, and the alternative has gone for ever.'

Still the man hesitated.

'I have not the inclination to parley,' said Mr. Brownlow, 'and, as I advocate the dearest interests of others, I have not the right.'

'Is there—' demanded Monks with a faltering tongue,—'is there—no middle course?'

'None.'

Monks looked at the old gentleman, with an anxious eye; but, reading in his countenance nothing but severity and determination, walked into the room, and, shrugging his shoulders, sat down.

'Lock the door on the outside,' said Mr. Brownlow to the attendants, 'and come when I ring.'

The men obeyed, and the two were left alone together.

'This is pretty treatment, sir,' said Monks, throwing down his hat and cloak, 'from my father's oldest friend.'

'It is because I was your father's oldest friend, young man,' returned Mr. Brownlow; 'it is because the hopes and wishes of young and happy years were bound up with him, and that fair creature of his blood and kindred who rejoined her God in youth, and left me here a solitary, lonely man: it is because he knelt with me beside his only sisters's death-bed when he was yet a boy, on the morning that would—but Heaven willed otherwise—have made her my young wife; it is because my seared heart clung to him, from that time forth, through all his trials and errors, till he died; it is because old recollections and associations filled my heart, and even the sight of you brings with it old thoughts of him; it is because of all these things that I am moved to treat you gently now—yes, Edward Leeford, even now—and blush for your unworthiness who bear the name.'

'What has the name to do with it?' asked the other, after contemplating, half in silence, and half in dogged wonder, the agitation of his companion. 'What is the name to me?'

'Nothing,' replied Mr. Brownlow, 'nothing to you. But it was hers, and even at this distance of time brings back to me, an old man, the glow and thrill which I once felt, only to hear it repeated by a stranger. I am very glad you have changed it—very—very.'

'This is all mighty fine,' said Monks (to retain his assumed designation) after a long silence, during which he had jerked himself in sullen defiance to and fro, and Mr. Brownlow had sat, shading his face with his hand. 'But what do you want with me?'

'You have a brother,' said Mr. Brownlow, rousing himself: 'a brother, the whisper of whose name in your ear when I came behind you in the street, was, in itself, almost enough to make you accompany me hither, in wonder and alarm.'

'I have no brother,' replied Monks. 'You know I was an only child. Why do you talk to me of brothers? You know that, as well as I.'

'Attend to what I do know, and you may not,' said Mr. Brownlow. 'I shall interest you by and by. I know that of the wretched marriage, into which family pride, and the most sordid and narrowest of all ambition, forced your unhappy father when a mere boy, you were the sole and most unnatural issue.'

'I don't care for hard names,' interrupted Monks with a jeering laugh. 'You know the fact, and that's enough for me.'

'But I also know,' pursued the old gentleman, 'the misery, the slow torture, the protracted anguish of that ill-assorted union. I know how listlessly and wearily each of that wretched pair dragged on their heavy chain through a world that was poisoned to them both. I know how cold formalities were succeeded by open taunts; how indifference gave place to dislike, dislike to hate, and hate to loathing, until at last they wrenched the clanking bond asunder, and retiring a wide space apart, carried each a galling fragment, of which nothing but death could break the rivets, to hide it in new society beneath the gayest looks they could assume. Your mother succeeded; she forgot it soon. But it rusted and cankered at your father's heart for years.'

'Well, they were separated,' said Monks, 'and what of that?'

'When they had been separated for some time,' returned Mr. Brownlow, 'and your mother, wholly given up to continental frivolities, had utterly forgotten the young husband ten good years her junior, who, with prospects blighted, lingered on at home, he fell among new friends. This circumstance, at least, you know already.'

'Not I,' said Monks, turning away his eyes and beating his foot upon the ground, as a man who is determined to deny everything. 'Not I.'

'Your manner, no less than your actions, assures me that you have never forgotten it, or ceased to think of it with bitterness,' returned Mr. Brownlow. 'I speak of fifteen years ago, when you were not more than eleven years old, and your father but one-and-thirty—for he was, I repeat, a boy, when his father ordered him to marry. Must I go back to events which cast a shade upon the memory of your parent, or will you spare it, and disclose to me the truth?'

'I have nothing to disclose,' rejoined Monks. 'You must talk on if you will.'

'These new friends, then,' said Mr. Brownlow, 'were a naval officer retired from active service, whose wife had died some half-a-year before, and left him with two children—there had been more, but, of all their family, happily but two survived. They were both daughters; one a beautiful creature of nineteen, and the other a mere child of two or three years old.'

'What's this to me?' asked Monks.

'They resided,' said Mr. Brownlow, without seeming to hear the interruption, 'in a part of the country to which your father in his wandering had repaired, and where he had taken up his abode. Acquaintance, intimacy, friendship, fast followed on each other. Your father was gifted as few men are. He had his sister's soul and person. As the old officer knew him more and more, he grew to love him. I would that it had ended there. His daughter did the same.'

The old gentleman paused; Monks was biting his lips, with his eyes fixed upon the floor; seeing this, he immediately resumed:

'The end of a year found him contracted, solemnly contracted, to that daughter; the object of the first, true, ardent, only passion of a guileless girl.'

'Your tale is of the longest,' observed Monks, moving restlessly in his chair.

'It is a true tale of grief and trial, and sorrow, young man,' returned Mr. Brownlow, 'and such tales usually are; if it were one of unmixed joy and happiness, it would be very brief. At length one of those rich relations to strengthen whose interest and importance your father had been sacrificed, as others are often—it is no uncommon case—died, and to repair the misery he had been instrumental in occasioning, left him his panacea for all griefs—Money. It was necessary that he should immediately repair to Rome, whither this man had sped for health, and where he had died, leaving his affairs in great confusion. He went; was seized with mortal illness there; was followed, the moment the intelligence reached Paris, by your mother who carried you with her; he died the day after her arrival, leaving no will—no will—so that the whole property fell to her and you.'

At this part of the recital Monks held his breath, and listened with a face of intense eagerness, though his eyes were not directed towards the speaker. As Mr. Brownlow paused, he changed his position with the air of one who has experienced a sudden relief, and wiped his hot face and hands.

'Before he went abroad, and as he passed through London on his way,' said Mr. Brownlow, slowly, and fixing his eyes upon the other's face, 'he came to me.'

'I never heard of that,' interrupted Monks in a tone intended to appear incredulous, but savouring more of disagreeable surprise.

'He came to me, and left with me, among some other things, a picture—a portrait painted by himself—a likeness of this poor girl—which he did not wish to leave behind, and could not carry forward on his hasty journey. He was worn by anxiety and remorse almost to a shadow; talked in a wild, distracted way, of ruin and dishonour worked by himself; confided to me his intention to convert his whole property, at any loss, into money, and, having settled on his wife and you a portion of his recent acquisition, to fly the country—I guessed too well he would not fly alone—and never see it more. Even from me, his old and early friend, whose strong attachment had taken root in the earth that covered one most dear to both—even from me he withheld any more particular confession, promising to write and tell me all, and after that to see me once again, for the last time on earth. Alas! That was the last time. I had no letter, and I never saw him more.'

'I went,' said Mr. Brownlow, after a short pause, 'I went, when all was over, to the scene of his—I will use the term the world would freely use, for worldly harshness or favour are now alike to him—of his guilty love, resolved that if my fears were realised that erring child should find one heart and home to shelter and compassionate her. The family had left that part a week before; they had called in such trifling debts as were outstanding, discharged them, and left the place by night. Why, or whither, none can tell.'

Monks drew his breath yet more freely, and looked round with a smile of triumph.

'When your brother,' said Mr. Brownlow, drawing nearer to the other's chair, 'When your brother: a feeble, ragged, neglected child: was cast in my way by a stronger hand than chance, and rescued by me from a life of vice and infamy—'

'What?' cried Monks.

'By me,' said Mr. Brownlow. 'I told you I should interest you before long. I say by me—I see that your cunning associate suppressed my name, although for ought he knew, it would be quite strange to your ears. When he was rescued by me, then, and lay recovering from sickness in my house, his strong resemblance to this picture I have spoken of, struck me with astonishment. Even when I first saw him in all his dirt and misery, there was a lingering expression in his face that came upon me like a glimpse of some old friend flashing on one in a vivid dream. I need not tell you he was snared away before I knew his history—'

'Why not?' asked Monks hastily.

'Because you know it well.'

'I!'

'Denial to me is vain,' replied Mr. Brownlow. 'I shall show you that I know more than that.'

'You—you—can't prove anything against me,' stammered Monks. 'I defy you to do it!'

'We shall see,' returned the old gentleman with a searching glance. 'I lost the boy, and no efforts of mine could recover him. Your mother being dead, I knew that you alone could solve the mystery if anybody could, and as when I had last heard of you-you were on your own estate in the West Indies—whither, as you well know, you retired upon your mother's death to escape the consequences of vicious courses here—I made the voyage. You had left it, months before, and were supposed to be in London, but no one could tell where. I returned. Your agents had no clue to your residence. You came and went, they said, as strangely as you had ever done: sometimes for days together and sometimes not for months: keeping to all appearance the same low haunts and mingling with the same infamous herd who had been your associates when a fierce ungovernable boy. I wearied them with new applications. I paced the streets by night and day, but until two hours ago, all my efforts were fruitless, and I never saw you for an instant.'

'And now you do see me,' said Monks, rising boldly, 'what then? Fraud and robbery are high-sounding words—justified, you think, by a fancied resemblance in some young imp to an idle daub of a dead man's Brother! You don't even know that a child was born of this maudlin pair; you don't even know that.'

840

'I did not,' replied Mr. Brownlow, rising too; 'but within the last fortnight I have learnt it all. You have a brother; you know it, and him. There was a will, which your mother destroyed, leaving the secret and the gain to you at her own death. It contained a reference to some child likely to be the result of this sad connection, which child was born, and accidentally encountered by you, when your suspicions were first awakened by his resemblance to your father. You repaired to the place of his birth. There existed proofs—proofs long suppressed—of his birth and parentage. Those proofs were destroyed by you, and now, in your own words to your accomplice the Jew, "the only proofs of the boy's identity lie at the bottom of the river, and the old hag that received them from the mother is rotting in her coffin." Unworthy son, coward, liar,—you, who hold your councils with thieves and murderers in dark rooms at night,—you, whose plots and wiles have brought a violent death upon the head of one worth millions such as you,—you, who from your cradle were gall and bitterness to your own father's heart, and in whom all evil passions, vice, and profligacy, festered, till they found a vent in a hideous disease which had made your face an index even to your mind—you, Edward Leeford, do you still brave me!'

'No, no, no!' returned the coward, overwhelmed by these accumulated charges.

'Every word!' cried the gentleman, 'every word that has passed between you and this detested villain, is known to me. Shadows on the wall have caught your whispers, and brought them to my ear; the sight of the persecuted child has turned vice itself, and given it the courage and almost the attributes of virtue. Murder has been done, to which you were morally if not really a party.'

'No, no,' interposed Monks. 'I—I knew nothing of that; I was going to inquire the truth of the story when you overtook me. I didn't know the cause. I thought it was a common quarrel.'

'It was the partial disclosure of your secrets,' replied Mr. Brownlow. 'Will you disclose the whole?'

'Yes, I will.'

'Set your hand to a statement of truth and facts, and repeat it before witnesses?'

'That I promise too.'

'Remain quietly here, until such a document is drawn up, and proceed with me to such a place as I may deem most advisable, for the purpose of attesting it?'

'If you insist upon that, I'll do that also,' replied Monks.

'You must do more than that,' said Mr. Brownlow. 'Make restitution to an innocent and unoffending child, for such he is, although the offspring of a guilty and most miserable love. You have not forgotten the provisions of the will. Carry them into execution so far as your brother is concerned, and then go where you please. In this world you need meet no more.'

While Monks was pacing up and down, meditating with dark and evil looks on this proposal and the possibilities of evading it: torn by his fears on the one hand and his hatred on the other: the door was hurriedly unlocked, and a gentleman (Mr. Losberne) entered the room in violent agitation.

'The man will be taken,' he cried. 'He will be taken to-night!'

'The murderer?' asked Mr. Brownlow.

'Yes, yes,' replied the other. 'His dog has been seen lurking about some old haunt, and there seems little doubt that his master either is, or will be, there, under cover of the darkness. Spies are hovering about in every direction. I have spoken to the men who are charged with his capture, and they tell me he cannot escape. A reward of a hundred pounds is proclaimed by Government to-night.'

'I will give fifty more,' said Mr. Brownlow, 'and proclaim it with my own lips upon the spot, if I can reach it. Where is Mr. Maylie?'

'Harry? As soon as he had seen your friend here, safe in a coach with you, he hurried off to where he heard this,' replied the doctor, 'and mounting his horse sallied forth to join the first party at some place in the outskirts agreed upon between them.'

'Fagin,' said Mr. Brownlow; 'what of him?'

'When I last heard, he had not been taken, but he will be, or is, by this time. They're sure of him.'

'Have you made up your mind?' asked Mr. Brownlow, in a low voice, of Monks.

'Yes,' he replied. 'You—you—will be secret with me?'

'I will. Remain here till I return. It is your only hope of safety.'

They left the room, and the door was again locked.

'What have you done?' asked the doctor in a whisper.

'All that I could hope to do, and even more. Coupling the poor girl's intelligence with my previous knowledge, and the result of our good friend's inquiries on the spot, I left him no loophole of escape, and laid bare the whole villainy which by these lights became plain as day. Write and appoint the evening after to-morrow, at seven, for the meeting. We shall be down there, a few hours before, but shall require rest: especially the young lady, who may have greater need of firmness than either you or I can quite foresee just now. But my blood boils to avenge this poor murdered creature. Which way have they taken?'

'Drive straight to the office and you will be in time,' replied Mr. Losberne. 'I will remain here.'

The two gentlemen hastily separated; each in a fever of excitement wholly uncontrollable.

CHAPTER L. THE PURSUIT AND ESCAPE

Near to that part of the Thames on which the church at Rotherhithe abuts, where the buildings on the banks are dirtiest and the vessels on the river blackest with the dust of colliers and the smoke of close-built low-roofed houses, there exists the filthiest, the strangest, the most extraordinary of the many localities that are hidden in London, wholly unknown, even by name, to the great mass of its inhabitants.

To reach this place, the visitor has to penetrate through a maze of close, narrow, and muddy streets, thronged by the roughest and poorest of waterside people, and devoted to the traffic they may be supposed to occasion. The cheapest and least delicate provisions are heaped in the shops; the coarsest and commonest articles of wearing apparel dangle at the salesman's door, and stream from the house-parapet and windows. Jostling with unemployed labourers of the lowest class, ballast-heavers, coal-whippers, brazen women, ragged children, and the raff and refuse of the river, he makes his way with difficulty along, assailed by offensive sights and smells from the narrow alleys which branch off on the right and left, and deafened by the clash of ponderous waggons that bear great piles of merchandise from the stacks of warehouses that rise from every corner. Arriving, at length, in streets remoter and less-frequented than those through which he has passed, he walks beneath tottering house-fronts projecting over the pavement, dismantled walls that seem to totter as he passes, chimneys half crushed half hesitating to fall, windows guarded by rusty iron bars that time and dirt have almost eaten away, every imaginable sign of desolation and neglect.

In such a neighborhood, beyond Dockhead in the Borough of Southwark, stands Jacob's Island, surrounded by a muddy ditch, six or eight feet deep and fifteen or twenty wide when the tide is in, once called Mill Pond, but known in the days of this story as Folly Ditch. It is a creek or inlet from the Thames, and can always be filled at high water by opening the sluices at the Lead Mills from which it took its old name. At such times, a stranger, looking from one of the wooden bridges thrown across it at Mill Lane, will see the inhabitants of the houses on either side lowering from their back doors and windows, buckets, pails, domestic utensils of all kinds, in which to haul the water up; and when his eye is turned from these operations to the houses themselves, his utmost astonishment will be excited by the scene before him. Crazy wooden galleries common to the backs of half a dozen houses, with holes from which to look upon the slime beneath; windows, broken and patched, with poles thrust out, on which to dry the linen that is never there; rooms so small, so filthy, so confined, that the air would seem too tainted even for the dirt and squalor which they shelter; wooden chambers thrusting themselves out above the mud, and threatening to fall into it—as some have done; dirt-besmeared walls and decaying foundations; every repulsive lineament of poverty, every loathsome indication of filth, rot, and garbage; all these ornament the banks of Folly Ditch.

In Jacob's Island, the warehouses are roofless and empty; the walls are crumbling down; the windows are windows no more; the doors are falling into the streets; the chimneys are blackened, but they yield no smoke. Thirty or forty years ago, before losses and chancery suits came upon it, it was a thriving place; but now it is a desolate island indeed. The houses have no owners; they are broken open, and entered upon by those who have the courage; and there they live, and there they die. They must have powerful motives for a secret residence, or be reduced to a destitute condition indeed, who seek a refuge in Jacob's Island.

In an upper room of one of these houses—a detached house of fair size, ruinous in other respects, but strongly defended at door and window: of which house the back commanded the ditch in manner already described—there were assembled three men, who, regarding each other every now and then with looks expressive of perplexity and expectation, sat for some time in profound and gloomy silence. One of these was Toby Crackit, another Mr. Chitling, and the third a robber of fifty years, whose nose had been almost beaten in, in some old scuffle, and whose face bore a frightful scar which might probably be traced to the same occasion. This man was a returned transport, and his name was Kags.

'I wish,' said Toby turning to Mr. Chitling, 'that you had picked out some other crib when the two old ones got too warm, and had not come here, my fine feller.'

'Why didn't you, blunder-head!' said Kags.

'Well, I thought you'd have been a little more glad to see me than this,' replied Mr. Chitling, with a melancholy air.

'Why, look'e, young gentleman,' said Toby, 'when a man keeps himself so very exclusive as I have done, and by that means has a snug house over his head with nobody a prying and smelling about it, it's rather a startling thing to have the honour of a wisit from a young gentleman (however respectable and pleasant a person he may be to play cards with at conweniency) circumstanced as you are.'

'Especially, when the exclusive young man has got a friend stopping with him, that's arrived sooner than was expected from foreign parts, and is too modest to want to be presented to the Judges on his return,' added Mr. Kags.

There was a short silence, after which Toby Crackit, seeming to abandon as hopeless any further effort to maintain his usual devil-may-care swagger, turned to Chitling and said,

'When was Fagin took then?'

'Just at dinner-time—two o'clock this afternoon. Charley and I made our lucky up the wash-us chimney, and Bolter got into the empty water-butt, head downwards; but his legs were so precious long that they stuck out at the top, and so they took him too.'

'And Bet?'

'Poor Bet! She went to see the Body, to speak to who it was,' replied Chitling, his countenance falling more and more, 'and went off mad, screaming and raving, and beating her head against the boards; so they put a strait-weskut on her and took her to the hospital—and there she is.'

'Wot's come of young Bates?' demanded Kags.

'He hung about, not to come over here afore dark, but he'll be here soon,' replied Chitling. 'There's nowhere else to go to now, for the people at the Cripples are all in custody, and the bar of the ken—I went up there and see it with my own eyes—is filled with traps.'

'This is a smash,' observed Toby, biting his lips. 'There's more than one will go with this.'

'The sessions are on,' said Kags: 'if they get the inquest over, and Bolter turns King's evidence: as of course he will, from what he's said already: they can prove Fagin an accessory before the fact, and get the trial on on Friday, and he'll swing in six days from this, by G—!'

'You should have heard the people groan,' said Chitling; 'the officers fought like devils, or they'd have torn him away. He was down once, but they made a ring round him, and fought their way along. You should have seen how he looked about him, all muddy and bleeding, and clung to them as if they were his dearest friends. I can see 'em now, not able to stand upright with the pressing of the mob, and draggin him along amongst 'em; I can see the people jumping up, one behind another, and snarling with their teeth and making at him; I can see the blood upon his hair and beard, and hear the cries with which the women worked themselves into the centre of the crowd at the street corner, and swore they'd tear his heart out!'

The horror-stricken witness of this scene pressed his hands upon his ears, and with his eyes closed got up and paced violently to and fro, like one distracted.

While he was thus engaged, and the two men sat by in silence with their eyes fixed upon the floor, a pattering noise was heard upon the stairs, and Sikes's dog bounded into the room.

They ran to the window, downstairs, and into the street. The dog had jumped in at an open window; he made no attempt to follow them, nor was his master to be seen.

'What's the meaning of this?' said Toby when they had returned. 'He can't be coming here. I—I—hope not.'

'If he was coming here, he'd have come with the dog,' said Kags, stooping down to examine the animal, who lay panting on the floor. 'Here! Give us some water for him; he has run himself faint.'

'He's drunk it all up, every drop,' said Chitling after watching the dog some time in silence. 'Covered with mud—lame—half blind—he must have come a long way.'

'Where can he have come from!' exclaimed Toby. 'He's been to the other kens of course, and finding them filled with strangers come on here, where he's been many a time and often. But where can he have come from first, and how comes he here alone without the other!'

'He'—(none of them called the murderer by his old name)—'He can't have made away with himself. What do you think?' said Chitling.

Toby shook his head.

'If he had,' said Kags, 'the dog 'ud want to lead us away to where he did it. No. I think he's got out of the country, and left the dog behind. He must have given him the slip somehow, or he wouldn't be so easy.'

This solution, appearing the most probable one, was adopted as the right; the dog, creeping under a chair, coiled himself up to sleep, without more notice from anybody.

It being now dark, the shutter was closed, and a candle lighted and placed upon the table. The terrible events of the last two days had made a deep impression on all three, increased by the danger and uncertainty of their own position. They drew their chairs closer together, starting at every sound. They spoke little, and that in whispers, and were as silent and awe-stricken as if the remains of the murdered woman lay in the next room.

They had sat thus, some time, when suddenly was heard a hurried knocking at the door below.

'Young Bates,' said Kags, looking angrily round, to check the fear he felt himself.

The knocking came again. No, it wasn't he. He never knocked like that.

Crackit went to the window, and shaking all over, drew in his head. There was no need to tell them who it was; his pale face was enough. The dog too was on the alert in an instant, and ran whining to the door.

'We must let him in,' he said, taking up the candle.

'Isn't there any help for it?' asked the other man in a hoarse voice.

'None. He must come in.'

'Don't leave us in the dark,' said Kags, taking down a candle from the chimney-piece, and lighting it, with such a trembling hand that the knocking was twice repeated before he had finished.

Crackit went down to the door, and returned followed by a man with the lower part of his face buried in a handkerchief, and another tied over his head under his hat. He drew them slowly off. Blanched face, sunken eyes, hollow cheeks, beard of three days' growth, wasted flesh, short thick breath; it was the very ghost of Sikes.

He laid his hand upon a chair which stood in the middle of the room, but shuddering as he was about to drop into it, and seeming to glance over his shoulder, dragged it back close to the wall—as close as it would go—and ground it against it—and sat down.

Not a word had been exchanged. He looked from one to another in silence. If an eye were furtively raised and met his, it was instantly averted. When his hollow voice broke silence, they all three started. They seemed never to have heard its tones before.

'How came that dog here?' he asked.

'Alone. Three hours ago.'

'To-night's paper says that Fagin's took. Is it true, or a lie?'

'True.'

They were silent again.

'Damn you all!' said Sikes, passing his hand across his forehead.

'Have you nothing to say to me?'

There was an uneasy movement among them, but nobody spoke.

'You that keep this house,' said Sikes, turning his face to Crackit, 'do you mean to sell me, or to let me lie here till this hunt is over?'

'You may stop here, if you think it safe,' returned the person addressed, after some hesitation.

Sikes carried his eyes slowly up the wall behind him: rather trying to turn his head than actually doing it: and said, 'Is—it—the body—is it buried?'

They shook their heads.

'Why isn't it!' he retorted with the same glance behind him. 'Wot do they keep such ugly things above the ground for?—Who's that knocking?'

Crackit intimated, by a motion of his hand as he left the room, that there was nothing to fear; and directly came back with Charley Bates behind him. Sikes sat opposite the door, so that the moment the boy entered the room he encountered his figure.

'Toby,' said the boy falling back, as Sikes turned his eyes towards him, 'why didn't you tell me this, downstairs?'

There had been something so tremendous in the shrinking off of the three, that the wretched man was willing to propitiate even this lad. Accordingly he nodded, and made as though he would shake hands with him.

'Let me go into some other room,' said the boy, retreating still farther.

'Charley!' said Sikes, stepping forward. 'Don't you—don't you know me?'

'Don't come nearer me,' answered the boy, still retreating, and looking, with horror in his eyes, upon the murderer's face. 'You monster!'

The man stopped half-way, and they looked at each other; but Sikes's eyes sunk gradually to the ground.

'Witness you three,' cried the boy shaking his clenched fist, and becoming more and more excited as he spoke. 'Witness you three—I'm not afraid of him—if they come here after him, I'll give him up; I will. I tell you out at once. He may kill me for it if he likes, or if he dares, but if I am here I'll give him up. I'd give him up if he was to be boiled alive. Murder! Help! If there's the pluck of a man among you three, you'll help me. Murder! Help! Down with him!'

Pouring out these cries, and accompanying them with violent gesticulation, the boy actually threw himself, single-handed, upon the strong man, and in the intensity of his energy and the suddenness of his surprise, brought him heavily to the ground.

The three spectators seemed quite stupefied. They offered no interference, and the boy and man rolled on the ground together; the former, heedless of the blows that showered upon him, wrenching his hands tighter and tighter in the garments about the murderer's breast, and never ceasing to call for help with all his might.

The contest, however, was too unequal to last long. Sikes had him down, and his knee was on his throat, when Crackit pulled him back with a look of alarm, and pointed to the window. There were lights gleaming below, voices in loud and earnest conversation, the tramp of hurried footsteps—endless they seemed in number—crossing the nearest wooden bridge. One man on horseback seemed to be among the crowd; for there was the noise of hoofs rattling on the uneven pavement. The gleam of lights increased; the footsteps came more thickly and noisily on. Then, came a loud knocking at the door, and then a hoarse murmur from such a multitude of angry voices as would have made the boldest quail.

'Help!' shrieked the boy in a voice that rent the air.

'He's here! Break down the door!'

'In the King's name,' cried the voices without; and the hoarse cry arose again, but louder.

'Break down the door!' screamed the boy. 'I tell you they'll never open it. Run straight to the room where the light is. Break down the door!'

Strokes, thick and heavy, rattled upon the door and lower window-shutters as he ceased to speak, and a loud huzzah burst from the crowd; giving the listener, for the first time, some adequate idea of its immense extent.

'Open the door of some place where I can lock this screeching Hell-babe,' cried Sikes fiercely; running to and fro, and dragging the boy, now, as easily as if he were an empty sack. 'That door. Quick!' He flung him in, bolted it, and turned the key. 'Is the downstairs door fast?'

'Double-locked and chained,' replied Crackit, who, with the other two men, still remained quite helpless and bewildered.

'The panels—are they strong?'

'Lined with sheet-iron.'

'And the windows too?'

'Yes, and the windows.'

'Damn you!' cried the desperate ruffian, throwing up the sash and menacing the crowd.

'Do your worst! I'll cheat you yet!'

Of all the terrific yells that ever fell on mortal ears, none could exceed the cry of the infuriated throng. Some shouted to those who were nearest to set the house on fire; others roared to the officers to shoot him dead. Among them all, none showed such fury as the man on horseback, who, throwing himself out of the saddle, and bursting through the crowd as if he were parting water, cried, beneath the window, in a voice that rose above all others, 'Twenty guineas to the man who brings a ladder!'

The nearest voices took up the cry, and hundreds echoed it. Some called for ladders, some for sledge-hammers; some ran with torches to and fro as if to seek them, and still came back and roared again; some spent their breath in impotent curses and execrations; some pressed forward with the ecstasy of madmen, and thus impeded the progress of those below; some among the boldest attempted to climb up by the water-spout and crevices in the wall; and all waved to and fro, in the darkness beneath, like a field of corn moved by an angry wind: and joined from time to time in one loud furious roar.

'The tide,' cried the murderer, as he staggered back into the room, and shut the faces out, 'the tide was in as I came up. Give me a rope, a long rope. They're all in front. I may drop into the Folly Ditch, and clear off that way. Give me a rope, or I shall do three more murders and kill myself.'

The panic-stricken men pointed to where such articles were kept; the murderer, hastily selecting the longest and strongest cord, hurried up to the house-top.

All the window in the rear of the house had been long ago bricked up, except one small trap in the room where the boy was locked, and that was too small even for the passage of his body. But, from this aperture, he had never ceased to call on those without, to guard the back; and thus, when the murderer emerged at last on the house-top by the door in the roof, a loud shout proclaimed the fact to those in front, who immediately began to pour round, pressing upon each other in an unbroken stream.

He planted a board, which he had carried up with him for the purpose, so firmly against the door that it must be matter of great difficulty to open it from the inside; and creeping over the tiles, looked over the low parapet.

The water was out, and the ditch a bed of mud.

The crowd had been hushed during these few moments, watching his motions and doubtful of his purpose, but the instant they perceived it and knew it was defeated, they raised a cry of triumphant execration to which all their previous shouting had been whispers. Again and again it rose. Those who were at too great a distance to know its meaning, took up the sound; it echoed and re-echoed; it seemed as though the whole city had poured its population out to curse him.

On pressed the people from the front—on, on, on, in a strong struggling current of angry faces, with here and there a glaring torch to lighten them up, and show them out in all their wrath and passion. The houses on the opposite side of the ditch had been entered by the mob; sashes were thrown up, or torn bodily out; there were tiers and tiers of faces in every window; cluster upon cluster of people clinging to every house-top. Each little bridge (and there were three in sight) bent beneath the weight of the crowd upon it. Still the current poured on to find some nook or hole from which to vent their shouts, and only for an instant see the wretch.

'They have him now,' cried a man on the nearest bridge. 'Hurrah!'

The crowd grew light with uncovered heads; and again the shout uprose.

'I will give fifty pounds,' cried an old gentleman from the same quarter, 'to the man who takes him alive. I will remain here, till he come to ask me for it.'

There was another roar. At this moment the word was passed among the crowd that the door was forced at last, and that he who had first called for the ladder had mounted into the room. The stream abruptly turned, as this intelligence ran from mouth to mouth; and the people at the windows, seeing those upon the bridges pouring back, quitted their stations, and running into the street, joined the concourse that now thronged pell-mell to the spot they had left: each man crushing and striving with his neighbor, and all panting with impatience to get near the door, and look upon the criminal as the officers brought him out. The cries and shrieks of those who were pressed almost to suffocation, or trampled down and trodden under foot in the confusion, were dreadful; the narrow ways were completely blocked up; and at this time, between the rush of some to regain the space in front of the house, and the unavailing struggles of others to extricate themselves from the mass, the immediate attention was distracted from the murderer, although the universal eagerness for his capture was, if possible, increased.

The man had shrunk down, thoroughly quelled by the ferocity of the crowd, and the impossibility of escape; but seeing this sudden change with no less rapidity than it had occurred, he sprang upon his feet, determined to make one last effort for his life by dropping into the ditch, and, at the risk of being stifled, endeavouring to creep away in the darkness and confusion.

Roused into new strength and energy, and stimulated by the noise within the house which announced that an entrance had really been effected, he set his foot against the stack of chimneys, fastened one end of the rope tightly and firmly round it, and with the other made a strong running noose by the aid of his hands and teeth almost in a second. He could let himself down by the cord to within a less distance of the ground than his own height, and had his knife ready in his hand to cut it then and drop.

At the very instant when he brought the loop over his head previous to slipping it beneath his arm-pits, and when the old gentleman before-mentioned (who had clung so tight to the railing of the bridge as to resist the force of the crowd, and retain his position) earnestly warned those about him that the man was about to lower himself down—at that very instant the murderer, looking behind him on the roof, threw his arms above his head, and uttered a yell of terror.

'The eyes again!' he cried in an unearthly screech.

Staggering as if struck by lightning, he lost his balance and tumbled over the parapet. The noose was on his neck. It ran up with his weight, tight as a bow-string, and swift as the arrow it speeds. He fell for five-and-thirty feet. There was a sudden jerk, a terrific convulsion of the limbs; and there he hung, with the open knife clenched in his stiffening hand.

The old chimney quivered with the shock, but stood it bravely. The murderer swung lifeless against the wall; and the boy, thrusting aside the dangling body which obscured his view, called to the people to come and take him out, for God's sake.

A dog, which had lain concealed till now, ran backwards and forwards on the parapet with a dismal howl, and collecting himself for a spring, jumped for the dead man's shoulders. Missing his aim, he fell into the ditch, turning completely over as he went; and striking his head against a stone, dashed out his brains.

CHAPTER LI. AFFORDING AN EXPLANATION OF MORE MYSTERIES THAN ONE, AND COMPREHENDING A PROPOSAL OF MARRIAGE WITH NO WORD OF SETTLEMENT OR PIN-MONEY

The events narrated in the last chapter were yet but two days old, when Oliver found himself, at three o'clock in the afternoon, in a travelling-carriage rolling fast towards his native town. Mrs. Maylie, and Rose, and Mrs. Bedwin, and the good doctor were with him: and Mr. Brownlow followed in a post-chaise, accompanied by one other person whose name had not been mentioned.

They had not talked much upon the way; for Oliver was in a flutter of agitation and uncertainty which deprived him of the power of collecting his thoughts, and almost of speech, and appeared to have scarcely less effect on his companions, who shared it, in at least an equal degree. He and the two ladies had been very carefully made acquainted by Mr. Brownlow with the nature of the admissions which had been forced from Monks; and although they knew that the object of their present journey was to complete the work which had been so well begun, still the whole matter was enveloped in enough of doubt and mystery to leave them in endurance of the most intense suspense.

The same kind friend had, with Mr. Losberne's assistance, cautiously stopped all channels of communication through which they could receive intelligence of the dreadful occurrences that so recently taken place. 'It was quite true,' he said, 'that they must know them before long, but it might be at a better time than the present, and it could not be at a worse.' So, they travelled on in silence: each busied with reflections on the object which had brought them together: and no one disposed to give utterance to the thoughts which crowded upon all.

But if Oliver, under these influences, had remained silent while they journeyed towards his birth-place by a road he had never seen, how the whole current of his recollections ran back to old times, and what a crowd of emotions were wakened up in his breast, when they turned into that which he had traversed on foot: a poor houseless, wandering boy, without a friend to help him, or a roof to shelter his head.

'See there, there!' cried Oliver, eagerly clasping the hand of Rose, and pointing out at the carriage window; 'that's the stile I came over; there are the hedges I crept behind, for fear any one should overtake me and force me back! Yonder is the path across the fields, leading to the old house where I was a little child! Oh Dick, Dick, my dear old friend, if I could only see you now!'

'You will see him soon,' replied Rose, gently taking his folded hands between her own. 'You shall tell him how happy you are, and how rich you have grown, and that in all your happiness you have none so great as the coming back to make him happy too.'

'Yes, yes,' said Oliver, 'and we'll—we'll take him away from here, and have him clothed and taught, and send him to some quiet country place where he may grow strong and well,—shall we?'

Rose nodded 'yes,' for the boy was smiling through such happy tears that she could not speak.

'You will be kind and good to him, for you are to every one,' said Oliver. 'It will make you cry, I know, to hear what he can tell; but never mind, never mind, it will be all over, and you will smile again—I know that too—to think how changed he is; you did the same with me. He said "God bless you" to me when I ran away,' cried the boy with a burst of affectionate emotion; 'and I will say "God bless you" now, and show him how I love him for it!'

As they approached the town, and at length drove through its narrow streets, it became matter of no small difficulty to restrain the boy within reasonable bounds. There was Sowerberry's the undertaker's just as it used to be, only smaller and less imposing in appearance than he remembered it—there were all the well-known shops and houses, with almost every one of which he had some slight incident connected—there was Gamfield's cart, the very cart he used to have, standing at the old public-house door—there was the workhouse, the dreary prison of his youthful days, with its dismal windows frowning on the street—there was the same lean porter standing at the gate, at sight of whom Oliver involuntarily shrunk back, and then laughed at himself for being so foolish, then cried, then laughed again—there were scores of faces at the doors and windows that he knew quite well—there was nearly everything as if he had left it but yesterday, and all his recent life had been but a happy dream.

But it was pure, earnest, joyful reality. They drove straight to the door of the chief hotel (which Oliver used to stare up at, with awe, and think a mighty palace, but which had somehow fallen off in grandeur and size); and here was Mr. Grimwig all ready to receive them, kissing the young lady, and the old one too, when they got out of the coach, as if he were the grandfather of the whole party, all smiles and kindness, and not offering to eat his head—no, not once; not even when he contradicted a very old postboy about the nearest road to London, and maintained he knew it best, though he had only come that way once, and that time fast asleep. There was dinner prepared, and there were bedrooms ready, and everything was arranged as if by magic.

Notwithstanding all this, when the hurry of the first half-hour was over, the same silence and constraint prevailed that had marked their journey down. Mr. Brownlow did not join them at dinner, but remained in a separate room. The two other gentlemen hurried in and out with anxious faces, and, during the short intervals when they were present, conversed apart. Once, Mrs. Maylie was called away, and after being absent for nearly an hour, returned with eyes swollen with weeping. All these things made Rose and Oliver, who were not in any new secrets, nervous and uncomfortable. They sat wondering, in silence; or, if they exchanged a few words, spoke in whispers, as if they were afraid to hear the sound of their own voices.

At length, when nine o'clock had come, and they began to think they were to hear no more that night, Mr. Losberne and Mr. Grimwig entered the room, followed by Mr. Brownlow and a man whom Oliver almost shrieked with surprise to see; for they told him it was his brother, and it was the same man he had met at the market-town, and seen looking in with Fagin at the window of his little room. Monks cast a look of hate, which, even then, he could not dissemble, at the astonished boy, and sat down near the door. Mr. Brownlow, who had papers in his hand, walked to a table near which Rose and Oliver were seated.

'This is a painful task,' said he, 'but these declarations, which have been signed in London before many gentlemen, must be in substance repeated here. I would have spared you the degradation, but we must hear them from your own lips before we part, and you know why.'

'Go on,' said the person addressed, turning away his face. 'Quick. I have almost done enough, I think. Don't keep me here.'

'This child,' said Mr. Brownlow, drawing Oliver to him, and laying his hand upon his head, 'is your half-brother; the illegitimate son of your father, my dear friend Edwin Leeford, by poor young Agnes Fleming, who died in giving him birth.'

'Yes,' said Monks, scowling at the trembling boy: the beating of whose heart he might have heard. 'That is the bastard child.'

'The term you use,' said Mr. Brownlow, sternly, 'is a reproach to those long since passed beyond the feeble censure of the world. It reflects disgrace on no one living, except you who use it. Let that pass. He was born in this town.'

'In the workhouse of this town,' was the sullen reply. 'You have the story there.' He pointed impatiently to the papers as he spoke.

'I must have it here, too,' said Mr. Brownlow, looking round upon the listeners.

'Listen then! You!' returned Monks. 'His father being taken ill at Rome, was joined by his wife, my mother, from whom he had been long separated, who went from Paris and took me with her—to look after his property, for what I know, for she had no great affection for him, nor he for her. He knew nothing of us, for his senses were gone, and he slumbered on till next day, when he died. Among the papers in his desk, were two, dated on the night his illness first came on, directed to yourself'; he addressed himself to Mr. Brownlow; 'and enclosed in a few short lines to you, with an intimation on the cover of the package that it was not to be forwarded till after he was dead. One of these papers was a letter to this girl Agnes; the other a will.'

'What of the letter?' asked Mr. Brownlow.

'The letter?—A sheet of paper crossed and crossed again, with a penitent confession, and prayers to God to help her. He had palmed a tale on the girl that some secret mystery—to be explained one day—prevented his marrying her just then; and so she had gone on, trusting patiently to him, until she trusted too far, and lost what none could ever give her back. She was, at that time, within a few months of her confinement. He told her all he had meant to do, to hide her shame, if he had lived, and prayed her, if he died, not to curse his memory, or think the consequences of their sin would be visited on her or their young child; for all the guilt was his. He reminded her of the day he had given her the little locket and the ring with her christian name engraved upon it, and a blank left for that which he hoped one day to have bestowed upon her—prayed her yet to keep it, and wear it next her heart, as she had done before—and then ran on, wildly, in the same words, over and over again, as if he had gone distracted. I believe he had.'

'The will,' said Mr. Brownlow, as Oliver's tears fell fast.

Monks was silent.

'The will,' said Mr. Brownlow, speaking for him, 'was in the same spirit as the letter. He talked of miseries which his wife had brought upon him; of the rebellious disposition, vice, malice, and premature bad passions of you his only son, who had been trained to hate him; and left you, and your mother, each an annuity of eight hundred pounds. The bulk of his property he divided into two equal portions—one for Agnes Fleming, and the other for their child, if it should be born alive, and ever come of age. If it were a girl, it was to inherit the money unconditionally; but if a boy, only on the stipulation that in his minority he should never have stained his name with any public act of dishonour, meanness, cowardice, or wrong. He did this, he said, to mark his confidence in the other, and his conviction—only strengthened by approaching death—that the child would share her gentle heart, and noble nature. If he were disappointed in this expectation, then the money was to come to you: for then, and not till then, when both children were equal, would he recognise your prior claim upon his purse, who had none upon his heart, but had, from an infant, repulsed him with coldness and aversion.'

'My mother,' said Monks, in a louder tone, 'did what a woman should have done. She burnt this will. The letter never reached its destination; but that, and other proofs, she kept, in case they ever tried to lie away the blot. The girl's father had the truth from her with every aggravation that her violent hate—I love her for it now—could add. Goaded by shame and dishonour he fled with his children into a remote corner of Wales, changing his very name that his friends might never know of his retreat; and here, no great while afterwards, he was found dead in his bed. The girl had left her home, in secret, some weeks before; he had searched for her, on foot, in every town and village near; it was on the night when he returned home, assured that she had destroyed herself, to hide her shame and his, that his old heart broke.'

There was a short silence here, until Mr. Brownlow took up the thread of the narrative.

'Years after this,' he said, 'this man's—Edward Leeford's—mother came to me. He had left her, when only eighteen; robbed her of jewels and money; gambled, squandered, forged, and fled to London: where for two years he had associated with the lowest outcasts. She was sinking under a painful and incurable disease, and wished to recover him before she died. Inquiries were set on foot, and strict searches made. They were unavailing for a long time, but ultimately successful; and he went back with her to France.'

'There she died,' said Monks, 'after a lingering illness; and, on her death-bed, she bequeathed these secrets to me, together with her unquenchable and deadly hatred of all whom they involved—though she need not have left me that, for I had inherited it long before. She would not believe that the girl had destroyed herself, and the child too, but was filled with the impression that a male child had been born, and was alive. I swore to her, if ever it crossed my path, to hunt it down; never to let it rest; to pursue it with the bitterest and most unrelenting animosity; to vent upon it the hatred that I deeply felt, and to spit upon the empty vaunt of that insulting will by draggin it, if I could, to the very gallows-foot. She was right. He came in my way at last. I began well; and, but for babbling drabs, I would have finished as I began!'

As the villain folded his arms tight together, and muttered curses on himself in the impotence of baffled malice, Mr. Brownlow turned to the terrified group beside him, and explained that the Jew, who had been his old accomplice and confidant, had a large reward for keeping Oliver ensnared: of which some part was to be given up, in the event of his being rescued: and that a dispute on this head had led to their visit to the country house for the purpose of identifying him.

'The locket and ring?' said Mr. Brownlow, turning to Monks.

'I bought them from the man and woman I told you of, who stole them from the nurse, who stole them from the corpse,' answered Monks without raising his eyes. 'You know what became of them.'

Mr. Brownlow merely nodded to Mr. Grimwig, who disappearing with great alacrity, shortly returned, pushing in Mrs. Bumble, and dragging her unwilling consort after him.

'Do my hi's deceive me!' cried Mr. Bumble, with ill-feigned enthusiasm, 'or is that little Oliver? Oh O-li-ver, if you know'd how I've been a-grieving for you—'

'Hold your tongue, fool,' murmured Mrs. Bumble.

'Isn't natur, natur, Mrs. Bumble?' remonstrated the workhouse master. 'Can't I be supposed to feel—I as brought him up porochially—when I see him a-setting here among ladies and gentlemen of the very affablest description! I always loved that boy as if he'd been my—my—my own grandfather,' said Mr. Bumble, halting for an appropriate comparison. 'Master Oliver, my dear, you remember the blessed gentleman in the white waistcoat? Ah! he went to heaven last week, in a oak coffin with plated handles, Oliver.'

'Come, sir,' said Mr. Grimwig, tartly; 'suppress your feelings.'

'I will do my endeavours, sir,' replied Mr. Bumble. 'How do you do, sir? I hope you are very well.'

This salutation was addressed to Mr. Brownlow, who had stepped up to within a short distance of the respectable couple. He inquired, as he pointed to Monks,

'Do you know that person?'

'No,' replied Mrs. Bumble flatly.

'Perhaps you don't?' said Mr. Brownlow, addressing her spouse.

'I never saw him in all my life,' said Mr. Bumble.

'Nor sold him anything, perhaps?'

'No,' replied Mrs. Bumble.

'You never had, perhaps, a certain gold locket and ring?' said Mr. Brownlow.

'Certainly not,' replied the matron. 'Why are we brought here to answer to such nonsense as this?'

Again Mr. Brownlow nodded to Mr. Grimwig; and again that gentleman limped away with extraordinary readiness. But not again did he return with a stout man and wife; for this time, he led in two palsied women, who shook and tottered as they walked.

'You shut the door the night old Sally died,' said the foremost one, raising her shrivelled hand, 'but you couldn't shut out the sound, nor stop the chinks.'

'No, no,' said the other, looking round her and wagging her toothless jaws. 'No, no, no.'

'We heard her try to tell you what she'd done, and saw you take a paper from her hand, and watched you too, next day, to the pawnbroker's shop,' said the first.

'Yes,' added the second, 'and it was a "locket and gold ring." We found out that, and saw it given you. We were by. Oh! we were by.'

'And we know more than that,' resumed the first, 'for she told us often, long ago, that the young mother had told her that, feeling she should never get over it, she was on her way, at the time that she was taken ill, to die near the grave of the father of the child.'

'Would you like to see the pawnbroker himself?' asked Mr. Grimwig with a motion towards the door.

'No,' replied the woman; 'if he'—she pointed to Monks—'has been coward enough to confess, as I see he has, and you have sounded all these hags till you have found the right ones, I have nothing more to say. I did sell them, and they're where you'll never get them. What then?'

'Nothing,' replied Mr. Brownlow, 'except that it remains for us to take care that neither of you is employed in a situation of trust again. You may leave the room.'

'I hope,' said Mr. Bumble, looking about him with great ruefulness, as Mr. Grimwig disappeared with the two old women: 'I hope that this unfortunate little circumstance will not deprive me of my porochial office?'

'Indeed it will,' replied Mr. Brownlow. 'You may make up your mind to that, and think yourself well off besides.'

'It was all Mrs. Bumble. She would do it,' urged Mr. Bumble; first looking round to ascertain that his partner had left the room.

'That is no excuse,' replied Mr. Brownlow. 'You were present on the occasion of the destruction of these trinkets, and indeed are the more guilty of the two, in the eye of the law; for the law supposes that your wife acts under your direction.'

'If the law supposes that,' said Mr. Bumble, squeezing his hat emphatically in both hands, 'the law is a ass—a idiot. If that's the eye of the law, the law is a bachelor; and the worst I wish the law is, that his eye may be opened by experience—by experience.'

Laying great stress on the repetition of these two words, Mr. Bumble fixed his hat on very tight, and putting his hands in his pockets, followed his helpmate downstairs.

'Young lady,' said Mr. Brownlow, turning to Rose, 'give me your hand. Do not tremble. You need not fear to hear the few remaining words we have to say.'

'If they have—I do not know how they can, but if they have—any reference to me,' said Rose, 'pray let me hear them at some other time. I have not strength or spirits now.'

'Nay,' returned the old gentleman, drawing her arm through his; 'you have more fortitude than this, I am sure. Do you know this young lady, sir?'

'Yes,' replied Monks.

'I never saw you before,' said Rose faintly.

'I have seen you often,' returned Monks.

'The father of the unhappy Agnes had two daughters,' said Mr. Brownlow. 'What was the fate of the other—the child?'

'The child,' replied Monks, 'when her father died in a strange place, in a strange name, without a letter, book, or scrap of paper that yielded the faintest clue by which his friends or relatives could be traced—the child was taken by some wretched cottagers, who reared it as their own.'

'Go on,' said Mr. Brownlow, signing to Mrs. Maylie to approach. 'Go on!'

'You couldn't find the spot to which these people had repaired,' said Monks, 'but where friendship fails, hatred will often force a way. My mother found it, after a year of cunning search—ay, and found the child.'

'She took it, did she?'

'No. The people were poor and began to sicken—at least the man did—of their fine humanity; so she left it with them, giving them a small present of money which would not last long, and promised more, which she never meant to send. She didn't quite rely, however, on their discontent and poverty for the child's unhappiness, but told the history of the sister's shame, with such alterations as suited her; bade them take good heed of the child, for she came of bad blood; and told them she was illegitimate, and sure to go wrong at one time or other. The circumstances countenanced all this; the people believed it; and there the child dragged on an existence, miserable enough even to satisfy us, until a widow lady, residing, then, at Chester, saw the girl by chance, pitied her, and took her home. There was some cursed spell, I think, against us; for in spite of all our efforts she remained there and was happy. I lost sight of her, two or three years ago, and saw her no more until a few months back.'

'Do you see her now?'

'Yes. Leaning on your arm.'

'But not the less my niece,' cried Mrs. Maylie, folding the fainting girl in her arms; 'not the less my dearest child. I would not lose her now, for all the treasures of the world. My sweet companion, my own dear girl!'

'The only friend I ever had,' cried Rose, clinging to her. 'The kindest, best of friends. My heart will burst. I cannot bear all this.'

'You have borne more, and have been, through all, the best and gentlest creature that ever shed happiness on every one she knew,' said Mrs. Maylie, embracing her tenderly. 'Come, come, my love, remember who this is who waits to clasp you in his arms, poor child! See here—look, look, my dear!'

'Not aunt,' cried Oliver, throwing his arms about her neck; 'I'll never call her aunt—sister, my own dear sister, that something taught my heart to love so dearly from the first! Rose, dear, darling Rose!'

Let the tears which fell, and the broken words which were exchanged in the long close embrace between the orphans, be sacred. A father, sister, and mother, were gained, and lost, in that one moment. Joy and grief were mingled in the cup; but there were no bitter tears: for even grief itself arose so softened, and clothed in such sweet and tender recollections, that it became a solemn pleasure, and lost all character of pain.

They were a long, long time alone. A soft tap at the door, at length announced that some one was without. Oliver opened it, glided away, and gave place to Harry Maylie.

'I know it all,' he said, taking a seat beside the lovely girl. 'Dear Rose, I know it all.'

'I am not here by accident,' he added after a lengthened silence; 'nor have I heard all this to-night, for I knew it yesterday—only yesterday. Do you guess that I have come to remind you of a promise?'

'Stay,' said Rose. 'You do know all.'

'All. You gave me leave, at any time within a year, to renew the subject of our last discourse.'

'I did.'

'Not to press you to alter your determination,' pursued the young man, 'but to hear you repeat it, if you would. I was to lay whatever of station or fortune I might possess at your feet, and if you still adhered to your former determination, I pledged myself, by no word or act, to seek to change it.'

'The same reasons which influenced me then, will influence me now,' said Rose firmly. 'If I ever owed a strict and rigid duty to her, whose goodness saved me from a life of indigence and suffering, when should I ever feel it, as I should to-night? It is a struggle,' said Rose, 'but one I am proud to make; it is a pang, but one my heart shall bear.'

'The disclosure of to-night,'—Harry began.

'The disclosure of to-night,' replied Rose softly, 'leaves me in the same position, with reference to you, as that in which I stood before.'

'You harden your heart against me, Rose,' urged her lover.

'Oh Harry, Harry,' said the young lady, bursting into tears; 'I wish I could, and spare myself this pain.'

'Then why inflict it on yourself?' said Harry, taking her hand. 'Think, dear Rose, think what you have heard to-night.'

'And what have I heard! What have I heard!' cried Rose. 'That a sense of his deep disgrace so worked upon my own father that he shunned all—there, we have said enough, Harry, we have said enough.'

'Not yet, not yet,' said the young man, detaining her as she rose. 'My hopes, my wishes, prospects, feeling: every thought in life except my love for you: have undergone a change. I offer you, now, no distinction among a bustling crowd; no mingling with a world of malice and detraction, where the blood is called into honest cheeks by aught but real disgrace and shame; but a home—a heart and home—yes, dearest Rose, and those, and those alone, are all I have to offer.'

'What do you mean!' she faltered.

'I mean but this—that when I left you last, I left you with a firm determination to level all fancied barriers between yourself and me; resolved that if my world could not be yours, I would make yours mine; that no pride of birth should curl the lip at you, for I would turn from it. This I have done. Those who have shrunk from me because of this, have shrunk from you, and proved you so far right. Such power and patronage: such relatives of influence and rank: as smiled upon me then, look coldly now; but there are smiling fields and waving trees in England's richest county; and by one village church—mine, Rose, my own!—there stands a rustic dwelling which you can make me prouder of, than all the hopes I have renounced, measured a thousandfold. This is my rank and station now, and here I lay it down!'

'It's a trying thing waiting supper for lovers,' said Mr. Grimwig, waking up, and pulling his pocket-handkerchief from over his head.

Truth to tell, the supper had been waiting a most unreasonable time. Neither Mrs. Maylie, nor Harry, nor Rose (who all came in together), could offer a word in extenuation.

'I had serious thoughts of eating my head to-night,' said Mr. Grimwig, 'for I began to think I should get nothing else. I'll take the liberty, if you'll allow me, of saluting the bride that is to be.'

Mr. Grimwig lost no time in carrying this notice into effect upon the blushing girl; and the example, being contagious, was followed both by the doctor and Mr. Brownlow: some people affirm that Harry Maylie had been observed to set it, originally, in a dark room adjoining; but the best authorities consider this downright scandal: he being young and a clergyman.

'Oliver, my child,' said Mrs. Maylie, 'where have you been, and why do you look so sad? There are tears stealing down your face at this moment. What is the matter?'

It is a world of disappointment: often to the hopes we most cherish, and hopes that do our nature the greatest honour.

Poor Dick was dead!

CHAPTER LII. FAGIN'S LAST NIGHT ALIVE

The court was paved, from floor to roof, with human faces. Inquisitive and eager eyes peered from every inch of space. From the rail before the dock, away into the sharpest angle of the smallest corner in the galleries, all looks were fixed upon one man—Fagin. Before him and behind: above, below, on the right and on the left: he seemed to stand surrounded by a firmament, all bright with gleaming eyes.

He stood there, in all this glare of living light, with one hand resting on the wooden slab before him, the other held to his ear, and his head thrust forward to enable him to catch with greater distinctness every word that fell from the presiding judge, who was delivering his charge to the jury. At times, he turned his eyes sharply upon them to observe the effect of the slightest featherweight in his favour; and when the points against him were stated with terrible distinctness, looked towards his counsel, in mute appeal that he would, even then, urge something in his behalf. Beyond these manifestations of anxiety, he stirred not hand or foot. He had scarcely moved since the trial began; and now that the judge ceased to speak, he still remained in the same strained attitude of close attention, with his gaze bent on him, as though he listened still.

A slight bustle in the court, recalled him to himself. Looking round, he saw that the juryman had turned together, to consider their verdict. As his eyes wandered to the gallery, he could see the people rising above each other to see his face: some hastily applying their glasses to their eyes: and others whispering their neighbours with looks expressive of abhorrence. A few there were, who seemed unmindful of him, and looked only to the jury, in impatient wonder how they could delay. But in no one face—not even among the women, of whom there were many there—could he read the faintest sympathy with himself, or any feeling but one of all-absorbing interest that he should be condemned.

As he saw all this in one bewildered glance, the deathlike stillness came again, and looking back he saw that the jurymen had turned towards the judge. Hush!

They only sought permission to retire.

He looked, wistfully, into their faces, one by one when they passed out, as though to see which way the greater number leant; but that was fruitless. The jailer touched him on the shoulder. He followed mechanically to the end of the dock, and sat down on a chair. The man pointed it out, or he would not have seen it.

He looked up into the gallery again. Some of the people were eating, and some fanning themselves with handkerchiefs; for the crowded place was very hot. There was one young man sketching his face in a little note-book. He wondered whether it was like, and looked on when the artist broke his pencil-point, and made another with his knife, as any idle spectator might have done.

In the same way, when he turned his eyes towards the judge, his mind began to busy itself with the fashion of his dress, and what it cost, and how he put it on. There was an old fat gentleman on the bench, too, who had gone out, some half an hour before, and now come back. He wondered within himself whether this man had been to get his dinner, what he had had, and where he had had it; and pursued this train of careless thought until some new object caught his eye and roused another.

Not that, all this time, his mind was, for an instant, free from one oppressive overwhelming sense of the grave that opened at his feet; it was ever present to him, but in a vague and general way, and he could not fix his thoughts upon it. Thus, even while he trembled, and turned burning hot at the idea of speedy death, he fell to counting the iron spikes before him, and wondering how the head of one had been broken off, and whether they would mend it, or leave it as it was. Then, he thought of all the horrors of the gallows and the scaffold—and stopped to watch a man sprinkling the floor to cool it—and then went on to think again.

At length there was a cry of silence, and a breathless look from all towards the door. The jury returned, and passed him close. He could glean nothing from their faces; they might as well have been of stone. Perfect stillness ensued—not a rustle—not a breath—Guilty.

The building rang with a tremendous shout, and another, and another, and then it echoed loud groans, that gathered strength as they swelled out, like angry thunder. It was a peal of joy from the populace outside, greeting the news that he would die on Monday.

The noise subsided, and he was asked if he had anything to say why sentence of death should not be passed upon him. He had resumed his listening attitude, and looked intently at his questioner while the demand was made; but it was twice repeated before he seemed to hear it, and then he only muttered that he was an old man—an old man—and so, dropping into a whisper, was silent again.

The judge assumed the black cap, and the prisoner still stood with the same air and gesture. A woman in the gallery, uttered some exclamation, called forth by this dread solemnity; he looked hastily up as if angry at the interruption, and bent forward yet more attentively. The address was solemn and impressive; the sentence fearful to hear. But he stood, like a marble figure, without the motion of a nerve. His haggard face was still thrust forward, his under-jaw hanging down, and his eyes staring out before him, when the jailer put his hand upon his arm, and beckoned him away. He gazed stupidly about him for an instant, and obeyed.

They led him through a paved room under the court, where some prisoners were waiting till their turns came, and others were talking to their friends, who crowded round a grate which looked into the open yard. There was nobody there to speak to him; but, as he passed, the prisoners fell back to render him more visible to the people who were clinging to the bars: and they assailed him with opprobrious names, and screeched and hissed. He shook his fist, and would have spat upon them; but his conductors hurried him on, through a gloomy passage lighted by a few dim lamps, into the interior of the prison.

Here, he was searched, that he might not have about him the means of anticipating the law; this ceremony performed, they led him to one of the condemned cells, and left him there—alone.

He sat down on a stone bench opposite the door, which served for seat and bedstead; and casting his blood-shot eyes upon the ground, tried to collect his thoughts. After awhile, he began to remember a few disjointed fragments of what the judge had said: though it had seemed to him, at the time, that he could not hear a word. These gradually fell into their proper places, and by degrees suggested more: so that in a little time he had the whole, almost as it was delivered. To be hanged by the neck, till he was dead—that was the end. To be hanged by the neck till he was dead.

As it came on very dark, he began to think of all the men he had known who had died upon the scaffold; some of them through his means. They rose up, in such quick succession, that he could hardly count them. He had seen some of them die,—and had joked too, because they died with prayers upon their lips. With what a rattling noise the drop went down; and how suddenly they changed, from strong and vigorous men to dangling heaps of clothes!

Some of them might have inhabited that very cell—sat upon that very spot. It was very dark; why didn't they bring a light? The cell had been built for many years. Scores of men must have passed their last hours there. It was like sitting in a vault strewn with dead bodies—the cap, the noose, the pinioned arms, the faces that he knew, even beneath that hideous veil.— Light, light!

At length, when his hands were raw with beating against the heavy door and walls, two men appeared: one bearing a candle, which he thrust into an iron candlestick fixed against the wall: the other dragging in a mattress on which to pass the night; for the prisoner was to be left alone no more.

Then came the night—dark, dismal, silent night. Other watchers are glad to hear this church-clock strike, for they tell of life and coming day. To him they brought despair. The boom of every iron bell came laden with the one, deep, hollow sound—Death. What availed the noise and bustle of cheerful morning, which penetrated even there, to him? It was another form of knell, with mockery added to the warning.

The day passed off. Day? There was no day; it was gone as soon as come—and night came on again; night so long, and yet so short; long in its dreadful silence, and short in its fleeting hours. At one time he raved and blasphemed; and at another howled and tore his hair. Venerable men of his own persuasion had come to pray beside him, but he had driven them away with curses. They renewed their charitable efforts, and he beat them off.

Saturday night. He had only one night more to live. And as he thought of this, the day broke—Sunday.

It was not until the night of this last awful day, that a withering sense of his helpless, desperate state came in its full intensity upon his blighted soul; not that he had ever held any defined or positive hope of mercy, but that he had never been able to consider more than the dim probability of dying so soon. He had spoken little to either of the two men, who relieved each other in their attendance upon him; and they, for their parts, made no effort to rouse his attention. He had sat there, awake, but dreaming. Now, he started up, every minute, and with gasping mouth and burning skin, hurried to and fro, in such a paroxysm of fear and wrath that even they—used to such sights—recoiled from him with horror. He grew so terrible, at last, in all the tortures of his evil conscience, that one man could not bear to sit there, eyeing him alone; and so the two kept watch together.

He cowered down upon his stone bed, and thought of the past. He had been wounded with some missiles from the crowd on the day of his capture, and his head was bandaged with a linen cloth. His red hair hung down upon his bloodless face; his beard was torn, and twisted into knots; his eyes shone with a terrible light; his unwashed flesh crackled with the fever that burnt him up. Eight—nine—then. If it was not a trick to frighten him, and those were the real hours treading on each other's heels, where would he be, when they came round again! Eleven! Another struck, before the voice of the previous hour had ceased to vibrate. At eight, he would be the only mourner in his own funeral train; at eleven—

Those dreadful walls of Newgate, which have hidden so much misery and such unspeakable anguish, not only from the eyes, but, too often, and too long, from the thoughts, of men, never held so dread a spectacle as that. The few who lingered as they passed, and wondered what the man was doing who was to be hanged to-morrow, would have slept but ill that night, if they could have seen him.

From early in the evening until nearly midnight, little groups of two and three presented themselves at the lodge-gate, and inquired, with anxious faces, whether any reprieve had been received. These being answered in the negative, communicated the welcome intelligence to clusters in the street, who pointed out to one another the door from which he must come out, and showed where the scaffold would be built, and, walking with unwilling steps away, turned back to conjure up the scene. By degrees they fell off, one by one; and, for an hour, in the dead of night, the street was left to solitude and darkness.

The space before the prison was cleared, and a few strong barriers, painted black, had been already thrown across the road to break the pressure of the expected crowd, when Mr. Brownlow and Oliver appeared at the wicket, and presented an order of admission to the prisoner, signed by one of the sheriffs. They were immediately admitted into the lodge.

'Is the young gentleman to come too, sir?' said the man whose duty it was to conduct them. 'It's not a sight for children, sir.'

'It is not indeed, my friend,' rejoined Mr. Brownlow; 'but my business with this man is intimately connected with him; and as this child has seen him in the full career of his success and villainy, I think it as well—even at the cost of some pain and fear—that he should see him now.'

These few words had been said apart, so as to be inaudible to Oliver. The man touched his hat; and glancing at Oliver with some curiousity, opened another gate, opposite to that by which they had entered, and led them on, through dark and winding ways, towards the cells.

'This,' said the man, stopping in a gloomy passage where a couple of workmen were making some preparations in profound silence—'this is the place he passes through. If you step this way, you can see the door he goes out at.'

He led them into a stone kitchen, fitted with coppers for dressing the prison food, and pointed to a door. There was an open grating above it, through which came the sound of men's voices, mingled with the noise of hammering, and the throwing down of boards. They were putting up the scaffold.

From this place, they passed through several strong gates, opened by other turnkeys from the inner side; and, having entered an open yard, ascended a flight of narrow steps, and came into a passage with a row of strong doors on the left hand. Motioning them to remain where they were, the turnkey knocked at one of these with his bunch of keys. The two attendants, after a little whispering, came out into the passage, stretching themselves as if glad of the temporary relief, and motioned the visitors to follow the jailer into the cell. They did so.

The condemned criminal was seated on his bed, rocking himself from side to side, with a countenance more like that of a snared beast than the face of a man. His mind was evidently wandering to his old life, for he continued to mutter, without appearing conscious of their presence otherwise than as a part of his vision.

'Good boy, Charley—well done—' he mumbled. 'Oliver, too, ha! ha! ha! Oliver too— quite the gentleman now—quite the—take that boy away to bed!'

The jailer took the disengaged hand of Oliver; and, whispering him not to be alarmed, looked on without speaking.

'Take him away to bed!' cried Fagin. 'Do you hear me, some of you? He has been the— the—somehow the cause of all this. It's worth the money to bring him up to it—Bolter's throat, Bill; never mind the girl—Bolter's throat as deep as you can cut. Saw his head off!'

'Fagin,' said the jailer.

'That's me!' cried the Jew, falling instantly, into the attitude of listening he had assumed upon his trial. 'An old man, my Lord; a very old, old man!'

'Here,' said the turnkey, laying his hand upon his breast to keep him down. 'Here's somebody wants to see you, to ask you some questions, I suppose. Fagin, Fagin! Are you a man?'

'I shan't be one long,' he replied, looking up with a face retaining no human expression but rage and terror. 'Strike them all dead! What right have they to butcher me?'

As he spoke he caught sight of Oliver and Mr. Brownlow. Shrinking to the furthest corner of the seat, he demanded to know what they wanted there.

'Steady,' said the turnkey, still holding him down. 'Now, sir, tell him what you want. Quick, if you please, for he grows worse as the time gets on.'

'You have some papers,' said Mr. Brownlow advancing, 'which were placed in your hands, for better security, by a man called Monks.'

'It's all a lie together,' replied Fagin. 'I haven't one—not one.'

'For the love of God,' said Mr. Brownlow solemnly, 'do not say that now, upon the very verge of death; but tell me where they are. You know that Sikes is dead; that Monks has confessed; that there is no hope of any further gain. Where are those papers?'

'Oliver,' cried Fagin, beckoning to him. 'Here, here! Let me whisper to you.'

'I am not afraid,' said Oliver in a low voice, as he relinquished Mr. Brownlow's hand.

'The papers,' said Fagin, drawing Oliver towards him, 'are in a canvas bag, in a hole a little way up the chimney in the top front-room. I want to talk to you, my dear. I want to talk to you.'

'Yes, yes,' returned Oliver. 'Let me say a prayer. Do! Let me say one prayer. Say only one, upon your knees, with me, and we will talk till morning.'

'Outside, outside,' replied Fagin, pushing the boy before him towards the door, and looking vacantly over his head. 'Say I've gone to sleep—they'll believe you. You can get me out, if you take me so. Now then, now then!'

'Oh! God forgive this wretched man!' cried the boy with a burst of tears.

'That's right, that's right,' said Fagin. 'That'll help us on. This door first. If I shake and tremble, as we pass the gallows, don't you mind, but hurry on. Now, now, now!'

'Have you nothing else to ask him, sir?' inquired the turnkey.

'No other question,' replied Mr. Brownlow. 'If I hoped we could recall him to a sense of his position—'

'Nothing will do that, sir,' replied the man, shaking his head. 'You had better leave him.'

The door of the cell opened, and the attendants returned.

'Press on, press on,' cried Fagin. 'Softly, but not so slow. Faster, faster!'

The men laid hands upon him, and disengaging Oliver from his grasp, held him back. He struggled with the power of desperation, for an instant; and then sent up cry upon cry that penetrated even those massive walls, and rang in their ears until they reached the open yard.

It was some time before they left the prison. Oliver nearly swooned after this frightful scene, and was so weak that for an hour or more, he had not the strength to walk.

Day was dawning when they again emerged. A great multitude had already assembled; the windows were filled with people, smoking and playing cards to beguile the time; the crowd were pushing, quarrelling, joking. Everything told of life and animation, but one dark cluster of objects in the centre of all—the black stage, the cross-beam, the rope, and all the hideous apparatus of death.

CHAPTER LIII. AND LAST

The fortunes of those who have figured in this tale are nearly closed. The little that remains to their historian to relate, is told in few and simple words.

Before three months had passed, Rose Fleming and Harry Maylie were married in the village church which was henceforth to be the scene of the young clergyman's labours; on the same day they entered into possession of their new and happy home.

Mrs. Maylie took up her abode with her son and daughter-in-law, to enjoy, during the tranquil remainder of her days, the greatest felicity that age and worth can know—the contemplation of the happiness of those on whom the warmest affections and tenderest cares of a well-spent life, have been unceasingly bestowed.

It appeared, on full and careful investigation, that if the wreck of property remaining in the custody of Monks (which had never prospered either in his hands or in those of his mother) were equally divided between himself and Oliver, it would yield, to each, little more than three thousand pounds. By the provisions of his father's will, Oliver would have been entitled to the whole; but Mr. Brownlow, unwilling to deprive the elder son of the opportunity of retrieving his former vices and pursuing an honest career, proposed this mode of distribution, to which his young charge joyfully acceded.

Monks, still bearing that assumed name, retired with his portion to a distant part of the New World; where, having quickly squandered it, he once more fell into his old courses, and, after undergoing a long confinement for some fresh act of fraud and knavery, at length sunk under an attack of his old disorder, and died in prison. As far from home, died the chief remaining members of his friend Fagin's gang.

Mr. Brownlow adopted Oliver as his son. Removing with him and the old housekeeper to within a mile of the parsonage-house, where his dear friends resided, he gratified the only remaining wish of Oliver's warm and earnest heart, and thus linked together a little society, whose condition approached as nearly to one of perfect happiness as can ever be known in this changing world.

Soon after the marriage of the young people, the worthy doctor returned to Chertsey, where, bereft of the presence of his old friends, he would have been discontented if his temperament had admitted of such a feeling; and would have turned quite peevish if he had known how. For two or three months, he contented himself with hinting that he feared the air began to disagree with him; then, finding that the place really no longer was, to him, what it had been, he settled his business on his assistant, took a bachelor's cottage outside the village of which his young friend was pastor, and instantaneously recovered. Here he took to gardening, planting, fishing, carpentering, and various other pursuits of a similar kind: all undertaken with his characteristic impetuosity. In each and all he has since become famous throughout the neighborhood, as a most profound authority.

Before his removal, he had managed to contract a strong friendship for Mr. Grimwig, which that eccentric gentleman cordially reciprocated. He is accordingly visited by Mr. Grimwig a great many times in the course of the year. On all such occasions, Mr. Grimwig plants, fishes, and carpenters, with great ardour; doing everything in a very singular and unprecedented manner, but always maintaining with his favourite asseveration, that his mode is the right one. On Sundays, he never fails to criticise the sermon to the young clergyman's face: always informing Mr. Losberne, in strict confidence afterwards, that he considers it an excellent performance, but deems it as well not to say so. It is a standing and very favourite joke, for Mr. Brownlow to rally him on his old prophecy concerning Oliver, and to remind him of the night on which they sat with the watch between them, waiting his return; but Mr. Grimwig contends that he was right in the main, and, in proof thereof, remarks that Oliver did not come back after all; which always calls forth a laugh on his side, and increases his good humour.

Mr. Noah Claypole: receiving a free pardon from the Crown in consequence of being admitted approver against Fagin: and considering his profession not altogether as safe a one as he could wish: was, for some little time, at a loss for the means of a livelihood, not burdened with too much work. After some consideration, he went into business as an informer, in which calling he realises a genteel subsistence. His plan is, to walk out once a week during church time attended by Charlotte in respectable attire. The lady faints away at the doors of charitable publicans, and the gentleman being accommodated with three-penny worth of brandy to restore her, lays an information next day, and pockets half the penalty. Sometimes Mr. Claypole faints himself, but the result is the same.

Mr. and Mrs. Bumble, deprived of their situations, were gradually reduced to great indigence and misery, and finally became paupers in that very same workhouse in which they had once lorded it over others. Mr. Bumble has been heard to say, that in this reverse and degradation, he has not even spirits to be thankful for being separated from his wife.

As to Mr. Giles and Brittles, they still remain in their old posts, although the former is bald, and the last-named boy quite grey. They sleep at the parsonage, but divide their attentions so equally among its inmates, and Oliver and Mr. Brownlow, and Mr. Losberne, that to this day the villagers have never been able to discover to which establishment they properly belong.

Master Charles Bates, appalled by Sikes's crime, fell into a train of reflection whether an honest life was not, after all, the best. Arriving at the conclusion that it certainly was, he turned his back upon the scenes of the past, resolved to amend it in some new sphere of action. He struggled hard, and suffered much, for some time; but, having a contented disposition, and a good purpose, succeeded in the end; and, from being a farmer's drudge, and a carrier's lad, he is now the merriest young grazier in all Northamptonshire.

And now, the hand that traces these words, falters, as it approaches the conclusion of its task; and would weave, for a little longer space, the thread of these adventures.

I would fain linger yet with a few of those among whom I have so long moved, and share their happiness by endeavouring to depict it. I would show Rose Maylie in all the bloom and grace of early womanhood, shedding on her secluded path in life soft and gentle light, that fell on all who trod it with her, and shone into their hearts. I would paint her the life and joy of the fire-side circle and the lively summer group; I would follow her through the sultry fields at noon, and hear the low tones of her sweet voice in the moonlit evening walk; I would watch her in all her goodness and charity abroad, and the smiling untiring discharge of domestic duties at home; I would paint her and her dead sister's child happy in their love for one another, and passing whole hours together in picturing the friends whom they had so sadly lost; I would summon before me, once again, those joyous little faces that clustered round her knee, and listen to their merry prattle; I would recall the tones of that clear laugh, and conjure up the sympathising tear that glistened in the soft blue eye. These, and a thousand looks and smiles, and turns of thought and speech—I would fain recall them every one.

How Mr. Brownlow went on, from day to day, filling the mind of his adopted child with stores of knowledge, and becoming attached to him, more and more, as his nature developed itself, and showed the thriving seeds of all he wished him to become—how he traced in him new traits of his early friend, that awakened in his own bosom old remembrances, melancholy and yet sweet and soothing—how the two orphans, tried by adversity, remembered its lessons in mercy to others, and mutual love, and fervent thanks to Him who had protected and preserved them—these are all matters which need not to be told. I have said that they were truly happy; and without strong affection and humanity of heart, and gratitude to that Being whose code is Mercy, and whose great attribute is Benevolence to all things that breathe, happiness can never be attained.

Within the altar of the old village church there stands a white marble tablet, which bears as yet but one word: 'AGNES.' There is no coffin in that tomb; and may it be many, many years, before another name is placed above it! But, if the spirits of the Dead ever come back to earth, to visit spots hallowed by the love—the love beyond the grave—of those whom they knew in life, I believe that the shade of Agnes sometimes hovers round that solemn nook. I believe it none the less because that nook is in a Church, and she was weak and erring.

About Author

Dickens's literary success began with the 1836 serial publication of The Pickwick Papers. Within a few years he had become an international literary celebrity, famous for his humour, satire, and keen observation of character and society. His novels, most published in monthly or weekly instalments, pioneered the serial publication of narrative fiction, which became the dominant Victorian mode for novel publication. Cliffhanger endings in his serial publications kept readers in suspense. The instalment format allowed Dickens to evaluate his audience's reaction, and he often modified his plot and character development based on such feedback. For example, when his wife's chiropodist expressed distress at the way Miss Mowcher in David Copperfield seemed to reflect her disabilities, Dickens improved the character with positive features. His plots were carefully constructed, and he often wove elements from topical events into his narratives. Masses of the illiterate poor chipped in ha'pennies to have each new monthly episode read to them, opening up and inspiring a new class of readers.

Dickens was regarded as the literary colossus of his age. His 1843 novella, A Christmas Carol, remains popular and continues to inspire adaptations in every artistic genre. Oliver Twist and Great Expectations are also frequently adapted, and, like many of his novels, evoke images of early Victorian London. His 1859 novel, A Tale of Two Cities, set in London and Paris, is his best-known work of historical fiction. Dickens has been praised by fellow writers—from Leo Tolstoy to George Orwell, G. K. Chesterton and Tom Wolfe—for his realism, comedy, prose style, unique characterisations, and social criticism. On the other hand, Oscar Wilde, Henry James, and Virginia Woolf complained of a lack of psychological depth, loose writing, and a vein of sentimentalism. The term Dickensian is used to describe something that is reminiscent of Dickens and his writings, such as poor social conditions or comically repulsive characters.

Early years

Charles John Huffam Dickens was born on 7 February 1812, at 1 Mile End Terrace (now 393 Commercial Road), Landport in Portsea Island (Portsmouth), the second of eight children of Elizabeth Dickens (née Barrow; 1789–1863) and John Dickens (1785–1851). His father was a clerk in the Navy Pay Office and was temporarily stationed in the district. He asked Christopher Huffam, rigger to His Majesty's Navy, gentleman, and head of an established firm, to act as godfather to Charles. Huffam is thought to be the inspiration for Paul Dombey, the owner of a shipping company in Dickens's novel Dombey and Son (1848).

In January 1815, John Dickens was called back to London, and the family moved to Norfolk Street, Fitzrovia. When Charles was four, they relocated to Sheerness, and thence to Chatham, Kent, where he spent his formative years until the age of 11. His early life seems to have been idyllic, though he thought himself a "very small and not-over-particularly-taken-care-of boy".

Charles spent time outdoors, but also read voraciously, including the picaresque novels of Tobias Smollett and Henry Fielding, as well as Robinson Crusoe and Gil Blas. He read and reread The Arabian Nights and the Collected Farces of Elizabeth Inchbald. He retained poignant memories of childhood, helped by an excellent memory of people and events, which he used in his writing. His father's brief work as a clerk in the Navy Pay Office afforded him a few years of private education, first at a dame school, and then at a school run by William Giles, a dissenter, in Chatham.

This period came to an end in June 1822, when John Dickens was recalled to Navy Pay Office headquarters at Somerset House, and the family (except for Charles, who stayed behind to finish his final term of work) moved to Camden Town in London. The family had left Kent amidst rapidly mounting debts, and, living beyond his means, John Dickens was forced by his creditors into the Marshalsea debtors' prison in Southwark, London in 1824. His wife and youngest children joined him there, as was the practice at the time. Charles, then 12 years old, boarded with Elizabeth Roylance, a family friend, at 112 College Place, Camden Town. Roylance was "a reduced [impoverished] old lady, long known to our family", whom Dickens later immortalised, "with a few alterations and embellishments", as "Mrs Pipchin" in Dombey and Son. Later, he lived in a back-attic in the house of an agent for the Insolvent Court, Archibald Russell, "a fat, good-natured, kind old gentleman... with a quiet old wife" and lame son, in Lant Street in Southwark. They provided the inspiration for the Garlands in The Old Curiosity Shop.

On Sundays—with his sister Frances, free from her studies at the Royal Academy of Music—he spent the day at the Marshalsea. Dickens later used the prison as a setting in Little Dorrit. To pay for his board and to help his family, Dickens was forced to leave school and work ten-hour days at Warren's Blacking Warehouse, on Hungerford Stairs, near the present Charing Cross railway station, where he earned six shillings a week pasting labels on pots of boot blacking. The strenuous and often harsh working conditions made a lasting impression on Dickens and later influenced his fiction and essays, becoming the foundation of his interest in the reform of socio-economic and labour conditions, the rigours of which he believed were unfairly borne by the poor. He later wrote that he wondered "how I could have been so easily cast away at such an age". As he recalled to John Forster (from The Life of Charles Dickens):

The blacking-warehouse was the last house on the left-hand side of the way, at old Hungerford Stairs. It was a crazy, tumble-down old house, abutting of course on the river, and literally overrun with rats. Its wainscoted rooms, and its rotten floors and staircase, and the old grey rats swarming down in the cellars, and the sound of their squeaking and scuffling coming up the stairs at all times, and the dirt and decay of the place, rise up visibly before me, as if I were there again. The counting-house was on the first floor, looking over the coal-barges and the river. There was a recess in it, in which I was to sit and work. My work was to cover the pots of paste-blacking; first with a piece of oil-paper, and then with a piece of blue paper; to tie them round with a string; and then to clip the paper close and neat, all round, until it looked as smart as a pot of ointment from an apothecary's shop. When a certain number of grosses of pots had attained this pitch of perfection, I was to paste on each a printed label, and then go on again with more pots. Two or three other boys were kept at similar duty down-stairs on similar wages. One of them came up, in a ragged apron and a paper cap, on the first Monday morning, to show me the trick of using the string and tying the knot. His name was Bob Fagin; and I took the liberty of using his name, long afterwards, in Oliver Twist.

When the warehouse was moved to Chandos Street in the smart, busy district of Covent Garden the boys worked in a room in which the window gave onto the street and little audiences gathered and watched them at work—in Dickens biographer Simon Callow's estimation, the public display was "a new refinement added to his misery".

A few months after his imprisonment, John Dickens's mother, Elizabeth Dickens, died and bequeathed him £450. On the expectation of this legacy, Dickens was released from prison. Under the Insolvent Debtors Act, Dickens arranged for payment of his creditors, and he and his family left Marshalsea, for the home of Mrs Roylance.

Charles's mother, Elizabeth Dickens, did not immediately support his removal from the boot-blacking warehouse. This influenced Dickens's view that a father should rule the family, and a mother find her proper sphere inside the home: "I never afterwards forgot, I never shall forget, I never can forget, that my mother was warm for my being sent back". His mother's failure to request his return was a factor in his dissatisfied attitude towards women.

Righteous indignation stemming from his own situation and the conditions under which working-class people lived became major themes of his works, and it was this unhappy period in his youth to which he alluded in his favourite, and most autobiographical, novel, David Copperfield: "I had no advice, no counsel, no encouragement, no consolation, no assistance, no support, of any kind, from anyone, that I can call to mind, as I hope to go to heaven!"

Dickens was eventually sent to the Wellington House Academy in Camden Town, where he remained until March 1827, having spent about two years there. He did not consider it to be a good school: "Much of the haphazard, desultory teaching, poor discipline punctuated by the headmaster's sadistic brutality, the seedy ushers and general run-down atmosphere, are embodied in Mr Creakle's Establishment in David Copperfield."

Dickens worked at the law office of Ellis and Blackmore, attorneys, of Holborn Court, Gray's Inn, as a junior clerk from May 1827 to November 1828. He was a gifted mimic and impersonated those around him: clients, lawyers, and clerks. He went to theatres obsessively—he claimed that for at least three years he went to the theatre every single day. His favourite actor was Charles Mathews, and Dickens learnt his monopolylogues, (farces in which Mathews played every character), by heart. Then, having learned Gurney's system of shorthand in his spare time, he left to become a freelance reporter. A distant relative, Thomas Charlton, was a freelance reporter at Doctors' Commons, and Dickens was able to share his box there to report the legal proceedings for nearly four years. This education was to inform works such as Nicholas Nickleby, Dombey and Son, and especially Bleak House—whose vivid portrayal of the machinations and bureaucracy of the legal system did much to enlighten the general public and served as a vehicle for dissemination of Dickens's own views regarding, particularly, the heavy burden on the poor who were forced by circumstances to "go to law".

In 1830, Dickens met his first love, Maria Beadnell, thought to have been the model for the character Dora in David Copperfield. Maria's parents disapproved of the courtship and ended the relationship by sending her to school in Paris.

Journalism and early novels

In 1832, at age 20, Dickens was energetic and increasingly self-confident. He enjoyed mimicry and popular entertainment, lacked a clear, specific sense of what he wanted to become, and yet knew he wanted fame. Drawn to the theatre—he became an early member of the Garrick — he landed an acting audition at Covent Garden, where the manager George Bartley and the actor Charles Kemble were to see him. Dickens prepared meticulously and decided to imitate the comedian Charles Mathews, but ultimately he missed the audition because of a cold. Before another opportunity arose, he had set out on his career as a writer.

In 1833, he submitted his first story, "A Dinner at Poplar Walk", to the London periodical Monthly Magazine. William Barrow, a brother of his mother, offered him a job on The Mirror of Parliament and he worked in the House of Commons for the first time early in 1832. He rented rooms at Furnival's Inn and worked as a political journalist, reporting on Parliamentary debates, and he travelled across Britain to cover election campaigns for the Morning Chronicle. His journalism, in the form of sketches in periodicals, formed his first collection of pieces, published in 1836: Sketches by Boz—Boz being a family nickname he employed as a pseudonym for some years. Dickens apparently adopted it from the nickname "Moses", which he had given to his youngest brother Augustus Dickens, after a character in Oliver Goldsmith's The Vicar of Wakefield. When pronounced by anyone with a head cold, "Moses" became "Boses"—later shortened to Boz. Dickens's own name was considered "queer" by a contemporary critic, who wrote in 1849: "Mr Dickens, as if in revenge for his own queer name, does bestow still queerer ones upon his fictitious creations." He contributed to and edited journals throughout his literary career. In January 1835, the Morning Chronicle launched an evening edition, under the editorship of the Chronicle's music critic, George Hogarth. Hogarth invited Dickens to contribute Street Sketches and Dickens became a regular visitor to his Fulham house, excited by Hogarth's friendship with a hero of his, Walter Scott, and enjoying the company of Hogarth's three daughters—Georgina, Mary, and nineteen-year-old Catherine.

Dickens made rapid progress both professionally and socially. He began a friendship with William Harrison Ainsworth, the author of the highwayman novel Rookwood (1834), whose bachelor salon in Harrow Road had become the meeting place for a set that included Daniel Maclise, Benjamin Disraeli, Edward Bulwer-Lytton, and George Cruikshank. All these became his friends and collaborators, with the exception of Disraeli, and he met his first publisher, John Macrone, at the house. The success of Sketches by Boz led to a proposal from publishers Chapman and Hall for Dickens to supply text to match Robert Seymour's engraved illustrations in a monthly letterpress. Seymour committed suicide after the second instalment, and Dickens, who wanted to write a connected series of sketches, hired "Phiz" to provide the engravings (which were reduced from four to two per instalment) for the story. The resulting story became The Pickwick Papers, and though the first few episodes were not successful, the introduction of the Cockney character Sam Weller in the fourth episode (the first to be illustrated by Phiz) marked a sharp climb in its popularity. The final instalment sold 40,000 copies.

In November 1836, Dickens accepted the position of editor of Bentley's Miscellany, a position he held for three years, until he fell out with the owner. In 1836 as he finished the last instalments of The Pickwick Papers, he began writing the beginning instalments of Oliver Twist—writing as many as 90 pages a month—while continuing work on Bentley's and also writing four plays, the production of which he oversaw. Oliver Twist, published in 1838, became one of Dickens's better known stories, and was the first Victorian novel with a child protagonist.

On 2 April 1836, after a one-year engagement, and between episodes two and three of The Pickwick Papers, Dickens married Catherine Thomson Hogarth (1816–1879), the daughter of George Hogarth, editor of the Evening Chronicle. They were married in St. Luke's Church, Chelsea, London. After a brief honeymoon in Chalk in Kent, the couple returned to lodgings at Furnival's Inn. The first of their ten children, Charley, was born in January 1837, and a few months later the family set up home in Bloomsbury at 48 Doughty Street, London, (on which Charles had a three-year lease at £80 a year) from 25 March 1837 until December 1839. Dickens's younger brother Frederick and Catherine's 17-year-old sister Mary, moved in with them. Dickens became very attached to Mary, and she died in his arms after a brief illness in 1837. Unusually for Dickens, as a consequence of his shock, he stopped working, and he and Kate stayed at a little farm on Hampstead Heath for a fortnight. Dickens idealised Mary—the character he fashioned after her, Rose Maylie, he found he could not now kill, as he had planned, in his fiction, and, according to Ackroyd, he drew on memories of her for his later descriptions of Little Nell and Florence Dombey. His grief was so great that he was unable to meet the deadline for the June instalment of Pickwick Papers and had to cancel the Oliver Twist instalment that month as well. The time in Hampstead was the occasion for a growing bond between Dickens and John Forster to develop and Forster soon became his unofficial business manager, and the first to read his work.

His success as a novelist continued. The young Queen Victoria read both Oliver Twist and Pickwick, staying up until midnight to discuss them. Nicholas Nickleby (1838–39), The Old Curiosity Shop (1840–41) and, finally, his first historical novel, Barnaby Rudge: A Tale of the Riots of 'Eighty, as part of the Master Humphrey's Clock series (1840–41), were all published in monthly instalments before being made into books.

In the midst of all his activity during this period, there was discontent with his publishers and John Macrone was bought off, while Richard Bentley signed over all his rights in Oliver Twist. Other signs of a certain restlessness and discontent emerge—in Broadstairs he flirted with Eleanor Picken, the young fiancée of his solicitor's best friend, and one night grabbed her and ran with her down to the sea. He declared they were both to drown there in the "sad sea waves". She finally got free but afterwards kept her distance. In June 1841 he precipitously set out on a two-month tour of Scotland and then, in September 1841, telegraphed Forster that he had decided to go to America. Master Humphrey's Clock was shut down, though Dickens was still keen on the idea of the weekly magazine, a form he liked, a liking that had begun with his childhood reading of the eighteenth-century magazines Tatler and The Spectator.

Dickens was perturbed by the return to power of the Tories, whom Dickens described as "people whom, politically, I despise and abhor." He had been tempted to stand for the Liberals in Reading, but decided against it due to financial straits. He wrote three anti-Tory verse satires ("The Fine Old English Gentleman", "The Quack Doctor's Proclamation", and "Subjects for Painters") which were published in The Examiner.

First visit to the United States

On 22 January 1842, Dickens and his wife arrived in Boston, Massachusetts aboard the RMS Britannia during their first trip to the United States and Canada. At this time Georgina Hogarth, another sister of Catherine, joined the Dickens household, now living at Devonshire Terrace, Marylebone, to care for the young family they had left behind. She remained with them as housekeeper, organiser, adviser, and friend until Dickens's death in 1870. Dickens modeled the character of Agnes Wickfield after Georgina and Mary.

He described his impressions in a travelogue, American Notes for General Circulation. Dickens includes in Notes a powerful condemnation of slavery, which he had attacked as early as

The Pickwick Papers, correlating the emancipation of the poor in England with the abolition of slavery abroad citing newspaper accounts of runaway slaves disfigured by their masters. In spite of the abolitionist sentiments gleaned from his trip to America, some modern commentators have pointed out inconsistencies in Dickens's views on racial inequality, for instance, he has been criticized for his subsequent acquiescence in Governor Eyre's harsh crackdown during the 1860s Morant Bay rebellion in Jamaica and his failure to join other British progressives in condemning it. From Richmond, Virginia, Dickens returned to Washington, D.C., and started a trek westward to St. Louis, Missouri. While there, he expressed a desire to see an American prairie before returning east. A group of 13 men then set out with Dickens to visit Looking Glass Prairie, a trip 30 miles into Illinois.

During his American visit, Dickens spent a month in New York City, giving lectures, raising the question of international copyright laws and the pirating of his work in America. He persuaded a group of twenty-five writers, headed by Washington Irving, to sign a petition for him to take to Congress, but the press were generally hostile to this, saying that he should be grateful for his popularity and that it was mercenary to complain about his work being pirated.

The popularity he gained caused a shift in his self-perception according to critic Kate Flint, who writes that he "found himself a cultural commodity, and its circulation had passed out his control", causing him to become interested in and delve into themes of public and personal personas in the next novels. She writes that he assumed a role of "influential commentator", publicly and in his fiction, evident in his next few books. His trip to the U.S. ended with a trip to Canada: Niagara Falls, Toronto, Kingston and Montreal where he appeared on stage in light comedies.

Soon after his return to England, Dickens began work on the first of his Christmas stories, A Christmas Carol, written in 1843, which was followed by The Chimes in 1844 and The Cricket on the Hearth in 1845. Of these, A Christmas Carol was most popular and, tapping into an old tradition, did much to promote a renewed enthusiasm for the joys of Christmas in Britain and America. The seeds for the story became planted in Dickens's mind during a trip to Manchester to witness the conditions of the manufacturing workers there. This, along with scenes he had recently witnessed at the Field Lane Ragged School, caused Dickens to resolve to "strike a sledge hammer blow" for the poor. As the idea for the story took shape and the writing began in earnest, Dickens became engrossed in the book. He later wrote that as the tale unfolded he "wept and laughed, and wept again" as he "walked about the black streets of London fifteen or twenty miles many a night when all sober folks had gone to bed."

After living briefly in Italy (1844), Dickens travelled to Switzerland (1846), where he began work on Dombey and Son (1846–48). This and David Copperfield (1849–50) mark a significant artistic break in Dickens's career as his novels became more serious in theme and more carefully planned than his early works.

At about this time, he was made aware of a large embezzlement at the firm where his brother, Augustus, worked (John Chapman & Co.). It had been carried out by Thomas Powell, a clerk, who was on friendly terms with Dickens and who had acted as mentor to Augustus when he started work. Powell was also an author and poet and knew many of the famous writers of the day. After further fraudulent activities, Powell fled to New York and published a book called The Living Authors of England with a chapter on Charles Dickens, who was not amused by what Powell had written. One item that seemed to have annoyed him was the assertion that he had based the character of Paul Dombey (Dombey and Son) on Thomas Chapman, one of the principal partners at John Chapman & Co. Dickens immediately sent a letter to Lewis Gaylord Clark, editor of the New York literary magazine The Knickerbocker, saying that Powell was a forger and thief. Clark published the letter in the New-York Tribune, and several other papers picked up on the story. Powell began proceedings to sue these publications, and Clark was arrested. Dickens, realising that he had acted in haste, contacted John Chapman & Co. to seek written confirmation of Powell's guilt. Dickens did receive a reply confirming Powell's embezzlement, but once the directors realised this information might have to be produced in court, they refused to make further disclosures. Owing to the difficulties of providing evidence in America to support his accusations, Dickens eventually made a private settlement with Powell out of court.

Philanthropy

Angela Burdett Coutts, heir to the Coutts banking fortune, approached Dickens in May 1846 about setting up a home for the redemption of fallen women of the working class. Coutts envisioned a home that would replace the punitive regimes of existing institutions with a reformative environment conducive to education and proficiency in domestic household chores. After initially resisting, Dickens eventually founded the home, named "Urania Cottage", in the Lime Grove section of Shepherds Bush, which he managed for ten years, setting the house rules, reviewing the accounts and interviewing prospective residents. Emigration and marriage were central to Dickens's agenda for the women on leaving Urania Cottage, from which it is estimated that about 100 women graduated between 1847 and 1859.

Death

On 8 June 1870, Dickens suffered another stroke at his home after a full day's work on Edwin Drood. He never regained consciousness, and the next day, five years to the day after the Staplehurst rail crash, he died at Gads Hill Place. Biographer Claire Tomalin has suggested Dickens was actually in Peckham when he suffered the stroke, and his mistress Ellen Ternan and her maids had him taken back to Gad's Hill so the public would not know the truth about their relationship. Contrary to his wish to be buried at Rochester Cathedral "in an inexpensive, unostentatious, and strictly private manner", he was laid to rest in the Poets' Corner of Westminster Abbey. A printed epitaph circulated at the time of the funeral reads:

To the Memory of Charles Dickens (England's most popular author) who died at his residence, Higham, near Rochester, Kent, 9 June 1870, aged 58 years. He was a sympathiser with the poor, the suffering, and the oppressed; and by his death, one of England's greatest writers is lost to the world.

His last words were: "On the ground", in response to his sister-in-law Georgina's request that he lie down. On Sunday, 19 June 1870, five days after Dickens was buried in the Abbey, Dean Arthur Penrhyn Stanley delivered a memorial elegy, lauding "the genial and loving humorist whom we now mourn", for showing by his own example "that even in dealing with the darkest scenes and the most degraded characters, genius could still be clean, and mirth could be innocent". Pointing to the fresh flowers that adorned the novelist's grave, Stanley assured those present that "the spot would thenceforth be a sacred one with both the New World and the Old, as that of the representative of literature, not of this island only, but of all who speak our English tongue."

In his will, drafted more than a year before his death, Dickens left the care of his £80,000 estate to his longtime colleague John Forster and his "best and truest friend" Georgina Hogarth who, along with Dickens's two sons, also received a tax-free sum of £8,000 (about £800,000 in present terms). Although Dickens and his wife had been separated for several years at the time of his death, he provided her with an annual income of £600 and made her similar allowances in his will. He also bequeathed £19 19s to each servant in his employment at the time of his death. (Source: Wikipedia)

CPSIA information can be obtained
at www.ICGtesting.com
Printed in the USA
LVHW111656230320
650904LV00002B/322